CENTURY READINGS

IN THE

AMERICAN SHORT STORY

EDITED AND ANNOTATED BY

FRED LEWIS PATTEE

PROFESSOR OF AMERICAN LITERATURE IN THE
PENNSYLVANIA STATE COLLEGE

APPLETON-CENTURY-CROFTS, INC.

NEW YORK

PREFACE

To illustrate the development of the American short story from its beginnings in *The Sketch Book* to its present-day form a century later, to make evident the fact that it has been a growth from peculiarly American conditions, and that, though it has been subject from decade to decade to the conditions and the literary fashions of the times, it has, in the mold of American life, gradually evolved into a distinct *genre,* the only art form that America has added to literature, has been the object of this volume. By presenting, so far as possible, the best and the most typical specimens of the form produced in each decade since Irving, the editor has sought to make not only a handbook historical illustrating the progress of American thought, American feeling, and American art, but a book of models showing specimens of every type of short story and making evident the various laws that have evolved to govern the form. Especially has this been true in the later and more crowded areas. To include *all* who have added distinctive work manifestly has been impossible. The result has been the inclusion only of the stronger typical figures and typical stories.

That the selections are not all of them precisely what the editor would have chosen had he possessed a free hand goes without saying. After reaching the early eighteen-seventies the anthologist in the field of American literature is at the command of publishers who often refuse to allow anything of certain of their standard authors to be used or else compel selection from inferior areas of their work. They are not to be blamed for thus protecting themselves, but their attitude joined with that of certain authors like Cabell, for instance, who permit nothing of their work to be republished in general miscellanies, renders the making of a perfect anthology impossible. But despite all these handicaps, the compiler feels that his collection needs no apology. Under the present conditions he feels that it is the best that can be made; it represents approximately the best work that America has produced in a difficult and distinctive field of literary creation.

To all those authors who have helped to make the collection richly representative by surrendering to it their best work, and to all who have helped him with the proof-reading and the various details of the editorial drudgery incident to such a volume the compiler renders his heartiest thanks. May the volume be the inspiration of a new generation of creators who shall bring the short story to higher levels than any reached by the authors who wrote during the pioneer century of its development.

F. L. P.

CONTENTS

PART I

The Early Short Story (1819-1865)

PART II

The Middle Period (1865-1890)

PART III

The Eighteen Nineties (1890-1900)

PART IV

Representative Contemporary Writers (1900-   )

CONTENTS

PART I

THE EARLY SHORT STORY, 1819–1865

I

WASHINGTON IRVING (1783–1859)

Every collection of American short stories that attempts at all to be chronological and inclusive must begin with Washington Irving's "Rip Van Winkle," which appeared in the first number of the *Sketch Book*, 1819. Irving's temperament, especially in his earlier days, inclined him to the literary form which he denominated "the sketch"—work to be done at a single dash with simple theme and not too elaborate plan. Character was to be made central and "materials" were to dominate plot. He was essentially a romanticist, infused abundantly with the German and the oriental romance of the early nineteenth century, yet he never forgot his early eighteenth century balance. He strove as earnestly as did Poe in later years for originality and he achieved it. His short story method and his short story product were something new in fiction. He was not only the "father of the American short story," he was also a pioneer and a dominating influence in the European area of shortened fiction. His conceptions as to the demands of "the tale" or the story-telling sketch he has set forth in full in a letter to Brevoort, December, 1824, the first critical document in the history of the American short story:

"I fancy much of what I value myself upon in writing, escapes the observation of the great mass of my readers: who are intent more upon the story than the way in which it is told. For my part I consider a story merely as a frame on which to stretch my materials. It is the play of thought, and sentiment and language; the weaving in of characters, lightly yet expressively delineated; the familiar and faithful exhibition of scenes in common life; and the half-concealed vein of humour that is often playing through the whole—these are among what I aim at, and upon which I felicitate myself in proportion as I think I succeed. I have preferred adopting a mode of sketches and short tales rather than long works, because I chose to take a line of writing peculiar to myself; rather than fall into the manner or school of any other writer: and there is a constant activity of thought and a nicety of execution required in writings of the kind, more than the world appears to imagine. It is comparatively easy to swell a story to any size when you have once the scheme and the characters in your mind; the mere interest of the story too carries the reader on through pages and pages of careless writing and the author may often be dull for half a volume at a time, if he has some striking scene at the end of it, but in these shorter writings every page must have its merit. The author must be continually piquant—woe to him if he makes an awkward sentence or writes a stupid page: the critics are sure to pounce upon it. Yet if he succeed: the very variety and piquancy of his writings; nay their very brevity; makes them frequently recurred to—and when the mere interest of the story is exhausted, he begins to get credit for his touches of pathos or humour; his points of wit or turns of language. I give these as some of the reasons that have induced me to keep on thus far in the way I had opened for myself—because I find by recent letters from E. I. that you are joining in the oft-repeated advice that I should write a novel. I believe the works I have written will be oftener re-read than any novel of the size that I could have written. It is true other writers have crowded into the same branch of literature, and I now begin to find myself elbowed by men who have followed my footsteps; but at any rate I have had the merit of adopting a line for myself instead of following others."

Again in another letter he speaks of his struggle for originality:

"There are such quantities of these legendary and romantic tales now littering from the press, both in England and in Germany, that one must take care not to fall into the commonplace of the day. Scott's manner must likewise be widely avoided. In short, I must strike out some way of my own, suited to my own way of thinking and writing."

Originality, therefore, may be placed as the first canon in Irving's short-story art. Characterization was the second, and perhaps the insistence that the tale was for entertainment and not for moral or didactic ends, was the third. He added also picturesque localization and humor.

3

RIP VAN WINKLE

Whoever has made a voyage up the Hudson must remember the Kaatskill Mountains. They are a dismembered branch of the great Appalachian family, and are seen away to the west of the river, swelling up to a noble height, and lording it over the surrounding country. Every change of season, every change of weather, indeed, every hour of the day, produces some change in the magical hues and shapes of these mountains, and they are regarded by all the good wives, far and near, as perfect barometers. When the weather is fair and settled, they are clothed in blue and purple, and print their bold outlines on the clear evening sky; but sometimes when the rest of the landscape is cloudless they will gather a hood of gray vapors about their summits, which, in the last rays of the setting sun, will glow and light up like a crown of glory.

At the foot of these fairy mountains, the voyager may have discried the light smoke curling up from a village, whose shingle-roofs gleam among the trees, just where the blue tints of the upland melt away into the fresh green of the nearer landscape. It is a little village of great antiquity, having been founded by some of the Dutch colonists in the early time of the province, just about the beginning of the government of the good Peter Stuyvesant, (may he rest in peace!) and there were some of the houses of the original settlers standing within a few years, built of small yellow bricks brought from Holland, having latticed windows and gable fronts, surmounted with weathercocks.

In that same village, and in one of these very houses (which, to tell the precise truth, was sadly time-worn and weather-beaten), there lived many years since, while the country was yet a province of Great Britain, a simple, good-natured fellow, of the name of Rip Van Winkle. He was a descendant of the Van Winkles who figured so gallantly in the chivalrous days of Peter Stuyvesant, and accompanied him to the siege of Fort Christina. He inherited, however, but little of the martial character of his ancestors. I have observed that he was a simple, good-natured man; he was, moreover, a kind neighbor, and an obedient henpecked husband. Indeed, to the latter circumstance might be owing that meekness of spirit which gained him such universal popularity; for those men are most apt to be obsequious and conciliating abroad, who are under the discipline of shrews at home. Their tempers, doubtless, are rendered pliant and malleable in the fiery furnace of domestic tribulation; and a curtain lecture is worth all the sermons in the world for teaching the virtues of patience and long-suffering. A termagant wife may, therefore, in some respects be considered a tolerable blessing, and if so, Rip Van Winkle was thrice blessed.

Certain it is, that he was a great favorite among all the good wives of the village, who, as usual with the amiable sex, took his part in all family squabbles; and never failed, whenever they talked those matters over in their evening gossipings, to lay all the blame on Dame Van Winkle. The children of the village, too, would shout with joy whenever he approached. He assisted at their sports, made their playthings, taught them to fly kites and shoot marbles, and told them long stories of ghosts, witches, and Indians. Whenever he went dodging about the village, he was surrounded by a troop of them, hanging on his skirts, clambering on his back, and playing a thousand tricks on him with impunity; and not a dog would bark at him throughout the neighborhood.

The great error in Rip's composition was an insuperable aversion to all kinds of profitable labor. It could not be from the want of assiduity or perseverance; for he would sit on a wet rock, with a rod as long and heavy as a Tartar's lance, and fish all day without a murmur, even though he should not be encouraged by a single nibble. He would carry a fowling-piece on his shoulder for hours together, trudging through woods and swamps, and up hill and down dale, to shoot a few squirrels or wild pigeons. He would never refuse to assist a neighbor, even in the roughest toil, and was a foremost man at all country frolics for husking Indian corn, or building stone-fences; the women of the village, too, used to employ him to run their errands, and to do such little odd jobs as their less obliging husbands would not do for them. In a word, Rip was ready to attend to anybody's business but his own; but as to doing family duty, and keeping his farm in order, he found it impossible.

In fact, he declared it was of no use to work on his farm; it was the most pestilent little piece of ground in the whole country; everything about it went wrong, and would go wrong, in spite of him. His fences were continually falling to pieces; his cow would either go astray or get among the cabbages; weeds were sure to grow quicker in his fields than anywhere else; the rain always made a point of setting in just as he had some out-door work to do; so that though his patrimonial estate had dwindled away under his management, acre by acre, until there was little more left than a mere patch of Indian corn and potatoes, yet it was the worst-conditioned farm in the neighborhood.

His children, too, were as ragged and wild as if they belonged to nobody. His son Rip, an urchin begotten in his own likeness, promised to inherit the habits, with the old clothes of his father. He was generally seen trooping like a colt at his mother's heels, equipped in a pair of his father's cast-off galligaskins, which he had much ado to hold up with one hand, as a fine lady does her train in bad weather.

Rip Van Winkle, however, was one of those happy mortals, of foolish, well-oiled dispositions, who take the world easy, eat white bread or brown, whichever can be got with least thought or trouble, and would rather starve on a penny than work for a pound. If left to himself, he would have whistled life away in perfect contentment; but his wife kept continually dinning in his ears about his idleness, his carelessness, and the ruin he was bringing on his family. Morning, noon, and night her tongue was incessantly going, and everything he said or did was sure to produce a torrent of household eloquence. Rip had but one way of replying to all lectures of the kind, and that, by frequent use, had grown into a habit. He shrugged his shoulders, shook his head, cast up his eyes, but said nothing. This, however, always provoked a fresh volley from his wife; so that he was fain to draw off his forces, and take to the outside of the house—the only side which, in truth, belongs to a henpecked husband.

Rip's sole domestic adherent was his dog Wolf, who was as much henpecked as his master; for Dame Van Winkle regarded them as companions in idleness, and even looked upon Wolf with an evil eye, as the cause of his master's going so often astray. True it is, in all points of spirit befitting an honorable dog, he was as courageous an animal as ever scoured the woods—but what courage can withstand the ever-during and all-besetting terrors of a woman's tongue? The moment Wolf entered the house his crest fell, his tail drooped to the ground, or curled between his legs, he sneaked about with a gallows air, casting many a sidelong glance at Dame Van Winkle, and at the least flourish of a broomstick or ladle he would fly to the door with yelping precipitation.

Times grew worse and worse with Rip Van Winkle as years of matrimony rolled on; a tart temper never mellows with age, and a sharp tongue is the only edged tool that grows keener with constant use. For a long while he used to console himself, when driven from home, by frequenting a kind of perpetual club of the sages, philosophers, and other idle personages of the village; which held its sessions on a bench before a small inn, designated by a rubicund portrait of His Majesty George the Third. Here they used to sit in the shade through a long lazy summer's day, talking listlessly over village gossip, or telling endless sleepy stories about nothing. But it would have been worth any statesman's money to have heard the profound discussions that sometimes took place, when by chance an old newspaper fell into their hands from some passing traveler. How solemnly they would listen to the contents, as drawled out by Derrick Van Bummel, the school-master, a dapper learned little man, who was not to be daunted by the most gigantic word in the dictionary; and how sagely they would deliberate upon public events some months after they had taken place.

The opinions of this junto were completely controlled by Nicholas Vedder, a patriarch of the village, and landlord of the inn, at the door of which he took his seat from morning till night, just moving sufficiently to avoid the sun and keep in the shade of a large tree; so that the neighbors could tell the hour by his movements as accurately as by a sun-dial. It is true he was rarely heard to speak, but smoked his pipe incessantly. His adherents, however (for every great man has his adherents), perfectly understood him and knew how to gather his opinions. When anything that was read or related displeased him, he was observed to smoke his pipe vehemently, and to send forth short, frequent and angry puffs; but when pleased, he would inhale the smoke slowly and tranquilly, and emit it in light and placid clouds; and sometimes, taking the pipe from his mouth, and letting the fragrant vapor curl about his nose, would gravely nod his head in token of perfect approbation.

From even this stronghold the unlucky Rip was at length routed by his termagant wife, who would suddenly break in upon the tranquillity of the assemblage and call the members all to naught; nor was that august personage, Nicholas Vedder himself, sacred from the daring tongue of this terrible virago, who charged him outright with encouraging her husband in habits of idleness.

Poor Rip was at last reduced almost to despair; and his only alternative, to escape from the labor of the farm and clamor of his wife, was to take gun in hand and stroll into the woods. Here he would sometimes seat himself at the foot of a tree, and share the contents of his wallet with Wolf, with whom he sympathized as a fellow-sufferer in persecution. "Poor Wolf," he would say, "thy mistress leads thee a dog's life of it; but never mind, my lad, whilst I live thou shalt never want a friend to stand by thee!" Wolf would wag his tail, look wistfully in his master's face, and if dogs can feel pity I verily believe he reciprocated the sentiment with all his heart.

In a long ramble of the kind on a fine autumnal day, Rip had unconsciously scrambled to one of the highest parts of the Kaatskill Mountains. He was after his favorite sport of squirrel shooting, and the still solitudes had echoed and reechoed with the reports of his gun. Panting and fatigued, he threw himself, late in the afternoon, on a green knoll, covered with mountain herbage, that crowned the brow of a precipice. From an opening between the trees he could overlook all the lower country for many a mile of rich woodland. He saw at a distance the lordly Hudson, far, far, below him, moving on its silent but majestic course, with the reflection of a purple cloud, or the sail of a lagging bark, here and there sleeping on its glassy bosom, and at last losing itself in the blue highlands.

On the other side he looked down into a deep mountain glen, wild, lonely, and shagged, the bottom filled with fragments from the impending cliffs, and scarcely lighted by the reflected rays of the setting sun. For some time Rip lay musing on this scene; evening was gradually advancing; the mountains began to throw their long blue shadows over the valleys; he saw that it would be dark long before he could reach the village, and he heaved a heavy sigh when he thought of encountering the terrors of Dame Van Winkle.

As he was about to descend, he heard a voice from a distance, hallooing, "Rip Van Winkle! Rip Van Winkle!" He looked round, but could see nothing but a crow winging its solitary flight across the mountain. He thought his fancy must have deceived him, and turned again to descend, when he heard the same cry ring through the still evening air: "Rip Van Winkle! Rip Van Winkle!"—at the same time Wolf bristled up his back, and giving a low growl, skulked to his master's side, looking fearfully down into the glen. Rip now felt a vague apprehension stealing over him; he looked anxiously in the same direction, and perceived a strange figure slowly toiling up the rocks, and bending under the weight of something he carried on his back. He was surprised to see any human being in this lonely and unfrequented place; but supposing it to be some one of the neighborhood in need of his assistance, he hastened down to yield it.

On nearer approach he was still more surprised at the singularity of the stranger's appearance. He was a short, square-built old fellow, with thick bushy hair, and a grizzled beard. His dress was of the antique Dutch fashion: a cloth jerkin strapped round the waist, several pair of breeches, the outer one of ample volume, decorated with rows of buttons down the sides, and bunches at the knees. He bore on his shoulder a stout keg, that seemed full of liquor, and made signs for Rip to approach and assist him with the load. Though rather shy and distrustful of this new acquaintance, Rip complied with his usual alacrity; and mutually relieving one another, they clambered up a narrow gully, apparently the dry bed of a mountain torrent. As they ascended, Rip every now and then heard long rolling peals like distant thunder that seemed to issue out of a deep ravine, or rather cleft, between lofty rocks, toward which their rugged path conducted. He paused for a moment, but supposing it to be the muttering of one of those transient thunder-showers which often take place in mountain heights, he proceeded. Passing through the ravine, they came to a hollow, like a small amphitheater, surrounded by perpendicular precipices, over the brinks of which impending trees shot their branches, so that you only caught glimpses of the azure sky and the bright evening cloud. During the whole time Rip and his companion had labored on in silence; for though the former marveled greatly what could be the object of carrying a keg of liquor up this wild mountain, yet there was something strange and incomprehensible about the unknown, that inspired awe and checked familiarity.

On entering the amphitheater, new objects of wonder presented themselves. On a level spot in the center was a company of odd-looking personages playing at ninepins. They were dressed in a quaint outlandish fashion; some wore short doublets, others jerkins, with long knives in their belts, and most of them had enormous breeches of similar style with that of the guide's. Their visages, too, were peculiar; one had a large beard, broad face, and small piggish eyes; the face of another seemed to consist entirely of nose, and was surmounted by a white sugar-loaf hat, set off with a little red cock's tail. They all had beards, of various shapes and colors. There was one who seemed to be the commander. He was a stout old gentleman, with a weather-beaten countenance; he wore a laced doublet, broad belt and hanger, high-crowned hat and feather, red stockings, and high-heeled shoes, with roses in them. The whole group reminded Rip of the figures in an old Flemish painting in the parlor of Dominie Van Shaick, the village parson, which had been brought over from Holland at the time of the settlement.

What seemed particularly odd to Rip was, that though these folks were evidently amusing themselves, yet they maintained the gravest faces, the most mysterious silence, and were, withal, the most melancholy party of pleasure he had ever witnessed. Nothing interrupted the stillness of the scene but the noise of the balls, which, whenever they were rolled, echoed along the mountains like rumbling peals of thunder.

As Rip and his companion approached them, they suddenly desisted from their play, and stared at him with such fixed, statue-like gaze, and such strange, uncouth, lack-luster countenances, that his heart turned within him and his knees smote together. His companion now emptied the contents of the keg into large flagons, and made signs to him to wait upon the company. He obeyed with fear and trembling; they quaffed the liquor in profound silence, and then returned to their game.

By degrees Rip's awe and apprehension subsided. He even ventured, when no eye was fixed upon him, to taste the beverage, which he found had much of the flavor of excellent Hollands. He was naturally a thirsty soul, and was soon tempted to repeat the draught. One taste provoked another; and he reiterated his visits to the flagon so often that at length his senses were overpowered, his eyes swam in his head, his head gradually declined, and he fell into a deep sleep.

On waking, he found himself on the green knoll whence he had first seen the old man of the glen. He rubbed his eyes—it was a bright, sunny morning. The birds were hopping and twittering among the bushes, and the eagle was wheeling aloft, and breasting the pure mountain breeze. "Surely," thought Rip, "I have not slept here all night." He recalled the occurrences before he fell asleep. The strange man with a keg of liquor—the mountain ravine—the wild retreat among the rocks—the woe-begone party at nine-pins—the flagon—"Oh! that flagon! that wicked flagon!" thought Rip—"what excuse shall I make to Dame Van Winkle?"

He looked round for his gun, but in place of the clean, well-oiled fowling-piece, he found an old firelock lying by him, the barrel incrusted with rust, the lock falling off, and the stock worm-eaten. He now suspected that the grave roisters of the mountain had put a trick upon him, and, having dosed him with liquor, had robbed him of his gun. Wolf, too, had disappeared, but he might have strayed away after a squirrel or partridge. He whistled after him, and shouted his name, but all in vain; the echoes repeated his whistle and shout, but no dog was to be seen.

He determined to revisit the scene of the

last evening's gambol, and if he met with any of the party, to demand his dog and gun. As he rose to walk, he found himself stiff in the joints, and wanting in his usual activity. "These mountain beds do not agree with me," thought Rip, "and if this frolic should lay me up with a fit of the rheumatism, I shall have a blessed time with Dame Van Winkle." With some difficulty he got down into the glen; he found the gully up which he and his companion had ascended the preceding evening; but to his astonishment a mountain stream was now foaming down it, leaping from rock to rock, and filling the glen with babbling murmurs. He, however, made shift to scramble up its sides, working his toilsome way through thickets of birch, sassafras, and witch-hazel, and sometimes tripped up or entangled by the wild grapevines that twisted their coils or tendrils from tree to tree, and spread a kind of network in his path.

At length he reached to where the ravine had opened through the cliffs to the amphitheater; but no traces of such opening remained. The rocks presented a high, impenetrable wall, over which the torrent came tumbling in a sheet of feathery foam, and fell into a broad, deep basin, black from the shadows of the surrounding forest. Here, then, poor Rip was brought to a stand. He again called and whistled after his dog; he was only answered by the cawing of a flock of idle crows, sporting high in air about a dry tree that overhung a sunny precipice; and who, secure in their elevation, seemed to look down and scoff at the poor man's perplexities. What was to be done? the morning was passing away, and Rip felt famished for want of his breakfast. He grieved to give up his dog and gun; he dreaded to meet his wife; but it would not do to starve among the mountains. He shook his head, shouldered the rusty firelock, and, with a heart full of trouble and anxiety, turned his steps homeward.

As he approached the village he met a number of people, but none whom he knew, which somewhat surprised him, for he had thought himself acquainted with every one in the country round. Their dress, too, was of a different fashion from that to which he was accustomed. They all stared at him with equal marks of surprise, and whenever they cast their eyes upon him, invariably stroked their chins. The constant

recurrence of this gesture induced Rip, involuntarily, to do the same, when, to his astonishment, he found his beard had grown a foot long!

5 He had now entered the skirts of the village. A troop of strange children ran at his heels, hooting after him, and pointing at his gray beard. The dogs, too, not one of which he recognized for an old acquaintance, 10 barked at him as he passed. The very village was altered; it was larger and more populous. There were rows of houses which he had never seen before, and those which had been his familiar 15 haunts had disappeared. Strange names were over the doors—strange faces at the windows,—everything was strange. His mind now misgave him; he began to doubt whether both he and the world 20 around him were not bewitched. Surely this was his native village, which he had left but the day before. There stood the Kaatskill Mountains—there ran the silver Hudson at a distance—there was every hill 25 and dale precisely as it had always been —Rip was sorely perplexed—"That flagon last night," thought he, "has addled my poor head sadly!"

It was with some difficulty that he found 30 the way to his own house, which he approached with silent awe, expecting every moment to hear the shrill voice of Dame Van Winkle. He found the house gone to decay—the roof fallen in, the windows 35 shattered, and the doors off the hinges. A half-starved dog that looked like Wolf was skulking about it. Rip called him by name, but the cur snarled, showed his teeth, and passed on. This was an unkind cut indeed 40 —"My very dog," sighed Rip, "has forgotten me!"

He entered the house, which, to tell the truth, Dame Van Winkle had always kept in neat order. It was empty, forlorn, and 45 apparently abandoned. This desolateness overcame all his connubial fears—he called loudly for his wife and children— the lonely chambers rang for a moment with his voice, and then again all was 50 silence.

He now hurried forth, and hastened to his old resort, the village inn—but it, too, was gone. A large rickety wooden building stood in its place, with great gaping 55 windows, some of them broken and mended with old hats and petticoats, and over the door was painted, "The Union Hotel, by Jonathan Doolittle." Instead of the great tree that used to shelter the quiet little Dutch inn of yore, there now was reared a tall naked pole, with something on the top that looked like a red night-cap, and from it was fluttering a flag, on which was a singular assemblage of stars and stripes—all this was strange and incomprehensible. He recognized on the sign, however, the ruby face of King George, under which he had smoked so many a peaceful pipe; but even this was singularly metamorphosed. The red coat was changed for one of blue and buff, a sword was held in the hand instead of a scepter, the head was decorated with a cocked hat, and underneath was painted in large characters, GENERAL WASHING-TON.

There was, as usual, a crowd of folk about the door, but none that Rip recollected. The very character of the people seemed changed. There was a busy, bustling, disputatious tone about it, instead of the accustomed phlegm and drowsy tranquillity. He looked in vain for the sage Nicholas Vedder, with his broad face, double chin, and fair long pipe, uttering clouds of tobacco-smoke instead of idle speeches; or Van Bummel, the school-master, doling forth the contents of an ancient newspaper. In place of these, a lean, bilious-looking fellow, with his pockets full of hand-bills, was haranguing vehemently about rights of citizens—elections—members of congress—liberty—Bunker's Hill—heroes of seventy-six—and other words, which were a perfect Babylonish jargon to the bewildered Van Winkle.

The appearance of Rip, with his long grizzled beard, his rusty fowling-piece, his uncouth dress, and an army of women and children at his heels, soon attracted the attention of the tavern-politicians. They crowded round him, eying him from head to foot with great curiosity. The orator bustled up to him, and, drawing him partly aside, inquired "on which side he voted?" Rip started in vacant stupidity. Another short but busy little fellow pulled him by the arm, and, rising on tiptoe, inquired in his ear, "Whether he was Federal or Democrat?" Rip was equally at a loss to comprehend the question; when a knowing, self-important old gentleman, in a sharp cocked hat, made his way through the crowd, putting them to the right and left with his elbows as he passed, and plant-ing himself before Van Winkle, with one arm akimbo, the other resting on his cane, his keen eyes and sharp hat penetrating, as it were, into his very soul, demanded in an austere tone, "what brought him to the election with a gun on his shoulder, and a mob at his heels, and whether he meant to breed a riot in the village?"—"Alas! gentlemen," cried Rip, somewhat dismayed, "I am a poor quiet man, a native of the place, and a loyal subject of the king, God bless him!"

Here a general shout burst from the by-standers—"A tory! a tory! a spy! a refugee! hustle him! away with him!" It was with great difficulty that the self-important man in the cocked hat restored order; and, having assumed a tenfold austerity of brow, demanded again of the unknown culprit what he came there for, and whom he was seeking? The poor man humbly assured him that he meant no harm, but merely came there in search of some of his neighbors, who used to keep about the tavern.

"Well—who are they?—name them."

Rip bethought himself a moment, and inquired, "Where's Nicholas Vedder?"

There was a silence for a little while, when an old man replied, in a thin, piping voice: "Nicholas Vedder! why, he is dead and gone these eighteen years! There was a wooden tombstone in the churchyard that used to tell all about him, but that's rotten and gone too."

"Where's Brom Dutcher?"

"Oh, he went off to the army in the beginning of the war; some say he was killed at the storming of Stony Point—others say he was drowned in a squall at the foot of Anthony's Nose. I don't know—he never came back again."

"Where's Van Bummel, the school-master?"

"He went off to the wars too, was a great militia general, and is now in Congress."

Rip's heart died away at hearing of these sad changes in his home and friends, and finding himself thus alone in the world. Every answer puzzled him too, by treating of such enormous lapses of time, and of matters which he could not understand: war—Congress—Stony Point; he had no courage to ask after any more friends, but cried out in despair, "Does nobody here know Rip Van Winkle?"

"Oh, Rip Van Winkle!" exclaimed two

or three, "Oh, to be sure! that's Rip Van Winkle yonder, leaning against the tree."

Rip looked, and beheld a precise counterpart of himself, as he went up the mountain: apparently as lazy, and certainly as ragged. The poor fellow was now completely confounded. He doubted his own identity, and whether he was himself or another man. In the midst of his bewilderment, the man in the cocked hat demanded who he was, and what was his name?

"God knows," exclaimed he, at his wit's end: "I'm not myself—I'm somebody else—that's me yonder—no—that's somebody else got into my shoes—I was myself last night, but I fell asleep on the mountain, and they've changed my gun, and everything's changed, and I'm changed, and I can't tell what's my name, or who I am!"

The bystanders began now to look at each other, nod, wink significantly, and tap their fingers against their foreheads. There was a whisper, also about securing the gun, and keeping the old fellow from doing mischief, at the very suggestion of which the self-important man in the cocked hat retired with some precipitation. At this critical moment a fresh, comely woman pressed through the throng to get a peep at the gray-bearded man. She had a chubby child in her arms, which, frightened at his looks, began to cry. "Hush, Rip," cried she, "hush, you little fool; the old man won't hurt you." The name of the child, the air of the mother, the tone of her voice, all awakened a train of recollections in his mind. "What is your name, my good woman?" asked he.

"Judith Gardenier."

"And your father's name?"

"Ah, poor man, Rip Van Winkle was his name, but it's twenty years since he went away from home with his gun, and never has been heard of since,—his dog came home without him; but whether he shot himself, or was carried away by the Indians, nobody can tell. I was then but a little girl."

Rip had but one question more to ask; and he put it with a faltering voice:—

"Where's your mother?"

"Oh, she too had died but a short time since; she broke a blood-vessel in a fit of passion at a New England peddler."

There was a drop of comfort at least, in this intelligence. The honest man could contain himself no longer. He caught his daughter and her child in his arms. "I am your father!" cried he—"Young Rip Van Winkle once—old Rip Van Winkle now! Does nobody know poor Rip Van Winkle?"

All stood amazed, until an old woman tottering out from among the crowd, put her hand to her brow, and peering under it in his face for a moment, exclaimed, "Sure enough it is Rip Van Winkle—it is himself! Welcome home again, old neighbor—Why, where have you been these twenty long years?"

Rip's story was soon told, for the whole twenty years had been to him but as one night. The neighbors stared when they heard it; some were seen to wink at each other, and put their tongues in their cheeks; and the self-important man in the cocked hat, who when the alarm was over, had returned to the field, screwed down the corners of his mouth, and shook his head—upon which there was a general shaking of the head throughout the assemblage.

It was determined, however, to take the opinion of old Peter Vanderdonk, who was seen slowly advancing up the road. He was a descendant of the historian of that name, who wrote one of the earliest accounts of the province. Peter was the most ancient inhabitant of the village, and well versed in all the wonderful events and traditions of the neighborhood. He recollected Rip at once, and corroborated his story in the most satisfactory manner. He assured the company that it was a fact, handed down from his ancestor the historian, that the Kaatskill Mountains had always been haunted by strange beings. That it was affirmed that the great Hendrick Hudson, the first discoverer of the river and country, kept a kind of vigil there every twenty years, with his crew of the Half-moon; being permitted in this way to revisit the scenes of his enterprise, and keep a guardian eye upon the river and the great city called by his name. That his father had once seen them in their old Dutch dresses playing at nine-pins in a hollow of the mountain; and that he himself had heard, one summer afternoon, the sound of their balls like distant peals of thunder.

To make a long story short, the company broke up, and returned to the more important concerns of the election. Rip's daughter took him home to live with her; she had a snug well-furnished house, and a stout cheery farmer for a husband, whom Rip recollected for one of the urchins that used to climb upon his back. As to Rip's son and heir, who was the ditto of himself, seen leaning against the tree, he was employed to work on the farm; but evinced an hereditary disposition to attend to anything else but his business.

Rip now resumed his old walks and habits; he soon found many of his former cronies, though all rather the worse for the wear and tear of time; and preferred making friends among the rising generation, with whom he soon grew into great favor.

Having nothing to do at home, and being arrived at that happy age when a man can be idle with impunity, he took his place once more on the bench at the inn door, and was reverenced as one of the patriarchs of the village, and a chronicle of the old times "before the war." It was some time before he could get into the regular track of gossip, or could be made to comprehend the strange events that had taken place during his torpor. How that there had been a revolutionary war—that the country had thrown off the yoke of old England—and that, instead of being a subject of his Majesty George the Third, he was now a free citizen of the United States. Rip, in fact, was no politician; the changes of states and empires made but little impression on him; but there was one species of despotism under which he had long groaned, and that was—petticoat government. Happily that was at an end; he had got his neck out of the yoke of matrimony, and could go in and out whenever he pleased, without dreading the tyranny of Dame Van Winkle. Whenever her name was mentioned, however, he shook his head, shrugged his shoulders, and cast up his eyes, which might pass either for an expression of resignation to his fate, or joy at his deliverance.

He used to tell his story to every stranger that arrived at Mr. Doolittle's hotel. He was observed, at first, to vary on some points every time he told it, which was, doubtless, owing to his having so recently awaked. It at last settled down precisely to the tale I have related, and not a man, woman, or child in the neighborhood but knew it by heart. Some always pretended to doubt the reality of it, and insisted that Rip had been out of his head, and that this was one point on which he always remained flighty. The old Dutch inhabitants, however, almost universally gave it full credit. Even to this day they never hear a thunder-storm of a summer afternoon about the Kaatskill, but they say Hendrick Hudson and his crew are at their game of nine-pins; and it is a common wish of all henpecked husbands in the neighborhood, when life hangs heavy on their hands, that they might have a quieting draught out of Rip Van Winkle's flagon.

THE STOUT GENTLEMAN

A STAGE-COACH ROMANCE

It was a rainy Sunday in the gloomy month of November. I had been detained, in the course of a journey, by a slight indisposition, from which I was recovering; but I was still feverish, and was obliged to keep within doors all day, in an inn of the small town of Derby. A wet Sunday in a country inn!—whoever has had the luck to experience one can alone judge of my situation. The rain pattered against the casements; the bells tolled for church with a melancholy sound. I went to the windows in quest of something to amuse the eye; but it seemed as if I had been placed completely out of the reach of all amusement. The windows of my bedroom looked out among tiled roofs and stacks of chimneys, while those of my sitting-room commanded a full view of the stable-yard. I know of nothing more calculated to make a man sick of this world than a stable-yard on a rainy day. The place was littered with wet straw that had been kicked about by travelers and stable-boys. In one corner was a stagnant pool of water, surrounding an island of muck; there were several half-drowned fowls crowded together under a cart, among which was a miserable, crest-fallen cock, drenched out of all life and spirit; his drooping tail matted, as it were, into a single feather, along which the water trickled from his back; near the cart was a half-dozing cow, chewing the cud, and standing patiently to be rained on, with wreaths of vapor rising from her reeking hide; a wall-eyed horse, tired of the loneliness of the stable, was poking his spectral head out of a window, with the rain dripping on it from the eaves; an unhappy cur, chained to a doghouse hard by, uttered something every now and then, between a bark and a yelp; a drab of a kitchen wench tramped backwards and forwards through the yard in pattens, looking as sulky as the weather itself; everything, in short, was comfortless and forlorn, excepting a crew of hard-drinking ducks, assembled like boon companions round a puddle, and making a riotous noise over their liquor.

I was lonely and listless, and wanted amusement. My room soon became insupportable. I abandoned it, and sought what is technically called the travelers'-room. This is a public room set apart at most inns for the accommodation of a class of wayfarers, called travelers, or riders; a kind of commercial knights-errant, who are incessantly scouring the kingdom in gigs, on horseback, or by coach. They are the only successors that I know of at the present day, to the knights-errant of yore. They lead the same kind of roving adventurous life, only changing the lance for a driving-whip, the buckler for a pattern-card, and the coat of mail for an upper Benjamin. Instead of vindicating the charms of peerless beauty, they rove about, spreading the fame and standing of some substantial tradesman, or manufacturer, and are ready at any time to bargain in his name; it being the fashion now-a-days to trade, instead of fight, with one another. As the room of the hostel, in the good old fighting times, would be hung round at night with the armor of way-worn warriors, such as coats of mail, falchions, and yawning helmets; so the travelers'-room is garnished with the harnessing of their successors, with box-coats, whips of all kinds, spurs, gaiters, and oil-cloth covered hats.

I was in hopes of finding some of these worthies to talk with, but was disappointed. There were, indeed, two or three in the room; but I could make nothing of them. One was just finishing his breakfast, quarreling with his bread and butter, and huffing the waiter; another buttoned on a pair of gaiters, with many execrations at Boots for not having cleaned his shoes well; a third sat drumming on the table with his fingers and looking at the rain as it streamed down the window-glass; they all appeared infected by the weather, and disappeared, one after the other, without exchanging a word.

I sauntered to the window, and stood gazing at the people, picking their way to church, with petticoats hoisted midleg high, and dripping umbrellas. The bell ceased to toll, and the streets became silent. I then amused myself with watching the daughters of a tradesman opposite; who, being confined to the house for fear of wetting their Sunday finery, played off their charms at the front windows, to fascinate the chance tenants of the inn. They at length were summoned away by a vigilant vinegar-faced mother, and I had nothing further from without to amuse me.

What was I to do to pass away the long-lived day? I was sadly nervous and lonely; and everything about an inn seems calculated to make a dull day ten times duller. Old newspapers, smelling of beer and tobacco smoke, and which I had already read half a dozen times—good-for-nothing books, that were worse than rainy weather. I bored myself to death with an old volume of the *Lady's Magazine*. I read all the commonplaced names of ambitious travelers scrawled on the panes of glass; the eternal families of the Smiths, and the Browns, and the Jacksons, and the Johnsons, and all the other sons; and I deciphered several scraps of fatiguing inn-window poetry which I have met with in all parts of the world.

The day continued lowering and gloomy; the slovenly, ragged, spongy clouds drifted heavily along; there was no variety even in the rain: it was one dull, continued, monotonous patter—patter—patter, excepting that now and then I was enlivened by the idea of a brisk shower, from the rattling of the drops upon a passing umbrella.

It was quite *refreshing* (if I may be allowed a hackneyed phrase of the day) when, in the course of the morning, a horn blew, and a stage-coach whirled through the street, with outside passengers stuck all over it, cowering under cotton umbrellas, and seethed together, and reeking with the steams of wet box-coats and upper Benjamins.

The sound brought out from their lurking-places a crew of vagabond boys, and vagabond dogs, and the carroty-headed hostler, and that nondescript animal y-cleped Boots, and all the other vagabond race that infest the purlieus of an inn; but the bustle was transient; the coach again whirled on its way; and boy and dog, and hostler and Boots, all slunk back again to their holes; the street again became silent, and the rain continued to rain on. In fact, there was no hope of its clearing up; the barometer pointed to rainy weather; mine hostess' tortoise-shell cat sat by the fire washing her face, and rubbing her paws over her ears, and on referring to the Almanac, I found a direful prediction stretching from the top of the page to the bottom through the whole month, "expect—much—rain—about—this —time!"

I was dreadfully hipped. The hours seemed as if they would never creep by. The very ticking of the clock became irksome. At length the stillness of the house was interrupted by the ringing of a bell. Shortly after I heard the voice of a waiter at the bar: "The stout gentleman in No. 13 wants his breakfast. Tea and bread and butter, with ham and eggs; the eggs not to be too much done."

In such a situation as mine every incident is of importance. Here was a subject of speculation presented to my mind, and ample exercise for my imagination. I am prone to paint pictures to myself, and on this occasion I had some materials to work upon. Had the guest up stairs been mentioned as Mr. Smith, or Mr. Brown, or Mr. Jackson, or Mr. Johnson, or merely as "the gentleman in No. 13," it would have been a perfect blank to me. I should have thought nothing of it; but "The stout gentleman!"—the very name had something in it of the picturesque. It at once gave the size; it embodied the personage to my mind's eye, and my fancy did the rest.

He was stout, or, as some term it, lusty; in all probability, therefore, he was advanced in life, some people expanding as they grow old. By his breakfasting rather late, and in his own room, he must be a man accustomed to live at his ease, and above the necessity of early rising; no doubt a round, rosy, lusty old gentleman.

There was another violent ringing. The stout gentleman was impatient for his breakfast. He was evidently a man of importance; "well to do in the world"; accustomed to be promptly waited upon; of a keen appetite, and a little cross when hungry; "perhaps," thought I, "he may be some London Alderman; or who knows but he may be a Member of Parliament?" The breakfast was sent up, and there was a short interval of silence; he was, doubtless, making the tea. Presently there was

a violent ringing; and before it could be answered, another ringing still more violent. "Bless me! what a choleric old gentleman!" The waiter came down in a huff. The butter was rancid, the eggs were overdone, the ham was too salt:—the stout gentleman was evidently nice in his eating; one of those who eat and growl, and keep the waiter on the trot, and live in a state militant with the household.

The hostess got into a fume. I should observe that she was a brisk, coquettish woman; a little of a shrew, and something of a slammerkin, but very pretty withal; with a nincompoop for a husband, as shrews are apt to have. She rated the servants roundly for their negligence in sending up so bad a breakfast, but said not a word against the stout gentleman; by which I clearly perceived that he must be a man of consequence, entitled to make a noise and to give trouble at a country inn. Other eggs, and ham, and bread and butter were sent up. They appeared to be more graciously received; at least there was no further complaint.

I had not made many turns about the travelers'-room, when there was another ringing. Shortly afterwards there was a stir and an inquest about the house. The stout gentleman wanted the *Times* or the *Chronicle* newspaper. I set him down, therefore, for a whig; or rather, from his being so absolute and lordly where he had a chance, I suspected him of being a radical. Hunt, I had heard, was a large man; "who knows," thought I, "but it is Hunt himself!"

My curiosity began to be awakened. I inquired of the waiter who was this stout gentleman that was making all this stir: but I could get no information: nobody seemed to know his name. The landlords of bustling inns seldom trouble their heads about the names or occupations of their transient guests. The color of a coat, the shape or size of the person, is enough to suggest a traveling name. It is either the tall gentleman, or the short gentleman, or the gentleman in black, or the gentleman in snuff-color; or, as in the present instance, the stout gentleman. A designation of the kind once hit on answers every purpose, and saves all further inquiry.

Rain — rain — rain! pitiless, ceaseless rain! No such thing as putting a foot out of doors, and no occupation nor amusement within. By and by I heard some one walking over head. It was in the stout gentleman's room. He evidently was a large man by the heaviness of his tread; and an old man from his wearing such creaking soles. "He is doubtless," thought I, "some rich old square-toes of regular habits, and is now taking exercise after breakfast."

I now read all the advertisements of coaches and hotels that were stuck about the mantel-piece. The *Lady's Magazine* had become an abomination to me; it was as tedious as the day itself. I wandered out, not knowing what to do, and ascended again to my room. I had not been there long, when there was a squall from a neighboring bedroom. A door opened and slammed violently; a chambermaid, that I had remarked for having a ruddy, good-humored face, went down stairs in a violent flurry. The stout gentleman had been rude to her!

This sent a whole host of my deductions to the deuce in a moment. This unknown personage could not be an old gentleman; for old gentleman are not apt to be so obstreperous to chambermaids. He could not be a young gentleman; for young gentlemen are not apt to inspire such indignation. He must be a middle-aged man, and confounded ugly into the bargain, or the girl would not have taken the matter in such terrible dudgeon. I confess I was sorely puzzled.

In a few minutes I heard the voice of my landlady. I caught a glance of her as she came tramping up stairs; her face glowing, her cap flaring, her tongue wagging the whole way. "She'd have no such doings in her house, she'd warrant. If gentlemen did spend money freely, it was no rule. She'd have no servant maids of hers treated in that way, when they were about their work, that's what she wouldn't."

As I hate squabbles, particularly with women, and above all with pretty women, I slunk back into my room, and partly closed the door; but my curiosity was too much excited not to listen. The landlady marched intrepidly to the enemy's citadel, and entered it with a storm: the door closed after her. I heard her voice in high windy clamor for a moment or two. Then it gradually subsided, like a gust of wind in a garret; then there was a laugh; then I heard nothing more.

After a little while my landlady came out with an odd smile on her face, adjusting her cap, which was a little on one side. As she went down stairs I heard the landlord ask her what was the matter; she said, "Nothing at all, only the girl's a fool."—I was more than ever perplexed what to make of this unaccountable personage, who could put a good-natured chambermaid in a passion, and send away a termagant landlady in smiles. He could not to be so old, nor cross, nor ugly either. I had to go to work at his picture again, and to paint him entirely different. I now set him down for one of those stout gentlemen that are frequently met with swaggering about the doors of country inns. Moist, merry fellows, in Belcher handkerchiefs, whose bulk is a little assisted by malt-liquors. Men who have seen the world, and been sworn at Highgate; who are used to tavern life; up to all the tricks of tapsters, and knowing in the ways of sinful publicans. Free-livers on a small scale; who are prodigal within the compass of a guinea; who call all the waiters by name, touzle the maids, gossip with the landlady at the bar, and prose over a pint of port, or a glass of negus, after dinner.

The morning wore away in forming these and similar surmises. As fast as I wove one system of belief, some movement of the unknown would completely overturn it, and throw all my thoughts again into confusion. Such are the solitary operations of a feverish mind. I was, as I have said, extremely nervous; and the continual meditation on the concerns of this invisible personage began to have its effect:—I was getting a fit of the fidgets.

Dinner-time came. I hoped the stout gentleman might dine in the travelers'-room, and that I might at length get a view of his person; but no—he had dinner served in his own room. What could be the meaning of this solitude and mystery? He could not be a radical; there was something too aristocratical in thus keeping himself apart from the rest of the world, and condemning himself to his own dull company throughout a rainy day. And then, too, he lived too well for a discontented politician. He seemed to expatiate on a variety of dishes, and to sit over his wine like a jolly friend of good living. Indeed, my doubts on this head were soon at an end; for he could not have finished his first bottle before I could faintly hear him humming a tune; and on listening, I found it to be "God save the King." 'Twas plain, then, he was no radical, but a faithful subject; one who grew loyal over his bottle, and was ready to stand by king and constitution, when he could stand by nothing else. But who could he be! My conjectures began to run wild. Was he not some personage of distinction traveling incog.? "God knows!" said I, at my wit's end; "it may be one of the royal family for aught I know, for they are all stout gentlemen!"

The weather continued rainy. The mysterious unknown kept his room, and, as far as I could judge, his chair, for I did not hear him move. In the meantime, as the day advanced, the travelers'-room began to be frequented. Some, who had just arrived, came in buttoned up in box-coats; others came home who had been dispersed about the town. Some took their dinners, and some their tea. Had I been in a different mood, I should have found entertainment in studying this peculiar class of men. There were two especially, who were regular wags of the road, and up to all the standing jokes of travelers. They had a thousand sly things to say to the waiting-maid, whom they called Louisa, and Ethelinda, and a dozen other fine names, changing the name every time, and chuckling amazingly at their own waggery. My mind, however, had become completely engrossed by the stout gentleman. He had kept my fancy in chase during a long day, and it was not now to be diverted from the scent.

The evening gradually wore away. The travelers read the papers two or three times over. Some drew round the fire and told long stories about their horses, about their adventures, their overturns, and breakings down. They discussed the credits of different merchants and different inns; and the two wags told several choice anecdotes of pretty chambermaids, and kind landladies. All this passed as they were quietly taking what they called their nightcaps, that is to say, strong glasses of brandy and water and sugar, or some other mixture of the kind; after which they one after another rang for "Boots" and the chambermaid, and walked off to bed in old shoes cut down into marvelously uncomfortable slippers.

There was now only one man left; a short-legged, long-bodied, plethoric fellow, with a very large, sandy head. He sat by himself, with a glass of port wine negus, and a spoon; sipping and stirring, and meditating and sipping, until nothing was left but the spoon. He gradually fell asleep bolt upright in his chair, with the empty glass standing before him; and the candle seemed to fall asleep too, for the wick grew long, and black, and cabbaged at the end, and dimmed the little light that remained in the chamber. The gloom that now prevailed was contagious. Around hung the shapeless, and almost spectral, box-coats of departed travelers, long since buried in deep sleep. I only heard the ticking of the clock, with the deep-drawn breathings of the sleeping topers, and the drippings of the rain, drop—drop—drop, from the eaves of the house. The church bells chimed midnight. All at once the stout gentleman began to walk over head, pacing slowly backwards and forwards. There was something extremely awful in all this, especially to one in my state of nerves. These ghastly great-coats, these guttural breathings, and the creaking footsteps of this mysterious being. His steps grew fainter and fainter, and at length died away. I could bear it no longer. I was wound up to the desperation of a hero of romance. "Be he who or what he may," said I to myself, "I'll have a sight of him!" I seized a chamber candle, and hurried up to No. 13. The door stood ajar. I hesitated—I entered: the room was deserted. There stood a large, broad-bottomed elbow-chair at a table, on which was an empty tumbler, and a *Times* newspaper, and the room smelt powerfully of Stilton cheese.

The mysterious stranger had evidently but just retired. I turned off, sorely disappointed, to my room, which had been changed to the front of the house. As I went along the corridor, I saw a large pair of boots, with dirty, waxed tops, standing at the door of a bed-chamber. They doubtless belonged to the unknown; but it would not do to disturb so redoubtable a personage in his den; he might discharge a pistol, or something worse, at my head. I went to bed, therefore, and lay awake half the night in a terribly nervous state; and even when I fell asleep, I was still haunted in my dreams by the idea of the stout gentleman and his wax-topped boots.

I slept rather late the next morning, and was awakened by some stir and bustle in the house, which I could not at first comprehend; until getting more awake, I found there was a mail coach starting from the door. Suddenly there was a cry from below, "The gentleman has forgot his umbrella! look for the gentleman's umbrella in No. 13!" I heard an immediate scampering of a chambermaid along the passage, and a shrill reply as she ran, "Here it is! here's the gentleman's umbrella!"

The mysterious stranger then was on the point of setting off. This was the only chance I should ever have of knowing him. I sprang out of bed, scrambled to the window, snatched aside the curtains, and just caught a glimpse of the rear of a person getting in at the coach-door. The skirts of a brown coat parted behind, and gave me a full view of the broad disk of a pair of drab breeches. The door closed—"all right!" was the word—the coach whirled off;—and that was all I ever saw of the stout gentleman!

II

WILLIAM AUSTIN (1778–1841)

The great popularity of Irving's *Sketch Book* had a tendency tŏ turn American literature toward native themes, especially to the legendary and the romantic. Charles Brockden Brown, whose somber novels with native backgrounds were the beginnings of American fiction, was also a strong influence. So great became the interest in native tradition and American legendary lore that in 1828 N. P. Willis could even issue two souvenir gift books bearing the title "The Legendary." New England, which for generations had lived in the shuddery atmosphere of the unseen world, made as her best contribution to this popular *genre* "Peter Rugg, the Missing Man," written by William Austin, Harvard College, 1798. The success of the first part, which had been issued in 1824, induced the author two years later to add the sequel with its "Wandering Jew," "Rip Van Winkle," "Man Without a Country" *motif*. Austin, who by profession was a lawyer, did no other literary work of any distinction.

In the history of the short-story form during the early period of its inoculation by German romance the "Peter Rugg" legend has a significant place. It was pioneer work of uncommon quality; it undoubtedly influenced Hawthorne; but measured by modern standards for the short story it has many grave defects.

PETER RUGG, THE MISSING MAN

I

From Jonathan Dunwell *of* New York *to* Mr. Herman Krauff.

Sir: Agreeably to my promise, I now relate to you all the particulars of the lost man and child which I have been able to collect. It is entirely owing to the humane interest you seemed to take in the report, that I have pursued the inquiry to the following result.

You may remember that business called me to Boston in the summer of 1820. I sailed in the packet to Providence, and when I arrived there I learned that every seat in the stage was engaged. I was thus obliged either to wait a few hours or accept a seat with the driver, who civilly offered me that accommodation. Accordingly, I took my seat by his side, and soon found him intelligent and communicative. When we had traveled about ten miles, the horses suddenly threw their ears on their necks, as flat as a hare's. Said the driver, "Have you a surtout with you?"

"No," said I; "why do you ask?"

"You will want one soon," said he. "Do you observe the ears of all the horses?"

"Yes; and was just about to ask the reason."

"They see the storm-breeder, and we shall see him soon."

At this moment there was not a cloud visible in the firmament. Soon after, a small speck appeared in the road.

"There," said my companion, "comes the storm-breeder. He always leaves a Scotch mist behind him. By many a wet jacket do I remember him. I suppose the poor fellow suffers much himself—much more than is known to the world."

Presently a man with a child beside him, with a large black horse, and a weather-beaten chair, once built for a chaise-body, passed in great haste, apparently at the rate of twelve miles an hour. He seemed to grasp the reins of his horse with firmness, and appeared to anticipate his speed. He seemed dejected, and looked anxiously at the passengers, particularly at the stage-driver and myself. In a moment after he passed us, the horses' ears were up, and bent themselves forward so that they nearly met.

"Who is that man?" said I; "he seems in great trouble."

"Nobody knows who he is, but his person and the child are familiar to me. I have met him more than a hundred times, and have been so often asked the way to Boston by that man, even when he was traveling directly from that town, that of late I have refused any communication with him; and that is the reason he gave me such a fixed look."

"But does he never stop anywhere?"

"I have never known him to stop anywhere longer than to inquire the way to Boston; and let him be where he may, he will tell you he cannot stay a moment, for he must reach Boston that night."

We were now ascending a high hill in Walpole; and as we had a fair view of the heavens, I was rather disposed to jeer the driver for thinking of his surtout, as not a cloud as big as a marble could be discerned.

"Do you look," said he, "in the direction whence the man came; that is the place to look. The storm never meets him; it follows him."

We presently approached another hill; and when at the height, the driver pointed out in an eastern direction a little black speck about as big as a hat. "There," said he, "is the seed-storm. We may possibly reach Polley's before it reaches us, but the wanderer and his child will go to Providence through rain, thunder and lightning."

And now the horses, as though taught by instinct, hastened with increased speed. The little black cloud came on rolling over the turnpike, and doubled and trebled itself in all directions. The appearance of this cloud attracted the notice of all the passengers, for after it had spread itself to a great bulk it suddenly became more limited in circumference, grew more compact, dark, and consolidated. And now the successive flashes of chain lightning caused the whole cloud to appear like a sort of irregular network, and displayed a thousand fantastic images. The driver bespoke my attention to a remarkable configuration in the cloud. He said every flash of lightning near its center discovered to him, distinctly, the form of a man sitting in an open carriage drawn by a black horse. But in truth I saw no such thing; the man's fancy was doubtless at fault. It is a very common thing for the imagination to paint for the senses, both in the visible and invisible world.

In the meantime the distant thunder gave notice of a shower at hand; and just as we reached Polley's tavern the rain poured down in torrents. It was soon over, the cloud passing in the direction of the turnpike toward Providence. In a few moments after, a respectable-looking man in a chaise stopped at the door. The man and child in the chair having excited some little sympathy among the passengers, the gentleman was asked if he had observed them. He said he had met them; that the man seemed bewildered, and inquired the way to Boston; that he was driving at great speed, as though he expected to outstrip the tempest; that the moment he had passed him, a thunderbolt broke directly over the man's head, and seemed to envelop both man and child, horse and carriage. "I stopped," said the gentleman, "supposing the lightning had struck him; but the horse only seemed to loom up and increase his speed; and as well as I could judge, he traveled just as fast as the thunder-cloud."

While this man was speaking, a peddler with a cart of tin merchandise came up, all dripping; and on being questioned, he said he had met that man and carriage, within a fortnight, in four different states; that at each time he had inquired the way to Boston; and that a thunder-shower like the present had each time deluged his wagon and his wares, setting his tin pots, etc., afloat, so that he had determined to get a marine insurance for the future. But that which excited his surprise most was the strange conduct of his horse, for long before he could distinguish the man in the chair his own horse stood still in the road, and flung back his ears. "In short," said the peddler, "I wish never to see that man and horse again; they do not look to me as though they belonged to this world."

This was all I could learn at that time; and the occurrence soon after would have become with me "like one of those things which had never happened," had I not, as I stood recently on the door-step of Bennett's hotel in Hartford, heard a man say, "There goes Peter Rugg and his child! He looks wet and weary, and farther from Boston than ever." I was satisfied it was the same man I had seen more than three years before; for whoever has once seen Peter Rugg can never after be deceived as to his identity.

"Peter Rugg!" said I; "and who is Peter Rugg?"

"That," said the stranger, "is more than

any one can tell exactly. He is a famous traveler, held in light esteem by all inn-holders, for he never stops to eat, drink, or sleep. I wonder why the government does not employ him to carry the mail."

"Aye," said a bystander, "that is a thought bright only on one side; how long would it take in that case to send a letter to Boston, for Peter has already, to my knowledge, been more than twenty years traveling to that place."

"But," said I, "does the man never stop anywhere; does he never converse with any one? I saw the same man more than three years since, near Providence, and I heard a strange story about him. Pray, sir, give me some account of this man."

"Sir," said the stranger, "those who know the most respecting that man say the least. I have heard it asserted that Heaven sometimes sets a mark on a man, either for judgment or a trial. Under which Peter Rugg now labors, I cannot say; therefore I am rather inclined to pity than to judge."

"You speak like a humane man," said I; "and if you have known him so long, I pray you will give me some account of him. Has his appearance much altered in that time?"

"Why, yes. He looks as though he never ate, drank or slept; and his child looks older than himself, and he looks like time broken off from eternity, and anxious to gain a resting-place."

"And how does his horse look?" said I.

"As for his horse, he looks fatter and gayer, and shows more animation and courage than he did twenty years ago. The last time Rugg spoke to me he in-quired how far it was to Boston. I told him just one hundred miles.

"'Why,' said he, 'how can you deceive me so? It is cruel to mislead a traveler. I have lost my way; pray direct me the nearest way to Boston.'

"I repeated, it was one hundred miles.

"'How can you say so?' said he; 'I was told last evening it was but fifty, and I have traveled all night.'

"'But,' said I, 'you are now traveling from Boston. You must turn back.'

"'Alas,' said he, 'it is all turn back! Boston shifts with the wind, and plays all around the compass. One man tells me it is to the east, another to the west; and the guide-posts too, they all point the wrong way.'

"'But will you not stop and rest?' said I; 'you seem wet and weary.'

"'Yes,' said he, 'it has been foul weather since I left home.'

"'Stop, then, and refresh yourself.'

"'I must not stop; I must reach home to-night, if possible: though I think you must be mistaken in the distance to Boston.'

"He then gave the reins to his horse, which he restrained with difficulty, and dis-appeared in a moment. A few days after-ward I met the man a little this side of Claremont, winding around the hills in Unity, at the rate, I believe, of twelve miles an hour."

"Is Peter Rugg his real name, or has he accidentally gained that name?"

"I know not, but presume he will not deny his name; you can ask him—for see, he has turned his horse, and is passing this way."

In a moment a dark-colored, high-spir-ited horse approached, and would have passed without stopping, but I had resolved to speak to Peter Rugg, or whoever the man might be. Accordingly I stepped into the street; and as the horse approached, I made a feint of stopping him. The man im-mediately reined in his horse. "Sir," said I, "may I be so bold as to inquire if you are not Mr. Rugg? for I think I have seen you before."

"My name is Peter Rugg," said he. "I have unfortunately lost my way; I am wet and weary, and will take it kindly of you to direct me to Boston."

"You live in Boston, do you; and in what street?"

"In Middle Street."

"When did you leave Boston?"

"I cannot tell precisely; it seems a con-siderable time."

"But how did you and your child become so wet? It has not rained here to-day."

"It has just rained a heavy shower up the river. But I shall not reach Boston to-night if I tarry. Would you advise me to take the old road or the turnpike?"

"Why, the old road is one hundred and seventeen miles, and the turnpike is ninety-seven."

"How can you say so? You impose on me; it is wrong to trifle with a traveler: you know it is but forty miles from New-buryport to Boston."

"But this is not Newburyport; this is Hartford."

"Do not deceive me, sir. Is not this town Newburyport, and the river that I have been following the Merrimack?"

"No, sir; this is Hartford, and the river, the Connecticut."

He wrung his hands and looked incredulous. "Have the rivers, too, changed their courses, as the cities have changed places? But see! the clouds are gathering in the south, and we shall have a rainy night. Ah, that fatal oath!"

He would tarry no longer; his impatient horse leaped off, his hind flanks rising like wings; he seemed to devour all before him, and to scorn all behind.

I had now, as I thought, discovered a clue to the history of Peter Rugg; and I determined, the next time my business called me to Boston, to make a further inquiry. Soon after, I was enabled to collect the following particulars from Mrs. Croft, an aged lady in Middle Street, who has resided in Boston during the last twenty years. Her narration is this:

Just at twilight last summer a person stopped at the door of the late Mrs. Rugg. Mrs. Croft on coming to the door perceived a stranger, with a child by his side, in an old weather-beaten carriage, with a black horse. The stranger asked for Mrs. Rugg, and was informed that Mrs. Rugg had died at a good old age, more than twenty years before that time.

The stranger replied, "How can you deceive me so? Do ask Mrs. Rugg to step to the door."

"Sir, I assure you Mrs. Rugg has not lived here these twenty years; no one lives here but myself, and my name is Betsy Croft."

The stranger paused, looked up and down the street, and said, "Though the paint is rather faded, this looks like my house."

"Yes," said the child, "that is the stone before the door that I used to sit on to eat my bread and milk."

"But," said the stranger, "it seems to be on the wrong side of the street. Indeed, everything here seems to be misplaced. The streets are all changed, the people are all changed, the town seems changed, and what is strangest of all, Catherine Rugg has deserted her husband and child. Pray," continued the stranger, "has John Foy come home from sea? He went a long voyage; he is my kinsman. If I could see

him, he could give me some account of Mrs. Rugg."

"Sir," said Mrs. Croft, "I never heard of John Foy. Where did he live?"

"Just above here, in Orange-tree Lane."

"There is no such place in this neighborhood."

"What do you tell me! Are the streets gone? Orange-tree Lane is at the head of Hanover Street, near Pemberton Hill."

"There is no such lane now."

"Madam, you cannot be serious! But you doubtless know my brother, William Rugg. He lives in Royal Exchange Lane, near King Street."

"I know of no such lane; and I am sure there is no such street as King Street in this town."

"No such street as King Street! Why, woman, you mock me! You may as well tell me there is no King George. However, madam, you see I am wet and weary, I must find a resting-place. I will go to Hart's tavern, near the market."

"Which market, sir? for you seem perplexed; we have several markets."

"You know there is but one market near the town dock."

"Oh, the old market; but no such person has kept there these twenty years."

Here the stranger seemed disconcerted, and uttered to himself quite audibly: "Strange mistake; how much this looks like the town of Boston! It certainly has a great resemblance to it; but I perceive my mistake now. Some other Mrs. Rugg, some other Middle Street. Then," said he, "madam, can you direct me to Boston?"

"Why, this is Boston, the city of Boston; I know of no other Boston."

"City of Boston it may be; but it is not the Boston where I live. I recollect now, I came over a bridge instead of a ferry. Pray, what bridge is that I just came over?"

"It is Charles River bridge."

"I perceive my mistake; there is a ferry between Boston and Charlestown; there is no bridge. Ah, I perceive my mistake. If I were in Boston my horse would carry me directly to my own door. But my horse shows by his impatience that he is in a strange place. Absurd, that I should have mistaken this place for the old town of Boston. It has been built long since Boston. I fancy Boston must lie at a distance from this city as the good woman seems ignorant of it."

At these words his horse began to chafe, and strike the pavement with his forefeet. The stranger seemed a little bewildered, and said, "No home to-night"; and giving the reins to his horse, passed up the street, and I saw no more of him.

It was evident that the generation to which Peter Rugg belonged had passed away.

This was all the account of Peter Rugg I could obtain from Mrs. Croft; but she directed me to an elderly man, Mr. James Felt, who lived near her, and who had kept a record of the principal occurrences for the last fifty years. At my request she sent for him; and after I had related to him the object of my inquiry, Mr. Felt told me he had known Rugg in his youth, and that his disappearance had caused some surprise; but as it sometimes happens that men run away—sometimes to be rid of others, and sometimes to be rid of themselves—and Rugg took his child with him, and his own horse and chair, and as it did not appear that any creditors made a stir, the occurrence soon mingled itself in the stream of oblivion; and Rugg and his child, horse, and chair were soon forgotten.

"It is true," said Mr. Felt, "sundry stories grew out of Rugg's affair, whether true or false I cannot tell; but stranger things have happened in my day, without even a newspaper notice."

"Sir," said I, "Peter Rugg is now living. I have lately seen Peter Rugg and his child, horse and chair; therefore I pray you to relate to me all you know or ever heard of him."

"Why, my friend," said James Felt, "that Peter Rugg is now a living man, I will not deny; but that you have seen Peter Rugg and his child, is impossible, if you mean a small child; for Jenny Rugg, if living, must be at least—let me see—Boston massacre, 1770—Jenny Rugg was about ten years old. Why, sir, Jenny Rugg, if living, must be more than sixty years of age. That Peter Rugg is living, is highly probable, as he was only ten years older than myself, and I was only eighty last March; and I am as likely to live twenty years longer as any man."

Here I perceived that Mr. Felt was in his dotage, and I despaired of gaining any intelligence from him on which I could depend.

I took my leave of Mrs. Croft, and proceeded to my lodging at the Marlborough Hotel.

"If Peter Rugg," thought I, "has been traveling since the Boston massacre, there is no reason why he should not travel to the end of time. If the present generation know little of him, the next will know less, and Peter and his child will have no hold on this world."

In the course of the evening, I related my adventure in Middle Street.

"Ha!" said one of the company, smiling, "do you really think you have seen Peter Rugg? I have heard my grandfather speak of him, as though he seriously believed his own story."

"Sir," said I, "pray let us compare your grandfather's story of Mr. Rugg with my own."

"Peter Rugg, sir—if my grandfather was worthy of credit—once lived in Middle Street, in this city. He was a man in comfortable circumstances, had a wife and one daughter, and was generally esteemed for his sober life and manners. But unhappily, his temper, at times, was altogether ungovernable, and then his language was terrible. In these fits of passion, if a door stood in his way, he would never do less than kick a panel through. He would sometimes throw his heels over his head, and come down on his feet, uttering oaths in a circle; and thus in a rage, he was the first who performed a somerset, and did what others have since learned to do for merriment and money. Once Rugg was seen to bite a tenpenny nail in halves. In those days everybody, both men and boys, wore wigs; and Peter, at these moments of violent passion, would become so profane that his wig would rise up from his head. Some said it was on account of his terrible language; others accounted for it in a more philosophical way, and said it was caused by the expansion of his scalp, as violent passion, we know, will swell the veins and expand the head. While these fits were on him, Rugg had no respect for heaven or earth. Except this infirmity, all agreed that Rugg was a good sort of a man; for when his fits were over, nobody was so ready to commend a placid temper as Peter.

"One morning, late in autumn, Rugg, in his own chair, with a fine large bay horse, took his daughter and proceeded to Concord. On his return a violent storm overtook him. At dark he stopped in Menotomy, now West Cambridge, at the door of a Mr. Cutter, a friend of his, who urged him to tarry the night. On Rugg's declining to stop, Mr. Cutter urged him vehemently. 'Why, Mr. Rugg,' said Cutter, 'the storm is overwhelming you. The night is exceedingly dark. Your little daughter will perish. You are in an open chair, and the tempest is increasing.' *'Let the storm increase,'* said Rugg, with a fearful oath, *'I will see home to-night, in spite of the last tempest, or may I never see home!'* At these words he gave his whip to his high-spirited horse and disappeared in a moment. But Peter Rugg did not reach home that night, nor the next; nor, when he became a missing man, could he ever be traced beyond Mr. Cutter's in Menotomy.

"For a long time after, on every dark and stormy night the wife of Peter Rugg would fancy she heard the crack of a whip, and the fleet tread of a horse, and the rattling of a carriage passing her door. The neighbors, too, heard the same noises, and some said they knew it was Rugg's horse; the tread on the pavement was perfectly familiar to them. This occurred so repeatedly that at length the neighbors watched with lanterns, and saw the real Peter Rugg, with his own horse and chair and the child sitting beside him, pass directly before his own door, his head turned toward his house, and himself making every effort to stop his horse, but in vain.

"The next day the friends of Mrs. Rugg exerted themselves to find her husband and child. They inquired at every public house and stable in town; but it did not appear that Rugg made any stay in Boston. No one, after Rugg had passed his own door, could give any account of him, though it was asserted by some that the clatter of Rugg's horse and carriage over the pavements shook the houses on both sides of the streets. And this is credible, if indeed Rugg's horse and carriage did pass on that night; for at this day, in many of the streets, a loaded truck or team in passing will shake the houses like an earthquake. However, Rugg's neighbors never afterward watched. Some of them treated it all as a delusion, and thought no more of it. Others of a different opinion shook their heads and said nothing.

"Thus Rugg and his child, horse, and chair were soon forgotten; and probably many in the neighborhood never heard a word on the subject.

"There was indeed a rumor that Rugg was seen afterward in Connecticut, between Suffield and Hartford, passing through the country at headlong speed. This gave occasion to Rugg's friends to make further inquiry; but the more they inquired, the more they were baffled. If they heard of Rugg one day in Connecticut, the next day they heard of him winding round the hills in New Hampshire; and soon after a man in a chair, with a small child, exactly answering the description of Peter Rugg, would be seen in Rhode Island inquiring the way to Boston.

"But that which chiefly gave a color of mystery to the story of Peter Rugg was the affair at Charlestown bridge. The toll-gatherer asserted that sometimes, on the darkest and most stormy nights, when no object could be discerned, about the time Rugg was missing, a horse and wheel-carriage, with a noise equal to a troop, would at midnight, in utter contempt of the rates of toll, pass over the bridge. This occurred so frequently that the toll-gatherer resolved to attempt a discovery. Soon after, at the usual time, apparently the same horse and carriage approached the bridge from Charlestown square. The toll-gatherer, prepared, took his stand as near the middle of the bridge as he dared, with a large three-legged stool in his hand; as the appearance passed, he threw the stool at the horse, but heard nothing except the noise of the stool skipping across the bridge. The toll-gatherer on the next day asserted that the stool went directly through the body of the horse, and he persisted in that belief ever after. Whether Rugg, or whoever the person was, ever passed the bridge again, the toll-gatherer would never tell; and when questioned, seemed anxious to waive the subject. And thus Peter Rugg and his child, horse, and carriage, remain a mystery to this day."

This, sir, is all that I could learn of Peter Rugg in Boston.

II

In the autumn of 1825 I attended the races at Richmond in Virginia. As two new horses of great promise were run, the race-ground was never better attended, nor was expectation ever more deeply excited. The partisans of Dart and Lightning, the two race-horses, were equally anxious and equally dubious of the result.

To an indifferent spectator, it was impossible to perceive any difference. They were equally beautiful to behold, alike in color and height, and as they stood side by side they measured from heel to forefeet within half an inch of each other. The eyes of each were full, prominent, and resolute; and when at times they regarded each other, they assumed a lofty demeanor, seemed to shorten their necks, project their eyes, and rest their bodies equally on their four hoofs. They certainly showed signs of intelligence, and displayed a courtesy to each other unusual even with statesmen.

It was now nearly twelve o'clock, the hour of expectation, doubt, and anxiety. The riders mounted their horses; and so trim, light, and airy they sat on the animals as to seem a part of them. The spectators, many deep in a solid column, had taken their places, and as many thousand breathing statues were there as spectators. All eyes were turned to Dart and Lightning and their two fairy riders. There was nothing to disturb this calm except a busy woodpecker on a neighboring tree. The signal was given, and Dart and Lightning answered it with ready intelligence. At first they proceed at a slow trot, then they quicken to a canter, and then a gallop; presently they sweep the plain. Both horses lay themselves flat on the ground, their riders bending forward and resting their chins between their horses' ears. Had not the ground been perfectly level, had there been any undulation, the least rise and fall, the spectator would now and then have lost sight of both horses and riders.

While these horses, side by side, thus appeared, flying without wings, flat as a hare, and neither gaining on the other, all eyes were diverted to a new spectacle. Directly in the rear of Dart and Lightning, a majestic black horse of unusual size, drawing an old weather-beaten chair, strode over the plain; and although he appeared to make no effort, for he maintained a steady trot, before Dart and Lightning approached the goal the black horse and chair had overtaken the racers, who, on perceiving this new competitor pass them, threw back their ears, and suddenly stopped in their course. Thus neither Dart nor Lightning carried away the purse.

The spectators now were exceedingly curious to learn whence came the black horse and chair. With many it was the opinion that nobody was in the vehicle. Indeed, this began to be the prevalent opinion; for those at a short distance, so fleet was the black horse, could not easily discern who, if anybody, was in the carriage. But both the riders, very near to whom the black horse passed, agreed in this particular—that a sad-looking man and a little girl were in the chair. When they stated this I was satisfied that the man was Peter Rugg. But what caused no little surprise, John Spring, one of the riders (he who rode Lightning), asserted that no earthly horse without breaking his trot could, in a carriage, outstrip his race-horse, and he persisted, with some passion, that it was not a horse—or, he was sure it was not a horse, but a large black ox. "What a great black ox can do," said John, "I cannot pretend to say; but no race-horse, not even flying Childers, could outtrot Lightning in a fair race."

This opinion of John Spring excited no little merriment, for it was obvious to every one that it was a powerful black horse that interrupted the race; but John Spring, jealous of Lightning's reputation as a horse, would rather have it thought that any other beast, even an ox, had been the victor. However, the "horse-laugh" at John Spring's expense was soon suppressed; for as soon as Dart and Lightning began to breathe more freely, it was observed that both of them walked deliberately to the track of the race-ground, and putting their heads to the earth, suddenly raised them again and began to snort. They repeated this till John Spring said, "These horses have discovered something strange; they suspect foul play. Let me go and talk with Lightning."

He went up to Lightning and took hold of his mane; and Lightning put his nose toward the ground and smelt of the earth without touching it, then reared his head very high, and snorted so loudly that the sound echoed from the next hill. Dart did the same. John Spring stooped down to examine the spot where Lightning had smelled. In a moment he raised himself up, and the countenance of the man was changed. His strength failed him, and he sidled against Lightning.

At length John Spring recovered from his stupor and exclaimed, "It was an ox! I told you it was an ox. No real horse ever yet beat Lightning."

And, now, on a close inspection of the

black horse's tracks in the path, it was evident to every one that the forefeet of the black horse were cloven. Notwithstanding these appearances, to me it was evident that the strange horse was in reality a horse. Yet when the people left the raceground, I presume one half of all those present would have testified that a large black ox had distanced two of the fleetest coursers that ever trod the Virginia turf. So uncertain are all things called historical facts.

While I was proceeding to my lodgings, pondering on the events of the day, a stranger rode up to me, and accosted me thus: "I think your name is Dunwell, sir."

"Yes, sir," I replied.

"Did I not see you a year or two since in Boston, at the Marlborough Hotel?"

"Very likely, sir, for I was there."

"And you heard a story about one Peter Rugg?"

"I recollect it all," said I.

"The account you heard in Boston must be true, for here he was to-day. The man has found his way to Virginia, and for aught that appears, has been to Cape Horn. I have seen him before to-day, but never saw him travel with such fearful velocity. Pray, sir, where does Peter Rugg spend his winters, for I have seen him only in summer, and always in foul weather except this time?"

I replied, "No one knows where Peter Rugg spends his winters; where or what he eats, drinks, sleeps, or lodges. He seems to have an indistinct idea of day and night, time and space, storm and sunshine. His only object is Boston. It appears to me that Rugg's horse has some control of the chair; and that Rugg himself is, in some sort, under the control of his horse."

I then inquired of the stranger where he first saw the man and horse.

"Why, sir," he said, "in the summer of 1824, I traveled to the North for my health; and soon after I saw you at the Marlborough Hotel I returned homeward to Virginia, and, if my memory is correct, I saw this man and horse in every state between here and Massachusetts. Sometimes he would meet me, but oftener overtake me. He never spoke but once, and that once was in Delaware. On his approach he checked his horse with some difficulty. A more beautiful horse I never saw; his hide was as fair and rotund and glossy as the skin of a Congo beauty. When Rugg's horse approached mine he reined in his neck, bent his ears forward until they met, and looked my horse full in the face. My horse immediately withered into half a horse, his hide curling up like a piece of burnt leather; spellbound, he was fixed to the earth as though a nail had been driven through each hoof.

" 'Sir,' said Rugg, 'perhaps you are traveling to Boston; and if so, I should be happy to accompany you, for I have lost my way, and I must reach home to-night. See how sleepy this little girl looks; poor thing, she is a picture of patience.'

" 'Sir,' I said, 'it is impossible for you to reach home to-night, for you are in Concord, in the county of Sussex, in the state of Delaware.'

" 'What do you mean,' said he, 'by state of Delaware? If I were in Concord, that is only twenty miles from Boston, and my horse Lightfoot could carry me to Charlestown ferry in less than two hours. You mistake, sir; you are a stranger here; this town is nothing like Concord. I am well acquainted with Concord. I went to Concord when I left Boston.'

" 'But,' said I, 'you are in Concord, in the state of Delaware.'

" 'What do you mean by state?' said Rugg.

" 'Why, one of the United States.'

" 'States'! said he, in a low voice; 'the man is a wag, and would persuade me I am in Holland.' Then, raising his voice, he said, 'You seem, sir, to be a gentleman, and I entreat you to mislead me not: tell me, quickly, for pity's sake, the right road to Boston, for you see my horse will swallow his bits; he has eaten nothing since I left Concord.'

" 'Sir,' said I, 'this town is Concord—Concord in Delaware, not Concord in Massachusetts; and you are now five hundred miles from Boston.'

"Rugg looked at me for a moment, more in sorrow than resentment, and then repeated, 'Five hundred miles! Unhappy man, who would have thought him deranged; but nothing in this world is so deceitful as appearances. Five hundred miles! This beats Connecticut River.'

"What he meant by Connecticut River, I know not; his horse broke away, and Rugg disappeared in a moment."

I explained to the stranger the meaning of Rugg's expression, "Connecticut River," and the incident respecting him that occurred at Hartford, as I stood on the doorstone of Mr. Bennett's excellent hotel. We both agreed that the man we had seen that day was the true Peter Rugg.

Soon after, I saw Rugg again, at the toll-gate on the turnpike between Alexandria and Middleburgh. While I was paying the toll, I observed to the toll-gatherer that the drought was more severe in his vicinity than farther south.

"Yes," said he, "the drought is excessive; but if I had not heard yesterday, by a traveler, that the man with the black horse was seen in Kentucky a day or two since, I should be sure of a shower in a few minutes."

I looked all around the horizon, and could not discern a cloud that could hold a pint of water.

"Look, sir," said the toll-gatherer, "you perceive to the eastward, just above that hill, a small black cloud not bigger than a blackberry, and while I am speaking it is doubling and trebling itself, and rolling up the turnpike steadily, as if its sole design was to deluge some object."

"True," said I, "I do perceive it; but what connection is there between a thunder-cloud and a man and horse?"

"More than you imagine, or I can tell you; but stop a moment, sir, I may need your assistance. I know that cloud; I have seen it several times before, and can testify to its identity. You will soon see a man and black horse under it."

While he was speaking, true enough, we began to hear the distant thunder, and soon the chain-lightning performed all the figures of a country-dance. About a mile distant we saw the man and black horse under the cloud; but before he arrived at the toll-gate, the thunder-cloud had spent itself, and not even a sprinkle fell near us.

As the man, whom I instantly knew to be Rugg, attempted to pass, the toll-gatherer swung the gate across the road, seized Rugg's horse by the reins, and demanded two dollars.

Feeling some little regard for Rugg, I interfered, and began to question the toll-gatherer, and requested him not to be wroth with the man. The toll-gatherer replied that he had just cause, for the man had run his toll ten times, and moreover that the horse had discharged a cannon-ball at him, to the great danger of his life; that the man had always before approached so rapidly that he was too quick for the

rusty hinges of the toll-gate; "but now I will have full satisfaction."

Rugg looked wistfully at me, and said, "I entreat you, sir, to delay me not; I have found at length the direct road to Boston, and shall not reach home before night if you detain me. You see I am dripping wet, and ought to change my clothes."

The toll-gatherer then demanded why he had run his toll so many times.

"Toll! Why," said Rugg, "do you demand toll? There is no toll to pay on the king's highway."

"King's highway! Do you not perceive this is a turnpike?"

"Turnpike! there are no turnpikes in Massachusetts."

"That may be, but we have several in Virginia."

"Virginia! Do you pretend I am in Virginia?"

Rugg then, appealing to me, asked how far it was to Boston.

Said I, "Mr. Rugg, I perceive you are bewildered, and am sorry to see you so far from home; you are, indeed, in Virginia."

"You know me, then, sir, it seems; and you say I am in Virginia. Give me leave to tell you, sir, you are the most impudent man alive; for I was never forty miles from Boston, and I never saw a Virginian in my life. This beats Delaware!"

"Your toll, sir, your toll!"

"I will not pay you a penny," said Rugg; "you are both of you highway robbers. There are no turnpikes in this country. Take toll on the king's highway! Robbers take toll on the king's highway!" Then in a low tone, he said, "Here is evidently a conspiracy against me; alas, I shall never see Boston! The highways refuse me a passage, the rivers change their courses, and there is no faith in the compass."

But Rugg's horse had no idea of stopping more than one minute; for in the midst of this altercation, the horse, whose nose was resting on the upper bar of the turnpike-gate, seized it between his teeth, lifted it gently off its staples, and trotted off with it. The toll-gatherer, confounded, strained his eyes after his gate.

"Let him go," said I, "the horse will soon drop your gate, and you will get it again."

I then questioned the toll-gatherer respecting his knowledge of this man; and he related the following particulars:

"The first time," said he, "that man ever

passed this toll-gate was in the year 1806, at the moment of the great eclipse. I thought the horse was frightened at the sudden darkness, and concluded he had run away with the man. But within a few days after, the same man and horse repassed with equal speed, without the least respect to the toll-gate or to me, except by a vacant stare. Some few years afterward, during the late war, I saw the same man approaching again, and I resolved to check his career. Accordingly I stepped into the middle of the road, and stretched wide both my arms, and cried, 'Stop, sir, on your peril!' At this the man said, 'Now, Lightfoot, confound the robber!' At the same time he gave the whip liberally to the flank of his horse, which bounded off with such force that it appeared to me two such horses, give them a place to stand, would overcome any check man could devise. An ammunition wagon which had just passed on to Baltimore had dropped an eighteen pounder in the road; this unlucky ball lay in the way of the horse's reels, and the beast, with the sagacity of a demon, clinched it with one of his heels and hurled it behind him. I feel dizzy in relating the fact, but so nearly did the ball pass my head, that the wind thereof blew off my hat; and the ball embedded itself in that gate-post, as you may see if you will cast your eye on the post. I have permitted it to remain there in memory of the occurrence—as the people of Boston, I am told, preserve the eighteen-pounder which is now to be seen half embedded in Brattle Street church."

I then took leave of the toll-gatherer, and promised him if I saw or heard of his gate I would send him notice.

A strong inclination had possessed me to arrest Rugg and search his pockets, thinking great discoveries might be made in the examination; but what I saw and heard that day convinced me that no human force could detain Peter Rugg against his consent. I therefore determined if I ever saw Rugg again to treat him in the gentlest manner.

In pursuing my way to New York, I entered on the turnpike in Trenton; and when I arrived at New Brunswick, I perceived the road was newly macadamized. The small stones had just been laid thereon. As I passed this piece of road, I observed that, at regular distances of about eight feet, the stones were entirely displaced from spots as large as the circumference of a half-bushel measure. This singular appearance induced me to enquire the cause of it at the turnpike-gate.

"Sir," said the toll-gatherer, "I wonder not at the question, but I am unable to give you a satisfactory answer. Indeed, sir, I believe I am bewitched, and that the turnpike is under a spell of enchantment; for what appeared to me last night cannot be a real transaction, otherwise a turnpike-gate is a useless thing."

"I do not believe in witchcraft or enchantment," said I; "and if you will relate circumstantially what happened last night, I will endeavor to account for it by natural means."

"You may recollect the night was uncommonly dark. Well, sir, just after I had closed the gate for the night, down the turnpike, as far as my eye could reach, I beheld what at first appeared to be two armies engaged. The report of the musketry, and the flashes of their firelocks, were incessant and continuous. As this strange spectacle approached me with the fury of a tornado, the noise increased; and the appearance rolled on in one compact body over the surface of the ground. The most splendid fireworks rose out of the earth and encircled this moving spectacle. The divers tints of the rainbow, the most brilliant dyes that the sun lays in the lap of spring, added to the whole family of gems, could not display a more beautiful, radiant, and dazzling spectacle than accompanied the black horse. You would have thought all the stars of heaven had met in merriment on the turnpike. In the midst of this luminous configuration sat a man, distinctly to be seen, in a miserable-looking chair, drawn by a black horse. The turnpike-gate ought, by the laws of nature and the laws of the state, to have made a wreck of the whole, and have dissolved the enchantment; but no, the horse without an effort passed over the gate, and drew the man and chair horizontally after him without touching the bar. This was what I call enchantment. What think you, sir?"

"My friend," said I, "you have grossly magnified a natural occurrence. The man was Peter Rugg, on his way to Boston. It is true, his horse traveled with unequaled speed, but as he reared high his forefeet, he could not help displacing the thousand small stones on which he trod, which flying in all directions struck one another, and resounded and scintillated. The top bar of your gate is not more than two feet from the ground, and Rugg's horse at every vault could easily lift the carriage over that gate."

This satisfied Mr. McDoubt, and I was pleased at that occurrence; for otherwise Mr. McDoubt, who is a worthy man, late from the Highlands, might have added to his calendar of superstitions. Having thus disenchanted the macadamized road and the turnpike-gate, and also Mr. McDoubt, I pursued my journey homeward to New York.

Little did I expect to see or hear anything further of Mr. Rugg, for he was now more than twelve hours in advance of me. I could hear nothing of him on my way to Elizabethtown, and therefore concluded that during the past night he had turned off from the turnpike and pursued a westerly direction; but just before I arrived at Powles's Hook, I observed a considerable collection of passengers in the ferry-boat, all standing motionless, and steadily looking at the same object. One of the ferry-men, Mr. Hardy, who knew me well, observing my approach, delayed a minute, in order to afford me a passage, and coming up, said, "Mr. Dunwell, we have a curiosity on board that would puzzle Dr. Mitchell."

"Some strange fish, I suppose, has found its way into the Hudson."

"No," said he, "it's a man who looks as if he had lain hidden in the ark, and had just now ventured out. He has a little girl with him, the counterpart of himself, and the finest horse you ever saw, harnessed to the queerest-looking carriage that ever was made."

"Ah, Mr. Hardy," said I, "you have, indeed, hooked a prize; no one before you could ever detain Peter Rugg long enough to examine him."

"Do you know the man?" said Mr. Hardy.

"No, nobody knows him, but everybody has seen him. Detain him as long as possible; delay the boat under any pretense, cut the gear of the horse, do anything to detain him."

As I entered the ferry-boat, I was struck at the spectacle before me. There, indeed, sat Peter Rugg and Jenny Rugg in the chair, and there stood the black horse, all as quiet as lambs, surrounded by more than fifty men and women, who seemed to have lost all their senses but one. Not a motion, not a breath, not a rustle. They were all eye. Rugg appeared to them to be a man not of this world; and they appeared to Rugg a strange generation of men. Rugg spoke not, and they spoke not; nor was I disposed to disturb the calm, satisfied to reconnoiter Rugg in a state of rest. Presently, Rugg observed in a low voice, addressed to nobody, "A new contrivance, horses instead of oars; Boston folks are full of notions."

It was plain that Rugg was of Dutch extraction. He had on three pairs of small clothes, called in former days of simplicity breeches, not much the worse for wear; but time had proved the fabric, and shrunk one more than another, so that they showed at the knees their different qualities and colors. His several waistcoats, the flaps of which rested on his knees, made him appear rather corpulent. His capacious drab coat would supply the stuff for half a dozen modern ones; the sleeves were like meal bags, in the cuffs of which you might nurse a child to sleep. His hat, probably once black, now of a tan color, was neither round nor crooked, but in shape much like the one President Monroe wore on his late tour. This dress gave the rotund face of Rugg an antiquated dignity. The man, though deeply sunburned, did not appear to be more than thirty years of age. He had lost his sad and anxious look, was quite composed, and seemed happy. The chair in which Rugg sat was very capacious, evidently made for service, and calculated to last for ages; the timber would supply material for three modern carriages. This chair, like a Nantucket coach, would answer for everything that ever went on wheels. The horse, too, was an object of curiosity; his majestic height, his natural mane and tail, gave him a commanding appearance, and his large open nostrils indicated inexhaustible wind. It was apparent that the hoofs of his forefeet had been split, probably on some newly macadamized road, and were now growing together again; so that John Spring was not altogether in the wrong.

How long this dumb scene would otherwise have continued I cannot tell. Rugg discovered no sign of impatience. But Rugg's horse having been quiet more than five minutes, had no idea of standing idle; he began to whinny, and in a moment after, with his right forefoot he started a plank. Said Rugg, "My horse is impatient, he sees the North End. You must be quick, or he will be ungovernable."

At these words, the horse raised his left forefoot; and when he laid it down every inch of the ferry-boat trembled. Two men immediately seized Rugg's horse by the nostrils. The horse nodded, and both of them were in the Hudson. While we were fishing up the men, the horse was perfectly quiet.

"Fret not the horse," said Rugg, "and he will do no harm. He is only anxious, like myself, to arrive at yonder beautiful shore; he sees the North Church, and smells his own stable."

"Sir," said I to Rugg, practising a little deception, "pray tell me, for I am a stranger here, what river is this, and what city is that opposite, for you seem to be an inhabitant of it?"

"This river, sir, is called Mystic River, and this is Winnisimmet ferry—we have retained the Indian names—and that town is Boston. You must, indeed, be a stranger in these parts, not to know that yonder is Boston, the capital of the New England provinces."

"Pray, sir, how long have you been absent from Boston?"

"Why, that I cannot exactly tell. I lately went with this little girl of mine to Concord, to see my friends; and I am ashamed to tell you, in returning lost the way, and have been traveling ever since. No one would direct me right. It is cruel to mislead a traveler. My horse, Lightfoot, has boxed the compass; and it seems to me he has boxed it back again. But, sir, you perceive my horse is uneasy; Lightfoot, as yet, has only given a hint and a nod. I cannot be answerable for his heels."

At these words Lightfoot reared his long tail, and snapped it as you would a whiplash. The Hudson reverberated with the sound. Instantly the six horses began to move the boat. The Hudson was a sea of glass, smooth as oil, not a ripple. The horses, from a smart trot, soon pressed into a gallop; water now ran over the gunwale; the ferry-boat was soon buried in an ocean of foam, and the noise of the spray was like the roaring of many waters. When we arrived at New York, you might see the beautiful white wake of the ferry-boat across the Hudson.

Though Rugg refused to pay toll at turnpikes, when Mr. Hardy reached his hand for the ferriage, Rugg readily put his hand into one of his many pockets, took out a piece of silver, and handed it to Hardy.

"What is this?" said Mr. Hardy.

"It is thirty shillings," said Rugg.

"It might once have been thirty shillings, old tenor," said Mr. Hardy, "but it is not at present."

"The money is good English coin," said Rugg; "my grandfather brought a bag of them from England, and had them hot from the mint."

Hearing this, I approached near to Rugg, and asked permission to see the coin. It was a half-crown, coined by the English Parliament, dated in the year 1649. On one side, "The Commonwealth of England," and St. George's cross encircled with a wreath of laurel. On the other, "God with us," and a harp and St. George's cross united. I winked at Mr. Hardy, and pronounced it good current money; and said loudly, "I will not permit the gentleman to be imposed on, for I will exchange the money myself."

On this, Rugg spoke: "Please to give me your name, sir."

"My name is Dunwell, sir," I replied.

"Mr. Dunwell," said Rugg, "you are the only honest man I have seen since I left Boston. As you are a stranger here, my house is your home; Dame Rugg will be happy to see her husband's friend. Step into my chair, sir, there is room enough; move a little, Jenny, for the gentleman, and we will be in Middle Street in a minute."

Accordingly I took a seat by Peter Rugg.

"Were you never in Boston before?" said Rugg.

"No," said I.

"Well, you will now see the queen of New England, a town second only to Philadelphia, in all North America."

"You forget New York," said I.

"Poh, New York is nothing; though I never was there. I am told you might put all New York in our mill-pond. No, sir, New York, I assure you, is but a sorry affair; no more to be compared with Boston than a wigwam with a palace."

As Rugg's horse turned into Pearl Street, I looked Rugg as fully in the face as good manners would allow, and said, "Sir, if this is Boston, I acknowledge New York is not worthy to be one of its suburbs."

Before we had proceeded far in Pearl Street, Rugg's countenance changed: his nerves began to twitch; his eyes trembled in their sockets; he was evidently bewildered. "What is the matter, Mr. Rugg; you seem disturbed."

"This surpasses all human comprehension; if you know, sir, where we are, I beseech you to tell me."

"If this place," I replied, "is not Boston, it must be New York."

"No, sir, it is not Boston; nor can it be New York. How could I be in New York, which is nearly two hundred miles from Boston?"

By this time we had passed into Broadway, and then Rugg, in truth, discovered a chaotic mind. "There is no such place as this in North America. This is all the effect of enchantment; this is a grand delusion, nothing real. Here is seemingly a great city, magnificent houses, shops and goods, men and women innumerable, and as busy as in real life, all sprung up in one night from the wilderness; or what is more probable, some tremendous convulsion of nature has thrown London or Amsterdam on the shores of New England. Or, possibly, I may be dreaming, though the night seems rather long; but before now I have sailed in one night to Amsterdam, bought goods of Vandogger, and returned to Boston before morning."

At this moment a hue-and-cry was heard, "Stop the madmen, they will endanger the lives of thousands!" In vain hundreds attempted to stop Rugg's horse. Lightfoot interfered with nothing; his course was straight as a shooting-star. But on my part, fearful that before night I should find myself behind the Alleghanies, I addressed Mr. Rugg in a tone of entreaty, and requested him to restrain the horse and permit me to alight.

"My friend," said he, "we shall be in Boston before dark, and Dame Rugg will be most exceeding glad to see us."

"Mr. Rugg," said I, "you must excuse me. Pray look to the west; see that thunder-cloud swelling with rage, as if in pursuit of us."

"Ah!" said Rugg, "it is in vain to attempt to escape. I know that cloud; it is collecting new wrath to spend on my head." Then checking his horse, he permitted me to descend, saying, "Farewell, Mr. Dunwell, I shall be happy to see you in Boston; I live in Middle Street."

It is uncertain in what direction Mr. Rugg pursued his course, after he disappeared in Broadway; but one thing is sufficiently known to everybody—that in course of two months after he was seen in New York, he found his way most opportunely to Boston.

It seems the estate of Peter Rugg had recently fallen to the Commonwealth of Massachusetts for want of heirs; and the Legislature had ordered the solicitor-general to advertise and sell it at public auction. Happening to be in Boston at the time, and observing his advertisement, which described a considerable extent of land, I felt a kindly curiosity to see the spot where Rugg once lived. Taking the advertisement in my hand, I wandered a little way down Middle Street, and without asking a question of any one, when I came to a certain spot I said to myself, "This is Rugg's estate; I will proceed no farther. This must be the spot; it is a counterpart of Peter Rugg." The premises, indeed, looked as if they had fulfilled a sad prophecy. Fronting on Middle Street, they extended in the rear to Ann Street, and embraced about half an acre of land. It was not uncommon in former times to have half an acre for a house-lot; for an acre of land then, in many parts of Boston, was not more valuable than a foot in some places at present. The old mansion-house had become a powder-post, and been blown away. One other building, uninhabited, stood ominous, courting dilapidation. The street had been so much raised that the bedchamber had descended to the kitchen and was level with the street. The house seemed conscious of its fate; and as though tired of standing there, the front was fast retreating from the rear, and waiting the next south wind to project itself into the street. If the most wary animals had sought a place of refuge, here they would have rendezvoused. Here, under the ridge-pole, the crow would have perched in security; and in the recesses below, you might have caught the fox and the weasel asleep. "The hand of destiny," said I, "has pressed heavy on this spot; still heavier on the former owners. Strange that so large a lot of land as this should want an heir! Yet Peter Rugg, at this day, might pass by his own door-stone, and ask, 'Who once lived here?'"

The auctioneer, appointed by the solicitor to sell this estate, was a man of eloquence, as many of the auctioneers of Boston are. The occasion seemed to warrant, and his duty urged, him to make a display. He addressed his audience as follows:

"The estate, gentlemen, which we offer you this day, was once the property of a family now extinct. For that reason it has escheated to the Commonwealth. Lest any one of you should be deterred from bidding on so large an estate as this for fear of a disputed title, I am authorized by the solicitor-general to proclaim that the purchaser shall have the best of all titles—a warranty-deed from the Commonwealth. I state this, gentlemen, because I know there is an idle rumor in this vicinity, that one Peter Rugg, the original owner of this estate, is still living. This rumor, gentlemen, has no foundation, and can have no foundation in the nature of things. It originated about two years since, from the incredible story of one Jonathan Dunwell, of New York. Mrs. Croft, indeed, whose husband I see present, and whose mouth waters for this estate, has countenanced this fiction. But, gentlemen, was it ever known that any estate, especially an estate of this value, lay unclaimed for nearly half a century, if any heir, ever so remote, were existing? For, gentlemen, all agree that old Peter Rugg, if living, would be at least one hundred years of age. It is said that he and his daughter, with a horse and chaise, were missed more than half a century ago; and because they never returned home, forsooth, they must be now living, and will some day come and claim this great estate. Such logic, gentlemen, never led to a good investment. Let not this idle story cross the noble purpose of consigning these ruins to the genius of architecture. If such a contingency could check the spirit of enterprise, farewell to all mercantile excitement. Your surplus money, instead of refreshing your sleep with the golden dreams of new sources of speculation, would turn to the nightmare. A man's money, if not employed, serves only to disturb his rest. Look, then, to the prospect before you. Here is half an acre of land —more than twenty thousand square feet —a corner lot, with wonderful capabilities; none of your contracted lots of forty feet by fifty, where, in dog-days, you can breathe only through your scuttles. On the contrary, an architect cannot contemplate this lot of land without rapture, for here

is room enough for his genius to shame the temple of Solomon. Then the prospect— how commanding! To the east, so near to the Atlantic that Neptune, freighted with the select treasures of the whole earth, can knock at your door with his trident. From the west, the produce of the river of Paradise—the Connecticut—will soon, by the blessings of steam, railways, and canals pass under your windows; and thus, on this spot, Neptune shall marry Ceres, and Pomona from Roxbury, and Flora from Cambridge, shall dance at the wedding.

"Gentlemen of science, men of taste, ye of the literary emporium—for I perceive many of you present—to you this is holy ground. If the spot on which in times past a hero left only the print of a footstep is now sacred, of what price is the birthplace of one who all the world knows was born in Middle Street, directly opposite to this lot; and who, if his birthplace were not well known, would now be claimed by more than seven cities. To you, then, the value of these premises must be inestimable. For ere long there will arise in full view of the edifice to be erected here, a monument, the wonder and veneration of the world. A column shall spring to the clouds; and on that column will be engraven one word which will convey all that is wise in intellect, useful in science, good in morals, prudent in counsel, and benevolent in principle—a name of one who, when living, was the patron of the poor, the delight of the cottage, and the admiration of kings; now dead, worth the whole seven wise men of Greece. Need I tell you his name? He fixed the thunder and guided the lightning.

"Men of the North End! Need I appeal to your patriotism, in order to enhance the value of this lot? The earth affords no such scenery as this; there, around that corner, lived James Otis; here, Samuel Adams; there, Joseph Warren; and around that other corner, Josiah Quincy. Here was the birthplace of Freedom; here Liberty was born, and nursed, and grew to manhood. Here man was newly created. Here is the nursery of American Independence—I am too modest—here began the emancipation of the world; a thousand generations hence millions of men will cross the Atlantic just to look at the North End of Boston. Your fathers— what do I say—yourselves—yes, this moment, I behold several attending this auction who lent a hand to rock the cradle of Independence.

"Men of speculation—ye who are deaf to everything except the sound of money—you, I know, will give me both your ears when I tell you the city of Boston must have a piece of this estate in order to widen Ann Street. Do you hear me—do you all hear me? I say the city must have a large piece of this land in order to widen Ann Street. What a chance! The city scorns to take a man's land for nothing. If it seizes your property, it is generous beyond the dreams of avarice. The only oppression is, you are in danger of being smothered under a load of wealth. Witness the old lady who lately died of a broken heart when the mayor paid her for a piece of her kitchen-garden. All the faculty agreed that the sight of the treasure, which the mayor incautiously paid her in dazzling dollars, warm from the mint, sped joyfully all the blood of her body into her heart, and rent it with raptures. Therefore, let him who purchases this estate fear his good fortune, and not Peter Rugg. Bid, then, liberally, and do not let the name of Rugg damp your ardor. How mucl. will you give per foot for this estate?"

Thus spoke the auctioneer, and gracefully waved his ivory hammer. From fifty to seventy-five cents per foot were offered in a few moments. The bidding labored from seventy-five to ninety. At length one dollar was offered. The auctioneer seemed satisfied; and looking at his watch, said he would knock off the estate in five minutes, if no one offered more.

There was a deep silence during this short period. While the hammer was suspended, a strange rumbling noise was heard, which arrested the attention of every one. Presently, it was like the sound of many shipwrights driving home the bolts of a seventy-four. As the sound approached nearer, some exclaimed, "The buildings in the new market are falling in promiscuous ruins." Others said, "No, it is an earthquake; we perceive the earth tremble." Others said, "Not so; the sound proceeds from Hanover Street, and approaches nearer;" and this proved true, for presently Peter Rugg was in the midst of us.

"Alas, Jenny," said Peter, "I am ruined; our house has been burned, and here are all our neighbors around the ruins. Heaven grant your mother, Dame Rugg, is safe."

"They don't look like our neighbors," said Jenny; "but sure enough our house is burned, and nothing left but the doorstone and an old cedar post. Do ask where mother is."

In the meantime more than a thousand men had surrounded Rugg and his horse and chair. Yet neither Rugg personally, nor his horse and carriage, attracted more attention than the auctioneer. The confident look and searching eyes of Rugg carried more conviction to every one present that the estate was his than could any parchment or paper with signature and seal. The impression which the auctioneer had just made on the company was effaced in a moment; and although the latter words of the auctioneer were, "Fear not Peter Rugg," the moment the auctioneer met the eye of Rugg his occupation was gone; his arm fell down to his hips, his late lively hammer hung heavy in his hand, and the auction was forgotten. The black horse, too, gave his evidence. He knew his journey was ended; for he stretched himself into a horse and a half, rested his head over the cedar post, and whinnied thrice, causing his harness to tremble from headstall to crupper.

Rugg then stood upright in his chair, and asked with some authority, "Who has demolished my house in my absence, for I see no signs of a conflagration? I demand by what accident this has happened, and wherefore this collection of strange people has assembled before my door-step. I thought I knew every man in Boston, but you appear to me a new generation of men. Yet I am familiar with many of the countenances here present, and I can call some of you by name; but in truth I do not recollect that before this moment I ever saw any one of you. There, I am certain, is a Winslow, and here a Sargent; there stands a Sewall, and next to him a Dudley. Will none of you speak to me,—or is this all a delusion? I see, indeed, many forms of men, and no want of eyes, but of motion, speech, and hearing, you seem to be destitute. Strange! Will no one inform me who has demolished my house?"

Then spake a voice from the crowd, but whence it came I could not discern: "There is nothing strange here but yourself, Mr. Rugg. Time, which destroys and renews all things, has dilapidated your house, and placed us here. You have suffered many years under an illusion. The tempest which you profanely defied at Menotomy has at length subsided; but you will never see home, for your house and wife and neighbors have all disappeared. Your estate, indeed, remains, but no home. You were cut off from the last age, and you can never be fitted to the present. Your home is gone, and you 5 can never have another home in this world."

III

JAMES KIRKE PAULDING (1779–1860)

The period from 1830 to 1850 in the history of American short story form is the period of the "gift-books" and "annuals," like *The Atlantic Souvenir, The Token,* and *The Gift.* The most sought-for contributors to these miscellanies seem to have been Catharine M. Sedgwick and James K. Paulding, each of whom produced a surprising number of shortened fictions. Miss Sedgwick, however, has small part in the history of the short story. She never awoke to the fact that the tale was at all different from the novel, and she wrote therefore nothing but truncated romances, stories handled in the first part as if she had unlimited space and then ended in a huddle. Paulding, however, despite a similar tendency to prolixity, at times achieved really distinctive short-story work. He had worked with Irving during the period when the *Salmagundi Papers* had been issued, and he had caught Irving's mannerisms and, unconsciously perhaps, had imitated them. There is wit abundant in his work, there is a play of sentiment often skilfully modulated, and at times there is careful attention to plot and dénouement. Most often, too, he used native themes. But he wrote always in a Scott-like, headlong haste, with little revision; he was often over-florid, and over-satiric; and seldom was he convincing. His tales, almost all of them, have been forgotten.

THE YANKEE SCHOOLMASTER

A LEGEND OF THE CITY OF HUDSON

The city of Hudson furnishes one of those examples of rapid growth so common and so peculiar to our country. It goes back no further than 1784, and is said now to contain nearly six thousand inhabitants. But towns, like children, are very apt to grow more in the first years, than all their lives after. But Hudson has a bank, which is a sort of wet-nurse to these little towns, giving them too often a precocious growth, which is followed by a permanent debility. The town is beautifully situated, and the environs of the most picturesque and romantic description. There are several pretty country-seats in the neighborhood. Here ends, according to the law of nature, the ship-navigation of the river; but by a law of the legislature, a company has been incorporated, with a capital of one million dollars—how easy it is to coin money in this way!—to make a canal to New Baltimore: for what purpose, only legislative wisdom can explain. There was likewise an incorporated company, to build a mud-machine for deepening the river. But the river is no deeper than it was, and the canal to New Baltimore is not made,

probably because the million of dollars is not forthcoming. One may pay too dear for a canal as well as a whistle. That canals are far better than rivers, is not 5 to be doubted; but as we get our rivers for nothing, and pay pretty dearly for our canals, I would beg leave to represent in behalf of the poor rivers, that they are entitled to some little consideration, if it is 10 only on the score of coming as free gifts. Hudson is said to be very much infested with politicians, a race of men, who, though they have never been classed among those who live by their own wits, 15 and the little wit of their neighbors, certainly belong to the genus.

Hence to Albany the Hudson gradually decreases in magnitude, changing its character of a mighty river for that of a pleas- 20 ant pastoral stream. The high banks gradually subside into rich flats, portentous of Dutchmen, who light on them as certainly as do the snipes and plovers. "Wisely despising," observes Alderman Janson,* "the 25 barren mountains, which are only made to look at, they passed up on the river from Fort Amsterdam, till they arrived here—

* Alderman Nicholas Nicodemus Janson was the flower of the magistracy of Coxsackie, and died full of years and honor, on St. Nicholas' day, in the year of our Lord, one thousand eight hundred and twenty-seven.—*Paulding's note.*

33

about, and here they pitched their tents. Their descendants still retain possession of the seats of their ancestors, though sorely beset by the march of the human mind, and the progress of public improvement on one hand, and on the other by interlopers from the modern Scythia, the cradle of the human race in the new world—Connecticut.[1] These last, by their pestilent scholarship, and mischievous contrivances of patent ploughs, patent threshing-machines, patent corn-shellers, and patent churns, for the encouragement of domestic industry, have gone near to overset all the statutes of St. Nicholas. The honest burghers of Coeymans, Coxsackie, and New Paltz, still hold out manfully; but alas! the women—the women are prone to backslidings and hankering after novelties. A Dutch damsel can't, for her heart, resist a Connecticut schoolmaster, with his rosy cheeks and store of scholarship, and even honest yffrow herself chuckles a little amatory Dutch at his approach; simpering mightily thereat, and stroking down her apron. A goose betrayed—no, I am wrong—a goose once saved the capitol of Rome; and it is to be feared a woman will finally betray the citadels of Coeymans, Coxsackie, and New Paltz, to the schoolmasters of Connecticut, who circumvent them with outlandish scholarship. These speculations," quoth the worthy alderman, "remind me of the mishap of my unfortunate great-uncle, Douw Van Wezel, who sunk under the star of one of these wandering Homers."

Douw, and little Alida Vander Speigle, had been playmates since their infancy—I was going to say schoolmates, but at that time there was no such thing as school, so far as I can learn, in the neighborhood, to teach the young varlets to chalk naughty words on walls and fences, which is all that learning is good for, for aught I see. Douw was no scholar, so there was no danger of his getting into the state prison for forgery; but it requires but little learning to fall in love. Alida had, however, stayed a whole winter in York, where she learned to talk crooked English, and cock her pretty little pug nose at our good old customs. They were the only offspring of their respective parents, whose farms lay side by side, squinting plainly at matrimony between the young people. Douw and Alida went to church together every Sunday; wandered into the church-

yard, where Alida read the epitaphs for him; and it was the talk of everybody that it would certainly be a match. Douw was a handsome fellow for a Dutchman, though he lacked that effeminate ruddiness which seduces poor ignorant women. He had a stout frame, a bluish complexion, straight black hair, eyes the color of indigo, and as honest a pair of old-fashioned bannister legs, as you would wish to see under a man. It was worth while to make good legs then, when every man wore breeches, and some of the women, too, if report is to be credited. Alida was the prettiest little Dutch damsel that ever had her stocking filled with cake on new year's eve, by the blessed St. Nicholas. I will not describe her, lest my readers should fall in love with her, or at all events weep themselves into Saratoga fountains, when they come to hear the disastrous fate of poor Douw, whose destiny it was—but let us have no anticipations; sufficient for the day is the evil thereof.

It was new year's eve, and Douw was invited to see out the old year at Judge Vander Speigle's, in the honest old Dutch way, under the especial patronage of St. Nicholas. There were glorious doings among the young folks, and the old ones too, for that matter, till one or two, or perhaps three in the morning, when the visitors got into their sleighs and skirred away home, leaving Douw and the fair Alida alone—or as good as alone, for the judge and the yffrow were as sound as a church, in the two chimney-corners. If wine and French liquors, and such trumpery, make a man gallant and adventurous, what will not hot-spiced Santa Cruz achieve? Douw was certainly a little flustered; perhaps it might be predicted of him that he was, as it were, a little tipsey. Certain it is, he waxed brave as a Dutch lion. I'll not swear but that he put his arm round her waist, and kissed the little Dutch girl; but I will swear positively, that before the parties knew whether they were standing on their heads or feet, they had exchanged vows, and had become irrevocably engaged. Whereupon Douw waked the old judge, and asked his consent on the spot. "Yaw, yaw," yawned the judge, and fell fast asleep again in a twinkling. Nothing but the last trumpet would rouse the yffrow till morning.

In the morning, the good yffrow was let into the affair, and began to bestir herself accordingly. I cannot count the sheets, and table-cloths, and towels, the good woman mustered out, nor describe the preparations made for the expected wedding. There was a cake baked as big as Kaatskill mountain, and mince-pies enough to cover it. There were cakes of a hundred nameless names, and sweetmeats enough to kill a whole village. All was preparation, anticipation, and prognostication. A Dutch tailor had constructed Douw a suit of snuff-color, that made him look like a great roll of leaf-tobacco; and a York milliner had exercised her skill in the composition of a wedding-dress for Alida, that made the hair of the girls of Coeymans and Coxsackie stand on end. All was ready, and the day appointed. But, alas! I wonder no one has yet had the sagacity to observe, and proclaim to the world, that all things in this life are uncertain, and that the anticipations of youth are often disappointed.

Just three weeks before the wedding, there appeared in the village of Coxsackie a young fellow, dressed in a three-cornered cocked hat, a queue at least a yard long hanging from under it, tied up in an eel-skin, a spruce blue coat, not much the worse for wear, a red waistcoat, corduroy breeches, handsome cotton stockings, with a pair of good legs in them, and pumps with silver buckles. His arrival was like the shock of an earthquake, he being the first stranger that had appeared within the memory of man. He was of a goodly height, well shaped, and had a pair of rosy cheeks, which no Dutch damsel ever could resist; for to say the truth, our Dutch lads are apt to be a little dusky in the epidermis.

He gave out that he was coming to set up a school, and teach the little chubby Dutch boys and girls English. The men set their faces against this monstrous innovation!—but the women! the women! they always will run after novelty, and they ran after the schoolmaster, his red cheeks, and his red waistcoat. Yffrow Vander Speigle contested the empire of the world within doors, with his honor the judge, and bore a divided reign. She was smitten with a desire to become a blue-stocking herself, or at least that her daughter should. The yffrow was the bell-wether of fashion in the village; of course, many other yffrows followed her example, and in a little time the lucky

schoolmaster was surrounded by half the grown-up damsels of Coxsackie.

Alida soon became distinguished as his favorite scholar; she was the prettiest, the 5 richest girl in the school—and she could talk English, which the others were only just learning. He taught her to read poetry —he taught her to talk with her eyes— to write love-letters—and at last to love. 10 Douw was a lost man the moment the schoolmaster came into the village. He first got the blind side of the daughter, then of the yffrow—but he found it a rather hard matter to get the blind side 15 of the judge, who had heard from his brother in Albany what pranks these Connecticut boys were playing there. He discouraged the schoolmaster, and he encouraged Douw to press his suit, which Alida 20 had put off, and put off, from time to time. She was sick—and not ready—and indifferent—and sometimes cross.

Douw smoked his pipe harder than ever at her; but she resisted like a hero- 25 ine.

In those times of cheap simplicity, it was the custom of the country for the schoolmaster to board alternately with the parents of his scholars a week or a fortnight 30 at a time; and it is recorded of these learned Thebans, that they always stayed longer where there was a pretty daughter, and plenty of pies and sweetmeats. The time at last came round, when it was the 35 schoolmaster's turn to sojourn with Judge Vander Speigle the allotted fortnight, sorely to the gloomy forebodings of Douw, who began to have a strong suspicion of the cause of Alida's coldness. The school- 40 master knew on which side his bread was buttered, and laid close siege to the yffrow, by praising her good things, exalting her consequence, and depressing that of her neighbors. Nor did he neglect the daugh- 45 ter, whom he plied with poetry, melting looks, and significant squeezes and all that; although all that was quite unnecessary, for she was ready to run away with him at any time. But this did not suit our Hom- 50 er; he might be divorced from the acres, if he married without the consent of the judge. He, however, continued to administer fuel to the flame, and never missed abusing poor Douw to his face, without 55 the latter being the wiser for it, he not understanding a word of English.

By degrees he opened the matter with the yffrow, who liked it exceedingly, for she was, as we said before, inclined to the mysteries of blue-stockingism, and was half in love with his red waistcoat and red cheeks. Finally, she told him, in a significant way, that as there were two to one in his favor, and the old judge would, she knew, never consent to the marriage while he could help it, the best thing he could do was to go and get married as soon as possible, and she would bear them out. That very night Douw became a disconsolate widower, although, poor fellow! he did not know of it till the next morning. The judge stormed and swore, and the yffrow talked; till at length he allowed them to come and live in the house, but with the proviso that they were never to speak to him, nor he to them. A little grandson, in process of time, healed all these internal divisions. They christened him Adrian Vander Speigle, after his grandfather; and when it came to pass that the old patriarch died, the estate passed from the Vander Speigles to the Longfellows, after the manner of men.

Poor Douw grew melancholy, and pondered sometimes whether he should not 5 bring his action for breach of promise, fly the country forever, turn Methodist, or marry under the nose of the faithless Alida, "on purpose to spite her." He finally decided on the latter, married a little 10 Dutch brunette from Kinderhook, and prospered mightily in posterity, as did also his neighbor, Philo Longfellow. But it was observed, that the little Van Wezels and the little Longfellows never met with- 15 out fighting; and that as they grew up, this hostility gathered additional bitterness. In process of time, the village became divided into two factions, which gradually spread wherever the Yankees 20 and the Dutch mixed together; and finally, like the feuds of the Guelphs and Ghibelines, divided the land for almost a hundred miles around.[2]

IV

NATHANIEL HAWTHORNE (1804-1864)

The apprenticeship of Nathaniel Hawthorne as a story-writer began while he was an undergraduate at Bowdoin College, 1821-1825. Under the influence of Scott and Irving, the two dominating forces in early American fiction, he planned and even partly completed before graduation, a book of "tales" and a novel. It was not until 1828 that the novel, *Fanshawe*, a shortened romance, appeared, shortened because of the shortness of its creator's pocket-book, and it was not until 1842 that the book of tales, with the final title of *Twice-Told Tales*, was published.

It was a discouraging period for writers of fiction in America. When publishers, in the absence of international copyright laws, could have for nothing their pick of all the famous new English books, why take the risk of publishing unknown writers and then in addition pay them copyright percentages? Novels, with a very few exceptions like Cooper's, were out of the question. But at this critical moment a new literary vehicle was found. In 1826 appeared *The Atlantic Souvenir*, a gift-book or souvenir made up of short pieces in prose and verse, and so highly successful was it that imitations sprang up on every side. *The Token, The Gift, The Diadem* and the hundreds of others that followed made it early a rule to use only native work and their success enabled them to pay prices that gave encouragement to the vigorous group of young writers who had just begun to find themselves. Fiction was in demand by all the editors of annuals, and to be publishable within the narrow compass of a book of miscellanies it must perforce be severely shortened. The new literary generation in America, therefore, was compelled to think constantly of condensation, of effects gained by suggestion and curtailment, of simplicity in plot and of fewness of characters and limitation of setting. It was the apprentice period, the seedtime, of the American short story. Hawthorne during those solitary years in which he mastered his art was compelled constantly to express himself in the one literary form for which he could find a market,—the condensed tale, with few characters, and a single intense situation. In *The Token* alone he published no less than twenty-six of his *Twice-Told Tales*. So long did he work with this shortened literary unit that it became a fixed literary habit. His longer romances, like *The Scarlet Letter*, show the influence of this habit. They are studies from several standpoints of a single intense situation.

Hawthorne added to the American short story depth and moral content. His tales are studies of intense moments and of situations involving those intangible elements which after all turn the currents of human life. Moreover he added beauty—the beauty of style and of artistic proportion, and in addition he did much to educate Puritan New England to a toleration of prose fiction.

THE WHITE OLD MAID

The moonbeams came through two deep and narrow windows, and showed a spacious chamber, richly furnished in an antique fashion. From one lattice the shadow of the diamond panes was thrown upon the floor; the ghostly light through the other slept upon a bed, falling between the heavy silken curtains, and illuminating the face of a young man. But how quietly the slumberer lay! how pale his features! and how like a shroud the sheet was wound about his frame! Yes; it was a corpse in its burial clothes.

Suddenly the fixed features seemed to move with dark emotion. Strange fantasy! It was but the shadow of the fringed curtain, waving betwixt the dead face and the moonlight as the door of the chamber 5 opened, and a girl stole softly to the bedside. Was there delusion in the moonbeams, or did her gesture and her eye betray a gleam of triumph, as she bent over the pale corpse—pale as itself—and 10 pressed her living lips to the cold ones of the dead? As she drew back from that long kiss her features writhed, as if a proud heart were fighting with its anguish. Again it seemed that the features of the corpse 15 had moved, responsive to her own. Still an illusion! The silken curtain had waved. a

37

second time, betwixt the dead face and the moonlight, as another fair young girl unclosed the door, and glided, ghost-like, to the bedside. There the two maidens stood, both beautiful, with the pale beauty of the dead between them. But she who had first entered was proud and stately; and the other a soft and fragile thing.

"Away!" cried the lofty one. "Thou hadst him living! The dead is mine!"

"Thine!" returned the other, shuddering. "Well hast thou spoken! The dead is thine!"

The proud girl started, and stared into her face with a ghastly look. But a wild and mournful expression passed across the features of the gentle one; and, weak and helpless, she sank down on the bed, her head pillowed beside that of the corpse, and her hair mingling with his dark locks. A creature of hope and joy, the first draught of sorrow had bewildered her.

"Edith!" cried her rival.

Edith groaned, as with a sudden compression of the heart, and removing her cheek from the dead youth's pillow, she stood upright, fearfully encountering the eyes of the lofty girl.

"Wilt thou betray me?" said the latter, calmly.

"Till the dead bid me speak, I will be silent," answered Edith. "Leave us alone together? Go, and live many years, and then return, and tell me of thy life. He, too, will be here! Then, if thou tellest of sufferings more than death, we will both forgive thee."

"And what shall be the token?" asked the proud girl, as if her heart acknowledged a meaning in these wild words.

"This lock of hair," said Edith, lifting one of the dark. clustering curls that lay heavily on the dead man's brow.

The two maidens joined their hands over the bosom of the corpse, and appointed a day and hour, far, far in time to come, for their next meeting in that chamber. The statelier girl gave one deep look at the motionless countenance, and departed—yet turned again and trembled, ere she closed the door, almost believing that her dead lover frowned upon her. And Edith, too! Was not her white form fading into the moonlight? Scorning her own weakness, she went forth, and perceived that a negro slave was waiting in the passage with a wax-light which he held between her face and his own, and regarded her, as she thought, with an ugly expression of merriment. Lifting his torch on high, the slave lighted her down the staircase, and undid the portal of the mansion. The young clergyman of the town had just ascended the steps, and bowing to the lady, passed in without a word.

Years, many years rolled on; the world seemed new again, so much older was it grown, since the night when those pale girls had clasped their hands across the bosom of the corpse. In the interval, a lonely woman had passed from youth to extreme age, and was known by all the town as the "Old Maid in the Winding-sheet." A taint of insanity had affected her whole life, but so quiet, sad, and gentle, so utterly free from violence, that she was suffered to pursue her harmless fantasies, unmolested by the world, with whose business or pleasures she had naught to do. She dwelt alone, and never came into the daylight, except to follow funerals. Whenever a corpse was borne along the street, in sunshine, rain, or snow, whether a pompous train of the rich and proud thronged after it, or few and humble were the mourners, behind them came the lonely woman, in a long, white garment, which the people called her shroud. She took no place among the kindred or the friends, but stood at the door to hear the funeral prayer, and walked in the rear of the procession, as one whose earthly charge it was to haunt the house of mourning, and be the shadow of affliction, and see that the dead were duly buried. So long had this been her custom, that the inhabitants of the town deemed her a part of every funeral, as much as the coffin-pall, or the very corpse itself, and augured ill of the sinner's destiny unless the "Old Maid in the Winding-sheet" came gliding like a ghost behind. Once, it is said, she affrighted a bridal party with her pale presence appearing suddenly in the illuminated hall just as the priest was uniting a false maid to a wealthy man, before her lover had been dead a year. Evil was the omen to that marriage! Sometimes she stole forth by moonlight, and visited the graves of venerable Integrity, and wedded Love, and virgin Innocence, and every spot where the ashes of a kind and faithful heart were moldering. Over the hillocks of those favored dead would she stretch out her arms, with a gesture, as if she were scattering seeds; and many believed that she brought them from the garden of Paradise; for the graves which she had visited were green beneath the snow, and covered with sweet flowers from April to November. Her blessing was better than a holy verse upon the tombstone. Thus wore away her long, sad, peaceful, and fantastic life, till few were so old as she, and the people of later generations wondered how the dead had ever been buried, or mourners had endured their grief, without the "Old Maid in the Winding-sheet."

Still years went on, and still she followed funerals, and was not yet summoned to her own festival of death. One afternoon, the great street of the town was all alive with business and bustle, though the sun now gilded only the upper half of the church-spire, having left the housetops and loftiest trees in shadow. The scene was cheerful and animated, in spite of the somber shade between the high brick buildings. Here were pompous merchants in white wigs and laced velvet; the bronzed faces of sea captains; the foreign garb and air of Spanish creoles; and the disdainful port of natives of Old England; all contrasted with the rough aspect of one or two back settlers, negotiating sales of timber from forests where ax had never sounded. Sometimes a lady passed, swelling roundly forth in an embroidered petticoat, balancing her steps in high-heeled shoes, and curtsying, with lofty grace, to the punctilious obeisances of the gentlemen. The life of the town seemed to have its very center not far from an old mansion that stood somewhat back from the pavement, surrounded by neglected grass, with a strange air of loneliness, rather deepened than dispelled by the throng so near it. Its site would have been suitably occupied by a magnificent Exchange, or a brick block, lettered all over with various signs; or the large house itself might have made a noble tavern, with the "King's Arms" swinging before it, and guests in every chamber, instead of the present solitude. But, owing to some dispute about the right of inheritance, the mansion had been long without a tenant, decaying from year to year, and throwing the stately gloom of its shadow over the busiest part of the town. Such was the scene, and such the time, when a figure, unlike any that have been described, was observed at a distance down the street.

"I espy a strange sail, yonder," re-

marked a Liverpool captain, "that woman in the long white garment!"

The sailor seemed much struck by the object, as were several others, who at the same moment, caught a glimpse of the figure that had attracted his notice. Almost immediately, the various topics of conversation gave place to speculations, in an under tone, on this unwonted occurrence.

"Can there be a funeral, so late this afternoon?" inquired some.

They looked for the signs of death at every door, the sexton, the hearse, the assemblage of black-clad relatives—all that makes up the woeful pomp of funerals. They raised their eyes, also, to the sun-gilt spire of the church, and wondered that no clang proceeded from its bell, which had always tolled till now, when this figure appeared in the light of day. But none had heard that a corpse was to be borne to its home that afternoon, nor was there any token of a funeral, except the apparition of the "Old Maid in the Winding-sheet."

"What may this portend?" asked each man of his neighbor.

All smiled as they put the question, yet with a certain trouble in their eyes, as if pestilence, or some other wide calamity, were prognosticated by the untimely intrusion among the living of one whose presence had always been associated with death and woe. What a comet is to the earth, was that sad woman to the town. Still she moved on, while the hum of surprise was hushed at her approach, and the proud and the humble stood aside, that her white garment might not wave against them. It was a long, loose robe of spotless purity. Its wearer appeared very old, pale, emaciated, and feeble, yet glided onward without the unsteady pace of extreme age. At one point of her course, a little rosy boy burst forth from a door, and ran with open arms towards the ghostly woman, seeming to expect a kiss from her bloodless lips. She made a slight pause, fixing her eye upon him with an expression of no earthly sweetness, so that the child shivered and stood awe-struck, rather than affrighted, while the Old Maid passed on. Perhaps her garment might have been polluted even by an infant's touch; perhaps her kiss would have been death to the sweet boy within the year.

"She is but a shadow," whispered the

superstitious. "The child put forth his arms and could not grasp her robe!"

The wonder was increased when the Old Maid passed beneath the porch of the deserted mansion, ascended the moss-covered steps, lifted the iron knocker, and gave three raps. The people could only conjecture that some old remembrance, troubling her bewildered brain, had impelled the poor woman hither to visit the friends of her youth; all gone from their home, long since and for ever, unless their ghosts still haunted it—fit company for the "Old Maid in the Winding-sheet." An elderly man approached the steps, and reverently uncovering his gray locks, essayed to explain the matter.

"None, madam," said he, "have dwelt in this house these fifteen years agone—no, not since the death of old Colonel Fenwicke, whose funeral you may remember to have followed. His heirs, being ill agreed among themselves, have let the mansion-house go to ruin."

The Old Maid looked slowly round, with a slight gesture of one hand, and a finger of the other upon her lip, appearing more shadow-like than ever in the obscurity of the porch. But again she lifted the hammer, and gave this time a single rap. Could it be that a footstep was now heard coming down the staircase of the old mansion which all conceived to have been so long untenanted? Slowly, feebly, yet heavily, like the pace of an aged and infirm person, the step approached, more distinct on every downward stair, till it reached the portal. The bar fell on the inside; the door was opened. One upward glance, towards the church-spire, whence the sunshine had just faded, was the last that the people saw of the "Old Maid in the Winding-sheet."

"Who undid the door?" asked many.

This question, owing to the depth of shadow beneath the porch, no one could satisfactorily answer. Two or three aged men, while protesting against an inference which might be drawn, affirmed that the person within was a negro, and bore a singular resemblance to old Cæsar, formerly a slave in the house, but freed by death some thirty years before.

"Her summons has waked up a servant of the old family," said one, half-seriously.

"Let us wait here," replied another. "More guests will knock at the door anon. But the gate of the graveyard should be thrown open!"

Twilight had overspread the town before the crowd began to separate, or the comments on this incident were exhausted. One after another was wending his way homeward, when a coach—no common spectacle in those days—drove slowly into the street. It was an old-fashioned equipage, hanging close to the ground, with arms on the panels, a footman behind, and a grave, corpulent coachman seated high in front—the whole giving an idea of solemn state and dignity. There was something awful in the heavy rumbling of the wheels. The coach rolled down the street, till, coming to the gateway of the deserted mansion, it drew up, and the footman sprang to the ground.

"Whose grand coach is this?" asked a very inquisitive body.

The footman made no reply, but ascended the steps of the old house, gave three raps with the iron hammer, and returned to open the coach door. An old man, possessed of the heraldic lore so common in that day, examined the shield of arms on the panel.

"Azure, a lion's head erased, between three flower de luces," said he; then whispered the name of the family to whom these bearings belonged. The last inheritor of its honors was recently dead, after a long residence amid the splendor of the British court, where his birth and wealth had given him no mean station. "He left no child," continued the herald, "and these arms, being in a lozenge, betoken that the coach appertains to his widow."

Further disclosures, perhaps, might have been made had not the speaker suddenly been struck dumb by the stern eye of an ancient lady who thrust forth her head from the coach, preparing to descend. As she emerged, the people saw that her dress was magnificent, and her dignified figure, in spite of age and infirmity—a stately ruin, but with a look at once of pride and wretchedness. Her strong and rigid features had an awe about them, unlike that of the white Old Maid, but as of something evil. She passed up the steps, leaning on a gold-headed cane; the door swung open as she ascended, and the light of a torch glittered on the embroidery of her dress, and gleamed on the pillars of the porch. After a momentary pause—a glance backwards—and then a desperate effort—she went in. The decipherer of the coat of arms had ventured up the lowest step, and shrinking back immediately, pale and tremulous, affirmed that the torch was held by the very image of old Cæsar.

"But such a hideous grin," added he, "was never seen on the face of mortal man, black or white! It will haunt me till my dying day."

Meantime the coach had wheeled round, with a prodigious clatter on the pavement, and rumbled up the street, disappearing in the twilight, while the ear still tracked its course. Scarcely was it gone when the people began to question whether the coach and attendants, the ancient lady, the specter of old Cæsar, and the Old Maid herself, were not all a strangely combined delusion, with some dark purport in its mystery. The whole town was astir, so that instead of dispersing, the crowd continually increased, and stood gazing up at the windows of the mansion, now silvered by the brightening moon. The elders, glad to indulge the narrative propensity of age, told of the long-faded splendor of the family, the entertainments they had given, and the guests, the greatest of the land, and even titled and noble ones from abroad, who had passed beneath that portal. These graphic reminiscences seemed to call up the ghosts of those to whom they referred. So strong was the impression on some of the more imaginative hearers, that two or three were seized with trembling fits, at one and the same moment protesting that they had distinctly heard three other raps of the iron knocker.

"Impossible!" exclaimed others. "See! The moon shines beneath the porch, and shows every part of it, except in the narrow shade of that pillar. There is no one there!"

"Did not the door open?" whispered one of these fanciful persons.

"Didst thou see it, too?" said his companion, in a startled tone.

But the general sentiment was opposed to the idea that a third visitant had made application at the door of the deserted house. A few, however, adhered to this new marvel, and even declared that a red gleam, like that of a torch, had shone through the great front window, as if the negro were lighting a guest up the staircase. This, too, was pronounced a mere fantasy. But, at once, the whole multitude started, and each man beheld his own terror painted in the face of all the rest.

"What an awful thing is this!" cried they.

A shriek, too fearfully distinct for doubt, had been heard within the mansion, breaking forth suddenly, and succeeded by a deep stillness, as if a heart had burst in giving it utterance. The people knew not whether to fly from the very sight of the house, or to rush trembling in, and search out the strange mystery. Amid their confusion and affright, they were somewhat reassured by the appearance of their clergyman, a venerable patriarch, and equally a saint, who had taught them and their fathers the way to heaven, for more than the space of an ordinary lifetime. He was a reverend figure, with long, white hair upon his shoulders, a white beard upon his breast, and a back so bent over his staff that he seemed to be looking downward continually, as if to choose a proper grave for his weary frame. It was some time before the good old man, being deaf, and of impaired intellect, could be made to comprehend such portions of the affair as were comprehensible at all. But when possessed of the facts, his energies assumed unexpected vigor.

"Verily," said the old gentleman, "it will be fitting that I enter the mansion-house of the worthy Colonel Fenwicke, lest any harm should have befallen that true Christian woman whom we call the 'Old Maid in the Winding-sheet.'"

Behold, then, the venerable clergyman ascending the steps of the mansion, with a torch-bearer behind him. It was the elderly man who had spoken to the Old Maid, and the same who had afterwards explained the shield of arms, and recognized the features of the negro. Like their predecessors, they gave three raps with the iron hammer.

"Old Cæsar cometh not," observed the priest. "Well, I wot, he no longer doth service in this mansion."

"Assuredly, then, it was something worse, in old Cæsar's likeness!" said the other adventurer.

"Be it as God wills," answered the clergyman. "See! my strength, though it be much decayed, hath sufficed to open this heavy door. Let us enter, and pass up the staircase."

Here occurred a singular exemplification of the dreamy state of a very old man's mind. As they ascended the wide flight of stairs, the aged clergyman appeared to move with caution, occasionally standing aside, and oftener bending his head, as it were in salutation, thus practising all the gestures of one who makes his way through a throng. Reaching the head of the staircase, he looked around with sad and solemn benignity, laid aside his staff, bared his hoary locks, and was evidently on the point of commencing a prayer.

"Reverend sir," said his attendant, who conceived this a very suitable prelude to their further search, "would it not be well that the people join with us in prayer?"

"Well-a-day!" cried the old clergyman, staring strangely around him. "Art thou here with me, and none other? Verily, past times were present to me, and I deemed that I was to make a funeral prayer, as many a time heretofore, from the head of this staircase. Of a truth, I saw the shades of many that are gone. Yea, I have prayed at their burials, one after another, and the 'Old Maid in the Winding-sheet' hath seen them to their graves!"

Being now more thoroughly awake to their present purpose, he took his staff and struck forcibly on the floor till there came an echo from each deserted chamber, but no menial to answer their summons. They therefore walked along the passage, and again paused, opposite to the great front window, through which was seen the crowd in the shadow and partial moonlight of the street beneath. On their right hand was the open door of a chamber, and a closed one on their left. The clergyman pointed his cane to the carved oak panel of the latter.

"Within that chamber," observed he, "a whole lifetime since, did I sit by the deathbed of a goodly young man, who, being now at the last gasp——"

Apparently there was some powerful excitement in the ideas which had now flashed across his mind. He snatched the torch from his companion's hand, and threw open the door with such sudden violence that the flame was extinguished, leaving them no other light than the moonbeams, which fell through two windows into the spacious chamber. It was sufficient to discover all that could be known. In a high-backed, oaken armchair, upright, with her hands clasped across her breast, and her head thrown back, sat the "Old Maid in the Winding-sheet." The stately dame had fallen on her knees, with her forehead on the holy knees of the Old Maid, one hand upon the floor, and the other pressed convulsively against her heart. It clutched a lock of hair, once sable, now discolored with a greenish mold. As the priest and layman advanced into the chamber, the Old Maid's features assumed such a semblance of shifting expression that they trusted to hear the whole mystery explained by a single word. But it was only the shadow of a tattered curtain waving betwixt the dead face and the moonlight.

"Both dead!" said the venerable man. "Then who shall divulge the secret? Methinks it glimmers to and fro in my mind, like the light and shadow across the Old Maid's face. And now 'tis gone!"

THE PROPHETIC PICTURES

"But this painter!" cried Walter Ludlow, with animation. "He not only excels in his peculiar art, but possesses vast acquirements in all other learning and science. He talks Hebrew with Dr. Mather, and gives lectures in anatomy to Dr. Boylston. In a word, he will meet the best instructed man among us, on his own ground. Moreover, he is a polished gentleman—a citizen of the world—yes, a true cosmopolite; for he will speak like a native of each clime and country on the globe, except our own forests, whither he is now going. Nor is all this what I most admire in him."

"Indeed!" said Elinor, who had listened with a woman's interest to the description of such a man. "Yet this is admirable enough."

"Surely it is," replied her lover, "but far less so than his natural gift of adapting himself to every variety of character, insomuch that all men—and all women too, Elinor—shall find a mirror of themselves in this wonderful painter. But the greatest wonder is yet to be told."

"Nay, if he have more wonderful attributes than these," said Elinor, laughing, "Boston is a perilous abode for the poor gentleman. Are you telling me of a painter, or a wizard?"

"In truth," answered he, "that question might be asked much more seriously than you suppose. They say that he paints not merely a man's features, but his mind and heart. He catches the secret sentiments and passions, and throws them upon the canvas, like sunshine—or perhaps, in the portraits of dark-souled men, like a gleam of infernal fire. It is an awful gift," added Walter, lowering his voice from its tone of enthusiasm. "I shall be almost afraid to sit to him."

"Walter, are you in earnest?" exclaimed Elinor.

"For Heaven's sake, dearest Elinor, do not let him paint the look which you now wear," said her lover, smiling, though rather perplexed. "There: it is passing away now, but when you spoke you seemed frightened to death, and very sad besides. What were you thinking of?"

"Nothing, nothing," answered Elinor, hastily. "You paint my face with your own fantasies. Well, come for me to-morrow, and we will visit this wonderful artist."

But when the young man had departed, it cannot be denied that a remarkable expression was again visible on the fair and youthful face of his mistress. It was a sad and anxious look, little in accordance with what should have been the feelings of a maiden on the eve of wedlock. Yes, Walter Ludlow was the chosen of her heart.

"A look!" said Elinor to herself. "No wonder that it startled him, if it expressed what I sometimes feel. I know, by my own experience, how frightful a look may be. But it was all fancy. I thought nothing of it at the time—I have seen nothing of it since—I did but dream it."

And she busied herself about the embroidery of a ruff, in which she meant that her portrait should be taken.

The painter of whom they had been speaking was not one of those native artists who, at a later period than this, borrowed their colors from the Indians, and manufactured their pencils of the furs of wild beasts. Perhaps, if he could have revoked his life and pre-arranged his destiny, he might have chosen to belong to that school without a master, in the hope of being at least original, since there were no works of art to imitate, nor rules to follow. But he had been born and educated in Europe. People said that he had studied the grandeur or beauty of conception, and every touch of the master-hand, in all the most famous pictures, in cabinets and galleries, and on the walls of churches, till there was nothing more for his powerful mind to learn. Art could add nothing to its lessons, but Nature might. He had therefore visited a world whither none of his professional brethren had preceded him, to feast his eyes on visible images that were noble and picturesque, yet had never been transferred to canvas. America was too poor to afford other temptations to an artist of eminence, though many of the colonial gentry, on the painter's arrival, had expressed a wish to transmit their lineaments to posterity by means of his skill. Whenever such proposals were made, he fixed his piercing eyes on the applicant, and seemed to look him through and through. If he beheld only a sleek and comfortable visage, though there were a gold-laced coat to adorn the picture, and golden guineas to pay for it, he civilly rejected the task and the reward. But if the face were the index of anything uncommon, in thought, sentiment, or experience; or if he met a beggar in the street, with a white beard and a furrowed brow; or if sometimes a child happened to look up and smile; he would exhaust all the art on them that he denied to wealth.

Pictorial skill being so rare in the colonies, the painter became an object of general curiosity. If few or none could appreciate the technical merit of his productions, yet there were points in regard to which the opinion of the crowd was as valuable as the refined judgment of the amateur. He watched the effect that each picture produced on such untutored beholders, and derived profit from their remarks, while they would as soon have thought of instructing Nature herself as him who seemed to rival her. Their admiration, it must be owned, was tinctured with the prejudices of the age and country. Some deemed it an offense against the Mosaic law, and even a presumptuous mockery of the Creator, to bring into existence such lively images of His creatures. Others, frightened at the art which could raise phantoms at will, and keep the form of the dead among the living, were inclined to consider the painter as a magician, or perhaps the famous Black Man, of old witch-times, plotting mischief in a new guise. These foolish fancies were more than half believed among the mob. Even in superior circles, his character was invested with a vague awe, partly rising like smoke-wreaths from the popular superstitions, but chiefly caused by the varied knowledge and talents which he made subservient to his profession.

Being on the eve of marriage, Walter Ludlow and Elinor were eager to obtain their portraits, as the first of what, they [5] doubtless hoped, would be a long series of family pictures. The day after the conversation above recorded, they visited the painter's rooms. A servant ushered them into an apartment, where, though the [10] artist himself was not visible, there were personages whom they could hardly forbear greeting with reverence. They knew, indeed, that the whole assembly were but pictures, yet felt it impossible to separate [15] the idea of life and intellect from such striking counterfeits. Several of the portraits were known to them, either as distinguished characters of the day, or their private acquaintances. There was Gov- [20] ernor Burnet, looking as if he had just received an undutiful communication from the House of Representatives, and were inditing a most sharp response. Mr. Cooke hung beside the ruler whom he opposed, [25] sturdy, and somewhat puritanical, as befitted a popular leader. The ancient lady of Sir William Phips eyed them from the wall, in ruff and farthingale, an imperious old dame, not unsuspected of witchcraft. [30] John Winslow, then a very young man, wore the expression of warlike enterprise which long afterward made him a distinguished general. Their personal friends were recognized at a glance. In most of [35] the pictures, the whole mind and character were brought out on the countenance, and concentrated into a single look, so that, to speak paradoxically, the originals hardly resembled themselves so strikingly as the [40] portraits did.

Among these modern worthies, there were two old bearded Saints, who had almost vanished into the darkening canvas. There was also a pale but unfaded Madonna, who had perhaps been worshiped in Rome, and now regarded the lovers with such a mild and holy look that they longed to worship too.

"How singular a thought," observed [50] Walter Ludlow, "that this beautiful face has been beautiful for above two hundred years! Oh, if all beauty would endure so well! Do you not envy her, Elinor?"

"If earth were heaven, I might," she replied. "But where all things fade, how miserable to be the one that could not fade!"

"This dark old St. Peter has a fierce and ugly scowl, saint though he be," continued Walter. "He troubles me. But the virgin looks kindly at us."

"Yes; but very sorrowful, methinks," [5] said Elinor. The easel stood beneath these three old pictures, sustaining one that had been recently commenced. After a little inspection, they began to recognize the features of their own minister, the Rev. [10] Dr. Colman, growing into shape and life as it were, out of a cloud.

"Kind old man!" exclaimed Elinor. "He gazes at me as if he were about to utter [15] a word of paternal advice."

"And at me," said Walter, "as if he were about to shake his head and rebuke me for some suspected iniquity. But so does the original. I shall never feel quite [20] comfortable under his eye, till we stand before him to be married."

They now heard a footstep on the floor, and turning, beheld the painter, who had been some moments in the room, and had [25] listened to a few of their remarks. He was a middle-aged man, with a countenance well worthy of his own pencil. Indeed, by the picturesque though careless arrangement of his rich dress, and, perhaps, be- [30] cause his soul dwelt always among painted shapes, he looked somewhat like a portrait himself. His visitors were sensible of a kindred between the artist and his works, and felt as if one of the pictures had [35] stepped from the canvas to salute them.

Walter Ludlow, who was slightly known to the painter, explained the object of their visit. While he spoke, a sunbeam was falling athwart his figure and Elinor's with so [40] happy an effect that they also seemed living pictures of youth and beauty, gladdened by bright fortune. The artist was evidently struck.

"My easel is occupied for several ensu- [45] ing days, and my stay in Boston must be brief," said he, thoughtfully; then, after an observant glance, he added, "but your wishes shall be gratified, though I disappoint the Chief-Justice and Madam Oliver. [50] I must not lose this opportunity, for the sake of painting a few ells of broadcloth and brocade."

The painter expressed a desire to introduce both their portraits into one picture, [55] and represent them engaged in some appropriate action. This plan would have delighted the lovers, but was necessarily rejected, because so large a space of canvas would have been unfit for the room which it was intended to decorate. Two half-length portraits were therefore fixed upon. After they had taken leave, Walter Ludlow asked Elinor, with a smile, whether she knew what an influence over their fates the painter was about to acquire.

"The old women of Boston affirm," continued he, "that after he has once got possession of a person's face and figure, he may paint him in any act or situation whatever—and the picture will be prophetic. Do you believe it?"

"Not quite," said Elinor, smiling. "Yet if he has such magic, there is something so gentle in his manner that I am sure he will use it well."

It was the painter's choice to proceed with both the portraits at the same time, assigning as a reason, in the mystical language which he sometimes used, that the faces threw light upon each other. Accordingly, he gave now a touch to Walter, and now to Elinor, and the features of one and the other began to start forth so vividly that it appeared as if his triumphant art would actually disengage them from the canvas. Amid the rich light and deep shade they beheld their phantom selves. But, though the likeness promised to be perfect, they were not quite satisfied with the expression; it seemed more vague than in most of the painter's works. He, however, was satisfied with the prospect of success, and being much interested in the lovers, employed his leisure moments, unknown to them, in making a crayon sketch of their two figures. During their sittings, he engaged them in conversation, and kindled up their faces with characteristic traits, which, though continually varying, it was his purpose to combine and fix. At length he announced that at their next visit both the portraits would be ready for delivery.

"If my pencil will but be true to my conception, in the few last touches which I meditate," observed he, "these two pictures will be my very best performances. Seldom, indeed, has an artist such subjects."

While speaking, he still bent his penetrative eye upon them, nor withdrew it till they had reached the bottom of the stairs.

Nothing, in the whole circle of human vanities, takes stronger hold of the imagination than this affair of having a portrait painted. Yet why should it be so? The looking-glass, the polished globes of the andirons, the mirror-like water, and all other reflecting surfaces, continually present us with portraits, or rather ghosts, of ourselves, which we glance at, and straightway forget them. But we forget them only because they vanish. It is the idea of duration—of earthly immortality—that gives such a mysterious interest to our own portraits. Walter and Elinor were not insensible to this feeling, and hastened to the painter's room, punctually at the appointed hour, to meet those pictured shapes which were to be their representatives with posterity. The sunshine flashed after them into the apartment, but left it somewhat gloomy, as they closed the door.

Their eyes were immediately attracted to their portraits, which rested against the furthest wall of the room. At the first glance, through the dim light and the distance, seeing themselves in precisely their natural attitudes, and with all the air that they recognized so well, they uttered a simultaneous exclamation of delight.

"There we stand," cried Walter, enthusiastically, "fixed in sunshine forever! No dark passions can gather on our faces!"

"No," said Elinor, more calmly; "no dreary change can sadden us."

This was said while they were approaching, and had yet gained only an imperfect view of the pictures. The painter, after saluting them, busied himself at a table in completing a crayon sketch, leaving his visitors to form their own judgment as to his perfected labors. At intervals, he sent a glance from beneath his deep eyebrows, watching their countenances in profile, with his pencil suspended over the sketch. They had now stood some moments, each in front of the other's picture, contemplating it with entranced attention, but without uttering a word. At length Walter stepped forward—then back—viewing Elinor's portrait in various lights, and finally spoke.

"Is there not a change?" said he, in a doubtful and meditative tone. "Yes; the perception of it grows more vivid, the longer I look. It is certainly the same picture that I saw yesterday; the dress—the features—all are the same; and yet something is altered."

"Is, then, the picture less like than it was yesterday?" inquired the painter, now drawing near, with irrepressible interest.

"The features are perfect, Elinor," answered Walter, "and, at the first glance, the expression seemed also hers. But, I could fancy that the portrait has changed countenance while I have been looking at it. The eyes are fixed on mine with a strangely sad and anxious expression. Nay, it is grief and terror! Is this like Elinor?"

"Compare the living face with the pictured one," said the painter.

Walter glanced sidelong at his mistress and stared. Motionless and absorbed—fascinated as it were—in contemplation of Walter's portrait, Elinor's face had assumed precisely the expression of which he had just been complaining. Had she practised for whole hours before a mirror, she could not have caught the look so successfully. Had the picture itself been a mirror, it could not have thrown back her present aspect with stronger and more melancholy truth. She appeared quite unconscious of the dialogue between the artist and her lover.

"Elinor," exclaimed Walter, in amazement, "what change has come over you?"

She did not hear him, nor desist from her fixed gaze, till he seized her hand, and thus attracted her notice; then, with a sudden tremor, she looked from the picture to the face of the original. "Do you see no change in your portrait?" asked she.

"In mine?—None!" replied Walter, examining it. "But let me see! Yes; there is a slight change—an improvement, I think, in the picture, though none in the likeness. It has a livelier expression than yesterday, as if some bright thought were flashing from the eyes, and about to be uttered from the lips. Now that I have caught the look, it becomes very decided."

While he was intent on these observations, Elinor turned to the painter. She regarded him with grief and awe, and felt that he repaid her with sympathy and commiseration, though wherefore she could but vaguely guess.

"That look!" whispered she, and shuddered. "How came it there?"

"Madam," said the painter, sadly, taking her hand, and leading her apart, "in both these pictures I have painted what I saw. The artist—the true artist—must look beneath the exterior. It is his gift—his proudest but often a melancholy one—to see the inmost soul, and by a power indefinable even to himself to make it glow or darken upon the canvas, in glances that express the thought and sentiment of years. Would that I might convince myself of error in the present instance!"

They had now approached the table, on which were heads in chalk, hands almost as expressive as ordinary faces, ivied church towers, thatched cottages, old thunder-stricken trees, Oriental and antique costume, and all such picturesque vagaries of an artist's idle moments. Turning them over, with seeming carelessness, a crayon sketch of two figures was disclosed.

"If I have failed," continued he, "if your heart does not see itself reflected in your own portrait, if you have no secret cause to trust my delineation of the other, it is not yet too late to alter them. I might change the action of these figures too. But would it influence the event?"

He directed her notice to the sketch. A thrill ran through Elinor's frame; a shriek was upon her lips; but she stifled it, with the self-command that becomes habitual to all who hide thoughts of fear and anguish within their bosoms. Turning from the table, she perceived that Walter had advanced near enough to have seen the sketch, though she could not determine whether it had caught his eye.

"We will not have the pictures altered," said she hastily. "If mine is sad, I shall but look the gayer for the contrast."

"Be it so," answered the painter, bowing. "May your griefs be such fanciful ones that only your picture may mourn for them! For your joys—may they be true and deep, and paint themselves upon this lovely face till it quite belie my art!"

After the marriage of Walter and Elinor, the pictures formed the two most splendid ornaments of their abode. They hung side by side, separated by a narrow panel, appearing to eye each other constantly, yet always returning the gaze of the spectator. Traveled gentlemen, who professed a knowledge of such subjects, reckoned these among the most admirable specimens of modern portraiture; while common observers compared them with the originals, feature by feature, and were rapturous in praise of the likeness. But it was on a third class—neither traveled connoisseurs nor common observers, but people of natural sensibility—that the pictures wrought their strongest effect. Such persons might gaze carelessly at first, but, becoming interested, would return day after day, and study these painted faces like the pages of a mystic volume. Walter Ludlow's portrait attracted their earliest notice. In the absence of himself and his bride, they sometimes disputed as to the expression which the painter had intended to throw upon the features; all agreeing that there was a look of earnest import, though no two explained it alike. There was less diversity of opinion in regard to Elinor's picture. They differed, indeed, in their attempts to estimate the nature and depth of the gloom that dwelt upon her face, but agreed that it was gloom, and alien from the natural temperament of their youthful friend. A certain fanciful person announced, as the result of much scrutiny, that both these pictures were parts of one design, and that the melancholy strength of feeling, in Elinor's countenance, bore reference to the more vivid emotion, or, as he termed it, the wild passion, in that of Walter. Though unskilled in art, he even began a sketch, in which the action of the two figures was to correspond with their mutual expression.

It was whispered among friends, that, day by day, Elinor's face was assuming a deeper shade of pensiveness, which threatened soon to render her too true a counterpart of her melancholy picture. Walter, on the other hand, instead of acquiring the vivid look which the painter had given him on the canvas, became reserved and downcast, with no outward flashes of emotion, however it might be smoldering within. In course of time, Elinor hung a gorgeous curtain of purple silk, wrought with flowers, and fringed with heavy golden tassels, before the pictures, under pretence that the dust would tarnish their hues, or the light dim them. It was enough. Her visitors felt that the massive folds of the silk must never be withdrawn, nor the portraits mentioned in her presence.

Time wore on; and the painter came again. He had been far enough to the north to see the silver cascade of the Crystal Hills, and to look over the vast round of cloud and forest, from the summit of New England's loftiest mountain. But he did not profane that scene by the mockery of his art. He had also lain in a canoe on the bosom of Lake George, making his soul the mirror of its loveliness and grandeur, till not a picture in the Vatican was more vivid than his recollection. He had gone with the Indian hunters to Niagara, and there, again, had flung his hopeless pencil down the precipice, feeling that he could as soon paint the roar as aught else that goes to make up the wondrous cataract. In truth, it was seldom his impulse to copy natural scenery, except as a framework for the delineations of the human form and face, instinct with thought, passion, or suffering. With store of such his adventurous ramble had enriched him; the stern dignity of Indian chiefs; the dusky loveliness of Indian girls; the domestic life of wigwams; the stealthy march; the battle beneath gloomy pine trees; the frontier fortress with its garrison; the anomaly of the old French partizan, bred in courts, but grown gray in shaggy deserts; such were the scenes and portraits that he had sketched. The glow of perilous moments; flashes of wild feeling; struggles of fierce power—love, hate, grief, frenzy—in a word, all the worn-out heart of the old earth had been revealed to him under a new form. His portfolio was filled with graphic illustrations of the volume of his memory, which genius would transmute into its own substance, and imbue with immortality. He felt that the deep wisdom in his art, which he had sought so far, was found.

But, amid stern or lovely nature, in the perils of the forest, or its overwhelming peacefulness, still there had been two phantoms, the companions of his way. Like all other men around whom an engrossing purpose wreathes itself, he was insulated from the mass of human kind. He had no aim—no pleasure—no sympathies—but what were ultimately connected with his art. Though gentle in manner, and upright in intent and action, he did not possess kindly feelings; his heart was cold; no living creature could be brought near enough to keep him warm. For these two beings, however, he had felt, in its greatest intensity, the sort of interest which always allied him to the subjects of his pencil. He had pried into their souls with his keenest insight, and pictured the result upon their features with his utmost skill, so as barely to fall short of that standard which no genius ever reached, his own severe conception. He had caught from the duskiness of the future—at least, so he fancied—a fearful secret, and had obscurely revealed it on the portraits. So much of himself—of his imagination and

all other powers—had been lavished on the
study of Walter and Elinor, that he almost
regarded them as creations of his own, like
the thousands with which he had peopled
the realms of Picture. Therefore did they 5
flit through the twilight of the woods,
hover on the mist of waterfalls, look
forth from the mirror of the lake, nor melt
away in the noontide sun. They haunted
his pictorial fancy, not as mockeries of 10
life, nor pale goblins of the dead, but in
the guise of portraits, each with the unal-
terable expression which his magic had
evoked from the caverns of the soul. He
could not recross the Atlantic, till he had 15
again beheld the originals of those airy
pictures.

"Oh, glorious Art!" thus mused the enthusiastic painter, as he trod the street.
"Thou art the image of the Creator's own. 20
The innumerable forms that wander in
nothingness start into being at thy beck.
The dead live again. Thou recallest them
to their old scenes, and givest their gray
shadows the luster of a better life, at once 25
earthly and immortal. Thou snatchest back
the fleeting moments of History. With
thee, there is no Past; for, at thy touch,
all that is great becomes forever present;
and illustrious men live through long ages, 30
in the visible performance of the very
deeds which made them what they are. Oh,
potent Art! as thou bringest the faintly
revealed Past to stand in that narrow strip
of sunlight which we call Now, canst thou 35
summon the shrouded Future to meet her
there? Have I not achieved it! Am I not
thy Prophet?"

Thus with a proud yet melancholy
fervor did he almost cry aloud, as he 40
passed through the toilsome street, among
people that knew not of his reveries, nor
could understand nor care for them. It is
not good for man to cherish a solitary ambition. Unless there be those around him 45
by whose example he may regulate himself, his thoughts, desires, and hopes will
become extravagant, and he the semblance,
perhaps the reality, of a madman. Reading
other bosoms, with an acuteness almost 50
preternatural, the painter failed to see the
disorder of his own.

"And this should be the house," said he,
looking up and down the front, before he
knocked. "Heaven help my brains! That 55
picture! Methinks it will never vanish.
Whether I look at the windows or the
door, there it is framed within them,

painted strongly, and glowing in the richest tints—the faces of the portraits—the
figures and action of the sketch!"

He knocked.

"The portraits! Are they within?" inquired he, of the domestic; then recollecting himself—"your master and mistress!
Are they at home?"

"They are, sir," said the servant, adding,
as he noticed that picturesque aspect of
which the painter could never divest himself, "and the Portraits too!"

The guest was admitted into a parlor,
communicating by a central door with an
interior room of the same size. As the
first apartment was empty, he passed to
the entrance of the second, within which
his eyes were greeted by those living personages, as well as their pictured representatives, who had long been the object
of so singular an interest. He involuntarily paused on the threshold.

They had not perceived his approach.
Walter and Elinor were standing before
the portraits, whence the former had just
flung back the rich and voluminous folds
of the silken curtain, holding its golden
tassel with one hand, while the other
grasped that of his bride. The pictures,
concealed for months, gleamed forth again
in undiminished splendor, appearing to
throw a somber light across the room
rather than to be disclosed by a borrowed
radiance. That of Elinor had been almost
prophetic. A pensiveness, and next a gentle
sorrow, had successively dwelt upon her
countenance, deepening, with the lapse of
time, into a quiet anguish. A mixture of
affright would now have made it the very
expression of the portrait. Walter's face
was moody and dull, or animated only by
fitful flashes, which left a heavier darkness
for their momentary illumination. He
looked from Elinor to her portrait, and
thence to his own, in the contemplation of
which he finally stood absorbed.

The painter seemed to hear the step of
Destiny approaching behind him, on its
progress toward its victims. A strange
thought darted into his mind. Was not his
own the form in which that Destiny had
embodied itself, and he a chief agent of
the coming evil which he had foreshadowed?

Still, Walter remained silent before the
picture, communing with it, as with his
own heart, and abandoning himself to the
spell of evil influence that the painter had

cast upon the features. Gradually his eye kindled; while, as Elinor watched the increasing wildness of his face, her own assumed a look of terror; and when at last he turned upon her, the resemblance of both to their portraits was complete.

"Our fate is upon us!" howled Walter. "Die!"

Drawing a knife, he sustained her, as she was sinking to the ground, and aimed it at her bosom. In the action and in the look and attitude of each, the painter beheld the figures of his sketch. The picture, with all its tremendous coloring, was finished.

"Hold, madman!" cried he, sternly.

He had advanced from the door, and interposed himself between the wretched beings, with the same sense of power to regulate their destiny as to alter a scene upon the canvas. He stood like a magician, controlling the phantoms which he had evoked.

"What!" muttered Walter Ludlow, as he relapsed from fierce excitement into silent gloom. "Does Fate impede its own decree?"

"Wretched lady!" said the painter. "Did I not warn you?"

"You did," replied Elinor, calmly, as her terror gave place to the quiet grief which it had disturbed. "But—I loved him!"

Is there not a deep moral in the tale? Could the result of one, or all our deeds, be shadowed forth and set before us— some would call it Fate and hurry onward, others be swept along by their passionate desires—and none to be turned aside by the Prophetic Pictures.

MRS. BULLFROG *

It makes me melancholy to see how like fools some very sensible people act, in the matter of choosing wives. They perplex their judgments by a most undue attention to little niceties of personal appearance, habits, disposition, and other trifles, which concern nobody but the lady herself. An unhappy gentleman, resolving to wed nothing short of perfection, keeps his heart and hand till both get so old and withered,

* "As to Mrs. Bullfrog, I give her up to the severest reprehension. The story was written as a mere experiment in that style; it did not come from any depth within me—neither my heart nor mind had anything to do with it."—*American Note-Books*, 1841.

that no tolerable woman will accept them. —Now, this is the very height of absurdity. A kind Providence has so skilfully adapted sex to sex, and the mass of individuals to each other, that, with certain obvious exceptions, any male and female may be moderately happy in the married state. The true rule is, to ascertain that the match is fundamentally a good one, and then to take it for granted that all minor objections, should there be such, will vanish, if you let them alone. Only put yourself beyond hazard, as to the real basis of matrimonial bliss, and it is scarcely to be imagined what miracles, in the way of reconciling smaller incongruities, connubial love will effect.

For my part, I freely confess, that, in my bachelorship, I was precisely such an over-cautious simpleton, as I now advise the reader not to be. My early habits had gifted me with a feminine sensibility, and too exquisite refinement.—I was the accomplished graduate of a dry-goods store, where, by dint of ministering to the whims of fine ladies, and suiting silken hose to delicate limbs, and handling satins, ribbons, chintzes, calicoes, tapes, gauze, and cambric needles, I grew up a very lady-like sort of a gentleman. It is not assuming too much, to affirm, that the ladies themselves were hardly so lady-like as Thomas Bullfrog. So painfully acute was my sense of female imperfection and such varied excellence did I require in the woman whom I could love, that there was an awful risk of my getting no wife at all, or of being driven to perpetuate matrimony with my own image in the looking-glass. Besides the fundamental principle, already hinted at, I demanded the fresh bloom of youth, pearly teeth, glossy ringlets, and the whole list of lovely items, with the utmost delicacy of habits and sentiments, a silken texture of mind and, above all, a virgin heart. In a word, if a young angel, just from Paradise, yet dressed in earthly fashion, had come and offered me her hand, it is by no means certain that I should have taken it. There was every chance of my becoming a most miserable old bachelor, when, by the best of luck in the world, I made a journey into another state, and was smitten by, and smote again, and wooed, won, and married the present Mrs. Bullfrog, all in the space of a fortnight. Owing to these extempore measures, I not only gave my bride credit for certain perfections, which have not as yet come to light, but also overlooked a few trifling defects, which, however, glimmered on my perception long before the close of the honey-moon. Yet, as there was no mistake about the fundamental principle aforesaid, I soon learned, as will be seen, to estimate Mrs. Bullfrog's deficiencies and superfluities at exactly their proper value.

The same morning that Mrs. Bullfrog and I came together as a unit, we took two seats in the stage-coach, and began our journey towards my place of business. There being no other passengers, we were as much alone, and as free to give vent to our raptures, as if I had hired a hack for the matrimonial jaunt. My bride looked charmingly, in a green silk calash, and riding-habit of pelisse cloth, and whenever her red lips parted with a smile, each tooth appeared like an inestimable pearl. Such was my passionate warmth, that—we had rattled out of the village, gentle reader, and were lonely as Adam and Eve in Paradise—I plead guilty to no less freedom than a kiss!—The gentle eye of Mrs. Bullfrog scarcely rebuked me for the profanation. Emboldened by her indulgence, I threw back the calash from her polished brow, and suffered my fingers, white and delicate as her own, to stray among those dark and glossy curls, which realized my day-dreams of rich hair.

"My love," said Mrs. Bullfrog, tenderly, "you will disarrange my curls."

"Oh, no, my sweet Laura!" replied I, still playing with the glossy ringlet. "Even your fair hand could not manage a curl more delicately than mine.—I propose myself the pleasure of doing up your hair in papers, every evening, at the same time with my own."

"Mr. Bullfrog," repeated she, "you must not disarrange my curls."

This was spoken in a more decided tone than I had happened to hear, until then, from my gentlest of all gentle brides. At the same time, she put up her hand and took mine prisoner, but merely drew it away from the forbidden ringlet, and then immediately released it. Now, I am a fidgety little man, and always love to have something in my fingers; so that, being debarred from my wife's curls, I looked about me for any other plaything. On the front seat of the coach, there was one of those small baskets in which travel-ing ladies, who are too delicate to appear at a public table, generally carry a supply of gingerbread, biscuits and cheese, cold ham, and other light refreshments, merely to sustain nature to the journey's end. Such airy diet will sometimes keep them in pretty good flesh, for a week together. Laying hold of this same little basket, I thrust my hand under the newspaper, with which it was carefully covered.

"What's this, my dear?" cried I; for the black neck of a bottle had popped out of the basket.

"A bottle of Kalydor, Mr. Bullfrog," said my wife, coolly taking the basket from my hands, and replacing it on the front seat.

There was no possibility of doubting my wife's word; but I never knew genuine Kalydor, such as I use for my own complexion, to smell so much like cherry-brandy. I was about to express my fears that the lotion would ruin her skin, when an accident occurred, which threatened more than a skin-deep injury. Our Jehu had carelessly driven over a heap of gravel, and fairly capsized the coach, with the wheels in the air, and our heels were where our heads should have been. What became of my wits I cannot imagine; they have always had a perverse trick of deserting me, just when they were most needed; but so it chanced, that, in the confusion of our overthrow I quite forgot that there was a Mrs. Bullfrog in the world. Like many men's wives, the good lady served her husband as a stepping-stone. I had scrambled out of the coach, and was instinctively settling my cravat, when somebody brushed roughly by me, and I heard a smart thwack upon the coachman's ear.

"Take that, you villain!" cried a strange, hoarse voice. "You have ruined me, you blackguard! I shall never be the woman I have been!"

And then came a second thwack, aimed at the driver's other ear, but which missed it, and hit him on the nose, causing a terrible effusion of blood. Now, who or what fearful apparition was inflicting this punishment on the poor fellow remained an impenetrable mystery to me. The blows were given by a person of grisly aspect, with a head almost bald, and sunken cheeks, apparently of the feminine gender, though hardly to be classed in the gentler sex. There being no teeth to modulate the, voice, it had a mumbled fierceness, not passionate, but stern, which absolutely made me quiver like calf's-foot jelly. Who could the phantom be? The most awful circumstance of the affair is yet to be told; for this ogre, or whatever it was, had a riding-habit like Mrs. Bullfrog's, and also a green silk calash, dangling down her back by the strings. In my terror and turmoil of mind, I could imagine nothing less, than that the old Nick, at the moment of our overturn, had annihilated my wife and jumped into her petticoats. This idea seemed the more probable, since I could nowhere perceive Mrs. Bullfrog alive, nor, though I looked very sharply about the coach, could I detect any traces of that beloved woman's dead body! There would have been a comfort in giving her Christian burial!

"Come, Sir, bestir yourself! Help this rascal to set up the coach," said the hobgoblin to me; then, with a terrific screech to three countrymen, at a distance—"Here, you fellows, ain't you ashamed to stand off, when a poor woman is in distress?"

The countrymen, instead of fleeing for their lives, came running at full speed, and laid hold of the topsy-turvy coach. I, also, though a small-sized man, went to work like a son of Anak. The coachman, too, with the blood still streaming from his nose, tugged and toiled most manfully, dreading, doubtless, that the next blow might break his head. And yet, bemauled as the poor fellow had been, he seemed to glance at me with an eye of pity, as if my case were more deplorable than his. But I cherished a hope that all would turn out a dream, and seized the opportunity, as we raised the coach, to jam two of my fingers under the wheel, trusting that the pain would awaken me.

"Why, here we are all to rights again!" exclaimed a sweet voice behind. "Thank you for your assistance, gentlemen. My dear Mr. Bullfrog, how you perspire! Do let me wipe your face. Don't take this little accident too much to heart, good driver. We ought to be thankful that none of our necks are broken!"

"We might have spared one neck out of the three," muttered the driver, rubbing his ear and pulling his nose, to ascertain whether he had been cuffed or not.—"Why, the woman's a witch!"

I fear that the reader will not believe, yet it is positively a fact, that there stood Mrs. Bullfrog, with her glossy ringlets curling on her brow, and two rows of orient pearls gleaming between her parted lips, which wore a most angelic smile. She had gained her riding-habit and calash from the grisly phantom, and was, in all respects the lovely woman who had been sitting by my side, at the instant of our overturn. How she had happened to disappear, and who had supplied her place, and whence did she now return, were problems too knotty for me to solve. There stood my wife. That was the one thing certain among a heap of mysteries. Nothing remained, but to help her into the coach, and plod on, through the journey of the day and the journey of life, as comfortably as we could. As the driver closed the door upon us, I heard his whisper to the three countrymen—

"How do you suppose a fellow feels, shut up in the cage with a she-tiger?"

Of course, this query could have no reference to my situation. Yet, unreasonable as it may appear, I confess that my feelings were not altogether so ecstatic, as when I first called Mrs. Bullfrog mine. True, she was a sweet woman, and an angel of a wife; but what if a gorgon should return, amid the transports of our connubial bliss, and take the angel's place! I recollected the tale of a fairy, who half the time was a beautiful woman, and half the time a hideous monster. Had I taken that very fairy to be the wife of my bosom? While such whims and chimeras were flitting across my fancy, I began to look askance at Mrs. Bullfrog, almost expecting that the transformation would be wrought before my eyes.

To divert my mind, I took up the newspaper which had covered the little basket of refreshments, and which now lay at the bottom of the coach, blushing with a deep-red stain, and emitting a potent spirituous fume, from the contents of the broken bottle of Kalydor. The paper was two or three years old, but contained an article of several columns, in which I soon grew wonderfully interested. It was the report of a trial for breach of promise of marriage, giving the testimony in full, with fervid extracts from both the gentleman's and lady's amatory correspondence. The deserted damsel had personally appeared in court, and had borne energetic evidence to her lover's perfidy, and the strength of her blighted affections.—On the defendant's part, there had been an attempt, though insufficiently sustained, to blast the plaintiff's character, and a plea in mitigation of damages, on account of her unamiable temper. A horrible idea was suggested by the lady's name.

"Madam," said I, holding the newspaper before Mrs. Bullfrog's eyes—and, though a small, delicate, and thin-visaged man, I feel assured that I looked very terrific— "Madam," repeated I, through my shut teeth, "were you the plaintiff in this case?"

"Oh, my dear Mr. Bullfrog," replied my wife, sweetly, "I thought all the world knew that!"

"Horror! horror!" exclaimed I, sinking back on the seat.

Covering my face with both hands, I emitted a deep and death-like groan, as if my tormented soul were rending me asunder. I, the most exquisitely fastidious of men, and whose wife was to have been of the most delicate and refined of women, with all the fresh dew-drops glittering on her virgin rosebud of a heart! I thought of the glossy ringlets and pearly teeth— I thought of the Kalydor—I thought of the coachman's bruised ear and bloody nose—I thought of the tender love-secrets, which she had whispered to the judge and jury, and a thousand tittering auditors—and gave another groan!

"Mr. Bullfrog," said my wife.

As I made no reply, she gently took my hands within her own, removed them from my face, and fixed her eyes steadfastly on mine.

"Mr. Bullfrog," said she, not unkindly, yet with all the decision of her strong character, "let me advise you to overcome this foolish weakness, and prove yourself, to the best of your ability, as good a husband as I will be a wife. You have discovered, perhaps, some little imperfections in your bride. Well—what did you expect? Women are not angels. If they were, they would go to Heaven for husbands—or, at least, be more difficult in their choice, on earth."

"But why conceal those imperfections?" interposed I, tremulously.

"Now, my love, are not you a most unreasonable little man?" said Mrs. Bullfrog, patting me on the cheek. "Ought a woman to disclose her frailties earlier than the wedding-day? Few husbands, I assure you, make the discovery in such good season, and still fewer complain that these trifles are concealed too long. Well, what a strange man you are! Poh! you are joking."

"But the suit for breach of promise!" groaned I.

"Ah! and is that the rub?" exclaimed my wife. "Is it possible that you view that affair in an objectionable light? Mr. Bullfrog, I never could have dreamt it! Is it an objection, that I have triumphantly defended myself against slander, and vindicated my purity in a court of justice? Or, do you complain, because your wife has shown the proper spirit of a woman, and punished the villain who trifled with her affections?"

"But," persisted I—shrinking into a corner of the coach, however; for I did not know precisely how much contradiction the proper spirit of a woman would endure— "but, my love, would it not have been more dignified to treat the villain with the silent contempt he merited?"

"That is all very well, Mr. Bullfrog," said my wife, slyly; "but in that case, where would have been the five thousand dollars which are to stock your dry-goods store?"

"Mrs. Bullfrog, upon your honor," demanded I, as if my life hung upon her words, "is there no mistake about those five thousand dollars?"

"Upon my word and honor, there is none," replied she. "The jury gave me every cent the rascal had—and I have kept it all for my dear Bullfrog!"

"Then, thou dear woman," cried I, with an overwhelming gust of tenderness, "let me fold thee to my heart! The basis of matrimonial bliss is secure, and all thy little defects and frailties are forgiven. Nay, since the result has been so fortunate, I rejoice at the wrongs which drove thee to this blessed law-suit. Happy Bullfrog that I am!"

V

EDGAR ALLAN POE (1809-1849)

During his earlier years Poe thought of a literary career always in terms of the making of poetry. His earliest volumes were collections of lyrics. When John P. Kennedy discovered him through a prize contest at Baltimore, Poe was at work on an ambitious poetic drama. Poetry to him "was a passion," a product almost sacred; prose was of secondary consideration, a marketable commodity that might be produced in cold blood simply to fill pages of a magazine or to replenish its creator's pocketbook. The winning of the Baltimore newspaper's prize and the resulting friendship of Kennedy which indirectly brought him the editorship of the *Southern Literary Messenger,* turned him into journalism as a profession. During the rest of his life he viewed literature more and more from the standpoint of the magazine editor.

From this viewpoint fiction became a thing to be considered in terms of space, of timeliness, of attractiveness to the general reader, of artistry. The call of the magazine was for short stories rather than for serials and the magazine was fast becoming a dominating force in America. In a letter to Professor Anthon, June, 1844, he wrote:

"I perceived that the country, from its very constitution, could not fail of affording in a few years a larger proportionate amount of readers than any upon earth. I perceived that the whole energetic, busy spirit of the age tended wholly to Magazine literature—to the curt, the terse, the well-timed, and the readily diffused, in preference to the old forms of the verbose and ponderous and inaccessible."

Again he wrote:

"We need now the light artillery rather than the "Peace-makers" of the intellect. I will not be sure that men at present think more profoundly than half a century ago, but without question they think with more rapidity, with more skill, with more tact, with more method and less of excrescence in the thought. Besides all this, they have a vast increase in the thinking material; they have more facts, more to think about. For this reason, they are disposed to put the greatest amount of thought in the smallest compass and disperse it with the utmost attainable rapidity. Hence the journalism of the age; hence, in especial, magazines."

Already in his review of Hawthorne's *Twice-Told Tales,* 1842, he had insisted that the short story is a distinct literary *genre* with rules of its own which he proceeded in a general way to codify—an enormously important study, the first document in short-story criticism.

Poe's approach to the short story was therefore from the standpoint of the journalist: the thing must be short so as to be read quickly; it must be fresh, timely, original, fascinating in its subject matter and startling in its climaxes; it must compel the author constantly to seek new materials and new *motifs,*—variety; and it must be divorced completely from message and from propaganda. To Poe the short story was a thing to be read for no other purpose than pleasure, entertainment, diversion. The more it could satisfy the reader's senses and hold him spellbound during the brief hour at the story teller's command the more valuable was it as a work of art. Poe added technique to the American short story.

HAWTHORNE'S TWICE-TOLD TALES

We said a few hurried words about Mr. Hawthorne in our last number, with the design of speaking more fully in the present. We are still, however, pressed for room, and must necessarily discuss his volumes more briefly and more at random than their high merits deserve.

The book professes to be a collection of *tales,* yet is, in two respects, misnamed. These pieces are now in their third re- publication, and, of course, are thrice-told. Moreover, they are by no means *all* tales, either in the ordinary or in the legitimate understanding of the term. Many of them 5 are pure essays; for example, "Sights from a Steeple," "Sunday at Home," "Little Annie's Ramble," "A Rill from the Town Pump," "The Toll-Gatherer's Day," "The Haunted Mind, "The Sister Years," 10 "Snow-Flakes," "Night Sketches," and "Foot-Prints on the Sea-Shore." We mention these matters chiefly on account of their discrepancy with that marked precision and finish by which the body of the work is distinguished.

Of the essays just named, we must be content to speak in brief. They are each and all beautiful, without being characterized by the polish and adaptation so visible in the tales proper. A painter would at once note their leading or predominant feature, and style it *repose*. There is no attempt at effect. All is quiet, thoughtful, subdued. Yet this repose may exist simultaneously with high originality of thought; and Mr. Hawthorne has demonstrated the fact. At every turn we meet with novel combinations; yet these combinations never surpass the limits of the quiet. We are soothed as we read; and withal is a calm astonishment that ideas so apparently obvious have never occurred or been presented to us before. Herein our author differs materially from Lamb or Hunt or Hazlitt—who, with vivid originality of manner and expression, have less of the true novelty of thought than is generally supposed, and whose originality, at best has an uneasy and meretricious quaintness, replete with startling effects unfounded in nature. and inducing trains of reflection which lead to no satisfactory result. The Essays of Hawthorne have much of the character of Irving, with more of originality, and less of finish; while, compared with the Spectator, they have a vast superiority at all points. The Spectator, Mr. Irving, and Mr. Hawthorne have in common that tranquil and subdued manner which we have chosen to denominate *repose:* but, in the case of the two former, this repose is attained rather by the absence of novel combination, or of originality, than otherwise, and consists chiefly in the calm, quiet, unostentatious expression of commonplace thoughts, in an unambitious, unadulterated Saxon. In them, by strong effort, we are made to conceive the absence of all. In the essays before us the absence of effort is too obvious to be mistaken, and a strong under-current of *suggestion* runs continuously beneath the upper stream of the tranquil thesis. In short, these effusions of Mr. Hawthorne are the product of a truly imaginative intellect, restrained, and in some measure repressed, by fastidiousness of taste, by constitutional melancholy and by indolence.

But it is of his tales that we desire principally to speak. The tale proper, in our opinion, affords unquestionably the fairest field for the exercise of the loftiest talent, which can be afforded by the wide domains of mere prose. Were we bidden to say how the highest genius could be most advantageously employed for the best display of its own powers, we should answer, without hesitation—in the composition of a rimed poem, not to exceed in length what might be perused in an hour. Within this limit alone can the highest order of true poetry exist. We need only here say, upon this topic, that, in almost all classes of composition, the unity of effect or impression is a point of the greatest importance. It is clear, moreover, that this unity cannot be thoroughly preserved in productions whose perusal cannot be completed at one sitting. We may continue the reading of a prose composition, from the very nature of prose itself, much longer than we can persevere, to any good purpose, in the perusal of a poem. This latter, if truly fulfilling the demands of the poetic sentiment, induces an exaltation of the soul which cannot be long sustained. All high excitements are necessarily transient. Thus a long poem is a paradox. And, without unity of impression, the deepest effects cannot be brought about. Epics were the offspring of an imperfect sense of Art, and their reign is no more. A poem *too* brief may produce a vivid, but never an intense or enduring impression. Without a certain continuity of effort—without a certain duration or repetition of purpose—the soul is never deeply moved. There must be the dropping of the water on the rock. De Béranger has wrought brilliant things—pungent and spirit-stirring—but, like all immassive bodies, they lack *momentum,* and thus fail to satisfy Poetic Sentiment. They sparkle and excite, but, from want of continuity, fail deeply to impress. Extreme brevity will degenerate into epigrammatism; but the sin of extreme length is even more unpardonable. *In medio tutissimus ibis.*

Were we called upon, however, to designate that class of composition which, next to such a poem as we have suggested, should best fulfil the demands of high genius— should offer it the most advantageous field of exertion—we should unhesitatingly speak of the prose tale, as Mr. Hawthorne has here exemplified it. We allude to the short prose narrative, requiring from a half-hour to one or two hours in its perusal. The ordinary novel is objectionable, from its length, for reasons already stated in substance. As it cannot be read at one sitting, it deprives itself, of course, of the immense force derivable from *totality*. Worldly interests intervening during the pauses of persual, modify, annul, or counteract, in a greater or less degree, the impressions of the book. But simple cessation in reading, would, of itself, be sufficient to destroy the true unity. In the brief tale, however, the author is enabled to carry out the fullness of his intention, be it what it may. During the hour of perusal the soul of the reader is at the writer's control. There are no external or extrensic influences—resulting from weariness or interruption.

A skilful literary artist has constructed a tale. If wise, he has not fashioned his thoughts to accommodate his incidents: but having conceived, with deliberate care, a certain unique or single *effect* to be wrought out, he then invents such incidents—he then combines such effects as may best aid him in establishing this preconceived effect. If his very initial sentence tend not to the outbringing of this effect, then he has failed in his first step. In the whole composition there should be no word written, of which the tendency, direct or indirect, is not to the one preestablished design. And by such means, with such care and skill, a picture is at length painted which leaves in the mind of him who contemplates it with a kindred art, a sense of the fullest satisfaction. The idea of the tale has been presented unblemished, because undisturbed; and this is an end unattainable by the novel. Undue brevity is just as exceptionable here as in the poem; but undue length is yet more to be avoided.

We have said that the tale has a point of superiority even over the poem. In fact, while the *rhythm* of this latter is an essential aid in the development of the poet's highest idea—the idea of the Beautiful—the artificialities of this rhythm are an inseparable bar to the development of all points of thought or expression which have their basis in *Truth*. But Truth is often, and in very great degree, the aim of the tale. Some of the finest tales are tales of ratiocination. Thus the field of this species of composition, if not in so elevated a region on the mountain of Mind, is a tableland of far vaster extent than the domain of the mere poem. Its products are never so rich, but infinitely more numerous, and more appreciable by the mass of mankind. The writer of the prose tale, in short, may bring to his theme a vast variety of modes or inflections of thought and expression—(the ratiocinative, for example, the sarcastic, or the humorous) which are not only antagonistical to the nature of the poem, but absolutely forbidden by one of its most peculiar and indispensable adjuncts; we allude, of course, to rhythm. It may be added here, *par parenthèse,* that the author who aims at the purely beautiful in a prose tale is laboring at great disadvantage. For Beauty can be better treated in the poem. Not so with terror, or passion, or horror, or a multitude of such other points. And here it will be seen how full of prejudice are the usual animadversions against those *tales of effect,* many fine examples of which were found in the earlier numbers of Blackwood. The impressions produced were wrought in a legitimate sphere of action, and constituted a legitimate although sometimes an exaggerated interest. They were relished by every man of genius: although there were found many men of genius who condemned them without just ground. The true critic will but demand that the design intended be accomplished, to the fullest extent, by the means most advantageously applicable.

We have very few American tales of real merit—we may say, indeed, none, with the exception of "The Tales of a Traveler" of Washington Irving, and these "Twice-Told Tales" of Mr. Hawthorne. Some of the pieces of Mr. John Neal abound in vigor and originality; but in general his compositions of this class are excessively diffuse, extravagant, and indicative of an imperfect sentiment of Art. Articles at random are, now and then, met with in our periodicals which might be advantageously compared with the best effusions of the British Magazines; but upon the whole, we are far behind our progenitors in this department of literature.

Of Mr. Hawthorne's "Tales" we would say, emphatically, that they belong to the highest region of Art—an Art subservient to genius of a very lofty order. We had supposed, with good reason for so supposing, that he had been thrust into his present position by one of the impudent *cliques* which beset our literature, and whose pretentions it is our full purpose to expose at the earliest opportunity; but we have been most agreeably mistaken. We know of few compositions which the critic can more honestly commend than these "Twice-Told Tales." As Americans, we feel proud of the book.

Mr. Hawthorne's distinctive trait is invention, creation, imagination, originality —a trait which, in the literature of fiction, is positively worth all the rest. But the nature of originality, so far as regards its manifestation in letters, is but imperfectly understood. The inventive or original mind as frequently displays itself in novelty of *tone* as in novelty of matter. Mr. Hawthorne is original at *all* points.

.   .   .   .   .   .

In the way of objection we have scarcely a word to say of these tales. There is, perhaps, a somewhat too general or prevalent *tone*—a tone of melancholy and mysticism. The subjects are insufficiently varied. There is not so much of *versatility* evinced as we might well be warranted in expecting from the high powers of Mr. Hawthorne. But beyond these trivial exceptions we have really none to make. The style is purity itself. Force abounds. High imagination gleams from every page. Mr. Hawthorne is a man of the truest genius. We only regret that the limits of our Magazine will not permit us to pay him that full tribute of commendation, which, under other circumstances, we should be so eager to pay.

THE FALL OF THE HOUSE OF USHER

Son cœur est un luth suspendu;
Sitôt qu'on le touche il résonne.[1]
              BÉRANGER.

During the whole of a dull, dark, and soundless day in the autumn of the year, when the clouds hung oppressively low in the heavens, I had been passing alone, on horseback, through a singularly dreary tract of country; and at length found myself, as the shades of the evening drew on, within view of the melancholy House of Usher. I know not how it was—but, with the first glimpse of the building, a sense of insufferable gloom pervaded my spirit. I say insufferable; for the feeling was unrelieved by any of that half-pleasurable, because poetic, sentiment with which the mind usually receives even the sternest natural images of the desolate or terrible. I looked upon the scene before me—upon the mere house, and the simple landscape features of the domain, upon the bleak walls, upon the vacant eye-like windows, upon a few rank sedges, and upon a few white trunks of decayed trees—with an utter depression of soul which I can compare to no earthly sensation more properly than to the after-dream of the reveler upon opium; the bitter lapse into every-day life, the hideous dropping off of the veil. There was an iciness, a sinking, a sickening of the heart, an unredeemed dreariness of thought which no goading of the imagination could torture into aught of the sublime. What was it—I paused to think— what was it that so unnerved me in the contemplation of the House of Usher? It was a mystery all insoluble; nor could I grapple with the shadowy fancies that crowded upon me as I pondered. I was forced to fall back upon the unsatisfactory conclusion, that while, beyond doubt, there *are* combinations of very simple natural objects which have the power of thus affecting us still the analysis of this power lies among considerations beyond our depth. It was possible, I reflected, that a mere different arrangement of the particulars of the scene, of the details of the picture, would be sufficient to modify, or perhaps to annihilate, its capacity for sorrowful impression; and acting upon this idea, I reined my horse to the precipitous brink of a black and lurid tarn that lay in unruffled luster by the dwelling, and gazed down—but with a shudder even more thrilling than before—upon the remodeled and inverted images of the gray sedge, and the ghastly tree-stems, and the vacant and eye-like windows.

Nevertheless, in this mansion of gloom I now proposed to myself a sojourn of some weeks. Its proprietor, Roderick Usher, had been one of my boon companions in boyhood; but many years had elapsed since our last meeting. A letter, however, had lately reached me in a distant part of the country—a letter from him—which in its wildly importunate nature had admitted of no other than a personal reply. The MS. gave evidence of nervous agitation. The writer spoke of acute bodily illness, of a mental disorder which oppressed him, and of an earnest desire to see me, as his best and indeed his only personal friend, with a view of attempting by the cheerfulness of my society, some alleviation of his malady. It was the manner in which all this, and much more, was said—it was the apparent *heart* that went with his request —which allowed me no room for hesitation; and I accordingly obeyed forthwith what I still considered a very singular summons.

Although as boys we had been even intimate associates, yet I really knew little of my friend. His reserve had been always excessive and habitual. I was aware, however, that his very ancient family had been noted, time out of mind, for a peculiar sensibility of temperament, displaying itself, through long ages, in many works of exalted art, and manifested of late in repeated deeds of munificent yet unobtrusive charity, as well as in a passionate devotion to the intricacies, perhaps even more than to the orthodox and easily recognizable beauties, of musical science. I had learned, too, the very remarkable fact that the stem of the Usher race, all time-honored as it was, had put forth at no period any enduring branch; in other words, that the entire family lay in the direct line of descent, and had always, with very trifling and very temporary variation, so lain. It was this deficiency, I considered, while running over in thought the perfect keeping of the character of the premises with the accredited character of the people, and while speculating upon the possible influence which the one, in the long lapse of centuries, might have exercised upon the other —it was this deficiency, perhaps, of collateral issue, and the consequent undeviating transmission from sire to son of the patrimony with the name, which had, at length, so identified the two as to merge the original title of the estate in the quaint and equivocal appellation of the "House of Usher"—an appellation which seemed to include, in the minds of the peasantry who used it, both the family and the family mansion.

I have said that the sole effect of my somewhat childish experiment, that of looking down within the tarn, had been to deepen the first singular impression. There can be no doubt that the consciousness of the rapid increase of my superstition—for why should I not so term it?—served mainly to accelerate the increase itself. Such, I have long known, is the paradoxical law of all sentiments having terror as a basis. And it might have been for this reason only, that, when I again uplifted my eyes to the house itself, from its image in the pool, there grew in my mind a strange fancy—a fancy so ridiculous, indeed, that I but mention it to show the vivid force of the sensations which oppressed me. I had so worked upon my imagination as really to believe that about the whole mansion and domain there hung an atmosphere peculiar to themselves and their immediate vicinity: an atmosphere which had no affinity with the air of heaven, but which had reeked up from the decayed trees, and the gray wall, and the silent tarn: a pestilent and mystic vapor, dull, sluggish, faintly discernible, and leaden-hued.

Shaking off from my spirit what *must* have been a dream, I scanned more narrowly the real aspect of the building. Its principal feature seemed to be that of an excessive antiquity. The discoloration of ages had been great. Minute fungi overspread the whole exterior, hanging in a fine tangled web-work from the eaves. Yet all this was apart from any extraordinary dilapidation. No portion of the masonry had fallen; and there appeared to be a wild inconsistency between its still perfect adaptation of parts and the crumbling condition of the individual stones. In this there was much that reminded me of the specious totality of old woodwork which has rotted for long years in some neglected vault, with no disturbance from the breath of the external air. Beyond this indication of excessive decay, however, the fabric gave little token of instability. Perhaps the eye of a scrutinizing observer might have discovered a barely perceptible fissure, which, extending from the roof of the building in front, made its way down the wall in a zigzag direction, until it became lost in the sullen waters of the tarn.

Noticing these things, I rode over a short causeway to the house. A servant in waiting took my horse, and I entered the Gothic archway of the hall. A valet, of stealthy step, thence conducted me, in silence, through many dark and intricate passages in my progress to the studio of his master. Much that I encountered on the way contributed, I know not how, to heighten the vague sentiments of which I have already spoken. While the objects around me—while the carvings of the ceilings, the somber tapestries of the walls, the ebon blackness of the floors, and the phantasmagoric armorial trophies which rattled as I strode, were but matters to which, or to such as which, I had been accustomed from my infancy—while I hesitated not to acknowledge how familiar was all this—I still wondered to find how unfamiliar were the fancies which ordinary images were stirring up. On one of the staircases, I met the physician of the family. His countenance, I thought, wore a mingled expression of low cunning and perplexity. He accosted me with trepidation and passed on. The valet now threw open a door and ushered me into the presence of his master.

The room in which I found myself was very large and lofty. The windows were long, narrow, and pointed, and at so vast a distance from the black oaken floor as to be altogether inaccessible from within. Feeble gleams of encrimsoned light made their way through the trellised panes, and served to render sufficiently distinct the more prominent objects around; the eye, however, struggled in vain to reach the remoter angles of the chamber, or the recesses of the vaulted and fretted ceiling. Dark draperies hung upon the walls. The general furniture was profuse, comfortless, antique, and tattered. Many books and musical instruments lay scattered about, but failed to give any vitality to the scene. I felt that I breathed an atmosphere of sorrow. An air of stern, deep, and irredeemable gloom hung over and pervaded all.

Upon my entrance, Usher arose from a sofa on which he had been lying at full length, and greeted me with a vivacious warmth which had much in it, I at first thought, of an overdone cordiality—of the constrained effort of the *ennuyé* man of the world. A glance, however, at his countenance, convinced me of his perfect sincerity. We sat down; and for some moments, while he spoke not, I gazed upon him with a feeling half of pity, half of awe. Surely man had never before so terribly altered, in so brief a period, as had Roderick Usher! It was with difficulty that I could bring myself to admit the identity of the wan being before me with the companion of my early boyhood. Yet the character of his face had been at all times remarkable. A cadaverousness of complexion; an eye large, liquid, and luminous beyond comparison; lips somewhat thin and very pallid, but of a sur-

passingly beautiful curve; a nose of a delicate Hebrew model, but with a breadth of nostril unusual in similar formations; a finely molded chin, speaking, in its want of prominence, of a want of moral energy; hair of a more than web-like softness and tenuity; these features, with an inordinate expansion above the regions of the temple, made up altogether a countenance not easily to be forgotten. And now in the mere exaggeration of the prevailing character of these features, and of the expression they were wont to convey, lay so much of change that I doubted to whom I spoke. The now ghostly pallor of the skin, and the now miraculous luster of the eye, above all things startled and even awed me. The silken hair, too, had been suffered to grow all unheeded, and as, in its wild gossamer texture, it floated rather than fell about the face, I could not, even with effort, connect its arabesque expression with any idea of simple humanity.

In the manner of my friend I was at once struck with an incoherence, an inconsistency; and I soon found this to arise from a series of feeble and futile struggles to overcome an habitual trepidancy, an excessive nervous agitation. For something of this nature I had indeed been prepared, no less by his letter than by reminiscences of certain boyish traits, and by conclusions deduced from his peculiar physical conformation and temperament. His action was alternatively vivacious and sullen. His voice varied rapidly from a tremulous indecision (when the animal spirits seemed utterly in abeyance) to that species of energetic concision—that abrupt, weighty, unhurried, and hollow-sounding enunciation—that leaden, self-balanced and perfectly modulated guttural utterance—which may be observed in the lost drunkard, or the irreclaimable eater of opium, during the periods of his most intense excitement.

It was thus that he spoke of the object of my visit, of his earnest desire to see me, and of the solace he expected me to afford him. He entered, at some length, into what he conceived to be the nature of his malady. It was, he said, a constitutional and a family evil, and one for which he despaired to find a remedy—a mere nervous affection, he immediately added, which would undoubtedly soon pass off. It displayed itself in a host of unnatural sensations. Some of these, as he detailed them, interested and bewildered me; although, perhaps, the terms and the general manner of the narration had their weight. He suffered much from a morbid acuteness of the senses; the most insipid food was alone endurable; he could wear only garments of a certain texture; the odors of all flowers were oppressive; his eyes were tortured by even a faint light; and there were but peculiar sounds, and these from stringed instruments, which did not inspire him with horror.

To an anomalous species of terror I found him a bounden slave. "I shall perish," said he, "I *must* perish in this deplorable folly. Thus, thus, and not otherwise, shall I be lost. I dread the events of the future, not in themselves, but in their results. I shudder at the thought of any, even the most trivial, incident, which may operate upon this intolerable agitation of soul. I have, indeed, no abhorrence of danger, except in its absolute effect—in terror. In this unnerved—in this pitiable condition, I feel that the period will sooner or later arrive when I must abandon life and reason together, in some struggle with the grim phantasm, FEAR."

I learned moreover at intervals, and through broken and equivocal hints, another singular feature of his mental condition. He was enchained by certain superstitious impressions in regard to the dwelling which he tenanted, and whence, for many years, he had never ventured forth—in regard to an influence whose supposititious force was conveyed in terms too shadowy here to be restated—an influence which some peculiarities in the mere form and substance of his family mansion, had, by dint of long sufferance, he said, obtained over his spirit—an effect which the physique of the gray walls and turrets, and of the dim tarn into which they all looked down, had, at length, brought about upon the morale of his existence.

He admitted, however, although with hesitation, that much of the peculiar gloom which thus afflicted him could be traced to a more natural and far more palpable origin—to the severe and long-continued illness, indeed to the evidently approaching dissolution, of a tenderly beloved sister— his sole companion for long years, his last and only relative on earth. "Her decease," he said, with a bitterness which I can never forget, "would leave him (him the hopeless and the frail) the last of the ancient race of the Ushers." While he spoke, the lady Madeline (for so was she called) passed slowly through a remote portion of the apartment, and, without having noticed my presence, disappeared. I regarded her with an utter astonishment not unmingled with dread, and yet I found it impossible to account for such feelings. A sensation of stupor oppressed me, as my eyes followed her retreating steps. When a door, at length, closed upon her, my glance sought instinctively and eagerly the countenance of the brother; but he had buried his face in his hands, and I could only perceive that a far more than ordinary wanness had overspread the emaciated fingers through which trickled many passionate tears.

The disease of the lady Madeline had long baffled the skill of her physicians. A settled apathy, a gradual wasting away of the person, and frequent although transient affections of a partially cataleptical character, were the unusual diagnosis. Hitherto she had steadily borne up against the pressure of her malady, and had not betaken herself finally to bed; but, on the closing in of the evening of my arrival at the house, she succumbed (as her brother told me at night with inexpressible agitation) to the prostrating power of the destroyer; and I learned that the glimpse I had obtained of her person would thus probably be the last I should obtain—that the lady, at least while living, would be seen by me no more.

For several days ensuing, her name was unmentioned by either Usher or myself; and during this period I was busied in earnest endeavors to alleviate the melancholy of my friend. We painted and read together; or I listened, as if in a dream, to the wild improvisation of his speaking guitar. And thus, as a closer and still closer intimacy admitted me more unreservedly into the recesses of his spirit, the more bitterly did I perceive the futility of all attempt at cheering a mind from which darkness, as if an inherent positive quality, poured forth upon all objects of the moral and physical universe, in one unceasing radiation of gloom.

I shall ever bear about me a memory of the many solemn hours I thus spent alone with the master of the House of Usher. Yet I should fail in any attempt to convey an idea of the exact character of the studies, or of the occupations, in which he involved me, or led me the way. An excited and highly distempered ideality threw a sulphureous luster over all. His long improvised dirges will ring forever in my ears. Among other things, I hold painfully in mind a certain singular perversion and amplification of the wild air of the last waltz of Von Weber. From the paintings over which his elaborate fancy brooded, and which grew, touch by touch, into vaguenesses at which I shuddered the more thrillingly because I shuddered knowing not why;—from these paintings (vivid as their images now are before me) I would in vain endeavor to educe more than a small portion which should lie within the compass of merely written words. By the utter simplicity, by the nakedness of his designs, he arrested and overawed attention. If ever mortal painted an idea, that mortal was Roderick Usher. For me at least, in the circumstances then surrounding me, there arose, out of the pure abstractions which the hypochondriac contrived to throw upon his canvas, an intensity of intolerable awe, no shadow of which felt I ever yet in the contemplation of the certainly glowing yet too concrete reveries of Fuseli.

One of the phantasmagoric conceptions of my friend, partaking not so rigidly of the spirit of abstraction, may be shadowed forth, although feebly, in words. A small picture presented the interior of an immensely long and rectangular vault or tunnel, with low walls, smooth, white, and without interruption or device. Certain accessory points of the design served well to convey the idea that this excavation lay at an exceeding depth below the surface of the earth. No outlet was observed in any portion of its vast extent, and no torch or other artificial source of light was discernible; yet a flood of intense rays rolled throughout, and bathed the whole in a ghastly and inappropriate splendor.

I have just spoken of that morbid condition of the auditory nerve which rendered all music intolerable to the sufferer, with the exception of certain effects of stringed instruments. It was, perhaps, the narrow limits to which he thus confined himself upon the guitar, which gave birth, in great measure, to the fantastic character of his performances. But the fervid *facility* of his impromptus could not be so accounted for. They must have been, and were, in the notes, as well as in the words of his wild

fantasias (for he not unfrequently accompanied himself with rhymed verbal improvisations), the result of that intense mental collectedness and concentration to which I have previously alluded to as observable only in particular moments of the highest artificial excitement. The words of one of these rhapsodies I have easily remembered. I was, perhaps, the more forcibly impressed with it, as he gave it, because, in the under or mystic current of its meaning, I fancied that I perceived, and for the first time, a full consciousness, on the part of Usher, of the tottering of his lofty reason upon her throne. The verses, which were entitled "The Haunted Palace," ran very nearly, if not accurately, thus:—

I

In the greenest of our valleys
  By good angels tenanted,
Once a fair and stately palace—
  Radiant palace—reared its head.
In the monarch Thought's dominion,
  It stood there;
Never seraph spread a pinion
  Over fabric half so fair.

II

Banners yellow, glorious, golden,
  On its roof did float and flow,
(This—all this—was in the olden
  Time long ago)
And every gentle air that dallied,
  In that sweet day,
Along the ramparts plumed and pallid,
  A wingèd odor went away.

III

Wanderers in that happy valley
  Through two luminous windows saw
Spirits moving musically
  To a lute's well-tunèd law,
Round about a throne where, sitting,
  Porphyrogene,
In state his glory well befitting,
  The ruler of the realm was seen.

IV

And all with pearl and ruby glowing
  Was the fair palace door,
Through which came flowing, flowing, flowing,
  And sparkling evermore,
A troop of Echoes whose sweet duty
  Was but to sing,
In voices of surpassing beauty,
  The wit and wisdom of their king.

V

But evil things, in robes of sorrow,
  Assailed the monarch's high estate;
(Ah, let us mourn, for never morrow
  Shall dawn upon him, desolate!)
And round about his home the glory
  That blushed and bloomed
Is but a dim-remembered story
  Of the old time entombed.

VI

And travellers now within that valley
  Through the red-litten windows see
Vast forms that move fantastically
  To a discordant melody;
While, like a ghastly rapid river,
  Through the pale door
A hideous throng rush out forever,
  And laugh—but smile no more.

I well remember that suggestions arising from this ballad led us into a train of thought, wherein there became manifest an opinion of Usher's which I mention not so much on account of its novelty, (for other men * have thought thus,) as on account of the pertinacity with which he maintained it. This opinion, in its general form, was that of the sentience of all vegetable things. But in his disordered fancy the idea had assumed a more daring character, and trespassed, under certain conditions, upon the kingdom of inorganization. I lack words to express the full extent, or the earnest *abandon* of his persuasion. The belief, however, was connected (as I have previously hinted) with the gray stones of the home of his forefathers. The conditions of the sentience had been here, he imagined, fulfilled in the method of collocation of these stones—in the order of their arrangement, as well as in that of the many fungi which overspread them, and of the decayed trees which stood around—above all, in the long undisturbed endurance of this arrangement, and in its reduplication in the still waters of the tarn. Its evidence —the evidence of the sentience—was to be seen, he said (and I here started as he spoke), in the gradual yet certain condensation of an atmosphere of their own about the waters and the walls. The result was discoverable, he added, in that silent, yet importunate and terrible influence which for centuries had molded the destinies of

* Watson, Dr. Percival, Spallanzani, and especially the Bishop of Landaff.—See "Chemical Essays," vol. v

his family, and which made *him* what I now saw him—what he was. Such opinions need no comment, and I will make none.

5 Our books—the books which, for years, had formed no small portion of the mental existence of the invalid—were, as might be supposed, in strict keeping with this character of phantasm. We pored together over such works as the Ververt and Chartreuse of Gresset; the Belphegor of Machiavelli; the Heaven and Hell of Swedenborg; the Subterranean Voyage of Nicholas Klimm by Holberg; the Chiromancy of Robert Flud, of Jean D'Indaginé, and of De la Chambre; the Journey into the Blue Distance of Tieck; and the City of the Sun of Campanella. One favorite volume was a small octavo edition of the *Directorium Inquisitorium*, by the Dominican Eymeric de Gironne; and there were passage in Pomponius Mela, about the old African Satyrs and Ægipans, over which Usher would sit dreaming for hours. His chief delight, however, was found in the perusal of an exceedingly rare and curious book in quarto Gothic—the manual of a forgotten church—the *Vigiliæ Mortuorum secundum Chorum Ecclesiæ Maguntinæ*.

I could not help thinking of the wild ritual of this work, and of its probable influence upon the hypochondriac, when one evening, having informed me abruptly that the lady Madeline was no more, he stated his intention of preserving her corpse for a fortnight, (previously to its final interment,) in one of the numerous vaults within the main walls of the building. The worldly reason, however, assigned for this singular proceeding, was one which I did not feel at liberty to dispute. The brother had been led to his resolution (so he told me) by consideration of the unusual character of the malady of the deceased, of certain obtrusive and eager inquiries on the part of her medical men, and of the remote and exposed situation of the burial-ground of the family. I will not deny that when I called to mind the sinister countenance of the person whom I met upon the staircase, on the day of my arrival at the house, I had no desire to oppose what I regarded as at best but a harmless, and by no means an unnatural, precaution.

At the request of Usher, I personally aided him in the arrangements for the temporary entombment. The body having been encoffined, we two alone bore it to its rest. The vault in which we placed it (and which had been so long unopened that our torches, half smothered in its oppressive atmosphere, gave us little opportunity for investigation) was small, damp, and entirely without means of admission for light; lying, at great depth, immediately beneath that portion of the building in which was my own sleeping apartment. It had been used, apparently, in remote feudal times, for the worst purposes of a donjon-keep, and in later days as a place of deposit for powder, or some other highly combustible substance, as a portion of its floor, and the whole interior of a long archway through which we reached it, were carefully sheathed with copper. The door, of massive iron, had been, also similarly protected. Its immense weight caused an unusually sharp grating sound, as it moved upon its hinges.

Having deposited our mournful burden upon tressels within this region of horror, we partially turned aside the yet unscrewed lid of the coffin, and looked upon the face of the tenant. A striking similitude between the brother and sister now first arrested my attention; and Usher divining, perhaps, my thoughts, I murmured out some few words from which I learned that the deceased and himself had been twins, and that sympathies of a scarcely intelligible nature had always existed between them. Our glances, however, rested not long upon the dead—for we could not regard her unawed. The disease which had thus entombed the lady in the maturity of youth, had left, as usual in all maladies of a strictly cataleptical character, the mockery of a faint blush upon the bosom and the face, and that suspiciously lingering smile upon the lip which is so terrible in death. We replaced and screwed down the lid, and, having secured the door of iron, made our way, with toil, into the scarcely less gloomy apartments of the upper portion of the house.

And now, some days of bitter grief having elapsed, an observable change came over the features of the mental disorder of my friend. His ordinary manner had vanished. His ordinary occupations were neglected or forgotten. He roamed from chamber to chamber with hurried, unequal, and objectless step. The pallor of his countenance had assumed, if possible, a more

ghastly hue—but the luminousness of his eye had utterly gone out. The once occasional huskiness of his tone was heard no more; and a tremulous quaver, as if of extreme terror, habitually characterized his utterance. There were times, indeed, when I thought his unceasingly agitated mind was laboring with some oppressive secret, to divulge which he struggled for the necessary courage. At times, again, I was obliged to resolve all into the mere inexplicable vagaries of madness, for I beheld him gazing upon vacancy for long hours, in an attitude of the profoundest attention, as if listening to some imaginary sound. It was no wonder that his condition terrified—that it infected me. I felt creeping upon me, by slow yet certain degrees, the wild influences of his own fantastic yet impressive superstitions.

It was, especially, upon retiring to bed late in the night of the seventh or eighth day after the placing of the lady Madeline within the donjon, that I experienced the full power of such feelings. Sleep came not near my couch, while the hours waned and waned away. I struggled to reason off the nervousness which had dominion over me. I endeavored to believe that much, if not all, of what I felt was due to the bewildering influence of the gloomy furniture of the room—of the dark and tattered draperies which, tortured into motion by the breath of a rising tempest, swayed fitfully to and fro upon the walls, and rustled uneasily about the decorations of the bed. But my efforts were fruitless. An irrepressible tremor gradually pervaded my frame; and at length there sat upon my very heart an incubus of utterly causeless alarm. Shaking this off with a gasp and a struggle, I uplifted myself upon the pillows, and, peering earnestly within the intense darkness of the chamber, hearkened —I know not why, except that an instinctive spirit prompted me—to certain low and indefinite sounds which came, through the pauses of the storm, at long intervals, I knew not whence. Overpowered by an intense sentiment of horror, unaccountable yet unendurable, I threw on my clothes with haste, (for I felt that I should sleep no more during the night,) and endeavored to arouse myself from the pitiable condition into which I had fallen, by pacing rapidly to and fro through the apartment.

I had taken but few turns in this manner, when a light step on an adjoining staircase arrested my attention. I presently recognized it as that of Usher. In an instant afterward he rapped with a gentle touch at my door, and entered, bearing a lamp. His countenance was, as usual, cadaverously wan—but, moreover, there was a species of mad hilarity in his eyes—an evidently restrained hysteria in his whole demeanor. His air appalled me—but anything was preferable to the solitude which I had so long endured, and I even welcomed his presence as a relief.

"And you have not seen it?" he said abruptly, after having stared about him for some moments in silence—"you have not then seen it?—but, stay! you shall." Thus speaking, and having carefully shaded his lamp, he hurried to one of the casements, and threw it freely open to the storm.

The impetuous fury of the entering gust nearly lifted us from our feet. It was, indeed, a tempestuous yet sternly beautiful night, and one wildly singular in its terror and its beauty. A whirlwind had apparently collected its force in our vicinity; for there were frequent and violent alterations in the direction of the wind; and the exceeding density of the clouds (which hung so low as to press upon the turrets of the house) did not prevent our perceiving the life-like velocity with which they flew careering from all points against each other, without passing away into the distance. I say that even their exceeding density did not prevent our perceiving this; yet we had no glimpse of the moon or stars, nor was there any flashing forth of the lightning. But the under surfaces of the huge masses of agitated vapor, as well as all terrestrial objects immediately around us, were glowing in the unnatural light of a faintly luminous and distinctly visible gaseous exhalation which hung about and enshrouded the mansion.

"You must not—you shall not behold this!" said I, shudderingly, to Usher, as I led him with a gentle violence from the window to a seat. "These appearances, which bewilder you, are merely electrical phenomena not uncommon—or it may be that they have their ghastly origin in the rank miasma of the tarn. Let us close this casement; the air is chilling and dangerous to your frame. Here is one of your favorite romances. I will read, and you shall listen; —and so we will pass away this terrible night together."

The antique volume which I had taken up was the "Mad Trist" of Sir Launcelot Canning; but I had called it a favorite of Usher's more in sad jest than in earnest; for, in truth, there is little in its uncouth and unimaginative prolixity which could have had interest for the lofty and spiritual ideality of my friend. It was, however, the only book immediately at hand; and I indulged a vague hope that the excitement which now agitated the hypochondriac might find relief (for the history of mental disorder is full of similar anomalies) even in the extremeness of the folly which I should read. Could I have judged, indeed, by the wild overstrained air of vivacity with which he harkened, or apparently harkened, to the words of the tale, I might well have congratulated myself upon the success of my design.

I had arrived at that well-known portion of the story where Ethelred, the hero of the Trist, having sought in vain for peaceable admission into the dwelling of the hermit, proceeds to make good an entrance by force. Here, it will be remembered, the words of the narrative run thus:—

"And Ethelred, who was by nature of a doughty heart, and who was now mighty withal, on account of the powerfulness of the wine which he had drunken, waited no longer to hold parley with the hermit, who, in sooth, was of an obstinate and maliceful turn, but, feeling the rain upon his shoulders, and fearing the rising of the tempest, uplifted his mace outright, and with blows made quickly room in the plankings of the door for his gauntleted hand; and now pulling therewith sturdily, he so cracked, and ripped, and tore all asunder, that the noise of the dry and hollow-sounding wood alarumed and reverberated throughout the forest."

At the termination of this sentence I started, and for a moment paused; for it appeared to me (although I at once concluded that my excited fancy had deceived me)—it appeared to me that from some very remote portion of the mansion there came, indistinctly, to my ears, what might have been, in its exact similarity of character, the echo (but a stifled and dull one certainly) of the very cracking and ripping sound which Sir Launcelot had so particularly described. It was, beyond doubt, the coincidence alone which had arrested my attention; for, amid the rattling of the sashes of the casements, and the ordinary commingled noises of the still increasing storm, the sound, in itself, had nothing, surely, which should have interested or disturbed me. I continued the story:—

"But the good champion Ethelred, now entering within the door, was sore enraged and amazed to perceive no signal of the maliceful hermit; but, in the stead thereof, a dragon of a scaly and prodigious demeanor, and of a fiery tongue, which sate in guard before a palace of gold, with a floor of silver; and upon the wall there hung a shield of shining brass with this legend enwritten—

Who entereth herein, a conqueror hath bin;
Who slayeth the dragon, the shield he shall win.

And Ethelred uplifted his mace, and struck upon the head of the dragon, which fell before him, and gave up his pesty breath, with a shriek so horrid and harsh, and withal so piercing, that Ethelred had fain to close his ears with his hands against the dreadful noise of it, the like whereof was never before heard."

Here again I paused abruptly, and now with a feeling of wild amazement; for there could be no doubt whatever that, in this instance, I did actually hear (although from what direction it proceeded I found it impossible to say) a low and apparently distant, but harsh, protracted, and most unusual screaming or grating sound —the exact counterpart of what my fancy had already conjured up for the dragon's unnatural shriek as described by the romancer.

Oppressed, as I certainly was, upon the occurrence of this second and most extraordinary coincidence, by a thousand conflicting sensations, in which wonder and extreme terror were predominant, I still retained sufficient presence of mind to avoid exciting, by any observation, the sensitive nervousness of my companion. I was by no means certain that he had noticed the sounds in question; although, assuredly, a strange alteration had during the last few minutes taken place in his demeanor. From a position fronting my own, he had gradually brought round his chair, so as to sit with his face to the door of the chamber; and thus I could but partially perceive his features, although I saw that his lips

trembled as if he were murmuring inaudibly. His head had dropped upon his breast —yet I knew that he was not asleep, from the wide and rigid opening of the eye as I caught a glance of it in profile. The motion of his body, too, was at variance with this idea—for he rocked from side to side with a gentle yet constant and uniform sway. Having rapidly taken notice of all this, I resumed the narrative of Sir Launcelot, which thus proceeded:—

"And now, the champion, having escaped from the terrible fury of the dragon, bethinking himself of the brazen shield, and of the breaking up of the enchantment which was upon it, removed the carcass from out of the way before him, and approached valorously over the silver pavement of the castle to where the shield was upon the wall; which in sooth tarried not for his full coming, but fell down at his feet upon the silver floor, with a mighty great and terrible ringing sound."

No sooner had these syllables passed my lips, than—as if a shield of brass had indeed, at the moment, fallen heavily upon a floor of silver—I became aware of a distinct, hollow, metallic and clangorous, yet apparently muffled reverberation. Completely unnerved, I leaped to my feet; but the measured rocking movement of Usher was undisturbed. I rushed to the chair in which he sat. His eyes were bent fixedly before him, and throughout his whole countenance there reigned a stony rigidity. But, as I placed my hand upon his shoulder, there came a strong shudder over his whole person; a sickly smile quivered about his lips; and I saw that he spoke in a low, hurried, and gibbering murmur, as if unconscious of my presence. Bending closely over him, I at length drank in the hideous import of his words.

"Not hear it?—yes, I hear it, and *have* heard it. Long—long—long—many minutes, many hours, many days, have I heard it—yet I dared not—oh, pity me, miserable wretch that I am!—I dared not —*I dared not speak! We have put her living in the tomb!* Said I not that my senses were acute? I *now* tell you that I heard her first feeble movements in the hollow coffin. I heard them—many, many days ago —yet I dared not—*I dared not speak!* And now—to-night—Ethelred—ha! ha! —the breaking of the hermit's door, and the death-cry of the dragon, and the clang-

or of the shield!—say, rather, the rending of her coffin, and the grating of the iron hinges of her prison, and her struggles within the coppered archway of the vault! Oh, whither shall I fly? Will she not be here anon? Is she not hurrying to upbraid me for my haste? Have I not heard her footstep on the stair? Do I not distinguish that heavy and horrible beating of her heart? Madman!"—here he sprang furiously to his feet, and shrieked out his syllables, as if in the effort he were giving up his soul—*"Madman! I tell you that she now stands without the door!"*

As if in the superhuman energy of his utterance there had been found the potency of a spell, the huge antique panels to which the speaker pointed threw slowly back, upon the instant, their ponderous and ebony jaws. It was the work of the rushing gust —but then without those doors there *did* stand the lofty and enshrouded figure of the lady Madeline of Usher. There was blood upon her white robes, and the evidence of some bitter struggle upon every portion of her emaciated frame. For a moment she remained trembling and reeling to and fro upon the threshold—then, with a low moaning cry, fell heavily inward upon the person of her brother, and, in her violent and now final death-agonies, bore him to the floor a corpse, and a victim of the terrors he had anticipated.

From that chamber, and from that mansion, I fled aghast. The storm was still abroad in all its wrath as I found myself crossing the old causeway. Suddenly there shot along the path a wild light, and I turned to see whence a gleam so unusual could have issued; for the vast house and its shadows were alone behind me. The radiance was that of the full, setting, and blood-red moon, which now shone vividly through that once barely-discernible fissure, of which I have before spoken as extending from the roof of the building, in a zig-zag direction, to the base. While I gazed, this fissure rapidly widened—there came a fierce breath of the whirlwind—the entire orb of the satellite burst at once upon my sight—my brain reeled as I saw the mighty walls rushing asunder—there was a long tumultuous shouting sound like the voice of a thousand waters—and the deep and dank tarn at my feet closed sullenly and silently over the fragments of the *"House of Usher."*

THE MURDERS IN THE RUE MORGUE

What song the Sirens sang, or what name Achilles assumed when he hid himself among women, although puzzling questions, are not beyond *all* conjecture.

SIR THOMAS BROWNE: *Urn-Burial.*

The mental features discoursed of as the analytical are, in themselves, but little susceptible of analysis. We appreciate them only in their effects. We know of them, among other things, that they are always to their possessor, when inordinately possessed, a source of the liveliest enjoyment. As the strong man exults in his physical ability, delighting in such exercises as call his muscles into action, so glories the analyst in that moral activity which *disentangles.* He derives pleasure from even the most trivial occupations bringing his talent into play. He is fond of enigmas, of conundrums, of hieroglyphics; exhibiting in his solutions of each a degree of acumen which appears to the ordinary apprehension preternatural. His results, brought about by the very soul and essence of method, have, in truth, the whole air of intuition.

The faculty of re-solution is possibly much invigorated by mathematical study, and especially by that highest branch of it, which, unjustly, and merely on account of its retrograde operations, has been called, as if *par excellence, analysis.* Yet to calculate is not in itself to analyze. A chess-player, for example, does the one, without effort at the other. It follows that the game of chess, in its effects upon mental character, is greatly misunderstood. I am not now writing a treatise, but simply prefacing a somewhat peculiar narrative by observations very much at random; I will, therefore, take occasion to assert that the higher powers of the reflective intellect are more decidedly and more usefully tasked by the unostentatious game of draughts than by all the elaborate frivolity of chess. In this latter, where the pieces have different and bizarre motions, with various and variable values, what is only complex is mistaken (a not unusual error) for what is profound. The *attention* is here called powerfully into play. If it flag for an instant, an oversight is committed, resulting in injury or defeat. The possible moves being not only manifold, but involute, the chances of such oversights are multiplied; and in nine cases out of ten, it is the more concentrative rather than the more acute player who conquers. In draughts, on the contrary, where the moves are unique and have but little variation, the probabilities of inadvertence are diminished, and the mere attention being left comparatively unemployed, what advantages are obtained by either party are obtained by superior acumen. To be less abstract: Let us suppose a game of draughts where the pieces are reduced to four kings, and where, of course, no oversight is to be expected. It is obvious that here the victory can be decided (the players being at all equal) only by some *recherché* movement, the result of some strong exertion of the intellect. Deprived of ordinary resources, the analyst throws himself into the spirit of his opponent, identifies himself therewith, and not unfrequently sees thus, at a glance, the sole methods (sometimes indeed absurdly simple ones) by which he may seduce into error or hurry into miscalculation.

Whist has long been noted for its influence upon what is termed the calculating power; and men of the highest order of intellect have been known to take an apparently unaccountable delight in it, while eschewing chess as frivolous. Beyond doubt there is nothing of a similar nature so greatly tasking the faculty of analysis. The best chess-player in Christendom may be little more than the best player of chess; but proficiency in whist implies capacity for success in all these more important undertakings where mind struggles with mind. When I say proficiency, I mean that perfection in the game which includes a comprehension of *all* the sources whence legitimate advantage may be derived. These are not only manifold, but multiform, and lie frequently among recesses of thought altogether inaccessible to the ordinary understanding. To observe attentively is to remember distinctly; and, so far, the concentrative chess-player will do very well at whist; while the rules of Hoyle (themselves based upon the mere mechanism of the game) are sufficiently and generally comprehensible. Thus to have a retentive memory, and to proceed by "the book," are points commonly regarded as the sum total of good playing. But it is in matters beyond the limits of mere rule that the skill of the analyst is evinced. He makes, in silence, a host of observations and inferences. So, perhaps, do his companions; and the difference in the extent of the information obtained lies, not so much in the validity of the inference, as in the quality of the observation. The necessary knowledge is that of *what* to observe. Our player confines himself not at all; nor, because the game is the object, does he reject deductions from things external to the game. He examines the countenance of his partner, comparing it carefully with that of each of his opponents. He considers the mode of assorting the cards in each hand; often counting trump by trump, and honor by honor, through the glances bestowed by their holders upon each. He notes every variation of face as the play progresses, gathering a fund of thought from the differences in the expression of certainty, of surprise, of triumph, or chagrin. From the manner of gathering up a trick he judges whether the person taking it can make another in the suit. He recognizes what is played through feint, by the air with which it is thrown upon the table. A casual or inadvertent word; the accidental dropping or turning of a card, with the accompanying anxiety or carelessness in regard to its concealment; the counting of the tricks, with the order of their arrangement; embarrassment, hesitation, eagerness or trepidation —all afford, to his apparently intuitive perception, indications of the true state of affairs. The first two or three rounds having been played, he is in full possession of the contents of each hand, and thenceforward puts down his cards with as absolute a precision of purpose as if the rest of the party had turned outward the faces of their own.

The analytical power should not be confounded with simple ingenuity; for while the analyst is necessarily ingenious, the ingenious man is often remarkably incapable of analysis. The constructive or combining power, by which ingenuity is usually manifested, and to which the phrenologists (I believe erroneously) have assigned a separate organ, supposing it a primitive faculty, has been so frequently seen in those whose intellect bordered otherwise upon idiocy, as to have attracted general observation among writers on morals. Between ingenuity and the analystic ability there exists a difference far greater, indeed, than that between the fancy and the imagination, but of a character very strictly analogous. It will be found, in fact, that the ingenious are always fanciful, and the truly imaginative never otherwise than analytic.

The narrative which follows will appear to the reader somewhat in the light of a commentary upon the propositions just advanced.

Residing in Paris during the spring and part of the summer of 18—, I there became acquainted with a Monsieur C. Auguste Dupin. This young gentleman was of an excellent—indeed of an illustrious—family, but, by a variety of untoward events, had been reduced to such poverty that the energy of his character succumbed beneath it, and he ceased to bestir himself in the world or to care for the retrieval of his fortunes. By courtesy of his creditors, there still remained in his possession a small remnant of his patrimony; and upon the income arising from this he managed, by means of a rigorous economy, to procure the necessities of life, without troubling himself about its superfluities. Books, indeed, were his sole luxuries, and in Paris these are easily obtained.

Our first meeting was at an obscure library in the Rue Montmartre, where the accident of our both being in search of the same very rare and very remarkable volume brought us into closer communion. We saw each other again and again. I was deeply interested in the little family history which he detailed to me with all that candor which a Frenchman indulges whenever mere self is the theme. I was astonished, too, at the vast extent of his reading; and, above all, I felt my soul enkindled within me by the wild fervor and the vivid freshness of his imagination. Seeking in Paris the objects I then sought, I felt that the society of such a man would be to me a treasure beyond price; and this feeling I frankly confided to him. It was at length arranged that we should live together during my stay in the city; and, as my wordly circumstances were somewhat less embarrassed than his own, I was permitted to be at the expense of renting, and furnishing in a style which suited the rather fantastic gloom of our common temper, a time-eaten and grotesque mansion, long deserted, through superstitions into which we did not inquire, and tottering to its fall in a retired and desolate portion of the Faubourg St. Germain.

Had the routine of our life at this place been known to the world, we should have been regarded as madmen—although, perhaps, as madmen of a harmless nature. Our seclusion was perfect. We admitted no visitors. Indeed, the locality of our retirement had been carefully kept a secret from my own former associates; and it had been many years since Dupin had ceased to know or be known in Paris. We existed within ourselves alone.

It was a freak of fancy in my friend (for what else shall I call it?) to be enamored of the night for her own sake; and into this bizarrerie, as into all his others, I quietly fell; giving myself up to his wild whims with a perfect abandon. The sable divinity would not herself dwell with us always; but we could counterfeit her presence. At the first dawn of the morning we closed all the massy shutters of our old building; lighted a couple of tapers which, strongly perfumed, threw out only the ghastliest and feeblest of rays. By the aid of these we then busied our souls in dreams—reading, writing, or conversing, until warned by the clock of the advent of the true Darkness. Then we sallied forth into the streets, arm and arm, continuing the topics of the day, or roaming far and wide until a late hour, seeking, amid the wild lights and shadows of the populous city, that infinity of mental excitement which quiet observation can afford.

At such times I could not help remarking and admiring (although from his rich ideality I had been prepared to expect it) a peculiar analytic ability in Dupin. He seemed, too, to take an eager delight in its exercise—if not exactly in its display—and did not hesitate to confess the pleasure thus derived. He boasted to me, with a low chuckling laugh, that most men, in respect to himself, wore windows in their bosoms, and was wont to follow up such assertions by direct and very startling proofs of his intimate knowledge of my own. His manner at these moments was frigid and abstract; his eyes were vacant in expression; while his voice, usually a rich tenor, rose into a treble which would have sounded petulantly but for the deliberateness and entire distinctness of the enunciation. Observing him in these moods, I often dwelt meditatively upon the old philosophy of the Bi-Part Soul, and amused myself with the fancy of a double Dupin—the creative and the resolvent.

Let it not be supposed from what I have just said that I am detailing any mystery, or penning any romance. What I have described in the Frenchman was merely the result of an excited, or perhaps of a diseased, intelligence. But of the character of his remarks at the periods in question an example will best convey the idea.

We were strolling one night down a long dirty street, in the vicinity of the Palais Royal. Being both, apparently, occupied with thought, neither of us had spoken a syllable for fifteen minutes at least. All at once Dupin broke forth with these words:

"He is a very little fellow, that's true, and would do better for the *Théâtre des Variétés.*"

"There can be no doubt of that," I replied unwittingly, and not at first observing (so much had I been absorbed in reflection) the extraordinary manner in which the speaker had chimed in with my meditations. In an instant afterward I recollected myself and my astonishment was profound.

"Dupin," said I, gravely, "this is beyond my comprehension. I do not hesitate to say that I am amazed, and can scarcely credit my senses. How was it possible you should know I was thinking of—?" Here I paused, to ascertain beyond a doubt whether he really knew of whom I thought.

"Of Chantilly," said he, "why do you pause? You were remarking to yourself that his diminutive figure unfitted him for tragedy."

This was precisely what had formed the subject of my reflections. Chantilly was a quondam cobbler of the Rue St. Denis, who, becoming stage-mad, had attempted the *rôle* of Xerxes, in Crébillon's tragedy so called, and been notoriously pasquinaded for his pains.

"Tell me, for Heaven's sake," I exclaimed, "the method—if method there is—by which you have been enabled to fathom my soul in this matter." In fact, I was even more startled than I would have been willing to express.

"It was the fruiterer," replied my friend, "who brought you to the conclusion that the mender of soles was not of sufficient height for Xerxes *et id genus omne.*"

"The fruiterer!—you astonish me—I know no fruiterer whomsoever."

"The man who ran up against you as we entered the street—it may have been fifteen minutes ago."

I now remembered that, in fact, a fruiterer, carrying upon his head a large basket of apples, had nearly thrown me down, by accident, as we passed from the Rue C—— into the thoroughfare where we stood; but what this had to do with Chantilly I could not possibly understand.

There was not a particle of *charlatanerie* about Dupin. "I will explain," he said, "and, that you may comprehend all clearly, we will first retrace the course of your meditations, from the moment in which I spoke to you until that of the *rencontre* with the fruiterer in question. The larger links of the chain run thus—Chantilly, Orion, Dr. Nichols, Epicurus, Stereotomy, the street stones, the fruiterer."

There are few persons who have not, at some period of their lives, amused themselves in retracing the steps by which particular conclusions of their own minds have been attained. The occupation is often full of interest; and he who attempts it for the first time is astonished by the apparently illimitable distance and incoherence between the starting-point and the goal. What, then, must have been my amazement when I heard the Frenchman speak what he had just spoken, and when I could not help acknowledging that he had spoken the truth? He continued:

"We had been talking of horses, if I remember aright, just before leaving the Rue C——. This was the last subject we discussed. As we crossed into this street, a fruiterer, with a large basket upon his head, brushing quickly past us, thrust you upon a pile of paving-stones collected at a spot where the causeway is undergoing repair. You stepped upon one of the loose fragments, slipped, slightly strained your ankle, appeared vexed or sulky, muttered a few words, turned to look at the pile, and then proceeded in silence. I was not particularly attentive to what you did; but observation has become with me, of late, a species of necessity.

"You kept your eyes upon the ground—glancing, with a petulant expression, at the holes and ruts in the pavement (so that I saw you were still thinking of the stones), until we reached the little alley called Lamartine, which had been paved, by way of experiment, with the overlapping and riveted blocks. Here your countenance brightened up, and, perceiving your lips move, I could not doubt that you murmured the word 'stereotomy,' a term very effectedly applied to this species of pavement. I knew that you could not say to yourself 'stereotomy' without being brought to think of atomies, and thus of the theories of Epicurus; and since, when we discussed this subject not very long ago, I mentioned to you how singularly, yet with how little notice, the vague guesses of that noble Greek had met with confirmation in the late nebular cosmogony, I felt that you could not avoid casting your eyes upward to the great nebula in Orion, and I certainly expected that you would do so. You did look up; and I was now assured that I had correctly followed your steps. But in that bitter tirade upon Chantilly, which appeared in yesterday's *Musée*, the satirist, making some disgraceful allusions to the cobbler's change of name upon assuming the buskin, quoted a Latin line about which we have often conversed. I mean the line

" 'Perdidit antiquum litera prima sonum.'

I had told you that this was in reference to Orion, formerly written Urion; and, from certain pungencies connected with this explanation, I was aware that you could not have forgotten it. It was clear, therefore, that you would not fail to combine the two ideas of Orion and Chantilly. That you did combine them I saw by the character of the smile which passed over your lips. You thought of the poor cobbler's immolation. So far, you had been stooping in your gait; but now I saw you draw yourself up to your full height. I was then sure that you reflected upon the diminutive figure of Chantilly. At this point I interrupted your meditations to remark that as, in fact, he *was* a very little fellow—that Chantilly—he would do better at the *Théâtre des Variétés.*"

Not long after this, we were looking over an evening edition of the *Gazette des Tribunaux,* when the following paragraphs arrested our attention:

"EXTRAORDINARY MURDERS.—This morning, about three o'clock, the inhabitants of the Quarter St. Roch were aroused from sleep by a succession of terrific shrieks, issuing apparently from the fourth story of a house in the Rue Morgue, known to be in the sole occupancy of one Madame L'Espanaye, and her daughter, Mademoiselle Camille L'Espanaye. After some delay, occasioned by a fruitless attempt to procure admission in the usual manner, the gateway was broken in with a crowbar, and eight or ten of the neighbors entered, accompanied by two gendarmes. By this time the cries had ceased; but, as the party rushed up the first flight of stairs, two or more rough voices, in angry contention, were distinguished, and seemed to proceed from the upper part of the house. As the second landing was reached, these sounds also had ceased, and everything remained perfectly quiet. The party spread themselves, and hurried from room to room. Upon arriving at a large back chamber in the fourth story (the door of which, being found locked, with the key inside, was forced open), a spectacle presented itself which struck every one present not less with horror than with astonishment.

"The apartment was in the wildest disorder—the furniture broken and thrown about in all directions. There was only one bedstead; and from this the bed had been removed, and thrown into the middle of the floor. On a chair lay a razor, besmeared with blood. On the hearth were two or three long and thick tresses of gray human hair, also dabbled in blood, and seeming to have been pulled out by the roots. Upon the floor were found four Napoleons, an ear-ring of topaz, three large silver spoons, three small of *métal d'Alger,* and two bags, containing nearly four thousand francs in gold. The drawers of a bureau, which stood in one corner, were open, and had been, apparently, rifled, although many articles still remained in them. A small iron safe was discovered under the *bed* (not under the bedstead). It was open, with the key still in the door. It had no contents beyond a few old letters, and other papers of little consequence.

"Of Madame L'Espanaye no traces were here seen; but an unusual quantity of soot being observed in the fireplace, a search was made in the chimney, and (horrible to relate!) the corpse of the daughter, head downward, was dragged therefrom; it having been thus forced up the narrow aperture for a considerable distance. The body was quite warm. Upon examining it, many excoriations were perceived, no doubt occasioned by the violence with which it had been thrust up and disengaged. Upon the face were many severe scratches, and upon the throat, dark bruises, and deep indentations of fingernails, as if the deceased had been throttled to death.

"After a thorough investigation of every portion of the house, without farther discovery, the party made its way into a small paved yard in the rear of the building, where lay the corpse of the old lady, with her throat so entirely cut that, upon an attempt to raise her, the head fell off. The body, as well as the head, was fearfully mutilated—the former so much so as scarcely to retain any semblance of humanity.

"To this horrible mystery there is not as yet, we believe, the slightest clew."

The next day's paper had these additional particulars.

"The Tragedy in the Rue Morgue. Many individuals have been examined in relation to this most extraordinary and frightful affair" [the word *"affaire"* has not as yet, in France, that levity of import which it conveys with us], "but nothing whatever has transpired to throw light upon it. We give below all the material testimony elicited.

"Pauline Dubourg, laundress, deposes that she has known both the deceased for three years, having washed for them during that period. The old lady and her daughter seemed on good terms—very affectionate towards each other. They were excellent pay. Could not speak in regard to their mode or means of living. Believed that Madame L. told fortunes for a living. Was reputed to have money put by. Never met any persons in the house when she called for the clothes or took them home. Was sure that they had no servant in employ. There appeared to be no furniture in any part of the building except in the fourth story.

"Pierre Moreau, tobacconist, deposes that he has been in the habit of selling small quantities of tobacco and snuff to Madame L'Espanaye for nearly four years. Was born in the neighborhood, and has always resided there. The deceased and her daughter had occupied the house in which the corpses were found, for more than six years. It was formerly occupied by a jeweller, who underlet the upper rooms to various persons. The house was the property of Madame L. She became dissatisfied with the abuse of the premises by her tenant, and moved into them herself, refusing to let any portion. The old lady was childish. Witness had seen the daughter some five or six times during the six years. The two lived an exceedingly retired life—were reputed to have money. Had heard it said among the neighbors that Madame L. told fortunes. Did not believe it. Had never seen any person enter the door except the old lady and her daughter, a porter once or twice, and a physician some eight or ten times.

"Many other persons, neighbors, gave evidence to the same effect. No one was spoken of as frequenting the house. It was not known whether there were any living connections of Madame L. and her daughter. The shutters of the front windows were seldom opened. Those in the rear were always closed, with the exception of the large back room, fourth story. The house was a good house—not very old.

"Isidore Musèt, gendarme, deposes that he was called to the house about three o'clock in the morning, and found some twenty or thirty persons at the gateway, endeavoring to gain admittance. Forced it open, at length, with a bayonet—not with a crowbar. Had but little difficulty in getting it open, on account of its being a double or folding gate, and bolted neither at bottom nor top. The shrieks were continued until the gate was forced—and then suddenly ceased. They seemed to be screams of some person (or persons) in great agony—were loud and drawn out, not short and quick. Witness led the way upstairs. Upon reaching the first landing, heard two voices in loud and angry contention: the one a gruff voice, the other much shriller—a very strange voice. Could distinguish some words of the former, which was that of a Frenchman. Was positive that it was not a woman's voice. Could distinguish the words *'sacré'* and *'diable.'* The shrill voice was that of a foreigner. Could not be sure whether it was the voice of a man or of a woman. Could not make out what was said, but believed the language to be Spanish. The state of the room and of the bodies was described by this witness as we described them yesterday.

"Henri Duval, a neighbor, and by trade a silversmith, deposed that he was one of the party who first entered the house. Corroborates the testimony of Musèt in general. As soon as they forced an entrance, they reclosed the door, to keep out the crowd, which collected very fast, notwithstanding the lateness of the hour. The shrill voice, this witness thinks, was that of an Italian. Was certain it was not French. Could not be sure that it was a man's voice. It might have been a woman's. Was not acquainted with the Italian language. Could not distinguish the words, but was convinced, by the intonation, that the speaker was an Italian. Knew Madame L. and her daughter. Had conversed with both frequently. Was sure that the shrill voice was not that of either of the deceased.

"—— Odenheimer, restaurateur. This witness volunteered his testimony. Not speaking French, was examined through an interpreter. Is a native of Amsterdam. Was passing the house at the time of the shrieks. They lasted for several minutes—probably ten. They were long and loud—very awful and distressing. Was one of those who entered the building. Corroborated the previous evidence in every respect but one. Was sure that the shrill voice was that of a man—of a Frenchman. Could not distinguish the words uttered. They were loud and quick—unequal—spoken apparently in fear as well as in anger. The voice was harsh—not so much shrill as harsh. Could not call it a shrill voice. The gruff voice said repeatedly, *'sacré,' 'diable,'* and once *'mon Dieu.'*

"Jules Mignaud, banker, of the firm of Mignaud et Fils, Rue Deloraine. Is the elder Mignaud. Madame L'Espanaye had some property. Had opened an account with his banking house in the spring of the year —— (eight years previously). Made frequent de-

posits in small sums. Had checked for nothing until the third day before her death, when she took out in person the sum of 4000 francs. This sum was paid in gold, and a clerk sent home with the money.

"*Adolphe Le Bon,* clerk to Mignaud et Fils, deposes that on the day in question, about noon, he accompanied Madame L'Espanaye to her residence with the 4000 francs, put up in two bags. Upon the door being opened, Mademoiselle L. appeared and took from his hands one of the bags, while the old lady relieved him of the other. He then bowed and departed. Did not see any person in the street at the time. It is a by-street—very lonely.

"*William Bird,* tailor, deposes that he was one of the party who entered the house. Is an Englishman. Has lived in Paris two years. Was one of the first to ascend the stairs. Heard the voices in contention. The gruff voice was that of a Frenchman. Could make out several words, but cannot now remember all. Heard distinctly '*sacré*' and '*mon Dieu.*' There was a sound at the moment as if of several persons struggling—a scraping and scuffling sound. The shrill voice was very loud—louder than the gruff one. Is sure that it was not the voice of an Englishman. Appeared to be that of a German. Might have been a woman's voice. Does not understand German.

"Four of the above-named witnesses, being recalled, deposed that the door of the chamber in which was found the body of Mademoiselle L. was locked on the inside when the party reached it. Everything was perfectly silent—no groans or noises of any kind. Upon forcing the door no person was seen. The windows, both of the back and front room, were down and firmly fastened from within. A door between the two rooms was closed, but not locked. The door leading from the front room into the passage was locked, with the key on the inside. A small room in the front of the house, on the fourth story, at the head of the passage, was open, the door being ajar. This room was crowded with old beds, boxes, and so forth. These were carefully removed and searched. There was not an inch of any portion of the house which was not carefully searched. Sweeps were sent up and down the chimneys. The house was a four-story one with garrets (*mansardes*). A trap-door on the roof was nailed down very securely—did not appear to have been opened for years. The time elapsing between the hearing of the voices in contention and the breaking open of the room door, was variously stated by the witnesses. Some made it as short as three minutes—some as long as five. The door was opened with difficulty.

"*Alfonzo Garcio,* undertaker, deposes that he resides in the Rue Morgue. Is a native of Spain. Was one of the party who entered the house. Did not proceed upstairs. Is nervous, and was apprehensive of the consequences of agitation. Heard the voices in contention. The gruff voice was that of a Frenchman. Could not distinguish what was said. The shrill voice was that of an Englishman—is sure of this. Does not understand the English language, but judges by the intonation.

"*Alberto Montani,* confectioner, deposes that he was among the first to ascend the stairs. Heard the voices in question. The gruff voice was that of a Frenchman. Distinguished several words. The speaker appeared to be expostulating. Could not make out the words of the shrill voice. Spoke quick and unevenly. Thinks it the voice of a Russian. Corroborates the general testimony. Is an Italian. Never conversed with a native of Russia.

"Several witnesses, recalled, here testified that the chimneys of all the rooms on the fourth story were too narrow to admit the passage of a human being. By 'sweeps' were meant cylindrical sweeping-brushes, such as are employed by those who clean chimneys. These brushes were passed up and down every flue in the house. There is no back passage by which any one could have descended while the party proceeded upstairs. The body of Mademoiselle L'Espanaye was so firmly wedged in the chimney that it could not be got down until four or five of the party united their strength.

"*Paul Dumas,* physician, deposes that he was called to view the bodies about daybreak. They were both then lying on the sacking of the bedstead in the chamber where Mademoiselle L. was found. The corpse of the young lady was much bruised and excoriated. The fact that it had been thrust up the chimney would sufficiently account for these appearances. The throat was greatly chafed. There were several deep scratches just below the chin, together with a series of livid spots which were evidently the impression of fingers. The face was fearfully discolored, and the eyeballs protruded. The tongue had been partially bitten through. A large bruise was discovered upon the pit of the stomach, produced, apparently, by the pressure of a knee. In the opinion of M. Dumas, Mademoiselle L'Espanaye had been throttled to death by some person or persons unknown. The corpse of the mother was horribly mutilated. All the bones of the right leg and arm were more or less shattered. The left *tibia* much splintered, as well as all the ribs of the left side. Whole body dreadfully bruised and discolored. It was not possible to say how the injuries had been inflicted. A heavy club of wood, or a broad bar of iron—a chair—any large, heavy, and obtuse weapon would have produced such results, if wielded by the hands of a very powerful man. No woman could have inflicted the blows with any weapon. The head of the deceased, when seen by witness, was entirely separated from the body, and was also greatly shattered. The throat had evidently been cut with some very sharp instrument—probably with a razor.

"*Alexandre Étienne,* surgeon, was called with M. Dumas to view the bodies. Corroborated the testimony, and the opinions of M. Dumas.

"Nothing farther of importance was elicited, although several other persons were examined. A murder so mysterious, and so perplexing in all its particulars, was never before committed in Paris—if indeed a murder has been committed at all. The police are entirely at fault—an unusual occurrence in affairs of this nature. There is not, however, the shadow of a clew apparent."

The evening edition of the paper stated that the greatest excitement still continued in the Quartier St. Roch—that the premises in question had been carefully researched, and fresh examinations of witnesses instituted, but all to no purpose. a postscript, however, mentioned that Adolphe Le Bon had been arrested and imprisoned, although nothing appeared to incriminate him, beyond the facts already detailed.

Dupin seemed singularly interested in the progress of this affair—at least so I judged from his manner, for he made no comments. It was only after the announcement that Le Bon had been imprisoned, that he asked me my opinion respecting the murders.

I could merely agree with all Paris in considering them an insoluble mystery. I saw no means by which it would be possible to trace the murderer.

"We must not judge of the means," said Dupin, "by this shell of an examination. The Parisian police, so much extolled for acumen, are cunning, but no more. There is no method in their proceedings, beyond the method of the moment. They make a vast parade of measures; but, not unfrequently, these are so ill adapted to the objects proposed, as to put us in mind of Monsieur Jourdain's calling for his *robe de chambre—pour mieux entendre la musique.* The results attained by them are not unfrequently surprising, but, for the most part, are brought about by simple diligence and activity. When these qualities are unavailing, their schemes fail. Vidocq, for example, was a good guesser, and a persevering man. But, without educated thought, he erred continually by the very intensity of his investigations. He impaired his vision by holding the object too close. He might see, perhaps, one or two points with unusual clearness, but in so doing he necessarily lost sight of the matter as a whole. Thus there is such a thing as being too profound. Truth is not always in a well. In fact, as regards the more important knowledge, I do believe that she is invariably superficial. The depth lies in the valleys where we seek her, and not upon the mountain-tops where she is found. The modes and sources of this kind of error are well typified in the contemplation of the heavenly bodies. To look at a star by glances—to view it in a sidelong way, by turning toward it the exterior portions of the retina (more susceptible of feeble impressions of light than the interior) is to behold the star distinctly—is to have the best appreciation of its luster: a luster which grows dim just in proportion as we turn our vision *fully* upon it. A greater number of rays actually fall upon the eye in the latter case, but, in the former, there is the more refined capacity for comprehension. By undue profundity we perplex and enfeeble thought; and it is possible to make even Venus herself vanish from the firmament by a scrutiny too sustained, too concentrated, or too direct.

"As for these murders, let us enter into some examinations for ourselves, before we make up an opinion respecting them. An inquiry will afford us amusement" [I thought this an odd term, so applied, but said nothing], "and, besides, Le Bon once rendered me a service for which I am not ungrateful. We will go and see the premises with our own eyes. I know G——, the Prefect of Police, and shall have no difficulty in obtaining the necessary permission."

The permission was obtained, and we proceeded at once to the Rue Morgue. This is one of those miserable thoroughfares which intervene between the Rue Richelieu and the Rue St. Roch. It was late in the afternoon when we reached it, as this quarter is at a great distance from that in which we resided. The house was readily found; for there were still many persons gazing up at the closed shutters, with an objectless curiosity, from the opposite side of the way. It was an ordinary Parisian house, with a gateway, on one side of which was a glazed watch-box, with a sliding panel in the window, indicating a *loge de concierge*. Before going in we walked up the street, turned down an alley, and then, again turning, passed in the rear of the building—Dupin, meanwhile, examining the whole neighborhood, as well as the house, with a minuteness of attention for which I could see no possible object.

Retracing our steps, we came again to the front of the dwelling, rang, and, having shown our credentials, were admitted by the agents in charge. We went upstairs —into the chamber where the body of Mademoiselle L'Espanaye had been found, and where both the deceased still lay. The disorders of the room had, as usual, been suffered to exist. I saw nothing beyond what had been stated in the *Gazette des Tribunaux*. Dupin scrutinized everything, not excepting the bodies of the victims. We then went into other rooms, and into the yard; a gendarme accompanying us throughout. The examination occupied us until dark, when we took our departure. On our way home my companion stepped in for a moment at the office of one of the daily papers.

I have said that the whims of my friend were manifold, and that *Je les ménagais:* —for this phrase there is no English equivalent. It was his humor, now, to decline all conversation on the subject of the murder, until about noon the next day. He then asked me, suddenly, if I had observed anything *peculiar* at the scene of the atrocity.

There was something in his manner of emphasizing the word "peculiar," which caused me to shudder, without knowing why.

"No, nothing *peculiar*," I said; "nothing more, at least, than we both saw stated in the paper."

"The *Gazette*," he replied, "has not entered, I fear, into the unusual horror of the thing. But dismiss the idle opinions of this print. It appears to me that this mystery is considered insoluble, for the very reason which should cause it to be regarded as easy of solution—I mean for the *outré* character of its features. The police are confounded by the seeming absence of motive: not for the murder itself, but for the atrocity of the murder. They are puzzled, too, by the seeming impossibility of reconciling the voices heard in contention, with the facts that no one was discovered upstairs but the assassinated Mademoiselle L'Espanaye, and that there were no means of egress without the notice of the party ascending. The wild disorder of the room; the corpse thrust, with the head downward, up the chimney; the frightful mutilation of the body of the old lady; these considerations, with those just mentioned, and others which I need not mention, have sufficed to paralyze the powers, by putting completely at fault the boasted acumen of the government agents. They have fallen into the gross but common error of confounding the unusual with the abstruse. But it is by these deviations from the plane of the ordinary that reason feels its way, if at all, in its search for the true. In investigations such as we are now pursuing, it should not be so much asked 'what has occurred,' as 'what has occurred that has never occurred before.' In fact, the facility with which I shall arrive, or have arrived, at the solution of this mystery, is in the direct ratio of its apparent insolubility in the eyes of the police."

I stared at the speaker in mute astonishment.

"I am now awaiting," continued he, looking toward the door of our apartment— "I am now awaiting a person who, although perhaps not the perpetrator of these butcheries, must have been in some measure implicated in their perpetration. Of the worst portion of the crimes committed, it is probable that he is innocent. I hope that I am right in this supposition; for upon it I build my expectation of reading the entire riddle. I look for the man here—in this room—every moment. It is true that he may not arrive; but the probability is that he will. Should he come, it will be necessary to detain him. Here are pistols; and we both know how to use them when occasion demands their use."

I took the pistols, scarcely knowing what I did, or believing what I heard, while Dupin went on, very much as if in a soliloquy. I have already spoken of his abstract manner at such times. His discourse was addressed to myself; but his voice, although by no means loud, had that intonation which is commonly employed in speaking to some one at a great distance. His eyes, vacant in expression, regarded only the wall.

"That the voices heard in contention," he said, "by the party upon the stairs, were not the voices of the women themselves, was fully proved by the evidence. This relieves us of all doubt upon the question whether the old lady could have first destroyed the daughter, and afterward have committed suicide. I speak of this point chiefly for the sake of method; for the strength of Madame L'Espanaye would have been utterly unequal to the task of thrusting her daughter's corpse up the chimney as it was found; and the nature of the wounds upon her own person entirely preclude the idea of self-destruction. Murder, then, has been committed by some third party; and the voices of this third party were those heard in contention. Let me now advert—not to the whole testimony respecting these voices—but to what was *peculiar* in that testimony. Did you observe anything peculiar about it?"

I remarked that, while all the witnesses agreed in supposing that gruff voice to be that of a Frenchman, there was much disagreement in regard to the shrill, or, as one individual termed it, the harsh voice.

"That was the evidence itself," said Dupin, "but it was not the peculiarity of the evidence. You have observed nothing distinctive. Yet there *was* something to be observed. The witnesses, as you remark, agreed about the gruff voice; they were here unanimous. But in regard to the shrill voice, the peculiarity is—not that they disagreed—but that, while an Italian, an Englishman, a Spaniard, a Hollander, and a Frenchman attempted to describe it, each one spoke of it as that *of a foreigner.* Each is sure that it was not the voice of one of his own countrymen. Each likens it—not to the voice of an individual of any nation with whose language he is conversant—but the converse. The Frenchman supposes it the voice of a Spaniard, and 'might have distinguished some words *had he been acquainted with the Spanish.*' The Dutchman maintains it to have been that of a Frenchman; but we find it stated that '*not understanding French, this witness was examined through an interpreter.*' The Englishman thinks it the voice of a German, and '*does not understand German.*' The Spaniard 'is sure' that it was that of an Englishman, but 'judges by the intonation' altogether, '*as he has no knowledge of the English.*' The Italian believes it the voice of a Russian, but '*has never conversed with a native of Russia.*' A second Frenchman differs, moreover, with the first, and is positive that the voice was that

of an Italian; but, *not being cognizant of that tongue,* is, like the Spaniard, 'convinced by the intonation.' Now, how strangely unusual must that voice have really been, about which such testimony as this *could* have been elicited!—in whose *tones,* even, denizens of the five great divisions of Europe could recognize nothing familiar! You will say that it might have been the voice of an Asiatic—of an African. Neither Asiatics nor Africans abound in Paris; but, without denying the inference, I will now merely call your attention to three points. The voice is termed by one witness 'harsh rather than shrill.' It is represented by two others to have been 'quick and *unequal.*' No words—no sounds resembling words—were by any witness mentioned as distinguishable.

"I know not," continued Dupin, "what impression I may have made, so far, upon your own understanding; but I do not hesitate to say that legitimate deductions even from this portion of the testimony—the portion respecting the gruff and shrill voices—are in themselves sufficient to engender a suspicion which should give direction to all farther progress in the investigation of the mystery. I said 'legitimate deductions'; but my meaning is not thus fully expressed. I designed to imply that the deductions are the *sole* proper ones, and that the suspicion arises *inevitably* from them as the single result. What the suspicion is, however, I will not say just yet. I merely wish you to bear in mind that, with myself, it was sufficiently forcible to give a definite form—a certain tendency—to my inquiries in the chamber.

"Let us now transport ourselves, in fancy, to this chamber. What shall we first seek here? The means of egress employed by the murderers. It is not too much to say that neither of us believe in preternatural events. Madame and Mademoiselle L'Espanaye were not destroyed by spirits. The doers of the deed were material, and escaped materially. Then how? Fortunately there is but one mode of reasoning upon the point, and that mode *must* lead us to a definite decision.—Let us examine, each by each, the possible means of egress. It is clear that the assassins were in the room where Mademoiselle L'Espanaye was found, or at least in the room adjoining, when the party ascended the stairs. It is then only from these two apartments that we have to seek issues. The police have laid bare the floors, the ceilings, and the masonry of the walls, in every direction. No *secret* issues could have escaped their vigilance. But, not trusting to their eyes, I examined with my own. There were, then, *no* secret issues. Both doors leading from the rooms into the passage were securely locked, with the keys inside. Let us turn to the chimneys. These, although of ordinary width for some eight or ten feet above the hearths, will not admit, throughout their extent, the body of a large cat. The impossibility of egress, by means already stated, being thus absolute, we are reduced to the windows. Through those of the front room no one could have escaped without notice from the crowd in the street. The murderers *must* have passed, then, through those of the back room. Now, brought to this conclusion in so unequivocal a manner as we are, it is not our part, as reasoners, to reject it on account of apparent impossibilities. It is only left for us to prove that these apparent 'impossibilities' are, in reality, not such.

"There are two windows in the chamber. One of them is unobstructed by furniture, and is wholly visible. The lower portion of the other is hidden from view by the head of the unwieldy bedstead which is thrust close up against it. The former was found securely fastened from within. It resisted the utmost force of those who endeavored to raise it. A large gimlet-hole had been pierced in its frame to the left, and a very stout nail was found fitted therein, nearly to the head. Upon examining the other window, a similar nail was seen similarly fitted in it; and a vigorous attempt to raise this sash failed also. The police were now entirely satisfied that egress had not been in these directions. And, *therefore,* it was thought a matter of supererogation to withdraw the nail and open the windows.

"My own examination was somewhat more particular, and was so for the reason I have just given; because here it was, I knew, that all apparent impossibilities *must* be proved to be not such in reality.

"I proceeded to think thus—*à posteriori.* The murderers *did* escape from one of these windows. This being so, they could not have refastened the sashes from the inside, as they were found fastened: the consideration which put a stop, through its obviousness, to the scrutiny of the police in this quarter. Yet the sashes *were* fastened. They *must,* then, have the power of fastening themselves. There was no escape from this conclusion. I stepped to the unobstructed casement, withdrew the nail with some difficulty, and attempted to raise the sash. It resisted all my efforts, as I had anticipated. A concealed spring must, I now knew, exist; and this corroboration of my idea convinced me that my premises, at least, were correct, however mysterious still appeared the circumstances attending the nails. A careful search soon brought to light the hidden spring. I pressed it, and, satisfied with the discovery, forbore to upraise the sash.

"I now replaced the nail and regarded it attentively. A person passing out through this window might have reclosed it, and the spring would have caught—but the nail could not have been replaced. The conclusion was plain, and again narrowed in the field of my investigations. The assassins *must* have escaped through the other window. Supposing, then, the springs upon each sash to be the same, as was probable, there *must* be found a difference between the nails, or at least between the modes of the fixture. Getting upon the sacking of the bedstead, I looked over the head-board minutely at the second casement. Passing my hand down behind the board, I readily discovered and pressed the spring, which was, as I had supposed, identical in character with its neighbor. I now looked at the nail. It was as stout as the other, and apparently fitted in the same manner—driven in nearly up to the head.

"You will say that I was puzzled; but, if you think so, you must have misunderstood the nature of the inductions. To use a sporting phrase, I had not been once 'at fault.' The scent had never for an instant been lost. There was no flaw in any link of the chain. I had traced the secret to its ultimate result,—and that result was *the* nail. It had, I say, in every respect, the appearance of its fellow in the other window; but this fact was an absolute nullity (conclusive as it might seem to be) when compared with the consideration that here, at this point, terminated the clue. 'There *must* be something wrong,' I said, 'about the nail.' I touched it; and the head, with about a quarter of an inch of the shank, came off in my fingers. The rest of the shank was in the gimlet-hole, where it had been broken off. The fracture was an old one (for its edges were incrusted with rust), and had apparently been accomplished by the blow of a hammer, which had partially embedded, in the top of the bottom sash, the head portion of the nail. I now carefully replaced this head portion in the indentation whence I had taken it, and the resemblance to a perfect nail was complete—the fissure was invisible. Pressing the spring, I gently raised the sash for a few inches; the head went up with it, remaining firm in its bed. I closed the window, and the semblance of the whole nail was again perfect.

"The riddle, so far, was now unriddled. The assassin had escaped through the window which looked upon the bed. Dropping of its own accord upon his exit (or perhaps purposely closed), it had become fastened by the spring; and it was the retention of this spring which had been mistaken by the police for that of the nail—further inquiry being thus considered unnecessary.

"The next question is that of the mode of descent. Upon this point I have been satisfied in my walk with you around the building. About five feet and a half from the casement in question there runs a lightning-rod. From this rod it would have been impossible for any one to reach the window itself, to say nothing of entering it. I observed, however, that the shutters of the fourth story were of the peculiar kind called by Parisian carpenters *ferrades*—a kind rarely employed at the present day, but frequently seen upon very old mansions at Lyons and Bordeaux. They are in the form of an ordinary door (a single, not a folding door), except that the lower half is latticed or worked in open trellis—thus affording an excellent hold for the hands. In the present instance these shutters are fully three feet and a half broad. When we saw them from the rear of the house, they were both about half open—that is to say, they stood off at right angles from the wall. It is probable that the police, as well as myself, examined the back of the tenement; but, if so, in looking at these *ferrades* in the line of their breadth (as they must have done), they did not perceive this great breadth itself, or, at all events, failed to take it into due consideration. In fact, having once satisfied themselves that no egress could have been made in this quarter, they would naturally bestow here a very cursory examination. It was clear to me, however, that the shutter belonging to the window at the head of the bed would, if swung fully back to

the wall, reach to within two feet of the lightning-rod. It was also evident that, by exertion to a very unusual degree of activity and courage, an entrance into the window, from the rod, might have been thus effected. By reaching to the distance of two feet and a half (we now suppose the shutter open to its whole extent), a robber might have taken a firm grasp upon the trellis-work. Letting go, then, his hold upon the rod, placing his feet securely against the wall, and springing boldly from it, he might have swung the shutter so as to close it, and, if we imagine the window open at the time, might even have swung himself into the room.

"I wish you to bear especially in mind that I have spoken of a *very* unusual degree of activity as requisite to success in so hazardous and so difficult a feat. It is my design to show you first, that the thing might possibly have been accomplished: but, secondly and *chiefly*, I wish to impress upon your understanding the *very extraordinary*, the almost preternatural, character of that agility which could have accomplished it.

"You will say, no doubt, using the language of the law, that 'to make out my case' I should rather undervalue than insist upon a full estimation of the activity required in this matter. This may be the practice in law, but it is not the usage of reason. My ultimate object is only the truth. My immediate purpose is to lead you to place in juxtaposition that *very unusual* activity, of which I have just spoken, with that *very peculiar* shrill (or harsh) and *unequal* voice, about whose nationality no two persons could be found to agree, and in whose utterance no syllabification could be detected."

At these words a vague and half-formed conception of the meaning of Dupin flitted over my mind. I seemed to be upon the verge of comprehension, without power to comprehend; as men, at times, find themselves upon the brink of remembrance, without being able, in the end, to remember. My friend went on with his discourse.

"You will see," he said, "that I have shifted the question from the mode of egress to that of ingress. It was my design to convey the idea that both were effected in the same manner, at the same point. Let us now revert to the interior of the room. Let us survey the appearances here. The drawers of the bureau, it is said, had been rifled, although many articles of apparel still remained within them. The conclusion here is absurd. It is a mere guess—a very silly one—and no more. How are we to know that the articles found in the drawers were not all these drawers had originally contained? Madame L'Espanaye and her daughter lived an exceedingly retired life—saw no company, seldom went out, had little use for numerous changes of habiliment. Those found were at least of as good quality as any likely to be possessed by these ladies. If a thief had taken any, why did he not take the best—why did he not take all? In a word, why did he abandon four thousand francs in gold to encumber himself with a bundle of linen? The gold *was* abandoned. Nearly the whole sum mentioned by Monsieur Mignaud, the banker, was discovered, in bags, upon the floor. I wish you, therefore, to discard from your thoughts the blundering idea of *motive*, engendered in the brains of the police by that portion of the evidence which speaks of money delivered at the door of the house. Coincidences ten times as remarkable as this (the delivery of the money, and murder committed within three days upon the party receiving it) happen to all of us every hour of our lives, without attracting even momentary notice. Coincidences, in general, are great stumbling-blocks in the way of that class of thinkers who have been educated to know nothing of the theory of probabilities: that theory to which the most glorious objects of human research are indebted for the most glorious of illustration. In the present instance, had the gold been gone, the fact of its delivery three days before would have formed something more than a coincidence. It would have been corroborative of this idea of motive. But, under the real circumstances of the case, if we were to suppose gold the motive of this outrage, we must also imagine the perpetrator so vacillating an idiot as to have abandoned his gold and his motive together.

"Keeping now steadily in mind the points to which I have drawn your attention—that peculiar voice, that unusual agility, and that startling absence of motive in a murder so singularly atrocious as this—let us glance at the butchery itself. Here is a woman strangled to death by manual strength, and thrust up a chimney, head downward. Ordinary assassins employ no such modes of murder as this. Least of all, do they thus dispose of the murdered. In the manner of thrusting the corpse up the chimney, you will admit that there was something *excessively outré*—something altogether irreconcilable with our common notions of human action, even when we suppose the actors the most depraved of men. Think, too, how great must have been that strength which could have thrust the body *up* such an aperture so forcibly that the united vigor of several persons was found barely sufficient to drag it *down!*

"Turn, now, to other indications of the employment of a vigor most marvelous. On the hearth were thick tresses—very thick tresses—of gray human hair. These had been torn out by the roots. You are aware of the great force necessary in tearing thus from the head even twenty or thirty hairs together. You saw the locks in question as well as myself. Their roots (a hideous sight!) were clotted with fragments of the flesh of the scalp; sure token of the prodigious power which had been exerted in uprooting perhaps half a million of hairs at a time. The throat of the old lady was not merely cut, but the head absolutely severed from the body: the instrument was a mere razor. I wish you also to look at the *brutal* ferocity of these deeds. Of the bruises upon the body of Madame L'Espanaye I do not speak. Monsieur Dumas, and his worthy coadjutor Monsieur Étienne, have pronounced that they were inflicted by some obtuse instrument; and so far these gentlemen are very correct. The obtuse instrument was clearly the stone pavement in the yard, upon which the victim had fallen from the window which looked in upon the bed. This idea, however simple it may now seem, escaped the police for the same reason that the breadth of the shutters escaped them—because, by the affair of the nails, their perceptions had been hermetically sealed against the possibility of the windows having ever been opened at all.

"If now, in addition to all these things, you have properly reflected upon the odd disorder of the chamber, we have gone so far as to combine the ideas of an agility astounding, a strength superhuman, a ferocity brutal, a butchery without motive, a *grotesquerie* in horror absolutely alien from humanity, and a voice foreign in tone to the ears of men of many nations, and devoid of all distinct or intelligible syllabification. What result, then, has ensued?

What impression have I made upon your fancy?"

I felt a creeping of the flesh as Dupin asked me the question. "A madman," I said, "has done this deed—some raving maniac, escaped from a neighboring *Maison de Santé*."

"In some respects," he replied, "your idea is not irrelevant. But the voices of madmen, even in their wildest paroxysms, are never found to tally with that peculiar voice heard upon the stairs. Madmen are of some nation, and their language, however incoherent in its words, has always the coherence of syllabification. Besides, the hair of a madman is not such as I now hold in my hand. I disentangled this little tuft from the rigidly clutched fingers of Madame L'Espanaye. Tell me what you can make of it."

"Dupin!" I said, completely unnerved; "this hair is most unusual—this is no *human* hair."

"I have not asserted that it is," said he; "but, before we decide this point, I wish you to glance at the little sketch I have here traced upon this paper. It is a fac-simile drawing of what has been described in one portion of the testimony as 'dark bruises, and deep indentations of finger nails,' upon the throat of Mademoiselle L'Espanaye, and in another (by Messrs. Dumas and Étienne), as a 'series of livid spots, evidently the impression of fingers.'

"You will perceive," continued my friend, spreading out the paper upon the table before us, "that this drawing gives the idea of a firm and fixed hold. There is no *slipping* apparent. Each finger has retained—possibly until the death of the victim—the fearful grasp by which it originally imbedded itself. Attempt, now, to place all your fingers, at the same time, in the respective impressions as you see them."

I made the attempt in vain.

"We are possibly not giving this matter a fair trial," he said. "The paper is spread out upon a plane surface; but the human throat is cylindrical. Here is a billet of wood, the circumference of which is about that of the throat. Wrap the drawing around it, and try the experiment again."

I did so; but the difficulty was even more obvious than before.

"This," I said, "is the mark of no human hand."

"Read now," replied Dupin, "this passage from Cuvier."

It was a minute anatomical and generally descriptive account of the large, fulvous Ourang-Outang of the East Indian Islands. The gigantic stature, the prodigious strength and activity, the wild ferocity, and the imitative propensities of these mammalia are sufficiently well known to all. I understood the full horrors of the murder at once.

"The description of the digits," said I, as I made an end of reading, "is in exact accordance with this drawing. I see that no animal but an Ourang-Outang, of the species here mentioned, could have impressed the indentations as you have traced them. This tuft of tawny hair, too, is identical in character with that of the beast of Cuvier. But I cannot possibly comprehend the particulars of this frightful mystery. Besides, there were *two* voices heard in contention, and one of them was unquestionably the voice of a Frenchman."

"True; and you will remember an expression attributed almost unanimously, by the evidence, to this voice,—the expression, '*mon Dieu*.' This, under the circumstances, has been justly characterized by one of the witnesses (Montani, the confectioner) as an expression of remonstrance or expostulation. Upon these two words, therefore, I have mainly built my hopes of a full solution of the riddle. A Frenchman was cognizant of the murder. It is possible —indeed it is far more than probable— that he was innocent of all participation in the bloody transactions which took place. The Ourang-Outang may have escaped from him. He may have traced it to the chamber; but, under the agitating circumstances which ensued, he could never have recaptured it. It is still at large. I will not pursue these guesses—for I have no right to call them more—since the shades of reflection upon which they are based are scarcely of sufficient depth to be appreciable by my own intellect, and since I could not pretend to make them intelligible to the understanding of another. We will call them guesses, then, and speak of them as such. If the Frenchman in question is indeed, as I suppose, innocent of this atrocity, this advertisement, which I left last night, upon our return home, at the office of *Le Monde* (a paper devoted to the shipping interest, and much sought by sailors), will bring him to our residence."

He handed me a paper, and I read thus:

"CAUGHT—*In the Bois de Boulogne, early in the morning of the —— inst.* [the morning of the murder], *a very large, tawny Ourang-Outang of the Bornese species. The owner (who is ascertained to be a sailor, belonging to a Maltese vessel) may have the animal again, upon identifying it satisfactorily, and paying a few charges arising from its capture and keeping. Call at No. ——, Rue ——, Faubourg St. Germain—au troisième.*"

"How was it possible," I asked, "that you should know the man to be a sailor, and belonging to a Maltese vessel?"

"I do *not* know it," said Dupin. "I am not *sure* of it. Here, however, is a small piece of ribbon, which, from its form, and from its greasy appearance, has evidently been used in tying the hair in one of those long *queues* of which sailors are so fond. Moreover, this knot is one which few besides sailors can tie, and is peculiar to the Maltese. I picked the ribbon up at the foot of the lightning-rod. It could not have belonged to either of the deceased. Now if, after all, I am wrong in my induction from this ribbon, that the Frenchman was a sailor belonging to a Maltese vessel, still I can have done no harm in saying what I did in the advertisement. If I am in error, he will merely suppose that I have been misled by some circumstance into which he will not take the trouble to inquire. But if I am right, a great point is gained. Cognizant, although innocent of the murder, the Frenchman will naturally hesitate about replying to the advertisement—about demanding the Ourang-Outang. He will reason thus: 'I am innocent; I am poor; my Ourang-Outang is of great value—to one in my circumstances a fortune of itself—why should I lose it through idle apprehensions of danger? Here it is, within my grasp. It was found in the Bois de Boulogne at a vast distance from the scene of that butchery. How can it ever be suspected that a brute beast should have done the deed? The police are at fault; they have failed to procure the slightest clue. Should they even trace the animal, it would be impossible to prove me cognizant of the murder, or to implicate me in guilt on account of that cognizance. Above all, *I am known*. The advertiser designates me as the possessor of the beast. I am not sure to what limit his knowledge may extend. Should I avoid claiming a property of so great value, which it is known that I possess, I will render the animal, at least, liable to suspicion. It is not my policy to attract attention either to myself or to the beast. I will answer the advertisement, get the Ourang-Outang, and keep it close until this matter has blown over.'"

At this moment we heard a step upon the stairs.

"Be ready," said Dupin, "with your pistols, but neither use them nor show them until at a signal from myself."

The front door of the house had been left open, and the visitor had entered, without ringing, and advanced several steps upon the staircase. Now, however, he seemed to hesitate. Presently we heard him descending. Dupin was moving quickly to the door, when we again heard him coming up. He did not turn back a second time, but stepped up with decision, and rapped at the door of our chamber.

"Come in," said Dupin, in a cheerful and hearty tone.

A man entered. He was a sailor, evidently,—a tall, stout, and muscular-looking person, with a certain dare-devil expression of countenance, not altogether unprepossessing. His face, greatly sunburnt, was more than half hidden by whisker and *mustachio*. He had with him a huge oaken cudgel, but appeared to be otherwise unarmed. He bowed awkwardly, and bade us "Good-evening," in French accents, which although somewhat Nefchâtelish, were still sufficiently indicative of a Parisian origin.

"Sit down, my friend," said Dupin. "I suppose you have called about the Ourang-Outang. Upon my word, I almost envy you the possession of him; a remarkably fine and no doubt a very valuable animal. How old do you suppose him to be?"

The sailor drew a long breath, with the air of a man relieved of some intolerable burden, and then replied, in an assured tone:

"I have no way of telling—but he can't be more than four or five years old. Have you got him here?"

"Oh, no; we had no conveniences for keeping him here. He is at a livery stable in the Rue Dubourg, just by. You can get him in the morning. Of course you are prepared to identify the property?"

"To be sure I am, sir."

"I shall be sorry to part with him," said Dupin.

"I don't mean that you should be at all this trouble for nothing, sir," said the man. "Couldn't expect it. Am very willing to pay a reward for the finding of the animal—that is to say, anything in reason."

"Well," replied my friend, "that is all very fair, to be sure. Let me think!—what should I have? Oh! I will tell you. My reward shall be this. You shall give me all the information in your power about these murders in the Rue Morgue."

Dupin said the last words in a very low tone, and very quietly. Just as quietly, too, he walked toward the door, locked it, and put the key in his pocket. He then drew a pistol from his bosom and placed it, without the least flurry, upon the table.

The sailor's face flushed up as if he were struggling with suffocation. He started to his feet and grasped his cudgel; but the next moment he fell back into his seat, trembling violently, and with the countenance of death itself. He spoke not a word. I pitied him from the bottom of my heart.

"My friend," said Dupin, in a kind tone, "you are alarming yourself unnecessarily —you are indeed. We mean you no harm whatever. I pledge you the honor of a gentleman, and of a Frenchman, that we intend you no injury. I perfectly well know that you are innocent of the atrocities in the Rue Morgue. It will not do, however, to deny that you are in some measure implicated in them. From what I have already said, you must know that I have had means of information about this matter—means of which you could never have dreamed. Now the thing stands thus. You have done nothing which you could have avoided—nothing, certainly, which renders you culpable. You were not even guilty of robbery, when you might have robbed with impunity. You have nothing to conceal. You have no reason for concealment. On the other hand, you are bound by every principle of honor to confess all you know. An innocent man is now imprisoned, charged with the crime of which you can point out the perpetrator."

The sailor had recovered his presence of mind, in a great measure, while Dupin uttered these words; but his original boldness of bearing was all gone.

"So help me God," said he, after a brief pause, "I *will* tell you all I know about this affair; but I do not expect you to believe one-half I say—I would be a fool indeed if I did. Still, I *am* innocent, and I will make a clean breast if I die for it."

What he stated was, in substance, this. He had lately made a voyage to the Indian Archipelago. A party, of which he formed one, landed at Borneo, and passed into the interior on an excursion of pleasure. Himself and a companion had captured the Ourang-Outang. This companion dying, the animal fell into his own exclusive possession. After great trouble, occasioned by the intractable ferocity of his captive during the home voyage, he at length succeeded in lodging it safely at his own residence in Paris, where, not to attract toward himself the unpleasant curiosity of his neighbors, he kept it carefully secluded, until such time as it should recover from a wound in the foot, received from a splinter on board ship. His ultimate design was to sell it.

Returning home from some sailors' frolic on the night, or rather in the morning, of the murder, he found the beast occupying his own bedroom, into which it had broken from a closet adjoining, where it had been, as was thought, securely confined. Razor in hand, and fully lathered, it was sitting before a looking-glass, attempting the operation of shaving, in which it had no doubt previously watched its master through the key-hole of the closet. Terrified at the sight of so dangerous a weapon in the possession of an animal so ferocious, and so well able to use it, the man for some moments was at a loss what to do. He had been accustomed, however, to quiet the creature, even in its fiercest moods, by the use of a whip, and to this he now resorted. Upon sight of it, the Ourang-Outang sprang at once through the door of the chamber, down the stairs, and thence, through a window, unfortunately open, into the street.

The Frenchman followed in despair; the ape, razor still in hand, occasionally stopping to look back and gesticulate at its pursuer, until the latter had nearly come up with it. It then again made off. In this manner the chase continued for a long time. The streets were profoundly quiet, as it was nearly three o'clock in the morning. In passing down an alley in the rear of the Rue Morgue, the fugutive's attention was arrested by a light gleaming from the open window of Madame L'Espanaye's chamber, in the fourth story of her house. Rushing to the building, it perceived the lightning-rod, clambered up with inconceivable agility, grasped the shutter, which was thrown fully back against the wall, and, by its means, swung itself directly upon the headboard of the bed. The whole feat did not occupy a minute. The shutter was kicked open again by the Ourang-Outang as it entered the room.

The sailor, in the meantime, was both rejoiced and perplexed. He had strong hopes of now recapturing the brute, as it could scarcely escape from the trap into which it had ventured, except by the rod, where it might be intercepted as it came down. On the other hand, there was much cause for anxiety as to what it might do in the house. This latter reflection urged the man still to follow the fugitive. A lightning-rod is ascended without difficulty, especially by a sailor; but, when he had arrived as high as the window, which lay far to his left, his career was stopped; the most that he could accomplish was to reach over so as to obtain a glimpse of the interior of the room. At this glimpse he nearly fell from his hold through excess of horror. Now it was that those hideous shrieks arose upon the night, which had startled from slumber the inmates of the Rue Morgue. Madame L'Espanaye and her daughter, habited in their night-clothes, had apparently been occupied in arranging some papers in the iron chest already mentioned, which had been wheeled into the middle of the room. It was open, and its contents lay beside it on the floor. The victims must have been sitting with their backs towards the windows; and, from the time elapsing between the ingress of the beast and the screams, it seems probable that it was not immediately perceived. The flapping-to of the shutter would naturally have been attributed to the wind.

As the sailor looked in, the gigantic animal had seized Madame L'Espanaye by the hair (which was loose, as she had been combing it), and was flourishing the razor about her face, in imitation of the motions of a barber. The daughter lay prostrate and motionless; she had swooned. The screams and struggles of the old lady (during which the hair was torn from her head) had the effect of changing the probably pacific purposes of the Ourang-Outang into those of wrath. With one determined sweep of its muscular arm it nearly severed her head from her body. The sight of blood inflamed its anger into frenzy.

Gnashing its teeth, and flashing fire from its eyes, it flew upon the body of the girl, and imbedded its fearful talons in her throat, retaining its grasp until she expired. Its wandering and wild glances fell at this moment upon the head of the bed, over which the face of its master, rigid with horror, was just discernible. The fury of the beast, who no doubt bore still in mind the dreaded whip, was instantly converted into fear. Conscious of having deserved punishment, it seemed desirous of concealing its bloody deeds, and skipped about the chamber in an agony of nervous agitation; throwing down and breaking the furniture as it moved, and dragging the bed from the bedstead. In conclusion, it seized first the corpse of the daughter, and thrust it up the chimney, as it was found; then that of the old lady, which it immediately hurled through the window headlong.

As the ape approached the casement with its mutilated burden, the sailor shrank aghast to the rod, and, rather gliding than clambering down it, hurried at once home —dreading the consequences of the butchery, and gladly abandoning, in his terror, all solicitude about the fate of the Ourang-Outang. The words heard by the party upon the staircase were the Frenchman's exclamations of horror and affright, commingled with the fiendish jabberings of the brute.

I have scarcely anything to add. The Ourang-Outang must have escaped from the chamber, by the rod, just before the breaking of the door. It must have closed the window as it passed through it. It was subsequently caught by the owner himself, who obtained for it a very large sum at the *Jardin des Plantes*. Le Bon was instantly released, upon our narration of the circumstances (with some comments from Dupin) at the bureau of the Prefect of Police. This functionary, however well disposed to my friend, could not altogether conceal his chagrin at the turn which affairs had taken, and was fain to indulge in a sarcasm or two, about the propriety of every person minding his own business.

"Let him talk," said Dupin, who had not thought it necessary to reply. "Let him discourse; it will ease his conscience. I am satisfied with having defeated him in his own castle. Nevertheless, that he failed in the solution of this mystery is by no means that matter for wonder which he supposes it; for, in truth, our friend the Prefect is somewhat too cunning to be profound. In his wisdom is no *stamen*. It is all head and no body, like the pictures of the Goddess Laverna,—or, at best, all head and shoulders, like a codfish. But he is a good creature after all. I like him especially for one master-stroke of cant, by which he has attained his reputation for ingenuity. I mean the way he has '*de nier ce qu'est et d'expliquer ce que n'est pas.*'"

VI

WILLIAM GILMORE SIMMS (1806–1870)

Before 1870, with the exception of Poe, the South produced but one writer of short stories worth mentioning,—William Gilmore Simms, and even he was first of all a novelist. Simms had been inspired by Irving and Cooper to work exclusively in native American materials,—legends, romanticized history, actual frontier characters. He did much excellent work, excellent when measured against the best work of his day. His tale "The Lazy Crow" is one of the earliest studies in fiction of the actual Southern negro. In the forties, when American fiction was dominated by Godey's *Lady's Book* and the feminized annuals, Simms seemed virile and vigorous and original, but viewed against the richer product of to-day he seems strangely old-fashioned and defective in art. In his preface to the second edition of *The Wigwam and the Cabin,* 1856, he expressed his opinion of the medium through which he had been forced to appear:

"These legends were mostly written for the annuals, in the period when annuals were supposed to be as essential to the Christmas and New Year's holidays as the egg-noggin or the mince pie. But the expensive form of the annual kept it from the great body of readers; and, besides, the annuals have gone the way of all mortal productions! Gold and glitter could not save them!—the pomp of heraldry, or the gorgeous blazonry of art. . . . When originally published, these stories were held to give signs of much more vitality than the medium in which they were so gorgeously encradled."

That Simms considered himself a pioneer in a new field there is little doubt, and that his influence was considerable during the formative period when good models were scarce, cannot be disputed. To him the materials of the story were more valuable than the art which worked with these materials. He was preserving, he believed, the history and the legends of his native land.

"One word for the material of these legends. It is local, sectional—and to be *national* in literature, one must needs be *sectional*. No one mind can fully or fairly illustrate the characteristics of any great country, and he who shall depict *one section* faithfully, has made his proper and sufficient contribution to the great work of national illustration. I can answer for it, confidently, that these legends represent, in large degree, the border history of the South. I can speak with confidence of the general truthfulness of its treatment."

GRAYLING; OR, "MURDER WILL OUT"

I

The world has become monstrous matter-of-fact in latter days. We can no longer get a ghost story, either for love or money. The materialists have it all their own way; and even the little urchin, eight years old, instead of deferring with decent reverence to the opinions of his grandmamma, now stands up stoutly for his own. He believes in every "ology" but pneumatology. "Faust" and the "Old Woman of Berkeley" move his derision only, and he would laugh incredulously, if he dared, at the Witch of Endor. The whole armory of modern reasoning is on his side; and, however he may admit at seasons that belief can scarcely be counted a matter of will, he yet puts his veto on all sorts of credulity. The cold-blooded demon called Science has taken the place of all the other demons. He has certainly cast out innumerable devils, however he may still spare the principal. Whether we are the better for his intervention is another question. There is reason to apprehend that in disturbing our human faith in shadows, we have lost some of those wholesome moral restraints which might have kept many of us virtuous, where the laws could not.

The effect, however, is much the more seriously evil in all that concerns the romantic. Our story-tellers are so resolute to deal in the real, the actual only, that they venture on no subjects the details of which are not equally vulgar and susceptible of proof. With this end in view, indeed, they too commonly choose their subjects among convicted felons, in order that they may avail themselves of the evidence which led to their conviction; and, to prove more conclusively their devoted adherence to nature and the truth, they depict the former not only in her condition of nakedness, but long before she has found out the springs of running water. It is to be feared that some of the coarseness of modern taste arises from the too great lack of that veneration which belonged to, and elevated to dignity, even the errors of preceding ages. A love of the marvelous belongs, it appears to me, to all those who love and cultivate either of the fine arts. I very much doubt whether the poet, the painter, the sculptor, or the romancer, ever yet lived, who had not some strong bias—a leaning, at least,—to a belief in the wonders of the invisible world. Certainly, the highest orders of poets and painters, those who create and invent, must have a strong taint of the superstitious in their composition. But this is digressive, and leads us from our purpose.

It is so long since we have been suffered to see or hear of a ghost, that a visitation at this time may have the effect of novelty, and I propose to narrate a story which I heard more than once in my boyhood, from the lips of an aged relative, who succeeded, at the time, in making me believe every word of it; perhaps, for the simple reason that she convinced me she believed every word of it herself. My grandmother was an old lady who had been a resident of the seat of most frequent war in Carolina during the Revolution. She had fortunately survived the numberless atrocities which she was yet compelled to witness; and, a keen observer, with a strong memory, she had in store a thousand legends of that stirring period, which served to beguile me from sleep many and many a long winter night. The story which I propose to tell was one of these; and when I say that she not only devoutly believed it herself, but that it was believed by sundry of her contemporaries, who were themselves privy to such of the circumstances as could be known to third parties, the gravity with which I repeat the legend will not be considered very astonishing.

The revolutionary war had but a little while been concluded. The British had left the country; but peace did not imply re-

pose. The community was still in that state of ferment which was natural enough to passions, not yet at rest, which had been brought into exercise and action during the protracted seven years' struggle through which the nation had just passed. The state was overrun by idlers, adventurers, profligates, and criminals. Disbanded soldiers, half-starved and reckless, occupied the highways,—outlaws, emerging from their hiding-places, skulked about the settlements with an equal sentiment of hate and fear in their hearts;—patriots were clamoring for justice upon the tories, and sometimes anticipating its course by judgments of their own; while the tories, those against whom the proofs were too strong for denial or evasion, buckled on their armor for a renewal of the struggle. Such being the condition of the country, it may easily be supposed that life and property lacked many of their necessary securities. Men generally traveled with weapons which were displayed on the smallest provocation: and few who could provide themselves with an escort ventured to travel any distance without one.

There was, about this time, said my grandmother, and while such was the condition of the country, a family of the name of Grayling, that lived somewhere upon the skirts of "Ninety-six" district. Old Grayling, the head of the family, was dead. He was killed in Buford's massacre. His wife was a fine woman, not so very old, who had an only son named James, and a little girl, only five years of age, named Lucy. James was but fourteen when his father was killed, and that event made a man of him. He went out with his rifle in company with Joel Sparkman, who was his mother's brother, and joined himself to Pickens's Brigade. Here he made as good a soldier as the best. He had no sort of fear. He was always the first to go forward; and his rifle was always good for his enemy's button at a long hundred yards. He was in several fights both with the British and Tories; and just before the war was ended he had a famous brush with the Cherokees, when Pickens took their country from them. But though he had no fear, and never knew when to stop killing while the fight was going on, he was the most bashful of boys that I ever knew; and so kind-hearted that it was almost impossible to believe all we heard of his fierce doings when he was in battle.

But they were nevertheless quite true for all his bashfulness.

Well, when the war was over, Joel Sparkman, who lived with his sister, Grayling, persuaded her that it would be better to move down into the low country. I don't know what reason he had for it, or what they proposed to do there. They had very little property, but Sparkman was a knowing man, who could turn his hand to a hundred things; and as he was a bachelor, and loved his sister and her children just as if they had been his own, it was natural that she should go with him wherever he wished. James, too, who was restless by nature—and the taste he had enjoyed of the wars had made him more so—he was full of it; and so, one sunny morning in April, their wagon started for the city. The wagon was only a small one, with two horses, scarcely larger than those that are employed to carry chickens and fruit to the market from the Wassamaws and thereabouts. It was driven by a negro fellow named Clytus, and carried Mrs. Grayling and Lucy. James and his uncle loved the saddle too well to shut themselves up in such a vehicle; and both of them were mounted on fine horses which they had won from the enemy. The saddle that James rode on,—and he was very proud of it,—was one that he had taken at the battle of Cowpens from one of the Tarleton's own dragoons, after he had tumbled the owner. The roads at that season were excessively bad, for the rains of March had been frequent and heavy, the track was very much cut up, and the red clay gullies of the hills of "Ninety-six" were so washed that it required all shoulders, twenty times a day, to get the wagon-wheels out of the bog. This made them travel very slowly,—perhaps, not more than fifteen miles a day. Another cause for slow traveling was, the necessity of great caution, and a constant look-out for enemies both up and down the road. James and his uncle took it by turns to ride ahead, precisely as they did when scouting in war, but one of them always kept along with the wagon. They had gone on this way for two days, and saw nothing to trouble and alarm them. There were few persons on the high-road, and these seemed to the full as shy of them as they probably were of strangers. But just as they were about to camp, the evening of the second day, while they were splitting light-wood, and getting out the kettles and the frying-pan, a person rode up and joined them without much ceremony. He was a short thick-set man, somewhere between forty and fifty: had on very coarse and common garments, though he rode a fine black horse of remarkable strength and vigor. He was very civil of speech, though he had but little to say, and that little showed him to be a person without much education and with no refinement. He begged permission to make one of the encampment, and his manner was very respectful and even humble; but there was something dark and sullen in his face—his eyes, which were of a light gray color, were very restless, and his nose turned up sharply, and was very red. His forehead was excessively broad, and his eyebrows thick and shaggy—white hairs being freely mingled with the dark, both in them and upon his head. Mrs. Grayling did not like this man's looks, and whispered her dislike to her son; but James, who felt himself equal to any man, said, promptly—

"What of that, mother! we can't turn the stranger off and say 'no'; and if he means any mischief, there's two of us, you know."

The man had no weapons—none, at least, which were then visible; and deported himself in so humble a manner, that the prejudice which the party had formed against him when he first appeared, if it was not dissipated while he remained, at least failed to gain any increase. He was very quiet, did not mention an unnecessary word, and seldom permitted his eyes to rest upon those of any of the party, the females not excepted. This, perhaps, was the only circumstance, that, in the mind of Mrs. Grayling, tended to confirm the hostile impression which his coming had originally occasioned. In a little while the temporary encampment was put in a state equally social and warlike. The wagon was wheeled a little way into the woods, and off the road; the horses fastened behind it in such a manner that any attempt to steal them would be difficult of success, even were the watch neglected which was yet to be maintained upon them. Extra guns, concealed in the straw at the bottom of the wagon, were kept well loaded. In the foreground, and between the wagon and the highway, a fire was soon blazing with a wild but cheerful gleam; and the worthy dame, Mrs. Grayling, assisted by the little girl, Lucy, lost no time in setting on the frying-pan, and cutting into slices the haunch of bacon, which they had provided at leaving home. James Grayling patrolled the woods, meanwhile for a mile or two round the encampment, while his uncle, Joel Sparkman, foot to foot with the stranger, seemed—if the absence of all care constitutes the supreme of human felicity—to realize the most perfect conception of mortal happiness. But Joel was very far from being the careless person that he seemed. Like an old soldier, he simply hung out false colors, and concealed his real timidity by an extra show of confidence and courage. He did not relish the stranger from the first, any more than his sister; and having subjected him to a searching examination, such as was considered, in those days of peril and suspicion, by no means inconsistent with becoming courtesy, he came rapidly to the conclusion that he was no better than he should be.

"You are a Scotchman, stranger," said Joel, suddenly drawing up his feet, and bending forward to the other with an eye like that of a hawk stooping over a covey of partridges. It was a wonder that he had not made the discovery before. The broad dialect of the stranger was not to be subdued; but Joel made slow stages and short progress in his mental journeyings. The answer was given with evident hesitation, but it was affirmative.

"Well, now, it's mighty strange that you should ha' fou't with us and not agin us," responded Joel Sparkman. "There was a precious few of the Scotch, and none that I knows on, saving yourself, perhaps,— that didn't go dead agin us, and for the tories, through thick and thin. That 'Cross Creek settlement' was a mighty ugly thorn in the sides of us whigs. It turned out a raal bad stock of varmints. I hope,—I reckon, stranger,—you ain't from that part."

"No," said the other; "oh no! I'm from over the other quarter. I'm from the Duncan settlement above."

"I've hearn tell of that other settlement, but I never know'd as any of the men fou't with us. What gineral did you fight under? What Carolina gineral?"

"I was at Gum Swamp when General Gates was defeated," was the still hesitating reply of the other.

"Well, I thank God, I warn't there, though I reckon things wouldn't ha' turned out quite so bad, if there had been a leetle sprinkling of Sumter's, or Pickens's, or Marion's men, among them two-legged critters that run that day. They did tell that some of the regiments went off without ever once emptying their rifles. Now, stranger, I hope you warn't among them fellows."

"I was not," said the other with something more of promptness.

"I don't blame a chap for dodging a bullet if he can, or being too quick for a bagnet, because, I'm thinking, a live man is always a better man than a dead one, or he can become so; but to run without taking a single crack at the inimy, is downright cowardice. There's no two ways about it, stranger."

This opinion, delivered with considerable emphasis, met with the ready assent of the Scotchman, but Joel Sparkman was not to be diverted, even by his own eloquence, from the object of his inquiry.

"But you ain't said," he continued, "who was your Carolina gineral. Gates was from Virginny, and he stayed a mighty short time when he come. You didn't run far at Camden, I reckon, and you joined the army ag'in, and come in with Greene? Was that the how?"

To this the stranger assented, though with evident disinclination.

"Then, mou'tbe, we sometimes went into the same scratch together? I was at Cowpens and Ninety-six, and seen sarvice at other odds and ends, where there was more fighting than fun. I reckon you must have been at 'Ninety-six,'—perhaps at Cowpens, too, if you went with Morgan?"

The unwillingness of the stranger to respond to these questions appeared to increase. He admitted, however, that he had been at "Ninety-six," though, as Sparkman afterwards remembered, in this case, as in that of the defeat of Gates at Gum Swamp, he had not said on which side he had fought. Joel, as he discovered the reluctance of his guest to answer his questions, and perceived his growing doggedness, forbore to annoy him, but mentally resolved to keep a sharper look-out than ever upon his motions. His examination concluded with an inquiry, which, in the plain-dealing regions of the south and southwest, is not unfrequently put first.

"And what mou't be your name, stranger?"

"Macnab," was the ready response. "Sandy Macnab."

"Well, Mr. Macnab, I see that my sister's got supper ready for us; so we mou't as well fall to upon the hoecake and bacon."

Sparkman rose while speaking, and led the way to the spot, near the wagon, where Mrs. Grayling had spread the feast. "We're pretty nigh on to the main road, here, but I reckon there's no great danger now. Besides, Jim Grayling keeps watch for us, and he's got two as good eyes in his head as any scout in the country, and a rifle that, after you once know how it shoots, 'twould do your heart good to hear its crack, if so be that twa'n't your heart that he drawed sight on. He's a perdigious fine shot, and as ready to shoot and fight as if he had a nateral calling that way."

"Shall we wait for him before we eat?" demanded Macnab, anxiously.

"By no sort o' reason, stranger," answered Sparkman. "He'll watch for us while we're eating, and after that I'll change shoes with him. So fall to, and don't mind what's a coming."

Sparkman had just broken the hoecake, when a distant whistle was heard. "Ha! That's the lad now!" he exclaimed, rising to his feet. "He's on trail. He's got a sight of an inimy's fire, I reckon. 'Twon't be onreasonable, friend Macnab, to get our we'pons in readiness;" and, so speaking, Sparkman bid his sister get into the wagon, where the little Lucy had already placed herself, while he threw open the pan of his rifle, and turned the priming over with his finger. Macnab, meanwhile, had taken from his holsters, which he had before been sitting upon, a pair of horseman's pistols, richly mounted with figures in silver. These were large and long, and had evidently seen service. Unlike his companion, his proceedings occasioned no comment. What he did seemed a matter of habit, of which he himself was scarcely conscious. Having looked at his priming, he laid the instruments beside him without a word, and resumed the bit of hoecake which he had just before received from Sparkman. Meanwhile, the signal whistle, supposed to come from James Grayling, was repeated. Silence ensued then for a brief space, which Sparkman employed in perambulating the grounds immediately contiguous. At length, just as he had returned to the fire, the sound of a horse's feet was heard, and a sharp quick halloo from Grayling informed his uncle that all was right. The youth made his appearance a moment after accompanied by a stranger on horseback; a tall, fine-looking young man, with a keen flashing eye, and a voice whose lively clear tones, as he was heard approaching, sounded cheerily like those of a trumpet after victory. James Grayling kept along on foot beside the newcomer; and his hearty laugh, and free, glib, garrulous tones, betrayed to his uncle, long ere he drew nigh enough to declare the fact, that he had met unexpectedly with a friend, or, at least, an old acquaintance.

"Why, who have you got there, James?" was the demand of Sparkman, as he dropped the butt of his rifle upon the ground.

"Why, who do you think, uncle? Who but Major Spencer—our own major?"

"You don't say so!—what!—well! Li'nel Spencer, for sartin! Lord bless you, major, who'd ha' thought to see you in these parts; and jest mounted too, for all natur, as if the war was to be fou't over ag'in. Well, I'm raal glad to see you. I am, that's sartin!"

"And I'm very glad to see you, Sparkman," said the other, as he alighted from his steed, and yielded his hand to the cordial grasp of the other.

"Well, I knows that, major, without you saying it. But you've jest come in the right time. The bacon's frying, and here's the bread;—let's down upon our haunches, in right good airnest, camp fashion, and make the most of what God gives us in the way of blessings. I reckon you don't mean to ride any further to-night, major?"

"No," said the person addressed, "not if you'll let me lay my heels at your fire. But who's in your wagon? My old friend, Mrs. Grayling, I suppose?"

"That's a true word, major," said the lady herself, making her way out of the vehicle with good-humored agility, and coming forward with extended hand.

"Really, Mrs. Grayling, I'm very glad to see you." And the stranger, with the blandness of a gentleman and the hearty warmth of an old neighbor, expressed his satisfaction at once more finding himself in the company of an old acquaintance. Their greetings once over, Major Spencer readily joined the group about the fire, while James Grayling—though with some reluctance—disappeared to resume his toils of the scout while the supper proceeded.

"And who have you here?" demanded Spencer, as his eye rested on the dark, hard features of the Scotchman. Sparkman told him all that he himself had learned of the name and character of the stranger, in a brief whisper, and in a moment after formally introduced the parties in this fashion—

"Mr. Macnab, Major Spencer. Mr. Macnab says he's true blue, major, and fou't at Camden, when General Gates run so hard to 'bring the d—d militia back.' He also fou't at Ninety-six, and Cowpens— so I reckon we had as good as count him one of us."

Major Spencer scrutinized the Scotchman keenly—a scrutiny which the latter seemed very ill to relish. He put a few questions to him on the subject of the war, and some of the actions in which he allowed himself to have been concerned; but his evident reluctance to unfold himself—a reluctance so unnatural to the brave soldier who has gone through his toils honorably —had the natural effect of discouraging the young officer, whose sense of delicacy had not been materially impaired amid the rude jostlings of military life. But, though he forbore to propose any other questions to Macnab, his eyes continued to survey the features of his sullen countenance with curiosity and a strangely increasing interest. This he subsequently explained to Sparkman, when, at the close of supper, James Grayling came in, and the former assumed the duties of the scout.

"I have seen that Scotchman's face somewhere, Sparkman, and I'm convinced at some interesting moment; but where, when, or how, I cannot call to mind. The sight of it is even associated in my mind with something painful and unpleasant; where could I have seen him?"

"I don't somehow like his looks myself," said Sparkman, "and I mislists he's been rether more of a tory than a whig; but that's nothing to the purpose now; and he's at our fire, and we've broken hoecake together; so we cannot rake up the old ashes to make a dust with."

"No, surely not," was the reply of Spencer. "Even though we knew him to be a tory, that cause of former quarrel should occasion none now. But it should produce watchfulness and caution. I'm glad to see that you have not forgotten your old business of scouting in the swamp."

"Kin I forget it. major?" demanded Sparkman, in tones which, though whispered, were full of emphasis, as he laid his ear to the earth to listen.

"James has finished supper, major— that's his whistle to tell me so; and I'll jest step back to make it cl'ar to him how we're to keep up the watch to-night."

"Count me in your arrangements, Sparkman, as I am one of you for the night," said the major.

"By no sort of means," was the reply. "The night must be shared between James and myself. Ef so be you wants to keep company with one or t'other of us, why, that's another thing, and, of course, you can do as you please."

"We'll have no quarrel on the subject, Joel," said the officer, good-naturedly, as they returned to the camp together.

II

The arrangements of the party were soon made. Spencer renewed his offer at the fire to take his part in the watch; and the Scotchman, Macnab, volunteered his services also; but the offer of the latter was another reason why that of the former should be declined. Sparkman was resolute to have everything his own way; and while James Grayling went out upon his lonely rounds, he busied himself in cutting bushes and making a sort of tent for the use of his late commander. Mrs. Grayling and Lucy slept in a wagon. The Scotchman stretched himself with little effort before the fire; while Joel Sparkman, wrapping himself up in his cloak, crouched under the wagon body, with his back resting partly against one of the wheels. From time to time he rose and thrust additional brands into the fire, looked up at the night, and round upon the little encampment, then sunk back to his perch and stole a few moments, at intervals, of uneasy sleep. The first two hours of the watch were over, and James Grayling was relieved. The youth, however, felt in no mood for sleep, and taking his seat by the fire, he drew from his pocket a little volume of Easy Reading Lessons, and by the fitful flame of the resinous light-wood, he prepared, in this rude manner, to make up for the precious time which his youth had lost of its legitimate employments, in the stirring events of the preceding seven years consumed in war. He was surprised at this employment by his late commander.

who, himself sleepless, now emerged from the bushes and joined Grayling at the fire. The youth had been rather a favorite with Spencer. They had both been reared in the same neighborhood, and the first military achievements of James had taken place under the eye, and had met the approbation of his officer. The difference of their ages was just such as to permit of the warm attachment of the lad without di- 10 minishing any of the reverence which should be felt by the inferior. Grayling was not more than seventeen, and Spencer was perhaps thirty four—the very prime of manhood. They sat by the fire and 15 talked of old times and told old stories with the hearty glee and good-nature of the young. Their mutual inquiries led to the revelation of their several objects in pursuing the present journey. Those of 20 James Grayling were scarcely, indeed, to be considered his own. They were plans and purposes of his uncle, and it does not concern this narrative that we should know more of their nature than has already been 25 revealed. But, whatever they were, they were as freely unfolded to his hearer as if the parties had been brothers, and Spencer was quite as frank in his revelations as his companion. He, too, was on 30 his way to Charleston, from whence he was to take passage for England.

"I am rather in a hurry to reach town," he said, "as I learn that the Falmouth packet is preparing to sail for England in 35 a few days, and I must go in her."

"For England, major!" exclaimed the youth with unaffected astonishment.

"Yes, James, for England. But why— what astonishes you?" 40

"Why, lord!" exclaimed the simple youth, "if they only knew there, as I do, what a cutting and slashing you did use to make among their red coats, I reckon they'd hang you to the first hickory." 45

"Oh, no! scarcely," said the other, with a smile.

"But I reckon you'll change your name, major?" continued the youth.

"No," responded Spencer, "if I did that, 50 I should lose the object of my voyage. You must know, James, that an old relative has left me a good deal of money in England, and I can only get it by proving that I am Lionel Spencer; so you see I 55 must carry my own name, whatever may be the risk."

"Well, major, you know best; but I do think if they could only have a guess of what you did among their sodgers at Hobkirk's and Cowpens, and Eutaw, and a dozen other places, they'd find some 5 means of hanging you up, peace or no peace. But I don't see what occasion you have to be going cl'ar away to England for money, when you've got a sight of your own already."

"Not so much as you think for," replied 10 the major, giving an involuntary and uneasy glance at the Scotchman, who was seemingly sound asleep on the opposite side of the fire. "There is, you know, but little money in the country at any time, and I 15 must get what I want for my expenses when I reach Charleston. I have just enough to carry me there."

"Well now, major, that's mighty strange. I always thought that you was about the 20 best off of any man in our parts; but if you're strained so close, I'm thinking, major,—if so be you wouldn't think me too presumptuous,—you'd better let me lend you a guinea or so that I've got to 25 spare, and you can pay me back when you get the English money."

And the youth fumbled in his bosom for a little cotton wallet, which, with its limited contents, was displayed in another 30 instant to the eyes of the officer.

"No, no, James," said the other, putting back the generous tribute; "I have quite enough to carry me to Charleston, and when there I can easily get a supply from 35 the merchants. But I thank you, my good fellow, for your offer. You *are* a good fellow, James, and I will remember you."

It is needless to pursue the conversation 40 farther. The night passed away without any alarms, and at dawn of the next day the whole party was engaged in making preparation for a start. Mrs. Grayling was soon busy in getting breakfast in readiness. 45 Major Spencer consented to remain with them until it was over; but the Scotchman, after returning thanks very civilly for his accommodation of the night, at once resumed his journey. His course seemed, 50 like their own, to lie below; but he neither declared his route nor betrayed the least desire to know that of Spencer. The latter had no disposition to renew those inquiries from which the stranger seemed to shrink 55 the night before, and he accordingly suffered him to depart with a quiet farewell, and the utterance of a good-natured wish, in which all the parties joined, that he might have a pleasant journey. When he was fairly out of sight, Spencer said to Sparkman,

"Had I liked that fellow's looks, nay, had I not positively disliked them, I should have gone with him. As it is, I will remain and share your breakfast."

The repast being over, all parties set forward; but Spencer, after keeping along with them for a mile, took his leave also. The slow wagon-pace at which the family traveled, did not suit the high-spirited cavalier; and it was necessary, as he assured them, that he should reach the city in two nights more. They parted with many regrets, as truly felt as they were warmly expressed; and James Grayling never felt the tedium of wagon traveling to be so severe as throughout the whole of that day when he separated from his favorite captain. But he was too stout-hearted a lad to make any complaint; and his dissatisfaction only showed itself in his unwonted silence, and an over-anxiety, which his steed seemed to feel in common with himself, to go rapidly ahead. Thus the day passed, and the wayfarers at its close had made a progress of some twenty miles from sun to sun. The same precautions marked their encampment this night as the last, and they rose in better spirits with the next morning, the dawn of which was very bright and pleasant, and encouraging. A similar journey of twenty miles brought them to the place of bivouac as the sun went down; and they prepared as usual for their securities and supper. They found themselves on the edge of a very dense forest of pines and scrubby oaks, a portion of which was swallowed up in a deep bay—so called in the dialect of the country—a swamp-bottom, the growth of which consisted of mingled cypresses and bay-trees, with tupola, gum, and dense thickets of low stunted shrubbery, cane grass, and dwarf willows, which filled up every interval between the trees, and to the eye most effectually barred out every human intruder. This bay was chosen as the background for the camping party. Their wagon was wheeled into an area on a gently rising ground in front, under a pleasant shade of oaks and hickories, with a lonely pine rising loftily in occasional spots among them. Here the horses were taken out, and James Grayling prepared to kindle up a fire; but, looking for his ax, it was unaccountably missing, and after

a fruitless search of half an hour, the party came to the conclusion that it had been left on the spot where they had slept last night. This was a disaster, and, while they meditated in what manner to repair it, a negro boy appeared in sight, passing along the road at their feet, and driving before him a small herd of cattle. From him they learned that they were only a mile or two from a farmstead where an ax might be borrowed; and James, leaping on his horse, rode forward in the hope to obtain one. He found no difficulty in his quest; and, having obtained it from the farmer, who was also a tavern-keeper, he casually asked if Major Spencer had not stayed with him the night before. He was somewhat surprised when told that he had not.

"There was one man stayed with me last night," said the farmer, "but he didn't call himself a major, and didn't look much like one."

"He rode a fine sorrel horse,—a tall, bright color, with white fore foot, didn't he?" asked James.

"No, that he didn't! he rode a powerful black, coal black, and not a bit of white about him."

"That was the Scotchman! But I wonder the major didn't stop with you. He must have rode on. Isn't there another house near you, below?"

"Not one. There's ne'er a house either above or below for a matter of fifteen miles. I'm the only man in all that distance that's living on this road; and I don't think your friend could have gone below, as I should have seen him pass. I've been all day out there in that field before your eyes, clearing up the brush."

III

Somewhat wondering that the major should have turned aside from the track, though without attaching to it any importance at that particular moment, James Grayling took up the borrowed ax and hurried back to the encampment, where the toil of cutting an extra supply of lightwood to meet the exigencies of the ensuing night, sufficiently exercised his mind as well as his body, to prevent him from meditating upon the seeming strangeness of the circumstance. But when he sat down to his supper over the fire that he had kindled, his fancies crowded thickly upon him, and he felt a confused doubt and suspicion that something was to happen, he knew not what. His conjectures and apprehensions were without form, though not altogether void; and he felt a strange sickness and a sinking at the heart which was very unusual with him. He had, in short, that lowness of spirits, that cloudy apprehensiveness of soul which takes the form of presentiment, and makes us look out for danger even when the skies are without a cloud, and the breeze is laden, equally and only, with balm and music. His moodiness found no sympathy among his companions. Joel Sparkman was in the best of humors, and his mother was so cheery and happy, that when the thoughtful boy went off into the woods to watch, he could hear her at every moment breaking out into little catches of country ditty, which the gloomy events of the late war had not yet obliterated from her memory.

"It's very strange!" soliloquized the youth, as he wandered along the edges of the dense bay or swamp-bottom, which we have passingly referred to,—"it's very strange what troubles me so! I feel almost frightened, and yet I know I'm not to be frightened easily, and I don't see anything in the woods to frighten me. It's strange the major didn't come along this road! Maybe he took another higher up that leads by a different settlement. I wish I had asked the man at the house if there's such another road. I reckon there must be, however, for where could the major have gone?"

The unphilosophical mind of James Grayling did not, in his farther meditations, carry him much beyond this starting point; and with its continual recurrence in soliloquy, he proceeded to traverse the margin of the bay, until he came to its junction with, and termination at, the highroad. The youth turned into this, and, involuntarily departing from it a moment after, soon found himself on the opposite side of the bay thicket. He wandered on and on, as he himself described it, without any power to restrain himself. He knew not how far he went; but, instead of maintaining his watch for two hours only, he was gone more than four; and, at length, a sense of weariness which overpowered him all of a sudden, caused him to seat himself at the foot of a tree, and snatch a few moments of rest. He denied that he slept in this time. He insisted to

the last moment of his life that sleep never visited his eyelids that night,—that he was conscious of fatigue and exhaustion, but not drowsiness,—and that this fatigue was so numbing as to be painful, and effectually kept him from any sleep. While he sat thus beneath the tree, with a body weak and nerveless, but a mind excited, he knew not how or why, to the most acute degree of expectation and attention, he heard his name called by the well-known voice of his friend, Major Spencer. The voice called him three times,—"James Grayling!—James!—James Grayling!" before he could muster strength enough to answer. It was not courage he wanted,—of that he was positive, for he felt sure, as he said, that something had gone wrong, and he was never more ready to fight in his life than at that moment, could he have commanded the physical capacity; but his throat seemed dry to suffocation,—his lips effectually sealed up as if with wax, and when he did answer, the sounds seemed as fine and soft as the whisper of some child just born.

"Oh! major, is that you?"

Such, he thinks, were the very words he made use of in reply; and the answer that he received was instantaneous, though the voice came from some little distance in the bay, and his own voice he did not hear. He only knows what he meant to say. The answer was to this effect.

"It is, James!—It is your own friend, Lionel Spencer, that speaks to you; do not be alarmed when you see me! I have been shockingly murdered!"

James asserts that he tried to tell him that he would not be frightened, but his own voice was still a whisper, which he himself could scarcely hear. A moment after he had spoken, he heard something like a sudden breeze that rustled through the bay bushes at his feet, and his eyes were closed without his effort, and indeed in spite of himself. When he opened them, he saw Major Spencer standing at the edge of the bay, about twenty steps from him. Though he stood in the shade of a thicket, and there was no light in the heavens save that of the stars, he was yet enabled to distinguish perfectly, and with great ease, every lineament of his friend's face.

He looked very pale, and his garments were covered with blood; and James said that he strove very much to rise from the place where he sat and approach him:—

"for, in truth," said the lad, "so far from feeling any fear, I felt nothing but fury in my heart; but I could not move a limb. My feet were fastened to the ground; my hands to my sides; and I could only bend forward and gasp. I felt as if I should have died with vexation that I could not rise; but a power which I could not resist, made me motionless, and almost speechless. I could only say, 'Murdered!'—and that one word I believe I must have repeated a dozen times.

"'Yes, murdered!—murdered by the Scotchman who slept with us at your fire the night before last. James, I look to you to have the murderer brought to justice! James!—do you hear me, James?'"

"These," said James, "I think were the very words, or near about the very words, that I heard; and I tried to ask the major to tell me how it was, and how I could do what he required; but I didn't hear myself speak, though it would appear that he did, for almost immediately after I had tried to speak what I wished to say, he answered me just as if I had said it. He told me that the Scotchman had waylaid, killed, and hidden him in that very bay; that his murderer had gone to Charleston; and that if I made haste to town, I would find him in the Falmouth packet, which was then lying in the harbor and ready to sail for England. He farther said that everything depended on my making haste,—that I must reach town by to-morrow night if I wanted to be in season, and go right on board the vessel and charge the criminal with the deed. 'Do not be afraid,' said he, when he had finished; 'be afraid of nothing, James, for God will help and strengthen you to the end.' When I heard all I burst into a flood or tears, and then I felt strong. I felt that I could talk, or fight, or do almost anything; and I jumped up to my feet, and was just about to run down to where the major stood, but, with the first step which I made forward, he was gone. I stopped and looked all around me, but I could see nothing; and the bay was just as black as midnight. But I went down to it, and tried to press in where I thought the major had been standing; but I couldn't get far, the brush and bay bushes were so close and thick. I was now bold and strong enough, and I called out, loud enough to be heard half a mile. I didn't exactly know what I called for, or what I wanted to learn, or I have forgotten. But I heard nothing more. Then I remembered the camp, and began to fear that something might have happened to mother and uncle, for I now felt, what I had not thought of before, that I had gone too far round the bay to be of much assistance, or, indeed, to be in time for any, had they been suddenly attacked. Besides, I could not think how long I had been gone; but it now seemed very late. The stars were shining their brightest, and the thin white clouds of morning were beginning to rise and run towards the west. Well, I bethought me of my course,—for I was a little bewildered and doubtful where I was; but, after a little thinking, I took the back track, and soon got a glimpse of the camp-fire, which was nearly burnt down; and by this I reckoned I was gone considerably longer than my two hours. When I got back into the camp, I looked under the wagon, and found uncle in a sweet sleep, and though my heart was full almost to bursting with what I had heard, and the cruel sight I had seen, yet I wouldn't waken him; and I beat about and mended the fire, and watched, and waited, until near daylight, when mother called to me out of the wagon, and asked who it was. This wakened my uncle, and then I up and told all that had happened, for if it had been to save my life, I couldn't have kept it in much longer. But though mother said it was very strange, Uncle Sparkman considered that I had been only dreaming; but he couldn't persuade me of it; and when I told him I intended to be off at daylight, just as the major had told me to do, and ride my best all the way to Charleston, he laughed, and said I was a fool. But I felt that I was no fool, and I was solemn certain that I hadn't been dreaming; and though both mother and he tried their hardest to make me put off going, yet I made up my mind to it, and they had to give up. For, wouldn't I have been a pretty sort of a friend to the major, if, after what he told me, I could have stayed behind, and gone on only at a wagon-pace to look after the murderer! I don't think if I had done so that I should ever have been able to look a white man in the face again. Soon as the peep of day, I was on horse-back. Mother was mighty sad, and begged me not to go, but Uncle Sparkman was mighty sulky, and kept calling me fool upon fool, until I was almost angry enough to forget that we were of blood kin. But all his talking did not stop me, and I reckon I was five miles on my way before he had his team in traces for a start. I rode as briskly as I could get on without hurting my nag. I had a smart ride of more than forty miles before me, and the road was very heavy. But it was a good two hours from sunset when I got into town, and the first question I asked of the people I met was, to show me where the ships were kept. When I got to the wharf they showed me the Falmouth packet, where she lay in the stream, ready to sail as soon as the wind should favor."

IV

James Grayling, with the same eager impatience which he has been suffered to describe in his own language, had already hired a boat to go on board the British packet, when he remembered that he had neglected all those means, legal and otherwise, by which alone his purpose might be properly effected. He did not know much about legal process but he had common sense enough, the moment that he began to reflect on the subject, to know that some such process was necessary. This conviction produced another difficulty; he knew not in which quarter to turn for counsel and assistance; but here the boatman who saw his bewilderment, and knew by his dialect and dress that he was a back-countryman, came to his relief, and from him he got directions where to find the merchants with whom his uncle, Sparkman, had done business in former years. To them he went, and without circumlocution, told the whole story of his ghostly visitation. Even as a dream, which these gentlemen at once conjectured it to be, the story of James Grayling was equally clear and curious; and his intense warmth and the entire absorption, which the subject had effected, of his mind and soul, was such that they judged it not improper, at least to carry out the search of the vessel which he contemplated. It would certainly, they thought, be a curious coincidence— believing James to be a veracious youth— if the Scotchman should be found on board. But another test of his narrative was proposed by one of the firm. It so happened that the business agents of Major Spencer, who was well known in Charleston, kept their office but a few rods distant from their own; and to them all

parties at once proceeded. But here the story of James was encountered by a circumstance that made somewhat against it. These gentlemen produced a letter from Major Spencer, intimating the utter impossibility of his coming to town for the space of a month, and expressing his regret that he should be unable to avail himself of the opportunity of the foreign vessel, of whose arrival in Charleston, and proposed time of departure, they had themselves advised him. They read the letter aloud to James and their brother merchants, and with difficulty suppressed their smiles at the gravity with which the former related and insisted upon the particulars of his vision.

"He has changed his mind," returned the impetuous youth; "he was on his way down, I tell you,—a hundred miles on his way,—when he camped with us. I know him well, I tell you, and talked with him myself half the night."

"At least," remarked the gentlemen who had gone with James, "it can do no harm to look into the business. We can procure a warrant for searching the vessel after this man, Macnab; and should he be found on board the packet, it will be a sufficient circumstance to justify the magistrates in detaining him, until we can ascertain where Major Spencer really is."

The measure was accordingly adopted, and it was nearly sunset before the warrant was procured, and the proper officer in readiness. The impatience of a spirit so eager and so devoted as James Grayling, under these delays, may be imagined; and when in the boat, and on his way to the packet where the criminal was to be sought, his blood became so excited that it was with much ado he could be kept in his seat. His quick, eager action continually disturbed the trim of the boat, and one of his mercantile friends, who had accompanied him, with that interest in the affair which curiosity alone inspired, was under constant apprehension lest he would plunge overboard in his impatient desire to shorten the space which lay between. The same impatience enabled the youth, though never on shipboard before, to grasp the rope which had been flung at their approach, and to mount her sides with cat-like agility. Without waiting to declare himself or his purpose, he ran from one side of the deck to the other, greedily staring, to the surprise of officers, passengers, and seamen, in the faces of all of them, and surveying them with an almost offensive scrutiny. He turned away from the search with disappointment. There was no face like that of the suspected man among them. By this time, his friend, the merchant, with the sheriff's officer, had entered the vessel, and were in conference with the captain. Grayling drew nigh in time to hear the latter affirm that there was no man of the name of Macnab, as stated in the warrant, among his passengers or crew.

"He is—he must be!" exclaimed the impetuous youth. "The major never lied in his life, and couldn't lie after he was dead. Macnab is here—he is a Scotchman—"

The captain interrupted him—

"We have, young gentleman, several Scotchmen on board, and one of them is named Macleod—"

"Let me see him—which is he?" demanded the youth.

By this time, the passengers and a goodly portion of the crew were collected about the little party. The captain turned his eyes upon the group, and asked,

"Where is Mr. Macleod?"

"He is gone below—he's sick!" replied one of the passengers.

"That's he! That must be the man!" exclaimed the youth. "I'll lay my life that's no other than Macnab. He's only taken a false name."

It was now remembered by one of the passengers, and remarked, that Macleod had expressed himself as unwell, but a few moments before, and had gone below even while the boat was rapidly approaching the vessel. At this statement, the captain led the way into the cabin, closely followed by James Grayling and the rest.

"Mr. Macleod," he said with a voice somewhat elevated, as he approached the berth of that person, "you are wanted on deck for a few moments."

"I am really too unwell, captain," replied a feeble voice from behind the curtains of the berth.

"It will be necessary," was the reply of the captain. "There is a warrant from the authorities of the town, to look after a fugitive of justice."

Macleod had already begun a second speech declaring his feebleness, when the fearless youth, Grayling, bounded before the captain and tore away, with a single grasp of his hand, the curtain which concealed the suspected man **from** their sight.

"It is he!" was the instant exclamation of the youth, as he beheld him. "It is he—Macnab, the Scotchman—the man that murdered Major Spencer!"

Macnab,—for it was he,—was deadly pale. He trembled like an aspen. His eyes were dilated with more than mortal apprehension, and his lips were perfectly livid. Still, he found strength to speak, and to deny the accusation. He knew nothing of the youth before him—nothing of Major Spencer—his name was Macleod, and he had never called himself by any other. He denied, but with great incoherence, everything which was urged against him.

"You must get up, Mr. Macleod," said the captain; "the circumstances are very much against you. You must go with the officer!"

"Will you give me up to my enemies?" demanded the culprit. "You are a countryman—a Briton. I have fought for the king, our master, against these rebels, and for this they seek my life. Do not deliver me into their bloody hands!"

"Liar!" exclaimed James Grayling— "Didn't you tell us at our own camp-fire that you were with us? that you were at Gates' defeat, and Ninety-six?"

"But I didn't tell you," said the Scotchman, with a grin, "which side I was on!"

"Ha! remember that!" said the sheriff's officer. "He denied, just a moment ago, that he knew this young man at all; now, he confesses that he did see and camp with him."

The Scotchman was aghast at the strong point which, in his inadvertence, he had made against himself; and his efforts to excuse himself, stammering and contradictory, served only to involve him more deeply in the meshes of his difficulty. Still he continued his urgent appeals to the captain of the vessel, and his fellow-passengers, as citizens of the same country, subjects to the same monarch, to protect him from those who equally hated and would destroy them all. In order to move their national prejudices in his behalf, he boasted of the immense injury which he had done, as a tory, to the rebel cause; and still insisted that the murder was only a pretext of the youth before him, by which to gain possession of his person, and wreak upon him the revenge which his own fierce performances during the war had naturally enough provoked. One or two of the passengers, indeed, joined with him in entreating the captain to set the accusers adrift and make sail at once; but the stout Englishman who was in command, rejected instantly the unworthy counsel. Besides, he was better aware of the dangers which would follow any such rash proceeding. Fort Moultrie, on Sullivan's Island, had been already refitted and prepared for an enemy; and he was lying, at that moment, under the formidable range of grinning teeth, which would have opened upon him, at the first moment, from the jaws of Castle Pinckney.

"No, gentlemen," said he, "you mistake your man. God forbid that I should give shelter to a murderer, though he were from my own parish."

"But I am no murderer," said the Scotchman.

"You look cursedly like one, however," was the reply of the captain. "Sheriff, take your prisoner."

The base creature threw himself at the feet of the Englishman, and clung, with piteous entreaties, to his knees. The latter shook him off, and turned away in disgust.

"Steward," he cried, "bring up this man's luggage."

He was obeyed. The luggage was brought up from the cabin and delivered to the sheriff's officer, by whom it was examined in the presence of all, and an inventory made of its contents. It consisted of a small new trunk, which, it afterwards appeared, he had bought in Charleston, soon after his arrival. This contained a few changes of raiment, twenty-six guineas in money, a gold watch, not in repair, and the two pistols which he had shown while at Joel Sparkman's camp fire; but, with this difference, that the stock of one was broken off short just above the grasp, and the butt was entirely gone. It was not found among his chattels. A careful examination of the articles in his trunk did not result in anything calculated to strengthen the charge of his criminality; but there was not a single person present who did not feel as morally certain of his guilt as if the jury had already declared the fact. That night he slept—if he slept at all—in the common jail of the city.

V

His accuser, the warm-hearted and resolute James Grayling, did not sleep. The excitement, arising from mingling and contradictory emotions,—sorrow for his brave young commander's fate, and the natural exultation of a generous spirit at the consciousness of having performed, with signal success, an arduous and painful task combined to drive all pleasant slumbers from his eyes; and with the dawn he was again up and stirring, with his mind still full of the awful business in which he had been engaged. We do not care to pursue his course in the ordinary walks of the city, nor account for his employments during the few days which ensued, until, in consequence of a legal examination into the circumstances which anticipated the regular work of the sessions, the extreme excitement of the young accuser had been renewed. Macnab or Macleod,— and it is possible that both names were fictitious,—as soon as he recovered from his first terrors, sought the aid of an attorney—one of those acute, small, chopping lawyers, to be found in almost every community, who are willing to serve with equal zeal the sinner and the saint, provided that they can pay with equal liberality. The prisoner was brought before the court under *habeas corpus,* and several grounds submitted by his counsel with the view to obtaining his discharge. It became necessary to ascertain, among the first duties of the state, whether Major Spencer, the alleged victim, was really dead. Until it could be established that a man should be imprisoned, tried, and punished for a crime, it was first necessary to show that a crime had been committed, and the attorney made himself exceedingly merry with the ghost story of young Grayling. In those days, however, the ancient Superstition was not so feeble as she has subsequently become. The venerable judge was one of those good men who had a decent respect for the faith and opinions of his ancestors; and though he certainly would not have consented to the hanging of Macleod under the sort of testimony which had been adduced, he yet saw enough, in all the circumstances, to justify his present detention. In the meantime, efforts were to be made, to ascertain the whereabouts of Major Spencer; though, were he even missing,—so the counsel for Macleod contended,—his death could be by no means assumed in consequence. To this the judge shook his head doubtfully. "'Fore God!" said he, "I would not have you be too sure of that." He was an Irishman, and proceeded after the fashion of his country. The reader will therefore *bear* with his *bull.* "A man may properly be hung for murdering another, though the murdered man be not dead; aye, before God, even though he be actually unhurt and uninjured, while the murderer is swinging by the neck for the bloody deed!"

The judge,—who it must be understood was a real existence, and who had no small reputation in his day in the south,—proceeded to establish the correctness of his opinions by authorities and argument, with all of which, doubtlessly, the bar were exceedingly delighted; but, to provide them in this place would only be to interfere with our own progress. James Grayling, however, was not satisfied to wait the slow processes which were suggested for coming at the truth. Even the wisdom of the judge was lost upon him, possibly, for the simple reason that he did not comprehend it. But the ridicule of the culprit's lawyer stung him to the quick, and he muttered to himself, more than once, a determination "to lick the life out of that impudent chap's leather." But this was not his only resolve. There was one which he proceeded to put into instant execution, and that was to seek the body of his murdered friend in the spot where he fancied it might be found—namely, the dark and dismal bay where the specter had made its appearance to his eyes.

The suggestion was approved—though he did not need this to prompt his resolution—by his mother and uncle, Sparkman. The latter determined to be his companion, and he was farther accompanied by the sheriff's officer who had arrested the suspected felon. Before daylight, on the morning after the examination before the judge had taken place, and when Macleod had been remanded to prison, James Grayling started on his journey. His fiery zeal received additional force at every added moment of delay, and his eager spurring brought him at an early hour after noon, to the neighborhood of the spot through which his search was to be made. When his companions and himself drew nigh, they were all at a loss in which direction first to proceed. The bay was one of those massed forests, whose wall of thorns, vines, and close tenacious shrubs, seemed to defy invasion. To the eye of the townsman it was so forbidding that he pronounced it absolutely impenetrable. But James was not to be baffled. He led them round it, taking the very course which he had pursued the night when the revelation was made him; he showed them the very tree at whose foot he had sunk when the supernatural torpor—as he himself esteemed it—began to fall upon him; he then pointed out the spot, some twenty steps distant, at which the specter made his appearance. To this spot they then proceeded in a body, and essayed an entrance, but were so discouraged by the difficulties at the outset that all, James not excepted, concluded that neither the murderer nor his victim could possibly have found entrance there.

But, lo! a marvel! Such it seemed, at the first blush, to all the party. While they stood confounded and indecisive, undetermined in which way to move, a sudden flight of wings was heard, even from the center of the bay, at a little distance above the spot where they had striven for entrance. They looked up, and beheld about fifty buzzards—those notorious domestic vultures of the south—ascending from the interior of the bay, and perching along upon the branches of the loftier trees by which it was overhung. Even were the character of these birds less known, the particular business in which they had just been engaged, was betrayed by huge gobbets of flesh which some of them had borne aloft in their flight, and still continued to rend with beak and bill, as they tottered upon the branches where they stood. A piercing scream issued from the lips of James Grayling as he beheld this sight, and strove to scare the offensive birds from their repast.

"The poor major! The poor major!" was the involuntary and agonized exclamation of the youth. "Did I ever think he would come to this!"

The search, thus guided and encouraged, was pressed with renewed diligence and spirit; and, at length, an opening was found through which it was evident that a body of considerable size had but recently gone. The branches were broken from the small shrub trees, and the undergrowth trodden into the earth. They followed this path, and, as is the case commonly with waste tracts of this description, the density of the growth diminished sensibly at every step they took, till they reached a little pond, which, though circumscribed in area, and full of cypresses, yet proved to be singularly deep. Indeed, it was an alligator-hole, where, in all probability, a numerous tribe of these reptiles had their dwelling. Here, on the edge of the pond, they discovered the object which had drawn the keen-sighted vultures to their feast, in the body of a horse, which James Grayling at once identified as that of Major Spencer. The carcass of the animal was already very much torn and lacerated. The eyes were plucked out, and the animal completely disemboweled. Yet, on examination, it was not difficult to discover the manner of his death. This had been effected by fire-arms. Two bullets had passed through his skull, just above the eyes, either of which must have been fatal. The murderer had led the horse to the spot, and committed the cruel deed where his body was found. The search was now continued for that of the owner, but for some time it proved ineffectual. At length, the keen eyes of James Grayling detected, amidst a heap of moss and green sedge that rested beside an overthrown tree, whose branches jutted into the pond, a whitish, but discolored object, that did not seem native to the place. Bestriding the fallen tree, he was enabled to reach this object, which, with a burst of grief, he announced to the distant party was the hand and arm of his unfortunate friend, the wristband of the shirt being the conspicuous object which had first caught his eye. Grasping this, he drew the corpse, which had been thrust beneath the branches of the tree, to the surface; and, with the assistance of his uncle, it was finally brought to the dry land. Here it underwent a careful examination. The head was very much disfigured; the skull was fractured in several places by repeated blows of some hard instrument, inflicted chiefly from behind. A closer inspection revealed a bullet-hole in the abdomen, the first wound, in all probability, which the unfortunate gentleman received, and by which he was, perhaps, tumbled from his horse. The blows on the head would seem to have been unnecessary, unless the murderer—whose proceedings appeared to have been singularly deliberate,—was resolved upon making "assurance doubly sure." But, as if the watchful Providence had meant that nothing should be left doubtful which might tend to the complete conviction of the criminal, the constable stumbled upon the butt of the broken pistol which had been found in Macleod's trunk. This he picked up on the edge of the pond in which the corpse had been discovered, and while James Grayling and his uncle, Sparkman, were engaged in drawing it from the water. The place where the fragment was discovered at once denoted the pistol as the instrument by which the final blows were inflicted. "'Fore God," said the judge to the criminal, as these proofs were submitted on the trial, "you may be a very innocent man after all, as, by my faith, I do think there have been many murderers before you; but you ought, nevertheless, to be hung as an example to all other persons who suffer such strong proofs of guilt to follow their innocent misdoings. Gentlemen of the jury, if this person, Macleod or Macnab, didn't murder Major Spencer, you or I did; and you must now decide which of us it is! I say, gentlemen of the jury, either you, or I, or the prisoner at the bar, murdered this man; and if you have any doubts which of us it was, it is but justice and mercy that you should give the prisoner the benefit of your doubts; and so find your verdict. But, before God, should you find him not guilty, Mr. Attorney there can scarcely do anything wiser than to put us all upon trial for the deed."

The jury, it may be scarcely necessary to add, perhaps under certain becoming fears of an alternative such as his honor had suggested, brought in a verdict of "Guilty," without leaving the panel; and Macnab, *alias* Macleod, was hung at White Point, Charleston, somewhere about the year 178—.

"And here," said my grandmother, devoutly, "you behold a proof of God's watchfulness to see that murder should not be hidden, and that the murderer should not escape. You see that he sent the spirit of the murdered man—since, by no other mode could the truth have been revealed—to declare the crime, and to discover the criminal. But for that ghost, Macnab would have got off to Scotland, and probably have been living to this very day on the money that he took from the person of the poor major."

As the old lady finished the ghost story, which, by the way, she had been tempted to relate for the fiftieth time in order to combat my father's ridicule of such superstitions, the latter took up the thread of the narrative.

"Now, my son," said he, "as you have heard all that your grandmother has to say on this subject, I will proceed to show you what you have to believe, and what not. It is true that Macnab murdered Spencer in the manner related; that James Grayling made the discovery and prosecuted the pursuit; found the body and brought the felon to justice; that MacNab suffered death, and confessed the crime; alleging that he was moved to do so, as well because of the money that he suspected Spencer to have in his possession, as because of the hate which he felt for a man who had been particularly bold and active in cutting up a party of Scotch loyalists to which he belonged, on the borders of North Carolina. But the appearance of the specter was nothing more than the work of a quick imagination, added to a shrewd and correct judgment. James Grayling saw no ghost, in fact, but such as was in his own mind; and, though the instance was one of a most remarkable character, one of singular combination, and well depending circumstances, still, I think it is to be accounted for by natural and very simple laws."

The old lady was indignant.

"And how could he see the ghost just on the edge of the same bay where the murder had been committed, and where the body of the murdered man even then was lying?"

My father did not directly answer the demand, but proceeded thus:—

"James Grayling, as we know, mother, was a very ardent, impetuous, sagacious man. He had the sanguine, the race-horse temperament. He was generous, always prompt and ready, and one who never went backward. What he did, he did quickly, boldly, and thoroughly! He never shrank from trouble of any kind: nay, he rejoiced in the constant encounter with difficulty and trial; and his was the temper which commands and enthralls mankind. He felt deeply and intensely whatever occupied his mind, and when he parted from his friend he brooded over little else than their past communion and the great distance by which they were to be separated. The dull traveling wagon-gait at which he himself was compelled to go, was a source of annoyance to him; and he became sullen, all the day, after the departure of his friend.

When, on the evening of the next day, he came to the house where it was natural to expect that Major Spencer would have slept the night before, and he learned the fact that no one stopped there but the Scotchman, Macnab, we see that he was struck with the circumstance. He mutters it over to himself, 'Strange, where the major could have gone!' His mind then naturally reverts to the character of the Scotchman;—to the opinions and suspicions which had been already expressed of him by his uncle, and felt by himself. They had all, previously, come to the full conviction that Macnab was, and had always been, a tory, in spite of his protestations. His mind next, and very naturally, reverted to the insecurity of the highways; the general dangers of traveling at that period; the frequency of crime, and the number of desperate men who were everywhere to be met with. The very employment in which he was then engaged, in scouting the woods for the protection of the camp, was calculated to bring such reflections to his mind. If these precautions were considered necessary for the safety of persons so poor, so wanting in those possessions which might prompt cupidity to crime, how much more necessary were precautions in the case of a wealthy gentleman like Major Spencer! He then remembered the conversation with the major at the camp-fire, when they fancied that the Scotchman was sleeping. How natural to think then, that he was all the while awake; and, if awake, he must have heard him speak of the wealth of his companion. True, the major, with more prudence than himself, denied that he had any money about him, more than would bear his expenses to the city; but such an assurance was natural enough to the lips of a traveler who knew the dangers of the country. That the man, Macnab, was not a person to be trusted, was the equal impression of Joel Sparkman and his nephew from the first. The probabilities were strong that he would rob and perhaps murder, if he might hope to do so with impunity; and as the youth made the circuit of the bay in the darkness and solemn stillness of the night, its gloomy depths and mournful shadows, naturally gave rise to such reflections as would be equally active in the mind of a youth, and of one somewhat familiar with the arts and usages of strife. He would see that the spot was just the one in which a practised partisan would delight to set an ambush for an unwary foe. There ran the public road, with a little sweep, around two-thirds of the extent of its dense and impenetrable thickets. The ambush could lie concealed, and at ten steps command the bosom of its victim. Here, then, you perceive the mind of James Grayling, stimulated by an active and sagacious judgment, had by gradual and reasonable stages come to these conclusions: that Major Spencer was an object to tempt a robber; that the country was full of robbers; that Macnab was one of them; that this was the very spot in which a deed of blood could be most easily committed, and most easily concealed; and, one important fact, that gave strength and coherence to the whole, that Major Spencer had not reached a well-known point of destination, while Macnab had.

"With these thoughts, thus closely linked together, the youth forgets the limits of his watch and his circuit. This fact, alone, proves how active his imagination had become. It leads him forward, brooding more and more on the subject, until, in the very exhaustion of his body, he sinks down beneath a tree. He sinks down and falls asleep; and in his sleep, what before was plausible conjecture, becomes fact, and the creative properties of his imagination give form and vitality to all his fancies. These forms are bold, broad, and deeply colored, in due proportion with the degree of force which they receive from probability. Here, he sees the image of his friend; but, you will remark—and this should almost conclusively satisfy any mind that all that he sees is the work of his imagination,—that, though Spencer tells him that he is murdered, and by Macnab, he does not tell him how, in what manner, or with what weapons. Though he sees him pale and ghost-like, he does not see, nor can he say, where his wounds are! He sees his pale features distinctly, and his garments are bloody. Now, had he seen the specter in the true appearances of death, as he was subsequently found, he would not have been able to discern his features, which were battered, according to his own account, almost out of all shape of humanity, and covered with mud; while his clothes would have streamed with mud and water, rather than with blood."

"Ah!" exclaimed the old lady, my grandmother, "it's hard to make you believe any-thing that you don't see; you are like Saint Thomas in the Scriptures; but how do you propose to account for his knowing that the Scotchman was on board the Falmouth packet? Answer to that!"

"That is not a more difficult matter than any of the rest. You forget that in the dialogue which took place between James and Major Spencer at the camp, the latter told him that he was about to take passage for Europe in the Falmouth packet, which then lay in Charleston harbor, and was about to sail. Macnab heard all that."

"True enough, and likely enough," returned the old lady; "but, though you show that it was Major Spencer's intention to go to Europe in the Falmouth packet, that will not show that it was also the intention of the murderer."

"Yet what more probable, and how natural for James Grayling to imagine such a thing! In the first place he knew that Macnab was a Briton; he felt convinced that he was a tory; and the inference was immediate, that such a person would scarcely have remained long in a country where such characters labored under so much odium, disfranchisement, and constant danger from popular tumults. The fact that Macnab was compelled to disguise his true sentiments, and affect those of the people against whom he fought so vindictively, shows what was his sense of the danger which he incurred. Now, it is not unlikely that Macnab was quite as well aware that the Falmouth packet was in Charleston, and about to sail, as Major Spencer. No doubt he was pursuing the same journey, with the same object, and had he not murdered Spencer, they would, very likely, have been fellow-passengers together to Europe. But, whether he knew the fact before or not, he probably heard it stated by Spencer while he seemed to be sleeping; and, even supposing that he did not then know, it was enough that he found this to be the fact on reaching the city. It was an after-thought to fly to Europe with his ill-gotten spoils; and whatever may have appeared a politic course to the criminal, would be a probable conjecture in the mind of him by whom he was suspected. The whole story is one of strong probabilities which happened to be verified; and if proving anything, proves only that which we know— that James Grayling was a man of remarkably sagacious judgment, and quick, daring imagination. This quality of imagination, by the way, when possessed very strongly in connection with shrewd common sense and well-balanced general faculties, makes that particular kind of intellect which, because of its promptness and powers of creation and combination, we call genius. It is genius only which can make ghosts, and James Grayling was a genius. He never, my son, saw any other ghosts than those of his own making!"

I heard my father with great patience to the end, though he seemed very tedious. 5 He had taken a great deal of pains to destroy one of my greatest sources of pleasure. I need not add that I continued to believe in the ghost, and, with my grandmother, to reject the philosophy. It was 10 more easy to believe the one than to comprehend the other.

VII

NATHANIEL PARKER WILLIS (1806–1867)

The influence of N. P. Willis upon the prose of the mid years of the nineteenth century has never been fully appreciated. He was a poet, a sentimentalist, a Byronic traveler through all the romantic areas of Europe, a yellow journalist two generations ahead of his time, an inspired special correspondent with a light and graceful pen in a period when most pens were leaden and iron-tipped. His short stories dealing with life in Europe and with social adventure in the few "civilized" areas of America, fill several volumes. In London he dashed off a series of "tales" over the pseudonym "Philip Slingsby," a hybrid pen-name most descriptive—a Greek sense of literary values joined to the pell-mell democratic pen of the society reporter for a *Smart Set* variety of journal. The titles of many of his books are also revealing touches: *Hurrygraphs, Dashes at Life with a Free Pencil, Inklings of Adventure, Fun Jottings.*

It is to be doubted if Willis ever looked upon the short story as anything but a curtailed novel—a thing to be deplored. He wished to write novels, but there was no market for novels, and accordingly he sold them in fragments. Or as he recorded it in the Preface to his *Dashes at Life with a Free Pencil:* "Like the sculptor who made toys of the fragments of his unsalable Jupiter, the author, in the following collection of brief tales, gives material, that, but for a single objection, would have been moulded into works of larger design. That objection is the unmarketableness of American books in America, owing to our defective law of copyright. The foreign author being allowed no property in his books, the American publisher gets for nothing every new novel brought out in England. Of course while he can have for publication, *gratis,* the new novels of Bulwer, D'Israeli, James, and others, he will not *pay* an American author for a new book, even if it were equally good. The consequence is, that we must either write books to give away, or take some vein of literature where the competition is more equal—an alternative that makes almost all American authors mere contributors of short papers to periodicals. . . . [He has therefore] gone on acquiring a habit of dashing off for a magazine any chance view of life that turned up to him, and selling in fragmentary chapters what should have been kept together and moulded into a proportionate work of imagination. So has gradually accumulated the large collection of tales which follow—literally *dashes at life with a free pencil*—each one, though a true copy of a part, conveying, of course, no portion of the meaning and moral of a whole. It is as a parcel of fragments—as a portfolio of sketches for a picture never painted—that he offers them to the public. The lack of what an English critic cleverly calls the 'ponderous goodness of a didactic purpose,' must be balanced, if at all, by their truth to life, for they have been drawn mostly from impressions freshly made, and with no record of what they were a part of. In proportion to his power of imagination, the reader will supply the back-ground and adjuncts—some, no doubt (if their author may judge by himself), preferring the sketch to the finished picture."

This preface to *Dashes at Life* is therefore an important document in the history of the short story form. It explains the causes that forced American writers to concentrate upon the short story until they brought it to its final perfection. It reveals also the fact that the short story is the child of the magazine and that its technique and laws came from the demand of the magazine for shortness, for a maximum of effectiveness within a minimum of limits, for material that should be fascinatingly attractive to the increasing public that found its literary bill of fare in periodicals.

Willis added lightness to the short story; even, at times, frothiness. Two generations before O. Henry, he had an O. Henry-like touch, an O. Henry-like *finesse.* He is one of the few short story writers of the mid-nineteenth century whose work—the best of it—can still be set as models for the use of the present generation.

THE SPIRIT-LOVE OF "IONE S——."

(Since discovered to be Miss Jones.)

Not long ago, but before poetry and pin-money were discovered to be cause and effect, Miss Phebe Jane Jones was one of the most charming contributors to a certain periodical now gone over "Lethe's wharf." Her signature was "Ione S——!" a neat anagram, out of which few would have picked the monosyllable engraved upon her father's brass knocker. She wrote mostly in verse; but her prose, of which you will presently see a specimen or two, was her better vein—as being more easily embroidered, and not cramped with the inexorable fetters of rime. Miss Jones abandoned authorship before the New Mirror[1] was established, or she would, doubtless, have been one of its *paid* contributors—as much ("we" flatter ourselves) as could well be said of her abilities.

The beauty of hectics and hollow chests has been written out of fashion; so I may venture upon the simple imagery of truth and nature. Miss Jones was as handsome as a prize heifer. She was a compact, plump, wholesome, clean-limbed, beautifully-marked animal, with eyes like inkstands running over, and a mouth that looked, when she smiled, as if it had never been opened before, the teeth seemed so fresh and unhandled. Her voice had a tone clear as the ring of a silver dollar; and her lungs must have been as sound as a pippin, for when she laughed (which she never did unless she was surprised into it, for she loved melancholy), it was like the gurgling of a brook over the pebbles. The bran-new people made by Deucalion and Pyrrha, when it cleared up after the flood, were probably in Miss Jones's style.

But do you suppose that "Ione S——" cared anything for her good looks! What —value the poor perishing tenement in which nature had chosen to lodge her intellectual and spiritual part! What—care for her covering of clay! What—waste thought on the chain that kept her from the Pleiades, of which, perhaps, she was the lost sister (who knows).? And, more than all—oh gracious!—to be *loved* for this trumpery-drapery of her immortal essence!

Yes—*infra dig.* as it may seem to record such an unworthy trifle—the celestial Phebe had the superfluity of an every-day lover. Gideon Flimmins was willing to take her on her outer inventory alone. He loved her cheeks—he did not hesitate to admit! He loved her lips—he could not help specifying! He had been known to name her shoulders! And, in taking out a thorn for her with a pair of tweezers one day, he had literally exclaimed with rapture that she had a heavenly little pink thumb. But of "Ione S——" he had never spoken a word. No, though she read him faithfully every effusion that appeared—asked his opinion of every separate stanza —talked of "Ione S——" as the person on earth she most wished to see (for she kept her literary incog.)—Gideon had never alluded to her a second time, and perseveringly, hatefully, atrociously, and with mundane motive only, he made industrious love to the outside and visible Phebe! Well! Well!

Contiguity is something, in love; and the Flimminses were neighbors of the Joneses. Gideon had another advantage—for Ophelia Flimmins, his eldest sister, was Miss Jones's eternally attached friend. To explain this, I must trouble the reader to take notice that there were two streaks in the Flimmins family. Fat Mrs. Flimmins, the mother (who had been dead a year), was a thorough "man of business," and it was to her downright and upright management of her husband's wholesale and retail hat-lining establishment, that the family owed its prosperity; for Heredotus Flimmins, whose name was on the sign, was a flimsyish kind of sighing-dying man, and nobody could ever find out what on earth he wanted. Gideon and the two fleshy Miss Flimminses took after their mother, but Ophelia, whose semi-translucent frame was the envy of her faithful Phebe, was, with very trifling exceptions, the perfect model of her sire. She devotedly loved the moon. She had her preferences among the stars of heaven. She abominated the garish sun. And she and Phebe met by night—on the sidewalk around their mutual nearest corner—deeply veiled to conceal their emotion from the intruding gaze of such stars as they were not acquainted with—and there they communed!

I never knew, nor have I any the remotest suspicion of the reasoning by which these commingled spirits arrived at the conclusion that there was a want in their delicious union. They might have known, indeed, that the chain of bliss, ever so far extended, breaks off at last with an imperfect link—that though mustard and ham may turn two slices of innocent bread into a sandwich, there will still be an unbuttered outside. But they were young—they were sanguine. Phebe, at least, believed that in the regions of space there existed—"wandering but not lost"— the aching worser half of which she was the "better"—some lofty intellect, capable of sounding the unfathomable abysses of hers—some male essence, all soul and romance, with whom she could soar finally, arm-in-arm, to their native star, with no changes of any consequence between their earthly and their astral communion. It occurred to her, at last, that a letter addressed to him, through her favorite periodical, might possibly reach his eye. The following (which the reader may very likely remember to have seen) appeared in the paper of the following Saturday:—

"To my spirit-husband, greeting:–

"Where art thou, bridegroom of my soul? Thy Ione S—— calls to thee from the aching void of her lonely spirit! What name bearest thou? What path walkest thou? How can I, glow-worm like, lift my wings and show thee my lamp of guiding love? Thus wing I these words to thy dwelling-place (for thou art, perhaps, a subscriber to the M—r). Go—truants! Rest not till ye meet his eye.

"But I must speak to thee after the manner of this world.

"I am a poetess of eighteen summers. Eighteen weary years have I worn this prison-house of flesh, in which, when torn from thee, I was condemned to wander. But my soul is untamed by its cage of darkness! I remember, and remember only, the lost husband of my spirit-world. I perform, coldly and scornfully, the unheavenly necessities of this temporary existence; and from the windows of my prison (black—like the glimpses of the midnight heaven they let in) I look out for the coming of my spirit-lord. Lonely! lonely!

"Thou wouldst know, perhaps, what semblance I bear since my mortal separation from thee. Alas! the rose, not the lily, reigns upon my cheek! I would not disappoint thee, though of that there is little fear, for thou lovest for the spirit only. But believe not, because health holds me rudely down, and I seem not fragile and ready to depart—believe not, oh bridegroom of my soul! that I bear willingly my fleshly fetter, or endure with patience the degrading homage to its beauty. For there are soulless worms who think me fair. Ay—in the strength and freshness of my corporeal covering, there are those who rejoice! Oh! mockery! mockery!

"List to me, Ithuriel (for I must have a name to call thee by, and, till thou breathest thy own seraphic name into my ear, be thou Ithuriel)! List! I would meet thee in the darkness only! Thou shalt not see me with thy mortal eyes! Penetrate the past, and remember the smoke-curl of wavy lightness in which I floated to thy embrace! Remember the sunset-cloud to which we retired; the starry lamps that hung over our slumbers! And on the softest whisper of our voices let thy thoughts pass to mine! Speak not aloud! Murmur! murmur! murmur!

"Dost thou know, Ithuriel, I would fain prove to thee my freedom from the trammels of this world! In what chance shape thy accident of clay may be cast, I know not. Ay, and I care not! I would thou wert a hunchback, Ithuriel! I would thou wert disguised as a monster, my spirit-husband! So would I prove to thee my elevation above mortality! So would I show thee, that in the range of eternity for which we are wedded, a moment's covering darkens thee not —that, like a star sailing through a cloud, thy brightness is remembered while it is eclipsed—that thy Ione would recognize thy voice, be aware of thy presence, adore thee, as she was celestially wont—ay, though thou wert imprisoned in the likeness of a reptile! Ione care for mortal beauty! Ha! ha! ha!— Ha! ha! ha!

"Come to me, Ithuriel! My heart writhes in its cell for converse with thee! I am sick-thoughted! My spirit wrings its thin fingers to play with thy ethereal hair! My earthly cheek, though it obstinately refuses to pale, tingles with fever for thy coming. Glide to me in the shadow of eve—softly! softly!

"Address 'P' at the M—r office.

"Thine,   "Ione S——"

*   *   *   *   *   *

There came a letter to "P."

*   *   *   *   *   *

It was an inky night. The moon was in her private chamber. The stars had drawn over their heads the coverlet of clouds and pretended to sleep. The street lamps heartlessly burned on.

Twelve struck with "damnable iteration."

On tiptoe and with beating heart, Phebe Jane left her father's area. Ophelia Flimmins followed her at a little distance, for Ione was going to meet her spirit-bridegroom, and receive a renewal of his antevital vows; and she wished her friend, the echo of her soul, to overhear and witness them. For oh—if words were anything—if the soul could be melted and poured, lava-like, upon "satin post"—if there was truth in feelings magnetic and prophetic—then was he who had responded to, and corresponded with, Ione S—— (she writing to "I," and he to "P"), the ideal for whom she had so long sighed— the lost half of the whole so mournfully incomplete—her soul's missing and once spiritually Siamesed twin! His sweet letters had echoed every sentiment of her heart. He had agreed with her that outside was nothing—that earthly beauty was poor, perishing, pitiful—that nothing that could be seen, touched, or described, had anything to do with the spiritually-passionate intercourse to which their respective essences achingly yearned—that, unseen, unheard, save in whispers faint as a rose's sigh when languishing at noon, they might meet in communion blissful, superhuman, and satisfactory.

Yet where fittingly to meet—oh agony! agony!

The street-lamps two squares off had been taken up to lay down gas. Ophelia Flimmins had inwardly marked it. Between No. 126 and No. 132, more particularly, the echoing sidewalk was bathed in unfathomable night—for there were vacant lots occupied as a repository for used-up omnibuses. At the most lonely point there stood a tree, and, fortunately, this night, in the gutter beneath the tree, stood a newly-disabled 'bus of the Knickerbocker line—and (sweet omen!) it was blue! In this covert could the witnessing Ophelia lie *perdu*, observing unseen through the open door; and beneath this tree was to take place the meeting of souls—the reinterchange of sky-born vows—the immaterial union of Ithuriel and Ione! Bliss! bliss!—exquisite to anguish.

But — oh incontinent vessel — Ophelia had blabbed. The two fat Miss Flimminses were in the secret—nay, more—they were in the omnibus! Aye—deeply in, and portentously silent, they sat, warm and wondering, on either side of the lamp, probably extinguished for ever! They knew not well what was to be. But whatever sort of thing was a "marriage of soul," and whether "Ithuriel" was body or nobody— mortal man or angel in a blue scarf—the Miss Flimminses wished to see him. Half an hour before the trysting-time they had fanned their way thither, for a thunderstorm was in the air and the night was intolerably close; and, climbing into the omnibus, they reciprocally loosened each other's upper hook, and with their moistened collars laid starchless in their laps, awaited the opening of the mystery.

Enter Ophelia, as expected. She laid her thin hand upon the leather string, and, drawing the door after her, leaned out of its open window in breathless suspense and agitation.

Ione's step was now audible, returning from 132. Slowly she came, but invisibly, for it had grown suddenly pitch-dark; and only the far-off lamps, up and down the street, served to guide her footsteps.

But hark! the sound of a heel! He came! They met! He passed his arm around her and drew her beneath the tree—and with whispers, soft and low, leaned breathing to her ear. He was tall. He was in a cloak. And oh, ecstasy, he was thin! But thinkest thou to know, oh reader of dust, what passed on those ethereal whispers? Futile —futile curiosity. Even to Ophelia's straining ear, those whispers were inaudible.

But hark! a rumble! Something wrong in the bowels of the sky! and pash! pash! —on the resounding roof of the omnibus —fell drops of rain—fitfully! fitfully!

"My dear!" whispered Ophelia (for Ione had borrowed her chip hat, the better to elude recognition), "ask Ithuriel to step in."

Ithuriel started to find a witness near, but a whisper from Ione reassured him, and gathering his cloak around his face, he followed his spirit-bride into the 'bus.

The fat Miss Flimminses contracted their orbed shapes, and made themselves small against the padded extremity of the vehicle; Ophelia retreated to the middle, and, next the door, on either side, sat the starry bride and bridegroom—all breathlessly silent. Yet there was a murmur—for five hearts beat within that 'bus duodecimal womb; and the rain pelted on the roof, pailsful-like and unpityingly.

But slap! dash! whew! heavens!—In rushed a youth, dripping, dripping!

"Get out!" cried Ione, over whose knees he drew himself like an eel pulled through a basket of contorted other eels.

"Come, come, young man!" said a deep bass voice, of which everybody had some faint remembrance.

"Oh!" cried one fat Miss Flimmins.

"Ah!" screamed the other.

"What—dad!" exclaimed Gideon Flimmins, who had dashed into the sheltering 'bus to save his new hat—"dad here with a girl!"

But the fat Flimminses were both in convulsions. Scream! scream! scream!

A moment of confusion! The next moment a sudden light! A watchman with his lantern stood at the door.

"Papa!" ejaculated three of the ladies. "Old Flimmins!—my heart will burst!" murmured Ione.

The two fat girls hurried on their collars; and Gideon, all amazement at finding himself in such a family party at midnight in a lonely 'bus, stepped out and entered into converse with the guardian of the night.

The rain stopped suddenly, and the omnibus gave up its homogeneous contents. Old Flimmins, who was in a violent perspiration, gave Gideon his cloak to carry, and his two arms to his two pinguid adult pledges. Gideon took Ophelia and Phebe, and they mizzled. Mockery! mockery!

Ione is not yet gone to the spirit-sphere —kept here partly by the fleshy fetter over which she mourned, and partly by the dove-tailed duties consequent upon annual Flimminses. Gideon loves her after the manner of this world—but she sighs "when she hears sweet music," that her better part is still unappreciated—unfathomed—"cabined, cribbed, confined!"

COUNT POTTS' STRATEGY

"L'Esprit est un faux monnayeur, qui change continuellement les gros sous en louis d'or, et qui souvent fait de ses louis d'or des gros sous."[2]

There were five hundred guardian angels (and of course as many evil spirits), in and about the merry premises of Congress Hall.[3] Each gay guest had his pair; but though each pair had their special ministry (and there were here and there a guest who would not have objected to transform his, for the time being, into a pair of trotting ponies), the attention of the cherubic troop, it may fairly be presumed, was directed mainly to the momentous flirtations of Miss. C. Sophy Onthank, the dread disposer of the destinies of eighty thousand innocent little dollars.

Miss Chittaline Sophy (though this is blabbing, for that mysterious "C." was generally condemned to travel in domino)— Miss Chittaline Sophy, besides her good

and evil spirit already referred to, was under the additional watch and ward of a pair of bombazine aunts, Miss Charity Onthank and Miss Sophy the same, of which she was the united namesake. "Chittaline" being the embellished diminutive of "Charity." These Hesperian dragons of old maids were cut after the common pattern of such utensils, and of course would not dignify a description; though this disparaging remark (we must stop long enough to say) is not at all to the prejudice of that occasional love-of-an-old-maid that one *does* sometimes see—that four-leaved clover of virginity—that star apart in the spilled milk of the Via Lactea:—

"For now and then you find one who could rally
  At forty, and go back to twenty-three—
A handsome, plump, affectionate 'Aunt Sally,'
With no rage for cats, flannel, and Bohea."

But the two elderly Misses Onthank were not of this category.

By the absence of that Junonic assurance, common to those ladies who are born and bred heiresses, Miss C. Sophy's autograph had not long been an object of interest at the bank. She had all the air of having been "brought up at the trough," as the French phrase it,

"Round as a cipher, simple as good day,"

and her belle-ship was still a surprise to her. Like the red-haired and freckled who find, when they get to Italy, that their flaming peculiarities are considered as captivating signs of a skin too delicate for exposure, she received with a slight incredulity the homage to her unseen charms—homage not the less welcome for exacting from the giver an exercise of faith and imagination. The same faith and imagination, she was free to suppose, might find a Venus within her girdle, as the sculptor sees one in the goodly block of marble, lacking only the removal of its clumsy covering by chisel and sand-paper. With no visible waist, she was as tall as a pump, and riotously rosy like a flowering rhododendron. Hair brown and plenty of it. Teeth white and all at home. And her voice, with but one semitone higher, would have been an approved contralto.

Having thus compressed into a couple of paragraphs what would have served a novelist for his first ten chapters, permit us, without the bother of intermediate mortar or moralizing (though this is rather a mixed figure), to lay on the next brick in the shape of a hint at the character of Miss Onthank's two prominent admirers.

Mr. Greville Seville was a New York beau. He had all the refinement that could possibly be imported. He had seen those who had seen all that is visible in the fashionable man of London and Paris, and he was well versed in the conduits through which their several peculiarities found their way across the Atlantic. Faultlessly booted, pantalooned, waistcoated, and shirted, he could afford to trust his coat and scarf to Providence, and his hat to Warnock or Leary. He wore a slightly restrained whisker, and a faint smut of an imperial, and his gloves fitted him inexorably. His figure was a matter of course. He was brought up in New York, and was one of the four hundred thousand results (more or less) of its drastic waters—washy and short. And he had as good a heart as is compatible with the above personal advantages.

It would very much have surprised the "company" at Congress Hall to have seen Mr. Chesterfield Potts put down as No. 2, in the emulous contest for the two hands of Miss Onthank. The count (he was commonly called "Count Potts," a compliment to good manners not unusual in America), was, by his own label, a man of "thirty and upward"—by the parish register possibly sixty-two. He was an upright, well preserved, stylish-looking man, with an expensive wig, fine teeth (commonly supposed not to be indigenous), and a lavish outlay of cotton batting, covering the retreat of such of his muscular forces as were inclined to retire from the field. What his native qualities might be was a branch of knowledge long since lost to the world. His politeness had superseded the necessity of any particular inquiry into the matter; indeed, we are inclined to believe his politeness had superseded his character altogether. He was as incapable of the impolite virtues (of which there are several) as of the impolite vices. Like cricketing, punning, political speech-making, and other mechanical arts, complimenting may be brought to a high degree of dexterity, and Count Potts, after a practice of many years, could, over most kinds of female platitude, spread a flattering unction humbugative to the most suspicious incredulity. As he told no sto-

ries, made no puns, volunteered but little conversation, and had the air of a modest man wishing to avoid notice, the blockheads and the very young girls stoutly denied his fascination. But in the memory of riper belles, as they went to sleep night after night, lay snugly lodged and carefully treasured, some timely compliment, some soothing word, and though credited to "old Potts," the smile with which it was gracefully re-acknowledged the next morning at breakfast, would have been warm enough for young Ascanius. "Nice old Potts!" was the faint murmur of many a bright lip turning downward to the pillow in the "last position."

And now, dear reader, you have an idea of the forces in the field, and you probably know how "the war is carried on" at Saratoga. Two aunts and a guardian angel versus an evil spirit and two lovers—Miss Onthank's hand, the (well-covered) bone of contention. Whether the citadel would speedily yield, and which of these two rival knights would bear away the palm of victory, were questions upon which the majority of lookers-on were doomed to make erroneous predictions. The reader, of course, is in the sagacious minority.

Mr. Potts' income was a net answer to his morning prayer. It provided his "daily bread" but no provender for a horse. He probably coveted Miss Onthank as much for her accompanying oats as for her personal avoirdupois, since the only complaint with which he ever troubled his acquaintances, was one touching his inability to keep an equipage. Man is instinctively a centaur, he used to say, and when you cut him off from his horse and reduce him to his simple trunk (and a trunk was all the count's worldly furniture), he is but a mutilated remainder, robbed of his natural locomotive.

It was not authenticated in Wall-street that Mr. Greville Seville was reasonably entitled to horse-flesh and caparison; but he had a trotting wagon and two delicious cropped sorrels; and those who drove in his company were obliged "to down with the dust" (a bon mot of Count Potts'). Science explains many of the enigmas of common life, however, and the secret of Mr. Seville's equipment and other means of going on swimmingly, lay in his unusually large organ of hope. He was simply anticipating the arrival of 1840, a year in which he had reason to believe that there would be paid in to the credit of the present Miss Onthank, a sufficient sum to cover his loosest expenditure. The intermediate transfer to himself of her rights to the same, was a mere filling up of an outline, his mind being entirely made up as to the conditional incumbrance of the lady's person. He was now paying her some attentions in advance, and he felt justified in charging his expenses on the estate. She herself would wish it, doubtless, if she could look into the future with *his* eyes.

By all the common data of matrimonial skirmishing, a lover with horses easily outstrips a lover with none. Miss C. Sophy, besides, was particularly fond of driving, and Seville was an accomplished whip. There was no lack of the "golden opportunity" of *tête-à-tête*, for, with a deaf aunt and somebody else on the back seat, he had Miss Onthank to himself on the driving box, and could talk to his horses in the embarrassing pauses. It looked a clear case to most observers; and as to Seville, he had studied out a livery for his future footman and tiger, and would not have taken an insurance at a quarter per cent.

But Potts—ah! Potts had traced back the wires of woman's weaknesses. The heiress had no conversation (why should she have it and money too?), and the part of her daily drive which she remembered with most pleasure, was the flourish of starting and returning—managed by Potts with a pomp and circumstance that would have done honor to the goings and comings of Queen Victoria. Once away from the portico, it was a monotonous drag through the dust for two or three hours, and as most ladies know, it takes a great deal of chit-chat to butter so large a slice of time; for there was no making love, *parbleu!* Miss Chittaline Onthank was of a stratum of human nature susceptible of no sentiment less substantial than a kiss, and when the news, and the weather, and the virtues of the sorrel ponies, were exhausted, the talk came to a stand-still. The heiress began to remember with alarm that her education had been neglected, and that it was a relief to get back to old Potts and the portico.

Fresh from his nap and warm bath, the perfumed count stepped out from the group he had purposely collected, gave her his hand with a deferential inquiry, spread the loungers to the right and left like an

"usher of the black rod," and with some well-studied impromptu compliment, waited on her to her chamber door. He received her again after her toilet, and for the remainder of the day devoted his utmost powers to her aggrandizement. If talking alone with her, it was to provoke her to some passage of school-girl autobiography, and listen like a charmed stone to the harp of Orpheus. If others were near, it was to catch her stupidities half uttered and twist them into sense before they came to the ground. His own clevernesses were prefaced with "As you remarked yesterday, Miss Onthank," or, "As you were about to say when I interrupted you." If he touched her foot, it was "so small he didn't see it." If she uttered an irredeemable and immitigable absurdity, he covered its retreat with some sudden exclamation. He called her pensive, when she was sleepy and vacant. He called her romantic, when he couldn't understand her. In short, her vanity was embodied—turned into a magician and slave—and in the shape of Count Chesterfield Potts ministered to her indefatigably.

But the summer solstice began to wane. A week more was all that was allotted to Saratoga by that great American commander, General Consent.

Count Potts came to breakfast, in a shawl cravat.

"Off, Potts?"

"Are you flitting, my dear count?"

"What—going away, dear Mr. Potts?"

"Gracious me! don't go, Mr. Potts!"

The last exclamation was sent across the table in a tone of alarm by Miss C. Sophy, and responded to only by a bow of obsequious melancholy.

Breakfast was over, and Potts arose. His baggage was at the door. He sought no interview with Miss Onthank. He did not even honor the two bombazinities with a farewell. He stepped up to the group of belles, airing their demi-toilets on the portico, said, "Ladies! au revoir!" took the heiress's hand and put it gallantly toward his lips, and walked off with his umbrella, requesting the driver to pick him up at the spring.

"He has been refused!" said one.

"He has given Seville a clear field in despair!" said another. And this was the general opinion.

The day crept on. But there was an emptiness without Potts. Seville had the field to himself, and as there was no fear of a new squatter, he thought he might dispense with tillage. They had a very dull drive and a very dull dinner, and in the evening, as there was no ball, Seville went off to play billiards. Miss Onthank was surrounded, as usual, by the belles and beaux, but she was down flat—unmagnetized, ungalvanized. The magician was gone. Her stupid things "stayed put." She was like a glass bead lost from a kaleidoscope.

That weary week was spent in lamentations over Potts. Everybody praised him. Everybody complimented Miss Onthank on her exclusive power of monopoly over such porcelain ware. The two aunts were his main glorifiers; for, as Potts knew, they were of that leathery toughness that only shines on you with rough usage.

We have said little, as yet, of Miss Onthank's capabilities in the love line. We doubt, indeed, whether she rightly understood the difference between loving and being born again. As to giving away her heart, she believed she could do what her mother did before her, but she would rather it would be one of her back teeth, if that would do as well. She liked Mr. Potts because he never made any difficulty about such things.

Seville considered himself accepted, though he had made no direct proposition. He had asked whether she preferred to live in country or town—she said "town." He had asked if she would leave the choice and management of horses and equipages to him—she said "be sure!" He had asked if she had any objection to his giving bachelor dinners occasionally—she said "la! no!" As he understood it, the whole thing was most comfortably arranged, and he lent money to several of his friends on the strength of it—giving his note, this is to say.

On a certain morning, some ten days after the departure of the count from Saratoga, Miss Onthank and her two aunts sat up in state in their parlor at the City Hotel. They always went to the City Hotel because Willard remembered their names, and asked after their uncle, the Major. Mr. Seville's ponies and wagon were at the door, and Mr. Seville's father, mother, seven sisters, and two small brothers, were in the progress of a betrothal visit—calling on the future Mrs. Greville Seville.

All of a sudden the door was thrown open, and enter Count Potts!

Up jumped the enchanted Chittaline Sophy.

"How *do* you do, Mr. Potts?"

"Good morning, Mr. Potts!" said the aunts in a breath.

"D'ye-do, Potts!" said Seville, giving him his fore-finger, with the air of a man rising from winning at cards.

Potts made his compliments all round. He was about sailing for Carolina, he said, and had come to ask permission of Miss Onthank to leave her sweet society for a few years of exile. But as this was the last of his days of pleasure, at least till he saw Miss Onthank again, he wished to be graced with the honor of her arm for a promenade in Broadway. The ladies and Mr. Seville doubtless would excuse her if she put on her bonnet without further ceremony.

Now Potts' politenesses had such an air of irresistible authority that people fell into their track like cars after a locomotive. While Miss Onthank was bonneting and shawling, the count entertained the entire party most gaily, though the Sevilles thought it rather unceremonious in the affianced miss to leave them in the midst of a first visit, and Mr. Greville Seville had arranged to send his mother home on foot, and drive Miss Onthank out to Harlem.

"I'll keep my horses here till you come back!" he shouted after them, as she tripped gaily down stairs on the count's arm.

And so he did. Though it was two hours before she appeared again, the impatient youth kept the old aunts company, and would have stayed till night, sorrels and all—for in that drive he meant to "name the day," and put his creditors at ease.

"I wouldn't even go up stairs, my dear!" said the count, handing her to the wagon, and sending up the groom for his master, "it's but an hour to dine, and you'll like the air after your fatigue. Ah, Seville, I've brought her back! Take good care of her for *my* sake, my good fellow!"

"What the devil has *his* sake to do with it, I wonder?" said Seville, letting his horses off like two rockets in harness.

And away they went toward Harlem; and in about an hour, very much to the surprise of the old aunts, who were looking out of the parlor window, the young lady dismounted from an omnibus! Count Potts had come to dine with them, and he tripped down to meet her with uncommon agility.

"Why, do you know, aunties!" she exclaimed, as she came up stairs out of breath, "do you know that Mr. Seville, when I told him I was married already to Mr. Potts, stopped his wagon, and p-p-put me into an omnibus!"

"Married to Mr. Potts!" screamed Aunt Charity.

"Married to Mr. Potts!" screamed Aunt Sophy.

"Why—yes, aunties; he said he must go south, if I didn't!" drawled out the bride, with only a *very* little blush indeed. "Tell aunties all about it, Mr. Potts!"

And Mr. Potts, with the same smile of infallible propriety, which seemed a warrant for everything he said or did, gave a very sketchy account of his morning's work, which, like all he undertook, had been exceedingly well done—properly witnessed, certified, etc., etc., etc. All of which shows the very sound policy of first making yourself indispensable to people you wish to manage. Or, put it receipt-wise:—

To marry a flat:—First, raise her up till she is giddy. Second, go away, and let her down. Third, come back, and offer to support her, if she will give you her hand. *"Simple comme bonjour!"* as Balzac says.

VIII

FITZ-JAMES O'BRIEN (1828–1862)

The brilliant cosmopolitan Irishman O'Brien ruled the short story of the fifties,—at least, he was the most significant influence between the death of Poe and the founding of *The Atlantic Monthly*. He had appeared unannounced in New York in 1852 with letters which admitted him at once to the metropolitan literary circles; he was soon a regular contributor to *Harper's Monthly* and other periodicals; and for ten years he was the leader of that "Bohemian group" of *littérateurs* which had as its gathering place Pfaff's *"rathskeller"* on Broadway.

To O'Brien literature was a thing to be thrown off in excited extempore to earn the wherewithal for Bohemian banquets and joyous luxuries to be shared with his friends. The "necessities" of life did not interest him. Like Poe, he was almost exclusively a magazinist looking at literature always as a thing to be thought of in terms of space, of the greatest effect in the smallest compass, of variety lest readers be repelled by sameness, of novel materials and unheard-of combinations. He was a lesser Poe, a Poe without the vividness and artistry and compelling power of the author of the *Tales of the Grotesque and the Arabesque*. Some of his tales, however, have survived and will survive. Among the best of them are "The Diamond Lens," "What Was It?," "The Wondersmith," "The Pot of Tulips," "The Golden Ingot," and "The Lost Room." In the advancement of the artistry of the short story, O'Brien stands as a midway figure between Hawthorne and Poe, and Harte and Aldrich.

WHAT WAS IT?

It is, I confess, with considerable diffidence that I approach the strange narrative which I am about to relate. The events which I purpose detailing are of so extraordinary a character that I am quite prepared to meet with an unusual amount of incredulity and scorn. I accept all such beforehand. I have, I trust, the literary courage to face unbelief. I have, after mature consideration, resolved to narrate, in as simple and straightforward a manner as I can compass, some facts that passed under my observation, in the month of July last, and which, in the annals of the mysteries of physical science, are wholly unparalleled.

I live at No. — Twenty-sixth Street, in New York. The house is in some respects a curious one. It has enjoyed for the last two years the reputation of being haunted. It is a large and stately residence, surrounded by what was once a garden, but which is now only a green enclosure used for bleaching clothes. The dry basin of what has been a fountain, and a few fruit-trees, ragged and unpruned, indicate that this spot in past year was a pleasant, shady retreat, filled with fruits and flowers and the sweet murmur of waters.

The house is very spacious. A hall of noble size leads to a large spiral staircase winding through its center, while the various apartments are of imposing dimensions. It was built some fifteen or twenty years since by Mr. A——, the well-known New York merchant, who five years ago threw the commercial world into convulsions by a stupendous bank fraud. Mr. A——, as every one knows, escaped to Europe, and died not long after, of a broken heart. Almost immediately, after the news of his decease reached this country and was verified, the report spread in Twenty-sixth Street that No. — was haunted. Legal measures had dispossessed the widow of its former owner, and it was inhabited merely by a caretaker and his wife, placed there by the house agent into whose hands it had passed for the purpose of renting or sale. These people declared that they were troubled with unnatural noises. Doors were opened without any visible agency. The remnants of furniture scattered through the various rooms were, during the night, piled one upon the other by unknown hands. Invisible feet passed up and down the stairs in broad daylight, accompanied by the rustle of unseen silk dresses, and the gliding of viewless hands along the massive balusters. The caretaker and his wife declared they would live there no longer. The house agent laughed, dismissed them, and put others in their place. The noises and supernatural manifestations continued. The neighborhood caught up the story, and the house remained untenanted for three years. Several persons negotiated for it; but, somehow, always before the bargain was closed they heard the unpleasant rumors, and declined to treat any further.

It was in this state of things that my landlady, who at that time kept a boarding-house in Bleecker Street, and who wished to move farther uptown, conceived the bold idea of renting No. —, Twenty-sixth Street. Happening to have in her house rather a plucky and philosophical set of boarders, she laid her scheme before us, stating candidly everything she had heard respecting the ghostly qualities of the establishment to which she wished to remove us. With the exception of two timid persons,—a sea-captain and a returned Californian, who immediately gave notice that they would leave,—all of Mrs. Moffat's guests declared that they would accompany her in her chivalric incursion into the abode of spirits.

Our removal was effected in the month of May, and we were charmed with our new residence. The portion of Twenty-Sixth Street where our house is situated, between Seventh and Eighth Avenues, is one of the pleasantest localities in New York. The gardens back of the houses, running down nearly to the Hudson, form, in the summer-time, a perfect avenue of verdure. The air is pure and invigorating, sweeping, as it does, straight across the river from the Weehawken heights, and even the ragged garden which surrounded the house, although displaying on washing days rather too much clothesline, still gave us a piece of greensward to look at, and a cool retreat in the summer evenings, where we smoked our cigars in the dusk, and watched the fireflies flashing their dark-lanterns in the long grass.

Of course we had no sooner established ourselves at No. — than we began to expect ghosts. We absolutely awaited their advent with eagerness. Our dinner conversation was supernatural. One of the boarders, who had purchased Mrs. Crowe's "Night Side of Nature" for his own private delectation, was regarded as a public enemy by the entire household for not having bought twenty copies. The man led a life of supreme wretchedness while he was reading this volume. A system of espionage was established, of which he was the victim. If he incautiously laid the book down for an instant and left the room, it was immediately seized and read aloud in secret places to a select few. I found myself a person of immense importance, it having leaked out that I was tolerably well versed in the history of supernaturalism, and had once written a story, the foundation of which was a ghost. If a table or a wainscoat panel happened to warp when we were assembled in the large drawing-room, there was an instant silence, and every one was prepared for an immediate clanking of chains and a spectral form.

After a month of psychological excitement, it was with the utmost dissatisfaction that we were forced to acknowledge that nothing in the remotest degree approaching the supernatural had manifested itself. Once the black butler asseverated that his candle had been blown out by some invisible agency while he was undressing himself for the night; but as I had more than once discovered this colored gentleman in a condition when one candle must have appeared to him like two, I thought it possible that by going a step further in his potations, he might have reversed this phenomenon, and seen no candle at all where he ought to have beheld one.

Things were in this state when an accident took place so awful and inexplicable in its character that my reason fairly reels at the bare memory of the occurrence. It was the tenth of July. After dinner was over I repaired, with my friend Dr. Hammond, to the garden to smoke my evening pipe. Independent of certain mental sympathies which existed between the Doctor and myself, we were linked together by a vice. We both smoked opium. We knew each other's secret, and respected it. We enjoyed together that wonderful expansion of thought, that marvelous intensifying of the perceptive faculties, that boundless feeling of existence when we seem to have points of contact with the whole universe, —in short, that unimaginable spiritual bliss, which I would not surrender for a throne, and which I hope you, reader, will never—never taste.

Those hours of opium happiness which the Doctor and I spent together in secret were regulated with a scientific accuracy. We did not blindly smoke the drug of paradise, and leave our dreams to chance. While smoking, we carefully steered our conversation through the brightest and calmest channels of thought. We talked of the East, and endeavored to recall the magical panorama of its glowing scenery. We criticized the most sensuous poets,—those who painted life ruddy with health, brimming with passion, happy in the possession of youth and strength and beauty. If we talked of Shakespeare's "Tempest," we lingered over Ariel, and avoided Caliban. Like the Guebers,[1] we turned our faces to the East, and saw only the sunny side of the world.

This skilful coloring of our train of thought produced in our subsequent visions a corresponding tone. The splendors of Arabian fairyland dyed our dreams. We paced the narrow strip of grass with the tread and port of kings. The song of the *rana arborea*,[2] while he clung to the bark of the ragged plum-tree, sounded like the strains of divine musicians. Houses, walls and streets melted like rain clouds, and vistas of unimaginable glory stretched away before us. It was a rapturous companionship. We enjoyed the vast delight more perfectly because, even in our most ecstatic moments, we were conscious of each other's presence. Our pleasures, while individual, were still twin, vibrating and moving in musical accord.

On the evening in question, the tenth of July, the doctor and myself drifted into an unusually metaphysical mood. We lit our large meerschaums, filled with fine Turkish tobacco, in the core of which burned a little black nut of opium, that, like the nut in the fairy-tale, held within its narrow limits wonders beyond the reach of kings; we paced to and fro, conversing. A strange perversity dominated the currents of our thought. They would *not* flow through the sunlit channels into which we strove to divert them. For some unaccountable reason, they constantly diverged into dark and lonesome beds, where a continual gloom brooded. It was in vain that, after our old fashion, we flung ourselves on the shores of the East, and talked of its gay bazaars, of the splendors of the time of Haroun, of harems and golden palaces. Black afreets continually arose from the depths of our talk, and expanded, like the one the fisherman released from the copper vessel, until they blotted everything bright from our vision. Insensibly, we yielded to the occult force that swayed us, and indulged in gloomy speculation. We had talked some time upon the proneness of the human mind to mysticism, and the almost universal love of the terrible, when Hammond suddenly said to me, "What do you consider to be the greatest element of terror?"

The question puzzled me. That many things were terrible, I knew. Stumbling over a corpse in the dark; beholding, as I once did, a woman floating down a deep and rapid river with wildly lifted arms, and awful, upturned face, uttering, as she drifted, shrieks that rent one's heart while we, spectators, stood frozen at a window which overhung the river at a height of sixty feet, unable to make the slightest effort to save her, but dumbly watching her last supreme agony and her disappearance. A shattered wreck, with no life visible, encountered floating listlessly on the ocean, is a terrible object, for it suggests a huge terror, the proportions of which are veiled. But it now struck me, for the first time, that there must be one great and ruling embodiment of fear,—a King of Terrors, to which all others must succumb. What might it be? To what train of circumstances would it owe its existence?

"I confess, Hammond," I replied to my friend, "I never considered the subject before. That there must be one Something more terrible than any other thing, I feel. I cannot attempt, however, even the most vague definition."

"I am somewhat like you, Harry," he answered. "I feel my capacity to experience a terror greater than anything yet conceived by the human mind;—something combining in fearful and unnatural amalgamation hitherto supposed incompatible elements. The calling of the voices in Brockden Brown's novel of 'Wieland' is awful; so is the picture of the Dweller of the Threshold, in Bulwer's 'Zanoni'; but," he added, shaking his head gloomily, "there is something more horrible still than those."

"Look here, Hammond," I rejoined, "let us drop this kind of talk, for Heaven's sake! We shall suffer for it, depend on it."

"I don't know what's the matter with me to-night," he replied, "but my brain is running upon all sorts of weird and awful thoughts. I feel as if I could write a story like Hoffmann, to-night, if I were only master of a literary style."

"Well, if we are going to be Hoffmannesque in our talk, I'm off to bed. Opium and nightmares should never be brought together. How sultry it is! Good-night, Hammond."

"Good-night, Harry. Pleasant dreams to you."

"To you, gloomy wretch, afreets, ghouls and enchanters."

We parted, and each sought his respective chamber. I undressed quickly and got into bed, taking with me, according to my usual custom, a book, over which I generally read myself to sleep. I opened the volume as soon as I had laid my head upon the pillow, and instantly flung it to the other side of the room. It was Goudon's "History of Monsters,"—a curious French work, which I had lately imported from Paris, but which, in the state of mind I had then reached, was anything but an agreeable companion. I resolved to go to sleep at once; so, turning down my gas until nothing but a little blue point of light glimmered on the top of the tube, I composed myself to rest.

The room was in total darkness. The atom of gas that still remained alight did not illuminate a distance of three inches round the burner. I desperately drew my arm across my eyes, as if to shut out even the darkness, and tried to think of nothing. It was in vain. The confounded themes touched on by Hammond in the garden kept obtruding themselves on my brain. I battled against them. I erected ramparts of would-be blankness of intellect to keep them out. They still crowded upon me. While I was lying still as a corpse, hoping that by a perfect physical inaction I should hasten mental repose, an awful incident occurred. A Something dropped, as it seemed, from the ceiling, plum upon my chest, and the next instant I felt two bony hands encircling my throat, endeavoring to choke me.

I am no coward, and am possessed of considerable physical strength. The suddenness of the attack, instead of stunning me, strung every nerve to its highest tension. My body acted from instinct, before my brain had time to realize the terrors of my position. In an instant I wound two muscular arms around the creature, and squeezed it, with all the strength of despair against my chest. In a few seconds the bony hands that had fastened on my throat loosened their hold, and I was free to breathe once more. Then commenced a struggle of awful intensity. Immersed in the most profound darkness, totally ignorant of the nature of the Thing by which I was so suddenly attacked, finding my grasp slipping every moment, by reason, it seemed to me, of the entire nakedness of my assailant, bitten with sharp teeth in the shoulder, neck, and chest, having every moment to protect my throat against a pair of sinewy, agile hands, which my utmost efforts could not confine,—these were a combination of circumstances to combat which required all the strength, skill, and courage that I possessed.

At last, after a silent, deadly, exhausting struggle, I got my assailant under by a series of incredible efforts of strength. Once pinned, with my knee on what I made out to be its chest, I knew that I was victor. I rested for a moment to breathe. I heard the creature beneath me panting in the darkness, and felt the violent throbbing of a heart. It was apparently as exhausted as I was! that was one comfort. At this moment I remembered that I usually placed under my pillow, before going to bed, a large yellow silk pocket handkerchief. I felt for it instantly; it was there. In a few seconds more I had, after a fashion, pinioned the creature's arms.

I now felt tolerably secure. There was nothing more to be done but to turn on the gas, and, having first seen what my midnight assailant was like, arouse the household. I will confess to being actuated by a certain pride in not giving the alarm before; I wished to make the capture alone and unaided.

Never losing my hold for an instant, I slipped from the bed to the floor, dragging my captive with me. I had but a few steps to make to reach the gasburner; these I made with the greatest caution, holding the creature in a grip like a vise. At last I got within arm's length of the tiny speck of blue light which told me where the gasburner lay. Quick as lightning I released my grasp with one hand and let on the full flood of light. Then I turned to look at my captive.

I cannot even attempt to give any definition of my sensations the instant after I turned on the gas. I suppose I must have shrieked with terror, for in less than a minute afterward my room was crowded with the inmates of the house. I shudder now as I think of that awful moment. *I saw nothing!* Yes; I had one arm firmly clasped round a breathing, panting, corporeal shape, my other hand gripped with all its strength a throat as warm, as apparently fleshy, as my own; and yet, with this living substance in my grasp, with its body pressed against my own, and all in the bright glare of a large jet of gas, I absolutely beheld nothing! Not even an outline, —a vapor!

I do not, even at this hour, realize the situation in which I found myself. I cannot recall the astounding incident thoroughly. Imagination in vain tries to compass the awful paradox.

It breathed. I felt its warm breath upon my cheek. It struggled fiercely. It had hands. They clutched me. Its skin was smooth, like my own. There it lay, pressed close up against me, solid as stone,—and yet utterly invisible!

I wonder that I did not faint or go mad, on the instant. Some wonderful instinct must have sustained me; for, absolutely, in place of loosening my hold on the terrible Enigma, I seemed to gain an additional strength in my moment of horror, and tightened my grasp with such wonderful force that I felt the creature shivering with agony.

Just then Hammond entered my room at the head of the household. As soon as he beheld my face—which, I suppose, must have been an awful sight to look at—he hastened forward, crying, "Great heaven, Harry! what has happened?"

"Hammond! Hammond!" I cried, "come here. Oh, this is awful! I have been attacked in bed by something or other, which I have hold of; but I can't see it,—can't see it!"

Hammond, doubtless struck by the unfeigned horror expressed in my countenance, made one or two steps forward with an anxious yet puzzled expression. A very audible titter burst from the remainder of my visitors. This suppressed laughter made me furious. To laugh at a human being in my position! It was the worst species of cruelty. *Now,* I can understand why the appearance of a man struggling violently, as it would seem, with an airy nothing, and calling for assistance against a vision, should have appeared ludicrous. *Then,* so

great was my rage against the mocking crowd that had I the power I would have stricken them dead where they stood.

"Hammond! Hammond!" I cried again, despairingly, "for God's sake, come to me. I can hold the—the thing but a short while longer. It is overpowering me. Help me! Help me!"

"Harry," whispered Hammond, approaching me, "you have been smoking too much opium."

"I swear to you, Hammond, that this is no vision," I answered, in the same low tone. "Don't you see how it shakes my whole frame with its struggles? If you don't believe me, convince yourself. Feel it,—touch it."

Hammond advanced and laid his hand in the spot I indicated. A wild cry of horror burst from him. He had felt it!

In a moment he had discovered somewhere in my room a long piece of cord, and was the next instant winding it and knotting it about the body of the unseen being that I clasped in my arms.

"Harry," he said, in a hoarse, agitated voice, for, though he preserved his presence of mind, he was deeply moved, "Harry, it's all safe now. You may let go, old fellow, if you're tired. The Thing can't move."

I was utterly exhausted, and I gladly loosed my hold.

Hammond stood holding the ends of the cord that bound the Invisible, twisted round his hand, while before him, self-supporting as it were, he beheld a rope laced and interlaced, and stretching tightly around a vacant space. I never saw a man look so thoroughly stricken with awe. Nevertheless his face expressed all the courage and determination which I knew him to possess. His lips, although white, were set firmly, and one could perceive at a glance, that, although stricken with fear, he was not daunted.

The confusion that ensued among the guests of the house who were witnesses of this extraordinary scene between Hammond and myself,—who beheld the pantomime of binding this struggling Something,—who beheld me almost sinking from physical exhaustion when my task of jailer was over,—the confusion and terror that took possession of the bystanders, when they saw all this, was beyond description. The weaker ones fled from the apartment. The few who remained clustered near the door and could not be induced to approach Hammond and his Charge. Still incredulity broke out through their terror. They had not the courage to satisfy themselves, and yet they doubted. It was in vain that I begged of some of the men to come near and convince themselves by touch of the existence in that room of a living being which was invisible. They were incredulous, but did not dare to undeceive themselves. How could a solid, living, breathing body be invisible, they asked. My reply was this. I gave a sign to Hammond, and both of us—conquering our fearful repugnance to touch the invisible creature—lifted it from the ground, manacled as it was, and took it to my bed. Its weight was about that of a boy of fourteen.

"Now, my friends," I said, as Hammond and myself held the creature suspended over the bed, "I can give you self-evident proof that here is a solid, ponderable body, which, nevertheless, you cannot see. Be good enough to watch the surface of the bed attentively."

I was astonished at my own courage in treating this strange event so calmly; but I had recovered from my first terror, and felt a sort of scientific pride in the affair, which dominated every other feeling.

The eyes of the bystanders were immediately fixed on my bed. At a given signal Hammond and I let the creature fall. There was a dull sound of a heavy body alighting on a soft mass. The timbers of the bed creaked. A deep impression marked itself distinctly on the pillow, and on the bed itself. The crowd who witnessed this gave a low cry, and rushed from the room. Hammond and I were left alone with our Mystery.

We remained silent for some time, listening to the low, irregular breathing of the creature on the bed, and watching the rustle of the bedclothes as it impotently struggled to free itself from confinement. Then Hammond spoke.

"Harry, this is awful."

"Aye, awful."

"But not unaccountable."

"Not unaccountable. What do you mean? Such a thing has never occurred since the birth of the world. I know not what to think, Hammond. God grant that I am not mad, and that this is not an insane fantasy!"

"Let us reason a little, Harry. Here is a solid body which we touch, but which we cannot see. The fact is so unusual that it strikes us with terror. Is there no parallel, though, for such a phenomenon? Take a piece of pure glass. It is tangible and transparent. A certain chemical coarseness is all that prevents its being so entirely transparent as to be totally invisible. It is not *theoretically impossible*, mind you, to make a glass which shall not reflect a single ray of light,—a glass so pure and homogeneous in its atoms that the rays from the sun will pass through it as they do through the air, refracted but not reflected. We do not see the air, and yet we feel it."

"That's all very well, Hammond, but these are inanimate substances. Glass does not breathe, air does not breathe. *This* thing has a heart that palpitates,—a will that moves it,—lungs that play, and inspire and respire."

"You forget the phenomena of which we have so often heard of late," answered the doctor, gravely. "At the meetings called 'spirit circles,' invisible hands have been thrust into the hands of those persons round the table,—warm, fleshly hands that seemed to pulsate with mortal life."

"What? Do you think, then, that this thing is—"

"I don't know what it is," was the solemn reply; "but please the gods I will, with your assistance, thoroughly investigate it."

We watched together, smoking many pipes, all night long, by the bedside of the unearthly being that tossed and panted until it was apparently wearied out. Then we learned by the low, regular breathing that it slept.

The next morning the house was all astir. The boarders congregated on the landing outside my room, and Hammond and myself were lions. We had to answer a thousand questions as to the state of our extraordinary prisoner, for as yet not one person in the house except ourselves could be induced to set foot in the apartment.

The creature was awake. This was evidenced by the convulsive manner in which the bedclothes were moved in its efforts to escape. There was something truly terrible in beholding, as it were, those second-hand indications of the terrible writhings and agonized struggles for liberty which themselves were invisible.

Hammond and myself had racked our brains during the long night to discover some means by which we might realize the shape and general appearance of the Enigma. As well as we could make out by passing our hands over the creature's form, its outlines and lineaments were human. There was a mouth, a round, smooth head without hair; a nose, which, however, was little elevated above the cheeks; and its hands and feet felt like those of a boy. At first we thought of placing the being on a smooth surface and tracing its outlines with chalk, as shoemakers trace the outline of the foot. This plan was given up as being of no value. Such an outline would give not the slightest idea of its conformation.

A happy thought struck me. We would take a cast of it in plaster of Paris. This would give us the solid figure, and satisfy all our wishes. But how to do it? The movements of the creature would disturb the setting of the plastic covering, and distort the mold. Another thought. Why not give it chloroform? It had respiratory organs,—that was evident by its breathing. Once reduced to a state of insensibility, we could do with it what we would. Doctor X—— was sent for; and after the worthy physician had recovered from the first shock of amazement, he proceeded to administer the chloroform. In three minutes afterward we were enabled to remove the fetters from the creature's body, and a modeler was busily engaged in covering the invisible form with the moist clay. In five minutes more we had a mold, and before evening a rough facsimile of the Mystery. It was shaped like a man,—distorted, uncouth, and horrible, but still a man. It was small, not over four feet and some inches in height, and its limbs revealed a muscular development that was unparalleled. Its face surpassed in hideousness anything I had ever seen. Gustav Doré, or Callot, or Tony Johannot, never conceived anything so horrible. There is a face in one of the latter's illustrations to *Un voyage où il vous plaira*,² which somewhat approaches the countenance of this creature, but does not equal it. It was the physiognomy of what I should fancy a ghoul might be. It looked as if it was capable of feeding on human flesh.

Having satisfied our curiosity, and bound every one in the house to secrecy, it became a question what was to be done with our Enigma? It was impossible that we should keep such a horror in our house; it was equally impossible that such an awful being should be let loose upon the world. I confess that I would have gladly voted for the creature's destruction. But who would shoulder the responsibility? Who would undertake the execution of this horrible semblance of a human being? Day after day this question was deliberated gravely. The boarders all left the house. Mrs. Moffat was in despair, and threatened Hammond and myself with all sorts of legal penalties if we did not remove the Horror. Our answer was, "We will go if you like, but we decline taking this creature with us. Remove it yourself, if you please. It appeared in your house. On you the responsibility rests." To this there was, of course, no answer. Mrs. Moffat could not obtain for love or money a person who would even approach the Mystery.

The most singular part of the affair was that we were entirely ignorant of what the creature habitually fed on. Everything in the way of nutriment that we could think of was placed before it, but was never touched. It was awful to stand by, day after day, and see the clothes toss, and hear the hard breathing, and know that it was starving.

Ten, twelve days, a fortnight passed, and it still lived. The pulsations of the heart, however, were daily growing fainter, and had now nearly ceased. It was evident that the creature was dying for want of sustenance. While this terrible life-struggle was going on, I felt miserable. I could not sleep. Horrible as the creature was, it was pitiful to think of the pangs it was suffering.

At last it died. Hammond and I found it cold and stiff one morning in the bed. The heart had ceased to beat, the lungs to inspire. We hastened to bury it in the garden. It was a strange funeral, the dropping of that viewless corpse into the damp hole. The cast of its form I gave to Doctor X——, who keeps it in his museum in Tenth Street.

As I am on the eve of a long journey from which I may not return, I have drawn up this narrative of an event the most singular that has ever come to my knowledge.

IX

HARRIET PRESCOTT SPOFFORD (1835-1920)

With *The Atlantic Monthly,* 1857, a new freshness and vigor began to appear in the American short story. The influence of Lowell, the first editor of the magazine, undoubtedly did much to free the fiction of the next decade from the mawkish sentimentality and tawdriness that a veritable "school" of feminine writers had thrown over it. Lowell preferred native themes and native tangs and actuality in our native fiction, and knowing this the younger writers for *The Atlantic* unconsciously began to write more naturally and more spontaneously. The first "discovery" of the new magazine was Harriet Prescott, a school girl who had read French fiction and had caught the style of it—that epigrammatic, crackling, concise style which we may describe only with the adjective *Gallic.* Her story "In a Cellar" was so unusual that for a time Lowell was suspicious of its authorship. She followed it with "The Amber Gods," a story of remarkable promise,—a promise, be it remarked, that she never fulfilled. She was a romanticist with a glowing pen, so glowing indeed and so superlative at times that Henry James in the mid-sixties used her novel *Azarian*—a flushed and hectic creation—as the best example he could find of the disease which was threatening American fiction.

But despite her purple patches Mrs. Spofford did in many of her short stories really distinctive work. In her use of dialogue she surpassed Hawthorne and Poe, and at times in her climaxes and her dramatic moments she had a power which, had it been always at her command, would have made her one of the greatest of American short-story writers.

CIRCUMSTANCE

She had remained, during all that day, with a sick neighbor—those eastern wilds of Maine in that epoch frequently making neighbors and miles synonymous—and so busy had she been with care and sympathy that she did not at first observe the approaching night. But finally the level rays, reddening the snow, threw their 10 gleam upon the wall, and, hastily donning cloak and hood, she bade her friends farewell and sallied forth on her return. Home lay some three miles distant, across a copse, a meadow, and a piece of woods— 15 the woods being a fringe on the skirts of the great forests that stretch far away into the North. That home was one of a dozen log-houses lying a few furlongs apart from each other, with their half-cleared 20 demesnes separating them at the rear from a wilderness untrodden save by stealthy native or deadly panther tribes.

She was in a nowise exalted frame of spirit—on the contrary, rather depressed 25 by the pain she had witnessed and the fatigue she had endured; but in certain temperaments such a condition throws open the mental pores, so to speak, and renders one receptive of every influence. Through the little copse she walked slowly, with her cloak folded about her, lingering to imbibe the sense of shelter, the sunset filtered 5 in purple through the mist of woven spray and twig, the companionship of growth not sufficiently dense to band against her, the sweet home-feeling of a young and tender winter wood. It was therefore just on the 10 edge of the evening that she emerged from the place and began to cross the meadowland. At one hand lay the forest to which her path wound; at the other the evening star hung over a tide of failing orange that 15 slowly slipped down the earth's broad side to sadden other hemispheres with sweet regret. Walking rapidly now, and with her eyes wide-open, she distinctly saw in the air before her what was not there a 20 moment ago, a winding-sheet—cold, white, and ghastly, waved by the likeness of four wan hands—that rose with a long inflation and fell in rigid folds, while a voice, shaping itself from the hollowness above, spectral 25 and melancholy, sighed, "The Lord have mercy on the people! The Lord have mercy on the people!" Three times the sheet with its corpse-covering outline waved beneath the pale hands, and the voice, awful in its solemn and mysterious depth, sighed, "The Lord have mercy on the people!" Then all was gone, the place was clear again, the gray sky was obstructed by no deathly blot; she looked about her, shook her shoulders decidedly, and, pulling on her hood, went forward once more.

She might have been a little frightened by such an apparition if she had led a life of less reality than frontier settlers are apt to lead; but dealing with hard fact does not engender a flimsy habit of mind, and this woman was too sincere and earnest in her character, and too happy in her situation to be thrown by antagonism, merely, upon superstitious fancies and chimeras of the second-sight. She did not even believe herself subject to an hallucination, but smiled simply, a little vexed that her thought could have framed such a glamour from the day's occurrences, and not sorry to lift the bough of the warder of the woods and enter and disappear in their somber path. If she had been imaginative, she would have hesitated at her first step into a region whose dangers were not visionary; but I suppose that the thought of a little child at home would conquer that propensity in the most habituated. So, biting a bit of spicy birch, she went along. Now and then she came to a gap where the trees had been partially felled, and here she found that the lingering twilight was explained by that peculiar and perhaps electric film which sometimes sheathes the sky in diffused light for many hours before a brilliant aurora. Suddenly, a swift shadow, like the fabulous flying-dragon, writhed through the air before her, and she felt herself instantly seized and borne aloft. It was that wild beast—the most savage and serpentine and subtle and fearless of our latitudes—known by hunters as the Indian Devil, and he held her in his clutches on the broad floor of a swinging fir-bough. His long sharp claws were caught in her clothing, he worried them sagaciously a little, then, finding that ineffectual to free them, he commenced licking her bare arm with his rasping tongue and pouring over her the wide streams of his hot, fetid breath. So quick had this flashing action been that the woman had had no time for alarm; moreover, she was not of the screaming kind; but now, as she felt him endeavoring to disentangle his claws, and the horrid sense

of her fate smote her, and she saw instinctively the fierce plunge of those weapons, the long strips of living flesh torn from her bones, the agony, the quivering disgust—itself a worse agony—while by her side and holding her in his great lithe embrace the monster crouched, his white tusks whetting and gnashing, his eyes glaring through all the darkness like balls of red fire—a shriek that rang in every forest hollow, that startled every winter-housed thing, that stirred and woke the least needle of the tasseled pines, tore through her lips. A moment afterward, the beast left the arm, once white, now crimson, and looked up alertly.

She did not think at this instant to call upon God. She called upon her husband. It seemed to her that she had but one friend in the world—that was he; and again the cry, loud, clear, prolonged, echoed through the woods. It was not the shriek that disturbed the creature at his relish; he was not born in the woods to be scared of an owl, you know—what then? It must have been the echo, most musical, most resonant, repeated and yet repeated, dying with long sighs of sweet sound, vibrated from rock to river and back again from depth to depth of cave and cliff. Her thought flew after it; she knew, that, even if her husband heard it, he yet could not reach her in time; she saw that while the beast listened he would not gnaw,—and this she *felt* directly, when the rough, sharp, and multiplied stings of his tongue retouched her arm. Again her lips opened by instinct, but the sound that issued thence came by reason. She had heard that music charmed wild beasts—just this point between life and death—intensified every faculty—and when she opened her lips the third time it was not for shrieking, but for singing.

A little thread of melody stole out, a rill of tremulous motion; it was the cradle-song with which she rocked her baby—how could she sing that? And then she remembered the baby sleeping rosily on the long settee before the fire; the father cleaning his gun, with one foot on the green wooden rundle; the merry light from the chimney dancing out and through the room, on the rafters of the ceiling with their tassels of onions and herbs, on the log walls painted with lichens and festooned with apples, on the king's-arm slung across the shelf with the old pirate's-cut-lass, on the snow-pile of the bed, and on the great brass clock,—dancing, too, and lingering on the baby, with his fringed gentian eyes, his chubby fists clenched on the pillow, and his fine breezy hair fanning with the motion of his father's foot. All this struck her in one, and made a sob of her breath, and she ceased.

Immediately the long red tongue was thrust forth again. Before it touched, a song sprang to her lips, a wild seasong, such as some sailor might be singing far out on trackless blue water that night, the shrouds whistling with frost and the sheets glued in ice—a song with the wind in its burden and the spray in its chorus. The monster raised his head and flared the fiery eyeballs upon her, then fretted the imprisoned claws a moment and was quiet; only the breath like the vapor from some hell-pit still swathed her. Her voice, at first faint and fearful, gradually lost its quaver, grew under her control and subject to her modulation; it rose on long swells, it fell in subtle cadences, now and then its tones pealed out like bells from distant belfries, on fresh sonorous mornings. She sung the song through, and, wondering lest his name of Indian Devil were not his true name, and if he would not detect her, she repeated it. Once or twice, now, indeed, the beast stirred uneasily, turned, and made the bough sway at his movement. As she ended, he snapped his jaws together, and tore away the fettered member, curling it under him with a snarl,—when she burst into the gayest reel that ever answered a fiddle-bow. How many a time she had heard her husband play it on the homely fiddle made by himself from birch and cherry-wood; how many a time she had seen it danced on the floor of their one room, to the patter of wooden clogs and the rustle of homespun petticoats; how many a time she had danced it herself;— and did she not remember once, as they joined clasps for right-hands-round, how it had lent its gay, bright measure to her life? And here she was singing it alone, in the forest, at midnight, to a wild beast! As she sent her voice trilling up and down its quick oscillations between joy and pain, the creature who grasped her uncurled his paw and scratched the bark from the bough; she must vary the spell, and her voice spun leaping along the projecting points of tune of a hornpipe. Still singing, she felt herself twisted about with a low growl and

a lifting of the red lip from the glittering teeth; she broke the hornpipe's thread, and commenced unraveling a lighter, livelier thing, an Irish jig. Up and **down and round** about her voice flew, the **beast threw** back his head so that the diabolical **face** fronted hers, and the torrent of his breath prepared her for his feast as the anaconda slimes his prey. Frantically she darted from tune to tune; his restless movements followed her. She tired herself with dancing and vivid national airs, growing feverish and singing spasmodically as she felt her horrid tomb yawning wider. Touching in this manner all the slogan and keen clan cries, the beast moved again, but only to lay the disengaged paw across her with heavy satisfaction. She did not dare to pause; through the clear cold air, the frosty starlight, she sang. If there were yet any tremor in the tone, it was not fear— she had learned the secret of sound at last; nor could it be chill—far too high a fever throbbed her pulses; it was nothing but the thought of the log-house and of what might be passing within it. She fancied the baby stirring in his sleep and moving his pretty lips—her husband rising and opening the door, looking out after her, and wondering at her absence. She fancied the light pouring through the chink and then shut in again with all the safety and comfort and joy, her husband taking down the fiddle and playing lightly with his head inclined, playing while she sang, while she sang for her life to an Indian Devil. Then she knew he was fumbling for and finding some shining fragment and scoring it down the yellowing hair, and unconsciously her voice forsook the wild war-tunes and drifted into the half-gay, half-melancholy *Rosin the Bow.*

Suddenly she woke pierced with a pang, and the daggered tooth penetrating her flesh—dreaming of safety, she had ceased singing and lost it. The beast had regained the use of all his limbs, and now, standing and raising his back, bristling and foaming, with sounds that would have been like hisses but for their deep and fearful sonority, he withdrew step by step toward the trunk of the tree, still with his flaming balls upon her. She was all at once free, on one end of the bough, twenty feet from the ground. She did not measure the distance, but rose to drop herself down, careless of any death, so that it were not this. Instantly, as if he scanned her thoughts, the creature bounded forward with a yell and caught her again in his dreadful hold. It might be that he was not greatly famished; for, as she suddenly flung up her voice again, he settled himself composedly on the bough, still clasping her with invincible pressure to his rough, ravenous breast, and listening in a fascination to the sad, strange, U-la-lu that now moaned forth in loud, hollow tones above him. He half closed his eyes, and sleepily reopened and shut them again.

What rending pains were close at hand! Death! and what a death! worse than any other that is to be named! Water, be it cold or warm, that which buoys up blue ice-fields, or which bathes tropical coasts with currents of balmy bliss, is yet a gentle conqueror, kisses as it kills, and draws you down gently through darkening fathoms to its heart. Death at the sword is the festival of trumpet and bugle and banner, with glory ringing out around you and distant hearts thrilling through yours. No gnawing disease can bring such hideous end as this; for that is a fiend bred of your own flesh, and this—is it a fiend, this living lump of appetites? What dread comes with the thought of perishing in flames! but fire, let it leap and hiss never so hotly, is something too remote, too alien, to inspire us with such loathly horror as a wild beast; if it have a life, that life is too utterly beyond our comprehension. Fire is not half ourselves; as it devours, arouses neither hatred nor disgust; is not to be known by the strength of our lower natures let loose; does not drip our blood into our faces from foaming chaps, nor mouth nor slaver above us with vitality. Let us be ended by fire, and we are ashes, for the winds to bear, the leaves to cover; let us be ended by wild beasts, and the base, cursed thing howls with us forever through the forest. All this she felt as she charmed him, and what force it lent to her song God knows. If her voice should fail! If the damp and cold should give her any fatal hoarseness! If all the silent powers of the forest did not conspire to help her! The dark, hollow night rose indifferently over her; the wide, cold air breathed rudely past her, lifted her wet hair and blew it down again; the great boughs swung with a ponderous strength, now and then clashed their iron lengths together and shook off a sparkle of icy spears or some long-lain weight of snow from their heavy shadows. The green

depths were utterly cold and silent and stern. These beautiful haunts that all the summer were hers and rejoiced to share with her their bounty, these heavens that had yielded their largess, these stems that had thrust their blossoms into her hands, all these friends of three moons ago forgot her now and knew her no longer.

Feeling her desolation, wild, melancholy, forsaken songs rose thereon from that frightful aerie—weeping, wailing tunes, that sob among the people from age to age, and overflow with otherwise unexpressed sadness—all rude, mournful ballads—old tearful strains, that Shakespeare heard the vagrants sing, and that rise and fall like the wind and tide—sailor-songs, to be heard only in lone mid-watches beneath the moon and stars—ghastly rhyming romances, such as that famous one of the *Lady Margaret*, when

She slipped on her gown of green
     A piece below the knee,—
And 'twas all a long, cold winter's night
     A dead corse followed she.

Still the beast lay with closed eyes, yet never relaxing his grasp. Once a half-whine of enjoyment escaped him,—he, fawned his fearful head upon her; once he scored her cheek with his tongue: savage caresses that hurt like wounds. How weary she was! and yet how terribly awake! How fuller and fuller of dismay grew the knowledge that she was only prolonging her anguish and playing with death! How appalling the thought that with her voice ceased her existence! Yet she could not sing forever; her throat was dry and hard, her very breath was a pain, her mouth was hotter than any desert-worn pilgrim's—if she could but drop upon her burning tongue one atom of the ice that glittered about her!—but both of her arms were pinioned in the giant's vice. She remembered the winding-sheet, and for the first time in her life shivered with spiritual fear. Was it hers? She asked herself, as she sang, what sins she had committed, what life she had led, to find her punishment so soon and in these pangs, and then she sought eagerly for some reason why her husband was not up and abroad to find her. He failed her—her one sole hope in life— and without being aware of it her voice forsook the songs of suffering and sorrow for old Covenanting hymns,—hymns with which her mother had lulled her, which the class-leader pitched in the chimney-corners—grand and sweet Methodist hymns, brimming with melody and with all fantastic involutions of tune to suit that ecstatic worship, hymns full of the beauty of holiness, steadfast, relying, sanctified by the salvation they had lent to those in worse extremity than hers, for they had found themselves in the grasp of hell, while she was but in the jaws of death. Out of this strange music, peculiar to one character of faith, and than which there is none more beautiful in its degree nor owning a more potent sway of sound, her voice soared into the glorified chants of churches. What to her was death by cold or famine or wild beasts? "Though He slay me, yet will I trust in Him," she sang. High and clear through the frore fair night, the level moonbeams splintering in the wood, the scarce glints of stars in the shadowy roof of branches, these sacred anthems rose—rose as a hope from despair, as some snowy spray of flower-bells from blackest mold. Was she not in God's hands? Did not the world swing at His will? If this were in His great plan of Providence, was it not best, and should she not accept it?

"He is the Lord our God; His judgments are in all the earth."

Oh, sublime faith of our fathers, where utter self-sacrifice alone was true love, the fragrance of whose unrequired subjection was pleasanter than that of golden censers swung in purple-vapored chancels!

Never ceasing in the rhythm of her thoughts, articulated in music as they thronged, the memory of her first communion flashed over her. Again she was in that distant place on that sweet spring morning. Again the congregation rustled out, and the few remained, and she trembled to find herself among them. How well she remembered the devout, quiet faces, too accustomed to the sacred feast to glow with their inner joy! how well the snowy linen at the altar, the silver vessels slowly and silently shifting! and as the cup approached and passed, how the sense of delicious perfume stole in and heightened the transport of her prayer, and she had seemed, looking up through the windows where the sky soared blue in constant freshness, to feel all heaven's balms dripping from the portals, and to scent the lilies of eternal peace! Perhaps another would not have felt so much ecstasy as satisfaction on that occasion; but it is a true, if a later dis-

ciple, who had said, "The Lord bestoweth his blessings there, where he findeth the vessels empty." "And does it need the walls of a church to renew my communion?" she 5 asked. "Does not every moment stand a temple four-square to God? And in that morning, with its buoyant sunlight, was I any dearer to the Heart of the World than now?" "My beloved is mine, and I am his," 10 she sang over and over again, with all varied inflection and profuse tune. How gently all the winter-wrapt things bent toward her then! Into what relation with her had they grown! How this common de- 15 pendence was the spell of their intimacy! How at one with Nature had she become! How all the night and the silence and the forest seemed to hold its breath, and to send its soul up to God in her singing! It 20 was no longer despondency, that singing. It was neither prayer nor petition. She had left imploring "How long wilt Thou forget me, O Lord?" "Lighten mine eyes, lest I sleep the sleep of death," "For in death 25 there is no remembrance of Thee," with countless other such fragments of supplication. She cried rather, "Yea, though I walk through the valley of the shadow of death, I will fear no evil, for Thou art 30 with me; Thy rod and Thy staff, they comfort me"; and lingered, and repeated, and sang again, "I shall be satisfied, when I awake, with Thy likeness."

Then she thought of the Great Deliver- 35 ance, when He drew her up out of many waters, and the flashing old psalm pealed forth triumphantly:

The Lord descended from above, and bow'd
    the heavens hie:
40 And underneath his feet he cast the darkness
    of the skie.
On cherubs and on cherubins full royally he
    road:
And on the wings of all the winds came
45   flying all abroad.

She forgot how recently, and with what a strange pity for her own shapeless form that was to be, she quaintly sung

50 Oh, lovely appearance of death!
    What sight upon earth is so fair?
Not all the gay pageants that breathe
    Can with a dead body compare!

55 She remembered instead, "In Thy presence is fullness of joy; at Thy right hand there are pleasures forevermore"; and, "God will redeem my soul from the power of the

grave: for He shall receive me"; "He will swallow up death in victory." Not once now did she say, "Lord, how long wilt Thou look on? Rescue my soul from their destructions, my darling from the lions," for she knew that "the young lions roar after their prey and seek their meat from God." "O Lord, Thou preservest man and beast!" she said.

She had no comfort or consolation in this season, such as sustained the Christian martyrs in the amphitheater. She was not dying for her faith, there were no palms in heaven for her to wave—but how many a time had she declared, "I had rather be a doorkeeper in the house of my God, than to dwell in the tents of wickedness!" And as the broad rays here and there broke through the dense covert of shade and lay in rivers of luster on crystal sheathing and frozen fretting of trunk and limb and on the great spaces of refraction, they builded up visibly that house, the shining city on the hill; and singing, "Beautiful for situation, the joy of the whole earth, is Mount Zion, on the sides of the North, the city of the Great King," her vision climbed to that higher picture where the angel shows the dazzling thing, the holy Jerusalem descending out of heaven from God, with its splendid battlements and gates of pearls, and its foundations—the eleventh a jacinth, the twelfth an amethyst—with its great white throne, and the rainbow round about it, in sight like unto an emerald—"And there shall be no night there, for the Lord God giveth them light," she sang.

What whisper of dawn now rustled through the wilderness? How the night was passing! And still the beast crouched upon the bough, changing only the posture of his head that again he migh⁺ command her with those charmed eyes. Half their fire was gone—she could almost have released herself from his custody—yet, had she stirred, no one knows what malevolent instinct might have dominated anew. But of that she did not dream; long ago stripped of any expectation, she was experiencing in her divine rapture how mystically true it is that "he that dwelleth in the secret place of the Most High shall abide under the shadow of the Almighty."

Slow clarion cries now wound from the distance as the cocks caught the intelligence of day and reëchoed it faintly from farm to farm—sleepy sentinels of night, sounding the foe's invasion, and translating that dim intuition to ringing notes of warning. Still she chanted on. A remote crash of brushwood told of some other beast on his depredations, or some night-belated traveler groping his way through the narrow path. Still she chanted on. The far, faint echoes of the chanticleers died into distance, the crashing of the branches grew nearer. No wild beast that, but a man's step, a man's form in the moonlight, stalwart and strong, on one arm slept a little child, in the other hand he held his gun. Still she chanted on.

Perhaps, when her husband last looked forth, he was half ashamed to find what a fear he felt for her. He knew she would never leave the child so long but for some direst need,—and yet he may have laughed at himself, as he lifted and wrapped it with awkward care, and, loading his gun and strapping on his horn, opened the door again and closed it behind him, going out and plunging into the darkness and dangers of the forest. He was more singularly alarmed than he would have been willing to acknowledge; as he had sat with his bow hovering over the strings, he had half believed to hear her voice mingling gaily with the instrument, till he paused and listened if she were not about to lift the latch and enter. As he drew nearer the heart of the forest, that intimation of melody seemed to grow more actual, to take body and breath, to come and go on long swells and ebbs of the night-breeze, to increase with tune and words, till a strange, shrill singing grew ever clearer, and, as he stepped into an open space of moonbeams, far up in the branches, rocked by the wind, and singing, "How beautiful upon the mountains are the feet of him that bringeth good tidings, that publisheth peace," he saw his wife—his wife—but, great God in heaven! how? Some mad exclamation escaped him, but without diverting her. The child knew the singing voice, though never heard before in that unearthly key, and turned toward it through the veiling dreams. With a celerity almost instantaneous, it lay, in the twinkling of an eye, on the ground at the father's feet, while his gun was raised to his shoulder and leveled at the monster covering his wife with shaggy form and flaming gaze—his wife so ghastly white, so rigid, so stained with blood, her eyes so fixedly bent above, and her lips, that had indurated into the chiseled pallor of marble, parted only with that flood of solemn song.

I do not know if it were the mother-instinct that for a moment lowered her eyes—those eyes, so lately rivited on heaven, now suddenly seeing all life-long bliss possible. A thrill of joy pierced and shivered through her like a weapon, her voice trembled in its course, her glance lost its steady strength, fever-flushes chased each other over her face, yet she never once ceased chanting. She was quite aware that if her husband shot now the ball must pierce her body before reaching any vital part of the beast—and yet better that death, by his hand, than the other. But this her husband also knew, and he remained motionless, just covering the creature with the sight. He dared not fire lest some wound not mortal should break the spell exercised by her voice, and the beast, enraged with pain, should rend her in atoms; moreover, the light was too uncertain for his aim. So he waited. Now and then he examined his gun to see if the damp were injuring its charge, now and then he wiped the great drops from his forehead. Again the cocks crowed with the passing hour— the last time they were heard on that night. Cheerful home sound then, how full of safety and all comfort and rest it seemed! What sweet morning incidents of sparkling fire and sunshine, of gay household bustle, shining dresser, and cooing baby, of steaming cattle in the yard, and brimming milk-pails at the door! What pleasant voices, what laughter, what security! And here—

Now as she sang on in the slow, endless, infinite moments, the fervent vision of God's peace was gone. Just as the grave had lost its sting, she was snatched back again into the arms of earthly hope. In vain she tried to sing, "There remaineth a rest for the people of God"—her eyes trembled on her husband's and she could think only of him, and of the child, and of happiness that yet might be, but with what a dreadful gulf of doubt between! She shuddered now in the suspense; all calm forsook her; she was tortured with dissolving heats or frozen with icy blasts; her face contracted, growing small and pinched; her voice was hoarse and sharp— every tone cut like a knife—the notes became heavy to lift—withheld by some hostile pressure—impossible. One gasp, a con-

vulsive effort, and there was silence—she had lost her voice.

The beast made a sluggish movement— stretched and fawned like one awakening— then, as if he would have yet more of the enchantment, stirred her slightly with his muzzle. As he did so a sidelong hint of the man standing below with the raised gun smote him; he sprung round furiously, and, seizing his prey, was about to leap into some unknown airy den of the topmost branches now waving to the slow dawn. The late moon had rounded through the sky so that her gleam at last fell full upon the bough with fairy frosting; the wintry morning light did not yet penetrate the gloom. The woman, suspended in mid-air an instant, cast only one agonized glance beneath, but across and through it, ere the lids could fall, shot a withering sheet of flame—a rifle-crack, half heard, was lost in the terrible yell of desperation that bounded after it and filled her ears with savage echoes, and in the wide arc of some eternal descent she was falling—but the beast fell under her.

I think that the moment following must have been too sacred for us, and perhaps the three have no special interest again till they issue from the shadows of the wilderness upon the white hills that skirt their home. The father carries the child hushed again to slumber, the mother follows with no such feeble step as might be anticipated. It is not time for reaction,—the tension not yet relaxed, the nerves still vibrant, she seems to herself like someone newly made; the night was a dream; the present stamped upon her in deep satisfaction, neither weighed nor compared with the past; if she has the careful tricks of former habit, it is as an automaton; and as they slowly climb the steep under the clear gray sky and the paling morning star, she stops to gather a spray of the red-rose berries or a feathery tuft of dead grasses for the chimney-piece of the log-house, or a handful of brown cones for the child's play,—and of these quiet, happy folk you would scarcely dream how lately they had stolen from under the banner and encampment of the great King Death. The husband proceeds a step or two in advance; the wife lingers over a singular foot-print in the snow, stoops and examines it, then looks up with a hurried word. Her husband stands alone on the hill, his arms folded across the babe, his gun fallen—stands defined against the pallid sky like a bronze. What is there in their home, lying below and yellowing in the light, to fix him with such a stare? She springs to his side. There is no home there. The log-house, the barns, the neighboring farms, the fences, are all blotted out and mingled in one smoking ruin. Desolation and death were indeed there, and benefi-cence and life in the forest. Tomahawk and scalping-knife, descending during that night, had left behind them only this work of their accomplished hatred and one subtle footprint in the snow.

For the rest—the world was all before them, where to choose.

X

EDWARD EVERETT HALE (1822–1909)

The successor of N. P. Willis as worker in the effervescent, the humorous, the daintily whimsical areas was Edward Everett Hale. Totally unlike as the two men were at almost every point, in their fiction they were of the same "school"—makers of the short story that depended largely for its effect upon the manner of the telling, possessors of that deft artistry which could hold its reader even through situations totally impossible and absurd, the school later to include in its membership Aldrich, Stockton, Bunner, and O. Henry.

Hale of late years has come to be regarded as almost a single-story creator, so completely does his "The Man Without a Country," a "propaganda story" of the Civil War period, dominate his work. His product, however, was voluminous, extending over four decades and filling half a dozen volumes. "My Double and How He Undid Me" shows, perhaps best of all his fictions, his peculiar style and mannerisms, his mastery of verisimilitude, his DeFoe-like multiplication of details until the reader's suspicions are completely lulled, and his surprising climaxes. Though subtly woven through the tale is a thread of satire upon existing conditions in church areas, the story, unlike "The Man Without a Country," cannot be classed as a "purpose creation." Moreover it is more compact, more observant of strict unity, better fitted to serve as a model than its more famous rival. His story "The Brick Moon," published in *The Atlantic* in 1869, created a sensation, but for modern uses it is too elaborate, too impossible even after its author's utmost efforts at verisimilitude. Undoubtedly Hale's fame must rest upon his "The Man Without a Country" and that largely because of its historical significance.

MY DOUBLE, AND HOW HE UNDID ME

It is not often that I trouble the readers of the *Atlantic Monthly*. I should not trouble them now, but for the importunities of my wife, who "feels to insist" that a duty to society is unfulfilled till I have told why I had to have a double, and how he undid me. She is sure, she says, that intelli- 10 gent persons cannot understand that pressure upon public servants which alone drives any man into the employment of a double. And while I fear she thinks, at the bottom of her heart, that my fortunes will 15 never be remade, she has a faint hope that, as another Rasselas, I may teach a lesson to future publics, from which they may profit, though we die. Owing to the behavior of my double or, if you please, to 20 that public pressure which compelled me to employ him, I have plenty of leisure to write this communication.

I am, or rather was, a minister of the Sandemanian connection.[1] I was settled in 25 the active, wide-awake town of Nagua-davick, on one of the finest water-powers in Maine. We used to call it a western town in the heart of the civilization of New England. A charming place it was and is. A spirited, brave young parish had I: and it seemed as if we might have all 5 "the joy of eventful living" to our heart's content.

Alas! how little we knew on the day of my ordination, and in those halcyon moments of our first housekeeping. To be the confidential friend in a hundred families in the town—cutting the social trifle, as my friend Haliburton says, "from the top of the whipped syllabub to the bottom of the sponge-cake, which is the foundation," —to keep abreast of the thought of the age in one's study, and to do one's best on Sunday to interweave that thought with the active life of an active town, and to inspirit both and make both infinite by 20 glimpses of the Eternal Glory, seemed such an exquisite forelook into one's life! Enough to do, and all so real and so grand! If this vision could only have lasted!

The truth is, that this vision was not in itself a delusion, nor, indeed, half bright enough. If one could only have been left to do his own business, the vision would have accomplished itself and brought out new paraheliacal visions, each as bright as the original. The misery was and is, as we found out, I and Polly, before long, that besides the vision, and besides the usual human and finite failures in life (such as breaking the old pitcher that came over in the *Mayflower,* and putting into the fire the alpenstock with which her father climbed Mount Blanc)—besides these, I say (imitating the style of *Robinson Crusoe*), there were pitchforked in on us a great rowen-heap of humbugs, handed down from some unknown seed-time, in which we were expected, and I chiefly, to fulfil certain public functions before the community, of the character of those fulfilled by the third row of supernumeraries who stand behind the Sepoys in the spectacle of the "Cataract of the Ganges." They were the duties, in a word, which one performs as members of one or another social class or subdivisions, wholly distinct from what one does as A. by himself A. What invisible power put these functions on me it would be very hard to tell. But such power there was and is. And I had not been at work a year before I found I was living two lives, one real and one merely functional,—for two sets of people, one my parish, whom I loved, and the other a vague public, for whom I did not care two straws. All this was in a vague notion, which everybody had and has, that this second life would eventually bring out some great results, unknown at present to somebody somewhere.

Crazed by this duality of life I first read Dr. Wigan on the *Duality of the Brain,* hoping that I could train one side of my head to do these outside jobs, and the other to do my intimate and real duties. For Richard Greenough once told me, that, in studying for the statue of Franklin, he found that the left side of the great man's face was philosophic and reflective, and the right side funny and smiling. If you will go and look at the bronze statue you will find he has repeated this observation there for posterity. The eastern profile is the portrait of the statesman Franklin, the western of poor Richard. But Dr. Wigan does not go into these niceties of this subject, and I failed. It was then that, on my wife's suggestion, I resolved to look out for a double.

I was, at first, singularly successful. We happened to be recreating at Stafford Springs that summer. We rode out one day, for one of the relaxations of that watering-place, to the great Monson Poorhouse. We were passing through one of the large halls, when my destiny was fulfilled! I saw my man!

He was not shaven. He had on no spectacles. He was dressed in a green baize roundabout and faded blue overalls, worn sadly at the knee. But I saw at once that he was of my height, five feet four and a half. He had black hair, worn off by his hat. So have and have not I. He stooped in walking. So do I. His hands were large, and mine. And—choicest gift of Fate in all —he had, not "a strawberry mark on his left arm," but a cut from a juvenile brickbat over his right eye, slightly affecting the play of that eyebrow. Reader, so have I! My fate was sealed!

A word with Mr. Holley, one of the inspectors, settled the whole thing. It proved that this Dennis Shea was a harmless, amiable fellow, of the class known as shiftless, who had sealed his fate by marrying a dumb wife, who was at that moment ironing in the laundry. Before I left Stafford I had hired both for five years. We had applied to Judge Pynchon, then the probate judge at Springfield, to change the name of Dennis Shea to Frederic Ingham. We had explained to the Judge what was the precise truth, that an eccentric gentleman wished to adopt Dennis, under this new name, into his family. It never occurred to him that Dennis might be more than fourteen years old. And thus, to shorten this preface, when we returned at night to my parsonage at Naguadavick, there entered Mrs. Ingham, her new dumb laundress, myself, who am Mr. Frederic Ingham, and my double, who was Mr. Frederic Ingham by as good right as I.

Oh, the fun we had the next morning in shaving his beard to my pattern, cutting his hair to match mine, and teaching him how to wear and how to take off gold-bowed spectacles! Really, they were electro-plate, and the glass was plain (for the poor fellow's eyes were excellent). Then in four successive afternoons I taught him four speeches. I had found these would be quite enough for the supernumerary-Sepoy line of life, and it was well for me they were; for though he was good-natured, he was very shiftless, and it was, as our national proverb says, "like pulling teeth" to teach him. But at the end of the next week he could say, with quite my easy and frisky air,—

1. "Very well, thank you. And you?" This for an answer to casual salutations.

2. "I am very glad you liked it."

3. "There has been so much said, and, on the whole, so well said, that I will not occupy the time."

4. "I agree, in general, with my friend the other side of the room."

At first I had a feeling that I was going to be at a great cost for clothing him. But it proved, of course, at once, that, whenever he was out, I should be at home. And I went, during the bright period of his success, to so few of those awful pageants which require a black dress-coat and what the ungodly call, after Mr. Dickens, a white choker, that in the happy retreat of my own dressing-gowns and jackets my days went by as happily and cheaply as those of another Thalaba. And Polly declares there was never a year when the tailoring cost so little. He lived (Dennis, not Thalaba) in his wife's room over the kitchen. He had orders never to show himself at that window. When he appeared in front of the house I retired to my sanctissimum and my dressing-gown. In short, the Dutchman and his wife, in the old weather-box, had not less to do with each other than he and I. He made the furnace-fire and split the wood before daylight; then he went to sleep again, and slept late; then came for orders, with a red silk bandanna tied round his head, with his overalls on, and his dresscoat and spectacles off. If we happened to be interrupted, no one guessed that he was Frederic Ingham as well as I; and, in the neighborhood, there grew up an impression that the minister's Irishman worked daytimes in the factory village at New Coventry. After I had given him his orders, I never saw him till the next day.

I launched him by sending him to a meeting of the Enlightenment Board. The Enlightenment Board consists of seventy-four members, of whom sixty-seven are necessary to form a quorum. One becomes a member under the regulations laid down in old Judge Dudley's will. I became one by being ordained pastor of a church in Naguadavick. You see you cannot help yourself if you would. At this particular time we had had four successive meetings, averaging four hours each,—wholly occupied in whipping in a quorum. At the first

only eleven men were present; at the next, by force of three circulars, twenty-seven; at the third, thanks to two days' canvassing by Auchmuty and myself, begging men to come, we had sixty. Half the others were in Europe. But without a quorum we could do nothing. All the rest of us waited grimly for our four hours, and adjourned without any action. At the fourth meeting we had flagged, and only got fifty-nine together. But on the first appearance of my double—whom I sent on this fatal Monday to the fifth meeting—he was the *sixty-seventh* man who entered the room. He was greeted by a storm of applause! The poor fellow had missed his way—read the street signs ill through his spectacles (very ill, in fact, without them)—and had not dared to inquire. He entered the room, finding the president and secretary holding to their chairs two judges of the Supreme Court, who were also members *ex officio* and were begging leave to go away. On his entrance all was changed. *Presto,* the by-laws were amended, and the western property was given away. Nobody stopped to converse with him. He voted, as I had charged him to do, in every instance, with the minority. I won new laurels as a man of sense, though a little unpunctual—and Dennis, *alias* Ingham, returned to the parsonage, astonished to see with how little wisdom the world is governed. He cut a few of my parishoners in the street; but he had his glasses off, and I am known to be near-sighted. Eventually he recognized them more readily than I.

I "set him again" at the exhibition of the New Coventry Academy; and here he undertook a "speaking part"—as, in my boyish, worldly days, I remember the bills used to say of Mlle. Celeste. We are all trustees of the New Coventry Academy; and there has lately been "a good deal of feeling" because the Sandemanians are leaning toward Free-Will, and that we have, therefore, neglected these semi-annual exhibitions, while there is no doubt that Auchmuty last year went to Commencement at Waterville. Now the head master at New Coventry is a real good fellow, who knows a Sanskrit root when he sees it, and often cracks etymologies with me; so that, in strictness, I ought to go to their exhibitions. But think, reader, of sitting through three long July days in that Academy chapel, following the program from

TUESDAY MORNING. *English Composition.* "SUNRISE." Miss Jones.

round to—

Trio on Three Pianos. Duel from the Opera of "Midshipman Easy." *Marryat.*

coming in at nine, Thursday evening! Think of this, reader, for men who know the world is trying to go backward, and who would give their lives if they could help it on! Well! The double had succeeded so well at the Board, that I sent him to the Academy. (Shade of Plato, pardon!) He arrived early on Tuesday, when, indeed, few but mothers and clergymen are generally expected, and returned in the evening to us, covered with honors. He had dined at the right hand of the chairman, and he spoke in high terms of the repast. The chairman had expressed his interest in the French conversation. "I am very glad you liked it," said Dennis; and the poor chairman, abashed, supposed the accent had been wrong. At the end of the day the gentlemen present had been called upon for speeches—the Rev. Frederic Ingham first, as it happened: upon which Dennis had risen, and had said: "There has been so much said, and, on the whole, so well said, that I will not occupy the time." The girls were delighted, because Dr. Dabney, the year before, had given them at this occasion a scolding on impropriety of behavior at lyceum lectures. They all declared Mr. Ingham was a love —and *so* handsome! (Dennis is good looking.) Three of them, with arms behind the others' waists, followed him up to the wagon he rode home in; and a little girl with a blue sash had been sent to give him a rosebud. After this *début* in speaking, he went to the exhibition for two days more, to the mutual satisfaction of all concerned. Indeed, Polly reported that he had pronounced the trustees' dinners of a higher grade than those of the parsonage. When the next term began I found six of the Academy girls had obtained permission to come across the river to attend our church. But this arrangement did not long continue.

After this he went to several Commencements for me, and ate the dinners provided. He sat through three of our Quarterly Conventions for me—always voting judiciously, by the simple rule mentioned above, of siding with the minority. And I,

meanwhile, who had before been losing caste among my friends, as holding myself aloof from the associations of the body, began to rise in everybody's favor. "Ingham's a good fellow, always on hand"; "never talks much, but does the right thing at the right time"; "is not as unpunctual as he used to be—he comes early, and sits through to the end." "He has got over his old talkative habit, too. I spoke to a friend of his about it once; and I think Ingham took it kindly," etc., etc.

This voting power of Dennis was particularly valuable at the quarterly meetings of the proprietors of the Naguadavick Ferry. My wife inherited from her father some shares in that enterprise, which is not yet fully developed, though it doubtless will become a very valuable property. The law of Maine then forbade stockholders to appear by proxy at such meetings. Polly disliked to go, not being, in fact, a "hens'-rights hen," and transferred her stock to me. I, after going once, disliked it more than she. But Dennis went to the next meeting, and liked it very much. He said the armchairs were good, the collation good, and the free rides to stockholders pleasant. He was a little frightened when they first took him upon one of the ferry-boats, but after two or three quarterly meetings he became quite brave.

Thus far I never had any difficulty with him. Indeed, being, as I implied, of that type which is called shiftless, he was only too happy to be told daily what to do, and to be charged not to be forthputting or in any way original in his discharge of that duty. He learned, however, to discriminate between the lines of his life, and very much preferred these stockholders' meetings and trustees' dinners and Commencement collations to another sort of occasions, from which he used to beg off most piteously. Our excellent brother, Dr. Fillmore, had taken a notion at this time that our Sandemanian churches needed more expression of mutual sympathy. He insisted upon it that we were remiss. He said that if the bishop came to preach at Naguadavick all the Episcopal clergy of the neighborhood were present; if Dr. Pond came, all the Congregational clergymen turned out to hear him; if Dr. Nichols, all the Unitarians; and he thought we owed it to each other, that, whenever there was an occasional service at a Sandemanian church, the other brethren should all, if possible, attend. "It looked well," if nothing more. Now this really meant that I had not been to hear one of Dr. Fillmore's lectures on the Ethnology of Religion. He forgot that he did not hear one of my courses on the "Sandemanianism of Anselm." But I felt badly when he said it; and afterwards I always made Dennis go to hear all the brethren preach, when I was not preaching myself. This was what he took exceptions to—the only thing, as I said, which he ever did except to. Now came the advantage of his long morning nap, and of the green tea with which Polly supplied the kitchen. But he would plead, so humbly, to be let off, only from one or two! I never excepted him, however. I knew the lectures were of value, and I thought it best he should be able to keep the connection.

Polly is more rash than I am, as the reader has observed in the outset of this memoir. She risked Dennis one night under the eyes of her own sex. Governor Gorges had always been very kind to us, and, when he gave his great annual party to the town, asked us. I confess I hated to go. I was deep in the new volume of Pfeiffer's *Mystics,* which Haliburton had just sent me from Boston. "But how rude," said Polly, "not to return the Governor's civility and Mrs. Gorges's, when they will be sure to ask why you are away!" Still I demurred, and at last she, with the wit of Eve and of Semiramis conjoined, let me off by saying that if I would go in with her, and sustain the initial conversations with the Governor and ladies staying there, we would risk Dennis for the rest of the evening. And that was just what we did. She took Dennis in training all that afternoon, instructed him in fashionable conversation, cautioned him against the temptations of the supper-table—and at nine in the evening he drove us all down in the carryall. I made the grand star *entrée* with Polly and the pretty Walton girls, who were staying with us. We had put Dennis into a great rough top-coat, without his glasses; and the girls never dreamed, in the darkness, of looking at him. He sat in the carriage, at the door, while we entered. I did the agreeable to Mrs. Gorges, was introduced to her niece, Miss Fernanda; I complimented Judge Jeffries on his decision in the great case of D'Aulnay *vs.* Laconia Mining Company; I stepped into the dressing-room for a

moment, stepped out for another, walked home after a nod with Dennis and tying the horse to a pump;—and while I walked home, Mr. Frederic Ingham, my double, stepped in through the library into the Gorges's grand saloon.

Oh! Polly died of laughing as she told me of it at midnight! And even here, where I have to teach my hands to hew the beech for stakes to fence our cave, she dies of laughing as she recalls it, and says that single occasion was worth all we have paid for it. Gallant Eve that she is! She joined Dennis at the library-door, and in an instant presented him to Dr. Ochterlong, from Baltimore, who was on a visit in town, and was talking with her as Dennis came in. "Mr. Ingham would like to hear what you were telling us about your success among the German population." And Dennis bowed and said, in spite of a scowl from Polly, "I'm very glad you liked it." But Dr. Ochterlong did not observe, and plunged into the tide of explanation; Dennis listening like a prime minister, and bowing like a mandarin, which is, I suppose, the same thing. Polly declared it was just like Haliburton's Latin conversation with the Hungarian minister, of which he is very fond of telling. *"Quæne sit historia Reformationis in Ungaria?"* quoth Haliburton, after some thought. And his confrère replied gallantly, *"In seculo decimo tertio,"* [2] etc., etc., and from *decimo tertio* to the nineteenth century and a half lasted till the oysters came. So was it that before Dr. Ochterlong came to the "success," or near it, Governor Gorges came to Dennis, and asked him to hand Mrs. Jeffries down to supper, a request which he heard with great joy.

Polly was skipping round the room, I guess, gay as a lark. Auchmuty came to her "in pity for poor Ingham," who was so bored by the stupid pundit; and Auchmuty could not understand why I stood so long. But when Dennis took Mrs. Jeffries down, Polly could not resist standing near them. He was a little flustered, till the sight of the eatables and drinkables gave him the same Mercian courage which it gave Diggory. A little excited then, he attempted one or two of his speeches to the judge's lady. But little he knew how hard it was to get in even a *promptu* there edgewise. "Very well, I thank you," said he, after the eating elements were adjusted; "and you?" And then did not he have to hear about the mumps, and the measles, and arnica, and belladonna, and camomile-flowers, and dodecatheon, till she changed oysters for salad; and then about the old practice and the new, and what her sister said, and what her sister's friend said, and what the physician to her sister's friend said, and then what was said by the brother of the sister of the physician of the friend of her sister, exactly as if it had been in Ollendorff? There was a moment's pause, as she declined champagne. "I am very glad you liked it," said Dennis again, which he never should have said but to one who complimented a sermon. "Oh! you are so sharp, Mr. Ingham! No! I never drink any wine at all, except sometimes in summer a little currant shrub, from our own currants, you know. My own mother, that is, I call her my own mother, because, you know, I do not remember," etc., etc., etc.; till they came to the candied orange at the end of the feast, when Dennis, rather confused, thought he must say something, and tried No. 4,—"I agree, in general, with my friend the other side of the room,"— which he never should have said but at a public meeting. But Mrs. Jeffries, who never listens expecting to understand, caught him up instantly with "Well, I'm sure my husband returns the compliment; he always agrees with you, though we do worship with the Methodists; but you know, Mr. Ingham," etc., etc., etc., till the move upstairs; and as Dennis led her through the hall, he was scarcely understood by any but Polly, as he said, "There has been so much said, and, on the whole, so well said, that I will not occupy the time."

His great resource the rest of the evening was standing in the library, carrying on animated conversations with one and another in much the same way. Polly had initiated him in the mysteries of a discovery of mine, that it is not necessary to finish your sentences in a crowd, but by a sort of mumble, omitting sibilants and dentals. This, indeed, if your words fail you, answers even in public extempore speech, but better where other talking is going on. Thus: "We missed you at the Natural History Society, Ingham." Ingham replies, "I am very gligloglum, that is, that you were mmmmmm." By gradually dropping the voice, the interlocutor is

compelled to supply the answer. "Mrs. Ingham, I hope your friend Augusta is better." Augusta has not been ill. Polly cannot think of explaining, however, and answers, "Thank you, ma'am; she is very rearason wewahwewoh," in lower and lower tones. And Mrs. Throckmorton, who forgot the subject of which she spoke as soon as she asked the question, is quite satisfied. Dennis could see into the card-room, and came to Polly to ask if he might not go and play all-fours. But, of course, she sternly refused. At midnight they came home delighted—Polly, as I said, wild to tell me the story of the victory; only both the pretty Walton girls said, "Cousin Frederic, you did not come near me all the evening."

We always called him Dennis at home, for convenience, though his real name was Frederic Ingham, as I have explained. When the election day came round, however, I found that by some accident there was only one Frederic Ingham's name on the voting list; and as I was quite busy that day in writing some foreign letters to Halle, I thought I would forego my privilege of suffrage, and stay quietly at home, telling Dennis that he might use the record on the voting-list, and vote, I gave him a ticket, which I told him he might use if he liked to. That was that very sharp election in Maine which the readers of the *Atlantic* so well remember, and it had been intimated in public that the ministers would do well not to appear at the polls. Of course, after that, we had to appear by self or proxy. Still, Naguadavick was not then a city, and this standing in a double queue at town-meeting several hours to vote was a bore of the first water; and so when I found that there was but one Frederic Ingham on the list, and that one of us must give up, I stayed at home and finished the letters (which, indeed, procured for Fothergill his coveted appointment as Professor of Astronomy at Leavenworth), and I gave Dennis, as we called him, the chance. Something in the matter gave a good deal of popularity to the Frederic Ingham name; and at the adjourned election, next week, Frederic Ingham was chosen to the legislature. Whether this was I or Dennis I never really knew. My friends seemed to think it was I; but I felt that as Dennis had done the popular thing, he was entitled to the honor; so I sent him to Augusta when the time came; and he took the oaths. And a very valuable member he made. They appointed him on the Committee on Parishes; but I wrote a letter for him, resigning, on the ground that he took an interest in our claim to the stumpage in the minister's sixteenths of Gore A, next to No. 7, in the 10th Range. He never made any speeches, and always voted with the minority, which was what he was sent to do. He made me and himself a great many good friends, some of whom I did not afterwards recognize as quickly as Dennis did my parishoners. On one or two occasions, when there was wood to saw at home, I kept him at home; but I took those occasions to go to Augusta myself. Finding myself often in his vacant seat at these times, I watched the proceedings with a great deal of care; and once was so much excited that I delivered my somewhat celebrated speech on the Central School-District question, a speech of which the *State of Maine* printed some extra copies. I believe there is no formal rule permitting strangers to speak; but no one objected.

Dennis, himself, as I said, never spoke at all. But our experience this session led me to think that if, by some such "general understanding" as the reports speak of in legislation daily, every member of Congress might leave a double to sit through those deadly sessions and answer to roll-calls and do the legitimate party-voting, which appears stereotyped in the regular list of Ash, Bocock, Black, etc., we should gain decidedly in working-power. As things stand, the saddest state prison I ever visit is that Representatives' Chamber in Washington. If a man leaves for an hour, twenty "correspondents" may be howling, "Where was Mr. Prendergast when the Oregon bill passed?" And if poor Prendergast stays there! Certainly the worst use you can make of a man is to put him in prison!

I know, indeed, that public men of the highest rank have resorted to this expedient long ago. Dumas' novel of the "Iron Mask" turns on the brutal imprisonment of Louis the Fourteenth's double. There seems little doubt, in our own history, that it was the real General Pierce who shed tears when the delegate from Lawrence explained to him the sufferings of the people there, and only General Pierce's double who had given the orders for the assault on that town, which was invaded the next day. My charming friend, George Withers, has, I am almost sure, a double, who preaches his afternoon sermons for him. This is the reason that the theology often varies so from that of the forenoon. But the double is almost as charming as the original. Some of the most well-defined men, who stand out most prominently on the background of history, are in this way stereoscopic men, who owe their distinct relief to the slight differences between the doubles. All this I know. My present suggestion is simply the great extension of the system, so that all public machine work may be done by it.

But I see I loiter on my story, which is rushing to the plunge. Let me stop an instant more, however, to recall, were it only to myself, that charming year while all was yet well. After the double had become a matter of course, for nearly twelve months before he undid me, what a year it was! Full of active life, full of happy love, of the hardest work, of the sweetest sleep, and the fulfilment of so many of the fresh aspirations and dreams of boyhood! Dennis went to every school-committee meeting, and sat through all those late wranglings which used to keep me up till midnight and awake till morning. He attended all the lectures to which foreign exiles sent me tickets, begging me to come for the love of Heaven and of Bohemia. He accepted and used all the tickets for charity concerts which were sent to me. He appeared everywhere where it was specially desirable that "our denomination," or "our party," or "our class," or "our family," or "our street," or "our town," or "our country," or "our state," should be fully represented. And I fell back to that charming life which in boyhood one dreams of, when he supposed he shall do his own duty and make his own sacrifices, without being tied up with those of other people. My rusty Sanskrit, Arabic, Hebrew, Greek, Latin, French, Italian, Spanish, German, and English began to take polish. Heavens! how little I had done with them while I attended to my *public* duties! My calls on my parishoners became the friendly, frequent, homelike sociabilities they were meant to be, instead of the hard work of a man goaded to desperation by the sight of his lists of arrears. And preaching! what a luxury preaching was when I had on Sunday the whole result of an individual, personal week, from which to speak to a people whom all that week I had been meeting as hand-to-hand-friends;—I, never tired on Sunday, and in condition to leave the sermon at home, if I chose, and preach it extempore, as all men should do always. Indeed, I wonder, when I think that a sensible people, like ours—really more attached to their clergy than they were in the lost days, when the Mathers and Nortons were noblemen—should choose to neutralize so much of their ministers' lives, and destroy so much of their early training, by this undefined passion for seeing them in public. It springs from our balancing of sects. If a spirited Episcopalian takes an interest in the almshouse, and is put on the Poor Board, every other denomination must have a minister there, lest the poorhouse be changed into St. Paul's Cathedral. If a Sandemanian is chosen president of the Young Men's Library, there must be a Methodist vice-president and a Baptist secretary. And if a Universalist Sunday-School Convention collects five hundred delegates, the next Congregationalist Sabbath-School Conference must be as large "lest 'they'—whoever *they* may be—should think 'we'—whoever *we* may be—are going down."

Freed from these necessities, that happy year I began to know my wife by sight. We saw each other sometimes. In those long mornings, when Dennis was in the study explaining to map-peddlers that I had eleven maps of Jerusalem already, she and I were at work together, as in those old dreamy days, and in these of our log-cabin again. But all this could not last; and at length poor Dennis, my double, overtasked in turn, undid me.

It was thus it happened. There is an excellent fellow, once a minister,—I will call him Isaacs,—who deserves well of the world till he dies, and after, because he once, in a real exigency, did the right thing, in the right way, at the right time, as no other man could do it. In the world's great football match, the ball by chance found him loitering on the outside of the field; he closed with it, "camped" it, charged it home—yes, right through the other side—not disturbed, not frightened by his own success—and, breathless, found himself a great man, as the Great Delta rang applause. But he did not find himself a rich man; and the football has

never come in his way again. From that moment to this moment he has been of no use, that one can see at all. Still, for that great act we speak of Isaacs grate-5 fully and remember him kindly; and he forges on, hoping to meet the football somewhere again. In that vague hope he had arranged a "movement" for a general organization of the human family into De-10 bating Clubs, County Societies, State Unions, etc., etc., with a view of inducing all children to take hold of the handles of their knives and forks, instead of the metal. Children have bad habits in that way. The 15 movement, of course, was absurd; but we all did our best to forward, not it, but him. It came time for the annual county meeting on this subject to be held at Naguadavick. Isaacs came round, good fellow! to ar-20 range for it—got the town-hall, got the Governor to preside (the saint!—he ought to have triplet doubles provided him by law), and then came to get me to speak. "No," I said, "I do not believe in the enter-25 prise. If I spoke it should be to say children should take hold of the prongs of the forks and the blades of the knives. I would subscribe ten dollars, but I would not speak a mill." So poor Isaacs went 30 his way sadly, to coax Auchmuty to speak, and Delafield. I went out. Not long after he came back, and told Polly that they had promised to speak, the Governor would speak, and he himself would close with 35 the quarterly report, and some interesting anecdotes regarding Miss Biffin's way of handling her knife and Mr. Nellis's way of footing his fork. "Now if Mr. Ingham will only come and sit on the platform, 40 he need not say one word; but it will show well in the paper—it will show that the Sandemanians take as much interest in the movement as the Armenians or the Meso-potamians, and will be a great favor to 45 me." Polly, good soul! was tempted, and she promised. She knew Mrs. Isaacs was starving, and the babies,—she knew Dennis was at home,—and she promised! Night came, and I returned. I heard his story. 50 I was sorry. I doubted. But Polly had promised to beg me, and I dared all! I told Dennis to hold his peace, under all circumstances, and sent him down.

It was not half an hour more before 55 he returned, wild with excitement,—in a perfect Irish fury,—which it was long before I understood. But I knew at once that he had undone me!

What happened was this. The audience got together, attracted by Governor Gorges's name. There were a thousand people. Poor Gorges was late from Augusta. They became impatient. He came in direct from the train, at last, really ignorant of the object of the meeting. He opened it in the fewest possible words, and said other gentlemen were present who would entertain them better than he. The audience were disappointed, but waited. The Governor, prompted by Isaacs, said, "The Honorable Mr. Delafield will address you." Delafield! He had forgotten the knives and forks, and was playing the Ruy Lopez opening at the chess-club. "The Rev. Mr. Auchmuty will address you." Auchmuty had promised to speak late, and was at the school-committee. "I see Dr. Stearns in the hall; perhaps he will say a word." Dr. Stearns said he had come to listen and not to speak. The Governor and Isaacs whispered. The Governor looked at Dennis, who was resplendent on the platform; but Isaacs, to give him his due, shook his head. But the look was enough. A miserable lad, ill-bred, who had once been in Boston, thought it would sound well to call for me, and peeped out, "Ingham!" A few more wretches cried, "Ingham! Ingham!" Still Isaacs was firm; but the Governor, anxious, indeed, to prevent a row, knew I would say something, and said, "Our friend Mr. Ingham is always prepared; and, though we had not relied upon him, he will say a word perhaps." Applause followed, which turned Dennis's head. He rose, fluttered, and tried No. 3. "There has been so much said, and, on the whole, so well said, that I will not occupy the time!" and sat down, looking for his hat; for things seemed squally. But the people cried, "Go on! go on!" and some applauded. Dennis, still confused, but flattered by the applause, to which neither he nor I are used, rose again, and this time tried No. 2: "I am very glad you liked it!" in a sonorous, clear delivery. My best friends stared. All the people who did not know me personally yelled with delight at the aspect of the evening; the Governor was beside himself, and poor Isaacs thought he was undone! Alas, it was I! A boy in the gallery cried in a loud tone, "It's all an infernal humbug," just as Dennis, waving his hand, commanded silence, and tried No. 4: "I agree, in general, with my friend the other side

of the room." The poor Governor doubted his senses and crossed to stop him—not in time, however. The same gallery-boy shouted, "How's your mother?" and Dennis, now completely lost, tried, as his last shot, No. 1, vainly: "Very well, thank you. And you?"

I think I must have been undone already. But Dennis, like another Lockhard, chose "to make sicker." The audience rose in a whirl of amazement, rage, and sorrow. Some other impertinence, aimed at Dennis, broke all restraint, and, in pure Irish, he delivered himself of an address to the gallery, inviting any person who wished to fight to come down and do so—stating, that they were all dogs and cowards, and the sons of dogs and cowards—that he would take any five of them single-handed. "Shure, I have said all this Riverence and the Misthress bade me say," cried he, in defiance; and, seizing the Governor's cane from his hand, brandished it, quarter-staff fashion, above his head. He was, indeed, got from the hall only with the greatest difficulty by the Governor, the city marshal, who had been called in, and the superintendent of my Sunday-School.

The universal impression, of course, was that the Rev. Frederic Ingham had lost all command of himself in some of those haunts of intoxication which for fifteen years I have been laboring to destroy. Till this moment, indeed, that is the impression in Naguadavick. This number of the *Atlantic* will relieve from it a hundred friends of mine who have been sadly wounded by that notion now for years; but I shall not be likely ever to show my head there again.

No! My double has undone me.

We left town at seven the next morning, I came to No. 9 in the Third Range, and settled on the Minister's Lot. In the new towns of Maine, the first settled minister has a gift of a hundred acres of land. I am the first settled minister in No. 9. My wife and little Paulina are my parish. We raise corn enough to live on in summer. We kill bear's meat enough to carbonize it in winter. I work on steadily on my *Traces of Sandemanianism in the Sixth and Seventh Centuries*, which I hope to persuade Phillips, Samson & Co. to publish next year. We are very happy, but the world thinks we are undone.

XI

HARRIET BEECHER STOWE (1812–1896)

Though very little of Mrs. Stowe's voluminous output of fiction is in short-story form, the little that she did produce was widely influential. It was her fortune to write when the short story was plastic and she wrote usually with life and her own feelings before her rather than books. As early as 1834 she had won a prize of $50 for her "New England Sketch," a study in black and white of the life she had known in her girlhood, and in later years after the fierce fire of *Uncle Tom's Cabin* had been quenched by the Civil War, she returned again to the same theme. For *The Atlantic Monthly* in 1870 she wrote a series of Yankee sketches centered about a somewhat idealized Connecticut "town character," Sam Lawson. The enormous publicity from *Uncle Tom's Cabin* gave her instantly a world-wide audience for anything she might write, and now everyone who could do so began to puzzle over the uncouthness of rural New England speech. It gave impetus to the new swing of fiction toward the natural, the locally peculiar, the lowly areas of life. Her dialect went to the extreme; seemingly it was presented as a thing to be shown off; to be laughed at and wondered at because of its uncouthness. But out of the midst of its impossibilities and its verbal monstrosities emerges Sam Lawson, alive, vibrant, humorous, convincing. No Yankee character in all literature up to that time, even Lowell's Hosea Biglow, had been so well presented. Instantly he became a type, one widely copied. In all of her stories minor faults abound, yet on the whole, her stories, even to-day, are remarkably good. They are well told, they hold the reader, they have a humor that time has not destroyed, their characters even to the most minor ones are alive, and always the subject seems adequate: they are woven of materials that are native grown, that wear and last.

THE GHOST IN THE CAP'N BROWN HOUSE

"Now, Sam, tell us certain true, is there any such things as ghosts?"

"Be there ghosts?" said Sam, immediately translating into his vernacular grammar; "wal, now, that are's jist the question, ye see."

"Well, grandma thinks there are, and Aunt Lois thinks it's all nonsense. Why, Aunt Lois don't even believe the stories in Cotton Mather's Magnolia."

"Wanter know?" said Sam, with a tone of slow, languid meditation.

We were sitting on a bank of the Charles River fishing. The soft melancholy red of evening was fading off in streaks on the glassy water, and the houses of Oldtown were beginning to loom through the gloom, solemn and ghostly. There are times and tones and moods of nature that make all the vulgar, daily real seem shadowy, vague, and supernatural, as if the outlines of this hard material present were fading into the invisible and unknown. So Oldtown with its elm-trees, its great square white houses, its meeting-house and tavern and blacksmith's shop and mill, which, at high noon, seem as real and as commonplace as possible, at this hour of the evening were dreamy and solemn. They rose up blurred, indistinct, dark; here and there winking candles sent long lines of light through the shadows, and little drops of unforeseen rain rippled the sheeny darkness of the water.

"Wal, you see, boys, in them things it's just as well to mind yer granny. There's a consid'able sight o' gumption in grandmas. You look at the folks that's allus tellin' you what they don't believe,—they don't believe this and they don't believe that,—and what sort o' folks is they? Why, like yer Aunt Lois, sort o' stringy and dry. There ain't no 'sorption got out o' not believin' nothin'.

"Lord a massy, we don't know nothin' 'bout them things. We hain't ben there, and can't say that there ain't no ghosts and sich, can we now?"

We agreed to that fact, and sat a little closer to Sam in the gathering gloom.

"Tell us about the Cap'n Brown house, Sam."

"Ye didn't never go over the Cap'n Brown house?"

No, we had not that advantage.

"Wal, yer see, Cap'n Brown he made all his money to sea, in furrin parts, and then come here to Oldtown to settle down.

"Now, there ain't no knowin' 'bout these 'ere old ship-masters, where they's ben or what they's ben a doin', or how they got their money. Ask me no questions and I'll tell ye no lies, is 'bout the best philosophy for them. Wal, it didn't do no good to ask Cap'n Brown questions too close, 'cause you didn't git no satisfaction. Nobody rightly knew 'bout who his folks was, or where they come from; and ef a body asked him, he used to say that the very fust he know'd about himself he was a young man walkin' the streets in London.

"But, yer see, boys, he hed money, and that's about all folks wanter know when a man comes to settle down. And he bought that are place, and built that are house. He built it all sea-cap'n fashion, so's to feel as much at home as he could. The parlor was like a ship's cabin. The table and chairs was fastened down to the floor, and the closets was made with holes to set the castors, and the decanters, and bottles in, jist's they be at sea; and there was stanchions to hold on by; and they say that blowy nights the Cap'n used to fire up pretty well with his grog, till he had about all he could carry, and then he'd set and hold on, and hear the wind blow, and kind o' feel out to sea right there to hum. There wasn't no Mis' Cap'n Brown, and there didn't seem likely to be none. And whether there ever had been one, nobody know'd. He had an old black Guinea nigger woman named Quassia, that did his work. She was shaped pretty much like one o' these 'ere great crookneck-squashes. She wa'n't no gret beauty, I can tell you, and she used to wear a gret red turban and a yaller short gown and red petticoat, and a gret string o' gold beads round her neck, and a gret big gold hoops in her ears, made right in the middle of Africa among the heathen there. For all she was black, she thought a heap o' herself, and was consid'able sort of predominative over the Cap'n. Lordy massy, boys, it's allus so. Get a man and a woman together,—any sort o' woman you're mind to, don't care who 't is,—and one way or another she gets the rule over him, and he jist has to train to her fife. Some does it one way and some does it another; some does it by jawin', and some does it by kissin', and some does it by faculty and contrivance; but one way or another they allers does it. Old Cap'n Brown was a good stout stocky kind o' John Bull sort o' fellow, and a good judge o' sperits, and allers kep' the best in them are cubboards o' hisn; but, fust and last, things in his house went pretty much as old Quassia said.

"Folks got to kind o' respectin' Quassia. She come to meetin' Sunday regular, and sot all fixed up in red and yaller and green, with glass beads and what not, lookin' for all the world like one o' them ugly Indian idols; but she was wal-behaved as any Christian. She was a master hand at cooking. Her bread and biscuits couldn't be beat, and no couldn't her pies, and there wa'n't no such pound-cake as she made nowhere. Wal, this 'ere story I'm a goin' to tell you was told me by Cinthy Pendleton. There ain't a more respectable gal, old or young, than Cinthy nowheres. She lives over to Sherburn now, and I hear tell she's sot up a manty-makin' business, but then she used to do tailorin' in Oldtown. She was a member o' the church, and a good Christian as ever was. Wal, ye see, Quassia she got Cinthy to come up and spend a week to the Cap'n Brown house, a doin' tailorin' and a fixin' over his close; 't was along toward the fust o' March. Cinthy she sot by the fire in the front parlor with her goose and her press-board and her work, for there wa'n't no company callin', and the snow was drifted four feet deep right across the front door; so there wa'n't much danger o' anybody comin' in, and the Cap'n he was a perlite man to wimmen, and Cinthy she liked it jist as well not to have company, 'cause the Cap'n he'd make himself entertainin' tellin' on her sea stories and all about his adventures among the Ammonites, and Perresites, and Jebusites, and all sorts o' heathen people he'd been among.

"Wal, that are week there come on the master snow-storm. Of all the snow-storms that hed ben that are was the beater, and I tell you the wind blew as if 't was the last chance it was ever goin' to have. Wal, it's kind o' scary like to be shut up in a lone house with all natur' a kind o' breakin' out, and goin' on so, and the snow a comin' down so thick ye can't see 'cross the street, and the wind a pipin' and a squallin' and a rumblin' and a tumblin' fust down this chimney and then down that. I tell you, it sort o' sets a feller thinkin' o' the three great things,—death, judgment, and etarnaty; and I don't care who the folks is, nor how good they be, there's times when they must be feelin' putty consid'able solemn.

"Wal, Cinthy she said she kind o' felt so along, and she had a sort o' queer feelin' come over her as if there was somebody or somethin' round the house more 'n appeared. She said she sort o' felt it in the air, but it seemed to her silly, and she tried to get over it. But two or three times, she said, when it got to be dusk, she felt somebody go by her up the stairs. The front entry wa'n't very light in the daytime, and in the storm, come five o'clock, it was so dark that all you could see was jist a gleam o' something, and two or three times when she started to go up stairs she see a soft white suthin' that seemed goin' up before her, and she stopped with her heart a beatin' like a trip-hammer, and she sort o' saw it go up and along the entry to the Cap'n's door, and then it seemed to go right through, 'cause the door didn't open.

"Wal, Cinthy says she to old Quassia, says she, 'Is there anybody lives in this house but us?'

"'Anybody lives here?' says Quassia; 'what you mean?' says she.

"Says Cinthy, 'I thought somebody went past me on the stairs last night and tonight.'

"Lordy massy, how old Quassia did screech and laugh. 'Good Lord!' says she, 'how foolish white folks is! Somebody went past you? Was 't the Captin?'

"'No, it wa'n't the Cap'n', says she; 'it was something soft and white, and moved very still; it was like somethin' in the air,' says she.

"Then Quassia she hawhawed louder. Says she, 'It's hiy-sterikes, Miss Cinthy; that's all it is.'

"Wal, Cinthy she was kind o' shamed, but for all that she couldn't help herself. Sometimes evenings she'd be a settin' with the Cap'n, and she'd think she'd hear somebody a movin' in his room overhead; and she knowed it wa'n't Quassia, 'cause Quassia was ironin' in the kitchen. She took pains once or twice to find out that are.

"Wal, ye see the Cap'n's room was the gret front upper chamber over the parlor and then right opposite to it was the gre[t] spare chamber where Cinthy slept. It wa[s] jist as grand as could be, with a gret four post mahogany bedstead and damask cur[-] tains brought over from England; but [it] was cold enough to freeze a white bea[r] solid,—the way spare chambers allers is[.] Then there was the entry between ru[n] straight through the house; one side wa[s] old Quassia's room, and the other was [a] sort o' store-room, where the old Cap'n kep[t] all sorts o' traps.

"Wal, Cinthy she kep' a hevin' thing[s] happen and a seein' things, till she didn'[t] railly know what was in it. Once whe[n] she come into the parlor jist at sundow[n] she was sure she see a white figure a van[-] ishing out o' the door that went toward[s] the side entry. She said it was so dus[k] that all she could see was jist this whit[e] figure, and it jist went out still as a ca[t] as she come in.

"Wal, Cinthy didn't like to speak to th[e] Cap'n about it. She was a close woman[,] putty prudent, Cinthy was.

"But one night 'bout the middle o' th[e] week this 'ere thing kind o' come to [a] crisis.

"Cinthy said she'd ben up putty late [a] sewin' and a finishin' off down in the par[-] lor, and the Cap'n he sot up with her an[d] was consid'able cheerful and entertainin['] tellin' her all about things over in the Ber[-] mudys, and off to Chiny and Japan, an[d] round the world ginerally. The storm tha[t] had ben a blowin' all the week was abou[t] as furious as ever, and the Cap'n he stirre[d] up a mess o' flip and hed it for her ho[t] to go to bed on. He was a good-nature[d] crittur, and allers had feelin's for lon[e] women, and I s'pose he knew 't was sor[t] o' desolate for Cinthy.

"Wal, takin' the flip so right the las[t] thing afore goin' to bed, she went righ[t] off to sleep as sound as a nut, and sle[pt] on till somewhere about mornin', when sh[e] said somethin' waked her broad awake i[n] a minute. Her eyes flew wide open like [a] spring, and the storm had gone down an[d] the moon come out, and there, standin['] right in the moonlight by her bed, was [a] woman jist as white as a sheet, with blac[k] hair hangin' down to her waist, and th[e] brightest, mournfullest black eyes you eve[r] see. She stood there lookin' right at Cin[-] thy, and Cinthy thinks that was wha[t] waked her up; 'cause, you know, ef any[-]

ody stands and looks steady at folks
sleep it's apt to wake 'em.

"Any way, Cinthy said she felt jist as
if she was turnin' to stone. She couldn't
move nor speak. She lay a minute, and
then she shut her eyes and begun to say
er prayers; and a minute after she opened
'm and it was gone.

"Cinthy was a sensible gal, and one that
llers hed her thoughts about her, and she
jist got up and put a shawl round her shoul-
ers and went first and looked at the doors,
and they was both on 'em locked jist as she
eft 'em when she went to bed. Then she
looked under the bed and in the closet, and
felt all round the room; where she couldn't
see she felt her way, and there wa'n't noth-
n' there.

"Wal, next mornin' Cinthy got up and
went home, and she kep' it to herself a
good while. Finally, one day when she was
workin' to our house she told Hepsy about
t, and Hepsy she told me."

"Well, Sam," we said, after a pause, in
which we heard only the rustle of leaves
and the ticking of branches against each
ther, "what do you suppose it was?"

"Wal, there 't is; you know jist as much
bout it as I do. Hepsy told Cinthy it
might 'a' ben a dream; so it might, but
Cinthy she was sure it wa'n't a dream,
ause she remembers plain hearin' the old
lock on the stairs strike four while she had
er eyes open lookin' at the woman; and
then she only shet 'em a minute, jist to say
'Now I lay me,' and opened 'em and she
as gone.

"Wal, Cinthy told Hepsy, and Hepsy she
ep' it putty close. She didn't tell it to
obody except Aunt Sally Dickerson and
the Widder Bije Smith and your grandma
Badger and the minister's wife, and they
very one o' 'em 'greed it ought to be
ep' close 'cause it would make talk. Wal,
ome spring somehow or other it seemed
o 'a' got all over Oldtown. I heard on 't
o the store and up to the tavern, and Jake
Marshall he says to me one day, 'What's
his 'ere about the Cap'n's house?' And the
Widder Loker she says to me, 'There's ben
ghost seen in the Cap'n's house'; and I
eard on 't clear over to Needham and
herburn.

"Some o' the women they drew them-
elves up putty stiff and proper. Your Aunt
Lois was one on 'em.

"'Ghost,' says she; 'don't tell me! Per-
aps it would be best ef 't was a ghost,'
says she. She didn't think there ought to
be no sich doin's in nobody's house; and
your grandma she shet her up, and told her
she didn't oughter talk so."

"Talk how!" said I, interrupting Sam,
with wonder. "What did Aunt Lois
mean?"

"Why, you see," said Sam, mysteriously,
"there allers is folks in every town that's
jist like the Sadducees in old times; they
won't believe in angel nor sperit, no way
you can fix it; and ef things is seen and
done in a house, why, they say it's 'cause
there's somebody there; there's some sort
o' deviltry or trick about it.

"So the story got round that there was
a woman kep' private in Cap'n Brown's
house, and that he brought her from furrin
parts; and it growed and growed, till there
was all sorts o' ways o' tellin' on 't.

"Some said they'd seen her a settin' at
an open winder. Some said that moonlight
nights they'd seen her a walkin' out in the
back garden kind o' in and out 'mong the
bean-poles and squash-vines.

"You see it come on spring and summer, and the winders o' the Cap'n Brown
house stood open, and folks was all a
watchin' on 'em day and night. Aunt Sally
Dickerson told the minister's wife that
she'd seen in plain daylight a woman a settin' at the chamber winder atween four and
five o'clock in the mornin',—jist a settin'
a lookin' out and a doin' nothin', like anybody else. She was very white and pale,
and had black eyes.

"Some said that it was a nun the Cap'n
had brought away from a Roman Catholic
convent in Spain, and some said he'd got
her out o' the Inquisition.

"Aunt Sally said she thought the minister ought to call and inquire why he
didn't come to meetin', and who she was,
and all about her; 'cause, you see, she said
it might be all right enough ef folks only
know'd jist how things was, but ef they
didn't, why, folks will talk."

"Well, did the minister do it?"

"What, Parson Lothrop? Wal, no, he
didn't. He made a call on the Cap'n in a
regular way, and asked arter his health and
all his family. But the Cap'n he seemed jist
as jolly and chipper as a spring robin, and
he gin the minister some o' his old Ja-
maicy; and the minister he come away and
said he didn't see nothin'; and no he didn't.
Folks never does see nothin' when they
ain't lookin' where 't is. Fact is, Parson

Lothrop wa'n't fond o' interferin'; he was a master hand to slick things over. Your grandma she used to mourn about it, 'cause she said he never gin no p'int to the doctrines; but 't was all of a piece, he kind o' took everything the smooth way.

"But your grandma she believed in the ghost, and so did Lady Lothrop. I was up to her house t' other day fixin' a door-knob, and says she, 'Sam, your wife told me a strange story about the Cap'n Brown house.'

"'Yes, ma'am, she did,' says I.

"'Well, what do you think of it?' says she.

"'Wal, sometimes I think, and then ag'in I don't know,' says I. 'There's Cinthy she's a member o' the church and a good pious gal,' says I.

"'Yes, Sam,' says Lady Lothrop, says she, 'and Sam,' says she, 'it is jist like something that happened once to my grandmother when she was livin' in the old Province House in Boston.' Says she, 'These 'ere things is the mysteries of Providence, and it's jist as well not to have 'em too much talked about.'

"'Jist so,' says I,—'jist so. That are's what every woman I've talked with says, and I guess, fust and last, I've talked with twenty,—good, safe church-members,—and they's every one o' opinion that this 'ere oughtn't to be talked about. Why, over to the Deacon's t' other night we went it all over as much as two or three hours, and we concluded that the best way was to keep quite still about it, and that's jist what they say over to Needham and Sherburn. I've been all round a hushin' this 'ere up, and I hain't found but a few people that hadn't the particulars one way or another. This 'ere was what I says to Lady Lothrop. The fact was, I never did see no report spread so, nor make sich sort o' surchings o' heart as this 'ere. It railly did beat all, 'cause ef 't was a ghost, why there was the p'int proved, ye see. Cinthy's a church-member, and she see it, and got right up and sarched the room; but then ag'in ef 't was a woman, why that are was kind o' aw-ful; it give cause, ye see, for thinkin' all sorts o' things. There was Cap'n Brown, to be sure, he wa'n't a church-member, but yet he was as honest and regular a man as any going, as fur as any on us could see. To be sure, nobody know'd where he come from, but that wa'n't no reason ag'in him; this 'ere might 'a' been a crazy sister

or some poor crittur that he took out o' the best o' motives, and the Scriptur says, 'Charity hopeth all things.' But then ye see folks will talk,—that are 's the pester of all these things,—and they did some on 'em talk consid'able strong about the Cap'n; but somehow or other there didn't nobody come to the p'int o' facin' on him down and sayin' square out, 'Cap'n Brown, have you got a woman in your house, or hain't you, or is it a ghost, or what is it?' Folks somehow never does come to that. Ye see there was the Cap'n so respectable, a settin' up every Sunday there in his pew, with his ruffles round his hands and his red broadcloth cloak and his cocked hat. Why, folks' hearts sort o' failed 'em when it come to sayin' anything right to him. They thought and kind o' whispered round that the minister or the deacons oughter to do it; but Lordy massy, ministers I s'pose has feelin's like the rest on us; they don't want to eat all the hard cheeses that nobody else won't eat. Anyhow, there wasn't nothin' said direct to the Cap'n, and jist for want o' that all the folks in Old-town kep' a bilin' and a bilin' like a kettle o' soap, till it seemed all the time as if they'd bile over.

"Some o' the wimmen tried to get somethin' out o' Quassy. Lordy massy, you might as well 'a' tried to get it out an old Tom-turkey, that'll strut and gobble and quitter and drag his wings on the ground and fly at you, but won't say nothing. Quassy she screeched her queer sort o' laugh, and she told 'em that they were a makin' fools o' themselves, and that the Cap'n's matters wa'n't none o' their bis'-ness; and that was true enough. As to goin' into Quassia's room, or into any o' the store-rooms, or closets she kep' the keys of, you might as well have gone into a lion's den; she kep' all her places locked up tight, and there was no gettin' at nothin' in the Cap'n Brown house, else I believe some o' the wimmen would 'a' sent a search-warrant."

"Well," said I, "what came of it? Didn't anybody ever find out?"

"Wal," said Sam, "it come to an end sort o', and didn't come to an end. It was jist this 'ere way. You see along in October, jist in the cider-makin' time, Abel Flint he was took down with dysentery and died. You 'member the Flint house; it stood on a little rise o' ground jist lookin' over towards the Brown house. Wal, there was Aunt Sally Dickerson and the Widder Bije Smith, they set up with the corpse. He was laid out in the back chamber, you see, over the milk-room and kitchen; but there was cold victuals and sich in the front chamber, where the watchers sot. Wal, now Aunt Sally she told me that between three and four o'clock she heard wheels a rumblin', and she went to the winder and it was clear starlight, and she see a coach come up to the Cap'n Brown house, and she see the Cap'n come out bringin' a woman all wrapped in a cloak, and old Quassy came after with her arms full of bundles, and he put her into the kerridge and shet her in and it driv off; and she see old Quassy stand lookin' over the fence arter it. She tried to wake up the widder, but 't was towards mornin', and the widder allers was a hard sleeper; so there wa'n't no witness but her.'

"Well, then it wasn't a ghost," said I, "after all, and it *was* a woman."

"Wall, there 't is, you see. Folks don't know that are yit, 'cause there it's jist as broad as 't is long. Now look at it. There's Cinthy, she's a good, pious gal; she locks her chamber doors, both on 'em, and goes to bed, and wakes up in the night and there's a woman there. She jist shets her eyes and the woman's gone. She gits up and looks and both doors is locked jist as she left 'em. That 'ere woman wa'n't 5 flesh and blood now, no way,—not such flesh and blood as we knows on, but then they say Cinthy might have dreamed it!

"Wal, now, look at it t'other way. There's Aunt Sally Dickerson,—she's a 10 good woman and a church-member; wal, she sees a woman in a cloak with all her bundles brought out o' Cap'n Brown's house and put into a kerridge and driv off, 15 atween three and four o'clock in the mornin'. Wal, that 'ere shows there must 'a' ben a real live woman kep' there privately, and so what Cinthy saw wasn't a ghost.

"Wal, now Cinthy says Aunt Sally 20 might 'a' dreamed it,—that she got her head so full o' stories about the Cap'n Brown house, and watched it till she got asleep and hed this 'ere dream; and as there didn't nobody else see it, it might 'a' 25 ben, you know. Aunt Sally's clear she didn't dream, and then ag'in Cinthy's clear *she* didn't dream; but which on 'em was awake or which on 'em was asleep is what ain't settled in Oldtown yet."

XII

ROSE TERRY COOKE (1827–1892)

Until well into the sixties and the seventies of the nineteenth century the America "female writers" lacked poise, control, and truth to the fundamentals of life. It was the er of *Godey's Lady's Book,* and Bonner's *New York Ledger,* and of the "best-sellers," *Unc Tom's Cabin, The Wide, Wide World,* and *The Lamp-Lighter,* books emotionally intense, over adjectived, sentimental to mawkishness—romance in black and white with no intermediat shades. Harriet Prescott had emerged from the group with several creations of real powe and with Lowell's hand to guide it the new *Atlantic Monthly* soon developed a veritable nev school of short-story writers. Lowell's second "find" as editor of the magazine was ur doubtedly Rose Terry, who, though her first stories and poems were of the prevailing fem nine type, rapidly adjusted herself to the new demand for "actuality." So promising was he work that Lowell published five of her tales in the first volume of *The Atlantic,* one in near every number. She was the first to exploit New England as a background for *genre* fictio in anything like the modern manner. She gave not, like Mrs. Stowe, the impression tha New England was inhabited by "Brahmins"; she dealt in a Dickens-like way with humb characters and "homey" people, and not always did she, like Harte, exploit them simpl because they were strange or picturesque. There is humor in her work and love of her mate rials. She did not stand apart and observe and record; and she knew of what she wrote. I her fidelity to the actualities of the Yankee dialect she is the peer even of Lowell: no on has rendered it better. She is distinctive, too, in that she constantly kept pace with her time shedding gradually her sentimentalism and conventionality, and with each story through thre decades making advances in her art and her "realism" and her convincingness. Her las volume, *Huckleberries Gathered from New England Hills,* published in 1892, the year o her death, contains much of her best work. Her strongest stories are "Grit," "Too Late, "Freedom Wheeler's Controversy with Providence," "Cal Culver and the Devil," "Th Deacon's Week," and "Miss Lucinda."

FREEDOM WHEELER'S CONTROVERSY WITH PROVIDENCE

A STORY OF OLD NEW ENGLAND

I

Aunt Huldy and Aunt Hannah sat in the kitchen: Aunt Huldah bolt upright in a straight-backed wooden chair, big silver-bowed spectacles astride her high nose, sewing carpet rags with such energy that her eyes snapped, and her brown, wrinkled fingers flew back and forth like the spokes of a rapid wheel; Aunt Hannah in a low, creaky old rocker, knitting diligently but placidly, and rocking gently; you could almost hear her purr, and you wanted to stroke her; but Aunt Huldah!—an electric machine could not be less desirable to handle than she, or a chestnut bur pricklier.

The back-log simmered and sputtered,

the hickory sticks in front shot up brigh soft flames, and through the two low green-paned windows the pallid sun o February sent in a pleasant shining on t 5 the clean kitchen floor. Cooking-stove were not made then, nor Merrimac cali coes: the two old women had stuff petti coats and homespun short gowns, clea mob-caps over their decent gray hair, an 10 big blue check aprons; hair dye, wig flowered chintz, and other fineries had no reached the lonely farms of Dorset in thos days. "Spinsters" was not a mere name the big wool-wheel stood in one corner o 15 the kitchen, and a little flax-wheel by th window; in summer both would be move to the great garret, where it was cool an out of the way.

"Curus, ain't it?" said Aunt Huldal 20 "Freedom never come home before, later' nine o'clock bell, and he was morta mighty then; kep' his tongue between hi eeth same way he did to breakfast this mornin'. There's suthin a-goin' on, Hanner, you may depend on 't."

"Mabbe he needs some wormwood tea," said Aunt Hannah, who like Miss Hannah More thought the only two evils in the world were sin and bile, and charitably referred to lay things first to the physical disorder.

"I du b'lieve, Hanner, you think 'riginal sin is nothin' but a bad stomick."

"Ef 'tain't 'riginal sin, it's actual transgression pretty often, Huldy," returned the placid old lady with a gentle cackle. The Assembly's Catechism had been ground into them both, as any old-fashioned New Englander will observe, and they quoted its forms of speech as Boston people do Emerson's essays, by "an automatic action of the unconscious nervous centers."

The door opened and Freedom walked in, scraping his boots upon the husk mat, as a man will who has lived all his days with two old maids, but nevertheless spreading abroad in that clean kitchen an odor of the barn that spoke of "chores," yet did not disturb the accustomed nostrils of his aunts. He was a middle-sized, rather "stocky" man, with a round head well covered with light-curling short hair, that revenged itself for being cut too short to curl by standing on end toward every point of the compass. You could not call him a common-looking man; something in his keen blue eye, abrupt nose, steady mouth, and square chin always made a stranger look at him twice. Rugged sense, but more rugged obstinacy, shrewdness, keen perception tempered somewhat by a certain kindliness that he himself felt to be his weak spot, all these were to be read in Freedom Wheeler's well-bronzed face, stury figure, positive speech, and blunt manner.

He strode up to the fire-place, sat down in an arm-chair rudely shaped out of wood by his own hands, and plunged, after his fashion, at once into the middle of things.

"Aunt Huldy and Aunt Hanner, I'm a-goin' to git married." The domestic bomb-shell burst in silence. Aunt Hannah dropped a stitch and couldn't see to pick it up for at least a minute. Aunt Huldah's scissors snipped at the rags with a vicious snap, as if they were responsible agents and she would end their proceedings then and there; presently she said, "Well, I am beat!" to which rather doubtful utterance

Freedom made no reply, and the scissors snipped harder yet.

Aunt Hannah recovered herself first: "Well, I'm real glad on 't!" purred she; it was her part to do the few amenities of the family.

"I dono whether I be or not, till I hear who 't is," dryly answered Aunt Huldah, who was obviously near akin to Freedom.

"It's Lowly Mallory," said the short-spoken nephew, who by this time was whittling busily at a peg for his ox-yoke.

"Du tell!" said Aunt Hannah in her lingering, deliberate tones, the words running into each other as she spoke. "She's jest 's clever 's the day is long; you've done a good thing, Freedom, 's sure 's you you live."

"He might ha' done wuss, that's a fact." And with this approval Freedom seemed satisfied, for he brushed his chips into the fire, ran his fingers through his already upright hair, eyed his peg with the keen aspect of a critic in pegs, and went off to the barn; he knew instinctively that his aunts must have a chance to talk the matter over.

"This is the beateree!" exclaimed Aunt Huldah as the door shut after him. "Lowly Mallory, of all creturs! Freedom's as masterful as though he was the Lord above, by natur, and ef he gets a leetle softly cretur like that, without no more grit 'n a November chicken, he'll ride right over everything, and she won't darst to peep nor mutter a mite. Good land!"

"Well, well," murmured Aunt Hannah, "she is a kind o' feeble piece, but she's real clever; an' I dono but what it 's as good as he could do; ef she was like to him, hard-headed 'n' sot in her way, I tell ye, Huldy, the fur 'd fly mightily, and it 's putty bad to have fight at home, when there's a fam'ly to fetch up."

"Well, you be forecastin' I must say, Hanner; but mabbe you're abaout right. Besides, I've observed that folks will marry to suit themselves, not other people; an' mabbe it's the best way, seein' it's their own loss or likin' more 'n anybody else's."

"But, Huldy, 'pears as if you'd forgot one thing: I expect we'd better be a-movin' out into the old house ef there's goin' to be more folks here."

"Well, I declare! I never thought on 't. 'Tis best, I guess. I wonder ef Freedom's got the idee!"

"I dono; but that hadn't oughter make

no difference; there never was a house big enough for two families, an' ef we go before we're obleeged to, it's a sight better 'n stayin' till we be."

"That's so, Hanner; you allers was a master-hand for takin' things right end foremost. I'll sort out our linen right off, 'nd set by our furnitoor into the back chamber. I guess the old house'll want a leetle paintin' an' scrapin'. It's dreadful lucky Amasy Flint's folks moved to Noppit last week; seems as though there was a Providence about it."

"I shouldn't wonder ef Freedom had give 'em a sort o' hint to go, Huldy."

"Well, you do beat all! I presume likely he did."

And Aunt Huldah picked up the rags at her feet, piled them into a splint basket, hung the shears on a steel chain by her side, and lifting her tall, gaunt figure from the chair betook herself upstairs. But Aunt Hannah kept on knitting; she was the thinker and Huldah the doer of the family; now her thoughts ran before her to the coming change, and she sighed, for she knew her nephew thoroughly, and she pitied the gentle, sweet nature that was to come in contact with his.

Dear Aunt Hannah! She had never had any romance in her own life; she did not know anything about love except as the placid and quite clear-eyed affection she felt for Freedom, who was her only near relation, and she saw little Lowly Mallory's future on its hardest side. But she could not help it, and her nature was one that never frets against a difficulty, any more than the green turf beats against the rock to whose edge it clings.

So the slow, sad New England spring, with storm and tempest, drifting snows and beating rains, worked its reluctant way into May; and when the lilacs were full of purple and white plumes, delicate as cut coral sprays and luscious with satiating odor, and the heavy-headed doffodils thrust golden locks upward from the sward, Aunt Huldah and Aunt Hannah moved their wool-wheel and their flax-wheel, the four stiff-backed chairs, the settle and big red chest, the high four-post bedstead, and the two rush-bottomed rockers that had been Grandsir Wheeler's, back into the small red house for which these furnishings had been purchased sixty years before, laid the rag carpet that Aunt Huldah had sewed and dyed and woven on the "settin'-room"

floor, and with a barrel of potatoes and a keg of salt pork went to housekeeping.

There was some home-made linen belonging to them, and a few cups and dishes; also a feather-bed and a pair of blankets. Freedom kept them supplied with what necessaries they wanted, and though he was called "dreadful near" in the town he was not an unjust man; his two aunts had taken him in charge, an orphan at six and been faithful and kind to him all his days; and he could do no less than care for them now. Besides, they owned half the farm; and though one was fifty-six and the other fifty-eight, there was much hard work left in them yet. Aunt Huldah was a skilful tailoress, in demand for miles about, and Aunt Hannah was the best sick-nurse in the county. They would not suffer and, truth to tell, they rather enjoyed the independence of their own house, for Freedom and Aunt Huldah were chips of the same block, and only Aunt Hannah's constant quiet restraint and peace-making kept the family tolerably harmonious. And in the farm-house a new reign began,—the reign of Queen Log!

Lowly Mallory was a fragile, slender delicate girl, with sweet gray eyes and plenty of brown hair; pale as a spring anemone, with just such faint pinkness in her lips and on her high cheek-bones as tints that pensile, egg-shaped bud when its

"Small flower layeth
Its fairy gem beneath some giant tree"

on the first warm days of May. She had already the line of care that marks New England women across the forehead like a mark of Cain, the signal of a life in which work has murdered health and joy and freedom; for Lowly was the oldest of ten children, and her mother was bedridden. Lovina was eighteen, now, and could take her place, and Lowly loved Freedom with the reticent, undemonstrative affection of her race and land; moreover, she was glad of change, of rest. Rest!—much of that awaited her! Freedom's first step after the decorous wedding and home-coming was to buy ten cows— he had two already—and two dozen new milk-pans.

"I calkerlate we can sell a good lot o' butter 'n' cheese down to Dartford, Lowly," he said, on introducing her to the new dairy he had fitted up at one end of the woodshed; and if the gentle creature's heart sank within her at the prospect, she did not say so, and Freedom never asked how she liked it. He was "masterful" indeed, and having picked out Lowly from all the other Dorset girls because she was a still and hard-working maiden, and would neither rebel against or criticize his edicts, he took it for granted things would go on as he wished.

Poor little Lowly! Her simple, tender heart went out to her husband like a vine feeling after a trellis, and even when she found it was only a boulder that chilled and repelled her slight ardors and timid caresses, she did still what the vine does, flung herself across and along the granite faces of the rock, and turned her trembling blossoms sunward, where life and light were free and sure.

Aunt Huldah and Aunt Hannah soon grew to be her ministering angels, and if they differed from the gold-haired, pink-enameled, straight-nosed creations of Fra Angelico, and would have figured ill, in their short gowns and mob-caps, bowing before an ideal Madonna, Lowly wanted no better tendance and providing that they gave her when in due season there appeared in the farm-house a red and roaring baby, evidently patterned after his father, morally as well as physically; the white down on his raw pink head twisting into tight kinks, and his stubby fists set in as firm a grasp as ever Freedom's big brown paws were. Lowly was a happy little woman: she had loved children always, and here was one all her own. Two weeks were dreamed away in rest and rapture, then Freedom began to bustle and fret and growl about the neglected dairy, and the rusty pork, and the hens that wanted care.

"Don't ye s'pose she'll git 'raound next week, Aunt Huldy? Things is gittin dredful behindhand!" Freedom had left the bedroom door open on purpose. Aunt Huldah got up and shut it with a slam, while he went on: "Them hens had oughter be set, 'n' I never git time to be a half a day prowlin' araound after 'em; they've stole their nests, I expect, the hull tribe; 'nd Hepsy don't make butter to compare along-side o' Lowly's; then there's that ere pork a-gittin rusty, 'n' Aunt Hanner, she's over to Mallory's nussin Loviny, so's I can't call on you, 'n' it doos seem 's though two weeks was a plenty for well folks to lie in bed!"

Here Aunt Huldah exploded: "Freedom Wheeler, you hain't got a mite o' compassion into ye! Lowly ain't over 'n' above powerful, any way; she'll break clear down ef she ain't real keerful; mabbe I ain't"—

The shutting of the back door stopped her tirade; while she hunted in a table drawer for her thimble, Freedom had coolly walked off; he did not choose to argue the subject, but next day Lowly got up and was dressed; there were two lines across the sad, low forehead now, but she went about her work in silence; there is a type of feminine character that can endure to the edge of death and endure silently, and that character was eminently hers.

"Good little feller, so he was, as ever was; there, there, there! should be cuddled up good 'n' warm; so he should!" Aunt Hannah purred to the small boy a month after, seeing him for the first time, as she had been taking care of Lovina Mallory through a low fever when he was born.

"What be ye a-goin' to call him, Freedom?"

"I calkerlate he'll be baptized Shearjashub.[1] There's allus ben a Shearjashub 'nd a Freedom amongst our folks; I've heered Grandsir Wheeler tell on 't more 'n forty times, how the' was them two names away back as fur as there's grave-stones to tell on 't down to Litchfield meetin'-house, 'nd back o' that in the old grave-yard to Har'ford. I expect this here feller'll be called Shearjashub 'nd the next one Freedom; that's the way they've allus run."

"For land's sakes!" sputtered Aunt Huldah. "I was in hopes you hadn't got that notion inter your head! Why can't ye call the child some kind o' pootty scripter name, like David, or Samwell, or Eber, 'nd not set him a-goin' with a kite's tail like that tied on to him?"

'I guess what's ben good 'nough for our folks time out o' mind 'll be good 'nough for him," stiffly answered Freedom; and Aunt Huldah, with inward rage, accepted the situation, and went out to the barn to help Lowly set some refractory hens, where she found the poor little woman, with suspiciously red eyes, counting eggs on a corner of the haymow.

"Hanner's come, Lowly," said she; "so she's got baby, 'nd I come out to give ye a lift about them hens. I've ben a-dealin' with Freedom about that there child's name, but you might jest as well talk to

White Rock; I will say for 't he's the sottest man I ever see! I b'lieve he'd set to to fight his own way out with the Lord above, if he hed to!"

Lowly gave a little plaintive smile, but, after the manner of her sex, took her husband's part: "Well, you see, Aunt Huldy, it's kind o' nateral he should want to foller his folks's ways. I don't say but what I did want to call baby Eddard, for my little brother that died. I set great store by Eddy,"—here Lowly's checked apron wiped a certain mist from her patient eyes, —"and 't would ha' been my mind to call him for Eddy; but Freedom don't feel to, and you know scripter says wives must be subject to husbands."

"Hm!" sniffed Aunt Huldah, who was lost to the strong-minded party of her sex by being born before its creation. "Scripter has a good deal to answer for!" with which enigmatical and shocking remark she turned and pounced upon the nearest hen. Poor old hen! she evidently represented a suffering and abject sex to Aunt Huldah, and exasperated her accordingly. Do I not know? Have not I, weakly and meekly protesting against their ways and works, also been hustled and bustled by the Right Women (?), even as this squawking, crawling, yellow biddy was pluffed and cuffed and shaken up by Aunt Huldah and plunged at last, in spite of nips and pecks and screaks, into the depths of a barrel, the head wedged on above her, and the unwilling matron condemned to solitary confinement, with hard labor, on thirteen eggs!

So Freedom had his way, of course; and Lowly went on, with the addition of a big naughty baby to take care of, waking before light to get her "chores" out of the way, prepare breakfast, skim cream, strain new milk and set it, scald pans, churn, work and put down butter, feed pigs and hens, bake, wash, iron, scrub, mend, make, nurse baby, fetch wood from the shed and water from the well; a delicate, bending, youthful figure, with hands already knotted and shoulders bowed by hard work; her sole variety of a week-day being when one kind of pie gave place to another, or when the long winter evenings, with dim light of tallow candles, made her spinning shorter and her sewing longer.

For Sundays were scarce a rest: breakfast was as early, milk as abundant, on that day as any other; and then there was a five-mile ride to meeting, for which ample lunch must be prepared, since the stayed at noon; there was baby to dres and her own Sunday clothes to put on, which stiff and unaccustomed finery she sa four mortal hours, with but the brief in terval of nooning, on a hard and comfort less seat; and then home again to get th real dinner of the day, to feed her pig and hens, to get the clamorous baby quiet this was hardly rest! And summer, tha brings to overstrained nerves and exhaust ed muscles the healing of sun, sweet winds fresh air, and the literal "balm of a thou sand flowers," only heralded to her th advent of six strong hungry men at hay ing, shearing, and reaping time, with ex tra meals, increased washing, and, o course, double fatigue. Yet this is the lif that was once the doom of all New Eng land farmers' wives; the life that sent thei to early graves, to mad-houses, to sui cide; the life that is so beautiful in th poet's numbers, so terrible in its stony bloomless, oppressive reality. It would hav been hard to tell if Lowly was glad o sorry when on a soft day in June Aun Hannah, this time at home, was hurriedl called from the red house to officiate a doctor and nurse both, at the arrival o another baby. This time Freedom growle and scowled by himself in the kitchen in stead of condescending to look at and ap prove the child; for it was a girl!

Aunt Hannah chuckled in her sleev Freedom had intimated quite frankly tha this child was to be called after himsel nothing doubting but that another boy wa at hand; and great was his silent rage a the disappointment.

"Imperdent, ain't it?" queried Aunt Hul dah, who sat by the kitchen fire stirring mess of Indian-meal porridge. "To think darst to be a girl when ye was so sot o its turnin' out a boy! Seems as thoug Providence got the upper hand on ye Freedom, arter all!"

But Freedom never gave retort to Aun Huldah: he had been brought up in cer tain superstitions, quite obsolete now, abou respecting his elders, and though the spiri was wanting sometimes, the letter of th law had observance; he could rage at Aun Huldah privately, but before her he hel his tongue; it was his wife who suffere as the sinner should for disturbing hi plans in this manner; he snubbed her, h despised the baby, and forthwith bougl

wo more cows with the grim remark,
"Ef I've got to fetch up a pack o' girls,
guess I'd better scratch around 'n' make
a leetle more money!"

But if the new baby was an eye-sore to
Freedom, she was a delight to Lowly. All
the more because her father ignored and
seemed to dislike her, the affluent mother
heart flowed out upon her. She was a cooing, clinging, lovely little creature, and
when, worn out with her day's work, Low-
y had at last coaxed her cross teething
boy to sleep, and she sat down in the old
creaky rocker to nurse and tend her baby,
the purest joy that earth knows stole over
her like the tranquil breath of heaven: the
touch of tiny fingers on her breast, the
warm shining head against her heart, the
vague baby smile and wandering eyes that
neither the wistfulness of doubt, the darkness of grief, nor the fire of passion cloud-
d as yet; the inarticulate murmurs of satisfaction, the pressure of the little help-
ess form upon her lap, the silent, ardent
tenderness that awoke and burned in her
own heart for this precious creature, all
made for the weary woman a daily oasis
of peace and beauty that perhaps saved
her brain from that common insanity we
all nervousness, and her body from ut-
er exhaustion; for happiness is a medicine of God's own sending; no quack has
ever pretended to dispense its potent and
beneficent cordial, and the true, honest
physician, he whose very profession is the
nearest approach to that of the Saviour
and Healer of men, knows well that one
drop of the only elixir he cannot bring
outweighs all he can. Shearjashub grew up
to the height of three years and the baby
toddled about and chattered like a merry
chipping-bird, when one Fast Day morn-
ng Lowly stayed at home from meeting
with a sinking heart, and Aunt Hannah
was sent for again. Freedom went off to
hear the usual sermon, on a pretense of
taking Shearjashub out of the way, he be-
ng irrepressible except by his father,
whom alone he feared. Mother and aunts
the youngster manfully defied and scorned,
out the very sound of his father's steps
reduced him to silence; shingles were not
out of fashion then as a means of discipline, and the hot tingle of the applica-
ion dwelt vividly in the boy's mind ever
since he had been "tuned mightily," as
his father phrased it, for disobedience and
obstinacy, Aunt Huldah's comment at the

first punishment being, "Hemlock all three
on 'em, man an' boy an' shingle; it's tough
to tell which'll beat!"

Little Love stayed at home with old Hep-
sey and prattled all day long in the kitchen;
Lowly could not spare the sweet voice from
her hearing, and she had need of all its
comfort, for when Freedom came home
from Dorset Center a great girl baby lay
by Lowly in the bed, and if its welcome
from the mother had been bitter tears
whose traces still shone on her wan face,
from the father came far bitterer words,
curses in all but the wording, for Freedom
was a "professor" and profanity was a sin.
Mint and anise and cumin he tithed scrupulously, but mercy and judgment fled from
him and hid their shamefaced heads. Aunt
Huldah and Aunt Hannah made their tansy
pudding that day after the custom of their
forefathers, and ate it with unflinching
countenances, but Lowly fasted in her secret soul; and since her husband grimly
remarked, " 'Tain't nothin' to me what ye
call her, gals ain't worth namin' anyhow!"
the new baby was baptized Marah, and behaved herself neither with the uproarious
misconduct of Shearjashub nor the gentle
sweetness of Love, but quite in defiance
of her name was the merriest, maddest
little grig that could be, afraid of nothing
and nobody, but as submissive to Lovey as
a lamb could be, and full of fight when
Shearjashub intruded himself on her domains. For this baby was a sturdy rosy
girl of three before the fourth appeared.
Lowly by this time had fallen into a listless carelessness toward her husband that
was simply the want of all spring in a long
down-trodden heart. Lovey alone could stir
her to tears or smiles. Marah tired and
tormented her with her restless and overflowing vitality, though she loved her dearly; and her boy was big enough now to
cling a little to "mother," and reward her
for her faithful patience and care; but
Lovey was the darling of her secret heart,
and being now five years old the little
maid waited on mother like a cherub on
a saint, ran of errands, wound yarn, and
did many a slight task in the kitchen that
saved Lowly's bent and weary fingers.

It was with an impotent rage beyond
speech that Freedom took the birth of another daughter; a frail, tiny creature,
trembling and weak as a new-born lamb
in a snow-drift, but for that very reason
rousing afresh in Lowly's breast the eter-

nal floods of mother-love, the only love that never fails among all earthly passions, the only patience that is never weary, the sole true and abiding trust for the helpless creatures who come into life as waifs from the great misty ocean, to find a shelter or a grave. Lowly was not only a mother according to the flesh,—for there are those whose maternity goes no further, and there are childless women who have the motherliness that could suffice for a countless brood,—but she had, too, the real heart; she clung to her weakling with a fervor and assertion that disgusted Freedom and astounded Aunt Huldah, who, like the old Scotch woman, sniffed at the idea of children in heaven: "No, no! a hantle o' weans there! an' me that could never abide bairns onywhere! I'll no believe it."

"It doos beat all, Hanner, to see her take to that skinny, miser'ble little crittur! The others was kind o' likely, all on 'em, but this is the dreadfullest weakly, peeked thing I ever see. I should think she'd be sick on 't!"

"I expect mothers—any way them that's real motherly, Huldy—thinks the most of them that needs it the most. I've seen women with children quite a spell now, bein' out nussin' 'round, an' I allers notice that the sickly ones gets the most lovin' an' cuddlin'. I s'pose it's the same kind o' feelin' the Lord hez for sinners; they want him a sight more 'n the righteous do."

"Why, Hanner Wheeler, what be you a-thinkin' of! Where's your catechis'? Ain't all men by nater under the wrath an cuss o' God 'cause they be fallen sinners? and here you be a-makin' out he likes 'em better 'n good folks."

"Well, Huldy, I warn't a-thinkin' of catechism, I was a-thinkin' about what it sez in the Bible."

Here the new baby cried, and Aunt Huldah, confounded but unconvinced, gave a loud sniff and carried off Shearjashub and Marah to the red house, where their fights and roars and general insubordination soon restored her faith in the catechism.

Lowly got up very slowly from little Phœbe's birth, and Freedom grumbled loud and long over the expense of keeping Hepsy a month in the kitchen, but his wife did not care now: a dumb and sudden endurance possessed her; she prayed night and morning with a certain monomaniac persistence that she and Lovey and the baby might die, but she did her work just

as faithfully and silently as ever, and stol away at night to lie down on the little co bed in the back chamber by Lovey an Marah, her hot cheek against the cool, sof face of her darling, and the little hand hi deep in her bosom, for an hour of res and sad peace.

Freedom, meanwhile, worked all day o the farm, and carried Shearjashub, whose oppressive name had lapsed into Bub, int wood and field with him; taught him t drive the oxen, to hunt hens' nests in th barn on the highest mow, to climb trees in short to risk his neck however he could "to make a man of him"; and the bo learned among other manly ways a sublim contempt for "gals," and a use of all th forcible words permitted to masculin tongues. But Shearjashub's scepter wa about to tremble; little Phœbe had lingere in this world through a year of flutterin; life when another baby was announced but this time it was a boy!—small even t Phœbe's first size, pallid, lifeless almost but still a boy.

"By Jinks!" exclaimed Freedom, hi hard face glowing with pleasure; "I tol ye so, Aunt Huldy! there's bound to be a Freedom Wheeler in this house whether o no!"

"Hm!" said Aunt Huldah, "you call t mind old Hepsy Tinker, don't ye? she tha was a-goin to Har'ford a Tuesday, Provi dence permittin', an' Wednesday whethe or no. Mabbe ye'll live to wish ye hadn' fit with the Lord's will the way ye hev."

"I've got a boy, anyhow," was the grim exultant answer. "And he'll be Freedom Wheeler afore night, for I'm a-goin' t fetch the parson right off."

Strenuously did Parson Pitcher objec to private baptism; but he was an old ma now, and Freedom threatened that he would go to Hartford and fetch the Epis copal minister, if Parson Pitcher refused and the old doctor knew he was quite sur to keep to his word; so, with a groan a the stiff-necked brother, he got out hi cloak and hat and rode home with victori ous Freedom to the farm-house. Here th punch-bowl was made ready on a stand i the parlor, and a fire kindled on the hearth for it was a chilly April day, and from th open door into Lowly's bedroom the wail ing day-old baby was brought and give into it's father's arms, a mere scrid an atom of humanity, but a boy!

The rite was over, the long prayer said

nd Freedom strode into the chamber to
ay his namesake beside its mother; but as
e stooped, the child quivered suddenly all
ver, gasped, opened its half-shut eyes
lazed with a fatal film, and then closed
he pallid, violet-shadowed lids forever.

The next entry in the family Bible
vas,—

"Freedom: born April 11th: died same
lay."

"Well, he hain't got nobody but the Lord
o querrel with this bout!" snapped Aunt
Iuldah. "He's had his way, 'nd now see
what come on 't!"

Lowly got up again after the fashion
f her kind, without a murmur: she felt
ler baby's death, she mourned her loss,
he was sorry for Freedom. She had loved
lim once, dearly; and if she had known
t Freedom loved her as much as he could
nything but himself, but it was not his
vay to show affection, even to his boy; as
luch of it as ever came to the surface was
rough caress offered now and then to
Lowly, a usage that had died out, and died
vith no mourning on either side. But as
here is a brief sweet season oftentimes, in
ur bitter climate, that comes upon the
our and angry November weather like a
espite of execution, a few soft, misty,
ensively sweet days, when the sun is red
nd warm in the heavens, the dead leaves
ive out their tender and melancholy odor,
nd the lingering birds twitter in the pine
oughs as if they remembered spring, so
here came to Lowly a late and last gleam
f tranquil pleasure.

Aunt Huldah brought it about, for her
ongue never failed her for fear; she
aught Freedom by himself one day, look-
ng like an ill-used bull-dog, all alone in
le barn, setting some new rake-teeth.

"I've hed it on my mind quite a spell,
'reedom," began the valorous old woman,
to tell ye that ef ye expect Lowly is ever
-goin' to hev a rousin' hearty child ag'in,
ou'll hev to cosset her up some. She ain't
ke our folks."

"That's pretty trew, Aunt Huldy," was
le bitter interruption.

"She ain't a nether millstone, thet's a
act," answered Aunt Huldah, with vigor.
Nor she ain't bend leather by a good
ight; she's one o' the weakly, meekly
ort, 'nd you can't make a whistle out o'
pig's tail, I've heerd father say, 'nd you
o need to try; no more can ye make a
tubbid, gritty cretur out o' Lowly; she's

good as gold, but she's one o' them that
hankers arter pleasantness, an' lovin', an'
sich; they're vittles an' drink to her, I tell
ye. You an' I can live on pork an' cabbage, and sass each other continooal, without turnin' a hair, but Lowly won't stan'
it; 'nd ef ye expect this next baby to git
along, I tell ye it's got to be easy goin'
with her. You want to keep your fight with
the Lord up, I s'pose; you're sot on hevin'
another Freedom Wheeler?"

"I be," was the curt response. But though
Aunt Huldah turned her back upon him
without further encouragement, and
marched through the ranks of "garden-
sass" back to the house, her apron over
her head and her nose high in air, like
one who snuffeth the battle from afar, her
pungent words fell not to the ground.
Freedom perceived the truth of what she
said, and his uneasy conscience goaded him
considerably as to past opportunities; but
he was an honest man, and when he saw
a thing was to be done, he did it. Next day
he brought Lowly a new rocking-chair
from the Center; he modified his manners
daily. He helped her lift the heavy milk-
pails, he kept her wood-pile by the shed
door well heaped, and was even known
to swing the heavy dinner pot off the
crane, if it was full and weighty.

"For the land sakes!" exclaimed Aunt
Hannah. "What's a-comin' to Freedom?
He does act half-way decent, Huldy."

Aunt Huldah shook her cap ruffle up and
down, and looked sagacious as an ancient
owl. "That's me! I gin it to him, I tell
ye, Hanner! Lowly wants cossetin' 'nd
handlin' tender-like, or we'll be havin'
more dyin' babies 'round. I up an' told him
so Wednesday mornin', out in the barn, 's
true's I'm alive."

"I'm glad on 't! I'm real glad on 't!"
exclaimed Aunt Hannah. "You done right,
Huldy; but massy to me! how darst
ye?"

"Ho!" sniffed Aunt Huldah, "ef you
think I'm afeared o' Freedom, you're clean
mistook. I've spanked him too often, 'n'
I wish to goodness I'd ha' spanked him a
heap more; he'd ha' ben a heap the better for 't. You reklect I had the tunin' of
him, Hanner? You was allus a nussin'
mother; Freedom come to us jest as she
got bedrid. Land! what a besom he was!
his folks never tuned him, nor never took
him to do, a mite. I hed it all to do, 'nd
my mind misgives me now I didn't half do

it; 'jest as the twig is bent the tree's inclined,' ye know it says in the speller."

"But, Huldy, 't ain't so easy bending a
white-oak saddle; 'specially ef it's got a
six years' growth."

"Well, I got the hang of him, anyhow,
'nd he'll hear to me most allus, whether
he performs accordin' or not."

"Mabbe it's too late, though, now,
Huldy."

"Law, don't ye croak, Hanner; the little cretur'll hev a pleasant spell anyhow
for a while."

And so she did. Lowly's ready heart responded to sunshine as a rain-drenched
bird will, preening its feathers, shaking its
weary wings, welcoming the warm gladness with faint chirps and tiny brightening eyes, and then—taking flight!

A long and peaceful winter passed away,
and in early May another boy was born;
alas, it was another waxen, delicate creature. The old parson was brought in haste
to baptize it; the pallid mother grew more
white all through the ceremony, but nobody noticed her; she took the child in her
arms with a wan smile and tried to call it
by name; "Free—" was all she said; her
arms closed about it with a quick shudder
and stringent grasp, her lips parted wide;
Lowly and her baby were both "free," for
its last breath fluttered upward with its
mother's; and in the family Bible there
was another record:—

"Lowly Wheeler, died May 3d.

"Freedom Wheeler, born May 3d, died
same day."

"Well," said Aunt Huldah, as they came
back to the ghastly quiet of the shut and
silent house, after laying Lowly and her
boy under the ragged turf of Dorset grave-
yard, "I guess Freedom'll give up his
wrastle with Providence, now, sence the
Lord's took wife 'nd baby 'nd all."

"I don't feel sure of that!" answered
Aunt Hannah, for once sarcastic.

II

Aunt Huldah and Aunt Hannah took
Love and Phœbe over to the red house
to live with them, for they found a little
note in Lowly's Bible requesting them
to take charge of these two, and their
father did not object. Phœbe was a baby
still; hopelessly feeble, she could not stand
alone, though she was more than two years

old, and Love was devoted to her. Bu[t]
and Marah could "fend for themselves[,]
and the old woman who came, as usua[l]
in Lowly's frequent absences from th[e]
kitchen, had promised to stay all summe[r.]
But before the summer was over Phœb[e]
faded away like a tiny snow-wreath in th[e]
sun, and made a third little grave at he[r]
mother's feet; and Lovey grieved for he[r]
so bitterly that Aunt Hannah insisted sh[e]
should stay with them still, and made he[r]
father promise she should be their littl[e]
girl always; certain forebodings of thei[r]
own as to the future prompting them to s[e]-
cure her a peaceful home while they live[d.]

As for Freedom, if he mourned Lowl[y]
it was with no soft or sentimental grie[f]
but with a certain resentful aching in h[is]
heart, and a defiant aspect of soul towar[d]
the divine will that had overset his inten[-]
tions and desires,—a feeling that deepene[d]
into savage determination, for this ma[n]
was made of no yielding stuff. Obstinac[y]
stood him in stead of patience, an acti[ve]
instead of a passive trait, and in less tha[n]
six months after Lowly's death he wa[s]
"published" according to the custom [of]
those days; the first intimation his aun[ts]
or his children had of the impending cris[is]
being this announcement from the pulp[it]
by Parson Pitcher, that "Freedom Whee[l-]
er, of this town, and Melinda Bassett, [of]
Hartland, intend marriage."

Aunt Huldah looked at Aunt Hanna[h]
from under her poke-bonnet with the loo[k]
of an enraged hen; her cap-frill trembl[ed]
with indignation, and Lovey shrank [up]
closer to Aunt Hannah than before, f[or]
she saw two tears rise to her kind o[ld]
eyes as they met Huldah's, and she love[d]
Aunt Hannah with all her gentle litt[le]
soul. As for Freedom he sat bolt uprig[ht]
and perfectly unmoved.

"Set his face as a flint!" raged Au[nt]
Huldah as soon as she got out of churc[h]
and went to take her "noon-spell" in t[he]
grave-yard, where the basket of dough[h-]
nuts, cheese, pie, cake, and early appl[es]
was usually unpacked on the stone-wa[ll]
on pleasant Sundays, and the aunts si[t]-
ting on a tombstone and the children o[n]
the grass ate their lunch. To-day Love[y]
and Marah were left on the stone to e[at]
their fill. Bub had gone to the spring fo[r]
water, and Freedom nobody knew wher[e]
while the aunts withdrew to "talk it over[."]

"Yis," repeated Aunt Huldah, "set h[is]
face like a flint! I tell ye he hain't got r[...]

ore feelin' than a cherub on a tomb-
tone, Hanner! She ain't cold in her grave
fore he's off to Hartland buyin' calves.
alves! I guess likely, comin' home jest
s plausible as a passnip: 'I shan't make
o butter this year, so I bought a lot o'
alves to raise.' Ho! heifer calves every
ne on 'em, mind ye. Ef we hadn't ha' ben
 pair o' fools we should ha' mistrusted
uthin. Ef that gal's Abigail Bassett's
arter, things'll fly, I tell ye." And here
unt Huldah blew a long breath out, as
 her steam was at high pressure and
ould not help opening a valve for relief,
nd wise Aunt Hannah seized the chance
 speak.

"Well, Huldy, I declare I'm beat, myself;
ut we can't help it. I must say I looked
orrard to the time when he would do it,
ut I didn't reelly expect it jest yet. We've
ot Lovey, any way; and ef Melindy ain't
 pootty capable woman she'll hev her
ands full with Bub and Marah."

"Thet's a fact," returned Aunt Huldah,
hose inmost soul rejoiced at the prospect
f Bub's contumaciousness under new rule,
or he was not a small boy any more, and
hingles were in vain; though he still
ade a certain outward show of obedience.
Iarah, too, was well calculated to be a
horn in the flesh of any meek step-mother,
ith her high spirits, untamed temper,
nd utter wilfulness; and Aunt Huldah,
hose soul was sore,—not because of Free-
om's marriage, for she recognized its ne-
essity, but because of its indecent haste,
hich not only seemed an insult to gentle
owly, whom Aunt Huldah had loved
early, but a matter of talk to all the town
here the Wheelers had been "respectit
ke the law" for many a long year,—Aunt
Iuldah rejoiced in that exasperated soul
f hers at a prospect of torment to the
oman who stepped into Lowly's place
uite unconscious of any evil design or
esire on the part of her new relatives.

But it was no meek step-mother whom
reedom brought home from a very in-
ormal wedding, in his old wagon, some
ree weeks after. Melinda Bassett was
uite capable of holding her own, even
ith Aunt Huldah; a strapping, buxom,
osy-faced girl, with abundant rough dark
air and a pair of bright, quick dark eyes,
n arm of might in the dairy, and a power
f work and management that would have
urnished forth at least five feeble pieces
ke Lowly. Freedom soon found he had

inaugurated Queen Stork. Bub was set to
rights as to his clotnes, and "pitched into,"
as he sulkily expressed it, in a way that
gave him a new and unwilling respect for
the other sex; and Marah entered at once
into an alliance, offensive and defensive,
with the new "mammy," for Melinda was
pleasant and cheerful when things went
right, and generally meant they should go
right. She was fond of children, too, when
they were "pretty behaved," and Marah
was bright enough to find out, with the
rapid perception of a keen-witted child,
that it was much better for her to *be* pretty
behaved than otherwise.

But Freedom!—it was new times to him
to have his orders unheeded and his ways
derided; he had been lord and master in
his house a long time, but here was a capable, plucky, courageous, and cheery creature who made no bones of turning him
out of her dominions when he interfered,
or ordering her own ways without his help
at all.

"Land of Goshen!" said Melinda to the
wondering Aunt Hannah. "Do you s'pose
I'm goin' to hev a man tewin' round in
my way all the time, jest cos he's my husband? I guess not. I know how to 'tend to
my business, and I expect to 'tend right
up to it; moreover, I expect he'll tend to
his 'n. When I get a holt of his plow, or
fodder his team, or do his choppin', 'll be
time enough for him to tell me how to
work butter 'n' scald pans. I ain't nobody's
fool, I tell ye, Aunt Hanner."

"I'm glad on 't,—I'm dredful glad on 't!"
growled Aunt Huldah, when she heard of
this manifesto.

"That's the talk; she'll straighten him
out, I'll bet ye! Ef poor Lowly'd had that
spunk she might ha' been livin' to-day.
But I guess she's better off," suddenly
wound up Aunt Huldah, remembering her
catechism, no doubt, as she walked off muttering, "Are at their death made perfect
in holiness, and do immediately pass into
glory,"—an assurance that has upheld
many a tired and weary soul more conversant with the language of the Assembly
of Divines than that of their Lord and
Head; for in those old days this formula
of the faith was ground into every infant
memory, though the tender gospel words
were comparatively unknown.

So the first year of the new reign passed
on, and in the next February Freedom was
mastered by a more stringent power than

Melinda, for he fell ill of old-fashioned typhus fever, a malign evil that lights down here and there in lonely New England farm-houses, utterly regardless of time or place; and in a week this strong man was helpless, muttering delirious speech, struggling for life with the fire that filled his veins and consumed his flesh. Aunt Hannah came to his aid, and the scarce neighbors did what they could for him; brother farmers snored away the night in a chair beside his bed, and said they had "sot up with Freedom Wheeler last night,"—ministrations worse than useless, but yet repeated as a sort of needful observance; and at the end of the first week Aunt Hannah was called away to the "up-chamber" room, where Melinda slept now, and a big boy was introduced into the Wheeler family; while Moll Thunder, an old woman skilled in "yarbs," as most of her race are,—for she was a half-breed Indian,—was sent for from Wingfield, and took command of the fever-patient, who raged and raved at his will, dosed with all manner of teas, choked with lukewarm porridge, smothered in blankets, bled twice a week, and kept as hot, as feeble, and as dirty as the old practice of medicine required, till disease became a mere question of "the survival of the fittest"; our grandfathers and grandmothers are vaunted to this day as a healthy, hard working race, because the weakly share of each generation was neatly eliminated according to law.

But if Freedom was helpless and wandering, Melinda was not; a week was all she spared to the rites and rights of the occasion: and when she first appeared in the kitchen, defying and horrifying Aunt Huldah, there ensued a brief and spicy conversation between the three women concerning this new baby, who lay sucking his fist in the old wooden cradle, looking round, hard and red as a Baldwin apple, and quite unconscious what a fire-brand he was about to be.

"It's real bad, ain't it?" purred Aunt Hannah, "to think Freedom shouldn't know nothin' about the baby? He'd be jest as tickled."

"I don' know what for," snapped Melinda. "I should think there was young uns enough 'round now, to suit him."

"But they wasn't boys," answered Aunt Hannah; "Freedom is sot on havin' a boy called for him; there's allus ben a Free-dom Wheeler amongst our folks, as well a a Shearjashub: and I never seen hi more pestered by a little thing than whe them two babies died, both on em bein' bap tized Freedom; and he's had a real cor troversy with Providence, Parson Pitche sez; his mind's so sot on this business."

"Well, this little feller isn't a-goin' t be called Freedom, now, I tell ye," ut tered Melinda with a look of positivenes that chilled Aunt Hannah to the hear "He's jest as much my baby 's he is hi pa's, and a good sight more, I b'lieve shan't I hev all the trouble on him? a jest as quick as he's big enough to hel instead o' hinder, won't he be snaked o into the lots to work? I've seen men folk afore; and I tell ye, Aunt Hanner, yo give 'em an inch 'n' they take a harf a yar certain!"

"Well, Melindy," interfered Aunt Hul dah, for once in her life essaying to mak peace, "Freedom's dreadful sick now; reel ly he's dangerous" (this is New Englan vernacular for in danger); "what ef h should up 'n' die? Wouldn't ye feel kin o' took aback to think on 't?"

"Things is right 'n' wrong jest the sam ef everybody dies; everybody doos, soone or later; I don't see what odds that makes Aunt Huldy. I ain't a-goin' to make n fuss about it; first Sunday in March i sacrament day, and children is allers pre sented for baptism then. I'll jest fix right, and ef his pa gits well, why ther 't is, 'nd he'll hev to git used to 't; an ef he don't, it ain't no matter, he won never know. I guess I've got folks as we as you, and names, too: there's old Grand sir Bassett; he sot a sight by me, 'nd h was ninety years old 'n' up'ards when h died; why, he fit the British out to Ticon derogy long o' Ethan Allen! He was dredful spry man, and had a kind o' poott name, too; smart-soundin', and I'm a-goin to call the boy for him. Freedom! Lan o' Goshen! tain't a half a name anyhow sounds like Fourth o' July oh-rations, 'n Hail Columby, 'nd fire-crackers, 'nd roo beer, 'nd Yankee Doodle thrown in! Nov Grandsir Bassett's name was Tyagustus That sounds well, I tell ye! kinder might an' pompous, 's though it come out o' then columns o' long proper names to the en of the speller."

Here Melinda got out of breath, and dis mayed Aunt Huldah followed Aunt Han nah, who had stolen off to Freedom's roon with a certain instinct of protecting him, as a hen who sees the circling wings of a hawk in the high blue heaven runs to brood her chicks.

Moll Thunder was smoking a clay pipe up the wide chimney, and Freedom lay on the bed with half-shut eyes, drawn and red visage, parched lips, and restless tossing head, murmuring wild words: here and there calls for Lowly, a tender word for Love, whom he scarce ever noticed in health, or a muttered profanity at some balky horse or stupid ox-team.

"Kinder pootty sick," grunted Moll Thunder, nodding to the visitants. "Plenty much tea-drink drown him ole debbil fever clear out 'fore long. He, he, he! Moll knows; squaw-vine, pep'mint, cohosh, fever-wort; pootty good steep." And from a pitcher of steaming herbs, rank of taste and evil of smell, she proceeded to dose her patient,—a heroic remedy that might have killed or cured but that now Aunt Hannah was no more needed up-stairs and could resume her place by Freedom; and Moll was sent home to Wingfield with a piece of pork, a bag of meal, and a jug of cider-brandy, a professional fee she much preferred to money.

But even Aunt Hannah could not arrest the fever; it had its sixty days of fight and fire. While yet it raged in Freedom's gaunt frame with unrelenting fierceness, Melinda carried out her program, and had her baby baptized Tyagustus Bassett. Parson Pitcher came now and then to visit the sick man; but even when recovery had proceeded so far that the reverend divine thought fit to exhort and catechise his weak brother in reference to his religious experience, the old gentleman shook his head and took numerous pinches of snuff at the result.

"There seems to be a root of bitterness, —a root of bitterness remaining, Huldy. His speritooal frame is cold and hard; there is a want of tenderness,—a want of tenderness."

"He didn't never have no great," dryly remarked Aunt Huldah.

"Grace has considerable of a struggle, no doubt, with the nateral man; it is so with all of us; but after such a dispensation, an amazing dispensation, brought into the jaws of death, Huldy, where death got hold of him and destruction made him afraid, in the words of scripter, I should expect, I did expect, to find him in a tender frame; but he seems to kick against the pricks,—to kick against the pricks."

"Well, Parson Pitcher, folks don't allus do jest as ye calc'late to have 'em, here below; and grace doos have a pootty hard clinch on 't with Freedom, I'm free to confess. He's dredful sot, dredful; and I don't mind tellin' ye, seein' we're on the subject, that he's ben kinder thwarted in suthin whilst he was sick, an' he hain't but jest found it out, and it doos rile him peskily; he dono how on earth to put up with 't."

"Indeed!—indeed! Well, Huldy, the heart knoweth its own bitterness. I guess I will pray with the family now, and set my face homeward without dealing with Freedom further to-day."

"I guess I would," frankly replied Aunt Huldah. "A little hullsome lettin' alone's 's good for grown folks as 't is for children; and after a spell he'll kinder simmer down; as Hanner sez, when ye can't fix a thing your way, you've got to swaller it some other way; but it doos choke ye awful sometimes."

There is no doubt that "Tyagustus" did choke Freedom, when he found that sonorous name tacked irremediably on to the great hearty boy he had hoped for so long, but never seen till it was six weeks old and solemnly christened after Grandsir Bassett. A crosser and a more disagreeable man than this convalescent never made a house miserable: the aunts went delicately in bitterness of soul, after Agag's fashion; Bub fled from before the paternal countenance, and almost lived in the barn; Marah had been for two months tyrannizing over Lovey at the red house, as happy and as saucy as a bobolink on a fence post; while Melinda, quite undaunted by the humors of her lord and master, went about her work with her usual zeal and energy, scolding Bub, working the hired man up to his extremest capacity, scrubbing, chattering, and cheery; now and then stopping to feed and hug the great good-tempered baby, or fetching some savory mess to Freedom, whose growls and groans disturbed her no more than the scrawks and croaks of the gossiping old hens about the doorstep.

By June he was about again, and things had found their level. If this were not a substantially true story, I should like to branch off here from the beaten track and reform my hero, make the gnarly oak into a fluent and facile willow-tree, and create a millennial peace and harmony in the old farm-house, just to make things pleasant for dear Aunt Hannah and gentle little Lovey; but facts are stubborn things, and if circumstances and the grace of God modify character, they do not change it; Peter and Paul were Paul and Peter still, though the end and aim of life was changed for them after conversion.

So Freedom Wheeler returned to his active life unchastened, indeed rather exasperated by his illness. The nervous irritation and general unhingeing of mind and body that follow a severe fever added, of course, to his disgust and rebellion against the state of things about him. His heart's desire had been refused him over and over, but it grew up again like a pruned shrub, the stronger and sturdier for every close cutting; and grinding his teeth against fate,—he dared not say against God,—he went his bitter way.

Melinda never feared him, but he was a terror to the children; and had there been any keen observer at hand, it would have been painful to see how "father" was a dreadful word instead of a synonym for loving protection and wise guidance. Aunt Hannah was shocked when Marah refused to say the Lord's prayer one night. "Me won't! me don't want father in heaven; fathers is awful cross; me won't say it, aunty."

"Now you jest clap down 'nd say 'Now I lay me' quick as a wink!" interposed Aunt Huldah. "Hanner, don't ye let that child talk so to ye. I'd tune her, afore I would, I tell ye."

But in the secrecy of her own apartment, Aunt Huldah explained: "You see, Hanner, I've took the measure of that young un's foot; she's pa all over; no more like Lowly 'n chalk is like cheese! Ef you'd ha' battled it out with her she'd ha' got the better of ye, 'nd more 'n likely gone home an' told the hull story, and then Freedom would nigh about ha' slartered her; 'nd I don't want the leetle cretur's sperit broke. Fact is, I feel jes' so myself; he is so all-fired ugly, seems as though I should bust, sometimes. Moreover 'nd above all 't ain't never best to let children git the better of ye. They don't never go back on their tracks ef they do. I put in my finger that time so's 't she shouldn't querrel with you, 'nd she said t' other thing jest like a cosset lamb; she was sort o' surprised into 't, ye see."

"I presume likely, I presume likely, Huldy; she's a masterful piece, Marah is; I'm afeard she'll taste trouble afore she dies. Sech as she has to have a lot of discipline to fetch 'em into the kingdom."

"Don't seem to be no use to Freedom, 'flictions don't, Hanner. Sometimes I declare for 't, I have my doubts ef he ever got religion, anyhow."

"Why, Huldy Wheeler!" Aunt Hannah's eyes glowed with mild wrath; "'nd he's ben a professor nigh on to thirty year. How can ye talk so? I'm clean overcome."

"Well, I can't help it. There's some things stand to reason, ef they be speritooal things, 'nd one on 'em is that ef a man's born again he's a new cretur. You're paowerful on Bible texts, so I won't sling no catechism at ye this time, but there is suthin somewhere, 'long in some o' the 'Pistles, about 'love, joy, peace, gentleness, goodness, meekness,' 'nd so on, for quite a spell; and if that cap fits Freedom, why I'm free to say I don't see it."

"Well, Huldy, we must make allowances; ye see he's dreadful disapp'inted."

"That's so! you'd better b'lieve *he* don't say the Lord's Prayer, no more 'n Marah; or ef he doos, it goes, 'My will be done:' he hain't learnt how to spell it t' other way." Aunt Hannah sighed; she was getting old now, and Freedom was as dear to her as an only child—wayward and wilful though it be—to a loving mother; but she rested her heart on its life-long comfort, a merciful presence that was her daily strength, and hoped for the best, for some future time, even if she did not live to see it, when this stubborn heart of her boy's should become flesh, and his soul accept a divine Master, with strong and submissive faith.

Poor Aunt Hannah! she had shed countless tears and uttered countless prayers to this end, but as yet in vain. Next year only brought fresh exasperation to Freedom in the birth of a daughter, as cross, noisy, and disagreeable as she was unwelcome. He flung out of the house and went to plowing the ten-acre lot, though the frost was only out of the surface; he broke his share, goaded his oxen till even those patient beasts rebelled, and at last left the plow in the furrow and took a last year's colt out to train. Melinda escaped a great deal through that poor colt, for what he dared not pour on her offending head in the way of reviling, he safely hurled at the wild creature he found so restive in harness; and many a kick and blow taught the brute how superior a being man is, particularly when he is out of temper!

"Keep that brat out o' my sight, Aunt Hanner," was his first greeting to the child. "Don't fetch it 'round here: it's nothin' but a noosance."

Aunt Hannah retreated in dismay, but she dared not tell Melinda, whose passion for fine-sounding names was mightily gratified at the opportunity to select a girl's appellation; before she issued from her sick room she made up her mind to call this child Chimera Una Vilda.

Dear reader, give me no credit for imagination here! These are actual names, registered on church records and tombstones; with sundry others of the like sort, such as Secretia, Luelle, Lorilla Allaroila, Lue, Plumy, Antha, Loruhama, Lophelia, Bethursda, and a host more. But it mattered little to Freedom; the child might have any name or no name as far as he cared; it was a naughty baby, and rent the air with cries of temper in a manner that was truly hereditary.

"I never see such a piece in all my days," sighed Aunt Hannah, whose belief in total depravity became an active principle under this dispensation. "I declare for 't, Huldy, you can hear her scream way over here."

"Well, I b'lieve you, Hanner: the winders is wide open, and we ain't but jest acrost the road. I guess you could hear her a good mile; an' she keeps it up the hull endurin' time. Makes me think o' them cherubims the Rev'lations tells about, that continooally do cry; only she ain't cryin' for praise."

"I expect she'd cry for suthin besides crossness ef she knew how her pa feels about her; it's awful, Huldy, it is awful to see him look at the child once in a while."

"She knows it in her bones, I tell ye. Talk about 'riginal sin! I guess she won't want no sin more 'riginal than what's come down pootty straight from him. She's jest another of 'em, now I tell ye."

But Melinda was equal to the situation: whether she picked up the last maple twig Marah brought in from driving the cows, or pulled the stiff wooden busk from her maternal bosom, or "ketched off her shoe," or even descended upon that chubby form with her own hard hand and pungently "reversed the magnetic currents," as they say in Boston, those currents were reversed so often it might have been matter of doubt which way they originally ran after a year or two! But the old Adam was strong, and when Chimera—no chimera to them, but a dreadful reality—was sent over to stay a while at the red house, the aunts were at their wits' ends, and Lovey both tired and tormented.

This time—for Chimera's visit to the aunts was occasioned by the immediate prospect of another baby—Aunt Hannah was not able to take care of Melindy: the dear old woman was getting old; a "shock-anum palsy," as Aunt Hulda called a slight paralytic stroke, had given her warning; her head shook perpetually, and her hands trembled; she could still do a little work about the house, but her whole failing body was weary with the perpetual motion, and she knew life was near its end for her. So they sent to Dorset Center for the village nurse, a fat, good-natural creature, and one morning, early, a boy—a rosy, sturdy, big boy—appeared on the stage.

Now Freedom exulted; he strode over to the red house to tell the news. "Fact, Aunt Hanner! I've got him now; a real stunner, too. You won't see no tricks played now, I tell ye! By jingo! I'm goin' off for Parson Pitcher quicker 'n lightnin'. I'll bet ye, Melindy won't git ahead o' me this time; that leetle feller'll be Freedom Wheeler in two hours' time, sure's ye live."

"Providence permitting," put in Aunt Hannah softly, as if to avert the omen of this loud and presumptuous rejoicing; but soft as the prayer was, Freedom heard it, and as he opened the door turned on his heel and answered, "Whether or no, this time."

Aunt Hannah lay back in her chair, utterly shocked; this was rank blasphemy in her ears; she did not remember the illustrative story Aunt Huldah told Freedom on a time long past about a certain old woman's intention to go to Hartford, or she might perhaps have been less horrified. Still, it was bad enough, for if the words were lightly spoken the spirit within the man accorded fully with his tone, and never was keener triumph rampant in any conqueror's heart than in this rough, self-willed farmer's as he drove his horse, full tilt, down the long hills and up the sharp ascents that lay between him and the parsonage. But Parson Pitcher had been called up higher than Freedom Wheeler's. That very morning he had fallen asleep in his bed, weak and wasted with a long influenza, and being almost ninety years old the sleep of weakness had slipped quietly into the deeper calm of death.

He had for a year past been obliged to have a colleague, so Freedom hunted the young man up at his boarding place, and took him instead; a little aggrieved, indeed, for long custom made Parson Pitcher seem the only valid authority for religious observances of this kind, and years after he ceased to preach the little children were always brought to him for baptism.

"But I s'pose one on 'em's reely as good as t' other for this puppus," hilariously remarked Freedom to the old lady who lodged the colleague, receiving a grim stare of disapproval for his answer, as he deserved. However, there was one advantage in having Mr. Brooks instead of the parson. Freedom was but slightly acquainted with the new-comer, so he poured out all his troubles, his losses, and his present rejoicing all the way home with a frankness and fluency strange enough; for New Englanders as a race are reticent both of their affairs and their feelings, and Freedom Wheeler was more so by nature than by race. This exultation seemed to have fused his whole character for the time into glowing, outpouring fervor; a deep and ardent excitement fired his eye and loosed his tongue, and Mr. Brooks, who had a tinge of the metaphysical and inquisitive about him, was mightily interested in the man; and being, as he phrased it, a "student of character," which is, being interpreted, an impertinent soul who makes puppets of his fellows to see how their wires work and discover the thoughts of their hearts for his own theories and speculations, he gently drew out this intoxicated man, "drunken, but not with wine," as he was, with judicious suggestions and inquiries, till he knew him to the core; a knowledge of use to neither party, and to the young clergyman only another apple off the tree from which Eve plucked sin and misery, and a sour one at that.

Once more the old china punch-bowl that had been a relic in the Wheeler family beyond their record, and would have crazed a china fancier with the lust of the eye, was filled from the spring and set on the claw-footed round table in the parlor, the door left open into Melinda's room so she could see all the ceremony, the aunts and nurses assembled in solemn array (all the children being sent over to Lovey's care, at the red house), and with due propriety the new baby, squirming and kicking with great vigor in his father's arms, was baptized Freedom Wheeler.

Why is it that "the curse of a granted prayer" comes sometimes immediately? Why do we pant and thirst, and find the draught poisonous? or after long exile come home, only to find home gone? alas! these are the conditions of humanity: the questions we all ask, the thwarting and despair we all endure; and also the mystery and incompleteness which tell us in hourly admonition that this life is a fragment and a beginning, and that its ends are not peace and rapture, but discipline and education. Freedom Wheeler was no apt pupil, but his sharpest lesson came to-day.

Full of exultation over fate, Melinda, and the aunts, chuckling to himself with savage satisfaction at the conscious feeling that it was no use for anybody—even the indefinite influence he dared not call God—to try to get the better of him, he strode across the room to give his boy back to Melinda, stumbled over a little stool that intruded from below the sofa, fell full length on the floor, with the child under him, and when he rose to his feet, dazed with the jar of the fall, it was but just in time to see those baby eyelids quiver once and close forever: the child was dead!

Melinda rose up in the bed with a dreadful face; shriek on shriek burst from her lips. The women crowded about Freedom and took the limp little body from his arms; he leaned against the door-way like a man in a dream; the torrents of reproach and agony that burst from Melinda's lips seemed not to enter his ears: "Now you've done it! you've killed him! you have! you have!" But why repeat the wild and bitter words of a mother bereft of her child in the first hours of its fresh, strong life? Melinda was not a cruel or ungenerous woman naturally, but now she was weak and nervous, and the shock was too much for her brain.

In this sudden stress Mr. Brooks forgot his metaphysics and fell back on the old formulas, which after all do seem to wear better than metaphysics in any real woe or want; he drew near to Freedom and put his hand on the wretched man's shoulder. "My brother," said he, gently, "this evil is from the hand of the Lord; bear it like a Christian."

"He ain't no Christian!" shouted Melinda, with accents of concentrated bitterness. "Christians ain't that sort, growlin' and scoldin' and fightin' with the Lord that made him, cos he couldn't hev his own way, and uplifted skyhigh when he got it; 'nd now look to where 't is! The hypocrite's hope is cut off, cut off! Oh, my baby! my baby! my baby!" Here she fell into piteous wailing and fainting, and Mr. Brooks led the passive, stricken man away, while Aunt Huldah dispatched Reuben Stark for the doctor, and Aunt Hannah and the nurse tried to calm and restore Melinda.

But it was idle to try to draw Freedom from his silent gloom; he would neither speak nor hear, apparently, and Mr. Brooks, seeing Reuben hitching the horse to the wagon, took his hat to leave. Aunt Huldah followed him to the door for politeness.

"Send for me when you are ready for the funeral, Miss Huldah," said he, in taking leave. "I feel deeply for you ali, especially for brother Wheeler; the Lord seems to have a controversy with him indeed."

"That's so," curtly replied Aunt Huldah; "an' I don't see but what he's kep' up his end on 't pootty well; but I guess he's got to let go. This makes three on 'em, and it's an old sayin', three times an' out."

A suddenly subdued smile curled the corners of Mr. Brooks's mouth for a second; poor man, he had a keen sense of the ludicrous and was minister in a country parish!

"Good day," nodded Aunt Huldah, quite unaware that she had said anything peculiar, and then she returned to Freedom; but he had gone out of the kitchen, nor did any one know where he was, till the horn called to supper, when he came in, swallowed a cup of tea, and went speechless to bed, not even asking about Melinda, whom the doctor found in the first stage of fever, and pronounced "dangerous."

But Melinda was strong and could bear a great deal yet; she was comparatively a young woman, and after a month's severe illness she began to improve daily, and in another month was like her old self again; perhaps a trifle less cheery, but still busy,

vivacious, and unsparing of herself or others. But Freedom was a changed man; the scornful and bitter words Melinda had uttered in her frantic passion burnt deep into his soul, though he gave no sign even of hearing them.

Kingsley speaks of "the still, deep-hearted Northern, whose pride breaks slowly and silently, but breaks once for all; who tells to God what he never will tell to man, and having told it is a new creature from that day forth forever;" and something after this fashion was Freedom Wheeler shaped. He had been brought up in the strictest Calvanism, had his "experience" in due form, and then united with the church; but Parson Pitcher never preached to anybody but unconverted sinners: hell fire drove him on to save from the consequences of sin; its conditions people who were once converted must look out for themselves; and Freedom's strong will, sullen temper, and undisciplined character grew up like the thorns in the parable and choked the struggling blades of grain that never reached an ear. Melinda's accusations were the first sermon that ever awoke his consciousness; he had always prided himself on his honesty, and here he saw that he had been an utter hypocrite.

With all his faults he had a simple faith in the truths of the Bible and a conscientious respect for ordinances, and now there fell upon him a deep conviction of heinous sin, a gloom, a despair that amounted almost to insanity; but he asked no counsel, he implored no divine aid; with the peculiar sophistry of religious melancholy he considered that his prayers would be an abomination to the Lord. So he kept silence, pouring more and more over his Bible, appropriating its dreadful texts all to himself, and turning his eyes away from every gracious and tender promise, as one unworthy to read them.

He worked more faithfully than ever; worked from day's first dawn into the edge of darkness, as if the suffering of a worn-out body had a certain counter-irritation for the tortured mind. There are many rods of stone-wall on that old farm to-day, laid up of such great stones, made so wide and strong and close, that the passer-by looks at it with wonder, little knowing that the dreadful struggles of a wandering and thwarted soul mark the layers of massive granite and record the exhaustion of flesh mastered by strong and strenuous spirit.

When Melinda was herself again, it was yet some time before she noticed the change in Freedom; there was a certain simple selfishness about her that made her own grief hide every other, and impelled her to try with all her might to forget her trouble, to get rid of the sharp memory that irked her soul like a rankling thorn. She hid all her baby clothes away in the garret, she sent the cradle out to the shed loft, and never opened her lips about that lost boy, whose name Aunt Huldah had recorded in the same record with the two who had preceded him, and whose little body lay under the mulleins and goldenrods, beside the others at Lowly's feet.

But as time wore on Melinda began to see that some change had passed over her husband. She had quite forgotten her own mad words, spoken in the first delirium of her anguish, and followed by the severe fever that had almost swept away life as well as memory; no remorse therefore softened her heart, but it was not needed. Though Melinda was an incisive, stirring, resolute woman, with her warm temper she had also a warm heart; she could not live in the house with a dog or a cat without feeling a certain kindly affection for the creature. Her step-children never suffered at her hands, but shared in all the care she gave her own, and loved her as well as shy, careless children of a healthy sort love anybody. She loved her husband truly. Her quick, stormy ways meant no more than the scolding of a wren; in her heart she held Freedom dear and honored, only he did not know it.

But she began now, in her anxiety about his sad and gloomy ways, to soften her manner toward him daily: she remembered the things he liked to eat and prepared them for the table; she made him a set of new shirts, and set the stitches in them with scrupulous neatness; she kept the house in trim and pleasant order, and sat up at night to mend his working-clothes, so that they were always whole,—homely services and demonstrations, no doubt, but having as much fitness to place and person as the scenic passion of a novel in high life, or a moral drama where the repentant wife throws herself into a stern husband's arms, and with flying tresses and flowing tears vows never to vex or misunderstand his noble soul again.

Freedom's conscious controversy with his Maker still went on within him, and raged between doubt and despair; but he was human, and the gentle ray of affection that stole from Melinda's "little candle" did its work in his "naughty world." He felt a certain comfort pervading home when he came in at night, sad and weary: the children's faces were clean, the hearth washed, the fire bright; warmth and peace brooded over the old kitchen, crackled softly from the back-log, purred in the cat, sang from the kettle-nose; Melinda's shining hair was smooth, her look quiet and wistful; the table was neatly spread,— little things, surely, but life is made up of them, and hope and happiness and success.

The dark cloud in this man's soul began to lift imperceptibly; and he was called out of himself presently to stand by Aunt Hannah's bed and see her die. A second shock of paralysis suddenly prostrated her, and she was laid on the pillows speechless and senseless; twenty-four hours of anxiety and tears passed, and then she seemed to revive; she stirred her hand, her face relaxed, her eyes opened, but the exhaustion was great and she was unable to speak. Conscious and patient she endured through a few days more, and then the final message came: another paralysis, a longer silence, and those grouped about her bed in the old red house, thinking every moment to see the shadow of death fall over those beloved features, beheld with surprise the soft brown eyes open and fix upon Freedom such a look of longing, tender, piteous affection as might have broken the heart of a stone; a long, long gaze, a very passion of love, pity, and yearning, and then those eyes turned heavenward, grew glorious with light and peace, and closed slowly, —closed forever.

Freedom went out and wept bitterly: he had denied his Lord, too, and it was a look that smote him to the heart, as that divine glance did Peter. But no man knew or saw it. Hidden in the barn, a dim and fragrant oratory that had seen more than one struggle of soul in the past and unknown records of New England, Freedom "gave up," and gave up finally.

He was no longer a young man, and he was not the stuff that saints are made of, but he had a stern honesty, an inward uprightness that held him to his new resolve like hooks of steel. If his temper softened a little, his obstinacy yielded here and there, his manner gave out now and then some scanty spark of affection and consideration, these were the outward signs of a mighty change within; for an old and weather-beaten tree does not bloom in its spring resurrection with the flowers and promise of a young and vigorous growth; it is much if the gnarled boughs put out their scanty share of verdure, if there is a blossom on a few branches, and shelter enough for a small bird's-nest from sun or rain. Lovey, grown by this time a tall and helpful girl, with her mother's delicate sweetness in face and figure, was first perhaps to feel this vital change in her father. Aunt Hannah's death was a woeful loss to her tender, clinging nature, and she turned to him with the instinct of a child, and found a shy and silent sympathy from him that was strangely dear and sweet and bound them together as never before. Aunt Huldah, too, noticed it. "Dear me!" said she to herself, as she sat alone by the fire, knitting red stockings for Chimera, who had begun to mend her ways a little under the steady birch and shingle discipline. "Dear me, I'm real afraid Freedom ain't long for this world. He is kinder mellerin', like a stone-apple in June; it's onnateral. I expect he's struck with death, Hanner, don't you? Oh, my land; what a old fool I be! Hanner's gone, 'nd here I be a-talkin' to her jest as though"—Aunt Huldah wiped her dimmed eyes with a red silk handkerchief, and rubbed her misty glasses before she went on, still leaving the sentence unfinished: "Mabbe it's a triumph o' grace; I s'pose grace can get the better o' Freedom: seems kinder doubtful, I must confess; but I don't see nothin' else that could fetch him, and he is a growin' soft, sure as ye live."

But Melinda, less sensitive or perceptive, perceived only that her efforts had "kinder sorter slicked him down," as she said.

It was reserved for the birth of another child to demonstrate how Freedom had laid down his arms and gone over to the king at last. Yes, two years after Aunt Hannah's death another fine and hearty boy entered the family, but not this time with such acclaim and welcome as the last. Melinda, weak. and happy, grew gentler than ever before, between present bliss and future fear, and Freedom, hiding his face in his hard brown hands, thanked God with shame and trembling for this undeserved mercy; and even while he shuddered, naturally enough, at the possibilities the past recalled, he could say humbly and fervently, "Thy will be done."

Nobody spoke of sending for the minister now, nor was even a name for baby suggested till two months after, when Melinda said to Freedom one night when the children were all in bed, and they sat alone by the fire waiting for the last brand to fall in two before it could be raked up, "Next Sunday but one is sacrament Sunday, Freedom. It's good weather now; hadn't the little feller better be presented fur baptism?"

"I guess so," answered he.

"What do ye calkerlate to call him?" asked Melinda, shyly, after a pause.

"Thet's for you to say, Melinda; I wish ye to do jest as ye're a mind to," he said, gently, with a stifled sigh.

"That's easy settled then," she replied, a pretty smile about her red lips, and laying her hand on her husband's knee; "I don't want to call him nothin' more nor less than Freedom."

He put his hand on hers for a moment, looked the other way, and then got up and went out silently.

So one bright June day baby was taken to the meeting-house and received his name, and was duly recorded in the family Bible, but with no ominous monosyllable added to his birth-date; and Aunt Huldah, as she went out of church, said to Mr. Brooks, by no means inaudibly, "I guess Freedom's gin up his controversy finally; he did keep up his end on 't quite a spell, but he's gin up for good now, I expect."

"Yes," answered the young parson, with a smile of mingled feeling and reverence. "The Lord was in the still small voice."

XIII

REBECCA HARDING DAVIS (1831–1910)

Lowell's taste for the original and the autochthonous led him to admit into one of the earliest numbers of *The Atlantic Monthly* (April, 1861) a piece of realism that would be noteworthy even if found new in one of the current magazines. With Rebecca Harding's "Life in the Iron Mills," realism, Russian-like, Zola-like in its remorseless depicting of unpleasant details, entered American fiction. Undoubtedly she had been influenced by the grim propaganda novels, *Alton Locke* and *Clara Barton,* and by *Uncle Tom's Cabin* with its puritanical, humanitarian *motif,* but nevertheless the story is to be rated as a new and original thing in American fiction, an important document in the history of the development of the short-story form. The impressionism that Harte a decade later was to use in his backgrounds and characterizations is here to be found, for the first time in American literature, distinctively used. Her delineations of the iron mills seen through the Pittsburgh smoke are like the hell-fire dabblings of Gustav Doré, and always the characters in the foreground are in keeping. No such grim ending, either, had ever before been given an American short story. The American Victorians had demanded the final triumph of right and justice with virtue rewarded after struggle, and marriage bells as the happy finale, but there was no yielding here to Victorian prejudice and squeamishness. The paragraphs recording the death of the central figure in the story might have been written by Gogol.

Miss Harding, afterwards Rebecca Harding Davis, mother of Richard Harding Davis, wrote nothing in later years comparable in strength and influence with this early effort of her pen.

LIFE IN THE IRON MILLS

"Is this the end?
O Life, as futile, then, as frail!
What hope of answer or redress?"

A cloudy day: do you know what that is in a town of iron-works? The sky sank down before dawn, muddy, flat, immovable. The air is thick, clammy with the breath of crowded human beings. It stifles me. I open the window, and, looking out, can scarcely see through the rain the grocer's shop opposite, where a crowd of drunken Irishmen are puffing Lynchburg tobacco in their pipes. I can detect the scent through all the foul smells ranging loose in the air.

The idiosyncrasy of this town is smoke. It rolls sullenly in slow folds from the great chimneys of the iron-foundries, and settles down in black, slimy pools on the muddy streets. Smoke on the wharves, smoke on the dingy boats, on the yellow river,—clinging in a coating of greasy soot to the house-front, the two faded poplars, the faces of the passers-by. The long train of mules, dragging masses of pig-iron through the narrow street, have a foul vapor hanging to their reeking sides. Here, inside, is a little broken figure of an angel pointing upward from the mantel-shelf; but even its wings are covered with smoke, clotted and black. Smoke everywhere! A dirty canary chirps desolately in a cage beside me. Its dream of green fields and sunshine is a very old dream,—almost worn out, I think.

From the back-window I can see a narrow brick-yard sloping down to the riverside, strewed with rain-butts and tubs. The river, dull and tawny-colored, (*la belle rivière!*) drags itself sluggishly along, tired of the heavy weight of boats and coal-barges. What wonder? When I was a child, I used to fancy a look of weary, dumb appeal upon the face of the negro-like river slavishly bearing its burden day after day. Something of the same idle notion comes to me to-day, when from the street-window I look on the slow stream of human life creeping past, night and morning, to the great mills. Masses of men, with dull, besotted faces bent to the ground, sharpened here and there by pain or cunning; skin and muscle and flesh begrimed with smoke and ashes; stooping all

158

night over boiling caldrons of metal, laired by day in dens of drunkenness and infamy; breathing from infancy to death an air saturated with fog and grease and soot, vileness for soul and body. What do you make of a case like that, amateur psychologist? You call it an altogether serious thing to be alive: to these men it is a drunken jest, a joke,—horrible to angels perhaps, to them commonplace enough. My fancy about the river was an idle one: it is no type of such a life. What if it be stagnant and slimy here? It knows that beyond there waits for it odorous sunlight— quaint old gardens, dusky with soft green foliage of apple-trees, and flushing crimson with roses,—air, and fields, and mountains. The future of the Welsh puddler, passing just now is not so pleasant. To be stowed away, after his grimy work is done, in a hole in the muddy graveyard, and after that,——*not* air, nor green fields, nor curious roses.

Can you see how foggy the day is? As I stand here, idly tapping the window-pane, and looking out through the rain at the dirty back-yard and the coal-boats below, fragments of an old story float up before me,—a story of this old house into which I happened to come to-day. You may think it a tiresome story enough, as foggy as the day, sharpened by no sudden flashes of pain or pleasure.—I know: only the outline of a dull life, that long since, with thousands of dull lives like its own, was vainly lived and lost: thousands of them,— massed, vile, slimy lives, like those of the torpid lizards in yonder stagnant water-butt.—Lost? There is a curious point for you to settle, my friend, who study psychology in a lazy, *dilettante* way. Stop a moment. I am going to be honest. This is what I want you to do. I want you to hide your disgust, take no heed to your clean clothes, and come right down with me,— here, into the thickest of the fog and mud and foul effluvia. I want you to hear this story. There is a secret down here, in this nightmare fog, that has lain dumb for centuries: I want to make it a real thing to you. You, Egoist, or Pantheist, or Arminian, busy in making straight paths for your feet on the hills, do not see it clearly,—this terrible question which men here have gone mad and died trying to answer. I dare not put this secret into words. I told you it was dumb. These men, going by with drunken faces and brains full of unawak-

ened power, do not ask it of Society or of God. Their lives ask it; their deaths ask it. There is no reply. I will tell you plainly that I have a great hope; and I bring it you to be tested. It is thus; that this terrible dumb question is its own reply; that it is not the sentence of death we think it, but, from the very extremity of its darkness, the most solemn prophecy which the world has known of the Hope to come. I dare make my meaning no clearer, but will only tell my story. It will, perhaps, seem to you as foul and dark as this thick vapor about us, and as pregnant with death; but if your eyes are free as mine are to look deeper, no perfume-tinted dawn will be so fair with promise of the day that shall surely come.

My story is very simple,—only what I remember of the life of one of these men, —a furnace-tender in one of Kirby & John's rolling-mills,—Hugh Wolfe. You know the mills? They took the great order for the Lower Virginia railroads there last winter; run usually with about a thousand men. I cannot tell why I choose the half-forgotten story of this Wolfe more than that of myriads of these furnace-hands. Perhaps because there is a secret underlying sympathy between that story and this day with its impure fog and thwarted sunshine,—or perhaps simply for the reason that this house is the one where the Wolfes lived. There were the father and son,— both hands, as I said, in one of Kirby & John's mills for making railroad-iron,— and Deborah, their cousin, a picker in some of the cotton-mills. The house was rented then to half a dozen families. The Wolfes had two of the cellar-rooms. The old man, like many of the puddlers and feeders of the mills, was Welsh,—had spent half of his life in the Cornish tin-mines. You may pick the Welsh emigrants, Cornish miners, out of the throng passing the windows, any day. They are a trifle more filthy; their muscles are not so brawny; they stoop more. When they are drunk, they neither yell, nor shout, nor stagger, but skulk along like beaten hounds. A pure, unmixed blood, I fancy: shows itself in the slight angular bodies and sharply-cut facial lines. It is nearly thirty years since the Wolfes lived here. Their lives were like those of their class: incessant labor, sleeping in kennel-like rooms, eating rank pork and molasses, drinking—God and the distillers only knew what; with an occasional night in jail, to atone for some drunken excess. Is that all of their lives?—of the portion given to them and these their duplicates swarming the streets to-day?—nothing beneath?—all? So many a political reformer will tell you,—and many a private reformer, too, who has gone among them with a heart tender with Christ's charity, and come out outraged, hardened.

One rainy night, about eleven o'clock, a crowd of half-clothed women stopped outside of the cellar-door. They were going home from the cotton-mill.

"Good-night, Deb," said one, a mulatto, steadying herself against the gas-post. She needed the post to steady her. So did more than one of them.

"Dah's a ball to Miss Potts' to-night. Ye'd best come."

"Inteet, Deb, if hur'll come, hur'll hef fun," said a shrill Welsh voice in the crowd.

Two or three dirty hands were thrust out to catch the gown of the woman, who was groping for the latch of the door.

"No."

"No? Where's Kit Small, then?"

"Begorra! on the spools. Alleys behint, though we helped her, we dud. An wid ye! Let Deb alone! It's ondacent frettin' a quiet body. Be the powers an' we'll have a night of it! there'll be lashin's o' drink,— the Vargent be blessed and praised for 't!"

They went on, the mulatto inclining for a moment to show fight, and drag the woman Wolfe off with them; but, being pacified, she staggered away.

Deborah groped her way into the cellar, and, after considerable stumbling, kindled a match, and lighted a tallow dip, that sent a yellow glimmer over the room. It was low, damp,—the earthen floor covered with a green, slimy moss,—a fetid air smothering the breath. Old Wolfe lay asleep on a heap of straw, wrapped in a torn horse-blanket. He was a pale, meek little man, with a white face and red rabbit-eyes. The woman Deborah was like him; only her face was even more ghastly, her lips bluer, her eyes more watery. She wore a faded cotton gown and a slouching bonnet. When she walked, one could see that she was deformed, almost a hunchback. She trod softly, so as not to waken him, and went through into the room beyond. There she found by the half-extinguished fire an iron saucepan filled with cold boiled potatoes, which she put upon a broken chair with a pint-cup of ale. Placing the old candlestick beside this dainty repast, she untied her bonnet, which hung limp and wet over her face, and prepared to eat her supper. It was the first food that had touched her lips since morning. There was enough of it, however: there is not always. She was hungry,—one could see that easily enough,—and not drunk, as most of her companions would have been found at this hour. She did not drink, this woman,—her face told that, too,—nothing stronger than ale. Perhaps the weak, flaccid wretch had some stimulant in her pale life to keep her up,—some love or hope, it might be, or urgent need. When that stimulant was gone, she would take to whisky. Man cannot live by work alone. While she was skinning the potatoes, and munching them, a noise behind her made her stop.

"Janey!" she called, lifting the candle and peering into the darkness. "Janey, are you there?"

A heap of ragged coats was heaved up, and the face of a young girl emerged, staring sleepily at the woman.

"Deborah," she said, at last, "I'm here the night."

"Yes, child. Hur's welcome," she said, quietly eating on.

The girl's face was haggard and sickly; her eyes were heavy with sleep and hunger: real Milesian eyes they were, dark, delicate blue, glooming out from black shadows with a pitiful fright.

"I was alone," she said, timidly.

"Where's the father?" asked Deborah, holding out a potato, which the girl greedily seized.

"He's beyant,—wid Haley,—in the stone house." (Did you ever hear the word jail from an Irish mouth?) "I came here. Hugh told me never to stay me-lone."

"Hugh?"

"Yes."

A vexed frown crossed her face. The girl saw it, and added quickly,—

"I have not seen Hugh the day, Deb. The old man says his watch lasts till the mornin'."

The woman sprang up, and hastily began to arrange some bread and flitch in a tin pail, and to pour her own measure of ale into a bottle. Tying on her bonnet, she blew out the candle.

"Lay ye down, Janey dear," she said, gently, covering her with the old rags.

"Hur can eat the potatoes, if hur's hungry."

"Where are ye goin', Deb? The rain's sharp."

"To the mill, with Hugh's supper."

"Let him bide till th' morn. Sit ye down."

"No, no,"—sharply pushing her off. "The boy'll starve."

She hurried from the cellar, while the child wearily coiled herself up for sleep. The rain was falling heavily, as the woman, pail in hand, emerged from the mouth of the alley, and turned down the narrow street, that stretched out, long and black, miles before her. Here and there a flicker of gas lighted an uncertain space of muddy footwalk and gutter; the long rows of houses, except an occasional lager-bier shop, were closed; now and then she met a band of mill-hands skulking to or from their work.

Not many even of the inhabitants of a manufacturing town know the vast machinery of system by which the bodies of workmen are governed, that goes on unceasingly from year to year. The hands of each mill are divided into watches that relieve each other as regularly as the sentinels of an army. By night and day the work goes on, the unsleeping engines groan and shriek, the fiery pools of metal boil and surge. Only for a day in the week, in half-courtesy to public censure, the fires are partially veiled; but as soon as the clock strikes midnight, the great furnaces break forth with renewed fury, the clamor begins with fresh, breathless vigor, the engines sob and shriek like "gods in pain."

As Deborah hurried down through the heavy rain, the noise of these thousand engines sounded through the sleep and shadow of the city like far-off thunder. The mill to which she was going lay on the river, a mile below the city-limits. It was far, and she was weak, aching from standing twelve hours at the spools. Yet it was her almost nightly walk to take this man his supper, though at every square she sat down to rest, and she knew she should receive small word of thanks.

Perhaps, if she had possessed an artist's eye, the picturesque oddity of the scene might have made her step stagger less, and the path seem shorter; but to her the mills were only "summat deilish to look at by night."

The road leading to the mills had been quarried from the solid rock, which rose abrupt and bare on one side of the cinder-covered road, while the river, sluggish and black, crept past on the other. The mills for rolling iron are simply immense tent-like roofs, covering acres of ground, open on every side. Beneath these roofs Deborah looked in on a city of fires, that burned hot and fiercely in the night. Fire in every horrible form: pits of flame waving in the wind; liquid metal-flames writhing in tortuous streams through the sand; wide caldrons filled with boiling fire, over which bent ghastly wretches stirring the strange brewing; and through all, crowds of half-clad men, looking like revengeful ghosts in the red light, hurried, throwing masses of glittering fire. It was like a street in Hell. Even Deborah muttered, as she crept through, " 'T looks like t' Devil's place !" It did,—in more ways than one.

She found the man she was looking for, at last, heaping coal on a furnace. He had not time to eat his supper; so she went behind the furnace, and waited. Only a few men were with him, and they noticed her only by a "Hyur comes t' hunchback, Wolfe."

Deborah was stupid with sleep; her back pained her sharply; and her teeth chattered with cold, with the rain that soaked her clothes and dripped from her at every step. She stood, however, patiently holding the pail, and waiting.

"Hout, woman! ye look like a drowned cat. Come near to the fire,"—said one of the men, approaching to scrape away the ashes.

She shook her head. Wolfe had forgotten her. He turned, hearing the man, and came closer.

"I did no' think; gi' me my supper, woman."

She watched him eat with a painful eagerness. With a woman's quick instinct, she saw that he was not hungry,—was eating to please her. Her pale, watery eyes began to gather a strange light.

"Is 't good, Hugh? T' ale was a bit sour, I feared."

"No, good enough." He hesitated a moment. "Ye're tired, poor lass! Bide here till I go. Lay down there on that heap of ash, and go to sleep."

He threw her an old coat for a pillow, and turned to his work. The heap was the refuse of the burnt iron, and was not a hard bed; the half-smothered warmth, too, penetrated her limbs, dulling their pain and cold shiver.

Miserable enough she looked, lying there on the ashes like a limp, dirty rag,—yet not an unfitting figure to crown the scene of hopeless discomfort and veiled crime: more fitting, if one looked deeper into the heart of things,—at her thwarted woman's form, her colorless life, her waking stupor that smothered pain and hunger,—even more fit to be a type of her class. Deeper yet if one could look, was there nothing worth reading in this wet, faded thing, half-covered with ashes? no story of a soul filled with groping passionate love, heroic unselfishness, fierce jealousy? of years of weary trying to please the one human being whom she loved, to gain one look of real heart-kindness from him? If anything like this were hidden beneath the pale, bleared eyes, and dull, washed-out-looking face, no one had ever taken the trouble to read its faint signs: not the half-clothed furnace-tender, Wolfe, certainly. Yet he was kind to her: it was his nature to be kind, even to the very rats that swarmed in the cellar: kind to her in just the same way. She knew that. And it might be that very knowledge had given to her face its apathy and vacancy more than her low, torpid life. One sees that dead, vacant look steal sometimes over the rarest, finest of women's faces,—in the very midst, it may be, of their warmest summer's day; and then one can guess at the secret of intolerable solitude that lies hid beneath the delicate laces and brilliant smile. There was no warmth, no brilliancy, no summer for this woman; so the stupor and vacancy had time to gnaw into her face perpetually. She was young, too, though no one guessed it; so the gnawing was the fiercer.

She lay quiet in the dark corner, listening, through the monotonous din and uncertain glare of the works, to the dull plash of the rain in the far distance,— shrinking back whenever the man Wolfe happened to look towards her. She knew, in spite of all his kindness, that there was that in her face and form which made him loathe the sight of her. She felt by instinct, although she could not comprehend it, the finer nature of the man, which made him among his fellow-workmen something unique, set apart. She knew, that, down under all the vileness and coarseness of his life, there was a groping passion for

whatever was beautiful and pure,—that his soul sickened with disgust at her deformity, even when his words were kindest. Through this dull consciousness, which never left her, came, like a sting, the recollection of the dark blue eyes and lithe figure of the little Irish girl she had left in the cellar. The recollection struck through even her stupid intellect with a vivid glow of beauty and of grace. Little Janey, timid, helpless, clinging to Hugh as her only friend: that was the sharp thought, the bitter thought, that drove into the glazed eyes a fierce light of pain. You laugh at it? Are pain and jealousy less savage realities down here in this place I am taking you to than in your own house or your own heart,—your heart, which they clutch at sometimes? The note is the same, I fancy, be the octave high or low.

If you could go into this mill where Deborah lay, and drag out from the hearts of these men the terrible tragedy of their lives, taking it as a symptom of the disease of their class, no ghost Horror would terrify you more. A reality of soul-starvation, of living death, that meets you every day under the besotted faces on the street, —I can paint nothing of this, only give you the outside outlines of a night, a crisis in the life of one man: whatever muddy depth of soul-history lies beneath you can read according to the eyes.God has given you.

Wolfe, while Deborah watched him as a spaniel its master, bent over the furnace with his iron pole, unconscious of her scrutiny, only stopping to receive orders. Physically, Nature had promised the man but little. He had already lost the strength and instinct vigor of a man, his muscles were thin, his nerves weak, his face (a meek, woman's face) haggard, yellow with consumption. In the mill he was known as one of the girl-men: "Molly Wolfe" was his *sobriquet*. He was never seen in the cockpit, did not own a terrier, drank but seldom; when he did, desperately. He fought sometimes, but was always thrashed, pommelled to a jelly. The man was game enough, when his blood was up: but he was no favorite in the mill; he had the taint of school-learning on him,— not to a dangerous extent, only a quarter or so in the free-school in fact, but enough to ruin him as a good hand in a fight.

For other reasons, too, he was not popular. Not one of themselves, they felt that, though outwardly as filthy and ash-covered; silent, with foreign thoughts and longings breaking out through his quietness in innumerable curious ways: this one, for instance. In the neighboring furnace-buildings lay great heaps of the refuse from the ore after the pig-metal is run. *Korl* we call it here: a light, porous substance, of a delicate, waxen, flesh-colored tinge. Out of the blocks of this korl, Wolfe, in his off-hours from the furnace, had a habit of chipping and molding figures,—hideous, fantastic enough, but sometimes strangely beautiful: even the millmen saw that, while they jeered at him. It was a curious fancy in the man, almost a passion. The few hours for rest he spent hewing and hacking with his blunt knife, never speaking, until his watch came again,—working at one figure for months, and, when it was finished, breaking it to pieces, perhaps, in a fit of disappointment. A morbid, gloomy man, untaught, unled, left to feed his soul in grossness and crime, and hard, grinding labor.

I want you to come down and look at this Wolfe, standing there among the lowest of his kind, and see him just as he is, that you may judge him justly when you hear the story of this night. I want you to look back, as he does every day, at his birth in vice, his starved infancy; to remember the heavy years he has groped through as boy and man,—the slow, heavy years of constant, hot work. So long ago he began, that he thinks sometimes he has worked there for ages. There is no hope that it will ever end. Think that God put into this man's soul a fierce thirst for beauty,—to know it, to create it; to be— something, he knows not what,—other than he is. There are moments when a passing cloud, the sun glinting on the purple thistles, a kindly smile, a child's face, will rouse him to a passion of pain,—when his nature starts up with a mad cry of rage against God, man, whoever it is that has forced this vile, slimy life upon him. With all this groping, this mad desire, a great blind intellect stumbling through wrong, a loving poet's heart, the man was by habit only a coarse, vulgar laborer, familiar with sights and words you would blush to name. Be just: when I tell you about this night, see him as he is. Be just,—not like man's law, which seizes on one isolated fact, but like God's judging angel, whose clear, sad eye saw all the countless cankering days of this man's life, all the countless nights, when, sick with starving, his soul fainted in him, before it judged him for this night, the saddest of all.

I called this night the crisis of his life. If it was, it stole on him unawares. These great turning-days of life cast no shadow before, slip by unconsciously. Only a trifle, a little turn of the rudder, and the ship goes to heaven or hell.

Wolfe, while Deborah watched him, dug into the furnace of melting iron with his pole, dully thinking only how many rails the lump would yield. It was late,—nearly Sunday morning; another hour, and the heavy work would be done,—only the furnaces to replenish and cover for the next day. The workmen were growing more noisy, shouting, as they had to do, to be heard over the deep clamor of the mills. Suddenly they grew less boisterous,—at the far end, entirely silent. Something unusual had happened. After a moment, the silence came nearer; the men stopped their jeers and drunken choruses. Deborah, stupidly lifting up her head, saw the cause of the quiet. A group of five or six men were slowly approaching, stopping to examine each furnace as they came. Visitors often came to see the mills after night: except by growing less noisy, the men took no notice of them. The furnace where Wolfe worked was near the bounds of the works; they halted there hot and tired: a walk over one of these great foundries is no trifling task. The woman, drawing out of sight, turned over to sleep. Wolfe, seeing them stop, suddenly roused from his indifferent stupor, and watched them keenly. He knew some of them: the overseer, Clarke,—a son of Kirby, one of the mill-owners,—and a Doctor May, one of the town-physicians. The other two were strangers. Wolfe came closer. He seized eagerly every chance that brought him into contact with this mysterious class that shone down on him perpetually with the glamour of another order of being. What made the difference between them? That was the mystery of his life. He had a vague notion that perhaps to-night he could find it out. One of the strangers sat down on a pile of bricks, and beckoned young Kirby to his side.

"This *is* hot, with a vengeance. A match, please?"—lighting his cigar. "But the walk is worth the trouble. If it were not that you must have heard it so often, Kirby, I would tell you that your works look like Dante's Inferno."

Kirby laughed.

"Yes. Yonder is Farinata himself in the burning tomb,"—pointing to some figure in the shimmering shadows.

"Judging from some of the faces of your men," said the other, "they bid fair to try the reality of Dante's vision, some day."

Young Kirby looked curiously around, as if seeing the faces of his hands for the first time.

"They're bad enough, that's true. A desperate set, I fancy. Eh, Clarke?"

The overseer did not hear him. He was talking of net profits just then,—giving, in fact, a schedule of the annual business of the firm to a sharp peering little Yankee, who jotted down notes on a paper laid on the crown of his hat: a reporter for one of the city-papers, getting up a series of reviews of the leading manufactories. The other gentlemen had accompanied them merely for amusement. They were silent until the notes were finished, drying their feet at the furnaces, and sheltering their faces from the intolerable heat. At last the overseer concluded with—

"I believe that is a pretty fair estimate, Captain."

"Here, some of you men!" said Kirby, "bring up those boards. We may as well sit down, gentlemen, until the rain is over. It cannot last much longer at this rate."

"Pig-metal,"—mumbled the reporter,— "um!—coal facilities,—um!—hands employed, twelve hundred,—bitumen,—um!— all right, I believe, Mr. Clarke;—sinking-fund,—what did you say was your sinking-fund?"

"Twelve hundred hands?" said the stranger, the young man who had first spoken. "Do you control their votes, Kirby?"

"Control? No." The young man smiled complacently. "But my father brought seven hundred votes to the polls for his candidate last November. No force-work, you understand,—only a speech or two, a hint to form themselves into a society, and a bit of red and blue bunting to make them a flag. The Invincible Roughs,—I believe that is their name. I forget the motto: 'Our country's hope,' I think."

There was a laugh. The young man talking to Kirby sat with an amused light in his cool gray eye, surveying critically the half-clothed figures of the puddlers, and the slow swing of their brawny muscles. He was a stranger in the city,—spending a couple of months in the borders of a Slave State, to study the institutions of the South,—a brother-in-law of Kirby's,— Mitchell. He was an amateur gymnast,— hence his anatomical eye; a patron, in a blasé way, of the prize-ring; a man who sucked the essence out of a science or philosophy in an indifferent, gentlemanly way; who took Kant, Novalis, Humboldt, for what they were worth in his own scales; accepting all, despising nothing, in heaven, earth, or hell, but one-ideaed men; with a temper yielding and brilliant as summer water, until his Self was touched, when it was ice, though brilliant still. Such men are not rare in the States.

As he knocked the ashes from his cigar, Wolfe caught with a quick pleasure the contour of the white hand, the blood-glow of a red ring he wore. His voice, too, that of Kirby's, touched him like music,— low, even, with chording cadences. About this man Mitchell hung the impalpable atmosphere belonging to the thorough-bred gentleman. Wolfe, scraping away the ashes beside him, was conscious of it, did obeisance to it with his artist sense, unconscious that he did so.

The rain did not cease. Clarke and the reporter left the mills; the others, comfortably seated near the furnace, lingered, smoking and talking in a desultory way. Greek would not have been more unintelligible to the furnace-tenders whose presence they soon forgot entirely. Kirby drew out a newspaper from his pocket and read aloud some article, which they discussed eagerly. At every sentence, Wolfe listened more and more like a dumb, hopeless animal, with a duller, more stolid look creeping over his face, glancing now and then at Mitchell, marking acutely every smallest sign of refinement, then back to himself, seeing as in a mirror his filthy body, his more stained soul.

Never! He had no words for such a thought, but he knew now, in all the sharpness of the bitter certainty, that between them there was a great gulf never to be passed. Never!

The bell of the mills rang for midnight. Sunday morning had dawned. Whatever hidden message lay in the tolling bells floated past these men unknown. Yet it was there. Veiled in the solemn music ushering the risen Saviour was a key-note to solve the darkest secrets of a world gone wrong,—even this social riddle which the brain of the grimy puddler grappled with madly to-night.

The men began to withdraw the metal from the caldrons. The mills were deserted on Sundays, except by the hands who fed the fires, and those who had no lodgings and slept usually on the ash-heaps. The three strangers sat still during the next hour, watching the men cover the furnaces, laughing now and then at some jest of Kirby's.

"Do you know," said Mitchell, "I like this view of the works better than when the glare was fiercest? These heavy shadows and the amphitheater of smothered fires are ghostly, unreal. One could fancy these red smouldering lights to be the half-shut eyes of wild beasts, and the spectral figures their victims in the den."

Kirby laughed. "You are fanciful. Come, let us get out of the den. The spectral figures, as you call them, are a little too real for me to fancy a close proximity in the darkness,—unarmed, too."

The others rose, buttoning their overcoats, and lighting cigars.

"Raining, still," said Doctor May, "and hard. Where did we leave the coach, Mitchell?"

"At the other side of the works.—Kirby, what's that?"

Mitchell started back, half-frightened, as, suddenly turning a corner, the white figure of a woman faced him in the darkness,—a woman, white, of giant proportions, crouching on the ground, her arms flung out in some wild gesture of warning.

"Stop! Make that fire burn there!" cried Kirby, stopping short.

The flame burst out, flashing the gaunt figure into bold relief.

Mitchell drew a long breath.

"I thought it was alive," he said, going up curiously.

The others followed.

"Not marble, eh?" asked Kirby, touching it.

One of the lower overseers stopped.

"Korl, Sir."

"Who did it?"

"Can't say. Some of the hands; chipped it out in off-hours."

"Chipped to some purpose, I should say. What a flesh-tint the stuff has! Do you see, Mitchell?"

"I see."

He had stepped aside where the light fell boldest on the figure, looking at it in silence. There was not one line of beauty or grace in it: a nude woman's form, muscular, grown coarse with labor, the powerful limbs instinct with some one poignant longing. One idea: there it was in the tense, rigid muscles, the clutching hands, the wild, eager face, like that of a starving wolf's. Kirby and Doctor May walked around it, critical, curious. Mitchell stood aloof, silent. The figure touched him strangely.

"Not badly done," said Doctor May. "Where did the fellow learn that sweep of the muscles in the arm and hand? Look at them! They are groping,—do you see? —clutching: the peculiar action of a man dying of thirst."

"They have ample facilities for studying anatomy," sneered Kirby, glancing at the half-naked figures.

"Look," continued the Doctor, "at this bony wrist, and the strained sinews of the instep! A working-woman,—the very type of her class."

"God forbid!" muttered Mitchell.

"Why?" demanded May. "What does the fellow intend by the figure? I cannot catch the meaning."

"Ask him," said the other, dryly. "There he stands,"—pointing to Wolfe, who stood with a group of men, leaning on his ash-rake.

The Doctor beckoned him with the affable smile which kind-hearted men put on, when talking to these people.

"Mr. Mitchell has picked you out as the man who did this,—I'm sure I don't know why. But what did you mean by it?"

"She be hungry."

Wolfe's eyes answered Mitchell, not the Doctor.

"Oh-h! But what a mistake you have made, my fine fellow! You have given no sign of starvation to the body. It is strong, —terribly strong. It has the mad, half-despairing gesture of drowning."

Wolfe stammered, glanced appealingly at Mitchell, who saw the soul of the thing, he knew. But the cool, probing eyes were turned on himself now,—mocking, cruel, relentless.

"Not hungry for meat," the furnace-tender said at last.

"What then? Whisky?" jeered Kirby, with a coarse laugh.

Wolfe was silent a moment, thinking.

"I dunno," he said, with a bewildered look. "It mebbe. Summat to make her live, I think,—like you. Whisky ull do it, in a way."

The young man laughed again. Mitchell flashed a look of disgust somewhere,—not at Wolfe.

"May," he broke out impatiently, "are you blind? Look at that woman's face! It asks questions of God, and says, 'I have a right to know.' Good God, how hungry it is!"

They looked a moment; then May turned to the mill-owner:—

"Have you many such hands as this? What are you going to do with them? Keep them at puddling iron?"

Kirby shrugged his shoulders. Mitchell's look had irritated him.

"*Ce n'est pas mon affaire.* I have no fancy for nursing infant geniuses. I suppose there are some stray gleams of mind and soul among these wretches. The Lord will take care of his own; or else they can work out their own salvation. I have heard you call our American system a ladder which any man can scale. Do you doubt it? Or perhaps you want to banish all social ladders, and put us all on a flat table-land, —eh, May?"

The Doctor looked vexed, puzzled. Some terrible problem lay hid in this woman's face, and troubled these men. Kirby waited for an answer, and, receiving none, went on, warming with his subject.

"I tell you, there's something wrong that no talk of '*Liberté*' or '*Egalité*' will do away. If I had the making of men, these men who do the lowest part of the world's work should be machines,—nothing more, —hands. It would be kindness. God help them! What are taste, reason, to creatures who must live such lives as that?" He pointed to Deborah, sleeping on the ash-heap. "So many nerves to sting them to pain. What if God had put your brain, with all its agony of touch, into your fingers, and bid you work and strike with that?"

"You think you could govern the world better?" laughed the Doctor.

"I do not think at all."

"That is true philosophy. Drift with the stream, because you cannot dive deep enough to find bottom, eh?"

"Exactly," rejoined Kirby. "I do not think. I wash my hands of all social problems,—slavery, caste, white or black. My duty to my operatives has a narrow limit, the pay-hour on Saturday night. Outside of that, if they cut korl, or cut each other's throats, (the more popular amusement of the two,) I am not responsible."

The Doctor sighed,—a good honest sigh, from the depths of his stomach.

"God help us! Who is responsible?"

"Not I, I tell you," said Kirby, testily. "What has the man who pays them money to do with their souls' concerns, more than the grocer or butcher who takes it?"

"And yet," said Mitchell's cynical voice, "look at her! How hungry she is!"

Kirby tapped his boot with his cane. No one spoke. Only the dumb face of the rough image looking into their faces with the awful question, "What shall we do to be saved?" Only Wolfe's face, with its heavy weight of brain, its weak, uncertain mouth, its desperate eyes, out of which looked the soul of his class,—only Wolfe's face turned towards Kirby's. Mitchell laughed,—a cool, musical laugh.

"Money has spoken!" he said, seating himself lightly on a stone with the air of an amused spectator at a play. "Are you answered?"—turning to Wolfe his clear, magnetic face.

Bright and deep and cold as Arctic air, the soul of the man lay tranquil beneath. He looked at the furnace-tender as he had looked at a rare mosaic in the morning; only the man was the more amusing study of the two.

"Are you answered? Why, May, look at him! '*De profundis clamavi.*' Or, to quote in English, 'Hungry and thirsty, his soul faints in him.' And so Money sends back its answer into the depths through you, Kirby! Very clear the answer, too!—I think I remember reading the same words somewhere:—washing your hands in Eau de Cologne, and saying, 'I am innocent of the blood of this man. See yet to it!'"

Kirby flushed angrily.

"You quote Scripture freely."

"Do I not quote correctly? I think I remember another line, which may amend my meaning: 'Inasmuch as ye did it unto one of the least of these, ye did it unto me.' Deist? Bless you, man, I was raised on the milk of the Word. Now, Doctor, the pocket of the world having uttered its voice, what has the heart to say? You are a philanthropist, in a small way,—*n'est ce pas?* Here, boy, this gentleman can show you how to cut korl better,—or your destiny. Go on, May!"

"I think a mocking devil possesses you to-night," rejoined the Doctor, seriously.

He went to Wolfe and put his hand kindly on his arm. Something of a vague idea possessed the Doctor's brain that much good was to be done here by a friendly word or two: a latent genius to be warmed into life by a waited-for sunbeam. Here it was: he had brought it. So he went on complacently:—

"Do you know, boy, you have it in you to be a great sculptor, a great man?—do you understand?" (talking down to the capacity of his hearer: it is a way people have with children, and men like Wolfe,) —"to live a better, stronger life than I, or Mr. Kirby here? A man may make himself anything he chooses. God has given you stronger powers than many men,—me, for instance."

May stopped, heated, glowing with his own magnanimity. And it was magnanimous. The puddler had drunk in every word, looking through the Doctor's flurry, and generous heat, and self-approval, into his will, with those slow, absorbing eyes of his.

"Make yourself what you will. It is your right."

"I know," quietly. "Will you help me?"

Mitchell laughed again. The Doctor turned now, in a passion,—

"You know, Mitchell, I have not the means. You know, if I had, it is in my heart to take this boy and educate him for"——

"The glory of God, and the glory of John May."

May did not speak for a moment; then, controlled, he said,—

"Why should one be raised, when myriads are left?—I have not the money, boy," to Wolfe, shortly.

"Money?" He said it over slowly, as one repeats the guessed answer to a riddle, doubtfully. "That is it? Money?"

"Yes, money,—that is it," said Mitchell, rising and drawing his furred coat about him. "You've found the cure for all the world's diseases.—Come, May, find your good-humor, and come home. This damp wind chills my very bones. Come and preach your Saint-Simonian doctrines to-morrow to Kirby's hands. Let them have a clear idea of the rights of the soul, and I'll venture next week they'll

strike for higher wages. That will be the end of it."

"Will you send the coach-driver to this side of the mills?" asked Kirby, turning to Wolfe.

He spoke kindly: it was his habit to do so. Deborah, seeing the puddler go, crept after him. The three men waited outside. Doctor May walked up and down, chafed. Suddenly he stopped.

"Go back, Mitchell! You say the pocket and the heart of the world speak without meaning to these people. What has its head to say? Taste, culture, refinement? Go!"

Mitchell was leaning against a brick wall. He turned his head indolently, and looked into the mills. There hung about the place a thick, unclean odor. The slightest motion of his hand marked that he perceived it, and his insufferable disgust. That was all. May said nothing, only quickened his angry tramp.

"Besides," added Mitchell, giving a corollary to this answer, "it would be of no use. I am not one of them."

"You do not mean"—— said May, facing him.

"Yes, I mean just that. Reform is born of need, not pity. No vital movement of the people's has worked down, for good or evil; fermented, instead, carried up the heaving, cloggy mass. Think back through history, and you will know it. What will this lowest deep,—thieves, Magdalens, negroes—do with the light filtered through ponderous Church creeds, Baconian theories, Goethe schemes? Some day, out of their bitter need will be thrown up their own light-bringer,—their Jean Paul, their Cromwell, their Messiah."

"Bah!" was the Doctor's inward criticism. However, in practice, he adopted the theory; for, when, night and morning, afterwards, he prayed that power might be given these degraded souls to rise, he glowed at heart, recognizing an accomplished duty.

Wolfe and the woman had stood in the shadow of the works as the coach drove off. The Doctor had held out his hand in a frank, generous way, telling him to "take care of himself, and to remember it was his right to rise." Mitchell had simply touched his hat, as to an equal, with a quiet look of thorough recognition. Kirby had thrown Deborah some money, which she found, and clutched eagerly enough. They were gone now, all of them. The man sat down on the cinder-road, looking up into the murky sky.

"'T be late, Hugh. Wunnot hur come?"

He shook his head doggedly, and the woman crouched out of his sight against the wall. Do you remember rare moments when a sudden light flashed over yourself, your world, God? when you stood on a mountain-peak, seeing your life as it might have been, as it is? one quick instant, when custom lost its force and every-day usage? when your friend, wife, brother, stood in a new light? your soul was bared, and the grave,—a foretaste of the nakedness of the Judgment-Day? So it came before him, his life, that night. The slow tides of pain he had borne gathered themselves up and surged against his soul. His squalid daily life, the brutal coarseness eating into his brain, as the ashes into his skin: before, these things had been a dull aching into his consciousness; to-night, they were reality. He gripped the filthy red shirt that clung, stiff with soot, about him, and tore it savagely from his arm. The flesh beneath was muddy with grease and ashes,—and the heart beneath that! And the soul? God knows.

Then flashed before his vivid poetic sense the man who had left him,—the pure face, the delicate, sinewy limbs, in harmony with all he knew of beauty or truth. In his cloudy fancy he had pictured a Something like this. He had found it in this Mitchell, even when he idly scoffed at his pain: a Man all-knowing, all-seeing, crowned by Nature, reigning,—the keen glance of his eye falling like a scepter on other men. And yet his instinct taught him that he too—— He! He looked at himself with sudden loathing, sick, wrung his hands with a cry, and then was silent. With all the phantoms of his heated, ignorant fancy, Wolfe had not been vague in his ambitions. They were practical, slowly built up before him out of his knowledge of what he could do. Through years he had day by day made this hope a real thing to himself,—a clear, projected figure of himself, as he might become. Able to speak, to know what was best, to raise these men and women working at his side up with him: sometimes he forgot this defined hope in the frantic anguish to escape,—only to escape,—out of the wet, the pain, the ashes, somewhere, anywhere, —only for one moment of free air on a hill-side, to lie down and let his sick soul throb itself out in the sunshine. But to-night he panted for life. The savage strength of his nature was aroused; his cry was fierce to God for justice.

"Look at me!" he said to Deborah, with a low, bitter laugh, striking his puny chest savagely. "What am I worth, Deb? Is it my fault that I am no better? My fault? My fault?"

He stopped, stung with a sudden remorse, seeing her hunchback shape writhing with sobs. For Deborah was crying thankless tears, according to the fashion of women.

"God forgi' me, woman! Things go harder wi' you nor me. It's a worse share."

He got up and helped her to rise; and they went doggedly down the muddy street, side by side.

"It's all wrong," he muttered, slowly,— "all wrong! I dunnot understan'. But it'll end some day."

"Come home, Hugh!" she said, coaxingly; for he had stopped, looking around bewildered.

"Home,—and back to the mill!" He went on saying this over to himself, as if he would mutter down every pain in this dull despair.

She followed him through the fog, her blue lips chattering with cold. They reached the cellar at last. Old Wolfe had been drinking since she went out, and had crept nearer the door. The girl Janey slept heavily in the corner. He went up to her, touching softly the worn white arm with his fingers. Some bitterer thought stung him, as he stood there. He wiped the drops from his forehead, and went into the room beyond, livid, trembling. A hope, trifling, perhaps, but very dear, had died just then out of the poor puddler's life, as he looked at the sleeping, innocent girl, —some plan for the future, in which she had borne a part. He gave it up that moment, then and forever. Only a trifle, perhaps, to us: his face grew a shade paler,— that was all. But, somehow, the man's soul, as God and the angels looked down on it, never was the same afterwards.

Deborah followed him into the inner room. She carried a candle, which she placed on the floor, closing the door after her. She had seen the look on his face, as he turned away: her own grew deadly. Yet, as she came up to him, her eyes glowed. He was seated on an old chest, quiet, holding his face in his hands.

"Hugh!" she said, softly.

He did not speak.

"Hugh, did hur hear what the man said, —him with the clear voice? Did hur hear? Money, money,—that it wud do all?"

He pushed her away,—gently, but he was worn out; her rasping tone fretted him.

"Hugh!"

The candle flared a pale yellow light over the cobwebbed brick walls, and the woman standing there. He looked at her. She was young, in deadly earnest; her faded eyes, and wet, ragged figure caught from their frantic eagerness a power akin to beauty.

"Hugh, it is true! Money ull do it! Oh, Hugh, boy, listen till me! He said it true! It is money!"

"I know. Go back! I do not want you here."

"Hugh, it is t' last time. I'll never worrit hur again."

There were tears in her voice now, but she choked them back.

"Hear till me only to-night! If one of t' witch people wud come, them we heard of t' home, and gif hur all hur wants, what then? Say, Hugh!"

"What do you mean?"

"I mean money."

Her whisper shrilled through his brain.

"If one of t' witch dwarfs wud come from t' lane moors to-night, and gif hur money, to go out,—out, I say,—out, lad, where t' sun shines, and t' heath grows, and t' ladies walk in silken gownds, and God stays all t' time,—where t' man lives that talked to us to-night,—Hugh knows, —Hugh could walk there like a king!"

He thought the woman mad, tried to check her, but she went on, fierce in her eager haste.

"If *I* were t' witch dwarf, if I had t' money, wud hur thank me? Wud hur take me out o' this place wid hur and Janey? I wud not come into the gran' house hur wud build, to vex hur wid t' hunch,—only at night, when t' shadows were dark, stand far off to see hur."

Mad? Yes! Are many of us mad in this way?

"Poor Deb! poor Deb!" he said, soothingly.

"It is here," she said, suddenly jerking into his hand a small roll. "I took it! I did it! Me, me!—not hur! I shall be hanged, I shall be burnt in hell, if anybody knows I took it! Out of his pock-

et, as he leaned against t' bricks. Hur knows?"

She thrust it into his hand, and then, her errand done, began to gather chips together to make a fire, choking down hysteric sobs.

"Has it come to this?"

That was all he said. The Welsh Wolfe blood was honest. The roll was a small green pocket-book containing one or two gold pieces, and a check for an incredible amount, as it seemed to the poor puddler. He laid it down, hiding his face again in his hands.

"Hugh, don't be angry wud me! It's only poor Deb,—hur knows?"

He took the long skinny fingers kindly in his.

"Angry? God help me, no! Let me sleep. I am tired."

He threw himself heavily down on the wooden bench, stunned with pain and weariness. She brought some old rags to cover him.

It was late on Sunday evening before he awoke. I tell God's truth, when I say he had then no thought of keeping this money. Deborah had hid it in his pocket. He found it there. She watched him eagerly, as he took it out.

"I must gif it to him," he said, reading her face.

"Hur knows," she said with a bitter sigh of disappointment. "But it is hur right to keep it."

His right! The word struck him. Doctor May had used the same. He washed himself, and went out to find this man Mitchell. His right! Why did this chance word cling to him so obstinately? Do you hear the fierce devils whisper in his ear, as he went slowly down the darkening street?

The evening came on, slow and calm. He seated himself at the end of an alley leading into one of the larger streets. His brain was clear to-night, keen, intent, mastering. It would not start back, cowardly, from any hellish temptation, but meet it face to face. Therefore the great temptation of his life came to him veiled by no sophistry, but bold, defiant, owning its own vile name, trusting to one bold blow for victory.

He did not deceive himself. Theft! That was it. At first the word sickened him; then he grappled with it. Sitting there on a broken cart-wheel, the fading day, the noisy groups, the church-bells' tolling, passed before him like a panorama, while the sharp struggle went on within. This money! He took it out, and looked at it. If he gave it back, what then? He was going to be cool about it.

People going by to church saw only a sickly mill-boy watching them quietly at the alley's mouth. They did not know that he was mad, or they would not have gone by so quietly: mad with hunger; stretching out his hands to the world, that had given so much to them, for leave to live the life God meant him to live. His soul within him was smothering to death; he wanted so much, thought so much, and *knew*—nothing. There was nothing of which he was certain, except the mill and things here. Of God and heaven he had heard so little, that they were to him what fairy-land is to a child: something real, but not here; very far off. His brain, greedy, dwarfed, full of thwarted energy and unused powers, questioned these men and women going by, coldly, bitterly, that night. Was it not his right to live as they, —a pure life, a good, true-hearted life, full of beauty and kind words? He only wanted to know how to use the strength within him. His heart warmed, as he thought of it. He suffered himself to think of it longer. If he took the money?

Then he saw himself as he might be, strong, helpful, kindly. The night crept on, as this one image slowly evolved itself from the crowd of other thoughts and stood triumphant. He looked at it. As he might be! What wonder, if it blinded him to delirium,—the madness that underlies all revolution, all progress, and all fall?

You laugh at the shallow temptation? You see the error underlying its argument so clearly,—that to him a true life was one of full development rather than self-restraint? that he was deaf to the higher tone in a cry of voluntary suffering for truth's sake than in the fullest flow of spontaneous harmony? I do not plead his cause. I only want to show you the mote in my brother's eye: then you can see clearly to take it out.

The money,—there it lay on his knee, a little blotted slip of paper, nothing in itself; used to raise him out of the pit; something straight from God's hand. A thief! Well, what was it to be a thief? He met the question at last, face to face,

wiping the clammy drops of sweat from his forehead. God made this money—the fresh air, too—for his children's use. He never made the difference between poor and rich. The Something who looked down on him that moment through the cool gray sky had a kindly face, he knew,—loved his children alike. Oh, he knew that!

There were times when the soft floods of color in the crimson and purple flames, or the clear depth of amber in the water below the bridge, had somehow given him a glimpse of another world than this,—of an infinite depth of beauty and of quiet somewhere,—somewhere,—a depth of quiet and rest and 'love. Looking up now, it became strangely real. The sun had sunk quite below the hills, but his last rays struck upward, touching the zenith. The fog had risen, and the town and river were steeped in its thick, gray damp; but overhead, the sun-touched smoke-clouds opened like a cleft ocean,—shifting, rolling seas of crimson mist, waves of billowy silver veined with blood-scarlet, inner depths unfathomable of glancing light. Wolfe's artist-eye grew drunk with color. The gates of that other world! Fading, flashing before him now! What, in that world of Beauty, Content, and Right, were the petty laws, the mine and thine, of mill-owners and mill-hands?

A consciousness of power stirred within him. He stood up. A man,—he thought, stretching out his hands,—free to work, to live, to love! Free! His right! He folded the scrap of paper in his hand. As his nervous fingers took it in, limp and blotted, so his soul took in the mean temptation, lapped it in fancied rights, in dreams of improved existences, drifting and endless as the cloud-seas of color. Clutching it, as if the tightness of his hold would strengthen his sense of possession, he went aimlessly down the street. It was his watch at the mill. He need not go, need never go again, thank God!— shaking off the thought with unspeakable loathing.

Shall I go over the history of the hours of that night? how the man wandered from one to another of his old haunts, with a half-consciousness of bidding them farewell,—lanes and alleys and back-yards where the mill-hands lodged,—noting, with a new eagerness, the filth and drunkenness, the pig-pens, the ash-heaps covered with potato-skins, the bloated, pimpled women at the doors,—with a new disgust, a new sense of sudden triumph, and, under all, a new, vague dread, unknown before, smothered down, kept under, but still there? It left him but once during the night, when, for the second time in his life, he entered a church. It was a somber Gothic pile, where the stained light lost itself in far-retreating arches; built to meet the requirements and sympathies of a far other class than Wolfe's. Yet it touched, moved him uncontrollably. The distances, the shadows, the still, marble figures, the mass of silent kneeling worshippers, the mysterious music, thrilled, lifted his soul with a wonderful pain. Wolfe forgot himself, forgot the new life he was going to live, the mean terror gnawing underneath. The voice of the speaker strengthened the charm; it was clear, feeling, full, strong. An old man, who had lived much, suffered much; whose brain was keenly alive, dominant; whose heart was summer-warm with charity. He taught it to-night. He held up Humanity in its grand total; showed the great world-cancer to his people. Who could show it better? He was a Christian reformer; he had studied the age thoroughly; his outlook at man had been free, world-wide, over all time. His faith stood sublime upon the Rock of Ages; his fiery zeal guided vast schemes by which the gospel was to be preached to all nations. How did he preach it to-night? In burning, light-laden words he painted the incarnate Life, Love, the universal Man: words that became reality in the lives of these people,—that lived again in beautiful words and actions, trifling, but heroic. Sin, as he defied it, was a real foe to them; their trials, temptations, were his. His words passed far over the furnace-tender's grasp, toned to suit another class of culture; they sounded in his ears a very pleasant song in an unknown tongue. He meant to cure this world-cancer with a steady eye that had never glared with hunger, and a hand that neither poverty nor strychinine-whisky had taught to shake. In this morbid, distorted heart of the Welsh puddler he had failed.

Wolfe rose at last, and turned from the church down the street. He looked up; the night had come on foggy, damp; the golden mists had vanished, and the sky lay dull and ash-colored. He wandered again aimlessly down the street, idly wondering what

had become of the cloud-sea of crimson and scarlet. The trial-day of this man's life was over, and he had lost the victory. What followed was mere drifting circumstance,—a quicker walking over the path, —that was all. Do you want to hear the end of it? You wish me to make a tragic story out of it? Why, in the police-reports of the morning paper you can find a dozen such tragedies: hints of shipwrecks unlike any that ever befell on the high seas; hints that here a power was lost to heaven,—that there a soul went down where no tide can ebb or flow. Commonplace enough the hints are,—jocose sometimes, done up in rime.

Doctor May, a month after the night I have told you of, was reading to his wife at breakfast from this fourth column of the morning-paper: an unusual thing,— these police-reports not being, in general, choice reading for ladies; but it was only one item he read.

"Oh, my dear! You remember that man I told you of, that we saw at Kirby's mill? —that was arrested for robbing Mitchell? Here he is; just listen:—'Circuit Court. Judge Day. Hugh Wolfe, operative in Kirby & John's Loudon Mills. Charge, grand larceny. Sentence, nineteen years hard labor in penitentiary.—Scoundrel! Serves him right! After all our kindness that night! Picking Mitchell's pocket at the very time!"

His wife said something about the ingratitude of that kind of people, and then they began to talk of something else.

Nineteen years! How easy that was to read! What a simple word for Judge Day to utter! Nineteen years! Half a lifetime!

Hugh Wolfe sat on the window-ledge of his cell, looking out. His ankles were ironed. Not usual in such cases; but he had made two desperate efforts to escape. "Well," as Haley, the jailer, said, "small blame to him! Nineteen years' imprisonment was not a pleasant thing to look forward to." Haley was very good-natured about it, though Wolfe had fought him savagely.

"When he was first caught," the jailer said afterwards, in telling the story, "before the trial, the fellow was cut down at once,—laid there on that pallet like a dead man, with his hands over his eyes. Never saw a man so cut down in my life. Time of the trial, too, came the queerest dodge

of any customer I ever had. Would choose
no lawyer. Judge gave him one, of course.
Gibson it was. He tried to prove the fellow crazy; but it wouldn't go. Thing was
plain as daylight: money found on him.
'Twas a hard sentence,—all the law allows; but it was for 'xample's sake. These
mill-hands are gettin' onbearable. When
the sentence was read, he just looked up,
and said the money was his by rights,
and that all the world had gone wrong.
That night, after the trial, a gentleman
came to see him here, name of Mitchell,
—him as he stole from. Talked to him
for an hour. Thought he came for curiosity, like. After he was gone, thought
Wolfe was remarkable quiet, and went
into his cell. Found him very low; bed
all bloody. Doctor said he had been bleeding at the lungs. He was as weak as a
cat; yet, if ye'll b'lieve me, he tried to
get a-past me and get out. I just carried
him like a baby, and threw him on the
pallet. Three days after, he tried it again:
that time reached the wall. Lord help you!
he fought like a tiger,—giv' some terrible
blows. Fightin' for life, you see; for he
can't live long, shut up in the stone crib
down yonder. Got a death-cough now. 'T
took two of us to bring him down that
day; so I just put the irons on his feet.
There he sits, in there. Goin' to-morrow,
with a batch more of 'em. That woman,
hunchback, tried with him,—you remember?—she's only got three years. 'Complice.
But *she's* a woman, you know. He's been
quiet ever since I put on irons: giv' up, I
suppose. Looks white, sick-lookin'. It acts
different on 'em, bein' sentenced. Most of
'em gets reckless, devilish-like. Some prays
awful, and sings them vile songs of the
mills, all in a breath. That woman, now,
she's desper't. Been beggin' to see Hugh,
as she calls him, for three days. I'm a-goin'
to let her in. She don't go with him. Here
she is in this next cell. I'm a-goin' now to
let her in."

He let her in. Wolfe did not see her.
She crept into a corner of the cell, and
stood watching him. He was scratching
the iron bars of the window with a piece
of tin which he had picked up, with an
idle, uncertain, vacant stare, just as a
child or idiot would do.

"Tryin' to get out, old boy?" laughed
Haley. "Them irons will need a crowbar beside your tin, before you can open
'em."

Wolfe laughed, too, in a senseless way.
"I think I'll get out," he said.

"I believe his brain's touched," said
Haley, when he came out.

The puddler scraped away with the tin
for half an hour. Still Deborah did not
speak. At last she ventured nearer, and
touched his arm.

"Blood?" she said, looking at some spots
on his coat with a shudder.

He looked up at her. "Why, Deb!" he
said, smiling,—such a bright, boyish smile,
that it went to poor Deborah's heart directly, and she sobbed and cried out loud.
"Oh, Hugh, lad! Hugh! dunnot look at
me, when it wur my fault! To think I
brought hur to it! And I loved hur so! Oh,
lad, I dud!"

The confession, even in this wretch,
came with the woman's blush through the
sharp cry.

He did not seem to hear her,—scraping
away diligently at the bars with the bit of
tin.

Was he going mad? She peered closely
into his face. Something she saw there
made her draw suddenly back,—something
which Haley had not seen, that lay beneath
the pinched, vacant look it had caught
since the trial, or the curious gray shadow
that rested on it. That gray shadow,—yes,
she knew what that meant. She had often
seen it creeping over women's faces for
months, who died at last of slow hunger
or consumption. That meant death, distant,
lingering: but this—— Whatever it was
the woman saw, or thought she saw, used
as she was to crime and misery, seemed to
make her sick with a new horror. Forgetting her fear of him, she caught his shoulders, and looked keenly, steadily, into his
eyes.

"Hugh!" she cried, in a desperate whisper,—"oh, boy, not that! for God's sake,
not *that!*"

The vacant laugh went off his face, and
he answered her in a muttered word or two
that drove her away. Yet the words were
kindly enough. Sitting there on his pallet,
she cried silently a hopeless sort of tears,
but did not speak again. The man looked
up furtively at her now and then. Whatever his own trouble was, her distress
vexed him with a momentary sting.

It was market-day. The narrow window of the jail looked down directly on
the carts and wagons drawn up in a long
line, where they had unloaded. He could

see, too, and hear distinctly the clink of money as it changed hands, the busy crowd of whites and blacks shoving, pushing one another, and the chaffering and swearing at the stalls. Somehow, the sound, more than anything else had done, wakened him up,—made the whole real to him. He was done with the world and the business of it. He let the tin fall, and looked out, pressing his face close to the rusty bars. How they crowded and pushed! And he,—he should never walk that pavement again! There came Neff Sanders, one of the feeders at the mill, with a basket on his arm. Sure enough, Neff was married the other week. He whistled, hoping he would look up; but he did not. He wondered if Neff remembered he was there,—if any of the boys thought of him up there, and thought that he never was to go down that old cinder-road again. Never again! He had not quite understood it before; but now he did. Not for days or years, but never!—that was it.

How clear the light fell on that stall in front of the market! and how like a picture it was, the dark-green heaps of corn, and the crimson beets, and golden melons! There was another with game: how the light flickered on that pheasant's breast, with the purplish blood dripping over the brown feathers! He could see the red shining of the drops, it was so near. In one minute he could be down there. It was just a step. So easy, as it seemed, so natural to go! Yet it could never be—not in all the thousands of years to come—that he should put his foot on that street again! He thought of himself with a sorrowful pity, as of some one else. There was a dog down in the market, walking after his master with such a stately, grave look!—only a dog, yet he could go backwards and forwards just as he pleased: he had good luck! Why, the very vilest cur, yelping there in the gutter, had not lived his life, had been free to act out whatever thought God had put into his brain; while he—— No, he would not think of that! He tried to put the thought away, and to listen to a dispute between a countryman and a woman about some meat; but it would come back. He, what had he done to bear this?

Then came the sudden picture of what might have been, and now. He knew what it was to be in the penitentiary,—how it went with men there. He knew how in these long years he should slowly die, but not until soul and body had become corrupt and rotten,—how, when he came out, if he lived to come, even the lowest of the mill-hands would jeer him,—how his hands would be weak, and his brain senseless and stupid. He believed he was almost that now. He put his hand to his head, with a puzzled, weary look. It ached, his head, with thinking. He tried to quiet himself. It was only right, perhaps; he had done wrong. But was there right or wrong for such as he? What was right? And who had ever taught him? He thrust the whole matter away. A dark, cold quiet crept through his brain. It was all wrong; but let it be! It was nothing to him more than the others. Let it be!

The door grated, as Haley opened it.

"Come, my woman! Must lock up for t' night. Come, stir yerself!"

She went up and took Hugh's hand.

"Good-night, Deb," he said, carelessly.

She had not hoped he would say more; but the tired pain on her mouth just then was bitterer than death. She took his passive hand and kissed it.

"Hur'll never see Deb again!" she ventured, her lips growing colder and more bloodless.

What did she say that for? Did he not know it? Yet he would not be impatient with poor old Deb. She had trouble of her own, as well as he.

"No, never again," he said, trying to be cheerful.

She stood just a moment, looking at him. Do you laugh at her, standing there, with her hunchback, her rags, her bleared, withered face, and the great despised love tugging at her heart?

"Come, you!" called Haley, impatiently.

She did not move.

"Hugh!" she whispered.

It was to be her last word. What was it?

"Hugh, boy, not THAT!"

He did not answer. She wrung her hands, trying to be silent, looking in his face in an agony of entreaty. He smiled again, kindly.

"It is best, Deb. I cannot bear to be hurted any more."

"Hur knows," she said, humbly.

"Tell my father good-by; and—and kiss little Janey."

She nodded, saying nothing, looked in

his face again, and went out of the door. As she went, she staggered.

"Drinkin' to-day?" broke out Haley, pushing her before him. "Where the Devil did you get it? Here, in with ye!" and he shoved her into her cell, next to Wolfe's, and shut the door.

Along the wall of her cell there was a crack low down by the floor, through which she could see the light from Wolfe's. She had discovered it days before. She hurried in now, and, kneeling down by it, listened, hoping to hear some sound. Nothing but the rasping of the tin on the bars. He was at his old amusement again. Something in the noise jarred on her ear, for she shivered as she heard it. Hugh rasped away at the bars. A dull old bit of tin, not fit to cut korl with.

He looked out of the window again. People were leaving the market now. A tall mulatto girl, following her mistress, her basket on her head, crossed the street just below, and looked up. She was laughing; but, when she caught sight of the haggard face peering out through the bars, suddenly grew grave, and hurried by. A free, firm, step, a clear-cut olive face, with a scarlet turban tied on one side, dark, shining eyes, and on the head the basket poised, filled with fruit and flowers, under which the scarlet turban and bright eyes looked out half-shadowed. The picture caught his eye. It was good to see a face like that. He would try to-morrow, and cut one like it. *To-morrow!* He threw down the tin, trembling, and covered his face with his hands. When he looked up again, the daylight was gone.

Deborah, crouching near by on the other side of the wall, heard no noise. He sat on the side of the low pallet, thinking. Whatever was the mystery which the woman had seen on his face, it came out now slowly, in the dark here, and became fixed, —a something never seen on his face before. The evening was darkening fast. The market had been over for an hour; the rumbling of the carts over the pavement grew more infrequent: he listened to each, as it passed, because he thought it was to be for the last time. For the same reason, it was, I suppose, that he strained his eyes to catch a glimpse of each passer-by, wondering who they were, what kind of homes they were going to, if they had children,— listening eagerly to every chance word in the street, as if—(God be merciful to the man! what strange fancy was this?)—as if he never should hear human voices again.

It was quite dark at last. The street was a lonely one. The last passenger, he thought, was gone. No,—there was a quick step: Joe Hill, lighting the lamps. Joe was a good old chap; never passed a fellow without some joke or other. He remembered once seeing the place where he lived with his wife. "Granny Hill," the boys called her. Bedridden she was; but so kind as Joe was to her! kept the room so clean! —and the old woman, when he was there, was laughing at "some of t' lad's foolishness." The step was far down the street; but he could see him place the ladder, run up, and light the gas. A longing seized him to be spoken to once more.

"Joe!" he called, out of the grating. "Good-by, Joe!"

The old man stopped a moment, listening uncertainly; then hurried on. The prisoner thrust his hand out of the window, and called again, louder; but Joe was too far down the street. It was a little thing; but it hurt him,—this disappointment.

"Good-by, Joe!" he called, sorrowfully enough.

"Be quiet!" said one of the jailers, passing the door, striking on it with his club.

Oh, that was the last, was it?

There was an inexpressible bitterness on his face, as he lay down on the bed, taking the bit of tin, which he had rasped to a tolerable degree of sharpness, in his hand,—to play with, it may be. He bared his arms, looking intently at their corded veins and sinews. Deborah, listening in the next cell, heard a slight clicking sound, often repeated. She shut her lips tightly, that she might not scream; the cold drops of sweat broke over her, in her dumb agony.

"Hur knows best," she muttered at last, fiercely clutching the boards where she lay.

If she could have seen Wolfe, there was nothing about him to frighten her. He lay quite still, his arms outstretched, looking at the pearly stream of moonlight coming into the window. I think in that one hour that came then he lived back over all the years that had gone before. I think that all the low, vile life, all his wrongs, all his starved hopes, came then, and stung him with a farewell poison that made him sick unto death. He made neither moan nor cry, only turned his worn face now and then to the pure light, that seemed so far off, as one that said, "How long, O Lord? how long?"

The hour was over at last. The moon, passing over her nightly path, slowly came nearer, and threw the light across his bed on his feet. He watched it steadily, as it crept up, inch by inch, slowly. It seemed to him to carry with it a great silence. He had been so hot and tired there always in the mills! The years had been so fierce and cruel! There was coming now quiet and coolness and sleep. His tense limbs relaxed, and settled in a calm languor. The blood ran fainter and slow from his heart. He did not think now with a savage anger of what might be and was not; he was conscious only of deep stillness creeping over him. At first he saw a sea of faces: the mill-men,—women he had known, drunken and bloated,—Janeys timid and pitiful,—poor old Debs: then they floated together like a mist, and faded away, leaving only the clear, pearly moonlight.

Whether, as the pure light crept up the stretched-out figure, it brought with it calm and peace, who shall say? His dumb soul was alone with God in judgment. A Voice may have spoken for it from far-off Calvary, "Father, forgive them, for they know not what they do!" Who dare say? Fainter and fainter the heart rose and fell, slower and slower the moon floated from behind a cloud, until, when at last its full tide of white splendor swept over the cell, it seemed to wrap and fold into a deeper stillness the dead figure that never should move again. Silence deeper than the Night! Nothing that moved, save the black, nauseous stream of blood dripping slowly from the pallet to the floor!

There was outcry and crowd enough in the cell the next day. The coroner and his jury, the local editors, Kirby himself, and boys with their hands thrust knowingly into their pockets and heads on one side, jammed into the corners. Coming and going all day. Only one woman. She came late, and outstayed them all. A Quaker, or Friend, as they call themselves. I think this woman was known by that name in heaven. A homely body, coarsely dressed in gray and white. Deborah (for Haley had let her in) took notice of her. She watched them all—sitting on the end of the pallet, holding his head in her arms

—with the ferocity of a watch-dog, if any of them touched the body. There was no meekness, or sorrow, in her face; the stuff out of which murderers are made, instead.

All the time Haley and the woman were laying straight the limbs and cleaning the cell, Deborah sat still, keenly watching the Quaker's face. Of all the crowd there that day, this woman alone had not spoken to her,—only once or twice had put some cordial to her lips. After they all were gone, the woman, in the same still, gentle way, brought a vase of wood-leaves and berries, and placed it by the pallet, then opened the narrow window. The fresh air blew in, and swept the woody fragrance over the dead face. Deborah looked up with a quick wonder.

"Did hur know my boy would like it? Did hur know Hugh?"

"I know Hugh now."

The white fingers passed in a slow, pitiful way over the dead, worn face. There was a heavy shadow in the quiet eyes.

"Did hur know where they'll bury Hugh?" said Deborah in a shrill tone, catching her arm.

This had been the question hanging on her lips all day.

"In t' town-yard? Under t' mud and ash? T' lad'll smother, woman! He wur born on t' lane moor, where t' air is frick and strong. Take hur out, for God's sake, take hur out where t' air blows!"

The Quaker hesitated, but only for a moment. She put her strong arm around Deborah and led her to the window.

"Thee sees the hills, friend, over the river? Thee sees how the light lies warm there, and the winds of God blow all the day? I live there,—where the blue smoke is, by the trees. Look at me." She turned Deborah's face to her own, clear and earnest. "Thee will believe me? I will take Hugh and bury him there to-morrow."

Deborah did not doubt her. As the evening wore on, she leaned against the iron bars, looking at the hills that rose far off, through the thick sodden clouds, like a bright, unattainable calm. As she looked, a shadow of their solemn repose fell on her face: its fierce discontent faded into a pitiful, humble quiet. Slow, solemn tears gathered in her eyes: the poor weak eyes turned so hopelessly to the place where Hugh was to rest, the grave heights looking higher and brighter and more solemn than ever before. The Quaker watched her keenly. She came to her at last, and touched her arm.

"When thee comes back," she said, in a low, sorrowful tone, like one who speaks from a strong heart deeply moved with remorse or pity, "thee shall begin thy life again,—there on the hills. I came too late; but not for thee,—by God's help, it may be."

Not too late. Three years after, the Quaker began her work. I end my story here. At evening-time it was light. There is no need to tire you with the long years of sunshine, and fresh air, and slow, patient Christ-love, needed to make healthy and hopeful this impure body and soul. There is a homely pine house, on one of these hills, whose windows overlook broad, wooded slopes and clover-crimsoned meadows,—niched into the very place where the light is warmest, the air freest. It is the Friends' meeting-house. Once a week they sit there, in their grave, earnest way, waiting for the Spirit of Love to speak, opening their simple hearts to receive His words. There is a woman, old, deformed, who takes a humble place among them: waiting like them: in her gray dress, her worn face, pure and meek, turned now and then to the sky. A woman much loved by these silent, restful people; more silent than they, more humble, more loving. Waiting: with her eyes turned to hills higher and purer than these on which she lives,—dim and far off now, but to be reached some day. There may be in her heart some latent hope to meet there the love denied her here,—that she shall find him whom she lost, and that then she will not be all-unworthy. Who blames her? Something is lost in the passage of every soul from one eternity to the other,— something pure and beautiful, which might have been and was not: a hope, a talent, a love, over which the soul mourns, like Esau deprived of his birthright. What blame to the meek Quaker, if she took her lost hope to make the hills of heaven more fair?

Nothing remains to tell that the poor Welsh puddler once lived, but this figure of the mill-woman cut in korl. I have it here in a corner of my library. I keep it hid behind a curtain,—it is such a rough, ungainly thing. Yet there are about it touches, grand sweeps of outline, that show a master's hand. Sometimes,—tonight, for instance,—the curtain is accidentally drawn back, and I see a bare arm stretched out imploringly in the darkness, and an eager, wolfish face watching mine: a wan, woeful face, through which the spirit of the dead korl-cutter looks out, with its thwarted life, its mighty hunger, its unfinished work. Its pale, vague lips seem to tremble with a terrible question. "Is this the End?" they say,—"nothing beyond?—no more?" Why, you tell me you have seen that look in the eyes of dumb brutes,—horses dying under the lash. I know.

The deep of the night is passing while I write. The gas-light wakens from the shadows here and there the objects which lie scattered through the room: only faintly, though: for they belong to the open sunlight. As I glance at them, they each recall some task or pleasure of the coming day. A half-molded child's head; Aphrodite; a bough of forest-leaves; music; work; homely fragments, in which lie the secrets of all eternal truth and beauty. Prophetic all! Only this dumb, woeful face seems to belong to and end with the night. I turn to look at it. Has the power of its desperate need commanded the darkness away? While the room is yet steeped in heavy shadow, a cool, gray light suddenly touches its head like a blessing hand, and its groping arm points through the broken cloud to the far East, where, in the flickering, nebulous crimson, God has set the promise of the Dawn.

PART II

THE MIDDLE PERIOD, 1865–1890

XIV

BRET HARTE (1836–1902)

In the decade following the Civil War came the earliest work of what we may term the second generation of short-story writers in America, that group born for the most part in the 1830's which had seen the earliest publications of the Hawthorne-Poe generation. Harte had been reared in the New York environment without any mixture of New Englandism. Cosmopolitanism was in his blood. On the paternal side his grandfather was Hebrew and his grandmother English, and his mother was Dutch. The early death of his father, a temperamental soul, a desultory scholar, unfixed, excited, artistic, changed completely the career of this boy. The widowed mother removed at length to California where her elder son had established himself, and the younger son, leaving the New York City environment where already he had dreams of literary triumphs, followed her into what seemed to him hopeless exile in a land utterly barbarous.

Harte was in California seventeen years and during practically the whole of this period he was employed in newspaper and magazine offices either as workman or editor. If ever he experienced the life of a miner it was only for the briefest of periods. He was a man of letters in almost constant practice of his art,—poet, essayist, parodist, tale writer, humorist, paragrapher, editorial writer: he learned his art as laboriously as did Hawthorne. It is an interesting study to follow the evolution of his peculiar type of short story from its Washington Irving beginnings, through its *Condensed Novels* period, through its wide area of Dickensism, until it emerged at last an original entity in "M'liss" and "The Luck of Roaring Camp."

Harte came at the one moment in American history when he could be a dominating influence on the short story. The intense interest of the whole world in the New Eldorado of California gave him from the very first a tremendous advantage and he used it to the full. He left California at the first possible moment and followed the applause and his market first to New England, then to New York, then to England where he spent his last years, an exile from his family and his country. His cosmopolitan ideals made of his art what Poe's had been: a thing almost wholly of the intellect rather than of the heart. He was concerned with the unique, the startling, the wildly picturesque; he fashioned with curious art gargoyles rather than living, breathing human beings; and he used sentimentalism as freely as did Dickens. Theatricality is in his work rather than truthfulness, paradox rather than simple fact, and melodrama rather than compelling human tragedy and comedy. His influence, however, was great. After his volume *The Luck of Roaring Camp and Other Sketches* (1870), there came a veritable flood of "local color" fiction that was not stemmed until near the close of the century.

Bret Harte's study of the American short story, contributed near the close of his career to an English magazine, is an excellent introduction to the shorter fiction of the new period which was started largely by his own work.

THE RISE OF THE "SHORT STORY"

As it has been the custom of good-natured reviewers to associate the present writer with the origin of the American "short story," he may have a reasonable excuse for offering the following reflections—partly the result of his own observations during the last thirty years, and partly from his experience in the introduction of this form of literature to the pages of the "Western Magazine,"[1] of which he was editor at the beginning of that period. But he is far from claiming the invention, or of even attributing its genesis to that particular occasion. The short story was familiar enough in form in America during the early half of the century; perhaps the proverbial haste of American life was some inducement to its brevity. It had been the medium through which some of the most characteristic work of the best American writers had won the approbation of the public. Poe—a master of the art, as yet unsurpassed—had written; Longfellow and Hawthorne had lent it the graces of the English classics. But it was not the American short story of to-day. It was not characteristic of American life, American habits, nor American thought. It was not vital and instinct with the experience and observation of the average American; it made no attempt to follow his reasoning or to understand his peculiar form of expression—which it was apt to consider vulgar; it had no sympathy with those dramatic contrasts and surprises which are the wonders of American civilization; it took no account of the modifications of environment and of geographical 'limitations; indeed, it knew little of American geography. Of all that was distinctly American it was evasive—when it was not apologetic. And even when graced by the style of the best masters, it was 'distinctly provincial.

It would be easier to trace the causes which produced this than to assign any distinct occasion or period for the change. What was called American literature was still limited to English methods and upon English models. The best writers either wandered far afield for their inspiration, or, restricted to home material, were historical or legendary; artistically contemplative of their own country, but seldom observant. Literature abode on a scant fringe of the Atlantic seaboard, gathering the drift from other shores, and hearing the murmur of other lands rather than the voices of its own; it was either expressed in an artificial treatment of life in the cities, or, as with Irving, was frankly satirical of provincial social ambition. There was much "fine" writing; there were American Addisons, Steeles, and Lambs—there were provincial "Spectators" and "Tatlers." The sentiment was English. Even Irving in the pathetic sketch of "The Wife" echoed the style of "Rosamond Grey."[2] There were sketches of American life in the form of the English Essayists, with no attempt to understand the American character. The literary man had little sympathy with the rough and half-civilized masses who were making his country's history; if he used them at all it was as a foil to bring into greater relief his hero of the unmistakable English pattern. In his slavish imitation of the foreigner, he did not succeed in retaining the foreigner's quick appreciation of novelty. It took an Englishman to first develop the humor and picturesqueness of American or "Yankee" dialect, but Judge Haliburton succeeded better in reproducing "Sam Slick's" speech than his character. Dr Judd's "Margaret"[4]—one of the early American stories—although a vivid picture of New England farm life and strongly marked with local color, was in incident and treatment a mere imitation of English rural tragedy. It would, indeed, seem that while the American people had shaken off the English yoke in government, politics and national progression, while they had already startled the old world with invention and originality in practical ideas, they had never freed themselves from the trammels of English literary precedent. The old sneer "Who reads an American book?" might have been answered by another "There are no *American* books."

But while the American literary imagination was still under the influence of English tradition, an unexpected factor was developing to diminish its power. It was *Humor*—of a quality as distinct and original as the country and civilization in which it was developed. It was at first noticeable in the anecdote or "story," and after the fashion of such beginnings, was orally transmitted. It was common in the bar-rooms, the gatherings in the "country store," and finally at public meetings in the mouths of "stump orators." Arguments were clenched, and political principles illustrated, by a "funny story." It invaded even the camp meeting and pulpit. It at last received the currency of the public press. But wherever met it was so distinctively original and novel, so individual and characteristic, that it was at once known and appreciated abroad as "an American story." Crude at first, it received a literary polish in the press, but its dominant quality remained. It was concise and condense, yet suggestive. It was delightfully extravagant—or a miracle of understatement. It voiced not only the dialect, but the habits of thought of a people or locality. It gave a new interest to slang. From a paragraph of a dozen lines it grew into a half column, but always retaining its conciseness and felicity of statement. It was a foe to prolixity of any kind, it admitted no fine writing nor affectation of style. It went directly to the point. It was burdened by no conscientiousness; it was often irreverent; it was devoid of all moral responsibility—but it was original! By de-

grees it developed character with its incident, often, in a few lines gave a striking photograph of a community or a sec-
ion, but always reached its conclusion
without an unnecessary word. It became—
and still exists—as an essential feature of
newspaper literature. It was the parent of
the American "short story."

But although these beginnings assumed
more of a national character than American serious or polite literature, they were
still purely comic, and their only immediate result was the development of a
number of humorists in the columns of the
daily press—all possessing the dominant
national quality with a certain individu-
ality of their own. For a while it seemed
as if they were losing the faculty of story-
telling in the elaboration of eccentric character—chiefly used as a vehicle for smart
sayings, extravagant incident, or political
satire. They were eagerly received by the
public and, in their day, were immensely
popular, and probably were better known
at home and abroad than the more aca-
demic but less national humorists of New
York or Boston. The national note was
always struck even in their individual
variations, and the admirable portraiture
of the shrewd and humorous showman in
"Artemus Ward" survived his more mechanical bad spelling. Yet they did not in-
vade the current narrative fiction; the short
and long story-tellers went with their old-
fashioned methods, their admirable morals,
their well-worn sentiments, their colorless
heroes and heroines of the first ranks of
provincial society. Neither did social and
political convulsions bring anything new
in the way of Romance. The Mexican war
gave us the delightful satires of Hosea
Biglow, but no dramatic narrative. The
anti-slavery struggle before the War of
the Rebellion produced a successful partizan political novel—on the old lines—with
only the purely American characters of the
negro "Topsy," and the New England
"Miss Ophelia." The War itself, prolific
as it was of poetry and eloquence—was
barren of romance, except for Edward
Everett Hale's artistic and sympathetic
The Man Without a Country. The tragedies enacted, the sacrifices offered, not
only on the battle-field but in the division
of families and households; the conflict of
superb Quixotism and reckless gallantry
against Reason and Duty fought out in
quiet border farmhouses and plantations;

the reincarnation of Puritan and Cavalier
in a wild environment of trackless wastes,
pestilential swamps and rugged mountains;
the patient endurance of both the conqueror and the conquered: all these found
no echo in the romance of the period. Out
of the battle smoke that covered half a
continent drifted into the pages of magazines shadowy but correct figures of blameless virgins of the North—heroines or
fashionable belles—habited as hospital
nurses, bearing away the deeply wounded
but more deeply misunderstood Harvard
or Yale graduate lover who had rushed to
bury his broken heart in the conflict. It
seems almost incredible that, until the last
few years, nothing worth of that tremendous episode has been preserved by the
pen of the romancer.

But if the war produced no characteristic American story it brought the literary
man nearer his work. It opened to him
distinct conditions of life in his own country, of which he had no previous conception; it revealed communities governed by
customs and morals unlike his own, yet
intensely human and American. The lighter side of some of these he had learned
from the humorists before alluded to; the
grim realities of war and the stress of
circumstances had suddenly given them a
pathetic or dramatic reality. Whether he
had acquired this knowledge of them with
a musket or a gilded strap on his shoulder, or whether he was later a peaceful
"carpet-bagger" into the desolate homes
of the South and South-West, he knew
something personally of their romantic and
picturesque value in story. Many cultivated aspirants for literature, as well as
many seasoned writers for the press, were
among the volunteer soldiery. Again, the
composition of the army was heterogeneous: regiments from the West rubbed
shoulders with regiments from the East;
spruce city clerks hobnobbed with back-
woodsmen, and the student fresh from college shared his rations with the half-edu-
cated western farmer. The Union, for the
first time, recognized its component parts;
the natives knew each other. The literary
man must have seen heroes and heroines
where he had never looked for them, situations that he had never dreamed of. Yet
it is a mortifying proof of the strength of
inherited literary traditions, that he never
dared till quite recently to make a test of
them. It is still more strange that he should

have waited for the initiative to be taken by a still more crude, wild, and more western civilization—that of California!

The gold discovery had drawn to the Pacific slope of the continent a still more heterogeneous and remarkable population. The immigration of 1849 and 1850 had taken farmers from the plow, merchants from their desks, and students from their books, while every profession was represented in the motley crowd of gold-seekers. Europe and her colonies had contributed to swell these adventurers—for adventurers they were whatever their purpose; the risks were great, the journey long and difficult—the nearest came from a distance of over a thousand miles; that the men were necessarily preëquipped with courage, faith and endurance was a foregone conclusion. They were mainly young: a gray-haired man was a curiosity in the mines in the early days, and an object of rude respect and reverence. They were consequently free from the trammels of precedent or tradition in arranging their lives and making their rude homes. There was a singular fraternity in this ideal republic into which all men entered free and equal. Distinction of previous condition or advantages was unknown, even record and reputation for ill or good were of little benefit or embarrassment to the possessor; men were accepted for what they actually were, and what they could do in taking their part in the camp or settlement. The severest economy, the direst poverty, the most menial labor carried no shame or disgrace with it; individual success brought neither envy nor jealousy. What was one man's fortune to-day might be the luck of another to-morrow. And to this Utopian simplicity of the people, the environment of magnificent scenery, a unique climate, and a vegetation that was marvelous in its proportions and spontaneity of growth; let it be further considered that the strongest relief was given to this picture by its setting among the crumbling ruins of early Spanish possession—whose monuments still existed in Mission and Presidio, and whose legitimate Castilian descendants still lived and moved in picturesque and dignified contrast to their energetic invaders—and it must be admitted that a condition of romantic and dramatic possibilities was created unrivaled in history.

But the earlier literature of the Pacific slope was, like that of the Atlantic seaboard, national and characteristic only in its humor. The local press sparkled with wit and satire, and, as in the East, developed its usual individual humorists. Of these should be mentioned the earliest pioneers of Californian humor—Lieut. Derby, a United States army engineer officer, author of a series of delightful extravagances known as the "Squibob Papers," and the later and universally known "Mark Twain," who contributed "The Jumping Frog of Calaveras" to the columns of the weekly press. "The San Francisco News Letter," whose whilom contributor, Major Bierce, has since written some of the most graphic romances of the Civil War; "The Golden Era," in which the present writer published his earlier sketches, and "The Californian," to which, as editor, in burlesque imitation of the enterprise of his journalistic betters, he contributed "The Condensed Novels," were the foremost literary weeklies. These were all more or less characteristically American, but it was again remarkable that the more literary, romantic, and imaginative romances had no national flavor. The better remembered serious work in the pages of the only literary magazine, "The Pioneer," was a romance of spiritualism, a psychological study, and a poem on the Chandos picture of Shakespeare.

With this singular experience before him, the present writer was called upon to take the editorial control of the "Overland Monthly," a much more ambitious magazine venture than had yet appeared in California. The best writers had been invited to contribute to its pages. But in looking over his materials on preparing the first number, he was discouraged to find the same notable lack of characteristic fiction. There were good literary articles, sketches of foreign travel, and some essays in description of the natural resources of California,—excellent from a commercial and advertising view-point. But he failed to discover anything of that wild and picturesque life which had impressed him, first as a truant schoolboy, and afterwards as a youthful schoolmaster among the mining population. In his perplexity he determined to attempt to make good the deficiency himself. He wrote "The Luck of Roaring Camp." However far short it fell of his ideal and his purpose, he conscientiously believed that he had painted much that "he saw, and part of which he was," that his subject and characters were distinctly Californian, as was equally his treatment of them. But an unexpected circumstance here intervened. The publication of the story was objected to by both printer and publisher, virtually for not being in the conventional line of subject, treatment, and morals! The introduction of the abandoned outcast mother of the foundling, "Luck," and the language used by the characters, received a serious warning and protest. The writer was obliged to use his right as editor to save his unfortunate contribution from oblivion. When it appeared at last, he saw with consternation that the printer and publisher had really voiced the local opinion; that the press of California was still strongly dominated by the old conservatism and conventionalism of the East, and that when "The Luck of Roaring Camp" was not denounced as "improper" and "corrupting," it was coldly received as being "singular" and "strange." A still more extraordinary instance of the "provincial note" was struck in the criticism of a religious paper that the story was strongly "unfavorable to immigration" and decidedly unprovocative of the "investment of foreign capital." However, its instantaneous and cordial acceptance as a new departure by the critics of the Eastern States and Europe, enabled the writer to follow it with other stories of like character. More than that, he was gratified to find a disposition on the part of his contributors to shake off their conservative trammels, and in an admirable and original sketch of a wandering circus attendant called "Centrepole Bill," he was delighted to recognize and welcome a convert. The term "Imitator," often used by the critics who, as previously stated, had claimed for the present writer the *invention* of this kind of literature, could not fairly apply to those who had cut loose from conventional methods, and sought to honestly describe the life around them, and he can only claim to have shown them that it could be done. How well it has since been done, what charm of individual flavor and style has been brought to it by such writers as Harris, Cable, Page, Mark Twain in "Huckleberry Finn," the author of "The Great Smoky Mountains," and Miss Wilkins, the average reader need not be told. It would seem evident, therefore, that the secret of the American short story was the treatment of characteristic American life, with absolute knowledge of its peculiarities and sympathy with its methods; with no fastidious ignoring of its habitual expression, or the inchoate poetry that may be found even hidden in its slang; with no moral determination except that which may be the legitimate outcome of the story itself; with no more elimination than may be necessary for the artistic conception, and never from the fear of the "fetish" of conventionalism. Of such is the American short story of to-day—the germ of American literature to come.

THE OUTCASTS OF POKER FLAT

As Mr. John Oakhurst, gambler, stepped into the main street of Poker Flat on the morning of the 23d of November, 1850, he was conscious of a change in its moral atmosphere since the preceding night. Two or three men, conversing earnestly together, ceased as he approached, and exchanged significant glances. There was a Sabbath lull in the air, which, in a settlement unused to Sabbath influences, looked ominous.

Mr. Oakhurst's calm, handsome face betrayed small concern in these indications. Whether he was conscious of any predisposing cause was another question. "I reckon they're after somebody," he reflected; "likely it's me." He returned to his pocket the handkerchief with which he had been whipping away the red dust of Poker Flat from his neat boots, and quietly discharged his mind of any further conjecture.

In point of fact, Poker Flat was "after somebody." It had lately suffered the loss of several thousand dollars, two valuable horses, and a prominent citizen. It was experiencing a spasm of virtuous reaction, quite as lawless and ungovernable as any of the acts that had provoked it. A secret committee had determined to rid the town of all improper persons. This was done permanently in regard of two men who were then hanging from the boughs of a sycamore in the gulch, and temporarily in the banishment of certain other objectionable characters. I regret to say that some of these were ladies. It is but due to the sex, however, to state that their impropriety was professional, and it was only in such easily established standards of evil that Poker Flat ventured to sit in judgment.

Mr. Oakhurst was right in supposing that he was included in this category. A few of the committee had urged hanging him as a possible example and a sure method of reimbursing themselves from his pockets the large sums he had won from them. "It's agin justice," said Jim Wheeler, "to let this yer young man from Roaring Camp—an entire stranger—carry away our money." But a crude sentiment of equity residing in the breasts of those who had been fortunate enough to win from Mr. Oakhurst overruled this narrowed local prejudice.

Mr. Oakhurst received his sentence with philosophic calmness, none the less coolly that he was aware of the hesitation of his judges. He was too much of a gambler not to accept fate. With him life was at best an uncertain game, and he recognized the usual percentage in favor of the dealer.

A body of armed men accompanied the deported wickedness of Poker Flat to the outskirts of the settlement. Besides Mr. Oakhurst, who was known to be a coolly desperate man, and for whose intimidation the armed escort was intended, the expatriated party consisted of a young woman familiarly known as "The Duchess;" another who had won the title of "Mother Shipton;" and "Uncle Billy," a suspected sluice-robber and confirmed drunkard. The cavalcade provoked no comments from the spectators, nor was any word uttered by the escort. Only when the gulch which marked the uttermost limit of Poker Flat was reached, the leader spoke briefly and to the point. The exiles were forbidden to return at the peril of their lives.

As the escort disappeared, their pent-up feelings found vent in a few hysterical tears from the Duchess, some bad language from Mother Shipton, and a Parthian volley of expletives from Uncle Billy. The philosophic Oakhurst alone remained silent. He listened calmly to Mother Shipton's desire to cut somebody's heart out, to the repeated statements of the Duchess that she would die in the road, and to the alarming oaths that seemed to be bumped out of Uncle Billy as he rode forward. With the easy good humor characteristic of his class, he insisted upon exchanging his own riding-horse, "Five-Spot," for the sorry mule which the Duchess rode. But even this act did not draw the party into any closer sympathy. The young woman readjusted her somewhat draggled plumes with a feeble, faded coquetry; Mother Shipton eyed the possessor of "Five-Spot" with malevolence, and Uncle Billy included the whole party in one sweeping anathema. The road to Sandy Bar—a camp that, not having as yet experienced the regenerating influences of Poker Flat, consequently seemed to offer some invitation to the emigrants—lay over a steep mountain range. It was distant a day's severe travel. In that advanced season the party soon passed out of the moist, temperate regions of the foothills into the dry, cold, bracing air of the Sierras. The trail was narrow and difficult. At noon the Duchess, rolling out of her saddle upon the ground, declared her intention of going no farther, and the party halted.

The spot was singularly wild and impressive. A wooded amphitheater, surrounded on three sides by precipitous cliffs of naked granite, sloped gently toward the crest of another precipice that overlooked the valley. It was, undoubtedly, the most suitable spot for a camp, had camping been advisable. But Mr. Oakhurst knew that scarcely half the journey to Sandy Bar was accomplished, and the party were not equipped or provisioned for delay. This fact he pointed out to his companions curtly, with a philosophic commentary on the folly of "throwing up their hand before the game was played out." But they were furnished with liquor, which in this emergency stood them in place of food, fuel, rest, and prescience. In spite of his remonstrances, it was not long before they were more or less under its influence. Uncle Billy passed rapidly from a bellicose state into one of stupor, the Duchess became maudlin, and Mother Shipton snored. Mr. Oakhurst alone remained erect, leaning against a rock, calmly surveying them.

Mr. Oakhurst did not drink. It interfered with a profession which required coolness, impassiveness, and presence of mind, and, in his own language, he "couldn't afford it." As he gazed at his recumbent fellow exiles, the loneliness begotten of his pariah trade, his habits of life, his very vices, for the first time seriously oppressed him. He bestirred himself in dusting his black clothes, washing his hands and face, and other acts characteristic of his studiously neat habits, and for a moment forgot his annoyance. The thought of deserting his weaker and more pitable companions never perhaps occurred to him. Yet he could not help feeling the want of that excitement which, singularly enough, was most conducive to that calm equanimity for which he was notorious. He looked at the gloomy walls that rose a thousand feet sheer above the circling pines around him, at the sky ominously clouded, at the valley below, already deepening into shadow; and, doing so, suddenly he heard his own name called.

A horseman slowly ascended the trail. In the fresh, open face of the newcomer Mr. Oakhurst recognized Tom Simson, otherwise known as "The Innocent," of Sandy Bar. He had met him some months before over a "little game," and had, with perfect equanimity, won the entire fortune —amounting to some forty dollars—of that guileless youth. After the game was finished, Mr. Oakhurst drew the youthful speculator behind the door and thus addressed him: "Tommy, you're a good little man, but you can't gamble worth a cent. Don't try it over again." He then handed him his money back, pushed him gently from the room, and so made a devoted slave of Tom Simson.

There was a remembrance of this in his boyish and enthusiastic greeting of Mr. Oakhurst. He had started, he said, to go to Poker Flat to seek his fortune. "Alone?" No, not exactly alone; in fact (a giggle), he had run away with Piney Woods. Didn't Mr. Oakhurst remember Piney? She that used to wait on the table at the Temperance House? They had been engaged a long time, but old Jake Woods had objected, and so they had run away, and were going to Poker Flat to be married, and here they were. And they were tired out, and how lucky it was they had found a place to camp, and company. All this the Innocent delivered rapidly, while Piney, a stout, comely damsel of fifteen, emerged from behind the pine-tree, where she had been blushing unseen, and rode to the side of her lover.

Mr. Oakhurst seldom troubled himself with sentiment, still less with propriety; but he had a vague idea that the situation was not fortunate. He retained, however, his presence of mind sufficiently to kick Uncle Billy, who was about to say something, and Uncle Billy was sober enough to recognize in Mr. Oakhurst's kick a superior power that would not bear trifling. He then endeavored to dissuade Tom Simson from delaying further, but in vain. He even pointed out the fact that there was no provision, nor means of making a camp. But, unluckily, the Innocent met this objection by assuring the party that he was provided with an extra mule loaded with provisions, and by the discovery of a rude attempt at a log house near the trail. "Piney can stay with Mrs. Oakhurst," said the Innocent, pointing to the Duchess, "and I can shift for myself."

Nothing but Mr. Oakhurst's admonishing foot saved Uncle Billy from bursting into a roar of laughter. As it was, he felt constrained to retire up the cañon until he could recover his gravity. There he confided the joke to the tall pine-trees, with many slaps of his leg, contortions of his face, and the usual profanity. But when he returned to the party, he found them seated by a fire—for the air had grown strangely chill and the sky overcast—in apparently amicable conversation. Piney was actually talking in an impulsive girlish fashion to the Duchess, who was listening with an interest and animation she had not shown for many days. The Innocent was holding forth, apparently with equal effect, to Mr. Oakhurst, and Mother Shipton, who was actually relaxing into amiability. "Is this yer a d—d picnic?" said Uncle Billy, with inward scorn, as he surveyed the sylvan group, the glancing firelight, and the tethered animals in the foreground. Suddenly an idea mingled with the alcoholic fumes that disturbed his brain. It was apparently of a jocular nature, for he felt impelled to slap his leg again and cram his fist into his mouth.

As the shadows crept slowly up the mountain, a slight breeze rocked the tops of the pine-trees and moaned through their long and gloomy aisles. The ruined cabin, patched and covered with pine boughs, was set apart for the ladies. As the lovers parted, they unaffectedly exchanged a kiss, so honest and sincere that it might have been heard above the swaying pines. The frail Duchess and the malevolent Mother Shipton were probably too stunned to remark upon this last evidence of simplicity, and so turned without a word to the hut. The fire was replenished, the men lay down before the door, and in a few minutes were asleep.

Mr. Oakhurst was a light sleeper. Toward morning he awoke benumbed and cold. As he stirred the dying fire, the wind, which was now blowing strongly, brought to his cheek that which caused the blood to leave it,—snow!

He started to his feet with the intention of awakening the sleepers, for there was no time to lose. But turning to where Uncle Billy had been lying, he found him gone. A suspicion leaped to his brain, and a curse to his lips. He ran to the spot where the mules had been tethered—they were no longer there. The tracks were already rapidly disappearing in the snow.

The momentary excitement brought Mr. Oakhurst back to the fire with his usual calm. He did not waken the sleepers. The Innocent slumbered peacefully, with a smile on his good-humored, freckled face; the virgin Piney slept beside her frailer sisters as sweetly as though attended by celestial guardians; and Mr. Oakhurst, drawing his blanket over his shoulders, stroked his mustaches and waited for the dawn. It came slowly in a whirling mist of snowflakes that dazzled and confused the eye. What could be seen of the landscape appeared magically changed. He looked over the valley, and summed up the present and future in two words, "Snowed in!"

A careful inventory of the provisions, which, fortunately for the party, had been stored within the hut, and so escaped the felonious fingers of Uncle Billy, disclosed the fact that with care and prudence they might last ten days longer. "That is," said Mr. Oakhurst, *sotto voce* to the Innocent, "if you're willing to board us. If you ain't —and perhaps you'd better not—you can wait till Uncle Billy gets back with provisions." For some occult reason, Mr. Oakhurst could not bring himself to disclose Uncle Billy's rascality, and so offered the hypothesis that he had wandered from the camp and had accidentally stampeded the animals. He dropped a warning to the Duchess and Mother Shipton, who of course knew the facts of their associate's defection. "They'll find out the truth about us *all* when they find out anything," he added significantly, "and there's no good frightening them now."

Tom Simson not only put all his worldly store at the disposal of Mr. Oakhurst, but seemed to enjoy the prospect of their enforced seclusion. "We'll have a good camp for a week, and then the snow'll melt, and we'll all go back together." The cheerful gaiety of the young man and Mr. Oakhurst's calm infected the others. The Innocent, with the aid of pine boughs, ex-temporized a thatch for the roofless cabin, and the Duchess directed Piney in the re-arrangement of the interior with a taste and tact that opened the blue eyes of that provincial maiden to their fullest extent. "I reckon now you're used to fine things at Poker Flat," said Piney. The Duchess turned away sharply to conceal something that reddened her cheeks through their professional tint, and Mother Shipton re-quested Piney not to "chatter." But when Mr. Oakhurst returned from a weary search for the trail, he heard the sound of happy laughter echoed from the rocks. He stopped in some alarm, and his thoughts first naturally reverted to the whisky, which he had prudently *cachéd*. "And yet it don't somehow sound like whisky," said the gambler. It was not until he caught sight of the blazing fire through the still blinding storm, and the group around it, that he settled to the conviction that it was "square fun."

Whether Mr. Oakhurst had *cachéd* his cards with the whiskey as something de-barred the free access of the community, I cannot say. It was certain that, in Mother Shipton's words, he "didn't say 'cards' once" during that evening. Haply the time was beguiled by an accordion, produced somewhat ostentatiously by Tom Simson from his pack. Notwithstanding some diffi-culties attending the manipulation of this instrument, Piney Woods managed to pluck several reluctant melodies from its keys, to an accompaniment by the Innocent on a pair of bone castanets. But the crown-ing festivity of the evening was reached in a rude camp-meeting hymn, which the lovers, joining hands, sang with great ear-nestness and vociferation. I fear that a certain defiant tone and Covenanter's swing to its chorus, rather than any devotional quality, caused it speedily to infect the others, who at last joined in the refrain:—

"I'm proud to live in the service of the Lord, And I'm bound to die in His army."

The pines rocked, the storm eddied and whirled above the miserable group, and the flames of their altar leaped heaven-ward, as if in token of the vow.

At midnight the storm abated, the rolling clouds parted, and the stars glittered keenly above the sleeping camp. Mr. Oakhurst, whose professional habits had enabled him to live on the smallest possible amount of sleep, in dividing the watch with Tom Simson somehow managed to take upon himself the greater part of that duty. He excused himself to the Innocent by saying that he had "often been a week without sleep." "Doing what?" asked Tom. "Poker!" replied Oakhurst sententiously. "When a man gets a streak of luck,— nigger-luck,—he don't get tired. The luck gives in first. Luck," continued the gambler reflectively, "is a mighty queer thing. All you know about it for certain is that it's bound to change. And it's finding out when it's going to change that makes you. We've had a streak of bad luck since we left Poker Flat,—you come along, and slap you get into it, too. If you can hold your cards right along you're all right. For," added the gambler, with cheerful irrelevance—

" 'I'm proud to live in the service of the Lord,
And I'm bound to die in His army.' "

The third day came, and the sun, looking through the white-curtained valley, saw the outcasts divide their slowly decreasing store of provisions for the morning meal. It was one of the peculiarities of that mountain climate that its rays diffused a kindly warmth over the wintry landscape, as if in regretful commiseration of the past. But it revealed drift on drift of snow piled high around the hut,—a hopeless, uncharted, trackless sea of white lying below the rocky shores to which the castaways still clung. Through the marvelously clear air the smoke of the pastoral village of Poker Flat rose miles away. Mother Shipton saw it, and from a remote pinnacle of her rocky fastness hurled in that direction a final malediction. It was her last vituperative attempt, and perhaps for that reason was invested with a certain degree of sublimity. It did her good, she privately informed the Duchess. "Just you go out there and cuss, and see." She then set herself to the task of amusing "the child," as she and the Duchess were pleased to call Piney. Piney was no chicken, but it was a soothing and original theory of the pair thus to account for the fact that she didn't swear and wasn't improper.

When night crept up again through the gorges, the reedy notes of the accordion rose and fell in fitful spasms and long-drawn gasps by the flickering camp-fire. But music failed to fill entirely the aching void left by insufficient food, and a new diversion was proposed by Piney,—story-telling. Neither Mr. Oakhurst nor his female companions caring to relate their personal experiences, this plan would have failed too, but for the Innocent. Some months before he had chanced upon a stray copy of Mr. Pope's ingenious translation of the Iliad. He now proposed to narrate the principal incidents of that poem—having thoroughly mastered the argument and fairly forgotten the words—in the current vernacular of Sandy Bar. And so for the rest of that night the Homeric demigods again walked the earth. Trojan bully and wily Greek wrestled in the winds, and the great pines in the cañon seemed to bow to the wrath of the son of Peleus. Mr. Oakhurst listened with quiet satisfaction. Most especially was he interested in the fate of "Ashheels," as the Innocent persisted in denominating the "swift-footed Achilles."

So, with small food and much of Homer and the accordion, a week passed over the heads of the outcasts. The sun again forsook them, and again from leaden skies the snowflakes were sifted over the land. Day by day closer around them drew the snowy circle, until at last they looked from their prison over drifted walls of dazzling white, that towered twenty feet above their heads. It became more and more difficult to replenish their fires, even from the fallen trees beside them, now half hidden in the drifts. And yet no one complained. The lovers turned from the dreary prospect and looked into each other's eyes, and were happy. Mr. Oakhurst settled himself coolly to the losing game before him. The Duchess, more cheerful than she had been, assumed the care of Piney. Only Mother Shipton—once the strongest of the party— seemed to sicken and fade. At midnight on the tenth day she called Oakhurst to her side. "I'm going," she said, in a voice of querulous weakness, "but don't say anything about it. Don't waken the kids. Take the bundle from under my head, and open it." Mr. Oakhurst did so. It contained Mother Shipton's rations for the last week, untouched. "Give 'em to the child," she said, pointing to the sleeping Piney. "You've starved yourself," said the gambler. "That's what they call it," said the woman querulously, as she lay down again, and, turning her face to the wall, passed quietly away.

The accordion and the bones were put

aside that day, and Homer was forgotten. When the body of Mother Shipton had been committed to the snow, Mr. Oakhurst took the Innocent aside, and showed him a pair of snowshoes, which he had fashioned from the old pack-saddle. "There's one chance in a hundred to save her yet," he said, pointing to Piney; "but it's there," he added, pointing toward Poker Flat. "If you can reach there in two days she's safe." "And you?" asked Tom Simson. "I'll stay here," was the curt reply.

The lovers parted with a long embrace. "You are not going, too?" said the Duchess, as she saw Mr. Oakhurst apparently waiting to accompany him. "As far as the cañon," he replied. He turned suddenly and kissed the Duchess, leaving her pallid face aflame, and her trembling limbs rigid with amazement.

Night came, but not Mr. Oakhurst. It brought the storm again and the whirling snow. Then the Duchess, feeding the fire, found that some one had quietly piled beside the hut enough fuel to last a few days longer. The tears rose to her eyes, but she hid them from Piney.

The women slept but little. In the morning, looking into each other's faces, they read their fate. Neither spoke, but Piney, accepting the position of the stronger, drew near and placed her arm around the Duchess's waist. They kept this attitude for the rest of the day. That night the storm reached its greatest fury, and, rending asunder the protecting vines, invaded the very hut.

Toward morning they found themselves unable to feed the fire, which gradually died away. As the embers slowly blackened, the Duchess crept closer to Piney, and broke the silence of many hours: "Piney, can you pray?" "No, dear," said Piney simply. The Duchess, without knowing exactly why, felt relieved, and, putting her head upon Piney's shoulder, spoke no more. And so reclining, the younger and purer pillowing the head of her soiled sister upon her virgin breast, they fell asleep.

The wind lulled as if it feared to waken them. Feathery drifts of snow, shaken from the long pine boughs, flew like white winged birds, and settled about them as they slept. The moon through the rifted clouds looked down upon what had been the camp. But all human stain, all trace of earthly travail, was hidden beneath the spotless mantle mercifully flung from above.

They slept all day that day and the next, nor did they waken when voices and footsteps broke the silence of the camp. And when pitying fingers brushed the snow from their wan faces, you could scarcely have told from the equal peace that dwelt upon them which was she that had sinned. Even the law of Poker Flat recognized this, and turned away, leaving them still locked in each other's arms.

But at the head of the gulch, on one of the largest pine-trees, they found the deuce of clubs pinned to the bark with a bowie-knife. It bore the following, written in pencil in a firm hand:—

†

BENEATH THIS TREE

LIES THE BODY

OF

JOHN OAKHURST,

WHO STRUCK A STREAK OF BAD LUCK

ON THE 23D OF NOVEMBER 1850,

AND

HANDED IN HIS CHECKS

ON THE 7TH DECEMBER, 1850.

⊥

And pulseless and cold, with a Derringer by his side and a bullet in his heart, though still calm as in life, beneath the snow lay he who was at once the strongest and yet the weakest of the outcasts of Poker Flat.

AN INGENUE OF THE SIERRAS *

I

We all held our breath as the coach rushed through the semi-darkness of Galloper's Ridge. The vehicle itself was only a huge, lumbering shadow; its side-lights were carefully extinguished, and Yuba Bill had just politely removed from the lips of an outside passenger even the cigar with which he had been ostentatiously exhibiting his coolness. For it had been rumored that the Ramon Martinez gang of "road agents" were "laying" for us on the second grade, and would time the passage of our lights across Galloper's in order to intercept us in the "brush" beyond. If we could cross the ridge without being seen, and so get through the brush before they reached it, we were safe. If they followed, it would only be a stern chase, with the odds in our favor.

The huge vehicle swayed from side to side, rolled, dipped, and plunged, but Bill kept the track, as if, in the whispered words of the expressman, he could "feel and smell" the road he could no longer see. We knew that at times we hung perilously over the edge of slopes that eventually dropped a thousand feet sheer to the tops of the sugar-pines below, but we knew that Bill knew it also. The half-visible heads of the horses, drawn wedgewise together by the tightened reins, appeared to cleave the darkness like a plowshare, held between his rigid hands. Even the hoof-beats of the six horses had fallen into a vague, monotonous, distant roll. Then the ridge was crossed, and we plunged into the still blacker obscurity of the brush. Rather, we no longer seemed to move—it was only the phantom night that rushed by us. The horses might have been submerged in some swift Lethean stream; nothing but the top of the coach and the rigid bulk of Yuba Bill arose above them. Yet even in that awful moment our speed was unslackened; it was as if Bill cared no longer to *guide*, but only to drive; or as if the direction of his huge machine was determined by other hands than his. An incautious whisper hazarded the paralyzing suggestion of our "meeting another team." To our great astonishment Bill overheard it; to our greater astonishment he replied. "It 'ud be only a neck and neck race which would get to h—ll first," he said quietly. But we were relieved—for he had *spoken!* Almost simultaneously the wider turnpike began to glimmer faintly as a visible track before us; the wayside trees fell out of line, opened up, and dropped off one after another; we were on the broader tableland, out of danger, and apparently unperceived and unpursued.

Nevertheless in the conversation that broke out again with the relighting of the lamps, and the comments, congratulations, and reminiscences that were freely exchanged, Yuba Bill preserved a dissatisfied and even resentful silence. The most generous praise of his skill and courage awoke no response. "I reckon the old man was just spilin' for a fight, and is feelin' disappointed," said a passenger. But those who knew that Bill had the true fighter's scorn for any purely purposeless conflict were more or less concerned and watchful of him. He would drive steadily for four or five minutes with thoughtfully knitted brows, but eyes still keenly observant under his slouched hat, and then, relaxing his strained attitude, would give way to a movement of impatience. "You ain't uneasy about anything, Bill, are you?" asked the expressman, confidentially. Bill lifted his eyes with a slightly contemptuous surprise. "Not about anything ter *come*. It's what *hez* happened that I don't exackly sabe. I don't see no signs of Ramon's gang ever havin' been out at all, and ef they were out I don't see why they didn't go for us."

"The simple fact is, that our ruse was successful," said an outside passenger. "They waited to see our lights on the ridge, and not seeing them, missed us until we had passed. That's my opinion."

"You ain't puttin' any price on that opinion, air ye?" inquired Bill politely.

"No."

"'Cos thar's a comic paper in 'Frisco pays for them things, and I've seen worse things in it."

"Come off, Bill!" retorted the passenger, slightly nettled by the tittering of his companions. "Then what did you put out the lights for?"

"Well," returned Bill, grimly, "it mout have been because I didn't keer to hev you chaps blazin' away at the first bush you *thought* you saw move in your skeer, and bringin' down their fire on us."

The explanation, though unsatisfactory, was by no means an improbable one, and we thought it better to accept it with a laugh. Bill, however, resumed his abstracted manner.

"Who got in at the Summit?" he at last asked abruptly of the expressman.

"Derrick and Simpson of Cold Spring, and one of the 'Excelsior' boys," responded the expressman.

"And that Pike County girl from Dow's Flat, with her bundles. Don't forget her," added the outside passenger, ironically.

"Does anybody here know her?" continued Bill, ignoring the irony.

"You'd better ask Judge Thompson; he

was mighty attentive to her, gettin' her a
seat by the off window, and lookin' after
her bundles and things."

"Gettin' her a seat by the *window?*" repeated Bill.

"Yes; she wanted to see everything, and
wasn't afraid of the shooting."

"Yes," broke in a third passenger, "and
he was so d—d civil that, when she dropped
her ring in the straw, he struck a match
ag'in' all your rules, you know, and held
it for her to find it. And it was just as we
were crossin' through the brush, too. I saw
the hull thing through the window, for I
was hanging over the wheels with my gun,
ready for action. And it wasn't no fault of
Judge Thompson's if his d—d foolishness
hadn't shown us up, and got us a shot
from the gang."

Bill gave a short grunt, but drove steadily on without further comment, or even
turning his eyes to the speaker.

We were now not more than a mile from
the station at the cross-roads where we
were to change horses. The lights already
glimmered in the distance, and there was
a faint suggestion of the coming dawn on
the summits of the ridge to the west. We
had plunged into a belt of timber, when
suddenly a horseman emerged at a sharp
canter from a trail that seemed to be parallel with our own. We were all slightly
startled; Yuba Bill alone preserving his
moody calm.

"Hullo!" he said.

The stranger wheeled to our side as Bill
slackened his speed. He seemed to be a
"packer," or freight muleteer.

"Ye didn't get 'held up' on the Divide?"
continued Bill, cheerfully.

"No," returned the packer, with a laugh;
"*I* don't carry treasure. But I see you're
all right, too. I saw you crossin' over
Galloper's."

"*Saw* us?" said Bill sharply. "We had
our lights out."

"Yes, but there was suthin' white, a
handkerchief or woman's veil, I reckon,
hangin' from the window. It was only a
movin' spot ag'in' the hillside, but ez I was
lookin' out for ye I knew it was you by
that. Good night!"

He cantered away. We tried to look at
each other's faces, and at Bill's expression
in the darkness, but he neither spoke nor
stirred until he threw down the reins when
we stopped before the station. The passengers quickly descended from the roof; the

expressman was about to follow, but Bill
plucked his sleeve.

"I'm goin' to take a look over this yer
stage and these yer passengers with ye,
afore we start."

"Why, what's up?"

"Well," said Bill, slowly disengaging
himself from one of his enormous gloves,
"when we waltzed down into the brush up
there, I saw a man, ez plain ez I see you,
rise up from it. I thought our time had
come and the band was goin' to play, when
he sorter drew back, made a sign, and we
just scooted past him."

"Well?"

"Well," said Bill, "it means that this
yer coach was *passed through free* to-
night."

"You don't object to *that*, surely? I think
we were deucedly lucky."

Bill slowly drew off his other glove.
"I've been riskin' my everlastin' life on
this d—d line three times a week," he said
with mock humility, "and I'm allus thankful for small mercies. *But*," he added
grimly, "when it comes down to being
passed free by some pal of a hoss-thief,
and thet called a speshal Providence, *I*
ain't in it! No, sir, I ain't in it!"

II

It was with mixed emotions that the
passengers heard that a delay of fifteen
minutes, to tighten certain screw-bolts, had
been ordered by the autocratic Bill. Some
were anxious to get their breakfast at
Sugar Pine, but others were not averse to
linger for the daylight that promised
greater safety on the road. The expressman, knowing the real cause of Bill's delay, was nevertheless at a loss to understand the object of it. The passengers were
all well known; any idea of complicity with
the road agents was wild and impossible;
and, even if there was a confederate of the
gang among them, he would have been
more likely to precipitate a robbery than
to check it. Again, the discovery of such a
confederate—to whom they clearly owed
their safety—and his arrest, would have
been quite against the Californian sense of
justice, if not actually illegal. It seemed
evident that Bill's quixotic sense of honor
was leading him astray.

The station consisted of a stable, a
wagon-shed, and a building containing
three rooms. The first was fitted up with

"bunks," or sleeping-berths, for the employees, the second was the kitchen, and the third and larger apartment was dining-room or sitting-room, and was used as general waiting-room for the passengers. It was not a refreshment station, and there was no "bar." But a mysterious command from the omnipotent Bill produced a demijohn of whisky, with which he hospitably treated the company. The seductive influence of the liquor loosened the tongue of the gallant Judge Thompson. He admitted to having struck a match to enable the fair Pike Countian to find her ring, which, however, proved to have fallen in her lap. She was "a fine, healthy young woman—a type of the Far West, sir; in fact, quite a prairie blossom, yet simple and guileless as a child." She was on her way to Marysville, he believed, "although she expected to meet friends—a friend, in fact—later on." It was her first visit to a large town— in fact, any civilized center—since she crossed the plains three years ago. Her girlish curiosity was quite touching, and her innocence irresistible. In fact, in a country whose tendency was to produce "frivolity and forwardness in young girls," he "found her a most interesting young person." She was even then out in the stable-yard watching the horses being harnessed, "preferring to indulge in a pardonable healthy young curiosity than to listen to the empty compliments of the younger passengers."

The figure which Bill saw thus engaged, without being otherwise distinguished, certainly seemed to justify the judge's opinion. She appeared to be a well-matured country girl, whose frank gray eyes and large laughing mouth expressed a wholesome and abiding gratification in her life and surroundings. She was watching the replacing of luggage in the boot. A little feminine start, as one of her own parcels was thrown somewhat roughly on the roof, gave Bill his opportunity. "Now, there," he growled to the helper, "ye ain't carting stone! Look out, will yer! Some of your things, miss?" he added with gruff courtesy, turning to her. "These yer trunks, for instance?"

She smiled a pleasant assent, and Bill, pushing aside the helper, seized a large, square trunk in his arms. But from excess of zeal, or some other mischance, his foot slipped, and he came down heavily, striking the corner of the trunk on the ground and

loosening its hinges and fastenings. It was a cheap, common-looking affair, but the accident discovered in its yawning lid a quantity of white, lace-edged feminine apparel of an apparently superior quality. The young lady uttered another cry and came quickly forward, but Bill was profuse in his apologies, himself girded the broken box with a strap, and declared his intention of having the company "make it good" to her with a new one. Then he casually accompanied her to the door of the waiting-room, entered, made a place for her before the fire by simply lifting the nearest and most youthful passenger by the coat-collar from the stool that he was occupying, and, having installed the lady in it, displaced another man who was standing before the chimney, and, drawing himself up to his full six feet of height in front of her, glanced down upon his fair passenger as he took his waybill from his pocket.

"Your name is down here as Miss Mullins?" he said.

She looked up, became suddenly aware that she and her questioner were the center of interest to the whole circle of passengers, and, with a slight rise of color, returned, "Yes."

"Well, Miss Mullins, I've got a question or two to ask ye. I ask it straight out afore this crowd. It's in my rights to take ye aside and ask it—but that ain't my style; I'm no detective. I needn't ask it at all, but act as ef I knowed the answer, or I might leave it to be asked by others. Ye needn't answer it ef ye don't like; ye've got a friend over ther—Judge Thompson— who is a friend to ye, right or wrong, jest as any other man here is—as though ye'd packed your own jury. Well, the simple question I've got to ask ye is this—Did you signal to anybody from the coach when we passed Galloper's an hour ago?"

We all thought that Bill's courage and audacity had reached its climax here. To openly and publicly accuse a "lady" before a group of chivalrous Californians, and that lady possessing the further attractions of youth, good looks, and innocence, was little short of desperation. There was an evident movement of adhesion towards the fair stranger, a slight muttering broke out on the right, but the very boldness of the act held them in stupefied surprise. Judge Thompson, with a bland propitiatory smile, began: "Really, Bill, I must protest on behalf of this young lady—" when the fair accused, raising her eyes to her accuser. to the consternation of everybody answered with the slight but convincing hesitation of conscientious truthfulness:

"*I did.*"

"Ahem!" interposed the judge, hastily, "er—that is—er—you allowed your handkerchief to flutter from the window. I noticed it myself casually—one might say even playfully—but without any partcular significance."

The girl, regarding her apologist with a singular mingling of pride and impatience, returned briefly:

"I signaled."

"Who did you signal to?" asked Bill, gravely.

"The young gentleman I'm going to marry."

A start, followed by a slight titter from the younger passengers, was instantly suppressed by a savage glance from Bill.

"What did you signal to him for?" he continued.

"To tell him I was here, and that it was all right," returned the young girl, with a steadily rising pride and color.

"Wot was all right?" demanded Bill.

"That I wasn't followed, and that he could meet me on the road beyond Cass's Ridge Station." She hesitated a moment, and then, with a still greater pride, in which a youthful defiance was still mingled, said: "I've run away from home to marry him. And I mean to! No one can stop me. Dad didn't like him just because he was poor, and dad's got money. Dad wanted me to marry a man I hate, and got a lot of dresses and things to bribe me."

"And you're taking them in your trunk to the other fellow?" said Bill, grimly.

"Yes; he's poor," returned the girl, defiantly.

"Then your father's name is Mullins?" asked Bill.

"It's not Mullins. I—I—took that name," she hesitated, with her first exhibition of self-consciousness.

"Wot *is* his name?"

"Eli Hemmings."

A smile of relief and significance went round the circle. The fame of Eli or "Skinner" Hemmings, as a notorious miser and usurer, had passed even beyond Galloper's Ridge.

"The step that you're taking, Miss Mullins, I need not tell you, is one of great gravity," said Judge Thompson, with a certain paternal seriousness of manner, in which, however, we were glad to detect a glaring affectation, "and I trust that you and your affianced have fully weighed it. Far be it from me to interfere with or question the natural affections of two young people; but may I ask you what you know of the—er—young gentleman for whom you are sacrificing so much, and, perhaps, imperiling your whole future? For instance, have you known him long?"

The slightly troubled air of trying to understand—not unlike the vague wonderment of childhood—with which Miss Mullins had received the beginning of this exordium, changed to a relieved smile of comprehension as she said quickly: "Oh, yes, nearly a whole year."

"And," said the judge, smiling, "has he a vocation—is he in business?"

"Oh, yes," she returned, "he's a collector."

"A collector?"

"Yes; he collects bills, you know, money," she went on, with childish eagerness; "not for himself—*he* never has any money, poor Charley—but for his firm. It's dreadful hard work, too; keeps him out for days and nights, over bad roads and baddest weather. Sometimes, when he's stole over to the ranch just to see me, he's been so bad he could scarcely keep his seat in the saddle, much less stand. And he's got to take mighty big risks, too. Times the folks are cross with him and won't pay; once they shot him in the arm, and he came to me, and I helped do it up for him. But he don't mind. He's real brave, jest as brave as he's good." There was such a wholesome ring of truth in this pretty praise that we were touched in sympathy with the speaker.

"What firm does he collect for?" asked the judge gently.

"I don't know exactly—he won't tell me —but I think it's a Spanish firm. You see" —she took us all into her confidence with a sweeping smile of innocent yet half-mischievous artfulness—"I only know because I peeped over a letter he once got from his firm, telling him he must hustle up and be ready for the road the next day; but I think the name was Martinez— yes, Ramon Martinez."

In the dead silence that ensued—a silence so profound that we could hear the horses in the distant stable-yard rattling their harness—one of the younger "Excelsior" boys burst into a hysteric laugh; but the fierce eye of Yuba Bill was down upon him, and seemed to instantly stiffen him into a silent, grinning mask. The young girl, however, took no note of it; following out, with loverlike diffusiveness, the reminiscences thus awakened, she went on:

"Yes, it's mighty hard work, but he says it's all for me, and as soon as we're married he'll quit it. He might have quit it before, but he won't take no money of me, nor what I told him I could get out of dad! That ain't his style. He's mighty proud—if he is poor—is Charley. Why, thar's all ma's money which she left me in the savin's bank that I wanted to draw out —for I had the right—and give it to him, but he wouldn't hear of it! Why, he wouldn't take one of the things I've got with me, if he knew it. And so he goes on ridin' and ridin', here and there and everywhere, and gettin' more and more played out and sad, and thin and pale as a spirit, and always so uneasy about his business, and startin' up at times when we're meetin' out in the south woods or in the far clearin', and sayin': 'I must be goin' now, Polly,' and yet always tryin' to be chiffle and chipper afore me. Why he must have rid miles and miles to have watched for me thar in the brush at the foot of Galloper's to-night, jest to see if all was safe, and Lordy! I'd have given him the signal and showed a light if I'd died for it the next minit. There! That's what I know of Charley—that's what I'm running away from home for—that's what I'm running to him for, and I don't care who knows it! And I only wish I'd done it afore—and I would—if—if—if—he'd only *asked me!* There now!" She stopped, panted, and choked. Then one of the sudden transitions of youthful emotion overtook the eager, laughing face; it clouded up with the swift change of childhood, a lightning quiver of expression broke over it—and—then came the rain!

I think this simple act completed our utter demoralization! We smiled feebly at each other with that assumption of masculine superiority which is miserably conscious of its own helplessness at such moments. We looked out of the window, blew our noses, said: "Eh—what?" and "I say," vaguely to each other, and were greatly relieved and yet apparently astonished when Yuba Bill, who had turned his back upon the fair speaker, and was kicking the logs in the fireplace, suddenly swept down upon us and bundled us all into the road, leaving Miss Mullins alone. Then he walked aside with Judge Thompson for a few moments; returned to us, autocratically demanded of the party a complete reticence towards Miss Mullins on the subject matter under discussion, reentered the station, reappeared with the young lady, suppressed a faint, idiotic cheer which broke from us at the spectacle of her innocent face once more cleared and rosy, climbed the box, and in another moment we were under way.

"Then she don't know what her lover is?" asked the expressman, eagerly.

"No."

"Are *you* certain it's one of the gang?"

"Can't say *for sure*. It mout be a young chap from Yolo who bucked ag'in' the tiger at Sacramento, got regularly cleaned out and busted, and joined the gang for a flier. They say thar was a new hand in that job over at Keeley's—and a mighty game one, too—and ez there was some buckshot onloaded that trip, he might hev got his share, and that would tally with what the girl said about his arm. See! Ef that's the man, I've heered he was the son of some big preacher in the States, and a college sharp to boot, who ran wild in 'Frisco, and played himself for all he was worth. They're the wust kind to kick when they once get a foot over the traces. For stiddy, comf'ble kempany," added Bill reflectively, "give *me* the son of a man that was *hanged!*"

"But what are you going to do about this?"

"That depends upon the feller who comes to meet her."

"But you ain't going to try to take him? That would be playing it pretty low down on them both."

"Keep your hair on, Jimmy! The judge and me are only going to rastle with the sperrit of that gay young galoot, when he drops down for his girl—and exhort him pow'ful! Ef he allows he's convicted of sin and will find the Lord, we'll marry him and the gal offhand at the next station, and the judge will officiate himself for nothin'. We're goin' to have this yer elopement done on the square—and our waybill clean —you bet!"

"But you don't suppose he'll trust himself in your hands?"

"Polly will signal to him that it's all square."

"Ah!" said the expressman. Nevertheless in those few moments the men seemed to have exchanged dispositions. The expressman looked doubtfully, critically, and even cynically before him. Bill's face had relaxed, and something like a bland smile beamed across it as he drove confidently and unhesitatingly forward.

Day, meantime, although full blown and radiant on the mountain summits around us, was yet nebulous and uncertain in the valleys into which we were plunging. Lights still glimmered in the cabins and few ranch buildings which began to indicate the thicker settlements. And the shadows were heaviest in a little copse, where a note from Judge Thompson in the coach was handed up to Yuba Bill, who at one slowly began to draw up his horses. The coach stopped finally near the junction of a small cross-road. At the same moment Miss Mullins slipped down from the vehicle, and, with a parting wave of her hand to the judge, who had assisted her from the steps, tripped down the crossroad, and disappeared in its semi-obscurity. To our surprise the stage waited, Bill holding the reins listlessly in his hands. Five minutes passed—an eternity of expectation—and, as there was that in Yuba Bill's face which forbade idle questioning, an aching void of silence also! This was at last broken by a strange voice from the road:

"Go on; we'll follow."

The coach started forward. Presently we heard the sound of other wheels behind us. We all craned our necks backward to get a view of the unknown, but by the growing light we could only see that we were followed at a distance by a buggy with two figures in it. Evidently Polly Mullins and her lover! We hoped that they would pass us. But the vehicle, although drawn by a fast horse, preserved its distance always, and it was plain that its driver had no desire to satisfy our curiosity. The expressman had recourse to Bill.

"Is it the man you thought of?" he asked, eagerly.

"I reckon," said Bill, briefly.

"But," continued the expressman, returning to his former skepticism, "what's to keep them both from levanting together now?"

Bill jerked his hand toward the boot with a grim smile.

"Their baggage."

"Oh!" said the expressman.

"Yes," continued Bill. "We'll hang on to that gal's little frills and fixin's until this yer job's settled, and the ceremony's over, jest as if we waz her own father. And, what's more, young man," he added, suddenly turning to the expressman, "*you'll* express them trunks of hers *through to Sacramento* with your kempany's labels, and hand her the receipts and checks for them so she *can get 'em there*. That'll keep *him* outer temptation and the reach o' the gang, until they get away among white men and civilization again. When your hoary-headed ole grandfather—or, to speak plainer, that partikler old whisky-soaker known as Yuba Bill, wot sits on this box," he continued, with a diabolical wink at the expressman—"waltzes in to pervide for a young couple jest startin' in life, thar's nothin' mean about his style, you bet. He fills the bill every time! Speshul Providences takes a back seat when he's around."

When the station hotel and straggling settlement of Sugar Pine, now distinct and clear in the growing light, at last rose within rifle-shot on the plateau, the buggy suddenly darted swiftly by us—so swiftly that the faces of the two occupants were barely distinguishable as they passed—and, keeping the lead by a dozen lengths, reached the door of the hotel. The young girl and her companion leaped down and vanished within as we drew up. They had evidently determined to elude our curiosity, and were successful.

But the material appetites of the passengers, sharpened by the keen mountain air, were more potent than their curiosity, and, as the breakfast-bell rang out at the moment the stage stopped, a majority of them rushed into the dining-room and scrambled for places without giving much heed to the vanished couple or to the Judge and Yuba Bill, who had disappeared also. The through coach to Marysville and Sacramento was likewise waiting, for Sugar Pine was the limit of Bill's ministration, and the coach which we had just left went no farther. In the course of twenty minutes, however, there was a slight and somewhat ceremonious bustling in the hall and on the veranda, and Yuba Bill and the judge reappeared. The latter was leading, with some elaboration of manner and detail, the shapely figure of Miss Mullins, and Yuba Bill was accompanying her companion to the buggy. We all rushed to the windows to get a good view of the mysterious stranger and probable ex-brigand whose life was now linked with our fair fellow-passenger. I am afraid, however, that we all participated in a certain impression of disappointment and doubt. Handsome and even cultivated looking he assuredly was; young and vigorous in appearance. But there was a certain half-shamed, half-defiant suggestion in his expression, yet coupled with a watchful, lurking uneasiness which was not pleasant, and hardly becoming in a bridegroom—and the possessor of such a bride. But the frank, joyous, innocent face of Polly Mullins, resplendent with a simple, happy confidence, melted our hearts again, and condoned the fellow's shortcomings. We waved our hands; I think we would have given three rousing cheers as they drove away if the omnipotent eye of Yuba Bill had not been upon us. It was well, for the next moment we were summoned to the presence of that soft-hearted autocrat.

We found him alone with the judge in a private sitting-room, standing before a table on which there was a decanter and glasses. As we filed expectantly into the room and the door closed behind us, he cast a glance of hesitating tolerance over the group.

"Gentlemen," he said slowly, "you was all present at the beginnin' of a little game this mornin', and the judge thar thinks that you oughter be let in at the finish. *I* don't see that it's any of *your* d—d business, so to speak; but ez the judge here allows you're all in the secret, I've called you in to take a partin' drink to the health of Mr. and Mrs. Charley Byng—ez is now comf'ably off on their bridal tower. What *you* know or what *you* suspects of the young galoot that's married the gal ain't worth shucks to anybody, and I wouldn't give it to a yaller pup to play with, but the judge'thinks you ought all to promise right here that you'll keep it dark. That's his opinion. Ez far as my opinion goes, gen'lemen," continued Bill, with greater blandness and apparent cordiality, "I wanter simply remark, in a keerless, offhand, gin'ral way, that ef I ketch any God-forsaken, lop-eared, chuckle-headed, blatherin' idjet airin' *his* opinion—"

"One moment, Bill," interposed Judge Thompson, with a grave smile, "let me explain.—You understand, gentlemen," he said, turning to us, "the singular, and I may say affecting, situation which our good-hearted friend here has done so much to bring to what we hope will be a happy termination. I want to give here, as my professional opinion, that there is nothing in his request which, in your capacity as good citizens and law-abiding men, you may not grant. I want to tell you, also, that you are condoning no offense against the statutes; that there is not a particle of legal evidence before us of the criminal antecedents of Mr. Charles Byng, except that which has been told you by the innocent lips of his betrothed, which the law of the land has now sealed forever in the mouth of his wife; and that our own actual experience of his acts has been in the main exculpatory of any previous irregularity, if not incompatible with it. Briefly, no judge would charge, no jury convict, on such evidence. When I add that the young girl is of legal age, that there is no evidence of any previous undue influence, but rather of the reverse, on the part of the bridegroom, and that I was content, as a magistrate, to perform the ceremony, I think you will be satisfied to give your promise, for the sake of the bride, and drink a happy life to them both."

I need not say that we did this cheerfully, and even extorted from Bill a grunt of satisfaction. The majority of the company, however, who were going with the through coach to Sacramento, then took their leave, and, as we accompanied them to the veranda, we could see that Miss Polly Mullins's trunks were already transferred to the other vehicle under the protecting seals and labels of the all-potent express company. Then the whip cracked, the coach rolled away, and the last traces of the adventurous young couple disappeared in the hanging red dust of its wheels.

But Yuba Bill's grim satisfaction at the happy issue of the episode seemed to suffer no abatement. He even exceeded his usual deliberately regulated potations, and, standing comfortably with his back to the center of the now deserted barroom, was more than usually loquacious with the expressman. "You see," he said, in bland reminiscence, "when your old Uncle Bill takes hold of a job like this, he puts it straight through without changin' hosses. Yet thar was a moment, young feller, when I thought I was stompt! It was when we'd made up our mind to make that chap tell the gal fust all what he was! Ef she'd rared or kicked in the traces, or hung back only ez much ez that, we'd hev given him jest five minits' law to get up and get and leave her, and we'd hev toted that gal and her fixin's back to her dad again! But she jest gave a little scream and start, and then went off inter hysterics, right on his buzzum, laughin' and cryin' and sayin' that nothin' should part 'em. Gosh! if I didn't think *he* woz more cut up than she about it; a minit it looked as ef *he* didn't allow to marry her arter all, but that passed, and they was married hard and fast—you bet! I reckon he's had enough of stayin' out o' nights to last him, and ef the valley settlements hevn't got hold of a very shining member, at least the foothills hev got shut of one more of the Ramon Martinez gang."

"What's that about the Ramon Martinez gang?" said a quiet, potential voice.

Bill turned quickly. It was the voice of the divisional superintendent of the express company—a man of eccentric determination of character, and one of the few whom the autocratic Bill recognized as an equal —who had just entered the barroom. His dusty pongee cloak and soft hat indicated that he had that morning arrived on a round of inspection.

"Don't care if I do, Bill," he continued, in response to Bill's invitatory gesture, walking to the bar. "It's a little raw out on the road. Well, what were you saying about the Ramon Martinez gang? You haven't come across one of 'em, have you?"

"No," said Bill, with a slight blinking of his eye, as he ostentatiously lifted his glass to the light.

"And you *won't*," added the superintendent, leisurely sipping his liquor. "For the fact is, the gang is about played out. Not from want of a job now and then, but from the difficulty of disposing of the results of their work. Since the new instructions to the agents to identify and trace all dust and bullion offered to them went into force, you see they can't get rid of their swag. All the gang are spotted at the offices, and it costs too much for them to pay a fence or a middleman of any standing. Why, all that flaky river gold they took from the Excelsior Company can

be identified as easy as if it was stamped with the company's mark. They can't melt it down themselves; they can't get others to do it for them; they can't ship it to the Mint or Assay Offices in Marysville and 'Frisco, for they won't take it without our certificate and seals, and *we* don't take any undeclared freight *within* the lines that we've drawn around their beat, except from people and agents known. Why, *you* know that well enough, Jim," he said, suddenly appealing to the expressman, "don't you?"

Possibly the suddenness of the appeal caused the expressman to swallow his liquor the wrong way, for he was overtaken with a fit of coughing, and stammered hastily, as he laid down his glass. "Yes—of course—certainly."

"No, sir," resumed the superintendent cheerfully, "they're pretty well played out. And the best proof of it is, that they've lately been robbing ordinary passengers' trunks. There was a freight wagon 'held up' near Dow's Flat the other day, and a lot of baggage gone through. I had to go down there to look into it. Darned if they hadn't lifted a lot o' woman's wedding things from that rich couple who got married the other day out at Marysville. Looks as if they were playing it rather low down, don't it? Coming down to hard pan and bed rock—eh?"

The expressman's face was turned anxiously toward Bill, who, after a hurried gulp of his remaining liquor, still stood staring at the window. Then he slowly drew on one of his large gloves. "Ye didn't," he said, with a slow, drawling, but perfectly distinct, articulation, "happen to know old 'Skinner' Hemmings when you were over there?"

"Yes."

"And his daughter?"

"He hasn't got any."

"A sort o' mild, innocent, guileless child of nature?" persisted Bill, with a yellow face, a deadly calm and satanic deliberation.

"No. I tell you he *hasn't* any daughter. Old man Hemmings is a confirmed old bachelor. He's too mean to support more than one."

"And you didn't happen to know any o' that gang, did ye?" continued Bill, with infinite protraction.

"Yes. Knew 'em all. There was French Pete, Cherokee Bob, Kanaka Joe, One-eyed Stillson, Softy Brown, Spanish Jack, and two or three Greasers."

"And ye didn't know a man by the name of Charley Byng?"

"No," returned the superintendent, with a slight suggestion of weariness and a distraught glance toward the door.

"A dark, stylish chap, with shifty black eyes and a curled-up merstache?" continued Bill, with dry, colorless persistence.

"No. Look here, Bill, I'm in a little bit of a hurry; but I suppose you must have your little joke before we part. Now, what *is* your little game?"

"Wot you mean?" demanded Bill, with sudden bruskness.

"Mean? Well, old man, you know as well as I do. You're giving me the very description of Ramon Martinez himself. Ha! ha! No, Bill, you didn't play me this time! You're mighty spry and clever, but you didn't catch on just then."

He nodded and moved away with a light laugh. Bill turned a stony face to the expressman. Suddenly a gleam of mirth came into his gloomy eyes. He bent over the young man, and said in a hoarse, chuckling whisper:

"But I got even after all!"

"How?"

"He's tied up to that lying little she-devil, hard and fast!"

XV

THOMAS BAILEY ALDRICH (1836–1907)

The first of the Eastern writers of the younger generation after the war to attract attention with a new and fresh variety of the short story was Thomas Bailey Aldrich, best known perhaps as our leading *artiste* in *vers de société*,—our "American Herrick." Born of an old Puritan family at Portsmouth, New Hampshire, he was early removed from the New England environment, and at New Orleans, where he lived for three years, and at New York City, where he spent his later youth and early manhood, he acquired that cosmopolitan view of life and culture that makes his work different from that of most of his New England contemporaries. Before he was twenty-one he was associate editor with N. P. Willis of the New York *Home Journal,* and soon he was boon companion with the brilliant Fitz-James O'Brien and in the full tide of the Broadway literary Bohemia of the fifties.

From the first, literature to Aldrich meant poetry. He published in his early years little else and all his life long poetry was to him supreme. But when after a brief war experience he settled in Boston as editor first of *The Illustrated News* and then of *Every Saturday,* he began to express himself more and more in prose. *Every Saturday* was an eclectic magazine made up almost wholly from European journals and reviews, and in editing it he was constantly in the atmosphere of foreign literature. The new French short story, which, influenced undoubtedly by Poe, had begun to be distinctive, early attracted him and soon he was himself writing short stories in the French manner—stories for entertainment solely, stories stripped of all moral or didactic or purpose ends, stories crisp, epigrammatic, sparkling, with surprising culminations and climaxes. Of these the most effective and characteristic was "Marjorie Daw" which gave the title to his best collection published in 1873. His short-story product may be called small—his entire list totals not over thirty—and distinctive, each story a highly finished product. Willis had been the first to add vivacity and brilliancy to the "light story" told for mere entertainment; Aldrich was the second; and then came Stockton, Bunner, O. Henry and the moderns. Never did Aldrich allow himself to go to the extremes of a Willis or of an O. Henry. In him there was the New England restraint, the awe of Boston standards, which kept constantly in leash the cosmopolitan and Bohemian impulses which always, we feel, were present when he wrote.

A STRUGGLE FOR LIFE

One morning last April, as I was passing through Boston Common, which lies pleasantly between my residence and my office, I met a gentleman lounging along The Mall. I am generally preoccupied when walking, and often thrid my way through crowded streets without distinctly observing a single soul. But this man's face forced itself upon me, and a very singular face it was. His eyes were faded, and his hair, which he wore long, was flecked with gray. His hair and eyes, if I may say so, were seventy years old, the rest of him not thirty. The youthfulness of his figure, the elasticity of his gait, and the venerable appearance of his head, were incongruities that drew more than one pair of curious eyes towards him. He was evi- dently an American,—the New England cut of countenance is unmistakable,—evidently a man who had seen something of the world; but strangely old and young.

Before reaching the Park Street gate, I had taken up the thread of thought which he had unconsciously broken; yet throughout the day this old young man, with his unwrinkled brow and silvered locks, glided in like a phantom between me and my duties.

The next morning I again encountered him on The Mall. He was resting lazily on the green rails, watching two little sloops in distress, which two ragged shipowners had consigned to the mimic perils of the Pond. The vessels lay becalmed in the middle of the ocean, displaying a tantalizing lack of sympathy with the frantic helplessness of the owners on shore. As the

entleman observed their dilemma, a light
me into his faded eyes, then died out,
aving them drearier than before. I won-
ered if he, too, in his time, had sent out
ips that drifted and drifted and never
me to port; and if these poor toys were
 him types of his own losses.

"I would like to know that man's story,"
said, half aloud, halting in one of those
inding paths which branch off from the
uietness of the Pond, and end in the rush
nd tumult of Tremont Street.

"Would you?" replied a voice at my
de. I turned and faced Mr. H——, a
eighbor of mine, who laughed heartily at
nding me talking to myself. "Well," he
lded, reflectively, "I can tell you this
an's story; and if you will match the nar-
tive with anything as curious, I shall be
lad to hear it."

"You know him then?"

"Yes and no. I happened to be in Paris
hen he was buried."

"Buried!"

"Well, strictly speaking, not buried; but
mething quite like it. If you've a spare
alf-hour," continued my interlocutor,
we'll sit on this bench, and I will tell you
ll I know of an affair that made some
oise in Paris a couple of years ago. The
entleman himself, standing yonder, will
erve as a sort of frontispiece to the ro-
ance,—a full-page illustration, as it
ere."

The following pages contain the story
at Mr. H—— related to me. While he
as telling it, a gentle wind arose; the
iniature sloops drifted feebly about the
cean; the wretched owners flew from
oint to point, as the deceptive breeze
romised to waft the barks to either shore;
e early robins trilled now and then from
e newly fringed elms; and the old young
an leaned on the rail in the sunshine,
earily, little dreaming that two gossips
ere discussing his affairs within twenty
ards of him.

Three people were sitting in a chamber
hose one large window overlooked the
lace Vendome. M. Dorine, with his back
alf turned on the other two occupants of
e apartment, was reading the *Moniteur*,
ausing from time to time to wipe his
lasses, and taking scrupulous pains not
 glance toward the lounge at his right,
n which were seated Mademoiselle Dorine
nd a young American gentleman, whose

handsome face rather frankly told his position in the family. There was not a hap-
pier man in Paris that afternoon than
Philip Wentworth. Life had become so
delicious to him that he shrunk from looking beyond to-day. What could the future
add to his full heart? what might it not
take away? In certain natures the deepest
joy has always something of melancholy
in it, a presentiment, a fleeting sadness, a
feeling without a name. Wentworth was
conscious of this subtle shadow, that night,
when he rose from the lounge, and thoughtfully held Julie's hand to his lip for a
moment before parting. A careless observer would not have thought him, as he
was, the happiest man in Paris.

M. Dorine laid down his paper and came
forward. "If the house," he said, "is such
as M. Martin describes it, I advise you to
close with him at once. I would accompany
you, Philip, but the truth is, I am too sad
at losing this little bird to assist you in
selecting a cage for her. Remember, the
last train for town leaves at five. Be sure
not to miss it; for we have seats for
M. Sardou's new comedy to-morrow night.
By to-morrow night," he added laughingly,
"little Julie here will be an old lady,—'tis
such an age from now until then."

The next morning the train bore Philip
to one of the loveliest spots within thirty
miles of Paris. An hour's walk through
green lanes brought him to M. Martin's
estate. In a kind of dream the young man
wandered from room to room, inspected
the conservatory, the stables, the lawns,
the strip of woodland through which a
merry brook sang to itself continually; and,
after dining with M. Martin, completed the
purchase, and turned his steps towards the
station, just in time to catch the express
train.

As Paris stretched out before him, with
its million lights twinkling in the early
dusk, and its sharp spires here and there
pricking the sky, it seemed to Philip as if
years had elapsed since he left the city. On
reaching Paris he drove to his hotel, where
he found several letters lying on the table.
He did not trouble himself even to glance
at their superscriptions as he threw aside
his traveling surtout for a more appropriate dress.

If, in his impatience to see Mademoiselle
Dorine, the cars had appeared to walk,
the fiacre which he had secured at the station appeared to creep. At last it turned

into the Place Vendome, and drew up before M. Dorine's residence. The door opened as Philip's foot touched the first step. The servant silently took his cloak and hat, with a special deference, Philip thought; but was he not now one of the family?

"Mr. Dorine," said the servant slowly, "is unable to see Monsieur at present. He wishes Monsieur to be shown up to the *salon.*"

"Is Mademoiselle—"

"Yes, Monsieur."

"Alone?"

"Alone, Monsieur," repeated the man, looking curiously at Philip, who could scarcely repress an exclamation of pleasure.

It was the first time that such a privilege had been accorded him. His interviews with Julie had always taken place in the presence of M. Dorine, or some member of the household. A well-bred Parisian girl has but a formal acquaintance with her lover.

Philip did not linger on the staircase; his heart sang in his bosom as he flew up the steps, two at a time. Ah! this wine of air which one drinks at twenty, and seldom after! He hastened through the softly lighted hall, in which he detected the faint scent of her favorite flowers, and stealthily opened the door of the *salon.*

The room was darkened. Underneath the chandelier stood a slim black casket on trestles. A lighted candle, a crucifix, and some white flowers were on a table near by. Julie Dorine was dead.

When M. Dorine heard the indescribable cry that rang through the silent house, he hurried from the library, and found Philip standing like a ghost in the middle of the chamber.

It was not until long afterwards that Wentworth learned the details of the calamity that had befallen him. On the previous night Mademoiselle Dorine had retired to her room in seemingly perfect health. She dismissed her maid with a request to be awakened early the next morning. At the appointed hour the girl entered the chamber. Mademoiselle Dorine was sitting in an arm-chair, apparently asleep. The candle had burnt down to the socket; a book lay half open on the carpet at her feet. The girl started when she saw that the bed had not been occupied, and that her mistress still wore an evening dress. She rushed to Mademoiselle Dorine's side. It was not slumber. It was death.

Two messages were at once despatched to Philip, one to the station at G——, the other to his hotel. The first missed him on the road, the second he had neglected to open. On his arrival at M. Dorine's house, the servant, under the supposition that Wentworth had been advised of Mademoiselle Dorine's death, broke the intelligence with awkward cruelty, by showing him directly to the *salon.*

Mademoiselle Dorine's wealth, her beauty, the suddenness of her death, and the romance that had in some way attached itself to her love for the young American, drew crowds to witness the final ceremonies which took place in the church in the Rue d'Aguesseau. The body was to be laid in M. Dorine's tomb, in the cemetery of Montmartre.

This tomb requires a few words of description. First, there was a grating of filigraned iron; through this you looked into a small vestibule or hall, at the end of which was a massive door of oak opening upon a short flight of stone steps descending into the tomb. The vault was fifteen or twenty feet square, ingeniously ventilated from the ceiling, but unlighted. It contained two sarcophagi; the first held the remains of Madame Dorine, long since dead; the other was new, and bore on one side the letters J. D., in monogram, interwoven with fleurs-de-lis.

The funeral train stopped at the gate of the small garden that enclosed the place of burial, only the immediate relatives following the bearers into the tomb. A slender wax candle, such as is used in Catholic churches, burnt at the foot of the uncovered sarcophagus, casting a dim glow over the center of the apartment, and deepening the shadows which seemed to huddle together in the corners. By this flickering light the coffin was placed in its granite shell, the heavy slab laid over it reverently and the oaken door revolved on its rusty hinges, shutting out the uncertain ray of sunshine that had ventured to peep in on the darkness.

M. Dorine, muffled in his cloak, threw himself on the back seat of the carriage too abstracted in his grief to observe that he was the only occupant of the vehicle. There was a sound of wheels grating on the graveled avenue, and then all was

ence again in the cemetery of Mont-
artre. At the main entrance the carriages
rted company, dashing off into various
reets at a pace that seemed to express a
nse of relief. The band plays a dead
arch going to the grave, but *Fra Diavolo*
ming from it.

It is not with the retreating carriages
at our interest lies. Nor yet wholly with
e dead in her mysterious dream; but with
ilip Wentworth.

The rattle of wheels had died out of the
r when Philip opened his eyes, bewil-
red, like a man abruptly roused from
mber. He raised himself on one arm
d stared into the surrounding blackness.
'here was he? In a second the truth
shed upon him. He had been left in the
mb! While kneeling on the farther side
the stone box, perhaps he had fainted,
d in the last solemn rites his absence
d been unnoticed.

His first emotion was one of natural
rror. But this passed as quickly as it
me. Life had ceased to be so very
ecious to him; and if it were his fate to
e at Julie's side, was not that the ful-
ment of the desire which he had ex-
essed to himself a hundred times that
orning? What did it matter, a few years
oner or later? He must lay down the
rden at last. Why not then? A pang of
lf-reproach followed the thought. Could
so lightly throw aside the love that had
nt over his cradle? The sacred name of
other rose involuntarily to his lips. Was
not cowardly to yield up without a strug-
le the life which he should guard for
er sake? Was it not his duty to the liv-
g and the dead to face the difficulties
f his position, and overcome them if it
ere within human power?

With an organization as delicate as a
oman's, he had that spirit which, how-
ver sluggish in repose, can leap with a
nd of exultation to measure its strength
ith disaster. The vague fear of the su-
ernatural, that would affect most men in
similar situation, found no room in his
eart. He was simply shut in a chamber
om which it was necessary that he should
btain release within a given period. That
is chamber contained the body of the
oman he loved, so far from adding to
e terror of the case, was a circumstance
om which he drew consolation. She was
beautiful white statue now. Her soul was
ar hence; and if that pure spirit could re-

turn, would it not be to shield him with
her love? It was impossible that the place
should not engender some thought of the
kind. He did not put the thought entirely
from him as he rose to his feet and
stretched out his hands in the darkness;
but his mind was too healthy and practical to indulge long in such speculations.

Philip chanced to have in his pocket a
box of wax-tapers which smokers use.
After several ineffectual attempts, he succeeded in igniting one against the dank
wall, and by its momentary glare perceived
that the candle had been left in the tomb.
This would serve him in examining the
fastenings of the vault. If he could force
the inner door by any means, and reach
the grating, of which he had an indistinct
recollection, he might hope to make himself
heard. But the oaken door was immovable,
as solid as the wall itself, into which it
fitted air-tight. Even if he had had the
requisite tools, there were no fastenings
to be removed: the hinges were set on the
outside.

Having ascertained this, he replaced the
candle on the floor, and leaned against
the wall thoughtfully, watching the blue
fan of flame that wavered to and fro,
threatening to detach itself from the wick.
"At all events," he thought, "the place is
ventilated." Suddenly Philip sprang forward and extinguished the light. His existence depended on that candle!

He had read somewhere, in some account
of shipwreck, how the survivors had lived
for days upon a few candles which one of
the passengers had insanely thrown into
the long-boat. And here he had been burning away his very life.

By the transient illumination of one of
the tapers, he looked at his watch. It had
stopped at eleven,—but at eleven that day,
or the preceding night? The funeral, he
knew, had left the church at ten. How
many hours had passed since then? Of
what duration had been his swoon? Alas!
It was no longer possible for him to measure those hours which crawl like snails
to the wretched, and fly like swallows over
the happy.

He picked up the candle, and seated himself on the stone steps. He was a sanguine
man, this Wentworth, but, as he weighed
the chances of escape, the prospect did
not seem encouraging. Of course he would
be missed. His disappearance under the
circumstances would surely alarm his

friends; they would instigate a search for him; but who would think of searching for a live man in the cemetery of Montmartre? The Prefect of Police would set a hundred intelligences at work to find him; the Seine might be dragged, *les misérables* turned over at the dead house; a minute description of him would be in every detective's pocket and he—in M. Dorine's family tomb!

Yet, on the other hand, it was here he was last seen; from this point a keen detective would naturally work up the case. Then might not the undertaker return for the candlestick, probably not left by design? Or, again, might not M. Dorine send fresh wreaths of flowers, to take the place of those which now diffused a pungent, aromatic odor throughout the chamber? Ah! what unlikely chances! But if one of these things did not happen speedily, it had better never happen. How long could he keep life in himself?

With unaccelerated pulse, he quietly cut the half-burned candle into four equal parts. "To-night," he meditated, "I will eat the first of these pieces; to-morrow, the second; to-morrow evening, the third; the next day, the fourth; and then—then I'll wait!"

He had taken no breakfast that morning, unless a cup of coffee can be called a breakfast. He had never been very hungry before. He was ravenously hungry now. But he postponed the meal as long as practicable. It must have been near midnight, according to his calculation, when he determined to try the first of his four singular repasts. The bit of white-wax was tasteless; but it served its purpose.

His appetite for the time appeased, he found a new discomfort. The humidity of the walls, and the wind that crept through the unseen ventilator, chilled him to the bone. To keep walking was his only resource. A sort of drowsiness, too, occasionally came over him. It took all his will to fight it off. To sleep, he felt was to die: and he had made up his mind to live.

Very strange fancies flitted through his head as he groped up and down the stone floor of the dungeon, feeling his way along the wall to avoid the sepulchers. Voices that had long been silent spoke words that had long been forgotten; faces he had known in childhood grew palpable against the dark. His whole life in detail was unrolled before him like a panorama: the

changes of a year, with its burden of love and death, its sweets and its bitternesses, were epitomized in a single second. The desire to sleep had left him. But the keen hunger came again.

It must be near morning now, he mused; perhaps the sun is just gilding the pinnacles and domes of the city; or, may be, a dull, drizzling rain is beating on Paris, sobbing on these mounds above me. Paris! it seems like a dream. Did I ever walk in its gay streets in the golden air? O the delight and pain and passion of that sweet human life!

Philip became conscious that the gloom, the silence, and the cold were gradually conquering him. The feverish activity of his brain brought on a reaction. He grew lethargic, he sunk down on the steps, and thought of nothing. His hand fell by chance on one of the pieces of candle; he grasped it and devoured it mechanically. This revived him. "How strange," he thought, "that I am not thirsty. It is possible that the dampness of the walls, which I must inhale with every breath, has supplied the need of water? Not a drop has passed my lips for two days, and still I experience no thirst. That drowsiness, thank Heaven, has gone. I think I was never wide awake until this hour. It would be an anodyne like poison that could weigh down by eyelids. No doubt the dread of sleep has something to do with this."

The minutes were like hours. Now he walked as briskly as he dared up and down the tomb; now he rested against the door. More than once he was tempted to throw himself upon the stone coffin that held Julie, and make no further struggle for his life.

Only one piece of candle remained. He had eaten the third portion, not to satisfy hunger, but from a precautionary motive. He had taken it as a man takes some disagreeable drug upon the result of which hangs safety. The time was rapidly approaching when even this poor substitute for nourishment would be exhausted. He delayed that moment. He gave himself a long fast this time. The half-inch of candle which he held in his hand was a sacred thing to him. It was his last defense against death.

At length, with such a sinking at heart as he had not known before, he raised it to his lips. Then he paused, then he hurled the fragment across the tomb, then the ken door was flung open, and Philip, ith dazzled eyes, saw M. Dorine's form arply outlined against the blue sky.

When they led him out, half blinded, to the broad daylight, M. Dorine noticed at Philip's hair, which a short time since as a black as a crow's wing, had actu-ly turned gray in places. The man's eyes, o, had faded; the darkness had spoiled eir luster.

"And how long was he really confined the tomb?" I asked, as Mr. H—— con-uded the story.

"Just one hour and twenty minutes!" plied Mr. H——, smiling blandly.

As he spoke, the little sloops, with their ils all blown out like white roses, came ating bravely into port, and Philip 'entworth lounged by us, wearily, in the easant April sunshine.

Mr. H——'s narrative made a deep im-ession on me. Here was a man who had dergone a strange ordeal. Here was a an whose sufferings were unique. His as no threadbare experience. Eighty min-es had seemed like two days to him!

he had really been immured two ys in the tomb, the story, from my int of view, would have lost its tragic ement.

After this it was but natural I should gard Mr. Wentworth with deepened in-rest. As I met him from day to day, ssing through the Common with that me abstracted air, 'here was something his loneliness which touched me. I won-red that I had not before read in his le meditative face some such sad his-

tory as Mr. H—— had confided to me. I formed the resolution of speaking to him, though with what purpose was not very clear to my mind. One May morning we met at the intersection of two paths. He courteously halted to allow me the prece-dence.

"Mr. Wentworth," I began, "——"

He interrupted me.

"My name, sir," he said, in an off-hand manner, "is Jones."

"Jo-Jo-Jones!" I gasped.

"Not Jo Jones," he returned coldly, "Frederick."

Mr. Jones, or whatever his name is, will never know, unless he reads these pages, why a man accosted him one morning as "Mr. Wentworth," and then abruptly rushed down the nearest path, and disap-peared in the crowd.

The fact is, I had been duped by Mr. H——, who is a gentleman of literary proclivities, and has, it is whispered, be-come somewhat demented in brooding over the Great American Novel—not yet hatched. He had actually tried the effect of one of his chapters on me!

My hero, as I subsequently learned, is no hero at all, but a commonplace young man who has some connection with the building of that pretty granite bridge which will shortly span the crooked little lake in the Public Garden.

When I think of the cool ingenuity and readiness with which Mr. H—— built up his airy fabric on my credulity, I am half inclined to laugh; though I feel not slight-ly irritated at having been the unresisting victim of his Black Art.

XVI

SAMUEL LANGHORNE CLEMENS (1835–1910)

Mark Twain bears out more completely than anyone else Bret Harte's theory as to th
American short story. His own short fiction, especially in the earlier years of his work, wa
almost wholly autobiographic in form, and seemingly a mere spontaneous overflow, withou
conscious art, of high spirits and youthful zest in life. Bret Harte was a widely read ma
a careful student of the art of other writers, but in Mark Twain there is no suggestion tha
he had ever read anything either in prose or poetry. He was as original as Walt Whitma
He had been a part of a veritable romance, the most stupendously magnificent one perhap
that the world has ever known, the opening of the great West of America, and he cou
write only what had passed under his own eye with all the native colors fresh upon i
All his earlier books are chaotic gatherings of anecdotes, pictures, special instances, whims
cal with the new western humor, and finished after the pattern of the *apropos* anecdote to
in gatherings of men. From every one of them breathes the personality of the narrator. The
are original, they are uniquely American, but first of all they are redolent with the whimsic
individualities of Samuel Langhorne Clemens. There is an unconscious drawl in the sty
that reminds us at every turn that the story was first orally given, and there is always
"nub," a carefully worked-up-to climax, an "explosion point" that often is found to be th
whole reason for the story. Never can he be taken as a model; Mark Twain is Mark Twai
  In his later years he changed somewhat the nature of his fiction. He used the short-stor
form more and more for humanitarian purposes, or for satiric or propagandic ends, as in th
case, for instance, of "The Man That Corrupted Hadleyburg." With him always form wa
secondary. If there is art to his somewhat chaotic fiction it is because he began his story on
when he had an end in view, and working constantly toward that end was able unconsciousl
to obey many of the so-called major canons of the critics.

THE CELEBRATED JUMPING FROG OF CALAVERAS COUNTY

In compliance with the request of a friend of mine, who wrote me from the East, I called on good-natured, garrulous old Simon Wheeler, and inquired after my friend's friend, *Leonidas W.* Smiley, as requested to do, and I hereunto append the result. I have a lurking suspicion that *Leonidas W.* Smiley is a myth; that my friend never knew such a personage; and that he only conjectured that, if I asked old Wheeler about him, that it would remind him of his infamous *Jim Smiley,* and he would go to work and bore me nearly to death with some infernal reminiscence of him as long and tedious as it would be useless to me. If that was the design, it certainly succeeded.

I found Simon Wheeler dozing comfortably by the bar-room stove of the old dilapidated tavern in the ancient mining camp of Angel's, and I noticed that he was fat and bald-headed, and had an expression of winning gentleness and simplicity upo his tranquil countenance. He roused up a gave me good-day. I told him a friend o mine had commissioned me to make som inquiries about a cherished companion o his boyhood named *Leonidas W.* Smiley *Rev. Leonidas W.* Smiley—a young min ister of the Gospel, who he had heard wa at one time a resident of Angel's Cam I added that, if Mr. Wheeler could tell m anything about this Rev. Leonidas W Smiley, I would feel under many obliga tions to him.

Simon Wheeler backed me into a corne and blockaded me there with his chai and then sat me down and reeled off th monotonous narrative which follows th paragraph. He never smiled, he neve frowned, he never changed his voice fro the gentle-flowing key to which he tune the initial sentence, he never betrayed th slightest suspicion of enthusiasm; but a through the interminable narrative ther ran a vein of impressive earnestness an sincerity, which showed me plainly tha so far from his imagining that there was anything ridiculous or funny about his story, he regarded it as a really important matter, and admitted its two heroes as men of transcendent genius in *finesse*. To me, the spectacle of a man drifting serenely along through such a queer yarn without ever smiling, was exquisitely absurd. As I said before, I asked him to tell me what he knew of Rev. Leonidas W. Smiley, and he replied as follows. I let him go on in his own way, and never interrupted him once:

There was a feller here once by the name of *Jim* Smiley, in the winter of '49 —or maybe it was the spring of '50—I don't recollect exactly, somehow, though what makes me think it was one or the other is because I remember the big flume wasn't finished when he first came to the camp; but anyway, he was the curiousest man about always betting on anything that turned up you ever see, if he could get anybody to bet on the other side; and if he couldn't, he'd change sides. Any way that suited the other man would suit him— any way just so's he got a bet, *he* was satisfied. But still he was lucky, uncommon lucky—he most always come out winner. He was always ready and laying for a chance; there couldn't be no solit'ry thing mentioned but that feller'd offer to bet on it, and take any side you please, as I was just telling you. If there was a horse-race, you'd find him flush, or you'd find him busted at the end of it; if there was a dog-fight, he'd bet on it; if there was a cat-fight, he'd bet on it; if there was a chicken-fight, he'd bet on it; why, if there was two birds setting on a fence, he would bet you which one would fly first; or if there was a camp-meeting, he would be there reg'lar, to bet on Parson Walker, which he judged to be the best exhorter about here, and so he was, too, and a good man. If he even seen a straddle-bug start to go anywheres, he would bet you how long it would take him to get wherever he was going to, and if you took him up, he would foller that straddle-bug to Mexico but what he would find out where he was bound for and how long he was on the road. Lots of the boys here has seen that Smiley, and can tell you about him. Why, it never made no difference to *him*—he would bet on *any*thing— the dangdest feller. Parson Walker's wife laid very sick once, for a good while, and it seemed as if they warn't going to save her; but one morning he came in, and Smiley asked how she was, and he said she was considerable better—thank the Lord for his inf'nit mercy—and coming on so smart that, with the blessing of Prov'-dence, she'd get well yet; and Smiley, before he thought, says, "Well, I'll risk two-and-a-half that she don't anyway."

Thish-yer Smiley had a mare—the boys called her the fifteen-minute nag, but that was only in fun, you know, because, of course, she was faster than that—and he used to win money on that horse, for all she was so slow and always had the asthma, or the distemper, or the consumption, or something of that kind. They used to give her two or three hundred yards start, and then pass her under way; but always at the fag-end of the race she'd get excited and desperate-like, and come cavorting and straddling up, and scattering her legs around limber, sometimes in the air, and sometimes out to one side amongst the fences, and kicking up m-o-r-e dust, and raising m-o-r-e racket with her coughing and sneezing and blowing her nose—and always fetch up at the stand just about a neck ahead, as near as you could cipher it down.

And he had a little small bull pup, that to look at him you'd think he wan't worth a cent but to set around and look ornery and lay for a chance to steal something. But as soon as money was up on him, he was a different dog; his under-jaw'd begin to stick out like the fo'castle of a steamboat, and his teeth would uncover, and shine savage like the furnaces. And a dog might tackle him, and bully-rag him, and bite him, and throw him over his shoulder two or three times, and Andrew Jackson—which was the name of the pup —Andrew Jackson would never let on but what *he* was satisfied, and hadn't expected nothing else—and the bets being doubled and doubled on the other side all the time, till the money was all up; and then all of a sudden he would grab that other dog jest by the j'int of his hind leg and freeze to it—not claw, you understand, but only jest grip and hang on till they throwed up the sponge, if it was a year. Smiley always come out winner on that pup, till he harnessed a dog once that didn't have no hind legs, because they'd been sawed off by a circular saw, and when the thing had gone along far enough, and the money was all up, and he come to make a snatch for his pet holt, he saw in a minute how he'd been imposed on, and how the other dog had him in the door, so to speak, and he 'peared surprised, and then he looked sorter discouraged-like, and didn't try no more to win the fight, and so he got shucked out bad. He give Smiley a look, as much to say his heart was broke and it was *his* fault for putting up a dog that hadn't no hind legs for him to take holt of, which was his main dependence in a fight, and then he limped off a piece and laid down and died. It was a good pup, was that Andrew Jackson, and would have made a name for hisself if he'd lived, for the stuff was in him, and he had genius—I know it, because he hadn't no opportunities to speak of, and it don't stand to reason that a dog could make such a fight as he could under them circumstances, if he hadn't no talent. It always makes me feel sorry when I think of that last fight of his'n, and the way it turned out.

Well, thish-yer Smiley had rat-tarriers, and chicken-cocks, and tom-cats, and all them kind of things, till you couldn't rest, and you couldn't fetch nothing for him to bet on but he'd match you. He ketched a frog one day, and took him home, and said he cal'klated to edercate him; and so he never done nothing for these three months but set in his back yard and learn that frog to jump. And you bet you he *did* learn him, too. He'd give him a little punch behind, and the next minute you'd see that frog whirling in the air like a doughnut—see him turn one summerset, or maybe a couple, if he got a good start, and come down flat-footed and all right, like a cat. He got him up so in the matter of catching flies, and kept him in practice so constant, that he'd nail a fly every time as far as he could see him. Smiley said all a frog wanted was education, and he could do most anything—and I believe him. Why, I've seen him set Dan'l Webster down here on this floor—Dan'l Webster was the name of the frog—and sing out, "Flies, Dan'l, flies!" and quicker'n you could wink, he'd spring straight up, and snake a fly off'n the counter there, and flop down on the floor again as solid as a gob of mud, and fall to scratching the side of his head with his hind foot as indifferent as if he hadn't no idea he's been doin' any more'n any frog might do. You never see a frog so modest and straight-

for'ard as he was, for all he was so gifted. And when it come to fair and square jumping on the dead level, he could get over more ground at one straddle than any animal of his breed you ever see. Jumping on a dead level was his strong suit, you understand; and when it come to that, Smiley would ante up money on him as long as he had a red. Smiley was monstrous proud of his frog, and well he might be, for fellers that had traveled and been everywhere all said he laid over any frog that ever *they* see.

Well, Smiley kept the beast in a little lattice box, and he used to fetch him downtown sometimes and lay for a bet. One day a feller—a stranger in the camp, he was—come across him with his box, and says:

"What might it be that you've got in the box?"

And Smiley says, sorter indifferent like "It might be a parrot, or it might be a canary, maybe, but it ain't—it's only just a frog."

An' the feller took it, and looked at it careful, and turned it round this way and that, and says, "H'm—so 'tis. Well, what's *he* good for?"

"Well," Smiley says, easy and careless "he's good enough for *one* thing, I should judge—he can outjump ary frog in Calaveras county."

The feller took the box again, and took another long, particular look, and give it back to Smiley, and says, very deliberate "Well, I don't see no p'ints about that frog that's any better'n any other frog."

"Maybe you don't," Smiley says. "Maybe you understand frogs, and maybe you don't understand 'em; maybe you've had experience, and maybe you ain't only a amature, as it were. Anyways, I've got *my* opinion, and I'll risk forty dollars that he can outjump any frog in Calaveras county."

And the feller studied a minute, and then says, kinder sad like, "Well, I'm only a stranger here, and I ain't got no frog but if I had a frog, I'd bet you."

And then Smiley says, "That's all right —that's all right—if you'll hold my box a minute, I'll go and get you a frog." And so the feller took the box, and put up his forty dollars along with Smiley's, and set down to wait.

So he set there a good while thinking and thinking to hisself, and then he got the frog out and prized his mouth open

nd took a teaspoon and filled him full of
uail shot—filled him pretty near up to
.is chin—and set him on the floor. Smiley
ιe went to the swamp and slopped
.round in the mud for a long time, and
'nally he ketched a frog, and fetched
ιim in, and give him to this feller, and
ays:

"Now, if you're ready, set him along-
ide of Dan'l, with his fore-paws just even
✓ith Dan'l, and I'll give the word." Then
ιe says, "One—two—three—jump!" and
ιim and the feller touched up the frogs
rom behind, and the new frog hopped off,
·ut Dan'l gave a heave, and hysted up his
houlders—so—like a Frenchman, but it
✓asn't no use—he couldn't budge; he was
·lanted as solid as an anvil, and he
·ouldn't no more stir than if he was an-
hored out. Smiley was a good deal sur-
·rised, and he was disgusted, too, but he
'idn't have no idea what the matter was,
·f course.

The feller took the money and started
·way; and when he was going out at the
·loor, he sorter jerked his thumb over his
houlder—this way—at Dan'l, and says
gain, very deliberate, "Well, _I_ don't see
ιo p'ints about that frog that's any bet-
·er'n any other frog."

Smiley he stood scratching his head and
ποoking down at Dan'l a long time, and at
ιst he says, "I do wonder what in the
.ation that frog throw'd off for—I wonder
f there ain't something the matter with
·im—he 'pears to look mighty baggy,
·omehow." And he ketched Dan'l by the
ιap of the neck, and lifted him up and
ays, "Why, blame my cats, if he don't
✓eight five pounds!" and turned him up-
·ide down, and he belched out a double
·andful of shot. And then he see how it
✓as, and he was the maddest man—he set
ιe frog down and took out after that fel-
·er, but he never ketched him. And—

(Here Simon Wheeler heard his name
·alled from the front yard, and got up to
·ee what was wanted.) And turning to me
·s he moved away, he said: "Just set where
·ou are, stranger, and rest easy—I ain't
·oing to be gone a second."

But, by your leave, I did not think that
·continuation of the history of the enter-
·rising vagabond _Jim_ Smiley would be like-
✓ to afford me much information concern-
ng the Rev. _Leonidas W._ Smiley, and so
started away.

At the door I met the sociable Wheeler

returning, and he buttonholed me and rec-
ommenced:

"Well, thish-yer Smiley had a yeller one-
eyed cow that didn't have no tail, only
jest a short stump like a bannanner, and—"

"Oh, hang Smiley and his afflicted cow!"
I muttered good-naturedly, and bidding the
old gentleman good-day, I departed.

THE FACTS CONCERNING THE RE-
CENT CARNIVAL OF CRIME
IN CONNECTICUT*

I was feeling blithe, almost jocund. I put
a match to my cigar, and just then the
morning's mail was handed in. The first
superscription I glanced at was in a handwriting that sent a thrill of pleasure
through and through me. It was aunt
Mary's; and she was the person I loved
and honored most in all the world, outside of my own household. She had been
my boyhood's idol; maturity, which is
fatal to so many enchantments, had not
been able to dislodge her from her pede-
stal; no, it had only justified her right to
be there, and placed her dethronement permanently among the impossibilities. To
show how strong her influence over me
was, I will observe that long after everybody else's _"do_-stop-smoking" had ceased
to affect me in the slightest degree, aunt
Mary could still stir my torpid conscience
into faint signs of life when she touched
upon the matter. But all things have their
limit, in this world. A happy day came at
last, when even aunt Mary's words could
no longer move me. I was not merely glad
to see that day arrive; I was more than
glad—I was grateful; for when its sun had
set, the one alloy that was able to mar my
enjoyment of my aunt's society was gone.
The remainder of her stay with us that
winter was in every way a delight. Of
course she pleaded with me just as earnestly as ever, after that blessed day, to quit
my pernicious habit, but to no purpose
whatever; the moment she opened the subject I at once became calmly, peacefully,
contentedly indifferent—absolutely, ada-
mantinely indifferent. Consequently the
closing weeks of that memorable visit melted away as pleasantly as a dream, they
were so freighted, for me, with tranquil
satisfaction. I could not have enjoyed my

* Published by permission of Harper and
Brothers, owners of the copyright.

pet vice more if my gentle tormentor had been a smoker herself, and an advocate of the practice. Well, the sight of her handwriting reminded me that I was getting very hungry to see her again. I easily guessed what I should find in her letter. I opened it. Good! just as I expected; she was coming! Coming this very day, too, and by the morning train; I might expect her any moment.

I said to myself, "I am thoroughly happy and content, now. If my most pitiless enemy could appear before me at this moment, I would freely right any wrong I may have done him."

Straightway the door opened, and a shriveled, shabby dwarf entered. He was not more than two feet high. He seemed to be about forty years old. Every feature and every inch of him was a trifle out of shape; and so, while one could not put his finger upon any particular part and say, "This is a conspicuous deformity," the spectator perceived that this little person was a deformity as a whole—a vague, general, evenly-blended, nicely-adjusted deformity. There was a fox-like cunning in the face and the sharp little eyes, and also alertness and malice. And yet, this vile bit of human rubbish seemed to bear a sort of remote and ill-defined resemblance to me! It was dully perceptible in the mean form, the countenance, and even the clothes, gestures, manner, and attitudes of the creature. He was a far-fetched, dim suggestion of a burlesque upon me, a caricature of me in little. One thing about him struck me forcibly, and most unpleasantly: he was covered all over with a fuzzy, greenish mold, such as one sometimes sees upon mildewed bread. The sight of it was nauseating.

He stepped along with a chipper air, and flung himself into a doll's chair in a very free and easy way, without waiting to be asked. He tossed his hat into the waste basket. He picked up my old chalk pipe from the floor, gave the stem a wipe or two on his knee, filled the bowl from the tobaccobox at his side, and said to me in a tone of pert command,—

"Gimme a match!"

I blushed to the roots of my hair; partly with indignation, but mainly because it somehow seemed to me that this whole performance was very like an exaggeration of conduct which I myself had sometimes been guilty of in my intercourse with familiar friends,—but never, never wit strangers, I observed to myself. I wante to kick the pygmy into the fire, but som incomprehensible sense of being legall and legitimately under his authority force me to obey his order. He applied the matc to the pipe, took a contemplative whiff o two, and remarked, in an irritatingly fa miliar way,—

"Seems to me it's devilish odd weathe for this time of year."

I flushed again, and in anger and hu miliation as before; for the language wa hardly an exaggeration of some that I hav uttered in my day, and moreover was de livered in a tone of voice and with an ex asperating drawl that had the seeming o a deliberate travesty of my style. Nov there is nothing I am quite so sensitiv about as a mocking imitation of my drawl ing infirmity of speech. I spoke up sharp ly and said,—

"Look here, you miserable ash-cat! yo will have to give a little more attentio to your manners, or I will throw you ou of the window!"

The manikin smiled a smile of maliciou content and security, puffed a whiff o smoke contemptuously toward me, and said with a still more elaborate drawl,—

"Come—go gently, now; don't put on to many airs with your betters."

This cool snub rasped me all over, but i seemed to subjugate me, too, for a moment The pygmy contemplated me a while wit his weasel eyes, and then said, in a pe culiarly sneering way,—

"You turned a tramp away from you door this morning."

I said crustily,—

"Perhaps I did, perhaps I didn't. Hov do *you* know?"

"Well, I know. It isn't any matter ho I know."

"Very well. Suppose I *did* turn a tram away from the door—what of it?"

"Oh, nothing; nothing in particula Only you lied to him."

"I *didn't!* That is, I"—

"Yes, but you did; you lied to him."

I felt a guilty pang,—in truth I had fe it forty times before that tramp had trav eled a block from my door,—but still resolved to make a show of feeling slan dered; so I said,—

"This is a baseless impertinence. I sai to the tramp"—

"There—wait. You were about to li

gain. *I* know what you said to him. You
aid the cook was gone down town and
here was nothing left from breakfast. Two
ies. You knew the cook was behind the
loor, and plenty of provisions behind *her*."

This astonishing accuracy silenced me;
nd it filled me with wondering specula-
ions, too, as to how this cub could have
ot his information. Of course he could
lave culled the conversation from the
ramp, but by what sort of magic had he
ontrived to find out about the concealed
ook? Now the dwarf spoke again:—

"It was rather pitiful, rather small, in
ou to refuse to read that poor young
voman's manuscript the other day, and
ive her an opinion as to its literary value;
nd she had come so far, too, and *so* hope-
ully. Now *wasn't* it?"

I felt like a cur! And I had felt so every
me the thing had recurred to my mind,
may as well confess. I flushed hotly and
aid,—

"Look here, have you nothing better to
o than prowl around prying into other
eople's business? Did that girl tell you
aat?"

"Never mind whether she did or not.
he main thing is, you did that contempti-
e thing. And you felt ashamed of it after-
ards. Aha! you feel ashamed of it *now!*"

This with a sort of devilish glee. With
ery earnestness I responded,—

"I told that girl, in the kindest, gentlest
ay, that I could not consent to deliver
idgment upon *any* one's manuscript, be-
ause an individual's verdict was worthless.
might underrate a work of high merit
id lose it to the world, or it might over-
te a trashy production and so open the
ay for its infliction upon the world. I said
at the great public was the only tribunal
mpetent to sit in judgment upon a lit-
ary effort, and therefore it must be best
lay it before that tribunal in the outset,
nce in the end it must stand or fall by
at mighty court's decision any way."

"Yes, you said all that. So you did, you
ggling, small-souled shuffler! And yet
ien the happy hopefulness faded out of
at poor girl's face, when you saw her
rtively slip beneath her shawl the scroll
e had so patiently and honestly scrib-
ed at,—so ashamed of her darling now,
proud of it before,—when you saw the
adness go out of her eyes and the tears
me there, when she crept away so hum-
y who had come so"—

"Oh, peace! peace! peace! Blister your
merciless tongue, haven't all these thoughts
tortured me enough, without *your* coming
here to fetch them back again?"

Remorse! remorse! It seemed to me that
it would eat the very heart out of me!
And yet that small fiend only sat there
leering at me with joy and contempt,
and placidly chuckling. Presently he began
to speak again. Every sentence was an
accusation, and every accusation a truth.
Every clause was freighted with sarcasm
and derision, every slow-dropping word
burned like vitriol. The dwarf reminded
me of times when I had flown at my children in anger and punished them for faults
which a little inquiry would have taught
me that others, and not they, had committed. He reminded me of how I had
disloyally allowed old friends to be tra-
duced in my hearing, and been too craven
to utter a word in their defense. He reminded me of many dishonest things which
I had done; of many which I had procured
to be done by children and other irrespon-
sible persons; of some which I had planned,
thought upon, and longed to do, and been
kept from the performance by fear of consequences only. With exquisite cruelty he
recalled to my mind, item by item, wrongs
and unkindnesses I had inflicted and humiliations I had put upon friends since
dead, "who died thinking of those injuries, maybe, and grieving over them,"
he added, by way of poison to the stab.

"For instance," said he, "take the case
of your younger brother, when you two
were boys together, many a long year
ago. He always lovingly trusted in you
with a fidelity that your manifold treach-
eries were not able to shake. He followed
you about like a dog, content to suffer
wrong and abuse if he might only be
with you; patient under these injuries
so long as it was your hand that inflicted
them. The latest picture you have of him
in health and strength must be such a
comfort to you! You pledged your honor
that if he would let you blindfold him no
harm should come to him; and then, gig-
gling and choking over the rare fun of the
joke, you led him to a brook thinly glazed
with ice, and pushed him in; and how you
did laugh! Man, you will never forget the
gentle, reproachful look he gave you as
he struggled shivering out, if you live a
thousand years! Oho! you see it now, you
see it *now!*"

"Beast, I have seen it a million times, and shall see it a million more! and may you rot away piecemeal, and suffer till doomsday what I suffer now, for bringing it back to me again!"

The dwarf chuckled contentedly, and went on with his accusing history of my career. I dropped into a moody, vengeful state, and suffered in silence under the merciless lash. At last this remark of his gave me a sudden rouse:—

"Two months ago, on a Tuesday, you woke up, away in the night, and fell to thinking, with shame, about a peculiarly mean and pitiful act of yours toward a poor ignorant Indian in the wilds of the Rocky Mountains in the winter of eighteen hundred and"—

"Stop a moment, devil! Stop! Do you mean to tell me that even my very *thoughts* are not hidden from you?"

"It seems to look like that. Didn't you think the thoughts I have just mentioned?"

"If I didn't, I wish I may never breathe again! Look here, friend—look me in the eye. Who *are* you?"

"Well, who do you think?"

"I think you are Satan himself. I think you are the devil."

"No."

"No? Then who *can* you be?"

"Would you really like to know?"

"*Indeed* I would."

"Well, I am your *Conscience!*"

In an instant I was in a blaze of joy and exultation. I sprang at the creature, roaring,—

"Curse you, I have wished a hundred million times that you were tangible, and that I could get my hands on your throat once! Oh, but I will wreak a deadly vengeance on"—

Folly! Lightning does not move more quickly than my Conscience did! He darted aloft so suddenly that in the moment my fingers clutched the empty air he was already perched on the top of the high bookcase, with his thumb at his nose in token of derision. I flung the poker at him, and missed. I fired the boot-jack. In a blind rage I flew from place to place, and snatched and hurled any missile that came handy; the storm of books, inkstands, and chunks of coal gloomed the air and beat about the manikin's perch relentlessly, but all to no purpose; the nimble figure dodged every shot; and not only that, but burst into a cackle of sarcastic and triumphant laughter as I sat down exhausted. While I puffed and gasped with fatigue and excitement, my Conscience talked to this effect:—

"My good slave, you are curiously witless—no, I mean characteristically so. In truth, you are always consistent, always yourself, always an ass. Otherwise it must have occurred to you that if you attempted this murder with a sad heart and a heavy conscience, I would droop under the burdening influence instantly. Fool, I should have weighed a ton, and could not have budged from the floor; but instead, you are so cheerfully anxious to kill me that your conscience is as light as a feather; hence I am away up here out of your reach. I can almost respect a mere ordinary sort of fool; but *you*—pah!"

I would have given anything, then, to be heavy-hearted, so that I could get this person down from there and take his life, but I could no more be heavy-hearted over such a desire than I could have sorrowed over its accomplishment. So I could only look longingly up at my master, and rave at the ill-luck that denied me a heavy conscience the one only time that I had ever wanted such a thing in my life. By and by I got to musing over the hour's strange adventure, and of course my human curiosity began to work. I set myself to framing in my mind some questions for this fiend to answer. Just then one of my boys entered, leaving the door open behind him and exclaimed,—

"My! what *has* been going on, here The book-case is all one riddle of"—

I sprang up in consternation, and shouted,—

"Out of this! Hurry! Jump! Fly! Shut the door! Quick, or my Conscience will get away!"

The door slammed to, and I locked it I glanced up and was grateful, to the bottom of my heart, to see that my own er was still my prisoner. I said,—

"Hang you, I might have lost you! Children are the heedlessest creatures. But look here, friend, the boy did not seem to notice you at all; how is that?"

"For a very good reason. I am invisible to all but you."

I made mental note of that piece of information with a good deal of satisfaction I could kill this miscreant now, if I got chance, and no one would know it. But this very reflection made me so light-hearted that my Conscience could hardly kee his seat, but was like to float aloft toward the ceiling like a toy balloon. I said, presently,—

"Come, my Conscience, let us be friendly. Let us fly a flag of truce for a while. I am suffering to ask you some questions."

"Very well. Begin."

"Well, then, in the first place, why were you never visible to me before?"

"Because you never asked to see me before; that is, you never asked in the right spirit and the proper form before. You were just in the right spirit this time, and when you called for your most pitiless enemy I was that person by a very large majority, though you did not suspect it."

"Well, did that remark of mine turn you into flesh and blood?"

"No. It only made me visible to you. I am unsubstantial, just as other spirits are."

This remark prodded me with a sharp misgiving. If he was unsubstantial, how was I going to kill him? But I dissembled, and said persuasively,—

"Conscience, it isn't sociable of you to keep at such a distance. Come down and take another smoke."

This was answered with a look that was full of derision, and with this observation added:—

"Come where you can get at me and kill me? The invitation is declined with thanks."

"All right," said I to myself; "so it seems a spirit *can* be killed, after all; there will be one spirit lacking in this world, presently, or I lose my guess." Then I said aloud,—

"Friend"—

"There; wait a bit. I am not your friend, I am your enemy; I am not your equal, I am your master. Call me 'my lord,' if you please. You are too familiar."

"I don't like such titles. I am willing to call you *sir*. That is as far as"—

"We will have no argument about this. Just obey; that is all. Go on with your chatter."

"Very well, my lord,—since nothing but my lord will suit you,—I was going to ask you how long you will be visible to me?"

"Always!"

I broke out with strong indignation: "This is simply an outrage. That is what I think of it. You have dogged, and dogged, and dogged me, all the days of my life, invisible. That was misery enough; now to

have such a looking thing as you tagging after me like another shadow all the rest of my days is an intolerable prospect. You have my opinion, my lord; make the most of it."

"My lad, there was never so pleased a conscience in this world as I was when you made me visible. It gives me an inconceivable advantage. *Now*, I can look you straight in the eye, and call you names, and leer at you, jeer at you, sneer at you; and *you* know what eloquence there is in visible gesture and expression, more especially when the effect is heightened by audible speech. I shall always address you henceforth in your o-w-n s-n-i-v-e-l-i-n-g d-r-a-w-l baby!"

I let fly with the coal-hod. No result. My lord said,—

"Come, come! Remember the flag of truce!"

"Ah, I forgot that. I will try to be civil; and *you* try it, too, for a novelty. The idea of a *civil* conscience! It is a good joke; an excellent joke. All the consciences *I* have ever heard of were nagging, badgering, fault-finding, execrable savages! Yes; and always in a sweat about some poor little insignificant trifle or other—destruction catch the lot of them, *I* say! I would trade mine for the small-pox and seven kinds of consumption, and be glad of the chance. Now tell me, why *is* it that a conscience can't haul a man over the coals once, for an offense, and then let him alone? Why is it that it wants to keep on pegging at him, day and night and night and day, week in and week out, forever and ever, about the same old thing? There is no sense in that, and no reason in it. I think a conscience that will act like that is meaner than the very dirt itself."

"Well, *we* like it; that suffices."

"Do you do it with the honest intent to improve a man?"

The question produced a sarcastic smile, and this reply:—

"No, sir. Excuse me. We do it simply because it is 'business.' It is our trade. The *purpose* of it *is* to improve the man, but *we* are merely disinterested agents. We are appointed by authority, and haven't anything to say in the matter. We obey orders and leave the consequences where they belong. But I am willing to admit this much: we *do* crowd the orders a trifle when we get a chance, which is most of the time. We enjoy it. We are instructed to remind a man a few times of an error; and I don't mind acknowledging that we try to give pretty good measure. And when we get hold of a man of a peculiarly sensitive nature, oh, but do we haze him! I have known consciences to come all the way from China and Russia to see a person of that kind put through his paces, on a special occasion. Why, I knew a man of that sort who had accidentally crippled a mulatto baby; the news went abroad, and I wish you may never commit another sin if the consciences didn't flock from all over the earth to enjoy the fun and help his master exercise him. That man walked the floor in torture for forty-eight hours, without eating or sleeping, and then blew his brains out. The child was perfectly well again in three weeks."

"Well, you are a precious crew, not to put it too strong. I think I begin to see, now, why you have always been a trifle inconsistent with me. In your anxiety to get all the juice you can out of a sin, you make a man repent of it in three or four different ways. For instance, you found fault with me for lying to that tramp, and I suffered over that. But it was only yesterday that I told a tramp the square truth, to wit, that, it being regarded as bad citizenship to encourage vagrancy, I would give him nothing. What did you do *then?* Why, you made me say to myself, 'Ah, it would have been so much kinder and blameless to ease him off with a little white lie, and send him away feeling that if he could not have bread, the gentle treatment was at least something to be grateful for!' Well, I suffered all day about *that.* Three days before, I had fed a tramp, and fed him freely, supposing it a virtuous act. Straight off you· said, 'O false citizen, to have fed a tramp!' and I suffered as usual. I gave a tramp work; you objected to it,—*after* the contract was made, of course; you never speak up beforehand. Next, I *refused* a tramp work; you objected to *that.* Next, I proposed to kill a tramp; you kept me awake all night, oozing remorse at every pore. Sure I was going to be right *this* time, I sent the next tramp away with my benediction; ·and I wish you may live as long as I do, if you didn't make me smart all night again because I didn't kill him. Is there *any* way of satisfying that malignant invention which is called a conscience?"

"Ha, ha! this is luxury! Go on!"

"But come, now, answer me that question. *Is* there any way?"

"Well, none that I propose to tell you, my son. Ass! I don't care *what* act you may turn your hand to, I can straightway whisper a word in your ear and make you think you have committed a dreadful meanness. It is my *business*—and my joy —to make you repent of *everything* you do. If I have fooled away any opportunities it was not intentional; I beg to assure you it was not intentional."

"Don't worry; you haven't missed a trick that *I* know of. I never did a thing in all my life, virtuous or otherwise, that I didn't repent of within twenty-four hours. In church last Sunday I listened to a charity sermon. My first impulse was to give three hundred and fifty dollars; I repented of that and reduced it a hundred; repented of that and reduced it another hundred; repented of that and reduced it another hundred; repented of that and reduced the remaining fifty to twenty-five; repented of that and came down to fifteen; repented of that and dropped to two dollars and a half; when the plate came around at last, I repented once more and contributed ten cents. Well, when I got home, I did wish to goodness I had that ten cents back again! You never *did* let me get through a charity sermon without having something to sweat about."

"Oh, and I never shall, I never shall. You can always depend on me."

"I think so. Many and many's the restless night I've wanted to take you by the neck. If I could only get hold of you now!"

"Yes, no doubt. But I am not an ass. I am only the saddle of an ass. But go on, go on. You entertain me more than I like to confess."

"I am glad of that. (You will not mind my lying a little, to keep in practice. Look here; not to be too personal, I think you are about the shabbiest and most contemptible little shriveled-up reptile that can be imagined. I am grateful enough that you are invisible to other people, for I should die with shame to be seen with such a mildewed monkey of a conscience as you are. Now if you were five or six feet high and"—

"Oh, come! who is to blame?"

"*I* don't know."

"Why, you are; nobody else."

"Confound you, I wasn't consulted about your personal appearance."

"I don't care, you had a good deal to do with it, nevertheless. When you were eight or nine years old, I was seven feet high and as pretty as a picture."

"I wish you had died young! So you have grown the wrong way, have you?"

"Some of us grow one way and some the other. You had a large conscience once; if you've a small conscience now, I reckon there are reasons for it. However, both of us are to blame, you and I. You see, you used to be conscientious about a great many things; morbidly so, I may say. It was a great many years ago. You probably do not remember it, now. Well, I took a great interest in my work, and I so enjoyed the anguish which certain pet sins of yours afflicted you with, that I kept pelting at you until I rather overdid the matter. You began to rebel. Of course I began to lose ground, then, and shrivel a little,—diminish in stature, get moldy, and grow deformed. The more I weakened, the more stubbornly you fastened on to those particular sins; till at last the places on my person that represent those vices became as callous as shark skin. Take smoking, for instance. I played that card a little too long, and I lost. When people plead with you at this late day to quit that vice, that old callous place seems to enlarge and cover me all over like a shirt of mail. It exerts a mysterious, smothering effect; and presently I, your faithful hater, your devoted Conscience, go sound asleep! Sound? It is no name for it. I couldn't hear it thunder at such a time. You have some few other vices—perhaps eighty, or maybe ninety—that affect me in much the same way."

"This is flattering; you must be asleep a good part of your time."

"Yes, of late years. I should be asleep all the time, but for the help I get."

"Who helps you?"

"Other consciences. Whenever a person whose conscience I am acquainted with tries to plead with you about the vices you are callous to, I get my friend to give his client a pang concerning some villainy of his own, and that shuts off his meddling and starts him off to hunt personal consolation. My field of usefulness is about trimmed down to tramps, budding authoresses, and that line of goods, now; but don't you worry—I'll harry you on *them* while they last! Just you put your trust in me."

"I think I can. But if you had only been good enough to mention these facts some thirty years ago, I should have turned my particular attention to sin, and I think 5 that by this time I should not only have had you pretty permanently asleep on the entire list of human vices, but reduced to the size of a homeopathic pill, at that. That is about the style of conscience *I* 10 am pining for. If I only had you shrunk down to a homeopathic pill, and I could get my hands on you, would I put you in a glass case for a keepsake? No, sir! I would give you to a yellow dog! That is 15 where *you* ought to be—you and all your tribe. You are not fit to be in society, in my opinion. Now another question. Do you know a good many consciences in this section?"

"Plenty of them." 20

"I would give anything to see some of them! Could you bring them here? And would they be visible to me?"

"Certainly not."

"I suppose I ought to have known that, without asking. But no matter, you can describe them. Tell me about my neighbor Thompson's conscience, please."

"Very well. I know him intimately; have 30 known him many years. I knew him when he was eleven feet high and of a faultless figure. But he is very rusty and tough and misshapen, now, and hardly ever interests himself about anything. As to his present 35 size—well, he sleeps in a cigar box."

"Likely enough. There are few smaller, meaner men in this region than Hugh Thompson. Do you know Robinson's conscience?"

40 "Yes. He is a shade under four and a half feet high; used to be a blond; is a brunette, now, but still shapely and comely."

"Well, Robinson is a good fellow. Do 45 you know Tom Smith's conscience?"

"I have known him from childhood. He was thirteen inches high, and rather sluggish, when he was two years old—as nearly all of us are, at that age. He is thirty-50 seven feet high, now, and the stateliest figure in America. His legs are still racked with growing-pains, but he has a good time, nevertheless. Never sleeps. He is the most active and energetic member of the 55 New England Conscience Club; is president of it. Night and day you can find him pegging away at Smith, panting with his labor, sleeves rolled up, countenance all alive with enjoyment. He has got his victim splendidly dragooned, now. He can make poor Smith imagine that the most innocent little thing he does is an odious sin; and then he sets to work and almost tortures the soul out of him about it."

"Smith is the noblest man in all this section, and the purest; and yet is always breaking his heart because he cannot be good! Only a conscience *could* find pleasure in heaping agony upon a spirit like that. Do you know my aunt Mary's conscience?"

"I have seen her at a distance, but am not acquainted with her. She lives in the open air altogether, because no door is large enough to admit her."

"I can believe that. Let me see. Do you know the conscience of that publisher who once stole some sketches of mine for a 'series' of his, and then left me to pay the law expenses I had to incur in order to choke him off?"

"Yes. He has a wide fame. He was exhibited, a month ago, with some other antiquities, for the benefit of a recent Member of the Cabinet's conscience, that was starving in exile. Tickets and fares were high, but I traveled for nothing by pretending to be the conscience of an editor, and got in for half price by representing myself to be the conscience of a clergyman. However, the publisher's conscience, which was to have been the main feature of the entertainment, was a failure—as an exhibition. He was there, but what of that? The management had provided a microscope with a magnifying power of only thirty thousand diameters, and so nobody got to see him, after all. There was great and general dissatisfaction, of course, but"—

Just here there was an eager footstep on the stair; I opened the door, and my aunt Mary burst into the room. It was a joyful meeting, and a cheery bombardment of questions and answers concerning family matters ensued. By and by my aunt said,—

"But I am going to abuse you a little now. You promised me, the day I saw you last, that you would look after the needs of the poor family around the corner as faithfully as I had done it myself. Well, I found out by accident that you failed of your promise. *Was* that right?"

In simple truth, I never had thought of that family a second time! And now such

a splintering pang of guilt shot through me! I glanced up at my Conscience. Plainly, my heavy heart was affecting him. His body was drooping forward; he seemed about to fall from the book-case. My aunt continued:—

"And think how you have neglected my poor *protégée* at the almshouse, you dear hard-hearted promise-breaker!" I blushed scarlet, and my tongue was tied. As the sense of my guilty negligence waxed sharper and stronger, my Conscience began to sway heavily back and forth; and when my aunt, after a little pause, said in a grieved tone, "Since you never once went to see her, maybe it will not distress you now to know that that poor child died months ago, utterly friendless and forsaken!" my Conscience could no longer bear up under the weight of my sufferings but tumbled headlong from his high perch and struck the floor with a dull, leaden thump. He lay there writhing with pain and quaking with apprehension, but straining every muscle in frantic efforts to get up. In a fever of expectancy I sprang to the door, locked it, placed my back against it, and bent a watchful gaze upon my struggling master. Already my fingers were itching to begin their murderous work.

"Oh, what *can* be the matter!" exclaimed my aunt, shrinking from me, and following with her frightened eyes the direction of mine. My breath was coming in short quick gasps now, and my excitement was almost uncontrollable. My aunt cried out,—

"Oh, do not look so! You appal me. Oh, what can the matter be? What is it you see? Why do you stare so? Why do you work your fingers like that?"

"Peace, woman!" I said, in a hoarse whisper. "Look elsewhere; pay no attention to me; it is nothing—nothing. I am often this way. It will pass in a moment. It comes from smoking too much."

My injured lord was up, wild-eyed with terror, and trying to hobble toward the door. I could hardly breathe, I was so wrought up. My aunt wrung her hands and said,—

"Oh, I knew how it would be; I knew it would come to this at last! Oh, I implore you to crush out that fatal habit while it may yet be time! You must not, you shall not be deaf to my supplication longer!" My struggling Conscience showed sudden signs of weariness! "Oh, promise me you will throw off this hateful slavery of tobacco!" My Conscience began to reel drowsily, and grope with his hands—enchanting spectacle! "I beg you, I beseech you, I implore you! Your reason is deserting you! There is madness in your eye! It flames with frenzy! Oh, hear me, hear me, and be saved! See, I plead with you on my very knees!" As she sank before me my Conscience reeled again, and then drooped languidly to the floor, blinking toward me a last supplication for mercy, with heavy eyes. "Oh, promise, or you are lost! Promise. and be redeemed! Promise! Promise and live!" With a long-drawn sigh my conquered Conscience closed his eyes and fell fast asleep!

With an exultant shout I sprang past my aunt, and in an instant I had my life-long foe by the throat. After so many years of waiting and longing, he was mine at last. I tore him to shreds and fragments. I rent the fragments to bits. I cast the bleeding rubbish into the fire, and drew into my nostrils the grateful incense of my burnt-offering. At last, and forever, my Conscience was dead!

I was a free man! I turned upon my poor aunt, who was almost petrified with error, and shouted,—

"Out of this with your paupers, your charities, your reforms, your pestilent morals! You behold before you a man whose life-conflict is done, whose soul is at peace; a man whose heart is dead to sorrow, dead to suffering, dead to remorse; a man WITHOUT A CONSCIENCE! In my joy I spare you, though I could throttle you and never feel a pang! Fly!"

She fled. Since that day my life is all bliss. Bliss, unalloyed bliss. Nothing in all the world could persuade me to have a conscience again. I settled all my old outstanding scores, and began the world anew. I killed thirty-eight persons during the first two weeks—all of them on account of ancient grudges. I burned a dwelling that interrupted my view. I swindled a widow and some orphans out of their last cow, which is a very good one, though not thoroughbred, I believe. I have also committed scores of crimes, of various kinds, and have enjoyed my work exceedingly, whereas it would formerly have broken my heart and turned my hair gray, I have no doubt.

In conclusion I wish to state, by way of advertisement, that medical colleges desiring assorted tramps for scientific purposes, either by the gross, by cord measurement, or per ton, will do well to examine the lot in my cellar before purchasing elsewhere, as these were all selected and prepared by myself, and can be had at a low rate, because I wish to clear out my stock and get ready for the spring trade.

XVII

HENRY JAMES (1843–1916)

The antithesis of Mark Twain in almost every respect was Henry James. Son of a re-tired philosopher, reared in a home where everything desired could be easily afforded, sur-rounded by English books and magazines and art, and, so far as it could be created in a New York City family circle, an atmosphere of the most refined European culture, from his child-hood years he was an aristocrat in tastes and inclination. To protect him from provincial nar-rowness and vulgarity his parents took him early to Europe where under tutors in various intellectual centers he learned languages and read the books that appealed to him and fol-lowed generally his growing fastidious inclinations. He was attracted first by painting as a life work, but abandoning it early, he settled down after a long period of hesitation and experi-ment to literary creation.

The influences directing him to fiction were first the early work of George Eliot, then the chaste individualistic art of Hawthorne, and finally the new younger generation "realism" of the Continental writers, especially those of France. He became our first professed "realist," the first to adopt the new *genre* deliberately after careful study, and a "realist"—after his own manner—he remained the rest of his life. Moreover, he may be grouped with the new "local colorists" who so dominated the two decades after 1870. For his background he chose the hitherto unexplored "no-man's land" that lay on the boundaries between Europe and America. He became our first distinctive "international novelist" dealing with Europeans visiting in America or Americans traveling in Europe, and picturing and interpreting with minuteness of detail each to each.

During his first decade as a writer of fiction he restricted himself to the short story, and at various times in his later years he returned to this literary form sometimes exclusively during a long period, but judging from many expressions in his later introductions he con-sidered it greatly inferior in value to the novel. In his final introduction to *Roderick Hudson,* for instance, he makes this significant remark:

"'Roderick Hudson' was my first attempt at a novel, a long fiction with a 'complicated' subject, and I recall again the quite uplifted sense with which my idea, such as it was, permitted me at last to put quite out to sea. I had but hugged the shore on sundry previous small occasions; bumping about, to acquire skill, in the shallow waters and sandy coves of the 'short story' and master as yet of no vessel constructed to carry a sail. The subject of 'Roderick Hudson' figured to me vividly this employment of canvas, and I have not for-gotten, even after long years, how the blue southern sea seemed to spread immediately before me and the breath of the spice-islands to be already in the breeze."

He demanded for his story leisurely development, multitudinous details, multiplicity of view-points, and he complained often that the restrictions as to space demanded by the magazines defeated the ends of his art. His story "The Middle Years," for instance, limited rigidly as to space by the magazine that had ordered it, gave him endless trouble:

"To get it right was to squeeze my subject into the five or six thousand words I had been invited to make it consist of—it consists, in fact, should the curious care to know, of some 5550—and I scarce perhaps recall another case . . . in which my struggle to keep com-pression rich, if not, better still, to keep accretions compressed, betrayed for me such community with the anxious effort of some warden of the insane engaged at a critical mo-ment in making fast a victim's straitjacket. The form of 'The Middle Years' is not that of the *nouvelle,* but that of the concise anecdote; whereas the subject treated would perhaps seem one comparatively demanding 'developments'—if indeed, amid these mysteries, distinc-tions were so absolute. (There is of course neither close nor fixed measure of the reach of a development, which in some connexions seems almost superfluous and then in others to represent the whole sense of the matter; and we should doubtless speak more thoroughly by book had we some secret for exactly tracing deflexions and returns.) However this may be it was as an anecdote, an anecdote only, that I was determined my little situation here should figure; to which end my effort was of course to follow it as much as possible from its outer edge in, rather than from its centre outwards."

216

This is an illuminating passage. It would seem that James considered that he was not a writer of what the French had denominated the *conte,* which to him was an elaborated anecdote, but of that more expanded form, the *nouvelle.* His "Short Stories," "The Abasement of the Northmores" and "The Tree of Knowledge" he considered "novels intensely compressed, and with that character in them, yet keeping at bay, under stress of their failing else to be good short stories, any air of mutilation. They had had to be good short stories, in order to earn, however precariously, their possible 'wage.' . . . They could but conceal the fact that they *were 'nouvelles';* they could but masquerade as little anecdotes."

When invited, he says, to contribute to the first number of the *Yellow Book* and told that no limits would be placed upon him as to space, it seemed to him that the millennium of the short story had come. The license granted by the editors seemed to him as "the fruit of the finest artistic intelligence."

"Among forms we had had, on the dimensional ground—for length and breadth—our ideal, the beautiful and blest *nouvelle;* the generous, the enlightened hour for which appeared thus at last to shine. It was under the star of the *nouvelle* that, in other languages, a hundred interesting and charming results, such studies on the minor scale as the best of Turgenieff's, of Balzac's, of Maupassant's, of Bourget's, and just lately, in our own tongue, of Kipling's, had been, all economically, arrived at—thanks to their authors', as 'contributors,' having been able to count, right and left, on a wise and liberal support. It had taken the blank misery of our Anglo-Saxon sense of such matters to organize, as might be said, the general indifference of this fine type of composition. In that dull view a 'short story' was a 'short story,' and that was the end of it. Shades and differences, varieties and styles, the value above all of the idea happily *developed,* languished, to extinction, under the hard and fast rule of the 'from six to eight thousand words'—when, for one's benefit, the rigour was a little relaxed. For myself, I delighted in the shapely *nouvelle*—as, for that matter, I had from time to time and here and there been almost encouraged to show."

As light upon the length of Henry James' short stories this indeed is valuable. There is implicit within it also his conception of the nature of the short-story form and its relative values as literature.

A DAY OF DAYS

Mr. Herbert Moore, a gentleman of some note in the scientific world, and a childless widower, finding himself at last unable to reconcile his sedentary habits with the management of a household, had invited his only sister to come and superintend his domestic affairs. Miss Adela Moore had assented the more willingly to his proposal, as by her mother's death she had recently been left without a formal protector. She was twenty-five years of age, and was a very active member of what she and her friends called society. She was almost equally at home in the very best company of three great cities, and she had encountered most of the adventures which await a young girl on the threshold of life. She had become rather hastily and imprudently engaged, but she had eventually succeeded in disengaging herself. She had spent a summer in Europe, and she had made a voyage to Cuba with a dear friend in the last stage of consumption, who had died at the hotel in Havana. Although by no means beautiful in person, she was yet thoroughly pleasing, rejoicing in what young ladies are fond of calling an *air.* That is, she was tall and slender, with a long neck, a low forehead and a handsome nose. Even after six years of "society," too, she still had excellent manners. She was, moreover, mistress of a very pretty little fortune, and was accounted clever without detriment to her amiability, and amiable without detriment to her wit. These facts, as the reader will allow, might have ensured her the very best prospects; but he has seen that she had found herself willing to forfeit her prospects and bury herself in the country. It seemed to her that she had seen enough of the world and of human nature, and that a couple of years of seclusion might not be unprofitable. She had begun to suspect that for a girl of her age she was unduly old and wise— and, what is more, to suspect that others suspected as much. A great observer of life and manners, so far as her opportunities went, she conceived that it behooved her to organize the results of her observation into principles of conduct and of belief. She was becoming—so she argued— too impersonal, too critical, too intelligent, too contemplative, too just. A woman had no business to be so just. The society of nature, of the great expansive skies and the primeval woods, would prove severely unpropitious to her excessive intellectual growth. She would spend her time in the fields and live in her feelings, her simple sense, and the perusal of profitable books from Herbert's library.

She found her brother very prettily housed at about a mile's distance from the nearest town, and about six miles' distance from another town, the seat of a small college, before which he delivered a weekly lecture. She had seen so little of him of late years that his acquaintance was almost to make; but it was very soon made. Herbert Moore was one of the simplest and least aggressive of men, and one of the most patient and delicate of students. He had a vague notion that Adela was a young woman of extravagant pleasures, and that, somehow, on her arrival, his house would be overrun with the train of her attendant revelers. It was not until after they had been six months together that he discovered that his sister was a model of diligence and temperance. By the time six months more had passed, Adela had brought back a delightful sense of youth and *naïveté*. She learned, under her brother's tuition, to walk—nay, to climb, for there were great hills in the neighborhood—to ride and to botanize. At the end of a year, in the month of August, she received a visit from an old friend, a girl of her own age, who, had been spending July at a watering-place, and who was about to be married. Adela had begun to fear that she had lapsed into an almost irreclaimable rusticity, and had suffered a permanent diminution of the social facility for which she had formerly been distinguished; but a week spent in *tête-à-tête* with her friend convinced her not only that she had not forgotten much that she had feared, but also that she had not forgotten much that she had hoped. For this, and other reasons, her friend's departure left her slightly depressed. She felt lonely and even a little elderly. She had lost another illusion. Laura B., for whom a year ago she had entertained a serious regard, now impressed her as a very flimsy little person, who talked about her lover with almost indecent flippancy.

Meanwhile, September was slowly running its course. One morning Mr. Moore took a hasty breakfast and started to catch the train for S., whither a scientific conference called him, which might, he said, release him that afternoon in time for dinner at home, and might, on the other hand, detain him until the evening. It was almost the first time during Adela's rustica-

tion that she had been left alone for several hours. Her brother's quiet presence was inappreciable enough; yet now that he was at a distance she nevertheless felt a singular sense of freedom; a sort of return of those days of early childhood, when, through some domestic catastrophe, she had for an infinite morning been left to her own devices. What should she do? she asked herself, half laughing. It was a fair day for work: but it was a still better one for play. Should she drive into town and pay a long-standing debt of morning calls? Should she go into the kitchen and try her hand at a pudding for dinner? She felt a delicious longing to do something illicit, to play with fire, to discover some Bluebeard's closet. But poor Herbert was no Bluebeard. If she were to burn down his house he would exact no amends. Adela went out to the veranda, and, sitting down on the steps, gazed across the country. It was apparently the last day of Summer. The sky was faintly blue; the woody hills were putting on the morbid colors of Autumn; the great pine grove behind the house seemed to have caught and imprisoned the protesting breezes. Looking down the road toward the village, it occurred to Adela that she might have a visit, and so kindly was her mood that she felt herself competent to a chat with one of her rustic neighbors. As the sun rose higher, she went in and established herself with a piece of embroidery in a deep, bow window in the second story, which, betwixt its muslin curtains and its external frame-work of vines, commanded most insidiously the principal approach to the house. While she drew her threads, she surveyed the road with a deepening conviction that she was destined to have a caller. The air was warm, yet not hot; the dust had been laid during the night by a gentle rain. It had been from the first a source of complaint among Adela's new friends that her courtesies were so thoroughly indiscriminating. Not only had she lent herself to no friendships, but she had committed herself to no preferences. Nevertheless, it was with a by no means impartial fancy that she sat thus expectant at her casement. She had very soon made up her mind that, to answer the exactions of the hour, her visitor should perforce be of the other sex, and as, thanks to the somewhat uncompromising indifference which, during her residence, she had exhibited to the *jeunesse dorée* of the county, her roll-call, in this her hour of need, was limited to a single name, so her thoughts were now centered upon the bearer of that name, Mr. Madison Perkins, the Unitarian minister. If, instead of being Miss Moore's story, this were Mr. Perkins's it might easily be condensed into one pregnant fact that he was very far gone in love for our heroine. Although of a different faith from his, she had been so well pleased with one of his sermons, to which she had allowed herself to lend a tolerant ear, that, meeting him some time afterward, she had received him with what she considered a rather knotty doctrinal question; whereupon, gracefully waiving the question, he had asked permission to call upon her and talk over her "difficulties." This short interview had enshrined her in the young minister's heart; and the half-dozen occasions on which he had subsequently contrived to see her had each contributed an additional taper to her shrine. It is but fair to add, however, that although a captive, Mr. Perkins was as yet no captor. He was simply an honorable young man, who happened at this moment to be the most sympathetic companion within reach. Adela, at twenty-five years of age, had both a past and a future. Mr. Perkins reëchoed the one, and foreshadowed the other.

So, at last, when, as the morning waned toward noon, Adela descried in the distance a man's figure treading the grassy margin of the road, and swinging his stick as he came, she smiled to herself with some complacency. But even while she smiled she became conscious of a most foolish acceleration of the process of her heart. She rose, and resenting her gratuitous emotion, stood for a moment half resolved to have herself denied. As she did so, she glanced along the road again. Her friend had drawn nearer, and, as the distance lessened, lo! it seemed to her that he was not her friend. Before many moments her doubts were removed. The gentleman was a stranger. In front of the house three roads diverged from a great spreading elm. The stranger came along the opposite side of the highway, and when he reached the elm stopped and looked about him as if to verify a direction. Then he deliberately crossed over. Adela had time to see, unseen, that he was a shapely young man, with a bearded chin and a straw hat. After the due

interval, Becky, the maid, came up with a card somewhat rudely superscribed in pencil:

THOMAS LUDLOW,
New York.

Turning it over in her fingers, Adela saw that the reverse of a card had been used, abstracted from the basket on her own drawing-room table. The printed name on the other side was dashed out; it ran: *Mr. Madison Perkins.*

"He asked me to give you this, ma'am," said Becky. "He helped himself to it out of the tray."

"Did he ask for me by name?"

"No, ma'am, he asked for Mr. Moore. When I told him Mr. Moore was away, he asked for some of the family. I told him you were all the family, ma'am."

"Very well," said Adela, "I will go down." But, begging her pardon, we will precede her by a few steps.

Tom Ludlow, as his friends called him, was a young man of twenty-eight, concerning whom you might have heard the most various opinions; for, as far as he was known (which, indeed, was not very far), he was at once one of the best liked and one of the best hated of men. Born in one of the lower *strata* of New York society, he was still slightly incrusted, if we may so express it, with his native soil. A certain crudity of manners and of aspect proved him to be one of the great majority of the ungloved. On this basis, however, he was a sufficiently good-looking fellow: a middle-sized, agile figure; a head so well shaped as to be handsome; a pair of inquisitive, responsive eyes, and a large, manly mouth, constituting his heritage of beauty. Turned upon the world at an early age, he had, in the pursuit of a subsistence, tried his head at everything in succession, and had generally found it to be quite as hard as the opposing substance; and his figure may have been thought to reflect this sweet assurance in a look of somewhat aggressive satisfaction with things in general, himself included. He was a man of strong faculties and a strong will, but it is doubtful whether his feelings were stronger than he. He was liked for his directness, his good humor, his general soundness and serviceableness; he was disliked for the same qualities under different names; that is, for his impudence, his offensive optimisms, and his inhuman avidity for facts. When his friends insisted upon his noble disinterestedness, his enemies were wont to reply it was all very well to ignore, to nullify oneself in the pursuit of science, but to that suppress the rest of mankind coincidentally betrayed an excess of zeal. Fortunately for Ludlow, on the whole, he was no great listener; and even if he had been, a certain plebeian thick-skinnedness would have been the guaranty of his equanimity; although it must be added that, if, like a genuine democrat, he was very insensitive, like a genuine democrat, too, he was amazingly proud. His tastes, which had always been for the natural sciences, had recently led him to paleontology, that branch of them cultivated by Herbert Moore; and it was upon business connected with this pursuit that, after a short correspondence, he had now come to see him.

As Adela went in to him, he came out with a bow from the window, whence he had been contemplating the lawn. She acknowledged his greeting.

"Miss Moore, I believe," said Ludlow.

"Miss Moore," said Adela.

"I beg your pardon for this intrusion, but as I had come from a distance to see Mr. Moore on business, I thought I might venture either to ask at headquarters how he may most easily be reached, or even to charge you with a message." These words were accompanied with a smile before which it was Adela's destiny to succumb—if this is not too forcible a term for the movement of feeling with which she answered them.

"Pray make no apologies," she said. "We hardly recognize such a thing as intrusion in the country. Won't you sit down? My brother went away only this morning, and I expect him back this afternoon."

"This afternoon? indeed. In that case I believe I'll wait. It was very stupid of me not to have dropped a word beforehand. But I have been in the city all Summer long, and I shall not be sorry to screw a little vacation out of this business. I'm prodigiously fond of the country, and I very seldom get a glimpse of it."

"It's possible," said Adela, "that my brother may not come home until the evening. He was uncertain. You might go to him at S."

Ludlow reflected a moment, with his eyes on his hostess. "If he does return in the afternoon, at what hour will he arrive?"

"At three."

"And my own train leaves at four. Allow him a quarter of an hour to come from town and myself a quarter of an hour to get there (if he would give me his vehicle, back), I should have half an hour to see him. We couldn't do much talk, but I could ask him the essential questions. I wish chiefly to ask him for some letters. It seems a pity to take two superflous—that is, possibly superfluous—railway journeys of an hour apiece, for I should probably come back with him. Don't you think so?" he asked, very frankly.

"You know best," said Adela. "I'm not particularly fond of the journey to S, even when it's absolutely necessary."

"Yes; and then this is such a lovely day for a good long ramble in the fields. That's a thing I haven't done since I don't know when. I'll stay." And he placed his hat on the floor beside him.

"I'm afraid, now that I think of it," said Adela, "that there is no train until so late an hour that you would have very little time left on your arrival to talk with my brother before the hour at which he himself might have determined to start for home. It's true that you might induce him to remain till the evening."

"Dear me! I shouldn't like to do that. It might be very inconvenient for him. Besides I shouldn't have time. And then I always like to see a man in his own home —or in my own home; a man, that is, whom I have any regard for—and I have a very great regard for your brother, Miss Moore. When men meet at a half-way house, neither feels at his ease. And then this is such an uncommonly pretty place of yours," pursued Ludlow, looking about him.

"Yes, it's a very pretty place," said Adela.

Ludlow got up and walked to the window. "I want to look at your view," said he. "A lovely view it is. You're a happy woman, Miss Moore, to live before such a prospect."

"Yes, if pretty scenery can make one happy, I ought to be happy." And Adela was glad to regain her feet and stand on the other side of the table, before the window.

"Don't you think it can?" asked Ludlow turning around. "I don't know, though, perhaps it can't. Ugly sights can't make you unhappy, necessarily. I've been working for a year in one of the narrowest, darkest, dirtiest, and busiest streets in New York, with rusty bricks and muddy gutters for scenery. But I think I can hardly set up to be miserable. I wish I could. It might be a claim on your favor." As he said these words, he stood leaning against the window shutter, without the curtain, with folded arms. The morning light covered his face, and, mingled with that of his broad laugh, showed Adela that it was a very pleasant face.

"Whatever else he may be," she said to herself as she stood within the shade of the other curtain, playing with the paper-knife which she had plucked from the table. "I think he is honest. I am afraid he isn't a gentleman—but he is not a simpleton."

She met his eye frankly for a moment. "What do you want of my favor?" she asked, with an abruptness of which she was acutely conscious. "Does he wish to make friends," she pursued, "or does he merely wish to pay me a vulgar compliment? There is bad taste, perhaps, in either case, but especially in the latter." Meanwhile her visitor had already answered her.

"What do I want of your favor? Why, I want to make the most of it." And Ludlow blushed at his own audacity.

Adela, however, kept her color. "I'm afraid it will need all your pulling and stretching," she said, with a little laugh.

"All right. I'm great at pulling and stretching," said Ludlow, with a deepening of his great masculine blush, and a broad laugh to match it.

Adela glanced toward the clock on the mantel. She was curious to measure the duration of her acquaintance with this breezy invader of her privacy, with whom she so suddenly found herself bandying florid personalities. She had known him some eight minutes.

Ludlow observed her movement. "I'm interrupting you and detaining you from your own affairs," he said; and he moved towards his hat. "I suppose I must bid you good-morning." And he picked it up.

Adela stood at the table and watched him cross the room. To express a very delicate feeling in terms comparatively broad, she was loath to have him go. She divined, too, that he was loath to go. The knowledge of this feeling on his part, however, affected her composure but slightly. The truth is—we say it with all respect—Adela was an old hand. She was modest, honest and wise; but, as we have said, she had a past—a past of which importunate swains in the guise of morning-callers had been no inconsiderable part; and a great dexterity in what may be called outflanking these gentlemen, was one of her registered accomplishments. Her liveliest emotion at present, therefore, was less one of annoyance at her companion than of surprise at her own gracious impulses, which were yet undeniable. "Am I dreaming?" she asked herself. She looked out of the window, and then back at Ludlow, who stood grasping his hat and stick, contemplating her face. Should she bid him remain? "He is honest," she repeated; "why should not I be honest for once?" "I'm sorry you are in a hurry," she said aloud.

"I am in no hurry," he answered.

Adela turned her face to the window again, and toward the opposite hills. There was a moment's pause.

"I thought you were in a hurry," said Ludlow.

Adela gave him her eyes. "My brother would be very glad to have you remain as long as you like. He would expect me to offer you what little hospitality is in my power."

"Pray, offer it then."

"That's easily done. This is the parlor, and there, beyond the hall, is my brother's study. Perhaps you would like to look at his books and his collections. I know nothing about them, and I should be a very poor guide. But you are welcome to go in and use your discretion in examining what may interest you."

"This, I take it, would be but another way of bidding you good-morning."

"For the present, yes."

"But I hesitate to take such liberties with your brother's treasures as you prescribe."

"Prescribe, sir? I prescribe nothing."

"But if I decline to penetrate into Mr. Moore's *sanctum,* what alternative remains?"

"Really—you must make your own alternative."

"I think you mentioned the parlor. Suppose I choose that."

"Just as you please. Here are some books, and, if you like, I will bring you some magazines. Can I serve you in any other way? Are you tired by your walk? Would you like a glass of wine?"

"Tired by my walk?—not exactly. You are very kind, but I feel no immediate desire for a glass of wine. I think you needn't trouble yourself about the magazines, either. I am in no mood to read." And Ludlow pulled out his watch and compared it with the clock. "I'm afraid your clock is fast."

"Yes;" said Adela, "very likely."

"Some ten minutes. Well, I suppose I had better be walking;" and, coming toward Adela, he extended his hand.

She gave him hers. "It's a day of days for a long, slow ramble," she said.

Ludlow's only rejoinder was his handshake. He moved slowly toward the door, half accompanied by Adela. "Poor fellow!" she said to herself. The lattice summerdoor admitted into the entry a cool, dusky light, in which Adela looked pale. Ludlow divided its wings with his stick, and disclosed a landscape, long, deep and bright, framed by the pillars of the veranda. He stopped on the threshold swinging his stick. "I hope I shan't lose my way," he said.

"I hope not. My brother will not forgive me if you do."

Ludlow's brows were slightly contracted by a frown, but he contrived to smile with his lips. "When shall I come back?" he asked abruptly.

Adela found but a low tone—almost a whisper—at her command, to answer. "Whenever you please," she said.

The young man turned about, with his back to the bright doorway, and looked into Adela's face, which was now covered with light. "Miss Moore," said he, "it's very much against my will that I leave you at all."

Adela stood debating within herself. What if her companion should stay? It would, under the circumstances, be an adventure; but was an adventure necessarily unadvisable? It lay wholly with herself to decide. She was her own mistress, and she had hitherto been a just mistress. Might she not for once be a generous one? The reader will observe in Adela's meditation the recurrence of this saving clause "for once." It rests upon the simple fact that she had begun the day in a romantic mood. She was prepared to be interested; and now that an interesting phenomenon had presented itself, that it stood before her in vivid human—nay, manly—shape, instinct with reciprocity, was she to close her hand to the liberality of fate? To do so would be to court mischance; for it would involve, moreover, a petty insult to human nature. Was not the man before her fairly redolent of honesty, and was that not enough? He was not what Adela had been used to call a gentleman. To this conviction she had made a swallow's flight; but from this assurance she would start. "I have seen" (she thus concluded) "all the gentlemen can show me; let us try something new."

"I see no reason why you should run away so fast, Mr. Ludlow," she said, aloud.

"I think," cried Ludlow, "it would be the greatest piece of folly I ever committed."

"I think it would be a pity," said Adela, with a smile.

"And you invite me into your parlor again? I come as your visitor, you know. I was your brother's before. It's a simple enough matter. We are old friends. We have a broad, common ground in your brother. Isn't that about it?"

"You may adopt whatever theory you please. To my mind, it is, indeed, a very simple matter."

"Oh, but I wouldn't have it too simple," said Ludlow, with a mighty smile.

"Have it as you please."

Ludlow leaned back against the doorway. "Your kindness is too much for me, Miss Moore," said he. "I am passive; I am in your hands; do with me what you please. I can't help contrasting my fate with what it might have been but for you. A quarter of an hour ago I was ignorant of your existence; you weren't in my program. I had no idea your brother had a sister. When your servant spoke of 'Miss Moore,' upon my word I expected something rather elderly—something venerable—some rigid old lady, who would say, 'exactly,' and 'very well, sir,' and leave me to spend the rest of the morning tilting back in a chair on the hotel piazza. It shows what fools we are to attempt to forecast the future."

"We must not let our imagination run away with us in any direction," said Adela.

"Imagination? I don't believe I have any. No, madam," and Ludlow straightened himself up, "I live in the present. I write my program from hour to hour—or, at any rate, I will in the future."

"I think you are very wise," said Adela. "Suppose you write a program for the present hour. What shall we do? It seems to me a pity to spend so lovely a morning in-doors. I fancy this is the last day of Summer. We ought to celebrate it. How would you like a walk?" Adela had decided that, to reconcile her favors with the proper maintenance of her dignity, her only course was to play the perfect hostess. This decision made, very naturally and gracefully she played her part. It was the one possible part. And yet it did not preclude those delicate sensations with which her novel episode seemed charged: it simply legitimated them. A romantic adventure on so classical a basis would assuredly hurt no one.

"I should like a walk very much," said Ludlow; "a walk with a halt at the end of it."

"Well, if you will consent to a short halt at the beginning of it," said Adela, "I will be with you in a very few minutes." When she returned in her little hat and shawl, she found her friend seated on the veranda steps. He arose and gave her a card.

"I have been requested, in your absence, to hand you this," he said.

Adela read with some compunction the name of Mr. Madison Perkins.

"Has he been here?" she asked. "Why didn't he come in?"

"I told him you were not at home. If it wasn't true then, it was going to be true so soon that the interval was hardly worth taking account of. He addressed himself to me, as I seemed from my position to be quite at home here; but I confess he looked at me as if he doubted my word. He hesitated as to whether he should confide his name to me, or whether he should confide it in that shape to the entry table. I think he wished to show me that he suspected my veracity, for he was making rather grimly for the table when I, fearing that once inside the house he might encounter the living truth, informed him in the most good-humored tone possible that I would take charge of his little tribute."

"I think, Mr. Ludlow, that you are a strangely unscrupulous man. How did you know that Mr. Perkins's business was not urgent?"

"I didn't know it. But I knew it could be no more urgent than mine. Depend upon it, Miss Moore, you have no case against me. I only pretend to be a man; to have admitted that charming young gentleman would have been heroic."

Adela was familiar with a sequestered spot, in the very heart of the fields, as it seemed to her, to which she now proposed to conduct her friend. The point was to select a goal neither too distant nor too near, and to adopt a pace neither too rapid nor too slow. But although Adela's happy valley was a good two miles away, and they had measured the interval with the very *minimum* of speed, yet most sudden seemed their arrival at the stile over which Adela was used to strike into the meadows. Once on the road, she felt a precipitate conviction that there could be no evil in an adventure so essentially wholesome as that to which she had lent herself, and that there could be no guile in a spirit so deeply sensitive to the sacred influences of Nature, and to the melancholy aspect of incipient Autumn as that of her companion. A man with an unaffected relish for small children is a man to inspire young women with a generous confidence; and so, in a lesser degree, a man with a genuine feeling for the simple beauties of a common New England landscape may not unreasonably be accepted by the daughters of the scene as a person worthy of their esteem. Adela was a great observer of the clouds, the trees and the streams, the sounds and colors, the echoes and reflections native to her adopted home; and she experienced an honest joy at the sight of Ludlow's keen appreciation of these modest facts. His enjoyment of them, deep as it was, however, had to struggle against that sensuous depression natural to a man who had spent the Summer in a close and fetid laboratory in the heart of a great city, and against a sensation of a less material color—the feeling that Adela was a delightful girl. Still, naturally a great talker, he celebrated his impressions in a generous flow of good-humored eloquence. Adela resolved within herself that he was decidedly a companion for the open air. He was a man to make use, even to abuse, of the wide horizon and the high ceiling of Nature. The freedom of his gestures, the sonority of his voice, the keenness of his vision, the general vivacity of his manners, seemed to necessitate and to justify a universal absence of barriers. They crossed the stile, and waded through the long grass of several successive meadows, until the ground began to rise, the stony surfaces to crop through the turf, when, after a short ascent, they reached a broad plateau, covered with boulders and shrubs, which lost itself on one side in a short, steep cliff, whence fields and marshes stretched down to the opposite river; and on the other, in scattered clumps of pine and maple, which gradually thickened and multiplied, until the horizon in that quarter was blue with a long line of woods. Here was both sun and shade—the unobstructed sky, or the whispering dome of a circle of pines. Adela led the way to a sunny seat among the rocks, which commanded the course of the river, and where a cluster of trees would lend an admonitory undertone to their conversion.

Before long, however, its muffled eloquence became rather importunate, and Adela remarked upon the essential melancholy of the phenomenon.

"It has always seemed to me," rejoined Ludlow, "that the wind in the pines expresses tolerably well man's sense of a coming change, simply *as* a change."

"Perhaps it does," said Adela. "The pines are forever rustling, and men are forever changing."

"Yes, but they can only be said to express it when there is some one there to hear them; and more especially some one in whose life a change is, to his own knowledge, going to take place. Then they are quite prophetic. Don't you know Longfellow says so?"

"Yes, I know Longfellow says so. But you seem to speak from your own feeling."

"I do."

"Is there a change pending in your life?"

"Yes, rather an important one."

"I believe that's what men say when they are going to be married," said Adela.

"I'm going to be divorced, rather. I'm going to Europe."

"Indeed! soon?"

"To-morrow," said Ludlow, after an instant's pause.

"Oh!" said Adela, "How I envy you!"

Ludlow, who sat looking over the cliff and tossing stones down into the plain, observed a certain inequality in the tone of his companion's two exclamations. The first was nature, the second art. He turned his eyes upon her, but she had turned hers away upon the distance. Then, for a moment, he retreated within himself and thought. He rapidly surveyed his position. Here was he, Tom Ludlow, a hard-headed son of toil, without fortune, without credit, without antecedents, whose lot was cast exclusively with vulgar males, and who had never had a mother, a sister nor a well-bred sweetheart to pitch his voice for the feminine tympanum; who had seldom come nearer an indubitable young lady than, in a favoring crowd, to receive a mechanical "thank you" (as if he were a policeman), for some ingeniously provoked service; here he found himself up to his neck in a sudden pastoral with the most ladyish young woman in the land. That it was in him to enjoy the society of such a woman (provided, of course, she were not a fool), he very well knew; but he had not yet suspected that it was possible for him (in the midst of more serious cares) to obtain it. Was he now to infer that this final gift was his—the gift of pleasing women who were worth the pleasing? The inference was at least logical. He had made a good impression. Why else should a modest and discerning girl have so speedily granted him her favor? It was with a little thrill of satisfaction that Ludlow reflected upon the directness of his course. "It all comes back," he said to himself, "to my old theory, that a process can't be too simple. I used no arts. In such an enterprise I shouldn't have known where to begin. It was my ignorance of the regulation method that served me. Women like a gentleman, of course; but they like a man better." It was the little touch of nature he had discerned in Adela's tone that had set him thinking; but as compared with the frankness of his own attitude it betrayed after all no undue emotion. Ludlow had accepted the fact of his adaptability to the idle mood of a cultivated woman in a thoroughly rational spirit, and he was not now tempted to exaggerate its bearings. He was not the man to be intoxicated by success—this or any other. "If Miss Moore," he pursued, "is so wise—or so foolish—as to like me half an hour for what I am, she is welcome. Assuredly," he added, as he gazed at her intelligent profile, "she will not like me for what I am not." It needs a woman, however, far more intelligent than (thank heaven!) most women are—more intelligent, certainly, than Adela was—to guard her happiness against a strong man's consistent assumption of her intelligence; and doubtless it was from a sense of this general truth, as Ludlow still gazed, he felt an emotion of manly tenderness. "I wouldn't offend her for the world," he thought. Just then, Adela, conscious of his gaze, looked about; and before he knew it, Ludlow had repeated aloud, "Miss Moore, I wouldn't offend you for the world."

Adela glanced at him for a moment with a little flush that subsided into a smile. "To what dreadful injury is that the prelude?" she asked.

"It's the prelude to nothing. It refers to the past—to any possible displeasure I may have caused you."

"Your scruples are unnecessary, Mr. Ludlow. If you had given me offense, I should not have left you to apologize for it. I should not have left the matter to occur to you as you sat dreaming charitably in the sun."

"What would you have done?"

"Done? nothing. You don't imagine I would have rebuked you—or snubbed you —or answered you back, I take it. I would have left undone—what, I can't tell you. Ask yourself what I have done. I'm sure I hardly know myself," said Adela, with some intensity. "At all events, here I am sitting with you in the fields, as if you were a friend of years. Why do you speak of offense?" And Adela (an uncommon accident with her) lost command of her voice, which trembled ever so slightly. "What an odd thought! why should you offend me? Do I invite it?" Her color had deepened again, and her eyes brightened. She had forgotten herself, and before speaking had not, as was her wont, sought counsel of that stanch conservative, her taste. She had spoken from a full heart— a heart which had been filling rapidly since the outset of their walk with a feeling almost passionate in its quality, and which that little blast of prose which had brought her Ludlow's announcement of his departure, had caused to overflow. The reader may give his feeling such a name as he pleases. We will content ourselves with saying that Adela had played with fire so effectually that she had been scorched. The slight vehemence of the speech just quoted had covered her sensation of pain.

"You pull me up rather short, Miss Moore," said Ludlow. "A man says the best he can."

Adela made no reply. For a moment she hung her head. Was she to cry out because she was hurt? Was she to introduce her injured soul as an impertinent third into the company? No! Here our reserved and contemplative heroine is herself again. Her part was still to be the perfect young lady. For our own part, we can imagine no figure more bewitching than that of the perfect young lady under these circumstances; and if Adela had been the most accomplished coquette in the world she could not have assumed a more becoming expression than the air of languid equanimity which now covered her features. But having paid this generous homage to propriety, she felt free to suffer. Raising her eyes from the ground, she abruptly addressed her companion with this injunction:

"Mr. Ludlow," said she, "tell me something about yourself."

Ludlow burst into a laugh. "What shall I tell you?"

"Everything."

"Everything? Excuse me, I'm not such a fool. But do you know that's a delicious request you make? I suppose I ought to blush and hesitate; but I never yet blushed or hesitated in the right place."

"Very good. There is one fact. Continue. Begin at the beginning."

"Well, let me see. My name you know. I'm twenty-eight years old."

"That's the end," said Adela.

"But you don't want the history of my babyhood, I take it. I imagine that I was a very big, noisy and ugly baby: what's called a 'splendid infant.' My parents were poor, and, of course, honest. They belonged to a very different set—or 'sphere,' I suppose you call it—from any you probably know. They were working people. My father was a chemist in a small way, and I fancy my mother was not above using her hands to turn a penny. But although I don't remember her, I am sure she was a good, sound woman; I feel her occasionally in my own sinews. I myself have been at work all my life, and a very good worker I am, let me tell you. I'm not patient, as I imagine your brother to be—although I have more patience than you might suppose—but I'm plucky. If you think I'm

over-egotistical, remember 'twas you began it. I don't know whether I'm clever,
and I don't much care; that word is used
only by unpractical people. But I'm clear-
headed, and inquisitive, and enthusiastic.
That's as far as I can describe myself. I
don't know anything about my character.
I simply suspect I'm a pretty good fellow.
I don't know whether I'm grave or gay,
lively or severe. I don't know whether
I'm high-tempered or low-tempered. I don't
believe I'm 'high-toned.' I fancy I'm good-
natured enough, inasmuch as I'm not
nervous. I should not be at all surprised to
discover I was prodigiously conceited;
but I'm afraid the discovery wouldn't cut
me down, much. I'm desperately hard to
snub, I know. Oh, you would think me a
great brute if you knew me. I should
hesitate to say whether I am of a loving
turn. I know I'm desperately tired of a
number of persons who are very fond of
me; I'm afraid I'm ungrateful. Of course
as a man speaking to a woman, there's
nothing for it but to say I'm selfish; but
I hate to talk about such windy abstractions. In the way of positive facts: I'm
not educated. I know no Greek and very
little Latin. But I can honestly say that
first and last I have read a great many
books—and, thank God, I have a memory!
And I have some tastes, too. I'm very fond
of music. I have a good old voice of my
own: *that* I can't help knowing; and I'm
not one to be bullied about pictures. Is
that enough? I'm conscious of an utter
inability to say anything to the point. To
put myself in a nutshell, I suppose I'm
simply a working man; I have his virtues
and I have his defects. I'm a very common fellow."

"Do you call yourself a very common
fellow because you really believe yourself
to be one, or because you are weakly
tempted to disfigure your rather flattering
catalogue with a great final blot?"

"I'm sure I don't know. You show more
subtlety in that one question that I have
shown in my whole string of affirmations.
You women are strong on asking witty
questions. Seriously, I believe I *am* a common fellow. I wouldn't make the admission to every one though. But to you, Miss
Moore, who sit there under your parasol
as impartial as the Muse of History, to you
I own the truth. I'm no man of genius.
There is something I miss; some final
distinction I lack; you may call it what you
please. Perhaps it's humility. Perhaps you
can find it in Ruskin, somewhere. Perhaps it's patience—perhaps it's imagination. I'm vulgar, Miss Moore. I'm the
vulgar son of vulgar people. I use the
word, of course, in its strictest sense. So
must I grant you at the outset, and then
I walk ahead."

"Have you any sisters?"

"Not a sister; and no brothers, nor
cousins, nor uncles, nor aunts."

"And you sail for Europe to-morrow?"

"To-morrow, at ten o'clock."

"To be away how long?"

"As long as I possibly can. Five years
if possible."

"What do you expect to do in those five
years?"

"Study."

"Nothing but study?"

"It will all come back to that, I fancy.
I hope to enjoy myself reasonably, and to
look at the world as I go. But I must not
waste time; I'm growing old."

"Where are you going?"

"To Berlin. I wanted to get letters from
your brother."

"Have you money? Are you well off?"

"Well off? Not I, no. I'm poor. I travel
on a little money that has just come to
me from an unexpected quarter: an old
debt owing my father. It will take me to
Germany and keep me for six months.
After that I shall work my way."

"Are you happy? Are you contented?"

"Just now I'm pretty comfortable, thank
you."

"But will you be so when you get to
Berlin?"

"I don't promise to be contented; but
I'm pretty sure to be happy."

"Well!" said Adela, "I sincerely hope
you may be."

"Amen!" said Ludlow.

Of what more was said at this moment,
no record may be given. The reader has
been put into possession of the key of our
friends' conversation; it is only needful
to say that substantially upon this key,
it was prolonged for half an hour more.
As the minutes elapsed, Adela found herself drifting further and further away
from her anchorage. When at last she compelled herself to consult her watch, and
remind her companion that there remained
but just time enough for them to reach
home, in anticipation of her brother's arrival, she knew that she was rapidly float-

ing seaward. As she descended the hill at her companion's side, she felt herself suddenly thrilled by an acute temptation. Her first instinct was to close her eyes upon it, in the trust that when she opened them again it would have vanished; but she found that it was not to be so uncompromisingly dismissed. It importuned her so effectually, that before she had walked a mile homeward, she had succumbed to it, or had at least given it the pledge of that quickening of the heart which accompanies a bold resolution. This little sacrifice allowed her no breath for idle words, and she accordingly advanced with a bent and listening head. Ludlow marched along, with no apparent diminution of his habitual buoyancy of mien, talking as fast and as loud as at the outset. He adventured a prophecy that Mr. Moore would not have returned, and charged Adela with a humorous message of regrets. Adela had begun by wondering whether the approach of their separation had wrought within him any sentimental depression at all commensurate with her own, with that which sealed her lips and weighed upon her heart; and now she was debating as to whether his express declaration that he felt "awfully blue" ought necessarily to remove her doubts. Ludlow followed up this declaration with a very pretty review of the morning, and a sober valedictory which, whether intensely felt or not, struck Adela as at least nobly bare of flimsy compliments. He might be a common fellow—but he was certainly a very uncommon one. When they reached the garden gate, it was with a fluttering heart that Adela scanned the premises for some accidental sign of her brother's presence. She felt that there would be an especial fitness in his not having returned. She led the way in. The hall table was bare of his hat and overcoat. The only object it displayed was Mr. Perkins's card, which Adela had deposited there on her exit. All that was represented by that little white ticket seemed a thousand miles away. Finally, Mr. Moore's absence from his study was conclusive against his return.

As Adela went back thence into the drawing-room, she simply shook her head at Ludlow, who was standing before the fire-place; and she did so, she caught her reflection in the mantel-glass. "Verily," she said to herself, "I have traveled far." She had pretty well unlearned the repose of the Veres of Vere. But she was to break with it still more completely. It was with a singular hardihood that she prepared to redeem the little pledge which had been extorted from her on her way home. She felt that there was no trial to which her generosity might now be called which she would not hail with enthusiasm. Unfortunately, her generosity was not likely to be challenged; although she nevertheless had the satisfaction of assuring herself at this moment that, like the mercy of the Lord, it was infinite. Should she satisfy herself of her friend's? or should she leave it delightfully uncertain? These had been the terms of what has been called her temptation, at the foot of the hill. But inasmuch as Adela was by no means strictly engaged in the pursuit of pleasure, and as the notion of a grain of suffering was by no means repugnant to her, she had resolved to obtain possession of the one essential fact of her case, even though she should be at heavy costs to maintain it.

"Well, I have very little time," said Ludlow; "I must get my dinner and pay my bill and drive to the train." And he put out his hand.

Adela gave him her own, and looked him full in the eyes. "You are in a great hurry," said she.

"It's not I who am in a hurry. It's my confounded destiny. It's the train and the steamer."

"If you really wished to stay you wouldn't be bullied by the train and the steamer."

"Very true—very true. But do I really wish to stay?"

"That's the question. That's what I want to know."

"You ask difficult questions, Miss Moore."

"I mean they shall be difficult."

"Then, of course, you are prepared to answer difficult ones."

"I don't know that that's of course, but I am."

"Well, then, do you wish me to stay? All I have to do is to throw down my hat, sit down and fold my arms for twenty minutes. I lose my train and my ship. I stay in America, instead of going to Europe."

"I have thought of all that."

"I don't mean to say it's a great deal. There are pleasures and pleasures."

"Yes, and especially the former. It is a great deal."

"And you invite me to accept it?"

"No, I ought not to say that. What I ask of you is whether, if I should so invite you, you would say 'yes.'"

"That makes the matter very easy for you, Miss Moore. What attractions do you hold out?"

"I hold out nothing whatever, sir."

"I suppose that means a great deal."

"It means what it seems to mean."

"Well, you are certainly a most interesting woman, Miss Moore—a charming woman."

"Why don't you call me 'fascinating' at once, and bid me good morning?"

"I don't know but that I shall have to come to that. But I will give you no answer that leaves you at an advantage. Ask me to stay—command me to stay, if that suits you better—and I will see how it sounds. Come, you must not trifle with a man." He still held Adela's hand, and they had been looking frankly into each other's eyes. He paused, waiting for an answer.

"Good-by, Mr. Ludlow," said Adela. "God bless you!" And she was about to withdraw her hand; but he held it.

"Are we friends?" said he.

Adela gave a little shrug of her shoulders. "Friends of three hours."

Ludlow looked at her with some sternness. "Our parting could at best hardly have been sweet," said he; "but why should you make it bitter, Miss Moore?"

"If it's bitter, why should you try to change it?"

"Because I don't like bitter things."

Ludlow had caught a glimpse of the truth—that truth of which the reader has had a glimpse—and he stood there at once thrilled and annoyed. He had both a heart and a conscience. "It's not my fault," he cried to the latter; but he was unable to add, in all consistency, that it was his misfortune. It would be very heroic, very poetic, very chivalric, to lose his steamer, and he felt that he could do so for sufficient cause—at the suggestion of a fact. But the motive here was less than a fact—an idea; less than an idea—a fancy. "It's a very pretty little romance as it is," he said to himself. "Why spoil it? She is an admirable girl: to have learned that is enough for me." He raised her hand to his lips, pressed them to it, dropped it, reached the door and bounded out of the garden gate.

The day was ended.

XVIII

FREDERIC BEECHER PERKINS (1828–1899)

Frederic Beecher Perkins, a grandson of Lyman Beecher, a native of Connecticut, librarian and editor in various cities, once as far west as San Francisco, is in many respects a minor figure in our literary history. His volume *Devil-Puzzlers and Other Studies,* 1877, however, when viewed in the light of its times is a distinctive volume. Its introduction is an important document in the history of the short-story *genre,* the first recognition of the form as a distinct entity since Poe's review of Hawthorne in 1842. To Perkins the short story was a thing distinct and apart. "A good short story possesses all the merits of a long one, and others of its own besides. A short story, in short, is to a long one what a diamond is to a mountain." He considered Poe and Hawthorne as our masters of this distinctive *genre,* with only Willis and Mrs. Stowe worthy among Americans of secondary mention. In Europe Hoffman, Fouque, Tieck, Novalis, and Zschokke had brought the short story to a high degree of excellence, but "with all of these, except the last, there is no English writer of short imaginative tales to compare at all, except Poe and Hawthorne; while a few of Zschokke's have a graceful genial fancifulness entirely their own."

"The claims of this particular kind of literature to artistic dignity as a class or department, have not been appreciated. Poe, whose critical observations are often worth careful consideration—though, indeed, they always require it—said that a poem, to be perfect, must be no longer than may be read at a single sitting, say of an hour. For, he reasoned, the impression produced by a poem, being very emotional, is necessarily transitory and indivisible. You cannot sustain such emotion for a long period. You cannot read in a poem until you reach a high pitch of feeling, then break off and transact an interlude of trade or other hard work, and then come back and finish your high emotion and your poem from the pitch and point where you dropped them, as one might go back to the cupboard and eat the other half of a pie.

"This is partly true and partly not. Poe begged the question by assuming that the only poems are those where a single pang of high and passionate emotion is their efficient cause, as it is their object and effect—that is that lyrics are the only poems. This is natural enough in Poe, who was a lyric poet and no other. But there is an abundance of poetry that is not intense, and whose soul is not any single impulse. Now the prose tale, or short story, is not the highest order of prose composition, any more than the lyric is of the poetical; but it is entitled, like the lyric, to high rank. It compares with other prose compositions as the lyric does with the epic, or narrative, or dramatic poem; as a melody with an opera or a sonata. A really fine short story (after the grade of Poe, Hawthorne, or the other masters I have named) is the product of a faculty lofty, unique and rare. It is a thing of power or beauty or fantastic pleasure, as fully as an oration, a melody, a picture, a statue, or an edifice. It is at least, as much as any of them, the visible, appreciable embodiment of the knowledge, wisdom, brightness and love which are in the writer's soul. It is intrinsically as valuable, and as much contains the seeds of usefulness and power, and has the signs and certificates of immortality and fame, as any other thing that is made. Will the pure, antique, tender beauty of the ancient Greek tale of *Cupid and Psyche* ever perish? It has lived seventeen hundred years. It will live as long as there is literature."

DEVIL-PUZZLERS

It will not do at all to disbelieve in the existence of a personal devil. It is not so many years ago that one of our profoundest divines remarked with indignation upon such disbelief. "No such person?" cried the doctor with energy. "Don't tell me! I can hear his tail snap and crack about amongst the churches any day!"

And if the enemy is, in truth, still as vigorously active among the sons of God as he was in the days of Job (that is to say, in the time of Solomon, when, as the 5 critics have found out, the Book of Job was written), then surely still more is he vigilant and sly in his tricks for foreclosing his mortgages upon the souls of the wicked.

10 And once more: still more than ever is

his personal appearance probable in these latter days. The everlasting tooting of the wordy Cumming has proclaimed the end of all things for a quarter of a century; and he will surely see his prophecy fulfilled if he can only keep it up long enough. But, though we discredit the sapient Second-Adventist as to the precise occasion of the diabolic avatar, has there not been a strange coincidence between his noisy declarations, and other evidences of an approximation of the spiritual to the bodily sphere of life? Is not this same quarter of a century that of the Spiritists? Has it not witnessed the development of Od? And of clairvoyance? And have not the doctrines of ghosts, and reappearances of the dead, and of messages from them, risen into a prominence entirely new, and into a coherence and semblance at least of fact and fixed law such as was never known before? Yea, verily. Of all times in the world's history, to reject out of one's beliefs either good spirits or bad, angelology or diabology, chief good being, or chief bad being, this is the most improper.

Dr. Hicok was trebly liable to the awful temptation, under which he had assuredly fallen, over and above the fact that he was a prig, which makes one feel the more glad that he was so handsomely come up with in the end; such a prig that everybody who knew him, invariably called him (when he wasn't by) Hicokalorum. This charming surname had been conferred on him by a crazy old fellow with whom he once got into a dispute. Lunatics have the most awfully tricky ways of dodging out of pinches in reasoning; but Hicok knew too much to know *that;* and so he acquired his fine title to teach him one thing more.

Trebly liable, we said. The three reasons are,—

1. He was foreign-born.
2. He was a Scotchman.
3. He was a physician and surgeon.

The way in which these causes operated was as follows (I wish it were allowable to use Artemus Ward's satisfactory vocable "thusly": like Mrs. Wiggle's soothing syrup, it "supplies a real want") :—

Being foreign-born, Dr. Hicok had not the unfailing moral stamina of a native American, and therefore was comparatively easily beset by sin. Being, secondly, a Scotchman, he was not only thoroughly conceited, with a conceit as immovable as the Bass Rock, just as other folks sometimes are, but, in particular, he was perfectly sure of his utter mastery of metaphysics, logic and dialectics, or, as he used to call it, with a snobbish Teutonicalization, *dialektik.* Now, in the latter two, the Scotch can do something, but in metaphysics they are simply imbecile; which quality, in the inscrutable providence of God, has been joined with an equally complete conviction of the exact opposite. Let not man, therefore, put those traits asunder —not so much by reason of any divine ordinance, as because no man in his senses would try to convince a Scotchman—or anybody else, for that matter.

Thirdly, he was a physician and surgeon; and gentlemen of this profession are prone to become either thoroughgoing materialists, or else implicit and extreme Calvinistic Presbyterians, "of the large blue kind." And they are, moreover, positive, hard-headed, bold, and self-confident. So they have good need to be. Did not Majendie say to his students, "Gentlemen, disease is a subject which physicians know nothing about"?

So the doctor both believed in the existence of a personal devil, and believed in his own ability to get the upper hand of that individual in a tournament of the wits. Ah, he learned better by terrible experience! The doctor was a dry-looking little chap, with sandy hair, a freckled face, small gray eyes, and absurd white eyebrows and eyelashes, which made him look as if he had finished off his toilet with just a light flourish from the dredging-box. He was erect of carriage, and of a prompt, ridiculous alertness of step and motion, very much like that of Major Wellington De Boots. And his face commonly wore a kind of complacent serenity such as the Hindoos ascribe to Buddha. I know a little snappish dentist's-goods dealer up town, who might be mistaken for Hicokalorum any day.

Well, well—what had the doctor done? Why—it will sound absurd, probably, to some unbelieving people—but really Dr. Hicok confessed the whole story to me himself: he had made a bargain with the Evil One! And indeed he was such an uncommonly disagreeable-looking fellow, that, unless on some such hypothesis, it is impossible to imagine how he could have prospered as he did. He gained patients, and cured them, too; made money; invested successfully; bought a brown-stone front—a house, not a wiglet—then bought other real estate; began to put his name on charity subscription lists, and to be made vice-president of various things.

Chiefest of all,—it must have been by some superhuman aid that Dr. Hicok married his wife, the then and present Mrs. Hicok. Dear me! I have described the doctor easily enough. But how infinitely more difficult it is to delineate Beauty than the Beast: did you ever think of it? All I can say is, that she is a very lovely woman now; and she must have been, when the doctor married her, one of the loveliest creatures that ever lived—a lively, graceful, bright-eyed brunette, with thick fine long black hair, penciled delicate eyebrows, little pink ears, thin high nose, great astonished brown eyes, perfect teeth, a little rosebud of a mouth, and a figure so extremely beautiful that nobody believed she did not pad—hardly even the artists who—those of them at least who work faithfully in the life-school—are the very best judges extant of truth in costume and personal beauty. But, furthermore, she was good, with the innocent unconscious goodness of a sweet little child; and of all feminine charms—even beyond her supreme grace of motion—she possessed the sweetest, the most resistless—a lovely voice; whose tones, whether in speech or song, were perfect in sweetness, and with a strange penetrating sympathetic quality and at the same time with the most wonderful half-delaying completeness of articulation and modulation, as if she enjoyed the sound of her own music. No doubt she did; but it was unconsciously, like a bird. The voice was so sweet, the great loveliness and kindness of soul it expressed were so deep, that, like every exquisite beauty, it rayed forth a certain sadness within the pleasure it gave. It awakened infinite, indiscreet emotions of beauty and perfection—infinite longings.

It's of no use to tell me that such a spirit—she really ought not to be noted so low down as amongst human beings—that such a spirit could have been made glad by becoming the yoke-fellow of Hicokalorum, by influences exclusively human. No!—I don't believe it—I won't believe it—it can't be believed. I can't convince you, of course, for you don't know her; but if you did, along with the rest of the evidence, and if your knowledge was like mine, that from the testimony of my own eyes and ears and judgment—you would know, just as I do, that the doctor's possession of his wife was the key-stone of the arch of completed proof on which I found my absolute assertion that he had made that bargain.

He certainly had! A most characteristic transaction too; for while, after the usual fashion, it was agreed by the "party of the first part," viz., Old Scratch—that Dr. Hicok should succeed in whatever he undertook during twenty years, and by the party of the second part, that at the end of that time the D—— should fetch him in manner and form as is ordinarily provided, yet there was added a peculiar clause. This was, that, when the time came for the doctor to depart, he should be left entirely whole and unharmed, in mind, body, and estate, provided he could put to the Devil three consecutive questions, of which either one should be such that that cunning spirit could not solve it on the spot.

So for twenty years Dr. Hicok lived and prospered, and waxed very great. He did not gain one single pound of avoirdupois however, which may perchance seem strange, but is the most natural thing in the world. Who ever saw a little dry, wiry, sandy, freckled man, with white eyebrows, that did grow fat? And besides, the doctor spent all his leisure time hunting up his saving trinity of questions; and hard study, above all for such a purpose, is as sure an anti-fattener as Banting.

He knew the Scotch metaphysicians by heart already, ex-officio as it were; but he very early gave up the idea of trying to fool the Devil with such mud-pie as that. Yet be it understood, that he found cause to except Sir William Hamilton from the muddle-headed crew. He chewed a good while, and pretty hopefully, upon the Quantification of the Predicate; but he had to give that up too, when he found out how small and how dry a meat rattled within the big, noisy nut-shell. He read Saint Thomas Aquinas, and Peter Dens, and a cart-load more of the old casuists, Romanist and Protestant.

He exhausted the learning of the Development Theory. He studied and experimented up to the existing limits of knowledge on the question of the Origin of Life, and then poked out alone, as much farther as he could, into the ineffable black darkness that is close at the end of our noses on that, as well as most other questions. He hammered his way through the whole controversy on the Freedom of the Will. He mastered the whole works of Mrs. Henry C. Carey on one side, and of two hundred and fifty English capitalists and American college professors on the other, on the question of Protection or Free Trade. He made, with vast pains, an extensive collection of the questions proposed at debating societies and college-students' societies with long Greek names. The last effort was a failure. Dr. Hicok had got the idea, that, from the spontaneous activity of so many free young geniuses, many wondrous and suggestive thoughts would be born. Having, however, tabulated his collection, he found, that, among all these innumerable gymnasia of intellect, there were only seventeen questions debated! The doctor read me a curious little memorandum of his conclusions on this unexpected fact, which will perhaps be printed some day.

He investigated many other things too; for a sharp-witted little Presbyterian Scotch doctor, working to cheat the Devil out of his soul, can accomplish an amazing deal in twenty years. He even went so far as to take into consideration mere humbugs; for, if he could cheat the enemy with a humbug, why not? The only pain, in that case, would be the mortification of having stooped to an inadequate adversary—a foeman unworthy of his steel. So he weighed such queries as the old scholastic *brocard, An chimæra bombinans in vacuo devorat secundas intentiones?*[1] and that beautiful moot point wherewith Sir Thomas More silenced the challenging school-men of Bruges, *An averia carrucæ capta in vetito nomio sint irreplegibilia?*[2]

He glanced a little at the subject of conundrums; and among the chips from his workshop is a really clever theory of conundrums. He has a classification and discussion of them, all his own, and quite ingenious and satisfactory, which divides them into answerable and unanswerable, and, under each of these, into resemblant and differential.

For instance: let the four classes be distinguished with the initials of those four terms, A. R., A. D., U. R., and U. D.; you will find that the Infinite Possible Conundrum (so to speak) can always be reduced under one of those four heads.

Using symbols, as they do in discussing syllogism—indeed, by the way, a conundrum is only a jocular variation in the syllogism, an intentional fallacy for fun (read Whately's *Logic*, Book III., and see if it isn't so)—using symbols, I say, you have these four "figures:"—

I. (A. R.) Why is A like B? (answerable): as, Why is a gentleman who gives a young lady a young dog, like a person who rides rapidly up hill? A. Because he gives a gallop up (gal-a-pup).

Sub-variety; depending upon a violation of something like the "principle of excluded middle," a very fallacy of a fallacy; such as the ancient "nigger-minstrel!" case, Why is an elephant like a brick? A. Because neither of them can climb a tree.

II. (A. D.) Why is A *unlike* B? (answerable) usually put thus: What is the difference between A and B? (Figure I., if worded in the same style, would become: "What is the similarity between A and B?") as, What is the difference between the old United-States Bank and the Fulton Ferry-boat signals in thick weather? A. One is a fog whistle, and the other is a Whig fossil.

III. (U. R.) Why is A like B? (unanswerable): as Charles Lamb's well-known question, Is that your own hare, or a wig?

IV. (U. D.) Why is A *unlike* B? (unanswerable): i. e., What is the difference, &c., as, What is the difference between a facsimile and a sick family; or between hydraulics and raw-hide licks?

But let me not diverge too far into frivolity. All the hopefully difficult questions Dr. Hicok set down and classified. He compiled a set of rules on the subject, and indeed developed a whole philosophy of it, by which he struck off, as soluble, questions or classes of them. Some he thought out himself; others were now and then answered in some learned book, that led the way through the very heart of one or another of his biggest mill-stones.

So it was really none too much time that he had; and, in truth, he did not actually decide upon his three questions, until just a week before the fearful day when he was to put them.

It came at last, as every day of reckoning surely comes; and Dr. Hicok, memorandum in hand, sat in his comfortable library about three o'clock on one beautiful warm summer afternoon, as pale as a sheet, his heart thumping away like Mr. Krupp's biggest steam-hammer at Essen, his mouth and tongue parched and feverish, a pitcher of cold water at hand from which he sipped and sipped, though it seemed as if his throat repelled it into "the globular state," or dispersed it into steam, as red-hot iron does. Around him were the records of the vast army of doubters and quibblers in whose works he had been hunting, as a traveler labors through a jungle, for the deepest doubts, the most remote inquiries.

Sometimes, with that sort of hardihood, rather than reason, which makes a desperate man try to believe by his will what he longs to know to be true, Dr. Hicok would say to himself, "I know I've got him!" And then his heart would seem to fall out of him, it sank so suddenly, and with so deadly a faintness, as the other side of his awful case loomed before him, and he thought, "But if——?" He would not finish *that* question; he could not. The furthest point to which he could bring himself was that of a sort of icy outer stiffening of acquiescence in the inevitable.

There was a ring at the street-door. The servant brought in a card, on a silver salver.

MR. APOLLO LYON

"Show the gentleman in," said the doctor. He spoke with difficulty; for the effort to control his own nervous excitement was so immense an exertion, that he hardly had the self-command and muscular energy even to articulate.

The servant returned, and ushered into the library a handsome, youngish, middle-aged and middle-sized gentleman, pale, with large melancholy black eyes, and dressed in the most perfect and quiet style.

The doctor arose, and greeted his visitor with a degree of steadiness and politeness that did him the greatest credit.

"How do you do, sir?" he said: "I am happy"—but it struck him that he wasn't, and he stopped short.

"Very right, my dear sir," replied the guest, in a voice that was musical but perceptibly sad, or rather patient in tone. "Very right; how hollow those formulas are! I hate all forms and ceremonies! But I am glad to see *you*, doctor. Now, that is really the fact."

No doubt! "Divil doubt him!" as an Irishman would say. So is a cat glad to see a mouse in its paw. Something like these thoughts arose in the doctor's mind; he smiled as affably as he could, and requested the visitor to be seated.

"Thanks!" replied he, and took the chair which the doctor moved up to the table for him. He placed his hat and gloves on the table. There was a brief pause, as might happen if any two friends sat down at their ease for a chat on matters and things in general. The visitor turned over a volume or two that lay on the table.

"The Devil," he read from one of them; "His Origin, Greatness, and Decadence. By the Rev. A. Réville, D. D."

"Ah!" he commented quietly. "A Frenchman, I observe. If it had been an Englishman, I should fancy he wrote the book for the sake of the rime in the title. Do you know, doctor, I fancy that incredulity of his will substitute one dash for the two periods in the reverend gentleman's degree! I know no one greater condition of success in some lines of operation, than to have one's existence thoroughly disbelieved in."

The doctor forced himself to reply. "I hardly know how I came to have the book here. Yet he does make out a pretty strong case. I confess I would like to be certified that he is right. Suppose you allow yourself to be convinced?" And the poor fellow grinned: it couldn't be called a smile.

"Why, really, I'll look into it. I've considered the point though, not that I'm sure I could choose. And you know, as the late J. Milton very neatly observed, one would hardly like to lose one's intellectual being, 'though full of pain;'" and he smiled, not unkindly but sadly, and then resumed: "A Bible too. Very good edition. I remember seeing it stated that a professional person made it his business to find errors of the press in one of the Bible Society's editions —this very one, I think; and the only one he could discover was a single 'wrong font.' Very accurate work—very!"

He had been turning over the leaves indifferently as he spoke, and laid the volume easily back. "Curious old superstition that," he remarked, "that certain personages were made uncomfortable by this work!" And he gave the doctor a glance, as much as to ask, in the most delicate manner in the world, "Did you put that there to scare me with?"

I think the doctor blushed a little. He had not really expected, you know,—still, in case there should be any prophy-lactic influence——? No harm done, in any event; and that was precisely the observation made by the guest.

"No harm done, my dear fellow!" he said, in his calm, quiet, musical voice. No good, either, I imagine they both of them added to themselves.

There is an often repeated observation, that people under the pressure of an im-measurable misery or agony seem to take on a preternaturally sharp vision for mi-nute details, such as spots in the carpet, and sprigs in the wall-paper, threads on a sleeve, and the like. Probably the doctor felt this influence. He had dallied a little, too, with the crisis; and so did his visitor—from different motives, no doubt; and, as he sat there, his eye fell on the card that had just been brought to him.

"I beg your pardon," he said; "but might I ask a question about your card?"

"Most certainly, doctor: what is it?"

"Why—it's always a liberty to ask ques-tions about a gentleman's name, and we Scotchmen are particularly sensitive on the point; but I have always been interested in the general subject of patronomatology."

The other, by a friendly smile and a deprecating wave of the hand, renewed his welcome to the doctor's question.

"Well, it's this: How did you come to decide upon that form of name—Mr. Apollo Lyon?"

"Oh! just a little fancy of mine. It's a newly-invented variable card, I believe they call it. There's a temporary ink ar-rangement. It struck me it was liable to abuse in case of an assumption of *aliases;* but perhaps that's none of my business. You can easily take off the upper name, and another one comes out underneath. I'm always interested in inventions. See."

And as the text, "But they have sought out many inventions," passed through Dr. Hicok's mind, the other drew forth a white handkerchief, and, rubbing the card in a careless sort of way, laid it down before the doctor. Perhaps the strain on the poor doctor's nerves was unsteadying him by this time: he may not have seen right; but he seemed to see only one name, as if compounded from the former two:

And it seemed to be in red ink instead of black; and the lines seemed to creep and throb and glow, as if the red were the red of fire, instead of vermilion. But red is an extremely trying color to the eyes. How-ever, the doctor, startled as he was, thought best not to raise any further queries, and only said, perhaps wih some difficulty, "Very curious, I'm sure!"

"Well, doctor," said Mr. Lyon, or what-ever his name was, "I don't want to hurry you, but I suppose we might as well have our little business over?"

"Why, yes. I suppose you would not care to consider any question of compromises or substitutes?"

"I fear it's out of the question, really," was the reply, most kindly in tone, but with perfect distinctness.

There was a moment's silence. It seemed to Dr. Hicok as if the beating of his heart must fill the room, it struck so heavily, and the blood seemed to surge with so loud a rush through the carotids up past his ears. "Shall I be found to have gone off with a rush of blood to the head?" he thought to himself. But—it can very often be done by a resolute effort—he gathered himself together as it were, and with one powerful exertion mastered his disordered nerves. Then he lifted his memorandum, gave one glance at the sad, calm face opposite him, and spoke.

"You know they're every once in a while explaining a vote, as they call it, in Con-gress. It don't make any difference, I know; but it seems to me as if I should put you more fully in possession of my meaning, if I should just say a word or two about the reasons for my selection."

The visitor bowed with his usual air of pleasant acquiescence.

"I am aware," said Dr. Hicok, "that my selection would seem thoroughly common-place to most people. Yet nobody knows better than you do, my dear sir, that the oldest questions are the newest. The same vitality which is so strong in them, as to raise them as soon as thought begins, is infinite, and maintains them as long as thought endures. Indeed, I may say to you frankly, that it is by no means on novelty, but rather on antiquity, that I rely."

The doctor's hearer bowed with an air of approving interest. "Very justly reasoned," he observed. The doctor went on—

"I have, I may say—and under the circumstances I shall not be suspected of conceit—made pretty much the complete circuit of unsolved problems. They class exactly as those questions do which we habitually reckon as solved: under the three subjects to which they relate—God, the intelligent creation, the unintelligent creation. Now, I have selected my questions accordingly—one for each of those divisions. Whether I have succeeded in satisfying the conditions necessarily will appear quickly. But you see that I have not stooped to any quibbling, or begging either. I have sought to protect myself by the honorable use of a masculine reason."

"Your observations interest me greatly," remarked the audience. "Not the less so, that they are so accurately coincident with my own habitual lines of thought—at least, so far as I can judge from what you have said. Indeed, suppose you had called upon me to help you prepare insoluble problems. I was bound, I suppose, to comply to the best of my ability; and, if I had done so, those statements of yours are thus far the very preface I supplied—I beg your pardon—should have supplied—you with. I fancy I could almost state the questions. Well?"—

All this was most kind and complimentary; but somehow it did not encourage the doctor in the least. He even fancied that he detected a sneer, as if his interlocutor had been saying, "Flutter away, old bird! That was *my bait* that you have been feeding on; you're safe enough; it is my net that holds you."

"*First Question*," said Dr. Hicok, with steadiness: "Reconcile the foreknowledge and the fore-ordination of God with the free will of man?"

"I thought so, of course," remarked the other. Then he looked straight into the doctor's keen little gray eyes with his deep melancholy black ones, and raised his slender forefinger. "Most readily. The reconciliation is *your own conscience*, doctor! Do what you know to be right, and you will find that there is nothing to reconcile—that you and your Maker have no debates to settle!"

The words were spoken with a weighty solemnity and conviction that were even awful. The doctor had a conscience, though he had found himself practically forced, for the sake of success, to use a good deal of constraint with it—in fact, to lock it up, as it were, in a private mad-house, on an unfounded charge of lunacy. But the obstinate thing would not die, and would not lose its wits; and now all of a sudden, and from the very last quarter where it was to be expected, came a summons before whose intensity of just requirement no bolts could stand. The doctor's conscience walked out of her prison and came straight up to the field of battle, and said—

"Give up the first question."

And he obeyed.

"I confess it," he said. "But how could I have expected a great basic truth both religiously and psychologically so, from— from *you?*"

"Ah! my dear sir," was the reply, "you have erred in *that* line of thought, exactly as many others have. The truth is one and the same, to God, man, and devil."

"*Second Question*," said Dr. Hicok. "Reconcile the development theory, connection of natural selection and sexual relation, with the responsible immortality of the soul."

"Unquestionably," assented the other, as if to say, "Just as I expected."

"No theory of creation has any logical connection with any doctrine of immortality. What was the motive of creation?— *that* would be a question! If you had asked me *that!* But the question, 'Where did men come from?' has no bearing on the question, 'Have they any duties now that they are here?' The two are reconciled, because they do not differ. You can't state any inconsistency between a yard measure and a fifty-six pound weight."

The doctor nodded; he sat down; he took a glass of water, and pressed his hand to his heart. "Now, then," he said to himself, "once more! If I have to stand this fifteen minutes I shall be in *some* other world!"

The door from the inner room opened; and Mrs. Hicok came singing in, carrying balanced upon her pretty pink fore-finger something or other of an airy boquet-like fabric. Upon this she was looking with much delight.

"See, dear!" she said; "how perfectly lovely!"

Both gentlemen started, and the lady started too. She had not known of the visit; and she had not, until this instant, seen that her husband was not alone.

Dr. Hicok, of course, had never given her the key to his skeleton-closet; for he was a shrewd man. He loved her too; and he thought he had provided for her absence during the ordeal. She had executed her shopping with unprecedented speed.

Why the visitor started, would be difficult to say. Perhaps her voice startled him. The happy music in it was enough like a beautified duplicate of his own thrilling sweet tones, to have made him acknowledge her for a sister—from heaven. He started, at any rate.

"Mr. Lyon, my wife," said the doctor, somewhat at a loss. Mr. Lyon bowed, and so did the lady.

"I beg your pardon, gentlemen, I am sure," she said. "I did not know you were busy, dear. There is a thundershower coming up. I drove home just in season."

"Oh!—only a little wager, about some conundrums," said the doctor. Perhaps he may be excused for his fib. He did not want to annoy her unnecessarily.

"Oh! do let me know!" she said, with much eagerness. "You know how I enjoy them!"

"Well," said the doctor, "not exactly the ordinary kind. I was to puzzle my friend here with one out of three questions; and he has beaten me in two of them already. I've but one more chance."

"Only one?" she asked, with a smile. "What a bright man your friend must be! I thought nobody could puzzle you, dear. Stay; let *me* ask the other question."

Both the gentlemen started again: it was quite a surprise.

"But you are a married man, Mr. Lyon?" she asked, with a blush.

"No, madam," was the reply, with a very graceful bow—"I have a mother, but no wife. Permit me to say, that, if I could believe there was a duplicate of yourself in existence, I would be as soon as possible."

"Oh, what a gallant speech!" said the lady. "Thank you, sir, very much;" and she made him a pretty little curtsy. "Then I am quite sure of my question, sir. Shall I, dear?"

The doctor quickly decided. "I am done for, anyhow," he reflected. "I begin to see that the old villain put those questions into my head himself. He hinted as much. I don't know but I'd rather she would ask it. It's better to have her kill me, I guess than to hold out the carving-knife to hir myself."

"With all my heart, my dear," said th doctor, "if Mr. Lyon consents."

Mr. Lyon looked a little disturbed; bu his manner was perfect, as he replied tha he regretted to seem to disoblige, but tha he feared the conditions of their little be would not allow it.

"Beg your pardon, I'm sure, for being s uncivil," said the lively little beauty, a she whispered a few words in her hus band's ear.

This is what she said—

"What's mine's yours, dear. Take i Ask him—buz, buzz, buzz."

The doctor nodded. Mrs. Hicok stood b him and smiled, still holding in her prett pink fore-finger the frail shimmering thin just mentioned; and she gave it a twirl, s that it swung quite round. "Isn't it a lov of a bonnet?" she said.

"Yes," the doctor said aloud. "I adop the question."

"*Third Question. Which is the front sid of this?*"

And he pointed to the bonnet. It mus have been a bonnet, because Mrs. Hico called it so. I shouldn't have known it fror the collection of things in a kaleidoscop bunched up together.

The lady stood before him, and twirle the wondrous fabric round and round, wit the prettiest possible unconscious rougis look of defiance. The doctor's very hear stood still.

"Put it on, please," said Mr. Lyon, in th most innocent way in the world.

"Oh, no!" laughed she. "I know I'r only a woman, but I'm not *quite* so silly But I'll tell you what: you men put it or if you think that will help you!" and sh held out the mystery to him.

Confident of his powers of discrimina tion, Mr. Lyon took hold of the fairy-lik combination of sparkles and threads an feathers and flowers, touching it with tha sort of timid apprehension that bachelor use with a baby. He stood before the glas over the mantel-piece. First he put i across his head with one side in fron and then with the other. Then he put i lengthways of his head, and tried the effec of tying one of the couples of strings unde each of his ears. Then he put it on, th other side up; so that it swam on his hea like a boat, with a high mounted bow an stern. More than once he did all this, with obvious care and thoughtfulness.

Then he came slowly back, and resumed his seat. It was growing very dark, though they had not noticed it; for the thunder-shower had been hurrying on, and already its advance guard of wind, heavy laden with the smell of rain, could be heard, and a few large drops splashed on the window.

The beautiful wife of the doctor laughed merrily to watch the growing discomposure of the visitor, who returned the bonnet, with undiminished courtesy, but with obvious constraint of manner.

He looked down; he drummed on the table; he looked up; and both the doctor and the doctor's wife were startled at the intense sudden anger in the dark, handsome face. Then he sprang up, and went to the window. He looked out a moment, and then said—

"Upon my word, that is going to be a very sharp squall! The clouds are *very* heavy. If I'm any judge, something will be struck. I can feel the electricity in the air."

While he still spoke, the first thunder-bolt crashed overhead. It was one of those close, sudden, overpoweringly awful explosions from clouds very heavy and very near, where the lightning and the thunder leap together out of the very air close about you, even as if you were in them. It was an unendurable burst of sound, and of the intense white sheety light of very near lightning. Dreadfully frightened, the poor little lady clung close to her husband.

He, poor man, if possible, yet more frightened, exhausted as he was by what he had been enduring, fainted dead away. Don't blame him: a cast-iron bull-dog might have fainted.

Mrs. Hicok, thinking that her husband was struck dead by the lightning, screamed terribly. Then she touched him; and, seeing what was really the matter, administered cold water from the pitcher on the table. Shortly he revived.

"Where is he?" he said.

"I don't know, love. I thought you were dead. He must have gone away. Did it strike the house?"

"Gone away? Thank God! Thank *you*, dear!" cried out the doctor.

Not knowing any adequate cause for so much emotion, she answered him—

"Now, love, don't you ever say women are not practical again. That was a practical question, you see. But didn't it strike the house? What a queer smell. Ozone: isn't that what you were telling me about? How funny, that lightning should have a smell."

"I believe there is no doubt of it," observed Dr. Hicok.

Mr. Apollo Lyon had really gone, though just how or when, nobody could say.

"My dear!" said Dr. Hicok, "I do so like that bonnet of yours! I don't wonder it puzzled him. It would puzzle the Devil himself. I firmly believe I shall call it your Devil-puzzler."

But he never told her what the puzzle had been.

XIX

GEORGE WASHINGTON CABLE (1844–1925)

The Civil War created for America new backgrounds and new *motifs* for fiction. The destruction by war of an old aristocracy founded on slavery, the peculiar characteristics of the freed negroes, and the vague hinterland of legend behind it all seemed to open up all at once a rich field for romance. The first native writer to use this new after-the-war material was George W. Cable whose New Orleans Creole story "Sieur George" appeared in *Scribner's Monthly* in 1873. To the North generally this story, like the others that followed it at timely intervals, was as strangely new as had been Bret Harte's California tales. New Orleans with its early strata of Spanish and French and American possessors, its semi-tropic backgrounds, its exotic race mixtures, and its unAmerican atmosphere was as unknown in 1870 to the generality of American readers as were the Steppes of Russia. Cable's *Old Creole Days*, 1878, became at once a widely influential book turning the current of the short story toward "local color" materials more than any other volume save *The Luck of Roaring Camp*.

Cable was not himself a Creole; he was not indeed an unqualified Southerner despite the fact that he had been born in New Orleans and had served for four years in the Confederate army. His parents were Northerners, his mother indeed a New England "Yankee." His pictures of Creole life, though written by one who knew his materials thoroughly from actual observation and who sought always truth to fact and background, are modified by strict Puritanic inhibitions and are tinted richly with romance. He was no more a realist than was Lafcadio Hearn who followed him. He was first of all an antiquarian desirous of preserving, though in a rich solution of romance, "the strange true stories of Louisiana." Then, secondly, he was an artist who had read widely in the current French fiction, the fiction of About and Merimée and Flaubert, who had read widely too in English fiction, especially Dickens. Like Harte, he learned his art from careful study of models and from incessant practice. There was in his pen a Celtic quality which, blended with the Puritanic and the Dickens elements, gave him at last a style peculiarly his own—a style highly individualistic and unmistakable. His first work was his best. His later fiction, done after the first glow of his enthusiasm had subsided, is markedly inferior. As a short-story writer he must stand or fall with his earliest collection, *Old Creole Days*, a book to be read in its later editions since to these have been appended the distinctive story "Madame Delphine."

"POSSON JONE'" *

To Jules St.-Ange—elegant little heathen —there yet remained at manhood a remembrance of having been to school, and of having been taught by a stony-headed Capuchin that the world is round—for example, like a cheese. This round world is a cheese to be eaten through, and Jules had nibbled quite into his cheese-world already at twenty-two.

He realized this as he idled about one Sunday morning where the intersection of Royal and Conti streets some seventy years ago formed a central corner of New Orleans. Yes, yes, the trouble was he had been wasteful and honest. He discussed the matter with that faithful friend and confidant, Baptiste, his yellow body-servant. They concluded that, papa's patience and *tante's*[1] pin-money having been gnawed away quite to the rind, there were left open only these few easily enumerated resorts: to go to work—they shuddered; to join Major Innerarity's filibustering expedition; or else—why not?—to try some games of confidence. At twenty-two one must begin to be something. Nothing else tempted; could that avail? One could but try. It is noble to try; and, besides, they were hungry. If one could "make the friendship" of some person from the country, for instance, with money, not expert at cards or dice, but, as one would say, willing to learn, one might find cause to say some "Hail Marys."

The sun broke through a clearing sky, and Baptiste pronounced it good for luck. There had been a hurricane in the night. The weed-grown tile-roofs were still dripping, and from lofty brick and low adobe walls a rising stream responded to the summer sunlight. Upstreet, and across the Rue du Canal, one could get glimpses of the gardens in Faubourg Ste.-Marie standing in silent wretchedness, so many tearful Lucretias, tattered victims of the storm. Short remnants of the wind now and then came down the narrow street in erratic puffs heavily laden with odors of broken boughs and torn flowers, skimmed the little pools of rain-water in the deep ruts of the unpaved street, and suddenly went away to nothing, like a juggler's butterflies or a young man's money.

It was very picturesque, the Rue Royale. The rich and poor met together. The locksmith's swinging key creaked next door to the bank; across the way, crouching, mendicant-like, in the shadow of a great importing-house, was the mud laboratory of the mender of broken combs. Light balconies overhung the rows of showy shops and stores open for trade this Sunday morning, and pretty Latin faces of the higher class glanced over their savagely pronged railings upon the passers below. At some windows hung lace curtains, flannel duds at some, and at others only the scraping and sighing one-hinged shutter groaning toward Paris after its neglectful master.

M. St.-Ange stood looking up and down the street for nearly an hour. But few ladies, only the inveterate mass-goers, were out. About the entrance of the frequent *cafés* the masculine gentility stood leaning on canes, with which now one and now another beckoned to Jules, some even adding pantomimic hints of the social cup.

M. St.-Ange remarked to his servant without turning his head that somehow he felt sure he should soon return those *bons*[2] that the mulatto had lent him.

"What will you do with them?"

"Me!" said Baptiste, quickly; "I will go and see the bull-fight in the Place Congo."

"There is to be a bull-fight? But where is M. Cayetano?"

"Ah, got all his affairs wet in the tornado. Instead of his circus, they are to have a bull-fight—not an ordinary bull-fight with sick horses, but a buffalo-and-tiger fight. I would not miss it——"

Two or three persons ran to the opposite corner, and commenced striking at something with their canes. Others followed. Can M. St.-Ange and servant, who hasten forward—can the Creoles, Cubans, Spaniards, San Domingo refugees, and other loungers—can they hope it is a fight? They hurry forward. Is a man in a fit? The crowd pours in from the side-streets. Have they killed a so-long snake? Bareheaded shopmen leave their wives, who stand upon chairs. The crowd huddles and packs. Those on the outside make little leaps into the air, trying to be tall.

"What is the matter?"

"Have they caught a real live rat?"

"Who is hurt?" asks some one in English.

"*Personne,*"[3] replies a shopkeeper; "a man's hat blow' in the gutter; but he has it now. Jules pick' it. See, that is the man, head and shoulders on top the res'."

"He in the homespun?" asks a second shopkeeper. "Humph! an *Américain*[4]—a West-Floridian; bah!"

"But wait; 'st! he is speaking; listen!"

"To who is he speak——?"

"Sh-sh-sh! to Jules."

"Jules who?"

"Silence, you! To Jules St.-Ange, what howe me a bill since long time. Sh-sh-sh!"

Then the voice was heard.

Its owner was a man of giant stature, with a slight stoop in his shoulders, as if he was making a constant, good-natured attempt to accommodate himself to ordinary doors and ceilings. His bones were those of an ox. His face was marked more by weather than age, and his narrow brow was bald and smooth. He had instantaneously formed an opinion of Jules St.-Ange, and the multitude of words, most of them lingual curiosities, with which he was rasping the wide-open ears of his listeners, signified, in short, that, as sure as his name was Parson Jones, the little Creole was a "plum gentleman."

M. St.-Ange bowed and smiled, and was about to call attention, by both gesture and speech, to a singular object on top of the still uncovered head, when the nervous motion of the *Américain* anticipated him, as, throwing up an immense hand, he drew down a large roll of bank-notes. The crowd laughed, the West-Floridian joining, and began to disperse.

"Why, that money belongs to Smyrny Church," said the giant.

"You are very dengerous to make your money expose like that, Misty Posson Jone'," said St.-Ange, counting it with his eyes.

The countryman gave a start and smile of surprise.

"How d'dyou know my name was Jones?" he asked; but, without pausing for the Creole's answer, furnished in his reckless way some further specimens of West-Floridian English; and the conciseness with which he presented full intelligence of his home, family, calling, lodging-house, and present and future plans, might have passed for consummate art, had it not been the most run-wild nature. "And I've done been to Mobile, you know, on business for Bethesdy Church. It's the on'yest time I ever been from home; now you wouldn't of believed that, would you? But I admire to have saw you, that's so. You've got to come and eat with me. Me and my boy ain't been fed yit. What might one call yo' name? Jools? Come on, Jools. Come on, Colossus. That's my niggah—his name's Colossus of Rhodes. Is that yo' yallah boy, Jools? Fetch him along, Colossus. It seems like a special providence.—Jools, do you believe in a special providence?"

Jules said he did.

The new-made friends moved briskly off, followed by Baptiste and a short, square, old negro, very black and grotesque, who had introduced himself to the mulatto, with many glittering and cavernous smiles, as "d'body-sarvant of d'Rev'n' Mr. Jones."

Both pairs enlivened their walk with conversation. Parson Jones descanted upon the doctrine he had mentioned, as illustrated in the perplexities of cotton-growing, and concluded that there would always be "a special providence again' cotton untell folks quits a-pressin' of it and haulin' of it on Sundays!"

"Je dis,"[5] said St.-Ange, in response, "I thing you is juz right. I believe, me, strong-strong in the improvidence, yes. You know my papa he hown a sugah-plantation, you know. 'Jules, me son,' he say one time to me, 'I goin' to make one baril sugah to fedge the moze high price in New Orleans.' Well, he take his bez baril sugah—I nevah see a so careful man like me papa always to make a so beautiful sugah et sirop. 'Jules, go at Father Pierre an' ged this lill pitcher fill with holy-water, an' tell him sen' his tin bucket, and I will make it fill

with quitte.'[6] I ged the holy-water; my papa sprinkle it over the baril, an' make one cross on the 'ead of the baril."

"Why, Jools," said Parson Jones, "that didn't do no good."

"Din do no good! Id broughd the so great value! You can strike me dead if thad baril sugah din fedge the more high cost than any other in the city. Parce-que,[7] the man what buy that baril sugah he make a mistake of one hundred pound"—falling back—"Mais[8] certainlee !"

"And you think that was growin' out of the holy-water?" asked the parson.

"Mais, what could make it else? Id could not be the quitte, because my papa keep the bucket, an' forget to sen' the quitte to Father Pierre."

Parson Jones was disappointed.

"Well, now, Jools, you know, I don't think that was right. I reckon you must be a plum Catholic."

M. St.-Ange shrugged. He would not deny his faith.

"I am a Catholique, mais"—brightening as he hoped to recommend himself anew—"not a good one."

"Well, you know," said Jones—"where's Colossus? Oh! all right. Colossus strayed off a minute in Mobile, and I plum lost him for two days. Here's the place; come in. Colossus and this boy can go to the kitchen.—Now, Colossus, what air you a-beckonin' at me faw?"

He let his servant draw him aside and address him in a whisper.

"Oh, go 'way!" said the parson with a jerk. "Who's goin' to throw me? What? Speak louder. Why, Colossus, you shayn't talk so, saw. 'Pon my soul, you're the mightiest fool I ever taken up with. Jest you go down that alley-way with this yalla boy, and don't show yo' face untell yo' called!"

The negro begged; the master wrathily insisted.

"Colossus, will you do ez I tell you, or shell I hev to strike you, saw?"

"O Mahs Jimmy, I—I's gwine; but"—he ventured nearer—"don't on no account drink nothin', Mahs Jimmy."

Such was the negro's earnestness that he put one foot in the gutter, and fell heavily against his master. The parson threw him off angrily.

"Thar, now! Why, Colossus, you most of been dosted with sumthin'; yo' plum crazy.—Humph, come on, Jools, let's eat !

Humph! to tell me that when I never taken a drop, exceptin' for chills, in my life—which he knows so as well as me!"

The two masters began to ascend a stair.

"*Mais*, he is a sassy; I would sell him, me," said the young Creole.

"No, I wouldn't do that," replied the parson; "though there is people in Bethesdy who says he is a rascal. He's a powerful smart fool. Why, that boy's got money, Jools; more money than religion, I reckon. I'm shore he fallen into mighty bad company"—they passed beyond earshot.

Baptiste and Colossus, instead of going to the tavern kitchen, passed to the next door and entered the dark rear corner of a low grocery, where, the law notwithstanding, liquor was covertly sold to slaves. There, in the quiet company of Baptiste and the grocer, the colloquial powers of Colossus, which were simply prodigious, began very soon to show themselves.

"For whilst," said he, "Mahs Jimmy has eddication, you know—whilst he has eddication, I has 'scretion. He has eddication and I has 'scretion, an' so we gits along."

He drew a black bottle down the counter, and, laying half his length upon the damp board, continued:

"As a p'inciple I discredits de imbimin' of awjus liquors. De imbimin' of awjus liquors, de wiolution of de Sabbaf, de playin' of de fiddle, and de usin' of by-words, dey is de fo' sins of de conscience; an' if any man sin de fo' sins of de conscience, de debble done sharp his fork fo' dat man.—Ain't that so, boss?"

The grocer was sure it was so.

"Neberdeless, mind you"—here the orator brimmed his glass from the bottle and swallowed the contents with a dry eye—"mind you, a roytious man, sech as ministers of de gospel and dere body-sarvants, can take a *leetle* for de weak stomach."

But the fascinations of Colossus's eloquence must not mislead us; this is the story of a true Christian; to wit, Parson Jones.

The parson and his new friend ate. But the coffee M. St.-Ange declared he could not touch; it was too wretchedly bad. At the French Market, near by, there was some noble coffee. This, however, would have to be bought, and Parson Jones had scruples.

"You see, Jools, every man has his conscience to guide him, which it does so in——"

"Oh, yes!" cried St.-Ange, "conscien'; thad is the bez, Posson Jone'. Certainlee! I am a *Catholique*, you is a *schismatique;* you thing it is wrong to dring some coffee—well, then, it *is* wrong; you thing it is wrong to make the sugah to ged the so large price—well, then, it *is* wrong; I thing it is right—well, then, it *is* right; it is all 'abit; *c'est tout.*[10] What a man thing is right, *is right;* 'tis all 'abit. A man muz nod go again' his conscien'. My faith! do you thing I would go again' my conscien'? *Mais allons,*[11] led us go and ged some coffee."

"Jools."

"W'at?"

"Jools, it ain't the drinkin' of coffee, but the buyin' of it on a Sabbath. You must really excuse me, Jools, it's again' conscience, you know."

"Ah!" said St.-Ange, "*c'est* very true. For you it would be a sin, *mais* for me it is only 'abit. Rilligion is a very strange; I know a man one time, he thing it was wrong to go to cock-fight Sunday evening. I thing it is all 'abit. *Mais,* come, Posson Jone'; I have got one friend, Miguel; led us go at his house and ged some coffee. Come; Miguel have no familie; only him and Joe—always like to see friend; *allons,* led us come yonder."

"Why, Jools, my dear friend, you know," said the shamefaced parson, "I never visit on Sundays."

"Never w'at?" asked the astounded Creole.

"No," said Jones, smiling awkwardly.

"Never visite?"

"Exceptin' sometimes amongst church-members," said Parson Jones.

"*Mais,*" said the seductive St.-Ange, "Miguel and Joe is church-member'—certainlee! They love to talk about rilligion. Come at Miguel and talk about some rilligion. I am nearly expire for me coffee."

Parson Jones took his hat from beneath his chair and rose up.

"Jools," said the weak giant, "I ought to be in church right now."

"*Mais,* the church is right yonder at Miguel', yes. Ah!" continued St.-Ange, as they descended the stairs, "I thing every man muz have the rilligion he like' the bez—me, I like the *Catholique* rilligion the bez—for me it *is* the bez. Every man will sure go to heaven if he like his rilligion the bez."

"Jools," said the West-Floridian, laying

his great hand tenderly upon the Creole's shoulder, as they stepped out upon the *banquette*,[12] "do you think you have any shore hopes of heaven?"

"Yass!" replied St.-Ange; "I am sure-sure. I thing everybody will go to heaven. I thing you will go, *et* I thing Miguel will go, *et* Joe—everybody, I thing—*mais*, hof course, not if they not have been christen'. Even I thing some niggers will go."

"Jools," said the parson, stopping in his walk—"Jools, I *don't* want to lose my niggah."

"You will not loose him. With Baptiste he *cannot* ged loose."

But Colossus's master was not reassured.

"Now," said he, still tarrying, "this is jest the way; had I of gone to church——"

"Posson Jone'," said Jules.

"What?"

"I tell you. We goin' to church!"

"Will you?" asked Jones, joyously.

"*Allons,* come along," said Jules, taking his elbow.

They walked down the Rue Chartres, passed several corners, and by and by turned into a cross street. The parson stopped an instant as they were turning and looked back up the street.

"W'at you lookin'?" asked his companion.

"I thought I saw Colossus," answered the parson, with an anxious face; "I reckon 'twa'n't him, though." And they went on.

The street they now entered was a very quiet one. The eye of any chance passer would have been at once drawn to a broad, heavy, white brick edifice on the lower side of the way, with a flag-pole standing out like a bowsprit from one of its great windows, and a pair of lamps hanging before a large closed entrance. It was a theater, honey-combed with gambling-dens. At this morning hour all was still, and the only sign of life was a knot of little barefoot girls gathered within its narrow shade, and each carrying an infant relative. Into this place the parson and M. St.-Ange entered, the little nurses jumping up from the sills to let them pass in.

A half-hour may have passed. At the end of that time the whole juvenile company were laying alternate eyes and ears to the chinks, to gather what they could of an interesting quarrel going on within.

"I did not, saw! I given you no cause of offence, saw! It's not so, saw! Mister Jools simply mistaken the house, thinkin' it was a Sabbath-school! No such thing, saw; I *ain't* bound to bet! Yes, I kin git out. Yes, without bettin'! I hev a right to my opinion; I reckon I'm *a white man,* saw! No, saw! I on'y said I didn't think you could get the game on them cards. 'Sno such thing, saw! I do *not* know how to play! I wouldn't hev a rascal's money ef I should win it! Shoot, ef you dare! You can kill me, but you cayn't scare me! No, I shayn't bet! I'll die first! Yes, saw; Mr. Jools can bet for me if he admires to; I ain't his mostah."

Here the speaker seemed to direct his words to St.-Ange.

"Saw, I don't understand you, saw. I never said I'd loan you money to bet for me. I didn't suspicion this from you, saw. No, I won't take any more lemonade; it's the most notorious stuff I ever drank, saw!"

M. St.-Ange's replies were in *falsetto* and not without effect; for presently the parson's indignation and anger began to melt. "Don't ask me, Jools, I can't help you. It's no use; it's a matter of conscience with me, Jools."

"*Mais* oui! 'tis a matt' of conscien' wid me, the same."

"But, Jools, the money's none o' mine, nohow; it belongs to Smyrny, you know."

"If I could make jus' *one* bet," said the persuasive St.-Ange, "I would leave this place, fas'-fas', yes. If I had thing—*mais* I did not soupspicion this from you, Posson Jone'——"

"Don't, Jools, don't!"

"No! Posson Jone'."

"You're bound to win?" said the parson, wavering.

"*Mais certainement!*[13] But it is not to win that I want; 'tis me conscien'—me honor!"

"Well, Jools, I hope I'm not a-doin' no wrong. I'll loan you some of this money if you say you'll come right out 'thout takin' your winnin's."

All was still. The peeping children could see the parson as he lifted his hand to his breast-pocket. There it paused a moment in bewilderment, then plunged to the bottom. It came back empty, and fell lifelessly at his side. His head dropped upon his breast, his eyes were for a moment closed, his broad palms were lifted and pressed against his forehead, a tremor seized him, and he fell all in a lump to the floor. The children ran off with their infant-loads, leaving Jules St.-Ange swearing by all his deceased relatives, first to Miguel and Joe, and then to the lifted parson, that he did not know what had become of the money "except if" the black man had got it.

In the rear of ancient New Orleans, beyond the sites of the old rampart, a trio of Spanish forts, where the town has since sprung up and grown old, green with all the luxuriance of the wild Creole summer, lay the Congo Plains. Here stretched the canvas of the historic Cayetano, who Sunday after Sunday sowed the sawdust for his circus-ring.

But to-day the great showman had fallen short of his printed promise. The hurricane had come by night, and with one fell swash had made an irretrievable sop of everything. The circus trailed away its bedraggled magnificence, and the ring was cleared for the bull.

Then the sun seemed to come out and work for the people. "See," said the Spaniards, looking up at the glorious sky with its great, white fleets drawn off upon the horizon—"see—heaven smiles upon the bullfight!"

In the high upper seats of the rude amphitheater sat the gaily-decked wives and daughters of the Gascons, from the *métaries* [14] along the Ridge, and the chattering Spanish women of the Market, their shining hair unbonneted to the sun. Next below were their husbands and lovers in Sunday blouses, milkmen, butchers, bakers, black-bearded fishermen, Sicilian fruiterers, swarthy Portuguese sailors, in little woolen caps, and strangers of the graver sort; mariners of England, Germany, and Holland. The lowest seats were full of trappers, smugglers, Canadian *voyageurs,* drinking and singing; *Américains,* too— more's the shame—from the upper rivers —who will not keep their seats—who ply the bottle, and who will get home by and by and tell how wicked Sodom is; broadbrimmed, silver-braided Mexicans, with their copper cheeks and bat's eyes, and their tinkling spurred heels. Yonder in that quieter section, are the quadroon women in their black lace shawls—and there is Baptiste; and below them are the turbaned black women, and there is—but he vanishes—Colossus.

The afternoon is advancing, yet the sport, though loudly demanded, does not begin. The *Américains* grow derisive and find pastime in gibes and raillery. They mock the various Latins with their national inflections, and answer their scowls with laughter. Some of the more aggressive shout pretty French greetings to the women of Gascony, and one bargeman, amid peals of applause, stands on a seat and hurls a kiss to the quadroons. The mariners of England, Germany, and Holland, as spectators, like the fun, while the Spaniards look black and cast defiant imprecations upon their persecutors. Some Gascons, with timely caution, pick their women out and depart, running a terrible fire of gallantries.

In hope of truce, a new call is raised for the bull: "The bull, the bull!—hush!" In a tier near the ground a man is standing and calling—standing head and shoulders above the rest—calling in the *Américaine* tongue. Another man, big and red, named Joe, and a handsome little Creole in elegant dress and full of laughter, wish to stop him, but the flat-boatmen, ha-ha-ing and cheering, will not suffer it. Ah, through some shameful knavery of the men, into whose hands he has fallen, he is drunk! Even the women can see that; and now he throws his arms wildly and raises his voice until the whole great circle hears it. He is preaching!

Ah! kind Lord, for a special providence now! The men of his own nation—men from the land of the open English Bible and temperance cup and song are cheering him on to mad disgrace. And now another call for the appointed sport is drowned by the flat-boatmen singing the ancient tune of Mear. You can hear the words—

"Old Grimes is dead, that good old soul"

—from ribald lips and throats turned brazen with laughter, from singers who toss their hats aloft and roll in their seats; the chorus swells to the accompaniment of a thousand brogans—

"He used to wear an old gray coat
All buttoned down before."

A ribboned man in the arena is trying to be heard, and the Latins raise one mighty cry for silence. The big red man gets a hand over the parson's mouth, and the ribboned man seizes his moment.

"They have been endeavoring for hours," he says, "to draw the terrible animals from their dens, but such is their strength and fierceness, that——"

His voice is drowned. Enough has been heard to warrant the inference that the beasts cannot be whipped out of the storm-drenched cages to which menagerie-life and long starvation have attached them, and from the roar of indignation the man of ribbons flies. The noise increases. Men are standing up by hundreds, and women are imploring to be let out of the turmoil. All at once, like the bursting of a dam, the whole mass pours down into the ring. They sweep across the arena and over the showman's barriers. Miguel gets a frightful trampling. Who cares for gates or doors? They tear the beasts' houses bar from bar, and, laying hold of the gaunt buffalo, drag him forth by feet, ears, and tail; and in the midst of the *mêlée*, still head and shoulders above all, wilder, with the cup of the wicked, than any beast, is the man of God from the Florida parishes!

In his arms he bore—and all the people shouted at once when they saw it—the tiger. He had lifted it high up with its back to his breast, his arms clasped under its shoulders; the wretched brute had curled up caterpillar-wise, with its long tail against its belly, and through its filed teeth grinned a fixed and impotent wrath. And Parson Jones was shouting:

"The tiger and the buffler *shell* lay down together! You dah to say they shayn't and I'll comb you with this varmint from head to foot! The tiger and the buffler *shell* lay down together. They *shell!* Now, you, Joe! Behold! I am here to see it done. The lion and the buffler *shell* lay down together!"

Mouthing these words again and again, the parson forced his way through the surge in the wake of the buffalo. This creature the Latins had secured by a lariat over his head, and were dragging across the old rampart and into a street of the city.

The northern races were trying to prevent, and there was pommeling and knocking down, cursing and knife-drawing, until Jules St.-Ange was quite carried away with the fun, laughed, clapped his hands, and swore with delight, and ever kept close to the gallant parson.

Joe, contrariwise, counted all this child's-play an interruption. He had come to find Colossus and the money. In an unlucky moment he made bold to lay hold of the parson, but a piece of the broken barriers in the hands of a flat-boatman felled him to the sod, the terrible crowd swept over him, the lariat was cut, and the giant parson hurled the tiger upon the buffalo's back. In another instant both brutes were dead at the hands of the mob; Jones was lifted from his feet, and prating of Scripture and the millennium, of Paul and Ephesus and Daniel in the "buffler's" den, was borne aloft upon the shoulders of the huzzaing *Américains*. Half an hour later he was sleeping heavily on the floor of a cell in the *calaboza*.[15]

When Parson Jones awoke, a bell was somewhat tolling for midnight. Somebody was at the door of his cell with a key. The lock grated, the door swung, the turnkey looked in and stepped back, and a ray of moonlight fell upon M. Jules St.-Ange. The prisoner sat upon the empty shackles and ring-bolt in the center of the floor.

"Misty Posson Jone'," said the visitor, softly.

"O Jools!"

"*Mais*, w'at de matter, Posson Jone'?"

"My sins, Jools, my sins!"

"Ah! Posson Jone', is that something to cry, because a man get sometime a litt' bit intoxicate? *Mais*, if a man keep *all the time* intoxicate, I think that is again' the conscien'."

"Jools, Jools, your eyes is darkened—oh! Jools, where's my pore old niggah?"

"Posson Jone', never min'; he is wid Baptiste."

"Where?"

"I don' know w'ere—*mais* he is wid Baptiste. Baptiste is a beautiful to take care of somebody."

"Is he as good as you, Jools?" asked Parson Jones, sincerely.

Jules was slightly staggered.

"You know, Posson Jone', you know, a nigger cannot be good as a w'ite man—*mais* Baptiste is a good nigger."

The parson moaned and dropped his chin into his hands.

"I was to of left for home to-morrow, sun-up, on the Isabella schooner. Pore Smyrny!" He deeply sighed.

"Posson Jone'," said Jules, leaning against the wall and smiling, "I swear you is the moz funny man I ever see. If I was you I would say, me, 'Ah! 'ow I am lucky! the money I los', it was not mine, anyhow!' My faith! shall a man make hisse'f to be the more sorry because the money he los' is not his? Me, I would say, 'it is a specious providence.'

"Ah! Misty Posson Jone'," he continued, "you make a so droll sermon ad the bull-ring. Ha! ha! I swear I think you can make money to preach thad sermon many time ad the theater St. Philippe. Hah! you is the moz brave dat I never see, *mais* ad the same time the moz rilligious man. Where I'm goin' to fin' one priest to make like dat? *Mais,* why you can't cheer up an' be 'appy? Me, if I should be miserabl' like that I would kill meself."

The countryman only shook his head.

"*Bien,* Posson Jone', I have the so good news for you."

The prisoner looked up with eager inquiry.

"Las' evening when they lock' you, I come right off at M. De Blanc's house to get you let out of de calaboose; M. De Blanc he is the judge. So soon I was entering—'Ah! Jules, me boy, juz the man to make complete the game!' Posson Jone', it was a specious providence. I win in t'ree hours more dan six hundred dollah! Look." He produced a mass of bank-notes, *bons,* and due-bills.

"And you got the pass?" asked the parson, regarding the money with a sadness incomprehensible to Jules.

"It is here; it take the effect so soon the daylight."

"Jools, my friend, your kindness is in vain."

The Creole's face became a perfect blank.

"Because," said the parson, "for two reasons: firstly, I have broken the laws, and ought to stand the penalty; and secondly—you must really excuse me, Jools, you know, but the pass has been got unfairly, I'm afeerd. You told the judge I was innocent; and in neither case it don't become a Christian (which I hope I can still say I am one) to 'do evil that good may come.' I muss stay."

M. St.-Ange stood up aghast, and for a moment speechless, at this exhibition of moral heroism; but an artifice was presently hit upon. "*Mais,* Posson Jone'!"—in his old *falsetto*—"de order—you cannot read it, it is in French—compel you to go hout, sir!"

"Is that so?" cried the parson, bounding up with radiant face—"is that so, Jools?"

The young man nodded, smiling; but, though he smiled, the fountain of his tenderness was opened. He made the sign of the cross as the parson knelt in prayer, and even whispered "Hail Mary," etc., quite through, twice over.

Morning broke in summer glory upon a cluster of villas behind the city, nestled under live-oaks and magnolias on the banks of a deep bayou, and known as Suburb St. Jean.

With the first beam came the West-Floridian and the Creole out upon the bank below the village. Upon the parson's arm hung a pair of antique saddle-bags. Baptiste limped wearily behind; both his eyes were encircled with broad, blue rings, and one cheek-bone bore the official impress of every knuckle of Colossus's left hand. The "beautiful to take care of somebody" had lost his charge. At mention of the negro he became wild, and, half in English, half in the "gumbo" dialect, said murderous things. Intimidated by Jules to calmness, he became able to speak confidently on one point; he could, would, and did swear that Colossus had gone home, to the Florida parishes; he was almost certain; in fact, he thought so.

There was a clicking of pulleys as the three appeared upon the bayou's margin, and Baptiste pointed out, in the deep shadow of a great oak, the Isabella, moored among the bulrushes, and just spreading her sails for departure. Moving down to where she lay, the parson and his friend paused on the bank, loath to say farewell.

"O Jools!" said the parson, "supposin' Colossus ain't gone home! O Jools, if you'll look him out for me, I'll never forget you—I'll never forget you, nohow, Jools. No, Jools, I never will believe he taken that money. Yes, I know all niggahs will steal"—he set foot upon the gang-plank—"but Colossus wouldn't steal from me. Good-by."

"Misty Posson Jone'," said St.-Ange, putting his hand on the parson's arm with genuine affection, "hol' on. You see dis money—w'at I win las' night? Well, I win' it by a specious providence, ain't it?"

"There's no tellin'," said the humbled Jones. "Providence

"'Moves in a mysterious way
His wonders to perform.'"

"Ah!" cried the Creole, "*c'est* very true. I ged this money in the mysterieuze way.

Mais, if I keep dis money, you know where it goin' be to-night?"

"I really can't say," replied the parson.

"Goin' to de dev'," said the sweetly-smiling young man.

The schooner-captain, leaning against the shrouds, and even Baptiste, laughed outright.

"O Jools, you mustn't!"

"Well, den, w'at I shall do wid *it?*"

"Any thing!" answered the parson; "better donate it away to some poor man——"

"Ah! Misty Posson Jone', dat is w'at I want You los' five hondred dollar'—'twas me fault."

"No, it wa'n't, Jools."

"*Mais,* it was!"

"No!"

"It *was* me fault! I *swear* it was me fault! *Mais,* here is five hondred dollar'; I wish you shall take it. Here! I don't got no use for money.—Oh, my faith! Posson Jone', you must not begin to cry some more."

Parson Jones was choked with tears. When he found voice he said:

"O Jools, Jools, Jools! my pore, noble, dear, misguidened friend! ef you hed of hed a Christian raisin'! May the Lord show you your errors better'n I kin, and bless you for your good intentions—oh, no! I cayn't touch that money with a ten-foot pole; it wa'n't rightly got; you must really excuse me, my dear friend, but I cayn't touch it."

St.-Ange was petrified.

"Good-by, dear Jools," continued the parson. "I'm in the Lord's haynds, and he's very merciful, which I hope and trust you'll find it out. Good-by!"—the schooner swang slowly off before the breeze—"good-by!"

St.-Ange roused himself.

"Posson Jone'! make me hany'ow *dis* promise: you never, never, *never* will come back to New Orleans."

"Ah, Jools, the Lord willin', I'll never leave home again!"

"All right!" cried the Creole; "I thing he's willin'. Adieu, Posson Jone'. My faith'! you are the so fighting an' moz rilligious man as I never saw! Adieu! Adieu!"

Baptiste uttered a cry and presently ran by his master toward the schooner, his hands full of clods.

St.-Ange looked just in time to see the sable form of Colossus of Rhodes emerge from the vessel's hold, and the pastor of Smyrna and Bethesda seize him in his embrace.

"O Colossus! you outlandish old nigger! Thank the Lord! Thank the Lord!"

The little Creole almost wept. He ran down the tow-path, laughing and swearing, and making confused allusion to the entire *personnel* and furniture of the lower regions.

By odd fortune, at the moment that St.-Ange further demonstrated his delight by tripping his mulatto into a bog, the schooner came brushing along the reedy bank with a graceful curve, the sails flapped, and the crew fell to poling her slowly along.

Parson Jones was on the deck, kneeling once more in prayer. His hat had fallen before him; behind him knelt his slave. In thundering tones he was confessing himself "a plum fool," from whom "the conceit had been jolted out," and who had been made to see that even his "nigger had the longest head of the two."

Colossus clasped his hands and groaned. The parson prayed for a contrite heart.

"Oh, yes!" cried Colossus.

The master acknowledged countless mercies.

"Dat's so!" cried the slave.

The master prayed that they might still be "piled on."

"Glory!" cried the black man, clapping his hands; "pile on!"

"An' now," continued the parson, "bring this pore, backslidin' jackace of a parson and this pore ole fool nigger back to thar home in peace!"

"Pray fo' de money!" called Colossus.

But the parson prayed for Jules.

"Pray fo' de *money!*" repeated the negro.

"And oh, give thy servant back that there lost money!"

Colossus rose stealthily, and tiptoed by his still shouting master. St.-Ange, the captain, the crew, gazed in silent wonder at the strategist. Pausing but an instant over the master's hat to grin an acknowledgment of his beholders' speechless interest, he softly placed in it the faithfully mourned and honestly prayed-for Smyrna fund; then, saluted by the gesticulative, silent applause of St.-Ange and the schooner-men, he resumed his first attitude behind his roaring master.

"Amen!" cried Colossus, meaning to bring him to a close.

"Onworthy though I be——" cried Jones.

"*Amen!*" reiterated the negro.

"A-a-amen!" said Parson Jones.

He rose to his feet, and, stooping to take up his hat, beheld the well-known roll. As one stunned, he gazed for a moment upon his slave, who still knelt with clasped hands and rolling eyeballs; but when he became aware of the laughter and cheers that greeted him from both deck and shore, he lifted eyes and hands to heaven, and cried like the veriest babe. And when he looked at the roll again, and hugged and kissed it, St.-Ange tried to raise a second shout, but choked, and the crew fell to their poles.

And now up runs Baptiste, covered with slime, and prepares to cast his projectiles. The first one fell wide of the mark; the schooner swung round into a long reach of water, where the breeze was in her favor; another shout of laughter drowned the maledictions of the muddy man; the sails filled; Colossus of Rhodes, smiling and bowing as hero of the moment, ducked as the main boom swept round, and the schooner, leaning slightly to the pleasant influence, rustled a moment over the bulrushes, and then sped far away down the rippling bayou.

M. Jules St.-Ange stood long, gazing at the receding vessel as it now disappeared, now reappeared beyond the tops of the high undergrowth; but, when an arm of the forest hid it finally from sight, he turned townward, followed by that fagged-out spaniel, his servant, saying, as he turned, "Baptiste."

"*Miché?*" [16]

"You know w'at I goin' do wid dis money?"

"*Non, m'sieur.*"

"Well, you can strike me dead if I don't goin' to pay hall my debts! *Allons!*" [17]

He began a merry little song to the effect that his sweetheart was a wine-bottle, and master and man, leaving care behind, returned to the picturesque Rue Royale. The ways of Providence are indeed strange. In all Parson Jones's after-life, amid the many painful reminiscences of his visit to the City of the Plain, the sweet knowledge was withheld from him that by the light of the Christian virtue that shone from him even in his great fall, Jules St.-Ange arose, and went to his father an honest man.

XX

CONSTANCE FENIMORE WOOLSON (1838–1894)

Constance Fenimore Woolson, a grandniece of James Fenimore Cooper, during the '70s was regarded generally as the most promising of all the younger feminine writers of fiction in America. Henry James could even include an appreciative study of her in his distinctive volume *Partial Portraits*, classing her with George Eliot, Stevenson, Daudet, Maupassant, and Turgenieff. She had been well trained for fiction: a girlhood spent in distinctive Eastern seminaries where among other studies she had read widely in French literature, then removal to the Middle West with summers spent in the wild regions of the upper lakes. Here she found her first backgrounds and her first distinctive characters: the old French *habitants*, survivors of the Canadian *ancien régime*. *Castle Nowhere*, 1875, a collection of tales of the Northern lakes, was the fruit of this period of her life. Then had come her sojourn in the South, in the critical period when the land was just awaking from the results of the war. She was the first Northern writer to perceive the literary possibilities of the region—the pathos of the desolated areas, the romantic side of the negro, the uniqueness of the wild Mountain Whites. Her collection of Southern tales, *Rodman the Keeper*, is a pioneer book. Then came the third period in her life, her final years in Italy where she wrote much, the best of it all in her collection *The Front Yard*. Thus she became a pioneer in three distinct regions.

Like all the women of the Civil War generation, Miss Woolson was fundamentally a romanticist. As she had been the first to catch for fiction the romance of the vanishing old French régime of the wild upper lakes, so also was she the first after the war distinctively to treat of the old régime in the South destroyed by the Civil War. Always was she dangerously near to sentimentalism, yet she had caught the new after-the-war spirit, the new demand for "truth," for actuality, for "local color" in new areas, and she is to be classed on the whole with the realists. She was a transition figure in the period of swift change, and viewed against the short-story work of the present she often seems childishly wanting in her art. Her dialogue at times is inflated and impossible, her effects often are overdrawn, but few in the '70s there were who equaled her command of the vital necessities of the short story. In artistry, in truth to the fundamentals of human character, in "soul," "The Lady of Little Fishing" so greatly surpasses Harte's "The Luck of Roaring Camp" that it arouses in its reader the suspicion that it was created as a protest against this melodramatic and superficial story that in 1874 was so sensationally taking possession of the reading world.*

THE LADY OF LITTLE FISHING

It was an island in Lake Superior.

I beached my canoe there about four o'clock in the afternoon, for the wind was against me, and a high sea running. The late summer of 1850, and I was coasting along the south shore of the great lake, hunting, fishing, and camping on the beach, under the delusion that in that way I was living "close to the great heart of nature," —whatever that may mean. Lord Bacon got up the phrase; I suppose he knew. Pulling the boat high and dry on the sand with the comfortable reflection that here were no tides to disturb her with their goings-out and comings-in, I strolled through the woods on a tour of exploration, expecting to find the blue-bells, Indian 5 pipes, juniper rings, perhaps a few agates along shore, possibly a bird or two for company. I found a town.

It was deserted; but none the less a town, with three streets, residences, a meeting-10 house, gardens, a little park, and an attempt at a fountain. Ruins are rare in the New World; I took off my hat. "Hail, homes of the past!" I said. (I cultivated the habit of thinking aloud when I was 15 living close to the great heart of nature.) "A human voice resounds through your arches" (there were no arches,—logs won't

* See Pattee's *Development of the American Short Story*, pp. 250-255.

arch; but never mind) "once more, a human hand touches your venerable walls, a
human foot presses your deserted hearthstones." I then selected the best half of the
meeting-house for my camp, knocked down
one of the homes for fuel, and kindled a
glorious bonfire in the park. "Now that
you are illuminated with joy, O Ruin," I
remarked, "I will go down to the beach and
bring up my supplies. It is long since I
have had a roof over my head; I promise
you to stay until your last residence is
well burned; then I will make a final cup
of coffee with the meeting-house itself, and
depart in peace, leaving your poor old
bones buried in decent ashes."

The ruin made no objection, and I took
up my abode there; the roof of the meeting-house was still water-tight (which is
an advantage when the great heart of
nature grows wet). I kindled a fire on the
sacerdotal hearth, cooked my supper, ate
it in leisurely comfort, and then stretched
myself on a blanket to enjoy an evening
pipe of peace, listening meanwhile to the
sounding of the wind through the great
pine-trees. There was no door to my sanc-
tuary, but I had the cozy far end; the
island was uninhabited, there was not a
boat in sight at sunset, nothing could disturb me unless it might be a ghost. Presently a ghost came in.

It did not wear the traditional gray tar-
latan armor of Hamlet's father, the only
ghost with whom I am well acquainted;
this specter was clad in substantial deer-
skin garments, and carried a gun and
loaded game-bag. It came forward to my
hearth, hung up its gun, opened its game-
bag, took out some birds, and inspected
them gravely.

"Fat?" I inquired.

"They'll do," replied the specter, and
forthwith set to work preparing them for
the coals. I smoked on in silence. The
specter seemed to be a skilled cook, and
after deftly broiling its supper, it offered
me a share; I accepted. It swallowed a huge
mouthful and crunched with its teeth; the
spell was broken, and I knew it for a
man of flesh and blood.

He gave his name as Reuben, and proved
himself an excellent camping companion;
in fact, he shot all the game, caught all
the fish, made all the fires, and cooked all
the food for us both. I proposed to him to
stay and help me burn up the ruin, with
the condition that when the last timber of

the meeting-house was consumed, we
should shake hands and depart, one to the
east, one to the west, without a backward
glance. "In that way we shall not infringe
upon each other's personality," I said.

"Agreed," replied Reuben.

He was a man of between fifty and
sixty years, while I was on the sunny side
of thirty; he was reserved, I was always
generously affable; he was an excellent
cook, while I—well, I wasn't; he was
taciturn, and so, in payment for the work
he did, I entertained him with conversation, or rather monologue, in my most brilliant style. It took only two weeks to burn
up the town, burned we never so slowly;
at last it came the turn of the meeting-
house, which now stood by itself in the
vacant clearing. It was a cool September
day; we cooked breakfast with the roof,
dinner with the sides, supper with the
odds and ends, and then applied a torch to
the frame-work. Our last camp-fire was a
glorious one. We lay stretched on our
blankets, smoking and watching the glow.
"I wonder, now, who built the old shanty,"
I said in a musing tone.

"Well," replied Reuben, slowly, "if you
really want to know, I will tell you. I did."

"You!"

"Yes."

"You didn't do it alone?"

"No; there were about forty of us."

"Here?"

"Yes; here at Little Fishing."

"Little Fishing?"

"Yes; Little Fishing Island. That is the
name of the place."

"How long ago was this?"

"Thirty years."

"Hunting and trapping, I suppose?"

"Yes; for the Northwest and Hudson
Bay Companies."

"Wasn't a meeting-house an unusual accompaniment?"

"Most unusual."

"Accounted for in this case by"—

"A woman."

"Ah!" I said in a tone of relish; "then
of course there is a story?"

"There is."

"Out with it, comrade. I scarcely expected to find the woman and her story
up here; but since the irrepressible creature
would come, out with her by all means.
She shall grace our last pipe together,
the last timber of our meeting-house, our
last night on Little Fishing. The dawn

will see us far from each other, to meet
no more this side heaven. Speak then, O
comrade mine! I am in one of my rare
listening moods!"

I stretched myself at ease and waited.
Reuben was a long time beginning, but I
was too indolent to urge him. At length
he spoke.

"They were a rough set here at Little
Fishing, all the worse for being all white
men; most of the other camps were full
of half-breeds and Indians. The island had
been a station away back in the early days
of the Hudson Bay Company; it was a
station for the Northwest Company while
that lasted; then it went back to the Hudson, and stayed there until the company
moved its forces farther to the north. It
was not at any time a regular post; only
a camp for the hunters. The post was
farther down the lake. Oh, but those were
wild days! You think you know the wilderness, boy; but you know nothing, absolutely nothing. It makes me laugh to see
the airs of you city gentlemen with your
fine guns, improved fishing-tackle, elaborate paraphernalia, as though you were
going to wed the whole forest, floating up
and down the lake for a month or two in
the summer! You should have seen the
hunters of Little Fishing going out gaily
when the mercury was down twenty degrees below zero, for a week in the woods.
You should have seen the trappers wading
through the hard snow, breast high, in
the gray dawn, visiting the traps and hauling home the prey. There were all kinds of
men here, Scotch, French, English, and
American; all classes, the high and the low,
the educated and the ignorant; all sorts,
the lazy and the hard-working. One thing
only they all had in common—badness.
Some had fled to the wilderness to escape
the law, others to escape order; some had
chosen the wild life because of its wilderness, others had drifted into it from sheer
lethargy. This far northern border did not
attract the plodding emigrant, the respectable settler. Little Fishing held none of
that trash; only a reckless set of fellows
who carried their lives in their hands, and
tossed them up, if need be, without a second thought."

"And other people's lives without a
third," I suggested.

"Yes; if they deserved it. But nobody
whined; there wasn't any nonsense here.
The men went hunting and trapping, got

the furs ready for the bateaux, ate when
they were hungry, drank when they were
thirsty, slept when they were sleepy, played
cards when they felt like it, and got angry
and knocked each other down whenever
they chose. As I said before, there wasn't
any nonsense at Little Fishing,—until *she*
came."

"Ah! the she!"

"Yes, the Lady,—our Lady, as we called
her. Thirty-one years ago; how long it
seems!"

"And well it may," I said. "Why, comrade, I wasn't born then!"

This stupendous fact seemed to strike
me more than my companion; he went on
with his story as though I had not spoken.

"One October evening, four of the boys
had got into a row over the cards; the rest
of us had come out of our wigwams to see
the fun, and were sitting around on the
stumps, chaffing them, and laughing; the
camp-fire was burning in front, lighting up
the woods with a red glow for a short distance, and making the rest doubly black all
around. There we all were, as I said before, quite easy and comfortable, when
suddenly there appeared among us, as
though she had dropped from heaven, a
woman!

"She was tall and slender, the firelight
shone full on her pale face and dove-
colored dress, her golden hair was folded
back under a little white cap, and a white
kerchief lay over her shoulders; she looked
spotless. I stared; I could scarcely believe
my eyes; none of us could. There was not
a white woman west of the Sault Ste.
Marie. The four fellows at the table sat as
if transfixed; one had his partner by the
throat, the other two were disputing over
a point in the game. The lily lady glided
up to their table, gathered the cards in
her white hands, slowly, steadily, without
pause or trepidation before their astonished eyes, and then, coming back, she
threw the cards into the center of the glowing fire. 'Ye shall not play away your
souls,' she said in a clear, sweet voice. 'Is
not the game sin? And its reward death?'
And then, immediately, she gave us a
sermon, the like of which was never heard
before; no argument, no doctrine, just
simple, pure entreaty. 'For the love of
God,' she ended, stretching out her hands
towards our silent, gazing group, 'for the
love of God, my brothers, try to do better.'

"We did try; but it was not for the

love of God. Neither did any of us feel like brothers.

"She did not give any name; we called her simply our Lady, and she accepted the title. A bundle carefully packed in birch-bark was found on the beach. 'Is this yours?' asked Black Andy.

"'It is,' replied the Lady; and removing his hat, the black-haired giant carried the package reverently inside her lodge. For we had given her our best wigwam, and fenced it off with pine saplings so that it looked like a miniature fortress. The Lady did not suggest this stockade; it was our own idea, and with one accord we worked at it like beavers, and hung up a gate with a ponderous bolt inside.

"'Mais, ze can nevare farsen eet wiz her leetle fingares,' said Frenchy, a sallow little wretch with a turn for handicraft; so he contrived a small spring which shot the bolt into place with a touch. The Lady lived in her fortress; three times a day the men carried food to her door, and, after tapping gently, withdrew again, stumbling over each other in their haste. The Flying Dutchman, a stolid Holland-born sailor, was our best cook, and the pans and kettles were generally left to him; but now all wanted to try their skill, and the results were extraordinary.

"'She's never touched that pudding, now,' said Nightingale Jack, discontentedly, as his concoction of berries and paste came back from the fortress door.

"'She will starve soon, I think,' remarked the Doctor, calmly; 'to my certain knowledge she has not had an eatable meal for four days.' And he lighted a fresh pipe. This was an aside, and the men pretended not to hear it; but the pans were relinquished to the Dutchman from that time forth.

"The Lady wore always her dove-colored robe, and little white cap, through whose muslin we could see the glimmer of her golden hair. She came and went among us like a spirit; she knew no fear; she turned our life inside out, nor shrank from its vileness. It seemed as though she was not of earth, so utterly impersonal was her interest in us, so heavenly her pity. She took up our sins, one by one, as an angel might; she pleaded with us for our own lost souls, she spared us not, she held not back one grain of denunciation, one iota of future punishment. Sometimes, for days, we would not see her; then, at twilight, she would glide out among us, and, standing in the light of the camp-fire, she would preach to us as though inspired. We listened to her; I do not mean that we were one whit better at heart, but still we listened to her, always. It was a wonderful sight, that lily face under the pine-trees, that spotless woman standing alone in the glare of the fire, while around her lay forty evil-minded, lawless men, not one of whom but would have killed his neighbor for so much as a disrespectful thought of her.

"So strange was her coming, so almost supernatural her appearance in this far forest, that we never wondered over its cause, but simply accepted it as a sort of miracle; your thoroughly irreligious men are always superstitious. Not one of us would have asked a question, and we should never have known her story had she not herself told it to us; not immediately, not as though it was of any importance, but quietly, briefly, and candidly as a child. She came, she said, from Scotland, with a band of God's people. She had always been in one house, a religious institution of some kind, sewing for the poor when her strength allowed it, but generally ill, and suffering much from pain in her head; often kept under the influence of soothing medicines for days together. She had no father or mother, she was only one of this band; and when they decided to send out missionaries to America, she begged to go, although but a burden; the sea voyage restored her health; she grew, she said, in strength and in grace, and her heart was as the heart of a lion. Word came to her from on high that she should come up into the northern lake-country and preach the gospel there; the band were going to the verdant prairies. She left them in the night, taking nothing but her clothing; a friendly vessel carried her north; she had preached the gospel everywhere. At the Sault the priests had driven her out, but nothing fearing, she went on into the wilderness, and so, coming part of the way in canoes, part of the way along shore, she had reached our far island. Marvelous kindness had she met with, she said; the Indians, the half-breeds, the hunters, and the trappers, had all received her, and helped her on her way from camp to camp. They had listened to her words also. At Portage they had begged her to stay through the winter, and offered to build her a little church for Sunday services. Our men looked at each other. Portage was the worst camp on the lake, notorious for its fights; it was a mining settlement.

"'But I told them I must journey on towards the west,' continued our Lady. 'I am called to visit every camp on this shore before the winter sets in; I must soon leave you also.'

"The men looked at each other again; the Doctor was spokesman. 'But, my Lady,' he said, 'the next post is Fort William, two hundred and thirty-five miles away on the north shore.'

"'It is almost November; the snow will soon be six and ten feet deep. The Lady could never travel through it—could she, now?' said Black Andy, who had begun eagerly, but in his embarrassment at the sound of his own voice, now turned to Frenchy and kicked him covertly into answering.

"'Nevare!' replied the Frenchman; he had intended to place his hand upon his heart to give emphasis to his word, but the Lady turned her calm eyes that way, and his grimy paw fell, its gallantry wilted.

"'I thought there was one more camp, —at Burnt-Wood River,' said our Lady in a musing tone. The men looked at each other a third time; there was a camp there, and they all knew it. But the Doctor was equal to the emergency.

"'That camp, my Lady,' he said gravely, 'that camp no longer exists!' Then he whispered hurriedly to the rest of us, 'It will be an easy job to clean it out, boys. We'll send over a party to-night; it's only thirty-five miles.'

"We recognized superior genius; the Doctor was our oldest and deepest sinner. But what struck us most was his anxiety to make good his lie. Had it then come to this,—that the Doctor told the truth?

"The next day we all went to work to build our Lady a church; in a week it was completed. There goes its last cross-beam now into the fire; it was a solid piece of work, wasn't it? It has stood this climate thirty years. I remember the first Sunday service: we all washed, and dressed ourselves in the best we had; we scarcely knew each other, we were so fine. The Lady was pleased with the church, but yet she had not said she would stay all winter; we were still anxious. How she preached to us that day! We had made a screen of young spruces set in boxes, and her figure stood out against the dark green background like a thing of light. Her silvery voice rang through the log temple, her face seemed to us like a star. She had no color in her cheeks at any time; her dress, too, was colorless. Although gentle, there was an iron inflexibility about her slight, erect form. We felt, as we saw her standing there, that if need be she would walk up to the lion's jaws, the cannon's mouth, with a smile. She took a little book from her pocket and read to us a hymn: 'Oh come, all ye faithful,' the old 'Adeste Fideles.' Some of us knew it; she sang, and gradually, shamefacedly, voices joined in. It was a sight to see Nightingale Jack solemnly singing away about 'choirs of angels'; but it was a treat to hear him, too, —what a voice he had! Then our Lady prayed, kneeling down on the little platform in front of the evergreens, clasping her hands, and lifting her eyes to heaven. We did not know what to do at first, but the Doctor gave us a severe look and bent his head, and we all followed his lead.

"When service was over and the door opened, we found that it had been snowing; we could not see out through the windows because white cloth was nailed over them in place of glass.

"'Now, my Lady, you will have to stay with us,' said the Doctor. We all gathered around with eager faces.

"'Do you really believe that it will be for the good of your souls?' asked the sweet voice.

"The Doctor believed—for us all.

"'Do you really hope?'

"The Doctor hoped.

"'Will you try to do your best?'

"The Doctor was sure he would.

"'I will,' answered the Flying Dutchman earnestly. 'I moost not fry de meat any more; I moost broil!'

"For we had begged him for months to broil, and he had obstinately refused; broil represented the good, and fry the evil, to his mind; he came out for the good according to his light; but none the less did we fall upon him behind the Lady's back, and cuff him into silence.

"She stayed with us all winter. You don't know what the winters are up here; steady, bitter cold for seven months, thermometer always below, the snow dry as dust, the air like a knife. We built a compact chimney for our Lady, and we cut cords of wood into small, light sticks, easy for her to lift, and stacked them in her shed; we lined her lodge with skins, and we made oil from bear's fat and rigged up a kind of lamp for her. We tried to make candles, I remember, but they would not run straight; they came out hump-backed and sidling, and burned themselves to wick in no time. Then we took to improving the town. We had lived in all kinds of huts and lean-to shanties; now nothing would do but regular log-houses. If it had been summer, I don't know what we might not have run to in the way of piazzas and fancy steps; but with the snow five feet deep, all we could accomplish was a plain, square log-house, and even that took our whole force. The only way to keep the peace was to have all the houses exactly alike; we laid out the three streets, and built the houses, all facing the meeting-house, just as you found them."

"And where was the Lady's lodge?" I asked, for I recalled no stockaded fortress, large or small.

My companion hesitated a moment. Then he said abruptly, "It was torn down."

"Torn down!" I repeated. "Why, what"—

Reuben waved his hand with a gesture that silenced me, and went on with his story. It came to me then for the first time, that he was pursuing the current of his own thoughts rather than entertaining me. I turned to look at him with a new interest. I had talked to him for two weeks, in rather a patronizing way; could it be that affairs were now, at this last moment, reversed?

"It took us almost all winter to build those houses," pursued Reuben. "At one time we neglected the hunting and trapping to such a degree, that the Doctor called a meeting and expressed his opinion. Ours was a voluntary camp, in a measure, but still we had formally agreed to get a certain amount of skins ready for the bateaux by early spring; this agreement was about the only real bond of union between us. Those whose houses were not completed scowled at the Doctor.

"'Do you suppose I'm going to live like an Injun when the other fellows has regular houses?' inquired Black Andy with a menacing air.

"'By no means,' replied the Doctor, blandly. 'My plan is this: build at night.'

"'At night?'

"'Yes; by the light of pine fires.'

"We did. After that, we faithfully went out hunting and trapping as long as daylight lasted, and then, after supper, we built up huge fires of pine logs, and went to work on the next house. It was a strange picture: the forest deep in snow, black with night, the red glow of the great fires, and our moving figures working on as complacently as though daylight, balmy air, and the best of tools, were ours.

"The Lady liked our industry. She said our new houses showed that the 'new cleanliness of our inner man required a cleaner tabernacle for the outer.' I don't know about our inner man, but our outer was certainly much cleaner.

"One day the Flying Dutchman made one of his unfortunate remarks. 'De boys t'inks you'll like dem better in nize houses,' he announced when, happening to pass the fortress, he found the Lady standing at her gate gazing at the work of the preceding night. Several of the men were near enough to hear him, but too far off to kick him into silence as usual; but they glared at him instead. The Lady looked at the speaker with her dreamy, far-off eyes.

"'De boys t'inks you like dem,' began the Dutchman again, thinking she did not comprehend; but at that instant he caught the combined glare of the six eyes, and stopped abruptly, not at all knowing what was wrong, but sure there was something.

"'Like them,' repeated the Lady dreamily; 'yea, I do like them. Nay, more, I love them. Their souls are as dear to me as the souls of brothers.'

"'Say, Frenchy, have you got a sister?' said Nightingale Jack confidentially, that evening.

"'Mais oui,' said Frenchy.

"'You think all creation of her, I suppose?'

"'We fight like four cats and one dog; she is the cats,' said the Frenchman concisely.

"'You don't say so!' replied Jack. 'Now, I never had a sister,—but I thought perhaps'— He paused, and the sentence remained unfinished.

"The Nightingale and I were house-mates. We sat late over our fire not long after that; I gave a gigantic yawn. 'This lifting logs half the night is enough to kill one,' I said, getting out my jug. 'Sing something, Jack. It's a long time since I've heard anything but hymns.'

"Jack always went off as easily as a music-box: you had only to wind him up;

the jug was the key. I soon had him in full blast. He was giving out

'The minute gun at sea—the minute gun at sea,'

with all the pathos of his tenor voice, when the door burst open and the whole population rushed in upon us.

" 'What do you mean by shouting this way, in the middle of the night?'

" 'Shut up your howling, Jack.'

" 'How do you suppose any one can sleep?'

" 'It's a disgrace to the camp!'

" 'Now then, gentlemen,' I replied, for my blood was up (whisky, perhaps), 'is this my house, or isn't it? If I want music, I'll have it. Time was when you were not so particular.'

"It was the first word of rebellion. The men looked at each other, then at me.

" 'I'll go and ask her if she objects,' I continued boldly.

" 'No, no. You shall not.'

" 'Let him go,' said the Doctor, who stood smoking his pipe on the outskirts of the crowd. 'It is just as well to have that point settled now. The Minute Gun at Sea is a good moral song in its way,—a sort of marine missionary affair.'

"So I started, the others followed; we all knew that the Lady watched late; we often saw the glimmer of her lamp far on towards morning. It was burning now. The gate was fastened, I knocked; no answer. I knocked again, and yet a third time; still, silence. The men stood off at a little distance and waited. 'She shall answer,' I said angrily, and going around to the side where the stockade came nearer to the wall of the lodge, I knocked loudly on the close-set saplings. For answer I thought I heard a low moan; I listened, it came again. My anger vanished, and with a mighty bound I swung myself up to the top of the stockade, sprung down inside, ran around, and tried the door. It was fastened; I burst it open and entered. There, by the light of the hanging lamp, I saw the Lady on the floor, apparently dead. I raised her in my arms; her heart was beating faintly, but she was unconscious. I had seen many fainting fits; this was something different; the limbs were rigid. I laid her on the low couch, loosened her dress, bathed her head and face in cold water, and wrenched up one of the warm hearthstones to apply to her feet. I did not hesitate; I saw that it was a dangerous case, something like a trance or an 'ecstasis.' Somebody must attend to her, and there were only men to choose from. Then why not I?

"I heard the others talking outside; they could not understand the delay; but I never heeded, and kept on my work. To tell the truth, I had studied medicine, and felt a genuine enthusiasm over a rare case. Once my patient opened her eyes and looked at me, then she lapsed away again into unconsciousness in spite of all my efforts. At last the men outside came in, angry and suspicious; they had broken down the gate. There we all stood, the whole forty of us, around the deathlike form of our Lady.

"What a night it was! To give her air, the men camped outside in the snow with a line of pickets in whispering distance from each other from the bed to their anxious group. Two were detailed to help me—the Doctor (whose title was a sarcastic D. D.) and Jimmy, a gentle little man, excellent at bandaging broken limbs. Every vial in the camp was brought in—astonishing lotions, drops, and balms; each man produced something; they did their best, poor fellows, and wore out the night with their anxiety. At dawn our Lady revived suddenly, thanked us all, and assured us that she felt quite well again; the trance was over. 'It was my old enemy,' she said, 'the old illness of Scotland, which I hoped had left me forever. But I am thankful that it is no worse; I have come out of it with a clear brain. Sing a hymn of thankfulness for me, dear friends, before you go.'

"Now, we sang on Sunday in the church; but then she led us, and we had a kind of an idea that after all she did not hear us. But now, who was to lead us? We stood awkwardly around the bed, and shuffled our hats in our uneasy fingers. The Doctor fixed his eyes upon the Nightingale; Jack saw it and cowered. 'Begin,' said the Doctor in a soft voice; but gripping him in the back at the same time with an ominous clutch.

" 'I don't know the words,' faltered the unhappy Nightingale.

" 'Now thank we all our God,
With hearts and hands and voices,'

began the Doctor, and repeated Luther's hymn with perfect accuracy from beginning to end. 'What will happen next? The

Doctor knows hymns!' we thought in profound astonishment. But the Nightingale had begun, and gradually our singers joined in; I doubt whether the grand old choral was ever sung by such a company before or since. There was never any further question, by the way, about that minute gun at sea; it stayed at sea as far as we were concerned.

"Spring came, the faltering spring of Lake Superior. I won't go into my own story, but such as it was, the spring brought it back to me with new force. I wanted to go,—and yet I didn't. 'Where,' do you ask? To see her, of course—a woman, the most beautiful—well, never mind all that. To be brief, I loved her; she scorned me; I thought I had learned to hate her—but—I wasn't sure about it now. I kept myself aloof from the others and gave up my heart to the old sweet, bitter memories; I did not even go to church on Sundays. But all the rest went; our Lady's influence was as great as ever. I could hear them singing; they sang better now that they could have the door open; the pent-up feeling used to stifle them. The time for the bateaux drew near, and I noticed that several of the men were hard at work packing the furs in bales, a job usually left to the *voyageurs* who came with the boats. 'What's that for?' I asked.

" 'You don't suppose we're going to have those bateaux rascals camping on Little Fishing, do you?' said Black Andy scornfully. 'Where are your wits, Reub?'

"And they packed every skin, rafted them all over to the mainland, and waited there patiently for days, until the train of slow boats came along and took off the bales; then they came back in triumph. 'Now we're secure for another six months,' they said, and began to lay out a park, and gardens for every house. The Lady was fond of flowers; the whole town burst into blossom. The Lady liked green grass; all the clearing was soon turfed over like a lawn. The men tried the ice-cold lake every day, waiting anxiously for the time when they could bathe. There was no end to their cleanliness; Black Andy had grown almost white again, and Frenchy's hair shone like oiled silk.

The Lady stayed on, and all went well. But, gradually, there came a discovery. The Lady was changing—had changed! Gradually, slowly, but none the less distinctly to the eyes that knew her every

eyelash. A little more hair was visible over the white brow, there was a faint color in the cheeks, a quicker step; the clear eyes were sometimes downcast now, the steady voice softer, the words at times faltering. In the early summer the white cap vanished, and she stood among us crowned only with her golden hair; one day she was seen through her open door sewing on a white robe! The men noted all these things silently; they were even a little troubled as at something they did not understand, something beyond their reach. Was she planning to leave them?

" 'It's my belief she's getting ready to ascend right up into heaven,' said Salem.

"Salem was a little 'wanting,' as it is called, and the men knew it; still, his words made an impression. They watched the Lady with an awe which was almost superstitious; they were troubled and knew not why. But the Lady bloomed on. I did not pay much attention to all this; but I could not help hearing it. My heart was moody, full of its own sorrows; I secluded myself more and more. Gradually I took to going off into the mainland forests for days on solitary hunting expeditions. The camp went on its way rejoicing; the men succeeded, after a world of trouble, in making a fountain which actually played, and they glorified themselves exceedingly. The life grew quite pastoral. There was talk of importing a cow from the East, and a messenger was sent to the Sault for certain choice supplies against the coming winter. But, in the late summer, the whisper went round again that the Lady had changed, this time for the worse. She looked ill, she drooped from day to day; the new life that had come to her vanished, but her former life was not restored. She grew silent and sad, she strayed away by herself through the woods, she scarcely noticed the men who followed her with anxious eyes. Time passed, and brought with it an undercurrent of trouble, suspicion, and anger. Everything went on as before; not one habit, not one custom was altered; both sides seemed to shrink from the first change, however slight. The daily life of the camp was outwardly the same, but brooding trouble filled every heart. There was no open discussion, men talked apart in twos and threes; a gloom rested over everything, but no one said, 'What is the matter?'

"There was a man among us—I have

not said much of the individual characters of our party, but this man was one of the least esteemed, or rather liked; there was not much esteem of any kind at Little Fishing. Little was known about him; although the youngest man in the camp, he was a mooning, brooding creature, with brown hair and eyes and a melancholy face. He wasn't hearty and whole-souled, and yet he wasn't an out and out rascal; he wasn't a leader, and yet he wasn't follower either. He wouldn't be; he was like a third horse, always. There was no goodness about him; don't go to fancying that that was the reason the men did not like him, he was as bad as they were, every inch! He never shirked his work, and they couldn't get a handle on him anywhere; but he was just —unpopular. The why and the wherefore are of no consequence now. Well, do you know what was the suspicion that hovered over the camp? It was this: our Lady loved that man!

"It took three months for all to see it, and yet never a word was spoken. All saw, all heard; but they might have been blind and deaf for any sign they gave. And the Lady drooped more and more.

"September came, the fifteenth; the Lady lay on her couch, pale and thin; the door was open and a bell stood beside her, but there was no line of pickets whispering tidings of her state to an anxious group outside. The turf in the three streets had grown yellow for want of water, the flowers in the little gardens had drooped and died, the fountain was choked with weeds, and the interiors of the houses were all untidy. It was Sunday, and near the hour for service; but the men lounged about, dingy and unwashed.

"'An't you going to church?' said Salem, stopping at the door of one of the houses; he was dressed in his best, with a flower in his button-hole.

"'See him now! See the fool,' said Black Andy. 'He's going to church, he is! And where's the minister, Salem? Answer me that!'

"'Why,—in the church, I suppose,' replied Salem vacantly.

"'No, she an't; not she! She's at home, a-weeping, and a-wailing, and a-ger-nashing of her teeth,' replied Andy with bitter scorn.

"'What for?' said Salem.

"'What for? Why, that's the joke! Hear him, boys; he wants to know what for!'

"The loungers laughed,—a loud, reckless laugh.

"'Well, I'm going any way,' said Salem, looking wonderingly from one to the other; he passed on and entered the church.

"'I say, boys, let's have a high old time,' cried Andy savagely. 'Let's go back to the old way and have a jolly Sunday. Let's have out the jugs and the cards and be free again!'

"The men hesitated; ten months and more of law and order held them back.

"'What are you afraid of?' said Andy. 'Not of a canting hypocrite, I hope. She's fooled us long enough, I say. Come on!' He brought out a table and stools, and produced the long unused cards and a jug of whisky. 'Strike up, Jack,' he cried; 'give us old Fiery-Eyes.'

"The Nightingale hesitated. Fiery-Eyes was a rollicking drinking song; but Andy put the glass to his lips and his scruples vanished in the tempting aroma. He began at the top of his voice, partners were chosen, and, trembling with excitement and impatience, like prisoners unexpectedly set free, the men gathered around, and made their bets.

"'What born fools we've been,' said Black Andy, laying down a card.

"'Yes,' replied the Flying Dutchman, 'porn fools!' And he followed suit.

"But a thin white hand came down on the bits of colored pasteboard. It was our Lady. With her hair disordered, and the spots of fever in her cheeks, she stood among us again; but not as of old. Angry eyes confronted her, and Andy wrenched the cards from her grasp. 'No, my Lady,' he said sternly; 'never again!'

"The Lady gazed from one face to the next, and so all around the circle; all were dark and sullen. Then she bowed her head upon her hands and wept aloud.

"There was a sudden shrinking away on all sides, the players rose, the cards were dropped. But the Lady glided away, weeping as she went; she entered the church door and the men could see her taking her accustomed place on the platform. One by one they followed; Black Andy lingered till the last, but he came. The service began, and went on falteringly, without spirit, with palpable fears of a total breaking down which never quite came; the Nightingale sang almost alone, and made sad work with the words; Salem joined in confidently, but did not improve the sense of the hymn. The Lady was silent. But when the time for the sermon came, she rose and her voice burst forth.

" 'Men, brothers, what have I done? A change has come over the town, a change has come over your hearts. You shun me! What have I done?'

"There was a grim silence; then the Doctor rose in his place and answered:

" 'Only this, madam. You have shown yourself to be a woman.'

" 'And what did you think me?'

" 'A saint.'

" 'God forbid!' said the lady, earnestly. 'I never thought myself one.'

" 'I know that well. But you were a saint to us; hence your influence. It is gone.'

" 'Is it all gone?' asked the Lady, sadly.

" 'Yes. Do not deceive yourself; we have never been one whit better save through our love for you. We held you as something high above ourselves; we were content to worship you.'

" 'Oh no, not me!' said the Lady, shuddering.

" 'Yes, you, you alone! But—our idol came down among us and showed herself to be but common flesh and blood! What wonder that we stand aghast? What wonder that our hearts are bitter? What wonder (worse than all!) that when the awe has quite vanished, there is strife for the beautiful image fallen from its niche?'

"The Doctor ceased, and turned away. The Lady stretched out her hands towards the others; her face was deadly pale, and there was a bewildered expression in her eyes.

" 'Oh, ye for whom I have prayed, for whom I have struggled to obtain a blessing,—ye whom I have loved so,—do *ye* desert me thus?' she cried.

" '*You* have deserted us,' answered a voice.

" 'I have not.'

" 'You have,' cried Black Andy, pushing to the front. 'You love that Mitchell! Deny it if you dare!'

"There was an irrepressible murmur, then a sudden hush. The angry suspicion, the numbing certainty had found voice at last; the secret was out. All eyes, which had at first closed with the shock, were now fixed upon the solitary woman before them; they burned like coals.

" 'Do I?' murmured the Lady, with a strange questioning look that turned from face to face. 'Do I?—Great God! I do. She sank upon her knees and buried her face in her trembling hands. 'The truth has come to me at last—I do!'

"Her voice was a mere whisper, but every ear heard it, and every eye saw the crimson rise to the forehead and redden the white throat.

"For a moment there was silence, broken only by the hard breathing of the men. Then the Doctor spoke.

" 'Go out and bring him in,' he cried. 'Bring in this Mitchell! It seems he has other things to do,—the blockhead!'

"Two of the men hurried out.

" 'He shall not have her,' shouted Black Andy. 'My knife shall see to that!' And he pressed close to the platform. A great tumult arose, men talked angrily and clenched their fists, voices rose and fell together: 'He shall not have her—Mitchell! Mitchell!'

" 'The truth is, each one of you wants her himself,' said the Doctor.

"There was a sudden silence, but every man eyed his neighbor jealously; Black Andy stood in front, knife in hand, and kept guard. The Lady had not moved; she was kneeling, with her face buried in her hands.

" 'I wish to speak to her,' said the Doctor, advancing.

" 'You shall not,' cried Andy, fiercely interposing.

" 'You fool! I love her this moment ten thousand times more than you do. But do you suppose I would so much as touch a woman who loved another man?'

"The knife dropped; the Doctor passed on and took his place on the platform by the Lady's side. The tumult began again, for Mitchell was seen coming in the door between his two keepers.

" 'Mitchell! Mitchell!' rang angrily through the church.

" 'Look, woman!' said the Doctor, bending over the kneeling figure at his side. She raised her head and saw the wolfish faces below.

" 'They have had ten months of your religion,' he said.

"It was his revenge. Bitter, indeed; but he loved her.

"In the meantime the man Mitchell was hauled and pushed and tossed forward to the platform by rough hands that longed to throttle him on the way. At last, angry himself, but full of wonder, he confronted them, this crowd of comrades suddenly turned madmen! 'What does this mean?' he asked.

"'Mean! mean!' shouted the men; 'a likely story! He asks what this means!' And they laughed boisterously.

"The Doctor advanced. 'You see this woman,' he said.

"'I see our Lady.'

"'Our Lady no longer; only a woman like any other,—weak and fickle. Take her, —but begone.'

"'Take her!' repeated Mitchell, bewildered. 'Take our Lady! And where?'

"'Fool! Liar! Blockhead!' shouted the crowd below.

"'The truth is simply this, Mitchell,' continued the Doctor, quietly. 'We herewith give you up our Lady,—ours no longer; for she has just confessed, openly confessed, that she loves you.'

"Mitchell started back. 'Loves me!'

"'Yes.'

"Black Andy felt the blade of his knife. 'He'll never have her alive,' he muttered.

"'But,' said Mitchell, bluntly confronting the Doctor, 'I don't want her.'

"'You don't want her?'

"'I don't love her.'

"'You don't love her?'

"'Not in the least,' he replied, growing angry, perhaps at himself. 'What is she to me? Nothing. A very good missionary, no doubt; but I don't fancy woman-preachers. You may remember that I never gave in to her influence; I was never under her thumb. I was the only man in Little Fishing who cared nothing for her!'

"'And that is the secret of her liking,' murmured the Doctor. 'O woman! woman! the same the world over!'

"In the meantime the crowd had stood stupefied.

"'He does not love her!' they said to each other; 'he does not want her!'

"Andy's black eyes gleamed with joy; he swung himself up on to the platform. Mitchell stood there with face dark and disturbed, but he did not flinch. Whatever his faults, he was no hypocrite. 'I must leave this to-night,' he said to himself, and turned to go. But quick as a flash our Lady sprang from her knees and threw herself at his feet. 'You are going,' she cried. 'I heard what you said,—you do not love me! But take me with you,—oh, take me with you! Let me be your servant—your slave—anything—anything, so that I am

not parted from you, my lord and master, my only, only love!'

"She clasped his ankles with her thin, white hands, and laid her face on his dusty shoes.

"The whole audience stood dumb before this manifestation of a great love. Enraged, bitter, jealous as was each heart, there was not a man but would at that moment have sacrificed his own love that she might be blessed. Even Mitchell, in one of those rare spirit-flashes when the soul is shown bare in the lightning, asked himself, 'Can I not love her?' But the soul answered, 'No.' He stooped, unclasped the clinging hands, and turned resolutely away.

"'You are a fool,' said the Doctor. 'No other woman will ever love you as she does.'

"'I know it,' replied Mitchell.

"He stepped down from the platform and crossed the church, the silent crowd making a way for him as he passed along; he went out into the sunshine, through the village, down towards the beach,—they saw him no more.

"The Lady had fainted. The men bore her back to the lodge and tended her with gentle care one week—two weeks—three weeks. Then she died.

"They were all around her; she smiled upon them all, and called them all by name, bidding them farewell. 'Forgive me,' she whispered to the Doctor. 'The Nightingale sang a hymn, sang as he had never sung before. Black Andy knelt at her feet. For some minutes she lay scarcely breathing; then suddenly she opened her fading eyes. 'Friends,' she murmured, 'I am well punished. I thought myself holy,— I held myself above my kind,—but God has shown me I am the weakest of them all.'

"The next moment she was gone.

"The men buried her with tender hands. Then, in a kind of blind fury against Fate, they tore down her empty lodge and destroyed its every fragment; in their grim determination they even smoothed over the ground and planted shrubs and bushes, so that the very location might be lost. But they did not stay to see the change. In a month the camp broke up of itself, the town was abandoned, and the island deserted for good and all; I doubt whether any of the men ever came back or even stopped when passing by. Probably I am the only one. Thirty years ago,—thirty years ago!"

"That Mitchell was a great fool," I said, after a long pause. "The Doctor was worth twenty of him; for that matter, so was Black Andy. I only hope the fellow was well punished for his stupidity."

"He was."

"Oh, you kept track of him, did you?"

"Yes. He went back into the world, and the woman he loved repulsed him a second time, and with even more scorn than before."

"Served him right."

"Perhaps so; but after all, what could he do? Love is not made to order. He loved one, not the other; that was his crime. Yet,—so strange a creature is man, —he came back after thirty years, just to see our Lady's grave."

"What! Are you"—

"I am Mitchell—Reuben Mitchell."

XXI

FRANK RICHARD STOCKTON (1834–1902)

The light, whimsical element had been introduced into the short story by Willis and the surprise ending and the *tour de force* creation of the impossible made plausible by skilful use of verisimilitude had been used by Aldrich and Hale, but it remained for Frank R. Stockton to bring whimsicality and unexpectedness to their extremes in fiction. In the early eighteen-eighties with such work as "The Transferred Ghost," "The Spectral Mortgage," "Negative Gravity," and the culminating "The Lady or the Tiger?" he became a veritable sensation. The ghost is haunted by living people and is terrified, gravity pulls not downward but upward, yet so plausible is the explanation with its Defoe-like multiplication of trivial details that the reader is carried to the end of the tale without protest only to awake suddenly aghast at the conclusion he has been forced to make or in a burst of laughter at the absolute nonsense he has been gravely swallowing. At the close of the last paragraph the reader is usually aware that the author stands chuckling in his sleeve at the success of his plot. No one has made more skilful use of verisimilitude, and no one has ever told tales with less of intention to instruct or moralize or uplift. Purely and simply is he an entertainer.

The influence of Stockton during a formative period in the history of the short-story form was considerable. He more than any one else taught later writers the uncanny possibilities of the literary instrument which they had in their hands, its adaptibility to the exploiting of paradox and unexpected culminations, and conundrum endings. Unquestionably Stockton was the forerunner of such later artists and literary contortionists as Bunner and O. Henry. Few stories have exerted a greater influence than "The Lady or the Tiger?"

THE LADY OR THE TIGER?*

In the very olden time, there lived a semi-barbaric king, whose ideas, though somewhat polished and sharpened by the progressiveness of distant Latin neighbors, were still large, florid, and untrammeled, as became the half of him which was barbaric. He was a man of exuberant fancy, and, withal, of an authority so irresistible that, at his will, he turned his varied fancies into facts. He was greatly given to self-communing, and when he and himself agreed upon anything, the thing was done. When every member of his domestic and political systems moved smoothly in its appointed course, his nature was bland and genial; but whenever there was a little hitch, and some of his orbs got out of their orbits, he was blander and more genial still, for nothing pleased him so much as to make the crooked straight, and crush down uneven places.

Among the borrowed notions by which

his barbarism had become semified was that of the public arena, in which, by exhibitions of manly and beastly valor, the minds of his subjects were refined and 5 cultured.

But even here the exuberant and barbaric fancy asserted itself. The arena of the king was built, not to give the people an opportunity of hearing the rhapsodies 10 of dying gladiators, nor to enable them to view the inevitable conclusion of a conflict between religious opinions and hungry jaws, but for purposes far better adapted to widen and develop the mental energies 15 of the people. This vast amphitheater, with its encircling galleries, its mysterious vaults, and its unseen passages, was an agent of poetic justice, in which crime was punished, or virtue rewarded, by the decrees 20 of an impartial and incorruptible chance.

When a subject was accused of a crime of sufficient importance to interest the king, public notice was given that on an 25 appointed day the fate of the accused person would be decided in the king's arena— a structure which well deserved its name;

* From *The Lady or the Tiger and Other Stories*, by Frank R. Stockton. Copyright, 1886, by Charles Scribner's Sons.

for, although its form and plan were borrowed from afar, its purpose emanated solely from the brain of this man, who, every barleycorn a king, knew no tradition to which he owed more allegiance than pleased his fancy, and who ingrafted on every adopted form of human thought and action the rich growth of his barbaric idealism.

When all the people had assembled in the galleries, and the king, surrounded by his court, sat high up on his throne of royal state on one side of the arena, he gave a signal, a door beneath him opened, and the accused subject stepped out into the amphitheater. Directly opposite him, on the other side of the enclosed space, were two doors, exactly alike and side by side. It was the duty and the privilege of the person on trial to walk directly to these doors and open one of them. He could open either door he pleased. He was subject to no guidance or influence but that of the aforementioned impartial and incorruptible chance. If he opened the one, there came out of it a hungry tiger, the fiercest and most cruel that could be procured, which immediately sprang upon him, and tore him to pieces, as a punishment for his guilt. The moment that the case of the criminal was thus decided, doleful iron bells were clanged, great wails went up from the hired mourners posted on the outer rim of the arena, and the vast audience, with bowed heads and downcast hearts, wended slowly their homeward way, mourning greatly that one so young and fair, or so old and respected, should have merited so dire a fate.

But if the accused person opened the other door, there came forth from it a lady, the most suitable to his years and station that his Majesty could select among his fair subjects; and to this lady he was immediately married, as a reward of his innocence. It mattered not that he might already possess a wife and family, or that his affections might be engaged upon an object of his own selection. The king allowed no such subordinate arrangements to interfere with his great scheme of retribution and reward. The exercises, as in the other instance, took place immediately, and in the arena. Another door opened beneath the king, and a priest, followed by a band of choristers, and dancing maidens blowing joyous airs on golden horns and treading an epithalamic measure, advanced to where the pair stood side by side, and the wedding was promptly and cheerily solemnized. Then the gay brass bells rang forth their merry peals, the people shouted glad hurrahs, and the innocent man, preceded by children strewing flowers on his path, led his bride to his home.

This was the king's semi-barbaric method of administering justice. Its perfect fairness is obvious. The criminal could not know out of which door would come the lady. He opened either door he pleased, without having the slightest idea whether, in the next instant, he was to be devoured or married. On some occasions the tiger came out of one door, and on some out of the other. The decisions of this tribunal were not only fair—they were positively determinate. The accused person was instantly punished if he found himself guilty, and if innocent he was rewarded on the spot, whether he liked it or not. There was no escape from the judgments of the king's arena.

The institution was a very popular one. When the people gathered together on one of the great trial days, they never knew whether they were to witness a bloody slaughter or a hilarious wedding. This element of uncertainty lent an interest to the occasion which it could not otherwise have attained. Thus the masses were entertained and pleased, and the thinking part of the community could bring no charge of unfairness against this plan; for did not the accused person have the whole matter in his own hands?

This semi-barbaric king had a daughter as blooming as his most florid fancies, and with a soul as fervent and imperious as his own. As is usual in such cases, she was the apple of his eye, and was loved by him above all humanity. Among his courtiers was a young man of that fineness of blood and lowness of station common to the conventional heroes of romance who love royal maidens. This royal maiden was well satisfied with her lover, for he was handsome and brave to a degree unsurpassed in all this kingdom, and she loved him with an ardor that had enough of barbarism in it to make it exceedingly warm and strong. This love affair moved on happily for many months, until, one day, the king happened to discover its existence. He did not hesitate nor waver in regard to his duty in the premises. The youth was immediately cast into prison, and a day was appointed for his trial in the king's arena. This, of course, was an especially important occasion, and his Majesty, as well as all the people, was greatly interested in the workings and development of this trial. Never before had such a case occurred—never before had a subject dared to love the daughter of a king. In after years such things became commonplace enough, but then they were, in no slight degree, novel and startling.

The tiger cages of the kingdom were searched for the most savage and relentless beasts, from which the fiercest monster might be selected for the arena, and the ranks of maiden youth and beauty throughout the land were carefully surveyed by competent judges, in order that the young man might have a fitting bride in case fate did not determine for him a different destiny. Of course, everybody knew that the deed with which the accused was charged had been done. He had loved the princess, and neither he, she, nor any one else thought of denying the fact. But the king would not think of allowing any fact of this kind to interfere with the workings of the tribunal, in which he took such great delight and satisfaction. No matter how the affair turned out, the youth would be disposed of, and the king would take an esthetic pleasure in watching the course of events which would determine whether or not the young man had done wrong in allowing himself to love the princess.

The appointed day arrived. From far and near the people gathered, and thronged the great galleries of the arena, while crowds, unable to gain admittance, massed themselves against its outside walls. The king and his court were in their places, opposite the twin doors—those fateful portals, so terrible in their similarity!

All was ready. The signal was given. A door beneath the royal party opened, and the lover of the princess walked into the arena. Tall, beautiful, fair, his appearance was greeted with a low hum of admiration and anxiety. Half the audience had not known so grand a youth had lived among them. No wonder the princess loved him! What a terrible thing for him to be there!

As the youth advanced into the arena, he turned, as the custom was, to bow to the king. But he did not think at all of that royal personage; his eyes were fixed upon the princess, who sat to the right of her father. Had it not been for the moiety of

barbarism in her nature, it is probable that lady would not have been there. But her intense and fervid soul would not allow her to be absent on an occasion in which she was so terribly interested. From the moment that the decree had gone forth that her lover should decide his fate in the king's arena, she had thought of nothing, night or day, but this great event and the various subjects connected with it. Possessed of more power, influence, and force of character than any one who had ever before been interested in such a case, she had done what no other person had done— she had possessed herself of the secret of the doors. She knew in which of the two rooms behind those doors stood the cage of the tiger, with its open front, and in which waited the lady. Through these thick doors, heavily curtained with skins on the inside, it was impossible that any noise or suggestion should come from within to the person who should approach to raise the latch of one of them. But gold, and the power of a woman's will, had brought the secret to the princess.

Not only did she know in which room stood the lady, ready to emerge, all blushing and radiant, should her door be opened, but she knew who the lady was. It was one of the fairest and loveliest of the damsels of the court who had been selected as the reward of the accused youth, should he be proved innocent of the crime of aspiring to one so far above him; and the princess hated her. Often had she seen, or imagined that she had seen, this fair creature throwing glances of admiration upon the person of her lover, and sometimes she thought these glances were perceived and even returned. Now and then she had seen them talking together. It was but for a moment or two, but much can be said in a brief space. It may have been on most unimportant topics, but how could she know that? The girl was lovely, but she had dared to raise her eyes to the loved one of the princess, and, with all the intensity of the savage blood transmitted to her through long lines of wholly barbaric ancestors, she hated the woman who blushed and trembled behind that silent door.

When her lover turned and looked at her, and his eye met hers as she sat there paler and whiter than any one in the vast ocean of anxious faces about her, he saw, by that power of quick perception which is given to those whose souls are one, that she knew behind which door crouched the tiger, and behind which stood the lady. He had expected her to know it. He understood her nature, and his soul was assured that she would never rest until she had made plain to herself this thing, hidden to all other lookers-on, even to the king. The only hope for the youth in which there was any element of certainty was based upon the success of the princess in discovering this mystery, and the moment he looked upon her, he saw she had succeeded.

Then it was that his quick and anxious glance asked the question, "Which?" It was as plain to her as if he shouted it from where he stood. There was not an instant to be lost. The question was asked in a flash; it must be answered in another.

Her right arm lay on the cushioned parapet before her. She raised her hand, and made a slight, quick movement toward the right. No one but her lover saw her. Every eye but his was fixed on the man in the arena.

He turned, and with a firm and rapid step he walked across the empty space. Every heart stopped beating, every breath was held, every eye was fixed immovably upon that man. Without the slightest hesitation, he went to the door on the right, and opened it.

Now, the point of the story is this: Did the tiger come out of that door, or did the lady?

The more we reflect upon this question, the harder it is to answer. It involves a study of the human heart which leads us through devious mazes of passion, out of which it is difficult to find our way. Think of it, fair reader, not as if the decision of the question depended upon yourself, but upon that hot-blooded, semi-barbaric princess, her soul at a white heat beneath the combined fires of despair and jealousy. She had lost him, but who should have him?

How often, in her waking hours and in her dreams, had she started in wild horror and covered her face with her hands as she thought of her lover opening the door on the other side of which waited the cruel fangs of the tiger!

But how much oftener had she seen him at the other door! How in her grievous reveries had she gnashed her teeth and torn her hair when she saw his start of rapturous delight as he opened the door of the lady! How her soul had burned in agony when she had seen him rush to meet that woman, with her flushing cheek and sparkling eye of triumph; when she had seen him lead her forth, his whole frame kindled with the joy of recovered life; when she had heard the glad shouts from the multitude, and the wild ringing of the happy bells; when she had seen the priest, with his joyous followers, advance to the couple, and make them man and wife before her very eyes; and when she had seen them walk away together upon their path of flowers, followed by the tremendous shouts of the hilarious multitude, in which her one despairing shriek was lost and drowned!

Would it not be better for him to die at once, and go to wait for her in the blessed regions of semi-barbaric futurity?

And yet, that awful tiger, those shrieks, that blood!

Her decision had been indicated in an instant, but it had been made after days and nights of anguished deliberation. She had known she would be asked, she had decided what she would answer, and, without the slightest hesitation, she had moved her hand to the right.

The question of her decision is one not to be lightly considered, and it is not for me to presume to set up myself as the one person able to answer it. So I leave it with all of you: Which came out of the opened door—the lady or the tiger?

XXII

BRANDER MATTHEWS (1852–   )

Brander Matthews, a native of New York City and for many years a professor of dramatic literature in Columbia University, is a noteworthy figure in the history of the American short story both as a critic of the form and as a writer of distinctive sketches and tales. Collaborating with H. C. Bunner, he issued in 1884 the collection *In Partnership: Studies in Story-Telling,* and in later years he published *Vignettes of Manhattan, Outlines in Local Color, Vistas of New York,* and other collections, all dealing with phases of life in the metropolis.

His most noteworthy contribution to the short story, however, has been in the field of criticism. His critique in the London *Saturday Review* in 1884 is a landmark in the critical history of short-story literature. The short story, he ruled, is a distinct literary form with laws peculiarly its own and to distinguish it from the story that is merely short he advocated the hyphenated form "short-story"—good advice that has not been followed. No criticism since Poe's review of Hawthorne in 1842 has been more important.

"The difference between a Novel and a Short-story is a difference of kind. A true Short-story is something other and something more than a mere story which is short. A true Short-story differs from the Novel chiefly in its essential unity of impression. In a far more exact and precise use of the word, a Short-story has unity as a Novel cannot have it. Often, it may be noted by the way, the Short-story fulfils the three false unities ot the French classic drama: it shows one action, in one place, on one day. A Short-story deals with a single character, a single event, a single emotion, or a series of emotions called forth by a single situation. Poe's paradox that a poem cannot greatly exceed a hundred lines in length under penalty of ceasing to be one poem and breaking into a string of poems, may serve to suggest the precise difference between the Short-story and the Novel. The Short-story is the single effect, complete and self-contained, while the Novel is of necessity broken into a series of episodes. Thus the Short-story has, what the Novel cannot have, the effect of 'totality,' as Poe called it, the unity of impression.

"Of a truth the Short-story is not only not a chapter out of a Novel, or an incident or an episode extracted from a longer tale, but at its best it impresses the reader with the belief that it would be spoiled if it were made larger, or if it were incorporated into a more elaborate work. The difference in spirit and in form between the Lyric and the Epic is scarcely greater than the difference between the Short-story and the novel. . . .

"Another great difference between the Short-story and the Novel lies in the fact that the Novel, nowadays at least, must be a love-tale, while the Short-story need not deal with love at all. . . .

"Other things are required of a writer of Short-stories which are not required of a writer of Novels. The Novelist may take his time; he has abundant room to turn about. The writer of Short-stories must be concise, and compression, a vigorous compression, is essential. For him, more than for any one else, the half is more than the whole. Again, the novelist may be commonplace, he may bend his best energies to the photographic reproduction of the actual; if he show us a cross-section of real life we are content; but the writer of Short-stories must have originality and ingenuity. If to compression, originality, and ingenuity he add also a touch of fantasy, so much the better. . . .

"I have written 'Short-stories' with a capital S and a hyphen because I wished to emphasise the distinction between the Short-story and the story that is merely short. The Short-story is a high and difficult department of fiction."

Matthews included this study, enlarged from its original limits, in his volume *Pen and Ink,* and in 1888 issued it as a volume with the title *The Philosophy of the Short-Story.*

ON AN ERRAND OF MERCY

The ambulance clanged along, now under the elevated railroad, and now wrenching itself outside to get ahead of a cable-car.

With his little bag in his hand, the young doctor sat wondering whether he would know just what to do when the time came. This was his first day of duty as ambulance surgeon, and now he was going to his first call. It was three in the afternoon of an August day, when the hot spell had lasted a week already, and yet the young physician was chill with apprehension as he took stock of himself, and as he had a realizing sense of his own inexperience.

The bullet-headed Irishman who was driving the ambulance as skilfully as became the former owner of a night-hawk cab glanced back at the doctor and sized up the situation.

"There's no knowin' what it is we'll find when we get there," he began. "There's times when it's no aisy job the doctor has. Say you give the man ether, now, or whatever it is you make him sniff, and maybe he's dead when he comes out of it. Where are you then?"

The young doctor decided instantly that if anything of that sort should happen to him that afternoon, he would go back to Georgia at once and try for a place in the country store.

"But nothing ever fazed Dr. Chandler," the driver went on. "It's Dr. Chandler's place you're takin' now, ye know that?"

It seemed to the surgeon that the Irishman was making ready to patronize him, or at least to insinuate the new-comer's inferiority to his predecessor, whereupon his sense of humor came to his rescue, and a smile relieved the tension of his nerves as he declared that Dr. Chandler was an honor to his profession.

"He is that!" the driver returned, emphatically, as with a dextrous jerk he swung the ambulance just in front of a cable-car, to the spluttering disgust of the gripman. "An' it's many a dangerous case we've had to handle together, him and me."

"I don't doubt that you were of great assistance," the young Southerner suggested.

"Many's the time he's tould me he never knew what he'd ha' done without me," the Irishman responded. "There was that night, now—the night when the big sailor come off the Roosian ship up in the North River there, an' he got full, an' he fell down the steps of a barber shop, an' he bruck his leg into three places, so he did; an' that made him mad, the pain of it, an' he was just wild when the ambulance come. Oh, it was a lovely jag he had on him, that Roosian—a lovely jag! An' it was a daisy scrap we had wid him!"

"What did he do?" asked the surgeon.

"What didn't he do?" the driver replied, laughing at the memory of the scene. "He tried to do the doctor—Dr. Chandler it was, as I tould you. He's a big knife—it's mortial long knives, too, them Roosians carry—an' he was so full he thought it was Dr. Chandler that was hurtin' him, and he med offer to put his knife in him, when, begorra, I kicked it out of his hand."

"I have often heard Dr. Chandler speak of you," said the doctor, with an involuntary smile, as he recalled several of the good stories that his predecessor had told him of the driver's peculiarities.

"An' why w'u'dn't he?" the Irishman replied. "It's more nor wanst I had to help him out of trouble. An' never a worrd we had in all the months he drove out wid me. But it'll be some aisy little job we'll have now, I'm thinkin'—a sun-stroke, maybe, or a kid that's got knocked down by a scorcher, or a trifle of that kind; you'll be able to attend to that yourself aisy enough, no doubt."

To this the young Southerner made no response, for his mind was busy in going over the antidotes for various poisons. Then he aroused himself and shook his shoulders, and laughed at his own preoccupation.

The Irishman did not approve of this. "An' of coorse," he continued, "it may be a scrap 'twixt a ginny and a Polander; or maybe, now, a coon has gone for a chink wid a razzer, and sliced him most in two, I dunno'."

Then he clanged the bell unexpectedly, and swerved off the track and down a side street toward the river.

The doctor soon found a curious crowd flattening their noses against the windows of a drug-store on a corner of a Boulevard. He sprang off as the driver slowed down to turn and back up.

A policeman stood in the doorway of the pharmacist's, swinging his club by its string as he kept the children outside. He drew back to let the young surgeon pass, saying, as he did so: "It's no use now, I think, Doctor. You are too late."

The body of the man lay flat on the tile pavement of the shop. He was decently dressed, but his shoes were worn and patched. He was a very large man, too, stout even for his length. His cravat had been untied and his collar had been opened. His face was covered with a torn handkerchief.

As the doctor dropped on his knees by the side of the body, the druggist's clerk came from behind the prescription counter —a thin, undersized, freckled youngster, with short red hair and a trembling voice.

"He's dead, ain't he?" asked the apparition.

The doctor finished his examination of the man on the floor, and then he answered, as he rose to his feet: "Yes, he's dead. How did it happen?"

The delivery of the young druggist was hesitating and broken. "Well, it was this way, you see. The boss was out, and I was in charge here, and there wasn't anything doing except at the fountain. Then this man came in; he was in a hurry, and he told me he was feeling faint—kind of suffocated, so he said—and couldn't I give him something. Well, I'm a graduate in pharmacy, you know, and so I fixed him up a little aromatic spirits of ammonia in a glass of soda-water. You know that won't hurt anybody. But just as he took the glass out of my hand his knees gave way and he squashed down on the floor there. The glass broke, and he hadn't paid for the spirits of ammonia either; and when I got round to him he was dead— at least I thought so, but I rang you up to make sure."

"Yes," the doctor returned, "apparently he died at once—heart failure. Probably he had fatty degeneration, and this heat has been too much for him."

"I don't think any man has a right to come in here and die like that without warning, heart failure or no heart failure, do you?" asked the red-headed assistant. "I don't know what the boss will say. That's the kind of thing that spoils trade, and it ain't any too good here, anyway, with a drug-store 'most every block."

"Do you know who he is?" the doctor inquired.

"I went through his pockets, but he hadn't any watch nor any letters," the druggist answered; "but he's got about a dollar in change in his pants."

The doctor looked around the shop. The policeman was still in the doorway, and a group of boys and girls blocked the entrance.

"Does anybody here know this man?" asked the surgeon.

A small boy twisted himself under the policeman's arm and slipped into the store. "I know him," he cried, eagerly. "I see him come in. I was here all the time, and I see it all. He's Tim McEcchran."

"Where does he live?" the doctor asked, only to correct himself swiftly—"where did he live?"

"I thought he was dead when I saw him go down like he was sandbagged," said the boy. "He lives just round the corner in Amsterdam Avenue—at least his wife lives there."

The doctor took the address, and with the aid of the policeman he put the body on the stretcher and lifted it into the ambulance. The driver protested against this as unprecedented.

"Sure it's none of our business to take a stiff home!" he declared. "That's no work at all, at all, for an ambulance. Dr. Chandler never done the like in all the months him an' me was together. Begob, I never contracted to drive hearses."

The young Southerner explained that this procedure might not be regular, but it revolted him to leave the body of a fellow-mortal lying where it had fallen on the floor of a shop. The least he could do, so it seemed to him, was to take it to the dead man's widow, especially since this was scarcely a block out of their way as they returned to the hospital.

The driver kept on grumbling as they drove off. "Sure, he give ye no chance at all, at all, Doctor, to go and croak afor iver ye got at him, and you only beginnin yer work! Dr. Chandler, now, he'd get 'em into the wagon ennyway, an' take chance of there bein' breath in 'em. Three times divil a less, they died on us on the stretcher there, an' me whippin' like the divil to get 'em into the hospital ennyhow where it was their own consarn whether they lived or died. That's the place for 'em to die in, an' not in the wagon; but the wagon's better than dyin' before we can get to 'em, an' the divil thank the begrudgers! It's unlucky, so it is; an' by the same token, to-day's Friday, so it is!"

The small boy who had identified the dead man ran alongside of them, accompanied by his admiring mates; and when the ambulance backed up again before a pretentious tenement-house with a brownstone front and beveled plate-glass doors, the small boy rang Mrs. McEcchran's bell.

"It's the third floor she lives on," he declared.

The janitor came up from the basement and he and the driver carried the stretcher up to Mrs. McEcchran's landing.

The doctor went up before them, and found an insignificant old woman waiting for him on the landing.

"Is this Mrs. McEcchran?" he asked.

"Yes," she answered; then, as she saw the burden the men were carrying, she cried: "My God! What's that? What are they bringing it here for?"

The young Southerner managed to withdraw her into the front room of the flat, and he noticed that it was very clean and very tidy.

"I am a doctor," he began soothingly, "and I am sorry to say that there has been an accident——"

"An accident?" she repeated. "Oh, my God! And is it Tim?"

"You must summon all your courage, Mrs. McEcchran," the doctor returned. "This is a serious matter—a very serious matter."

"Is he hurt very bad?" she cried. "Is it dangerous?"

"I may as well tell you the truth, Mrs. McEcchran," said the physician. "I cannot say that your husband will ever be able to be out again."

By that time the stretcher had been brought into the room, with the body on it entirely covered by a blanket.

"You don't mean to tell me that he is going to die?" she shrieked, wringing her hands. "Don't say that, Doctor! don't say that!"

The bearers set the stretcher down, and the woman threw herself on her knees beside it.

"Tim!" she cried. "Speak to me, Tim!" Getting no response, she got to her feet and turned to the surgeon. "You don't mean he is dead?" And the last word died away in a wail.

"I'm afraid there is no hope for him," the doctor replied.

"He's dead! Tim's dead! Oh, my God!" she said, and then she dropped into a chair and threw her apron over her head and rocked to and fro, sobbing and mourning.

The young Southerner was not yet hardened to such sights, and his heart was sore with sympathy. Yet it seemed to him that the woman's emotion was so violent that it would not last long.

While he was getting ready to have the body removed from the stretcher to a bed in one of the other rooms, Mrs. McEcchran unexpectedly pulled the apron from her head.

"Can I look at him?" she asked, as she slipped to the side of the body and stealthily lifted a corner of the covering to peek in. Suddenly she pulled it back abruptly. "Why, this ain't Tim!" she cried.

"That is not your husband?" asked the doctor, in astonishment. "Are you sure?"

"Of course I'm sure!" she answered hysterically. "Of course I'm sure. As if I didn't know Tim, the father of my children! Why, this ain't even like him!"

The doctor did not know what to say. "Allow me to congratulate you, madam," he began. "No doubt Mr. McEcchran is still alive and well; no doubt he will return to you. But if this is not your husband, whose husband is he?"

The room had filled with the neighbors, and in the crowd the small boy who had brought them there made his escape.

"Can any one tell me who this is?" the surgeon asked.

"I knew that weren't Mr. McEcchran as soon as I see him," said another boy. "That's Mr. Carroll."

"And where does—did Mr. Carroll live?" the doctor pursued, repenting already of his zeal as he foresaw a repetition of the same painful scene in some other tenement-house.

"It's only two blocks off—on the Boulevard," explained the second boy. "It's over a saloon on the corner. I'll show you if I can ride on the wagon."

"Very well," agreed the doctor; and the body was carried down and placed again in the ambulance.

As the ambulance started he overheard one little girl say to another: "He was killed in a blast! My! ain't it awful? It blew his legs off!"

To which the other little girl answered, "But I saw both his boots as they carried him out."

And the first little girl then explained: "Oh, I guess they put his legs back in place so as not to hurt his wife's feelings. Turrible, ain't it?"

When the ambulance started, the driver began grumbling again. "It's not Dr. Chandler that 'ud have a thing like this happen to him. Him an' me never went traipsing round wid a corp that didn't belong to nobody. We knew enough to take it where the wake was waitin'."

The boy on the box with the driver guided the ambulance to a two-story wooden shanty with a rickety stairway outside leading up to the second floor.

He sprang down as the ambulance backed up, and he pointed out to the doctor the sign at the foot of these external steps—"Martin Carroll, Photographer."

"That's where he belongs," the boy explained. "He sleeps in the gallery up there. The saloon belongs to a Dutchman that married his sister. This is the place all right, if it really is Mr. Carroll."

"What do you mean by that?" shouted the doctor. "Are you not sure about it?"

"I ain't certain sure," the fellow replied. "I ain't as sure as I was first off. But I think it is Mr. Carroll. Leastways, if it ain't, it looks like him!"

It was with much dissatisfaction at this doubtfulness of his guide that the doctor helped the driver slide out the stretcher.

Then the side door of the saloon under the landing of the outside stairs opened and a stocky little German came out.

"What's this? What's this?" he asked.

The young surgeon began his explanation again. "This is where Mr. Carroll lived, isn't it? Well, I am sorry to say there has been an accident, and—"

"Is that Martin there?" interrupted the German.

"Yes," the Southerner replied, "and I'm afraid it is a serious case—a pretty serious case—"

"Is he dead?" broke in the saloon-keeper again.

"He is dead," the doctor answered.

"Then why didn't you say so?" asked the short man harshly. "Why waste all that time talking if he's dead?"

The Southerner was inclined to resent his rudeness, but he checked himself.

"I understand that you are Mr. Carroll's brother-in-law," he began again, "so I suppose I can leave the body in your charge—"

The German went over to the stretcher and turned down the blanket.

"No, you don't leave him here," he declared. "I'm not going to take him. This ain't my sister's husband!"

"This is not Mr. Carroll?" and this time 5 the doctor looked around for the boy who had misinformed him. "I was told it was."

"The man who told you was a liar, that's all. This ain't Martin Carroll, and the sooner you take him away the better. That's what I say," declared the saloon-10 keeper, going back to his work.

The doctor looked around in disgust. What he had to do now was to take the body to the morgue, and that revolted him. It seemed to him an insult to the dead and 15 an outrage toward the dead man's family. Yet he had no other course of action open to him, and he was beginning to be impatient to have done with the thing. The week of hot weather had worn on his 20 nerves also, and he wanted to be back again in the cool hospital out of the oven of the streets.

As he and the driver were about to lift 25 up the stretcher again, a man in overalls stepped up to the body and looked at it attentively.

"It's Dick O'Donough!" he said at once. "Poor old Dick! It's a sad day for her— 30 and her that excitable!"

"Do you know him?" asked the doctor.

"Don't I?" returned the man in overalls, a thin, elderly man, with whisps of hair beneath his chin and a shrewd, weazened 35 face. "It's Dick O'Donough!"

"But are you sure of it?" the young surgeon insisted. "We've had two mistakes already."

"Sure of it?" repeated the other. "Of 40 course I'm sure of it! Didn't I work alongside of him for five years? And isn't that the scar on him he got when the wheel broke?" And he lifted the dead man's hair and showed a cicatrix on the temple.

"Very well," said the doctor. "If you 45 are sure, where did he live?"

"It's only a little way."

"I'm glad of that. Can you show us?"

"I can that," replied the man in overalls. "Then jump in front," said the doctor. 50

As they started again, the driver grumbled once more. "Begorra, April Day's a fool to ye," he began. "Them parvarse gossoons, now, if I got howld of 'em, 55 they'd know what it was hurt 'em, I'm thinkin'."

The man in overalls directed them to a shabby double tenement in a side street swarming with children. There was a Chinese laundry on one side of the doorway, and on the other side a bakery. The door stood open, and the hallway was dark and dirty.

"It's a sad day it'll be for Mrs. O'Donough," sighed the man in overalls. "I don't know what it is she's got, but she's very queer, now, very queer."

He went into the bakery and got a man to help the driver carry up the stretcher. Women came out of the shops on both sides of the street, and leaned out of their windows with babies in their arms, and stepped out on the fire-escapes. There were banana peelings and crumpled newspapers and rubbish of one sort or another scattered in the street, and the savor of it all was unpleasant even to a man who was no stranger to the casual ward of a hospital.

The man in overalls went up stairs with the doctor, warning him where a step was broken or where a bit of the hand-rail was missing. They groped their way along the passage on the first floor and knocked.

The door opened suddenly, and they saw an ill-furnished room, glaring with the sun reflected from its white walls. Two women stood just within the door. One was tall and spare, with gray streaks in her coal-black hair, and with piercing black eyes; the other was a comfortable body with a cheerful smile.

"That's Mrs. O'Donough," said the doctor's guide—"the tall one. See the eyes of her now! The other's a neighbor woman, who's with her a good deal, she's that excitable."

The doctor stepped into the room, and began once more to break the news. "This is Mrs. O'Donough, is it not?" he said. "I'm a doctor, and I am sorry to have to say there has been an accident, and Mr. O'Donough is—is under treatment."

Here the driver and the man from the bakery brought in the stretcher.

When the tall woman saw this she gripped the arm of the other and hissed out, "Is it *it?*" Then she turned her back on the body and sank her head on her friend's shoulder.

The other woman made signs to the doctor to say little or nothing.

The driver and the baker took a thin counterpane off the bed, which stood against the wall. Then they lifted the body from the stretcher to the bed, and covered it with the counterpane.

The doctor did not know what to say in the face of the signals he was receiving from the widow's friend.

"In case I can be of any assistance at any time," he suggested—and then Mrs. O'Donough lifted her head and looked at him with her burning eyes—"if I can be of service, do not hesitate to call on me. Here is my card."

As he felt his way down-stairs again he heard a hand-organ break out suddenly into a strident waltz.

When he came out into the street a few little children were dancing in couples, although most of them stood around the ambulance, gazing with morbid curiosity at the driver as he replaced the stretcher. At the door of the baker's shop stood a knot of women talking it over; but in the Chinese laundry the irons went back and forth steadily, with no interest in what might happen in the street outside.

As the doctor took his seat in the vehicle a shriek came from the room he had just left—a shuddering, heartrending wail—then another—and then there was silence. The ambulance started forward, the bell clanged to clear the way, the horse broke into a trot, and in a minute they turned into the broad avenue.

Then the driver looked at the doctor. "The widdy's takin' it harrd, I'm thinkin', but she'll get over it before the wake," he said. "An' it's good lungs she has, ennyhow."

XXIII

LAFCADIO HEARN (1850–1904)

The strange, exotic work of Lafcadio Hearn fell often into short-story form, especially in his early American period when he was on the contributing staff of the Cincinnati and the New Orleans papers. No more picturesque figure than he may be found in any literary history. Born in the island of Leucadia of a Greek mother and an Irish soldier father, reared in Ireland by his father's people, sent to a monastic school in England to be fitted for the priesthood, he escaped to Paris where for months he lived as a street waif and picked up that knowledge of French which so colored his later writings. After many adventures he migrated to America, and in New York City for months again was a waif living as he could. An emigrant train at length took him west, to Cincinnati where for some years he lived as a vagrant supporting himself by contributions to the newspapers. For a time he was a staff reporter enriching the Sunday issues with exotic materials from his reading and his vividly recounted experiences as a reporter. Then migrating to New Orleans, he again became a reporter and picturesque correspondent, tremendously interested in the exotic elements in the romantic old tropic city. But nowhere could he stay long. For two years he was in the French West Indies, his experiences recorded in a book lurid with color and reeking with tropic odors, then he was off to Japan where he shook from himself as far as possible every vestige of the western world and lived and died an oriental. Surely one looks not for the ordinary in Lafcadio Hearn.

His short-story work is, first of all, original. His attraction to the strange, the morbid the uniquely individual was with him well-nigh pathological. Always he sought the sensuous, the colorful, the unique. His work is full of color words,—gorgeous and often horrific adjectives. Always was he lawless. Short-story art concerned him not at all. He wrote as he willed, as he felt, as he lived. His story *Chita,* a novelette perhaps, has in it all the profusion and paradox of the tropics. It is an orgy in color and sensation, and as lawless as the storm that it records. One reads him for his atmospheres, his lurid picturings, the exotic Poe-like moods he can induce, and the joy one feels always in the presence of the rich and precisely chosen vocabulary and the mastery of a style that is original and compelling. As a model for beginners, however, he is not to be commended. It is only the genius who can disregard all rules and still produce classics.

BANJO JIM'S STORY

Melancholy, indeed, is the river-view when a rainy day dawns in dull gray light upon the levee—the view of a rapid yellow river under an ashen sky; of distant hills looming dimly through pallid mist; of steamboat smoke hanging sluggishly over the sickly-hued current; and, drearier yet, the ancient fronts of weather-stained buildings on the Row, gloomy masses of discolored brick and stone with gaping joints and shattered windows. Yet of rainy nights the voice of wild merriment echoes loudest along the levee,—the shouts of the lithe dancers and the throbbing of bass viols and the thrumming of banjos and the shrieking of fiddles seem to redouble in volume.

On breezy, bright nights, when the stars glow overhead, and the ruffled breast of the river reflects the sky-purple or the rich silver of a full moon, the dusky folks seek mirth for mirth's sake. But in night of foul weather and fog, some say the merriment of the Row is attributable to the same strange cause which prompts solitary men in desolate houses or desert places by night to seek relief from loneliness by waking echoes in the gloom with shout or song.

Ghostly at all times, especially to those who live in old dwellings, are rainy nights full of creeping sounds and awesome hoes and unaccountable knockings and ysterious noises, as of foot-falls upon ιcient floors, that groan when walked ιon. Now, the old Row is faced with old)uses, and they say that of rainy nights e dead hide in the shadowy old doorways ιd haunt the dark nooks of the deserted ιncing halls, which have been closed up ιce the great flood. And the habitants of e levee fear the dead with an unutter- ιle fear.

"Look-a-hyar, old gal," cried Banjo Jim Mary Pearl, when the poor woman was ving in her dance-house on the Row,— f you's a-gwine to die, don't you be a ιmin' back hyar after you's done dead, s' I'se a gwine ober the ribber—*I is.*" nd when Mary died, Jim went over the ver with several of the levee girls. For e dead may not pass over water, accord- g to the faith of the roustabout; and to e haunted the steamboat offers a safe ylum from the haunters. But it is said αt Mary came back notwithstanding, and mes back ever and anon on rainy nights, inging with her the ghosts of many dead iends—Winnie, the pretty-faced little hite girl who died at Pickett's dance-ιuse; and Horseheaded Em, the tall, icked-eyed mulatto who drank herself to αth; and Mattie Phillips, the young ιadroon who died at the Workhouse, ιks say for want of morphine. There is long, deep basement under the building ιere Mary kept house, with a great brick chway at the further end, behind which a dark bedroom.

It happened one night not long after the ι dance-house had changed hands, that a ιnken levee girl wandered into that ιm to return, wholly sobered by terror, th a weird tale of how she had seen by e flickering light of a tallow-dip three αd women seated at a table—Mary Pearl, d Jane Goodrich and Horseheaded Em, d how Mary had "gobbled at her." Since en no one dare sleep in that room alone. αggie Sperlock, who lives there, can also l you about a little woman who comes ck sometimes to watch over her children the waifs that Maggie named and opted, Sis and Tom and Howard. Sis is ver whipped, for Maggie says that ιenever the child is punished the dead ιther will come in the night to haunt the αstiser. Sis is a pretty brown child, with ʒ, dreamful eyes, and a strange habit of ιndering in solitary places, whispering

to herself or to Somebody invisible to all others—perhaps the frail, fond, dark mother, who came back silently in the night to protect her little one. Maggie has become afraid of the child's elfish ways, and vows that old Jot, the Obi-man, must have bewitched her. But all attempts, kindly or unkindly, to make the child speak of the viewless beings she held converse with, or of the spectral fancies that seemed to haunt her little brain, proved useless; the old foster-mother dared not whip her for fear of the Shadowy Woman whom she had seen one night bending over the sleeping child, as though to bestow a ghostly kiss; and Sis was finally sent to a kind relative in Bucktown, in the desperate hopes of exorcising her.

While Sis was whispering to herself in shadowy places, and while that hideous story about dead Mary coming back to "gobble" at lonely people in the dark, was being discussed along the levee, folks began to remember that there had been an extraordinary mortality in the Row during the past twelve months. There was Dave Whitton, the tall, thin violin-player of Pickett's dance-house; and Uncle Dan Booker, the withered old "piker," who used to wander about the levee bent crescent-wise with age, and finally died in the Workhouse, serving out a sentence of vagrancy; and pretty Winnie, the little dance-house cook; and Matt Phillips, the morphine-eater; and Horseheaded Em; and the supple quadroon, Dancing Sis; and clumsy Jane Goodrich; and poor Mary Pearl, who died vainly trying to whisper some awful confession to Judge Fox—all had departed from the life of the Row in one brief year. Some said that it must have been the great flood, which left its yellow slime and death dampness in the dance-houses, that had thus depopulated the Row. Some whispered that if one who could no longer cast a shadow in the moonlight had indeed returned to haunt the levee, other unwelcome people would surely follow to revisit their old friends and old resorts. Then folks began to talk about going over the river.

"Tain't no use a-sayin' dem tings am unpossible," gravely observed Judge Fox; "I b'lebes in de Bible, I does; an' I knows dar am folks roun' hyar a-talkin' to folks dat am done dead, an' a sinnin' awful sins agin de Lord." Perhaps the Judge was referring to old Jot.

At last, one stormy night—a night of black ragged clouds fleeing before the face of a gibbous moon—there came a spectral shock which paralyzed the Row with fright—Banjo Jim's story.

Since Pickett after the last foundation removed his establishment from No. 17 to his present location, the old dance-house has remained untenanted. By standing upon a chair or barrel one can obtain a good view of the interior through the narrow panes of dingy glass in the upper part of the door. It can then be perceived that the plaster has fallen away from the ceiling in great irregular patches; the bare walls still betray faintly verdant traces of the last flood; the door of the wooden partition in the rear lies unhinged upon the floor near a row of empty barrels; spiders monstrous enough to serve for the deadliest of Jot's Voodoo decoctions have spun vast webs in the dark corners; and a veil of pallid dust, thick enough to muffle the echo of a heavy footstep, masks the planking of the dance-room. Now, for some time previous to the occurrence which we are about to relate, Matt. Adams (who was born with a veil, they say), had been telling people that strange noises shook the old dance-house on rainy nights —the booming of a ghostly bass-viol, the heavy sound of dancers' feet, and the echo of strange laughter, "like the laughing of people long dead." "I listened at the door one night," said Matt., "and I heard them talking; I heard Dancing Sis and Dave Whitton, and they laughed in the dark, but I could not hear what they were saying." After the girl told that story, Banjo Jim seldom passed along the Row at night without a rabbit's foot in the breast pocket of his woolen shirt.

Whether he forgot the rabbit's foot on a certain Friday night, has not been recorded; but it is most likely that he did, for he had managed to get very drunk at Maggie Sperlock's, where the folks had been having a big dance. It was nearly two in the morning when the ball broke up, and Jim lingered last at the bar. When he went out, the gloomy Row and the silent steamboats at the wharf, and the great posts by the broken curb, seemed to reel about fantastically to the music of the last set—Big Ball Up Town. It was a hot, feverish night; the wild sky was thronged with the oddest clouds, moving in phantasmagorial procession before a warm breeze that seemed to blow from some volcanic land; and the horizon seemed to pulsate with lightning flashes. Jim listened for a friendly police whistle, the wanton laughter of a levee girl—even the footfall of a roustabout. But everything was silent as the silent boats; the voices of the levee were hushed; the windows were all dark.

"I b'leebe the Row am dead," muttered Jim. "I'll make de old gal talk all de same." He seized his banjo, and staggered along the broken sidewalk toward Pickett's, thrumming furiously to the negro melody:

"Ole Joe kickin' up ahind an' afore,
An' a yaller gal a-kickin' up ahind ole Joe."

Suddenly he arrived at the broken steps opposite the deserted dance-house, tripped and fell headlong, his banjo clattering on the uneven pavement with a dying twang of musical reproach.

"Hell an' d—tion," observed Jim.

A burst of unearthly laughter followed the remark. Jim looked around him for the laughers, but saw nobody. He held his breath and listened. Sounds of negro merriment seemed to issue from the old dance-house—the "Kee-yah, kee-yah!" of roustabout laughter, the tramp of dancing feet, and the rapid melody of The Arkansaw Traveler, furiously played upon a shrieking violin. Jim was too drunk to observe just where he was; the levee seemed to have grown a mile long, and probably he thought himself at the new ballroom. He staggered to the door, and found it fast; he rapped, and none responded. Then he rolled an ash-barrel, filled with garbage and cinders, under the window, climbed upon it, and peered in.

The old hall was filled with a pale, sea-green light—such an unsteady radiance as illumes the path of a diver in deep water —a light that seemed to ripple up from the floor, along the walls, and against the shattered ceiling, though reflected by no visible flame. The room was filled with dancers, dancing wildly with goblin gestures, while upon the broken partition-door, placed across a row of empty barrels, stood the tall, thin figure of Dave Whitton, the dead violin player, furiously fiddling The Arkansaw Traveler, his favorite air. And among the dancers Jim could recognize the familiar faces of many dead friends—Winnie and Dancing Sis, En and Matt Phillips, and all the dead girls of the Row, with withered Dan Booker sitting in a corner, sleeping over his basket as in the old days.

They laughed and seemed to speak to one another, but Jim could not understand what was being said, whether that they spoke in some unknown tongue or that the noise of the music drowned the voices of the throng. He observed also that the thick layer of dust upon the floor remained undisturbed by the feet of the eerie crew, and that the figures of the dancers cast no shadows. Dave Whitton's eyes flamed with an elfish light, and a faint streak of pale fire seemed to follow each stroke of the fiddle bow.

Jim thinks that he had been watching the dance for an hour when the scene commenced slowly to assume a new character. The weird figure of the phantom fiddler grew taller and weirder; his violin lengthened and broadened until its tones deepened into a hoarse roar, and the phosphoric light which followed his bow shone brighter. Simultaneously the figures of the ghostly dancers lengthened and commenced to tower toward the ceiling. Then the music ceased to play *The Arkansaw Traveler;* the dance continued to the goblin air of *The Devil Among the Tailors.* Jim began to fancy that the figures of the dancers were blurring and blending into one another, so rapidly did the phantoms elongate and twine about in the nightmare dance. He instinctively looked up at the musician to see whether he had grown to the roof. But that climax of ghastliness must have been reached while Jim was watching the nearest dancers. The long fiddler had not only grown to the ceiling, but was actually growing *along the ceiling* toward the window over the door, bending horribly over the crowd below. The terrified roustabout involuntarily reckoned that at this frightful rate of growth the specter's head would touch the window-pane in about sixty seconds. He began to wonder whether the goblin would then commence to lengthen downward, and coil about the ballroom like an anaconda. The rippling light on the wall brightened from pale green to a livid corpse-light, and Jim felt that matters were approaching a crisis. From the moment he had peeped through the window some hideous fascination held him there; he lacked even the power to scream. He felt that he could free himself by one audible yell of terror, but he could not even whisper; some ghastly influence had deprived him of motion and voice. Suddenly his ear caught the silvery sound of a patrolman's whistle on Lawrence street—the police Lieutenant was making his early round, and the spell was broken.

"Gorramighty!" gasped Jim in horror, when a flood of light burst over the levee —a sheet of white fire, followed by an abysmal crash.

.   .   .   .   .

Five minutes afterward two police officers found an apparently dead negro lying in the rain, opposite the old dance-house, together with an overturned ash-barrel and a broken banjo.

"That flash struck right near here," said Officer Brazil. "It's Banjo Jim; wonder if he got struck?"

Officer Knox bent over, opened the roustabout's woolen shirt, and laid his hand over the man's heart.

"Guess he must have got struck," observed Knox, with a satisfied expression of countenance.

"By lightning?" queried Patsy Brazil, stooping to make an observation.

"Lightning whisky," said Officer Knox.

Jim says otherwise, and the levee folks no longer lounge about the battered doors of No. 17 during the night hours.

XXIV

SARAH ORNE JEWETT (1849-1905)

The local color work of Mrs. Stowe and Harte and Cable and Eggleston was followed in the mid-seventies by the New England stories of Sarah Orne Jewett. Born in Berwick, Maine, the daughter of a country physician, in her childhood frail of physique and threatened possibly with tuberculosis, she was taken by her wise doctor father on his round of visits to his country patients, riding miles daily in the open air and becoming intimately acquainted with the people and the characteristics of a wide area. Awakened to the desire for literary expression over a copy of Mrs. Stowe's *The Pearl of Orr's Island*, she began in 1875 to write sketches of the Maine village life she knew so intimately, issuing them as a collected volume, *Deephaven*, in 1877. Following it came a steady but not hurried series of tales and sketches during the next two decades, her best collection being perhaps *A White Heron and Other Stories*, 1886, and *A Native of Winby and Other Tales*, 1893.

With these short stories Miss Jewett added a new territory to the American literary map, the "Sarah Orne Jewett country," an area extending along the Atlantic coast from Berwick to Portsmouth, N. H., and to some extent into the hinterland beyond. She was a realist to the extent that she used always the materials and the backgrounds that she intimately knew, but one reads not far before one discovers that it is a modified realism. Over all her work there is the mellow atmosphere that transfigures and beautifies. All ugliness and unrelieved tragedy are absent from her picture. One sees only the best that is in her homely characters and backgrounds. She is not a showman exhibiting the strange and unique: she loved her people and her country and she was of it herself. One feels, however, that she does not identify herself with her characters. There is a patrician air always in her work. She is like the gracious lady of the noble house visiting her poor tenants and delighting in them.

She is at her best in her character painting, her depictings of old sea captains who in their prime have trod with authority the quarter decks of great East Indiamen but now in their senile days are sitting on the long wharf looking wistfully and reminiscently out to sea of interesting remnants of better days,—old maids, widows of sailors lost at sea pathetic survivals of "the old governor's set" once regnant at Berwick, of honest old fisher men and farmers. Her style, simple, beautifully finished, chaste, unadorned, has been likened even to Hawthorne's. She stands as a transition figure between the Irving-Hawthorne early period of romanticism and style and the later period of realism and conscious technique.

A NATIVE OF WINBY *

On the teacher's desk, in the little roadside school-house, there was a bunch of May-flowers, beside a dented and bent brass bell, a small Worcester's Dictionary without any cover, and a worn morocco-covered Bible. These were placed in an orderly row, and behind them was a small wooden box which held some broken pieces of blackboard crayon. The teacher, whom no timid new scholar could look at boldly, wore her accustomed air of authority and importance. She might have been nineteen years old,—not more,—but for the time being she scorned the frivolities of youth.

* Copyright by Houghton Mifflin Co.

The hot May sun was shining in at the smoky small-paned windows; sometime an outside shutter swung to with a crea and eclipsed the glare. The narrow doc 5 stood wide open, to the left as you face the desk, and an old spotted dog lay aslee on the step, and looked wise and old enoug to have gone to school with several gen erations of children. It was half past thre 10 o'clock in the afternoon, and the prim class, settled into the apathy of afte recess fatigue, presented a stragglin front, as they stood listlessly on the floo As for the big boys and girls, they al 15 were longing to be at liberty, but the pret teacher, Miss Marilla Hender, seem quite as energetic as when school w begun in the morning.

274

The spring breeze blew in at the open door, and even fluttered the primer leaves, at the back of the room felt hot and close, if it were midsummer. The children in e class read their lessons in those high-yed, droning voices which older teachers arn to associate with faint powers of erception. Only one or two of them had a awakened human look in their eyes, ch as Matthew Arnold delighted himself in finding so often in the school-children France. Most of these poor little stu-nts were as inadequate, at that weary oment, to the pursuit of letters as if they ad been woolly spring lambs on a sunny llside. The teacher corrected and admon-hed with great patience, glancing now d then towards points of danger and in-rrection, whence came a suspicious buzz whispering from behind a desk-lid or pair of widespread large geographies. ow and then a toiling child would rise d come down the aisle, with his fore-ger firm upon a puzzling word as if it ere an unclassified insect. It was a lovely ckoning day out-of-doors. The children lt like captives; there was something at provoked rebellion in the droning ices, the buzzing of an early wild bee ainst the sunlit pane, and even in the uffy familiar odor of the place—the odor apples and crumbs of doughnuts and ngerbread in the dinner pails on the high try nails, and of all the little gowns and ousers that had brushed through junipers d young pines on their way to school. The bee left his prisoning pane at last, d came over to the Mayflowers, which ere in full bloom, although the season as very late, and deep in the woods there ere still some gray-backed snowdrifts, eckled with bits of bark and moss from e trees above. "Come, come, Ezra!" urged the young acher, rapping her desk sharply. "Stop atchin' that common bee! You know ell enough what those letters spell. You n't learn to read at this rate until you e a grown man. Mind your book now; u ought to remember who went to this hool when he was a little boy. You've ard folks tell about the Honorable Jo-ph K. Laneway? He used to be in primer st as you are now, and 't wasn't long fore he was out of it, either, and was lled the smartest boy in school. He's got be a general and a Senator, and one of e richest men out West. You don't seem

to have the least mite of ambition to-day, any of you!"

The exhortation, entirely personal in the beginning, had swiftly passed to a general rebuke. Ezra looked relieved, and the other children brightened up as they recognized a tale familiar to their ears. Anything was better than trying to study in that dull last hour of afternoon school.

"Yes," continued Miss Hender, pleased that she had at last roused something like proper attention, "you all ought to be proud that you are schoolmates of District Number Four, and can remember that the celebrated General Laneway had the same early advantages as you, and think what he has made of himself by perseverance and ambition."

The pupils were familiar enough with the illustrious history of their noble pred-ecessor. They were sure to be told, in lawless moments, that if Mr. Laneway were to come in and see them he would be mortified to death; and the members of the school committee always referred to him, and said that he had been a poor boy, and was now a self-made man,—as if every man were not self-made as to his character and reputation!

At this point, young Johnny Spencer showed his next neighbor, in the back of his *Colburn's Arithmetic*, an imaginary portrait of their district hero, which caused them both to chuckle derisively. The Hon-orable Mr. Laneway figured on the flyleaf as an extremely cross-eyed person, with strangely crooked legs and arms and a terrific expression. He was outlined with red and blue pencils as to coat and trousers, and held a reddened scalp in one hand and a blue tomahawk in the other; being closely associated in the artist's mind with the early settlements of the far West.

There was a noise of wheels in the road near by, and, though Miss Hender had much more to say, everybody ceased to listen to her, and turned toward the win-dows, leaning far forward over their desks to see who might be passing. They caught a glimpse of a shiny carriage; the old dog bounded out, barking, but nothing passed the open door. The carriage had stopped; some one was coming to the school; some-body was going to be called out! It could not be the committee, whose pompous and uninspiring spring visit had taken place only the week before.

Presently a well-dressed elderly man,

with an expectant, masterful look, stood on the doorstep, glanced in with a smile, and knocked. Miss Marilla Hender blushed, smoothed her pretty hair anxiously with both hands, and stepped down from her little platform to answer the summons. There was hardly a shut mouth in the primer class.

"Would it be convenient for you to receive a visitor to the school?" the stranger asked politely, with a fine bow of deference to Miss Hender. He looked much pleased and a little excited, and the teacher said,—

"Certainly; step right in, won't you, sir?" in quite another tone from that in which she had just addressed the school.

The boys and girls were sitting straight and silent in their places, in something like a fit of apprehension and unprepared-ness at such a great emergency. The guest represented a type of person previously unknown in District Number Four. Everything about him spoke of wealth and authority. The old dog returned to the doorstep, and after a careful look at the invader, approached him, with a funny doggish grin and a desperate wag of the tail, to beg for recognition.

The teacher gave her chair on the platform to the guest, and stood beside him with very red cheeks, smoothing her hair again once or twice, and keeping the hardwood ruler fast in hand, like a badge of office. "Primer class may now retire!" she said firmly, although the lesson was not more than half through; and the class promptly escaped to their seats, waddling and stumbling, until they all came up behind their desks, face foremost, and added themselves to the number of staring young countenances. After this there was silence, which grew more and more embarrassing.

"Perhaps you would be pleased to hear our first class in geography, sir?" asked the fair Marilla, recovering her presence of mind; and the guest kindly assented.

The young teacher was by no means willing to give up a certainty for an uncertainty. Yesterday's lesson had been well learned; she turned back to the questions about the State of Kansota, and at the first sentence the mysterious visitor's dignity melted into an unconscious smile. He listened intently for a minute, and then seemed to reoccupy himself with his own thoughts and purposes, looking eagerly about the old school-house, and sometimes gazing steadily at the children. The lesson went on finely, and when it was finished Miss Hender asked the girl at the head of the class to name the States and Territories, which she instantly did, mispronouncing nearly all the names of the latter; then others stated boundaries and capitals, and the resources of the New England States, passing on finally to the names of the Presidents. Miss Hender glowed with pride; she had worked hard over the geography class in the winter term, and it did not fail her on this great occasion. When she turned bravely to see if the gentleman would like to ask any questions, she found that he was apparently lost in a deep reverie, so she repeated her own question more distinctly.

"They have done very well,—very well indeed," he answered kindly; and then, to every one's surprise, he rose, went up the aisle, pushed Johnny Spencer gently along his bench, and sat down beside him. The space was cramped, and the stranger looked huge and uncomfortable, so that everybody laughed, except one of the big girls, who turned pale with fright, and thought he must be crazy. When this girl gave a faint squeak Miss Hender recovered herself, and rapped twice with the ruler to restore order; then became entirely tranquil. There had been talk of replacing the hacked and worn old school-desks with patent desks and chairs; this was probably an agent connected with that business. At once she was resolute and self-reliant, and said, "No whispering!" in a firm tone that showed she did not mean to be trifled with. The geography class was dismissed, but the elderly gentleman, in his handsome overcoat, sat still there wedged in at John Spencer's side.

"I presume, sir, that you are canvassing for new desks," said Miss Hender with dignity. "You will have to see the supervisor and the selectmen." There did not seem to be any need of his lingering, but she had an ardent desire to be pleasing to a person of such evident distinction. "We always tell strangers—I thought, sir, you would be gratified to know—that this is the schoolhouse where the Honorable Joseph K. Laneway first attended school. All do not know that he was born in this town and went West very young; it is only about a mile from here where his folks used to live."

At this moment the visitor's eyes fell

He did not look at pretty Marilla any more, but opened Johnny Spencer's arithmetic, and, seeing the imaginary portrait of the great General Laneway, laughed a little,—a very deep-down comfortable laugh it was,—while Johnny himself turned cold with alarm, he could not have told why.

It was very still in the school-room; the bee was buzzing and bumping at the pane again; the moment was one of intense expectation.

The stranger looked at the children right and left. "The fact is this, young people," said he, in a tone that was half pride and half apology, "I am Joseph K. Laneway myself."

He tried to extricate himself from the narrow quarters of the desk, but for an embarrassing moment found that he was stuck fast. Johnny Spencer instinctively gave him an assisting push, and once freed the great soldier, statesman, and millionaire took a few steps forward to the open floor; then, after hesitating a moment, he mounted the little platform and stood in the teacher's place. Marilla Hender was as pale as ashes.

"I have thought many times," the great guest began, "that some day I should come back to visit this place, which is so closely interwoven with the memories of my childhood. In my counting-room, on the fields of war, in the halls of Congress, and most of all in my Western home, my thoughts have flown back to the hills and brooks of Winby and to this little old school-house. I could shut my eyes and call back the buzz of voices, and fear my teacher's frown, and feel my boyish ambitions waking and stirring in my breast. On that bench where I just sat I saw some notches that I cut with my first jack-knife fifty-eight years ago this very spring. I remember the faces of the boys and girls who went to school with me, and I see their grandchildren before me. I know that one is a Goodsoe and another a Winn by the old family look. One generation goes and another comes.

"There are many things that I might say to you. I meant, even in those early restricted days, to make my name known, and I dare say that you too have ambitions. Be careful what you wish for in this world, for if you wish hard enough you are sure to get it. I once heard a very wise man say this, and the longer I live the more firmly I believe it to be true.

But wishing hard means working hard for what you want, and the world's prizes wait for the men and women who are ready to take pains to win them. Be careful and set your minds on the best things. I meant to be a rich man when I was a boy here, and I stand before you a rich man, knowing the care and anxiety and responsibility of wealth. I meant to go to Congress, and I am one of the Senators from Kansota. I say this as humbly as I say it proudly. I used to read of the valor and patriotism of the old Greeks and Romans with my youthful blood leaping along my veins, and it came to pass that my own country was in danger, and that I could help to fight her battles. Perhaps some one of these little lads has before him a more eventful life than I have lived, and is looking forward to activity and honor and the pride of fame. I wish him all the joy that I have had, all the toil that I have had, and all the bitter disappointments even; for adversity leads a man to depend upon that which is above him, and the path of glory is a lonely path, beset by temptations and a bitter sense of the weakness and imperfections of man. I see my life spread out like a great picture, as I stand here in my boyhood's place. I regret my failures. I thank God for what in his kind providence has been honest and right. I am glad to come back, but I feel, as I look in your young faces, that I am an old man, while your young lives are just beginning. When you remember in years to come, that I came here to see the old school-house, remember that I said: Wish for the best things and work hard to win them; try to be good men and women, for the honor of the school and the town, and the noble young country that gave you birth; be kind at home and generous abroad. Remember that I, an old man who had seen much life, begged you to be brave and good."

The Honorable Mr. Laneway had rarely felt himself so moved in any of his public speeches, but he was obliged to notice that for once he could not hold his audience. The primer class especially had begun to flag in attention, but one or two faces among the elder scholars fairly shone with vital sympathy and a lovely prescience of their future. Their eyes met his as if they struck a flash of light. There was a sturdy boy who half rose in his place unconsciously, the color coming and going in his cheeks; something in Mr. Laneway's words lit the altar flame in his reverent heart.

Marilla Hender was pleased and a little dazed; she could not have repeated what her illustrious visitor had said, but she longed to tell everybody that he was in town, and had come to school to make an address. She had never seen a great man before, and really needed time to reflect upon him and to consider what she ought to say. She was just quivering with the attempt to make a proper reply and thank Mr. Laneway for the honor of his visit to the school, when he asked her which of the boys could be trusted to drive back his hired horse to the Four Corners. Eight boys, large and small, nearly every boy in the school, rose at once and snapped insistent fingers; but Johnny Spencer alone was desirous not to attract attention to himself. The *Colburn's Intellectual Arithmetic* with the portrait had been well secreted between his tight jacket and his shirt. Miss Hender selected a trustworthy freckled person in long trousers, who was half way to the door in an instant, and was heard almost immediately to shout loudly at the quiet horse.

Then the Hero of District Number Four made his acknowledgments to the teacher. "I fear that I have interrupted you too long," he said with pleasing deference.

Marilla replied that it was of no consequence; she hoped he would call again. She may have spoken primly, but her pretty eyes said everything that her lips forgot. "My grandmother will want to see you, sir," she ventured to say. "I guess you will remember her,—Mis' Hender, she that was Abby Harran. She has often told me how you used to get your lessons out of the same book."

"Abby Harran's granddaughter?" Mr. Laneway looked at her again with fresh interest. "Yes, I wish to see her more than any one else. Tell her that I am coming to see her before I go away, and give her my love. Thank you, my dear," as Marilla offered his missing hat. "Good-by, boys and girls." He stopped and looked at them once more from the boys' entry, and turned again to look back from the very doorstep.

"Good-by, sir—good-by," piped two or three of the young voices; but most of the children only stared, and neither spoke nor moved.

"We will omit the class in Fourth Reader this afternoon. The class in gram-mar may recite," said Miss Hender in he[r] most contained and official manner.

The grammar class sighed like a singl[e] pupil, and obeyed. She was very ster[n] with the grammar class, but every one i[n] school had an inner sense that it was [a] great day in the history of District Num[ber] ber Four.

The Honorable Mr. Laneway found th[e] outdoor air very fresh and sweet afte[r] the closeness of the school-house. It ha[d] just that same odor in his boyhood, an[d] as he escaped he had a delightful sens[e] of playing truant or of having an unex[-] pected holiday. It was easier to think [of] himself as a boy, and to slip back into boy[-] ish thoughts, than to bear the familia[r] burden of his manhood. He climbed th[e] tumble-down stone wall across the roa[d] and went along a narrow path to th[e] spring that bubbled up clear and col[d] under a great red oak. How many time[s] he had longed for a drink of that wate[r] and now here it was, and the thirst [of] that warm spring day was hard to quench[.] Again and again he stooped to fill th[e] birchbark dipper which the school-childre[n] had made, just as his own comrades mad[e] theirs years before. The oak-tree was dy[-] ing at the top. The pine woods beyon[d] had been cut and had grown again sinc[e] his boyhood, and looked much as he re[-] membered them. Beyond the spring an[d] away from the woods the path led acros[s] overgrown pastures to another road, per[-] haps three quarters of a mile away, an[d] near this road was the small farm whic[h] had been his former home. As he walke[d] slowly along, he was met again and aga[in] by some reminder of his youthful day[s.] He had always liked to refer to his ear[ly] life in New England in his political ad[-] dresses, and had spoken more than on[ce] of going to find the cows at nightfall i[n] the autumn evenings, and being glad [to] warm his bare feet in the places whe[re] the sleepy beasts had lain, before he fo[l-] lowed their slow steps homeward throug[h] bush and brier. The Honorable Mr. Lan[e-] way had a touch of true sentiment whi[ch] added much to his really stirring an[d] effective campaign speeches. He had oft[en] been called the "king of the platform" [in] his adopted State. He had long ago grow[n] used to saying "Go" to one man, a[nd] "Come" to another, like the ruler of ol[d,] but all his natural power of leadersh[ip] and habit of authority disappeared at once as he trod the pasture slopes, calling back the remembrance of his childhood. Here was the place where two lads, older than himself, had killed a terrible woodchuck at bay in the angle of a great rock; and just beyond was the sunny spot where he had picked a bunch of pink and white anemones under a prickly barberry thicket, to give to Abby Harran in morning school. She had put them into her desk, and let them wilt there, but she was pleased when she took them. Abby Harran, the little teacher's grandmother, was a year older than he, and had wakened the earliest thought of love in his youthful breast.

It was almost time to catch the first sight of his birthplace. From the knoll just ahead he had often seen the light of his mother's lamp, as he came home from school on winter afternoons; but when he reached the knoll the old house was gone, and so was the great walnut-tree that grew beside it, and a pang of disappointment shot through his devout pilgrim's heart. He never had doubted that the old farm was somebody's home still, and had counted upon the pleasure of spending a night there, and sleeping again in that room under the roof, where the rain sounded loud, and the walnut branches brushed to and fro when the wind blew, as if they were the claws of tigers. He hurried across the worn-out fields, long ago turned into sheep pastures, where the last year's tall grass and golden-rod stood gray and winter-killed; tracing the old walls and fences, and astonished to see how small the fields had been. The prosperous owner of Western farming lands could not help remembering those widespread luxuriant acres, and the broad outlooks of his Western home.

It was difficult at first to find exactly where the house had stood; even the foundations had disappeared. A last in the long, faded grass he discovered the doorstep, and near by was a little mound where the great walnut-tree stump had been. The cellar was a mere dent in the sloping ground; it had been filled in by the growing grass and slow processes of summer and winter weather. But just at the pilgrim's right were some thorny twigs of an old rosebush. A sudden brightening of memory brought to mind the love that his mother—dead since his fifteenth year —had kept for this sweet-brier. How often

she had wished that she had brought it to her new home! So much had changed in the world, so many had gone into the world of light, and here the faithful blooming thing was yet alive! There was one slender branch where green buds were starting, and getting ready to flower in the new year.

The afternoon wore late, and still the gray-haired man lingered. He might have laughed at some one else who gave himself up to sad thoughts, and found fault with himself, with no defendant to plead his cause at the bar of conscience. It was an altogether lonely hour. He had dreamed all his life, in a sentimental, self-satisfied fashion, of this return to Winby. It had always appeared to be a grand affair, but so far he was himself the only interested spectator at his poor occasion. There was even a dismal consciousness that he had been undignified, perhaps even a little consequential and silly, in the old schoolhouse. The picture of himself on the warpath, in Johnny Spencer's arithmetic, was the only tribute that his longed-for day had held, but he laughed aloud delightedly at the remembrance and really liked that solemn little boy who sat at his own old desk. There was another older lad, who sat at the back of the room, who reminded Mr. Laneway of himself in his eager youth. There was a spark of light in that fellow's eyes. Once or twice in the earlier afternoon, as he drove along, he had asked people in the road if there was a Laneway family in that neighborhood, but everybody had said no in an indifferent fashion. Somehow he had been expecting that every one would know him and greet him, and give him credit for what he had tried to do, but old Winby had her own affairs to look after, and did very well without any of his help.

Mr. Laneway acknowledged to himself at this point that he was weak and unmanly. There must be some old friends who would remember him, and give him as hearty a welcome as the greeting he had brought for them. So he rose and went his way westward toward the sunset. The air was growing damp and cold, and it was time to make sure of shelter. This was hardly like the visit he had meant to pay to his birthplace. He wished with all his heart he had never come back. But he walked briskly away, intent upon wider thoughts as the fresh evening breeze quickened his steps. He did not consider where he was going, but was for a time the busy man of affairs, stimulated by the unconscious influence of his surroundings. The slender gray birches and pitch pines of that neglected pasture had never before seen a hat and coat exactly in the fashion. They may have been abashed by the presence of a United States Senator and Western millionaire, though a piece of New England ground that had often felt the tread of his bare feet was not likely to quake because a pair of smart shoes stepped hastily along the school-house path.

There was an imperative knock at the side door of the Hender farmhouse, just after dark. The young school-mistress had come home late, because she had stopped all the way along to give people the news of her afternoon's experience. Marilla was not coy and speechless any longer, but sat by the kitchen stove telling her eager grandmother everything she could remember or could imagine.

"Who's that knocking at the door?" inquired Mrs. Hender. "No, I'll go myself; I'm nearest."

The man outside was cold and foot-weary. He was not used to spending a whole day unrecognized, and, after being first amused, and even enjoying a sense of freedom at escaping his just dues of consideration and respect, he had begun to feel as if he were old and forgotten, and was hardly sure of a friend in the world. Old Mrs. Hender came to the door, with her eyes shining with delight, in great haste to dismiss whoever had knocked, so that she might hear the rest of Marilla's story. She opened the door wide to whoever might have come on some country errand, and looked the tired and faint-hearted Mr. Laneway full in the face.

"Dear heart, come in!" she exclaimed, reaching out and taking him by the shoulder, as he stood humbly on a lower step. "Come right in, Joe. Why, I should know you anywhere! Why, Joe Laneway, *you same boy!*"

In they went to the warm, bright, country kitchen. The delight and kindness of an old friend's welcome and her instant sympathy seemed the loveliest thing in the world. They sat down in two straight-backed kitchen chairs. They still held each other by the hand, and looked into each other's face. The plain old room was aglow

with heat and cheerfulness; the tea-kettle was singing; a drowsy cat sat on the wood-box with her paws tucked in; and the house dog came forward in a friendly way, wagging his tail, and laid his head on their clasped hands.

"And to think I haven't seen you since your folks moved out West, the next spring after you were thirteen in the winter," said the good woman. "But I s'pose there ain't been anybody that has followed your career closer than I have, accordin' to their opportunities. You've done a great work for your country, Joe. I'm proud of you clean through. Sometimes folks has said, 'There, there, Mis' Hender, what be you goin' to say now?' but I've always told 'em to wait. I knew you saw your reasons. You was always an honest boy." The tears started and shone in her kind eyes. Her face showed that she had waged a bitter war with poverty and sorrow, but the look of affection that it wore, and the warm touch of her hard hand, misshapen and worn with toil, touched her old friend in his inmost heart, and for a minute neither could speak.

"They do say that women folks have got no natural head for politics, but I always could seem to sense what was goin' on in Washington, if there was any sense to it," said grandmother Hender at last.

"Nobody could puzzle you at school, I remember," answered Mr. Laneway, and they both laughed heartily. "But surely this granddaughter does not make your household? You have sons?"

"Two beside her father. He died, but they're both away, up toward Canada, buying cattle. We are getting along considerable well these last few years, since they got a mite of capital together; but the old farm wasn't really able to maintain us, with the heavy expenses that fell on us unexpected year by year. I've seen a great sight of trouble, Joe. My boy John, Marilla's father, and his nice wife, —I lost 'em both early, when Marilla was but a child. John was the flower of my family. He would have made a name for himself. You would have taken to John."

"I was sorry to hear of your loss," said Mr. Laneway. "He was a brave man. I know what he did at Fredericksburg. You remember that I lost my wife and my only son?"

There was a silence between the friends,

who had no need for words now; they understood each other's heart only too well. Marilla, who sat near them, rose and went out of the room.

"Yes, yes, daughter," said Mrs. Hender, calling her back. "We ought to be thinking about supper."

"I was going to light a little fire in the parlor," explained Marilla, with a slight tone of rebuke in her clear girlish voice.

"Oh, no, you ain't,—not now, at least," protested the elder woman decidedly. "Now, Joseph, what should you like to have for supper? I wish to my heart I had some fried turnovers, like those you used to come after when you was a boy. I can make 'em just about the same as mother did. I'll be bound you've thought of some old-fashioned dish that you would relish for your supper."

"Rye drop-cakes, then, if they wouldn't give you too much trouble," answered the Honorable Joseph, with prompt seriousness, "and don't forget some cheese." He looked up at his old playfellow as she stood beside him, eager with affectionate hospitality.

"You've no idea what a comfort Marilla's been," she stooped to whisper. "Always took right hold and helped me when she was a baby. She's as good as made up already for my having no daughter. I want you to get acquainted with Marilla."

The granddaughter was still awed and anxious about the entertainment of so distinguished a guest when her grandmother appeared at last in the pantry.

"I ain't goin' to let you do no such a thing, darlin'," said Abby Hender, when Marilla spoke of making something that she called "fairy gems" for tea, after a new and essentially feminine recipe. "You just let me get supper to-night. The Gen'ral has enough kickshaws to eat; he wants a good, hearty, old-fashioned supper,—the same country cooking he remembers when he was a boy. He went so far himself as to speak of rye dropcakes, an' there ain't one in a hundred, nowadays, knows how to make the kind he means. You go an' lay the table just as we always have it, except you can get out them old big sprigged cups o' my mother's. Don't put on none o' the parlor cluset things."

Marilla went off crestfallen and demurring. She had a noble desire to show Mr. Laneway that they knew how to have things as well as anybody, and was sure that he would consider it more polite to be asked into the best room, and to sit there alone until tea was ready; but the illustrious Mr. Laneway was allowed to stay in the kitchen, in apparent happiness, and to watch the proceedings from beginning to end. The two old friends talked industriously, but he saw his rye dropcakes go into the oven and come out, and his tea made, and his piece of salt fish broiled and buttered, a broad piece of honeycomb set on to match some delightful thick slices of brown-crusted loaf bread, and all the simple feast prepared. There was a sufficient piece of Abby Hender's best cheese; it must also be confessed that there were also some baked beans, and, as one thing after appeared, the Honorable Joseph K. Laneway grew hungrier and hungrier, until he fairly looked pale with anticipation and delay, and was bidden at that very moment to draw up his chair and make himself a supper if he could. What cups of tea, what uncounted rye drop-cakes, went to the making of that successful supper! How gay the two old friends became, and of what old stories they reminded each other, and how late the dark spring evening grew, before the feast was over and the straight-backed chairs were set against the kitchen wall!

Marilla listened for a time with more or less interest, but at last she took up one of her school-books, with slight ostentation, and went over to study by the lamp. Mrs. Hender had brought her knitting-work, a blue woolen stocking, out of a drawer, and sat down serene and unruffled, prepared to keep awake as late as possible. She was a woman who had kept her youthful looks through the difficulties of farm life as few women can, and this added to her guest's sense of home-likeness and pleasure. There was something that he felt to be sisterly and comfortable in her strong figure; he even noticed the little plaid woolen shawl that she wore about her shoulders. Dear, uncomplaining heart of Abby Hender! The appealing friendliness of the good woman made no demands except to be allowed to help and to serve everybody who came in her way.

Now began in good earnest the talk of old times, and what had become of this and that old schoolmate; how one family had come to want and another to wealth.

The changes and losses and windfalls of good fortune in that rural neighborhood were made tragedy and comedy. by turns in Abby Hender's dramatic speech. She grew younger and more entertaining hour by hour, and beguiled the grave Senator into confidential talk of national affairs. He had much to say to which she listened with rare sympathy and intelligence. She astonished him by her comprehension of difficult questions of the day, and by her simple good sense. Marilla grew hopelessly sleepy, and departed, but neither of them turned to notice her as she lingered a moment to say good-night. When the immediate subjects of conversation were fully discussed, however, there was an unexpected interval of silence, and, after making sure that her knitting stitches counted exactly right, Abby Hender cast a questioning glance at the Senator to see if he had it in mind to go to bed. She was reluctant to end her evening so soon, but determined to act the part of considerate hostess. The guest was as wide awake as ever: eleven o'clock was the best part of his evening.

"Cider?" he suggested, with an expectant smile, and Abby Hender was on her feet in a moment. When she had brought a pitcher from the pantry, he took a candle from the high shelf and led the way.

"To think of your remembering our old cellar candlestick all these years!" laughed the pleased woman, as she followed him down the steep stairway, and then laughed still more at his delight in the familiar look of the place.

"Unchanged as the pyramids!" he said. "I suppose those pound sweetings that used to be in that farthest bin were eaten up months ago?"

It was plain to see that the household stores were waning low, as befitted the time of the year, but there was still enough in the old cellar. Care and thrift and gratitude made the poor farmhouse a rich place. This woman of real ability had spent her strength from youth to age, and had lavished as much industry and power of organization in her narrow sphere as would have made her famous in a wider one. Joseph Laneway could not help sighing as he thought of it. How many things his good friend had missed, and yet how much she had been able to win that makes everywhere the very best of life. Poor and

early widowed, there must have been a constant battle with poverty on that stony Harran farm, whose owners had been pitied even in his early boyhood, when the best of farming land was none too easy. But Abby Hender had always been one of the leaders of the town.

"Now, before we sit down again, I want you to step into my best room. Perhaps you won't have time in the morning, and I've got something to show you," she said persuasively.

It was a plain, old-fashioned best room, with a look of pleasantness in spite of the spring chill and the stiffness of the best chairs. They lingered before the picture of Mrs. Hender's soldier son, a poor work of a poorer artist in crayons, but the spirit of the young face shone out appealingly. Then they crossed the room and stood before some bookshelves, and Abby Hender's face brightened into a beaming smile of triumph.

"You didn't expect we should have all those books, now, did you, Joe Laneway?" she asked.

He shook his head soberly, and leaned forward to read the titles. There were no very new ones, as if times had been hard of late; almost every volume was either history, or biography, or travel. Their owner had reached out of her own narrow boundaries into other lives and into far countries. He recognized with gratitude two or three congressional books that he had sent her when he first went to Washington, and here was a life of himself, written from a partizan point of view, and issued in one of his most exciting campaigns; the sight of it touched him to the heart, and then she opened it, and showed him the three or four letters that he had written her,—one, in boyish handwriting, describing his adventures on his first Western journey.

"There are a hundred and six volumes now," announced the proud owner of such a library. "I lend 'em all I can, or most of them would look better. I have had to wait a good while for some, and some weren't what I expected 'em to be, but most of 'em's as good books as there is in the world. I've never been so situated that it seemed best for me to indulge in a daily paper, and I don't know but it's just as well; but stories were never any great of a temptation. I know pretty well what's goin' on about me, and I can make that do. Real life's interestin' enough for me."

Mr. Laneway was still looking over the books. His heart smote him for not being thoughtful; he knew well enough that the overflow of his own library would have been delightful to this self-denying, eager-minded soul. "I've been a very busy man all my life, Abby," he said impulsively, as if she waited for some apology for his forgetfulness, "but I'll see to it now that you have what you want to read. I don't mean to lose hold of your advice on state matters." They both laughed, and he added, "I've always thought of you, if I haven't shown it."

"There's more time to read than there used to be; I've had what was best for me," answered the woman gently, with a grateful look on her face, as she turned to glance at her old friend. "Marilla takes hold wonderfully and helps me with the work. In the long winter evenings you can't think what a treat a new book is. I wouldn't change places with the queen."

They had come back to the kitchen, and she stood before the cupboard, reaching high for two old gaily striped crockery mugs. There were some doughnuts and cheese at hand; their early supper seemed quite forgotten. The kitchen was warm, and they had talked themselves thirsty and hungry; but with what an unexpected tang the cider freshened their throats! Mrs. Hender had picked the apples herself that went to the press; they were all chosen from the old russet tree and the gnarly, red-cheeked, ungrafted fruit that grew along the lane. The flavor made one think of frosty autumn mornings on high hillsides, of north winds and sunny skies. "It 'livens one to the heart," as Mrs. Hender remarked proudly, when the Senator tried to praise it as much as it deserved, and finally gave a cheerful laugh, such as he had not laughed for many a day.

"Why, it seems like drinking the month of October," he told her; and at this the hostess reached over, protesting that the striped mug was too narrow to hold what it ought, and filled it up again.

"Oh, Joe Laneway, to think that I see you at last, after all these years !" she said. "How rich I shall feel with this evening to live over ! I've always wanted to see somebody that I'd read about, and now I've got that to remember; but I've always known I should see you again, and I believe 't was the Lord's will."

Early the next morning they said goodby. The early breakfast had to be hurried, and Marilla was to drive Mr. Laneway to the station three miles away. It was Saturday morning, and she was free from school.

Mr. Laneway strolled down the lane before breakfast was ready, and came back with a little bunch of pink anemones in his hand. Marilla thought that he meant to give them to her, but he laid them beside her grandmother's plate. "You mustn't put those in your desk," he said with a smile, and Abby Hender blushed like a girl.

"I've got those others now, dried and put away somewhere in one of my books," she said quietly, and Marilla wondered what they meant.

The two old friends shook hands warmly at parting. "I wish you could have stayed another day, so that I could have had the minister come and see you," urged Mrs. Hender regretfully.

"You couldn't have done any more for me. I have had the best visit in the world," he answered, a little shaken, and holding her hand a moment longer, while Marilla sat, young and impatient, in the high wagon. "You're a dear good woman, Abby. Sometimes when things have gone wrong I've been sorry that I ever had to leave Winby."

The woman's clear eyes looked straight into his; then fell. "You wouldn't have done everything you have for the country," she said.

"Give me a kiss; we're getting to be old folks now," said the General; and they kissed each other gravely.

A moment later Abby Hender stood alone in her dooryard, watching and waving her hand again and again, while the wagon rattled away down the lane and turned into the highroad.

Two hours after Marilla returned from the station, and rushed into the kitchen. "Grandma !" she exclaimed, "you never did see such a crowd in Winby as there was at the depot ! Everybody in town had got word about General Laneway, and they were pushing up to shake hands, and cheering same as at election, and the cars waited as much as ten minutes, and all the folks was lookin' out of the windows, and came out on the platforms when they heard who it was. Folks say that he'd been to see the selectmen yesterday before he came to school, and he's goin' to build an elegant town hall, and have the names put up in it of all the Winby men that went to the war." Marilla sank into a chair, flushed with excitement. "Everybody was asking me about his being here last night and what he said to the school. I wished that you'd gone down to the depot instead of me."

"I had the best part of anybody," said Mrs. Hender, smiling and going on with her Saturday morning work. "I'm real glad they showed him proper respect," she added a moment afterward, but her voice faltered.

"Why, you ain't been cryin', grandma?" asked the girl. "I guess you're tired. You had a real good time, now, didn't you?"

"Yes, dear heart!" said Abby Hender. "'T ain't pleasant to be growin' old, that's all. I couldn't help noticin' his age as he rode away. I've always been lookin' forward to seein' him again, an' now it's all over."

XXV

MARY NOAILLES MURFREE (1850-1922)

Charles Egbert Craddock, the pen name of Mary N. Murfree of Murfreesboro, Tennessee, first attracted the attention of readers in 1878 with her story in *The Atlantic Monthly*, entitled "Tha Dancin' Party at Harrison's Cove." Dialect and strange geographical setting were in the very title, and the style and treatment of materials were fully as novel. Not only did she bring into fiction a new wild background and people, the Southern mountaineers, but she brought what seemed at that time a uniqueness of method—an impressionistic handling of landscape and a making of it what really was one of the characters in the tragedy. Moreover her style had an eighteenth century tang. There is a peculiar Dr. Johnson inflation of diction and an intensity of phrase and apparently of feeling that impressed for a time readers of fiction. But her style has not worn well. Read in the coldness and leisure of later days it is found that she was artificial, and not always true to life. She exaggerated her effects: her mountains which she made veritable Alps are in reality but respectable hills and her characters are subject to the same criticism.

The influence of Charles Egbert Craddock, however, at a critical moment, was considerable. A peculiar bit of advertising gave her work wings. During all of the period from 1878 to 1884 T. B. Aldrich, editor of *The Atlantic Monthly*, and the whole reading public supposed she was a man. Their astonishment when she appeared at the editorial office and announced that she was Charles Egbert Craddock was flashed over the country as major news and its effect upon the sale and the influence of the collection *In the Tennessee Mountains* was instant and influential.

After the success of her first collection she turned to the novel and the greater part of her later work was in the longer rather than the shorter forms of fiction. Gradually her vogue declined and even before she died she had become a figure of the past, an episode in the history of American fiction. To spend a literary lifetime depicting a single crude environment is to court failure and oblivion. Such an environment may produce one volume of vivid, worth-while work, but seldom more. *In the Tennessee Mountains* is such a volume. Its place among the collections of short-story classics of America has not as yet been seriously disputed.

'WAY DOWN IN LONESOME COVE *

One memorable night in Lonesome Cove the ranger of the county entered upon a momentous crisis in his life. What hour it was he could hardly have said, for the primitive household reckoned time by the sun when it shone, by the domestic routine when no better might be. It was late. The old crone in the chimney-corner nodded over her knitting. In the trundle-bed at the further end of the shadowy room were transverse billows under the quilts, which intimated that the small children were numerous enough for the necessity of sleeping crosswise. He had smoked out many pipes, and at last knocked the cinder from the bowl. The great hickory logs had

burned asunder and fallen from the stones that served as andirons. He began to slowly cover the embers with ashes, that the fire might keep till morning.

His wife, a faded woman, grown early old, was bringing the stone jar of yeast to place close by the hearth, that it might not "take a chill" in some sudden change of the night. It was heavy, and she bent in carrying it. Awkward, and perhaps nervous, she brought it sharply against the shovel in his hands.

The clash roused the old crone in the corner. She recognized the situation instantly, and the features that sleep had relaxed into inexpressiveness took on a weary apprehension, which they wore like a habit. The man barely raised his surly black eyes, but his wife drew back humbly with a mutter of apology.

The next moment the shovel was almost thrust out of his grasp. A tiny barefooted girl, in a straight unbleached cotton nightgown and a quaint little cotton night-cap, cavalierly pushed him aside, that she might cover in the hot ashes a burly sweet-potato, destined to slowly roast before morning. A long and careful job she made of it, and unconcernedly kept him waiting while she pottered back and forth about the hearth. She looked up once with an authoritative eye, and he hastily helped to adjust the potato with the end of the shovel. And then he glanced at her, incongruously enough, as if waiting for her autocratic nod of approval. She gravely accorded it, and pattered nimbly across the puncheon floor to the already well-filled bed.

"Now," he drawled, in gruff accents, "ef you-uns hev all hed yer fill o' foolin' with this hyar fire, I'll kiver it, like I hev started out ter do."

At this moment there was a loud trampling upon the porch without. The batten door shook violently. The ranger sprang up. As he frowned, the hair on his scalp, drawn forward, seemed to rise like bristles. "Dad burn that thar fresky filly!" he cried, angrily. "Jes' brung her noisy bones up on that thar porch again, an' her huffs will bust spang through the planks o' the floor, the fust thing ye know."

The narrow aperture, as he held the door ajar, showed outlined against the darkness the graceful head of a young mare, and once more hoof-beats resounded on the rotten planks of the porch.

Clouds were adrift in the sky. No star gleamed in the wide space high above the somber mountains. On every side they encompassed Lonesome Cove, which seemed to have importunately thrust itself into the darkling solemnities of their intimacy.

All at once the ranger let the door fly from his hand, and stood gazing in blank amazement. For there was a strange motion in the void vastnesses of the wilderness. They were creeping into view. How, he could not say, but the summit of the great mountain opposite was marvellously distinct against the sky. He saw the naked, gaunt December woods. He saw the grim gray crags. And yet Lonesome Cove below and the spurs on the other side were all benighted. A pale flickering light was dawning in the clouds; it brightened, faded, glowed again, and their sad gray folds assumed a vivid vermilion reflection, for there was a fire in the forest below. Only these reactions of color on the clouds betokened its presence and its progress. Sometimes a fluctuation of orange crossed them, then a glancing line of blue, and once more that living red hue which only a pulsating flame can bestow.

"Air it the comin' o' the Jedgmint Day, Tobe?" asked his wife, in a meek whisper.

"I'd be afraid so if I war ez big a sinner ez you-uns," he returned.

"The woods air afire," the old woman declared, in a shrill voice.

"They be a-soakin' with las' night's rain," he retorted, gruffly.

The mare was standing near the porch. Suddenly he mounted her and rode hastily off, without a word of his intention to the staring women in the doorway.

He left freedom of speech behind him. "Take yer bones along, then, ye tongue-tied catamount!" his wife's mother apostrophied him, with all the acrimony of long repression. "Got no mo' politeness 'n a settin' hen," she muttered, as she turned back into the room.

The young woman lingered wistfully. "I wisht he wouldn't go a-ridin' off that thar way 'thout lettin' we-uns know whar he air bound fur, an' when he'll kem back. He mought git hurt some ways roun' that thar fire—git overtook by it, mebbe."

"Ef he war roasted, 'twould be mighty peaceful round in Lonesome," the old crone exclaimed, rancorously.

Her daughter stood for a moment with the bar of the door in her hand, still gazing out at the flare in the sky. The unwonted emotion had conjured a change in the stereotyped patience in her face—even anxiety, even the acuteness of fear, seemed a less pathetic expression than that meek monotony bespeaking a broken spirit. As she lifted her eyes to the mountain, one might wonder to see that they were so blue. In the many haggard lines drawn upon her face, the effect of the straight lineaments was lost; but just now, embellished with a flush, she looked young—as young as her years.

As she buttoned the door and put up the bar, her mother's attention was caught by the change. Peering at her critically, and shading her eyes with her hand from the uncertain flicker of the tallow dip, she broke out, passionately: "Wa'al, Madeliny, who would ever hev thought ez yer cake would be *all* dough? Sech a laffin', plump, spry gal ez ye useter be—fur all the worl' like a fresky young deer! An' sech a pack 'o men ez ye hed the ch'ice amongst! An' ter pick out Tobe Gryce an' marry him, an' kem 'way down hyar ter live along o' him in Lonesome Cove!"

She chuckled aloud, not that she relished her mirth, but the harlequinade of fate constrained a laugh for its antics. The words recalled the past to Madeline; it rose visibly before her. She had had scant leisure to reflect that her life might have been ordered differently. In her widening eyes were new depths, a vague terror, a wild speculation, all struck aghast by its own temerity.

"Ye never said nuthin ter hender," she faltered.

"I never knowed Tobe, sca'cely. How's ennybody goin' ter know a man ez lived 'way off down hyar in Lonesome Cove?" her mother retorted, acridly, on the defensive. "He never courted *me*, nohows. All the word he gin me war, 'Howdy,' an' I gin him no less."

There was a pause.

Madeline knelt on the hearth. She placed together the broken chunks, and fanned the flames with a turkey wing. "I won't kiver the fire yit," she said, thoughtfully. "He mought be chilled when he gits home."

The feathery flakes of the ashes flew; they caught here and there in her brown hair. The blaze flared up, and flickered over her flushed, pensive face and glowed in her large and brilliant eyes.

"Tobe said 'Howdy,'" her mother bickered on. "I knowed by that ez he hed the gift o' speech, but he spent no mo' words on me." Then, suddenly: "I war a fool, though, ter gin my cornsent ter yer marryin' him, bein' ez ye war the only child I hed, an' I knowed I'd hev ter live with ye 'way down hyar in Lonesome Cove. I wish now ez ye hed abided by yer fust ch'ice, an' married Luke Todd."

Madeline looked up with a gathering frown. "I hev no call ter spen' words 'bout Luke Todd," she said, with dignity, "ez me an' him are both married ter other folks."

"I never said ye hed," hastily replied the old woman, rebuked and embarrassed. Presently, however, her vagrant speculation went recklessly on. "Though ez ter Luke's marryin', 'tain't wuth while ter set store on sech. The gal he found over thar in Big Fox Valley favors ye ez close ez two black-eyed peas. That's why he married her. She looks percisely like ye useter look. An' she laffs the same. An' I reckon *she* 'ain't hed no call ter quit laffin', 'kase he air a powerful easy-goin' man. Leastways he uster be when we-uns knowed him."

"That ain't no sign," said Madeline. "A saafter-spoken body I never seen than Tobe war when he fust kem a-courtin' round the settlemint."

"Sech ez that ain't goin' ter las' noways," dryly remarked the philosopher of the chimney-corner.

This might seem rather a reflection upon the courting gentry in general than a personal observation. But Madeline's consciousness lent it point.

"Laws-a-massy," she said, "Tobe ain't so rampagious, nohows, ez folks make him out. He air toler'ble peaceable, cornsiderin' ez nobody hev ever hed grit enough ter make a stand agin him, 'thout 'twar the Cunnel thar."

She glanced around at the little girl's face framed in the frill of her night-cap, and peaceful and infantile as it lay on the pillow.

"Whenst the Cunnel war born," Madeline went on, languidly reminiscent, "Tobe war powerful outed 'kase she war a gal. I reckon ye 'members ez how he said he hed no use for sech cattle ez that. An' when she tuk sick he 'lowed he seen no differ. 'Jes ez well die ez live,' ez he said. An' bein' ailin', the Cunnel tuk it inter her head ter holler. Sech hollerin' we-uns hed never hearn with none o' the t'other chil'ren. The boys war nowhar. But a-fust it never 'sturbed Tobe. He jest yelled out same ez he useter do at the tothers, 'Shet up, ye pop-eyed buzzard!' Wa'al, sir, the Cunnel jes blinked at him, an' braced herself as stiff, an' yelled! I 'lowed 'twould take off the roof. An' Tobe said he'd wring her neck ef she warn't so mewlin'-lookin' an' peakèd. An' he tuk her up an' walked across the floor with her, an' she shet up; an' he walked back agin, an' she staid shet up. Ef he sot down fur a minit, she yelled so ez ye'd think ye'd be deef fur life, an' ye 'most hoped ye would be. So Tobe war obleeged ter tote her agin ter git shet o' the noise. He got started on that thar 'forced march,' ez he calls it, an' he never could git off'n it. Trot, he must when the

Cunnel pleased. He 'lowed she reminded him o' that thar old Cunnel that he sarved under in the wars. Ef it killed the regiment, he got thar on time. Sence then the Cunnel jes gins Tobe her orders, an' he moseys ter do 'em quick, jes like he war obleeged ter obey. I b'lieve he air, somehows."

"Wa'al, some day," said the disaffected old woman, assuming a port of prophetic wisdom, "Tobe will find a differ. Thar ain't no man so headin' ez don't git treated with perslimness by somebody some time. I knowed a man wunst ez owned fower horses an' cattle-critters quarryspondin', an' he couldn't prove ez he war too old ter be summonsed ter work on the road an' war fined by the overseer 'cordin' ter law. Tobe will git his wheel scotched yit, sure ez ye air born. Somebody besides the Cunnel will skeer up grit enough ter make a stand agin him. I don' know how other men kin sleep o' night, knowin' how he be always darin' folks ter differ with him, an' how brigaty he be. The Bible 'pears ter me ter hev Tobe in special mind when it gits ter mournin' bout'n the stiff-necked ones."

The spirited young mare that the ranger rode strove to assert herself against him now and then, as she went at a break-neck speed along the sandy bridle-path through the woods. How was she to know that the white-wanded young willow by the wayside was not some spiritual manifestation as it suddenly materialized in a broken beam from a rift in the clouds? But as she reared and plunged, she felt his heavy hand and his heavy heel, and so forward again at a steady pace. The forests served to screen the strange light in the sky, and the lonely road was dark, save where the moonbeam was splintered and the mists loitered.

Presently there were cinders flying in the breeze, a smell of smoke pervaded the air, and the ranger forgot to curse the mare when she stumbled.

"I wonder," he muttered, "what them no' count half-livers o' town folks hev hed the insurance ter let ketch afire thar?"

The infirmities of his pronunciation must be duly considered; he was not sufficiently sophisticated to appreciate the necessity of insurance before letting things catch fire.

As he neared the brink of the mountain he saw a dense column of smoke against the sky, and a break in the woods showed the little town—the few log houses, the "gyarden spots" about them, and in the center of the Square a great mass of coals, a flame flickering here and there, two gaunt and tottering chimneys where once the court-house had stood. At some distance—for the heat was still intense—were grouped the slouching, spiritless figures of the mountaineers. On the porches of the houses, plainly visible in the unwonted red glow, were knots of women and children—here and there a brat in the scantiest of raiment ran nimbly in and out. The clouds still borrowed the light from below, and the solemn leafless woods on one side were outlined distinctly against the reflection in the sky. The flare showed, too, the abrupt precipice on the other side, the abysmal gloom of the valley, the austere summit-line of the mountain beyond, and gave the dark mysteries of the night a somber revelation, as in visible blackness it filled the illimitable space.

The little mare was badly blown as the ranger sprang to the ground. He himself was panting with amaze and eagerness.

"The stray-book!" he cried. "Whar's the stray-book?"

One by one the slow group turned, all looking at him with a peering expression as he loomed distorted through the shimmer of the heat above the bed of live coals and the hovering smoke.

"Whar's the stray-book?" he reiterated, imperiously.

"Whar's the court-house, I reckon ye mean ter say," replied the sheriff—a burly mountaineer in brown jeans and high boots on which the spurs jingled; for in his excitement he had put them on as mechanically as his clothes, as if they were an essential part of his attire.

"Naw, I *ain't* meanin' ter say whar's the court-house," said the ranger, coming up close, with the red glow of the fire on his face, and his eyes flashing under the broad brim of his wool hat. He had a threatening aspect, and his elongated shadow, following him and repeating the menace of his attitude, seemed to back him up.

"Ye air sech a triflin', slack-twisted tribe hyar in town, ez ennybody would know ef a spark cotched fire ter suthin' ye'd set an' suck yer paws, an' eye it till it bodaciously burnt up the court-house—sech a dad-burned lazy set o' half-livers ye be! I never axed 'bout'n the court-house. I want ter know whar's that thar stray-book," he concluded, inconsequently.

"Tobe Gryce, ye air fairly demented," exclaimed the register—a chin-whiskered, grizzled old fellow, sitting on a stump and hugging his knee with a desolate, bereaved look—"talkin' 'bout the *stray-book,* an' all the records gone! What will folks do 'bout thar deeds, an' mortgages, an' sech? An' that thar keerful index ez I hed made—ez straight ez a string—all cinders!"

He shook his head, a forlorn masculine Rachel, mourning alike for the party of the first part and the party of the second part, and the vestiges of all that they had agreed together.

"An' ye ter kem mopin' hyar this time o' night arter the *stray-book!*" said the sheriff. "Shucks!" And he turned aside and spat disdainfully on the ground.

"I want that thar stray-book!" cried Gryce, indignantly. "Ain't nobody seen it?" Then realizing the futility of the question, he yielded to a fresh burst of anger, and turned upon the bereaved register. "An' did ye jes set thar an' say, 'Good Mister Fire, don't burn the records; what 'll folks do 'bout thar deeds an' sech?' an' hold them claws o' yourn, an' see the court-house burn up, with that thar stray-book in it?"

Half a dozen men spoke up. "The fire tuk inside, an' the court-house war haffen gone 'fore 'twar seen," said one, in sulky extenuation.

"Leave Tobe be—let him jaw!" said another, cavalierly.

"Tobe 'pears ter be spilin fur a fight," said a third, impersonally, as if to direct the attention of any belligerent in the group to the opportunity.

The register had an expression of slow cunning as he cast a glance up at the overbearing ranger.

"What ailed the stray-book ter bide hyar in the court-house all night, Tobe? Couldn't ye gin it house-room? Thar warn't no special need fur it to be hyar."

Tobe Gryce's face showed that for once he was at a loss. He glowered down at the register and said nothing.

"Ez ter me," resumed that worthy, "by the law o' the land my books war obligated ter be thar." He quoted mournfully, " 'shall at all times be and remain in his office.' "

He gathered up his knee again and subsided into silence.

All the freakish spirits of the air were a-loose in the wind. In fitful gusts they rushed up the gorge, and suddenly the boughs would fall still again, and one could hear the eerie rout a-rioting far off down the valley. Now and then the glow of the fire would deepen, the coals tremble, and with a gleaming fibrous swirl, like a garment of flames, a sudden animation would sweep over it, as if an apparition had passed, leaving a line of flying coals to mark its trail.

"I'm goin' home," drawled Tobe Gryce presently. "I don't keer a frog's toe-nail ef the whole settlement burns bodaciously up; 'tain't nuthin ter me. I hev never hankered ter live in towns an' git tuk up with town ways, an' set an' view the court-house like the apple o' my eye. We-uns don't ketch fire down in the Cove, though mebbe we ain't so peart ez folks ez herd tergether like sheep an' sech."

The footfalls of the little black mare annotated the silence of the place as he rode away into the darkling woods. The groups gradually disappeared from the porches. The few voices that sounded at long intervals were low and drowsy. The red fire smoldered in the center of the place, and sometimes about it appeared so doubtful a shadow that it could hardly argue substance. Far away a dog barked, and then was still.

Presently the great mountains loom aggressively along the horizon. The black abysses, the valleys and coves, show dun-colored verges and grow gradually distinct, and on the slopes the ash and the pine and the oak are all lustrous with a silver rime. The mists are rising, a wind springs up, the clouds set sail, and a beam slants high.

"What I want ter know," said a mountaineer newly arrived on the scene, sitting on the verge of the precipice, and dangling his long legs over the depths beneath, "air how do folks ez live 'way down in Lonesome Cove, an' who nobody knowed nuthin about noways, ever git 'lected ranger o' the county ennyhow. I ain't s'prised none ter hear 'bout Tobe Gryce's goin's-on hyar las' night. I hev looked fur more'n that."

"Wa'al, I'll tell ye," replied the register. "Nuthin but favoritism in the county court. Ranger air 'lected by the jestices. Ye know," he added, vainglorious of his own tenure of office by the acclaiming voice of the sovereign people, "ranger ain't 'lected, like the register, by pop'lar vote."

A slow smoke still wreathed upward from the charred ruins of the court-house. Gossiping groups stood here and there, mostly the jeans-clad mountaineers, but there were a few who wore "store clothes," being lawyers from more sophisticated regions of the circuit. Court had been in session the previous day. The jury, serving 10 in a criminal case—still strictly segregated, and in charge of an officer—were walking about wearily, waiting with what patience they might their formal discharge.

The sheriff's dog, a great yellow cur, 15 trotted in the rear. When the officer was first elected, this animal, observing the change in his master's habits, deduced his own conclusions. He seemed to think the court-house belonged to the sheriff, and 20 thenceforward guarded the door with snaps and growls: being a formidable brute, his idiosyncrasies invested the getting into and getting out of law with abnormal difficulties. Now, as he followed 25 the disconsolate jury, he bore the vigilant mien with which he formerly drove up the cows, and if a juror loitered or stepped aside from the path, the dog made a slow detour as if to round him in, and the melan- 30 choly cortége wandered on as before. More than one looked wistfully at the group on the crag, for it was distinguished by that sprightly interest which scandal excites so readily.

"Ter my way of thinkin'," drawled Sam Peters, swinging his feet over the giddy depths of the valley, "Tobe ain't sech ez oughter be set over the county ez a ranger, noways. 'Pears not ter me, an' I hev been 40 keepin' my eye on him mighty sharp."

A shadow fell among the group, and a man sat down on a boulder hard by. He, too, had just arrived, being lured to the town by the news of the fire. His slide had 45 been left at the verge of the clearing, and one of the oxen had already lain down; the other, although hampered by the yoke thus diagonally displaced, stood meditatively gazing at the distant blue moun- 50 tains. Their master nodded a slow, grave salutation to the group, produced a plug of tobacco, gnawed a fragment from it, and restored it to his pocket. He had a pensive face, with an expression which 55 in a man of wider culture we should discriminate as denoting sensibility. He had long yellow hair that hung down to his

shoulders, and a tangled yellow beard. There was something at once wistful and searching in his gray eyes, dull enough too, at times. He lifted them heavily, and they 5 had a drooping lid and lash. There seemed an odd incongruity between this sensitive weary face and his stalwart physique. He was tall and well proportioned. A leather belt girded his brown jeans coat. The ends 10 of his trousers were stuffed into great cowhide boots. His pose, as he leaned on the rock, had a muscular picturesqueness.

"Who be ye a-talkin' about?" he drawled.

Peters relished his opportunity. He 15 laughed in a distorted fashion, his pipe-stem held between his teeth.

"*You-uns* ain't wantin' ter swop lies 'bout sech ez him, Luke! We war a-talkin' 'bout Tobe Gryce."

The color flared into the new-comer's 20 face. A sudden animation fired his eye.

"Tobe Gryce air jes the man I'm always wantin' ter hear a word about. Jes perceed with yer rat-killin'. I'm with ye." 25 And Luke Todd placed his elbows on his knees and leaned forward with an air of attention.

Peters looked at him, hardly comprehending this ebullition. It was not what 30 he had expected to elicit. No one laughed. His fleer was wide of the mark.

"Wa'al"—he made another effort— "Tobe, we war jes sayin', ain't fitten fur ter be ranger o' the county. He be ez peart 35 in gittin' ter own other folkses' stray cattle ez he war in courtin' other folkses' sweetheart, an', ef the truth mus' be knowed, in marryin' her." He suddenly twisted round, in some danger of falling from his 40 perch. "I want ter ax one o' them thar big-headed lawyers a question on a p'int o' law," he broke off abruptly.

"What be Tobe Gryce a-doin' of now?" asked Luke Todd, with eager interest in 45 the subject.

"Wa'al," resumed Peters, nowise loath to return to the gossip, "Tobe, ye see, air the ranger o' this hyar county, an' by law all the stray horses ez air tuk up by folks 50 hev ter be reported to him, an' appraised by two householders, an' swore to afore the magistrate an' be advertised by the ranger, an' ef they ain't claimed 'fore twelve months, the taker-up kin pay into 55 the county treasury one-haffen the appraisement an' hev the critter fur his'n. An' the owner can't prove it away arter that."

"Thanky," said Luke Todd, dryly. "S'pose ye teach yer gran'mammy ter suck aigs. I knowed all that afore."

Peters was abashed, and with some difficulty collected himself.

"An' I knowed ye knowed it, Luke," he hastily conceded. "But hyar be what I'm a-lookin' at—the law 'ain't got no pervision fur a stray horse ez kem of a dark night, 'thout nobody's percuremint, ter the ranger's own house. Now, the p'int o' law ez I wanted ter ax the lawyers 'bout air this—kin the ranger be the ranger an' the taker-up too?"

He turned his eyes upon the great landscape lying beneath, flooded with the chill matutinal sunshine, and flecked here and there with the elusive shadows of the fleecy drifting clouds. Far away the long horizontal lines of the wooded spurs, converging on either side of the valley and rising one behind the other, wore a subdued azure, all unlike the burning blue of summer, and lay along the calm, passionless sky, that itself was of a dim, repressed tone. On the slopes nearer, the leafless boughs, massed together, had purplish-garnet depths of color wherever the sunshine struck aslant, and showed richly against the faintly tinted horizon. Here and there among the boldly jutting gray crags hung an evergreen vine, and from a gorge on the opposite mountain gleamed a continuous flash, like the waving of a silver plume, where a cataract sprang down the rocks. In the depths of the valley, a field in which crab-grass had grown in the place of the harvested wheat showed a tiny square of palest yellow, and beside it a red clay road, running over a hill, was visible. Above all a hawk was flying.

"Afore the winter fairly set in las' year," Peters resumed, presently, "a stray kem ter Tobe's house. He 'lowed ter me ez he fund her a-standin' by the fodder-stack a-pullin' off'n it. An' he 'quired round, an' he never hearn o' no owner. I reckon he never axed outside o' Lonesome," he added, cynically. He puffed industriously at his pipe for a few moments; then continued: "Wa'al, he 'lowed he couldn't feed the critter fur fun. An' he couldn't work her till she war appraised an' sech, that bein' again the law fur strays. So he jes ondertook ter be ranger an' taker-up too—the bangedest consarn in the kentry! Ef the leetle mare hed been wall-eyed, or lame, or ennything, he wouldn't hev wanted ter be ranger an'

taker-up too. But she air the peartest little beastis—she war jes bridle-wise when she fust kem—young an' spry!"

Luke Todd was about to ask a question, but Peters, disregarding him, persisted:

"Wa'al, Tobe tuk up the beastis, an' I reckon he reported her ter hisself, bein' the ranger—the critter makes me laff—an' he hed that thar old haffen-blind uncle o' his'n an' Perkins Bates, ez be never sober, ter appraise the vally o' the mare, an' I s'pose he delivered thar certificate ter hisself, an' I reckon he tuk oath that she kem 'thout his procuremint ter his place, in the presence o' the ranger."

"I reckon thar ain't no law again the ranger's bein' a ranger an' a taker-up too," put in one of the by-standers. 'Tain't like a sher'ff's buyin' at his own sale. An' he hed ter pay haffen her vally into the treasury o' the county arter twelve months, ef the owner never proved her away."

"Thar ain't no sign he ever paid a cent," said Peters, with a malicious grin, pointing at the charred remains of the court-house, "an' the treasurer air jes dead."

"Wa'al, Tobe hed ter make a report ter the jedge o' the county court every six months."

"The papers of his office air cinders," retorted Peters.

"Wa'al, then," argued the optimist, "the stray-book will show ez she war reported an' sech."

"The ranger took mighty partic'lar pains ter hev his stray-book in that thar court-house when 'twar burnt."

There was a long pause while the party sat ruminating upon the suspicions thus suggested.

Luke Todd heard them, not without a thrill of satisfaction. He found them easy to adopt. And he, too, had a disposition to theorize.

"It takes a mighty mean man ter steal a horse," he said. "Stealin' a horse air powerful close to murder. Folkses' lives fairly depend on a horse ter work that corn an' sech, an' makes a support fur 'em. I hev knowed folks ter kem mighty close ter starvin' through hevin thar horse stole. Why, even that thar leetle filly of our'n, though she hedn't been fairly bruk ter the plow, war mightily missed. We-uns hed ter make out with the old sorrel, ez air nigh fourteen year old, ter work the crap, an' we war powerful disapp'inted. But we ain't never found no trace o' the filly since

she war tolled off one night las' fall a
year ago."

The hawk and its winged shadow disappeared together in the dense glooms of
a deep gorge. Luke Todd watched them as
they vanished.

Suddenly he lifted his eyes. They were
wide with a new speculation. An angry
flare blazed in them. "What sort'n beastis
is this hyar mare ez the ranger tuk up?"
he asked.

Peters looked at him, hardly comprehending his tremor of excitement. "Seems
sorter sizable," he replied, sibilantly, sucking his pipe-stem.

Todd nodded meditatively several times,
leaning his elbows on his knees, his eyes
fixed on the landscape. "Hev she got enny
partic'lar marks, ez ye knows on?" he
drawled.

"Wa'al, she be ez black ez a crow, with
the nigh fore-foot white. An' she hev got
a white star spang in the middle o' her
forehead, an' the left side o' her nozzle is
white too."

Todd rose suddenly to his feet. "By
gum!" he cried, with a burst of passion,
"she air *my* filly! An' 'twar that thar
durned horse-thief of a ranger ez tolled
her off!"

Deep among the wooded spurs Lonesome Cove nestles, sequestered from the
world. Naught emigrates thence except an
importunate stream that forces its way
through a rocky gap, and so to freedom
beyond. No stranger intrudes; only the
moon looks in once in a while. The roaming wind may explore its solitudes; and
it is but the vertical sun that strikes to the
heart of the little basin, because of the
massive mountains that wall it round and
serve to isolate it. So nearly do they meet
at the gap that one great assertive crag,
beetling far above, intercepts the view of
the wide landscape beyond, leaving its sub-
stituted profile jaggedly serrating the
changing sky. Above it, when the weather
is fair, appear vague blue lines, distant
mountain summits, cloud strata, visions.
Below its jutting verge may be caught
glimpses of the widening valley without.
But preëminent, gaunt, somber, it sternly
dominates "Lonesome," and is the salient
feature of the little world it limits.

Tobe Gryce's house, gray, weather-beat-
en, moss-grown, had in comparison an
ephemeral, modern aspect. For a hundred
years its inmates had come and gone and
lived and died. They took no heed of the
crag, but never a sound was lost upon it.
Their drawling iterative speech the iterative echoes conned. The ringing blast of
a horn set astir some phantom chase in
the air. When the cows came lowing home,
there were lowing herds in viewless company. Even if one of the children sat on
a rotting log crooning a vague, fragmentary ditty, some faint-voiced spirit in the
rock would sing. Lonesome Cove?—home
of invisible throngs!

As the ranger trotted down the winding road, the multitudinous hoof-beats, as
of a troop of cavalry, heralded his approach to the little girl who stood on the
porch of the log cabin and watched for
him.

"Hy're, Cunnel!" he cried, cordially.

But the little "Colonel" took no heed.
She looked beyond him at the vague blue
mountains, on which the great grim rock
was heavily imposed, every ledge, every
waving dead crisp weed, distinct.

He noticed the smoke curling briskly
up in the sunshine from the clay and stick
chimney. He strode past her into the house,
as Madeline, with all semblance of youth
faded from her countenance, haggard and
hollow-eyed in the morning light, was hurrying the corn-dodgers and venison steak
on the table.

Perhaps he did not appreciate that the
women were pining with curiosity, for he
vouchsafed no word of the excitements in
the little town; and he himself was ill at
ease.

"What ails the Cunnel, Madeliny?" he
asked presently, glancing up sharply from
under his hat brim, and speaking with his
mouth full.

"The cat 'pears ter hev got her tongue,"
said Madeline, intending the "Colonel"
should hear, and perhaps profit. "She ain't
able ter talk none this mornin'."

The little body cast so frowning a glance
upon them as she stood in the doorway
that her expression was but slightly less
lowering than her father's. It was an incongruous demonstration, with her infantile features, her little yellow head, and
the slight physical force she represented.
She wore a blue cotton frock, fastened up
the back with great horn buttons; she had
on shoes laced with leather strings; one
of her blue woolen stockings fell over
her ankle, disclosing the pinkest of plump

calves; the other stocking was held in place by an unabashed cotton string. She had a light in her dark eyes and a color in her cheeks, and albeit so slight a thing, she wielded a strong coercion.

"Laws-a-massy, Cunnel!" said Tobe, in a harried manner, "couldn't ye find me nowhar? I'm powerful sorry. I couldn't git back hyar no sooner."

But not in this wise was she to be placated. She fixed her eyes upon him, but made no sign.

He suddenly rose from his half-finished breakfast. "Look-a-hyar, Cunnel," he cried, joyously, "don't ye want ter ride the filly? —ye know ye hanker ter ride the filly."

Even then she tried to frown, but the bliss of the prospect overbore her. Her cheek and chin dimpled, and there was a gurgling display of two rows of jagged little teeth as the doughty "Colonel" was swung to his shoulder, and he stepped out of the door.

He laughed as he stood by the glossy black mare, and lifted the child to the saddle. The animal arched her neck and turned her head and gazed back at him curiously. "Hold on tight, Cunnel," he said as he looked up at her, his face strangely softened almost beyond recognition. And she gurgled and laughed and screamed with delight as he began to slowly lead the mare along.

The "Colonel" had the gift of continuance. Some time elapsed before she exhausted the joys of her exaltation. More than once she absolutely refused to dismount. Tobe patiently led the beast up and down, and the "Colonel" rode in state. It was only when the sun had grown high, and occasionally she was fain to lift her chubby hands to her eyes, imperiling her safety on the saddle, that he ventured to seriously remonstrate, and finally she permitted herself to be assisted to the ground. When, with the little girl at his heels, he reached the porch, he took off his hat, and wiped the perspiration from his brow with his great brown hand.

"I tell ye, jouncin' round arter the Cunnel air powerful hot work," he declared.

The next moment he paused. His wife had come to the door, and there was a strange expression of alarm among the anxious lines of her face.

"Tobe," she said, in a bated voice, "who war them men?"

He stared at her, whirled about, surveyed the vacant landscape, and once more turned dumfounded toward her. "What men?" he asked.

"Them men ez acted so cur'ous," she said. "I couldn't see thar faces plain, an' I don't know who they war."

"Whar war they?" And he looked over his shoulder once more.

"Yander along the ledges of the big rock. Thar war two of 'em, hidin' ahint that thar jagged aidge. An' ef yer back war turned they'd peep out at ye an' the Cunnel ridin'. But whenst ye would face round again, they'd drap down ahint the aidge o' the rock. I 'lowed wunst ez I'd holler ter ye, but I war feared ye moughtn't keer ter know." Her voice fell in its deprecatory cadence.

He stood in silent perplexity. "Ye air a fool, Madeliny, an' ye never seen nuthin. Nobody hev got enny call ter spy on me."

He stepped in-doors, took down his rifle from the rack, and went out frowning into the sunlight.

The suggestion of mystery angered him. He had a vague sense of impending danger. As he made his way along the slope toward the great beetling crag, all his faculties were on the alert. He saw naught when he stood upon its dark seamed summit, and he went cautiously to the verge and looked down at the many ledges. They jutted out at irregular intervals, the first only six feet below, and all accessible enough to an expert climber. A bush grew in a niche. An empty nest, riddled by the wind, hung disheveled from a twig. Coarse withered grass tufted the crevices, and lichens clung. Far below he saw the depths of the Cove—the tops of the leafless trees, and glimpsed through the interlacing boughs were piles of rocks, the rush of a mountain rill, and a white flash as a sunbeam slanted on the foam.

He was turning away, all incredulous, when with a sudden start he looked back. On one of the ledges was a slight depression. It was filled with sand and earth. Imprinted upon it was the shape of a man's foot. The ranger paused and gazed fixedly at it. "Wa'al, by the Lord!" he exclaimed, under his breath. Presently, "But they hev no call!" he argued. Then once more, softly, "By the Lord!"

The mystery baffled him. More than once that day he went up to the crag and stood and stared futilely at the foot-print. Conjecture had license and limitations too.

As the hours wore on he became harassed by the sense of espionage. He was a bold man before the foes he knew, but this idea of inimical lurking, of furtive scrutiny for unknown purposes, preyed upon him. He brooded over it as he sat idle by the fire. Once he went to the door and stared speculatively at the great profile of the cliff. The sky above it was all a lustrous amber, for the early sunset of the shortest days of the year was at hand. The mountains, seen partly above and partly below it, wore a glamorous purple. There were clouds, and from their rifts long divergent lines of light slanted down upon the valley, distinct among their shadows. The sun was not visible—only in the western heavens was a half-veiled effulgence too dazzlingly white to be gazed upon. The ranger shaded his eyes with his hand. No motion, no sound; for the first time in his life the unutterable loneliness of the place impressed him.

"Madeliny," he said, suddenly, looking over his shoulder within the cabin, "be you-uns *sure* ez they war—*folks?*"

"I don't know what ye mean," she faltered, her eyes dilated. "They *looked* like folks."

"I reckon they war," he said, re-assuring himself. "The Lord knows I hope they war."

That night the wind rose. The stars all seemed to have burst from their moorings, and were wildly adrift in the sky. There was a broken tumult of billowy clouds, and the moon tossed hopelessly among them, a lunar wreck, sometimes on her beam ends, sometimes half submerged, once more gallantly struggling to the surface, and again sunk. The bare boughs of the trees beat together in a dirge-like monotone. Now and again a leaf went sibilantly whistling past. The wild commotion of the heavens and earth was visible, for the night was not dark. The ranger, standing within the rude stable of unhewn logs, all undaubed, noted how pale were the horizontal bars of gray light alternating with the black logs of the wall. He was giving the mare a feed of corn, but he had not brought his lantern as was his custom. That mysterious espionage had in some sort shaken his courage, and he felt the obscurity a shield. He had brought instead his rifle.

The equine form was barely visible among the glooms. Now and then, as the mare noisily munched, she lifted a hoof and struck it upon the ground with a dull thud. How the gusts outside were swirling up the gorge! The pines swayed and sighed. Again the boughs of the chestnut-oak above the roof crashed together. Did a fitful blast stir the door?

He lifted his eyes mechanically. A cold thrill ran through every fiber. For there, close by the door, somebody—something—was peering through the space between the logs and the wall. The face was invisible but the shape of a man's head was distinctly defined. He realized that it was no supernatural manifestation when a husky voice began to call the mare, in a hoarse whisper, "Cobe! Cobe! Cobe!" With a galvanic start he was about to spring forward to hold the door. A hand was laid upon it.

He placed the muzzle of the rifle between the logs, a jet of red light was suddenly projected into the darkness, the mare was rearing and plunging violently, the little shanty was surcharged with roar and reverberation, and far and wide the crags and chasms echoed the report of the rifle.

There was a vague clamor outside, an oath, a cry of pain. Hasty footfalls sounded among the dead leaves, and died in the distance.

When the ranger ventured out he saw the door of his house wide open, and the fire-light flickering out among the leafless bushes. His wife met him half-way down the hill.

"Air ye hurt, Tobe?" she cried. "Did yer gun go off suddint?"

"Mighty suddint," he replied, savagely.

"Ye didn't fire it a-purpose?" she faltered.

"Edzactly so," he declared.

"Ye never hurt nobody, did ye, Tobe?" She had turned very pale. "I 'lowed it couldn't be the wind ez I hearn a-hollerin'."

"I hopes an' prays I hurt 'em," he said, as he replaced the rifle in the rack. He was shaking the other hand, which had been jarred in some way by the hasty discharge of the weapon. "Some dad-burned horse-thief war arter the mare. Jedgin' from the sound o' thar runnin', 'peared like to me ez thar mought be two o' 'em."

The next day the mare disappeared from the stable. Yet she could not be far off, for Tobe was about the house most of the time, and when he and the "Colonel" came in-doors in the evening the little girl held in her hand a half-munched ear of corn, evidently abstracted from the mare's supper.

"Whar be the filly hid, Tobe?" Madeline asked, curiosity overpowering her.

"Ax me no questions an' I'll tell ye no lies," he replied, gruffly.

In the morning there was a fall of snow, and she had some doubt whether her mother, who had gone several days before to a neighbor's on the summit of the range, would return; but presently the creak of unoiled axles heralded the approach of a wagon, and soon the old woman, bundled in shawls, was sitting by the fire. She wore heavy woolen socks over her shoes as protection against the snow. The incompatibility of the shape of the hose with the human foot was rather marked, and as they were somewhat inelastic as well, there was a muscular struggle to get them off only exceeded by the effort which had been required to get them on. She shook her head again and again, with a red face, as she bent over the socks, but plainly more than this discomfort vexed her.

"Laws-a-massy, Madeliny! I hearn a awful tale over yander 'mongst them Jenkins folks. Ye oughter hev married Luke Todd, an' so I tole ye an' fairly beset ye ter do ten year ago. *He* keered fur ye. An' Tobe—shucks! Wa'al, laws-as-massy, child! I hearn a awful tale 'bout Tobe up yander at Jenkinses'."

Madeline colored.

"Folks hed better take keer how they talk 'bout Tobe," she said, with a touch of pride. "They be powerful keerful ter do it out'n rifle range."

With one more mighty tug the sock came off, the red face was lifted, and Mrs. Pearce shook her head ruefully.

"The Bible say 'words air foolishness.' Ye don't know what ye air talkin' 'bout, child."

With this melancholy preamble she detailed the gossip that had arisen at the county town and pervaded the country-side. Madeline commented, denied, flashed into rage, then lapsed into silence. Although it did not constrain credulity, there was something that made her afraid when her mother said:

"Ye hed better not be talkin' 'bout rifle range so brash, Madeliny, nohows. They 'lowed ez Luke Todd an' Sam Peters kem

hyar—'twar jes night before las'—aimin' ter take the mare away 'thout no words an' no lawin', 'kase they didn't want ter wait. Luke hed got a chance ter view the mare, an' knowed ez she war his'n. An' Tobe war hid in the dark beside the mare, an' fired at 'em, an' the rifle-ball tuk Sam right through the beam o' his arm. I reckon, though, ez that warn't true, else ye would hev knowed it."

She looked up anxiously over her spectacles at her daughter.

"I hearn Tobe shoot," faltered Madeline. "I seen blood on the leaves."

"Laws-a-massy!" exclaimed the old woman, irritably. "I be fairly feared ter bide hyar; 'twouldn't s'prise me none ef they kem hyar an' hauled Tobe out an' lynched him an' sech, an' who knows who mought git hurt in the scrimmage?"

They both fell silent as the ranger strode in. They would need a braver heart than either bore to reveal to him the suspicions of horse-stealing sown broadcast over the mountain. Madeline felt that this in itself was coercive evidence of his innocence. Who dared so much as say a word to his face?

The weight of the secret asserted itself, however. As she went about her accustomed tasks, all bereft of their wonted interest, vapid and burdensome, she carried so woe-begone a face that it caught his attention, and he demanded, angrily, "What ails ye ter look so durned peaked?"

This did not abide long in his memory, however, and it cost her a pang to see him so unconscious.

She went out upon the porch late that afternoon to judge of the weather. Snow was falling again. The distant summits had disappeared. The mountains near at hand loomed through the myriads of serried white flakes. A crow flew across the Cove in its midst. It heavily thatched the cabin, and tufts dislodged by the opening of the door fell down upon her hair. Drifts lay about the porch. Each rail of the fence was laden. The ground, the rocks, were deeply covered. She reflected with satisfaction that the red splotch of blood on the dead leaves was no longer visible. Then a sudden idea struck her that took her breath away. She came in, her cheeks flushed, her eyes bright with an excited dubitation.

Her husband commented on the change.

"Ye air a powerful cur'ous critter, Made-liny," he said: "a while ago ye looked some fower or five hundred year old— now ye favors yerself when I fust kem a-courtin' round the settlement."

She hardly knew whether the dull stir in her heart were pleasure or pain. Her eyes filled with tears, and the irradiated iris shone through them with a liquid luster. She could not speak.

Her mother took ephemeral advantage of his softening mood. "Ye useter be mighty perlite and saaft-spoken in them days, Tobe," she ventured.

"I hed ter be," he admitted, frankly, " 'kase thar war sech a many o' them mealy-mouthed cusses a-waitin' on Made-liny. The kentry 'peared ter me ter bristle with Luke Todd; he 'minded me o' brum saidge—*everywhar* ye seen his yaller head, ez homely an' ez onwel-come."

"I never wunst gin Luke a thought arter ye tuk ter comin' round the settlement," Madeline said, softly.

"I wisht I hed knowed that then," he replied; "else I wouldn't hev been so all-fired oneasy an' beset. I wasted mo' time a-studyin' 'bout ye an' Luke Todd 'n ye war both wuth, an' went 'thout my vittles an' sot up a nights. Ef I hed spent that time a-moanin' fur my sins an' settin' my soul at peace, I'd be 'quirin' roun' the throne o' Grace now! Young folks air powerful fursaken fools."

Somehow her heart was warmer for this allusion. She was more hopeful. Her resolve grew stronger and stronger as she sat and knitted, and looked at the fire and saw among the coals all her old life at the settlement newly aglow. She was remembering now that Luke Todd had been as wax in her hands. She recalled that when she was married there was a gleeful "sayin'" going the rounds of the mountain that he had taken to the woods with grief, and he was heard of no more for days. The gossips relished his despair as the corollary of the happy bridal. He had had no reproaches for her. He had only looked the other way when they met, and she had not spoken to him since.

"He set store by my word in them days," she said, her lips vaguely moving. "I mis-doubts ef he hev furgot."

All through the long hours of the winter night she silently canvassed her plan. The house was still noiseless and dark when she softly opened the door and softly closed it behind her.

It had ceased to snow and the sky had cleared. The trees, all the limbs whitened, were drawn distinctly upon it, and through the boughs overhead a brilliant star, aloof and splendid, looked coldly down. Along the chill east Orion had drawn his glittering blade. Above the snowy mountains a melancholy waning moon was swinging. The valley was full of mist, white and shining where the light fell upon it, a vaporous purple where the shadows held sway. So still it was! the only motion in all the world the throbbing stars and her palpitating heart. So solemnly silent! It was a relief, as she trudged on and on, to note a gradual change; to watch the sky withdraw, seeming fainter; to see the moon grow filmy, like some figment of the frost; to mark the gray mist steal on apace, swathe mountain, valley, and heaven with mystic folds, shut out all vision of things familiar. Through it only the sense of dawn could creep.

She recognized the locality; her breath was short; her step quickened. She appeared, like an apparition out of the mists, close to a fence, and peered through the snow-laden rails. A sudden pang pierced her heart.

For there, milking the cow, she saw, all blooming in the snow—herself; the azalea-like girl she had been!

She had not known how dear to her was that bright young identity she remembered. She had not realized how far it had gone from her. She felt a forlorn change-ling looking upon her own estranged estate.

A faint cry escaped her.

The cow, with lifted head and a mut-tered low of surprise, moved out of reach of the milker, who, half kneeling upon the ground, stared with wide blue eyes at her ghost in the mist.

There was a pause. It was a moment before Madeline spoke; it seemed years, so charged it was with retrospect.

"I kem over hyar ter hev a word with ye," she said.

At the sound of a human voice Luke Todd's wife struggled to her feet. She held the piggin with one arm encircled about it, and with the other hand she clutched the plaid shawl around her throat.

Her bright hair was tossed by the rising wind.

"I 'lowed I'd find ye hyar a-milkin' 'bout now."

The homely allusion reassured the younger woman.

"I hev ter begin toler'ble early," she said. "Spot gins 'bout a gallon a milkin' now."

Spot's calf, which subsisted on what was left over, seemed to find it cruel that delay should be added to hls hardships, and he lifted up his voice in a plaintive remonstrance. This reminded Mrs. Todd of his existence; she turned and let down the bars that served to exclude him.

The stranger was staring at her very hard. Somehow she quailed under that look. Though it was fixed upon her in unvarying intensity, it had a strange impersonality. This woman was not seeing her, despite that wide, wistful, yearning gaze; she was thinking of something else, seeing some one else.

And suddenly Luke Todd's wife began to stare at the visitor very hard, and to think of something that was not before her.

"I be the ranger's wife," said Madeline. "I kem over hyar ter tell ye he never tuk yer black mare nowise but honest, bein' the ranger."

She found it difficult to say more. Under that speculative, unseeing look she too faltered.

"They tell me ez Luke Todd air powerful outed 'bout'n it. An' I 'lowed ef he knowed from me ez 'twar tuk fair, he'd b'lieve me."

She hesitated. Her courage was flagging; her hope had fled. The eyes of the man's wife burned upon her face.

"We-uns useter be toler'ble well 'quainted 'fore he ever seen ye, an' I 'lowed he'd b'lieve my word," Madeline continued.

Another silence. The sun was rising; long liquescent lines of light of purest amber-color were streaming through the snowy woods; the shadows of the fence rails alternated with bars of dazzling glister; elusive prismatic gleams of rose and lilac and blue shimmered on every slope—thus the winter flowered. Tiny snowbirds were hopping about; a great dog came down from the little snow-thatched cabin, and was stretching himself elastically and yawning most portentously.

"An' I 'lowed I'd see ye an' git you-uns ter tell him that word from me, an' then he'd b'lieve it," said Madeline.

The younger woman nodded mechanically, still gazing at her.

And was this her mission! Somehow it had lost its urgency. Where was its potency, her enthusiasm? Madeline realized that her feet were wet, her skirts draggled; that she was chilled to the bone and trembling violently. She looked about her doubtfully. Then her eyes came back to the face of the woman before her.

"Ye'll tell him, I s'pose?"

Once more Luke Todd's wife nodded mechanically, still staring.

There was nothing further to be said. A vacant interval ensued. Then, "I 'lowed I'd tell ye," Madeline reiterated, vaguely, and turned away, vanishing with the vanishing mists.

Luke Todd's wife stood gazing at the fence through which the apparition had peered. She could see yet her own face, grown old and worn. The dog wagged his tail and pressed against her, looking up and claiming her notice. Once more he stretched himself elastically and yawned widely, with shrill variations of tone. The calf was frisking about in awkward bovine elation, and now and then the cow affectionately licked its coat with the air of making its toilet. An assertive chanticleer was proclaiming the dawn within the hen-house, whence came a clamor of sounds, for the door, which served to exclude any marauding fox, was closed upon the imprisoned poultry. Still she looked steadily at the fence where the ranger's wife had stood.

"That thar woman favors me," she said presently. And suddenly she burst into tears.

Perhaps it was well that Madeline could not see Luke Todd's expression as his wife recounted the scene. She gave it truly, but without, alas! the glamour of sympathy.

"She 'lowed ez ye'd b'lieve her, bein' ez ye useter be 'quainted."

His face flushed. "Wa'al, sir! the insurance o' that thar woman!" he exclaimed. "I war 'quainted with her; I war mighty well 'quainted with her." He had a casual remembrance of those days when "he tuk ter the woods ter wear out his grief." "She never gin me no promise, but me an' her kep' company some. Sech dependence ez I put on her war mightily wasted. I dunno what ails the critter ter 'low ez I set store by her word."

Poor Madeline! There is nothing so dead as ashes. His flame had clean burned out. So far afield were all this thoughts that he stood amazed when his wife, with a sudden burst of tears, declared passionately that she knew it—she saw it—she favored Madeline Gryce. She had found out that he had married her because she looked like another woman.

"Madeliny Gryce hev got powerful little ter do ter kem a-jouncin' through the snow over hyar ter try ter set ye an' me agin one another," he exclaimed, angrily. "Stealin' the filly ain't enough ter sati'fy her!"

His wife was in some sort mollified. She sought to reassure herself.

"Air we-uns of a favor?"

"I dunno," he replied, sulkily. "I 'ain't seen the critter fur nigh on ter ten year. I hev furgot the looks of her. 'Pears like ter me," he went on, ruminating, "ez 'twar in my mind when I fust seen ye ez thar war a favor 'twixt ye. But I misdoubts now. Do she 'low ez I hev hed nuthin ter study 'bout sence?"

Perhaps Madeline is not the only woman who overrates the strength of a sentimental attachment. A gloomy intuition of failure kept her company all the lengthening way home. The chill splendors of the wintry day grated upon her dreary mood. How should she care for the depth and richness of blue deepening toward the zenith in those vast skies? What was it to her that the dead vines, climbing the grim rugged crags, were laden with tufts and corollated shapes wherever these fantasies of flowers might cling, or that the snow flashed with crystalline scintillations? She only knew that they glimmered and dazzled upon the tears in her eyes, and she was moved to shed them afresh. She did not wonder whether her venture had resulted amiss. She only wondered that she had tried aught. And she was humbled.

When she reached Lonesome Cove she found the piggin where she had hid it, and milked the cow in haste. It was no great task, for the animal was going dry. "Their'n gins a gallon a milkin'," she said, in rueful comparison.

As she came up the slope with the piggin on her head, her husband was looking down from the porch with a lowering brow. "Why n't ye spen' the day a-milkin' the

cow?" he drawled. "Dawdlin' yander in the cow-pen till this time in the mornin'! An' ter-morrer's Chrismus!"

The word smote upon her weary heart with a dull pain. She had no cultured phrase to characterize the sensation as a presentiment, but she was conscious of the prophetic process. To-night "all the mounting" would be riotous with that dubious hilarity known as "Chrismus in the bones," and there was no telling what might come from the combined orgy and an inflamed public spirit.

She remembered the familiar doom of the mountain horse-thief, the men lurking on the cliff, the inimical feeling against the ranger. She furtively watched him with forebodings as he came and went at intervals throughout the day.

Dusk had fallen when he suddenly looked in and beckoned to the "Colonel," who required him to take her with him whenever he fed the mare.

"Let me tie this hyar comforter over the Cunnel's head," Madeline said, as he bundled the child in a shawl and lifted her in his arms.

"'Tain't no use," he declared. "The Cunnel ain't travelin' fur."

She heard him step from the creaking porch. She heard the dreary wind without.

Within, the clumsy shadows of the warping-bars, the spinning-wheel, and the churn were dancing in the fire-light on the wall. The supper was cooking on the live coals. The children, popping corn in the ashes, were laughing; as her eye fell upon the "Colonel's" vacant little chair her mind returned to the child's excursion with her father, and again she wondered futilely where the mare could be hid. The next moment she was heartily glad that she did not know.

It was like the fulfilment of some dreadful dream when the door opened. A man entered softly, slowly; the flickering fire showed his shadow—was it?—nay, another man, and still another, and another.

The old crone in the corner sprang up, screaming in a shrill, tremulous, cracked voice. For they were masked. Over the face of each dangled a bit of homespun, with great empty sockets through which eyes vaguely glanced. Even the coarse fiber of the intruders responded to that quavering, thrilling appeal. One spoke instantly:

"Laws-a-massy! Mis' Pearce, don't ye

feel interrupted none—nor Mis' Gryce nuther. We-uns ain't harmful nowadays —jes want ter know whar that thar black mare hev disappeared to. She ain't in the stable."

He turned his great eye-sockets on Madeline. The plaid homespun mask dangling about his face was grotesquely incongruous with his intent, serious gaze.

"I don' know," she faltered; "I don' know."

She had caught at the spinning-wheel for support. The fire crackled. The baby was counting aloud the grains of corn popping from the ashes. "Six, two, free," he babbled. The kettle merrily sang.

The man still stared silently at the ranger's wife. The expression in his eyes changed suddenly. He chuckled derisively. The others echoed his mocking mirth. "Ha! ha! ha!" they laughed aloud; and the eye-sockets in the homespun masks all glared significantly at each other. Even the dog detected something sinister in this laughter. He had been sniffing about the heels of the strangers; he bristled, showed his teeth, and growled. The spokesman hastily kicked him in the ribs, and the animal fled yelping to the further side of the fire-place behind the baby, where he stood and barked defiance. The rafters rang with the sound.

Some one on the porch without spoke to the leader in a low voice. This man, who seemed to have a desire to conceal his identity which could not be served by a mask, held the door with one hand that the wind might not blow it wide open. The draught fanned the fire. Once the great bowing, waving white blaze sent a long, quivering line of light through the narrow aperture, and Madeline saw the dark lurking figure. He had one arm in a sling. She needed no confirmation to assure her that this was Sam Peters, whom her husband had shot at the stable door.

The leader instantly accepted his suggestion. "Wa'al, Mis' Gryce, I reckon ye don't know whar Tobe be, nuther?"

"Naw, I don' know," she said, in a tremor.

The homespun fragment swayed with the distortions of his face as he sneered: "Ye mean ter say ye don't 'low ter tell us."

"I don' know whar he be." Her voice had sunk to a whisper.

Another exchange of glances.

"Wa'al, ma'am, jes gin us the favor of a light by yer fire, an' we-uns'll find him."

He stepped swiftly forward, thrust a pine torch into the coals, and with it all whitely flaring ran out into the night; the others followed his example; and the terror-stricken women, hastily barring up the door, peered after them through the little batten shutter of the window.

The torches were already scattered about the slopes of the Lonesome Cove like a fallen constellation. What shafts of white light they cast upon the snow in the midst of the dense blackness of the night! Somehow they seemed endowed with volition, for their brilliancy almost canceled the figures of the men that bore them—only an occasional erratic shapeless shadow was visible. Now and then a flare pierced the icicle-tipped holly bushes, and again there was a fibrous glimmer in the fringed pines.

The search was terribly silent. The snow deadened the tread. Only the wind was loud among the muffled trees, and sometimes a dull thud sounded when the weight of snow fell from the evergreen laurel as the men thrashed through the foliage. They separated after a time, and here and there an isolated stellular light illuminated the snow, and conjured white mystic circles into the wide spaces of the darkness. The effort flagged at last, and its futility only sharpened the sense of injury in Luke Todd's heart.

He was alone now, close upon the great rock, and looking at its jagged ledges all cloaked with snow. Above those soft white outlines drawn against the deep clear sky the frosty stars scintillated. Beneath were the abysmal depths of the valley masked by the darkness.

His pride was touched. In the old quarrel his revenge had been hampered, for it was the girl's privilege to choose, and she had chosen. He cared nothing for that now, but he felt it indeed a reproach to tamely let this man take his horse when he had all the mountain at his back. There was a sharp humiliation in his position. He felt the pressure of public opinion.

"Dad burn him!" he exclaimed. "Ef I kin make out ter git a glimpse o' him, I'll shoot him dead—dead!"

He leaned the rifle against the rock. It struck upon a stone. A metallic vibration rang out. Again and again the sound was repeated—now loud, still clanging; now faint, but clear; now soft and away to a doubtful murmur which he hardly was sure that he heard. Never before had he known such an echo. And suddenly he recollected that this was the great "Talking Rock," famed beyond the limits of Lonesome. It had traditions as well as echoes. He remembered vaguely that beneath this cliff there was said to be a cave which was utilized in the manufacture of saltpeter for gunpowder in the war of 1812.

As he looked down the slope below he thought the snow seemed broken—by footprints, was it? With the expectation of a discovery strong upon him, he crept along a wide ledge of the crag, now and then stumbling and sending an avalanche of snow and ice and stones thundering to the foot of the cliff. He missed his way more than once. Then he would turn about, laboriously retracing his steps, and try another level of the ledges. Suddenly before him was the dark opening he sought. No creature had lately been here. It was filled with growing bushes and dead leaves and brambles. Looking again down upon the slope beneath, he felt very sure that he saw foot-prints.

"The old folks useter 'low ez thar war two openings ter this hyar cave," he said. "Tobe Gryce mought hev hid hyar through a opening down yander on the slope. But *I'll* go the way ez I hev hearn tell on, an' peek in, an' ef I kin git a glimpse o' him, I'll make him tell me whar that thar filly air, or I'll let daylight through him, sure!"

He paused only to bend aside the brambles, then he crept in and took his way along a low, narrow passage. It had many windings, but was without intersections or intricacy. He heard his own steps echoed like a pursuing footfall. His labored breathing returned in sighs from the inanimate rocks. It was an uncanny place, with strange, sepulchral, solemn effects. He shivered with the cold. A draught stole in from some secret crevice known only to the wild mountain winds. The torch flared, crouched before the gust, flared again, then darkness. He hesitated, took one step forward, and suddenly—a miracle!

A soft aureola with gleaming radiations, a low, shadowy chamber, a beast feeding from a manger, and within it a child's golden head.

His heart gave a great throb. Somehow he was smitten to his knees. Christmas Eve! He remembered the day with a rush of emotion. He stared again at the vouchsafed vision. He rubbed his eyes. It had changed.

Only hallucination caused by an abrupt transition from darkness to light; only the most mundane facts of the old troughs and ash-hoppers, relics of the industry that had served the hideous carnage of battle; only the yellow head of the ranger's brat, who had climbed into one of them, from which the mare was calmly munching her corn.

Yet this was Christmas Eve. And the Child did lie in a manger.

Perhaps it was well for him that his ignorant faith could accept the illusion as a vision charged with all the benignities of peace on earth, good-will toward men. With a keen thrill in his heart, on his knees he drew the charge from his rifle, and flung it down a rift in the rocks. "Christmas Eve," he murmured. He leaned his empty weapon against the wall, and strode out to the little girl who was perched up on the trough.

"Chrismus gift, Cunnel!" he cried, cheerily. "Ter-morrer's Chrismus."

The echoes caught the word. In vibratory jubilance they repeated it. "Chrismus!" rang from the roof, scintillating with calc-spar; "Chrismus!" sounded from the colonnade of stalactites that hung down to meet the uprising stalagmites; "Chrismus!" repeated the walls incrusted with roses that, shut in from the light and the fresh air of heaven, bloomed forever in the stone. Was ever chorus so sweet as this?

It reached Tobe Gryce, who stood at his improvised corn bin. With a bundle of fodder still in his arms he stepped forward. There beside the little Colonel and the black mare he beheld a man seated upon an inverted half-bushel measure, peacefully lighting his pipe with a bunch of straws which he kindled at the lantern on the ash-hopper.

The ranger's black eyes were wide with wonder at this intrusion, and angrily flashed. He connected it at once with the attack on the stable. The hair on his low forehead rose bristlingly as he frowned. Yet he realized with a quaking heart that he was helpless. He, although the crack shot of the county, would not have fired while the Colonel was within two yards of his mark, for the State of Tennessee.

He stood his ground with stolid courage —a target.

Then, with a start of surprise, he perceived that the intruder was unarmed. Twenty feet away his rifle stood against the wall.

Tobe Gryce was strangely shaken. He experienced a sudden revolt of credulity. This was surely a dream.

"Ain't that thar Luke Todd? Why air e a-waitin' thar?" he called out in a husky undertone.

Todd glanced up, and took his pipe from his mouth; it was now fairly alight.

"Kase it be Chrismus Eve, Tobe," he said, gravely.

The ranger stared for a moment; then came forward and gave the fodder to the mare, pausing now and then and looking with oblique distrust down upon Luke as he smoked his pipe.

"I want ter tell ye, Tobe, ez some o' the mounting boys air a-sarchin fur ye outside."

"Who air they?" asked the ranger, calmly.

His tone was so natural, his manner so unsuspecting, that a new doubt began to stir in Luke Todd's mind.

"What ails ye ter keep the mare down yar, Tobe?" he asked, suddenly. " 'Pears like ter me ez that be powerful comical."

"Kase," said Tobe, reasonably, "some durned horse-thieves kem arter her one night. I fired at 'em. I hain't hearn on em sence. An' so I jes hid the mare."

Todd was puzzled. He shifted his pipe in his mouth. Finally he said: "Some folks lowed ez ye hed no right ter take up that mare, bein' ez ye war the ranger."

Tobe Gryce whirled round abruptly. "What war I a-goin' ter do, then? Feed he critter fur nuthin till the triflin' scamp ez owned her kem arter her? I couldn't vork her 'thout takin' her up an' hevin her appraised. Thar's a law agin sech. An' I couldn't git somebody ter toll her off an' ake her up. That ain't fair. What ought I er hev done?"

"Wa'al," said Luke, drifting into argument, "the town-folks 'low ez ye hev got nuthin ter prove it by, the stray-book an' ecords bein' burnt. The town-folks 'low ez ye can't prove by writin' an' sech ez ye ever tried ter find the owner."

"The town-folks air fairly sodden in foolishness," exclaimed the ranger, indignantly.

He drew from his ample pockets a roll of ragged newspapers, and pointed with his great thumb at a paragraph. And Luke Todd read by the light of the lantern the advertisement and description of the estray printed according to law in the nearest newspaper.

The newspaper was so infrequent a factor in the lives of the mountain gossips that this refutation of their theory had never occurred to them.

The sheet was trembling in Luke Todd's hand; his eyes filled; the cavern with its black distances, its walls close at hand sparkling with delicate points of whitest light; the yellow flare of the lantern; the grotesque shadows on the ground; the fair little girl with her golden hair; the sleek black mare; the burly figure of the ranger—all the scene swayed before him. He remembered the gracious vision that had saluted him; he shuddered at the crime from which he was rescued. Pity him because he knew naught of the science of optics; of the bewildering effects of a sudden burst of light upon the delicate mechanism of the eye; of the vagaries of illusion.

"Tobe," he said, in a solemn voice—all the echoes were bated to awed whispers —"I hev been gin ter view a vision this night, bein' 'twar Chrismus Eve. An' now I want ter shake hands on it fur peace."

Then he told the whole story, regardless of the ranger's demonstration, albeit they were sometimes violent enough. Tobe sprang up with a snort of rage, his eyes flashing, his thick tongue stumbling with the curses crowding upon it, when he realized the suspicions rife against him at the county town. But he stood with his clinched hand slowly relaxing, and with the vague expression which one wears who looks into the past, as he listened to the recital of Madeline's pilgrimage in the snowy wintry dawn. "Mighty few folks hev got a wife ez set store by 'em like that," Luke remarked, impersonally.

The ranger's rejoinder seemed irrelevant.

"Madeliny be a-goin' ter see a powerful differ arter this," he said, and fell to musing.

Snow, fatigue, and futility destroyed the ardor of the lynching party after a time, and they dispersed to their homes. Little was said of this expedition afterward, and it became quite impossible to find a man who would admit having joined it. For

the story went the rounds of the mountain that there had been a mistake as to
unfair dealing on the part of the ranger,
and Luke Todd was quite content to accept
from the county treasury half the sum of
the mare's appraisement—with the deduc-
tion of the stipulated per cent, which Tobe
Gryce had paid, the receipt for which he
produced.

The gossips complained, however, that
after all this was settled according to law,
Tobe wouldn't keep the mare, and insisted
that Luke should return to him the money
he had paid into the treasury, half her
value, "bein' so brigaty he wouldn't own
Luke Todd's beast. An' Luke agreed ter
so do; but he didn't wanter be outdone, so
fur the keep o' the filly he gin the Cunnel

a heifer. An' Tobe war mighty nigh tickled
ter death fur the Cunnel ter hev a cow
o' her own."

And now when December skies darken
above Lonesome Cove, and the snow in
dizzying whirls sifts softly down, and the
gaunt brown leafless heights are clothed
with white as with a garment, and the
wind whistles and shouts shrilly, and above
the great crag loom the distant mountains,
and below are glimpsed the long stretches
of the valley, the two men remember the
vision that illumined the cavernous solitudes that night, and bless the gracious
power that sent salvation 'way down to
Lonesome Cove, and cherish peace and
good-will for the sake of a little Child
that lay in the manger.

XXVI

THOMAS NELSON PAGE (1853-1922)

What Miss Jewett did for her native New England area Thomas Nelson Page did for his Virginia. A member of the most exclusive Southern aristocracy, old enough at the time of the war to have seen and understood the plantation life in its prime, and yet young enough at the close of the struggle to accept defeat without bitterness and to become an active part of the new reconstructed republic, he was peculiarly well fitted to present in fiction the old régime which had perished. Law had become at length his profession and he was practising it with success in the North before he had thought seriously of literary work. Influenced by the work of Irwin Russell, he had made a few dialect poems which at length in conjunction with Armisted Gordon he had issued as a volume with the title *Befo' de War*. Then to *The Century Magazine* he had submitted a war tale, "Marse Chan," representing it as the pathetic story told by a faithful old body servant. The magazine hesitated. Strong as the story undoubtedly was and popular as was dialect fiction at the time, it seemed hazardous to issue a story told *wholly* in the uncouth language of the negro. They held it for months, finally issuing it, however, in 1884. Success was instant. Other stories in the same manner followed and finally in 1887 these were issued in a collection entitled *In Ole Virginia*, a book that has taken its place alongside *The Luck of Roaring Camp, Old Creole Days, In the Tennessee Mountains*, and a few others as undoubted classics in their field.

Never again did Page reach the level of these earlier tales, but these, few as they are, are enough to establish his fame. Like Miss Jewett, he threw a glamour of romance over his seemingly genuine characters and seemingly realistic details: like her he is more romanticist than realist. It is only on returning to his beautiful narratives that one begins to perceive their artificiality. Only a negro with an art equal to Page's own could tell such finished stories as "Marse Chan" and "Unc' Edinburg." Moreover, one feels at last that the author is giving a glorified view of his South, romance not reality, golden-tinted memories of a long-ago-destroyed old régime. As one reads story after story, one is forced to the conclusion that the chivalry of the South and its young manhood was of superman texture and that almost to a man these young Bayards and Sydneys perished in the war.

The stories, however, are exquisitely told and they are becoming a part of the great American legend: tales of the enchanted "befo'-de-war" South and the old régime forever vanished now, legends to place beside the vanished California of Bret Harte, the vanished old times on the Mississippi of Mark Twain, the vanished Oregon trail of Parkman, the vanished golden West of the desperado and cow-boy of Owen Wister.

"UNC' EDINBURG'S DROWNIN'"

A PLANTATION ECHO

"Well, suh, dat's a fac—dat's what Marse George al'ays said. 'Tis hard to spile Christmas anyways."

The speaker was "Unc' Edinburg," the driver from Werrowcoke, where I was going to spend Christmas; the time was Christmas Eve, and the place the muddiest road in eastern Virginia—a measure which, I feel sure, will to those who have any experience establish its claim to distinction.

A half-hour before, he had met me at the station, the queerest-looking, raggedest old darky conceivable, brandishing a cedar-staffed whip of enormous proportions in one hand, and clutching a calico letter-bag with a twisted string in the other; and with the exception of a brief interval of temporary suspicion on his part, due to the unfortunate fact that my luggage consisted of only a hand-satchel instead of a trunk, we had been steadily progressing in mutual esteem.

"Dee's a boy standin' by my mules; I got de ker-idge heah for you," had been his first remark on my making myself known to him. "Mistis say as how you might bring a trunk."

303

I at once saw my danger, and muttered something about "a short visit," but this only made matters worse.

"Dee don' nobody nuver pay short visits dyah," he said, decisively, and I fell to other tactics.

"You couldn' spile Christmas den noways," he repeated, reflectingly, while his little mules trudged knee-deep through the mud. "Twuz Christmas den, sho' 'nough," he added, the fires of memory smoldering, and then, as they blazed into sudden flame, he asserted, positively: "Dese heah free-issue niggers don' know what Christmas is. Hog meat an' pop crackers don' meck Christmas. Hit tecks ole times to meck a sho-'nough, tyahin'-down Christmas. Gord! I's seen 'em! But de wuss Christmas I ever seen tunned out de best in de een," he added, with sudden warmth, "an' dat wuz de Christmas me an' Marse George an' Reveller all got drownded down at Braxton's Creek. You's hearn 'bout dat?"

As he was sitting beside me in solid flesh and blood, and looked as little ethereal in his old hat and patched clothes as an old oak stump would have done, and as Colonel Staunton had made a world-wide reputation when he led his regiment through the Chickahominy thickets against McClellan's intrenchments, I was forced to confess that I had never been so favored, but would like to hear about it now; and with a hitch of the lap blanket under his outside knee, and a supererogatory jerk of the reins, he began:

"Well, you know, Marse George was jes eighteen when he went to college. I went wid him, 'cause me an' him wuz de same age; I was born like on a Sat'day in de Christmas, an' he wuz born in de new year on a Chuesday, an' my mammy nussed us bofe at one breast. Dat's de reason maybe huccome we took so to one nurr. He sutney set a heap o' sto' by me; an' I 'ain' nuver see nobody yit wuz good to me as Marse George."

The old fellow, after a short reverie, went on:

"Well, we growed up togerr, jes as to say two stalks in one hill. We cotch ole hyahs togerr, an' we hunted 'possums togerr, an' 'coons. Lord! he wuz a climber! I 'member a fight he had one night up in de ve'y top of a big poplar-tree wid a 'coon, whar he done gone up after, an' he flung he hat over he head; an' do' de varmint leetle mo' tyah him all to pieces, he fotch him down dat tree 'live; an' me an' him had him at Christmas. 'Coon meat mighty good when dee fat, you know?"

As this was a direct request for my judgment, I did not have the moral courage to raise an issue, although my views on the subject of 'coon meat are well known to my family, so I grunted something which I doubt not he took for assent, and he proceeded:

"Dee warn' nuttin he didn' lead de row in; he wuz de bes' swimmer I ever see, an' he handled a skiff same as a fish handle heself. An' I wuz wid him constant; wharever you see Marse George, dyah Edinburg sho, jes like he shadow. So twuz, when he went to de university; 'twarn' nuttin would do but I got to go too. Marster he didn't teck much to de notion, but Marse George wouldn' have it no urr way, an' co'se mistis she teck he side. So I went 'long as he body-servant to teck keer on him an' help meck him a gent'man. An' he wuz, too. From time he got dyah tell he come 'way he wuz de head man.

"Dee warn' but one man dyah didn' compliment him, an' dat wuz Mr. Darker. But he warn' nuttin! not dat he didn' come o' right good fambly—'cep' dee politics; but he wuz sutney pitted, jes like sometimes you see a weevly runty pig in a right good litter. Well, Mr. Darker he al'ays 'ginst Marse George; he hate me an' him bofe, an' he sutney act mischeevous todes us; 'cause he know he warn' as we all. De Stauntons dee wuz de populariitiest folks in Virginia; an' dee wuz high-larnt besides. So when Marse George run for de medal, an' wuz to meck he gret speech, Mr. Darker he speak 'ginst him. Dat's what Marse George whip him 'bout. 'Ain' nobody nuver told you 'bout dat?"

I again avowed my misfortune; and although it manifestly aroused new doubts, he worked it off on the mules, and once more took up his story:

"Well, you know, dee had been speakin' 'ginst one nurr ev'y Sat'dy night; an' ev'ybody knowed Marse George wuz de bes' speaker, but dee give him one mo' sho', an' dee was bofe gwine spread deeselves, an' dee wuz two urr gent'mens also gwine speak. An' dat night when Mr. Darker got up he meck sich a fine speech ev'ybody wuz s'prised; an' some on 'em say Mr. Darker done beat Marse George. But shuh! I know better'n dat; an' Marse

eorge face look so curious; but, suh,
hen he riz I knowed der wuz somen
wine happen—I wuz leanin' in de winder.
[e jes step out in front an' throwed up he
ead like a horse wid a rank kyurb on
[m, an' den he begin; an' twuz jes like de
ver when hit gits out de bank. He swep'
'ything. When he fust open he mouf I
nowed twuz comin'; he face wuz pale, an'
e wuds tremble like a fiddle-string, but he
yes wuz blazin', an' in a minute he wuz
es reshin'. He voice soun' like a bell; an'
e jes wallered dat turr man, an' wared
im out; an' when he set down dee all
elled an' hollered so you couldn' heah you'
ars. Gent'mans, twuz royal!

"Den dee tuck de vote, an' Marse George
ot it munanimous, an' dee all hollered
gin, all 'cep' a few o' Mr. Darker friends.
An' Mr. Darker he wuz de second. An'
en dee broke up. An' jes den Marse
George walked thoo de crowd straight up
o him, an' lookin' him right in de eyes,
ays to him, 'You stole dat speech you
aade to-night.' Well, suh, you ought to
. hearn 'em; hit soun' like a mill-dam.
'ou couldn' heah nuttin 'cep' roarin', an'
ou couldn' see nutting 'cep' shovin'; but,
ig as he wuz, Marse George beat him; an'
vhen dee pull him off, do' he face wuz
nighty pale, he stan' out befo' 'em all, dem
rhar wuz 'ginst him, an' all, an' as straight
s an arrow, an' say: 'Dat speech wuz
vritten an' printed years ago by somebody
r nurr in Congress, an' this man stole it;
ad he beat me only, I should not have
aid one word; but as he has beaten others,
shall show him up!' Gord, suh, he voice
vuz clear as a game rooster. I sutney wuz
roud on him.

"He did show him up, too, but Mr.
Darker ain' wait to see it; he lef' dat night.
An' Marse George he wuz de popularest
ent'man at dat university. He could
aandle dem students dyah same as a man
aandle a hoe.

"Well, twuz de next Christmas we meet
Miss Charlotte an' Nancy. Mr. Braxton
nvite we all to go down to spen' Christ-
nas wid him at he home. An' sich a time
.s we had!

"We got dyah Christmas Eve night—
lis very night—jes befo' supper, an' jes
aatchelly froze to death," he pursued, deal-
ng in his wonted hyperbole, "an' we jes
aad time to git a apple toddy or two when
supper was ready, an' wud come dat dee
vuz waitin' in de hall. I had done fix

Marse George up gorgeousome, I tell you;
an' when he walked down dem stairs in dat
swaller-tail coat, an' dem paten'-leather
pumps on, dee warn nay one dyah could
tetch him; he looked like he own 'em all.
I jes rest my mind. I seen him when he
shake hands wid 'em all roun', an' I say,
'Um-m-m! he got 'em.'

"But he ain' teck noticement o' none
much tell Miss Charlotte come. She didn'
live dyah, had jes come over de river dat
evenin' from her home, 'bout ten miles off,
to spen' Christmas like we all, an' she come
down de stairs jes as Marse George finish
shakin' hands. I seen he eye light on her
as she come down de steps smilin', wid her
dim blue dress trainin' behind her, an' her
little blue foots peepin' out so pretty, an'
holdin' a little hankcher, lookin' like a
spider-web, in one hand, an' a gret blue
fan in turr, spread out like a peacock tail.
an' jes her roun' arms an' th'oat white, an'
her gret dark eyes lightin' up her face. I
say, 'Dyah 'tis!' an' when de ole Cun'l
stan' aside an' interduce 'em, an' Marse
George step for'ard an' meck he grand bow,
an' she sort o' swing back an' gin her
curtchy, wid her dress sort o' dammed up
'ginst her, an' her arms so white, an' her
face sort o' sunsetty, I say, 'Yes, Lord!
Edinburg, dyah you mistis.' Marse George
look like he thinks she done come down
right from de top o' de blue sky an' bring
piece on it wid her. He ain' nuver took he
eyes from her dat night. Dee glued to her,
mun! an' she—well, do' she mighty rosy,
an' look mighty unconsarned, she sutney
ain' hender him. Hit look like kyarn nobody else tote dat fan an' pick up dat
hankcher skuzin o' him; an' after supper,
when dee all playin' blindman's-buff in de
hall—I don' know how twuz—but do' she
jes as nimble as a filly, an' her ankle jes
as clean, an' she kin git up her dress an'
dodge out de way o' ev'ybody else, somehow or nurr she kyarn help him ketchin'
her to save her life; he always got her
cornered; an' when dee'd git fur apart,
dat ain' nuttin, dee jes as sure to come
togerr again as water is whar you done run
you hand thoo. An' do' he kiss ev'ybody
else under de mestletow, 'cause dee be sort
o' cousins, he ain' nuver kiss her, nor nobody else nurr, 'cep' de ole Cun'l. I wuz
standin' down at de een de hall wid de
black folks, an' I notice it 'tic'lar, 'cause
I done meck de 'quintance o' Nancy; she
wuz Miss Charlotte's maid; a mighty likely

young gal she wuz den, an' jes as impident as a fly. She see it too, do' she ain' 'low it. Fust thing I know I seen a mighty likely light-skinned gal standin' dyah by me, wid her hyah mos' straight as white folks, an' a mighty good frock on, an' a clean apron, an' her hand mos' like a lady, only it brown, an' she keep on 'vidin' her eyes twix me an' Miss Charlotte; when I watchin' Miss Charlotte she watchin' me, an' when I steal my eye roun' on her she noticin' Miss Charlotte; an' presney I sort o' sidle 'longside her, an' I say, 'Lady, you mighty sprightly to-night.' An' she say, she 'bleeged to be sprightly, her mistis look so good; an' I ax her which one twuz, an' she tell me, 'Dat queen one over dyah,' an' I tell her dee's a king dyah too, she got her eye set for; an' when I say her mistis tryin' to set her cap for Marse George, she fly up, an' say she an' her mistis don' have to set dee cap for nobody; *dee* got to set dee cap an' all de clo'es for dem, an' den dee ain' gwine cotch 'em, 'cause dee ain' study-in' 'bout no up-country folks whar dee ain' nobody know nuttin 'bout.

"Well, dat oudaciousness so aggrivate me, I lite into dat nigger right dyah. I tell her she ain' been nowhar 'tall ef she don' know we all; dat we wuz de bes' of quality, de ve'y top de pot; an' den I tell her 'bout how gret we wuz; how de ker'idges wuz al'ays hitched up night an' day, an' niggers jes thick as weeds; an' how Unc' Torm he wared he swaller-tail ev'y day when he wait on de table; an' Marse George he won' wyah a coat mo'n once or twice anyways, to save your life. Oh! I sutney 'stonish dat nigger, 'cause I wuz teckin up for de fambly, an' I meck out like dee use gold up home like urr folks use wood, an' sow silver like urr folks sow wheat; an' when I got thoo dee wuz all on 'em listenin', an' she 'lowed dat Marse George he were ve'y good, sho 'nough, ef twarn for he nigger; but I ain' tarrifyin' myself none 'bout dat, 'cause I know she jes projickin, an' she couldn' help bein' impident ef you wuz to whup de frock off her back.

"Jes den dee struck up de dance. Dee had wheel de pianer out in de hall, an' somebody say Jack Forester had come 'cross de river, an' all on 'em say dee mus' git Jack; an' presney he come in wid he fiddle, grinnin' an' scrapin', 'cause he wuz a notable fiddler, do' I don' think he may equal to we all's Tubal, an' I know he couldn' tetch Marse George, 'cause Mars George wuz a natchel fiddler, jes lik 'coons is natchel pacers, an' mules i natchel kickers. Howsomever, he sutne jucked a jig sweet, an' when he shake da bow you couldn' help you foot switchin' a leetle—not ef you wuz a member of d chutch. He wuz a mighty sinful man, Jac wuz, an' dat fiddle had done drawed man souls to torment.

"Well, in a minute dee wuz all flyin', ar Jack he wuz rockin' like boat rockin' on d water, an' he face right shiny, an' he tee look like ear o' corn he got in he mouf an' he big foot set 'way out keepin' time an' Marse George he wuz in de lead ro dyah too; ev'y chance he git he tunne Miss Charlotte—'petchel motion, righ hand across, an' cauliflower, an' coquette— dee coquette plenty o' urrs, but I notice de ain' nuver fail to tun one nurr, an' ev' tun he gin she wrappin' de chain roun him; once when dee wuz 'prominadin-all down we all's een o' de hall, as he tunne her somebody step on her dress an' to' it I heah de screech o' de silk, an' Nancy say 'O Lord!' den she say, 'Nem mine! nov I'll git it!' an' dee stop for a minute fo Marse George to pin it up, while turrer went on, an' Marse George wuz down o he knee, an' she look down on him might sweet out her eyes, an' say, 'Hit don' mec no difference,' an' he glance up an' cotc her eye, an', jest dout a wud, he tyah a gre piece right out de silk an' slipt it in h bosom, an' when he got up, he say, righ low, lookin' in her eyes right deep, 'I gwin wyah dis at my weddin',' an' she jes lool sweet as candy; an' ef Nancy ever wya dat frock I ain' see it.

"Den presney dee wuz talkin' 'bout stop pin'. De ole Cun'l say hit time to hav prars, an' dee wuz beggin' him to wait leetle while; an' Jack Forester lay he fiddl down nigh Marse George, an' he picked up an' drawed de bow 'cross it jes to tr it, an' den jes projickin' he struck da chune 'bout 'You'll ermember me.' H hadn' mo'n tetch de string when you coul heah a pin drop. Marse George he war noticin', an' he jes lay he face on de fiddle wid he eyes sort o' half shet, an' drawe her out like he'd do some nights at home in de moonlight on de gret porch, tell on sudden he looked up an' cotch Miss Char lotte eye leanin' for'ards so earnest, an' all on 'em list'nin', an' he stopt, an' dee al clapt dee hands, an' he sudney drapt into

jig. Jack Forester ain' had to play no mo'
at night; even de ole Cun'l ketched de
ver, an' he stept out in de flo', in he long-
il coat an' high collar, an' knocked 'em
ff de 'Snow-bud on de Ash-bank,' an'
'hicken in de Bread-tray,' right natchel.
h, he could jes plank 'em down!

"Oh, dat wuz a Christmas like you been
ead 'bout! An' twuz hard to tell which
ittin cotch most, Marse George or me,
ause dat nigger she jes as confusin' as
Iiss Charlotte. An' she sutney wuz sp'ilt
m days; ev'y nigger on dat place got he
ye on her, an' she jes as oudacious an'
ggrivatin as jes womens kin be. Dees
ionsus 'ceivin' critters, womens is, jes as
nreliable as de hind-leg of a mule; a
an got to watch 'em all de time; you
yarn break 'em like you kin horses. Now
at off mule dyah" (indicating, by a lazy
ut not light lash of his whip the one se-
cted for his illustration), "dee ain' no
untin' on her at all; she go 'long all day,
r maybe a week, jes dat easy an' sociable,
n' fust thing you know you ain' know
n' fust thing you know you ain' know
uttin, she done knock you brains out; dee
in' no 'pendence to be placed in 'em 'tall,
h; she jes as sweet as a kiss one minute,
n' next time she come out de house she
ot her head up in de air, an' her ears
acked, an' goin' 'long switchin' herself
ke I ain' good 'nough for her to walk
n.

"'Fox-huntin's?' oh, yes, suh, ev'y day
ios'; an' when Marse George didn' git
e tail, twuz 'cause twuz a bob-tail fox—
ou heah me! He play de fiddle for he pas-
me, but he fotched up in de saddle—dat
e cradle.

"De fust day dee went out I heah Nancy
uoilin 'bout de tail layin' on Miss Char-
tte dressin'-table gittin' hyahs over ev'y-
iing.

"One day de ladies went out too, Miss
harlotte 'mongst 'em, on Miss Lucy gray
ayah Switchity, an' Marse George he rid
Ir. Braxton's chestnut Willful. Well, suh,
e stick so close to dat gray myah, he leetle
o' los' dat fox; but, Lord! he know what
e 'bout—he monsus 'ceivin' 'bout dat!—
e know de way de fox gwine jes as well
s he know heself; an' all de time he leadin'
Iiss Charlotte whar she kin heah de music,
ut he watchin' him too, jes as narrow as
ole hound. So, when de fox tun de head
' de creek, Marse George had Miss Char-
tte on de aidge o' de flat, an' he de fust
ian see de fox tun down on turr side wid

de hounds right rank after him. Dat sort
o' set him back, 'cause by rights de fox
ought to 'a double an' come back dis side;
he kyarn git out dat way, an' two or three
gent'mens dee had see it too, an' wuz jes
layin' de horses to de groun' to git roun'
fust, 'cause de creek wuz heap too wide
to jump, an' wuz 'way over you head, an'
hit cold as Christmas, sho 'nough; well,
suh, when dee tunned, Mr. Clarke he wuz
in de lead (he wuz ridin' for Miss Charlotte too), an' hit fyah set Marse George
on fire; he ain' said but one wud, 'Wait,'
an' jes set de chestnut's head straight for
de creek, whar de fox comin' wid he tail
up on he back, an' de dogs ravlin mos' on
him. De ladies screamed, an' some de gent'-
mens hollered for him to come back, but
he ain' mind; he went 'cross dat flat like a
wild-duck; an' when he retch de water he
horse try to flinch, but dat hand on de
bridle, an' dem rowels in he side, an' he
'bleeged to teck it. Lord, suh, sich a screech
as dee set up! But he wuz swimmin' for
life, an' he wuz up de bank an' in de
middle o' dogs time dee tetched ole
Gray Jacket; an' when Mr. Clarke got
dyah Marse George wuz stanin' holdin'
up de tail for Miss Charlotte to see, turrer
side de creek, an' de hounds wuz wallerin'
all over de body, an' I don' think Mr.
Clarke don got up wid 'em yit.

"He cotch de fox, an' he cotch some'n'
else besides, in my 'pinion, 'cause when de
ladies went upstairs dat night Miss Charlotte had to wait on de steps for a glass
o' water, an' couldn' nobody git it but
Marse George; an' den when she tell him
good-night over de banisters, he couldn' say
it good enough; he got to kiss her hand;
an' she ain' do nuttin but jes peep upstairs
ef anybody dyah lookin'; an' when I come
thoo de do' she juck her hand 'way an' ran
upstairs jes as farst as she could. Marse
George look at me sort o' laughin', an'
say: 'Confound you! Nancy couldn' been
very good to you.' An' I say, 'She le' me
squench my thirst kissin' her hand'; an'
he sort o' laugh an' tell me to keep my
mouf shet.

"But dat ain' de on'y time I come on
'em. Dee al'ays gittin' corndered; an' de
evenin' befo' we come 'way I wuz gwine in
thoo de conservity, an' dyah dee wuz sort
o' hide 'way. Miss Charlotte she wuz settin' down, an' Marse George he wuz leanin'
over her, got her hand to he face, talkin'
right low an' lookin' right sweet, an' she

ain' say nuttin; an' presney he dropt on one knee by her, an' slip he arm roun' her, an' try to look in her eyes, an' she so 'shamed to look at him she got to hide her face on he shoulder, an' I slipt out.

"We come 'way next mornin'. When marster heah 'bout it he didn' teck to de notion at all, 'cause her pa—dat is, he warn' her own pa, 'cause he had married her ma when she wuz a widder after Miss Charlotte pa died, an' he politics warn' same as ourn. 'Why, you kin never stand him, suh,' he said to Marse George. 'We won't mix any mo'n fire and water; you ought to have found that out at college; dat fellow Darker is his son.'

"Marse George he say he know dat; but he on'y de step-brurr of de young lady, an' ain' got a drap o' her blood in he veins, an' he didn' know it when he meet her, an' anyhow hit wouldn' meck any diffence; an' when de mistis see how sot Marse George is on it she teck he side, an' dat fix it; 'cause when ole mistis warn marster to do a thing, hit jes good as done. I don' keer how much he rar roun' an' say he ain' gwine do it, you jes well go 'long an' put on you hat; you gwine see him presney doin' it jes peaceable as a lamb. She tun him jes like she got bridle on him, an' he ain' nuver know it.

"So she got him jes straight as a string. An' when de time come for Marse George to go, marster he mo' consarned 'bout it 'n Marse George; he ain' say nuttin 'bout it befo', but now he walkin' roun' an' roun' axin mistis mo' questions 'bout he cloes an' he horse an' all; an' dat mornin' he gi' him he two Sunday razors, an' gi' me a pyah o' boots an' a beaver hat, 'cause I wuz gwine wid him to kyar he portmanteau, an' git he shavin' water, sence marster say ef he wuz gwine marry a Locofoco, he at least must go like a gent'man; an' me an' Marse George had done settle it 'twixt us, 'cause we al'ays set bofe we traps on de same hyah parf.

"Well, we got 'em, an' when I ax dat gal out on de wood-pile at night, she say bein' as her mistis gwine own me, an' we bofe got to be in de same estate, she reckon she ain' nuver gwine to be able to git shet o' me; an' den I clamp her. Oh, she wuz a beauty!"

A gesture and guffaw completed the recital of his conquest.

"Yes, suh, we got 'em sho!" he said, presently. "Dee couldn' persist us; we crowd 'em into de fence an' run 'em off dee foots.

"Den come de 'gagement' an' ev'ything wuz smooth as silk. Marse George an' me wuz ridin' over dyah constant, on'y we nuver did git over bein' skeered when we wuz ridin' up dat turpentine road facin' all dem winders. Hit 'pear like ev'ybody in de wull 'mos' wuz lookin' at us.

"One evenin' Marse George say, 'Edinburg, d'you ever see as many winders p'intin' one way in you' life? When I git a house,' he say, 'I gwine have all de winders lookin' turr way.' But dat evenin', when I see Miss Charlotte come walkin' out de gret parlor wid her hyah sort o' rumpled over her face, an' some yaller roses on her bres, an' her gret eyes so soft an' sweet, an' Marse George walkin' 'long hinst her, so peaceable, like she got chain roun' him, I say, 'Winders ain' nuttin.' Oh, twuz jes like holiday all de time! An' den Miss Charlotte come over to see mistis, an' of co'se she bring her maid wid her, 'cause she 'bleeged to have her maid, you know, an' dat wuz de bes' of all. Dat evenin', 'bout sunset, dee come drivin' up in de big ker'idge, wid dee gret hyah trunk stropped on de seat behind, an' Nancy she settin' by Billy, an' Marse George settin' inside by he rose-bud, 'cause he had done gone down to bring her up; an' marster he done been drest in he blue coat an' yallow westket ever sence dinner, an' walkin' roun', watchin' up de road all de time, an' tellin' de mistis he reckon dee ain' comin' an' ole mistis she try to pacify him, an' she come out presney drest, an' rustlin' in her stiff black silk an' all, an' when de ker'idge come in sight, ev'ybody wuz runnin'; an' when dee draw up to de do', Marse George he help her out an' 'duce her to marster an ole mistis; an' marster he start to meck her a gret bow, an' she jes put up her mout like a little gal to be kissed, an' dat got him. An' mistis teck her right in her arm an' kiss her twice, an' de servants dee wuz all peepin' an' grinnin'. Ev'ywhar you tur you see a nigger teef, 'cause dee all war see de young mistis whar good 'nougl for Marse George. Dee ain' gwine b married tell de next fall, 'count o' Mis Charlotte bein' so young; but she jes goo as b'longst to we all now; an' ole marste an' mistis dee jes as much in love wid he as Marse George. Hi! dee warn pull d house down an' buil' it over for her! An ev'y han' on de place he peepin' to try t

it a look at he young mistis whar he
wine b'longst to. One evenin' dee all on
m come roun' de porch an' send for
Marse George, an' when he come out,
Charley Brown (he al'ays de speaker,
'cause he got so much mouf, kin talk pretty
s white folks), he say dee warn interduce
de young mistis, an' pay dee bespects to
er; an' presney Marse George lead her
ut on de porch laughin' at her, wid her
ace jes rosy as a wine-sap apple, an' she
meck 'em a beautiful bow, an' speak to
'm ev'y one, Marse George namin' de
ames; an' Charley Brown he meck her a
retty speech, an' tell her we mighty proud
) own her; an' one o' dem impident gals
x her to gin her dat white frock when she
it married; an' when she say, 'Well, what
m I goin' weah?' Sally say, 'Lord, honey,
Marse George gwine dress you in pure
ool'!' an' she look up at him wid sparks
ashin' out her eyes, while he look like
at ain' good 'nough for her. An' so twuz,
hen she went 'way, Sally Marshall got
at frock, an' proud on it I tell you.

"Oh yes; he sutney mindin' her tender.
Hi! when she go to ride in evenin' wid
im, de ain' no horseblock good 'nough for
er! Marse George got to have her step in
e hand; an' when dee out walkin' he got
e umbreller holdin' 't over her all de time,
e so feared de sun'll kiss her; an' dee
'alk so slow down dem walks in de shade
ou got to sight 'em by a tree to tell ef dee
novin' 'tall. She use' to look like she used
) it too, I tell you, 'cause she wuz quality,
ne de white-skinned ones; an' she'd set
a dem big cheers, wid her little foots on
e cricket whar Marse George al'ays set
or her, he so feared dee'd tetch de groun',
es like she on her throne; an' ole marster
e'd watch her 'mos' edmirin as Marse
George; an' when she went 'way hit sutney
was lonesome. Hit look like daylight gone
vid her. I don' know which I miss mos',
Miss Charlotte or Nancy.

"Den Marse George was 'lected to de
Legislature, an' ole Jedge Darker run for
e Senator, an' Marse George vote gin him
n' beat him. An' dat commence de fuss;
n' den dat man gi' me de whuppin, an'
lat breck 'tup an' breck he heart.

"You see, after Marse George wuz
lected ('lections wuz 'lections dem days;
lee warn' no bait-gode 'lections, wid ev'y
ort o' worms squirmin' up 'ginst one nurr,
vid piece o' paper d' ain' know what on,
trappin' in a chink; didn' nuttin but gent'-

mens vote den, an' dee took dee dram, an'
vote out loud, like gent'mens)—well, arter
Marse George wuz 'lected, de parties wuz
jes as even balanced as stilyuds, an' wen
dee ax Marse George who wuz to be de
Senator, he vote for de Whig, 'ginst de
ole jedge, an' dat beat him, of co'se. An'
dee ain' got sense to know he 'bleeged to
vote wid he politics. Dat he sprinciple; he
kyarn vote for Locofoco, I don' keer ef he
is Miss Charlotte pa, much less her step-
pa. Of co'se de ole jedge ain' speak to him
arter dat, nur is Marse George ax him to.
But who dat gwine s'pose women-folks got
to put dee mouf in too? Miss Charlotte
she write Marse George a letter dat pester
him mightily; he set up all night answerin'
dat letter, an' he mighty solemn, I tell you.
An' I wuz gittin' right grewsome myself,
'cause I studyin' 'bout dat gal down dyah
whar I done gi' my wud to, an' when dee
ain' no letters come torectly hit hard to tell
which one de anxiouser, me or Marse
George. Den presney I so 'straughted 'long
o' it I ax Aunt Haly 'bouten it: she know
all sich things, 'cause she 'mos' a hunderd
years ole, an' seed evil sperits, an' got
skoripins up her chimney, an' knowed cun-
jure; an' she ax me what wuz de signica-
tion, an' I tell her I ain't able nuther to eat
nor to sleep, an' dat gal come foolin' 'long
me when I sleep jes like as natchel as ef I
see her sho 'nough. An' she say I done conjured; dat de gal done tricked me. Oh,
Gord; dat skeered me. You white folks,
marster, don' b'lieve nuttin like dat; y' all
got too much sense, 'cause y' all kin read;
but niggers dee ain' know no better, an' I
sutney wuz skeered, 'cause Aunt Haly say
my coffin done seasoned, de planks up de
chimney. Well, I got so bad Marse George
ax me 'bout it, an' he sort o' laugh an'
sort o' cuss, an' he tell Aunt Haly ef she
don' stop dat foolishness skeerin' me he'll
sell her an' teah her ole skoripin house
down. Well, co'se he jes talkin', an' he ax
me next day how'd I like to go an' see my
sweetheart. Gord! suh, I got well torectly.
So I set off next evenin', feelin' jes big as
ole marster, wid my pass in my pocket,
which I warn' to show nobody 'douten I
'bleeged to, 'cause Marse George didn'
warn nobody to know he le' me go. An'
den dat rascallion teck de shut off my back.
But ef Marse George didn' pay him de
wuth o' it!

"I done git 'long so good, too. When
Nancy see me she sutney was 'stonished.

She come roun' de cornder in de back yard whar I settin' in Nat's do' (he wuz de gardener) wid her hyah all done untwist, an' breshed out mighty fine, an' a clean ap'on wid fringe on it, meckin' out she so s'prised to see me (whar wuz all a lie, 'cause some on 'em done notify her I dyah), an' she say, 'Hi! what dis black nigger doin' heah?'

"An' I say, 'Who you callin' nigger, vou impident kercumber-faced thing you?' Den we shake hands, an' I tell her Marse George done set me free—dat I done buy myself; dat's de lie I done lay off to tell her.

"An' when I tole her dat, she bust out laughin', an' say, well, I better go 'long 'way, den, dat she don' warn no free nigger to be comp'ny for her. Dat sort o' set me back, an' I tell her she kickin' 'fo' she spurred, dat I ain' got her in my mine; I got a nurr gal at home, whar grievin' 'bout me dat ve'y minute. An' after I tell her all sich lies as dat, presney she ax me ain' I hongry; an' ef dat nigger didn' git her mammy to gi' me de bes' supper! Umm-m! I kin 'mos' tas'e it now. Wheat bread off de table, an' zerves, an' fat bacon, tell I couldn' 'a put a nurr moufful nowhar sep'n' I'd teck my hat. Dat night I tote Nancy water for her, an' I tell her all 'bout ev'ything an' she jes sweet as honey. Next mornin', do', she done sort o' tunned some, an' ain' so sweet. You know how milk gits sort o' bonnyclabberish? An' when she see me she 'gin to 'buse me—say I jes tryin' to fool her, an' all de time got nurr wife at home, or gittin' ready to git one, for all she know, an' she ain' know wherr Marse George ain' jes 'ceivin' as I is; an' nem mine, she got plenty warn marry her; an' as to Miss Charlotte, she got de whole wull; Mr. Darker he ain' got nobody in he way now, dat he deah all de time, an' ain' gwine West no mo'. Well, dat aggrivate me so I tell her ef she say dat 'bout Marse George I gwine knock her; an' wid dat she got so oudacious I meck out I gwine 'way, an' lef' her, an' went up todes de barn; an' up dyah, fust thing I know, I come across dat ar man Mr. Darker. Soon as he see me he begin to cuss me, an' he ax me what I doin' on dat land, an' I tell him nuttin. An' he say, well, he gwine to gi' me some'n; he gwine teach me to come prowlin' round gent'men's houses. An' he meck me go in de barn an' teck off my shut, an' he beat me wid he whup tell de blood run out my back. He sutney did

beat me scandalous, 'cause he done hate me an' Marse George ever since we wuz at college togurr. An' den he say: 'Now you git right off dis land. Ef either you or you marster ever put you foot on it, you'll git de same thing agin.' An' I tell you, Edinburg he come 'way, 'cause he sutney had worry me. I ain't stop to see Nancy or nobody; I jes come 'long, shakin' de dust, I tell you. An' as I come 'long de road I pass Miss Charlotte walkin' on de lawn by herself, an' she call me: 'Why, hi! ain' dat Edinburg?'

"She look so sweet, an' her voice soun' so cool, I say, 'Yes'm; how you do, missis?' An' she say, she ve'y well, an' how I been, an' whar I gwine? I tell her I ain' feelin' so well, dat I gwine home. 'Hi!' she say, 'is anybody treat you bad?' An' I tell her, 'Yes'm.' An' she say, 'Oh! Nancy don' mean nuttin by dat; dat you mus'n mine what womens say an' do, 'cause dee feel sorry for it next minute; an' sometimes dee kyarn help it, or maybe hit you fault; an', anyhow, you ought to be willin' to overlook it; an' I better go back an' wait till to-morrow—ef—ef I ain' 'bleeged to git home to-day.'

"She got mighty mixed up in de een part o' dat, an' she looked mighty anxious 'bout me an' Nancy; an' I tell her, 'Nor'm, I 'bleeged to git home.'

"Well, when I got home Marse George he warn know all dat gwine on; but I mighty sick—dat man done beat me so an' he ax me what de marter, an' I upped an' tell him.

"Gord! I nuver see a man in sich a rage He call me in de office an' meck me teck off my shut, an' he fyah bust out cryin'. He walked up an' down dat office like a caged lion. Ef he had got he hand on Mr Darker den, he'd 'a kilt him, sho!

"He wuz most 'stracted. I don' know what he'd been ef I'd tell him what Nancy tell me. He call for Peter to git he horse torectly, an' he tell me to go an' git some'n from mammy to put on my back, an' to go to bed torectly, an' not to say nuttin to nobody, but to tell he pa he'd be away for two days, maybe; an' den he got on Reveller an' galloped 'way hard as he could wid he jaw set farst, an' he heaviest whip clamped in he hand. Gord! I wuz mos hopin' he wouldn' meet dat man, 'cause feared ef he did he'd kill him; an' h would, sho, ef he had meet him right den dee say he leetle mo' did when he fine hin next day, an' he had done been ridin' den all night; he cotch him at a sto' on de road, an' dee say he leetle mo' cut him all to pieces; he drawed a weepin on him, but Marse George wrench it out he hand an' flung it over de fence; an' when dee got him 'way he had weared he whup out on him; an' he got dem whelps on him now, ef he ain' dead. Yes, suh, he ain' let nobody else do dat he ain' do heself, sho!

"Dat done de business! He sont Marse George a challenge, but Marse George sont him he'll cowhide him agin ef he ever meah any mo' from him, an' he 'ain't. Dat perrify him, so he shet he mouf. Den come he ring an' all he pictures an' things back —a gret box on 'em, and not a wud wid em. Marse George, I think he know'd dee wuz comin', but dat ain' keep it from huttin him, 'cause he done been 'gaged to Miss Charlotte, an' got he mine riveted to her; an' do' befo' dat dee had stop writin', an' a riff done git 'twixt 'em, he ain't satisfied n he mine dat she ain't gwine 'pologizee —I know by Nancy; but now he got de confirmation dat he done for good, an' dat le gret gulf fixed 'twix him an' Abraham bosom. An', Gord, suh, twuz torment, sho nough! He ain' say nuttin 'bout it, but I see de light done pass from him, an' de darkness done wrap him up in it. In a eetle while you wouldn' 'a knowed him. Den ole mistis died. B'lieve me, ole marster me 'most much hut by Miss Charlotte as Marse George. He meck a 'tempt to buy Nancy for me, so I find out arterward, an' vrite Jedge Darker he'll pay him anything he'll ax for her, but he letter wuz sont back 'dout any answer. He sutney was mad 'bout it—he say he'd horsewhip him as Marse George did dat urr young puppy, but ole mistis wouldn' le' him do nuttin, nd den he grieve heself to death. You see e mighty ole, anyways. He nuver got over le mistis death. She had been failin' a ong time, an' he ain' tarry long 'hinst her; it sort o' like breckin up a holler—de ole coon goes 'way soon arter dat; an' marster uver could pin he own collar or buckle he wn stock—mistis she al'ays do dat; an' do' Marse George do de bes' he kin, an' mighty villin', he kyarn handle pin like a woman; e hand tremble like a p'inter dog; an' nyways he ain' ole mistis. So old marster oller her dat next fall, when dee wuz itting in de corn, an' Marse George he in' got nobody in de wull left; he all alone a dat gret house, an' I wonder sometimes

he ain' die too, 'cause he sutney wuz fond o' ole marster. When ole mistis wuz dyin' she tell him to be good to ole marster, an' patient wid him, 'cause he ain' got nobody but him now (ole marster he had jes step out de room to cry); an' Marse George he lean over her an' kiss her an' promise her faithful he would. An' he sutney wuz tender wid him as a woman; an' when ole marster die he set by him an' hol' he hand an' kiss him sorf, like he wuz ole mistis. But, Gord! twuz lonesome arter dat, an' Marse George eyes look wistful, like he al'ays lookin' far 'way; an' Aunt Haly say he see harnts whar walk 'bout in de gret house. She say dee walk dyah constant of nights sence ole marster done alternate de rooms from what dee wuz when he gran'pa buil' 'em, an' dat dee huntin' for dee ole chambers an' kyarn git no rest 'cause dee kyarn fine 'em. I don't know how dat wuz. I know Marse George he used to walk about heself mightily of nights. All night long, all night long, I'd heah him tell de chickens crowin' dee second crow, an' some mornin's I'd go dyah an' he ain' even rumple de bed. I thought sho he wuz gwine die, but I suppose he done 'arn he days to be long in de land, an' dat save him. But hit sutney wuz lonesome, an' he nuver went off de plantation, an' he got older an' older, tell we all thought he wuz gwine die. An' one day come jes befo' Christmas, 'bout night two year after marster die, Mr. Braxton ride up to de do'. He had done come to teck Marse George home to spen' Christmas wid him. Marse George warn git out it, but Mr. Braxton won' teck no disapp'intment; he say he gwine baptize he boy, an' he done name him after Marse George (he had marry Marse George cousin, Miss Peggy Carter, an' he 'vite Marse George to de weddin', but he wouldn' go, do' I sutney did want him to go, 'cause I heah Miss Charlotte was nominated to marry Mr. Darker, an' I warn know what done 'come o' dat brightskinned nigger gal whar I used to know down dyah); an' he say Marse George got to come an' stan' for him, an' gi' him a silver cup an' a gol' rattle. So Marse George he finally promise to come an' spend Christmas Day, an' Mr. Braxton went 'way next mornin', an' den hit tun in an' rain so I feared we couldn' go, but hit cler off de day befo' Christmas Eve an' tun cold. Well, suh, we ain' been nowhar for so long I wuz skittish as a young filly;

an' den you know twuz de same ole place. We didn' git dyah till supper-time, an' twuz a good one too, 'cause seventy miles dat cold a weather hit whet a man's honger jes like a whetstone. Dee sutney wuz glad to see we all. We rid roun' by de back yard to gi' Billy de horses, an' we see dee wuz havin' gret fixin's; an' den we went to de house, jes as some o' de folks run in an' tell 'em we wuz come When Marse George stept in de hall dee all clustered roun' him like dee gwine hug him, dee faces fyah dimplin' wid pleasure, an' Miss Peggy she jes retched up an' teck him in her arms an' hug him.

"Dee tell me in de kitchen dat dee wuz been 'spectin' of Miss Charlotte over to spend Christmas too, but de river wuz so high dee s'pose dee couldn' git 'cross. Chile, dat sutney disapp'int me!

"Well, after supper de niggers had a dance. Hit wuz down in de laundry, an' de table wuz set in de carpenter shop jes by. Oh, hit sutney wuz beautiful! Miss Lucy an' Miss Ailsy dee had superintend' ev'ything wid dee own hands. So dee wuz down dyah wid dee ap'ons up to dee chins, an' dee had de big silver strandeliers out de house, two on each table, an' some o' ole mistiss's best damas' table-clothes, an' ole marster's gret bowl full o' eggnog; hit look big as a mill-pond settin' dyah in de cornder; an' dee had flowers out de greenhouse on de table, an' some o' de chany out de gret house, an' de dinin'-room cheers set roun' de room. Oh! oh! nuttin warn too good for niggers dem times; an' de little niggers wuz runnin' roun' right 'stracted, squealin' an' peepin' an' gittin in de way onder you foots; an' de mens dee wuz totin' in de wood—gret hickory logs, look like stock whar you gwine saw—an' de fire so big hit look like you gwine kill horgs, 'cause hit sutney wuz cold dat night. Dis nigger ain' nuver gwine forgit it! Jack Forester he had come 'cross de river to lead de fiddlers, an' he say he had to put he fiddle onder he coat an' poke he bow in he breeches leg to keep de strings from poppin', an' dat de river would freeze over sho ef twarn so high; but twuz jes snortin', an' he had hard wuck to git over in he skiff, an' Unc' Jeems say he ain' gwine come out he boat-house no mo' dat night— he done tempt Providence often 'nough dat day. Den ev'ything wuz ready, an' de fiddlers got dee dram an' chuned up, an' twuz lively, I tell you! Twuz jes as thick in dyah as blackberries on de blackberry bush, 'cause ev'y gal on de plantation wuz dyah shakin' her foot for some young buck, an' back-steppin' for to go 'long. Dem ole sleepers wuz jes a-rockin', an' Jack Forester he wuz callin' de figgers for to wake 'em up. I warn' dancin', 'cause I done got 'ligion an' longst to de chutch since de trouble done tetch us up so rank; but I tell you my foots wuz pintedly eechchin for a leetle sop on it, an' I had to come out to keep from crossin' 'em onst, anyways. Den, too, I had a tetch o' misery in my back, an' I lay off to git a tas'e o' dat eggnog out dat big bowl wid snow-drift on it from Miss Lucy—she al'ays mighty fond o' Marse George; so I slip into de carpenter shop, an' ax her kyarn I do nuttin for her, an' she laugh an' say, yes, I kin drink her health, an' gi' me a gret gobletful, an' jes den de white folks come in to 'spec' de tables, Marse George in de lead, an' dee all fill up dee glasses an' pledge dee health, an' all de servants', an' a merry Christmas; an' den we went in de laundry to see de dancin', an' maybe to teck a hand deeself, 'cause white folks' 'ligion ain' like niggers', you know; dee got so much larnin dee kin dance an' fool de devil too. An' I stay roun' a little while, an' den went in de kitchen to see how supper gittin on, 'cause I wuz so hongry when I got dyah I ain' able to eat 'nough at one time to 'commodate it, an' de smell o' de turkeys an' de gret saddlers o' mutton in de two kitchens wuz mos' 'nough by deeself to feed a right hongry man; an' dyah wuz a whole parcel o' niggers cookin' an' tunnin 'bout for life, an' dee faces jes as shiny as ef dee done bas'e 'em wid gravy; an' dyah, settin' back in a cheer out de way, wid her clean frock up off de flo', wuz dat gal. I sutney did feel curious.

"I say, 'Hi! name o' Gord, whar'd you come from?' She say, 'Oh, Marster! er heah ain' dat free nigger!' An' ev'ybody laughed. Well, presney we come out 'cause Nancy warn see de dancin', an' we stop a leetle while 'hind de cornder out de wind while she tell me 'bout ev'ything. An she say dat's all a lie she tell me dat da 'bout Mr. Darker an' Miss Charlotte; an he done gone 'way now for good, 'caus he so low-down an' wuthless dee kyarn no body stand him; an' all he warn marr Miss Charlotte for is to git her niggers But Nancy say Miss Charlotte nuver coul abide him, he so 'sateful, spressly sence sn fine out what a lie he told 'bout Marse George. You know, Mr. Darker he done meck 'em think Marse George sont me dyah to fine out ef he done come home, an' den dat he fall on him wid he weepin when he ain' noticin' him, an' sort o' out de way too, an' git two urr mens to hold him while he beat him, all 'cause he in love wid Miss Charlotte. D'you ever, ever heah sich a lie? An' Nancy say, do' Miss Charlotte ain' b'lieve it all togerr, hit look so reasonable she done le' de ole jedge an' her ma, who wuz 'pending on what she heah, 'duce her to send back he things; an' dee ain' know no better not tell after de ole jedge die; den dee fine out 'bout de whuppin me, an' all; an' den Miss Charlotte know huccome I ain' gwine stay dat day; an' she say dee wuz sutney outdone 'bout it, but it too late den, an' Miss Charlotte kyarn do nuttin but cry 'bout it, an' dat she did, pintedly, 'cause she done lost Marse George, an' done 'stroy he life; an' she nuver keer 'bout nobody else sep Marse George, Nancy say. Mr. Clarke he hangin' on, but Miss Charlotte she done tell him pintedly she ain' nuver gwine marry nobody. An' dee jes done come, she say, 'cause dee had to go 'way round by de rope-ferry 'long o' de river bein' so high, an' dee ain' know tell dee done git out de ker'idge an' in de house dat we all wuz heah; an' Nancy say she glad dee ain', 'cause she 'feared ef dee had, Miss Charlotte wouldn' 'a come.

"Den I tell her all 'bout Marse George, 'cause I know she 'bleeged to tell Miss Charlotte. Twuz powerful cold out dyah, but I ain' mine dat, chile. Nancy she done had to wrop her arms up in her ap'on, an' she kyarn meck so zistance 'tall, an' dis nigger ain' keerin nuttin' bout cold den.

"An' jes den two ladies come out de carpenter shop an' went 'long to de laundry, an' Nancy say, 'Dyah Miss Charlotte now'; an' twuz Miss Lucy an' Miss Charlotte; an' we heah Miss Lucy coaxin' Miss Charlotte to go, tellin' her she kin come right out; an' jes den dee wuz a gret shout, an' we went in hinst 'em. Twuz Marse George had done teck de fiddle, an' ef he warn' natchelly layin' hit down! He wuz up at de urr een o' de room, 'way from we all, 'cause we wuz at de do', nigh Miss Charlotte to go, tellin' her she kin come on 'em, wid her eyes on him mighty timid, like she hidin' from him, an' ev'y nigger in de room wuz on dat flo'. Gord! suh, dee wuz grinnin' so dee warn' a toof in dat

room you couldn' git you tweezers on; an' you couldn' heah a wud, dee so proud o' Marse George playin' for 'em.

"Well, dee danced tell you couldn' tell which wuz de clappers an' which de back-steppers; de whole house look like it wuz rockin'; an' presney somebody say supper, an' dat stop 'em, an' dee wuz a spell for a minute, an' Marse George standin' dyah wid de fiddle in he hand. He face wuz tunned away, an' he wuz studyin'—studyin' 'bout dat urr Christmas so long ago—an' sudney he face drapt down on de fiddle, an' he drawed he bow 'cross de strings, an' dat chune begin to whisper right sorf. Hit begin so low ev'ybody had to stop talkin' an' hold dee mouf to heah it; an' Marse George he ain' know 'bout it, he done gone back, an' standin' dyah in de gret hall playin' it for Miss Charlotte whar done come down de steps wid her little blue foots an' gret fan, an' standin' dyah in her dim blue dress an' her fyah arms, an' her gret eyes lookin' in he face so earnest, whar he ain' gwine nuver speak to no mo'. I see it by de way he look—an' de fiddle wuz jes pleadin'. He drawed it out jes as fine as a stran' o' Miss Charlotte's hyah.

"Hit so sweet, Miss Charlotte, mun, she couldn' stan' it; she made to de do'; an' jes while she watchin' Marse George to keep him from seein' her he look dat way, an' he eyes fall right into hern.

"Well, suh, de fiddle drapt down on de flo', an' he face wuz white as a sycamore limb. Dee say twuz a swimmin' in de head he had; an' Jack say de whole fiddle warn' wuff de five dollars.

"Me an' Nancy followed 'em tell dee went in de house, an' den we come back to de shop whar de supper wuz gwine on, an' got we all supper an' a leetle sop o' dat yaller gravy out dat big bowl, an' den we all rejourned to de laundry agin, an' got onder de big bush o' misseltow whar hangin' from de jice, an' ef you ever see scufflin' dat's de time.

"Well, me an' she had jes done lay off de whole Christmas, when wud come dat Marse George want he horses.

"I went, but it sutney breck me up; an' I wonder whar de name o' Gord Marse George gwine sen' me dat cold night, an' jes as I got to de do' Marse George an' Mr. Braxton come out, an' I know torectly Marse George wuz gwine home. I seen he face by de light o' de lantern, an' twuz set jes rigid as a rock. Mr. Braxton he wuz beggin' him to stay; he tell him he ruinin' he life, dat he sho dee's some mistake, an' 'twill be all right. An' all de answer Marse George meck wuz to swing heself up in de saddle, an' Reveller he look like he gwine fyah 'stracted. He al'ays mighty fool anyways when he git cold, dat horse wuz.

"Well, we come 'long 'way, an' Mr. Braxton an' two mens come down to de river wid lanterns to see us cross, 'cause twuz dark as pitch, sho 'nough. An' jes 'fo' I started I got one o' de mens to hol' my horses, an' I went in de kitchen to git warm, an' dyah Nancy wuz. An' she say Miss Charlotte upsteirs cryin' right now, 'cause she think Marse George gwine cross de river 'count o' her, an' she whimper a little herself when I tell her good-by. But twuz too late den. Well, de river wuz jes natchelly b'ilin', an' hit soun' like a mill-dam roarin' by; an' when we got dyah Marster George tunned to me an' tell me he reckon I better go back. I ax him whar he gwine, an' he say, 'Home.' 'Den I gwine wid you,' I says. I wuz mighty skeered, but me an' Marse George wuz boys togerr; an' he plunged right in, an' I after him.

"Gord! twuz cold as ice; an' we hadn' got in befo' bofe horses wuz swimmin' for life. He holler to me to byah de myah head up de stream; an' I did try, but what's a nigger to dat water! Hit jes pick me up an' dash me down like I ain' no mo'n a chip, an' de fust thing I know I gwine down de stream like a piece of bark, an' water washin' all over me. I knowed den I gone, an' I hollered for Marse George for help. I heah him answer me not to git skeered, but to hold on; but de myah wuz lungin' an' de water wuz all over me like ice, an' den I washed off de myah back, an' got drownded. I 'member comin' up an' hollerin' agin for help, but I know den 'tain' no use, dee ain' no help den, an' I got to pray to Gord, an' den some'n hit me an' I went down again, an'—de next thing I know, I wuz in de bed, an' I heah 'em talkin' 'bout wherr I dead or not, an' I ain' know myself tell I taste o' whisky dee po'rin' down my jugular. An' den dee tell me 'bout how when I hollered Marse George tun back an' struck out for me for life, an' how jes as I went down de last time he cotch me an' helt on to me tell we wash down to whar de bank curve, an' dyah de current wuz so rapid hit yuck him off Reveller back, but he helt on to do reins tell de horse lunge

so he hit him wid he fo'-foot an' breck he collar-bone, an' den he had to let him go, an' jest helt on to me; an' jes den we wash up agin de bank an' cotch in a tree, an' de mens got dyah quick as dee could, an' when dee retched us Marse George wuz holdin' on to me, an' had he arm wropped roun' a limb, an' we wuz lodged in de crotch, an' bofe jes as dead as a nail; an' de myah she got out, but Reveller he wuz drownded, wid his foot cotch in de rein an' de saddle tunned onder he side; an' dee ain' know wherr Marse George ain' dead too, 'cause he not only drownded, but he lef' arm broke up nigh de shoulder. An' dee say Miss Charlotte she 'most 'stracted; dat de fust thing anybody know 'bout it wuz when some de servants bust in de hall an' holler, and say Marse George an' me done bofe washed 'way an' drownded, an' dat she drapt down dead on de flo', an' when dee bring her to she 'low to Miss Lucy dat she de 'casion on he death; an' dee say dat when de mens wuz totin' him in de house, an' wuz shufflin' de feets not to meck no noige, an' a little piece o' blue silk drapt out he breast whar somebody picked up an' gin Miss Lucy, Miss Charlotte breck right down agin; an' some on 'em say she sutney did keer for him; an' now when he layin' upsteairs dyah dead, hit too late for him ever to know it.

"Well, suh, I couldn' teck it in dat Marse George and Reveller wuz dead, an' jes den somebody say Marse George done comin' to, an' dee gi' me so much whisky I went to sleep. An' next mornin' I got up an' went to Marse George room, an' see him layin' dyah in de bed, wid he face so white an' he eyes so tired-lookin', an' he ain' know me no mo' 'n ef he nuver see me, an' I couldn' stan' it; I jes drap down on de flo' an' bust out cryin'. Gord! suh, I couldn' help it, 'cause Reveller wuz drownded, an' Marse George he wuz mos' gone. An' he came nigher goin' yit, 'cause he had sich a strain, an' been so long in de water, he heart got numbed, an' he got 'lirium, an' all de time he thought he tryin' to git 'cross de river to see Miss Charlotte, an' hit so high he kyarn git dyah. Hit sutney wuz pitiful to see him layin' dyah tossin' an' pitchin', not knowin' whar he wuz, tell it took all Mr. Braxton an' me could do to keep him in de bed, an' de doctors say he kyarn hol' out much longer.

"An' all dis time Miss Charlotte she wuz gwine 'bout de house wid her face right white, an' Nancy say she don' do nuttin all day long in her room but cry an' say her pra'rs, prayin' for Marse George, whar dyin' upsteirs by 'count o' not knowin' she love him, an' I tell Nancy how he honin' all de time to see her, an' how he constant callin' her name. Well, so twuz, tell he mos' done weah heself out; an' jes lay dyah wid his face white as de pillow an' he gret pitiful eyes rollin' 'bout so restless, like he still lookin' for her whar he all de time callin' her name, an' kyarn git 'cross dat river to see; an' one evenin' 'bout sunset he 'peared to be gwine; he weaker'n he been at all, he ain' able to scuffle no mo', an' jes layin' dyah so quiet, an' presney he say, lookin' mighty wistful,

" 'Edinburg, I'm goin' to-night; ef I don' git 'cross dis time, I'll gin' it up.'

"Mr. Braxton wuz standin' nigh de head o' de bed, an' he say, 'Well, by Gord! he shall see her!'—jes so. An' he went out de room, an' to Miss Charlotte do', an' call her, an' tell her she got to come, ef she don', he'll die dat night; an' fust thing I know, Miss Lucy bring Miss Charlotte in, wid her face right white, but jes as tender as a angel's, an' she come an' stan' by the side de bed, an' lean down over him, an' call he name, 'George!'—jes so.

"An' Marse George he ain' answer; he jes look at her studdy for a minute, an' den he forehead got smooth, an' he tun he eyes to me, an' say, 'Edinburg, I'm 'cross.' "

XXVII

ELIZABETH GRACE KING (1852–   )

The early work of Grace King came as a protest against what she considered the false impressions of the Creoles and of Creole society given by George W. Cable. She was herself of Creole birth, she had been educated with the finest types of Creole femininity in a school such as she has depicted in "Monsieur Motte," and she felt that Cable, a Puritan, though of Southern birth, had *exhibited* his Creoles as curiosities, had been guilty at times of positive errors concerning them, had given only the surface of their life without understanding it fully, and she set out deliberately to depict her people from the inner life outward. Her first story, "Monsieur Motte," is exquisitely told. It is French in atmosphere and art. As one approaches its strong climax, one feels not only the coming inevitable tragedy, as remorseless as a creation of Euripides, but one feels as if one had actually lived in the presence of the two helpless victims. They are alive; we see them, we feel them. Everything, the very atmosphere, is redolent of Creolism; yet the story is far more than a mere exhibition of Creoles. It rests on characteristics fundamentally human: it is a fragment torn from real life and one sees the blood. It ends with dramatic *finesse,* yet the final paragraph does not end the tale. And that is the crowning touch of art.

In the same vein, though never again with equal power, Miss King told other Creole tales, collecting them into volumes entitled *Tales of a Time and Place,* 1892, and *Balcony Stories,* 1893. In her art she is Gallic—impassioned yet always within leash—chaste, finished, epigrammatic. She is one of the few who have mastered the technique of the short-story form.

MONSIEUR MOTTE

It was near mid-day in June. A dazzling stream of vertical sun-rays fell into the quadrangular court-yard of the Institute St. Denis and filled it to suffocation with light and heat. The flowers which grew in little beds, dotting the gray-flagged surface, bowed their heads under their leaves for shelter.

A thin strip of shadow, stretching from the side of the school-house, began to creep over the garden, slowly following the sun in its progress past the obtruding walls of neighboring buildings, until he should disappear behind a certain square steeple far off in the distance; then the shade would entirely cover the yard; then the stars would be coming out, languid and pale; and then the fragrance of oleander and jasmine, traveling from yard to yard, would burden the air, soothing the senses in order to seduce the imagination.

Along the narrow shaded strip, quite filling it up, moved a class of girls in Indian-file, their elbows scraping against the rugged bricks of the wall as they held their books up to the openings of their sun-bonnets. A murmur of rapidly articulated words, like the murmur of boiling water in a closed kettle, came from the leaves of their books, while from their [5] hidden lips dropped disjointed fragments of *l'Histoire de France.*

The foundation, as well as key-stone, of St. Denisian education, it was but natural that the examination in *l'Histoire de [10] France, par D. Lévi Alvares, père,*[1] should fill the last days of the scholastic term; and as a prize in that exercise set the brightest crown upon the head of the victor, it was not strange that it should [15] be conducted with such rigidity and impartiality as to demoralize panic-stricken contestants whose sex usually warranted justice in leaving one eye at least unbound.

Under the circumstances, a trust in luck [20] is the most reliable source of comfort. If experience proved anything, if the study of the history of France itself made one point clear, it was the dependence of great events on trifles, the unfailing interposi- [25] tion of the *inattendu,*[2] and, consequently, the utter futility of preparation. The graduating class of 1874 turned their pages with clammy fingers, and repeated mechanically, with unwearied tongues, any passage upon which Fate should direct their eyes. None dared be slighted with impunity, the most insignificant being perhaps the very one to trip them up, the most familiar, the traitor to play them false. A laggard church clock in the neighborhood gave them each eleven separate, distinct shocks. It warned them that two minutes and a half had already been consumed on the road from one class-room to the other, and reminded them of Monsieur Mignot's diabolical temper.

A little girl, also in a large sun-bonnet, with a placard marked *"Passe-Partout"* [3] around her neck, turned an angle of the building suddenly and threw the nervous ranks into dire confusion; the books went down, the bonnets up.

"Seigneur! qu'est-ce que c'est?" [4]

"Ma chère! [5] how you frightened me!"

"Mon Dieu! [6] I thought it was Monsieur Mignot!"

"I am trembling all over!"

"I can hardly stand up!"

"Just feel how my heart beats."

"You had better hurry up, *mes enfants,"* [7] replied the little one, in the patronizing tone of personal disinterestedness; "it is past eleven."

"But we don't know one word," they groaned in unison—"not one single word."

"Ah, bah! you are frightened, that's all; you always say that." She gave one of them a good-natured push in the direction of the door about which they were standing in distressful hesitation.

"I tell you, old Mignot is in a horrible temper. *Il a fait les quatre cent coups* [8] in our class; threw his inkstand at Stéphanie Morel's head."

The door, with startling coincidence, was violently pulled open at these words, and a gray-haired, spectacled old gentleman thrust out an irate face in quest of his dilatory class. Thrown by the catastrophe into a state of complete nescience of all things historical, from Clovis to Napoleon, the young ladies jerked off their sun-bonnets and entered the room, while the little girl escaped at full speed. A drowsy, quiet, peaceful half-hour followed in the yard. A surprising silence for the center of a busy city considering the close proximity of two hundred school-girls. It was a mocking contrast to the scene of doubt, hesitation, and excitement on the other side of the closed door—a contrast advantageous to the uneducated happiness of the insects and flowers.

A door-bell rang; not the bell of the pretty little gate which admitted visitors to the rose-hedged, violet-bordered walk leading to Madame's *antichambre;* [9] but the bell of the capacious *porte-cochère* [10] which was reserved for the exits and entrances of scholars and domestics. After a carefully measured pause, the ring was repeated, then again, and again. The rusty organ of intercommunication squeaked and creaked plaintively after each disturbance as if forced from a sick-bed to do painful and useless service. A gaunt, red-haired woman finally came out in obedience to the summons, with an elaboration of slowness which the shuffling sabots clearly betrayed to the outsider, as evidenced by a last superfluous, unnecessarily energetic pull of the bell-knob.

She carefully unrolled her sleeves as she sauntered along, and stood until she loosened the cord which reefed her dress to an unconventional height. Then she opened the *grille* [11] and looked out.

"Ah, je le savais bien," [12] she muttered, with strong Gascon [13] accent.

There was a diminutive door cut into the large gate. It looked, with its coat of fresh paint, like a barnacle on the weather-beaten exterior. Opening with the facility of greased hinges, it was an unavoidable compromise between the heavy cypress timber and iron fastenings, prescribed by the worldly, or heavenly, experience of St. Denis as the proper protection of a young ladies' boarding-school, and the almost incessant going and coming which secluded femininity and excluded shops made necessary.

"But I can't get in there!" said a woman outside.

"Tant pis." [14] and the little door was closed.

"But I must come in with my basket."

A shrug of the shoulders was the only reply through the *grille.*

"It is Mamzelle Marie's toilet for the exhibition."

The little gate was again held open.

"Don't you see I can't get in there?"

"Ça m'est égal." [15]

A snort of exasperation was heard on the outside, and a suppressed *"C'est un peu fort!"* [16]

"Will you open the big gate for me so

that I can bring in Mamzelle Marie's dress?"

No answer.

"Well, then, I shall ring at Madame's bell."

The white woman did not lack judgment. She was maintaining her own in a quarrel begun years ago; a quarrel involving complex questions of the privileges of order and the distinctions of race; a quarrel in which hostilities were continued, year by year, with no interruptions of courtesy or mitigation by truce. This occasion was one of the perquisites of Jeanne's position of *femme de ménage*.[17] Slight compensation enough when compared to the indignities put upon her as a white woman, and the humiliations as a sensitive one by *"cette négresse Marcélite."*[18] But the duration of triumph must be carefully measured. Marcélite's ultimatum, if carried out, would quickly reverse their relative positions by a bonus to Marcélite in the shape of a reprimand to Jeanne. She allowed her foe, however, to carry her basket in the hot sun as far as the next bell, and even waited until she put her hand on it before the iron bar fell and the massive structure was allowed to swing open.

"Ristocrate!"[19] she muttered, without looking at either woman or basket.

"Canaille!"[20] whispered the other, with her head thrown back and her nose in the air.

Glancing at the line of shade in the yard to see how near it was to twelve o'clock, for want of other accommodation she went into an open arbor, put her basket on the floor, and wiped her face with a colored foulard handkerchief. *"Fait chaud mo dit toi,"*[21] she said aloud in creole, her language for self-communion. She pulled her skirts out on each side, and sat down with a force that threatened the stability of the bench; then, careless of creeping and crawling possibilities, leaned her head back against the vine-covered wall. The green leaves formed a harmonious frame for the dark-brown face, red and yellow *tignon*,[22] and the large gold earrings hanging beneath two glossy *coqs*[23] of black wool. Her features were regular and handsome according to the African type, with a strong, sensuous expression, subdued but not obliterated. Her soft black eyes showed in their voluptuous depths intelligence and strength and protecting tenderness. Her stiff purple calico dress settled in defining folds about her portly limbs. A white handkerchief was pinned over her untrammeled bosom; her large, full, supple waist was encircled by the strings of her apron, which were tied in a careful bow at her side.

Besides the large basket, she carried on her arm a small covered one, which, if opened, would reveal her calling to be that of hairdressing. She was the *coiffeuse*[24] of the school, and, as such, the general *chargée d'affaires, confidante,*[25] messenger, and adviser of teachers and scholars. Her discretion was proven beyond suspicion. Her judgment, or rather her intuition, was bold, quick, and effective. In truth, Marcélite was as indispensable as a lightning-rod to the boarding-school, conducted as it was under the austere discipline of the old régime. Her smooth, round hands and taper fingers had been polished by constant friction with silken locks; her familiar, polite, gentle, servile manners were those contracted during a courtly life of dependent intimacy with superiors. *On dit*[26] that her basket carried other articles besides combs, brushes, and cosmetics, and that her fingers had been found preferable to the post-office, for the delivery of certain implicative missives, written in the prose or verse of irresistible emotion. Even without her basket, any one, from her hands, *démarche,*[27] and language would recognize a *coiffeuse* of the élite, while in New Orleans, in the *Quartier Créole,*[28] there was hardly a man, woman, or child who did not call her by name: Marcélite Gaulois.

She lifted a palmetto fan, bound and tied to her waist with black ribbon, and holding it up between her and observation, betook herself in quiet and privacy to slumber. A nap of delicious relaxation, so gentle that the bite of a mosquito, the crawling of an ant, an incipient snore, startled it; but so tenacious, that the uplifted hand and dropping head resettled themselves without breaking its delicate filaments. A little, thin, rusty-voiced bell had now one of its three important daily announcements to make—Recreation Time. From all over the city came corroborative evidence of the fact, by chronometers, some a little ahead, and some a little behind meridian. This want of unanimity proclaimed the notorious and distressing difference of two minutes and a half between church and state—

a difference in which the smallest watch in the school could not avoid participation.

It was the same little girl with the "*Passe-Partout*" who published the truce to study. The rope of the bell and she were both too short, so she had to stand on tiptoe and jerk it in little quick jumps. The operation involved a terrible disproportion between labor invested and net profit, for which nothing but the gladsome nature of her mission, and the honorary distinction implied in it, could have compensated her. A moment of stillness, during which both the rope and the little girl quieted themselves, and then—a shower of little girls fell into the yard—all of them little girls, but not all of them children, and as much alike as drops of different colored water.

They were all dressed in calico dresses made in the same way, with very full, short skirts, and very full, short waists, fastened, matron-fashion, in front. They all wore very tight, glossy, fresh, black French kid boots, with tassels or bows hanging from the top. With big sun-bonnets, or heavily veiled hats on their heads, thick gloves on their hands, and handkerchiefs around their necks, they were walking buttresses against the ardent sun. They held their lunch baskets like bouquets, and their heads as if they wore crowns. They carried on conversations in sweet, low voices, with interrupting embraces and apostrophic tendernesses:

"*Chère!*" [29]
"*Chérie!*" [30]
"*Ange!*" [31]
"*M'amie!*" [32]

They had a grace of ease, the gift of generations; a self-composure and polish, dating from the cradle. Of course they did not romp, but promenaded arm in arm, measuring their steps with dainty particularity; moving the whole body with rhythmic regularity, displaying and acquiring at the same time a sinuosity of motion. Their hair hung in plaits so far below their waists that it threatened to grow into a measuring-tape for their whole length.

The angular Jeanne appeared, holding a waiter at arm's-length over her head. She had no need to cluck or chirp; the sound of her sabots was enough to call around her in an instant an eager brood of hungry boarders, jumping and snatching for their portion of lunch. There was the usual moment of obstruction over the point of etiquette whether they should take heir own piece of bread and butter or receive it from Jeanne. The same useless sacrifice of a test slice was made, and the obstinate servant had to give in with the same consolatory satisfaction of having been again true to her fixed principle to make herself as disagreeable as possible under any circumstances that the day might bring forth. There is great field for choice, even in slices of bread and butter. The ends, or knots of the loaves, split longitudinally, offer much more appetizing combinations of crust and crumb than the round inside slices. Knots, however, were the prerogative of the big girls; inside slices the grievance of the little ones. To-day, "*comme toujours,*" [33] as they said, with a shrug, the primary classes had to take what was left them. But, their appetite was so good, they ate their homely fare with so much gusto that the day scholars looked on enviously and despised their own epicurean baskets, which failed to elicit such expectations, and never afforded them similar gratification. *A la fin des fins!* [34] The door which concealed the terrible struggle going on with the history of France was opened. All rushed forward for news, with eager sympathy. It was a dejected little army that filed out after so protracted a combat, with traces of tears in their eyes and all over their flushed cheeks. Tired and nervous, not one would confess to a ray of hope. Certainty of defeat had succeeded to certainty of failure. The history of France, with its disastrous appliances of chronology, dynasties, conquests, and revolutions, had gained, according to them, a complete and unquestioned victory.

"Marie Modeste, look at Marcélite," said one of the girls, hailing the diversion.

The *bonne* [35] was coming out of the garden-house with her basket. One of the graduating class rushed forward to meet her, and both together disappeared in the direction of the dormitory stairway. "It is her toilet for the exhibition," was whispered, and curious eyes followed the basket invested with such preternatural importance. "They say *le vieux* [36] is going to give her a superb one."

The *Grand Concert Musicale et Distribution de Prix* [37] was to take place the next evening. All parents and friends had, for two weeks, been invited to "assist" by their presence. This annual fête wa; preëminently *the* fête of St. Denis. [38] It was the goal of the scholastic course, the beginning of vacation, and the set term to the young ladies' aspirations if not ambition. A fair share of books, laurel crowns, in green and gold paper, and a possible real gold medal was with them, the end if not the aim of study from the opening of the school in September. Personally they could not imagine any state or condition in life when knowledge of French history would be a comfort or cosmography an assistance; but prizes were so many concrete virtues which lasted fresh into grandmotherhood. *Noblesse oblige,*[39] that the glory of maternal achievements be not dimmed in these very walls where their mothers, little creoles like themselves, strove for laurel crowns culled from the same imperishable tree in Rue Royale.

Marcélite followed Marie through the dormitory, down the little aisle, between the rows of beds with their veils of mosquito netting, until they came to the farthest corner; which, when one turned one's back to the rest of the chamber, had all the seclusion and "sociability" of a private apartment. The furniture, however, did not include chairs, so Marie seated herself on the side of the bed, and, taking off her bonnet, awaited Marcélite's pleasure to initiate her into the delightful mysteries of the basket.

She wondered where Marcélite had picked up the artistic expedient of heightening the effect by playing on the feelings of the spectators; and she wondered if carrying that basket up the stairs had really tired those strong shoulders and made her so dreadfully hot; and if it were really necessary that each one of those thousand pins should be quilted into the front of that white handkerchief; and if Marcélite had made a vow not to open her mouth until she got out the last pin; and if . . .

She was naturally nervous and impatient, and twisted and turned ceaselessly on the bed during the ordeal of assumed procrastination. Her black eyes were oversized for her face, oversized and overweighted with expression; and most of the time, as to-day, they were accompanied by half-moon shadows which stretched half-way down her cheek. Over her forehead and temples the hieroglyphic tracery of blue veins might be seen, until it became obscured under the masses of black hair whose heavy plaits burdened the delicate

head and strained the slender neck. The exterior of a girl of seventeen! That frail mortal encasement which precocious inner life threatens to rend and destroy. The appealing languor, the uncomplaining lassitude, the pathetic apathy, the transparent covering through which is seen the growth of the woman in the body of the child.

Marcélite saw upon the bed the impatient figure of a petulant girl, wild for the sight of her first *toilette de bal.*[40] There lay on the bed, in reality, a proud, reserved, eager, passionate spirit, looking past toilettes, past graduating, past studies and examinations; looking from the prow of an insignificant vessel into the broad prospect, so near, so touchingly near, reserved for her, and all girls of seventeen, that unique realm, called: "Woman's Kingdom."

Romances and poetry had been kept from her like wine and spices. But the flowers bloomed, and music had chords, and moonlight rays, and were the bars of the school never so strong and the rules never so rigid, they could not prevent her heart from going out toward the rays, nor from listening to the music, nor from inhaling the breath of the flowers. And what they said is what they always say to the girl of seventeen. It is the love-time of life, when the heart first puts forth its flowers; and what boarding-school can frustrate spring? Her mouth, like her eyes, was encircled with a shadow, faint, almost imperceptible, like the timid suggestion of nascent passion which it gave to the thin, sad lips.

She had been four years old when she came to this school; so Marcélite told her, for she could not remember. Now she was seventeen. She looked at the strong, full maturity of Marcélite. Would she, Marie, ever be like that? Had Marcélite ever been like her? At seventeen, did she ever feel this way? This—oh, this longing! Could Marcélite put her finger on the day, as Marie could, when this emotion broke into her heart, that thought into her brain? Did Marcélite know the origin of blushes, the cause of tremors? Did Marcélite ever pray to die to be relieved from vague apprehensions, and then pray to live in the faith of some great unknown, but instinctive prophecy?

She forbore to ask. If she had had a mother! . . . But did girls even ask their mothers these things? But she had no mother! Good, devoted, loyal as she was,

Marcélite was not a mother—not her mother. She had stopped at the boundary where the mother ceases to be a physical and becomes a psychical necessity. The child still clung to Marcélite, but the young woman was motherless. She had an uncle, however, who might become a father. . . .

"Là!"[41] Marcélite had exhausted her last devisable subterfuge, and made known her readiness to begin the show.

"Là! mon bébé! là, ma mignonne![42] what do you think of that?" She turned it around by the belt, it seemed all covered over with bubbles of muslin and frostings of lace.

"Just look at that! Ah ha! I thought you would be astonished! You see that lace? Ça c'est du vrai,[43] no doubt about that—real Valenciennes. You think I don't know real lace, hein?[44] and mousseline des Indes?[45] You ask Madame Treize—you know what she said? 'Well, Marcélite, that is the prettiest pattern of lace and the finest piece of muslin I almost ever saw.' Madame Treize told me that herself, and it's true, for I know it myself."

"Madame Treize, Marcélite?"

Madame Treize was the ou ne peut plus[46] of New Orleans for fashion and extravagance.

"Yes, Madame Treize. Who do you think was going to make your dress, hein? Madame N'importe-qui?"[47]

"Marcélite, it must have cost so much!"

"Eh bien,[48] it's all paid for. What have you got to do with that? All you have got to do is to put it on and wear it. Oh, mon bébé! ma petite chérie![49]—what tones of love her rich voice could carry—"if it had cost thousands and thousands of dollars it would not be too fine for you, nor too pretty."

"But, Marcélite, I will be ashamed to wear it; it is too beautiful."

But the eyes sparkled joyfully, and the lips trembled with delightful anticipations.

"Here's the body! You see those bows? that was my taste. I said to myself, 'she must have blue ribbons on the shoulder,' and I went back and made Madame Treize put them on. Oh, I know Madame Treize; and Madame Treize, she knows me!"

"And the shoes, Marcélite?"

Hands and voice fell with utter disgust.

"Now you see, mamzelle, you always do that. Question, question, question all the time. Why didn't you wait? Now you have spoiled it all—all the surprise!"

"Pardon, Marcélite, I did not mean; but I was afraid you had forgotten——"

"Oh, mon bébé! when did Marcélite ever forget anything you wanted?"

Marie blushed with shame at a self-accusation of ingratitude.

"Ma bonne Marcélite! I am so impatient, I cannot help it."

A bundle of shoes was silently placed in her lap.

"White satin boots! Mar-cé-lite! White satin boots for me? Oh, I can't believe it! And I expected black leather!—how shall I ever thank my uncle for them—and all this? How can I ever do it?"

The radiant expression faded away from the nurse's face at these words.

"Oh, but I know it was your idea, Marcélite! My good, kind, dear Marcélite! I know it was all your idea. He never could have thought of all these beautiful things —a man!"

She put her arms around the bonne's neck and laid her head on the broad, soft shoulder, as she used to do when she was a little, little girl.

"Ah, Marcélite, my uncle can never be as kind to me as you are. He gives me the money, but you——"

She felt the hands patting her back and the lips pressed against her hair; but she could not see the desperate, passionate, caressing eyes, "savoring" her like the lips of an eager dog.

"Let us try them on."

She knelt on the floor and stripped off one shoe and stocking. When the white foot on its fragile ankle lay in her dark palm, her passion broke out afresh. She kissed it over and over again; she nestled it in her bosom; she talked baby-talk to it in creole; she pulled on the fine stocking as if every wrinkle were an offense, and slackness an unpardonable crime. How they both labored over the boot; straining, pulling, smoothing the satin, coaxing, urging, drawing the foot! What patience on both sides! What precaution that the glossy white should meet with no defilement! Finally the button-holes were caught over the buttons, and to all intents and purposes a beautiful, symmetrical, solidified satin foot lay before them.

"Too tight?"

It might have been a question, but it sounded more like the laying of a doubt.

"Too tight! just look!"

The little toes made a vigorous demonstration of contempt and denial.

"I can change them if they are."

"Do you want me to wear sabots like Jeanne?"

"They will stretch, anyhow."

Marcélite preferred yielding to her own rather than to another's conviction, even when they both were identical.

The boots were taken off, rolled in tissue-paper, and put away in the *armoire*,[50] which was now opened to its fullest extent to receive the dress.

Marie leaned against the pillow of the bed and clasped her hands over her head. She listened dreamily and contentedly to her praises thrown off by Marcélite's fluent tongue. What would the reality be, if the foretaste were so sweet?

"I wonder what he will say, Marcélite?"

"*Qui ça?*"[51]

"My uncle. Do you think he will be pleased?"

"What makes you so foolish, *bébé?*"

"But that's not foolish, Marcélite."

"Hum!"

"Say, Marcélite, do you think he will be satisfied?"

"Satisfied with what?"

"Oh, you know, Marcélite—satisfied with me?"

The head was thrust too far into the *armoire*[52] for an immediate answer.

"How can I tell, mamzelle?"

"Mamzelle! mamzelle! Madame Marcélite!"

"Well then, *bébé.*"

"Anyway, he will come to the concert —*Hein,* Marcélite?"

"What is it, Zozo?"

"My uncle; he is coming to the concert, isn't he?"

Marcélite shrugged her shoulders; her mouth was filled with pins.

"*Ma bonne!* do not be so mean; tell me if he is coming, and what he said."

"Poor gentleman! he is so old."

"Did he tell you that?"

Marie laughed; this was a standing joke between them.

"But, my child, what do you want him to say? You bother me so with your questions, I don't know what I am doing."

"But, Marcélite, it is only natural for me to want him to come to the concert and see me in my pretty dress that he gave me."

"Well, when one is old and sick——"

"Sick! ah, you did not tell me that."

"But I tell it to you all the time!"

"Oh, Marcélite!"

There is no better subject on which to exercise crude eloquence than the delinquencies of laundresses. A heinous infraction had been committed against the integrity of one of Marie's garments, and Marcélite threatened to consume the rest of the day in expressions of disgust and indignation.

"So he is *not* coming to the concert?" the girl demanded, excitedly.

"Ah! there's the bell, you had better run quick before they send for you."

"No, I am excused until time to practise my duet. Marcélite"—the voice lost its excited tone and became pleading, humble, and timid—"Marcélite, do you think my uncle will like me?"

"*Mon Dieu!* yes, yes, yes."

"*Mais ne t'impatientes pas, ma bonne,*[53] I can't help thinking about it. He has never seen me—since I was a baby, I mean—and I don't recollect him at all, at all. Oh, Marcélite! I have tried so often, so often to recall him, and my *maman*"[54]—she spoke it as shyly as an infant does the name of God in its first prayer. "If I could only go just one little point farther back, just that little bit"—she measured off a demi-centimeter on her finger—"but impossible. Maybe it will all come back to me when I see him, and the house, and the furniture. Perhaps, if I had been allowed to see it only once or twice, I might be able to remember something. It *is* hard, Marcélite, it is very hard not even to be able to recollect a mother. To-morrow evening!" she gave a long, long sigh—"only to-morrow evening more!"

The depravity of the washerwoman must have got beyond even Marcélite's powers of description, for she had stopped talking, but held her head inside the shelf.

"One reason I want him to come to the concert is to take me home with him. In the first place, Madame wouldn't let me go unless he came for me; and—and I want the girls to see him; they have teased me so much about him. I believe, Marcélite, that if my graduating were put off one day longer, or if my uncle did not come for me to-morrow evening, I would die. How foolish! Just think of all these years I have been here, summer after summer, the only boarder left during vacation! I didn't seem to mind it then, but now it's all different;

everything has become so different this last year." The tears had been gathering in her eyes for some time, and she had been smearing them with her finger off the side of her face to escape Marcélite's notice; but now they came too fast for that, so she was forced to turn over and hide her face flat in the pillow.

"Crying, *mon bébé?* what is the matter with you—oh, oh!—you do not feel well! something you do not like about your toilet, *hein?* Tell Marcélite, *chérie;* tell your *bonne.* There! there!"

Sobs were added to tears, until she seemed in conflict with a tornado of grief. She pressed her head tighter and tighter against the pillow to stifle the noise, but her narrow, high shoulders shook convulsively, and her feet twisted and turned, one over the other, in uncontrollable agitation. Marcélite stood by her side, a look of keen torture on her emotional face. If the child had only been larger, or stronger! if she did not writhe so helplessly before her! if she had fought less bravely against the rending sobs! Ah! and if the shrouded form of a dead mother had not intervened with outstretched arms and reproachful eyes fixed upon Marcélite. She could hold out no longer, but fell on her knees by the bed, and clasped her arms around the little one to hold her quiet. With her face on the pillow, and her lips close to the red, burning ear, she whispered the soothing tendernesses of a maternal heart. There was a balsam which never failed; a story she had often told, but which repetition had only made more difficult, more hesitating; to-day the words fell like lead. About the father Marie had never seen, the mother she had never known, the home-shelter of her baby years, beyond even her imagination, and the guardian uncle, the question of whose coming to the concert had so excited her.

"Is Marie Modeste here?" asked a little voice through a far-off door.

Marie started. "Yes." Her voice was rough, weak, and trembling.

"They want you for the 'Cheval de Bronze.'" [55]

She sat up and let the nurse smooth her hair and bathe her face, keeping her lips tightly shut over the ebbing sobs.

"Thank you, Marcélite. Thank you for everything—for my beautiful dress, and my shoes—and thank my uncle too; and try and persuade him to come to-morrow evening, won't you, Marcélite? Do not tell him about my crying, though. Oh, I want to go home so much! and to see him. You know if you want you can get him to come. Won't you promise me, *ma bonne?*"

"You know I would kill myself for you, *mon bébé.*"

The good little Paula was waiting outside the door. Uncontrollable tears are too common in a girls' school to attract attention. They were crises which, though not to be explained, even the smallest girl understood intuitively, and for which were tacitly employed convenient convential excuses.

"The *concours* [56] was very difficult, *chère?*"

"Yes, very difficult."

"And Monsieur Mignot is so trying. I think he gets more *exigeant* [57] every day." And they kissed each other sympathetically on the stair-way.

"*Grand Dieu Seigneur!*" [58] groaned Marcélite, when Marie had left the room, holding her head with both hands.

"What am I going to do now! I believe I am turning fool!"

Life was changing from a brilliant path in white muslin dresses to a hideous dilemma. And for once she did not know what to do. A travail seemed going on in her brain, her natural strength and audacity had completely oozed away from her. She began a vehement monologue in creole reiterating assertions and explanations, stopping short always at one point.

"My God! I never thought of that."

She looked towards the ceiling with violent reproaches to the *bon Dieu, doux Jésus* and *Sainte-Vierge.* [59] Why had they left her alone to manage this? They knew she was a "nigger, nigger, nigger" (trying to humiliate and insult herself). Why hadn't they done something? Why couldn't they do something now? And all she had done for them, and that ungrateful patron saint, the recipient of so much attention, so many favors. She never had asked them anything for herself, thank God! Marcélite could always manage her own affairs without the assistance of any one. But her *bébé!* for whom she had distinctly prayed and burned candles, and confessed and communed, and worked, and toiled, and kept straight! She clasped her flesh in her sharp, long nails, and the pain did her good. She could have dashed her head against the wall. She would gladly have stripped her shoulders to the lash, if, if it would do any good. She would kill herself for the matter of that, but what would that prevent or remedy? The church was not far off, perhaps a miracle! But what miracle can avert the inevitable? She shoved her empty basket under the bed and went out upon the covered gallery that spanned the garden and led to Madame Lareveillère's bedchamber.

The quadrangle lay half overspread now by shadow. The gay *insouciante* [60] flowers moved gently in an incipient breeze, the umbrella top of the little summer-house warded the rays from the benches beneath, and kept them cool and pleasant. Her own face was not more familiar, more matter-of-fact to Marcélite, and yet she saw in the yard things she had never remarked before. There was a different expression to it all. Flowers, summer-house, even the gray flags, depressed her and made her sad; as if they, or she, were going to die soon. She caught the balustrade in her hand, but it was not vertigo. What was it, then, that made her feel so unnatural and everything so portentous? This morning, life was so comfortable and small, everything just under her hand. She was mistress of every day, and night was the truce, if not the end of all trouble. But to-day had united itself to past and future in such a way that night was but a transparent veil that separated but could not isolate them one from the other. Time was in revolt against her, her own powers betrayed her; flight was impossible, resistance useless, death even, futile.

"What was the matter with her head, anyhow? She must be *voudoued.*" [61] If she could only feel as she did this morning! The slatternly Jeanne shuffled underneath on her way to the bell, an augur of ill omen. She would go and see Madame Lareveillère. Madame (as she was commonly called) sat at her *secrétaire* [62] writing. Her pen, fine pointed as a cambric needle, scratched under her fingers as if it worked on steel instead of paper. She was very busy, transferring the names from a list before her into the gilt-edged prize books piled up in glowing heaps all around her. A strict observer would have noticed many inaccuracies which would have invalidated any claim to correctness on the part of her copy. There were not only liberties taken with the prize itself, but entire names were involved in transactions which the original list by no means war-

ranted. These inaccuracies always occurred after consultation of another list kept in madame's little drawer—a list whose columns carried decimals instead of good and bad marks for lessons. A single ray of light, filtered through various intermedial shades and curtains, had been manœuvered so as to fall on the small desk at a safe distance from madame's sensitive complexion. At difficult calculations, she would screw up her eyes and peer at both lists brought into the focus of illumination, then would sink back into obscurity for advisory reflection.

There are so many calculations to be made, so many fine distinctions drawn in a distribution of prizes! No one but a schoolmistress knows the mental effort requisite for the working out of an equation which sets good and bad scholars against good and bad pay. Why could not the rich girls study more, or the poor less? Oh, the simple beauty of strict, injudicious impartiality! Cursed be the inventor or originator of these annual rehearsals, where every one was rewarded except the rewarder!

On occasions like these any interruption is a deliverance; madame heard with glad alacrity a knock at the door.

"*Ah! c'est toi,*" [63] Marcélite!"

Marcélite represented another matter of yearly consideration, another question of paramount importance, a suspensive judgment, involving, however, madame alone. With the assistance of the *coiffeuse,* many years ago (the date is not essential, and women are sensitive about such things), the principal of the Institute St. Denis had engaged in one of those struggles against Time to which pretty, unmarried women seem pledged during a certain period, the fighting age, of their lives. It was purely a defensive struggle on her part, and consisted in a protest against that uglifying process by which women are coaxed into resignation to old age and death. So far, she had maintained her own perfectly, and Time, for all the progress he had made in the sweet, delicate face of Eugénie Lareveillère, might just as well have been tied for ten years past to one of the four posts of the bedstead. The musical concert and distribution of prizes and its consequent indispensable new toilet furnished an excellent date for an annual review and consultation, when old measures were discussed, new ones adopted, and the next campaign planned. Madame, however, did not feel this year the same buoyant courage, the same irrepressible audacity as heretofore. In fact, there was a vague suspicion in her breast, hitherto unacknowledged, that in spite of facial evidence she herself, *dans son intérieur,*[64] was beginning to grow the least, little, tiny bit old. She felt like capitulating with the enemy, and had almost made up her mind to surrender—her hair. *L'incertitude est le pire des maux, jusqu'au moment ou la réalité nous fait regretter l'incertitude.*[65] Should the conditions be proven too hard for mortal beauty, she could at least revolt again. Thank Heaven! over there in Paris worked devoted emissaries for women, and the last word had not yet been said by the artists of hair-dyes and cosmetics.

"*Eh, bien, qu'en dis-tu,*[66] Marcélite?"

The artistically arranged head, with its curls and puffs and frisettes clustered like brown silken flowers above the fair skin, was directly in the line of Marcélite's vision. Who would have suspected that these were but transplanted exotics from the hot head of foreign youth? that under their adorning luxuriance lay, fastened by inflexible hair-pins, the legitimate but deposed possessors of this crown? But they were old, gray, almost white, and madame was suggesting for them a temporary and empirical resurrection. That head which daily for years she had molded according to her comprehension of fashion; that inert little ball for which Marcélite, in her superb physical strength, had almost felt a contempt; she looked at it now, and like the flowers in the garden, it was changed to her, was pregnant with subtle, portentous meaning. She was beginning faintly to suspect the truth. All this buzzing, whirling, thought, fear, calculation, retrospection, and prevision, which had come into her great, big, strong head only an hour ago, had been going on in this little, fragile, delicate handful of skull for years, ever since it was born. She saw it now, she knew it: the difference between madame's head and hers, between a consciousness limited by eternity and one limited by a nightly sleep, between an intelligence looking into immortality and one looking into the eyes of a confessor.

The room would have been quite dark but for that one useful ray which, after enlightening the path of distributive justice for madame, fell on and was absorbed by a picture opposite. Out of the obscurity arose one by one the features of the bedchamber, the supreme model of bedchambers in the opinion of the impressionable loyalists of St. Denis. A bedchamber, the luxury of which could never be surpassed, the mysterious solemnity never equaled. A bedchamber, in fact, created to satisfy the majestic coquettishness of the autocratic superior of an artistic school for girls.

Indistinct, undefined, vague fragments of color struggled up through the floor of somber carpet. The windows, made to exclude the light, hung with their mantles of lace and silk from gigantic, massive, convoluted gilt cornices. The grand fourposted mahogany bedstead, with its rigging of mosquito netting and cords and tassels, looked like some huge vessel that by accident had lodged in this small harbor. So stupendous, so immeasurable, so gloomily, grandly, majestically imposing, this dark, crimson-housed bedstead looked in the small, dimly-lighted room, that little girls sent on occasional messages to madame felt a tremor of awe at the sight of it, and understood instinctively, without need of explanation or elucidation, that here, indeed, was one of those *lits de justice*[67] which caused such dismay in the pages of their French history. The bureau was as coquettish, as volatile, as petulant an article of furniture as was ever condemned to bedchamber companionship with a *lit de justice.*

The *prie-dieu*[68] in front of the altar granted the occupant an encouraging view into all the visible appliances for stimulating faith in the things not seen. The willing heart, as by an ascending scale, rose insensibly from the humanity to the divinity of sacrifice and suffering. Reliquaries, triply consecrated beads, palms, and crucifixes, pictures of sainted martyrs and martyresses (which contradicted the fallacious coincidence of homeliness and virtue), statuettes, prayer books, pendant flasks of holy water, and an ecclesiastical flash of still holier liquid, impregnated with miraculous promises. A taper, in a red globe, burned with subdued effulgence below it all. Ghastly white and black bead wreaths, hanging under faded miniatures, set the bounds of mural consecration, and kept madame mournfully reminded of her deceased husband and mother.

Marcélite stood, like a threatening idol, in the center of the room, her eyes glaring through the gloom with fierce doggedness. Her feet were planted firmly apart, her hands doubled up on her high, round, massive hips. The cords of her short, thick neck stood out, and her broad, flexible nostrils rose and fell with passion. Her untamed African blood was in rebellion against the religion and civilization whose symbols were all about her in that dim and stately chamber; a civilization which had tampered with her brain, had enervated her will, and had duped her with false assurances of her own capability.

She felt a crushing desire to tear down, split, destroy, to surround herself with ruins, to annihilate the miserable, little, weak devices of intelligence, and reassert the proud supremacy of brute force. She longed to humiliate that meek Virgin Mother—and if the form on the crucifix had been alive she would have gloated over the blood and agony. She thirsted to get her thin, taper, steel-like fingers but once more on that pretty, shapely, glossy head. . . . "*Pauvre petite chatte!*[69] I shall miss her very much; you know, Marcélite, it seems only a year or two since you brought her here a little baby, and now she is a young lady of seventeen. Thirteen years ago! What a *chétive*[70] little thing she was! You were as much of a scholar here then as she; you had to stay with her so much. You have been a faithful nurse to her, *ma bonne femme.*[71] A mother could not have been more devoted, and very few would have done all you have for that child. Ah! that's a thing money can never pay for: love. I hope Marie will always remember what you have been to her, and repay it with affection. But she will; she is a good girl—a good, good, girl, *pauvre petite!*[72] It is Monsieur Motte, though, who should give you a handsome present, something really valuable. I would like to know what he would have done for a *bonne* for his niece without you. You remember that summer when she had the fever? Eh, well she would have died but for you; I shall never forget her sad little face and her big black eyes. You see, her mother must see all that; I can never believe, Marcélite, that a mother cannot come back, sometimes, to see her children, particularly a little girl. . . ."

Marcélite listened with head averted. Her hands had fallen from her hips, her mouth slowly relaxed, and the lips opened moist and red. As if drawn by strains of music, she came nearer and nearer madame's chair.

"She was always such a quiet little thing, *ma foi!*"[73] Madame's reminiscence was an endless chain. "I used to forget her entirely; but now she is going away, I know I shall miss her, yes, very much. I hope the world will be kind to her. She will be handsome, too, some day, when she does not have to study so hard, and can enjoy the diversions of society a little. By the time she is twenty you will see she will be *une belle femme.*[74] Ah, Monsieur Motte, you will be satisfied, *allez!*"[75]

The little pen commenced scratching away again, and this time registered the deed of prize of French history to *l'elève,*[76] Marie Modeste Motte.

Marcélite, with wistful eyes, listened for some more of the soft, sweet tones. She made the movement of swallowing two or three times to get the swelling and stiffness out of her throat.

"Mamzelle Marie, too, she will be sorry to leave madame." Her voice was thick and unsteady.

"Oh no, girls are always glad to quit school. Very naturally, too. When one is young, one does not like to stay in-doors and study, when there is so much outside— dancing, music, beaux." A sigh interrupted madame. "It is all past for me now, but I can recollect how I felt when I was seventeen. *Apropos,*[77] Marcélite, did you give my invitation to Monsieur Motte?"

"Yes, madame."

The answer came after an interval of hesitation. At one moment Marcélite's eyes flashed as if she would brave all results and refuse to respond.

"And what did he say?"

"He, he sent his compliments to madame."

Madame looked around to see what the good-natured *coiffeuse* meant by such sullen tones. "Yes, but did he say he would come to the concert? I wanted particularly to know that."

"He is so old, madame."

"*Là, là,* the same old excuse! I am so tired of it."

"But when one is old, madame."

"Ah bah, I do not believe he is too old for his own pleasure. I know men; old age is a very convenient excuse at times."

Marcélite appeared to have no reply at the end of her ready tongue.

"But this time he must come, *par ex-*

mple![78] even if he is so old. I think he might subject himself to some little inconvenience and trouble to see his niece graduate. He has not put himself out much about her for twelve or thirteen years."

"God knows! madame."

"God knows? Mais,[79] Marcélite, how silly you talk! Don't you see that Monsieur Motte must come to-morrow night, at least to take Marie home? God does know, and so should he."

Marcélite spoke as if galvanized by an aspiration. "Perhaps he wants Miss Marie to stay another year, madame; you see, she so young, and, and, there is so much to learn, enfin."[80]

"He wants that, does he? he wants that! Ah, l'egoïste![81] That is like a man; oh, I know them like a b c. No, if Marie is not too young to graduate, she is not too young to leave school; and besides, if she had not learned everything, how could she graduate? There is an end to learning, enfin.[82] You tell Monsieur Motte that. But no, tiens, it is better I shall write it."

She seized some note paper and put her message in writing with the customary epistolary embellishment of phrase at the expense of sincerity and truth.

"I hope he will be kind to her, and look out for a good parti[83] for her. Of course she will have a dot—his only relative. Did you not tell me she was his only relative, Marcélite? He has absolutely no one else besides her?"

"No, madame."

"Well, then, she will get it all when he dies, unless"—with a shrug—"I do not know; one is never sure about men."

Madame bethought herself of the time, and looked at her watch just as Marcélite, by a sudden resolution, made a desperate movement towards her.

"Nearly three o'clock! I must go and make my tour. Au revoir, ma bonne,[84] be sure and give Monsieur Motte my note, and come early to-morrow morning; and do not forget to think about what I told you, you know." She tapped her head significantly and left the room. On the short passage to the Salle des Classes[85] she put off her natural manner, and assumed the conventional disguise supposed to be more fitting her high position. When the door opened and the little girls started up to drop their curtseys and their "Je vous salue, madame,"[86] her stately tread and severe mien could hardly have been dis-

tinguished from those of her predecessor, the aristocratic old refugée[87] from the Island of St. Domingo. After dinner, when the shadow had entirely enveloped the yard, and the fragrance of the oleander and jasmine had fastened itself on the air, the girls were allowed their evening recreation. Relieved from the more or less restraining presence of the day scholars, the boarders promenaded in the cordial intimacy of home life. The laughter of the children in the street, the music of the organs (there seemed to be one at each corner), the gay jingle of the ice-cream cart came over the wall to them. To-morrow there would be no wall between them and the world, the great, gay, big world of New Orleans. The thought was too exhilarating for their fresh blood; they danced to the music and laughed to the laughter outside, they kissed their hands to invisible friends, and made révérences[88] and complimentary speeches to the crescent moon up in the blue sky. The future would soon be here now! only to-morrow evening: the future, which held for them a début[89] in society, a box at the opera, beautiful toilets, balls, dancing, music. No more study, routine, examinations, scoldings, punishments, and bread-and-butter lunches. The very idea of it was intoxicating, and each girl felt guilty of a maudlin effusion of sentiment and nonsense to her best friend. A "best friend" is an institution in every girl's school. Every class book when opened would direct you to a certain page on which was to be found the name of "celle que j'aime," or "celle que j'adore," or "mon amie chérie,"[90] or "ma toute dévouée."[91] The only source of scandal that flourished in their secluded circle was the formation or disrupting of these ties through the intermeddling officiousness of "rapporteuses"[92] and "mauvaises langues."[93] But the approaching dissolution of all ties drew them together, each one to each one's best friend, and, as usual, the vows exchanged became more fervent and passionate just before breaking. Marcélite was outside, leaning against the wall. Close over her head hung the pink oleanders through their green leaves, and on their strong perfume were wafted the merry voices of the boarders. How glad, how happy they were! She could hear her bébé above the others, and, strange to say, her laughter made her sadder even than her tears to-day. She lifted up her black, passionate face. If she could only see them! if she could only look over the wall and catch one more glimpse of the girl whom as a baby she had held to her bosom, and whom she had carried in her arms through that gate when. . . . *"Ah, mon Dieu, ayez pitié de moi, pauvre négresse!"* [94]

"Dansez, Chantez," [95] they were singing and making a *ronde.* [96] She heard some one at the gate, Jeanne, probably, coming out. She turned her back quickly and walked away around the corner, making the tour of the square. When she turned the corner coming the other way, she was quite out of breath with walking fast; as there was no one in the street, she increased her pace still, to a run, and reached the oleanders panting; but all was now still inside; the boarders had been summoned to supper. She stretched her arms out and leaned her head against the rough bricks. She turned and looked at the sky; her eyes gleamed through her tears like the hot stars through the blue air. She moved away a few steps, hesitated, returned; then went again, only to be drawn back under the oleanders. She sat down close to the wall, threw her apron over her head and drew her feet up out of the way of the passers-by.

Daylight found her still there. When the early carts began to pass, laden for the neighboring market, she rose stiff and sore and walked in the direction of the river, where the morning breeze was just beginning to ripple the waters, and drive away the fog.

The great day of the concert commenced very early. Fête days always get up before the sun. The boarders in the dormitory raised their heads from their pillows and listened to the pushing and dragging going on underneath them: the men arranging the chairs for that night. Their heads, done up in white paper *papillotes,* [97] looked like so many branched porcupines. This was one of the first of those innumerable degrees of preparation by which they expected to transform themselves into houris of loveliness by concert time. As there can be no beauty without curls, in a school-girl's opinion, and as a woman's first duty is to be beautiful, they felt called upon to roll lock after lock of their hair around white paper, which was then twisted to the utmost limit of endurance; and on occasions when tightness of

curl is regulated by tightness of twist, endurance may safely be said to have no limits. Fear of the unavoidable ensuing disappointment forced Marie to renounce, reluctantly, beauty in favor of discretion. When her companions saw the omission they screamed in dismay.

"Oh, Marie!"

"Ah! Why didn't you put your hair up?"

"What a pity!"

"And you won't have curls for this evening?"

"Do it now!"

"Mais je t'assure," [98] it will curl almost as tight."

"Let me do it for you, *chère.*"

"No, me."

"But it is better to have it a little *frisè,* than straight, so."

Marie, from practice accomplished in excuses, persisted that she had a *migraine.* [100]

"Oh, *la migraine,* poor thing!"

"I implore you, don't be ill to-night."

"Try my *eau de Cologne.*" [101]

"No, my *eau sédative* [102] is better."

"Put this on your head."

"Tie this around your neck."

"Carry this in your pocket."

"Some water from Notre Dame de Lourdes." [103]

"Some smelling salts."

Madame Lareveillère opened *her* eyes that morning as from an unsuccessful experiment. She cared little about sleep as a restorative, but it was invaluable to her in this emergency as a cosmetic.

Jeanne brought in her morning cup of coffee, with the news that the men had almost finished in the *Salle de Concert.*

"C'est bon; [104] tell Marcélite to come as soon as she is ready."

The eyes closed again on the pillow in expectation of speedy interruption. But sleep, the coquette, courted and coaxed in vain all night, came now with blandishment, lullaby, and soft caress, and fastened the already heavy lids down over the brown eyes, and carried the occupant of the big bed away out on pretty dreams of youth and pleasure; away, beyond all distractions, noises, interruptions; beyond the reach of matutinal habits, duties, engagements, rehearsals, prizes; beyond even the practising of the *"Cheval de Bronze"* on four pianos just underneath her. She slept as people sleep only on the field of battle or amid the ruins of broken promises; and

anks to her exalted position, she slept
disturbed.

"*Mais,* come in *donc,*[105] Marcélite!" she
xclaimed, as a perseverant knocking at
e door for the past five minutes had the
fect of balancing her in a state of uncer-
in wakefulness. "You are a little early
is morning, it seems."

She rubbed her hands very softly over
er still-closed eyes; that last dream was
sweet, so clinging, what a pity to open
em!

"It is not Marcélite; it is I, Madame
ubert."

"You! Madame Joubert!"

The excellent, punctilious, cold, austere,
flexible French teacher by her bed-side!

"I thought it was Marcélite."

She still was hardly awake.

"No, it is I."

"But what is the matter, Madame
ubert?"

"It is twelve o'clock, madame."

"Twelve o'clock! Impossible!"

"You hear it ringing, Madame."

"But where is Marcélite?"

"Marcélite did not come this morning."

"Marcélite did not come this morning!"
he was again going to say "Impossible!"
ut she perceived Madame Joubert's head,
nd was silent.

Instead of her characteristic, formal, but
onventionally fashionable coiffure, Ma-
ame Joubert had returned to, or assumed,
nat most primitive and innocent way of
ombing her hair called *la sauvagesse.*[106]
Unrelieved by the soft perspective of Mar-
élite's handiwork, her plain, prominent
eatures stood out with the savage boldness
f rocks on a shrubless beach. "How
rightfully ugly!" thought Madame Lare-
eillère.

"Marcélite did not come this morning?
Vhy?"

"How should I know, madame?"

"She must be ill; send Jeanne to see."

"I did that, madame, five hours ago; she
vas not in her room."

"But what can have become of her?"

Madame Joubert had early in life elim-
nated the consideration of supposititious
ases from the catalogue of her salaried
uties; but she answered gratuitously:

"I cannot imagine, madame."

"But I must have some one to comb my
air."

"The music teacher is waiting for you.
The French professor says he will be here
again in a half-hour; he has been here
twice already. Madame Criard says that it
is indispensable for her to consult you
about the choruses."

"*Mais, mon Dieu!*[107] Madame Joubert, I
must have a hair-dresser!"

Madame Joubert waived all participation
in this responsibility by continuing her
communication.

"The girls are all very tired; they say
they will be worn out by to-night if they
are kept much longer. *They* have been up
ever since six o'clock."

"I know, I know, Madame Joubert; it
was an accident. I also was awake at six
o'clock."

"*J'ai fait la nuit blanche.*"[108]

"Then I fell asleep again. Ah! that miserable Marcélite! I beg of you, tell Jeanne
to go for some one, no matter whom—
Henriette, Julie, Artémise. I shall be ready
in a moment."

In a surprisingly short while she was
quite ready, all but her hair, and stood in
her white muslin peignoir, tied with blue
ribbons, before her toilet, waiting impatiently for some one to come to her
assistance.

How terrible it is not to be able to comb
your own hair! Her hands had grown completely unaccustomed to the exercise of the
comb and brush.

"Madame," said Jeanne at the door, "I
have been everywhere. I cannot find a
coiffeuse at home; I have left word at
several places, and Madame Joubert says
they are waiting for you."

What could she do? She looked in the
glass at her gray, spare locks; she looked
on her toilet at her beautiful brown curls
and plaits. "How in the world did Marcélite manage to secure all *that* on *this?*"

There was a knock at the door.

"Perhaps that was a *coiffeuse!*" She
hastened to unfasten it.

"Madame," said a little girl, trying to
speak distinctly, despite a nervous shortness of breath, "Madame Joubert sent me
to tell you they were waiting."

"Very well, *mon enfant,* very well. I am
coming."

"I shall be a greater fright than Madame
Joubert," she murmured to herself.

The drops of perspiration disfiguring the
clear tissue of the muslin peignoir were
the only visible results of her conscientious
efforts.

"I will never be able to fix my hair."

There was another knock at the door, another "Madame Joubert *vous fait dire,*[109] etc., etc.

"Tell Madame Joubert I am coming in a moment."

How impatient Madame Joubert was this morning. Oh, for Marcélite!

She knew nothing about hair, that was evident; but she remembered that she knew something about lace. Under the pressure of accelerating summonses from Madame Joubert, she fashioned a fichu, left on a chair from last night, into a very presentable substitute for curls and puffs.

"*Mais ce n'est pas mal, en effet,*"[110] she muttered; but hearing the sound of footsteps again in the corridor, she rushed from the mirror and met the messenger just as her hand was poised to give a knock at the door. The "*Sa . . . lu . . . t! mois de va . . . can . . . ces!*" and the "*Vi . . . er . . . ge, Ma . . . ri . . . e*"[111] had been chorused and re-chorused; the "*Cheval de Bronze*" had been hammered into durable perfection; the solos and duos, dialogues and scenes, the salutatory and valedictory had been rehearsed *ad nauseam.*[112]

Madame finally dismissed the tired actors, with the recommendation to collect all their *petites affaires,*[113] so that their trunks could be sent away very early the next morning.

"I suppose Marcélite will be sure to come this evening?" she asked Madame Joubert.

"Oh, *that* is sure, madame," Madame Joubert replied, as if this were one of the few rules of life without exceptions; and Madame Lareveillère believed her as confidently as if Noël and Chapsal had passed upon her answer, and the *Dictionnaire de l'Académie*[114] had endorsed it.

The girls scattered themselves all over the school, effacing with cheerful industry every trace of their passage through the desert of education. "*Dieu merci!*[115] that was all past." Marie had emptied her desk of everything belonging to her except her name, dug out of the black lid with a dull knife. That had to remain, with a good so many other Marie Modeste Mottes on the different desks that had harbored her books during her sojourn in the various classes. This was all that would be left of her in the rooms where she had passed thirteen years of her life. The vacant teacher's desk, the throne of so many tyrants (the English teachers were all hateful!), the

white walls, with their ugly protecting dado of black; the rows of pegs, where the hats and cloaks hung; the white marble mantel, with its carving of naked cherubs which the stove had discreetly clothed in soot: she could never forget them. Sitting in her future home, the house of her uncle, she knew that these homely objects would come to her memory, as through sunset clouds of rose and gold.

"What will you do when you quit school, Marie?" her companions would ask, after detailing with ostentatious prolixity their own pleasant prospects.

"Ah, you know that depends entirely upon my uncle," she would reply, shrugging her thin shoulders under her calico waist.

This rich old uncle, an obstinate recluse, was the traditional *le vieux* of the school.

"How is *le vieux*[116] to-day?" they would call to Marcélite.

"Give my love to *le vieux.*"

"*Dis donc,*[117] why doesn't *le vieux* take Marie away in the summer?"

"Did you see the beautiful *étrennes*[118] *le vieux* has sent Marie?"

"They say he has sent her *une toilette superbe*[119] for the exhibition, made at Madame Treize's, and white satin boots."

Her trunk had been brought down with the others, and placed at her bedside. What more credible witness than a coffin or a trunk? It stood there as it might have stood thirteen years ago, when her baby wardrobe was unpacked. Her dear, ugly little, old trunk! It had belonged to her mother, and bore three faded M's on its leather skin. She leaned her head against the top as she knelt on the floor before it, to pack her books. How much that trunk could tell her if it could only speak! If she were as old as that trunk she would have known a father, a mother, and a home. She wrinkled her forehead in a concentrated effort to think a little farther back, to push her memory just a little, a little beyond that mist out of which it arose. In vain! The big bell at the gate, with its clanging orders, remained the boundary of consciousness.

And Marcélite did not come, not even when the lamps were lighted, to comb their hair, fasten their dresses, and tie their sashes; did not even come at the very last minute to see how their toilets became them. The young ladies had waited until the very last moment, dressed to the last

in, taken their hair out of the last *papil-
ote*,[120] and then looked at one another in
despair, indignation, and grief.

"Just look at my head, I ask you?"

"But mine is worse than yours."

"I shall never be able to do anything
with mine."

"The more I brush, the more like a
ègre I look."

"Ah, Marie, how wise you were not to
ut your hair in *papillottes!*"

"And all that trouble for nothing, *hein!*"

"And the pain."

"I didn't sleep a wink last night."

"See how nice Marie looks with her hair
noothly plaited."

"I will never forgive Marcélite."

"Nor I."

"Nor I."

"Nor I."

Marie's heart sank when she thought
ow difficult it would be for Marcélite to
fface this disappointment from the re-
nembrance of her *clientèle;*[121] and she felt
uilty, as being in a measure responsible
or it all. Marcélite was evidently de-
ined, or prevented from coming by prep-
rations for Marie's return. Who knows?
-perhaps the eccentric old uncle had
omething to do with it! Madame Joubert
ositively refused to mitigate the injury or
ondone the offense by the employment of
nother hair-dresser. As she had com-
nenced, so she closed the day, *à la sau-
agesse;* and so she wore her hair to the
nd of her life, maintaining, logically, that
hat one hair-dresser had done, all were
able to do; life should never serve this
isappointment to her a second time; she
ould employ no more of them.

The being deserted in a critical moment
y a trusted servitor, dropped without
arning by a confidante, left with an in-
ifference, which amounted to heartless-
ess, to the prying eyes and gossiping
ongue of a stranger; this, not the mere
rivial combing, was what isolated and
istinguished Madame Lareveillère in her
ffliction. The question had been lifted be-
ond material consequences. Morally, it
pproached tragic seriousness. Marcélite
ould naturally have suggested, whether
he thought so or not, that the color of the
ew gray moire-antique was a trifle *in-
rate,* and madame at least might have
ad the merit of declining propitiatory
ompromises between it and her com-
lexion. . . . Julie was an idiot, there was

no doubt about that; and the length of her
tongue was notorious. By to-morrow evening the delicate mysteries of the youthful-
looking Madame Lareveillère's toilet
would be unveiled to satisfy the sensational cravings of her malicious *clientèle.*

The young ladies were placed on a high
platform of steps, and rose tier above tier
like flowers in a horticultural show—the
upper classes at the top and the best-
looking girls well in the center, as if the
product of their beauty as well as their
study went to the credit of the institute.
When anything particular arrested their
attention they whispered behind their fans,
and it was as if a hive of bees had been
let loose; when they laughed it was like
a cascade rippling from step to step; when
they opened their white, blue, and rose-
colored fans (school-girls always do the
same thing at the same time) and fluttered them, then they looked like a cloud
of butterflies hovering and coquetting
about their own lips.

The *Externes*[122] were radiant in toilets
unmarred by accident or omission; the
flattering compliments of their mirrors at
home had turned their heads in the direction of perfect self-content. Resignation
was the only equivalent the unfortunate
Internes[123] could offer in extenuation of
the unfinished appearance of their heads.

"*Mais, dis donc, chère,*[124] what is the
matter with your hair?"

"Marcélite did not come."

"Why, *doudouce,*[125] how could you allow
your hair to be combed that way?"

"Marcélite did not come."

"*Chérie,* I think your hair is curled a
little tight this evening."

"I should think so; that *diable* Marcélite
did not come."

"*Mon Dieu,* look at Madame Joubert *à
la sauvagesse!*"

"And Madame *à la grand maman!*"[126]

"Marcélite did not come, you see."

Not only was the room filled, but an
eager audience crowded the yard and
peeped in through the windows. The stair-
ways, of course, were filled with the colored servants, an enthusiastic, irrepressible
claque. When it was all over and the last
bis[127] and *encore*[127] had subsided, row after
row of girls was gleaned by the parents,
proud possessors of such shawlfuls of
beauty, talent, and prizes. Marie's class,
the last to leave, were picked off one by
one. She helped the others to put on their

wraps, gather up their prizes, and kissed one after another good-by.

Each man that came up was, by a glance, measured and compared with her imaginary standard. "He is too young." "He is too fat." "I hope he is not that cross-looking one." "Maybe it is he." "What a funny little one that is." "Ah, he is very nice-looking." "Is it he?" "No, he is Co-rinne's father." "I feel sure he is that ugly, disagreeable one." "Ah, here he is at last! at last!" "No; he only came to say good-night to madame." "He is afraid of the crowd." "He is waiting outside." "He is at the gate in a carriage." "After all he has only sent Marcélite." "I saw her here on the steps a while ago." She looked at the steps; they were deserted. There was but one person left in the room besides herself; madame and her suite had gone to partake of their yearly exhibitional refreshments: lemonade and *masse-pain*,[128] served in the little parlor. Her uncle must be that man. The person walked out after finding a fan he had returned to seek.

She remained standing so by the piano a long while, her gold crown on her head, her prizes in her arms, and a light shawl she had thoughtfully provided to wear home. Home! She looked all around very slowly once more. She heard Jeanne crossing the yard, but before the servant could enter the door, the white muslin dress, blue sash and satin boots had bounded into the darkness of the stairway. The white-veiled beds which the night before had nestled the gay *papillotted* heads were deserted and silent in the darkness. What a shelter the darkness was! She caught hold of the bedpost, not thinking, but feeling. Then Madame Joubert came tripping across the gallery with a candle, on her way to bed. The prizes and shawl dropped to the floor, and Marie crouched down close behind the bar. "Oh, God," she prayed, "keep her from seeing me!" The teacher after a pause of reflection passed on to her room; the child on the floor gave herself up to the full grief of a disappointment which was not childish in its bitterness. The events of the evening kept slipping away from her while the contents of her previous life were poured out with never-ending detail, and as they lay there, before and all around her, she saw for the first time how bare, how denuded, of pleasure and comfort it had been. What had her weak little body not

endured in patient ignorance? But th others were not ignorant—the teachers Marcélite, her uncle! How had they im posed upon the orphan in their hands She saw it now, and she felt a woman' indignation and pity over it. The materna instinct in her bosom was aroused by th contemplation of her own infancy. "Mar célite! Marcélite!" she called out, "hov could you? for you knew, you knew i all!" The thought of a mother compelle to leave her baby on such an earth, th betrayal of the confidence of her ow mother by her uncle, drew the first tear from her eyes. She leaned her head agains the side of her bed and wept, not fo herself, but for all women and all orphans Her hand fell on the lace of her dress and she could not recall at first what i was. She bounded up, and with eager trembling fingers, tearing open the fasten ings, she threw the grotesque masquerade boots and all, far from her on the floor and stood clasping her naked arms ove her panting breast; she had forgotten th gilt wreath on her head. "If she could di then and there! that would hurt her uncl who cared so little for her, Marcélite wh had deserted her!" Living she had no one but dead, she felt she had a mother. Be fore getting into bed, she mechanically fell on her knees, and her lips repeate the formula of a prayer, an uncorrected rude tradition of her baby days, belongin to the other side of her memory. It con sisted of one simple petition for her ow welfare, but the blessings of peace, pros perity, and eternal salvation of her uncl and Marcélite were insisted upon wit pious determination.

"I know I shall not sleep, I canno sleep." Even with the words she san into the oblivion of tired nature at seven teen years; an oblivion which blotted ou everything—toilet, prizes scattered on th floor, graduation, disappointment, and dis comfort from the gilt-paper crown sti encircling her black plaits.

"Has Marcélite come?" demanded ma dame, before she tasted her coffee

"Not yet, madame."

"I wonder what has become of her?"

Jeanne sniffed a volume of unspeakab probabilities.

"Well, then, I will not have that *sotte* Julie; tell her so when she comes. I wou rather dress myself."

"Will madame take her breakfast alone, with Madame Joubert?"

The pleasure of vacation was tempered the companionship of Madame Joubert at her daily meals—a presence imposed by that stern tyrant, common courtesy.

"Not to-day, Jeanne; tell madame I have *migraine*. I shall eat breakfast alone."

"And Mamzelle Marie Modeste?"

"Marie Modeste!"

"Yes, madame; where must she take her breakfast?"

The Gasconne's eyes flamed suddenly from under her red lashes and her voice ventured on its normal loud tones in these sacred precincts.

"It's a shame of that *négresse!* She ought to be punished well for it, too, ha! Not to come for that poor young lady last night; to leave her in that big dormitory all by herself; and all the other young ladies to go home and have their pleasure, and she all by herself, just because she is an orphan. You think she doesn't feel that, *hein?* If I had known it I would have helped her undress, and stayed with her, too; I would have slept on the floor. A delicate, little, nervous thing like that. And a great big, fat, lazy, good-for-nothing *négresse* like Marcélite. *Mais, c'est infâme!*[130] It is enough to give her *des crises.* Ah, I would not have done that! *tenez,*[131] not to go back to France would I have done that. And when I got up this morning, and saw her sitting in the *tonnelle,*[132] so pale, I was frightened myself. . . . I . . ."

"What is all this you are telling me? Jeanne, Jeanne, go immediately; run, I tell you—run and fetch that poor child here. Oh, *mon Dieu! égoïste* that I am to forget her! *Pauvre petite chatte!* What must she think of me?"

She jumped out of bed, threw on a wrapper, and waited at the door, peeping out.

"*Ma fille;* I did not know—Jeanne has just told me."

The pale little figure made an effort to answer with the old pride and indifference.

"It seems my uncle . . ."

"*Mais qu'est-ce que c'est donc, mon enfant?*[133] Do not cry so! What is one night more in your old school? It is all my fault; the idea that I should forget you. Leave you all alone while we were enjoying our lemonade and *masse-pain!*[134] But why did you not come to me? Oh! oh! if you cry so, I shall think you are sorry not to leave me; besides, it will spoil your pretty eyes."

"If Marcélite had only come . . ."

"Ah, my dear! *n'en parles pas!*[135] do not mention her name to me. We are *quittes*[136] from this day; you hear me? We are *quittes.* But, Marie, my child, you will make yourself ill if you cry so. *Vraiment,*[137] you must try and compose yourself. What is it that troubles you so? Come here, come sit by me; let me confess you. I shall play that I am your *maman.* There, there, put your head here, my *bébé,* so. Oh, I know how you feel. I have known what disappointment was; but *enfin*[138] my child, that will all pass; and one day, when you are old and gray-headed like me, you will laugh well over it."

The tender words, the caresses, the enfolding arms, the tears that she saw standing in the august school-mistress's eyes, the sympathetic movement of the soft, warm bosom;—her idea of a mother was not a vain imagining. This was it; this was what she had longed for all her life. And she did confess to her—confessed it all from the first childish trouble to the last disappointment. Oh, the delicious relief of complete, entire confession to a sympathetic ear!

The noble heart of madame, which had frittered itself away over puny distributions of prizes and deceiving cosmetics, beat young, fresh, and impulsive as in the days when the gray hairs were *chatains clair,*[139] and the cheeks bloomed natural roses. Tears fell from her eyes on the little black head lying so truthful, so confiding on her bosom. *Grand Dieu!* and they had been living thirteen years under the same roof! the poor, insignificant, abandoned, suffering little Marie, and the gay, beautiful, rich, envied Madame Lareveillère. This was their first moment of confidence. Would God ever forgive her? Could she ever forgive herself? How good it feels to have a child in your arms! so. She went to the stand by her bed and filled a small gilded glass with *eau des carmes*[140] and water.

"There, drink that, my child; it will compose you. I must make my toilet, it is breakfast-time. You see, *ma fille,* this is a lesson. You must not expect too much of the men; they are not like us. Oh, I know them well. They are *égoïstes.* They take a great deal of trouble for you when you do not want it, if it suits them; and then they refuse to raise their little finger for you, though you get down on your knees to them. Now, there's your uncle. You see he has sent you to the best and most expensive school in the city, and he has dressed you well; oh, yes, very well; look at your toilet last night! real lace, I r marked it. Yet he would not come for you and take you home, and spare you this disappointment. I wrote him a note myself and sent it by Marcélite."

"He *is* old, madame," said Marie, loyally.

"Ah, bah! *Plus les hommes sont vieux plus ils sont méchants.*[141] Oh, I have done that so often; I said: 'If you do not do this, I will not do that.' And what was the result? they did not do this, and I had *tout simplement et bonnement*[142] to do that. I write to Monsieur Motte, 'Your niece shall not leave the Pension until you come for her'; he does not come, and I take her to him. *Voilà la politique féminine.*"[143]

After breakfast, when they had dressed, bonneted, and gloved themselves, madame said:

"*Ma foi!* I do not even know where the old Diogène lives. Do you remember the name of the street, Marie?"

"No, madame; somewhere in the *Faubourg d'en bas.*"[144]

"Ah, well! I must look for it here."

She went to the table and quickly turned over the leaves of a ledger.

"Marie Modeste Motte, niece of Monsieur Motte. *Mais, tiens,*[145] there is no address!"

Marie looked with interest at her name written in red ink.

"No; it is not there."

"*Ah, que je suis bête.*[146] It is in the other one. This one is only for the last ten years. There, *ma fille*, get on a chair; can you reach that one? No, not that, the other one. How warm it is! You look it out for me!"

"I do not see any address here either, madame."

"Impossible! There must be an address there. True, nothing but Marie Modeste Motte, niece of Monsieur Motte, just like the other one. Now, you see, that's Marcélite again; that's all her fault. It was her duty to give that address thirteen years ago. In thirteen years she has not had the time to do that!"

They both sat down warm and vexed.

"I shall send Jeanne for her again!"

But Jeanne's zeal had anticipated orders.

"I have already been there, madame; I beat on her door, I beat on it as hard as I

could, and the neighbors opened their windows and said they didn't think she had been there all night."

"Well, then, there is nothing for me to do but send for Monsieur le Notaire! Here Jeanne; take this note to Monsieur Goupilleau."

All unmarried women, widows or maids if put to the torture, would reveal some secret, unsuspected sources of advisory assistance—a subterranean passage for friendship which sometimes offers a retreat into matrimony—and the last possible wrinkle, the last resisting gray hair is added to other female burdens at the death of this secret counsellor or the closing up of the hidden passage. Therefore, how dreadful it is for women to be condemned to a life of such logical exactions where a reason is demanded for everything, even for a *statu quo*[147] affection of fifteen years or more. Madame Lareveillère did not possess courage enough to defy logic, but her imagination and wit could seriously embarrass its conclusions. The *raison d'être*[148] of a Goupilleau in her life had exercised both into athletic proportions.

"An old friend, *ma mignonne;*[149] I look upon him as a father, and he treats me just as if I were his daughter. I go to him as to a confessor. And a great institute like this requires so much advice; oh so much! He is very old, as old as Monsieur Motte himself. We might just as well take off our things; he will not come before evening. You see, he is so discreet he would not come in the morning for *rien au monde.*[150] He is just exactly like a father, I assure you, and very, very old.'

The graduate and young lady of a day sat in the *berceuse*[151] quiet, almost happy. She was not in the home she had looked forward to; but madame's tenderness, the beautiful room in its soothing twilight, and the patronizing majesty of the *lit de justice*[152] made this a very pleasant abiding place in her journey—the journey so long and so difficult from school to her real home, from girlhood to real young ladyhood. It was nearly two days now since she had seen Marcélite. How she longed for her, and what a scolding she intended to give her when she arrived at her uncle's where, of course, Marcélite was waiting for her. How silly she acted about the address! But, after all, procrastination is so natural. As for madame, Marie smiled as she thought how easily a reconciliation could be effected between them, *quittes* though they were.

It is hard to wean young hearts from hoping and planning; they will do it in the very presence of the angel of death, and with their shrouds in full view.

Monsieur Goupilleau came: a Frenchman of small stature but large head. He had the eyes of a poet and the smile of a woman.

The prelude of compliments, the tentative flourish to determine in which key the ensuing variation on their little romance should be played, was omitted. Madame came brusquely to the *motif,*[153] not personal to either of them.

"Monsieur Goupilleau, I take pleasure in presenting you to Mademoiselle Marie Motte, one of our young lady graduates. *Mon ami,* we are in the greatest trouble imaginable. *Figurez-vous,*[154] Monsieur Motte, the uncle of mademoiselle, could not come for her last night to take her home. He is so old and infirm," added madame, considerately, "so you see mademoiselle could not leave last night; I want to take her home myself—a great pleasure it is, and not a trouble, I assure you, Marie —but we do not know where he lives."

"Ah! you have not his address."

"No, it should be in the ledger; but an accident—in fact, the laziness of her *bonne,* who never brought it, not once in thirteen years."

"Her *bonne?*"

"Yes, her *bonne* Marcélite; you know Marcélite *la coiffeuse;* what, you do not know Marcélite, that great, fat . . ."

"Does Marcélite know where he lives?"

"But of course, my friend, Marcélite knows, she goes there every day."

"Well, send for Marcélite."

"Send for Marcélite! but I have sent for Marcélite at least a dozen times! she is never at her room. Marcélite! ha! my friend, I am done with Marcélite. What do you think? After combing my hair for fifteen years!—fifteen years, I tell you— she did not come yesterday at all, not once; and the concert at night! You should have seen our heads last night! we were frights, frights! I assure you."

It was a poetical license, but the eyes of Monsieur Goupilleau disclaimed any such possibility for the head before him.

"Does not mademoiselle know the address of her uncle?"

"Ah, *that,* no. Mademoiselle has been a *pensionnaire*[155] at the Institute St. Denis for thirteen years, and she has never been anywhere except to church; she has seen no one without a chaperon; she has received no letter that has not passed through Madame Joubert's hands. Ah! for that I am particular, and it was Monsieur Motte himself who requested it."

"Then you need a directory."

"A what?"

"A directory."

"But what is that—a directory?"

"It's a volume, madame, a book containing the addresses of all the residents of the city."

"*Quelle bonné idée!*[156] If I had only known that! I shall buy one. Jeanne! Jeanne! run quick, *ma bonne,* to Morel's and buy me a directory."

"Pardon, madame, I think it would be quicker to send to Bâle's, the *pharmacien*[157] at the corner, and borrow one. Here, Jeanne, take my card."

"*À la bonne heure!*[158] now we shall find our affair."

But the M's which started so many names in the directory were perfectly innocent of any combination applicable to an old uncle by the name of Motte.

"You see, your directory is no better than my books!"

Monsieur Goupilleau looked mortified, and shrugged his shoulders.

"He must live outside the city limits, madame."

"Marcélite always said, 'in the *Faubourg d'en bas.*'"[159]

Jeanne interrupted stolidly:

"Monsieur Bâle told me to bring the book right back, it is against his rules to lend it out of his store."

"Here, take it! take it! Tell him I am infinitely obliged. It was of no use anyway. Ah, *les hommes!*"[160]

"Madame," began Monsieur Goupilleau in precautionary deprecation.

A sudden noise outside! Apparently an assault at the front door! A violent struggle in the antechamber!

"*Grand Dieu!* what can that be!" Madame's lips opened for a shrill *Au secours! Voleurs!*[161] but seeing the notary rush to the door, she held him fast with her two little white hands on his arm.

"*Mon ami,* I implore you!"

The first recognition; the first expression of a fifteen years' secret affection! The first thrill (old as he was) of his first passion! But danger called him outside; he unloosed the hands and opened the door.

A heavy body propelled by Jeanne's strong hands fell on the floor of the room, accompanied by a shower of leaves from Monsieur Bâle's directory.

"Misérable! Infâme! Effrontée![162] Ah, I have caught you! Scélérate!"[163]

"Marcélite!"

"Marcélite!"

"Marcélite?"

"Sneaking outside the gate! Like an animal! like a thief! like a dog! Ha! I caught you well!"

The powerful arms seemed ready again to crush the unresisting form rising from the floor.

"Jeanne! hush! How dare you speak to Marcélite like that? Oh, ma bonne, what is the matter with you?"

Shaking, trembling, she cowered before them silent.

"Ah! she didn't expect me, la fière négresse.[164] Just look at her!"

They did, in painful, questioning surprise. Was this their own clean, neat, brave, honest, handsome Marcélite? This panting, tottering, bedraggled wretch before them? Threatening to fall on the floor again, not daring to raise even her eyes?

"Marcélite! Marcélite! who has done this to you! Tell me, tell your bébé, Marcélite."

"Is she drunk?" whispered madame to the notary.

Her tignon[165] had been dragged from her head. Her calico dress torn and defaced, showed her skin in naked streaks. Her black woolly hair, always so carefully packed away under her handkerchief, stood in grotesque masses around her face; scratched and bleeding like her exposed bosom. She jerked herself violently away from Marie's clasp.

"Send them away! Send them away!" she at last said to Monsieur Goupilleau, in a low, unnatural voice. "I will talk to you, but send them all away."

Madame and Marie immediately obeyed his look; but outside the door Marie stopped firmly.

"Madame, Marcélite can have nothing to say which I should not hear. . . ."

"Hush! . . ." Madame put her finger to her lips; the door was still a little open and the voices came to them.

Marcélite, from the corner of her bleared eyes, watched them retire, and then with a great heave of her naked chest she threw herself on the floor at the notary's feet.

"Master! Oh master! Help me!"

All the suffering and pathos of a woman's heart were in the tones, all the weakness, dependence, and abandonment in the words.

The notary started at the unexpected appeal. His humanity, his manhood, his chivalry, answered it.

"Ma fille, speak; what can I do for you?"

He bent over her as she lay before him, and put his thin, white, wrinkled hand on her shoulder, where it had burst through her dress. His low voice promised the willing devotion of a savior.

"But don't tell my bébé, don't let her know! My God! it will kill her! She's got no uncle! no Monsieur Motte! It was all a lie. It was me, me a nigger, that sent her to school and paid for her. . . ."

"You! Marcélite! You!"

Marcélite jumped and tried to escape from the room. Monsieur Goupilleau quickly advanced before her to the door.

"You fooled me! It was you fooled me!" she screamed to madame. "God will never forgive you for that! My bébé has heard it all!"

Marie clung to her; Monsieur Goupilleau caught her by the arm.

"Marcélite! It was you, you who sent me to school, who paid for me! And I have no uncle?"

Marcélite looked at the notary; a prayer for help. The girl fell in a chair and hid her face in her hands.

"Oh, my God! I knew it would kill her! I knew it would! To be supported by a nigger!" She knelt by the chair. "Speak to me, Mamzelle Marie. Speak to me just once! Pardon me, my little mistress! Pardon me! I did not know what I was doing; I am only a fool nigger, anyhow! I wanted you to go to the finest school with ladies, and, and, oh! my bébé won't speak to me; she won't even look at me."

Marie raised her head, put both hands on the nurse's shoulders, and looked her straight in the eyes.

"And that also was all a lie about" (she sank her trembling voice) "about my mother?"

"That a lie! That a lie! 'Fore God in Heaven, that was the truth; I swear it. I will kiss the crucifix. What do you take

ne for, Mamzelle Marie? Tell a lie
bout . . ."

Marie fell back in the chair with a
despairing cry.

"I cannot believe any of it."

"Monsieur! Madame! I swear to you
t's the truth! God in Heaven knows it is.
wouldn't lie about that, about my poor,
dead young mistress. Monsieur! Madame!
ell Miss Marie for me; can't you believe
me?" She shrieked in desperation to Monsieur Goupilleau.

He came to her unhesitatingly. "I believe you, Marcélite." He put his hand
again on her shoulder; his voice faltered
"Poor Marcélite."

"God bless you, master! God bless you
for that. Let me tell you; you believe me
when my bébé won't. My young mistress,
he died; my young master, he had been
killed in the war. My young mistress was
all alone by herself, with nobody but me,
and I didn't take her poor little baby out
of her arms till she was dead, as she told
me. Mon bébé, mon bébé! don't you know
that's the truth? Can't you feel that's the
truth? You see that; she will never speak
to me again; I knew it; I told you so. I
heard her last night, in that big room, all
by herself, crying for Marcélite. Marcélite!
my God! I was afraid to go to her, and
I was just under a bed; you think that
didn't most kill me?" She hid her face in
her arms, and swayed her body back and
forth.

"Marcélite," said Monsieur Goupilleau.
The voice of the champion trembled, and
his eyes glistened with tears at the distress
he had pledged himself to relieve. "Marcélite, I believe you, my poor woman, I
believe you. Tell me the name of the lady,
the mother of mademoiselle."

"Ha! her name! I am not ashamed to
tell her name before anybody. Her name!
I will tell you her name." She sprang to
her feet. "You ask anybody from the Paroisse St. Jacques if they ever heard the
name of Mamzelle Marie Modeste Viel and
Monsieur Alphonse Motte. That was the
name of her mother and her father, and
I am not ashamed of it that I shouldn't
tell, ha! Yes, and I am Marcélite Gaulois,
and when my mother was sold out the
parish, who took me and brought me up
and made me sleep on the foot of her bed,
and fed me like her own baby, hein?
Mamzelle Marie Viel's mother, and mamzelle was the other baby, and she nursed

us like twins, hein? You ask anybody from
the Paroisse St. Jacques. They know; they
can tell you."

Marie stood up.

"Come, Marcélite, let us go. Madame,
monsieur." She evidently struggled to say
something else, but she only reiterated, "I
must go; we must go; come, Marcélite,
let us go."

No one would have remarked now that
her eyes were too old for her face.

"Go! My Lord! Where have you got
to go to?"

"I want to go home to Marcélite; I want
to go away with her; come, Marcélite, let
us go. Oh! don't you all see I can't stay
here any longer? Let me go! Let me go!"

"Go with me! Go to my home! A white
young lady like you go live with a nigger
like me!"

"Come, Marcélite; please come, go with
me; I don't want to stay here."

"You stand there! You hear that! Monsieur! Madame! You hear that!"

"Marcélite, I want to go with you; I
want to live with you; I am not too good
for that."

"What! You don't think you ain't white!
Oh, God! Strike me dead!"

She raised her naked arms over her head,
imploring destruction.

"Marcélite, ma fille, do not forget, I
have promised to help you. Marcélite, only
listen to me a moment. Mademoiselle, do
not fear; mademoiselle shall not leave us.
I shall protect her; I shall be a father to
her. . . ."

"And I," said madame, drawing Marie
still closer to her, "I shall be her mother."

"Now, try, Marcélite," continued Monsieur Goupilleau, "try to remember somebody, anybody who knows you, who knew
your mistress; I want their names. Anybody, anybody will do, my poor Marcélite!
Indeed I believe you; we all believe you;
we know you are telling the truth; but
is there not a person, even a book,
a piece of paper, anything, you can remember?"

He stood close to her; his head did not
reach above her shoulders, but his eyes
plead into her face as if petitioning for his
own honor; and then they followed the
hands of the woman fumbling, feeling,
passing, repassing inside her torn dress
waist. He held his hands out, the kind, tender, little hands that had rested so gently
on her bruised black skin.

"If I have not lost it, if I have not dropped it out of my gown since last night, I never have dropped it, and I have carried it round inside my body now for seventeen years; but I was most crazy last night. . . ."

She put a small package, all wrapped up in an old bandanna handkerchief in his hands.

"I was keeping that for my *bébé;* I was going to give it to her when she graduated, just to remind her of her own mother. She gave it to me when she died."

It was only a little worn-out prayer-book, but all filled with written papers and locks of hair and dates and certificates, frail fluttering scraps that dropped all over the table, but unanswerable champions for the honor of dead men and the purity of dead women.

"Par la grâce de Dieu!" [160] exclaimed the notary, while the tears fell from his eyes 5 on the precious relics, discolored and worn from bodily contact. Marie sank on her knees by the table, holding Marcélite tight by the hand.

"Par la grâce de Dieu! Nothing is want- 10 ing here, nothing, nothing except the forgiveness of this good woman, and the assurances of our love and gratitude. And they say," turning to madame, he hazarded the bold step of taking both her hands in 15 his, "they say," recollecting the tender pressure on his arm, he ventured still further, "they say, Eugénie, that the days of heroism are past, and they laugh at our chivalry."

XXVIII

ARTHUR SHERBURNE HARDY (1847–)

Though of Boston birth, trained at West Point, professor of mathematics at Dartmouth, and Ambassador at various times to important European nations, Arthur Sherburne Hardy has won for himself a place among the American novelists of distinction. Beginning with the novel *But Yet a Woman*, 1884, he did work during his early period only in the longer forms of fiction, but in later years he took up the short-story form and in it in many ways surpassed his earlier achievements. As with Miss King, there is a French tip to his pen. He is brilliant, concise, epigrammatic, and his art has always *finesse* and a precision almost mathematical. He too does not finish his tale with the concluding sentence. The reader carries away always a haunting suspicion; a drop of red lifeblood has fallen upon him as it did on M. Joly's volume and it will not let him rest. The reader has been brought for a moment face to face with the tragedy inherent in all human life, and he is sent away in the same mood that an old Greek might have been in after witnessing a tragedy by Æschylus.

Mr. Hardy's short-story product is small, included for the most part in the single volume *Diane and Her Friends*, 1914, but it is distinctive. With his experience in many arts and many nations he has been able to shake off provincialism and to give his work a cosmopolitan content and a breadth and depth not frequently found in American fiction.

THE MYSTERY OF CÉLESTINE

In the farthest recess of Belon's bookshop M. Joly, ex-Inspector of Police, was endeavoring to get rid of one of those hours which since his retirement hung so heavily on his hands. His eyes, wandering over the musty volumes on the shelf, had been caught by the title, *Criminal Responsibility*.

"Come, now," he said to himself; "let us see what web these gentlemen of the robe have spun for my children;" for M. Joly, in spite of his respect for the law, entertained a certain affectionate regard for those he pursued. Spread open on his knee, the book itself, apart from its contents, appealed to him. Bound in flexible covers, its every page, flat and obedient to his touch, invited him.

Except for Belon on his high stool, writing with his stub pencil on the fly-leaves of a new invoice the characters with which he disguised his profits, the shop was empty. A mournful silence hung like a pall over the dusty shelves and encumbered counters. For Belon's wares consisted chiefly of first editions in contemporary bindings and presentation volumes, books to be neither "tasted, swallowed, chewed, nor digested," but gloated over by those whose chief interests is found in the joy of acquisition.

"Belon," said M. Joly one day, "the sign over your door annoys me. Your bookshop 5 is a mausoleum."

In this mournful silence, his attention diverted only by a large spider whose tranquillity had been disturbed by the extraction from its resting-place of *Criminal* 10 *Responsibility*, an event which had not occurred in its lifetime, M. Joly read on in the feeble light of the dark window, thick with the accumulated dust of years. "Retribution is instinctive in all animal life. 15 This instinct is the expression of the Will to Live. All life is the constant overcoming of things that would hinder or destroy it. Vengeance is biologically necessary for survival. Retributive punishment is the or-20 der of all nature." Here M. Joly turned over the leaf. On the page which followed three dull-red spots broke the thread of the argument. Reading on mechanically, they constantly obtruded themselves on his 25 attention.

It is impossible to admit that the purpose of punishment is to prevent the criminal from doing further injury to society or to prevent others from committing the like offense. 30 Equality before the law is a cardinal tenet of our legal faith. Two persons who commit

339

exactly the same crime must be punished equally, no matter whether the judge is certain that for the one case a hundredth part of the punishment for the other would be just as efficacious in deterring from further crime.

These spots have certainly fallen from a certain height. Even without a microscope one readily detects minute specks—the spatter of a liquid which drops from a distance.

If the one criminal were sent to prison for one week and the other for two years, there would arise a storm of protest from the outraged sense of retributive justice.

What was that liquid? A viscous one, for the words on which it fell are entirely obscured. A drop of wine would not render the text illegible.

The general principle that penal suffering should be graduated according to the magnitude of the crime goes to show that retribution is the proper basis for punishment.

One must be on one's guard against jumping at conclusions. If Pichon were to see these spots he would pronounce them blood offhand. Pichon sees blood in everything which is red. Yet they made him Inspector! Do I complain? Not at all. Pichon is an excellent fellow. Nature abhors a vacuum. I retire—enter Pichon!

Equally significant is the principle that punishment must not overstep the limits set down by moral disapproval. We are more indignant over the murder of a great man than over that of a worthless drunkard. So, too, courage, genius, worth of the criminal, constitute alleviating circumstances. These facts show that punishment is intended to pay back for wrong-doing in proportionate measure—is, in other words, for retribution.

Yet that property of the blood which we call clotting would produce precisely such spots as these. When withdrawn from the veins it becomes converted into a stiff jelly, which in times becomes solid. On the other hand, when old, the identity of blood-stains is not readily determined.

But is the motive of punishment for retribution worthy of a moral person? If the proper aim of punishment were retributive, the returning of evil for evil in proportionate measure, how could the amount of punishment

be determined in case of such offenses as perjury, deception, or treason? Must society lie to the liar, deceive the deceiver, and betray the traitor? Seneca wittily asks, "Would any one think himself in his right mind if he were to return kicks to a mule or bites to a dog?"

"Belon," said M. Joly, closing the book on his knee, "of whom did you buy this amusing treatise?"

His pencil behind his ear under his bushy hair, Belon came down from his stool.

"From the library of Monsieur Vidal."

"How astonishing! You know the former owners of all these volumes"—M. Joly waved his hand in an embracing gesture—"without referring to your records?"

"It is my trade," replied Belon, simply.

"In asking its price—"

"Oh," interrupted Belon, contemptuously, "it is of no value. In every library the worthless outnumber the valuable. One buys the lot for the few treasures known only to the connoisseur like myself. I make you a present of it, Monsieur Joly."

"Thank you," said M. Joly; and to Belon's amazement he added, "I also am a connoisseur."

Belon surveyed him anxiously over his spectacles. "Is it possible," he said to himself, "that I have overlooked something!"

M. Joly went on thinking. "A nose-bleed is out of the question." Then, aloud, "This Vidal, he is dead, then, since you possess his treasures."

"Not at all. He has simply moved away."

Folding his hands over his waistcoat, M. Joly played his card of silence. "Naturally you are ignorant of this detail since you came to Passy after Monsieur Vidal changed his domicile. Formerly he lived in the house of the curé—the little house in the trees, in the Impasse St.-Jean."

"Yes," assented M. Joly. "A pleasant spot. One must have had good reasons for abandoning it."

"As to that, they were excellent," said Belon, remounting his stool and plunging into his calculations.

"Can you explain to me, Belon," said M. Joly, reflectively, "how it happens that for one hundred people who insist upon talking of what they know nothing there is only one, on the contrary, who—"

"Ha, ha! You are curious, Monsieur Joly!"

"Why should I deny it? This Vidal who

inds the maxims of the law in flexible
1orocco interests me."

"You gentry of the police"—Belon
cratched his ear with the point of his
encil—"twenty per cent. of thirty is six, 5
which added to thirty makes thirty-six—
n impossible figure"—and he wrote forty
n the fly-leaf—"I was saying that you
entry of the police—"

"Formerly," interposed M. Joly.   10

"It is the same thing. Habit is tenacious
-have always a nose for what does not
xist."

"Come, come," objected M. Joly, "you
re thinking of Monsieur le Curé."   15

"Monsieur Vidal was an honest man—
nd most unfortunate," said Belon, return-
ng to his figures.

"Ah, well," said M. Joly to himself, put-
ing on his hat, "I will ask my wife. Good 20
lay, Belon."

On the way to the "little house in the
rees" M. Joly communed with himself.
Solitude had no terrors for him. He had 25
given instant absolution to his little Dor-
inte, who, when chided for leaving the
garden of Monrepos alone, had replied,
"I was not alone; I was with myself."

Yet Belon's accusation of curiosity had 30
penetrated below the skin, since it put him
on his defense. "Why not?" he was repeating to himself. "Has not a great philosopher said curiosity is the desire to know
how and why—a trait which distinguishes 35
man from all other animals?" It must be
admitted also that a visit to the curé of
St.-Médard promised other felicities. The
curé possessed for him the fascination
which a mollusk has for a mischievous boy 40
who loves to poke it with a stick "to see
what it would do." M. Joly adored his wife.
Never in his most captious mood would he
dream of disturbing the placid pool of her
beliefs. Grounded in faith, even to provoke 45
a momentary ripple would be a crime. But
the roots of the curé's beliefs were deep
down in dogma, geological strata, fixed,
rigid, immovable, full of dead men's bones.

He was sitting in his easy chair when 50
M. Joly opened the door, two fat, nerveless hands crossed over his paunch, eyelids
heavy with sleep. "What is this mollusk
thinking of?" M. Joly asked himself. At
the sound of the opening door the mollusk 55
stirred, jelly-wise, suspicious. If the ex-
Inspector was in a friendly mood this
morning, as his open face betokened, yet

it was in these playful moods that he often
asked the most embarrassing questions.
Smiling, the curé watched him as the
mouse watches the cat.

"What a restful place!" said M. Joly.
Beyond the open window a thrush was
singing on a swaying branch. Reassured,
the curé nodded. "But the shade is too
dense. A house should stand in the sun."

"True," echoed the curé, "in the sun."

"Monsieur Vidal, the former owner—"

"Pardon me, Monsieur Vidal is still the
owner. Every month I send him the rent—
a mere pittance. He is so generous."

"And it is here you compose your sermons."

"At this desk, in this chair. All you see
here belongs to Monsieur Vidal," he added,
changing the subject warily.

"One would say he expected some day
to return."

The curé shook his head. "I think not.
This house is full of painful recollections.
Monsieur Vidal, already a widower, had
the misfortune also to lose a beloved
daughter."

"Ah!"

"Yes, a daughter who disappeared suddenly."

"Gossip," suggested M. Joly.

"Oh no; the fact is well known. Her
name was Célestine."

M. Joly repressed a smile. The curé's
logic was a perennial source of amusement.

"You would be astonished," he added,
reflectively, "if you knew how many such
disappearances are recorded every year at
the Prefecture. One would say a gulf
which opens. A young girl, an old man,
vanish, without a trace. It is mortifying. I
speak professionally. To be sure there are
cases in which it is better not to explore
the gulf."

"Monsieur Vidal was not of your opinion. A father prefers to know the truth.
Uncertainty is the worst of tortures."

"Undoubtedly," sighed M. Joly. "Certainty is the panacea the church offers to
humanity." A dull flush colored the curé's
cheeks, but to his relief M. Joly added,
"Next to owning a property is to have
a good landlord."

The flush disappeared in a smile of placid
contentment. "God has been good to me.
Before going away Monsieur Vidal had
this room done over—"

"I observed it. A new ceiling—"

"Tinted—fresh paper on the walls, and in the room above a new flooring, which I am told was decaying—but that was unnecessary. I sleep here, a little room next the kitchen, out of consideration for Babette, who is rheumatic."

And all this time above the droning voice M. Joly heard the sound of something dropping—one—two—three—on the book lying open on the desk where the sermons were written. "What a wild colt is this imagination!" he muttered. "Positively I must see Pichon. There is no antidote like Pichon."

"You were saying?" asked the curé.

"That if you have no objection I would like the address of your landlord."

"You think of purchasing the property!" gasped the curé.

"Not until Madame Joly receives another legacy," said M. Joly.

That afternoon M. Joly wrote a letter:

DEAR COMRADE: If your service permits, dine with Madame to-morrow. It will delight her. Monrepos has on its summer dress. We will dine on the little terrace under the arbor and renew our youth. There still remains a bottle of Romanée from the cellar of the Fountain of Health.

By the way, it appears that a young girl, Célestine Vidal, disappeared from the Impasse St.-Jean, Passy, in the year which you will ascertain if it appears on your record.

He read this invitation, omitting the last paragraph, to Madame Joly, who was sewing beside him.

"Very well," she said.

"That is all you have to say, Marie?"

"You know very well what I think, if I do not say it."

"What is it you think and do not say, Marie?"

"That you are restless."

"I restless! What an idea!"

"But you asked for it."

M. Joly laid down his cigar.

"You have no fault to find with Pichon, Marie?"

"No more than you have."

"Oh, Marie, Marie!" exclaimed M. Joly, taking her hand, "you know well there is only one person with whom I find no fault."

The head bent over the work, a faint color stole into the cheeks, and the hand was withdrawn gently. Did she know she

was never more bewitching than when shy? M. Joly wondered.

"The old masters," he said, "did well to paint their angels in the clouds. I like them best so—even in my garden."

"We dine at the same hour?" asked Madame Joly, in a matter-of-fact voice which nevertheless trembled a little.

"Since it is only Pichon," assented M. Joly, relighting his cigar, which in this interlude had gone out.

The sun hung edgewise on the horizon. For the third time Pichon's glass was empty, but at this moment Madame Joly brought the *fine champagne* and coffee. In the softened glow of the sun her hair, drawn smoothly behind the ears, shone like strands of gold. In spite of the Romanée, the aroma of the coffee, and the *fine champagne* mounting in his glass under the white wrist, Pichon sighed. His circumstances did not permit either of domestic felicity or table delicacies. Her slim figure outlined against the sky, there emanated from this woman, as from the garden of Monrepos, an atmosphere of fragrance—of promise and fulfilment.

"What luck!" thought Pichon. "And to think with such a woman there was also a legacy!"

M. Joly waited. It was never necessary to intimate anything to Marie. She had long since ceased the attempt to reconcile her husband's profession with his character. Certainly these two men were going to talk shop, a subject repugnant to her gentle nature. Pichon could not have told at what instant of the deepening shadows she vanished. The light of two cigars, like glow-worms, punctured the dark, and the murmur of voices mingled with the hum of insects.

Madame Joly closed her window.

Yes, Pichon was saying, it was the year 18—, the 13th of May, that M. Vidal applied to the police. His daughter had disappeared three days before. He explained that he had not applied at once, thinking Célestine had gone to visit an aunt who lived in Reuil. Pichon had the record of the Prefecture by heart: Age twenty—height 1m 70c, approximate—weight about 59k—complexion fair—eyes and hair brown—wearing when last seen a dark-blue dress. The hat usually worn, missing. M. Vidal could offer no explanation. Célestine was of a retiring disposition. Nothing had occurred to furnish a reason for her departure. "She had no lover," added Pichon, skeptically. Then, as a cat thrusts its claws forward, he asked, negligently, "You are interested in Monsieur Vidal?"

"As a bibliophile," said M. Joly.

Pichon's curiosity rose to fever pitch, but he remained silent. Pichon was aggressive only with inferiors.

"It is far easier to lose sight of the living than to dispose of the dead," said M. Joly, after a long pause.

"You are right," nodded Pichon, completely mystified, "and invariably they bungle it terribly."

M. Joly rose, throwing his cigar in the lilacs.

"Well, good night, my friend. It is a pleasure to see you. I will go to the gate with you. Listen to that nightingale"— his hand paused on the latch—"a soul that rejoices when evil is abroad. Did you ever think of that? Another cigar, Pichon."

Outside the gate, striking a match on the lamp-post as he listened to the retreating footsteps on the gravel of Monrepos, Pichon was saying to himself:

"What the devil is the old fox after?"

Pichon would have been astounded had he known M. Joly was asking the same question. Often in the past perplexed, he had rarely been undecided. Indecision and rashness hunt in couples. Was he growing old—or rusty? Was leisure robbing him of his faculties? In every crunch of his foot on the gravel he heard the word *Justice! Justice!* Yet something, like a ball and chain, clogged his every movement. He even went so far as to consult Madame Joly—indirectly.

"Marie, suppose that by chance you became aware of circumstances—"

"By chance, you say."

"Well, yes, for the most part. Of circumstances, I was saying, which, let us suppose, proved that a grave crime had been committed against society—that a neighbor who passed for an honest man was in reality a great criminal."

"You ask what I would do?"

"Yes, I ask you."

Madame Joly reflected a moment before lifting her face to her husband's.

"Not being of the police, I should close my eyes," she said firmly.

"There is something in that," replied M. Joly, noting the delicate use of the personal pronoun.

Nevertheless, the next day he called a cab and gave the address confided him by the curé. In his pocket was the morocco-bound volume. Beyond indulging in one of those searching conversations for which he was famous at the Prefecture, his intentions were of the vaguest. In the hoof-beats on the asphalt he heard again the word *Justice! Justice!* In the glass behind the bent form of the coachman he also saw the faun eyes of Marie. Between these two his mind swayed like a pendulum.

The cab stopped before a wooden gate on which was inscribed the name Vidal.

No, said the maid who answered his summons, M. Vidal was not at home. Would Monsieur wait? He was expected shortly.

"We will wait," said M. Joly to himself; "since time is no longer of any value, let us enjoy a luxury which costs nothing."

Entering, he saw that he was in a garden—less formal than that of Monrepos, but still a garden. Evidently, like himself, M. Vidal was a lover of nature.

Under a mulberry-tree a table was spread. The remains of a breakfast, abandoned to the bees, still encumbered it. M. Joly noted there were two covers.

Would Monsieur prefer to go into the house, or would he repose in the garden? Monsieur would wait in the open air.

From the adjoining shrubbery a little girl ran out, eying him suspiciously from behind the skirts of the maid removing the dishes. M. Joly took the book from his pocket. It was difficult, however, to read in the presence of this child, for he adored children. From time to time his gaze wandered to the innocent face on which suspicion was gradually yielding to curiosity. Wisps of thin brown hair, the thin hair of childhood, strayed over the brown eyes. At last, having completed its survey of this silent stranger, the little figure toddled unsteadily on its fat legs toward the house, crying: "Mamma! Mamma!"

"The wretch has married again," thought M. Joly, opening to a page at random.

"No validity can be ascribed to the theory of expiation so far as social protection is concerned. Let injuries to the gods be the concern of the gods. No man must be the viceregent of God to avenge—"

"Mamma! Mamma!" cried the voice again.

"History abounds in mistakes of this

nature. As to the theory of retribution, like that of deterrence, it is justified only as it is socially useful."

At this moment the present generation intervened. Clinging to the folds of a dark-blue dress, it babbled up into the face of a woman whose eyes smiled down upon it.

"Monsieur Vidal must be detained. I am sorry."

"It is of no consequence," said M. Joly. "My business can wait."

Fortified by the presence of the blue dress, the child began to climb upon his knee. The woman bent forward to restrain it.

"No, no," cried M. Joly; "if I do not lift her it is because effort is good for the young." Firmly ensconced at last on his knees, the child's chubby fingers began to rumple the leaves of *Criminal Responsibility.* "Unfortunately, there are no pictures," smiled M. Joly. What an amiable gentleman! the woman was saying to herself. "One has only to look at this face to perceive you are its mother."

The woman flushed with pleasure. M. Joly watched the color disappearing among the fine roots of the brown hair and beneath the lace fichu of the bosom. Nothing in this woman really reminded him of Marie, yet he thought of her.

The gate creaked on its hinges.

"Ah, here he is! Papa, a gentleman who wishes to see you."

"Leave us, Célestine," said M. Vidal.

"Your daughter's name is Célestine!" said M. Joly, dumfounded.

Amazed at this pronouncement, M. Vidal's face betrayed surprise—but nothing more.

"After her mother," he replied, staring at his singular visitor.

"Pardon me," said M. Joly, completely taken back, "but I thought that it was her sister's."

M. Vidal drew himself up stiffly. "Célestine never had the good fortune to possess a sister. Célestine is my only child. To what have I the honor—"

"A mere trifle." M. Joly had recovered himself. "Recently, in the bookshop of Belon, in Passy, I purchased this volume. Afterward, I observed from the fly-leaf that it had been given to you with the author's compliments. It occurred to me that —being a presentation copy—by some error—"

M. Vidal unbent a little. "Your consideration does you honor. I thank you. But you are mistaken. I take no interest in either the writer or his subject."

M. Joly replaced the book in his pocket. Not within his memory had he experienced so embarrassing a moment. Not within his memory had the solitude of a cab proved so agreeable.

"It is true," he muttered, "that when the dead return and the lost are found there is no need to trouble the Prefecture. They keep no fatted calves there. Pichon was probably right. There was a lover, since there is now that little cherub. At all events, it appears Monrepos is not the only Eden. Ah, Pichon, Pichon, if it had been you astride that Barbary colt Imagination you would certainly have gone over the precipice."

With this consoling reflection, M. Joly lowered the window and called to the coachman, "The Fountain of Health, rue Dauphiné."

After his luncheon he strolled along the river. On reaching a quiet spot he took the book from his pocket and laid it on the parapet. By a perverse fate it opened in the breeze to the three sinister spots. Looking about to see if he was observed, M. Joly dropped *Criminal Responsibility* gently into the Seine.

"*Ma foi,*" he said, watching it swirling in the eddy under the bridge, "I take no more interest in it than you do"—and hailed the tram for Passy.

Dorante came running down the path before he could lock the gate behind him. He caught her in his arms, to deposit her in the lap of Marie, sewing in the arbor. One of Madame Joly's charms was her silences. She knew how to refrain. Yet it was natural under the circumstances—for M. Joly had gone out that morning without saying a word—to look up into his face inquiringly.

"Marie," he whispered, indulging in one of those white lies permitted by conscience, "since we are no longer in the police, I shut my eyes as you do."

PART III

THE EIGHTEEN NINETIES, 1890–1900

XXIX

HENRY CUYLER BUNNER (1855-1896)

During the eighteen nineties a younger generation, born for the most part in the Civil War decade, began to influence the short-story product. The local color strangeness and the selective realism of the work of Harte and Cable and the rest of the writers of the seventies were to this vigorous young group, headed by Frank Norris and Hamlin Garland, "old stuff." In tune with the new tendencies in fiction everywhere, especially in France, they demanded a more inclusive definition of "realism." "Veritism," "naturalism," "actuality," "truth," came out as terms in the new criticism. The influence of Zola and the Russians brought materials into fiction that had been carefully shunned by the earlier writers. Truth to life was to be the only standard, truth to *all* life with nothing omitted. The decade also stands for a swift formulation of the laws governing short-story art, for demands for more and more careful technique. Textbooks and treatises began to appear, soon to be swelled into a veritable library, and short-story courses were offered in schools and colleges. The age of conscious art had begun.

A pioneer in the new period undoubtedly was H. C. Bunner, whose entire life after he was twenty-one was centered about the humorous journal *Puck,* of which until his death he was the only editor. Practically all he ever wrote appeared first in the columns of *Puck.* Like Poe, he viewed the short story primarily from the editorial standpoint. The first demand, from this viewpoint, always concerned space: he wrote always with a definite space to fill, one inexorably limited. To him, therefore, the short story meant condensation, nothing too much. Moreover, written for a periodical like *Puck,* the story must be light, alive, entertaining, unfettered with the didactic or the moralistic. It must also be original, and as far as possible different from anything that had hitherto proceeded from its author's pen. The short story, Poe had ruled, must first of all be original; and secondly the author must possess variety. That Bunner for two decades delighted the readers of his whimsical journal is all we need to say about the man's art. Like all entertainers he wrought for his own time, and therefore must be content to perish with his time, and yet in many of his tales there is far more than mere ephemeral stuff. They are founded on universal characteristics, the fundamentals of human life, and therefore are likely to endure. That he was influenced by French art is evident to all readers, especially those who have read his *Made in France* collection, which is a deliberate adaptation to American conditions of some of Maupassant's most characteristic *contes.* His best collection is his *Short Sixes, Stories to be Read While the Candle Burns.* Two series. 1891.

THE LOVE-LETTERS OF SMITH *

When the little seamstress had climbed to her room in the story over the top story of the great brick tenement house in which she lived, she was quite tired out. If you do not understand what a story over a top story is, you must remember that there are no limits to human greed, and hardly any to the height of tenement houses. When the man who owned that seven-story tenement found that he could rent another floor, he found no difficulty in persuading the guardians of our building laws to let him clap another story on the

* Published by arrangement with Charles Scribner's Sons, owners of the copyright.

roof, like a cabin on the deck of a ship; and in the southeasterly of the four apartments on this floor the little seamstress lived. You could just see the top of her window from the street—the huge cornice that had capped the original front, and that served as her window-sill now, quite hid all the lower part of the story on top of the top story.

The little seamstress was scarcely thirty years old, but she was such an old-fashioned little body in so many of her looks and ways that I had almost spelled her sempstress, after the fashion of our grandmothers. She had been a comely body, too; and would have been still, if she had not been thin and pale and anxious-eyed.

347

She was tired out to-night because she had been working hard all day for a lady who lived far up in the "New Wards" beyond Harlem River, and after the long journey home, she had to climb seven flights of tenement-house stairs. She was too tired both in body and in mind to cook the two little chops she had brought home. She would save them for breakfast, she thought. So she made herself a cup of tea on the miniature stove, and ate a slice of dry bread with it. It was too much trouble to make toast.

But after dinner she watered her flowers. She was never too tired for that; and the six pots of geraniums that caught the south sun on the top of the cornice did their best to repay her. Then she sat down in her rocking-chair by the window and looked out. Her eyrie was high above all the other buildings, and she could look across some low roofs opposite, and see the further end of Tompkins Square, with its sparse Spring green showing faintly through the dusk. The eternal roar of the city floated up to her and vaguely troubled her. She was a country girl, and although she had lived for ten years in New York, she had never grown used to that ceaseless murmur. To-night she felt the languor of the new season as well as the heaviness of the physical exhaustion. She was almost too tired to go to bed.

She thought of the hard day done and the hard day to be begun after the night spent on the hard little bed. She thought of the peaceful days in the country, when she taught school in the Massachusetts village where she was born. She thought of a hundred small slights that she had to bear from people better fed than bred. She thought of the sweet green fields that she rarely saw nowadays. She thought of the long journey forth and back that must begin and end her morrow's work, and she wondered if her employer would think to offer to pay her fare. Then she pulled herself together. She must think of more agreeable things, or she could not sleep. And as the only agreeable things she had to think about were her flowers, she looked at the garden on top of the cornice.

A peculiar gritting noise made her look down, and she saw a cylindrical object that glittered in the twilight, advancing in an irregular and uncertain manner toward her flower-pots. Looking closer, she saw that it was a pewter beer-mug, which somebody

in the next apartment was pushing with a two-foot rule. On top of the beer-mug was a piece of paper, and on this paper was written, in a sprawling, half-formed hand:

porter
pleas excuse the libberty And
drink it

The seamstress started up in terror, and shut the window. She remembered that there was a man in the next apartment. She had seen him on the stairs, on Sundays. He seemed a grave, decent person; but— he must be drunk. She sat down on her bed, all a-tremble. Then she reasoned with herself. The man was drunk, that was all. He probably would not annoy her further. And if he did, she had only to retreat to Mrs. Mulvaney's apartment in the rear, and Mr. Mulvaney, who was a highly respectable man and worked in a boiler-shop, would protect her. So, being a poor woman who had already had occasion to excuse—and refuse—two or three "libberties" of like sort, she made up her mind to go to bed like a reasonable seamstress, and she did. She was rewarded, for when her light was out, she could see in the moonlight that the two-foot rule appeared again, with one joint bent back, hitched itself into the mug-handle, and withdrew the mug.

The next day was a hard one for the little seamstress, and she hardly thought of the affair of the night before until the same hour had come around again, and she sat once more by her window. Then she smiled at the remembrance. "Poor fellow," she said in her charitable heart, "I've no doubt he's *awfully* ashamed of it now. Perhaps he was never tipsy before. Perhaps he didn't know there was a lone woman in here to be frightened."

Just then she heard a gritting sound. She looked down. The pewter pot was in front of her, and the two-foot rule was slowly retiring. On the pot was a piece of paper, and on the paper was:

porter
good for the helth
it makes meet

This time the little seamstress shut her window with a bang of indignation. The color rose to her pale cheeks. She thought that she would go down to see the janitor at once. Then she remembered the seven flights of stairs; and she resolved to see the janitor in the morning. Then she went to bed and saw the mug drawn back just as it had been drawn back the night before.

The morning came, but, somehow, the seamstress did not care to complain to the janitor. She hated to make trouble—and the janitor might think—and—and—well, if the wretch did it again she would speak to him herself, and that would settle it.

And so, on the next night, which was a Thursday, the little seamstress sat down by her window, resolved to settle the matter. And she had not sat there long, rocking in the creaking little rocking-chair which she had brought with her from her old home, when the pewter pot hove in sight, with a piece of paper on the top.

This time the legend read:

> Perhaps you are afrade i will adress you
> i am not that kind

The seamstress did not quite know whether to laugh or cry. But she felt that the time had come for speech. She leaned out of her window and addressed the twilight heaven.

"Mr.—Mr.—sir—I—will you *please* put your head out of the window so that I can speak to you?"

The silence of the other room was undisturbed. The seamstress drew back, blushing. But before she could nerve herself for another attack, a piece of paper appeared on the end of the two-foot rule.

> when i Say a thing i mene it
> i have Sed i would not Adress you and i Will not

What was the little seamstress to do? She stood by the window and thought hard about it. Should she complain to the janitor? But the creature was perfectly respectful. No doubt he meant to be kind. He certainly was kind, to waste these pots of porter on her. She remembered the last time—and the first—that she had drunk porter. It was at home, when she was a young girl, after she had had the diphtheria. She remembered how good it was, and how it had given her back her strength. And without one thought of what she was doing, she lifted the pot of porter and took one little reminiscent sip—two little reminiscent sips—and became aware of her utter fall and defeat. She blushed now as she had never blushed before, put the pot down, closed the window, and fled to her bed like a deer to the woods.

And when the porter arrived the next night, bearing the simple appeal:

> Dont be atrade of it
> drink it all

the little seamstress arose and grasped the pot firmly by the handle, and poured its contents over the earth around her largest geranium. She poured the contents out to the last drop, and then she dropped the pot, and ran back and sat on her bed and cried, with her face hid in her hands.

"Now," she said to herself, "you've done it! And you're just as nasty and hardhearted and suspicious and mean as—as pusley!"

And she wept to think of her hardness of heart. "He will never give me a chance to say I am sorry," she thought. And, really, she might have spoken kindly to the poor man, and told him that she was much obliged to him, but that he really mustn't ask her to drink porter with him.

"But it's all over and done now," she said to herself as she sat at her window on Saturday night. And then she looked at the cornice, and saw the faithful little pewter pot traveling slowly toward her.

She was conquered. This act of Christian forbearance was too much for her kindly spirit. She read the inscription on the paper:

> porter is good for Flours
> but better for Fokes

and she lifted the pot to her lips, which were not half so red as her cheeks, and took a good, hearty, grateful draught.

She sipped in thoughtful silence after this first plunge, and presently she was surprised to find the bottom of the pot in full view.

On the table at her side a few pearl buttons were screwed up in a bit of white paper. She untwisted the paper and smoothed it out, and wrote in a tremulous hand— she *could* write a very neat hand—

> Thanks.

This she laid on the top of the pot, and in a moment the bent two-foot rule appeared and drew the mail-carriage home. Then she sat still, enjoying the warm glow of the porter, which seemed to have permeated her entire being with a heat that was not at all like the unpleasant and oppressive heat of the atmosphere, an atmosphere heavy with the Spring damp. A gritting on the tin aroused her. A piece of paper lay under her eyes.

> fine groing weather
>   Smith

it said.

Now it is unlikely that in the whole round and range of conversational commonplaces there was one other greeting that could have induced the seamstress to continue the exchange of communications. But this simple and homely phrase touched her country heart. What did *"groing weather"* matter to the toilers in this waste of brick and mortar? This stranger must be like herself, a country-bred soul, longing for the new green and the upturned brown mold of the country fields. She took up the paper, and wrote under the first message:

> Fine

But that seemed curt; *for* she added: *"for"* what? She did not know. At last in desperation she put down *potatoes*. The piece of paper was withdrawn and came back with an addition:

> Too mist for potatos

And when the little seamstress had read this, and grasped the fact that *m-i-s-t* represented the writer's pronunciation of "moist," she laughed softly to herself. A man whose mind, at such a time, was seriously bent upon potatoes, was not a man to be feared. She found a half-sheet of note-paper, and wrote:

> I lived in a small village before I came to New York, but I am afraid I do not know much about farming. Are you a farmer?

The answer came:

> have ben most Every thing
> farmed a Spel in Maine
>   Smith

As she read this, the seamstress heard a church clock strike nine.

"Bless me, is it so late?" she cried, and she hurriedly penciled *Good Night,* thrust the paper out, and closed the window. But a few minutes later, passing by, she saw yet another bit of paper on the cornice, fluttering in the evening breeze. It said only *good nite,* and after a moment's hesitation, the little seamstress took it in and gave it shelter.

* * * * *

After this, they were the best of friends. Every evening the pot appeared, and while the seamstress drank from it at her window, Mr. Smith drank from its twin at his; and notes were exchanged as rapidly as Mr. Smith's early education permitted. They told each other their histories, and Mr. Smith's was one of travel and variety, which he seemed to consider quite a matter of course. He had followed the sea, he had farmed, he had been a logger and a hunter in the Maine woods. Now he was foreman of an East River lumber yard, and he was prospering. In a year or two he would have enough laid by to go home to Bucksport and buy a share in a ship-building business. All this dribbled out in the course of a jerky but variegated correspondence, in which autobiographic details were mixed with reflections, moral and philosophical.

A few samples will give an idea of Mr. Smith's style:

> i was one trip to van demens
> land

To which the seamstress replied:

> It must have been very interesting

But Mr. Smith disposed of this subject very briefly:

> it wornt

Further he vouchsafed:

> i seen a chinese cook in
> hong kong could cook flapjacks
> like your Mother

> a mishnery that sells Rum
> is the menest of Gods crechers

> a bulfite is not what it is
> cract up to Be

> the dagos are wussen the
> brutes

i am 6 1¾
but my Father was 6 foot 4

The seamstress had taught school one
Winter, and she could not refrain from
making an attempt to reform Mr. Smith's
orthography. One evening, in answer to
this communication:

i killd a Bare in Maine 600
lbs waight

she wrote:

Isn't it generally spelled Bear?

but she gave up the attempt when he responded:

a bare is a mene animle any
way you spel him

The Spring wore on, and the Summer
came, and still the evening drink and the
evening correspondence brightened the
close of each day for the little seamstress.
And the draught of porter put her to sleep
each night, giving her a calmer rest than
she had ever known during her stay in the
noisy city; and it began, moreover, to make
a little *"meet"* for her. And then the
thought that she was going to have an
hour of pleasant companionship somehow
gave her courage to cook and eat her little
dinner, however tired she was. The seamstress's cheeks began to blossom with the
June roses.

And all this time Mr. Smith kept his
vow of silence unbroken, though the seamstress sometimes tempted him with little
ejaculations and exclamations to which he
might have responded. He was silent and
invisible. Only the smoke of his pipe, and
the clink of his mug as he set it down
on the cornice, told her that a living, material Smith was her correspondent. They
never met on the stairs, for their hours
of coming and going did not coincide. Once
or twice they passed each other in the
street—but Mr. Smith looked straight
ahead of him, about a foot over her head.
The little seamstress thought he was a very
fine-looking man, with his six feet one and
three-quarters and his thick brown beard.
Most people would have called him plain.
Once she spoke to him. She was coming home one Summer evening, and a gang
of corner-loafers stopped her and demanded money to buy beer, as is their custom.

Before she had time to be frightened, Mr.
Smith appeared—whence, she knew not—
scattered the gang like chaff, and, collaring
two of the human hyenas, kicked them with
deliberate, ponderous, alternate kicks until
they writhed in ineffable agony. When he
let them crawl away, she turned to him
and thanked him warmly, looking very
pretty now, with the color in her cheeks.
But Mr. Smith answered no word. He
stared over her head, grew red in the face,
fidgeted nervously, but held his peace until his eyes fell on a rotund Teuton, passing
by.

"Say, Dutchy!" he roared.

The German stood aghast.

"I ain't got nothing to write with!"
thundered Mr. Smith, looking him in the
eye. And then the man of his word passed
on his way.

And so the Summer went on, and the
two correspondents chatted silently from
window to window, hid from sight of all
the world below by the friendly cornice.
And they looked out over the roof, and
saw the green of Tompkins Square grow
darker and dustier as the months went on.

Mr. Smith was given to Sunday trips
into the suburbs, and he never came back
without a bunch of daisies or black-eyed
Susans or, later, asters or golden-rod for
the little seamstress. Sometimes, with a
sagacity rare in his sex, he brought
her a whole plant, with fresh loam for
potting.

He gave her also a reel in a bottle, which,
he wrote, he had *"maid"* himself, and some
coral, and a dried flying-fish, that was
somewhat fearful to look upon, with its
sword-like fins and its hollow eyes. At
first, she could not go to sleep with that
flying-fish hanging on the wall.

But he surprised the little seamstress
very much one cool September evening,
when he shoved this letter along the cornice:

Respected and Honored Madam:
Having long and vainly sought an oppor-
tunity to convey to you the expression of my
sentiments, I now avail myself of the privi-
lege of epistolary communication to acquaint
you with the fact that the Emotions, which
you have raised in my breast, are those which
should point to Connubial Love and Affection
rather than to simple Friendship. In short,
Madam, I have the Honor to approach you
with a Proposal, the acceptance of which will
fill me with ecstatic Gratitude, and enable me

to extend to you those Protecting Cares,
which the Matrimonial Bond makes at once
the Duty and the Privilege of him, who
would, at no distant date, lead to the Hyme-
neal Altar one whose charms and virtues
should suffice to kindle its Flames, without
extraneous Aid.

  I remain, Dear Madam,
   Your Humble Servant and
    Ardent Adorer, J. Smith

The little seamstress gazed at his letter a long time. Perhaps she was wondering in what Ready Letter-Writer of the last century Mr. Smith had found this form. Perhaps she was amazed at the results of his first attempt at punctuation. Perhaps she was thinking of something else, for there were tears in her eyes and a smile on her small mouth.

But it must have been a long time, and Mr. Smith must have grown nervous, for presently another communication came along the line where the top of the cornice was worn smooth. It read:

If not understood will you mary me?

The little seamstress seized a piece of paper and wrote:

If I say Yes, will you speak to me?

Then she rose and passed it out to him, leaning out of the window, and their faces met.

XXX

MARY ELEANOR WILKINS FREEMAN (1862–   )

Until the late eighties, when the grim stories of Mary E. Wilkins began to appear, New England had for the most part been reported in fiction by golden-tipped pens. Mrs. Stowe and Mrs. Cooke and Miss Jewett had been inclined to throw over their native region an Indian-summer, Washington Irving-like atmosphere. Even the most realistic attempts of these writers were touched at times with romance. But with the fading years of the century it was realized more and more that the old New England had as surely been destroyed by the Civil War as had been the old régime in the South. The westward migration following the war had drained the rural districts of their younger generation and the new industrial readjustments caused by the war had brought swarms of immigrants into the manufacturing cities. The readjustment in many of its phases was tragic. The exodus left behind it many wrecks and incongruities and curious survivals, and the depicter of this tragic abandoned area was Mary E. Wilkins, a puritan of the puritans herself, the last survivor of a line that had originated in Old Salem, Massachusetts, contemporary with Hawthorne's earliest American ancestor.

To understand Mrs. Freeman one must first of all realize her frail health that compelled her to be educated at home, that gave her the point of view of the recluse who looks out upon life but does not share it, and that made her a Hawthorne-like brooder over problems and special cases. The death of her parents left her alone with an old aunt whom she must support in a great house her father had built at Randolph, Mass. She had no means; her precarious health forbade teaching or other employment open to women, and she turned perforce to fiction. Without models or helpful counsel from older writers, she began to make short stories from the only materials she knew,—small-town characters of the Massachusetts and Vermont environments. Plain as veritable puritans these earliest stories are, unornamented, almost unadjectived, short of sentence and unconnected, staccato in style, and dealing almost wholly with thwarted lives, with pathetic remnants and failures, with tragic survivals and inherited warpings of character, left-overs from the iron-bound generations that had once ruled New England. To leaf through her earlier collections of tales brings the same feeling as does Masters' *Spoon River Anthology* of a later day. It is depressed realism; it is overemphasis of the tragedy and the drabness and the unbeautiful in the small-town areas of life.

Her first volume, *A Humble Romance*, 1887, despite the efforts of the Harpers publishing house, fell unnoticed, but her second volume, *A New England Nun*, 1891, made something like a sensation, first in England and then at home. Little by little she outgrew her earlier bareness of style and crudeness until at last in such collections as *Six Trees*, a work of pure symbolism, and *The Wind in the Rose Bush*, one of the best collections of ghost stories of modern times, she achieved even beauty of expression. Yet in all her work there is emphasis upon the unlovely. She is the recorder of the last act of the New England drama; the exhibitor of the moraines and gnarled human boulders of the puritan glacial period. She is the grimmest and perhaps the truest of all the recorders of the New England decline.

A VILLAGE SINGER*

The trees were in full leaf, a heavy south wind was blowing, and there was a loud murmur among the new leaves. The people noticed it, for it was the first time that year that the trees had so murmured in the wind. The spring had come with a rush during the last few days.

The murmur of the trees sounded loud in the village church, where the people sat waiting for the service to begin. The windows were open; it was a very warm Sunday for May.

The church was already filled with this soft sylvan music—the tender harmony

* Published by arrangement with Harper & Brothers, owners of the copyright.

353

of the leaves and the south wind, and the sweet, desultory whistles of birds—when the choir arose and began to sing.

In the center of the row of women singers stood Alma Way. All the people stared at her, and turned their ears critically. She was the new leading soprano. Candace Whitcomb, the old one, who had sung in the choir for forty years, had lately been given her dismissal. The audience considered that her voice had grown too cracked and uncertain on the upper notes. There had been much complaint, and after long deliberation the church-officers had made known their decision as mildly as possible to the old singer. She had sung for the last time the Sunday before, and Alma Way had been engaged to take her place. With the exception of the organist, the leading soprano was the only paid musician in the large choir. The salary was very modest, still the village people considered it large for a young woman. Alma was from the adjoining village of East Derby; she had quite a local reputation as a singer.

Now she fixed her large, solemn blue eyes; her long, delicate face, which had been pretty, turned paler; the blue flowers on her bonnet trembled; her little thin gloved hands, clutching the singing-book, shook perceptibly; but she sang out bravely. That most formidable mountain-height of the world, self-distrust and timidity, arose before her, but her nerves were braced for its ascent. In the midst of the hymn she had a solo; her voice rang out piercingly sweet; the people nodded admiringly at each other; but suddenly there was a stir; all the faces turned toward the windows on the south side of the church. Above the din of the wind and the birds, above Alma Way's sweetly straining tones, arose another female voice, singing another hymn to another tune.

"It's her," the women whispered to each other; they were half aghast, half smiling.

Candace Whitcomb's cottage stood close to the south side of the church. She was playing on her parlor organ, and singing, to drown out the voice of her rival.

Alma caught her breath; she almost stopped; the hymn-book waved like a fan; then she went on. But the long husky drone of the parlor organ and the shrill clamor of the other voice seemed louder than anything else.

When the hymn was finished, Alma sat down. She felt faint; the woman next her slipped a peppermint into her hand. "It ain't worth minding," she whispered, vigorously. Alma tried to smile; down in the audience a young man was watching her with a kind of fierce pity.

In the last hymn Alma had another solo. Again the parlor organ droned above the carefully delicate accompaniment of the church organ, and again Candace Whitcomb's voice clamored forth in another tune.

After the benediction, the other singers pressed around Alma. She did not say much in return for their expressions of indignation and sympathy. She wiped her eyes furtively once or twice, and tried to smile. William Emmons, the choir leader, elderly, stout, and smooth-faced, stood over her, and raised his voice. He was the old musical dignitary of the village, the leader of the choral club and the singing-schools. "A most outrageous proceeding," he said. People had coupled his name with Candace Whitcomb's. The old bachelor tenor and old maiden soprano had been wont to walk together to her home next door after the Saturday night rehearsals, and they had sung duets to the parlor organ. People had watched sharply her old face, on which the blushes of youth sat pitifully, when William Emmons entered the singing-seats. They wondered if he would ever ask her to marry him.

And now he said further to Alma Way that Candace Whitcomb's voice had failed utterly of late, that she sang shockingly, and ought to have had sense enough to know it.

When Alma went down into the audience-room, in the midst of the chattering singers, who seem to have descended like birds, from song flights to chirps, the minister approached her. He had been waiting to speak to her. He was a steady-faced, fleshy old man, who had preached from that one pulpit over forty years. He told Alma, in his slow way, how much he regretted the annoyance to which she had been subjected, and intimated that he would endeavor to prevent a recurrence of it. "Miss Whitcomb — must be — reasoned with," said he; he had a slight hesitation of speech, not an impediment. It was as if his thoughts did not slide readily into his words, although both were present. He walked down the aisle with Alma, and bade her good-morning when he saw Wilson Ford waiting for her in the doorway.

Everybody knew that Wilson Ford and Alma were lovers; they had been for the last ten years.

Alma colored softly, and made a little imperceptible motion with her head; her silk dress and the lace on her mantle fluttered, but she did not speak. Neither did Wilson, although they had not met before that day. They did not look at each other's faces—they seemed to see each other without that—and they walked along side by side.

They reached the gate before Candace Whitcomb's little house. Wilson looked past the front yard, full of pink and white spikes on flowering bushes, at the lace-curtained windows; a thin white profile, stiffly inclined, apparently over a book, was visible at one of them. Wilson gave his head a shake. He was a stout man, with features so strong that they overcame his flesh. "I'm going up home with you, Alma," said he; "and then—I'm just coming back, to give Aunt Candace one blowing up."

"Oh, don't, Wilson."

"Yes, I shall. If you want to stand this kind of a thing you may; I sha'n't."

"There's no need of your talking to her. Mr. Pollard's going to."

"Did he say he was?"

"Yes. I think he's going in before the afternoon meeting, from what he said."

"Well, there's one thing about it, if she does that thing again this afternoon, I'll go in there and break that old organ up into kindling-wood." Wilson set his mouth hard, and shook his head again.

Alma gave little side glances up at him, her tone was deprecatory, but her face was full of soft smiles. "I suppose she does feel dreadfully about it," said she. "I can't help feeling kind of guilty, taking her place."

"I don't see how you're to blame. It's outrageous, her acting so."

"The choir gave her a photograph album last week, didn't they?"

"Yes. They went there last Thursday night, and gave her an album and a surprise-party. She ought to behave herself."

"Well, she's sung there so long, I suppose it must be dreadful hard for her to give it up."

Other people going home from church were very near Wilson and Alma. She spoke softly that they might not hear; he did not lower his voice in the least. Presently Alma stopped before a gate.

"What are you stopping here for?" asked Wilson.

"Minnie Lansing wanted me to come and stay with her this noon."

"You're going home with me."

"I'm afraid I'll put your mother out."

"Put mother out! I told her you were coming, this morning. She's got all ready for you. Come along; don't stand here."

He did not tell Alma of the pugnacious spirit with which his mother had received the announcement of her coming, and how she had stayed at home to prepare the dinner, and make a parade of her hard work and her injury.

Wilson's mother was the reason why he did not marry Alma. He would not take his wife home to live with her, and was unable to support separate establishments. Alma was willing enough to be married and put up with Wilson's mother, but she did not complain of his decision. Her delicate blond features grew sharper, and her blue eyes more hollow. She had had a certain fine prettiness, but now she was losing it, and beginning to look old, and there was a prim, angular, old maiden carriage about her narrow shoulders.

Wilson never noticed it, and never thought of Alma as not possessed of eternal youth, or capable of losing or regretting it.

"Come along, Alma," said he; and she followed meekly after him down the street.

Soon after they passed Candace Whitcomb's house, the minister went up the front walk, and rang the bell. The pale profile at the window had never stirred as he opened the gate and came up the walk. However, the door was promptly opened, in response to his ring. "Good-morning, Miss Whitcomb," said the minister.

"Good-morning." Candace gave a sweeping toss of her head as she spoke. There was a fierce upward curl to her thin nostrils and her lips, as if she scented an adversary. Her black eyes had two tiny cold sparks of fury in them, like an enraged bird's. She did not ask the minister to enter, but he stepped lumberingly into the entry, and she retreated rather than led the way into her little parlor. He settled into the great rocking-chair and wiped his face. Candace sat down again in her old place by the window. She was a tall woman, but very slender and full of pliable motions, like a blade of grass.

"It's a—very pleasant day," said the minister.

Candace made no reply. She sat still, with her head drooping. The wind stirred the looped lace-curtains; a tall rose-tree outside the window waved; soft shadows floated through the room. Candace's parlor organ stood in front of an open window that faced the church; on the corner was a pitcher with a bunch of white lilacs. The whole room was scented with them. Presently the minister looked over at them and sniffed pleasantly.

"You have — some beautiful — lilacs there."

Candace did not speak. Every line of her slender figure looked flexible, but it was a flexibility more resistant than rigor.

The minister looked at her. He filled up the great rocking-chair; his arms in his shiny black coat-sleeves rested squarely and comfortably upon the hair-cloth arms of the chair.

"Well, Miss Whitcomb, I suppose I— may as well come to—the point. There was —a little—matter I wished to speak to you about. I don't suppose you were—at least I can't suppose you were—aware of it, but —this mornin', during the singing by the choir, you played and—sung a little too— loud. That is, with—the windows open. It —disturbed us—a little. I hope you won't feel hurt—my dear Miss Candace, but I knew you would rather I would speak of it, for I knew—you would be more disturbed than anybody else at the idea of such a thing."

Candace did not raise her eyes; she looked as if his words might sway her through the window. "I ain't disturbed at it," said she. "I did it on purpose; I meant to."

The minister looked at her.

"You needn't look at me. I know jest what I'm about. I sung the way I did on purpose, an' I'm going to do it again, an' I'd like to see you stop me. I guess I've got a right to set down to my own organ, an' sing a psalm tune on a Sabbath day, 'f I want to; an' there ain't no amount of talkin' an' palaverin' a-goin' to stop me. See there!" Candace swung aside her skirts a little. "Look at that!"

The minister looked. Candace's feet were resting on a large red-plush photograph album.

"Makes a nice footstool, don't it?" said she.

The minister looked at the album, then at her; there was a slowly gathering alarm in his face; he began to think she was losing her reason.

Candace had her eyes full upon him now, and her head up. She laughed, and her laugh was almost a snarl. "Yes; I thought it would make a beautiful footstool," said she. "I've been wantin' one for some time." Her tone was full of vicious irony.

"Why, miss—" began the minister; but she interrupted him:

"I know what you're a-goin' to say, Mr. Pollard, an' now I'm goin' to have my say; I'm a-goin' to speak. I want to know what you think of folks that pretend to be Christians treatin' anybody the way they've treated me? Here I've sung in those singin'-seats forty year. I 'ain't never missed a Sunday, except when I've been sick, an' I've gone an' sung a good many times when I'd better been in bed, an' now I'm turned out without a word of warnin'. My voice is jest as good as ever 'twas; there can't anybody say it ain't. It wa'n't ever quite so high-pitched as that Way girl's, mebbe; but she flats the whole durin' time. My voice is as good an' high to-day as it was twenty year ago; an' if it wa'n't, I'd like to know where the Christianity comes in. I'd like to know if it wouldn't be more to the credit of folks in a church to keep an old singer an' an old minister, if they didn't sing an' hold forth quite so smart as they used to, ruther than turn 'em off an' hurt their feelin's. I guess it would be full as much to the glory of God. S'pose the singin' an' the preachin' wa'n't quite so good, what difference would it make? Salvation don't hang on anybody's hittin' a high note, that I ever heard of. Folks are gettin' as high-steppin' an' fussy in a meetin'-house as they are in a tavern, nowadays. S'pose they should turn you off, Mr. Pollard, come an' give you a photograph album, an' tell you to clear out, how'd you like it? I ain't findin' any fault with your preachin'; it was always good enough to suit me; but it don't stand to reason folks'll be as took up with your sermons as when you was a young man. You can't expect it. S'pose they should turn you out in your old age, an' call in some young bob squirt, how'd you feel? There's William Emmons, too; he's three years older'n I am, if he does lead the choir an' run all the singin' in town. If my voice has gi'en out, it stan's to reason his has. It ain't, though. William Emmons sings jest as well as he ever did. Why don't they turn him out the way they have me, an' give him a photograph album? I dun know but it would be a good idea to send everybody, as soon as they get a little old an' gone by, an' young folks begin to push, onto some desert island, an' give 'em each a photograph album. Then they can sit down an' look at pictures the rest of their days. Mebbe government'll take it up.

"There they come here last week Thursday, all the choir, jest about eight o'clock in the evenin', an' pretended they'd come to give me a nice little surprise. Surprise! h'm! Brought cake an' oranges, an' was jest as nice as they could be, an' I was real tickled. I never had a surprise-party before in my life. Jenny Carr she played, an' they wanted me to sing alone, an' I never suspected a thing. I've been mad ever since to think what a fool I was, an' how they must have laughed in their sleeves.

"When they'd gone I found this photograph album on the table, all done up as nice as you please, an' directed to Miss Candace Whitcomb from her many friends, an' I opened it, an' there was the letter inside givin' me notice to quit.

"If they'd gone about it any decent way, told me right out honest that they'd got tired of me, an' wanted Alma Way to sing instead of me, I wouldn't minded so much; I should have been hurt 'nough, for I'd felt as if some that had pretended to be my friends wa'n't; but it wouldn't have been as bad as this. They said in the letter that they'd always set great value on my services, an' it wa'n't from any lack of appreciation that they turned me off, but they thought the duty was gettin' a little too arduous for me. H'm! I hadn't complained. If they'd turned me right out fair an' square, showed me the door, an' said, 'Here, you get out,' but to go an' spill molasses, as it were, all over the threshold, tryin' to make me think it's all nice an' sweet—

"I'd sent that photograph album back quick's I could pack it, but I didn't know who started it, so I've used it for a footstool. It's all it's good for, 'cordin' to my way of thinkin'. An' I ain't been particular to get the dust off my shoes before I used it neither."

Mr. Pollard, the minister, sat staring. He did not look at Candace; his eyes were fastened upon a point straight ahead. He had a look of helpless solidity, like a block of granite. This country minister, with his steady, even temperament, treading with heavy precision his one track for over forty years, having nothing new in his life except the new sameness of the seasons, and desiring nothing new, was incapable of understanding a woman like this, who had lived as quietly as he, and all the time held within herself the elements of revolution. He could not account for such violence, such extremes, except in a loss of reason. He had a conviction that Candace was getting beyond herself. He himself was not a typical New-Englander; the national elements of character were not pronounced in him. He was aghast and bewildered at this outbreak, which was tropical, and more than tropical, for a New England nature has a floodgate, and the power which it releases is an accumulation. Candace Whitcomb had been a quiet woman, so delicately resolute that the quality had been scarcely noticed in her, and her ambition had been unsuspected. Now the resolution and the ambition appeared raging over her whole self.

She began to talk again. "I've made up my mind that I'm goin' to sing Sundays the way I did this mornin', an' I don't care what folks say," said she. "I've made up my mind that I'm goin' to take matters into my own hands. I'm goin' to let folks see that I ain't trod down quite flat, that there's a little rise left in me. I ain't goin' to give up beat yet a while; an' I'd like to see anybody stop me. If I ain't got a right to play a psalm tune on my organ an' sing, I'd like to know. If you don't like it, you can move the meetin'-house."

Candace had had an inborn reverence for clergymen. She had always treated Mr. Pollard with the utmost deference. Indeed, her manner toward all men had been marked by a certain delicate stiffness and dignity. Now she was talking to the old minister with the homely freedom with which she might have addressed a female gossip over the back fence. He could not say much in return. He did not feel competent to make headway against any such tide of passion; all he could do was to let it beat against him. He made a few expostulations, which increased Candace's vehemence; he expressed his regret over the whole affair, and suggested that they should kneel and ask the guidance of the

Lord in the matter, that she might be led to see it all in a different light.

Candace refused flatly. "I don't see any use prayin' about it," said she. "I don't think the Lord's got much to do with it, anyhow."

It was almost time for the afternoon service when the minister left. He had missed his comfortable noontide rest, through this encounter with his revolutionary parishioner. After the minister had gone, Candace sat by the window and waited. The bell rang, and she watched the people file past. When her nephew Wilson Ford with Alma appeared, she grunted to herself. "She's thin as a rail," said she; "guess there won't be much left of her by the time Wilson gets her. Little soft-spoken nippin' thing, she wouldn't make him no kind of a wife, anyway. Guess it's jest as well."

When the bell had stopped tolling, and all the people entered the church, Candace went over to her organ and seated herself. She arranged a singing-book before her, and sat still, waiting. Her thin, colorless neck and temples were full of beating pulses; her black eyes were bright and eager; she leaned stiffly over toward the music-rack, to hear better. When the church organ sounded out she straightened herself; her long skinny fingers pressed her own organ-keys with nervous energy. She worked the pedals with all her strength; all her slender body was in motion. When the first notes of Alma's solo began, Candace sang. She had really possessed a fine voice, and it was wonderful how little she had lost it. Straining her throat with jealous fury, her notes were still for the main part true. Her voice filled the whole room; she sang with wonderful fire and expression. That, at least, mild little Alma Way could never emulate. She was full of steadfastness and unquestioning constancy, but there were in her no smoldering fires of ambition and resolution. Music was not to her what it had been to her older rival. To this obscure woman, kept relentlessly by circumstances in a narrow track, singing in the village choir had been as much as Italy was to Napoleon—and now on her island of exile she was still showing fight.

After the church service was done, Candace left the organ and went over to her old chair by the window. Her knees felt weak, and shook under her. She sat down.

and leaned back her head. There were red spots on her cheeks. Pretty soon she heard a quick slam of her gate, and an impetuous tread on the gravel-walk. She looked up, and there was her nephew Wilson Ford hurrying up to the door. She cringed a little, then she settled herself more firmly in her chair.

Wilson came into the room with a rush. He left the door open, and the wind slammed it to after him.

"Aunt Candace, where are you?" he called out, in a loud voice.

She made no reply. He looked around fiercely, and his eyes seemed to pounce upon her.

"Look here, Aunt Candace," said he, "are you crazy?" Candace said nothing. "Aunt Candace!" She did not seem to see him. "If you don't answer me," said Wilson, "I'll just go over there and pitch that old organ out of the window!"

"Wilson Ford!" said Candace, in a voice that was almost a scream.

"Well, what say! What have you got to say for yourself, acting the way you have? I tell you what 'tis, Aunt Candace, I won't stand it."

"I'd like to see you help yourself."

"I will help myself. I'll pitch that old organ out of the window, and then I'll board up the window on that side of your house. Then we'll see."

"It ain't your house, and it won't never be."

"Who said it was my house? You're my aunt and I've got a little lookout for the credit of the family. Aunt Candace, what are you doing this way for?"

"It don't make no odds what I'm doin' so for. I ain't bound to give my reasons to a young fellar like you, if you do act so mighty toppin'. But I'll tell you one thing, Wilson Ford, after the way you've spoke to-day, you sha'n't never have one cent of my money, an' you can't never marry that Way girl if you don't have it. You can't never take her home to live with your mother, an' this house would have been mighty nice an' convenient for you some day. Now you won't get it. I'm goin' to make another will. I'd made one, if you did but know it. Now you won't get a cent of my money, you nor your mother neither. An' I ain't goin' to live a dreadful while longer, neither. Now I wish you'd go home; I want to lay down. I'm 'bout sick."

Wilson could not get another word from

his aunt. His indignation had not in the least cooled. Her threat of disinheriting him did not cow him at all; he had too much rough independence, and indeed his aunt Candace's house had always been too much of an air-castle for him to contemplate seriously. Wilson, with his burly frame and his headlong common-sense, could have little to do with air-castles, had he been hard enough to build them over graves. Still, he had not admitted that he never could marry Alma. All his hopes were based upon a rise in his own fortunes, not by some sudden convulsion, but by his own long and steady labor. Some time, he thought, he should have saved enough for the two homes.

He went out of his aunt's house still storming. She arose after the door had shut behind him, and got out into the kitchen. She thought that she would start a fire and make a cup of tea. She had not eaten anything all day. She put some kindling-wood into the stove and touched a match to it; then she went back to the sitting-room, and settled down again into the chair by the window. The fire in the kitchen-stove roared, and the light wood was soon burned out. She thought no more about it. She had not put on the teakettle. Her head ached, and once in a while she shivered. She sat at the window while the afternoon waned and the dusk came on. At seven o'clock the meeting bell rang again, and the people flocked by. This time she did not stir. She had shut her parlor organ. She did not need to out-sing her rival this evening; there was only congregational singing at the Sunday-night prayer-meeting.

She sat still until it was nearly time for meeting to be done; her head ached harder and harder, and she shivered more. Finally she arose. "Guess I'll go to bed," she muttered. She went about the house, bent over and shaking, to lock the doors. She stood a minute in the back door, looking over the fields to the woods. There was a red light over there. "The woods are on fire," said Candace. She watched with a dull interest the flames roll up, withering and destroying the tender green spring foliage. The air was full of smoke, although the fire was half a mile away.

Candace locked the door and went in. The trees with their delicate garlands of new leaves, with the new nests of song birds, might fall, she was in the roar of an intenser fire; the growths of all her springs and the delicate wontedness of her whole life were going down in it. Candace went to bed in her little room off the parlor, but she could not sleep. She lay awake all night. In the morning she crawled to the door and hailed a little boy who was passing. She bade him go for the doctor as quickly as he could, then to Mrs. Ford's, and ask her to come over. She held on to the door while she was talking. The boy stood staring wonderingly at her. The spring wind fanned her face. She had drawn on a dress skirt and put her shawl over her shoulders, and her gray hair was blowing over her red cheeks.

She shut the door and went back to her bed. She never arose from it again. The doctor and Mrs. Ford came and looked after her, and she lived a week. Nobody but herself thought until the very last that she would die; the doctor called her illness merely a light run of fever; she had her senses fully.

But Candace gave up at the first. "It's my last sickness," she said to Mrs. Ford that morning when she first entered; and Mrs. Ford had laughed at the notion; but the sick woman held to it. She did not seem to suffer much physical pain; she only grew weaker and weaker, but she was distressed mentally. She did not talk much, but her eyes followed everybody with an agonized expression.

On Wednesday William Emmons came to inquire for her. Candace heard him out in the parlor. She tried to raise herself on one elbow that she might listen better to his voice.

"William Emmons come in to ask how you was," Mrs. Ford said, after he was gone.

"I—heard him," replied Candace. Presently she spoke again. "Nancy," said she, "where's that photograph album?"

"On the table," replied her sister, hesitatingly.

"Mebbe—you'd better—brush it up a little."

"Well."

Sunday morning Candace wished that the minister should be asked to come in at the noon intermission. She had refused to see him before. He came and prayed with her, and she asked his forgiveness for the way she had spoken the Sunday before. "I

—hadn't ought to—spoke so," said she. "I was—dreadful wrought up."

"Perhaps it was your sickness coming on," said the minister, soothingly.

Candace shook her head. "No—it wa'n't. I hope the Lord will—forgive me."

After the minister had gone, Candace still appeared unhappy. Her pitiful eyes followed her sister everywhere with the mechanical persistency of a portrait.

"What is it you want, Candace?" Mrs. Ford said at last. She had nursed her sister faithfully, but once in a while her impatience showed itself.

"Nancy!"

"What say?"

"I wish—you'd go out when—meetin's done, an'—head off Alma an' Wilson, an'—ask 'em to come in. I feel as if—I'd like to—hear her sing."

Mrs. Ford stared. "Well," said she.

The meeting was now in session. The windows were all open, for it was another warm Sunday. Candace lay listening to the music when it began, and a look of peace came over her face. Her sister had smoothed her hair back, and put on a clean cap. The white curtain in the bedroom window waved in the wind like a white sail. Candace almost felt as if she were better, but the thought of death seemed easy.

Mrs. Ford at the parlor window watched for the meeting to be out. When the people appeared, she ran down the walk and waited for Alma and Wilson. When they came she told them what Candace wanted, and they all went in together.

"Here's Alma an' Wilson, Candace," said Mrs. Ford, leading them to the bedroom door.

Candace smiled. "Come in," she said, feebly. And Alma and Wilson entered and stood beside the bed. Candace continued to look at them, the smile straining her lips. "Wilson!"

"What is it, Aunt Candace?"

"I ain' altered that—will. You an' Alma can—come here an'—live—when I'm—gone. Your mother won't mind livin' alone. Alma can have—all—my things."

"Don't, Aunt Candace." Tears were running over Wilson's cheeks, and Alma's delicate face was all of a quiver.

"I thought—maybe—Alma'd be willin' to—sing for me," said Candace.

"What do you want me to sing?" Alma asked, in a trembling voice.

"'Jesus, lover of my soul.'"

Alma, standing there beside Wilson, began to sing. At first she could hardly control her voice, then she sang sweetly and clearly.

Candace lay and listened. Her face had a holy and radiant expression. When Alma stopped singing it did not disappear, but she looked up and spoke, and it was like a secondary glimpse of the old shape of a forest tree through the smoke and flame of the transfiguring fire the instant before it falls. "You flatted a little on—'soul'," said Candace.

XXXI

HAMLIN GARLAND (1861–   )

The new realism, or "veritism," was expressed for the Middle West by Hamlin Garland, a native of Wisconsin and a pioneer with his father in the settlement of the Iowa prairie lands in the eighteen-seventies. He had broken at length from his frontier environment, and had lived for several years in Boston, supporting and educating himself as best he could with the smallest of material resources. A summer visit to his "Middle Border" home after his Eastern experiences astonished and maddened him. He saw his native West,—its rawness and primitive vulgarity and its grinding toil—with new eyes, and was swept suddenly with passion into the new "populist" movement of the area, that rising of the agricultural West against the Eastern capitalist and the unscrupulous landowner who were making life all too often a veritable hell for the moneyless tenant. His revolt, his love for the West, his eager literary enthusiasm he threw into a series of short stories later collected in three volumes, *Main-Travelled Roads,* first and second series, 1891-1899, and *Prairie Folks,* 1893, stories hot with propagandic fire like "Under the Lion's Paw" or grim with a Zola-like soddenness of realism like "Lucretia Burns," or reminiscent of boyhood on the prairies like "A Branch Road," or tinted with what was really innate within him, a sense of the romantic and the idyllic, like "Among the Corn Rows."

In his later years Garland's work ran oftenest to longer fiction but his most enduring work, excepting perhaps his late "Middle Border" trilogy—part fiction, part biography, part autobiography,—is to be found in these tense short stories of the 90's. They so intimately reveal the life of the pioneer in the vital early days of the first settlement that they are not likely to be forgotten.

AMONG THE CORN-ROWS *

A cornfield in July is a sultry place. The soil is hot and dry; the wind comes across the lazily murmuring leaves laden with a warm, sickening smell drawn from the rapidly growing, broad-flung banners of the corn. The sun, nearly vertical, drops a flood of dazzling light upon the field, over which the cool shadows run, only to make the heat seem the more intense.

Julia Peterson, faint with hunger, was toiling back and forth between the corn-rows, holding the handles of the double-shovel corn-plow, while her little brother Otto rode the steaming horse. Her heart was full of bitterness, her face flushed with heat, and her muscles aching with fatigue. The heat grew terrible. The corn came to her shoulders, and not a breath seemed to reach her, while the sun, nearing the noon mark, lay pitilessly upon her shoulders, protected only by a calico dress. The dust

rose under her feet, and as she was wet with perspiration it soiled her, till, with a woman's instinctive cleanliness, she shuddered. Her head throbbed dangerously. 5 What matter to her that the kingbird pitched jovially from the maples to catch a wandering bluebottle fly, that the robin was feeding its young, that the bobolink was singing? All these things, if she saw 10 them, only threw her bondage to labor into greater relief.

Across the field, in another patch of corn, she could see her father—a big, gruff-voiced, wide-bearded Norwegian—at 15 work also with a plow. The corn must be plowed, and so she toiled on, the tears dropping from the shadow of the ugly sun-bonnet she wore. Her shoes, coarse and square-toed, chafed her feet; her hands, 20 large and strong, were browned, or, more properly, *burnt,* on the backs by the sun. The horse's harness "*creak*-cracked" as he swung steadily and patiently forward, the moisture pouring from his sides, his nos- 25 trils distended.

The field bordered on a road, and on the

other side of the road ran a river—a broad, clear, shallow expanse at that point, and the eyes of the boy gazed longingly at the pond and the cool shadow each time that he turned at the fence.

"Say, Jule, I'm goin' in! Come, can't I? Come—say!" he pleaded, as they stopped at the fence to let the horse breathe.

"I've let you go wade twice."

"But that don't do any good. My legs is all smarty, 'cause ol' Jack sweats so." The boy turned around on the horse's back and slid back to his rump. "I can't stand it!" he burst out, sliding off and darting under the fence. "Father can't see."

The girl put her elbows on the fence and watched her little brother as he sped away to the pool, throwing off his clothes as he ran, whooping with uncontrollable delight. Soon she could hear him splashing about in the water a short distance up the stream, and caught glimpses of his little shiny body and happy face. How cool that water looked! And the shadows there by the big basswood! How that water would cool her blistered feet. An impulse seized her, and she squeezed between the rails of the fence, and stood in the road looking up and down to see that the way was clear. It was not a main-traveled road; no one was likely to come; why not?

She hurriedly took off her shoes and stockings—how delicious the cool, soft velvet of the grass!—and sitting down on the bank under the great basswood, whose roots formed an abrupt bank, she slid her poor blistered, chafed feet into the water, and bare head leaned against the huge tree-trunk.

And now, as she rested, the beauty of the scene came to her. Over her the wind moved the leaves. A jay screamed far off, as if answering the cries of the boy. A kingfisher crossed and recrossed the stream with dipping sweep of his wings. The river sang with its lips to the pebbles. The vast clouds went by majestically, far above the tree-tops, and the snap and buzzing and ringing whir of July insects made a ceaseless, slumberous undertone of song solvent of all else. The tired girl forgot her work. She began to dream. This would not last always. Some one would come to release her from such drudgery. This was her constant, tenderest, and most secret dream. *He* would be a Yankee, not a Norwegian. The Yankees didn't ask their wives to work in the field. He would have a home.

Perhaps he'd live in town—perhaps a merchant! And then she thought of the drug clerk in Rock River who had looked at her—A voice broke in on her dream, a fresh, manly voice.

"Well, by jinks! if it ain't Julia! Just the one I wanted to see!"

The girl turned, saw a pleasant-faced young fellow in a derby hat and a cutaway suit of diagonals.

"Bob Rodemaker! How come—"

She remembered her situation and flushed, looking down at the water, and remained perfectly still.

"Ain't you goin' to shake hands? Y' don't seem very glad t' see me."

She began to grow angry. "If you had any eyes, you'd see."

Rob looked over the edge of the bank, whistled, turned away. "Oh, I see! Excuse *me!* Don't blame yeh a bit, though. Good weather f'r corn," he went on, looking up at the trees. "Corn seems to be pretty well forward," he continued, in a louder voice, as he walked away, still gazing into the air. "Crops is looking first-class in Boom-town. Hello! This Otto? H'yare, y' little scamp! Get on to that horse ag'in. Quick, 'r I'll take y'r skin off an' hang it on the fence. What y' been doin'?"

"Ben in swimmin'. Jimminy, ain't it fun! When 'd y' get back?" said the boy, grinning.

"Never you mind!" replied Rob, leaping the fence by laying his left hand on the top rail. "Get on to that horse, and hung his coat on the fence. "I s'pose the ol' man makes her plow, same as usual?"

"Yup," said Otto.

"Dod ding a man that'll do that! I don't mind if it's necessary, but it ain't necessary in his case." He continued to mutter in this way as he went across to the other side of the field. As they turned to come back, Rob went up and looked at the horse's mouth. "Gettin' purty near of age. Say, who's sparkin' Julia now—anybody?"

"Nobody 'cept some ol' Norwegians. She won't have them. Por wants her to, but she won't."

"Good f'r her. Nobody comes t' see her Sunday nights, eh?"

"Nope; only 'Tias Anderson an' Ole Hoover; but she goes off and leaves 'em."

"Chk!" said Rob, starting old Jack across the field.

It was almost noon, and Jack moved reluctantly. He knew the time of day as well as the boy. He made this round after distinct protest.

In the meantime Julia, putting on her shoes and stockings, went to the fence and watched the man's shining white shirt as he moved across the cornfield. There had never been any special tenderness between them, but she had always liked him. They had been at school together. She wondered why he had come back at this time of the year, and wondered how long he would stay. How long had he stood looking at her? She flushed again at the thought of it. But he wasn't to blame; it was a public road. She might have known better. She stood under a little popple-tree, whose leaves shook musically at every zephyr, and her eyes, through half-shut lids, roved over the sea of deep-green, glossy leaves, dappled here and there by cloud shadows, stirred here and there like water by the wind; and out of it all a longing to be free from such toil rose like a breath, filling her throat and quickening the motion of her heart. Must this go on forever, this life of heat and dust and labor? What did it all mean?

The girl laid her chin on her strong red wrists, and looked up into the blue spaces between the vast clouds—aërial mountains dissolving in a shoreless azure sea. How cool and sweet and restful they looked! If she might only lie out on the billowy, snow-white, sunlit edge! The voices of the driver and the plowman recalled her, and she fixed her eyes again upon the slowly nodding head of the patient horse, on the boy turned half about on his saddle, talking to the white-sleeved man, whose derby hat bobbed up and down quite curiously, like the horse's head. Would she ask him to dinner? What would her people say?

"Phew! it's hot!" was the greeting the young fellow gave as he came up. He smiled in a frank, boyish way, as he hung his hat on the top of a stake and looked up at her. "D'y' know, I kind o' enjoy gettin' at it again? Fact. It ain't no work for a girl, though," he added.

"When 'd you get back?" she asked, the flush not yet out of her face.

Rob was looking at her thick, fine hair and full Scandinavian face, rich as a rose in color, and did not reply for a few seconds. She stood with her hideous sun-bonnet pushed back on her shoulders. A kingbird was chattering overhead.

"Oh, a few days ago."

"How long y' goin' t' stay?"

"Oh, I d' know. A week, mebbe."

A far-off halloo came pulsing across the shimmering air. The boy screamed "Dinner!" and waved his hat with an answering whoop, then flopped off the horse like a turtle off a stone into the water. He had the horse unhooked in an instant, and had flung his toes up over the horse's back, in act to climb on, when Rob said:

"H'yare, young feller! Wait a minute. Tired?" he asked the girl, with a tone that was more than kindly. It was almost tender.

"Yes," she replied, in a low voice. "My shoes hurt me."

"Well, here y' go," he replied, taking his stand by the horse, and holding out his hand like a step. She colored and smiled a little as she lifted her foot into his huge, hard, sun-burned hand.

"Oop-a-daisy!" he called. She gave a spring, and sat on the horse like one at home there.

Rob had a deliciously unconscious, abstracted, business-like air. He really left her nothing to do but enjoy his company, while he went ahead and did precisely as he pleased.

"We don't raise much corn out there, an' so I kind o' like to see it once more."

"I wish I didn't have to see another hill of corn as long as I live!" replied the girl, bitterly.

"Don't know as I blame yeh a bit. But all the same, I'm glad you was working in it to-day," he thought to himself, as he walked beside her horse toward the house.

"Will you stop to dinner?" she inquired bluntly, almost surlily. It was evident there were reasons why she didn't mean to press him to do so.

"You bet I will," he replied; "that is, if you want I should."

"You know how we live," she replied evasively. "If you can stand it, why—" She broke off abruptly.

Yes, he remembered how they lived in that big, square, dirty, white frame house. It had been three or four years since he had been in it, but the smell of the cabbage and onions, the penetrating, peculiar mixture of odors, assailed his memory as something unforgettable.

"I guess I'll stop," he said, as she hesitated.

She said no more, but tried to act as if she were not in any way responsible for what came afterward.

"I guess I c'n stand f'r one meal what you stand all the while," he added.

As she left them at the well and went to the house, he saw her limp painfully, and the memory of her face so close to his lips as he helped her down from the horse gave him pleasure at the same time that he was touched by its tired and gloomy look. Mrs. Peterson came to the door of the kitchen, looking just the same as ever. Broad-faced, unwieldy, flabby, apparently wearing the same dress he remembered to have seen her in years before,—a dirty, drab-colored thing,—she looked as shapeless as a sack of wool. Her English was limited to, "How de do, Rob?"

He washed at the pump, while the girl, in the attempt to be hospitable, held the clean towel for him.

"You're purty well used up, eh?" he said to her.

"Yes; it's awful hot out there."

"Can't you lay off this afternoon? It ain't right."

"No. *He* won't listen to that."

"Well, let me take your place."

"No; there ain't any use o' that."

Peterson, a brawny, wide-bearded Norwegian, came up at this moment, and spoke to Rob in a sullen, gruff way.

"Hallo, whan yo' gaet back?"

"To-day. He ain't *very* glad to see me," said Rob, winking at Julia. "He ain't b'ilin' over with enthusiasm; but I c'n stand it, for your sake," he added, with amazing assurance; but the girl had turned away, and it was wasted.

At the table he ate heartily of the "bean swaagen,"which filled a large wooden bowl in the center of the table, and which was ladled into smaller wooden bowls at each plate. Julia had tried hard to convert her mother to Yankee ways, and had at last given it up in despair. Rob kept on safe subjects, mainly asking questions about the crops of Peterson, and when addressing the girl, inquired of the schoolmates. By skilful questioning, he kept the subject of marriage uppermost, and seemingly was getting an inventory of the girls not yet married or engaged.

It was embarrassing for the girl. She was all too well aware of the difference between her home and the home of her schoolmates and friends. She knew that it was not pleasant for her "Yankee" friends to come to visit her when they could not feel sure of a welcome from the tireless, silent, and grim-visaged old Norse, if, indeed, they could escape insult. Julia ate her food mechanically, and it could hardly be said that she enjoyed the brisk talk of the young man, his eyes were upon her so constantly and his smile so obviously addressed to her. She rose as soon as possible and, going outside, took a seat on a chair under the trees in the yard. She was not a coarse or dull girl. In fact, she had developed so rapidly by contact with the young people of the neighborhood that she no longer found pleasure in her own home. She didn't believe in keeping up the old-fashioned Norwegian customs, and her life with her mother was not one to breed love or confidence. She was more like a hired hand. The love of the mother for her "Yulyie" was sincere, though rough and inarticulate, and it was her jealousy of the young "Yankees" that widened the chasm between the girl and herself—an inevitable result.

Rob followed the girl out into the yard, and threw himself on the grass at her feet, perfectly unconscious of the fact that this attitude was exceedingly graceful and becoming to them both. He did it because he wanted to talk to her, and the grass was cool and easy; there wasn't any other chair, anyway.

"Do they keep up the ly-ceum and the sociables same as ever?"

"Yes. The others go a good 'eal, but I don't. We're gettin' such a stock round us, and father thinks he needs me s' much, I don't get out often. I'm gettin' sick of it."

"I sh'd think y' would," he replied, his eyes on her face.

"I c'd stand the churnin' and housework, but when it comes t' workin' outdoors in the dirt an' hot sun, gettin' all sunburned and chapped up, it's another thing. An' then it seems as if he gets stingier 'n' stingier every year. I ain't had a new dress in—I d'-know-how-long. He says it's all nonsense, an' mother's just about as bad. *She* don't want a new dress, an' so she thinks I don't." The girl was feeling the influence of a sympathetic listener and was making up for the long silence. "I've tried t' go out t' work, but they won't let me. They'd have t' pay a hand twenty dollars a month f'r the work I do, an' they like cheap help; but I'm not goin' t' stand it much longer, I can tell you that."

Rob thought she was very handsome as she sat there with her eyes fixed on the horizon, while these rebellious thoughts found utterance in her quivering, passionate voice.

"Yulie! Kom haar!" roared the old man from the well.

A frown of anger and pain came into her face. She looked at Rob. "That means more work."

"Say! let me go out in your place. Come, now; what's the use—"

"No; it wouldn't do no good. It ain't t'-day s' much; it's every day, and—"

"Yulie!" called Peterson again, with a string of impatient Norwegian. "Batter yo' kom pooty hal quick."

"Well, all right, only I'd like to—" Rob submitted.

"Well, good-by," she said, with a little touch of feeling. "When d' ye go back?"

"I don't know. I'll see y' again before I go. Good-by."

He stood watching her slow, painful pace till she reached the well, where Otto was standing with the horse. He stood watching them as they moved out into the road and turned down toward the field. He felt that she had sent him away; but still there was a look in her eyes which was not altogether—

He gave it up in despair at last. He was not good at analyses of this nature; he was used to plain, blunt expressions. There was a woman's subtlety here quite beyond his reach.

He sauntered slowly off up the road after his talk with Julia. His head was low on his breast; he was thinking as one who is about to take a decided and important step.

He stopped at length, and, turning, watched the girl moving along in the deeps of the corn. Hardly a leaf was stirring; the untempered sunlight fell in a burning flood upon the field; the grasshoppers rose, snapped, buzzed, and fell; the locust uttered its dry, heat-intensifying cry. The man lifted his head.

"It's a d——n shame!" he said, beginning rapidly to retrace his steps. He stood leaning on the fence, awaiting the girl's coming very much as she had waited his on the round he had made before dinner. He grew impatient at the slow gait of the horse, and drummed on the rail while he whistled. Then he took off his hat and dusted it nervously. As the horse got a little nearer he wiped his face carefully, pushed his hat back on his head, and climbed over the fence, where he stood with elbows on the middle rail as the girl and boy and horse came to the end of the furrow.

"Hot, ain't it?" he said, as she looked up. "Jimminy Peters, it's awful!" puffed the boy.

The girl did not reply till she swung the plough about after the horse, and set it upright into the next row. Her powerful body had a superb swaying motion at the waist as she did this—a motion which affected Rob vaguely but massively.

"I thought you'd gone," she said gravely, pushing back her bonnet till he could see her face dewed with sweat, and pink as a rose. She had the high cheek-bones of her race, but she had also their exquisite fairness of color.

"Say, Otto," asked Rob, alluringly, "wan' to go swimmin'?"

"You bet," replied Otto.

"Well, I'll go a round if—"

The boy dropped off the horse, not waiting to hear any more. Rob grinned, but the girl dropped her eyes, then looked away.

"Got rid o' him mighty quick. Say, Julyie, I hate like thunder t' see you out here; it ain't right. I wish you'd—I wish—"

She could not look at him now, and her bosom rose and fell with a motion that was not due to fatigue. Her moist hair matted around her forehead gave her a boyish look.

Rob nervously tried again, tearing splinters from the fence. "Say, now, I'll tell yeh what I came back here for—t' git married; and if you're willin', I'll do it to-night. Come, now, whaddy y' say?"

"What 've I got t' do 'bout it?" she finally asked, the color flooding her face, and a faint smile coming to her lips. "Go ahead, I ain't got anything—"

Rob put a splinter in his mouth and faced her. "Oh, looky here, now, Julyie! You know what I mean! I've got a good claim out near Boomtown—a *rattlin'* good claim; a shanty on it fourteen by sixteen—no tarred paper about it, and a suller to keep butter in, and a hundred acres o' wheat just about ready to turn now. I need a wife."

Here he straightened up, threw away

the splinter, and took off his hat. He was a very pleasant figure as the girl stole a look at him. His black laughing eyes were especially earnest just now. His voice had a touch of pleading. The popple-tree over their heads murmured applause at his eloquence, then hushed to listen. A cloud dropped a silent shadow down upon them, and it sent a little thrill of fear through Rob, as if it were an omen of failure. As the girl remained silent, looking away, he began, man-fashion, to desire her more and more, as he feared to lose her. He put his hat on the post again and took out his jack-knife. Her calico dress draped her supple and powerful figure simply but naturally. The stoop in her shoulders, given by labor, disappeared as she partly leaned upon the fence. The curves of her muscular arms showed through her sleeves.

"It's all-fired lonesome f'r me out there on that claim, and it ain't no picnic f'r you here. Now, if you'll come out there with me, you needn't do anything but cook f'r me, and after harvest we can git a good layout o' furniture, an' I'll lath and plaster the house and put a little hell [ell] in the rear." He smiled, and so did she. He felt encouraged to say: "An' there we be, as snug as y' please. We're close t' Boomtown an' we can go down there to church sociables an' things, and they're a jolly lot there."

The girl was still silent, but the man's simple enthusiasm came to her charged with passion and a sort of romance, such as her hard life had known little of. There was something enticing about this trip to the West.

"What'll my folks say?" she said at last.

A virtual surrender, but Rob was not acute enough to see it. He pressed on eagerly:

"I don't care. Do you? They'll jest keep y' plowin' corn and milkin' cows till the day of judgment. Come, Julyie, I ain't got no time to fool away. I've got t' get back t' that grain. It's a whoopin' old crop, sure's y'r born, an' that means sompin' purty scrumptious in furniture this fall. Come, now." He approached her and laid his hand on her shoulder very much as he would have touched Albert Seagraves or any other comrade. "Whaddy y' say?"

She neither started nor shrunk nor looked at him. She simply moved a step away. "They'd never let me go," she replied bitterly. "I'm too cheap a hand. I do a man's work an' get no pay at all."

"You'll have half o' all I c'n make," he put in.

"How long c'n you wait?" she asked, looking down at her dress.

"Just two minutes," he said, pulling out his watch. "It ain't no use t' wait. The old man'll be jest as mad a week from now as he is to-day. Why not go now?"

"I'm of age in a few days," she mused, wavering, calculating.

"You c'n be of age to-night if you'll jest call on old Squire Hatfield with me."

"All right, Rob," the girl said, turning and holding out her hand.

"That's the talk!" he exclaimed, seizing it. "And now a kiss, to bind the bargain, as the fellah says."

"I guess we c'n get along without that."

"No, we can't. It won't seem like an engagement without it."

"It ain't goin' to seem much like one, anyway," she answered, with a sudden realization of how far from her dreams of courtship this reality was.

"Say, now, Julyie, that ain't fair; it ain't treatin' me right. You don't seem to understand that I *like* you, but I do."

Rob was carried quite out of himself by the time, the place, and the girl. He had said a very moving thing.

The tears sprang involuntarily to the girl's eyes. "Do you mean it? If y' do, you may."

She was trembling with emotion for the first time. The sincerity of the man's voice had gone deep.

He put his arm around her almost timidly, and kissed her on the cheek, a great love for her springing up in his heart. "That settles it," he said. "Don't cry, Julyie. You'll never be sorry for it. Don't cry. It kind o' hurts me to see it."

He hardly understood her feelings. He was only aware that she was crying, and tried in a bungling way to soothe her. But now that she had given way, she sat down in the grass and wept bitterly.

"*Yulyie!*" yelled the vigilant old Norwegian, like a distant foghorn.

The girl sprang up; the habit of obedience was strong.

"No; you set right there, and I'll go round," he said. "*Otto!*"

The boy came scrambling out of the wood, half dressed. Rob tossed him up on the horse, snatched Julia's sun-bonnet, put his own hat on her head, and moved off down the corn-rows, leaving the girl smiling through her tears as he whistled and chirped to the horse. Farmer Peterson, seeing the familiar sunbonnet above the corn-rows, went back to his work, with a sentence of Norwegian trailing after him like the tail of a kite—something about lazy girls who didn't earn the crust of their bread, etc.

Rob was wild with delight. "Git up there, Jack! Hay, you old corncrib! Say, Otto, can you keep your mouth shet if it puts money in your pocket?"

"Jest try me 'n' see," said the keen-eyed little scamp.

"Well, you keep quiet about my bein' here this afternoon, and I'll put a dollar on y'r tongue — hay? — what? — understand?"

"Show me y'r dollar," said the boy, turning about and showing his tongue.

"All right. Begin to practise now by not talkin' to me."

Rob went over the whole situation on his way back, and when he got in sight of the girl his plan was made. She stood waiting for him with a new look on her face. Her sullenness had given way to a peculiar eagerness and anxiety to believe in him. She was already living that free life in a far-off, wonderful country. No more would her stern father and sullen mother force her to tasks which she hated. She'd be a member of a new firm. She'd work, of course, but it would be because she wanted to, and not because she was forced to. The independence and the love promised grew more and more attractive. She laughed back with a softer light in her eyes, when she saw the smiling face of Rob looking at her from her sunbonnet.

"Now you mustn't do any more o' this," he said. "You go back to the house an' tell y'r mother you're too lame to plow any more to-day, and it's gettin' late, anyhow. To-night!" he whispered quickly. "Eleven! Here!"

The girl's heart leaped with fear. "I'm afraid."

"Not of me, are yeh?"

"No, I'm not afraid of you, Rob."

"I'm glad o' that. I—I want you—to *like* me, Julyie; won't you?"

"I'll try," she answered, with a smile.

"To-night, then," he said, as she moved away.

"To-night. Good-by."

"Good-by."

He stood and watched her till her tall figure was lost among the drooping corn-leaves. There was a singular choking feeling in his throat. The girl's voice and face had brought up so many memories of parties and picnics and excursions on far-off holidays, and at the same time held suggestions of the future. He already felt that it was going to be an unconscionably long time before eleven o'clock.

He saw her go to the house, and then he turned and walked slowly up the dusty road. Out of the May-weed the grasshoppers sprang, buzzing and snapping their dull red wings. Butterflies, yellow and white, fluttered around moist places in the ditch, and slender, striped water-snakes glided across the stagnant pools at sound of footsteps.

But the mind of the man was far away on his claim, building a new house, with a woman's advice and presence.

.   .   .   .   .   .

It was a windless night. The katydids and an occasional cricket were the only sounds Rob could hear as he stood beside his team and strained his ear to listen. At long intervals a little breeze ran through the corn like a swift serpent, bringing to his nostrils the sappy smell of the growing corn. The horses stamped uneasily as the mosquitoes settled on their shining limbs. The sky was full of stars, but there was no moon.

"What if she don't come?" he thought. "Or *can't* come? I can't stand that. I'll go to the old man an' say, 'Looky here—' Sh!"

He listened again. There was a rustling in the corn. It was not like the fitful movement of the wind; it was steady, slower, and approaching. It ceased. He whistled the wailing sweet cry of the prairie-chicken. Then a figure came out into the road—a woman—Julia!

He took her in his arms as she came panting up to him.

"Rob!"

"Julyie!"

.   .   .   .   .   .

A few words, the dull tread of swift horses, the rising of a silent train of dust, and then—the wind wandered in the growing corn, the dust fell, a dog barked down the road, and the katydids sang to the liquid contralto of the river in its shallows.

XXXII

AMBROSE BIERCE (1842–1914)

From the standpoint of age Ambrose Bierce belongs with the writers of the preceding period, with Harte and Aldrich and Howells and Cable. As a short-story writer, however, he did not attract attention until there appeared his collection, *Tales of Soldiers and Civilians,* 1891. Like Howells, he was Ohio-born of Eastern ancestry and like him, too, he was un-schooled though not uneducated. The Civil War took four years of his young manhood, years in which he encountered every experience and saw every horror that warfare can bring. He emerged disillusioned, cynical as to all things, old to senility when scarcely out of his adolescence. Drifting to California, he took up at length newspaper work as his profession and soon his pen was widely known and feared. His criticism was keen and sardonic and his satire was merciless. Later he lived in London, a companion of the wits and satirists of the Bohemian set led by Tom Hood the younger and Captain Reid. Here, too, his caustic criticism and cynical outpourings became notable. He was alluded to as "Bitter Bierce" and he gloried in his notoriety. Again he removed to California, now as columnist for the *Examiner,* in which his column "Prattle" was merciless and brilliant. He disappeared in Mexico early in the World War period and it is believed that he fell into the power of the bandit Villa and was executed. The best samples of his cynicism one may find now in his volume entitled *The Devil's Dictionary.* His complete works have been issued in twelve volumes.

His two short-story volumes came late. In the preface to the first of these he makes the statement that most of the stories had been written earlier than 1891 when the volume appeared, but that they were so true to the actualities of war that no magazine and no publisher dared to print them. They never would have appeared, he believed, had not a wealthy friend donated the money that allowed him to issue them privately. The stories are indeed gruesome, often with mere repulsive recitals of physical horror. They were manu-factured, as were Poe's, deliberately and with thorough knowledge of short-story technique, with no other thought than to bring sensation to the reader. With all their art, however, they fall far below the level of the highest short-story requirements. They are like artificial flowers, beautiful but lifeless; they are theatric and melodramatic; and they are not always true to the fundamentals of human life. Bierce may be summed up in a single phrase: "he wrought with intellect in the materials of horror."

AN OCCURRENCE AT OWL CREEK BRIDGE

I

A man stood upon a railroad bridge in Northern Alabama, looking down into the swift waters twenty feet below. The man's hands were behind his back, the wrists bound with a cord. A rope loosely encir- cled his neck. It was attached to a stout cross-timber above his head, and the slack fell to the level of his knees. Some loose boards laid upon the sleepers supporting the metals of the railway supplied a foot-ing for him and his executioners—two private soldiers of the Federal army, directed by a sergeant, who in civil life may have been a deputy sheriff. At a short remove upon the same temporary platform was an officer in the uniform of his rank, armed. He was a captain. A sentinel at each end of the bridge stood with his rifle in the position known as "support," that is to say, vertical in front of the left shoulder, the hammer resting on the forearm thrown straight across the chest—a formal and unnatural position enforcing an erect carriage of the body It did not appear to be the duty of these two men to know what was occurring at the center of the bridge; they merely blockaded the two ends of the foot-plank which traversed it.

Beyond one of the sentinels nobody was in sight; the railroad ran straight away to a forest for a hundred yards, then, rving, was lost to view. Doubtless there is an outpost further along. The other nk of the stream was open ground—a ntle acclivity crowned with a stockade vertical tree-trunks, loopholed for rifles, ith a single embrasure through which otuded the muzzle of a brass cannon mmanding the bridge. Midway up the ope between the bridge and fort were e spectators—a single company of intry in line, at "parade rest," the butts the rifles on the ground, the barrels clining slightly backward against the ght shoulder, the hands crossed upon the ock. A lieutenant stood at the right of e line, the point of his sword upon the ound, his left hand resting upon his ght. Excepting the group of four at the nter of the bridge not a man moved. The mpany faced the bridge, staring stonily, otionless. The sentinels, facing the banks the stream, might have been statues to lorn the bridge. The captain stood with lded arms, silent, observing the work his subordinates, but making no sign. eath is a dignitary who, when he comes nounced, is to be received with formal anifestations of respect, even by those ost familiar with him. In the code of ilitary etiquette silence and fixity are rms of deference.

The man who was engaged in being anged was apparently about thirty-five ars of age. He was a civilian, if one ight judge from his dress, which was at of a planter. His features were good —a straight nose, firm mouth, broad forehead, from which his long, dark hair was ombed straight back, falling behind his ars to the collar of his well-fitting frock oat. He wore a mustache and pointed eard, but no whiskers; his eyes were arge and dark gray, and had a kindly exression which one would hardly have exected of one whose neck was in the hemp. vidently this was no vulgar assassin. The beral military code makes provision for anging many kinds of people, and gentlemen are not excluded.

The preparations being complete, the wo private soldiers stepped aside, and ach drew away the plank upon which he ad been standing. The sergeant turned o the captain, saluted, and placed himself mmediately behind that officer, who in urn moved apart one pace. These movements left the condemned man and the

sergeant standing on the two ends of the same plank, which spanned three of the cross-ties of the bridge. The end upon which the civilian stood almost, but not 5 quite, reached a fourth. This plank had been held in place by the weight of the captain; it was now held by that of the sergeant. At a signal from the former the latter would step aside, the plank would 10 tilt, and the condemned man go down between two ties. The arrangement commended itself to his judgment as simple and effective. His face had not been covered nor his eyes bandaged. He looked a 15 moment at his "unsteadfast footing," then let his gaze wander to the swirling water of the stream racing madly beneath his feet. A piece of dancing driftwood caught his attention, and his eyes followed it 20 down the current. How slowly it appeared to move! What a sluggish stream!

He closed his eyes in order to fix his last thoughts upon his wife and children. The water, touched to gold by the early 25 sun, the brooding mists under the banks at some distance down the stream, the fort, the soldiers, the piece of drift—all had distracted him. And now he became conscious of a new disturbance. Striking 30 through the thought of his dear ones was a sound he could neither ignore nor understand, a sharp, distinct, metallic percussion like the stroke of a blacksmith's hammer upon the anvil; it had the same 35 ringing quality. He wondered what it was, and whether immeasurably distant or near by—it seemed both. Its recurrence was regular, but as slow as the tolling of a death-knell. He awaited each stroke with 40 impatience and—he knew not why—apprehension. The intervals of silence grew progressively longer; the delays maddening. With their greater infrequency the sounds increased in strength and sharp- 45 ness. They hurt his ear like the thrust of a knife; he feared he would shriek. What he heard was the ticking of his watch.

He unclosed his eyes and saw again the water below him. "If I could free my 50 hands," he thought, "I might throw off the noose and spring into the stream. By diving, I could evade the bullets, and, swimming vigorously, reach the bank, take to the woods, and get away home. My 55 home, thank God, is as yet outside their lines; my wife and little ones are still beyond the invaders' farthest advance."

As these thoughts, which have here to be

set down in words, were flashed into the doomed man's brain rather than evolved from it, the captain nodded to the sergeant. The sergeant stepped aside.

II

Peyton Farquhar was a well-to-do planter, of an old and highly respected Alabama family. Being a slave-owner, and, like other slave-owners, a politician, he was naturally an original secessionist and ardently devoted to the Southern cause. Circumstances of an imperious nature which it is unnecessary to relate here had prevented him from taking service with the gallant army which had fought the disastrous campaigns ending with the fall of Corinth, and he chafed under the inglorious restraint, longing for the release of his energies, the larger life of the soldier, the opportunity for distinction. That opportunity, he felt, would come, as it comes to all in war-time. Meanwhile, he did what he could. No service was too humble for him to perform in aid of the South, no adventure too perilous for him to undertake if consistent with the character of a civilian who was at heart a soldier, and who in good faith and without too much qualification assented to at least a part of the frankly villainous dictum that all is fair in love and war.

One evening while Farquhar and his wife were sitting on a rustic bench near the entrance to his grounds, a gray-clad soldier rode up to the gate and asked for a drink of water. Mrs. Farquhar was only too happy to serve him with her own white hands. While she was gone to fetch the water, her husband approached the dusty horseman and inquired eagerly for news from the front.

"The Yanks are repairing the railroads," said the man, "and are getting ready for another advance. They have reached the Owl Creek Bridge, put it in order, and built a stockade on the other bank. The commandant has issued an order, which is posted everywhere, declaring that any civilian caught interfering with the railroad, its bridges, tunnels, or trains, will be summarily hanged. I saw the order."

"How far is it to the Owl Creek Bridge?" Farquhar asked.

"About thirty miles."

"Is there no force on this side the creek?"

"Only a picket post half a mile out, on the railroad, and a single sentinel at this end of the bridge."

"Suppose a man—a civilian and student of hanging—should elude the picket post and perhaps get the better of the sentinel," said Farquhar, smiling, "what could he accomplish?"

The soldier reflected. "I was there a month ago," he replied. "I observed that the flood of last winter had lodged a great quantity of driftwood against the wooden pier at this end of the bridge. It is now dry, and would burn like tow."

The lady had now brought the water, which the soldier drank. He thanked her ceremoniously, bowed to her husband, and rode away. An hour later, after nightfall, he repassed the plantation, going northward in the direction from which he had come. He was a Federal scout.

III

As Peyton Farquhar fell straight downward through the bridge, he lost consciousness and was as one already dead. From this state he was awakened—ages later, it seemed to him—by the pain of a sharp pressure upon his throat, followed by a sense of suffocation. Keen, poignant agonies seemed to shoot from his neck downward through every fiber of his body and limbs. These pains seemed to flash along well-defined lines of ramification, and to beat with an inconceivably rapid periodicity. They seemed like streams of pulsating fire, heating him to an intolerable temperature. As to his head, he was conscious of nothing but a feeling of fulness —of congestion. These sensations were unaccompanied by thought. The intellectual part of his nature was already effaced; he had power only to feel, and feeling was torment. He was conscious of motion. Encompassed in a luminous cloud, of which he was now merely the fiery heart, without material substance, he swung through unthinkable arcs of oscillation, like a vast pendulum. Then all at once, with terrible suddenness, the light about him shot upward with the noise of a loud splash, a frightful roaring was in his ears, and all was cold and dark. The power of thought was restored; he knew that the rope had broken and he had fallen into the stream. There was no additional strangulation; the noose about his neck was already suffocating him, and kept the water from his lungs. To die hanging at the bottom of a river—the idea seemed to him ludicrous. He opened his eyes in the blackness and saw above him a gleam of light, but how distant, how inaccessible! He was still sinking, for the light became fainter and fainter until it was a mere glimmer. Then it began to grow and brighten, and he knew that he was rising toward the surface—knew it with reluctance, for he was now very comfortable. "To be hanged and drowned," he thought, "that is not so bad; but I do not wish to be shot. No; I will not be shot; that is not fair."

He was not conscious of an effort, but a sharp pain in his wrists apprized him that he was trying to free his hands. He gave the struggle his attention, as an idler might observe the feat of a juggler, without interest in the outcome. What splendid effort—what magnificent, what superhuman strength! Ah, that was a fine endeavor! Bravo! The cord fell away; his arms parted and floated upward, the hands dimly seen on each side in the growing light. He watched them with a new interest as first one and then the other pounced upon the noose at his neck. They tore it away and thrust it fiercely aside, its undulations resembling those of a water-snake. "Put it back! put it back!" He thought he shouted these words to his hands, for the undoing of the noose had been succeeded by the direst pang which he had yet experienced. His neck ached horribly; his brain was on fire; his heart, which had been fluttering faintly, gave a great leap, trying to force itself out of his mouth. His whole body was racked and wrenched with an insupportable anguish! But his disobedient hands gave no heed to the command. They beat the water vigorously with quick, downward strokes, forcing him to the surface. He felt his head emerge; his eyes were blinded by the sunlight; his chest expanded convulsively, and with a supreme and crowning agony his lungs engulfed a great draught of air, which instantly he expelled in a shriek!

He was now in full possession of his physical senses. They were, indeed, preternaturally keen and alert. Something in the awful disturbance of his organic system had so exalted and refined them that they made record of things never before perceived. He felt the ripples upon his face and heard their separate sounds as they struck. He looked at the forest on the bank of the stream, saw the individual trees, the leaves and the veining of each leaf—saw the very insects upon them, the locusts, the brilliant-bodied flies, the gray spiders stretching their webs from twig to twig. He noted the prismatic colors in all the dewdrops upon a million blades of grass. The humming of the gnats that danced above the eddies of the stream, the beating of the dragonflies' wings, the strokes of the waterspiders' legs, like oars which have lifted their boat—all these made audible music. A fish slid along beneath his eyes, and he heard the rush of its body parting the water.

He had come to the surface facing down the stream; in a moment the visible world seemed to wheel slowly round, himself the pivotal point, and he saw the bridge, the fort, the soldiers on the bridge, the captain, the sergeant, the two privates, his executioners. They were in silhouette against the blue sky. They shouted and gesticulated, pointing at him; the captain had drawn his pistol, but did not fire; the others were unarmed. Their movements were grotesque and horrible, their forms gigantic.

Suddenly he heard a sharp report, and something struck the water smartly within a few inches of his head, spattering his face with spray. He heard a second report, and saw one of the sentinels with his rifle at his shoulder, a light cloud of blue smoke rising from the muzzle. The man in the water saw the eye of the man on the bridge gazing into his own through the sights of the rifle. He observed that it was a gray eye, and remembered having read that gray eyes were keenest, and that all famous marksmen had them. Nevertheless, this one had missed.

A counter-swirl had caught Farquhar and turned him half round; he was again looking into the forest on the bank opposite the fort. The sound of a clear, high voice in a monotonous sing-song now rang out behind him and came across the water with a distinctness that pierced and subdued all other sounds, even the beating of the ripples in his ears. Although no soldier, he had frequented camps enough to know the dread significance of that deliberate, drawling, aspirated chant; the lieutenant on shore was taking a part in the morning's work. How coldly and pitilessly—with what an even, calm intonation, presaging and enforcing tranquillity in the men—with what accurately measured intervals fell those cruel words: "Attention, company. Shoulder arms. Ready. Aim. Fire!"

Farquhar dived—dived as deeply as he could. The water roared in his ears like the voice of Niagara, yet he heard the dulled thunder of the volley, and rising again toward the surface, met shining bits of metal, singularly flattened, oscillating slowly downward. Some of them touched him on the face and hands, then fell away, continuing their descent. One lodged between his collar and neck; it was uncomfortably warm, and he snatched it out.

As he rose to the surface, gasping for breath, he saw that he had been a long time under water; he was perceptibly farther down-stream—nearer to safety! The soldiers had almost finished reloading; the metal ramrods flashed all at once in the sunshine as they were drawn from the barrels, turned in the air, and thrust into their sockets. The two sentinels fired again, independently and ineffectually.

The hunted man saw all this over his shoulder; he was now swimming vigorously with the current. His brain was as energetic as his arms and legs; he thought with the rapidity of lightning.

"The officer," he reasoned, "will not make that martinet's error a second time. It is as easy to dodge a volley as a single shot. He has probably already given the command to fire at will. God help me, I cannot dodge them all!"

An appalling plash within two yards of him, followed by a loud rushing sound, diminuendo, which seemed to travel back through the air to the fort and died in an explosion which stirred the very river to its deeps. A rising sheet of water, which curved over him, fell down upon him, blinded him, strangled him. The cannon had taken a hand in the game. As he shook his head free from the commotion of the smitten water, he heard the deflected shot humming through the air ahead, and in an instant it was cracking and smashing the branches in the forest beyond.

"They will not do that again," he thought; "the next time they will use a charge of grape. I must keep my eye upon the gun; the smoke will apprize me—the report arrives too late; it lags behind the missile. It is a good gun."

Suddenly he felt himself whirled round and around—spinning like a top. The water, the banks, the forest, the now distant bridge, fort and men—all were commingled and blurred. Objects were represented by their colors only; circular horizontal streaks of color—that was all he saw. He had been caught in a vortex, and was being whirled on with a velocity of advance and gyration which made him giddy and sick. In a few moments he was flung upon the gravel at the foot of the left bank of the stream—the southern bank —and behind a projecting point which concealed him from his enemies. The sudden arrest of his motion, the abrasion of one of his hands on the gravel, restored him, and he wept with delight. He dug his fingers into the sand, threw it over himself in handfuls and audibly blessed it. It looked like gold, like diamonds, rubies, emeralds; he could think of nothing beautiful which it did not resemble. The trees upon the bank were giant garden plants; he noted a definite order in their arrangement, inhaled the fragrance of their blooms. A strange, roseate light shone through the spaces among their trunks and the wind made in their branches the music of Æolian harps. He had no wish to perfect his escape, was content to remain in that enchanting spot until retaken.

A whizz and rattle of grapeshot among the branches high above his head roused him from his dream. The baffled cannoneer had fired him a random farewell. He sprung to his feet, rushed up the sloping bank, and plunged into the forest.

All that day he traveled, laying his course by the rounding sun. The forest seemed interminable; nowhere did he discover a break in it, not even a woodman's road. He had not known that he lived in so wild a region. There was something uncanny in the revelation.

By nightfall he was fatigued, footsore, famishing. The thought of his wife and children urged him on. At last he found a road which led him in what he knew to be the right direction. It was as wide and straight as a city street, yet it seemed untraveled. No fields bordered it, no dwelling anywhere. Not so much as the barking of a dog suggested human habitation. The black bodies of the great trees formed a straight wall on both sides, terminating on e horizon in a point, like a diagram in lesson in perspective. Overhead, as he oked up through this rift in the wood, one great golden stars looking unfamil-r and grouped in strange constellations. e was sure they were arranged in some der which had a secret and malign sig-ficance. The wood on either side was full singular noises, among which—once, rice, and again—he distinctly heard whis-rs in an unknown tongue.

His neck was in pain, and, lifting his nd to it, he found it horribly swollen. e knew that it had a circle of black here the rope had bruised it. His eyes lt congested; he could no longer close em. His tongue was swollen with thirst; relieved its fever by thrusting it for-ard from between his teeth into the cool r. How softly the turf had carpeted the traveled avenue! He could no longer el the roadway beneath his feet!

Doubtless, despite his suffering, he fell leep while walking, for now he sees another scene—perhaps he has merely re-covered from a delirium. He stands at the gate of his own home. All is as he left it, and all bright and beautiful in the 5 morning sunshine. He must have traveled the entire night. As he pushes open the gate and passes up the wide white walk, he sees a flutter of female garments; his wife, looking fresh and cool and sweet, 10 steps down from the veranda to meet him. At the bottom of the steps she stands wait-ing, with a smile of ineffable joy, an at-titude of matchless grace and dignity. Ah, how beautiful she is! He springs forward 15 with extended arms. As he is about to clasp her, he feels a stunning blow upon the back of the neck; a blinding white light blazes all about him, with a sound like the shock of a cannon—then all is 20 darkness and silence!

Peyton Farquhar was dead; his body, with a broken neck, swung gently from side to side beneath the timbers of the Owl Creek Bridge.

XXXIII

RICHARD HARDING DAVIS (1864–1916)

Another element that came prominently into the short story during the eighteen nineties may be characterized with the term "journalistic." The demand of readers more and more seemed to be for work containing special correspondence features: stories that seemingly had been dissected out of actual life by a man on the spot. If the story concerned the theater it should be written by one who had lived behind the scenes and who knew all the secrets of that mysterious area; if it concerned the New York City idle rich or the slums or the South Sea islands or the lands where defaulters escape justice, the writer of the tale should himself have been a part of the materials in which he worked—that seemed to be the demand of the time. A new school arose—Stephen Crane, Jack London, Sydney Porter, Owen Wister, and others—as the result of this new demand for actuality.

The pioneer figure and perhaps the most important member of this reporter short-story group was Richard Harding Davis, from the day of his graduation from Lehigh University to the day of his death a newspaper man of Philadelphia and New York City. His cosmopolitan ramblings in both hemispheres, his reportings of many world-famous events like the coronation of the Czar and the Queen's Jubilee, we need not follow. When he died at the age of fifty-two he had been practically everywhere, he had seen everything and everybody, and he had written a five-foot shelf of books in half a dozen different fields. His short-story work came first of all and it is remarkably varied. Like the true journalist he was, he was sensitive always to the demands of the hour. He wrote adventure stories of New York City life and studies of the idle rich; he wrote "Zenda" romance; he painted veritistic pictures of many lands; and he found areas unique for fiction, like the no-man's land beyond extradition where live the American colony of escaped defaulters. His earlier volume, *Gallegher and Other Stories*, 1891, is held to be his best, but *Van Bibber and Others*, 1892, and *The Exiles and Other Stories*, 1894, fall not far behind. He was distinctively of the school of art for entertainment's sake. Seldom did he strike deep notes. With remarkable lightness he skimmed over the surface of things, but he avoided the deeper currents. He was a brilliant journalist and he satisfied his day.

A LEANDER OF THE EAST RIVER *

"Hefty" Burke was one of the best swimmers in the East River. There was no regular way open for him to prove this, as the gentlemen of the Harlem boat-clubs, under whose auspices the annual races were given, called him a professional, and would not swim against him. "They won't keep company with me on land," Hefty complained, bitterly, "and they can't keep company with me in the water; so I lost both ways." Young Burke held these gentlemen of the rowing clubs in great contempt, and their outriggers and low-necked and picturesque rowing clothes as well. They were fond of lying out of the current, with the oars pulled across at their backs for support, smoking and commenting audibly upon the other oarsmen who passed them by perspiring uncomfortably, 5 and conscious that they were being criticized. Hefty said that these amateur oarsmen and swimmers were only pretty boys, and that he could give them two hundred yards start in a mile of rough or smooth 10 water and pass them as easily as a tug passes a lighter.

He was quite right in this latter boast; but, as they would call him a professional and would not swim against him, there 15 was no way for him to prove it. His idea of a race and their idea of a race differed. They had a committee to select prizes and open a book for entries, and when the day of the races came they had a judges'

* Published by arrangement with Harper and Brothers, owners of the copyright.

boat with gay bunting all over it, and a badly frightened referee and a host of reporters, and police boats to keep order. But when Hefty swam, his two backers, who had challenged some other young man through a sporting paper, rowed in a boat behind him and yelled and swore directions, advice, warnings, and encouragement at him, and in their excitement drank all the whiskey that had been intended for him. And the other young man's backers, who had put up ten dollars on him, and a tugboat filled with other rough young men, kegs of beer, and three Italians with two fiddles and one harp, followed close in the wake of the swimmers. It was most exciting, and though Hefty never had any prizes to show for it, he always came in first, and so won a great deal of local reputation. He also gained renown as a life-saver; for if it had not been for him many a venturesome lad would have ended his young life in the waters of the East River.

For this he received ornate and very thin gold medals, with very little gold spread over a large extent of medal, from grateful parents and admiring friends. These were real medals, and given to him, and not paid for by himself as were "Rags" Raegan's, who always bought himself a medal whenever he assaulted a reputable citizen and the case was brought up before the Court of General Sessions. It was the habit of Mr. Raegan's friends to fall overboard for him whenever he was in difficulty of this sort, and allow themselves to be saved, and to present Raegan with the medal he had prepared; and this act of heroism would get into the papers, and Raegan's lawyers would make the most of it before the judges. Rags had been Hefty's foremost rival among the swimmers of the East Side, but since the retirement of the former into reputable and private life Hefty was the acknowledged champion of the river front.

Hefty was not at all a bad young man— that is, he did not expect his people to support him—and he worked occasionally, especially about election time, and what he made in bets and in backing himself to swim supplied him with small change. Then he fell in love with Miss Casey, and the trouble and happiness of his life came to him hand in hand together; and as this human feeling does away with class distinctions, I need not feel I must apologize for him any longer, but just tell his story.

He met her at the Hon. P. C. McGovern's Fourth Ward Association's excursion and picnic, at which he was one of the twenty-five vice-presidents. On this occasion Hefty had jumped overboard after one of the Rag Gang whom the members of the Half-Hose Social Club had, in a spirit of merriment, dropped over the side of the boat. This action and the subsequent rescue and ensuing intoxication of the half-drowned member of the Rag Gang had filled Miss Casey's heart with admiration, and she told Hefty he was a good one and ought to be proud of himself.

On the following Sunday he walked out Avenue A to Tompkins Square with Mary, and he also spent a great deal of time every day on her stoop when he was not working, for he was working now and making ten dollars a week as an assistant to an ice-driver. They had promised to give him fifteen dollars a week and a seat on the box if he proved steady. He had even dreamed of wedding Mary in the spring. But Casey was a particularly objectionable man for a father-in-law, and his objections to Hefty were equally strong. He honestly thought the young man no match for his daughter, and would only promise to allow him to "keep company" with Mary on condition of his living steadily.

So it became Hefty's duty to behave himself. He found this a little hard to do at first, but he confessed that it grew easier as he saw more of Miss Casey. He attributed his reform to her entirely. She had made the semi-political, semisocial organizations to which he belonged appear stupid, and especially so when he lost his money playing poker in the clubroom (for the club had only one room), when he might have put it away for her. He liked to talk with her about the neighbors in the tenement, and his chance of political advancement to the position of a watchman at the Custom-house Wharf, and hear her play "Mary and John" on the melodeon. He boasted that she could make it sound as well as it did on the barrel-organ.

He was very polite to her father and very much afraid of him, for he was a most particular old man from the North of Ireland, and objected to Hefty because he was a good Catholic and fond of street fights. He also asked pertinently how

Hefty expected to support a wife by swimming from one pier to another on the chance of winning ten dollars, and pointed out that even this precarious means of livelihood would be shut off when the winter came. He much preferred "Patsy" Moffat as a prospective son-in-law, because Moffat was one of the proprietors in a local express company with a capital stock of three wagons and two horses. Miss Casey herself, so it seemed to Hefty, was rather fond of Moffat; but he could not tell for whom she really cared, for she was very shy, and would as soon have thought of speaking a word of encouragement as of speaking with unkindness.

There was to be a ball at the Palace Garden on Wednesday night, and Hefty had promised to call for Mary at nine o'clock. She told him to be on time, and threatened to go with her old love, Patsy Moffat, if he were late.

On Monday night the foreman at the livery stable of the ice company appointed Hefty a driver, and, as his wages would now be fifteen dollars a week, he concluded to ask Mary to marry him on Wednesday night at the dance.

He was very much elated and very happy.

His fellow-workmen heard of his promotion and insisted on his standing treat, which he did several times, until the others became flippant in their remarks and careless in their conduct. In this innocent but somewhat noisy state they started home, and on the way were injudicious enough to say, "Ah there!" to a policeman as he issued from the side door of a saloon. The policeman naturally pounded the nearest of them on the head with his club, and as Hefty happened to be that one, and as he objected, he was arrested. He gave a false name, and the next morning pleaded guilty to the charge of "assaulting an officer and causing a crowd to collect."

His sentence was thirty days in default of three hundred dollars, and by two o'clock he was on the boat to the Island, and by three he had discarded the blue shirt and red suspenders of an iceman for the gray stiff cloth of a prisoner. He took the whole trouble terribly to heart. He knew that if Old Man Casey, as he called him, heard of it there would no winning his daughter with his consent, and he feared that the girl herself would have grave doubts concerning him. He was especially cast down when he thought of the dance on Wednesday night, and of how she would go off with Patsy Moffat. And what made it worse was the thought that if he did not return he would lose his position at the ice company's stable, and then marriage with Mary would be quite impossible. He grieved over this all day, and speculated as to what his family would think of him. His circle of friends was so well known to other mutual friends that he did not dare to ask any of them to bail him out, for this would have certainly come to Casey's ears.

He could do nothing but wait. And yet thirty was a significant number to his friends, and an absence of that duration would be hard to explain. On Wednesday morning, two days after his arrest, he was put to work with a gang of twenty men breaking stone on the roadway that leads from the insane quarters to the penitentiary. It was a warm, sunny day, and the city, lying just across the narrow channel, never looked more beautiful. It seemed near enough for him to reach out his hand and touch it. And the private yachts and big excursion-boats that passed, banging out popular airs and alive with bunting, made Hefty feel very bitter. He determined that when he got back he would go look up the policeman who had assaulted him and break his head with a brick in a stocking. This plan cheered him somewhat, until he thought again of Mary Casey at the dance that night with Patsy Moffat, and this excited him so that he determined madly to break away and escape. His first impulse was to drop his crowbar and jump into the river on the instant, but his cooler judgment decided him to wait.

At the northern end of the Island the grass runs high, and there are no houses of any sort upon it. It reaches out into a rocky point, where it touches the still terribly swift eddies of Hell Gate, and its sharp front divides the water and directs it towards Astoria on the east and the city on the west. Hefty determined to walk off from the gang of workmen until he could drop into this grass and to lie there until night. This would be easy, as there was only one man to watch them, for they were all there for only ten days or one month, and the idea that they should try to escape was hardly considered. So Hefty edged off farther from the gang, and then, while the guard was busy lighting his pipe, dropped into the long grass and lay there quietly, after having ridden himself of his shoes and jacket. At six o'clock a bell tolled and the guard marched away, with his gang shambling after him. Hefty guessed that they would not miss him until they came to count heads at supper-time; but even now it was already dark, and lights were showing on the opposite bank. He had selected the place he meant to swim for—a green bank below a row of new tenements, a place where a few bushes still stood, and where the boys of Harlem hid their clothes when they went in swimming.

At half-past seven it was quite dark, so dark, in fact, that the three lanterns which came tossing towards him told Hefty that his absence had been discovered. He rose quickly and stepped cautiously, instead of diving, into the river, for he was fearful of hidden rocks. The current was much stronger than he had imagined, and he hesitated for a moment, with the water pulling at his knees, but only for a moment; for the men were hunting for him in the grass.

He drew the gray cotton shirt from his shoulders, and threw it back of him with an exclamation of disgust, and of relief at being a free man again, and struck his broad, bare chest and the biceps of his arms with a little gasp of pleasure in their perfect strength, and then bent forward and slid into the river.

The current from the opening at Hell Gate caught him as though he had been a plank. It tossed him and twisted him and sucked him down. He bent his way for a second to the surface and gasped for breath and was drawn down again, striking savagely at the eddies which seemed to twist his muscles into useless, heavy masses of flesh and muscle. Then he dived down and down, seeking a possibly less rapid current at the muddy bottom of the river; but the current drew him up again until he reached the top, just in time, so it seemed to him, to breathe the pure air before his lungs split with the awful pressure. He was gloriously and fiercely excited by the unexpected strength of his opponent and the probably fatal outcome of his adventure. He stopped struggling that he might gain fresh strength, and let the current bear him along the bottom, clutching with his hands at the soft, thick mud, and rising only to gasp for breath and sink again. His eyes were smarting hotly, and his head and breast ached with pressure that seemed to come from the inside and threatened to burst its way out. His arms had grown like lead and had lost their strength, and his legs were swept and twisted away from his control and were numb and useless. He assured himself fiercely that he could not have been in the water for more than five minutes at the longest, and reminded himself that he had often before lived in it for hours, and that this power, which was so much greater than his own, could not outlast him. But there was no sign of abatement in the swift, cruel uncertainty of its movement, and it bore him on and down or up as it pleased. The lights on the shore became indistinct, and he finally confused the two shores, and gave up hope of reaching the New York side, except by accident, and hoped only to reach some solid land alive. He did not go over all of his past life, but the vision of Mary Casey did come to him, and how she would not know that he had been innocent. It was a little thing to distress himself about at such a time, but it hurt him keenly. And then the lights grew blurred, and he felt that he was making heavy mechanical strokes that barely kept his lips above the water-line. He felt the current slacken perceptibly, but he was too much exhausted to take advantage of it, and drifted forward with it, splashing feebly like a dog, and holding his head back with a desperate effort. A huge, black shadow, only a shade blacker than the water around him, loomed up suddenly on his right, and he saw a man's face appear in the light of a hatchway and disappear again.

"Help!" he cried, "help!" but his voice sounded far away and barely audible. He struck out desperately against the current, and turned on his back and tried to keep himself afloat where he was. "Help!" he called again, feebly, grudging the strength it took to call even that. "Help! Quick, for God's sake! help me!"

Something heavy, black, and wet struck him sharply in the face and fell with a splash on the water beside him. He clutched for it quickly, and clasped it with both hands and felt it grow taut, and then gave up thinking, and they pulled him on board.

When he came to himself, the captain of the canal-boat stooped and took a fold of the gray trousers between his thumb and finger. Then he raised his head and glanced across at the big black island, where lights were still moving about on the shore, and whistled softly. But Hefty looked at him so beseechingly that he arose and came back with a pair of old boots and a suit of blue jeans.

"Will you send these back to me to-morrow?" he asked.

"Sure," said Hefty.

"And what'll I do with these?" said the captain, holding up the gray trousers.

"Anything you want, except to wear 'em," said Mr. Burke, feebly, with a grin.

One hour later Miss Casey was standing up with Mr. Patsy Moffat for the grand march of the grand ball of the Jolly Fellows' Pleasure Club of the Fourteenth Ward, held at the Palace Garden. The band was just starting the "Boulanger March," and Mr. Moffat was saying wittily that it was warm enough to eat ice, 5 when Mr. Hefty Burke shouldered in between him and Miss Casey. He was dressed in his best suit of clothes, and his hair was conspicuously damp.

"Excuse me, Patsy," said Mr. Burke, as 10 he took Miss Casey's arm in his, "but this march is promised to me. I'm sorry I was late, and I'm sorry to disappoint you; but you're like the lad that drives the hansom cab, see?—you're not in it."

15 "But indeed," said Miss Casey, later, "you shouldn't have kept me a-waiting. It wasn't civil."

"I know," assented Hefty, gloomily, "but I came as soon as I could. I even went 20 widout me supper so's to get here; an' they wuz expectin' me to stay to supper, too."

XXXIV

MARGARET WADE DELAND (1857–   )

With most writers of fiction the short story comes first, an apprenticeship exercise before attempting the more elaborate art of the novel or the long romance. With Margaret Deland the novel came first. With her *John Ward, Preacher,* 1888, she won immediate and international recognition and until the present time her leading literary achievements have been in the longer forms of fiction. Not until 1898, when appeared her *Old Chester Tales,* was she accorded a place with the short-story writers. The volume was a distinctive one, and with two others which followed it—*Dr. Lavendar's People,* 1903, and *Around Old Chester,* 1915, —has won its way to what seems like a permanent place among the best products of American short-story art.

The "Old Chester" of the series is the birthplace of Mrs. Deland, the village of Manchester, now a part of greater Pittsburgh, Pennsylvania. She had been privately educated, had studied design and then had taught it in New York art schools, had written and published a volume of poems, and then had become the wife of Lorin F. Deland, professor in Harvard University. Her "Old Chester" series of tales are idealized pictures of the little Main Street village of her childhood. In all of them is the dominating figure of Dr. Lavendar, a charming character, romanticized somewhat, undoubtedly, yet vivid and intensely alive, a real addition to the small gallery of American fictional types. Beneath all her work runs a deep undercurrent of tragedy. She is not a preacher, but always she faces the moral issues of life, always the complexing tangles of the common lot. No writer of the decade added more of depth to the short story or more of serious thought. Never are her stories finished with the final paragraph: hers is the art provocative of thought, the art that allies the problem of her characters with the problems of the reader's own soul.

AT THE STUFFED-ANIMAL HOUSE *

I

Willy King's buggy, splashed to the top of the hood with mud and sagging sidewise on its worn old springs, came pulling up the hill past the burial-ground. The doctor himself, curled in one corner, rested a leg on the dash-board and hung his reins on the hook over his head. He was very sleepy, for he had been up until three with an old woman who thought she was sick, and he had been routed out of bed again at five because she told her family that she was going to die. William King was not given to sarcasm, but he longed to say to the waiting relatives, "There is no hope!—she'll live." Instead, he looked seriously sympathetic and kept his thoughts to himself. When he got home to breakfast, his wife told him how foolish he was to take so much trouble. "There's nothing

the matter with Mrs. Drayton," said Mrs. King; "and I should tell her so, flatly and frankly. It would do her good."

William said that he would like another cup of coffee.

"It wouldn't be good for you," said his Martha; "you are drinking too much coffee. You can have shells if you want to. Shall I have some shells warmed up?"

William said "No," and went trudging off to his office; and then, at ten, started on his round of calls, his old buggy still unwashed from the morning jaunt to the hypochondriac's death-bed. The day was still and sunny, the road quite deserted and full of pleasant shadows under the May foliage. But the sleepy doctor saw it all through half-closed eyes, and yawned, and rested one plump leg on the dash-board, and let the reins hang swaying from the hook in the roof of the buggy. Then, suddenly, his mare stopped and William opened his eyes.

"Caught you napping, Willy!" said a loud, hearty voice. And the doctor sat up and drew his leg in and laughed.

"Well, Miss Harriet, how do you know but what I was worrying over a case?"

"Much worrying you do, young man!" She sat down on a log on the road-bank and smiled at him. She was a big, vigorous woman with a fresh, brown face and a keen, kind eye. She had a gun in her hand, and a rabbit's white tail stuck out of the hunting-wallet slung over her shoulder. She had broken through the underbrush on the hill-side just as Willy's buggy jogged into the shadow of a sycamore that stretched its mottled arms over the deserted road.

"Willy," she went on, in her loud, cheerful voice, "do you doctor-men smile at one another when you meet, like the Augurs, because you fool us so easily with your big words? You call a scratched finger an 'abrasion of the epidermis'—and then you send a bill. And, bless me! what a serious air you put on at a minute's notice!—I saw you pull your leg in, Willy. Come, now; you were in my Sunday-school class —why don't you just admit to me that that piercing look over your eye-glasses is one of the tricks of the trade? I won't tell."

William King chuckled. "You just get a touch of lumbago, Miss Harriet, and you'll believe in my tricks."

"Lumbago!" said his reviler. "Not I; a day's shooting would cure it quicker than a barrel of your pills."

"Been shooting this morning?"

"No; I set a trap in Dawson's hollow." She pulled out the rabbit and held it up. "Not a bone broken. Handsome, isn't he? Poor little thing!"

William looked at the soft, furry creature, limp in the big brown hand, with critical appreciation. "Yes, beautiful. Miss Annie didn't find him, to let him out?"

The hunter's face changed to amused impatience. "Willy, she opened three traps last week. And she was so shrewd about it; you would never believe how clever she is. Of course it's no use to scold."

"Of course not. What excuse does she make?"

"Oh, just the same thing: 'Sister, it hurts me to think they can't get out.'"

"Poor thing!" said the doctor.

"I have tried to make her promise not to interfere with the traps. You know, if I could once get a promise out of her I would be all right; Annie never broke a promise in her life. But she is too shrewd to be led into it. She always says, 'I'm the oldest, and you mustn't order me round.' It would be funny if it weren't so provoking."

"Poor thing!" said the doctor again.

"She follows me and takes the bait out of the traps once in a while; but she prefers to let things go. And she is certainly wonderfully bright about it," Miss Harriet said. "Now, why can't she be sensible in other things?"

"Well, you know she has always been about twelve; it's the young head on old shoulders."

"I must tell you her last performance," Miss Harriet said. "You know that picture of Aunt Gordon that hung in the dining-room? Dreadful thing! I never saw the poor woman, but I believe she wasn't quite as ugly as that portrait, though Alex looks just like her, Dr. Lavendar says; and Alex is dreadfully ugly, with those pale eyes of his. Well, I happened to say—it was last Tuesday, at tea, and Matty Barkley was there: 'That picture of Aunt Gordon is awful! I can't bear it.' Of course I never thought of it again, until I came home the next day—and what do you suppose?"

Willy began to grin.

"Yes! she had got up on a chair, if you please, and cut it out of the frame and slashed it all to pieces."

"Well done!" said Willy King, slapping his thigh.

"No such thing. It was ugly, but it was a family portrait."

"What did she say?"

"Oh, she had her excuse. . . . Willy, I can't understand her mind; it is so unreasonably reasonable: 'Sister, you said you couldn't bear it, so what was the use of having it?' After all, that was sense, William."

"So it was," said the doctor, and unhooked his reins and nodded. "Well," he said——

But Miss Harriet laughed awkwardly. "Wait a minute, can't you? It won't kill anybody to do without a pill for five minutes."

"Well, no, I suppose it won't," William admitted; "but with a view to getting home in time for dinner——"

"Oh, let Martha wait. Willy, you are the meekest being—let her wait. Tell her you'll have your dinner when you're good and ready."

"Martha is only concerned on my own account," the loyal William protested.

"Well, I'm not going to keep you long," his old friend said, roughly; "I—I just want to ask you a question." Her face grew suddenly a dull red. "Not that I believe in your pills and potions—just please remember that. But I suppose you do know a little something."

"I could diagnose a scratched finger," said the doctor, meekly.

"Well—" she said, and looked at the lock of her rifle; "there's nothing in the world the matter with me, but——"

"You don't look like a confirmed invalid," the doctor assured her.

"No!—do I?" she said, eagerly. "I really am very well, William—very well. Dear me, when I get home after a round of my traps (when Annie hasn't teased me by letting things out) and eat a good dinner, and sit down with a taxidermy magazine, I—I wouldn't thank King George to be my uncle. Yes, I am *very* well."

Her emphasis had in it a certain agitation that caught the doctor's eye. "Your out-of-door life is calculated to keep you well," he said.

Miss Harriet got up and thrust the rabbit back into the pouch at her side. "Of course; and, anyhow, I'm not the sick kind. Imagine me shut up between four walls! I should be like Sterne's starling. Do you remember?—'I want to get out, I want to get out.' No, there's nothing the matter with me. Absolutely nothing."

She did look very well, the big, brown woman, towering up at the road-side, with her rifle in her hand and the good color in her cheeks and lips. Yet her eyes had a worn look, William thought. "Pain somewhere," said the doctor to himself.

"You know, I don't believe in your pills and truck," she insisted, frowning.

"Of course not," he assured her easily. "Come, now, Miss Harriet, what's wrong?"

"Nothing, I tell you," she said, sharply; and then, with impatient brevity, she spoke of some special discomfort which had annoyed her. "It began about six months ago."

"Probably you've taken cold," William King said, and then he asked a question or two. She answered with irritable flippancy:

"Now don't put on airs, Willy. There's no use trying to impress me; I know you.

Remember, you were in my Sunday-school class."

"Why didn't you make a better boy of me, then? You had your chance. Miss Harriet, would you mind coming into my office and just letting me look you over? Come, now, why shouldn't I get a job out of you for once? Here you tackle me on the road-side and get an opinion for nothing."

She chuckled, but retorted that she hated doctors and their offices. "I'm not that Drayton cat," she said, "always wanting a doctor to fuss over me. No, you can give me a pill right here—though I haven't a bit of faith in it."

"I wouldn't waste a good pill on you," the doctor defended himself. "You've got to come and see me."

But when she had promised to come, and William, slapping a rein down on the mare's flank, was jogging along under the sycamore branches, he did not fall into his pleasant drowse again. "She looks so well," he said to himself, "she must be all right——"

II

Miss Harriet's house, called by Old Chester children "The Stuffed-Animal House," was on the hill-road a stone's-throw beyond the burial-ground. It was of weather-worn brick, and its white lintels, carved in thin festoons of fruit and flowers, were nearly hidden by ivy that stretched dark figures over the marble, and, thickening with the years across the tops of the windows, made the rooms within dim with wavering leaf shadows. A brick path, damp and faintly green with moss, ran down to a green gate set in a ragged privet hedge that was always dusty and choked with dead twigs. The house itself was so shaded by horse-chestnuts that grass refused to grow in the door-yard. A porch shadowed the front door, which opened into a dark, square hall, full of dim figures that hung from the ceiling and stood in cases against the walls. A dusty crocodile stretched overhead, almost the width of the hall; a shark, with varnished belly splitting a little under one fin and showing a burst of cotton, lurked in a dim corner; over the parlor door a great snake, coiled about a branch, looked down with glittering yellow eyes; and along the walls were cases of very beautiful birds, their plumage dulled now, for it was forty years since Miss Harriet's father had made his collection. But all around the hall were glistening eyes that stared and stared, until sometimes an Old Chester child, clinging to a mother's protecting hand, felt sure they moved, and that in another moment the crocodile's jaws would snap together, or the eagle's wings would flap horribly in the darkness.

Yet there was an awful joy to Old Chester youth in being allowed to accompany a mother when she made a polite call on Miss Harriet. This hall, that was dark and still and full of the smell of dead fur and feathers and some acrid preservative, had all the fascination of horror. If we were very good we were allowed to walk from case to case with old Miss Annie, while our mothers sat in the parlor and talked to Miss Harriet. Miss Annie could not tell us much of the creatures in the cases, and for all she used to laugh and giggle just as we did, she never really knew how to play that the hall was a desert island and the wild beasts were lurking in the forest to fall upon us. "It isn't a forest, it's our front hall," Miss Annie would say; "and you must do what I tell you, because I'm the oldest, and I don't want to play desert island. But I'll show you my chickens," she would add, with eager politeness.

Sometimes, if Miss Annie were not in the room, we would hear Miss Harriet tell some story about her mischievousness, and our mothers would sigh and smile and say, "Poor dear!" Our mothers never said "poor dear!" about us when we did such things. If one of us Old Chester children had spoken out in church as Miss Harriet said Miss Annie did once, and told Dr. Lavendar that he was telling a story when he read in the morning lesson that the serpent talked to Eve—"because," said Miss Annie, "snakes can't talk"—if we had done such a dreadful thing, we should have been taken home and whipped and sent to bed without any supper, and probably have the whole of the third chapter of Genesis to learn by heart. *We* should not have been "poor things!" This was very confusing to Old Chester youth until we grew older and understood. Then, instead of being puzzled, we shrunk a little and stayed close to our mothers, listening to Miss Harriet's stories of Miss Annie with strange interest and repulsion, or staring furtively at the little old woman, who laughed often and had a way of running about like a girl, and of smoothing back her gray hair from her temples with a fluttering gesture, and of putting up her lip and crying when she was angry or frightened or when she saw anything being hurt. Miss Annie could never bear to see anything hurt; she would not let us kill spiders, and she made us walk in the grass instead of on the brick path, because the ants came up between the bricks, and she was afraid we would step on them.

"Annie is very kind-hearted," Miss Harriet used to tell our mothers. "She can't bear my traps."

Miss Harriet's traps were her passion; her interest in taxidermy had come to her from her father, and though she had not been able to add anything of real value to Mr. Hutchinson's collection, her work was thoroughly well done; and she even made a fair sum of money each year by sending her squirrels and doves to town for the Christmas trade.

But more important than the money was the wholesome out-of-door life her little business entailed, which had given her her vigorous body and sane mind. She needed both to live with this gray-haired woman, whose mind was eleven or twelve years old. It was not a bad mind for eleven or twelve, Willy King used to say. Old Miss Annie had a sort of crude common-sense; she could reason and determine as well as any other twelve-year-old child—indeed, with an added shrewdness of experience that sixty years of bodily age made inevitable. She knew, innocently, much of life that other children were guarded from knowing; she knew death, too, but with no horror—perhaps as we were meant to know it—something as natural as life itself, and most of all as a release from pain. For old Annie knew pain and feared it as only the body in which the soul is not awake can fear it. She wept at the sight of blood and moaned when she heard a squirrel squeak in the trap; she shivered with passionate expectation of relief when Miss Harriet's kindly chloroform brought peace to fluttering wings or beating claws. When some soft, furry creature, hurt in the trap, relaxed into happy sleep in the thick, sweet smell that came out of Miss Harriet's big bottle, Miss Annie would laugh for joy, the tears of misery still wet upon her wrinkled cheeks.

"Don't come into my shop," Miss Harriet used to say, laughing and impatient, when Miss Annie would follow her into the room in the barn where she did her work—"don't come in here, and then you won't see things that hurt your feelings."

But Annie, smoothing her hair back from her temples with a curious, girlish gesture, would only shake her head and sidle closer to her sister, the young, guileless eyes in the withered face full of protest and appeal. Her horror of pain lost Miss Harriet many a fine specimen; for, in her pity for the trapped creatures, Annie, noiselessly, like some Indian hunter, used to follow on her sister's footsteps through the woods, lifting the baits out of the traps, or if she found a snared creature unhurt, letting it go, and then creeping home, frightened at Miss Harriet's anger, which, if she discovered the old child's naughtiness, fell like a thunderbolt, and then cleared into patient amusement, as a black shower brightens into sunshine. The big, kind woman with a man's mind could not be angry at this poor creature; so she did her duty by her and tried not to think about her. She went her way, and set her traps, and prepared her few specimens, brushing Annie or any other annoyance aside with careless good-nature.

"Don't think about unpleasant things," she used to say, in her loud, cheerful voice. "The trouble with you doctors and ministers," she told Dr. Lavendar, "is that you make people think about their insides. It's stomachs with Willy and souls with you. Nobody ought to know that they have a stomach or a soul. I don't. A tree don't. And there isn't an oak in Old Chester that isn't pleasanter than Mrs. Drayton. Yet she's always fussing about her insides —spiritual and material."

"It's when you don't have 'em that you fuss," Dr. Lavendar said: "the trouble isn't too much soul, it's too little. And I guess it's the same with stomachs."

"Then you say Mrs. Drayton has no soul?" Miss Harriet said, pleasantly.

"I never said anything of the sort," said Dr. Lavendar.

As for Miss Harriet, she went on to Willy King's office, prepared, as usual, to make him as uncomfortable as she could. But she never put Willy out. Her flings at his profession tickled him immensely, and if now and then the good, honest William practised, as Miss Harriet said, a few of the tricks of his trade, he was not averse to sharing their humor with some one who could appreciate it.

"So you have that Drayton cat on your hands again?" Miss Harriet said, plumping herself down in William's own chair in front of his office table so that she could pick up and examine what she called his "riffraff." ("Do open your windows, William. I don't see how you can be so shut up. Po-o-o! how can people live so much in-doors?")

"Well," said William, doing as he was bid, "she enjoys my visits and I enjoy her checks. I don't complain."

"That's like the profession," said Miss Harriet; "you put your hands in our pockets whenever you get a chance. Well, you'll get nothing out of my pocket, William, for there's nothing in it."

"Miss Harriet," said William, chuckling —"you won't tell anybody, will you? But Mrs.—well, I won't name names; that's not professional——"

"Call her a 'Female,'" said Miss Harriet.

"Well, a Female sent for me on Tuesday, in a dreadful hurry; I must come, 'right off! quick!' I was just sitting down to breakfast, but of course I ran——"

"Martha must have been pleased?"

"I ran; and arrived, winded. There was —the Female, at her breakfast. 'Oh,' she said, 'doctor, the baby has slept right through from six last night, and he hasn't wakened up yet. I am afraid there is something the matter with his little brain.'"

"William, if you didn't say that there was something the matter with her little brain—"

"I didn't," William said, grimly, "because she hasn't any. Now, Miss Harriet, let's talk about yourself; it's pleasanter."

"Oh, there was not the slightest occasion to come to see you. But I said I would, and here I am. I suppose you'll send me a bill as long as my arm. Do you have a system of charges, Willy? So much for a look over your glasses? So much for that solemn cough? I suppose you grade all your tricks. Now work off the most expensive ones on me; I propose to get the worth of my money, young man."

"Thought you said you weren't going to pay any bills?" William reminded her; and then refused to be side-tracked any longer, but asked question after question, bringing her up once or twice with a sharp turn. "Don't joke now, please, Miss Harriet. Be as exact as you can. Is this condition thus, or so—?" And when he got through with his questions, he took up the joking rather heavily.

"You're so faithless about pills," he said, "that I'm not going to give you any."

"What! no pills?" said Miss Harriet.

William King laughed awkwardly. "Not a pill! I don't see any condition which warrants them; but—"

"What did I tell you? There's nothing the matter, and you just dragged me here to give your office a busy look."

"I didn't suppose you'd see through it," said Willy King. "But, Miss Harriet, I—I don't feel *quite* satisfied. I—do you know I've a great mind to get a man in Mercer to look you over? I want you to go up with me to-morrow and see him."

"Nonsense!"

"No, truly," he said; "I am not satisfied, Miss Harriet."

"But what do you mean?" she insisted, sharply. "There's nothing the matter with me. You said yourself I didn't need any medicine. Give me some opiate to stop this—this discomfort when it comes on, and I'll be all right."

"You can't bear opiates," he said, bluntly; "your heart won't stand them. Don't you remember the time you broke your ankle and I tried morphine—a baby dose—to give you some relief? You gave me a scare, I can tell you."

Miss Harriet was silent. Then: "I've known my heart wasn't right for two years. But—"

"Oh, your heart doesn't give me any concern—if you don't take liberties with it. Perhaps it isn't quite as good as it was thirty years ago, but—"

"Ah, I lost it to you then, Willy. You were a sweet little fellow when you came into my class. Do you remember once when—"

"Miss Harriet, you've got to go to Mercer with me to-morrow," William King interrupted, quietly. "I hope there's nothing much out of the way. I hope not. I—I believe not. But I'm not sure. We'll go up and see Greylord and find out. He'll give you some pills, maybe," he ended, and laughed and got up. "Now I'm off to the cat, Miss Harriet."

And Miss Harriet, to her astonishment, found herself dismissed before she had made the boy tell her what he was afraid of. "He *is* a boy," she said to herself. "Of course he wouldn't be apt to know what was the matter. I ought to have gone to see some Mercer man to begin with. I remember when Willy was born."

III

When they came out of the Mercer doctor's door William King's fresh face had gone white, but Miss Harriet walked smiling. At the foot of the steps the doctor paused and stood an instant leaning on the hand-rail, as though for support and to get his breath. Miss Harriet looked at him with concern. "Why, Willy!" she said.

"Miss Harriet," William said, hoarsely, "he may be mistaken. It's perfectly possible that he is mistaken."

"I guess not, Willy," she said, simply. "Come, now, don't be such a wet string." She struck him a friendly blow on the shoulder that made the doctor take a quick step forward to keep his balance; but it gave him the grip upon himself that for a single instant he had lost.

"And, anyhow," he said, "even if he is right, it may not develop. I've known a case where it was checked for two years; and then the patient died of small-pox."

"Pleasant alternative," said Miss Harriet; she was smiling, her face full of color, her shoulders back, her head up. "Come, Willy, let's have a spree. Here we are for a day, and Martha's at home. We'll have a good dinner, and we'll do something interesting. *Hurrah!*" said Harriet Hutchinson.

And the doctor could do no less than fall into step at that martial note and march at her side proudly. And by some spiritual contagion his courage met hers like the clash of swords. They went to get their good dinner, and Miss Harriet ate it with appetite. Afterwards she declared they would go to the circus. "It's in town; I saw the tents. I haven't been to a circus for forty years," she said; "but I know just how the pink lemonade tastes. You've got to treat, Willy."

"I'll throw in pea-nuts," said William King; and with that they left the restaurant and went sauntering along the hot, grimy street in the direction of the open lots beyond the blast-furnaces, where, under a deep June sky, dazzling even though it was smudged by coils of smoke, were stretched the circus tents, brave with flags and slapping and billowing in a joyous wind. William King held on to his hat and looked at the great, white clouds, domed and shining, piled all along the west. "We'll get a shower, I'm afraid, Miss Harriet."

"Well, take a pill, Willy, and then it won't hurt you," she told him, with a laugh that belonged to the sun and wind, to the flags whipping out on their halyards and the signs of the side-shows bellying from their guy-ropes, to the blare of music and the eager circus crowd—that crowd that never changes with changing generations. Still there is the old man gaping with excited eyes; still the lanky female in spectacles; the cross elder sister afraid of crushing her fresh skirts; the little boy absorbed in thought; the little girl who would like to ride on the Shetland pony when the clown offers any miss in the audience an opportunity. We know them all, and doubtless they know us, the patronizing, amused on-lookers, who suddenly become as eager and absorbed as any graybeard or child in the crowd. We know the red boxes, too, where men with hard faces and wearied eyes shout mechanically the same words of vociferous invitation to the side-shows. Children, pulled along by their elders, would stop, open-mouthed, before these men; but somehow they never see the wild man or the fat lady. Ah, the regret for the unseen side-shows!—the lady with the snakes; the skeleton man; the duel between the educated hyena and his trainer—that hyena of whom the man in the red box speaks with such convincing enthusiasm. *"I have been,"* cries the strident voice—*"I have been connected with circuses all my life—all my life, ladies and gentlemen!—and I give you my sacred word of honor that this is the most magnificent specimen of the terrible grave-robbing hyena that I have ever seen!"* Why did we never see that hyena? Why, why did we always hurry on to the main tent? It is the pang that even paradise must know, of the lost experience of earth —or perhaps of hell.

"We ought to see the fat lady," said Dr. King.

"I'm afraid we'll be late," Miss Harriet objected, eagerly.

So they pushed on with the impatient, good-natured crowd. The smell of tan-bark and matted pelts and stale pea-nut shells came in a gust as they jostled under the flap of the outer tent and found themselves inside the circle of gilded cages. "Shall we go right in and get our seats?" William said.

"What! and not look at the animals? Willy, you're crazy. I want to feed the elephants. Why, there are a lot of them, six or seven."

So they trudged around the ring, their feet sinking deep into the loose, trampled earth. Miss Harriet poked the monkeys clinging to the grating of their car, with her big umbrella, and examined the elephant's hide with professional interest. "Imagine curing that proboscis," she said. And then they stopped in front of a miserable, magnificent lion, turning, turning, turning in a cage hardly more than his own length. Miss Harriet drew in her breath. "It's being trapped that is so awful, Willy. The consciousness that *you can't get out.* It isn't the—the pain of it; it's being trapped."

William King, looking at the poor tawny creature of the desert and free winds and life that dealt death with passion, blinked suddenly behind his glasses. "But you trap things yourself," he protested, a moment afterwards.

"Oh, but I don't keep 'em trapped; I kill 'em," she defended herself. "I couldn't keep things shut up. I'd be as bad as Annie if I saw any living creature that wasn't free to get out-of-doors." And then she pushed on to the next cage, and the next; then suddenly feared that they would not get good seats if they wasted any more time among the animals. "For we won't have any reserved doings," she said. "I want to sit on those boards that I sat on forty years ago."

She was as excited as she might have been forty years ago; and pushed ahead into the big tent, dragging William by the hand, and climbing up tier after tier, to get a good view of the ring. When they sat down, she made haste to spread open the flimsy pink sheet of the programme with its pale type, and read to William, in a loud, ecstatic voice, just what was going to happen:

"*Display No. 1. Gigantic Pageantric Prelude—presenting Equitational Exercises, Hippodromatical Revivals, Pachydermical Aggregations—the only terpsichorean Pachyderms ever taught to tread the mazes of the Quadrille.*

"*Display No. 2. Claire St. Jeal and her*

company—the loveliest daughters of Italy, and world-famous bareback equestriennes—"

"You are sure you are not getting tired?" William King interrupted.

"Tired?" she repeated, scornfully. "William, as Matty Barkley would say, you are a perfect fool. Why should I be tired? I feel first rate—never better. I wouldn't thank King George to be my uncle! I've wanted to come to the circus for years. Willy, what will your wife say?"

"Nothing," said William, significantly.

At which Miss Harriet laughed until the tears stood in her eyes. "William, you have more sense than I gave you credit for. But I am not sure that, as your Sunday-school teacher, I ought not to tell you to confess. Hullo! look what's coming."

Flare of banners! Prancing horses! Roman soldiers in rumbling gold-and-crimson chariots! Elephants bearing, throned upon their backs, goddesses of liberty and queens of beauty! Miss Harriet was leaning forward, her lips parted with excitement. William King looked at her and drew in his breath.

"'Not more than six months'; God grant not!—I wish it might not be more than two."

"Willy, read what comes next," she said, shoving the programme at him; "I can't stop looking."

The canvas was darkening a little overhead, so that William had to put on his glasses and hold the printed sheet at arm's-length to decipher the blurred, smudged text sufficiently to say that "Mademoiselle Orinda, Queen of the Flying Trapeze, would give her marv—"

"William—what shall I do about Annie?" Miss Harriet said.

"You know we will all take care of Miss Annie," he said, tenderly; "and—"

"Oh, Willy, there's the red lemonade," she interrupted, standing up and beckoning with her crumpled programme. "Did you ever see so deadly a drink? You forgot the pea-nuts," she reminded him, reproachfully. And when William secured his hot, brown-paper bag, she ate the pea-nuts and watched the changing wonders of the ring with intent eyes. She laughed aloud at the clown's endeavors to ride a kicking donkey, and when the educated dogs carried one another about in a wheelbarrow she applauded generously. "They are wonderful!" she said.

William King looked at her keenly; it was all real. Miss Harriet was incapable of pretence.

The brilliant day, that had showed between lacings of the tent like strings of sapphires, had dimmed and dimmed; and by-and-by, unnoticed at first, there was the drip of rain. Here and there an umbrella was raised, and once or twice a bedraggled man or woman led out a reluctant child—"For I ain't a-goin' to have you catch your death of cold for no trained elephants," a mother said, decidedly, pulling a whining boy from beside Miss Harriet.

"Perhaps," ventured the doctor, "we really ought to go. I can't have you 'catch your death of cold,' Miss Harriet."

"I won't die of a cold, William," she said, her eyes narrowing.

And William swore at himself under his breath, but said, with clumsy jocularity: "Well, not if I can help it. But I don't know why you should be so sure; it might give you bronchitis for a year."

"I won't have bronchitis for a year," Miss Harriet said, gazing at the clowns.

And William King swore at himself again.

The rain increased to a downpour; little streams at first dripped, then poured, upon the thinning benches. The great centre pole was streaming wet; the clown stood in a puddle, and the red triangle on his chalk-white forehead melted into a pink smear.

"Really, Miss Harriet," William said, anxiously, "I'm afraid—"

"If you're afraid for yourself, I'll go," she said; "but we ought to wait for the grand concert. (Ah! there's the man with the red balloons. If you had a half-dozen children, Willy, as you ought to have, I'd buy him out.) Well, are you sugar or salt, to be so scared of a drop of rain?"

She did not look afraid of rain herself when she got up and pushed past the scattered spectators, her hair glistening with drops, her cheeks red, her eyes clear. "William," she said, when they got outside and were hurrying along to catch the stage for Old Chester—"William, that has done me good. I feel superbly. Do you know, I haven't had an instant's pain since I first spoke of the thing to you? That's three days entirely free. Why, such a thing hasn't happened in—in three months. Just think of that—entirely free. William, I'll cheat you doctor-men yet." She looked at him with glowing courage. "I feel so well," she said.

She held out her hand, there in the rain on the black cinder-path, and William King struck his into it with a sort of shout.

"Hurrah!" he said, as she had said when they had come out from hearing the sentence in the Mercer doctor's office.

The long ride home in the stage, in which they were the only passengers, was perhaps a descending scale. . . . At first they talked of the circus. "I liked the man and the bear best," William said.

"Oh, he wasn't as fine as that beautiful lady in pink petticoats who rode the fat, white horse. Did you ever see a horse with so broad a back, Willy? Why, I could have ridden him myself."

"He would need a broad back," William said; and Miss Harriet told him to hold his tongue and not be impudent. The rain was pattering on the roof and streaming down the windows, and in the dark, damp cavern of the stage they could not see each other's face very well; but the stretches of tense silence in the circus talk made William King's heart beat heavily, although he burst out gayly that the afternoon had brought back his youth. "Miss Harriet, when you were a child, didn't you always want to poke around under the seats when it was over and find things? William Rives once found five cents. But William would find five cents in the Desert of Sahara. I never had his luck, but I was confident that watches were dropped freely by the spectators."

"Of course," cried Miss Harriet. "Or diamond-rings. My fancy led me towards diamond-rings. But I suppose you never knew the envy of the ladies' clothes? Dear me—those petticoats!"

"The ring-master's boots were very bitter to me; but my greatest desire was—"

"Willy," Miss Harriet said, hoarsely, "I don't want anybody to know."

"Of course not," William King said. "Why should they? We may hold this thing at bay for—"

"We will hold it at bay," she said, with passion. "I will! I *will!* Do you hear me?"

Willy King murmured something inarticulately; his eyes suddenly smarted.

The ride to Old Chester seemed to him interminable; and when, after wandering snatches of talk about the circus, the stage at last drew up at the green gate in Miss Harriet's privet hedge, his nerves were tense and his face haggard with fatigue.

At home, at his belated supper-table, his good Martha was very severe with him. You oughtn't to allow yourself to get so tired; it's wrong. You could just as well as not have ordered your things by mail. I must say, William, flatly and frankly, that a doctor ought to have more sense. I hope there was nobody in the stage you knew to talk you to death?"

"Miss Harriet came down," William said, "but she hadn't much to say."

"I suppose she went to buy some of her horrid supplies?" Martha said. "I can't understand that woman—catching things in traps. How would she like to be caught in a trap? I asked her once—because I am always perfectly frank with people. 'How would you like to be caught in a trap, Miss Harriet?' I said. And she said, 'Oh, Annie would let me out.' You can never get a straight answer out of Harriet Hutchinson."

"My dear, I'll take another cup of tea. Stronger, please."

"My dear, strong tea isn't good for you," Martha said.

IV

When Miss Harriet woke the next morning the blue June day was flooding her room. At first she could not remember. . . . What was the something behind her consciousness? It came in an instant. *"Trapped,"* she said, aloud, and turned her head to see Miss Annie at her bedside.

"What is trapped, sister?" said Miss Annie, her little old face crumpling with distress.

"I am," Harriet said; and laughed at the absurdity of telling Annie in such a fashion. But of course there was no use in telling Annie. She couldn't understand, and all that there was for her to know, the ultimate fact, she would find out soon enough. The younger sister felt a sick distaste of dealing with this poor mind; she wanted to be kind to Annie; she had always wanted to be kind to her—but she didn't want her round, that was all. And so she sent her off, patiently and not ungently: "Don't bother me, Annie, that's a good girl. No—I don't want any roses; take them away. No—I don't want to look at pictures. You go away now, that's a good girl."

And the wrinkled child obeyed meekly. But she told the deaf Augustine that Harriet was cross. "I'm the oldest, and she oughtn't to order me round," she whimpered.

Poor Miss Annie was constantly being told to be a good girl and go away, in the days that followed—days, to Miss Harriet, of that amazement and self-concentration which belong to such an experience as hers. There had been no leading up to this knowledge that had come to her—no gradual preparation of apprehension or suspicion. The full speed of living had come, *crash!* against the fact of dying. The recoil, the pause, the terrible astonishment of that moment when Life, surging ahead with all his banners flying, flings himself in an instant against the immovable face of Death—leaves the soul dazed by the shock—dazed, and unbelieving. "*It cannot be.*" That is the first clear thought. It is impossible; there is a mistake somewhere. A day ago, an hour ago, Death was lying hidden far, far off in the years. Sometime, of course, he would arrive—solemn, inevitable, but beneficent, or at least serene. He would send soft warnings before him —faint tollings of fatigue, vague mists of sunset shadows. The soul will be ready for him when he comes then; will even welcome him, for after a while Life grows a little tired and is ready to grasp that cool hand and rest. We all know how to meet Death then, with dignity and patience. But to meet him to-morrow—to-day, even, when we are full of our own business, of our own urgent affairs—the mere interruption of it is maddening. Across the solemnity of the thought comes with grotesque incongruity an irritated consciousness of the *inconvenience* of dying.

As for Harriet Hutchinson—"I don't believe it," she said to herself, that first morning. And then, breathlessly, "Why, I can't—die!"

She was not afraid, as one counts fear, but she was absorbed; for there is a dreadful and curiously impersonal interest in the situation that takes possession of the mind in moments like this. No wonder she could not think about Annie. She could not think about anything except that that man in Mercer had said that in a very short time—

"Why, but it's perfectly ridiculous!" she told herself; "it *can't* be. I'm not sick—"

As she lay there in her bed that morning, after she had sent Miss Annie away, she lifted her hand—a large hand, with strong, square fingers, brown with weather and rough with her work, and looked at it curiously. It was a little thin —she had not noticed that before; but there it was, eager, vital, quick to grip and hold, life in every line. And it would be—still? No; she did not believe it. And, besides, it couldn't be, it mustn't be. She had a hundred things to do. She must do them; she couldn't suddenly—*stop.* Life surged up in a great wave of passionate determination. She got up, eager to go on living, and to deny, deny, deny! It was the old human experience which is repeated and repeated until Life can learn the fulfilment of Death. Poor Life, beaten by the whips of pain, it takes so long sometimes to learn its lesson!

In those weeks that followed—weeks of refusal, and then struggle, and then acceptance, and last of all adjustment—Miss Harriet found old Annie's companionship almost intolerable. She was very unreasonable with her, very harsh even; but all she asked was solitude, and solitude Annie would not give. She ran at her sister's heels like a dog; sat looking at her with frightened eyes in the bad hours that came with relentlessly increasing frequency; came whimpering to her bedside on those exhausted mornings when Harriet would scourge her poor body onto its feet and announce that she was going out. "These four walls smother me," she used to say; "I must get out-of-doors."

Sometimes it seemed as if the big, kind nature that had borne the pin-pricks so patiently all these years had reached the breaking-point, and another day or another hour of poor old Annie's foolish love would cause it to burst out in frantic anger:

"It hurts, sister?"

"Yes, Annie; but never mind. If I could only get out-of-doors I wouldn't mind."

"Oh, sister, don't let it hurt."

"Can't help it, Annie. Now, don't think about it, that's a good girl. Maybe I can get out to-morrow a little while."

"But I can't bear it."

"Got to, my dear. Come, now, run away. Go and see your chickens."

"Sister, I can't bear it."

"Annie, you drive me wild. Augustine— oh, she can't hear. *Augustine!* you must take Miss Annie away. Annie, if you say another word—"

"I'm the oldest and I have a right to talk. Why don't you smell your big bottle? When the squirrels smell it they are not hurt."

"Well, I'm not a squirrel. Annie, if you stay another minute, I'll—I'll— Oh, for Heaven's sake, let me alone!"

She could stand it, she told herself, if she was alone. For though she finally accepted the fact, her own weakness she could not accept. "I am ashamed," she told William King, angrily.

"But there's nothing to be ashamed of," Willy King protested, in his kind way. "Dear Miss Harriet—"

"Hold your tongue. Nothing to be ashamed of? I guess if your body had put your soul in a corner, with its face to the wall—I guess you'd be ashamed. Yesterday I—I— Well, never mind. But my body got me down, I tell you—got my soul down. Isn't that something to be ashamed of? Don't be an ass, William. I'm ashamed."

It was this consciousness of her own weakness that made her hold herself aloof from her friends.

In those days people did not have trained nurses; they nursed one another. It was not skilful nursing: it frequently was not wise, as we count wisdom to-day; but it was very tender and loving, and it was very bracing. In these softer times, when we run so easily to relief from pain, we do not feel the presence of the professional nurse a check upon our weakness; if we suffer, we are willing that this skilful, noiseless machine, who will know exactly how to relieve us, shall see the suffering. We are neither mortified nor humiliated by our lack of endurance or of courage. But in Old Chester, when we were ill, and some friend or relative came to sit by our bedside, we had—for their sakes— to make an effort to control ourselves. If the effort failed, our souls blushed. Miss Harriet would not run the risk of failure; her body, as she said, got the better of her soul when she was alone; it should not have the chance to humiliate her publicly; so, roughly, she refused the friendly assistance so eagerly offered: "Thank you; Augustine can look after me. I don't want anybody. And besides, I'm perfectly comfortable. (William, I won't have anybody. Do you understand? It's bad enough to

disgrace myself in my own eyes; I won't have Matty Barkley sit and look on.)"

And William King put people off as well as he could: "I go in two or three times a day, just to say how do you do; and Miss Annie is about and can bring her anything she needs. And Augustine is very faithful. Of course, she is deaf as a post, but she seems to know what Miss Harriet wants."

So the situation was accepted. "Here I am," she told the doctor, grimly, "dying like a rat in a hole. If I could only get out-of-doors!—or if I had anything to do! —I think it's the having nothing to do that is the worst. But I'll tell you one thing, Willy—I won't be pitied. Don't have people mourning over me, or pretending that I'm going to get well. They know better, and so do I."

Those who dared to pity her or who ventured some futile friendly lie about recovery were met by the fiercest impatience. "How do I feel? Very well, thank you. And if I didn't, I hope I wouldn't say so. I hope I'm well enough bred not to ask or answer questions about feelings. There is nothing in the world so vulgar," she said, and braced herself to one or another imprudence that grieved and worried all the kind hearts that stood by, eager to show their love.

"It breaks my heart to see her, and there's nothing anybody can do for her," Mrs. Barkley told Dr. Lavendar, snuffling and wiping her eyes. "She positively turned Rachel King out of the house; and Maria Welwood cried her eyes out yesterday because she was so sharp with her when Maria said she was sorry she had had a bad night and hoped she'd soon feel better."

The old man nodded silently. "Poor Miss Harriet!" he said.

"Don't say 'poor Miss Harriet!' to her. Dr. Lavendar, Harriet and I have been friends since we were put in short dresses —and she spoke to me to-day in a way—! Well, of course, I shall go back; but I was ready to say I wouldn't. And she treats poor old Annie outrageously."

Dr. Lavendar nodded again. He himself had seen her several times, but she had never let him be personal: "Was Mrs. Drayton still gossiping about her soul?" "Wasn't it nearly time to get a new carpet for the chancel?" etc., etc. It was her way of defending herself—and Dr. Lavendar understood. So he only brought her his kindly gossip or his church news, and he never looked at her mournfully; but neither did he ever once refer to a possible recovery—that poor, friendly pretence that so tries the soul absorbed in its own solemn knowledge!

But in the afternoon, after his talk with Mrs. Barkley, the old man went plodding up the hill to the Stuffed-Animal House, with tender and relentless purpose in his face. It was a serene September day, full of pulsing light and fragrant with the late mowing. William King's mare was hitched to a post by the green gate in the hedge, and the doctor was giving her a handful of grass as Dr. Lavendar came up. "How is Miss Harriet, Willy?" the old man said.

William climbed into the buggy and flicked with his whip at the ironweed by the road-side. "Oh—about the same. Dr. Lavendar, it's cruel—it's cruel!"

"What's cruel, William?"

"I can't give her any opiate—to amount to anything."

"Why?"

"Her heart."

"But you can't let her suffer!"

"If I stopped the suffering," the doctor said, laconically, "it would be murder."

"You mean—"

"Depressants, to amount to anything, would kill her."

Dr. Lavendar looked up into the sky silently. Willy King gathered up the reins. "And Annie?" Dr. Lavendar said.

"She is just a poor, frantic child. I can't make her understand why Miss Harriet shouldn't have two powders, when one 'sugar,' as she calls it, gives her a little comfort for a little while. She says, 'Harriet wouldn't let a squirrel stay hurt.' Miss Harriet says she told her the other day that she wasn't a squirrel; but it didn't seem to make any difference to Miss Annie. She has a queer elemental reasonableness about her, hasn't she? Well, I must go. Dr. Lavendar, I—I hope you won't mind if I say that perhaps—I mean she doesn't want anybody to refer to—to anything religious."

"William," said the old man, mildly, "if you can mention anything which is not religious to a woman who is going to die within a very few weeks, I will consider it."

And William King had the grace to blush and stammer something about Miss Harriet's hating anything personal. Dr.

Lavendar listened silently; then he went on up the path to the Stuffed-Animal House. Old Miss Annie let him into the darkened hall, a burst of western sunshine flooding in behind him and making the grim, dead creatures dart out of their shadows for a moment, and sink back into them again when the door was shut. The old child had been crying, for Miss Harriet had turned her out of her room, and so he had to sit there in the hall, under the shark, and try to comfort her and bid her go out and see her chickens. But for once Miss Annie would not be diverted:

"Harriet wants to go out-of-doors, and she can't. And she is hurt; and Willy King won't give her sugar in a paper to stop the hurting. He is wicked."

"By-and-by," said Dr. Lavendar, "Harriet will fall asleep and not be hurt any more."

"Not till she is dead," Miss Annie said; "Augustine told me so."

"I meant that," Dr. Lavendar said, stroking the poor, gray head groveling against his knee.

"Then why didn't you say so? It is a story to say sleep when you mean dead."

"I ought to have said dead," he acknowledged, gently, "so that you could understand. But I want you to remember that death is a happy sleep. Will you remember that?"

"A happy sleep," Miss Annie repeated; "yes; I will remember. A happy sleep." She lifted her head from his knee and smiled. "I'll go and see my chickens," she said.

And Dr. Lavendar took his way upstairs, past the cases of birds, to Miss Harriet's room. She received him with elaborate cheerfulness.

As for Dr. Lavendar, he lost no time in pretence. "Miss Harriet," he said, "I am not going to stay and talk and tire you. You've seen people enough to-day—"

"I'm not tired in the least."

"But I have a word to say to you."

She looked at him angrily. I would rather not talk about myself, Dr. Lavendar, please."

"I don't want to talk about yourself," he said.

Her face cleared a little. "That's a relief. I was afraid you were going to talk to me about 'preparing,' and so forth."

A sudden smile twinkled into Dr. Lavendar's old eyes. "My dear Miss Harriet, ou've been 'preparing' for fifty years—or it fifty-one? I've lost count, Harriet. o; you haven't got anything to do about ing; dying is not your business. In fact, sometimes think it never is our business. ur business is living. Dying is God's fair."

"I haven't any business, that's the worst it," Miss Harriet said, bitterly. "I've thing to do—nothing to do but just lie re and wait. I don't mind dying; but be here in this trap, waiting. And I've ways been so busy, I don't know how do nothing."

"That's what I wanted to say to you. here is something you can do. In fact, ere's something you must do."

"Something I must do?" Miss Harriet id, puzzled.

"My dear friend, you must meet this fliction; you can't escape; we can't save ou from it. But there is one thing you n do; you can try to spare the pain of to other people. Set yourself, Miss Har- et, to make it as easy as you can for ose who stand by."

Harriet Hutchinson looked at him in nazement. No pity? No condolences? othing but the high charge to spare hers. "You mean my temper?" she said last, slowly.

"Yes," said Dr. Lavendar. Miss Harriet blushed hotly. "It is bad; know it's bad. But—"

"Mine would be worse," said Dr. Laven- ir, thoughtfully. "But look out for it, arriet. It's getting ahead of you."

Miss Harriet nodded. "You're right."

"You see, when you are out of temper shows you are suffering; and that's ird for us to bear—not the temper, of urse, but the knowledge. So you've got spare us, Harriet. Understand?"

"I understand."

"It will be hard work for you," he said, eerfully; and somehow the words meant, t pity, but "Shoulder arms!"

For an instant they gazed, eye to eye— e woman devoured by pain, the old man ith his calm demand; and then the soul her rose with a shout. What! there was mething left for her to do? She need t merely sit still and die? She need not ait idly for the end? It was a splendid mmons to the mind—a challenge to the dy that had dogged and humiliated the ul, that had wrung from her good- mored courage irritability and unjust

anger, that had dragged her pride in the dust of shame, yes, even—even (alone, and in the dark), but even of tears.

"*Make it as easy as possible for those that stand by.*"

Some might say that that austere com- mand was the lash of the whip; but to Miss Harriet it was the rod and the staff. The Spartan old man had suddenly re- vealed to her that as long as the body does not compel the soul, there is no shame. As long as she could hold her tongue, she said to herself, she need not be ashamed. Let the body whimper as it may, if the soul is silent it is master. Miss Harriet saw before her, not humiliation and idle- ness and waiting, but fierce struggle. . . . And it was a struggle. It was no easy thing to be amiable when good Maria Welwood wept over her; or when Martha King told her, flatly and frankly, that she was doing very wrong not to make more effort to eat; or even when Mrs. Dale hoped that she had made her peace with Heaven.

"Heaven had better try to make its peace with me, considering," said Miss Harriet, grimly; but when she saw how she had shocked Mrs. Dale, she made haste to apologize. "I didn't mean it, of course. But I am nervous, and say things to let off steam." Such an admission meant much from Miss Harriet, and it certainly soothed Mrs. Dale.

But most of all, Harriet Hutchinson for- bade her body to dictate to her soul when Miss Annie hung whimpering about her with frantic persistence of pity. Never in all their years together had Miss Harriet shown such tenderness to Annie as now, when the poor old child's mere presence was maddening to her. For Annie could think of nothing but the pain which could not be hidden, and her incessant entreaty was that it should be stopped. "Wouldn't you rather be dead, sister?"

"Yes, Annie."

"Well, then, be dead."

"I can't, Annie. Now let us talk of something else. Tell me what the black hen did when the speckled hen stole her nest."

Annie joyously told her story, as she had told it dozens of times before; while Har- riet Hutchinson turned her face to the wall. Annie sat on her heels on the floor beside the bed, rocking back and forth, and talking: "And so the speckled hen flew off. Sister, I'll get you your big bottle?"

No answer.

"Sister, don't you want to smell the bottle?"

"No, Annie. No—no—no! Oh, Annie, don't you want to go and see your chickens?"

"Why not?"

"Because it wouldn't be right, Annie."

"Why wouldn't it be right, sister?"

"Because," said Harriet Hutchinson—because I suppose that's one of the things that would 'make it harder for those that stand by.'"

"I don't understand," poor old Annie said, timidly.

"Well, Annie, that's the only reason I know of. Oh, Annie, Annie! it is the only reason there is; it is the root of its being wrong." . . . And then the long moan. When Miss Annie heard that sound she shivered all over; it was the elemental protest of the flesh, which cannot understand the regal and unconquered soul.

Those were hard days for Willy King, what with his affection and his sympathy and his daily struggles with Miss Annie; "for she is frantic," he told Dr. Lavendar. They were walking up the hill together in the late afternoon. Miss Harriet had sent for the old man, on whom now she leaned even more than on William King, for Dr. Lavendar gave her granite words instead of Willy's tenderer sympathy. "She insists that I shall give Miss Harriet something— 'stuff out of Harriet's bottle,' she says. I suppose she means chloroform. I wish to God I could."

"God will do His own work, William."

"Yes, sir; but it's such a waste—this courage that fairly breaks our hearts."

"Waste! William, what are you talking about? We are every one of us richer for it. I told her so yesterday."

"Well," said William King, thoughtfully, "perhaps so; in this case we are richer, I admit. But suppose it were a baby that was suffering—or a dog? Only, we wouldn't let the dog suffer. Dr. Lavendar, one of these days—you and I won't live to see it, but one of these days—"

"There is Miss Annie now," said Dr. Lavendar. "Why—look at her!"

The old woman came fluttering down the path towards the green gate in the privet hedge; she was smoothing her hair back from her temples, with her strange, girlish gesture, and she was smiling, but there was a new and solemn age in her face that made the two men look at each other, startled and wondering.

"Dr. Lavendar! Willy!" she said, her voice breaking with joy, "Harriet is dead —oh, Harriet is dead!"

They stopped short in the pathway. "What—what?" stammered William King.

"Oh, Harriet is dead!" the old woman said; "and I'm so happy." She came and leaned on the closed gate at the foot of the path, smiling up into their faces. "She isn't hurt any more. Oh, I can breathe—I can breathe, now," said Miss Annie, laying her withered hands upon her throat and drawing a deep breath.

"When?" said the doctor.

"Oh, just a little while ago. As soon as she got dead I opened the windows and let the air blow in; she likes the wind when she isn't hurt."

William King said, suddenly, "My God!" and turned and ran up the path, into the house, into the room, where, indeed, there was no more hurting.

"Annie," Dr. Lavendar said, "were you with her?"

"Yes," Miss Annie said. "Harriet was hurt very much. But when she smelled her bottle she stopped being hurt."

Dr. Lavendar leaned against the gate, his breath wavering; then he sat down on the grass, and rested his forehead on his hands clasped on the top of his stick. He was unable to speak. Miss Annie came out into the road and looked at him curiously. After a while he said, feebly, "Annie, tell me about it."

"Willy wouldn't give Harriet sugar a paper to stop the hurting. And Harriet said she couldn't get her bottle. She said it would be wrong for her to get it."

Dr. Lavendar lifted his head with a quick gesture of relief. "What! Harriet didn't get it herself?"

"Oh no," Miss Annie said. "I got it. And I went into Harriet's room. Harriet's eyes were shut, and she was—was moaning," said Miss Annie, shivering. "So I put some stuff out of the bottle on a towel and held it for Harriet to smell. And Harriet opened her eyes and looked frightened, and she said, 'No, no!' And I said, 'Yes; I'm the oldest and you must do what I say.' And she said, 'Augustine! Augustine!' But Augustine can't hear. And I held it down and I said, 'You won't be hurt any more.' And Harriet pushed it away and said 'No.' And then she shut her

es. And after a while she didn't say
ything more. And I held it, oh, a long
ne. And then I looked, and Harriet's
es were shut. And now she's dead! And
doesn't hurt any more. You come and
ok at her, and you'll see it doesn't hurt
y more. *Now* she wouldn't thank King
eorge to be her uncle! Oh, she's dead,"
id Miss Annie, nodding her head and
ughing; "a happy sleep." She was stand-
g there in the dusty road in front of
m, telling the story, her hands behind her,
cking slightly backward and forward,
e a child repeating a lesson. The long
ternoon shadows stretched from the trees
ross the road, and, swaying lightly,
cked her gray head with sunshine.

"Annie," said Dr. Lavendar, "come here
d sit beside me."

She came, happily enough, and let him
ke her hand and hold it, patting it softly
r a moment before he spoke.

"Annie, it was not right to give Harriet
e stuff out of the bottle; our Heavenly
ather stops the hurting when He thinks
st. So it does not please Him for us to
it when we think best."

"But Willy gave Harriet one sugar in a
per, and that stopped it a little," Miss
nnie said, puzzled; "and if he stopped it
little, why shouldn't it all be stopped?"
he obvious logic of the poor mind ad-
itted of no answer—certainly no argu-
ent.

Dr. Lavendar said, gravely, stroking the
nd, as wrinkled as his own: "It was not
ght, my child. You will believe me when
say so? And I do not want any one to
ow that you did a thing that was not
ght. So I want you to promise me now
at you will not tell any one that you did
Will you promise me?"

"Willy knows it, I guess," Miss Annie
id.

Dr. Lavendar was silent. Just what had
William heard her say? Only that Miss
Harriet was "dead." "I am pretty sure that
Willy doesn't *know* it," he said, slowly.
"And I am quite sure he would prefer not
to know it; so you mustn't tell him. But
you can't understand about that, Annie.
You'll just have to believe me. Will you
promise me?"

"Why, yes," Miss Annie said, indifferently, smiling up at the moving leaves. "Oh,
Harriet isn't hurt now!"

Dr. Lavendar trembled with anxiety. "I
want a solemn promise, Annie. What do
the children do when they make a solemn
promise?"

Miss Annie was instantly interested.
"Why, they cross their breast and say
'*honest and true*'; don't you know?" . . .

"Well, then," said Dr. Lavendar, slowly,
"you will make a promise to me in that
way." He stood up and took her hand, his
face very pale. "Promise me that never,
so long as you live, will you tell any
one—any one, Annie—that you made
Harriet fall asleep by giving her the big
bottle to smell. Now, make the promise,
Annie."

Miss Annie slowly crossed her breast.
"I promise," she said, in a low voice; her
eyes, widening with awe, were fixed on his
face. "I promise:

"Honest and true,
Black and black and blue,
Lay me down
And cut me in two—

if I do."

"*Amen!*" said Dr. Lavendar; and took
off his hat, and stood looking up into the
sky, his lip trembling. "Father," he said,
"I don't even say 'forgive her!' She is Thy
little child." And then they stood for a
moment hand in hand in the sunny silence.

XXXV

MARY HARTWELL CATHERWOOD (1847–1902)

Mrs. Catherwood, a native of Ohio and the first woman writer of any prominence t gain a degree from an American college, first attracted the attention of readers with he colorful and headlong serial in the *Century Magazine,* entitled "The Romance of Dollar 1888. She had chosen as her field for fiction the same area that Parkman had covere in his histories, the old French régime of Canada and the North-west, and she had saturate herself with his histories until her fiction had all of his picturesqueness, his vivid descriptio his swift-moving narrative, his romantic subject matter. Primarily was she a romancer, ar for the most part her work is in the longer forms where she could have freedom and swee and unlimited canvass. Often, however, she threw her French and Indian adventure in the short-story form. Four collections in all she published, the most noteworthy being he *The Chase of Saint Castin, and Other Stories of the French in the New World,* 1894, ar *Mackinac and Lake Stories,* 1899.

Mrs. Catherwood had the historian's type of imagination; seemingly she worked wit the sources before her, using actual characters found in Parkman, and actual historic backgrounds and happenings. Whether true or not, her stories and her characters carr conviction: they are compellingly alive. Often, as in "The Windigo," she dramatizes a pla and makes it in reality a character in the tragedy. Her art, however, is not her strong poir She is often careless in her construction, admitting much that should have been blue-per ciled out: her strength is her vividness and her mastery of action.

THE WINDIGO *

The cry of those rapids in Sainte Marie's River called the Sault could be heard at all hours through the settlement on the rising shore and into the forest beyond. Three quarters of a mile of frothing billows, like some colossal instrument, never ceased playing music down an in-lined channel until the trance of winter locked it up. At August dusk, when all that shaggy world was sinking to darkness, the gushing monotone became very distinct.

Louizon Cadotte and his father's young seignior, Jacques de Repentigny, stepped from a birch canoe on the bank near the fort, two Chippewa Indians following with their game. Hunting furnished no small addition to the food-supply of the settlement, for the English conquest had brought about scarcity at this as well as other Western posts. Peace was declared in Europe; but soldiers on the frontier, waiting orders to march out at any time, were not abundantly supplied with stores,

* Reprinted by permission of James S. Catherwood, Poughkeepsie, N. Y., owner of the copyright.

and they let season after season go b reluctant to put in harvests which migl be reaped by their successors.

Jacques was barely nineteen, and Lou 5 zon was considerably older. But the Repe tignys had gone back to France after tl fall of Quebec; and five years of Europea life had matured the young seignior a decades of border experience would neve 10 mature his half-breed tenant. Yet Louizc was a fine dark-skinned fellow, well mac for one of short stature. He trod close l his tall superior with visible fondness; e joying this spectacle of a man the like c 15 whom he had not seen on the frontier.

Jacques looked back, as he walked, at tl long zigzag shadows on the river. Fore fire in the distance showed a leaning co umn, black at base, pearl-colored in tl 20 primrose air, like smoke from some g gantic altar. He had seen islands in tl lake under which the sky seemed to sli throwing them above the horizon i mirage, and trees standing like detache 25 bushes on a world rim of water. Tl Sainte Marie River was a beautiful lig green in color, and sunset and twiligl played upon it all the miracles of chang

"I wish my father had never left this country," said young Repentigny, feeling that spell cast by the wilderness. "Here is this place. He should have withdrawn to the Sault, and accommodated himself to the English, instead of returning to France. The service in other parts of the world does not suit him. Plenty of good men have held to Canada and their honor also."

"Yes, yes," assented Louizon. "The English cannot be got rid of. For my part, shall be glad when this post changes hands. I am sick of our officers."

He scowled with open resentment. The seigniory house faced the parade ground, and they could see against its large low mass, lounging on the gallery, one each side of a window, the white uniforms of two French soldiers. The window sashes, screened by small curtains across the middle, were swung into the room; and Louizon's wife leaned on her elbows across the sill, the rosy atmosphere of his own fire projecting to view every ring of her bewitching hair, and even her long eyelashes as she turned her gaze from side to side.

It was so dark, and the object of their regard was so bright, that these buzzing bees of Frenchmen did not see her husband until he ran up the steps facing them. Both of them greeted him heartily. He felt it a peculiar indignity that his wife's danglers forever passed their good-will on to him; and he left them in the common hall, with his father and the young seignior, and the two or three Indians who congregated there every evening to ask for presents or to smoke.

Louizon's wife met him in the middle of the broad low apartment where he had been so proud to introduce her as a bride, and turned her cheek to be kissed. She was not fond of having her lips touched. Her hazel-colored hair was perfumed. She was so supple and exquisite, so dimpled and aggravating, that the Chippewa in him longed to take her by the scalp-lock of her light head; but the Frenchman bestowed the salute. Louizon had married the prettiest woman in the settlement. Life overflowed in her, so that her presence spread animation. Both men and women paid homage to her. Her very mother-in-law was her slave. And this was the stranger spectacle because Madame Cadotte, the senior, though born a Chippewa, did not easily make herself subservient to anybody.

The time had been when Louizon was proud of any notice this siren conferred on him. But so exacting and tyrannical is the nature of man that when he got her he wanted to keep her entirely to himself. From his Chippewa mother, who, though treated with deference, had never dared to disobey his father, he inherited a fond and jealous nature; and his beautiful wife chafed it. Young Repentigny saw that she was like a Parisian. But Louizon felt that she was a spirit too fine and tantalizing for him to grasp, and she had him in her power.

He hung his powder-horn behind the door, and stepped upon a stool to put his gun on its rack above the fireplace. The fire showed his round figure, short but well muscled, and the boyish petulance of his shaven lip. The sun shone hot upon the Sault of an August noon, but morning and night were cool, and a blaze was usually kept in the chimney.

"You found plenty of game?" said his wife; and it was one of this woman's wickedest charms that she could be so interested in her companion of the moment.

"Yes," he answered, scowling more, and thinking of the brace on the gallery whom he had not shot, but wished to.

She laughed at him.

"Archange Cadotte," said Louizon, turning around on the stool before he descended; and she spread out her skirts, taking two dancing steps to indicate that she heard him. "How long am I to be mortified by your conduct to Monsieur de Repentigny?"

"Oh—Monsieur de Repentigny. It is now that boy from France, at whom I have never looked."

"The man I would have you look at, madame, you scarcely notice."

"Why should I notice him? He pays little attention to me."

"Ah, he is not one of your danglers, madame. He would not look at another man's wife. He has had trouble himself."

"So will you have if you scorch the backs of your legs," observed Archange.

Louizon stood obstinately on the stool and ignored the heat. He was in the act of stepping down, but he checked it as she spoke.

"Monsieur de Repentigny came back to this country to marry a young English lady of Quebec. He thinks of her, not of you."

"I am sure he is welcome," murmured

Archange. "But it seems the young English lady prefers to stay in Quebec."

"She never looked at any other man, madame. She is dead."

"No wonder. I should be dead, too, if I looked at one stupid man all my life."

Louizon's eyes sparkled. "Madame, I will have you know that the seignior of Sault Sainte Marie is entitled to your homage."

"Monsieur, I will have you know that I do not pay homage to any man."

"You, Archange Cadotte? You are in love with a new man every day."

"Not in the least, monsieur. I only desire to have a new man in love with me every day."

Her mischievous mouth was a scarlet button in her face, and Louison leaped to the floor, and kicked the stool across the room.

"The devil himself is no match at all for you!"

"But I married him before I knew that," returned Archange; and Louizon grinned in his wrath.

"I don't like such women."

"Oh, yes, you do. Men always like women whom they cannot chain."

"I never tried to chain you." Her husband approached, shaking his finger at her. "There is not another woman in the settlement who has her way as you have. And see how you treat me!"

"How do I treat you?" inquired Archange, sitting down and resigning herself to statistics.

"Saint Marie! Saint Joseph!" shouted the Frenchman. "How does she treat me! And every man in the seigniory dangling at her apron string!"

"You are mistaken. There is the young seignior; and there is the new English commandant, who must be now within the seigniory, for they expect him at the post to-morrow morning. It is all the same: if I look at a man you are furious, and if I refuse to look at him you are more furious still."

Louizon felt that inward breaking up which proved to him that he could not stand before the tongue of this woman. Groping for expression, he declared:

"If thou wert sickly or blind, I would be just as good to thee as when thou wert a bride. I am not the kind that changes if a woman loses her fine looks."

"No doubt you would like to see me with the smallpox," suggested Archange. "But it is never best to try a man too far."

"You try me too far—let me tell you that. But you shall try me no further."

The Indian appeared distinctly on his softer French features, as one picture may be stamped over another.

"Smoke a pipe, Louizon," urged the thorn in his flesh. "You are always so much more agreeable when your mouth is stopped."

But he left the room without looking at her again. Archange remarked to herself that he would be better-natured when his mother had given him his supper; and she yawned, smiling at the maladroit creature whom she made her sport. Her husband was the best young man in the settlement. She was entirely satisfied with him, and grateful to him for taking the orphan niece of a poor post commandant, without prospects and conquest, and giving her sumptuous quarters and comparative wealth; but she could not forbear amusing herself with his masculine weaknesses.

Archange was by no means a slave in the frontier household. She did not spin or draw water, or tend the oven. Her mother-in-law, Madame Cadotte, had a hold on perennially destitute Chippewa women who could be made to work for longer or shorter periods in a Frenchman's kitchen or loom-house instead of with savage implements. Archange's bed had ruffled curtains, and her pretty dresses, carefully folded, filled a large chest.

She returned to the high window-sill and watched the purple distances growing black. She could smell the tobacco the men were smoking in the open hall, and hear their voices. Archange knew what her mother-in-law was giving the young seignior and Louizon for their supper. She could fancy the officers laying down their pipes to draw to the board, also, for the Cadottes kept open house all the year round.

The thump of the Indian drum was added to the deep melody of the rapids. There were always a few lodges of Chippewas about the Sault. When the trapping season and the maple-sugar-making were over and his profits drunk up, time was the largest possession of an Indian. He spent it around the door of his French brother ready to fish or to drink whenever invited. If no one cared to go on the river, he turned to his hereditary amusements

ery night that the rapids were void of
ches showing where the canoes of white
hers darted, the thump of the Indian
um and the yell of Indian dancers could
heard.

Archange's mind was running on the
w English garrison who were said to be
near taking possession of the picketed
rt, when she saw something red on the
rade ground. The figure stood erect and
tionless, gathering all the remaining
ht on its indistinct coloring, and Ar-
ange's heart gave a leap at the hint of
military man in a red uniform. She was
alive, like a whitefisher casting the net
a hunter sighting game. It was Ar-
ange's nature, without even taking
ught, to turn her head on her round
ck so that the illuminated curls would
ow against a background of wall, and
eathe her half-bare arms across the sill.
be looked at, to lure and tantalize, was
re than pastime. It was a woman's chief
vilege. Archange held the secret convic-
n that the priest himself could be made
give her lighter penances by an angelic
pression she could assume. It is conven-
t to have large brown eyes and the trick
casting them sidewise in sweet distress.
But the Chippewa widow came in earlier
n usual that evening, being anxious to
back to the lodges to watch the dancing.
change pushed the sashes shut, ready
r other diversions, and Michel Penson-
au never failed to furnish her that. The
tle boy was at the widow's heels. Michel
s an orphan.

"If Archange had children," Madame
dotte had said to Louizon, "she would
t seek other amusement. Take the little
nsonneau lad that his grandmother can
rdly feed. He will give Archange some-
ing to do."

So Louizon brought home the little Pen-
nneau lad. Archange looked at him, and
nsidered that here was another person
wait on her. As to keeping him clean
d making clothes for him, they might
well have expected her to train the
dge dogs. She made him serve her, but
r mothering he had to go to Madame
dotte. Yet Archange far outweighed
adame Cadotte with him. The labors put
on him by the autocrat of the house were
eeter than mococks full of maple sugar
om the hand of the Chippewa house-
eper. At first Archange would not let
m come into her room. She dictated to

him through door or window. But when
he grew fat with good food and was decently clad under Madame Cadotte's hand,
the great promotion of entering that sacred
5 apartment was allowed him. Michel came
in whenever he could. It was his nightly
habit to follow the Chippewa widow there
after supper, and watch her brush Archange's hair.

10 Michel stood at the end of the hearth
with a roll of pagessanung, or plum-
leather, in his fist. His cheeks had a hard
garnered redness like polished apples. The
Chippewa widow set her husband carefully
15 against the wall. The husband was a bundle about two feet long, containing her
best clothes tied up in her dead warrior's
sashes and rolled in a piece of cloth. His
arm-bands and his necklace of bear's claws
20 appeared at the top as a grotesque head.
This bundle the widow was obliged to
carry with her everywhere. To be seen
without it was a disgrace, until that time
when her husband's nearest relations
25 should take it away from her and give her
new clothes, thus signifying that she had
mourned long enough to satisfy them. As
the husband's relations were unable to
cover themselves, the prospect of her re-
30 lease seemed distant. For her food she
was glad to depend on her labor in the
Cadotte household. There was no hunter
to supply her lodge now.

The widow let down Archange's hair
35 and began to brush it. The long mass was
too much for its owner to handle. It spread
around her like a garment, as she sat on
her chair, and its ends touched the floor.
Michel thought there was nothing more
40 wonderful in the world than this glory of
hair, its rings and ripples shining in the
firelight. The widow's jaws worked in unobtrusive rumination on a piece of pleasantly bitter fungus, the Indian substitute
45 for quinine, which the Chippewas called
waubudone. As she consoled herself much
with this medicine, and her many-syllabled
name was hard to pronounce, Archange
called her Waubudone, an offense against
50 her dignity which the widow might not
have endured from anybody else, though
she bore it without a word from this soft-
haired magnate.

As she carefully carded the mass of hair
55 lock by lock, thinking it an unnecessary
nightly labor, the restless head under her
hands was turned towards the portable
husband. Archange had not much imagina-

tion, but to her the thing was uncanny. She repeated what she said every night:

"Do stand him in the hall and let him smell the smoke, Waubudone."

"No," refused the widow.

"But I don't want him in my bedroom. You are not obliged to keep that thing in your sight all the time."

"Yes," said the widow.

A dialect of mingled French and Chippewa was what they spoke, and Michel knew enough of both tongues to follow the talk.

"Are they never going to take him from you? If they don't take him from you soon, I shall go to the lodges and speak to his people about it myself."

The Chippewa widow usually passed over this threat in silence; but, threading a lock with the comb, she now said:

"Best not go to the lodges awhile."

"Why?" inquired Archange. "Have the English already arrived? Is the tribe dissatisfied?"

"Don't know that."

"Then why should I not go to the lodges?"

"Windigo at the Sault now."

Archange wheeled to look at her face. The widow was unmoved. She was little older than Archange, but her features showed a stoical harshness in the firelight. Michel, who often went to the lodges, widened his mouth and forgot to fill it with plum-leather. There was no sweet which Michel loved as he did this confection of wild plums and maple sugar boiled down and spread on sheets of birch bark. Madame Cadotte made the best pagessanung at the Sault.

"Look at the boy," laughed Archange. "He will not want to go to the lodges any more after dark."

The widow remarked, noting Michel's fat legs and arms:

"Windigo like to eat him."

"I would kill a windigo," declared Michel, in full revolt.

"Not so easy to kill a windigo. Bad spirits help windigos. If man kill windigo and not tear him to pieces, he come to life again."

Archange herself shuddered at such a tenacious creature. She was less superstitious than the Chippewa woman, but the Northwest had its human terrors as dark as the shadow of witchcraft.

Though a Chippewa was bound to dip his hand in the war kettle and taste th flesh of enemies after victory, there wa nothing he considered more horrible tha a confirmed cannibal. He believed that person who had eaten human flesh to sa isfy hunger was never afterwards cor tented with any other kind, and, bein deranged and possessed by the spirit of beast, he had to be killed for the safet of the community. The cannibal usuall became what he was by stress of starva tion: in the winter when hunting faile and he was far from help, or on a journe when provisions gave out, and his onl choice was to eat a companion or di But this did not excuse him. As soon as I was detected, the name of "windigo" wa given him, and if he did not betake himse again to solitude he was shot or knocke in the head at the first convenient oppo tunity. Archange remembered one suc wretched creature who had haunted th settlement awhile, and then disappeare His canoe was known, and when it hovere even distantly on the river every child ra to its mother. The priest was less succes ful with this kind of outcast than with an other barbarian on the frontier.

"Have you seen him, Waubudone?" i quire Archange. "I wonder if it is th same man who used to frighten us?"

"This windigo a woman. Porcupine her. She lie down and roll up and hic her head when you drive her off."

"Did you drive her off?"

"No. She only come past my lodge the night."

"Did you see her?"

"No, I smelt her."

Archange had heard of the atmosphe which windigos far gone in cannibalis carried around them. She desired to kno nothing more about the poor creature, the class to which the poor creature b longed, if such isolated beings may b classed. The Chippewa widow talked wit out being questioned, however, preparin to reduce Archange's mass of hair to th compass of a nightcap.

"My grandmother told me there was man dreamed he had to eat seven person He sat by the fire and shivered. If h squaw wanted meat, he quarreled with he 'Squaw, take care. Thou wilt drive me far that I shall turn windigo.'"

People who did not give Archange th keen interest of fascinating them wer a great weariness to her. Humble

retched human life filled her with dis-
ust. She could dance all night at the
eekly dances, laughing in her sleeve at
rls from whom she took the best part-
ers. But she never helped nurse a sick
ild, and it made her sleepy to hear of
indigos and misery. Michel wanted to
quat by the chimney and listen until
ouizon came in; but she drove him out
rly. Louizon was kind to the orphan,
ho had been in some respects a failure,
d occasionally let him sleep on blankets
skins by the hearth instead of groping
the dark attic. And if Michel ever
anted to escape the attic, it was to-night,
hen a windigo was abroad. But Louizon
d not come.

It must have been midnight when Ar-
ange sat up in bed, startled out of sleep
her mother-in-law, who held a candle
tween the curtains. Madame Cadotte's
atures were of a mild Chippewa type,
t the restless aboriginal eye made Ar-
ange uncomfortable with its anxiety.

"Louizon is still away," said his mother.
"Perhaps he went whitefishing after he
d his supper." The young wife yawned
d rubbed her eyes, beginning to notice
at her husband might be doing some-
ing unusual.

"He did not come to his supper."

"Yes, mama. He came in with Monsieur
Repentigny."

"I did not see him. The seignior ate
one."

Archange stared, fully awake. "Where
es the seignior say he is?"

"The seignior does not know. They
rted at the door."

"Oh, he has gone to the lodges to watch
e dancing."

"I have been there. No one has seen him
nce he set out to hunt this morning."

"Where are Louizon's canoemen?"

"Jean Boucher and his son are at the
ncing. They say he came into this
ouse."

Archange could not adjust her mind to
xiety without the suspicion that her
other-in-law might be acting as the in-
rument of Louizon's resentment. The
ge feather bed was a tangible comfort
terposed betwixt herself and calamity.

"He was sulky to-night," she declared.
"He has gone up to sleep in Michel's attic
frighten me."

"I have been there. I have searched the
ouse."

"But are you sure it was Michel in the
bed?"

"There was no one. Michel is here."

Archange snatched the curtain aside,
and leaned out to see the orphan sprawled
on a bearskin in front of the collapsing logs.
He had pushed the sashes inward from the
gallery and hoisted himself over the high
sill after the bed drapery was closed for
the night, for the window yet stood open.
Madame Cadotte sheltered the candle she
carried, but the wind blew it out. There was
a rich glow from the fireplace upon Michel's
stuffed legs and arms, his cheeks, and the
full parted lips through which his breath
audibly flowed. The other end of the
room, lacking the candle, was in shadow.
The thump of the Indian drum could still
be heard, and distinctly and more distinctly, as if they were approaching the
house, the rapids.

Both women heard more. They had not
noticed any voice at the window when they
were speaking themselves, but some offensive thing scented the wind, and they
heard, hoarsely spoken in Chippewa from
the gallery:

"How fat he is!"

Archange, with a gasp, threw herself
upon her mother-in-law for safety, and
Madame Cadotte put both arms and the
smoking candle around her. A feeble yet
dexterous scramble on the sill resulted
in something dropping into the room. It
moved toward the hearth glow, a gaunt
vertebrate body scarcely expanded by ribs,
but covered by a red blanket, and a head
with deathlike features overhung by strips
of hair. This vision of famine leaned forward and indented Michel with one finger,
croaking again:

"How fat he is!"

The boy roused himself, and, for one
instant stupid and apologetic, was going
to sit up and whine. He saw what bent
over him, and, bristling with unimaginable
revolutions of arms and legs, he yelled a
yell which seemed to sweep the thing back
through the window.

Next day no one thought of dancing or
fishing or of the coming English. Frenchmen and Indians turned out together to
search for Louizon Cadotte. Though he
never in his life had set foot to any expedition without first notifying his household, and it was not the custom to hunt
alone in the woods, his disappearance
would not have roused the settlement in so

short a time had there been no windigo hanging about the Saulte. It was told that the windigo, who entered his house again in the night, must have made way with him.

Jacques Repentigny heard this with some amusement. Of windigos he had no experience, but he had hunted and camped much of the summer with Louizon.

"I do not think he would let himself be 10 knocked on the head by a woman," said Jacques.

"White chief doesn't know what helps a windigo," explained a Chippewa; and the canoeman, Jean Boucher, interpreted him. 15 "Bad spirit makes a windigo strong as a bear. I saw this one. She stole my whitefish and ate them raw."

"Why didn't you give her cooked food when you saw her?" demanded Jacques.

"She would not eat that now. She likes offal better."

"Yes, she was going to eat me," declared Michel Pensonneau. "After she finished Monsieur Louizon, she got through the 25 window to carry me off."

Michel enjoyed the windigo. Though he strummed on his lip and mourned aloud whenever Madame Cadotte was by, he felt so comfortably full of food and horror, 30 and so important with his story, that life threatened him with nothing worse than satiety.

While parties went up the river and down the river, and talked about the 35 chutes in the rapids where a victim could be sucked down to death in an instant, or about tracing the windigo's secret camp, Archange hid herself in the attic. She lay upon Michel's bed and wept, or walked 40 the plank floor. It was no place for her. At noon the bark roof heated her almost to fever. The dormer windows gave her little air, and there was dust as well as something like an individual sediment of 45 the poverty from which the boy had come. Yet she could endure the loft dungeon better than the face of the Chippewa mother who blamed her, or the bluff excitement of Monsieur Cadotte. She could 50 hear his voice from time to time, as he ran in for spirits or provisions for parties of searchers. And Archange had aversion, like the instinct of a maid, to betraying fondness for her husband. She was furious 55 with him, also, for causing her pain. When she thought of the windigo, of the rapids, of any peril which might be working him

limitless absence, she set clenched han in her loosened hair and trembled wi hysterical anguish. But the enormity his behavior if he were alive made h hiss at the rafters. "Good, monsieur! Ne time I will have four officers. I will ha the entire garrison sitting along the ga lery! Yes, and they shall be English, tc And there is one thing you will nev know, besides." She laughed through h weeping. "You will never know I ma eyes at a windigo."

The preenings and posings of a creatu whose perfections he once thought we the result of a happy chance had ma Louizon roar. She remembered all the life together, and moaned, "I will say thi he was the best husband that any girl ev had. We scarcely had a disagreement B to be the widow of a man who is eat up—O Sainte Marie!"

In the clear August weather the wi river seemed to bring its opposite shor nearer. Islands within a stone's throw the settlement, rocky drops in a boiliı current, vividly showed their rich foliaç of pines. On one of these islands Fathı Dablon and Father Marquette had bui their first mission chapel; and though the afterwards removed it to the mainland, tl old tracery of foundation stones could sti be seen. The mountains of Lake Superio showed like a cloud. On the ridge abo• fort and houses the Chippewa lodges we• pleasant in the sunlight, sending ribboı of smoke from their camp-fires far abov the serrated edge of the woods. Nake Indian children and their playmates of tl settlement shouted to one another, as the ran along the river margin, threats of iı stant seizure by the windigo. The Chiı pewa widow, holding her husband in he arms, for she was not permitted to han him on her back, stood and talked wit her red-skinned intimates of the lodge The Frenchwomen collected at the sei niory house. As for the men of the garr son, they were obliged to stay and receiv the English then on the way from Detoı But they came out to see the boats off wit the concern of brothers, and Archange uncle, the post commandant, embrace Monsieur Cadotte.

The priest and Jacques Repentigny di not speak to each other about that wretche creature whose hoverings around the Sau were connected with Louizon Cadotte disappearance. But the priest went wit

uizon's father down the river, and
cques led the party which took the op-
site direction. Though so many years had
ssed since Father Dablon and Father
arquette built the first bark chapel, their
ccessor found his work very little easier
an theirs had been.

A canoe was missing from the little fleet
ually tied alongshore, but it was not the
e belonging to Louizon. The young seig-
r took that one, having Jean Boucher
d Jean's son to paddle for him. No other
an of Sault Sainte Marie could pole up
e rapids or paddle down them as this
pert Chippewa could. He had been bap-
ed with a French name, and his son
ter him, but no Chippewa of pure blood
d name looked habitually as he did into
ose whirlpools called the chutes, where
e slip of a paddle meant death. Yet no-
dy feared the rapids. It was common for
ys and girls to flit around near shore in
ch canoes, balancing themselves and ex-
rtly dipping up whitefish.

Jean Boucher thrust out his boat from
hind an island, and, turning it as a fish
des, moved over thin sheets of water
raying upon rocks. The fall of the Sainte
arie is gradual, but even at its upper end
ere is a little hill to climb. Jean set his
le into the stone floor of the river, and
ted the vessel length by length from
est to crest of foam. His paddles lay bend him, and his arms were bare to the
ows, showing their strong red sinews.
e had let his hair grow like a French-
an's, and it hung forward shading his
tless brow. A skin apron was girded in
ont of him to meet waves which frothed
over the canoe's high prow. Blacksmith
the waters, he beat a path between juts
rocks; struggling to hold a point with
e pole, calling a quick word to his helper,
d laughing as he forged his way. Other
yagers who did not care to tax them-
lves with this labor made a portage with
eir canoes alongshore, and started above
e glassy curve where the river bends
wn to its leap.

Gros Cap rose in the sky, revealing its
ak in bolder lines as the searchers pushed
the Sainte Marie, exploring mile after
le of pine and white birch and fantastic
ck. The shaggy bank stooped to them,
e illimitable glory of the wilderness wit-
ssing a little procession of boats like
ips floating by.

It was almost sunset when they came
back, the tired paddlers keeping near that
shore on which they intended to land. No
trace of Louizon Cadotte could be found;
and those who had not seen the windigo
were ready to declare that there was no
such thing about the Sault, when, just
above the rapids, she appeared from the
dense up-slope of forest.

Jacques Repentigny's canoe had kept the
lead, but a dozen light-bodied Chippewas
sprung on shore and rushed past him into
the bushes.

The woman had disappeared in underbrush, but, surrounded by hunters in full
chase, she came running out, and fell on
her hands, making a hoarse noise in her
throat. As she looked up, all the marks
in her aged aboriginal face were distinct
to Jacques Repentigny. The sutures in her
temples were parted. She rolled herself
around in a ball, and hid her head in her
dirty red blanket. Any wild beast was in
harmony with the wilderness, but this sick
human being was a blot upon it. Jacques
felt the compassion of a god for her. Her
pursuers were after her, and the thud of
stones they threw made him heartsick, as
if the thing were done to the woman he
loved.

"Let her alone!" he commanded fiercely.

"Kill her!" shouted the hunters. "Hit
the windigo on the head!"

All that world of Northern air could not
sweeten her, but Jacques picked her up
without a thought of her offensiveness and
ran to his canoe. The bones resisted him;
the claws scratched at him through her
blanket. Jean Boucher lifted a paddle to
hit the creature as soon as she was down.

"If you strike her, I will kill you!"
warned Jacques, and he sprung into the
boat.

The superstitious Chippewas threw
themselves madly into their canoes to
follow. It would go hard, but they would
get the windigo and take the young seignior out of her spell. The Frenchmen, with
man's instinct for the chase, were in full
cry with them.

Jean Boucher laid down his paddle sulkily, and his son did the same. Jacques took
a long pistol from his belt and pointed it
at the old Indian.

"If you don't paddle for life, I will
shoot you." And his eyes were eyes which
Jean respected as he never had respected
anything before. The young man was a
beautiful fellow. If he wanted to save a

windigo, why, the saints let him. The priest might say a good word about it when you came to think, also.

"Where shall I paddle to?" inquired Jean Boucher, drawing in his breath. The canoe leaped ahead, grazing hands stretched out to seize it.

"To the other side of the river."

"Down the rapids?"

"Yes."

"Go down rough or go down smooth?"

"Rough—rough—where they cannot catch you."

The old canoeman snorted. He would like to see any of them catch him. They were straining after him, and half a dozen canoes shot down that glassy slide which leads to the rocks.

It takes three minutes for a skilful paddler to run that dangerous race of three quarters of a mile. Jean Boucher stood at the prow, and the waves boiled as high as his waist. Jacques dreaded only that the windigo might move and destroy the delicate poise of the boat; but she lay very still. The little craft quivered from rock to rock without grazing one, rearing itself over a great breaker or sinking under a crest of foam. Now a billow towered up, and Jean broke it with his paddle, shouting his joy. Showers fell on the woman coiled in the bottom of the boat. They were going down very rough indeed. Yells from the other canoes grew less distinct. Jacques turned his head, keeping a true balance, and saw that their pursuers were skirting toward the shore. They must make a long detour to catch him after he reached the foot of the fall.

The roar of awful waters met him as he looked ahead. Jean Boucher drove the paddle down and spoke to his son. The canoe leaned sidewise, sucked by the first chute, a caldron in the river bed where all Sainte Marie's current seemed to go down, and whirl, and rise, and froth, and roar.

"Ha!" shouted Jean Boucher. His face glistened with beads of water and the glory of mastering Nature.

Scarcely were they past the first pit when the canoe plunged on the verge of another. This sight was a moment of madness. The great chute, lined with moving water walls and floored with whirling foam, bellowed as if it were submerging the world. Columns of green water sheeted in white rose above it and fell forward on the current. As the canoemen held on with their paddles and shot by through spur and rain, every soul in the boat exulted except the woman who lay flat on its keel. The rapids gave a voyager the illusion that they were running uphill to meet him, that they were breasting and opposing him instead of carrying him forward. There was scarcely a breath between riding the edge of the bottomless pit and shooting out on clear water. The rapids were past, and they paddled for the other shore, a mile away.

On the west side the green water seemed turning to fire, but as the sunset went out shadows sank on the broad surface. The fresh evening breath of a primitive world blew across it. Down-river the channel turned, and Jacques could see nothing of the English or of the other party. His pursuers had decided to land at the settlement.

It was twilight when Jean Boucher brought the canoe to pine woods which met them at the edge of the water. The young Repentigny' had been wondering what he should do with his windigo. There was no settlement on this shore, and had there been one it would offer no hospitality to such as she was. His canoemen would hardly camp with her, and he had no provisions. To keep her from being stoned or torn to pieces he had made an inconsiderate flight. But his perplexity dissolved in a moment before the sight of Louizo Cadotte coming out of the woods toward them, having no hunting equipments and looking foolish.

"Where have you been?" called Jacques.

"Down this shore," responded Louizon.

"Did you take a canoe and come out here last night?"

"Yes, monsieur. I wished to be by myself. The canoe is below. I was coming home."

"It is time you were coming home, when all the men in the settlement are searching for you, and all the women trying to console your mother and your wife."

"My wife—she is not then talking with any one on the gallery?" Louizon's voice betrayed gratified revenge.

"I do not know. But there is a woman in this canoe who might talk on the gallery and complain to the priest against a man who has got her stoned on her account."

Louizon did not understand this, even

when he looked at the heap of dirty blanket in the canoe.

"Who is it?" he inquired.

"The Chippewas call her a windigo. They were all chasing her for eating you up. But now we can take her back to the priest, and they will let her alone when they see you. Where is your canoe?"

"Down here among the bushes," answered Louizon. He went to get it, ashamed to look the young seignior in the face. He was light-headed from hunger and exposure, and what followed seemed to him afterwards a piteous dream.

"Come back!" called the young seignior, and Louizon turned back. The two men's eyes met in a solemn look.

"Jean Boucher says this woman is dead."

Jean Boucher stood on the bank, holding the canoe with one hand, and turning her unresisting face with the other. Jacques and Louizon took off their hats.

They heard the cry of the whip-poor-will. The river had lost all its green and was purple, and purple shadows lay on the distant mountains and opposite ridge. Darkness was mercifully covering this poor demented Indian woman, overcome by the burdens of her life, aged without being venerable, perhaps made hideous by want and sorrow.

When they had looked at her in silence, respecting her because she could no longer be hurt by anything in the world, Louizon whispered aside to his seignior:

"What shall we do with her?"

"Bury her," the old canoeman answered for him.

One of the party yet thought of taking her back to the priest. But she did not belong to priests and rites. Jean Boucher said they could dig in the forest mold with a paddle, and he and his son would make her a grave. The two Chippewas left the burden to the young men.

Jacques Repentigny and Louizon Cadotte took up the woman who, perhaps, had never been what they considered a woman; who had missed the good, and got for her portion the ignorance and degradation of the world; yet who must be something to the Almighty, for he had sent youth and love to pity and take care of her in her death. They carried her into the woods between them.

XXXVI

KATE CHOPIN (1851–1904)

The Louisiana Creoles and the Acadians of the cane-brakes appeared again in this dec:
in the temperamental and very original tales of Kate Chopin, an Irish woman who had m.
ried a Louisiana cotton factor and had lived for years in an isolated French village in t
heart of the Red River lowlands. Though she had been educated in a St. Louis conv<
school until she was nineteen, she had had little contact with literature and her later isola<
life and her growing family had given her little time for reading or for culture. The de:
of her husband when she was thirty-six left her without means of support and in sh<
desperation she turned to fiction as a possible help to her income. The result was a ser
of short stories as primitively original as the first work of Mary E. Wilkins. She worl
without models and with small recollection of other writers, for she had read but lit<
Her stories, therefore, are redolent only of herself—her temperamental Irish soul, her Ce<
wit and humor, and her romanticism and sentiment. Redolent they are also of the pecu<
environment and people of the strange land where she had lived. Her collections *Bay*
Folk, 1894, and *A Night in Acadie,* 1897, contain the sum of her short-story product. S
was a meteoric figure disappearing as suddenly as she had appeared. Piqued by harsh cri
cism of her technique, she vowed suddenly and temperamentally that she would write
more and she kept her word.

A few of her stories undoubtedly will endure. They have an intensity, a feminine chai
an aura of strangeness, and at times a gripping reality that are all their own. In many wa
they are unique.

MADAME CÉLESTIN'S DIVORCE

Madame Célestin always wore a neat and snugly fitting calico wrapper when she went out in the morning to sweep her small gallery. Lawyer Paxton thought she looked very pretty in the gray one that was made with a graceful Watteau fold at the back, and with which she invariably wore a bow of pink ribbon at the throat. She was always sweeping her gallery when Lawyer Paxton passed by in the morning on his way to his office at St. Denis Street.

Sometimes he stopped and leaned over the fence to say good morning at his ease; to criticize or admire her rosebushes; or, when he had time enough, to hear what she had to say. Madame Célestin usually had a good deal to say. She would gather up the train of her calico wrapper in one hand, and balancing the broom gracefully in the other, would go tripping down to where the lawyer leaned, as comfortably as he could, over her picket fence.

Of course she had talked to him of her troubles. Everyone knew of Madame Célestin's troubles.

"Really, madame," he told her once, his deliberate, calculating, lawyer-to: "It's more than human nature—woma: nature—should be called upon to endu: Here you are, working your fingers o —she glanced down at two rosy fing: tips that showed through the rents of l baggy doeskin gloves—"taking in se ing; giving music lessons; doing G knows what in the way of manual lal to support yourself and those two lit ones"—Madame Célestin's pretty f: beamed with satisfaction at this enumei tion of her trials.

"You right, Judge. Not a picayune, : one, not one, have I lay my eyes on in t pas' fo' months that I can say Céles give it to me or sen' it to me."

"The scoundrel!" muttered lawyer Pa ton in his beard.

"An' *pourtant*," she resumed, "they s he is making money down round Alexa dria w'en he wants to work."

"I daresay you haven't seen him : months?" suggested the lawyer.

"It's good six month' since I see a sig of Célestin," she admitted.

"That's it, that's what I say; he has pr:

404

:ally deserted you; fails to support you.
wouldn't surprise me a bit to learn that
: has ill treated you."

"Well, you know, Judge," with an
/asive cough, "a man that drinks—w'at
.n you expec'? An' if you would know
e promises he has made me! Ah, if I
.d as many dolla' as I had promise from
élestin, I would n' have to work, *je vous
.rantis.*"

"And in my opinion, madame, you would
: a foolish woman to endure it longer,
.en the divorce court is there to offer you
.dress."

"You spoke about that befo', Judge; I'm
)in' think about that divo'ce. I believe
)u right."

Madame Célestin thought about the di-
)rce and talked about it, too; and lawyer
.axton grew deeply interested in the
.eme.

"You know, about that divo'ce, Judge,"
.adame Célestin was waiting for him that
)rning, "I been talking to my family an'
y frien's, an' it's me that tells you, they
I plumb agains' that divo'ce."

"Certainly, to be sure; that's to be ex-
:cted, madame, in this community of
:reoles. I warned you that you would meet
.ith opposition, and would have to face it
.d brave it."

"Oh, don't fear, I'm going to face it!
.aman says it's a disgrace like it's neva
.en in the family. But it's good for Maman
talk, her. W'at trouble she ever had?
.e says I mus' go by all means consult
.ith Père Duchéron—it's my confessor,
)u undastan'—Well, I'll go, Judge, to
.ease Maman. But all the confessor' in
.e world' ent goin' make me put up with
at conduc' of Célestin any longa."

A day or two later, she was there wait-
.g for him again. "You know, Judge,
)out that divo'ce."

"Yes, yes," responded the lawyer, well
.eased to trace a new determination in her
.own eyes and in the curves of her pretty
)uth. "I suppose you saw Père Duchéron
.d had to brave it out with him, too."

"Oh, fo' that, a perfec' sermon, I assho'
)u. A talk of giving scandal an' bad ex-
.nple that I thought would neva en'! He
.ys, fo' him, he wash' his hands; I mus'
) see the bishop."

"You won't let the bishop dissuade you,
trust," stammered the lawyer more
.xiously than he could well understand.

"You don't know me yet, Judge," laughed

Madame Célestin with a turn of the head
and a flirt of the broom which indicated
that the interview was at an end.

"Well, Madame Célestin! And the
bishop!" Lawyer Paxton was standing there
holding to a couple of shaky pickets. She
had not seen him. "Oh, it's you, Judge?"
and she hastened towards him with an
empressement that could not but have been
flattering.

"Yes, I saw Monseigneur," she began.
The lawyer had already gathered from her
expressive countenance that she had not
wavered in her determination. "Ah, he's a
eloquent man. It's not a mo' eloquent man
in Natchitoches Parish. I was fo'ced to cry,
the way he talked to me about my troubles;
how he undastan's them, an' feels for me.
It would move even you, Judge, to hear
how he talk' about that step I want to take;
its danga, its temptation. Now it is the
duty of a Catholic to stan' everything till
the las' extreme. An' that life of retirement an' self-denial I would have to lead
—he tole me all that."

"But he hasn't turned you from your
resolve, I see," laughed the lawyer complacently.

"For that, no," she returned emphatically. "The bishop don't know w'at it is
to be married to a man like Célestin, an'
have to endu' that conduc' like I have to
endu' it. The Pope himse'f can't make
me stan' that any longer, if you say I
got the right in the law to sen' Célestin
sailing."

A noticeable change had come over lawyer Paxton. He discarded his work-day
coat and began to wear his Sunday one
to the office. He grew solicitous as to the
shine of his boots, his collar, and the set
of his tie. He brushed and trimmed his
whiskers with a care that had not before
been apparent. Then he fell into a stupid
habit of dreaming as he walked the streets
of the old town. It would be good to take
unto himself a wife, he dreamed. And he
could dream of no other than pretty
Madame Célestin filling that sweet and
sacred office as she filled his thoughts, now.
Old Natchitoches would not hold them
comfortably, perhaps; but the world was
surely wide enough to live in, outside of
Natchitoches town.

His heart beat in a strangely irregular
manner as he neared Madame Célestin's
house one morning, and discovered her behind the rose-bushes, as usual plying her

broom. She had finished the gallery and steps and was sweeping the little brick walk along the edge of the violet border.

"Good morning, Madame Célestin."

"Ah, it's you, Judge? Good-morning." He waited. She seemed to be doing the same. Then she ventured, with some hesitancy. "You know, Judge, about that divo'ce. I been thinking—I reckon you betta neva mine about that divo'ce." She was making deep rings in the palm of h gloved hand with the end of her broo handle, and looking at them critically. H face seemed to the lawyer to be unusua rosy; but maybe it was only the reflecti of the pink bow at the throat. "Yes, reckon you need n' mine. You see, Judg Célestin came home las' night. An' h promise me on his word an' honor h going to turn ova a new leaf."

XXXVII

STEPHEN CRANE (1871–1900)

The genius of the decade of the nineties was undoubtedly Stephen Crane. After his course at Lafayette College, Pennsylvania, he turned, like so many others of his generation, to journalism, but not at all with the intention of making it his profession. He had literary dreams that soared. His genius first manifested itself in his poetry,—strange, amorphic forms now crowned as the beginnings of the "free verse" movement. Under the temporary influence of Zola he wrote a "naturalistic" novel, *Maggie, a Girl of the Streets,* a novel so brutally sordid in its setting and so specific in its revealings that it found no publisher, and when at length it was issued at the author's expense it found no readers. The day for such work had not arrived.

Crane himself may be said to have "arrived" when was published his war novel, *The Red Badge of Courage,* 1895, a remarkable piece of *tour de force* realism. With no actual experience of war, he produced a narrative with a DeFoe-like minuteness of detail that seemingly could have come only from the observations of a veteran, the survivor of many battles. His short-story work was for the most part incidental to his larger literary plans, mere intervals in his creative work. His much-praised "The Open Boat" is a piece of clever journalism thrown off during the war in Cuba. He deals with his characters as if they were *x, y,* and *z* in a problem. He does not even give them names. But he concentrates on seemingly trivial details, multiplying them until the feeling of actuality has been created in the reader to the overpowering of all suspicion and apathy. In his descriptions he sought always familiar comparisons easily visualized by his reader: "cotton flannel gulls" sat on the water; the sun was pasted on the sky "like a wafer," and the like. He was a journalist with a poet's pen; a poet who awoke to find himself in a scientific age, an age of realism and prose.

A GRAY SLEEVE *

I

"It looks as if it might rain this afternoon," remarked the lieutenant of artillery.

"So it does," the infantry captain assented. He glanced casually at the sky. When his eyes had lowered to the green-shadowed landscape before him, he said fretfully: "I wish those fellows out yonder would quit pelting at us. They've been at it since noon."

At the edge of a grove of maples, across wide fields, there occasionally appeared little puffs of smoke of a dull hue in this gloom of sky which expressed an impending rain. The long wave of blue and steel in the field moved uneasily at the eternal barking of the far-away sharpshooters, and the men, leaning upon their rifles, stared at the grove of maples. Once a private turned to borrow some tobacco from a comrade in the rear rank, but, with his hand still stretched out, he continued to twist his head and glance at the distant trees. He was afraid the enemy would shoot him at a time when he was not looking.

Suddenly the artillery officer said: "See what's coming!"

Along the rear of the brigade of infantry a column of cavalry was sweeping at a hard gallop. A lieutenant, riding some yards to the right of the column, bawled furiously at the four troopers just at the rear of the colors. They had lost distance and made a little gap, but at the shouts of the lieutenant they urged their horses forward. The bugler, careering along behind the captain of the troop, fought and tugged like a wrestler to keep his frantic animal from bolting far ahead of the column.

On the springy turf the innumerable hoofs thundered in a swift storm of sound. In the brown faces of the troopers their eyes were set like bits of flashing steel.

The long line of the infantry regiments standing at ease underwent a sudden movement at the rush of the passing squadron.

The foot soldiers turned their heads to gaze at the torrent of horses and men.

The yellow folds of the flag fluttered back in silken, shuddering waves, as if it were a reluctant thing. Occasionally a giant spring of a charger would rear the firm and sturdy figure of a soldier suddenly head and shoulders above his comrades. Over the noise of the scudding hoofs could be heard the creaking of leather trappings, the jingle and clank of steel, and the tense, low-toned commands or appeals of the men to their horses. And the horses were mad with the headlong sweep of this movement. Powerful under jaws bent back and straightened so that the bits were clamped as rigidly as vises upon the teeth, and glistening necks arched in desperate resistance to the hands at the bridles. Swinging their heads in rage at the granite laws of their lives, which compelled even their angers and their ardours to chosen directions and chosen paces, their flight was as a flight of harnessed demons.

The captain's bay kept its pace at the head of the squadron with the lithe bounds of a thoroughbred, and this horse was proud as a chief at the roaring trample of his fellows behind him. The captain's glance was calmly upon the grove of maples whence the sharpshooters of the enemy had been picking at the blue line. He seemed to be reflecting. He stolidly rose and fell with the plunges of his horse in all the indifference of a deacon's figure seated plumply in church. And it occurred to many of the watching infantry to wonder why this officer could remain imperturbable and reflective when his squadron was thundering and swarming behind him like the rushing of a flood.

The column swung in a sabre-curve toward a break in a fence, and dashed into a roadway. Once a little plank bridge was encountered, and the sound of the hoofs upon it was like the long roll of many drums. An old captain in the infantry turned to his first lieutenant and made a remark which was a compound of bitter disparagement of cavalry in general and soldierly admiration of this particular troop.

Suddenly the bugle sounded, and the column halted with a jolting upheaval amid sharp, brief cries. A moment later the men had tumbled from their horses and, carbines in hand, were running in a swarm toward the grove of maples. In the road one of every four of the troopers was standing with braced legs, and pulling and hauling at the bridles of four frenzied horses.

The captain was running awkwardly in his boots. He held his saber low, so that the point often threatened to catch in the turf. His yellow hair ruffled out from under his faded cap. "Go in hard now!" he roared, in a voice of hoarse fury. His face was violently red.

The troopers threw themselves upon the grove like wolves upon a great animal. Along the whole front of woods there was the dry crackling of musketry, with bitter, swift flashes and smoke that writhed like stung phantoms. The troopers yelled shrilly and spanged bullets low into the foliage.

For a moment, when near the woods, the line almost halted. The men struggled and fought for a time like swimmers encountering a powerful current. Then with a supreme effort they went on again. They dashed madly at the grove, whose foliage, from the high light of the field, was as inscrutable as a wall.

Then suddenly each detail of the calm trees became apparent, and with a few more frantic leaps the men were in the cool gloom of the woods. There was a heavy odor as from burned paper. Wisps of gray smoke wound upward. The men halted; and, grimy, perspiring, and puffing, they searched the recesses of the woods with eager, fierce glances. Figures could be seen flitting afar off. A dozen carbines rattled at them in an angry volley.

During this pause the captain strode along the line, his face lit with a broad smile of contentment. "When he sends this crowd to do anything, I guess he'll find we do it pretty sharp," he said to the grinning lieutenant.

"Say, they didn't stand that rush a minute, did they?" said the subaltern. Both officers were profoundly dusty in their uniforms, and their faces were soiled like those of two urchins.

Out in the grass behind them were three tumbled and silent forms.

Presently the line moved forward again. The men went from tree to tree like hunters stalking game. Some at the left of the line fired occasionally, and those at the right gazed curiously in that direction. The men still breathed heavily from their scramble across the field.

Of a sudden a trooper halted and said:

"Hello! there's a house!" Every one paused. The men turned to look at their leader.

The captain stretched his neck and swung his head from side to side. "By George, it is a house!" he said.

Through the wealth of leaves there vaguely loomed the form of a large white house. These troopers, brown-faced from many days of campaigning, each feature of them telling of their placid confidence and courage, were stopped abruptly by the appearance of this house. There was some subtle suggestion—some tale of an unknown thing—which watched them from they knew not what part of it.

A rail fence girded a wide lawn of tangled grass. Seven pines stood along a driveway which led from two distant posts of a vanished gate. The blue-clothed troopers moved forward until they stood at the fence, peering over it.

The captain put one hand on the top rail and seemed to be about to climb the fence, when suddenly he hesitated and said in a low voice: "Watson, what do you think of it?"

The lieutenant stared at the house. "Derned if I know!" he replied.

The captain pondered. It happened that the whole company had turned a gaze of profound awe and doubt upon this edifice which confronted them. The men were very silent.

At last the captain swore and said: "We are certainly a pack of fools. Derned old deserted house halting a company of Union cavalry, and making us gape like babies!"

"Yes, but there's something—something——" insisted the subaltern in a half stammer.

"Well, if there's 'something—something' in there, I'll get it out," said the captain. "Send Sharpe clean around to the other side with about twelve men, so we will sure bag your 'something—something,' and I'll take a few of the boys and find out what's in the damned old thing!"

He chose the nearest eight men for his "storming party," as the lieutenant called it. After he had waited some minutes for the others to get into position, he said "Come ahead" to his eight men, and climbed the fence.

The brighter light of the tangled lawn made him suddenly feel tremendously apparent, and he wondered if there could be some mystic thing in the house which was regarding his approach. His men trudged silently at his back. They stared at the windows and lost themselves in deep speculations as to the probability of there being, perhaps, eyes behind the blinds—malignant eyes, piercing eyes.

Suddenly a corporal in the party gave vent to a startled exclamation and half threw his carbine into position. The captain turned quickly, and the corporal said: "I saw an arm move the blinds. An arm with a gray sleeve!"

"Don't be a fool, Jones, now," said the captain sharply.

"I swear t'——" began the corporal, but the captain silenced him.

When they arrived at the front of the house, the troopers paused, while the captain went softly up the front steps. He stood before the large front door and studied it. Some crickets chirped in the long grass, and the nearest pine could be heard in its endless sighs. One of the privates moved uneasily, and his foot crunched the gravel. Suddenly the captain swore angrily and kicked the door with a loud crash. It flew open.

II

The bright lights of the day flashed into the old house when the captain angrily kicked open the door. He was aware of a wide hallway carpeted with matting and extending deep into the dwelling. There was also an old walnut hatrack and a little marble-topped table with a vase and two books upon it. Farther back was a great venerable fireplace containing dreary ashes.

But directly in front of the captain was a young girl. The flying open of the door had obviously been an utter astonishment to her, and she remained transfixed there in the middle of the floor, staring at the captain with wide eyes.

She was like a child caught at the time of a raid upon the cake. She wavered to and fro upon her feet, and held her hands behind her. There were two little points of terror in her eyes, as she gazed up at the young captain in dusty blue, with his reddish, bronze complexion, his yellow hair, his bright saber held threateningly.

These two remained motionless and silent, simply staring at each other for some moments.

The captain felt his rage fade out of him and leave his mind limp. He had been violently angry, because this house had made him feel hesitant, wary. He did not like to be wary. He liked to feel confident, sure. So he had kicked the door open, and had been prepared to march in like a soldier of wrath.

But now he began, for one thing, to wonder if his uniform was so dusty and old in appearance. Moreover, he had a feeling that his face was covered with a compound of dust, grime, and perspiration. He took a step forward and said: "I didn't mean to frighten you." But his voice was coarse from his battle-howling. It seemed to him to have hempen fibers in it.

The girl's breath came in little, quick gasps, and she looked at him as she would have looked at a serpent.

"I didn't mean to frighten you," he said again.

The girl, still with her hands behind her, began to back away.

"Is there any one else in the house?" he went on, while slowly following her. "I don't wish to disturb you, but we had a fight with some rebel skirmishers in the woods, and I thought maybe some of them might have come in here. In fact, I was pretty sure of it. Are there any of them here?"

The girl looked at him and said, "No!" He wondered why extreme agitation made the eyes of some women so limpid and bright.

"Who is here besides yourself?"

By this time his pursuit had driven her to the end of the hall, and she remained there with her back to the wall and her hands still behind her. When she answered this question, she did not look at him, but down at the floor. She cleared her voice and then said: "There is no one here."

"No one?"

She lifted her eyes to him in that appeal that the human being must make even to falling trees, crashing boulders, the sea in a storm, and said, "No, no, there is no one here." He could plainly see her tremble.

Of a sudden he bethought him that she continually kept her hands behind her. As he recalled her air when first discovered, he remembered she appeared precisely as a child detected at on of the crimes of childhood. Moreover, she had always backed away from him. He thought now that she was concealing something which was an evidence of the presence of the enemy in the house.

"What are you holding behind you?" he said suddenly.

She gave a little quick moan, as if some grim hand had throttled her.

"Oh, nothing—please. I am not holding anything behind me; indeed I'm not."

"Very well. Hold your hands out in front of you, then."

"Oh, indeed, I'm not holding anything behind me. Indeed I'm not."

"Well," he began. Then he paused, and remained for a moment dubious. Finally, he laughed. "Well, I shall have my men search the house, anyhow. I'm sorry to trouble you, but I feel that there is some one here whom we want." He turned to the corporal, who, with the other men, was gaping quietly in at the door, and said: "Jones, go through the house."

As for himself, he remained planted in front of the girl, for she evidently did not dare to move and allow him to see what she held so carefully behind her back. So she was his prisoner.

The men rummaged around on the ground floor of the house. Sometimes the captain called to them, "Try that closet," "Is there any cellar?" But they found no one, and at last they went trooping toward the stairs which led to the second floor.

But at this movement on the part of the men the girl uttered a cry—a cry of such fright and appeal that the men paused. "Oh, don't go up there! Please don't go up there!—ple-ease! There is no one there! Indeed—indeed there is not! Oh, ple-ease!"

"Go on, Jones," said the captain calmly. The obedient corporal made a preliminary step, and the girl bounded toward the stairs with another cry.

As she passed him, the captain caught sight of that which she had concealed behind her back, and which she had forgotten in this supreme moment. It was a pistol.

She ran to the first step and, standing there, faced the men, one hand extended with perpendicular palm, and the other holding the pistol at her side. "Oh, please, don't go up there! Nobody is there—indeed, there is not! P-l-e-a-s-e!" Then suddenly she sank swiftly down upon the step and, huddling forlornly, began to weep in the agony and with the convulsive tremors of an infant. The pistol fell from her fingers and rattled down to the floor.

The astonished troopers looked at their

astonished captain. There was a short silence.

Finally, the captain stooped and picked up the pistol. It was a heavy weapon of the army pattern. He ascertained that it was empty.

He leaned toward the shaking girl and said gently: "Will you tell me what you were going to do with this pistol?"

He had to repeat the question a number of times, but at last a muffled voice said, "Nothing."

"Nothing!" He insisted quietly upon a further answer. At the tender tones of the captain's voice, the phlegmatic corporal turned and winked gravely at the man next to him.

"Won't you tell me?"

The girl shook her head.

"Please tell me!"

The silent privates were moving their feet uneasily and wondering how long they were to wait.

The captain said: "Please, won't you tell me?"

Then this girl's voice began in stricken tones, half coherent, and amid violent sobbing: "It was grandpa's. He—he—he said he was going to shoot anybody who came in here—he didn't care if there were thousands of 'em. And—and I know he would, and I was afraid they'd kill him. And so—and—so I stole away his pistol—and I was going to hide it when you—you kicked open the door."

The men straightened up and looked at each other. The girl began to weep again.

The captain mopped his brow. He peered down at the girl. He mopped his brow again. Suddenly he said: "Ah, don't cry like that."

He moved restlessly and looked down at his boots. He mopped his brow again.

Then he gripped the corporal by the arm and dragged him some yards back from the others. "Jones," he said, in an intensely earnest voice, "will you tell me what in the devil I am going to do?"

The corporal's countenance became illuminated with satisfaction at being thus requested to advise his superior officer. He adopted an air of great thought, and finally said: "Well, of course, the feller with the gray sleeve must be upstairs, and we must get past the girl and up there somehow. Suppose I take her by the arm and lead her——"

"What!" interrupted the captain from between his clinched teeth. As he turned away from the corporal, he said fiercely over his shoulder: "You touch that girl and I'll split your skull!"

III

The corporal looked after his captain with an expression of mingled amazement, grief, and philosophy. He seemed to be saying to himself that there unfortunately were times, after all, when one could not rely upon the most reliable of men. When he returned to the group he found the captain bending over the girl and saying: "Why is it that you don't want us to search upstairs?"

The girl's head was buried in her crossed arms. Locks of her hair had escaped from their fastenings, and these fell upon her shoulder.

"Won't you tell me?"

The corporal here winked again at the man next to him.

"Because," the girl moaned—"because—there isn't anybody up there."

The captain at last said timidly: "Well, I'm afraid—I'm afraid we'll have to——"

The girl sprang to her feet again, and implored him with her hands. She looked deep into his eyes with her glance, which was at this time like that of the fawn when it says to the hunter, "Have mercy upon me!"

These two stood regarding each other. The captain's foot was on the bottom step, but he seemed to be shrinking. He wore an air of being deeply wretched and ashamed. There was a silence.

Suddenly the corporal said in a quick, low tone: "Look out, captain!"

All turned their eyes swiftly toward the head of the stairs. There had appeared there a youth in a gray uniform. He stood looking coolly down at them. No word was said by the troopers. The girl gave vent to a little wail of desolation, "Oh, Harry!"

He began slowly to descend the stairs. His right arm was in a white sling, and there were some fresh blood-stains upon the cloth. His face was rigid and deathly pale, but his eyes flashed like lights. The girl was again moaning in an utterly dreary fashion, as the youth came slowly down toward the silent men in blue.

Six steps from the bottom of the flight

he halted and said: "I reckon it's me you're looking for."

The troopers had crowded forward a trifle and, posed in lithe, nervous attitudes, were watching him like cats. The captain remained unmoved. At the youth's question he merely nodded his head and said, "Yes."

The young man in gray looked down at the girl, and then, in the same even tone, which now, however, seemed to vibrate with suppressed fury, he said: "And is that any reason why you should insult my sister?"

At this sentence, the girl intervened, desperately, between the young man in gray and the officer in blue. "Oh, don't, Harry; don't! He was good to me! He was good to me, Harry—indeed he was!"

The youth came on in his quiet, erect fashion until the girl could have touched either of the men with her hand, for the captain still remained with his foot upon the first step. She continually repeated: "Oh, Harry! Oh, Harry!"

The youth in gray manœuvred to glare into the captain's face, first over one shoulder of the girl and then over the other. In a voice that rang like metal, he said: "You are armed and unwounded, while I have no weapons and am wounded; but——"

The captain had stepped back and sheathed his saber. The eyes of these two men were gleaming fire, but otherwise the captain's countenance was imperturbable. He said: "You are mistaken. You have no reason to——'

"You lie!"

All save the captain and the youth in gray started in an electric movement. These two words crackled in the air like shattered glass. There was a breathless silence.

The captain cleared his throat. His look at the youth contained a quality of singular and terrible ferocity, but he said in his stolid tone: "I don't suppose you mean what you say now."

Upon his arm he had felt the pressure of some unconscious little fingers. The girl was leaning against the wall as if she no longer knew how to keep her balance, but those fingers—he held his arm very still. She murmured: "Oh, Harry, don't! He was good to me—indeed he was!"

The corporal had come forward until he in a measure confronted the youth in gray, for he saw those fingers upon the captain's arm, and he knew that sometimes very strong men were not able to move hand or foot under such conditions.

The youth had suddenly seemed to become weak. He breathed heavily and clung to the rail. He was glaring at the captain, and apparently summoning all his will power to combat his weakness. The corporal addressed him with profound straightforwardness: "Don't you be a derned fool!" The youth turned toward him so fiercely that the corporal threw up a knee and an elbow like a boy who expects to be cuffed.

The girl pleaded with the captain. "You won't hurt him, will you? He don't know what he's saying. He's wounded, you know. Please don't mind him!"

"I won't touch him," said the captain, with rather extraordinary earnestness; "don't you worry about him at all. I won't touch him!"

Then he looked at her, and the girl suddenly withdrew her fingers from his arm.

The corporal contemplated the top of the stairs, and remarked without surprise: "There's another of 'em coming!"

An old man was clambering down the stairs with much speed. He waved a cane wildly. "Get out of my house, you thieves! Get out! I won't have you cross my threshold! Get out!" He mumbled and wagged his head in an old man's fury. It was plainly his intention to assault them.

And so it occurred that a young girl became engaged in protecting a stalwart captain, fully armed, and with eight grim troopers at his back, from the attack of an old man with a walking-stick!

A blush passed over the temples and brow of the captain, and he looked particularly savage and weary. Despite the girl's efforts, he suddenly faced the old man.

"Look here," he said distinctly; "we came in because we had been fighting in the woods yonder, and we concluded that some of the enemy were in this house, especially when we saw a gray sleeve at the window. But this young man is wounded, and I have nothing to say to him. I will even take it for granted that there are no others like him upstairs. We will go away, leaving your damned old house just as we found it! And we are no more thieves and rascals than you are!"

The old man simply roared: "I haven't got a cow nor a pig nor a chicken on the place! Your soldiers have stolen everything they could carry away. They have torn down half my fences for firewood. This afternoon some of your accursed bullets even broke my window panes!"

The girl had been faltering: "Grandpa! Oh, grandpa!"

The captain looked at the girl. She returned his glance from the shadow of the old man's shoulder. After studying her face a moment, he said: "Well, we will go now." He strode toward the door, and his men clanked docilely after him.

At this time there was the sound of harsh cries and rushing footsteps from without. The door flew open, and a whirlwind composed of blue-coated troopers came in with a swoop. It was headed by the lieutenant. "Oh, here you are!" he cried, catching his breath. "We thought— Oh, look at the girl!"

The captain said intensely: "Shut up, you fool!"

The men settled to a halt with a clash and a bang. There could be heard the dulled sound of many hoofs outside of the house.

"Did you order up the horses?" inquired the captain.

"Yes. We thought——"

"Well, then, let's get out of here," interrupted the captain morosely.

The men began to filter out into the open air. The youth in gray had been hanging dismally to the railing of the stairway. He now was climbing slowly up to the second floor. The old man was addressing himself directly to the serene corporal.

"Not a chicken on the place!" he cried.

"Well, I didn't take your chickens, did I?"

"No, maybe you didn't, but——"

The captain crossed the hall and stood before the girl in rather a culprit's fashion. "You are not angry at me, are you?" he asked timidly.

"No," she said. She hesitated a moment, and then suddenly held out her hand. "You were good to me—and I'm—much obliged."

The captain took her hand, and then he blushed, for he found himself unable to formulate a sentence that applied in any way to the situation.

She did not seem to heed that hand for a time.

He loosened his grasp presently, for he was ashamed to hold it so long without saying anything clever. At last, with an air of charging an entrenched brigade, he contrived to say: "I would rather do anything than frighten or trouble you."

His brow was warmly perspiring. He had a sense of being hideous in his dusty uniform and with his grimy face.

She said, "Oh, I'm so glad it was you instead of somebody who might have— might have hurt brother Harry and grandpa!"

He told her, "I wouldn't have hurt 'em for anything!"

There was a little silence.

"Well, good-by!" he said at last.

"Good-by!"

He walked toward the door past the old man, who was scolding at the vanishing figure of the corporal. The captain looked back. She had remained there watching him.

At the bugle's order, the troopers standing beside their horses swung briskly into the saddle. The lieutenant said to the first sergeant:

"Williams, did they ever meet before?"

"Hanged if I know!"

"Well, say——"

The captain saw a curtain move at one of the windows. He cantered from his position at the head of the column and steered his horse between two flower-beds.

"Well, good-by!"

The squadron trampled slowly past.

"Good-by!"

They shook hands.

He evidently had something enormously important to say to her, but it seems that he could not manage it. He struggled heroically. The bay charger, with his great mystically solemn eyes, looked around the corner of his shoulder at the girl.

The captain studied a pine tree. The girl inspected the grass beneath the window. The captain said hoarsely: "I don't suppose—I don't suppose—I'll ever see you again!"

She looked at him affrightedly and shrank back from the window. He seemed to have woefully expected a reception of this kind for his question. He gave her instantly a glance of appeal.

She said: "Why, no, I don't suppose we will."

"Never?"

"Why, no, 'tain't possible. You—you are a—Yankee!"

"Oh, I know it, but——" Eventually he

continued: "Well, some day, you know, when there's no more fighting, we might——" He observed that she had again withdrawn suddenly into the shadow, so he said: "Well, good-by!"

When he held her fingers she bowed her head, and he saw a pink blush steal over the curves of her cheek and neck.

"Am I never going to see you again?" She made no reply.

"Never?" he repeated.

After a long time, he bent over to hear a faint reply: "Sometime—when there are no troops in the neighborhood—grandpa don't mind if I—walk over as far as that old oak tree yonder—in the afternoons."

It appeared that the captain's grip was very strong, for she uttered an exclamation and looked at her fingers as if she expected to find them mere fragments. He rode away.

The bay horse leaped a flower-bed. They were almost to the drive, when the girl uttered a panic-stricken cry.

The captain wheeled his horse violently, and upon his return journey went straight through a flower-bed.

The girl had clasped her hands. She beseeched him wildly with her eyes. "Oh, please, don't believe it! I never walk to the old oak tree. Indeed I don't! I never—never—never walk there."

The bridle drooped on the bay charger's neck. The captain's figure seemed limp. With an expression of profound dejection and gloom he stared off at where the leaden sky met the dark green line of the woods. The long-impending rain began to fall with a mournful patter, drop and drop. There was a silence.

At last a low voice said, "Well—I might —sometimes I might—perhaps—but only once in a great while—I might walk to the old tree—in the afternoons."

XXXVIII

ALICE BROWN (1857–   )

Of the quintette of feminine writers who have done distinctive work in the short story with New England background—Mrs. Stowe, Mrs. Cooke, Miss Jewett, Mrs. Freeman, and Alice Brown—Miss Brown is the latest to continue writing. Few literary creators have maintained a perennial freshness and a continuance of originality during so long a period as she. Her variety has been remarkable. Beginning with short stories, *Meadow Grass,* 1895, she has written biography, travel sketches, juveniles, poems—a volume of them—criticism, historical romance, and drama even to the winning of a ten thousand dollar prize in 1915. Moreover, she is one of the few whose first short-story collections are not her best work. Nearly thirty years after her first volume of tales she won the distinctive Harpers' short-story contest in competition with the best writers of the younger generation. Steadily has her work improved in technique and in power. Her earlier stories were inclined to the faults of the eighties: they were prone to the exhibition of dialect curiosities and local oddities, they were sometimes over-sentimental, and always were they somewhat loosely constructed. But her work with the drama reacted upon her stories; more and more can her later tales be studied for their dramatic values. She has even retold some of the earlier ones in one-act play form decidedly to their improvement. Her latest work is her best.

Miss Brown's short stories can most effectively be described with the adjective "human." Her characters are alive; they are natural; they are like the people we have known. They have not been looked at from the elevation of a patronizing, even though sympathizing and understanding, onlooker like Miss Jewett; they have not been heightened and idealized like Mrs. Stowe's characters; not viewed from a depressed and carefully selected standpoint like Mrs. Freeman's. She is herself a part of her own materials: one looks neither up nor down as one is introduced to them. Her characters and their little tragedies and comedies appeal to us like actual life: we live with them and know them.

OLD LEMUEL'S JOURNEY *

Old Lemuel Wood was stretched on his bed in the best bedroom. He was going to die. He was not really old, though his neighbors called him so, half in derision, half in pity; but he looked like death and age together, as he lay there, his eyes screwed up, his thin mouth tightly shut, and his whole wrinkled face somehow conveying the impression that it had gone out of business, so far as any evidence it might give, and that nobody was to find out anything about Lemuel Wood any more.

Lemuel was a miser. He had worked hard and pared thin, and his wife, a sweet, plump, blonde woman, had not been able to sway him an inch from the rigor of his ways. They were well to do, inheriting prosperity from the beginning, and yet they had always lived "nigh the wind." The neighbors said Lemuel even begrudged his

wife's plumpness to her. He suspected she ate more than she'd a right to, or she never could have gained so persistently. He was thin as a rail, and so was Dan, their son, who took after his mother in every inner characteristic and went about from childhood with a seeking look because he never could have things the other boys had, never even time to play with them. Lemuel made it known in the boy's babyhood that he was not named Daniel, simply Dan, and the neighbors again opined that this was because it would take less ink to write it, if he had to sign a document; they furthermore asserted that his father, when he met a man named Ai, from a neighboring town, was heard to express regret that he hadn't known there was a proper name of two letters instead of three.

Lemuel himself was never called by his actual name except in direct address. He had renamed himself by a shady transaction the neighborhood had not been slow at noting, and thenceforth he carried the label of it in every slightest allusion to him. A lawyer in Sudleigh had bought several cords of wood of him, to be delivered "split and stove-wood length," which, in this case, was twelve inches; and Lemuel had sawed and split the cord-wood sticks himself, with the result that all the lawyer's sticks were slightly short. From each four-foot stick Lemuel had thrown out a "nubbins" from the end.

Little Dana West, who had gone over to buy a peck of potatoes for his mother and tagged after Mrs. Wood when she ran down to the lower barn to ask her husband what bin she should get the potatoes from, stood by while she asked her question, and then saw her eye fall on the pile of nubbins thrown to one side.

"Lemuel," said she, "what are them little chunks?"

"You take some of 'em in your apron," said Lemuel. "They'll be good to brash up the fire with."

"You don't mean," said she, "you're sawin' them off the ends o' Lawyer Trumbull's wood?"

" 'Tain't so easy as you might think to saw off twelve-inch wood by your eye," said Lemuel. "You take a handful of 'em with you when you go."

But Mrs. Wood shut her mouth like a steel trap, Dana said, and went back to the house, and she carried no handful of chunks; and a few days after that, when Lemuel had gone to market and Dana came over to see if he could get Dan to go coltsfootin', he came on Mrs. Wood kneeling by the back veranda, a half-bushel basket of the nubbins beside her. And she had loosened a slat of the lattice, and was throwing the nubbins under, fast and furious. And again her mouth was like a steel trap.

No one ever knew what Lawyer Trumbull said, when the wood was delivered; but Dan and his mother knew that Lemuel came home "mad as a hornet" and scarcely spoke for days. And there was no butter on the table for the period of his displeasure; and when Mrs. Wood brought it out, as she did three times a day, she was ordered to "take that stuff away." This continued until, as she and Dan judged, Lemuel concluded that the discount Lawyer Trumbull had caused him to accept on the wood had been worked out. But not here did Nemesis leniently pause. Dana had told his mother and his mother told her cronies,

and Lemuel, whose middle name was Ingersoll and who signed himself, in a crabbed hand, "L. I. Wood," was known thereafter as "old 'Leven-Inch Wood." Did he 5 know it? No one could say. Nobody would have taxed him with it, for he was, it was owned, a good-natured old cuss, after all, if you'd only give him the last cent.

And now old 'Leven-Inch was dying, 10 and, against his will, in the best bedroom. The doctor had ordered him in there because the little dark room where he had slept all his life had scant air even for a man in health, and not a ray of sun. 15 Lemuel was carried in protesting, and when he had been settled in the white sheets, he looked up at Mary, his wife, whose compassion for him made this crossing of his will even more terrible than 20 death itself, and said:

"Don't you s'pose you could have the bed moved whilst you take up the straw mattin'?"

"What you want the mattin' up for, 25 dear?" she asked tenderly.

The little love word she had not used to him since the first year of their marriage. She had grown satirical, in a mild, hidden way, and she would have judged 30 that he thought it wasted breath.

"That mattin' 's over forty years old," said Lemuel, "an' the doctor's boots are terrible heavy. Anyways, if Dan has to lift me, you make him come in in his stockin' 35 feet."

Two tears trickled out of his eyes, and his wife wiped them away. By long habit of living with him she knew exactly how he felt, and the things she had all their 40 lives fought in him, with a bitter resolution, seemed to her now his terrible misfortune, the bruises and stabs self-inflicted on a suffering child.

One day, when he was feeling a little 45 stronger, he called her to sit down by the bed.

"Don't you hitch your chair when you git up," he cautioned her. "There's nothin' easier in the world than marrin' a mop-50 board, an' doctor alone's enough to call for a new coat o' paint. Now I want to tell you about my will."

She begged him to settle down and take a nap. She didn't want to hear about a will. 55 But he went on:

"I've cut Dan off with a hundred dollars. That's in case he marries the Tolman gal."

"Why?" said his wife, "what makes you think he wants to marry Lyddy Tolman?" She thought the secret had been well kept. "I guess I found it out as soon as anybody," said Lemuel shrewdly. "There's that day I come from market 'fore you expected me, an' you was b'ilin' molasses candy over the stove. An' that night I see him slip out with that little checkered box in his hand, the one in the upper cupboard, and I says to myself, 'That's candy,' an' I walked a step or two arter him and see where he went."

He ended in triumph, but Mary turned her eyes from him, she felt such shame.

"Next day I had it out with him," said Lemuel. "I told him she's no more fit for a farm like this than a chiny doll."

"She's real strong, Lemuel," his wife pleaded. "She's slim-lookin', I know, but she can do her part."

"Well," said Lemuel, "be that as it may, I ain't a-goin' to take the resk. But, in case he marries Isabel Flagg within two years after my demise, then the heft o' the property goes to him. You're provided for anyways. Seemed to me at your age you wouldn't start out squanderin' things right an' left as a younger woman might."

"Why, Lemuel," said his wife, "Isabel Flagg's no more idea o' marryin' our Dan than the man in the moon. She's all took up with Sam Towle. An' as for Dan, he wouldn't look at her if she's the last woman on earth—a great strammin' creatur' that can milk ten cows an' set down to her supper afterwards an' not wash her hands."

"She's a good strong worker," said Lemuel. "Now you go off an' let me see 'f I can get me a wink o' sleep 'fore doctor comes. I've got suthin' to thrash out with him."

Mary ventured one word more.

"Lemuel," said she, "about Isabel Flagg: if you put that in your will, same's you said, you'll make Dan a laughin'-stock all over the county, an' her, too. I shouldn't wonder if it got into the Boston papers. They're terrible smart pickin' things up."

"Better laugh than cry," said Lemuel, shutting his eyes so tight that he seemed to shut his whole face with them. "I guess when Dan's as old as I be an' layin' here,—don't you set that tumbler on the table less'n you put a piece o' newspaper under it,—I guess then he'll be glad he had a father that knew enough to provide for

him, if he didn't know himself. You put that curtain up as fur's 't will go. That kind o' green's terrible easy to fade."

Lemuel had managed a comfortable nap before the doctor came. He seemed to know ways of saving his strength, Mary thought, in wonder at him, as unerringly as he knew the roads to hoarding money.

The doctor was an old man, a giant in size and still strong, with heavy black eyebrows and thick white hair. He came stooping into the low bedroom and Lemuel snapped his eyes open and greeted him: "Now, doctor, I want to ask ye one question, an' if it's yes you can look at my tongue an' feel my pulse. If it's no, ye can't. Be I goin' to git well?"

The doctor sat down and regarded him from under heavy brows.

"Well," said he, "not right off."

"Don't you beat about the bush," said Lemuel. "I won't have it. I pay you for comin' here, an' I've got a right to see 't you earn your money. Now, be I goin' to git well or be I goin' to die?"

The doctor still regarded him. He was a merciful man, but old 'Leven-Inch was, he told himself, enough to try a saint.

"Come, come," said Lemuel, "don't you set there studyin' how you can screw two dollars more out o' me. Be I goin' to git well?"

"No," said the doctor shortly. He rose to his feet. "You're not."

"Ah!" said Lemuel, as if he were supremely satisfied. "That's the talk. Now how soon be I goin' to die?"

"I don't know," said the doctor. "It might be a matter of three weeks."

"Ah!" said Lemuel again. "Then you needn't come here no more. If I was goin' to git well, I'd let ye come to see if you couldn't for'ard the v'y'ge an' git me up 'fore hayin'. But if I'm goin' to die, I guess I can die full as easy without a doctor as with one. No, no." He put his hand under the sheet. The doctor had taken a step toward the bed. "I ain't a-goin' to have my pulse felt nor no thermometers in my mouth. An' you see't you don't charge this call up to me, for you ain't done an endurin' thing an' you know it."

The doctor turned away from him, but at the door he stopped. He had to be sorry for the wretched bundle of mortality that could not take its riches with it.

"You poor old fool!" he said; "you don't

know what you're talking about. You'd better let me come in once in a while. I won't charge you for it."

"Aha!" said Lemuel, with an actual crow of delighted laughter, he felt himself so clever. "Mebbe ye wouldn't charge me whilst I'm here to chalk it up. You'd charge it to the estate. I know ye!"

And the doctor, being human, swore mildly at him and left. Mary followed him down to the gate. She had been listening and knew.

"O doctor!" she said; "I don't see what under the sun I'm goin' to do if he won't have you no more. I never can go through with it in the world."

"Don't you worry," said the doctor. He lifted his weight into the carriage and then stepped back to shake hands with her. "If he gets uneasy you just send round and I'll come in. Maybe I can take a look at him when he's asleep or something. I don't want to hound the poor old devil—Well, maybe we can do something for him when the time comes."

He drove away rather wishing he had not called Lemuel a poor old devil to his wife. But Mary understood. To her, also, he was a poor old devil in the terms of compassion she knew how to translate. Mary understood Lemuel very well after these married years. She knew how he had been tangled in the snarl of his mortality, and she hardly saw how he was to undertake this journey into the mystery he seemed to regard as lightly as a trip to market: that is, she wished he need not prepare to enter on it so unfriended and alone.

Lemuel lay there for three weeks, demanding nothing but precautions against the wear and tear of house and furniture, and speaking seldom. Mary took care of him night and day, and Dan, the big, sad-faced son, lifted him and tried to take his turn with the nursing at night. But Lemuel fought this off with a terse authority of tone.

"I ain't goin' to have him lazin' round in here, pullin' an' haulin'," he said to Mary, "lettin' the farm work git all behind-hand. Don't you fetch him in here less'n I tell you to, in case I have to give him some orders about the stock."

At the end of the three weeks, on a day when his breath had shortened more and more, until it seemed to Mary it was only a flutter in his throat, she told Dan the

time had come. He could stay out in the sitting-room, not to worry father, but presently she would need him.

Dan sat there by the west window, looking out at the orchard where the birds were loud, and even he could not tell what he was thinking. Was he sad because his father was dying, or did some tightened spring inside him unroll with a great relief at the prospect of freedom after all his life of meager living? He could not tell. All he knew was that it was a beautiful day, and his heart ached hard.

Suddenly, with a little swift rush, unlike her dragging step of the last weeks, his mother came, put a hand on his shoulder and supported herself by it. She was breathing fast. Dan turned under the touch and stared up at her. He had never seen his mother look like this, and a slow wonder came over him. Father had always been the grit in the wheels, the boulder in the path. Was it possible mother had forgotten all that because father was on his way to some other place, to stay forever? Dan was very like his mother, and suddenly, after that thought, to his renewed wonder he felt an unaccustomed choke in his own throat.

"He's gone," said she, in the instant of getting her breath. "You run right over to Ezra's an' tell him to come, quick's he can. Tell him you an' I'll help."

Dan sprang to his feet. Death was new to him and he felt it was all hurry. But his mother, glancing from the window at the sound of wheels, cried out:

"My Lord 'a' mercy! there's doctor. You run an' git him in."

The doctor had drawn up at the gate, and now he got out and hitched his horse; and he came along the path and into the sitting-room, where Dan and Mary waited for him, the tale of Lemuel's going on their faces.

"He's gone, doctor," said Mary. "I'm terrible glad you've come."

"When?" asked the doctor.

"Just now."

He went on into the bedroom, and took up Lemuel's nerveless hand.

"Yes," he said. And then, because he was on the point of adding, "Poor old devil!" he checked himself and held the flaccid wrist, and suddenly a look of curiosity and eagerness came into his face. He made himself busy about the body, and Mary felt a sick anticipation that did not seem like hope, and Dan, with that overwhelming misery of realizing the piteousness of things mortal in decay, thought how horrible it all was. The doctor turned to them, hesitated a moment, and walked past them out of the bedroom, and they followed him. He was frowning so that his black brows met.

"He's given up the ghost," he said, in a tone of unwilling conviction. "But, by thunder!" he added, as if another conviction struck him full in the face, "that man ain't dead!"

All day he stayed with them and fought against the forces of dissolution to bring Lemuel back to life. But the man resisted him. The ghost he had given up refused to come back, and at night the doctor went away for a necessary visit, disheartened. "Don't you leave him," he told them. "Don't you get Ezra Hines over here, laying him out. If there's any change, you send for me."

Old Lemuel, from being a poor old devil, of no use to himself or anybody else, as the doctor had always characterized him in his own mind when he saw him about on his ant-like delvings, had become to him his dearest concern. The passion of the scientist enveloped the poor old body, and he would have welcomed him back as the sisters welcomed Lazarus.

On the morning of the third day, while Mary sat beside the bed and Dan continued his terrible watch in the next room, old Lemuel opened his eyes. Hour after hour, while Mary sat there, she had wondered at intervals what she should do if he really did open them. She thought it probable she should scream. But now she felt no impulse of amazement or of joy. She took the covered glass from the table at her side and poised the spoon.

"I guess," she said, "I'll give you a little mite o' this." She had almost said, "Doctor told me to"; but that she discarded as likely to annoy him in any state of mind he might have kept.

Lemuel was looking directly at her with a strange glance of certainty and even brightness.

"Mary," said he, "where d' you s'pose I've been?"

Mary put back the spoon into the glass. She saw the contents trembling with her hand. But she answered him quietly with another question:

"Where have you been?"

He screwed up his eyes and smiled a little.

"You take my keys out o' my trowsis pocket," said he, "an' go an' unlock the top left-hand little drawer o' my desk. My will's in there. You bring it here to me."

Mary set down the glass and went out of the room. As she passed Dan she said to him in a steady voice he wondered at, "Your father's come to. You run over an' tell doctor an' ask him to git here quick's he can. Tell him to come in as if he happened to be goin' by."

She went on to the sitting-room, unlocked the little drawer, took out the paper, and carried it back to Lemuel.

"You tear it," said he, "right through the middle. No, don't ye do it, neither. I dunno but the law could git hold o' ye if Lawyer Trumbull happened to tell ye old 'Leven-Inch left a will, an' ask ye where 't was. You give it here an' I'll fix it."

Mary took up the tumbler and spoon again.

"You let me give you a little mite o' this," she said; and he took it willingly, his busy hands tearing slowly at the will. It took him a long time to tear it into the fragments he judged small enough, and half way through the task he bade Mary bring a newspaper, so that he might know no fragments had escaped him. And there in a few minutes the doctor found him lying placidly on the pillows, a little heap of torn paper under his hovering palms.

Old Lemuel put out his hand. "You can feel my pulse if you want to," he said, "an' then you can give me suthin' to keep me goin' a spell. I've got consid'able to do."

"You've had a good long sleep," said the doctor speciously. "Feel stronger for it, don't you?"

"I ain't been asleep," said Lemuel, with a queer little smile neither Mary nor the doctor had seen on his face before.

"Well, I s'pose," said the doctor jocosely, his hand on the sinewy old wrist, "I s'pose you'll be telling us next you've heard every word that's been said in this room, since you dropped off."

"No," said Lemuel. "I ain't been here."

"Where have you been?"

Again Lemuel smiled and screwed up his eyes. But he opened them at once.

"You bear witness, doctor," said he, "these here papers on my chist is what's left o' my will. I tore it up. I tore it up myself. There ain't nobody else had the leastest thing to do with it. Now, you take them papers an' go out an' put 'em in the kitchen stove."

And the doctor, not being troubled by imaginative hypotheses of the legality of the act, did it. When Lemuel had been made comfortable,—and for the first time Mary could remember he accepted comfort with an alert responsiveness, objecting only to spoon victuals as not sustaining enough for a man with work before him,— the doctor went away, and Lemuel, who was supposed now to settle down to sleep, put his hand on Mary's wrist.

"You se' down here side o' me," he bade her, "an' we'll plan it all out. I've got consid'able to do."

Mary sat down and he kept his hand on her wrist.

"What day's to-day?" he asked her.

"Sunday."

"That's what I thought. Well, you can't do nothin' 'fore Monday. Now Tuesday arternoon I want you should give a party."

"A party?" said Mary; and in her wonder she felt as if, though she had received him quietly when he came back, the moment was perhaps here when she must make some outcry from the strangeness of it all. "What kind of a party?"

"A tea-party," said Lemuel, smacking his lips. "Ain't that 'bout the only kind there is this season o' the year?"

"Why," said Mary, and then paused. She had been about to say, "You never would let me have a party. It cost too much." But she ended, "I don't think it's any time for a party, you sick an' all."

"What kind o' cake was that your mother used to stir up," said Lemuel, "an' we used to have it out on the front porch with lemonade when I come courtin' you?"

"One-two-three-four," said Mary, "with raisins in it an' citron."

"Terrible nice cake that was," said Lemuel. "Monday you make up a lot of it; cookies, too, an' sugar ginger-bread. Ain't you got mother's cooky-cutters, leaf-patterns an' hearts an' rounds?"

"But Lemuel," said she, "them things are terrible expensive, high as everything is now."

She saw no way of stopping him but that of appealing to his dearest vice.

"You can bile a ham," said he, luxuriating in his flights. "You do as I tell ye.

If you don't help me out, I dunno how I shall git through with it."

He looked worried now, and this frightened her.

"Course I'll help you out, Lemuel," she said. "Who do you want to your party?"

"Everybody in the neighborhood," said Lemuel, "old an' young. I'd ruther have the whole county, but there ain't no time. Plague take it all! why didn't I know sooner about there bein' no time. But the neighborhood I guess we can manage. You tell Dan to fix up some trestles an' boards on em' out under the old elm. There'll be too many to eat indoor."

"Lemuel," said his wife, "I dunno how I can. I don't b'lieve I could carry it through. An' if I could, I guess every-body'd think I was out o' my head, you sick an' all."

Lemuel considered for a moment.

"Well, then," said he, "you might scare up some kind of a reason for 't. Dan could git married, if he felt like it, an' I kinder think he does. There's that gal he carried the candy to in the checkered box. You say she's a likely gal. I dunno how long 't'll take him to git his license, as the law directs; but you tell him to harness up an' ask the gal, an' ride right off an' see to it this arternoon."

Mary felt the sickness of apprehension born out of the unknown.

"But Lemuel," she said, "folks can't git married like that, all of a whew. Even if they've talked it over,—an' I s'pose they have,—she ain't begun to think o' gittin' her clo'es."

"Then let her turn to an git 'em now," said Lemuel, "'fore she's a day older. You gi' me my bank-book, out o' that same drawer, an' I'll sign an order so's Dan can draw out as much as he needs—the whole business, if he wants to. You take the gal over to Sudleigh an' fit her out. An' while you're about it, you git suthin' for yourself, too. Kind of a stiff silk, same's your mother used to wear, the sort that'll stand alone."

"I don't want—" said Mary; but her voice failed her and she went blindly out of the room.

Lemuel called after her:

"An' you tell him to git his name se' down Dan'el, in the license, same as his gran'ther's. I al'ays mistrusted he never took to bein' called Dan."

Mary hesitated there by the door, her face turned from him.

"Lemuel," she said, "it's jest as I told you; I ain't got the heart to set out makin' cake. I dunno's I've got the strength, neither. I've been terrible worried about you, an' it's told on me. I never should ha' brought it up, never in the world, only I dunno how I can, Lemuel, I dunno how I can."

"Course you can't," said Lemuel, jovially. "You hire Mis' Buell an' Nancy Towle to come in an' do the heft on 't. Lay the things out afore 'em, the eggs an' the butter an' the citron an' raisins,"—Mary never forgot the childlike delight of his tone while he enumerated these,—"an' give 'em the receipts an' tell 'em to go ahead, an' then you come in here an' set with me. Mis' Buell's a terrible extravagant cook. She uses tea by the handful, an' I heard the thrashers say, that week she boarded 'em, her pie-crust'd melt in your mouth."

Then something in Mary's bowed shoulders seemed to speak to him, and he added, in a softened tone she had not heard from him since the days of their courtship: "But she can't hold a candle to you, Mary. Any woman can cook if you give 'em things enough to do with, but there's one or two that can git pie off a rock, as ye might say. I ain't seen but one, but mebbe there's another some'er's, same's there's more'n one pea in a pod. They al'ays set out suthin' to make your mouth water, no matter 'f you do keep 'em sailin' nigh the wind."

"Lemuel," said his wife. She was troubled beyond measure by this incursion into the delights of the palate. "Be you hungry?"

Lemuel laughed. "Hungry?" said he. "Lor', no, I guess I ain't. All I want is to have doctor see 't I have suthin' to keep me up, what time I'm here."

The doctor came in that afternoon and found him very much alive. Mary waylaid him at the gate and besought him to discourage the strange project of the party, or the wedding, as it might prove. He listened to her gravely, nodding from time to time, but when she asked him: "Doctor, what'd he mean by sayin' to me, that first minute he opened his eyes, 'Mary, where d'you s'pose I've been?'"

"Well," said the doctor, looking at her sharply, "where d'you suppose he'd been? Didn't he tell you? I s'pose you asked him."

"Oh, yes, I asked him, but he never said a word—only kinder screwed up his eyes an' laughed. No, he didn't really laugh, only looked as if he could if he'd a mind to. As if he knew suthin' he didn't think best to tell."

"Mary," said the doctor, and made it all the more serious by using her Christian name, "I shouldn't worry him, if I were you, by going against his little fancies. If he wanted anything, I should let him have it. And if he says any more about where he's been, I hope you'll remember it just as it was, and, if you think you can't remember it, put it down on paper. I'd like mighty well to know where he's been."

And it seemed as if the doctor had not only been fascinated by the problem of persuading old Lemuel back to this earth, but was doubly attracted, now he had him alive. He came in once, and sometimes twice, a day, and they talked, old Lemuel carrying on his side of it as if he were in health; only not as he would have done before he went away. The doctor reminded him at the outset that these were not professional visits: there would be no fee. But Lemuel smiled at him shrewdly and said:—

"Charge it up! charge it up! the estate's good for it."

The doctor never questioned him about his mysterious going away, and Lemuel never once referred to it. Mary, dazed and unremonstrating, found herself putting the party through. She let Lemuel, lying there in his bed, plan the manner of it, and she and Dan carried it out. Mrs. Buell came and cooked, and Nancy helped her, and there was a rich odor of good things about the house.

Dan walked as one in a dream. He had obeyed his father implicitly, and Lydia Tolman had allowed herself to be caught up on the wings of their will, and her mother, dazed by the strangeness of it all, drove over to Sudleigh with her and bought her white garments and a wedding dress.

It was the day before the wedding, when the house was smelling of meats and spices and there was a vague air of excitement, not only through its rooms, but through all the neighborhood as well, that Lemuel demanded to be bolstered up in bed.

"I want to set up on end a spell," said he. And Dan managed it without trouble. "There," said Lemuel, "now you fetch me the Bible."

Mary did it, wondering. She came back with the great family Bible in her hand.

"Don't you think," she said, hesitatingly, because it was an implication of his extremity, "you better let me read some out loud? It's kinder heavy to hold."

"No," said Lemuel briskly, "I don't want no readin'. I ain't got time. I want to look up suthin'. You bring me a pencil."

So she left him there, with the Bible propped against his knees, frowning through his spectacles, and peering while he turned page after page. This was in the morning, and at three o'clock in the afternoon he had found what he sought.

"Where's Dan?" he called to Mary, who was making herself busy in the next room, to be near him. "You tell him to come here."

In a few minutes Dan came slouching in. He was timid before his father, and especially since Lemuel had come back so strangely changed. As he went past his mother, through the outer room, she thought what a beautiful young man he was, with the strength and sadness of his face and his wonderful frame, made to work and also to beguile the eye with its ease and suppleness. He came in and stood looking down at his father in a pathetic distrust and questioning, and with this a great compassion.

"What is it, father?" he asked.

"You listen to this," said Lemuel, his lean forefinger on the page. "I've had a terrible time findin' it, but I knew 'twas some'r's here. Now you listen. 'Remember now thy Creator in the days of thy youth.'" He read it slowly with emphasis and a certain delight—either in the verse or in his own cleverness in finding it. Then he read it again. "I've put a line under it," he said, "an' I'm goin' to put in a mark, too, so's you can turn to it. You hand me that piece o' newspaper there on the bureau. I'll lay that in."

Dan gave him the paper, and he laid it carefully between the pages and closed the book.

"There," said he, "you can carry this off."

"Don't you want I should leave it so's you can have some read—"

Dan paused there. His father's bright eyes made him feel as if he had said something strangely beside the question.

"No," said Lemuel alertly, "I'm through with it. Look here," he called when Dan, carrying the Bible, had reached the door, "d'you buy yourself a weddin' suit?"

Dan turned and looked at him. His young face grew stern. Was his father going to take it all back?

"Yes," he said, "I did."

"That's right," said Lemuel, chuckling. "That's right. What color?"

"Blue."

"Ha! that's jest what I'd ha' picked out myself. Ye can't do better'n blue."

The day of the party, or the wedding, —they hardly knew which to call it,— was set for Thursday; not quite so soon as Lemuel had planned, because there was so much to do. But when the sun rose fresh from lightest morning clouds and shone divinely, the house was in holiday dress, and Lemuel, from his bedroom, gave out orders and emanated cheer. Mary wanted the ceremony in the front room so that he could look on from his open door and be in a manner present; but Lemuel forbade it, and ordered that it should be out under the old elm. And he was to be left alone, to rest, he said speciously, though with the gleam in his eye that made Mary and Dan suspect he was laughing at them, and after it they were to sing,—"Coronation," for one,— and then they were to dance. Ezra Hines was to play his fiddle.

It all fell out exactly as Lemuel had planned. There was merry-making and much eating, and everybody forgot how strange it all was, with old 'Leven-Inch lying in the house there, perhaps getting well and perhaps near his end, and let themselves go in a gay abandon. And when the party was over, the little bride came shyly in to let Lemuel see her in her white dress, and he said to her—:

"You're as pretty as a picter in them frill-de-dills—though you ain't a mite handsomer—nor so handsome—as Mary was when she walked out a bride."

Lydia was a little frightened, because this must, after all, be old 'Leven-Inch; but it looked like a man she had never seen, and she stepped up to him and laid her hand timidly on his and ran away.

The next morning Lemuel seemed quite strong and untired, but he said to Mary, when she came in at sunrise—:

"You tell Dan to kinder stay round this forenoon. He can be takin' down the tables an' rakin' up the clutter if there is any."

"Don't you feel so well?" she asked. "You think you better see doctor?"

"No," said Lemuel, "I don't want no doctor. You have your breakfast an' then you se' down here side o' me an' stay a spell. 'T won't be long."

Mary hurried through her breakfast and came back to him. She felt in haste, as if there was something to be asked him and she must ask it and make sure. Then she thought what it was.

"Lemuel," said she, "what was it you meant when you said, 'Where do you s'pose I've been?'"

Lemuel turned his head on the pillow and smiled at her. He looked very secretive and knowing, but not at that moment, she thought with a kind of terror, old. The marks of his hard life and his penury had fallen away from him and he was young.

"You let me take hold o' your hand," said he. "So. There, that's right."

He shut his eyes, and while she watched him his face seemed to her to grow more secretive and certainly more still. In an hour, perhaps, the doctor came in and she looked up at him.

"Why," said he, without a pause to make sure of it, "he's gone!"

"But, doctor," said Mary, with a cry, "you know before—"

"No," said the doctor; "this time he's gone for good."

The week after his father was buried, Dan went into the front room by himself and opened the Bible where his father had put the mark. He thought he would do it every week while he lived, but he had not told anybody. His father was only one he wished he could tell, and somehow he felt his father knew. And when he was about to close the book, it fell open at the Family Record, and under the deaths he saw a new entry, and stared at it until he could bear his own solitary discovery of it no longer and went to the door and called—:

"Mother! Lyddy! you come here."

They came hurrying, and he showed them the record. It was in pencil in his father's crabbed hand.

"He put that down there himself, the day before the weddin'," said Dan. "An' that was the day before his death."

"Yes," said his mother, "he put it down, date an' all, day o' the month an' day o' the week."

"Yes," said Lyddy, in awe, peering at the record, her pretty head against Dan's arm to bring her nearer, but really because she liked it there.

"O Dan'el," said his mother, in a great burst of yearning hope, "where do you s'pose he'd been?"

XXXIX

EDITH WHARTON (1862–   )

To classify Edith Wharton as a disciple of Henry James is conventional, yet it is unavoidable if one is to weigh critically her work. Like James she has looked upon life from the patrician standpoint. Born in New York City in a family of wealth and distinctive traditions, she was educated by private tutors both at home and abroad, with art, architecture, literature,—everything cultural—constantly a part of her living and thinking. Much of her early life she spent in Italy and in France: none of our writers has been more cosmopolitan. Like Henry James, she was much influenced by the artistic ideals of France. James, too, was a veritable master for her: for weeks at a time he was a guest at her home in France and the correspondence between them when he was away, as presented in the volume edited by William James, is distinctive and illuminating.

It is natural, then, that her conception of the short story should be French rather than American. In France, she declares, "it was made a neat thing," a thing of finished art. The Russians added depth and feeling. "The result has been to give to the short story, as French and Russian art have combined to shape it, great closeness of texture with profundity of form. Instead of a loose web spread over the surface of life they have made it, at its best, a shaft driven straight into the heart of human experience."

Clearly does this describe her own art. When at her best, as in her long short stories, "Madame de Treymes" and "Ethan Frome," she creates situations that in their grip and their inevitableness and their haunting power are like Greek tragedy, but, like James, she is repressed, finished, brilliant, Gallic in her lightness of touch. She is a scientist viewing life, but like George Eliot she views it as a woman in whom science has not extinguished pity and even passion.

In the opinion of Mrs. Wharton the first requirement of the short story is the winning of the reader to "an immediate sense of security." In order to lead him where the writer wills he must be most carefully handled at the start. "The next rule of the game is to avoid distracting and splintering up his attention." "There must be unity and totality of impression," to use Poe's term. In the short story this is not easy to gain. "Situation is the main concern of the short story; character of the novel; and it follows that the effect produced by the short story depends entirely on its form, or presentation." The maker of this *genre*, therefore, must be an artist knowing at every moment what he is accomplishing, exceedingly careful with opening "exposition" and with closing effects, avoiding with watchfulness the ever-present temptation "to make a mere sketch of the episode selected" or else to overdo a series of minor details.

All of the fifty-two or more short stories that Mrs. Wharton has written have stood with refinement and restraint and artistic finish upon moral bases and upon a Hawthorne-like knowledge of the human heart. "To call her a feminine Henry James is perhaps fanciful, is possibly ludicrous, but the comparison certainly works no injustice to Henry James and certainly it does not attribute too much to Mrs. Wharton."

THE CHOICE *

I

Stilling, that night after dinner, had surpassed himself. He always did, Wrayford reflected, when the small fry from Highfield came to dine. He, Cobham Stilling, who had to find his bearings, keep to his level, in the big, heedless, oppressive

* From *Xingu. and Other Stories.* 1916. Published by arrangement with Charles Scribner's Sons, owners of the copyright.

world of New York, dilated and grew vast in the congenial medium of Highfield. The Red House was the biggest house of the Highfield summer colony, as Cobham Stilling was its biggest man. No one else within a radius of a hundred miles (on a conservative estimate) had as many horses, as many greenhouses, as many servants, and assuredly no one else had two motors, or a motor-boat for the lake.

The motor-boat was Stilling's latest hobby, and he rode—or sailed—it in and out of the conversation all the evening, to the obvious edification of every one present save his wife and his visitor, Austin Wrayford. The interest of the latter two, who, from opposite ends of the drawing-room, exchanged a fleeting glance when Stilling again launched his craft on the thin current of the talk—the interest of Mrs. Stilling and Wrayford, had already lost its edge by protracted conversational contact with the subject.

But the dinner-guests—the Rector, Mr. Swordsley, and Mrs. Swordsley, Lucy and Agnes Granger and their brother Addison, and young Jack Emmerton from Harvard —were all, for divers reasons, stirred to the proper pitch of feeling. Mr. Swordsley, no doubt, was saying to himself: "If my good parishioner here can afford to buy a motor-boat, in addition to all the other expenditures which an establishment like this must entail, I certainly need not scruple to appeal to him again for a contribution toward our Galahad Club." The Granger girls, meanwhile, were evoking visions of lakeside picnics, not unadorned with the presence of young Mr. Emmerton; while that youth himself speculated as to whether his affable host would let him, when he came back on his next vacation, "learn to run the thing himself"; and Mr. Addison Granger, the elderly bachelor brother of the volatile Lucy and Agnes, mentally formulated the precise phrase in which, in his next letter to his cousin Professor Spildyke of the University of East Latmos, he should allude to "our last delightful trip in my old friend Cobham Stilling's ten-thousand-dollar motor-launch"—for East Latmos was still in that primitive stage of social culture on which such figures impinge.

Isabel Stilling, sitting beside Mrs. Swordsley, her head slightly bent above the needlework with which, on such occasions, it was her old-fashioned habit to be engaged—Isabel also had doubtless her reflections to make. As Wrayford leaned back in his corner, and looked at her across the bright, flower-filled drawing-room, he noted first of all—for the hundredth time —the flexible play of her hands above the embroidery-frame, the shadow of the dusky, wavy hair on her forehead, the tired droop of the lids over her somewhat full gray eyes. He noted this, taking in unconsciously, at the same time, the indescribable quality in her attitude, in the fall of

her dress and the turn of her head, that set her, for him, in a separate world; then he said to himself: "She's certainly thinking 'Where on earth will he get the money to pay for it?'"

But at the same moment, from his inevitable position on the hearth-rug, cigar in mouth, his hands in his waistcoat pockets, Stilling was impressively perorating.

"I said, 'If I have the thing at all, I want the best that can be got.' That's my way, you know, Swordsley; I suppose I'm what you'd call fastidious. Always was, about everything, from cigars to wom-"— his eye met the apprehensive glance of Mrs. Swordsley, who looked, in evening dress, like her husband with his clerical coat cut slightly lower—"so I said, 'If I have the thing at all, I want the best that can be got.' Nothing makeshift for me, no second-best. I never cared for the cheap and showy. I always say frankly to a man, 'If you can't give me a first-rate cigar, for the Lord's sake, let me smoke my own.' Well, if you want my standards, you can't buy a thing in a minute. You must look round, compare, select. I found there were lots of motor-boats on the market, just as there's lots of stuff called champagne. But I said to myself, 'Ten to one there's only one fit to buy, just as there's only one champagne fit for a gentleman to drink.' Argued like a lawyer, eh, Austin?" He tossed this jovially toward Wrayford. "Take me for one of your own trade, wouldn't you? Well, I'm not such a fool as I look. I suppose you fellows who are tied to the treadmill,—oh, excuse me, Swordsley, but work's work, isn't it?—I suppose you think a man like me has nothing to do but take it easy—loll through life like a woman. By George, sir, I'd like either of you to see the time it takes—I won't say the brains—but just the *time* it takes to pick out a good motor-boat. Why, I went—"

Mrs. Stilling set her embroidery-frame noiselessly on the low table at her side, and turned her head toward Wrayford. "Would you mind ringing for the tray?"

The interruption helped Mrs. Swordsley to waver to her feet. "I think we really ought to be going; my husband has an early service to-morrow."

Her host sounded an immediate protest. "Going already? Nothing of the sort! Why, the night's still young, as the poet says. Long way from here to the rectory? Nonsense! In our little twenty-horse motor we do it in five minutes—don't we, Belle? Ah, you're walking, to be sure—" Stilling's indulgent gesture seemed to concede that, in such a case, allowances must be made, and that he was the last man not to make them. "Well, then, Swordsley—" He held out a thick, red hand that seemed to exude beneficence, and the clergyman, pressing it, ventured to murmur a suggestion.

"What, that Galahad Club again? Why, I thought my wife— Isabel, didn't we— No? Well, it must have been my mother, then. And of course, you know, anything my good mother gives is—well—virtually— You haven't asked her? Sure? I could have sworn; I get so many of these appeals. And in these times, you know, we have to go cautiously. I'm sure you recognize that yourself, Swordsley. With my obligations—here now, to show you don't bear malice, have a brandy and soda before you go. Nonsense, man! This brandy isn't liquor; it's *liqueur*. I picked it up last year in London—last of a famous lot from Lord St. Oswyn's cellar. Laid down here, it stood me at— Eh?" he broke off as his wife moved toward him. "Ah, yes, of course. Miss Lucy, Miss Agnes—a drop of soda-water? Look here, Addison, *you* won't refuse my tipple, I know. Well, take a cigar, at any rate, Swordsley. And, by the way, I'm afraid you'll have to go round the long way by the avenue to-night. Sorry, Mrs. Swordsley, but I forgot to tell them to leave the gate on the lane unlocked. Well, it's a jolly night, and I daresay you won't mind the extra turn along the lake. And, by Jove! if the moon's out, you can get a glimpse of the motor-boat as you turn the point. She's moored just out beyond our boat-house; and it's a privilege to look at her, I can tell you!"

The dispersal of the remaining guests carried Stilling out into the hall, where his pleasantries echoed genially under the oak rafters while the Granger girls were being muffled for the drive and the carriages summoned from the stables.

By a common impulse Mrs. Stilling and Wrayford had moved together toward the hearth, which was masked from the door into the hall by a tall screen of lacquer. Wrayford leaned his elbow against the chimney-piece, and Mrs. Stilling stood motionless beside him, her clasped hands hanging down before her. The rose on her breast stirred slightly.

"Have you any more work to do with him to-night?" she asked below her breath.

Wrayford shook his head. "We wound it all up before dinner. He doesn't want to talk about it any more than he can help."

"It's so bad?"

"No; but he's got to pull up."

She paused, looking down at her clasped hands. He listened a moment, catching Stilling's farewell shout; then he changed his position slightly, and laid his hand on her arm.

"In an hour?"

She made a faint motion of assent.

"I'll tell you all about it then. The key's in the usual place?"

She nodded again, and walked away with her long, drifting motion as her husband came in from the hall. He went up to the tray, and poured himself a tall glass of brandy and soda.

"The weather's turning queer—black as pitch out now. I hope the Swordsleys won't walk into the lake—involuntary immersion, eh? He'd come out a Baptist, I suppose. What'd the Bishop do in such a case? There's a problem for a lawyer, my boy!"

He clapped Wrayford resoundingly on the thin shoulder and then walked over to his wife, who was gathering up her embroidery silks and dropping them into an old-fashioned work-bag. Stilling took her by the arms and swung her playfully about so that she faced the lamplight.

"What's the matter with you to-night?"

"The matter?" she echoed, blushing a little, and standing very erect in her desire not to appear to shrink from his touch.

"You never opened your lips. Left me the whole job of entertaining those blessed people. Didn't she, Austin?"

Wrayford laughed and lighted a cigarette. "She wasn't quite up to the mark."

"There! You see even Austin noticed it. What's the matter? Aren't they good enough for you? I don't pretend they're particularly exciting; but, hang it! I like to ask them here—I like to give pleasure."

"I didn't mean to be dull," said Isabel, appealingly.

"Well, you must learn to make an effort. Don't treat people as if they weren't in the room just because they don't happen to amuse you. Do you know what they'll think? They'll think it's because you've got a bigger house and more cash. Shall I tell you something? My mother said she'd noticed the same thing in you lately. She said she sometimes felt you looked down on her for living in a small house. Oh, she was half joking, of course; but you see you do give people that impression. I can't understand treating any one in that way. The more I have myself, the more I want to make other people happy."

Isabel gently freed herself and laid the work-bag on her embroidery-frame. "I have a headache; perhaps that made me stupid. I'm going to bed." She turned toward Wrayford and held out her hand. "Good night."

"Good night," he answered, opening the door for her.

When he turned back into the room, his host was pouring himself a third glass of brandy and soda.

"Here, have a nip? Gad, I need it badly, after the shaking up you gave me this afternoon." Stilling gave a short laugh, and carried his glass to the hearth, where he took up his usual commanding position. "Why the deuce don't you drink something, Austin? You look as glum as Isabel. One would think *you* were the chap that had been hit."

Wrayford threw himself into the chair from which Mrs. Stilling had lately risen. It was the one she habitually sat in, and to his fancy a faint scent of her always clung to it. He leaned back and looked up at Stilling.

"Want a cigar?" the latter continued. "Shall we go into the den and smoke?"

Wrayford hesitated. "If there's anything more you want to ask me about—"

"Gad, no! I had full measure and running over this afternoon. The deuce of it is, I don't see where the money's all gone to. Luckily I've got plenty of nerve; I'm not the kind of man to sit down and snivel because he's been touched in Wall Street."

Wrayford rose again. "Then, if you don't want me, I think I'll go up to my room and put some finishing touches to a brief before I turn in. I must get back to town to-morrow afternoon."

"All right, then." Stilling set down his empty glass, and held out his hand with a tinge of alacrity. "Good night, old man."

They shook hands, and Wrayford moved toward the door.

"I say, Austin—stop a minute!" his host called after him.

Wrayford turned, and the two men faced each other across the hearth-rug. Stilling's eyes shifted uneasily in his flushed face.

"There's one thing more you *can* do for me, like a good chap, before you go. Tell Isabel about that loan; explain to her she's got to sign a note for it."

Wrayford, in his turn, flushed slightly. "You want *me* to tell her?"

"Hang it! I'm soft-hearted—that's the worst of me." Stilling moved toward the tray, and lifted the brandy decanter. "And she'll take it better from you; she'll *have* to take it from you. She's proud. You can take her out for a row to-morrow morning—you can take her out in the motor-launch, if you like. I meant to have a spin in it myself in the morning; but if you'll tell her—"

Wrayford hesitated. "All right. I'll tell her."

"Thanks a lot, my dear fellow. And you'll make her see it wasn't my fault, eh? Women are awfully vague about money, and if you appear to back me up, you know—"

Wrayford nodded. "As you please. Good night."

"Good night. Here, Austin—there's just one more thing. You needn't say anything to Isabel about the other business—I mean my mother's securities."

"Ah?" said Wrayford.

Stilling shifted from one foot to the other. "I'd rather put that to the old lady myself. I can make it clear to her. She idolizes me, you know—and, hang it! I've got a good record. Up to now, I mean. My mother's been in clover since I married; I may say she's been my first thought. And I don't want her to hear of this from Isabel. Isabel's a little harsh at times—and of course this isn't going to make her any easier to live with."

"Very well," Wrayford assented.

Stilling, with a look of relief, walked toward the window which opened on the terrace. "Gad! what a queer night! Hot as the kitchen-range. Shouldn't wonder if we had a squall before morning. I wonder if that infernal skipper took in the launch's awnings before he went home."

Wrayford paused a moment in the doorway. "Yes, I saw him do it. She's shipshape for the night."

"Good! That saves me a run down to the shore." Stilling strolled back into the room, whistling cheerfully.

"Good night then," said Wrayford.

"Good night, old man. You'll tell her?"
"I'll tell her," Wrayford answered from the threshold.

"And mum about my mother!" his host called after him.

II

The darkness had thinned a little when Wrayford scrambled down the steep path to the shore. Though the air was heavy, the threat of a storm seemed to have vanished, and now and then the moon's edge showed above a torn slope of cloud.

But in the densely massed shrubbery about the boat-house the night was still black, and Wrayford had to strike a match before he could find the lock and insert his key. He left the door unlatched, and groped his way in. How often he had crept into this warm pine-scented obscurity, guiding himself cautiously by the edge of the bench along the side wall, and hearing the stealthy lap of water through the gaps in the floor-ing! He knew just where one had to duck one's head to avoid the two canoes swung from the rafters, and just where to put his hand on the latch of the door that led to the balcony above the lake.

The boat-house represented one of Still-ing's abandoned whims. He had built it some seven years before, and for a time it had been the scene of incessant nautical exploits. Stilling had rowed, sailed, paddled indefatigably, and all Highfield had been impressed to bear him company and admire his versatility. Then motors had come in, and he had forsaken aquatic sports for the guidance of the flying chariot. The canoes of birch-bark and canvas had been hoisted to the roof, the little sail-boat had rotted at her moorings, and the movable floor of the boat-house, ingeniously contrived to slide back on noiseless runners, had lain undisturbed through several seasons. Even the key of the boat-house had been mis-laid,—by Isabel's fault, her husband as-serted,—and the locksmith had to be called in to make a new one when the purchase of the motor-boat made the lake once more the center of Stilling's activity.

As Wrayford entered he noticed that a strange oily odor overpowered the usual scent of dry pine-wood; and at the next step his foot struck an object that rolled noisily across the boards. He lighted a match, and found he had overturned a can of grease which the boatman had no doubt been using to oil the runners of the sliding-floor.

Wrayford felt his way down the length of the boat-house, and softly opening the balcony door, looked out on the lake. A few yards off the launch lay motionless in the veiled moonlight; and just below him, on the black water, he saw the dim outline of the skiff which Stilling used to paddle out to her. The silence was so intense that Wrayford fancied he heard a faint rustling in the shrubbery on the high bank behind the boat-house, and the crackle of gravel on the path descending to it.

He closed the door again and turned back; and as he did so the other door, on the land-side, swung inward, and a figure darkened the dim opening. Just enough light entered through the round holes above the respective doors to reveal it as Mrs. Stilling's cloaked outline, and to guide her to him as he advanced. But be-fore they met she stumbled and gave a little cry.

"What is it?" he exclaimed, springing toward her.

"My foot caught; the floor seemed to give way under me. Ah, of course—" She bent down in the darkness— "I saw the men oiling it this morning."

Wrayford caught her to him. "Be care-ful, darling! It might be dangerous if it slid too easily. The water's deep under here."

"Yes; the water's very deep. I some-times wish—" She leaned against him with-out finishing her sentence, and he tight-ened his arms about her.

"Hush!" he whispered, his lips on her hair.

Suddenly she threw back her head and seemed to listen.

"What's the matter?" he asked, listening also. "What did you hear?"

"I don't know." He felt her trembling. "I'm not sure this place is as safe as it used to be—"

Wrayford held her to him reassuringly. "But the boatman sleeps down at the vil-lage; and who else should come here at this hour?"

"My husband might. He thinks of noth-ing but the launch."

"He won't to-night, for I told him I'd seen the skipper roll up the awning, and put the launch shipshape, and that satis-fied him."

"Ah, he did think of coming, then?"

"Only for a minute, when the sky looked so black half an hour ago, and he was afraid of a squall. It's clearing now, and there's no danger."

He drew her down on the bench, and they sat a moment or two in silence, her hands in his. Then she said wearily: "You'd better tell me."

Wrayford gave a faint laugh. "Yes, I suppose I had. In fact, he asked me to."

"He asked you to?"

"Yes."

She sounded a sharp note of contempt. "The coward! he's afraid!"

Wrayford made no reply, and she went on: "*I'm* not. Tell me everything, please."

"Well, he's chucked away a pretty big sum again—"

"How has he done it?"

"He says he doesn't know. He's been speculating, I suppose. The madness of making him your trustee!"

She drew her hands away quickly. "You know why I did it. When we married I didn't want to put him in the false position of the man who accepts everything; I wanted people to think the money was partly his."

"I don't know what you've made *people* think; but you've been eminently successful in one respect. *He* thinks it's his—and he loses it as if it were."

She shivered a little, drawing her cloak closer. "There are worse things. Go on."

"Isabel!" He bent over her. "Give me your hand again." He lifted it and laid a long kiss on it.

"What was it—exactly—that he wished you to tell me?" she asked.

"That you've got to sign another promissory note—for fifty thousand this time."

She drew a deep breath. "Is that all?"

Wrayford hesitated; then he said: "Yes —for the present."

She sat motionless, her head bent, her hand resting passively in his.

He leaned nearer. "What did you mean, just now, by worse things?"

She paused a moment. "Haven't you noticed that he's been drinking a great deal lately?"

"Yes; I've noticed."

They were both silent again; then Wrayford said with sudden vehemence: "And *yet* you won't—"

"Won't?"

"Put an end to it. Good God! Save what's left of your life."

She made no answer, and in the deep stillness the *throb-throb* of the water underneath them was like the anxious beat of a heart.

"Isabel—" Wrayford murmured. He bent over to kiss her, and felt the tears on her face. "Isabel! I can't stand it! Listen to me—"

She interrupted him. "No; no. I've thought of everything. There's the boy— the boy's fond of him. He's not a bad father."

"Except in the trifling matter of ruining his son."

"And there's his poor old mother. He's a good son, at any rate; he's never hurt *her*. And I know her. If I left him she'd never touch a penny. What she has of her own is not enough to live on; and how could *he* provide for her? If I put him out of doors, I should be putting his mother out, too—out of the little house she's so happy in."

"But surely you could arrange—there are always ways."

"Not for her! She's proud. And then she believes in him. Lots of people believe in him, you know. It would kill her if she ever found out."

Wrayford made an impatient movement: "It will kill you, if you stay with him to prevent her finding out."

She turned toward him and laid her other hand on his. "Not while I have you."

"Have me? In this way?" he echoed with an exasperated laugh.

"In any way."

"My poor girl—poor child!"

She drew back from him suddenly, with a quick movement of fear. "You mean that *you'll* grow tired—your patience will give out soon?"

He answered her only by saying: "My poor Isabel!"

But she went on insistently: "Don't you suppose I've thought of that—foreseen it?"

"Well—and then?" he exclaimed with sudden passion.

"I've accepted that, too," she said.

He dropped her hands with a despairing gesture. "Then, indeed, I waste my breath!"

She made no answer, and for a time they sat silent, side by side, but with a space between. At length he asked in a contrite voice: "You're not crying, Isabel?"

"No."

"I can't see your face, it's grown so dark again."

"Yes. I hadn't noticed. The storm must be coming, after all." She made a motion as if to rise.

He drew close, and put his arm about her again. "Don't leave me yet, dear! You know I must go to-morrow." He broke off with a laugh. "I'm to break the news to you to-morrow morning, by the way; I'm to take you out in the motor-launch and break it to you." He dropped her hands and stood up. "Good God! How can I go away and leave you here alone with him?"

"You've done it often before."

"Yes; but each time it's more damnable. And then I've always had a hope—"

"A hope?" She rose also. "Give it up! Give it up!" she moaned.

"You've none, then, yourself?"

She was silent, drawing the folds of her cloak about her.

"None—none?" he insisted.

"Only one," she broke out passionately. He bent over and sought for her in the darkness. "What is it, my dearest? What is it?"

"Don't touch me! That he may die!" she shuddered back.

He dropped his hands, and they drew apart instinctively, hearing each other's quick breathing through the obscurity.

"*You* wish that sometimes, too?" he said at length in a low voice.

"Sometimes? I wish it always—every day, every hour, every moment!" She paused, and then let the quivering words break out. "You'd better know it; you'd better know the worst of me. I'm not the saint you suppose; the duty I do is poisoned by the thoughts I think. Day by day, hour by hour, I wish him dead. When he goes out I pray for something to happen; when he comes back I say to myself: 'Are you here again?' When I hear of people being killed in accidents I think: 'Why wasn't he there?' When I read the death-notices in the paper I say: 'So-and-so was just his age.' When I see him taking such care of his health and his diet—as he does, you know, except when he gets reckless and begins to drink too much—when I see him exercising and resting, and eating only certain things, and weighing himself, and feeling his muscles, and boasting that he hasn't gained a pound, I think of the men who die from overwork, who throw their lives away for some big ob-

ject, and I say to myself: 'What can kill a man who thinks only of himself?' And night after night I keep myself from going to sleep for fear I may dream that he's dead. When I dream that, and wake and find him there, it's worse than ever —and my thoughts are worse than ever, too!"

She broke off on a stifled sob, and the *thump-thump* of the water under the floor was like the beat of a loud, rebellious heart.

"There, you know the truth! Is it too bad for you?"

He answered in a low voice, as if unconscious of her question: "Such things do sometimes happen, you know."

"Do they?" She laughed. "Yes, I've seen it happen—in happy marriages!"

They were silent again, not approaching each other. Abruptly Isabel turned, feeling her way toward the door. As she did so, the profound stillness of the night was broken by the sound of a man's voice, caroling out somewhat unsteadily the refrain of a music-hall song.

The two in the boat-house darted toward each other with a simultaneous movement, clutching hands as they met.

"He's coming!" Isabel breathed.

Wrayford detached himself hastily from her hold.

"He may only be out for a turn before he goes to bed. Wait a minute. I'll see if I can make out." He felt his way to the bench, scrambled up on it, and stretching his body forward, managed to bring his eyes in line with the opening above the door.

"It's as black as pitch. I can't see anything."

The refrain rang out nearer.

"Wait! I saw something twinkle. There it is again. It's coming this way—down the path. It's his cigar."

There was a long rattle of thunder through the stillness.

"It's the storm!" Isabel gasped. "He's coming to see about the launch."

Wrayford dropped noiselessly from the bench to her side.

"He's coming—yes."

She caught him by the arm.

"Isn't there time to get up the path and slip under the shrubbery?" she whispered.

"No, no; he's in the path now. He'll be here in two minutes. He'll find us."

He felt her hand tighten on his arm.

"You must go in the skiff, then. It's the only way."

"And let him find you here? And hear my oars? Isabel, listen—there's something I must say."

She flung herself against him, shaken with dry sobs.

"Isabel, just now I didn't tell you everything. He's ruined his mother—taken everything of hers, too. And he's got to tell her; it can't be kept from her."

She uttered a startled sound and drew away.

"Is this the truth? Why didn't you tell me before?"

"He forbade me. You were not to know."

Close above them, in the shrubbery, Stilling rolled out:

"Nita, Juanita,
Ask thy soul if we must part!"

Wrayford caught her wrist in a hard grasp. "Understand this—if he comes in, he'll find us. And if there's a scandal you'll lose your boy."

She seemed not to hear him. "You—you—you—he'll kill you!" she cried out.

Wrayford laughed and released her. She drew away and stood shrinking close against the wall, her hands pressed to her breast. Wrayford straightened himself and listened intently. Then he dropped to his knees and laid his hands against the boards of the sliding-floor. It yielded at once with a kind of evil alacrity; and at their feet they saw, in the night, another night that moved and shimmered. Wrayford sprang up, and threw himself back against the wall, behind the door.

A key rattled, and after a moment's fumbling the door swung open noisily. Wrayford and Isabel saw a black bulk against the obscurity. It moved a step, lurched forward, and vanished from them. In the depths there was a long cry and a splash.

"Go! go!" Wrayford cried out, feeling blindly for Isabel in the blackness.

"Go?" she shuddered back, wrenching herself away from him with horror.

He stood still a moment, as if dazed; then she saw him suddenly plunge from her side, and heard another splash far down, and a tumult in the beaten water.

In the darkness she cowered close to the opening, pressing her face over the edge, and frantically crying out the name of each in turn. Suddenly she began to see; the obscurity was less opaque, a faint moon-pallor diluted it. Isabel vaguely discerned the two shapes struggling in the black pit below her; once she saw the gleam of a face. Then she glanced up desperately for some means of rescue, and caught sight of the oars ranged on brackets against the wall. She snatched down the nearest, bent over the opening, and pushed the oar down into the blackness, calling her husband's name.

The clouds had swallowed up the moon again, and she could see nothing below her, but she still heard a tumult in the beaten water.

"Cobham! Cobham!" she screamed.

As if in answer, she felt a mighty clutch on the oar, a clutch that strained her arms to the breaking-point as she tried to brace her knees against the runners of the sliding-floor.

"Hold on! hold on! hold on!" a voice gasped out from below; and she held on, with racked muscles, with bleeding palms, with eyes straining from their sockets, and a heart that tugged at her like the weight on the oar.

Suddenly the weight relaxed, and the oar slipped up through her lacerated hands. She felt a wet bulk scrambling over the edge of the opening, and Stilling's voice, raucous and strange, groaned out, close to her: "God! I thought I was done for."

He staggered to his knees, coughing and sputtering, and the water dripped on her from his clothes.

She flung herself down, straining over the pit. Not a sound came up from it.

"Austin! Austin! Quick! Another oar!" she shrieked.

Stilling gave a cry. "My God! Was it Austin? What in hell— Another oar? No, no; untie the skiff, I tell you. But it's no use. Nothing's any use. I felt him lose hold as I came up."

After that she remembered nothing more till, hours later, as it appeared to her, she became dimly aware of her husband's voice, high, hysterical and important, haranguing a group of scared lantern-struck faces that seemed to have sprung up mysteriously about them in the night.

"Poor Austin! Poor fellow . . . terrible loss to me . . . mysterious dispensation. Yes, I do feel gratitude—miraculous escape—but I wish he could have known that I was saved!"

XL

JACK LONDON (1876–1916)

During the closing years of the decade American fiction was running mainly in tw channels: the short and abortive Spanish war had caused a widespread demand for his torical romance of the swashbuckling variety, not much of it, however, expressed in short story lengths; and the rise of the out-of-doors cult with its demand for Nature, for th "god of things as they are" in the forests and the open fields, had produced the "red-blooded school of writers, makers of fiction that dealt with "men with the bark on," and adventur in the raw wilds expressed in all its primitive details. It was Bret-Harteism modified b "naturalism" and the new scientific spirit, and its vehicle was for the most part the short story form.

And this brings us to Jack London, the typical product of the movement, Jack Londor California waif, water-front street gamin, bar-room "tough" and hoodlum, leader of th oyster pirates, deck-hand on a North Pacific sealer, mill worker, hobo, college student for time, gold-seeker in Alaska during the first wild days of the Klondike rush, adventure among the islands of the South Seas. The stories of London, first published in the Sa Francisco *Overland Monthly*, dealt first with his Alaska experiences—wild tales of super men in an environment as strange and elemental as any produced by Harte a generatior before. Once accepted by the publishers, he began upon a literary career little short o amazing,—in sixteen years upwards of forty volumes, all of them fundamentally autobio graphic, all of them presenting his superman dreams of himself.

A typical Jack London story plunges the reader at the start into a picturesque environ ment utterly new to him—Alaska usually or the South Sea islands, always superlatives usually extremes of savagery and blood and brutal adventure, always as characters supermer with passions as powerful as their bodies, always headlong action that hurls the reade excitedly to a climax. It is melodrama, one feels, and yet one is inclined to accept it un questioned as the truth. One is made to feel that the author is recording actuality, that h has been to the place described and is picturing it from notes taken on the spot, that it i perhaps an adventure of his own that he is recording. It is the triumph of verisimilitude In the age of Roosevelt, the era of the "strenuous life" that yelled shame on the "molly coddle" and exalted "red blood" and life in the open air, Jack London was the leader of th "best sellers," the best paid of all the short-story writers of one whole decade in America.

THE MADNESS OF JOHN HARNED *

I tell this for a fact. It happened in the bull-ring at Quito. I sat in the box with John Harned, and with Maria Valenzuela, and with Luis Cervallos. I saw it happen. I saw it all from first to last. I was on the steamer *Ecuadore* from Panama to Guaya-quil. Maria Valenzuela is my cousin. I have known her always. She is very beau-tiful. I am a Spaniard—an Ecuadoriano, true, but I am descended from Pedro Patino, who was one of Pizarro's captains. They were brave men. They were heroes. Did not Pizarro lead three hundred and

fifty Spanish cavaliers and four thousand Indians into the far Cordilleras in search of treasure? And did not all the four thou sand Indians and three hundred of the 5 brave cavaliers die on that vain quest But Pedro Patino did not die. He it wa: that lived to found the family of the Patinc I am Ecuadoriano, true, but I am Spanish I am Manuel de Jesus Patino. I own many 10 haciendas, and ten thousand Indians are my slaves, though the law says they are free men who work by freedom of con tract. The law is a funny thing. We Ecua dorianos laugh at it. It is our law. W 15 make it for ourselves. I am Manuel de Jesus Patino. Remember that name. It wil be written some day in history. There are revolutions in Ecuador. We call them elec

* Republished from *The Night-Born*. Copyright by the Century Co., 1913.

tions. It is a good joke, is it not?—what you call a pun?

John Harned was an American. I met him first at the Tivoli hotel in Panama. He had much money—this I have heard. He was going to Lima, but he met Maria Valenzuela in the Tivoli hotel. Maria Valenzuela is my cousin, and she is beautiful. It is true, she is the most beautiful woman in Ecuador. But also is she most beautiful in every country—in Paris, in Madrid, in New York, in Vienna. Always do all men look at her, and John Harned looked long at her at Panama. He loved her, that I know for a fact. She was Ecuadoriano, true—but she was of all countries; she was of all the world. She spoke many languages. She sang—ah! like an artiste. Her smile—wonderful, divine. Her eyes—ah! have I not seen men look in her eyes? They were what you English call amazing. They were promises of paradise. Men drowned themselves in her eyes.

Maria Valenzuela was rich—richer than I, who am accounted very rich in Ecuador. But John Harned did not care for her money. He had a heart—a funny heart. He was a fool. He did not go to Lima. He left the steamer at Guayaquil and followed her to Quito. She was coming home from Europe and other places. I do not see what she found in him, but she liked him. This I know for a fact, else he would not have followed her to Quito. She asked him to come. Well do I remember the occasion. She said:

"Come to Quito and I will show you the bull-fight—brave, clever, magnificent!"

But he said: "I go to Lima, not Quito. Such is my passage engaged on the steamer."

"You travel for pleasure—no?" said Maria Valenzuela; and she looked at him as only Maria Valenzuela could look, her eyes warm with the promise.

And he came. No; he did not come for the bull-fight. He came because of what he had seen in her eyes. Women like Marie Valenzuela are born once in a hundred years. They are of no country and no time. They are what you call universal. They are goddesses. Men fall down at their feet. They play with men and run them through their pretty fingers like sand. Cleopatra was such a woman they say; and so was Circe. She turned men into swine. Ha! ha! It is true—no?

It all came about because Maria Valenzuela said:

"You English people are—what shall I say?—savage—no? You prize-fight. Two men each hit the other with their fists till their eyes are blinded and their noses are broken. Hideous! And the other men who look on cry out loudly and are made glad. It is barbarous—no?"

"But they are men," said John Harned; "and they prize-fight out of desire. No one makes them prize-fight. They do it because they desire it more than anything else in the world."

Maria Valenzuela—there was scorn in her smile as she said:

"They kill each other often—is it not so? I have read it in the papers."

"But the bull," said John Harned. "The bull is killed many times in the bull-fight, and the bull does not come into the ring out of desire. It is not fair to the bull. He is compelled to fight. But the man in the prize-fight—no; he is not compelled."

"He is the more brute therefore," said Maria Valenzuela. "He is savage. He is primitive. He is animal. He strikes with his paws like a bear from a cave, and he is ferocious. But the bull-fight—ah! You have not seen the bull-fight—no? The toreador is clever. He must have skill. He is modern. He is romantic. He is only a man, soft and tender, and he faces the wild bull in conflict. And he kills with a sword, a slender sword, with one thrust, so, to the heart of the great beast. It is delicious. It makes the heart beat to behold—the small man, the great beast, the wide level sand, the thousands that look on without breath; the great beast rushes to the attack, the small man stands like a statue; he does not move, he is unafraid, and in his hand is the slender sword flashing like silver in the sun; nearer and nearer rushes the great beast with its sharp horns, the man does not move, and then—so—the sword flashes, the thrust is made, to the heart, to the hilt, the bull falls to the sand and is dead, and the man is unhurt. It is brave. It is magnificent! Ah!—I could love the toreador. But the man of the prize-fight—he is the brute, the human beast, the savage primitive, the maniac that receives many blows in his stupid face and rejoices. Come to Quito and I will show you the brave sport, the sport of men, the toreador and the bull."

But John Harned did not go to Quito

for the bull-fight. He went because of Maria Valenzuela. He was a large man, more broad of shoulder than we Ecuadorianos, more tall, more heavy of limb and bone. True, he was larger even than most men of his own race. His eyes were blue, though I have seen them gray, and, sometimes, like cold steel. His features were large, too—not delicate like ours, and his jaw was very strong to look at. Also, his face was smooth-shaven like a priest's. Why should a man feel shame for the hair on his face? Did not God put it there? Yes, I believe in God. I am not a pagan like many of you English. God is good. He makes me an Ecuadoriano with ten thousand slaves. And when I die I shall go to God. Yes, the priests are right.

But John Harned. He was a quiet man. He talked always in a low voice, and he never moved his hands when he talked. One would have thought his heart was a piece of ice; yet did he have a streak of warm in his blood, for he followed Maria Valenzuela to Quito. Also, and for all that he talked low without moving his hands, he was an animal, as you shall see—the beast primitive, the stupid, ferocious savage of the long ago that dressed in wild skins and lived in the caves along with the bears and wolves.

Luis Cervallos is my friend, the best of Ecuadorianos. He owns three cacao plantations at Naranjito and Chobo. At Milagro is his big sugar plantation. He has large haciendas at Ambato and Latacunga, and down the coast is he interested in oil-wells. Also has he spent much money in planting rubber along the Guayas. He is modern, like the Yankee; and, like the Yankee, full of business. He has much money, but it is in many ventures, and ever he needs more money for new ventures and for the old ones. He has been everywhere and seen everything. When he was a very young man he was in the Yankee military academy, what you call West Point. There was trouble. He was made to resign. He does not like Americans. But he did like Maria Valenzuela, who was of his own country. Also, he needed her money for his ventures and for his gold mine in Eastern Ecuador where the painted Indians live. I was his friend. It was my desire that he should marry Maria Valenzuela. Further, much of my money had I invested in his ventures, more so in his gold mine which was very rich but which first re-

quired the expense of much money before it would yield forth its riches. If Luis Cervallos married Maria Valenzuela I should have more money very immediately.

But John Harned followed Maria Valenzuela to Quito, and it was quickly clear to us—to Luis Cervallos and me—that she looked upon John Harned with great kindness. It is said that a woman will have her will, but this is a case not in point, for Maria Valenzuela did not have her will —at least not with John Harned. Perhaps it would all have happened as it did, even if Luis Cervallos and I had not sat in the box that day at the bull-ring in Quito. But this I know: we *did* sit in the box that day. And I shall tell you what happened.

The four of us were in the one box, guests of Luis Cervallos. I was next to the Presidente's box. On the other side was the box of General José Eliceo Salazar. With him were Joaquin Endara and Urcisino Castillo, both generals, and Colonel Jacinto Fierro and Captain Baltazar de Echeverria. Only Luis Cervallos had the position and the influence to get that box next to the Presidente. I know for a fact that the Presidente himself expressed the desire to the management that Luis Cervallos should have that box.

The band finished playing the national hymn of Ecuador. The procession of the toreadors was over. The Presidente nodded to begin. The bugles blew, and the bull dashed in—you know the way, excited, bewildered, the darts in its shoulder burning like fire, itself seeking madly whatever enemy to destroy. The toreadors hid behind their shelters and waited. Suddenly they appeared forth, the capadors, five of them, from every side, their colored capes flinging wide. The bull paused at sight of such a generosity of enemies, unable in his own mind to know which to attack. Then advanced one of the capadors alone to meet the bull. The bull was very angry. With its fore-legs it pawed the sand of the arena till the dust rose all about it. Then it charged, with lowered head, straight for the lone capador.

It is always of interest, the first charge of the first bull. After a time it is natural that one should grow tired, a trifle, that the keenness should lose its edge. But the first charge of the first bull! John Harned was seeing it for the first time, and he could not escape the excitement—the sight of the man, armed only with a piece of cloth, and of the bull rushing upon him across the sand with sharp horns, widespreading.

"See!" cried Marie Valenzuela. "Is it not superb?"

John Harned nodded, but did not look at her. His eyes were sparkling, and they were only for the bull-ring. The capador stepped to the side, with a twirl of the cape eluding the bull and spreading the cape on his own shoulders.

"What do you think?" asked Maria Valenzuela. "Is it not a—what-you-call—sporting proposition—no?"

"It is certainly," said John Harned. "It is very clever."

She clapped her hands with delight. They were little hands. The audience applauded. The bull turned and came back. Again the capador eluded him, throwing the cape on his shoulders, and again the audience applauded. Three times did this happen. The capador was very excellent. Then he retired, and the other capador played with the bull. After that they placed the banderillos in the bull, in the shoulders, on each side of the back-bone, two at a time. Then stepped forward Ordonez, the chief matador, with the long sword and the scarlet cape. The bugles blew for the death. He is not so good as Matestini. Still he is good, and with one thrust he drove the sword to the heart, and the bull doubled his legs under him and lay down and died. It was a pretty thrust, clean and sure; and there was much applause, and many of the common people threw their hats into the ring. Maria Valenzuela clapped her hands with the rest, and John Harned, whose cold heart was not touched by the event, looked at her with curiosity.

"You like it?" he asked.

"Always," she said, still clapping her hands.

"From a little girl," said Luis Cervallos. "I remember her first fight. She was four years old. She sat with her mother, and just like now she clapped her hands. She is a proper Spanish woman."

"You have seen it," said Maria Valenzuela to John Harned, as they fastened the mules to the dead bull and dragged it out. "You have seen the bull-fight and you like it—no? What do you think?"

"I think the bull had no chance," he said. "The bull was doomed from the first. The issue was not in doubt. Every one knew, before the bull entered the ring, that it was to die. To be a sporting proposi-tion, the issue must be in doubt. It was one stupid bull who had never fought a man against five wise men who had fought many bulls. It would be possibly a little bit fair if it were one man against one bull."

"Or one man against five bulls," said Maria Valenzuela; and we all laughed, and Luis Cervallos laughed loudest.

"Yes," said John Harned, "against five bulls, and the man, like the bulls, never in the bull-ring before—a man like yourself, Senor Cervallos."

"Yet we Spanish like the bull-fight," said Luis Cervallos; and I swear the devil was whispering then in his ear, telling him to do that which I shall relate.

"Then must it be a cultivated taste," John Harned made answer. "We kill bulls by the thousand every day in Chicago, yet no one cares to pay admittance to see."

"That is butchery," said I; "but this—ah, this is an art. It is delicate. It is fine. It is rare."

"Not always," said Luis Cervallos. "I have seen clumsy matadors, and I tell you it is not nice."

He shuddered, and his face betrayed such what-you-call disgust, that I knew, then, that the devil was whispering and that he was beginning to play a part.

"Senor Harned may be right," said Luis Cervallos. "It may not be fair to the bull. For is it not known to all of us that for twenty-four hours the bull is given no water, and that immediately before the fight he is permitted to drink his fill?"

"And he comes into the ring heavy with water?" said John Harned quickly; and I saw that his eyes were very gray and very sharp and very cold.

"It is necessary for the sport," said Luis Cervallos. "Would you have the bull so strong that he would kill the toreadors?"

"I would that he had a fighting chance," said John Harned, facing the ring to see the second bull come in.

It was not a good bull. It was frightened. It ran around the ring in search of a way to get out. The capadors stepped forth and flared their capes, but he refused to charge upon them.

"It is a stupid bull," said Maria Valenzuela.

"I beg pardon," said John Harned; "but it would seem to me a wise bull. He knows he must not fight man. See! He smells death there in the ring."

True. The bull, pausing where the last one had died, was smelling the wet sand and snorting. Again he ran around the ring, with raised head, looking at the faces of the thousands that hissed him, that threw orange-peel at him and called him names. But the smell of blood decided him, and he charged a capador, so without warning that the man just escaped. He dropped his cape and dodged into the shelter. The bull struck the wall of the ring with a crash. And John Harned said, in a quiet voice, as though he talked to himself:

"I will give one thousand sucres to the lazar-house of Quito if a bull kills a man this day."

"You like bulls?" said Maria Valenzuela with a smile.

"I like such men less," said John Harned. "A toreador is not a brave man. He surely cannot be a brave man. See, the bull's tongue is already out. He is tired and he has not yet begun."

"It is the water," said Luis Cervallos.

"Yes, it is the water," said John Harned. "Would it not be safer to hamstring the bull before he comes on?"

Maria Valenzuela was made angry by this sneer in John Harned's words. But Luis Cervallos smiled so that only I could see him, and then it broke upon my mind surely the game he was playing. He and I were to be banderilleros. The big American bull was there in the box with us. We were to stick the darts in him till he became angry, and then there might be no marriage with Maria Valenzuela. It was a good sport. And the spirit of bull-fighters was in our blood.

The bull was now angry and excited. The capadors had great game with him. He was very quick, and sometimes he turned with such sharpness that his hind legs lost their footing and he plowed the sand with his quarter. But he charged always the flung capes and committed no harm.

"He has no chance," said John Harned. "He is fighting wind."

"He thinks the cape is his enemy," explained Maria Valenzuela. "See how cleverly the capador deceives him."

"It is his nature to be deceived," said John Harned. "Wherefore he is doomed to fight wind. The toreadors know it, the audience knows it, you know it, I know it —we all know from the first that he will fight wind. He only does not know it. It is his stupid beast-nature. He has no chance."

"It is very simple," said Luis Cervallos. "The bull shuts his eyes when he charges. Therefore—"

"The man steps out of the way and the bull rushes by," John Harned interrupted.

"Yes," said Luis Cervallos; "that is it. The bull shuts his eyes, and the man knows it."

"But cows do not shut their eyes," said John Harned. "I know a cow at home that is a Jersey and gives milk, that would whip the whole gang of them."

"But the toreadors do not fight cows," said I.

"They are afraid to fight cows," said John Harned.

"Yes," said Cervallos; "they are afraid to fight cows. There would be no sport in killing toreadors."

"There would be some sport," said John Harned, "if a toreador were killed once in a while. When I become an old man, and mayhap a cripple, and should I need to make a living and be unable to do hard work, then would I become a bull-fighter. It is a light vocation for elderly gentlemen and pensioners."

"But see!" said Maria Valenzuela, as the bull charged bravely and the capador eluded it with a fling of his cape. "It requires skill so to avoid the beast."

"True," said John Harned. "But believe me, it requires a thousand times more skill to avoid the many and quick punches of a prize-fighter who keeps his eyes open and strikes with intelligence. Furthermore, this bull does not want to fight. Behold, he runs away."

It was not a good bull, for again it ran around the ring, seeking to find a way out.

"Yet these bulls are sometimes the most dangerous," said Luis Cervallos. "It can never be known what they will do next. They are wise. They are half cow. The bull-fighters never like them.—See! He has turned!"

Once again, baffled and made angry by the walls of the ring that would not let him out, the bull was attacking his enemies valiantly.

"His tongue is hanging out," said John Harned. "First, they fill him with water. Then they tire him out, one man and then another, persuading him to exhaust himself by fighting wind. While some tire him, others rest. But the bull they never let rest."

fterward, when he is quite tired and no
onger quick, the matador sticks the sword
into him."

The time had now come for the ban-
erillos. Three times one of the fighters
endeavored to place the darts, and three
times did he fail. He but stung the bull
and maddened it. The banderillos must go
in, you know, two at a time, into the shoul-
ers, on each side the backbone and close
to it. If but one be placed, it is a failure.
The crowd hissed and called for Ordonez.
And then Ordonez did a great thing. Four
times he stood forth, and four times, at
the first attempt, he stuck in the banderil-
os, so that eight of them, well placed,
stood out of the back of the bull at one
time. The crowd went mad, and a rain of
hats and money fell upon the sand of the
ring.

And just then the bull charged unex-
ectedly one of the capadors. The man
slipped and lost his head. The bull caught
him—unfortunately, between his wide
horns. And while the audience watched,
breathless and silent, John Harned stood
up and yelled with gladness. Alone, in that
hush of all of us, John Harned yelled. And
he yelled for the bull. As you see yourself,
John Harned wanted the man killed. His
was a brutal heart. This bad conduct made
those angry that sat in the box of General
Salazar, and they cried out against John
Harned. And Urcisino Castillo told him
to his face that he was a dog of a Gringo
and other things. Only it was in Spanish,
and John Harned did not understand. He
stood and yelled, perhaps for the time of
ten seconds, when the bull was enticed into
charging the other capadors and the man
rose unhurt.

"The bull has no chance," John Harned
said with sadness as he sat down. "The
man was uninjured. They fooled the bull
way from him." Then he turned to Maria
Valenzuela and said: "I beg your pardon.
I was excited."

She smiled and in reproof tapped his
arm with her fan.

"It is your first bull-fight," she said.
"After you have seen more you will
not cry for the death of the man. You
Americans, you see, are more brutal
than we. It is because of your prize-
fighting. We come only to see the bull
killed."

"But I would the bull had some chance,"
he answered. "Doubtless, in time, I shall

cease to be annoyed by the men who take
advantage of the bull."

The bugles blew for the death. Ordonez
stood forth with the sword and the scarlet
cloth. But the bull had changed again, and
did not want to fight. Ordonez stamped his
foot in the sand, and cried out, and waved
the scarlet cloth. Then the bull charged,
but without heart. There was no weight
to the charge. It was a poor thrust. The
sword struck a bone and bent. Ordonez
took a fresh sword. The bull, again stung
to the fight, charged once more. Five times
Ordonez essayed the thrust, and each time
the sword went but part way in or struck
bone. The sixth time, the sword went in
to the hilt. But it was a bad thrust. The
sword missed the heart and stuck out half
a yard through the ribs on the opposite
side. The audience hissed the matador. I
glanced at John Harned. He sat silent,
without movement; but I could see his
teeth were set, and his hands were clenched
tight on the railing of the box.

All fight was now out of the bull, and,
though it was no vital thrust, he trotted
lamely what of the sword that stuck
through him, in one side and out the other.
He ran away from the matador and the
capadors, and encircled the edge of the
ring, looking up at the many faces.

"He is saying: 'For God's sake let me
out of this; I don't want to fight,'" said
John Harned.

That was all. He said no more, but sat
and watched, though sometimes he looked
sideways at Maria Valenzuela to see how
she took it. She was angry with the matador. He was awkward, and she had desired
a clever exhibition.

The bull was now very tired, and weak
from loss of blood, though far from dying.
He walked slowly around the wall of the
ring, seeking a way out. He would not
charge. He had had enough. But he must
be killed. There is a place, in the neck
of a bull behind the horns, where the cord
of the spine is unprotected and where a
short stab will immediately kill. Ordonez
stepped in front of the bull and lowered
his scarlet cloth to the ground. The bull
would not charge. He stood still and
smelled the cloth, lowering his head to do
so. Ordonez stabbed between the horns
at the spot in the neck. The bull jerked his
head up. The stab had missed. Then the
bull watched the sword. When Ordonez
moved the cloth on the ground, the bull

forgot the sword and lowered his head to smell the cloth. Again Ordonez stabbed, and again he failed. He tried many times. It was stupid. And John Harned said nothing. At last a stab went home, and the bull fell to the sand, dead immediately, and the mules were made fast and he was dragged out.

"The Gringos say it is a cruel sport—no?" said Luis Cervallos. "That it is not humane. That it is bad for the bull. No?"

"No," said John Harned. "The bull does not count for much. It is bad for those that look on. It is degrading to those that look on. It teaches them to delight in animal suffering. It is cowardly for five men to fight one stupid bull. Therefore those that look on learn to be cowards. The bull dies, but those that look on live and the lesson is learned. The bravery of men is not nourished by scenes of cowardice."

Maria Valenzuela said nothing. Neither did she look at him. But she heard every word and her cheeks were white with anger. She looked out across the ring and fanned herself, but I saw that her hand trembled. Nor did John Harned look at her. He went on as though she were not there. He, too, was angry, coldly angry.

"It is the cowardly sport of a cowardly people," he said.

"Ah," said Luis Cervallos softly, "you think you understand us."

"I understand now the Spanish Inquisition," said John Harned. "It must have been more delightful than bull-fighting."

Luis Cervallos smiled but said nothing. He glanced at Maria Valenzuela, and knew that the bull-fight in the box was won. Never would she have further to do with the Gringo who spoke such words. But neither Luis Cervallos nor I was prepared for the outcome of the day. I fear we do not understand the Gringos. How were we to know that John Harned, who was so coldly angry, should go suddenly mad? But mad he did go, as you shall see. The bull did not count for much—he said so himself. Then why should the horse count for so much? That I cannot understand. The mind of John Harned lacked logic. That is the only explanation.

"It is not usual to have horses in the bull-ring at Quito," said Luis Cervallos, looking up from the program. "In Spain they always have them. But to-day, by special permission we shall have them. When the next bull comes on there will be horses and picadors—you know, the men who carry lances and ride the horses."

"The bull is doomed from the first," said John Harned. "Are the horses then likewise doomed?"

"They are blindfolded so that they may not see the bull," said Luis Cervallos. "I have seen many horses killed. It is a brave sight."

"I have seen the bull slaughtered," said John Harned. "I will now see the horse slaughtered, so that I may understand more fully the fine points of this noble sport."

"They are old horses," said Luis Cervallos, "that are not good for anything else."

"I see," said John Harned.

The third bull came on, and soon against it were both capadors and picadors. One picador took his stand directly below us. I agree, it was a thin and aged horse he rode, a bag of bones covered with mangy hide.

"It is a marvel that the poor brute can hold up the weight of the rider," said John Harned. "And now that the horse fights the bull, what weapons has it?"

"The horse does not fight the bull," said Luis Cervallos.

"Oh," said John Harned, "then is the horse there to be gored? That must be why it is blindfolded, so that it shall not see the bull coming to gore it."

"Not quite so," said I. "The lance of the picador is to keep the bull from goring the horse."

"Then are horses rarely gored?" asked John Harned.

"No," said Luis Cervallos. "I have seen at Seville, eighteen horses killed in one day, and the people clamored for more horses."

"Were they blindfolded like this horse?" asked John Harned.

"Yes," said Luis Cervallos.

After that we talked no more, but watched the fight. And John Harned was going mad all the time, and we did not know. The bull refused to charge the horse. And the horse stood still, and because it could not see it did not know that the capadors were trying to make the bull charge upon it. The capadors teased the bull with their capes, and when it charged them they ran toward the horse and into their shelters. At last the bull was well angry, and it saw the horse before it.

"The horse does not know, the horse

does not know," John Harned whispered like to himself, unaware that he voiced his thought aloud.

The bull charged, and of course the horse knew nothing till the picador failed and the horse found himself impaled on the bull's horns from beneath. The bull was magnificently strong. The sight of its strength was splendid to see. It lifted the horse clear into the air; and as the horse fell to its side on the ground the picador landed on his feet and escaped, while the capadors lured the bull away. The horse was emptied of its essential organs. Yet did it rise to its feet screaming. It was the scream of the horse that did it, that made John Harned completely mad; for he, too, started to rise to his feet. I heard him curse low and deep. He never took his eyes from the horse, which, still screaming, strove to run, but fell down instead and rolled on its back so that all its four legs were kicking in the air. Then the bull charged it and gored it again and again until it was dead.

John Harned was now on his feet. His eyes were no longer cold like steel. They were blue flames. He looked at Maria Valenzuela, and she looked at him, and in his face was a great loathing. The moment of his madness was upon him. Everybody was looking, now that the horse was dead; and John Harned was a large man and easy to be seen.

"Sit down," said Luis Cervallos, "or you will make a fool of yourself."

John Harned replied nothing. He struck out his fist. He smote Luis Cervallos in the face so that he fell like a dead man across the chairs and did not rise again. He saw nothing of what followed. But I saw much. Urcisino Castillo, leaning forward from the next box, with his cane struck John Harned full across the face. And John Harned smote him with his fist so that in falling he overthrew General Salazar. John Harned was now in what-you-call Berserker rage—no? The beast primitive in him was loose and roaring—the beast primitive of the holes and caves of the long ago.

"You came for a bull-fight," I heard him say, "and by God I'll show you a man-fight!"

It was a fight. The soldiers guarding the Presidente's box leaped across, but from one of them he took a rifle and beat them on their heads with it. From the other box Colonel Jacinto Fierro was shooting at him with a revolver. The first shot killed a soldier. This I know for a fact. I saw it. But the second shot struck John Harned in the side. Whereupon he swore, and with a lunge drove the bayonet of his rifle into Colonel Jacinto Fierro's body. It was horrible to behold. The Americans and the English are a brutal race. They sneer at our bull-fighting, yet do they delight in the shedding of blood. More men were killed that day because of John Harned than were ever killed in all the history of the bull-ring of Quito, yes, and of Guayaquil and all Ecuador.

It was the scream of the horse that did it. Yet why did not John Harned go mad when the bull was killed? A beast is a beast, be it bull or horse. John Harned was mad. There is no other explanation. He was blood-mad, a beast himself. I leave it to your judgment. Which is worse—the goring of the horse by the bull, or the goring of Colonel Jacinto Fierro by the bayonet in the hands of John Harned? And John Harned gored others with that bayonet. He was full of devils. He fought with many bullets in him, and he was hard to kill. And Maria Valenzuela was a brave woman. Unlike the other women, she did not cry out nor faint. She sat still in her box, gazing out across the bull-ring. Her face was white and she fanned herself, but she never looked around.

From all sides came the soldiers and officers and the common people bravely to subdue the mad Gringo. It is true—the cry went up from the crowd to kill all the Gringos. It is an old cry in Latin-American countries, what of the dislike for the Gringos and their uncouth ways. It is true, the cry went up. But the brave Ecuadorianos killed only John Harned, and first he killed seven of them. Besides, there were many hurt. I have seen many bull-fights, but never have I seen anything so abominable as the scene in the boxes when the fight was over. It was like a field of battle. The dead lay around everywhere, while the wounded sobbed and groaned and some of them died. One man, whom John Harned had thrust through the belly with the bayonet, clutched at himself with both his hands and screamed. I tell you for a fact it was more terrible than the screaming of a thousand horses.

No, Maria Valenzuela did not marry Luis Cervallos. I am sorry for that. He was my friend, and much of my money was invested in his ventures. It was five weeks before the surgeons took the bandages from his face. And there is a scar there to this day, on the cheek, under the eye. Yet John Harned struck him but once and struck him only with his naked fist. Maria Valenzuela is in Austria now. It is said she is to marry an Arch-Duke or some high nobleman. I do not know. I think she liked John Harned before he followed her to Quito to see the bull-fight. But why the horse? That is what I desire to know. Why 5 should he watch the bull and say that it did not count, and then go immediately and most horribly mad because a horse screamed? There is no understanding the Gringos. They are barbarians.

XLI

WILLIAM SYDNEY PORTER (O. HENRY) (1862–1921)

Like Mark Twain, William Sydney Porter has made a pen name so familiar to the reading world that his real name has become all but forgotten. "O. Henry" published his earliest short story within a month of the time when Jack London's first tale appeared in print (1899). Both were hailed as unique discoveries—crude, wild adventurers, "men with the bark on," who had lived in the wild places and had had adventures numberless and wilder than romance—veritable Sindbads turned author and, miracle of miracles, able to write in a graphic way with reasonable regard to the requirements of grammar. O. Henry had been, it was whispered, a Texas cow-boy, then a tramp, then an adventurer in South America. Swiftly had come another sensation: the man was in New York City and he was writing now tales of "the little old Bagdad on the Hudson," tales that seemed on the face of them to prove that he had lived all his life within the shadow of Madison Square Garden. He had been engaged, it was found, by the New York *World* to write a story each week for the Sunday edition and surely he was giving the paper its money's worth. Then as suddenly as he had appeared he was gone, dead after a literary career of a single decade, but leaving behind him what became a set of twelve volumes of tales.

In later years, with the biography of Professor Smith, the true facts as to his life came to light. He had been an employee in a Texas bank, had "borrowed" funds from the bank expecting soon to restore them, had been detected by the bank examiner and in a panic had run away to South America. After a year or more he had returned, had been apprehended and tried for embezzlement, and had been sentenced to serve a term of years at the Columbus Federal prison. It was in prison that he learned to write short stories, his first model being Bret Harte, and his later one Maupassant. When his earliest stories began to appear in the magazines, sensational indeed would it have been to their readers could they have known that they were being served fiction that was prison made. His sentence served, he continued to make short stories at first with South American and Wild West backgrounds, but it was not until he went to New York City that he discovered the full compass of his powers.

O. Henry stands for deliberate art. Like Poe, he aimed only to interest and thrill and hold his reader. Humor he used in profusion, much of it expressed in the current slang of the period, and surprise endings, trick endings, startling incongruities of structure—every device known to the literary juggler, he used until they became veritable "O. Henryisms." His characters, despite the skill with which he dressed them, are mere marionettes, artificial creations with which to amuse his readers. His style is colloquial, over-familiar,—democratic, the style of a skilful *reconteur* of anecdotes. His vocabulary, however, when he wishes to describe or to bring out quaintnesses in locality or in characters, is wide and remarkable, and his handling of plot is often irresistible. His influence has been wide and on the whole it has been deplorable. A single O. Henry one could enjoy for a time, but a generation of O. Henrys, all of them trying to practise his peculiar "O. Henryism," became nauseating. His influence has waned, but even yet it is affecting a wide area of the contemporary short story.

THE COUNT AND THE WEDDING GUEST*

One evening when Andy Donovan went to dinner at his Second Avenue boarding-house, Mrs. Scott introduced him to a new boarder, a young lady, Miss Conway. Miss

* From *The Trimmed Lamp.* Copyright, 1907, by Doubleday Page & Company.

Conway was small and unobtrusive. She wore a plain, snuffy-brown dress, and bestowed her interest, which seemed languid, upon her plate. She lifted her diffident eyelids and shot one perspicuous, judicial glance at Mr. Donovan, politely murmured his name, and returned to her mutton. Mr. Donovan bowed with the grace and beaming smile that were rapidly winning for him social, business and political advancement, and erased the snuffy-brown one from the tablets of his consideration.

Two weeks later Andy was sitting on the front steps enjoying his cigar. There was a soft rustle behind and above him, and Andy turned his head—and had his head turned.

Just coming out the door was Miss Conway. She wore a night-black dress of crêpe de—crêpe de—oh, this thin black goods. Her hat was black, and from it drooped and fluttered an ebon veil, filmy as a spider's web. She stood on the top step and drew on black silk gloves. Not a speck of white or a spot of color about her dress anywhere. Her rich golden hair was drawn, with scarcely a ripple, into a shining, smooth knot low on her neck. Her face was plain rather than pretty, but it was now illuminated and made almost beautiful by her large gray eyes that gazed above the houses across the street into the sky with an expression of the most appealing sadness and melancholy.

Gather the idea, girls—all black, you know, with the preference for crêpe de— oh, crêpe de Chine—that's it. All black, and that sad, faraway look, and the hair shining under the black veil (you have to be a blonde, of course), and try to look as if, although your young life had been blighted just as it was about to give a hop-skip-and-a-jump over the threshold of life, a walk in the park might do you good, and be sure to happen out the door at the right moment, and—oh, it'll fetch 'em every time. But it's fierce, now, how cynical I am, ain't it?—to talk about mourning costumes this way.

Mr. Donovan suddenly reinscribed Miss Conway upon the tablets of his consideration. He threw away the remaining inch-and-a-quarter of his cigar, that would have been good for eight minutes yet, and quickly shifted his center of gravity to his low-cut patent leathers.

"It's a fine, clear evening, Miss Conway," he said; and if the Weather Bureau could have heard the confident emphasis of his tones it would have hoisted the square white signal and nailed it to the mast.

"To them that has the heart to enjoy it, it is, Mr. Donovan," said Miss Conway, with a sigh.

Mr. Donovan in his heart cursed fair weather. Heartless weather! It should hail and blow and snow to be consonant with the mood of Miss Conway.

"I hope none of your relatives—I hope you haven't sustained a loss?" ventured Mr. Donovan.

"Death has claimed," said Miss Conway, hesitating—"not a relative, but one who— but I will not intrude my grief upon you, Mr. Donovan."

"Intrude?" protested Mr. Donovan. "Why, say, Miss Conway, I'd be delighted, that is, I'd be sorry—I mean I'm sure nobody could sympathize with you truer than I would."

Miss Conway smiled a little smile. And oh, it was sadder than her expression in repose.

"'Laugh, and the world laughs with you; weep, and they give you the laugh,'" she quoted.

"I have learned that, Mr. Donovan. I have no friends or acquaintances in this city. But you have been kind to me. I appreciate it highly."

He had passed her the pepper twice at the table.

"It's tough to be alone in New York— that's a cinch," said Mr. Donovan. "But, say—whenever this little old town does loosen up and get friendly it goes the limit. Say you took a little stroll in the park, Miss Conway—don't you think it might chase away some of your mully-grubs? And if you'd allow me—"

"Thanks, Mr. Donovan. I'd be pleased to accept of your escort if you think the company of one whose heart is filled with gloom could be anyways agreeable to you."

Through the open gates of the iron-railed, old, downtown park, where the elect once took the air, they strolled and found a quiet bench.

There is this difference between the grief of youth and that of old age: youth's burden is lightened by as much of it as another shares; old age may give and give, but the sorrow remains the same.

"He was my fiancé," confided Miss Conway, at the end of an hour. "We were going to be married next spring. I don't want you to think that I am stringing you, Mr. Donovan, but he was a real Count. He had an estate and a castle in Italy. Count Fernando Mazzini was his name. I never saw the beat of him for elegance. Papa objected, of course, and once we eloped, but papa overtook us, and took us back. I thought sure papa and Fernando would fight a duel. Papa has a livery business—in P'kipsee, you know.

"Finally, papa came around all right, and said we might be married next spring. Fernando showed him proofs of his title and wealth, and then went over to Italy to get the castle fixed up for us. Papa's very proud, and when Fernando wanted to give me several thousand dollars for my trousseau he called him down something awful. He wouldn't even let me take a ring or any presents from him. And when Fernando sailed I came to the city and got a position as cashier in a candy store.

"Three days ago I got a letter from Italy, forwarded from P'kipsee, saying that Fernando had been killed in a gondola accident.

"That is why I am in mourning. My heart, Mr. Donovan, will remain forever in his grave. I guess I am poor company, Mr. Donovan, but I can not take any interest in no one. I should not care to keep you from gaiety and your friends who can smile and entertain you. Perhaps you would prefer to walk back to the house?"

Now, girls, if you want to observe a young man hustle out after a pick and shovel, just tell him that your heart is in some other fellow's grave. Young men are grave-robbers by nature. Ask any widow. Something must be done to restore that missing organ to weeping girls in *crêpe de Chine*. Dead men certainly get the worse of it from all sides.

"I'm awful sorry," said Mr. Donovan gently. "No, we won't walk back to the house just yet. And don't say you haven't no friends in this city, Miss Conway. I'm awful sorry, and I want you to believe I'm your friend, and that I'm awful sorry."

"I've got his picture here in my locket," said Miss Conway, after wiping her eyes with her handkerchief. "I never showed it to anybody, but I will to you, Mr. Donovan, because I believe you to be a true friend."

Mr. Donovan gazed long and with much interest at the photograph in the locket that Miss Conway opened for him. The face of Count Mazzini was one to command interest. It was a smooth, intelligent, bright, almost a handsome face—the face of a strong, cheerful man who might well be a leader among his fellows.

"I have a larger one, framed, in my room," said Miss Conway. "When we return I will show you that. They are all I have to remind me of Fernando. But he ever will be present in my heart, that's a sure thing."

A subtle task confronted Mr. Donovan—that of supplanting the unfortunate Count in the heart of Miss Conway. This his admiration for her determined him to do. But the magnitude of the undertaking did not seem to weigh upon his spirits. The sympathetic but cheerful friend was the rôle he essayed, and he played it so successfully that the next half-hour found them conversing pensively across two plates of ice-cream, though yet there was no diminution of the sadness in Miss Conway's large gray eyes.

Before they parted in the hall that evening she ran upstairs and brought down the framed photograph wrapped lovingly in a white silk scarf. Mr. Donovan surveyed it with inscrutable eyes.

"He gave me this the night he left for Italy," said Miss Conway. "I had one for the locket made from this."

"A fine-looking man," said Mr. Donovan heartily. "How would it suit you, Miss Conway, to give me the pleasure of your company to Coney next Sunday afternoon?"

A month later they announced their engagement to Mrs. Scott and the other boarders. Miss Conway continued to wear black.

A week after the announcement the two sat on the same bench in the downtown park, while the fluttering leaves of the trees made a dim kinetoscopic picture of them in the moonlight. But Donovan had worn a look of abstracted gloom all day. He was so silent to-night that love's lips could not keep back any longer the questions that love's heart propounded.

"What's the matter, Andy, you are so solemn and grouchy to-night?"

"Nothing, Maggie."

"I know better. Can't I tell? You never acted this way before. What is it?"

"It's nothing much, Maggie."

"Yes it is, and I want to know. I'll bet it's some other girl you are thinking about. All right. Why don't you go and get her if you want her? Take your arm away, if you please."

"I'll tell you then," said Andy wisely; "but I guess you won't understand it exactly. You've heard of Mike Sullivan, haven't you? 'Big Mike' Sullivan, everybody calls him."

"No, I haven't," said Maggie. "And I don't want to, if he makes you act like this. Who is he?"

"He's the biggest man in New York," said Andy, almost reverently. "He can do about anything he wants to with Tammany or any other old thing in the political line. He's a mile high and as broad as East River. You say anything against Big Mike and you'll have a million men on your collarbone in about two seconds. Why, he made a visit over to the old country awhile back, and the kings took to their holes like rabbits.

"Well, Big Mike's a friend of mine. I ain't more than deuce-high in the district as far as influence goes, but Mike's as good a friend to a little man, or a poor man, as he is to a big one. I met him to-day on the Bowery, and what do you think he does? Comes up and shakes hands. 'Andy,' says he, 'I've been keeping cases on you. You've been putting in some good licks over on your side of the street, and I'm proud of you. What'll you take to drink?' He takes a cigar, and I take a highball. I told him I was going to get married in two weeks. 'Andy,' says he, 'send me an invitation, so I'll keep in mind of it, and I'll come to the wedding.' That's what Big Mike says to me; and he always does what he says.

"You don't understand it, Maggie, but I'd have one of my hands cut off to have Big Mike Sullivan at our wedding. It would be the proudest day of my life. When he goes to a man's wedding there's a guy being married that's made for life. Now, that's why I've maybe been looking sore to-night."

"Why don't you invite him, then, if he's so much to the mustard?" said Maggie lightly.

"There's a reason why I can't," said Andy sadly. "There's a reason why he mustn't be there. Don't ask me what it is, for I can't tell you."

"Oh, I don't care," said Maggie. "It's something about politics, of course. But it's no reason why you can't smile at me."

"Maggie," said Andy presently, "do you think as much of me as you did of your— as you did of the Count Mazzini?"

He waited a long time, but Maggie did not reply. And then, suddenly she leaned against his shoulder and began to cry— to cry and shake with sobs, holding his arm tightly and wetting the *crêpe de Chine* with tears.

"There, there, there!" soothed Andy, putting aside his own trouble. "And what is it now?"

"Andy," sobbed Maggie, "I've lied to you and you'll never marry me, or love me any more. But I feel that I've got to tell. Andy, there never was so much as the little finger of a count. I never had a beau in my life. But all the other girls had, and they talked about 'em, and that seemed to make the fellows like 'em more. And, Andy, I look swell in black—you know I do. So I went out to a photograph store and bought that picture, and had a little one made for my locket, and made up all that story about the Count and about his being killed, so I could wear black. And nobody can love a liar and you'll shake me, Andy, and I'll die for shame. Oh, there never was anybody I liked but you—and that's all."

But instead of being pushed away she found Andy's arm folding her closely. She looked up and saw his face cleared and smiling.

"Could you—could you forgive me, Andy?"

"Sure," said Andy. "It's all right about that. Back to the cemetery for the Count. You've straightened everything out, Maggie. I was in hopes you would before the wedding day. Bully girl!"

"Andy," said Maggie with a somewhat shy smile, after she had been thoroughly assured of forgiveness, "did you believe all that story about the Count?"

"Well, not to any large extent," said Andy, reaching for his cigar-case; "because it's Big Mike Sullivan's picture you've got in that locket of yours."

THE LAST LEAF *

In a little district west of Washington Square the streets have run crazy and broken themselves into small strips called "places." These "places" make strange angles and curves. One street crosses itself a time or two. An artist once discovered a valuable possibility in this street. Suppose a collector with a bill for paints, paper and canvas should, in traversing this route, suddenly meet himself coming back,

* From *The Trimmed Lamp*. Copyright, 1907, by Doubleday Page & Company.

without a cent having been paid on account!

So, to quaint old Greenwich Village the art people soon came prowling, hunting for north windows and eighteenth-century gables and Dutch attics and low rents. Then they imported some pewter mugs and a chafing dish or two from Sixth Avenue and became a "colony."

At the top of a squatty, three-story brick Sue and Johnsy had their studio. "Johnsy" was familiar for Joanna. One was from Maine; the other from California. They had met at the *table d'hote* of an Eighth Street "Delmonico's," and found their tastes in art, chicory salad and sleeves so congenial that the joint studio resulted.

That was in May. In November a cold, unseen stranger, whom the doctors called Pneumonia, stalked about the colony, touching one here and there with his icy fingers. Over on the east side this ravager strode boldly, smiting his victims by scores, but his feet trod slowly through the maze of the narrow and moss-grown "places."

Mr. Pneumonia was not what you would call a chivalric old gentleman. A mite of a little woman with blood thinned by California zephyrs was hardly fair game for the red-fisted, short-breathed old duffer. But Johnsy he smote; and she lay, scarcely moving, on her painted iron bedstead, looking through the small Dutch window-panes at the blank side of the next brick house.

One morning the busy doctor invited Sue into the hallway with a shaggy, gray eyebrow.

"She has one chance in—let us say, ten," he said, as he shook down the mercury in his clinical thermometer. "And that chance is for her to want to live. The way people have of lining up on the side of the undertaker makes the entire pharmacopeia look silly. Your little lady has made up her mind that she's not going to get well. Has she anything on her mind?"

"She—she wanted to paint the Bay of Naples some day," said Sue.

"Paint?—bosh! Has she anything on her mind worth thinking about twice—a man, for instance?"

"A man?" said Sue, with a jew's-harp twang in her voice. "Is a man worth—but, no, doctor; there is nothing of the kind."

"Well, it is the weakness, then," said the doctor. "I will do all that science, so far as it may filter through my efforts, can accomplish. But whenever my patient begins to count the carriages in her funeral procession I subtract 50 per cent. from the curative power of medicines. If you will get her to ask one question about the new winter styles in cloak sleeves, I will promise you a one-in-five chance for her, instead of one in ten."

After the doctor had gone, Sue went into the workroom and cried a Japanese napkin to a pulp. Then she swaggered into Johnsy's room with her drawing-board, whistling ragtime.

Johnsy lay, scarcely making a ripple under the bedclothes, with her face toward the window. Sue stopped whistling, thinking she was asleep.

She arranged her board and began a pen-and-ink drawing to illustrate a magazine story. Young artists must pave their way to Art by drawing pictures for magazine stories that young authors write to pave their way to Literature.

As Sue was sketching a pair of elegant horse-show riding trousers and a monocle on the figure of the hero, an Idaho cowboy, she heard a low sound, several times repeated. She went quickly to the bedside.

Johnsy's eyes were open wide. She was looking out the window and counting—counting backward.

"Twelve," she said, and a little later "eleven"; and then "ten," and "nine"; and then "eight" and "seven," almost together.

Sue looked solicitously out the window. What was there to count? There was only a bare, dreary yard to be seen, and the blank side of the brick house twenty feet away. An old, old ivy vine, gnarled and decayed at the roots, climbed half way up the brick wall. The cold breath of autumn had stricken its leaves from the vine until its skeleton branches clung, almost bare, to the crumbling bricks.

"What is it, dear?" asked Sue.

"Six," said Johnsy, in almost a whisper. "They're falling faster now. Three days ago there were almost a hundred. It made my head ache to count them. But now it's easy. There goes another one. There are only five left now."

"Five what, dear? Tell your Sudie."

"Leaves. On the ivy vine. When the last one falls I must go, too. I've known that for three days. Didn't the doctor tell you?"

"Oh, I never heard of such nonsense," complained Sue, with magnificent scorn. "What have old ivy leaves to do with your getting well? And you used to love that vine so, you naughty girl. Don't be a goosey. Why, the doctor told me this morning that your chances for getting well real soon were—let's see exactly what he said —he said the chances were ten to one! Why, that's almost as good a chance as we have in New York when we ride on the street cars or walk past a new building. Try to take some broth now, and let Sudie go back to her drawing, so she can sell the editor man with it, and buy port wine for her sick child, and pork chops for her greedy self."

"You needn't get any more wine," said Johnsy, keeping her eyes fixed out the window. "There goes another. No, I don't want any broth. That leaves just four. I want to see the last one fall before it gets dark. Then I'll go, too."

"Johnsy, dear," said Sue, bending over her, "will you promise me to keep your eyes closed, and not look out the window until I am done working? I must hand those drawings in by to-morrow. I need the light, or I would draw the shade down."

"Couldn't you draw in the other room?" asked Johnsy, coldly.

"I'd rather be here by you," said Sue. "Besides, I don't want you to keep looking at those silly ivy leaves."

"Tell me as soon as you have finished," said Johnsy, closing her eyes, and lying white and still as a fallen statue, "because I want to see the last one fall. I'm tired of waiting. I'm tired of thinking. I want to turn loose my hold on everything, and go sailing down, down, just like one of those poor, tired leaves."

"Try to sleep," said Sue. "I must call Behrman up to be my model for the old hermit miner. I'll not be gone a minute. Don't try to move 'till I come back."

Old Behrman was a painter who lived on the ground floor beneath them. He was past sixty and had a Michael Angelo's Moses beard curling down from the head of a satyr along the body of an imp. Behrman was a failure in art. Forty years he had wielded the brush without getting near enough to touch the hem of his Mistress's robe. He had been always about to paint a masterpiece, but had never yet begun it. For several years he had painted nothing except, now and then, a daub in the line of commerce or advertising. He earned a little by serving as a model to those young artists in the colony who could not pay the price of a professional. He drank gin to excess, and still talked of his coming masterpiece. For the rest he was a fierce little old man, who scoffed terribly at softness in any one, and who regarded himself as especial mastiff-in-waiting to protect the two young artists in the studio above.

Sue found Behrman smelling strongly of juniper berries in his dimly lighted den below. In one corner was a blank canvas on an easel that had been waiting there for twenty-five years to receive the first line of the masterpiece. She told him of Johnsy's fancy, and how she feared she would, indeed, light and fragile as a leaf herself, float away when her slight hold upon the world grew weaker.

Old Behrman, with his red eyes plainly streaming, shouted his contempt and derision for such idiotic imaginings.

"Vass!" he cried. "Is dere people in de world mit der foolishness to die because leafs dey drop off from a confounded vine? I haf not heard of such a thing. No, I will not bose as a model for your fool hermit-dunderhead. Vy do you allow dot silly pusiness to come in der prain of her? Ach, dot poor leetle Miss Johnsy."

"She is very ill and weak," said Sue, "and the fever has left her mind morbid and full of strange fancies. Very well, Mr. Behrman, if you do not care to pose for me, you needn't. But I think you are a horrid old—old flibbertigibbet."

"You are just like a woman!" yelled Behrman. "Who said I vill not bose? Go on. I come mit you. For half an hour I haf been trying to say dot I am ready to bose. Gott! dis is not any blace in which one so goot as Miss Yohnsy shall lie sick. Some day I vill baint a masterpiece, and ve shall all go away. Gott! yes."

Johnsy was sleeping when they went upstairs. Sue pulled the shade down to the window-sill, and motioned Behrman into the other room. In there they peered out the window fearfully at the ivy vine. Then they looked at each other for a moment without speaking. A persistent, cold rain was falling, mingled with snow. Behrman, in his old blue shirt, took his seat as the hermit-miner on an upturned kettle for a rock.

A Struggle for Life

70
32
——
(38)

120
/ 6
——
72.0

's sleep
sy with
drawn

ordered, 5

d fierce
hrough
od out 10

It was
en near
s tinted
decay,
twenty 15

asy. "I
ng the
to-day,

20

ig her
ink of
What

lone- 25
a soul
on its
seemed
by one
ip and 30

The day wore away, and even through the twilight they could see the lone ivy leaf clinging to its stem against the wall. And then, with the coming of the night the north wind was again loosed, while the rain still beat against the windows and pattered down from the low Dutch eaves.

When it was light enough Johnsy, the merciless, commanded that the shade be raised.

The ivy leaf was still there.

Johnsy lay for a long time looking at it. And then she called to Sue, who was stirring her chicken broth over the gas stove.

"I've been a bad girl, Sudie," said Johnsy. "Something has made that last

leaf stay there to show me how wicked I was. It is a sin to want to die. You may bring me a little broth now, and some milk with a little port in it, and—no; bring me a hand-mirror first, and then pack some pillows about me, and I will sit up and watch you cook."

An hour later she said.

"Sudie, some day I hope to paint the Bay of Naples"

The doctor came in the afternoon, and Sue had an excuse to go into the hallway as he left.

"Even chances," said the doctor, taking Sue's thin, shaking hand in his. "With good nursing, you'll win. And now I must see another case I have downstairs. Behrman, his name is—some kind of an artist, I believe. Pneumonia, too. He is an old, weak man, and the attack is acute. There is no hope for him; but he goes to the hospital to-day to be made more comfortable."

The next day the doctor said to Sue: "She's out of danger. You've won."

And that afternoon Sue came to the bed where Johnsy lay, contentedly knitting a very blue and very useless woolen shoulder scarf, and put one arm around her, pillows and all.

"I have something to tell you, white mouse," she said. "Mr. Behrman died of pneumonia to-day in the hospital. He was ill only two days. The janitor found him on the morning of the first day in his room downstairs helpless with pain. His shoes and clothing were wet through and icy cold. They couldn't imagine where he had been on such a dreadful night. And then they found a lantern, still lighted, and a ladder that had been dragged from its place, and some scattered brushes, and a palette with green and yellow colors mixed on it, and—look out the window, dear, at the last ivy leaf on the wall. Didn't you wonder why it never fluttered or moved when the wind blew? Ah, darling, it's Behrman's masterpiece—he painted it there the night that the last leaf fell."

PART IV

REPRESENTATIVE CONTEMPORARY WRITERS, 1900–

XLII

KATHERINE FULLERTON GEROULD (1879–

Katherine Fullerton Gerould, a native of Massachusetts, a graduate of Radcliffe College, and a teacher of English for nearly a decade at Bryn Mawr College, first came into prominence in 1914 with her collection of short stories entitled *Vain Oblations*. She is of the Henry James-Mrs. Wharton group of writers; her stories for the most part are not confined to the New England environment but often are cosmopolitan, and they deal always with fundamental problems of society and life. She is a careful artisan; she knows the rules of the short-story art like a professor of literature, and seldom does her work fall short of their requirements. Moreover she is a critic of discernment, especially in the field of fiction. Her *causerie* on the present-day state of the American short story in *The Yale Review* of July, 1924, should be read by all students of the short story. Her summaries may be taken as an introduction to the work of the modern era.

"The astonishing thing about the contemporary short story in America," she declares, "is that there is so much of it, and that it is, on the whole, so clever. I don't say 'good'; I say 'clever.' Full of 'pep'; amusing or thrilling incident; surprise. The plots over which our grandparents—our parents, even—grew excited, would not suffice nowadays to lift the eyebrows of a ten-year-old child, in the dark. To be sure, we have a more complicated mechanism of life, to help out the thrill; and many of the thrills come from that mere mechanism. We have airplanes, and motor-cars, and poison gas, and soviets, and Hollywood, and flappers, and radio, and bootleggers—to say nothing of highjackers. The habit of wonder has been atrophied in us. Stories that once were classics could not achieve that position now."

In her opinion the present-day requirements may be summed up in a paragraph:

"To be first rate, a short story must first of all be well made. It must give us situation, suspense, and climax. The incident that informs and creates the story must be a significant one; either truly momentous for one person, or vividly typical of the lives of many people, or—if you like—suggestively symbolic. It must carry more than its own weight. It cannot, that is, be simple anecdote, however trenchant. If it but chronicles an absurdity, the absurdity must carry implications concerning fate or human character. A short story that does not do this may be readable, and often is, but it is not a great short story."

EMMA BLAIR *

I was excited and depressed, the last night out—excited because at dawn we should lift that wondrous headland of which I had heard; depressed because I was looking for health, and health, which is the most decent thing in the world to possess, is the least decent thing in the world to look for. Or, at least, so I've always felt. Travel for pleasure, for gain, for idleness, for revenge—all these motives are plausible. But to crawl about, expecting the planet to resolve itself into a pill—no, that's not done. It jaundices the beauty of high heaven. A sick man should stop in his hole. But, like every one else, I had obeyed physicians; and

there I was. The vast, inhuman wastes of the Pacific were supposed to be tonic, and even more tonic the haven where I should presently be. I am not prepared to say that the Pacific was not tonic, but that night there was fever in me. I spent the long hours on deck, fully dressed; and before dawn I had fought my disgust to a finish—sent it to the mat in a bloody crumple. I would not pretend that my illness was interesting, but I would fight for exceeding fitness. Then I would fold my arms and nod, comrade-wise, at the wonders of nature. I would mix in crowds again and shrink from no man.

We landed in the very early morning, and I found myself liking it almost as a healthy man may. Never mind the island or the port; if you'll permit me, I'll be geographically vague. You may think of me as anywhere between the equator and the Tropic of Capricorn. Tahiti, Samoa, Fiji, the Cook Islands—anywhere will do. Plain, seaworthy little steamers go to all of those places, as you know. I betook myself to the hotel, and a very decent place it was—small, and by no means vacuum-cleaned, but comfortable and airy and extremely well victualed. It was kept by a Frenchwoman, the widow of the late landlord, who had been, I believe, a British subject—with a touch of the tar-brush. The place had improved, I was told, since his death. I do not know whether my destination had been guesswork on the part of my physician. If so, it was a guess of genius. After three nights I began to sleep under my mosquito-bar as in many a long month I had not slept at home.

Curious what the tropics do to you! If you know that you don't have to stay forever, that is. As an interlude they are very convincing. I found myself ready to recline on the bosom of Nature in almost Wordsworthian fashion, though before long I began to understand . . . and I sat up straight very quickly. Of course, if Wordsworth had ever seen the tropics, he would have run away at once. It is easier, you see, to find God a little above Tintern Abbey than in Polynesia—if only because He was put there a long time ago. I soon realized that my favorite poets had met Nature only at afternoon tea, and that it was too idiotic of them to pretend to know her character. Her character, I have come to believe, is very unsavory. That is why I said, just now, that the tropics were all right if you knew you weren't going to stay—if you didn't intend to make it a permanent relation. White men have arrived in the South Seas; they have even lingered there; they have left strange and touching monuments to themselves; but they have not been there long or numerously enough to tinge the atmosphere. Nature is still dominant, and she is no more to be trusted than the obscure Venus of the Hollow Hill.

That is a digression, of course. And yet it isn't, wholly. If I had not come to my adventure by just the ways I took, it would have tasted differently to me. That I know. I was eventually ripe for the encounter with an old acquaintance—two, you might say, except that I never, thank Heaven, really encountered him.

Sleep soaked me through and through, then turned me over to the sun to saturate me again. For days and weeks I walked about, heavy with sun and sleep. Then the buoyancy of my reviving body made me eager, alert. I began to cast an eye on humankind. I was no longer content to lie in a palm-grove on the beach, idly filling and refilling my lungs with the Trade. I became curious once more. I had not been curious for a very long time. The native idiom intrigued me, and I bribed men to stop mending their nets and talk to me. I grew adept in Polynesian beauty, disdaining to watch any girl over fifteen. I dined out with consuls, and gathered in the news that beats about such ports as this— opera-bouffe news, a lot of it, but true. It was always one of two *données*—the comic one of the brown man trying to be white, or the tragic one of the white man trying to be brown. As stories, they went off into nothing, because they were too absurd. But some of them were exciting enough, to a semi-invalid. Never, though, did I get a hint of this story. I had to discover that for myself. I stood beach-combers to drinks in villainous bars, and followed conch-shells at dusk to the outskirts of festival. The lovely, frowsy little town became known to me in detail. Then, human-fashion, I began to get tired of it. The natives were incredible; and in so far as the few white people conscientiously stayed white, they were permanently provincial—always thinking of the little European towns they had come from. The only people who tried to understand were missionaries, and they were rather a scratch lot. When a missionary doesn't manage to understand, he is the poorest company in the world. Of course I ran into the usual sleek Sydney trader, but he wasn't a very interesting breed—except as there is always drama to be had when a man is doing a little business in pearls on the side. I always kept away from pearls and talk about pearls, because I expected to need all my money for an infirm old age; and the things the small trader drinks don't agree with me. Copra and trepang were the rest of it.

It didn't, as I say, take me many weeks to feel that I had exhausted the resources of the capital—exhausted them, that is, as far as one of my temperament and condition was able to. And, though I distrusted Nature, I thought that, forearmed by my distrust, I could perhaps afford to see her a little more intimately. The town was lovely; but it was a port, a trading-center, and there were too many mongrel faces and voices. I wanted to push on into the interior of the island, find an enchanted gorge, and pitch my camp above a rainbow torrent—with perhaps a palm-smothered village to hum a few hundred feet below me. The climate made hardship very improbable. I applied for aid and advice to the man most likely to help me. He put his back into it and made excellent arrangements. He named the gorge, the torrent, and the village for me, dragged the town for a couple of natives to make up my little caravan, and discovered, engaged, and haled to my feet a weazened, one-eyed Chinaman who, he said, could cook and was anxious, for reasons of his own, to flee temptation. The proud possessor, for a term, by contract, of these mixed dregs of humanity, I started for my waterfall. The island is small, of course; and, whatever happened, I should not be too far away from what called itself civilization. The wonder was that, twenty miles from the capital, I should be able to find the lonely gorge of my dreams. But I was.

All known indolence is hectic compared with the life I lived for a week on the upper slope of my cañon. I had only to lie among the fern and look, look, look until the world swam into a parti-colored blur. Sleep? I have never known sleep like that. I descended into it as into a bath of cool wine, waking into an air heady with flowers and fruit. More than once I scrambled down to the stream and bathed at dawn, then clambered back and plaited myself a cap of fern stuck over with orchids, all before breakfast. A green parrot in the pandanus-tree above my tent roof screeched to the sun while I drank my coffee. I had no great use for my two natives after I had once arrived, and as I failed to invent any services for them, they often crept away into the fern on business of their own. They brought fruits, and things for the Chinaman to cook—fowls for which I paid through the nose, and fresh-water fish for which I thanked them with elaborate facial contortions. Except for foraging, though, there was little for them to do, and I believe they spent quite half their time in the village below. Sometimes I could feel a dozen eyes peering at me out of the foliage, and then I knew that they were exhibiting me to friends. I did my best, on such occasions,

to show off properly, without noticing them. The Chinaman, true to type, asked nothing better than to work, and he took the sole care of me. His name, amusingly enough, sounded like nothing but "Chink," and "Chink" I called him. Nature herself lightened his tasks considerably; it was impossible to complicate life very much. For a week I moved in a restricted and perfect dream. I sought no other vistas; I did not even make my way to the head of the gorge, or yet pass back again along the trail up which we had come. I hollowed myself a fragrant retreat about a hundred yards from the camp, and there I drowsed and lay for long hours, my whole heart fallow to the sun. I knew what Nature's tender moods were worth; but while they endured, I was ready, like any other male, to flirt.

Of course it could not last. Such an experience is unreal, an artificial gesture on the part of life. I have never believed those men who pretended that they had really prolonged such an existence. The goat's horns and the cleft hoof always gleam through their accounts at some point or other. Whereas my relations with Nature were perfectly innocent. No, of course it could not last. My paradise was bound to be shattered over my head. One night in my second week I sat in my retreat after the sun had gone down. The crimson crash of his setting was my dinner-gong; but sometimes I waited for Chink's sibilant echo before I made for my tent and dinner. The tropic twilight, as you know, hardly exists; night is rung down like a quick curtain; and I had just time to pace my hundred yards between sunset and dark. On this occasion Chink uttered no refrain to the sunset, and for a few moments I stayed on lazily where I was. I had to hurry to reach the camp before the undergrowth should trip me in the dusk. I saw the ashy glow of a forsaken fire in the cooking-place, but my own tent was dark. So, too, was the little shack the natives had put up. I hunted about for the cook, and found him, at last, dead drunk among the fern at a discreet distance. By match-flare, he was a horrid sight—with a trickle of what had once been food from the corner of his mouth—and I left him where he was, then proceeded to cook my supper. I had never learned the secret of cooking over hot stones, and I let it go at tea and eggs. I was thoroughly disgusted with

Chink, and, as I splashed myself at dessert with mango juice, I greatly wondered.

There were no spirits in the camp, except for a flask of whiskey which at that moment I drew forth from my pocket safe and undepleted. Kava, of course, and probably square-face, were going, down in the village near the stream, but I knew that Chink did not share my natives' habit of descending to collogue with the villagers. I kicked about in the grass of the little clearing, by torch-light, but I found nothing that could have held strong drink. I could have rifled the man's shapeless garments while he slept, but a complete and perfect repugnance prevented me. I lay cradled in the fern outside my tent all the evening, face upturned, hunting the stars through waving banana-fronds. The native boys returned, softly chattering, and soon slept in their absurd hut. Toward midnight there was still no sound from the cook; I judged him safe then to sleep it off and wake sober, and I turned in. I had brought no fire-arms into Eden, and I wanted to be quite sure.

Chink's weazened face, as he served me my breakfast the next morning, was impassive and shameless. True, I do not know what emotion would have been powerful enough to work upheaval among those secular features. He might have been the cunning enemy of dinosaurs, one who had survived their defeat and his own prime. There was no point in expecting expression to prick through that hard, yellow glaze. He intimidated me; it was so inconceivable that my opinion of him and his opinion of me should ever encounter each other. And of course I had only pidgin-talk to probe him with. I couldn't get at the situation, and I am ashamed to say that, with the morning well advanced, I still had made no beginning—not the first word of a reproach. I poked about for a cache with large, exploring gestures, but I found nothing. Luncheon came, and still I said no word to Chink. My rest-cure, so far, had been no preparation for the kind of scene I ought to make. If it had been merely the drunken sleep I could have ignored it; but the failure to cook my dinner I could not ignore. Before night I must assert myself and tell that grotesque creature he was a sinner. I assure you Chink's conduct and my own pusillanimity blackened the day for me.

A nap after luncheon was part of my ritual, and I turned in conscientiously. I did not sleep very long, though; and when I woke, the sun, which by rights should have been high in the heavens and still torrid, was temporarily obscured by clouds. I came out of my tent and saw Chink busy, with a monstrous industry, over pots and pans. Of course I must speak to him. No shaft of mine could reach his soul, which was at least a thousand years away; but I must register for him the fact that I knew I had had to cook my own dinner. He was a creature who might have waited on you in a dream; he had nothing to do with life. Yet there we were, on the map, you might say; and latitude and longitude, our eternal masters, forbade the plausible dream hypothesis. I must reprove and question him—now: my conscience told me.

My reply to conscience was to turn my back on Chink and strike off through the bushes toward the head of the gorge. I had never gone in that direction before, though a trail of sorts snaked through the trees. After I had put twenty minutes between myself and Chink I stopped and reflected, sitting on a rotted tree-trunk. What should I do then? I had stuck out my tongue at my conscience, and I might as well get any benefit I could from my impudence. The trail wound on and on ahead of me, leading, I inferred, to the waterfall at the head of the gorge. Probably a religious trail, I mused—trodden by men and women bearing queer little vegetable gifts to some unpronounceable god. I knew already something of their habits. Well, I decided to follow it up myself and see what the head of the gorge was like. Probably at the end the trail would wind down, and perhaps I should find a rock pool beneath the fall to bathe in. Chink would simply have to wait, focusing his single eye upon the pots and pans.

After half an hour of very slow walking —for of course the path was constantly impeded by the irrepressible jungle growth —I reached a point where the trail forked. I could see nothing through the thick fern, like green jalousies let down on every side of me; but the trail itself turned downward among bamboo clumps, while there was unmistakably a little smear going off in an easterly direction, higher up the slope. The trail would take me to the waterfall, I felt sure; indeed, I could hear a faint, watery rumble off there to the northwest, where the fall must be. But somehow I wanted to follow the slug-track, up. So I embarked on the sketchier path, beating the fronds and stalks away from my face with my outstretched hands —an awkward swimming motion that was very tiring. After about fifteen minutes of slow climbing I found the path widening. Nor had it been widened only by the passage of bodies; the growth had been lopped off by a knife or a hatchet. I pressed onward, much intrigued.

Suddenly I heard something that made me turn; I could not have identified the sound; I almost more felt it than heard it. I was only aware, and sharply, that it was something other than the constant little stir of vegetable life. It had a direct human clumsiness. I caught a glint of blue about twenty yards behind me; it wriggled once in the streaky light and then was motionless.

At that instant, drama entered into my experience. Chink, for reasons of his own, was stalking me. I cared little enough what became of Chink, either in this world or the next—his adventures could probably be neither phrased by my language nor conceived by my brain. But none the less that little blue wriggle among the fern seemed to me part less of Chink's life than of mine. My own spine wriggled in sympathy. Then I felt something nearer home than Chink's illegal presence; and I looked down to see a tiny pig caroming off my left ankle. A few steps more, and the path widened into a clearing, within which, about fifty yards ahead of me, I perceived a house, half wood and half thatch, boasting a rude veranda. Dirty chickens pecked round it, and there were more pigs on the veranda. Indescribable heaps of junk lay about the compound—things half decayed, half rusted, or half torn. There was a rude outdoor oven near a spring, and dirty white curtains at the windows of the house. A few chairs huddled together on the veranda, in the unsociable attitude of furniture that a slatternly maid has flung about while sweeping. Various little plots at the outer edges of the clearing were under cultivation and showed the uneven green tops of their different crops.

I hardly knew, after the first survey, what to do—whether to turn in my tracks or go forward and wait among the pigs and poultry until I could have speech with the occupants. I decided to wait a few moments, anyhow, and give Chink time to evade me. I had no desire to make the return journey with Chink. So I halted where I was, etching that scene of complicated desolation on my mind. The hens squawked in their universal tongue, and the baby pigs paid no attention to me whatever except when they collided with my feet. They ran about like blind things. I did not quite want to sit down where I was, nor did I want to go up on the veranda. Finally I rolled myself a cigarette and stood with my back against a tree, politely staring. A blue smock came round the corner of the house, and I started. By what devious way had Chink got to the back of the house? The blue smock, which had evidently been making for the spring, wheeled sharply at sight of me, and ducked again behind the house. I had just time to see that it was a foot taller than Chink and therefore not he, when it disappeared. I settled myself comfortably down into my drama, but rather wished I had something better than a slight stick to play my part with. I do not know why two one-eyed Chinamen are so much more than twice as bad as one, but the green patch over the left eye of this apparition turned me quite sick. I decided to go away; to get back to my friendly, feckless Polynesians. They might be devils, though I didn't believe it, but they were at least good-looking. I do not know what inward impertinence moved me to pick a custard-banana off a near-by tree and eat it before I went; but at all events it gave time to Chink's compeer to carry his news within the house. Just as I flung the peel away and started to go, a woman came out on the veranda and down the steps toward me. That, of course, stopped me in mid-flight. My feet seemed to have entered the earth and changed into roots.

The woman was tall, with stooped shoulders. So much of her figure only could I make out, for all the lines of her body were heavily hidden by one loose garment of no cut or mode. She looked as if a pink calico curtain had been hung round her. Chinese straw sandals flopped on her white-stockinged feet. Her hair was a straight, faded yellow, and she wore it in a frowsy plait over one shoulder—a kind of parody of pre-Raphaelite tresses. As she moved across the disheveled compound toward me I saw that she was naturally of an almost Scandinavian fairness, though her features were those of our own race. The pink curtain that hid her body from the world was very dirty, but she had rings on her fingers—a wedding-ring, and guarding it—I think—an emerald.

She did not speak for a moment, as she faced me; nor did I find any word to greet her with. My tongue seemed suddenly to have turned vegetable like my body. For one thing, I had no notion, for all she looked so like a misused compatriot, what language to try. For another, I had a tortured sense of having seen her before, and not in a dream, nor yet in a previous existence. Those features, I could not but believe, were known to me; that mouth had spoken to me; yet I could not place her anywhere within my experience of space or time. My shadowy memories wheeled about in a confusing, batlike flutter. Whether she belonged to my childhood or to my maturity, I could not have told; yet I was sure that I had seen her, somewhere across the world, in the flesh. Meanwhile her opaque blue eyes searched my face.

Desperately I decided on French, and began to apologize for my intrusion.

She cut me short. "You are English, aren't you?"

"No. American."

"Oh, American."

"I am camping down near the mouth of the gorge. I somehow think my Chinese cook comes up here to see yours. In fact, I believe he has followed me this afternoon. He was very drunk last night—I don't know on what. But I mustn't trouble you. I stumbled on your place—didn't dream it was here. I'll be going now. Very sorry to have intruded."

My speech, which had begun firmly enough, ran out in a little, ineffectual trickle of words. She was appalling in her degeneration, her familiarity, her silence.

"It's all right." And she turned her back on me.

I lifted my hat and turned, then, resolute if ever. Luckily my feet politely consented to move. I would go back to camp, pack up my kit, and leave on the morrow; and I would never, never speak to Chink about his misdemeanors. I felt curiosity to be as dangerous as pearls. I had got perhaps ten paces out of the clearing when a voice behind me pulled me up short.

"Mr. Kirwin!"

My own name, ringing out of that unkempt compound on the edge of the world!

What was a guilty blue smock in the fern, to that? I wheeled, of course. I came back into the clearing almost at a run. Against the significance of that cry my mere will was about as powerful as a bent bodkin.

I came close to where she stood, looking into her face. Her arms were folded tensely across her breast. Her stooped shoulders gave her a crouching look. She spoke at once, almost in a whisper:

"I knew you at once, of course. I didn't mean to let you know, but when I saw you going—going off, away—I had to bring you back. I must talk to you."

"But how do you know me? Where did you know me?" At a gesture from her I brought my eager voice down to an explosive whisper. "Your face—I know I've seen it; but I can't place you. You must forgive me. I knew I knew you; that was why I stood and stared like a stuck pig."

"You really don't know me?" Her face was so close to mine that I could hardly make out the features. Why were we whispering intimately to each other in all that tropic emptiness? "You don't remember?" Her low murmur was as tragically hurt as though she were Helen of Troy.

"No." I was ashamed, but I stuck to the truth.

"Then I will talk. I will have it out. You *shall* remember!" Her voice seemed torn in her throat. Then she flung her arms wide and looked down the length of them to her hands; surveyed the dirty, pink wrapper, the flapping sandals, the white stockings—with a hole in one of the toes. I was still struggling among my memories—searching the ground at my feet as if I could find her name written there.

"Of course, of course," I muttered. Nothing in the litter underfoot gave back her name to me.

"Look at me!"

Stupidly I lifted my chin and looked at her.

"You don't remember? Look hard."

I looked hard. My eyes bored obediently into her peevish, thrust-out countenance, though that dirty sallowness still said nothing to me. Her mouth had gone slack, but the nose was very beautiful. Surely one must remember such an aristocrat among noses. I looked at it—focused my eyes on the high bridge and the delicate nostrils. It brought back no name, no scene, however; and I could not stand there forever gazing at a woman's nose, two feet from mine, as if I were a beauty-doctor. I wriggled a little, then wrenched my eyes away from the lovely masterpiece of bone and cartilage, and directed them at her own opaque blue ones.

"No," I breathed, uncomfortably.

"Oh, it's too much—not to remember *me!*" She seemed actually to speak of herself with awe. Then she bit her lip and changed her tone. I fancied then I was hearing the voice that her one-eyed Chinaman was wont to hear. "When can I see you? Can you wait until I'm a little more civilized? I can't talk to you like this." She glanced scornfully down again at her pink curtain and her sandals.

"But why not?" I tried to suggest by my own tone that she was, if she liked, Helen of Troy.

She did not answer the direct question. "Can you wait for twenty minutes?"

"I'm afraid, if I don't get back before dark, I can't. It's not much of a trail unless you're used to it."

"I am used to it. I'll take you back."

"Oh, thank you . . ." And I now had my turn at feeling that it was "too much." But the matter was apparently settled. "Does your Chinaman give my Chinaman liquor, do you think?"

She shrugged her shoulders contemptuously. "Very likely. Lung is a vicious beast. But he cooks well. Only it would be more likely to be opium, I should think. Lung smokes it, I know."

"No; my man was drunk. It wasn't the black smoke. Besides, there was no apparatus about. Perhaps he gave him some to eat."

She shook her head. "They don't eat it much, you know. But Lung would have had plenty of square-face—or would have known where to find it—and he gets kava from the natives, I imagine. He can stand any amount, though. He's never really drunk, though stupid, sometimes, after the black smoke." She spoke very indifferently, as if the subject were quite irrelevant. But irrelevant to what? "If you are going to be about here for some time, I'll speak to Lung, if you like—tell him not to give stuff to yours. Only, you know, they are probably 'brothers' of some kind. In that case, no interference would do any good." The lady seemed very bored— afternoon tea bored, within her dirty pink curtain.

"I shall strike camp as soon as I can—

to-morrow, if possible. I only hired Chink for a few weeks. He doesn't belong to me, thank God."

She started toward the house. "I'll get a chair for you. Please don't come up on the veranda."

But I was not going to have her fetching chairs for me, and I followed. She looked at me, a little helpless for all her truculence, and did not protest. She only jerked a grass curtain across one of the open doors, and handed me down one of the light chairs. Then she leaned over the rail. "I can't talk to you here. We should wake my husband. Go over in the banana-grove. I'll come." And she disappeared.

I fetched a second chair, averting my eyes discreetly from the grass curtain, and passed across to the indicated spot. I do not know how long I sat in the banana-grove, waiting. Long enough, anyhow, for plenty of lurid conjectures to take up their abode within me. I no longer wondered who she was, for I knew that she would presently tell me, and I gave up trying to think. But I was very curious about the sleeping husband. She hadn't the air of a woman who has married a native. Still . . . if he had been a white man, shouldn't I have heard of him, down yonder, with my consuls? Anyhow, he was not expected to assist at the conference. He was—asleep. Then suddenly, from behind a banana-tree, Chink appeared, salaaming. Here was my chance for a scene. Chink's wickedness, however, was no longer so very important to me. There was other drama afoot. Matched up with the mystery inside the house—Caucasian, and a woman—he had shrunk into a vague, yellow blot. Within twenty-four hours I hoped to return Chink politely to the temptations of the capital; meanwhile I was not going to wrestle either for Chink's soul or for my own dignity. Doubtless I could have got comedy out of it by keeping him on for a few moments; but the imminent hint of tragedy sours the laugh in one's mouth. I looked at him contemptuously and waved him away. He slobbered a little, inarticulately, then made off behind the house to join, I suppose, his one-eyed brother. It was a hectic life for a semi-invalid, and I was feeling a little tired.

The lady did not keep me waiting, certainly, beyond the twenty minutes mentioned. Presently I saw her come out of the house and down the veranda steps, toward me. I rose and faced her as she approached. The pink curtain was gone, and the sandals; in their place she had donned slippers and a garment of faded blue that looked like a long-superannuated tea-gown. It was creased and spotted, but both the creases and the spots looked to be of very ancient date. The dress linked itself to none of my recent memories of female attire. I know nothing of fashions, but it looked quaint; it might have been something she was in the habit of wearing at the unremembered period when I had "known" her. Her hair was dressed high on her head and skewered through with imitation jade hair-pins such as low-caste Chinese women wear. She looked singularly battered; more so, I suppose, because she was now unmistakably an American woman, though a shoddy and shabby one. Nothing, probably, could give her back beauty—or neatness; but at least she looked extraordinarily out of place in that filthy clearing at the hidden head of that exotic gorge. She turned and gazed at me silently as she sat down. Evidently she thought that, once more in the garb of her class, I should know her. But I didn't, though scenes began to shape themselves vaguely behind her—rooms full of people, and city streets, mistily encroaching on bamboo and palm. I shook my head, and the tears came into her eyes.

"Of course I never knew you well, but I am Emma Blair. I used to see you at your cousin's—Gerty Fox."

Emma Blair! I cursed myself then with more than orthodox fervor. No wonder! no wonder! Of all the brutal things my merely average personality had ever achieved, this was the most brutal. Not to have recognized her—it was the *Urdummheit*, no less. Perhaps I blamed myself at the moment too much. It had been ten years since I or mine had set eyes on Mrs. Blair, or heard of her. Still, it was hard on her. In a state of contrition that would almost have sufficed for Lucifer, I laid my hand on hers, though I stared straight ahead of me into the cluster of banana-trunks.

"Mrs. Blair! How could I? But I've had many misfortunes. I've been out of the world, wandering in my own inner jungle. I've lost touch with them all."

They were poor words, but they seemed to hearten her. She put a shy and stealthy hand up to her hair, straightened one of the fantastic hair-pins. "Then you think others may not have forgotten?"

Indescribable, the fanatic eagerness of her voice!

"They've forgotten what your husband did, I believe."

I meant it, Heaven knows, for reassurance—what kinder thing could one say to Blair's wife than that the world had forgotten Blair's crime?—but it did not have that effect.

"Forgotten? Why, people can't forget a thing like that—forging, and then absconding! Or do you mean that they think my husband is dead? I hope they don't think *I* am dead."

I remembered so much, now—comments, gestures, the expressions of frowning, averted faces, social and moral attitudes publicly struck, a coruscating heap of detail. Incredible that, up to the utterance of her name, I should have had that visual aphasia. Out of the heap of detail, one fact glimmered most brightly—that never, at any moment, from her marriage on, had Mrs. Blair pretended to care the snap of her finger for her husband. That she should leave the country with him had been the breath-taking fact—not that Rupert Blair should have done any one of the thousand things that aren't "done." There were those who had said that she had stuck by him when the crash came, for the loot. They had soon found out, however, that there couldn't have been much loot; and it was then that Mrs. Blair's accompanying him in his flight had turned to a nine-days' wonder. A few dowagers had praised her nobility into one another's ear-trumpets, but most of them were dead by this time. Other people had given it up and gone on to other things. You can't be intrigued forever, if there is no promise of the riddle's being solved. If a person goes down at once, and never rises again, that is. . . .

"People forget everything. And, as it happens—if I remember rightly—no one suffered much who couldn't afford to suffer."

"Perhaps not. That's one thing *I* have forgotten." She smiled bitterly. "But it was a dirty, disgraceful act, dirtily and disgracefully done."

It was not a pleasant line for her to take, and I hardly knew how to meet her words.

"You haven't forgiven him—even now?"

"Forgiven him? What do you mean? Surely people don't think that of me! Do I look as if I would forgive that sort of thing?"

She looked—*pace* the unforgetable vision of her—as if she would forgive anything; as if the sun had corrupted her to its own indifferentism. So I only stammered.

"And yet," she went on, "that was no worse than a dozen other things, for his wife. It was no revelation to me. He was always a beast."

The "beast," please remember, was just over yonder, in the house, hidden from the veranda by a grass curtain pulled across a door.

"Do you mean that you always hated him?"

"Always. I didn't happen to be in love with any one else, but I certainly never pretended to be in love with him."

"Why didn't you divorce him?"

Mrs. Blair drew the loose, faded folds of her gown around her, then let them fall across her knees. I noticed again the beautiful line of her nose.

"One has to stand by the cards, don't you think? I married for what I could get out of it. Of course, if I had expected to get this"—her voice harshened a little with disgust—"I shouldn't have sat in. But if you play the game, you must play it, mustn't you? I thought my friends realized—" Again the questing agony in her voice.

"Not if the man you're playing with cheats," I answered, slowly.

"Oh, the law—! I'm talking about one's marriage vow."

"You mean you think it's a sacrament?"

"I've forgotten about the sacraments. It's a long time since I've seen one. I mean that I was brought up to be a sport."

The words fell oddly from her lips; I can hardly explain how oddly. They didn't sound spontaneous. They weren't vivid; they might have been an old formula dragged out of a trunk like the creased tea-gown. The formula was stale on her lips. It has been invented years ago for a moment that never came. When the moment did come, there was no time to furbish and freshen. Her phrase was musty—and not clean. . . . This is important, for the whole situation was Emma Blair's. Except hers, there was none. My coming there at all, my ill-health and the doctor's guess, my little "affair" with Nature, my troubles with Chink, were only part of her delayed fate. I assure you I felt all that, very humbly, as I sat there beside this terrible person. It was perhaps her greatest misfortune—yes, her greatest —that when her big scene came she couldn't put it through any better than she did. The footlights only picked flaws in her make-up. Or shall I say that her obsession had gnawed her into an impossible shape? But I had to go on.

"You were magnificent."

"Was I? Is that what they say of me?" She crossed her hands on her breast and breathed hard. I tell you her eagerness was not decent. No one has a right to want anything—even good report—for himself with such a bestial intensity. I began to see my difficult part in it all. For the truth was that no one said anything, any longer, and the mention of Emma Blair would awake only yawns. No; a nine-days' wonder mustn't ape immortality.

"I tell you I'm out of the world. But that is what they did say. It was very fine of you to stand by. And finer than ever, when one considers this." I lashed myself into admiration, looking round at the desolate dirtiness of her home.

She drank in my words, lips wide apart over her yellow teeth. "They don't know, I suppose, what has become of me," she panted.

"No, of course not. Even the people in T——"—I mentioned the capital of the archipelago—"didn't tell me there were white folk up here. You've kept it all awfully quiet."

"We never go down." And again her voice dropped to indifference. "Lung does our buying. That is—he gets the square-face and the brandy. Otherwise, we live on the land." She crooked a scornful finger at the fuzzy crops that girdled the compound. "They've forgotten about us down there, I don't doubt. It must be years since either of us has crossed the island."

"What do you find to do?" And indeed my curiosity on that point was vivid.

"I live." With a turn of the hand she shut off my curiosity, pressed it back to its source.

"But—"

I got no further, for then Emma Blair began to talk, like a resuscitated actress of the old school. Her tones and gestures had been learned long ago, and the world had gone on. I cannot reproduce for you her harangue—all her out-dated phrases and her occasional old-fashioned slang. Points of view don't change much—the blessed old world has always held them all. You can't out-date tragedy, but a given expression of it can be laid on the shelf. The real tragedy of Emma Blair was her belief in her own heroism. She didn't mind suffering in her apathetic way, if her name were only a sacred symbol in certain drawing-rooms of our Atlantic seaboard. I made it all out, sooner or later; and her false stresses, her bad (artistically bad) egotism, were, you might say, smelly torches to light me to the truth. There had been a glimmer of a fine idea in the beginning —that of "standing by the cards"; of sticking to a disgraced husband whom she detested, because she had taken him originally for what she could get out of it. The trouble was that the fine idea hadn't been genuine. She hadn't really conceived it to be her duty; she had only conceived it to be a showily beautiful act. If you choose to object that she had at all events really done it, for whatever reason, and that she was really "paying"—well, I can't deny that. But she was counting very heavily on praise. She was a sentimentalist, and you can't be more rotten than that. She was stiff with histrionism still. I dare say, more than once, in the years, she had wished that she hadn't originally burned her boats. But now and then, in a phrase, I saw the secret ambition that had kept her alive.

She expected, sooner or later, to lay him in six feet of disgusted earth, and return to find her shrine waiting. With a moral preëminence like that, losing her looks wouldn't count. She would have stolen a march on her contemporaries who, when *their* looks went, would have no striking moral beauty to show. I don't say she had worked it all out when she left hastily by night, with Blair, for parts unknown. Working it out had probably been the one solace of her unspeakable days. Unlike her husband, she had abstained from square-face, and refreshed herself from this hidden spring. Once or twice she said the most overweening things—as if she expected people to model her in marble and set her in a public square with an appropriate inscription. (How was I to tell her that they would be much more likely to put her in an old-ladies' home?)

She had hoped that people talked of her constantly; she had held her breath across the world, in her leafy retreat, imagining what they were saying. And I had frightened her terribly by not even knowing her; not knowing her even· when she had put on real shoes and done her hair on top of her head. That, she just couldn't bear. It all came out, pell-mell—what she had expected of her friends at home, and what she felt about them if they hadn't lived up to her expectations. Her moral beauty was about as real as the ·sapphires in a fifty-cent bracelet. But one thing was real enough—her idea of her moral beauty and of what it merited. People who didn't appreciate it, feed on it as gospel, were serving the devil; they would get no quarter from her.

There were moments, as I sat there listening to her, when I loathed her. She was a model of idealistic greed. I wanted to break in, to tell her that no one gave a hang for her; that I hadn't heard her mentioned for years; and that, if I spoke of her on my return, the subject wouldn't last twenty minutes. But on the heels of that desire came always a horrified wonder at what she had actually borne, in however bad a cause. And on· the heels of *that* came the fear that she would have it all out of me before I could leave the enchanted gorge behind me. A sentimentalist can usually be put off with a lie; but she was greedy, too, and the greedy man knows whether his mouth· is filled or not. She had broken down, you see, before my insulting failure to recognize her. Her myth had been stabbed. . . . I don't suppose she really thought her old acquaintances were forever tiptoeing round the earth, hoping at each instant to surprise her in her hiding-place—not really. But I am sure she felt that to discover her would be a climax to any adventure. Well, it was a climax, Heaven knows, to mine! I was very tired.

With that sudden weariness, I realized that I must be getting back. The sky was being hastily prepared for sunset. I didn't know where Chink was; and, in any case, had not Mrs. Blair said that she would accompany me? I would much rather have taken my chances alone in the fern, but I did not expect to be let off. I rose at last.

"I've got to get back, Mrs. Blair. Is there anything in the world I can do for you?"

She got up, too. "Nothing, thank you.

am afraid I can't give you the pleasure
f meeting my husband. He's always drunk
n the afternoon. He's drunk now—up
here." She nodded at the house.

"But—but what a life!"

"You may well say it. But it won't last
much longer. He has delirium tremens,
believe."

"Couldn't a doctor do anything? There's
decent one down yonder."

"It's not very easy to get a doctor up
here. And I'm sure he would hate being
cured. What is there left in life for him
but drink? I tell you it won't last much
longer."

"But you— How hideous—how dangerous for you!"

She shook her head. "I stay out of the
way when it's bad. Lung is very strong.
He looks after him. If Lung is far gone
with the black smoke, I simply hide in the
bush until it's over. I don't intend to be
killed in that way. It's not as if I had
ever loved him."

"No, of course not," I stammered. "Does
he love you?"

She stopped, with one foot on the lower
step of the veranda. "Are most people at
home as stupid as you are?"

I met her in like temper. "Just about, I
think."

"There used to be quarrels. There aren't,
any more." Leaving my question thus quite
unanswered, she passed into the house.
tiptoed up on the veranda and listened—
did not look—through the grass curtain. There was no doubt that Blair was
within.

"Your man has gone." Mrs. Blair's voice
sounded sharply in my ear. "I'll see you
home."

I protested, with all the fervor my
shaken nerves could muster. But it was
of no use. Mrs. Blair kilted up the soiled
folds of her dress and led the way. I gave
one look back at the clearing and the house,
and then we started out, in full sunlight,
with a lighted lantern. In the gloom of the
trail it was not useless, and before half an
hour dusk was upon us and we picked our
way only by its light.

Mrs. Blair walked ahead, carrying the
lantern. She was shapeless as some monster there ahead in the gloom—a monster
with a blue skin, as you could tell from
the occasional patch of her that the swinging lantern illumined. Our conversation
was very slight and quite scrappy. I ven-

tured once, "This is a heavenly beautiful
place."

"Is it?" She did not turn, and her words
came to me muffled. It seemed an interminable walk. I was dripping with sweat
and aching in every sinew; and how I
longed to be out of her custody! The trail
to the clearing behind me, the jungle on
either side, and the swaying blue monster
in front of me— Never was a man more
vilely imprisoned than that. Toward the
end of our journey it became too much
for me.

"I know it's not very far, now. Please
don't go farther. I really can get there
safely. Unless you'll come all the way and
have supper with me, then let me send
some one back with you?"

I fancy she, too, had had enough of it.
She turned to me. "Well—if you can find
your way." And we stood there for a moment, facing each other in the narrow path.

"Of course I can. And I can't tell you—"
I searched desperately for a fitting final
word, but it was not easily come by.

She swung the lantern back and forth
viciously. "Of course you can't tell me,"
she broke out suddenly. "Who could? Even
I, getting my chance after all these years,
can't tell *you.*"

"You don't need to. Think of what
you've put through." Yes, she had put
through unspeakable things, and I must
keep my mind on that fact. I could see her
beautiful nostrils quiver faintly as they
met that incense.

Then, abruptly, she held out her hand.
"Good-by. I've done what no other
woman in the world has ever done—and
it hasn't been worth it. I haven't even a
child to be proud of me."

"May I tell them at home about it?"

"Some day I'll tell them myself. But you
can tell them what you like. Only—if they
are all like you—they'll never understand.
Why, you had forgotten me!"

"I never shall again."

"No?" There was irony in her tone—
and yet a last little spent eagerness, too.
Then she passed me in the narrow trail
and faced homeward. "But it would take
a great genius to understand me—to explain. People like you forget."

Without another word she started up the
trail. I watched the blue glimmer of her
figure until, in the near distance, the path
took a turn. Then I stumbled on home,
infinitely glad to be rid of her, convinced

that she was a little mad, my pity mitigated by the knowledge that no one would ever pity her for the right things. For the more obvious blows of circumstance, Emma Blair had developed a kind of anæsthesia—though, no doubt, she bled inwardly from strange wounds.

The rest is—nothing much. I made up my mind, in those last strides down the trail, not to question Chink. He had prepared for me a remarkable dinner. I ate it appreciatively, but in silence; then announced to my caravan that we should leave on the morrow. Impossible, they said. On the day after, then, at dawn; and to that they agreed. Chink, so far as I know, did not journey back to his fellow-countryman at the head of the gorge; and, certainly, all the long day no word came down the trail for me. I do not suppose that Mrs. Blair told her husband of my visit. It would not, at least, have been in character.

I was in twenty minds as to whether or not to make inquiries when I got back to T——. It was rather stupid of me, I think, to decide not to; but at the time I did not really crave more information than I had. I held my tongue about the Blairs and praised the beauty of my camping-place. Before many weeks I started for home.

Of course I brought my nine-days' wonder out on the first possible occasion. I had been even more right than I knew. I found that unless I was prepared to lie about Emma Blair I could not make her the talk of the town. The women wanted to know how she looked; the men yawned when I said I had not seen Blair himself. If I could have painted a *grande passion* in an enchanted valley, I might have brought a few tears to the gentlest eyes. But my memory was inexorable. I could not force any false splendors into my phrase. The pigs, the poultry, the junk-heaps, and the sordid hatred that brooded over that compound got in my way. Only my cousin, Gerty Fox, made any practical suggestion. She spoke vaguely of sending paper dress-patterns to poor Emma. I doubt, though, if she ever did. I was never able to hold any one for more than half an evening with the tale. To be sure, I did not have a chance at any great genius.

Blair may not yet be dead, for Mrs. Blair has never turned up. When she does, she will do her own work better than apparently I can do it for her. Yet as the years go on and she doesn't appear, I cannot help suspecting that she has renounced her reward. Blair can't have lasted so long as this—not if she spoke the truth. Then I am stabbed with fear—fear lest it should really have been I who spoiled her life, for I had not been reassuring about her fame. There may, of course, have been some hideous Oriental *débâcle* at the end. Yet I sometimes wish I had lied better— for though she may have been a little mad, it was a very discouraged monster that faded away from me in the gloom of that hidden trail.

XLIII

WILLA SEIBERT CATHER (1875-   )

A new voicing of the Middle West came early in the new century from Willa Seibert Cather, who united the new spirit of realism with the new conception of short-story art as taught in university classes with a dash of the poetic and the idealistic peculiar to herself alone. As with almost all the American fiction writers, she is the interpreter and depicter of a geographical area,—in her case Nebraska of the early frontier period. She combines realism—"naturalism" often, avoiding nothing as her generation demanded—with sympathy and optimism. She herself had been borne into Nebraska on the first wave of the settlement. Too young to remember much of the Virginia where her ancestors for generations had made their homes, she had grown up among the Bohemian and Scandinavian immigrants and had learned not only to know intimately her wild prairie environment but to love it with all the passion of a native. In later days she had gone to the University of Nebraska where she had taken the full course prescribed, then she had gone into newspaper work in Pittsburgh and editorial work in New York, at one time holding the editorship of *McClure's Magazine.* Thus outside her home environment she had learned the technique of literary art. Materials she had now, and artistry, and moreover she had acquired that rarest of all accomplishments of the realist—detachment, objectivity. A turning point in her literary career came during her early period in the East: "I had the good fortune to meet Sarah Orne Jewett, who had read all of my early stories and had very clear and definite opinions about them and about where my work fell short. She said, 'Write it as it is, don't try to make it like this or that. You can't do it in anybody else's way; you will have to make a way of your own. If the way happens to be new, don't let that frighten you. Don't try to write the kind of short story that this or that magazine wants; write the truth and let them take it or leave it.' It is that kind of honesty, that earnest endeavor to tell truly the thing that haunts the mind, that I love in Miss Jewett's own work. I dedicated *O Pioneers!* to her because I had talked over some of the characters with her, and in this book I tried to tell the story of the people as truthfully and simply as if I were telling it to her by word of mouth."

The greater part of Miss Cather's work has been novels rather than short stories, and she must be classed first of all as a novelist. Like Alice Brown, she has grown constantly in power and her short stories, whenever she has expressed herself in this form, have become increasingly more valuable. She stands for honest realism tempered with sympathy and poetic beauty.

THE SCULPTOR'S FUNERAL*

A group of the townspeople stood on the station siding of a little Kansas town, awaiting the coming of the night train, which was already twenty minutes overdue. The snow had fallen thick over everything; in the pale starlight the line of bluffs across the wide, white meadows south of the town made soft, smoke-colored curves against the clear sky. The men on the siding stood first on one foot and then on the other, their hands thrust deep into their trousers pockets, their overcoats open, their shoulders screwed up with the cold; and they glanced from time to time toward the southeast, where the railroad track wound along the river shore. They conversed in low tones and moved 5 about restlessly, seeming uncertain as to what was expected of them. There was but one of the company who looked as though he knew exactly why he was there, and he kept conspicuously apart, walking 10 to the far end of the platform, returning to the station door, then pacing up the track again, his chin sunk in the high collar of his overcoat, his burly shoulders drooping forward, his gait heavy and 15 dogged. Presently he was approached by a tall, spare, grizzled man clad in a faded Grand Army suit, who shuffled out from

463

the group and advanced with a certain deference, craning his neck forward until his back made the angle of a jack-knife three-quarters open.

"I reckon she's a-goin' to be pretty late agin to-night, Jim," he remarked in a squeaky falsetto. "S'pose it's the snow?"

"I don't know," responded the other man with a shade of annoyance, speaking from out an astonishing cataract of red beard which grew fiercely and thickly in all directions.

The spare man shifted the quill toothpick he was chewing to the other side of his mouth. "It ain't likely that anybody from the East will come with the corpse, I s'pose?" he went on reflectively.

"I don't know," responded the other, more curtly than before.

"It's too bad he didn't belong to some lodge or other. I like an order funeral myself. They seem more appropriate for people of some repytation," the spare man continued, with an ingratiating concession in his shrill voice, as he carefully placed his toothpick in his vest pocket. He always carried the flag at the G. A. R. funerals in the town.

The heavy man turned on his heel without replying, and walked up the siding. The spare man shuffled back to the uneasy group. "Jim's ez full ez a tick, ez ushel," he commented commiseratingly.

Just then a distant whistle sounded, and there was a shuffling of feet on the platform. A number of lanky boys of all ages appeared as suddenly and slimily as eels wakened by the crack of thunder; some came from the waiting-room, where they had been warming themselves by the red stove, or half asleep on the slat benches; others uncoiled themselves from baggage trucks or slid out of express wagons. Two clambered down from the driver's seat of a hearse that stood backed up against the siding. They straightened their stooping shoulders and lifted their heads, and a flash of momentary animation kindled their dull eyes at that cold, vibrant scream, the world-wide call for men. It stirred them like the note of a trumpet, just as it had often stirred in his boyhood the man who was coming home to-night.

The night express shot, red as a rocket, out of the eastward marsh lands, and wound along the river shore under the long lines of shivering poplars that sentineled the meadows, the escaping steam hanging in gray masses against the still, pale sky and blotting out the Milky Way. In a moment the red glare from the headlight streamed up the snow-covered track before the siding and glittered on the wet, black rails. The burly man with the disheveled red beard walked swiftly up the platform toward the approaching train, uncovering his head as he went. The group of men behind him hesitated, glanced questioningly at one another, and awkwardly followed his example. The train stopped, and the crowd shuffled up to the express car just as the door was thrown open, the spare man in the G. A. R. suit thrusting his head forward with curiosity. The express messenger appeared in the doorway, accompanied by a young man in a long ulster and traveling-cap.

"Are Mr. Merrick's friends here?" inquired the young man.

The group on the platform swayed and shuffled uneasily. Philip Phelps, the banker, responded with dignity: "We have come to take charge of the body. Mr. Merrick's father is very feeble and can't be about."

"Send the agent out here," growled the express messenger, "and tell the operator to lend a hand."

The coffin was got out of its rough box and down on the snowy platform. The townspeople drew back enough to make room for it and then formed a close semi-circle about it, looking curiously at the palm-leaf which lay across the black cover. No one said anything. The baggageman stood by his truck, waiting to get at the trunks. The engine panted heavily, and the fireman dodged in and out among the wheels with his yellow torch and long oil-can, snapping the spindle boxes. The young Bostonian, one of the dead sculptor's pupils, who had come with the body, looked about him helplessly. He turned to the banker, the only one of that black, uneasy, stoop-shouldered group who seemed enough of an individual to be addressed.

"None of Mr. Merrick's brothers are here?" he asked uncertainly.

The man with the red beard for the first time stepped up and joined the group. "No, they have not come yet; the family is scattered. The body will be taken directly to the house." He stooped and took hold of one of the handles of the coffin.

"Take the long hill road up, Thompson; it will be easier on the horses," called the liveryman, as the undertaker snapped the door of the hearse and prepared to mount to the driver's seat.

Laird, the red-bearded lawyer, turned again to the stranger: "We didn't know whether there would be any one with him or not," he explained. "It's a long walk, so you'd better go up in the hack." He pointed to a single battered conveyance, but the young man replied stiffly: "Thank you, but I think I will go up with the hearse. If you don't object," turning to the undertaker, "I'll ride with you."

They clambered up over the wheels and drove off in the starlight up the long, white hill toward the town. The lamps in the still village were shining from under the low, snow-burdened roofs; and beyond, on every side, the plains reached out into emptiness, peaceful and wide as the soft sky itself, and wrapped in a tangible, white silence.

When the hearse backed up to a wooden sidewalk before a naked, weather-beaten frame house, the same composite, ill-defined group that had stood upon the station siding was huddled about the gate. The front yard was an icy swamp, and a couple of warped planks, extending from the sidewalk to the door, made a sort of rickety foot-bridge. The gate hung on one hinge, and was opened wide with difficulty. Steavens, the young stranger, noticed that something black was tied to the knob of the front door.

The grating sound made by the casket, as it was drawn from the hearse, was answered by a scream from the house; the front door was wrenched open, and a tall, corpulent woman rushed out bareheaded into the snow and flung herself upon the coffin, shrieking: "My boy, my boy! And this is how you've come home to me!"

As Steavens turned away and closed his eyes with a shudder of unutterable repulsion, another woman, also tall, but flat and angular, dressed entirely in black, darted out of the house and caught Mrs. Merrick by the shoulders, crying sharply: "Come, come, mother; you mustn't go on like this!" Her tone changed to one of obsequious solemnity as she turned to the banker: "The parlor is ready, Mr. Phelps."

The bearers carried the coffin along the narrow boards, while the undertaker ran ahead with the coffin-rests. They bore it into a large, unheated room that smelled of dampness and disuse and furniture polish, and set it down under a hanging lamp ornamented with jingling glass prisms and before a "Rogers group" of John Alden and Priscilla, wreathed with smilax. Henry Steavens stared around him with the sickening conviction that there had been some horrible mistake, and that he had somehow arrived at the wrong destination. He looked painfully about over the clover-green Brussels, the fat plush upholstery; among the hand-painted china plaques and panels and vases, for some mark of identification, for something that might once have conceivably belonged to Harvey Merrick. It was not until he recognized his friend in the crayon portrait of a little boy in kilts and curls, hanging over the piano, that he felt willing to let any of these people approach the coffin.

"Take the lid off, Mr. Thompson; let me see my boy's face," wailed the elder woman between her sobs. This time Steavens looked fearfully, almost beseechingly, into her face, red and swollen under its masses of strong, black, shiny hair. He flushed, dropped his eyes, and then, almost incredulously, looked again. There was a kind of power about her face—a kind of brutal handsomeness, even; but it was scarred and furrowed by violence, and so colored and coarsened by fiercer passions that grief seemed never to have laid a gentle finger there. The long nose was distended and knobbed at the end, and there were deep lines on either side of it; her heavy, black brows almost met across her forehead, her teeth were large and square, and set far apart—teeth that could tear. She filled the room; the men were obliterated, seemed tossed about like twigs in an angry water, and even Steavens felt himself being drawn into the whirlpool.

The daughter—the tall, raw-boned woman in crêpe, with a mourning-comb in her hair which curiously lengthened her long face—sat stiffly upon the sofa, her hands, conspicuous for their large knuckles, folded in her lap, her mouth and eyes drawn down, solemnly awaiting the opening of the coffin. Near the door stood a mulatto woman, evidently a servant in the house, with a timid bearing and an emaciated face pitifully sad and gentle. She was weeping silently, the corner of her calico apron lifted to her eyes, occasionally suppressing a long, quivering sob. Steavens walked over and stood beside her.

Feeble steps were heard on the stairs, and an old man, tall and frail, odorous of pipe smoke, with shaggy, unkempt gray hair and a dingy beard, tobacco-stained about the mouth, entered uncertainly. He went slowly up to the coffin and stood rolling a blue cotton handkerchief between his hands, seeming so pained and embarrassed by his wife's orgy of grief that he had no consciousness of anything else.

"There, there, Annie, dear, don't take on," he quavered timidly, putting out a shaking hand and awkwardly patting her elbow. She turned with a cry, and sank upon his shoulder with such violence that he tottered a little. He did not even glance toward the coffin, but continued to look at her with a dull frightened, appealing expression, as a spaniel looks at the whip. His sunken cheeks slowly reddened and burned with miserable shame. When his wife rushed from the room, her daughter strode after her with set lips. The servant stole up to the coffin, bent over it for a moment, and then slipped away to the kitchen, leaving Steavens, the lawyer, and the father to themselves. The old man stood trembling and looking down at his dead son's face. The sculptor's splendid head seemed even more noble in its rigid stillness than in life. The dark hair had crept down upon the wide forehead; the face seemed strangely long, but in it there was not that beautiful and chaste repose which we expect to find in the faces of the dead. The brows were so drawn that there were two deep lines above the beaked nose, and the chin was thrust forward defiantly. It was as though the strain of life had been so sharp and bitter that death could not at once wholly relax the tension and smooth the countenance into perfect peace—as though he were still guarding something precious and holy which might even yet be wrested from him.

The old man's lips were working under his stained beard. He turned to the lawyer with timid deference: "Phelps and the rest are comin' back to set up with Harve, ain't they?" he asked. "Thank 'ee, Jim, thank 'ee." He brushed the hair back gently from his son's forehead. "He was a good boy, Jim; always a good boy. He was ez gentle ez a child and the kindest of 'em all—only we didn't none of us ever onderstand him." The tears trickled slowly down his beard and dropped upon the sculptor's coat.

"Martin, Martin—Oh, Martin! come here," his wife wailed from the top of th stairs. The old man started timorously "Yes, Annie, I'm coming." He turne away, hesitated, stood for a moment i miserable indecision; then reached bac and patted the dead man's hair softly, an stumbled from the room.

"Poor old man, I didn't think he ha any tears left. Seems as if his eyes woul have gone dry long ago. At his age nothin cuts very deep," remarked the lawyer.

Something in his tone made Steaven glance up. While the mother had been i the room the young man had scarcely see any one else; but now, from the momen he first glanced into Jim Laird's florid fac and blood-shot eyes, he knew that he ha found what he had been heart-sick at no finding before—the feeling, the under standing, that must exist in some one, eve here.

The man was red as his beard, with fea tures swollen and blurred by dissipation and a hot, blazing blue eye. His face wa strained—that of a man who is controllin himself with difficulty—and he kept pluck ing at his beard with a sort of fierce re sentment. Steavens, sitting by the window watched him turn down the glaring lamp still its jangling pendants with an angr gesture, and then stand with his hand locked behind him, staring down into th master's face. He could not help wonder ing what link there could have been be tween the porcelain vessel and so sooty lump of potter's clay.

From the kitchen an uproar was sound ing; when the dining-room door opened the import of it was clear. The mother wa abusing the maid for having forgotte to make the dressing for the chicken sala which had been prepared for the watchers Steavens had never heard anything in th least like it; it was injured, emotional dramatic abuse, unique and masterly in it excruciating cruelty, as violent and unre strained as had been her grief of twent minutes before. With a shudder of disgust the lawyer went into the dining-room an closed the door into the kitchen.

"Poor Roxy's getting it now," he re marked when he came back. "The Mer ricks took her out of the poor-house year ago; and if her loyalty would let her, guess the poor old thing could tell tale that would curdle your blood. She's th mulatto woman who was standing in her a while ago, with her apron to her eyes

The old woman is a fury; there never was anybody like her for demonstrative piety and ingenious cruelty. She made Harvey's life a hell for him when he lived at home; he was so sick ashamed of it. I never could see how he kept himself so sweet."

"He was wonderful," said Steavens lowly, "wonderful; but until to-night I have never known how wonderful."

"That is the true and eternal wonder of it, anyway; that it can come even from such a dung-heap as this," the lawyer cried, with a sweeping gesture which seemed to indicate much more than the four walls within which they stood.

"I think I'll see whether I can get a little air. The room is so close I am beginning to feel rather faint," murmured Steavens, struggling with one of the windows. The sash was stuck, however, and would not yield, so he sat down dejectedly and began pulling at his collar. The lawyer came over, loosened the sash with one blow of his red fist, and sent the window up a few inches. Steavens thanked him, but the nausea which had been gradually climbing into his throat for the last half hour left him with but one desire—a desperate feeling that he must get away from this place with what was left of Harvey Merrick. Oh, he comprehended well enough now the gentle bitterness of the smile that he had seen so often on his master's lips!

He remembered that once, when Merrick returned from a visit home, he brought with him a singularly feeling and suggestive bas-relief of a thin, faded old woman, sitting and sewing something pinned to her knee; while a full-lipped, full-blooded little urchin, his trousers sustained by a single gallows, stood beside her impatiently twitching her gown to call her attention to a butterfly he had caught. Steavens, impressed by the tender and delicate modeling of the thin, tired face, had asked him if it were his mother. He remembered the dull flush that had burned up in the sculptor's face.

The lawyer was sitting in a rocking-chair beside the coffin, his head thrown back and his eyes closed. Steavens looked at him earnestly, puzzled at the line of the chin, and wondering why a man should conceal a feature of such distinction under that disfiguring shock of red beard. Suddenly, as though he felt the young sculptor's keen glance, he opened his eyes.

"Was he always a good deal of an oyster?" he asked abruptly. "He was terribly shy as a boy."

"Yes, he was an oyster, since you put it so," rejoined Steavens. "Although he could be very fond of people, he always gave one the impression of being detached. He disliked violent emotion; he was reflective, and rather distrustful of himself —except, of course, as regarded his work. He was sure-footed enough there. He distrusted men pretty thoroughly, and women even more, yet somehow without believing ill of them. He was determined, indeed, to believe the best, but he seemed afraid to investigate."

"A burnt dog dreads the fire," said the lawyer grimly, and closed his eyes.

Steavens went on and on, reconstructing that whole miserable boyhood. All this raw, biting ugliness had been the portion of the man whose tastes were refined beyond the limits of the reasonable—whose mind was an exhaustless gallery of beautiful impressions, so sensitive that the mere shadow of a poplar leaf flickering against a sunny wall would be etched and held there forever. Surely, if ever a man had the magic wand in his finger-tips, it was Merrick. Whatever he touched, he revealed its holiest secret; liberated it from enchantment and restored it to its pristine loveliness, like the Arabian prince who fought the enchantress, spell for spell. Upon whatever he had come in contact with, he had left a beautiful record of the experience—a sort of ethereal signature; a scent, a sound, a color that was his own.

Steavens understood now the real tragedy of his master's life; neither love nor wine, as many had conjectured, but a blow which had fallen earlier and cut deeper than these could have done—a shame not his, and yet so unescapably his, to hide in his heart from his very boyhood. And without, the frontier warfare; the yearning of a boy, cast ashore upon a desert of newness and ugliness and sordidness, for all that is chastened and old, and noble with traditions.

At eleven o'clock the tall, flat woman in black crêpe entered and announced that the watchers were arriving, and asked them "to step into the dining-room." As Steavens rose, the lawyer said dryly: "You go on—it'll be a good experience for you, doubtless; as for me, I'm not equal to that crowd to-night; I've had twenty years of them."

As Steavens closed the door after him, he glanced back at the lawyer, sitting by the coffin in the dim light, with his chin resting on his hand.

The same misty groups that had stood before the door of the express-car shuffled into the room. In the light of the kerosene lamp they separated and became individuals. The minister, a pale, feeble-looking man with white hair and blond chin-whiskers, took his seat beside a small table, and placed his Bible upon it. The Grand Army man took a seat behind the stove and tilted his chair back comfortably against the wall, fishing his quill toothpick from his waistcoat pocket. The two bankers, Phelps and Elder, sat off in a corner behind the dinner-table, where they could finish their discussion of the new usury law and its effect on chattel security loans. The real estate agent, an old man with a smiling, hypocritical face, soon joined them. The coal and lumber dealer and the cattle shipper sat on opposite sides of the hard coal burner, their feet on the nickel-work. Steavens took a book from his pocket and began to read. The talk around him ranged through various topics of local interest while the house was quieting down. When it was clear that the members of the family were in bed, the Grand Army man hitched his shoulders, and untangling his long legs, caught his heels on the rounds of his chair.

"S'pose there'll be a will, Phelps?" he queried in his weak falsetto.

The banker laughed disagreeably, and began trimming his nails with a pearl-handled pocket-knife.

"There'll scarcely be any need for one, will there?" he queried in his turn.

The restless Grand Army man shifted his position again, getting his knees still nearer his chin. "Why, the ole man says Harve's done right well lately," he chirped.

The other banker spoke up. "I reckon he means by that Harve ain't asked him to mortgage any more farms lately so as he could go on with his education."

"Seems like my mind don't reach back to a time when Harve wasn't bein' edycated," tittered the Grand Army man.

There was a general chuckle. The minister took out his handkerchief and blew his nose sonorously. Banker Phelps closed his knife with a snap. "It's too bad the

old man's sons didn't turn out better,' remarked, with reflective authority. "I never hung together. He spent mc enough on Harve to stock a dozen ci farms, and he might as well have por it into Sand Creek. If Harve had sti at home and helped nurse what little t had, and gone into stock on the old m bottom farm, they might all have been fixed. But the old man had to trust eve thing to tenants and was cheated right left."

"Harve never could have handled st none," interposed the cattleman. hadn't it in him to be sharp. Do you member when he bought Sander's m for eight-year olds, when everybody town knew that Sander's father-in-give 'em to his wife for a wedding pre eighteen years before, an' they was i grown mules then?"

Everyone chuckled, and the Gr Army man rubbed his knees with a sp of childish delight.

"Harve never was much account anything practical, and he shore was ne fond of work," began the coal and lum dealer. "I mind the last time he was ho the day he left, when the old man was to the barn helpin' his hand hitch up take Harve to the train, and Cal. M was patchin' up the fence, Harve, he co out on the step and sings out, in his la like voice: 'Cal. Moots, Cal. Moots! ple come cord my trunk.'"

"That's Harve for you," approved Grand Army man gleefully. "I kin l him howlin' yet, when he was a big fe in long pants, and his mother used to wl him with a rawhide in the barn for let the cows git foundered in the corn when he was drivin' 'em home from j ture. He killed a cow of mine that-a-v onct—a pure Jersey and the best mi I had, an' the ole man had to put up her. Harve, he was watchin' the sun acrost the marshes when the anamile away; he argued that sunset was onc mon fine."

"Where the old man made his mist was in sending the boy East to scho said Phelps, stroking his goatee and spe ing in a deliberate, judicial tone. "Tl was where he got his head full of tra ing to Paris and all such folly. W Harve needed, of all people, was a co in some first-class Kansas City busi college."

The letters were swimming before Stevens's eyes. Was it possible that these men did not understand, that the palm on the coffin meant nothing to them? The very name of their town would have remained forever buried in the postal guide, had it not been now and again mentioned in the world in connection with Harvey Merrick's. He remembered what his master had said to him on the day of his death, after the congestion of both lungs had shut off any probability of recovery, and the sculptor had asked his pupil to send his body home. "It's not a pleasant place to be lying while the world is moving and doing and bettering," he said, with a feeble smile: "but it rather seems as though we ought to go back to the place we came from in the end. The townspeople will come in for a look at me; and after they have had their say, I shan't have much to fear from the judgment of God. The wings of the Victory, in there"—with a weak gesture towards his studio—"will not shelter me."

The cattleman took up the comment. "Forty's young for a Merrick to cash in; they usually hang on pretty well. Probably he helped it along with whisky."

"His mother's people were not long-lived, and Harvey never had a robust constitution," said the minister mildly. He would have liked to say more. He had been the boy's Sunday-school teacher, and had been fond of him; but he felt that he was not in a postion to speak. His own sons had turned out badly, and it was not a year since one of them had made his last trip home in the express-car, shot in a gambling-house in the Black Hills.

"Nevertheless, there is no disputin' that Harve frequently looked upon the wine when it was red, also variegated, and it hore made an oncommon fool of him," moralized the cattleman.

Just then the door leading into the parlor rattled loudly, and everyone started involuntarily, looking relieved when only Jim Laird came out. His red face was convulsed with anger, and the Grand Army man ducked his head when he saw the park in his blue, blood-shot eye. They were all afraid of Jim; he was a drunkard, but he could twist the law to suit his client's needs as no other man in all Western Kansas could do; and there were many who tried. The lawyer closed the door gently behind him, leaned back against it, and folded his arms, cocking his head a little to one side. When he assumed this attitude in the court-room, ears were always pricked up, as it usually foretold a flood of withering sarcasm.

"I've been with you gentlemen before," he began in a dry, even tone, "when you've sat by the coffins of boys born and raised in this town; and, if I remember rightly, you were never any too well satisfied when you checked them up. What's the matter, anyhow? Why is it that reputable young men are as scarce as millionaires in Sand City? It might almost seem to a stranger that there was some way something the matter with your progressive town. Why did Reuben Sayer, the brightest young lawyer you ever turned out, after he had come home from the university as straight as a die, take to drinking, and forge a check and shoot himself? Why did Bill Merrit's son die of the shakes in a saloon in Omaha? Why was Mr. Thomas's son, here, shot in a gambling-house? Why did young Adams burn his mill to beat the insurance companies, and go to the pen?"

The lawyer paused and unfolded his arms, laying one clenched fist quietly on the table. "I'll tell you why: because you drummed nothing but money and knavery into their ears from the time they wore knickerbockers; because you carped away at them as you've been carping here tonight, holding our friends Phelps and Elder up to them for their models, as our grandfathers held up George Washington and John Adams. But the boys, worse luck, were young, and raw at the business you put them to; and how could they match coppers with such artists as Phelps and Elder? You wanted them to be successful rascals; they were only unsuccessful ones—that's all the difference. There was only one boy ever raised in this borderland between ruffianism and civilization who didn't come to grief, and you hated Harvey Merrick more for winning out than you hated all the other boys who got under the wheels. Lord, Lord, how you did hate him! Phelps, here, is fond of saying that he could buy and sell us all out any time he's a mind to; but he knew Harve wouldn't have given a tinker's damn for his bank and all his cattle-farms put together; and a lack of appreciation, that way, goes hard with Phelps.

"Old Nimrod, here, thinks Harve drank too much; and this from such as Nimrod and me!

"Brother Elder says Harve was too free with the old man's money—fell short in filial consideration, maybe. Well, we can all remember the very tone in which Brother Elder swore his own father was a liar, in the county court; and we all know that the old man came out of that partnership with his son as bare as a sheared lamb. But maybe I'm getting personal, and I'd better be driving ahead at what I want to say."

The lawyer paused a moment, squared his heavy shoulders, and went on: "Harvey Merrick and I went to school together, back East. We were in dead earnest, and we wanted you all to be proud of us some day. We meant to be great men. Even I, and I haven't lost my sense of humor, gentlemen, I meant to be a great man. I came back here to practise, and I found you didn't in the least want me to be a great man. You wanted me to be a shrewd lawyer—oh, yes! Our veteran here wanted me to get him an increase of pension, because he had dyspepsia; Phelps wanted a new county survey that would put the widow Wilson's little bottom farm inside his south line; Elder wanted to lend money at five per cent a month and get it collected; old Stark here wanted to wheedle old women up in Vermont into investing their annuities in real-estate mortgages that are not worth the paper they are written on. Oh, you needed me hard enough, and you'll go on needing me; and that's why I'm not afraid to plug the truth home to you this once.

"Well, I came back here and became the damned shyster you wanted me to be. You pretend to have some sort of respect for me; and yet you'll stand up and throw mud at Harvey Merrick, whose soul you couldn't dirty, and whose hands you couldn't tie. Oh, you're a discriminating lot of Christians! There have been times when the sight of Harvey's name in some Eastern paper has made me hang my head

like a whipped dog; and, again, times when I liked to think of him off there in the world, away from all this hog-wallow, doing his great work, and climbing the big, clean up-grade he'd set for himself.

"And we? Now that we've fought and lied and sweated and stolen and hated, as only the disappointed strugglers in a bitter, dead little Western town know how to do, what have we got to show for it? Harvey Merrick wouldn't have given one sunset over your marshes for all you've got put together, and you know it. It's not for me to say why, in the inscrutable wisdom of God, a genius should ever have been called from this place of hatred and bitter waters; but I want this Boston man to know that the drivel he's been hearing here to-night is the only tribute any truly great man could ever have from such a lot of sick, side-tracked, burnt-dog, land-poor sharks as the here-present financiers of Sand City—upon which town may God have mercy!"

The lawyer thrust out his hand to Steavens as he passed him, caught up his overcoat in the hall, and had left the house before the Grand Army man had found time to lift his ducked head and crane his long neck about at his fellows.

Next day Jim Laird was drunk and unable to attend the funeral services. Steavens called twice at his office, but was compelled to start East without seeing him. He had a presentiment that he would hear from him again, and left his address on the lawyer's table; but if Laird found it, he never acknowledged it. The thing in him that Harvey Merrick had loved must have gone under ground with Harvey Merrick's coffin; for it never spoke again, and Jim got the cold he died of driving across the Colorado mountains to defend one of Phelps's sons, who had got into trouble out there by cutting government timber.

XLIV

THEODORE DREISER (1871–   )

The movement started by Norris and Hamlin Garland and Stephen Crane during the closing years of the nineteenth century in revolt against the "parlor realism" of Howells and James, reached its full tide in the work of Theodore Dreiser, a native of Indiana. We may take him as the leader and the extreme example of the new school of depressed and disillusioned, embittered realists of the latest manner, "veritists," "naturalists," that the new century poured out of the Middle West. Like Miss Cather, he had been graduated from a state university, and like her he had taken up newspaper work as his profession. With success came a widening of his field. He was made editor of influential magazines in New York City and remained in editorial work until it became possible to devote his whole time to fiction.

Novels have been for the most part his product, novels of bulk and ponderous intent. Working in the age of O. Henryism, the age of conscious art and of manner, he has been the antipodes of O. Henry. Of compression, finesse, lightness and grace of style, he apparently cares nothing. He is a Millet working coarsely with peasants, modeling them in their native clay with all their commonness and vulgarity and dirt. In marble he works not at all. To elaborate his plot he requires the space of a *Tom Jones*. He omits nothing, he avoids nothing, he interprets nothing: he presents the mere facts as he finds them, usually in the coarser areas of life. The meaning of it all he does not know. Unlike Garland he has no propaganda, no theory, no Q. E. D., and unlike Willa Cather, he has no golden light to throw over his picturings. He settles nothing, he teaches nothing, he means nothing.

Not often has he essayed the short-story form, and whenever he has done so he has produced only miniatures of his novels: creations elephantine in movement and style, but elephantine also in strength, for they leave impressions upon the reader that remain, they burn and sere the soul like a visit to the morgue or the madhouse. Always his plots center in low living and in the drab areas of life; always his characters are inhabitants of the mean streets of the small town or city or else wolves from the dens of corrupt industrialism; and his *motifs* involve always adultery and sexual license and sordid ideals,—the Spoon River population on its tragic, revolting way to disillusion, death, and the potter's field. The best of his shorter fictions are in his volume entitled *Free and Other Stories*, 1918.

OLD ROGAUM AND HIS THERESA*

In all Bleecker Street was no more comfortable doorway than that of the butcher Rogaum, even if the first floor was given over to meat market purposes. It was to one side of the main entrance, which gave ingress to the butcher shop, and from it led up a flight of steps, at least five feet wide, to the living rooms above. A little portico stood out in front of it, railed on either side, and within was a second or final door, forming, with the outer or storm door, a little area, where Mrs. Rogaum and her children frequently sat of a summer's evening. The outer door was never locked, owing to the inconvenience it would

inflict on Mr. Rogaum, who had no other way of getting upstairs. In winter, when all had gone to bed, there had been cases in which belated travelers had taken refuge 5 there from the snow or sleet. One or two newsboys occasionally slept there, until routed out by Officer Maguire, who, seeing it half open one morning at two o'clock, took occasion to look in. He jogged the 10 newsboy sharply with his stick, and then, when they were gone, tried the inner door, which was locked.

"You ought to keep that outer door locked, Rogaum," he observed to the phleg- 15 matic butcher the next evening, as he was passing, "people might get in. A couple o' kids was sleepin' in there last night."

"Ach, dot iss no difference," answered Rogaum pleasantly. "I haf der inner door

* From *Free and Other Stories*, 1918. Published by arrangement with Boni and Liveright.

locked, yet. Let dem sleep. Dot is no difference."

"Better lock it," said the officer, more to vindicate his authority than anything else. "Something will happen there yet."

The door was never locked, however, and now of a summer evening Mrs. Rogaum and the children made pleasant use of its recess, watching the rout of street cars and occasionally belated trucks go by. The children played on the sidewalk, all except the budding Theresa (eighteen just turning), who, with one companion of the neighborhood, the pretty Kenrihan girl, walked up and down the block, laughing, glancing, watching the boys. Old Mrs. Kenrihan lived in the next block, and there, sometimes, the two stopped. There, also, they most frequently pretended to be when talking with the boys in the intervening side street. Young "Connie" Almerting and George Goujon were the bright particular mashers who held the attention of the maidens in this block. These two made their acquaintance in the customary bold, boyish way, and thereafter the girls had an urgent desire to be out in the street together after eight, and to linger where the boys could see and overtake them.

Old Mrs. Rogaum never knew. She was a particularly fat, old German lady, completely dominated by her liege and portly lord, and at nine o'clock regularly, as he had long ago deemed meet and fit, she was wont to betake her way upward and so to bed. Old Rogaum himself, at that hour, closed the market and went to his chamber.

Before that all the children were called sharply, once from the doorstep below and once from the window above, only Mrs. Rogaum did it first and Rogaum last. It had come, because of a shade of lenience, not wholly apparent in the father's nature, that the older of the children needed two callings and sometimes three. Theresa, now that she had "got in" with the Kenrihan maiden, needed that many calls and even more.

She was just at that age for which mere thoughtless, sensory life holds its greatest charm. She loved to walk up and down in the as yet bright street where were voices and laughter, and occasionally moonlight streaming down. What a nuisance it was to be called at nine, anyhow. Why should one have to go in then, anyhow. What old fogies her parents were, wishing to go to

bed so early. Mrs. Kenrihan was not so strict with her daughter. It made her pettish when Rogaum insisted, calling as he often did, in German, "Come you now," in a very hoarse and belligerent voice.

She came, eventually, frowning and wretched, all the moonlight calling her, all the voices of the night urging her to come back. Her innate opposition due to her urgent youth made her coming later and later, however, until now, by August of this, her eighteenth year, it was nearly ten when she entered, and Rogaum was almost invariably angry.

"I vill lock you oudt," he declared, in strongly accented English, while she tried to slip by him each time. "I vill show you. Du sollst come ven I say, yet. Hear now."

"I'll not," answered Theresa, but it was always under her breath.

Poor Mrs. Rogaum troubled at hearing the wrath in her husband's voice. It spoke of harder and fiercer times which had been with her. Still she was not powerful enough in the family councils to put in a weighty word. So Rogaum fumed unrestricted.

There were other nights, however, many of them, and now that the young sparks of the neighborhood had enlisted the girls' attention, it was a more trying time than ever. Never did a street seem more beautiful. Its shabby red walls, dusty pavements and protruding store steps and iron railings seemed bits of the ornamental paraphernalia of heaven itself. These lights, the cars, the moon, the street lamps! Theresa had a tender eye for the dashing Almerting, a young idler and loafer of the district, the son of a stationer farther up the street. What a fine fellow he was, indeed! What a handsome nose and chin! What eyes! What authority! His cigarette was always cocked at a high angle, in her presence, and his hat had the least suggestion of being set to one side. He had a shrewd way of winking one eye, taking her boldly by the arm, hailing her as "Hey, Pretty!" and was strong and athletic and worked (when he worked) in a tobacco factory. His was a trade, indeed, nearly acquired, as he said, and his jingling pockets attested that he had money of his own. Altogether he was very captivating.

"Aw, whaddy ya want to go in for?" he used to say to her, tossing his head gayly on one side to listen and holding her by the arm, as old Rogaum called. "Tell him yuh didn't hear."

"No, I've got to go," said the girl, who was soft and plump and fair—a Rhine maiden type.

"Well, yuh don't have to go just yet. Stay another minute. George, what was that fellow's name that tried to sass us the other day?"

"Theresa!" roared old Rogaum forcefully. "If you do not now come! Ve vill see!"

"I've got to go," repeated Theresa with a faint effort at starting. "Can't you hear? Don't hold me. I haf to."

"Aw, whaddy ya want to be such a coward for? Y' don't have to go. He won't do nothin' tuh yuh. My old man was always hollerin' like that up tuh a coupla years ago. Let him holler! Say, kid, but yuh got sweet eyes! They're as blue! An' your mouth—"

"Now stop! You hear me!" Theresa would protest softly, as, swiftly, he would slip an arm about her waist and draw her to him, sometimes in a vain, sometimes in a successful effort to kiss her.

As a rule she managed to interpose an elbow between her face and his, but even then he would manage to touch an ear or a cheek or her neck—sometimes her mouth, full and warm—before she would develop sufficient energy to push him away and herself free. Then she would protest mock earnestly or sometimes run away.

"Now, I'll never speak to you any more, if that's the way you're going to do. My father don't allow me to kiss boys, anyhow," and then she would run, half ashamed, half smiling herself as he would stare after her, or if she lingered, develop a kind of anger and even rage.

"Aw, cut it! Whaddy ya want to be so shy for? Dontcha like me? What's gettin' into yuh, anyhow? Hey?"

In the meantime George Goujon and Myrtle Kenrihan, their companions, might be sweeting and going through a similar contest, perhaps a hundred feet up the street or near at hand. The quality of old Rogaum's voice would by now have become so raucous, however, that Theresa would have lost all comfort in the scene and, becoming frightened, hurry away. Then it was often that both Almerting and Goujon as well as Myrtle Kenrihan would follow her to the corner, almost in sight of the irate old butcher.

"Let him call," young Almerting would insist, laying a final hold on her soft white fingers and causing her to quiver thereby.

"Oh, no," she would gasp nervously. "I can't."

"Well, go on, then," he would say, and with a flip of his heel would turn back, leaving Theresa to wonder whether she had alienated him forever or no. Then she would hurry to her father's door.

"Muss ich all my time spenden calling, mit you on de streeds oudt?" old Rogaum would roar wrathfully, the while his fat hand would descend on her back. "Take dot now. Vy don't you come ven I call? In now. I vill show you. Und come you yussed yunce more at dis time—ve vill see if I am boss in my own house, aber! Komst du vun minute nach ten to-morrow und you vill see vot you vill get. I vill der door lock. Du sollst not in kommen. Mark! Oudt sollst du stayen—oudt!" and he would glare wrathfully at her retreating figure.

Sometimes Theresa would whimper, sometimes cry or sulk. She almost hated her father for his cruelty, "the big, fat, rough thing," and just because she wanted to stay out in the bright streets, too! Because he was old and stout and wanted to go to bed at ten, he thought every one else did. And outside was the dark sky with its stars, the street lamps, the cars, the tinkle and laughter of eternal life!

"Oh!" she would sigh as she undressed and crawled into her small neat bed. To think that she had to live like this all her days! At the same time old Rogaum was angry and equally determined. It was not so much that he imagined that his Theresa was in bad company as yet, but he wished to forefend against possible danger. This was not a good neighborhood by any means. The boys around here were tough. He wanted Theresa to pick some nice sober youth from among the other Germans he and his wife knew here and there—at the Lutheran Church, for instance. Otherwise she shouldn't marry. He knew she only walked from his shop to the door of the Kenrihans and back again. Had not his wife told him so? If he had thought upon what far pilgrimage her feet had already ventured, or had even seen the dashing Almerting hanging near, then had there been wrath indeed. As it was, his mind was more or less at ease.

On many, many evenings it was much the same. Sometimes she got in on time, sometimes not, but more and more "Connie" Almerting claimed her for his "steady," and bought her ice-cream. In the range of the short block and its confining corners it was all done, lingering by the curbstone and strolling a half block either way in the side streets, until she had offended seriously at home, and the threat was repeated anew. He often tried to persuade her to go on picnics or outings of various kinds, but this, somehow, was not to be thought of at her age—at least with him. She knew her father would never endure the thought, and never even had the courage to mention it, let alone run away. Mere lingering with him at the adjacent street corners brought stronger and stronger admonishments—even more blows and the threat that she should not get in at all.

Well enough she meant to obey, but on one radiant night late in June the time fled too fast. The moon was so bright, the air so soft. The feel of far summer things was in the wind and even in this dusty street. Theresa, in a newly starched white summer dress, had been loitering up and down with Myrtle when as usual they encountered Almerting and Goujon. Now it was ten, and the regular calls were beginning.

"Aw, wait a minute," said "Connie." "Stand still. He won't lock yuh out."

"But he will, though," said Theresa. "You don't know him."

"Well, if he does, come on back to me. I'll take care of yuh. I'll be here. But he won't though. If you stayed out a little while he'd letcha in all right. That's the way my old man used to try to do me but it didn't work with me. I stayed out an' he let me in, just the same. Don'tcha let him kidja." He jingled some loose change in his pocket.

Never in his life had he had a girl on his hands at any unseasonable hour, but it was nice to talk big, and there was a club to which he belonged, The Varick Street Roosters, and to which he had a key. It would be closed and empty at this hour, and she could stay there until morning, if need be or with Myrtle Kenrihan. He would take her there if she insisted. There was a sinister grin on the youth's face.

By now Theresa's affections had carried her far. This youth with his slim body, his delicate strong hands, his fine chin, straight mouth and hard dark eyes—how wonderful he seemed. He was but nineteen to her

eighteen but cold, shrewd, daring. Yet how tender he seemed to her, how well worth having! Always, when he kissed her now she trembled in the balance. There was something in the iron grasp of his fingers that went through her like fire. His glance held hers at times when she could scarcely endure it.

"I'll wait, anyhow," he insisted.

Longer and longer she lingered, but now for once no voice came.

She began to feel that something was wrong—a greater strain than if old Rogaum's voice had been filling the whole neighborhood.

"I've got to go," she said.

"Gee, but you're a coward, yuh are!" said he derisively. "What 'r yuh always so scared about? He always says he'll lock yuh out, but he never does."

"Yes, but he will," she insisted nervously. "I think he has this time. You don't know him. He's something awful when he gets real mad. Oh, Connie, I must go!" For the sixth or seventh time she moved and once more he caught her arm and waist and tried to kiss her, but she slipped away from him.

"Ah, yuh!" he exclaimed. "I wish he would lock yuh out!"

At her own doorstep she paused momentarily, more to soften her progress than anything. The outer door was open as usual, but not the inner. She tried it, but it would not give. It was locked! For a moment she paused, cold fear racing over her body, and then knocked.

No answer.

Again she rattled the door, this time nervously, and was about to cry out.

Still no answer.

At last she heard her father's voice hoarse and indifferent, not addressed to her at all, but to her mother.

"Let her go, now," it said savagely, from the front room where he supposed she could not hear. "I vill her a lesson teach."

"Hadn't you better let her in now, yet?" pleaded Mrs. Rogaum faintly.

"No," insisted Mr. Rogaum. "Nefer Let her go now. If she vill alvays stay oud let her stay now. Ve vill see how she like dot."

His voice was rich in wrath; and he was saving up a good beating for her into the bargain, that she knew. She would have to wait and wait and plead, and when she was thoroughly wretched and subdued h would let her in and beat her—such a beating as she had never received in all her born days.

Again the door rattled, and still she got no answer. Not even her call brought a sound.

Now, strangely, a new element, not heretofore apparent in her nature, but nevertheless wholly there, was called into life, springing in action as Diana, full formed. Why should he always be so harsh? She hadn't done anything but stay out a little later than usual. He was always so anxious to keep her in and subdue her. For once the cold chill of her girlish fears left her, and she wavered angrily.

"All right," she said, some old German stubbornness springing up, "I don't knock. You don't need to let me in, then."

A suggestion of tears was in her eyes, but she backed firmly out onto the stoop and sat down, hesitating. Old Rogaum saw her, lowering down from the lattice, but said nothing. He would teach her for once what were proper hours! At the corner, standing, Almerting also saw her. He recognized the simple white dress and paused steadily, a strange thrill racing over him. Really they had locked her out. Gee, this was new. It was great in a way. There she was, white, quiet, shut out, waiting at her father's doorstep.

Sitting thus, Theresa pondered a moment, her girlish rashness and anger dominating her. Her pride was hurt and she felt revengeful. They would shut her out, would they? All right, she would go out and they should look to it how they would get her back—the old curmudgeons. For the moment the home of Myrtle Kenrihan came to her as a possible refuge, but she decided that she need not go there yet. She had better wait about awhile and see —or walk and frighten them. He would beat her, would he? Well, maybe he would and maybe he wouldn't. She might come back, but still that was a thing afar off. Just now it didn't matter so much. "Connie" was still there on the corner. He loved her dearly. She felt it.

Getting up, she stepped to the now quieting sidewalk and strolled up the street. It was a rather nervous procedure, however. There were street cars still, and stores lighted and people passing, but soon these would not be, and she was locked out. The side streets were already little more than long silent walks and gleaming rows of lamps.

At the corner her youthful lover almost pounced upon her.

"Locked out, are yuh?" he asked, his eyes shining.

For the moment she was delighted to see him, for a nameless dread had already laid hold of her. Home meant so much. Up to now it had been her whole life.

"Yes," she answered feebly.

"Well, let's stroll on a little," said the boy. He had not as yet quite made up his mind what to do, but the night was young. It was so fine to have her with him—his.

At the farther corner they passed Officers Maguire and Delahanty, idly swinging their clubs and discussing politics.

" 'Tis a shame," Officer Delahanty was saying, "the way things are run now," but he paused to add, "Ain't that old Rogaum's girl over there with young Almerting?"

"It is," replied Maguire, looking after.

"Well, I'm thinkin' he'd better be keepin' an eye on her," said the former. "She's too young to be runnin' around with the likes o' him."

Maguire agreed. "He's a young tough," he observed. "I never liked him. He's too fresh. He works over here in Myer's tobacco factory, and belongs to The Roosters. He's up to no good, I'll warrant that."

"Teach 'em a lesson, I would," Almerting was saying to Theresa as they strolled on. "We'll walk around a while an' make 'em think yuh mean business. They won't lock yuh out any more. If they don't let yuh in when we come back I'll find yuh a place, all right."

His sharp eyes were gleaming as he looked around into her own. Already he had made up his mind that she should not go back if he could help it. He knew a better place than home for this night, anyhow—the club room of The Roosters, if nowhere else. They could stay there for a time, anyhow.

By now old Rogaum, who had seen her walking up the street alone, was marveling at her audacity, but thought she would soon come back. It was amazing that she should exhibit such temerity, but he would teach her! Such a whipping! At half-past ten, however, he stuck his head out of the open window and saw nothing of her. At eleven, the same. Then he walked the floor.

At first wrathful, then nervous, then nervous and wrathful, he finally ended all nervous, without a scintilla of wrath. His stout wife sat up in bed and began to wring her hands.

"Lie down!" he commanded. "You make me sick. I know vot I am doing!"

"Is she still at der door?" pleaded the mother.

"No," he said. "I don't tink so. She should come ven I call."

His nerves were weakening, however, and now they finally collapsed.

"She vent de stread up," he said anxiously after a time. "I vill go after."

Slipping on his coat, he went down the stairs and out into the night. It was growing late, and the stillness and gloom of midnight were nearing. Nowhere in sight was his Theresa. First one way and then another he went, looking here, there, everywhere, finally groaning.

"Ach, Gott!" he said, the sweat bursting out on his brow, "vot in Teufel's name iss dis?"

He thought he would seek a policeman, but there was none. Officer Maguire had long since gone for a quiet game in one of the neighboring saloons. His partner had temporarily returned to his own beat. Still old Rogaum hunted on, worrying more and more.

Finally he bethought him to hasten home again, for she must have got back. Mrs. Rogaum, too, would be frantic if she had not. If she were not there he must go to the police. Such a night! And Theresa—— This thing could not go on.

As he turned into his own corner he almost ran, coming up to the little portico wet and panting. At a puffing step he turned, and almost fell over a white body at his feet, a prone and writhing woman.

"Ach, Gott!" he cried aloud, almost shouting in his distress and excitement. "Theresa, vot iss dis? Wilhelmina, a light now. Bring a light now, I say, for himmel's sake! Theresa hat sich *umgebracht*. Help!"

He had fallen to his knees and was turning over the writhing, groaning figure. By the pale light of the street, however, he could make out that it was not his Theresa, fortunately, as he had at first feared, but another and yet there was something very like her in the figure.

"Um!" said the stranger weakly. "Ah!"

The dress was gray, not white as was his Theresa's, but the body was round and plump. It cut the fiercest cords of his intensity, this thought of death to a young woman, but there was something else about the situation which made him forget his own troubles.

Mrs. Rogaum, loudly admonished, almost tumbled down the stairs. At the foot she held the light she had brought—a small glass oil-lamp—and then nearly dropped it. A fairly attractive figure, more girl than woman, rich in all the physical charms that characterize a certain type, lay near to dying. Her soft hair had fallen back over a good forehead, now quite white. Her pretty hands, well decked with rings, were clutched tightly in an agonized grip. At her neck a blue silk shirtwaist and light lace collar were torn away where she had clutched herself, and on the white flesh was a yellow stain as of one who had been burned. A strange odor reeked in the area, and in one corner was a spilled bottle.

"Ach, Gott!" exclaimed Mrs. Rogaum. "It iss a vooman! She haf herself gekilt. Run for der police! Oh, my! oh, my!"

Rogaum did not kneel for more than a moment. Somehow, this creature's fate seemed in some psychic way identified with that of his own daughter. He bounded up, and jumping out his front door, began to call lustily for the police. Officer Maguire, at his social game nearby, heard the very first cry and came running.

"What's the matter here, now?" he exclaimed, rushing up full and ready for murder, robbery, fire, or, indeed, anything in the whole roster of human calamities.

"A vooman!" said Rogaum excitedly. "She haf herself *umgebracht*. She iss dying. Ach, Gott! in my own doorstep, yet!"

"Vere iss der hospital?" put in Mrs. Rogaum, thinking clearly of an ambulance, but not being able to express it. "She iss gekilt, sure. Oh! Oh!" and bending over her the poor old motherly soul stroked the tightened hands, and trickled tears upon the blue shirtwaist. "Ach, vy did you do dot?" she said. "Ach, for vy?"

Officer Maguire was essentially a man of action. He jumped to the sidewalk, amid the gathering company, and beat loudly with his club upon the stone flagging. Then he ran to the nearest police phone, returning to aid in any other way he might. A milk wagon passing on its way from the Jersey ferry with a few tons of fresh milk aboard, he held it up and demanded a helping.

"Give up a quart there, will you?" he

said authoritatively. "A woman's swallowed acid in here."

"Sure," said the driver, anxious to learn the cause of the excitement. "Got a glass, anybody?"

Maguire ran back and returned, bearing a measure. Mrs. Rogaum stood looking nervously on, while the stocky officer raised the golden head and poured the milk.

"Here, now, drink this," he said. "Come on. Try an' swallow it."

The girl, a blonde of the type the world too well knows, opened her eyes, and looked, groaning a little.

"Drink it," shouted the officer fiercely. "Do you want to die? Open your mouth!"

Used to a fear of the law in all her days, she obeyed now, even in death. The lips parted, the fresh milk was drained to the end, some spilling on neck and cheek.

While they were working old Rogaum came back and stood looking on, by the side of his wife. Also Officer Delahanty, having heard the peculiar wooden ring of the stick upon the stone in the night, had come up.

"Ach, ach," exclaimed Rogaum rather distractedly, "und she iss oudt yet. I could not find her. Oh, oh!"

There was a clang of a gong up the street as the racing ambulance turned rapidly in. A young hospital surgeon dismounted, and seeing the woman's condition, ordered immediate removal. Both officers and Rogaum, as well as the surgeon, helped place her in the ambulance. After a moment the lone bell, ringing wildly in the night, was all the evidence remaining that a tragedy had been here.

"Do you know how she came here?" asked Officer Delahanty, coming back to get Rogaum's testimony for the police.

"No, no," answered Rogaum wretchedly. "She vass here alretty. I vass for my daughter loog. Ach, himmel, I haf my daughter lost. She iss avay."

Mrs. Rogaum also chattered, the significance of Theresa's absence all the more painfully emphasized by this.

The officer did not at first get the import of this. He was only interested in the facts of the present case.

"You say she was here when you come? Where was you?"

"I say I vass for my daughter loog. I come here, und der vooman vass here now alretty."

"Yes. What time was this?"

"Only now yet. Yussed a half-hour."

Officer Maguire had strolled up, after chasing away a small crowd that had gathered with fierce and unholy threats. For the first time now he noticed the peculiar perturbation of the usually placid German couple.

"What about your daughter?" he asked, catching a word as to that.

Both old people raised their voices at once.

"She haf gone. She haf run avay. Ach, himmel, ve must for her loog. Quick—she could not get in. Ve haf der door shut."

"Locked her out, eh?" inquired Maguire after a time, hearing much of the rest of the story.

"Yes," exclaimed Rogaum. "It was to schkare her a liddle. She vould not come ven I called."

"Sure, that's the girl we saw walkin' with young Almerting, do ye mind? The one in the white dress," said Delahanty to Maguire.

"White dress, yah!" echoed Rogaum, and then the fact of her walking with some one came home like a blow.

"Did you hear dot?" he exclaimed even as Mrs. Rogaum did likewise. "Mein Gott, hast du das gehoert?"

He fairly jumped as he said it. His hands flew up to his stout and ruddy head.

"Whaddy ya want to let her out for nights?" asked Maguire roughly, catching the drift of the situation. "That's no time for young girls to be out, anyhow, and with these toughs around here. Sure, I saw her, nearly two hours ago."

"Ach," groaned Rogaum. "Two hours yet. Ho, ho, ho!" His voice was quite hysteric.

"Well, go on in," said Officer Delahanty. "There's no use yellin' out here. Give us a description of her an' we'll send out an alarm. You won't be able to find her walkin' around."

Her parents described her exactly. The two men turned to the nearest police box and then disappeared, leaving the old German couple in the throes of distress. A time-worn old Church-clock nearby now chimed out one and then two. The notes cut like knives. Mrs. Rogaum began fearfully to cry. Rogaum walked and blustered to himself.

"It's a queer case, that," said Officer Delahanty to Maguire after having reported the matter of Theresa, but referring solely to the outcast of the doorway so recently sent away and in whose fate they were much more interested. She being a part of the commercialized vice of the city, they were curious as to the cause of her suicide. "I think I know that woman. I think I know where she came from. You do, too—Adele's around the corner, eh? She didn't come into that doorway by her-self, either. She was put there. You know how they do."

"You're right," said Maguire. "She was put there, all right, and that's just where she come from, too."

The two of them now tipped up their noses and cocked their eyes significantly.

"Let's go around," added Maguire.

They went, the significant red light over the transom at 68 telling its own story. Strolling leisurely up, they knocked. At the very first sound a painted denizen of the half-world opened the door.

"Where's Adele?" asked Maguire as the two, hats on as usual, stepped in.

"She's gone to bed."

"Tell her to come down."

They seated themselves deliberately in the gaudy mirrored parlor and waited, conversing between themselves in whispers. Presently a sleepy-looking woman of forty in a gaudy robe of heavy texture, and slippered in red, appeared.

"We're here about that suicide case you had to-night. What about it? Who was she? How'd she come to be in that doorway around the corner? Come, now," Maguire added, as the madam assumed an air of mingled injured and ignorant innocence, "you know. Can that stuff! How did she come to take poison?"

"I don't know what you're talking about," said the woman with the utmost air of innocence. "I never heard of any suicide."

"Aw, come now," insisted Delahanty, "the girl around the corner. You know. We know you've got a pull, but we've got to know about this case, just the same. Come across now. It won't be published. What made her take the poison?"

Under the steady eyes of the officers the woman hesitated, but finally weakened.

"Why—why—her lover went back on her—that's all. She got so blue we just couldn't do anything with her. I tried to, but she wouldn't listen."

"Lover, eh?" put in Maguire as though

that were the most unheard-of-thing in the world. "What was his name?"

"I don't know. You never can tell that."

"What was her name—Annie?" asked Delahanty wisely, as though he knew but was merely inquiring for form's sake.

"No—Emily."

"Well, how did she come to get over there, anyhow?" inquired Maguire most pleasantly.

"George took her," she replied, referring to a man-of-all-work about the place.

Then little by little as they sat there the whole miserable story came out, miserable as all the wilfulness and error and suffering of the world.

"How old was she?"

"Oh, twenty-one."

"Well, where'd she come from?"

"Oh, here in New York. Her family locked her out one night, I think."

Something in the way the woman said this last brought old Rogaum and his daughter back to the policemen's minds. They had forgotten all about her by now, although they had turned in an alarm. Fearing to interfere too much with this well-known and politically controlled institution, the two men left, but outside they fell to talking of the other case.

"We ought to tell old Rogaum about her sometime," said Maguire to Delahanty cynically. "He locked his kid out to-night."

"Yes, it might be a good thing for him to hear that," replied the other. "We'd better go round there an' see if his girl's back yet. She may be back by now," and so they returned but little disturbed by the joint miseries.

At Rogaum's door they once more knocked loudly.

"Is your daughter back again?" asked Maguire when a reply was had.

"Ach, no," replied the hysterical Mrs. Rogaum, who was quite alone now. "My husband he haf gone oudt again to loog vunce more. Oh, my! Oh, my!"

"Well, that's what you get for lockin' her out," returned Maguire loftily, the other story fresh in his mind. "That other girl downstairs here to-night was locked out too, once." He chanced to have a girl-child of his own and somehow he was in the mood for pointing a moral. "You oughtn't to do anything like that. Where d'yuh expect she's goin' to if you lock her out?"

Mrs. Rogaum groaned. She explained that it was not her fault, but anyhow it was carrying coals to Newcastle to talk to her so. The advice was better for her husband.

The pair finally returned to the station to see if the call had been attended to.

"Sure," said the sergeant, "certainly. Whaddy ya think?" and he read from the blotter before him:

"'Look out for girl, Theresa Rogaum. Aged 18; height, about 5, 3; light hair, blue eyes, white cotton dress, trimmed with blue ribbon. Last seen with lad named Almerting, about 19 years of age, about 5, 9; weight, 135 pounds.'"

There were other details even more pointed and conclusive. For over an hour now, supposedly, policemen from the Battery to Harlem, and far beyond, had been scanning long streets and dim shadows for a girl in a white dress with a youth of nineteen,—supposedly.

Officer Halsey, another of this region, which took in a portion of Washington Square, had seen a good many couples this pleasant summer evening since the description of Theresa and Almerting had been read to him over the telephone, but none that answered to these. Like Maguire and Delahanty, he was more or less indifferent to all such cases, but idling on a corner near the park at about three a. m., a brother officer, one Paisly by name, came up and casually mentioned the missing pair also.

"I bet I saw that couple, not over an hour ago. She was dressed in white, and looked to me as if she didn't want to be out. I didn't happen to think at the time, but now I remember. They acted sort o' funny. She did, anyhow. They went in this park down at the Fourth Street end there."

"Supposing we beat it, then," suggested Halsey, weary for something to do.

"Sure," said the other quickly, and together they began a careful search, kicking around in the moonlight under the trees. The moon was leaning moderately toward the west, and all the branches were silvered with light and dew. Among the flowers, past clumps of bushes, near the fountain, they searched, each one going his way alone. At last, the wandering Halsey paused beside a thick clump of flaming bushes, ruddy, slightly, even in the light. A murmur of voices greeted him, and something very much like the sound of a sob.

"What's that?" he said mentally, drawing near and listening.

"Why don't you come on now?" said the first of the voices heard. "They won't let you in any more. You're with me, ain't you? What's the use cryin'?"

No answer to this, but no sobs. She must have been crying silently.

"Come on. I can take care of yuh. We can live in Hoboken. I know a place where we can go to-night. That's all right."

There was a movement as if the speaker were patting her on the shoulder.

"What's the use cryin'? Don't you believe I love yuh?"

The officer who had stolen quietly around to get a better view now came closer. He wanted to see for himself. In the moonlight, from a comfortable distance, he could see them seated. The tall bushes were almost all about the bench. In the arms of the youth was the girl in white, held very close. Leaning over to get a better view, he saw him kiss her and hold her—hold her in such a way that she could but yield to him, whatever her slight disinclination.

It was a common affair at earlier hours, but rather interesting now. The officer was interested. He crept nearer.

"What are you two doin' here?" he suddenly inquired, rising before them, as though he had not seen.

The girl tumbled out of her compromising position, speechless and blushing violently. The young man stood up, nervous, but still defiant.

"Aw, we were just sittin' here," he replied.

"Yes? Well, say, what's your name? I think we're lookin' for you two, anyhow. Almerting?"

"That's me," said the youth.

"And yours?" he added, addressing Theresa.

"Theresa Rogaum," replied the latter brokenly, beginning to cry.

"Well, you two'll have to come along with me," he added laconically. "The Captain wants to see both of you," and he marched them solemnly away.

"What for?" young Almerting ventured to inquire after a time, blanched with fright.

"Never mind," replied the policeman irritably. "Come along, you'll find out at the station house. We want you both. That's enough."

At the other end of the park Paisly

joined them, and, at the station-house, the girl was given a chair. She was all tears and melancholy with a modicum possibly of relief at being thus rescued from the world. Her companion, for all his youth, was defiant if circumspect, a natural animal defeated of its aim.

"Better go for her father," commented the sergeant, and by four in the morning old Rogaum, who had still been up and walking the floor, was rushing stationward. From an earlier rage he had passed to an almost killing grief, but now at the thought that he might possibly see his daughter alive and well once more he was overflowing with a mingled emotion which contained rage, fear, sorrow, and a number of other things. What should he do to her if she were alive? Beat her? Kiss her? Or what? Arrived at the station, however, and seeing his fair Theresa in the hands of the police, and this young stranger lingering near, also detained, he was beside himself with fear, rage, affection.

"You! You!" he exclaimed at once, glaring at the imperturbable Almerting, when told that this was the young man who was found with his girl. Then, seized with a sudden horror, he added, turning to Theresa, "Vot haf you done? Oh, oh! You! You!" he repeated again to Almerting angrily, now that he felt that his daughter was safe. "Come not near my tochter any more! I vill preak your effery pone, du teufel, du!"

He made a move toward the incarcerated lover, but here the sergeant interfered.

"Stop that, now," he said calmly. "Take your daughter out of here and go home, or I'll lock you both up. We don't want any fighting in here. D'ye hear? Keep your daughter off the streets hereafter, then she won't get into trouble. Don't let her run around with such young toughs as this." Almerting winced. "Then there won't anything happen to her. We'll do whatever punishing's to be done."

"Aw, what's eatin' him!" commented Almerting dourly, now that he felt himself reasonably safe from a personal encounter. "What have I done? He locked her out, didn't he? I was just keepin' her company till morning."

"Yes, we know all about that," said the sergeant, "and about you, too. You shut up, or you'll go down town to Special Sessions. I want no guff out o' you." Still he ordered the butcher angrily to be gone.

Old Rogaum heard nothing. He had his daughter. He was taking her home. She was not dead—not even morally injured in so far as he could learn. He was a compound of wondrous feelings. What to do was beyond him.

At the corner near the butcher shop they encountered the wakeful Maguire, still idling, as they passed. He was pleased to see that Rogaum had his Theresa once more. It raised him to a high, moralizing height.

"Don't lock her out any more," he called significantly. "That's what brought the other girl to your door, you know!"

"Vot iss dot?" said Rogaum.

"I say the other girl was locked out. That's why she committed suicide."

"Ach, I know," said the husky German under his breath, but he had no intention of locking her out. He did not know what he would do until they were in the presence of his crying wife, who fell upon Theresa, weeping. Then he decided to be reasonably lenient.

"She vass like you," said the old mother to the wandering Theresa, ignorant of the seeming lesson brought to their very door. "She vass loog like you."

"I vill not vip you now," said the old butcher solemnly, too delighted to think of punishment after having feared every horror under the sun, "aber, go not oudt any more. Keep off de streeds so late. I von't haf it. Dot loafer, aber—let him yussed come here some more! I fix him!"

"No, no," said the fat mother tearfully, smoothing her daughter's hair. "She vouldn't run avay no more yet, no, no." Old Mrs. Rogaum was all mother.

"Well, you wouldn't let me in," insisted Theresa, "and I didn't have any place to go. What do you want me to do? I'm not going to stay in the house all the time."

"I fix him!" roared Rogaum, unloading all his rage now on the recreant lover freely. "Yussed let him come some more! Der penitentiary he should haf!"

"Oh, he's not so bad," Theresa told her mother, almost a heroine now that she was home and safe. "He's Mr. Almerting, the stationer's boy. They live here in the next block."

"Don't you ever bother that girl again," the sergeant was saying to young Almerting as he turned him loose an hour later. "If you do, we'll get you, and you won't get off under six months. Y' hear me, do you?"

"Aw, I don't want 'er," replied the boy truculently and cynically. "Let him have his old daughter. What's he want to lock 'er out for? They'd better not lock 'er out again though, that's all I say. I don't want 'er."

"Beat it!" replied the sergeant, and 5 away he went.

XLV

IRVIN SHREWSBURY COBB (1876–   )

Irvin S. Cobb is peculiarly a product of modern journalism. With him we enter again th
South which after the first generation following the war lay bare of literary recorders
Paducah, Kentucky, was his birthplace. After slight schooling he found employment as ;
mere boy on one of the local papers and since that time he has filled about every positio
possible to find on a newspaper, urban or metropolitan. Early he became a "columnist" editing
as part of his day's work, the column "Sour Mash" in the Louisville, Ky., *Evening Post*
and the training engendered turned him first to humor as his field of expression. In 1904 h
became a humorist on New York papers and it was as a humorist that he first made hi.
name known to the reading public. It was soon found, however, that he was much mor
than a mere fun-maker. His story "The Belled Buzzard," 1912, placed him at a bound amon
the best story-tellers of the time and he followed it with others in rich variety. He is at hi
best in his *genre* studies of Southern life and character. In such gruesome tales as "Fish
head" he shows a mastery of impressionistic detail and a suggestiveness of horror that mak
him comparable even with Poe. In all of his work, however, there is humor—a qualit
that Poe sadly lacked—sometimes boisterous and unrestrained, more often subdued and atmos
pheric. He is an artist with Southern sensibilities and a strong predilection for the uncouth
the paradoxical, the autochthonic. He was the winner in 1922 of the O. Henry short-story
award. Perhaps his most distinctive collection is his *Mr. Trimm*, 1913.

A LADY AND A GENTLEMAN *

There were the hotel lobbies; they roared and spun like whirlpools with the crowds that were in them. But the streets outside were more like mill-races, and the exits from the railroad stations became flumes down which all morning and all afternoon the living torrents unceasingly had poured. Every main crossing was in a twist of opposing currents. Overhead, on cornices and across window-ledges and against house-fronts and on ropes which passed above the roadway from one building to another, hung buntings and flags and streamers, the prevalent colors being red and white; and also many great goggle-eyed and bewhiskered portraits of dead warriors done on sail-cloth in the best styles of two domestic schools—sign-painting and election-bannering. Numbers of brass bands marched to and fro, playing this, that and the next appropriate air, but when in doubt playing "Dixie"; and the musicians waded knee-deep through an accumulating wreckage of abandoned consonants—softly dropped *g's*, eliminated *r's*.

* Published by arrangement with Irvin S. Cobb, owner of the copyright.

In short, the United Confederate Veterans were holding their annual reunion, this being the evening of the opening day.

For absolute proof that this really was a reunion of his kind, there was visible here and there a veteran. His average age was eighty-three years and some odd months. He was feeble or he was halt or sometimes he was purblind. Only very rarely did he carry his years and his frame straight. He was near to being swept away and drowned in a vast and fragrant sea of gracious, chattering femininity. His daughters and his granddaughters and his nieces and his younger sisters and, very rarely, his wife—they collectively were as ten to one against him. They were the sponsors and the maids of honor and the matrons of honor and the chaperons; they represented such-and-such a camp or such-and-such a state, wearing flowing badges to attest their queenly distinctions; wearing, also, white summery gowns, the most of them, with touches of red. But the older women nearly always were in black.

Here and there moved the Amazonian figure of one among them who had decked herself for this great occasion in a gray uniform with bullet buttons of brass in twin rows down the front of the jacket and with a soldier cap on her bobbed hair —nearly always it was bobbed—and gold braid at the seams of her short walking skirt. A crafty stylist even had thought out the added touches of epaulets for her straight shoulders and a pair of black cavalry boots; and she went about much admired by herself and the rest.

You see, it was like this: In the days when there were many of them, the veterans had shared their reunions with their women. Now that they were so few and so weakly, their women were letting the veterans share the reunions with them. It was very much like this—a gorgeous social event, the whole South participating, with sentiment for its half-erased background, with the memories of a war that ended nearly sixty years before for its fainting, fading excuse; with the splendid promise of balls and parties and receptions and flirting and love-making and matchmaking for its assembly call to the campaigning, rampaging young of the species.

Only over by the river at the big yellow pine auditorium did the puny veteran element yet hold its own against the dominant attendant tides of the newer generations of its descendants. "General Van Brunk of Texas, honored head of the Trans-Mississippi Department, will now present the important report of the Committee on History," the octogenarian commander-in-chief was announcing to those fifteen hundred white heads that nodded before him like so much ripened cotton in the bolls. So General Van Brunk, holding the typewritten fruitage of one year's hard work in his palsied hands, took the platform and cleared a shrunken throat and began.

But just then the members of the Orphan Brigade of Kentucky—thirty-two of them, no less—marched down the middle aisle with a fife-and-drum corps at their head and a color-bearer bearing a tattered rag on a scarred staff, and everybody rose up shakily to give the Rebel yell, and nobody, not even General Van Brunk, ever heard a word of General Van Brunk's report. It was ordered spread upon the minutes, though, while the commander-in-chief stood up there with his arms outstretched and wept a welcome to the straggly incoming column. He was an Orphan himself.

The proceedings were proceeding according to custom. The orator chosen to deliver the annual oration would have an easy time of it when his hour came next day. "Comrades of my father," he would say, and they would applaud for five minutes. He would mention Jackson and they would whoop for seven minutes; mention Lee and that would mean ten minutes of the same. And so on.

At a quarter to ten a certain portly churchman—lately a chaplain with the A.E.F.—who by invitation had come down from Minneapolis to bear an affectionate message to these old men in behalf of the American Legion, wormed his way out of a side door of the auditorium, his job done. Inside his black garments he was perspiring heavily. The air of the packed hall had been steaming hot. He stood for a minute on the sidewalk, grateful for the cooling wind of the May night and trying to decide whether he ought to turn east or west to get back to his hotel. He was a bishop of the Episcopal Church and he had the bishop's look and manner. On his arm he felt a bony clutch, like the clutch of a parrot's foot.

A bent shell of a man was alongside him; it was this shell had fastened its skeleton fingers upon his sleeve. Out of a head that was just a skull with a brown hard skin stretched over it, a pair of filmed eyes looked up into his face, and from behind an ambush of dense white whiskers came a piping voice saying:

"Howdy, son."

The bishop was startled and secretly amused. He was used to being called "Father"—frequently his collar and vest deceived Romanists—but he couldn't remember when anyone had addressed him as "son."

"Good evening, sir," he answered.

"Son," quavered the other—he must be all of ninety, the bishop decided—"say, son, I heared you back thar—part of whut you said. You done fust-rate—yep, fust-rate, fur a Yankee. You air a Yankee, ain't you?"

"Well, I was born in Nebraska, but I live now in Minnesota," said the bishop.

"That so? Well, I'm an Alabama boy!"

All at once the bishop ceased to be amused. As the talon released its fumbling hold on him and the remnant tottered away, the bishop's right arm came up smartly but involuntarily in a military salute.

"He calls himself a boy!" quoth the bishop, addressing no one in particular. "I know now why they fought four years down here against such odds!"

Suddenly he was prouder than ever of being an American. And he, a stranger to these parts, felt the pathos of it all—the pathos of age and decrepitude, the pathos of the thronging shadows of an heroic Lost Cause, the gallant pathos of these defeated men who even now at their time of life would never admit they had been defeated—these things, thrown out in relief against this screen of blaring brass and pretty young girls and socially ambitious mothers and general hullabaloo.

But this story, such as it is, is not concerned with this particular reunion so much as it is concerned with the reactions to the reunion of one surviving Confederate who attended it. He was not an imported orator nor a thwarted deliverer of historical reports, nor yet the commander of some phantom division whose main camp ground now was a cemetery. He was still what he had been back yonder in '65—a high private of the rear rank. He was fond of saying so. With him it was one favorite little joke which never staled.

He was a very weary high private as he trudged along. An exceedingly young and sleepy Boy Scout was his guide, striving to keep in stride with him. First the old man would tote his small valise, then the Scout would take it over for a spell.

They had ridden together on a streetcar. At a corner which the guide thought must be their corner, they got off. They were entering an outlying part of the city, that much was certain, at least. The last high-dangled example of the art preservative as practised by local masters of outdoor advertising service—it was labeled with the name of President Jefferson Davis, so it must be a likeness of President Davis—was swinging aloft far behind them. Those thin broken sounds of distant band-music no longer came to their ears. The houses were getting scarcer, getting to be farther apart. They stumbled in the darkness across railroad tracks, thence passed on through a sort of tunnel that was as black inside as a pocket. When they came out from under the culvert they found themselves in a desert so far as stirring life went.

"Shore you're not lost, sonny?" asked the old man for the second or third time.

"No, suh, I think not." But the youngster's tone had lost its earlier manful conviction. "It oughter be right down this way somewhere. I guess we'll strike it soon."

So they went ahead. The veteran's trudge became a shamble. The Scout's step became a drowsy stagger. That Scout was growing very tired in his legs; they were such short legs. He had been on duty since breakfast time and it must be nearly eleven o'clock by now.

It was the high private's turn to carry the grip. He halted and put it down to ease his cramped hand and to breathe. His companion lurched with a bump against the telephone pole and gave a comatose grunt.

"Look here, little pardner," said the old man, "you act like to me you're mighty near played out. Whereabouts do you live?"

"Clean over—over—on the other side of town from here." The child spoke between jaw-stretching yawns. "That car-line back there goes right past our house though." His voice was very wistful as he said that last.

"Tell you what, then. It'd be wrong to keep you up any longer. But me, I'm one of these here old-time campaigners. You hand me over that piece of paper with the name and the number and all on it, and then you put out for home and get yourself a good night's rest. By myself I'll be shore to locate the place we're hunting for. Anyway, you've done enough good deeds for one day."

That Scout might be sleepy, but sleepy or not he had a bounden service to perform and would have so stated. But the veteran cut short those plucky semiconscious protests of his, and being outargued the boy surrendered a scrap of cardboard and bade his late charge good-by and good night and set out on his return to civilization.

Under a near-by electric this old-time campaigner adjusted his glasses and studied the scribbled face of the card. Immediately above his head a street-marker showed on the lamp-post where the light would fall on it, and next he looked up and spelled out the lettering there. He merely was reconfirming a fact already confirmed.

"This is certainly the right street," he said to himself. "But the question is—which-a-way is the right house? The thing for me to do, I reckin, is to roust up somebody and ask—if I can find anybody awake."

Diagonally opposite, he made out the square bulk of a sizable two-story structure. It must be a dwelling, for it had a bit of lawn in front of it; it must be tenanted because a patchy dullish crescent of illumination made outlines for a transom above the door. Maybe somebody over there might be smart enough to tell him.

He went across, moving very slowly, and toiled up a flight of porch steps. There were only four of the steps; he would have taken his oath there were a full dozen of them. He fumbled at the door-jamb until he found a knocker.

To his knocking the response was immediate. From the inner side there was the scraping sound as of a heavy bolt being withdrawn. Next a lock clicked, and then discreetly, almost cautiously, the door opened a few inches and the face of a negro girl was revealed to him in the dim glow of a heavily hooded light burning behind her in the entry hall. She squinted hard at him.

"Whut you want yere this time o' night, mista?" she demanded. Her manner was not hospitable; it bordered on the suspicious.

"I'm looking for an address," he began.

"Dis can't be it."

"I know that. But I thought maybe somebody here might help direct me." From his growing exhaustion the intruder fairly was panting. "I'm sort of lost."

"Oh, so tha's it? Wait a minute, then." Still holding the door slightly ajar, she called rearward over her shoulder: "Miss Sissie! Oh, Miss Sissie!"

"What is it?" The answer came from back of her.

"They's a ole, kinder feebled-up lookin' w'ite gen'elman out yere w'ich he think he's lost his way."

"Wait, I'll come talk to him."

A middle-aged tall woman, who was dressed, so the stranger decided, as though expecting stylish company, appeared now at the door and above the servant's shoulder eyed him appraisingly. He tried to tell her his mission, but his voice weakened on him and trailed off. He caught at the door-casing; he felt dizzy.

The white woman elbowed the black one aside. She caught him about the waist.

"Come on in," she ordered. "Get out of the way, can't you, Pansy?" She threw this second command at her maid. "Don't you see he's about ready to drop? Pick up his valise. There, that's it, mister. Just put your weight on me."

She half lifted him across the threshold and eased him down upon a sofa in the hall. The negress closed and barred the door.

"Run make some hot coffee," her employer bade her. "Or maybe you'd rather have a little liquor? I've got plenty of it in the house." She addressed the slumped intruder.

"Nome, I never touch anything strong. But I reckin a cup of coffee would taste good to me—if I'm not putting you out too much? You'll please have to excuse me, ma'am, for breaking in on you this way, but I—" Remembering his manners, he got his hat off in a little flurry of confusion.

"Where were you trying to get to?"

With difficulty he brought his card forth from his pocket and she took it from him and read what was written upon it.

"You're a good long two miles and a half from where you belong," she told him sharply.

"But ain't this Bonaventure Avenue?"

"Yes, North Bonaventure. You came out Lawes Drive, didn't you?—the wide street where the trolley-line is? Well, you should have gone south when you turned off. Instead of that you came north. These people"—she consulted the card again—"Philipson or whatever the name is—are they friends of yours?"

"Well, yes, ma'am, and nome. I've never met them. But they're taking in one old soldier during the reunion, the hotels and the boarding-houses and all being so full up. And a gentleman at Tennessee Headquarters—that's my headquarters, 'ma'am —he gave me that card and sent me there."

"Send you alone?" Her angular shoulders, bare above a low-cut evening gown, shrugged impatiently.

"Oh, nome, one of these here little Boy Scouts he came with me to show me the way. You see, ma'am, it's rightly my own fault, not being all settled before dark. But I didn't get in on the steam-cars till about six o'clock this evening and I didn't want to miss the opening session at the big hall. So I went right there, packing my baggage along with me, just as soon as I'd got me a snack of supper, me not wanting to miss anything, as I was saying to you, ma'am. Then when the speechmaking and all was over, me and this little Boy Scout —he'd stayed right along with me at the hall—we put out to find where I was to stay. But he couldn't hardly drag one foot behind the other. Poor little wore-out fellow, I reckin he'd been running around all day. So a few minutes ago I made him go on home, me figuring I could find the house my own self. And—well, here I am, ma'am, imposing on your kindness and mighty sorry to do it, too."

"Never mind that part of it."

"But just as soon as I can get a dram of hot coffee in me I expect I'll feel stronger and then I'll be shoving along and not bother you any more. I reckin that long train ride and the excitement and everything must 'a' took it out of me, some way. There was a time when it wouldn't have bothered me at all—not a bit. Still, I'll have to confess I'm getting along, ma'am. I'll be eighty-four this coming ninth of August."

"Listen to me: You're not going to stir another inch to-night. You stay right here and to-morrow morning I'll decide myself whether you're fit to go trapesing off across to the other side of town."

"Oh, ma'am, I couldn't do that!"

"Why couldn't you?"

"But, ma'am, are you taking in any visitors during the reunion?"

"I wasn't aiming to." Her voice was grim. "But I'm fixing now to do that very little thing, whether or no."

"But honest, now—I—" He scuffled with his tired feet. "It's mighty good and mighty sweet of you, ma'am, but I'd hate to impose on you like that."

"No imposition. There're five spare bedrooms in this house—and nobody in any of them. And nobody going to be in any of them, either, while you're here —except you. I think you'll be comfortable."

"I know I'd be comfortable but—"

"Then it's all settled. By the way, I don't know your name yet?"

"My name is Braswell—Nathan Braswell, late high private of the rear rank in the Eighteenth Tennessee Infantry. But up at Forks of Hatchie—that's my home town, ma'am, a little town up in West Tennessee—they call me the Reverend Braswell, sometimes."

"Reverend?" Her eyelids narrowed. "Are you a minister?"

"Oh, nome. But sometimes when we're short on a preacher I make out to take the pulpit and read the Scriptures and make a little kind of a talk—not a regular sermon—just a little kind of a religious talk. And I'm purty active in church work generally. So I reckin that's why some people call me the Reverend Braswell. But I never use the entitlement myself—it wouldn't be becoming in a layman."

"I see. You preach but you're not a preacher. I guess you practise what you preach, too. You look like a good man, to me—and a good man can be set down anywhere and not suffer by it; at least that's my opinion. So, Mr. Braswell, right here is where you camp."

"Just as you say, ma'am." His surrender was complete now, his weariness was, too. "Probably you're right—if I tried to go any further to-night it's likely I wouldn't be much good to-morrow and I want to be spry and fresh so I can knock around and see if I can't run across some of my old pardners in the army. But excuse me again —you got my name but you ain't told me yours?"

"Call me Miss Sissie, if you want to. That's what nearly everybody does call me. Or else just plain Sis."

"All right, Miss Sissie, just as you say." He bowed to her with a grave simplicity. "And I'm sure I'm very much beholden to you, ma'am. It ain't every day that an old fellow like me is lucky enough to run into such a lovely nice lady as you."

He drank his coffee and, being helped to his feet, he went upstairs with some aid from the lovely nice lady and presently was sound asleep in a clean bed in what he regarded as a very fine bedroom indeed. Its grandeur impressed him even through his tiredness.

Coming back down after seeing him properly bestowed, the mistress of the house hailed the colored girl. "Pansy," she said, "this place is out of business until further orders, understand?"

At that, Pansy seemed deeply puzzled. "But, Miss Sissie," she expostulated, "don't you remember 'at a suttin party—you know, Mista J. W. B.—is 'spectin' to be yere most any time wid—"

"Did you hear what I told you?" A quality of metallic harshness in •Miss Sissie's voice was emphasized.

"Yessum, but you know yo'se'f how that there party, Mista J. W. B., is. He'll shore be dis'p'inted. He's liable raise Cain. He's—"

"Get him on the telephone; you know his number. Tell him this place is closed for to-night and for every day and every night until further notice from me. And tell the same thing to everybody else who calls up or stops by during the reunion. Get me?" By her tone she menaced the darky.

"Yassum."

"Then turn that hall light out."

For three days Mr. Braswell abided under that roof. Frequently during that time he remarked that he couldn't remember when he'd had a pleasanter stay anywhere. Nor could it be said that Miss Sissie failed in any possible effort to make the visit pleasant for him.

He limped down to breakfast next morning; to limp was the best he could do. His entertainer gave her household staff a double surprise, first by coming down to join him at the meal instead of taking her coffee and rolls in her room and second by appearing not in negligée but in a plain dark house-gown which accentuated rather than softened the square contours of her face and the sharp lines in it. By daylight the two had better opportunity to study each other than the somewhat hurried meeting of the night before had afforded.

She saw in him a gentle tottery relic of a man with a pair of faded unworldly old eyes looking out from a bland, wrinkly, rather empty face. He saw in her a most kindly and considerate hostess. Privately he decided she must have had plenty of sorrow in her time—something or other about her told him that life had bestowed upon her more than her proper share of hard knocks. He figured that living here alone in such a big house—except for the servants she seemed to be quite alone—must be lonesome for her, too.

As they sat down, just the two of them, he said, not apologetically exactly but a bit timidly:

"I hope, ma'am, you don't mind if I say a grace at your table? I always like to invoke the divine blessing before I break bread—seems like to me it makes the victuals taste better. Or maybe"—he hesitated politely—"maybe it's your custom to ask the blessing your own.self?"

"You say it, please," she urged him in a curious strained fashion, which, however, he did not notice, and lowered her head. She lifted it once—to shoot a quick venomous glance at Pansy, who stood to serve, and a convulsive giggle which had formed in Pansy's throat died instantly. Then she bowed it again and kept it bowed while he asked God to sanctify this food to their uses and to be merciful to all within those walls and to all His children everywhere. For Jesus' sake. Amen!

She plied his plate abundantly and, for all his bodily infirmity, he showed her a healthy appetite. He talked freely, she encouraging him by proving a good listener. He was a widower with one married daughter. Since his wife's death he had made his home with this daughter. Her husband was a mighty fine man—not religious, but high-principled and doing very well indeed as a banker, considering that Forks of Hatchie was such a small town. He himself had been in the grain and feed business for most of his life but was retired now. He'd never been much of a hand for gadding over the world. Going to reunions once a year was about the extent of his traveling around. In all the time since the United Confederate Veterans had been formed he'd missed but one reunion —that was the spring when his wife died.

"Minty—that's my daughter, ma'am— Minty, she didn't want me to come to this one," he went on. "She was afraid for me to be putting out alone on such a long trip 'way down here; she kept saying, Minty did, she was afraid the excitement might be too much for me at my age. But I says to her, I says, 'Minty, child, when my time comes for me to go I don't ask anything better than that it should be whilst I'm amongst my old comrades, with the sound of one of our old battle songs ringing in my ears!' I says to her, 'Shucks, but what's the use of talking that way! Nothing's going to happen to me. I can get there and I can get back!' I says to her. 'Going to reunion makes me feel young and spry all over again.' But, ma'am, I'm afraid Minty was right about it, this time anyhow. I actually don't believe I'm going to be able to get back downtown for to-day's doings —not for the morning's session anyway. I have to own up to you that I feel all kind of let-down and no-account, someway."

So through the forenoon he sat in an easy chair in an inner sitting-room and Miss Sissie, abandoning whatever else she might have had to do, read to him the accounts of the great event which filled column after column of the morning paper. He dozed off occasionally but she kept on reading, her voice droning across the placid quiet. Following the dinner which came at midday, she prevailed on him to take a real nap, and he stretched out on a sofa under a light coverlid which she tucked about him and slept peacefully until four o'clock. Late in the afternoon a closed car containing a couple—a man and a woman—stopped in the alleyway behind the house and the driver came to the back door, but Miss Sissie went out and gave him a message for his passengers and he returned to his car and drove away. There were no other callers that day.

Mr. Braswell fretted a little after supper over his inability to muster up strength for getting to the auditorium, but somewhat was consoled by her assurances that a good night's rest should put him in proper trim for marching in the big parade next morning. By nine o'clock he was in bed and Miss Sissie had a silent idle evening at home and seemed not ungrateful for it.

On the second morning the ancient greeted her in what plainly was his official wardrobe for parading. A frayed and threadbare butternut jacket, absurdly short, with a little peaked tail sticking out behind and a line of tarnished brass buttons spaced down its front, hung grotesquely upon his withered framework. Probably it had fitted him once; now it was acres too loose. Pinned to the left breast was a huge badge, evidently home-made, of yellowed white silk, and lengthwise of it in straggled letters worked with faded red floss ran the number and name of his regiment. In his hand he carried a slouch-hat which had been black once but now was a rusty brown, with a scrap of black ostrich-plume fastened to its band by a brass token.

With trembling fingers he proudly caressed the badge.

"My wife made it for me out of a piece of her own wedding-dress nearly thirty years ago," he explained. "I've worn it to every reunion since then. It's funny how you put me in mind of my wife. Not that you look like her nor talk like her either. She was kind of small and she had a low voice and you're so much taller and your way of speaking is deeper and carries further than hers did. And of course you can't be more than half as old as she'd be if she'd lived. Funny, but you do remind

me of her, though. Still, I reckin that's easy to explain. All good women favor each other some way even when they don't look alike. It's something inside of them that does it, I judge—goodness and purity and thinking Christian thoughts."

If she winced at that last his innocent weakened old eyes missed it. Anyhow the veteran very soon had personal cause for distress. He had to confess that he wasn't up to marching. Leaving the dining-room, he practically collapsed. He was heart-broken.

"Don't you worry," said Miss Sissie, in that masterful way of hers. "Even if you're not able to turn out with the rest of them you're going to see the parade. I can't send you down town in my own car—it's—it's broken down—and I can't go with you myself—I—I'm going to be busy. But I can send you in a taxicab with a careful man to drive you and you can see the parade from it."

"That's mighty sweet of you—but then, I reckin it's your nature to be sweet and thoughtful for other folks," he said gratefully. "But, ma'am"—and doubt crept into his voice—"but ain't all the public hacks likely to be engaged beforehand for to-day?"

"I happen to know the manager of the leading taxicab company here," she told him. "He'll do what I say even if he has to take a rig away from somebody else. I'll telephone him."

"But with the streets all crowded the way they'll be, won't it be hard to find a place where I can watch the other boys marching by?" In his eagerness he was childish.

"That'll be arranged, too," she stated. "As it so happens, I also know the chief of police. I'll call him up and give him the number of the taxi you're in and I'll guarantee one of his policemen will be on the special lookout for you at the far end of the Drive to see to it that you get a good place somewhere along the route."

"Seems like to me the most important people in this town must respect you mighty highly!" he exclaimed happily. "Well, I guess it's that same way everywhere—all kinds of people are bound to recognize a real lady when they meet her and look up to her!"

"Oh, yes, there's one thing more." She added this as if by an afterthought. "You needn't tell anybody you meet—any of your old friends or any of the committeemen or anybody—where you're stopping. You see, I didn't arrange to take in any visitors for the reunion—there were reasons why I didn't care to take in anyone—and now that I have you with me I wouldn't care for anybody connected with the local arrangements to know about it. You understand, don't you?—they might think I was presuming on their rights."

"Oh, yes'm, I understand," he said unsuspectingly. "It'll just be a little secret between us if that's the way you'd rather it was. But I couldn't rightly tell anybody anyhow—seeing that you ain't ever told me what your last name is. I'd like to know it, too—I aim to write you a letter after I get home."

"My name is Lamprey," she said. "Cecelia Lamprey. I don't hear it very often myself—at least, not spoken out in full. And now I'd better be ringing up those influential friends of mine—you mustn't be late getting started."

The same taxicab driver who drove him on this day came again on the third day to take Miss Sissie's venerable house guest to his train. It would appear that her car still was out of commission.

She did not accompany him to the station. Domestic cares would hold her, she told him. She did not go to the front of the house to see him off, either. Indeed a more observant person than Mr. Braswell might have marveled that so constantly she had secluded herself indoors during his visit; and not only indoors, but behind windows curtained against the bright, warm Southern sunshine. They exchanged their farewells in her living-room.

"I ain't never going to forget you," he told her. "If you'd been my own daughter you couldn't 'a' treated me any nicer than what you have—and me just an old stove-up spavined country-jake that you never saw before in your life and probably never will see again. You ain't seen fit, ma'am, to tell me much about yourself—seems like you let me do most of the talking, and that suited me—but old as I am I know a perfect lady when I see one and that's what you are, ma'am, and what always you must have been and always will be—good-by and God bless you!"

Saying nothing, she bent in the attitude of one accepting a benediction, and a moment later she was following him to the door and watching him as he crept in his labored, faltering gait along the entrance-hall. Under his arm was his luncheon to be eaten on the train; she had with her own hands prepared and boxed it. She waited there on the threshold until the hooded front door clicked behind him.

"Pansy," she called then toward the back of the house, and now her voice had in it a customary rasping quality which, strangely, had been almost altogether lacking from it these past two or three days. "You, Pansy!"

"Yassum."

"You might call up that party that we turned down the other night and tell him this place has reopened for business as usual."

Approximately two weeks later, Mr. Randolph Embury, president of the Forks of Hatchie People's Bank, wrote as follows to the mayor of that city where the veterans had met:

"Dear Mr. Mayor: You may possibly recall that we met in 1922 while serving as delegates for our respective states at the Inter-Southern Commercial Congress in Norfolk? I am therefore taking advantage of our slight acquaintance and am trespassing upon your patience to ask a favor which means a great deal to my wife.

"Her aged father, the late Nathan Braswell, attended the recent Confederate Reunion in your city. Almost immediately upon his arrival back at this place he suffered a stroke of paralysis. Within ten days a second stroke resulted fatally to him. The interment took place yesterday, the twenty-ninth inst. His loss in this community is very deeply mourned. He was the last old soldier left here.

"Although rendered entirely helpless by the first stroke, he remained almost entirely rational and coherent until the second one occurred. In this stage of his illness he spoke repeatedly of his experiences while at the reunion. He was a guest in the private home of one who must have been a most cultured and charming lady—undoubtedly a lady of position and affluence. By her graciousness and her zealous care of him and her constant ministrations to his comfort she made a deep impression upon him. He was most anxious that she should know of his gratitude, and repeatedly he charged us to write her, telling how much he appreciated the attentions shown him.

"Naturally, during his illness and until after the interment neither my wife nor myself had much time for letter-writing. But this morning Mrs. Embury wrote to this lady, thanking her in her dead father's name and in ours and telling her that with practically his last conscious breath he spoke affectionately of her and paid tribute to her splendid womanly qualities and even uttered a little prayer for her well-being. He was a very devout man. That letter I enclose with this one, but in an unaddressed envelop. Mrs. Embury, of course, is most anxious that it should reach the intended recipient promptly.

"The reason for not addressing it you will understand when I tell you that my father-in-law could not remember his benefactress's last name except that it began with an 'L' and sounded something like 'Lampey' or 'Lambry.' He referred to her always as 'Miss Sissie,' which I would judge was her familiar name among more intimate friends. He could not remember the name of the street upon which she resided. However, he did describe the residence as being a very large and very handsome one, standing in a somewhat secluded part of the outskirts and not far from where a railroad track and an overhead viaduct were.

"This, then, is the favor I would ask of you: If the lady is as prominently connected as I had reason to believe from Mr. Braswell's statements, I assume you know her already. If not, I take it that it should not be a very difficult matter to locate one whose character and attainments must have given her a high standing among your good citizens. So I am asking you to see to it that this letter is put at once into her hands.

"Thanking you in advance for any trouble or inconvenience to which you may be put in carrying out our wishes, I remain,
"Yours most sincerely,
        "RANDOLPH EMBURY."

And within four days got back the following reply:

"Mayor's Office, June 2.
"Dear Sir:
"Yours received and contents carefully noted. In reply to same would say that while ready at any time to serve you and your good wife in every way possible, yet in this case I am put in a delicate attitude and fear you also may be put in one should I undertake to fulfill your desire.

"Undoubtedly the person that your late father-in-law had in mind was one Cecelia Lamprey, better known as 'Sis.' But not by the widest stretch of imagination could anyone think of her as a 'lady.' She is the proprietress of a most notorious assignation house located on North Bonaventure Avenue, this city, and according to my best information and belief, has always been a woman of loose morals and bad repute. I might add that having been elected on a reform ticket and being committed to the task of ridding our city of evil, I am at present setting on foot an effort to close up her establishment, which has until lately enjoyed secret 'protection,' and to drive her from our midst.

"Accordingly, I am constrained to believe that, being probably semi-delirious, the lately deceased, your esteemed father-in-law, must have made a mistake. I assume that he had 'Sis' Lamprey's house pointed out to him and in his ravings got it confused with the domicile where he was housed during his sojourn among us. It is not conceivable to me that a man such as you describe would, while in his sober senses, set foot inside an establishment so readily recognizable at a glance as being absolutely disreputable, let alone remain there for any appreciable period of time. It is equally incredible to think of 'Sis' opening her doors to any decent person or for any worthy purpose.

"In view of these facts I am constrained to believe that your wife would shrink from any contact or any communication with such an individual. I am therefore taking the liberty of holding her letter on my desk until you and she have had opportunity to consider this embarrassing situation and to decide what you should do. My advice is that you instruct me to return the letter to you at once and consider the incident closed. However, I await your further instruction.
(Signed)   "JASON BRODERICK, Mayor."

To which the following reply was immediately dispatched by wire:

"Nevertheless, on behalf of my wife and myself, kindly be so good as immediately to deliver the letter in question to the lady in question."

XLVI

SHERWOOD ANDERSON (1876–   )

The most original writer of fiction who has come out of the Middle West in later years has been Sherwood Anderson, a native of Ohio. Like most of the western group of writers—Dreiser, Lewis, Masters, Sandburg, and the rest—he came from the laboring class with little inheritance of culture. During his formative years his area of observation was a depressing one: a childhood pinched and sordid, with little of schooling, with manual labor in the factory or the fields imperative from early boyhood, and with entertainment furnished largely by country store groups, by bar-rooms, and livery stables. As a result, much of the material for his tales, coming from the actuality of his own observation, is drab and depressing. His *Winesburg, Ohio,* is a prose *Spoon River Anthology.*

Anderson's literary life has been a struggle for self-expression, for an interpretation of life that shall look beyond the surfaces into the primal verities. He is an "expressionist," and expressionism has thus been explained by Professor Perry:

"The author's concern with his character is with the latter's mind rather than with his outer life, with the sick man's dream rather than with the sick man. . . . The objective world is of secondary value to the expressionists. . . . They would break the old molds of thought and action and feeling, and liberate the spirit from the restraint of institutions and intellectual, moral, emotional, esthetic conventions. . . . This constrains the artists in the new movement to make war on all accepted standards, on sentimentality, prejudice, hypocrisy, on all second-hand pretensions to genuine preferences and refusals. The extremists in their campaign of disruption and inversion attack whatever is sacrosanct; they advocate whatever is different, not that it is in itself necessarily better, but that custom, habit, is paralyzing, tending towards stagnation, petrification, death, and must be ruthlessly demolished. In the resulting topsy-turvydom our honored faculties are debased, our vices are sublimated into virtues."

Like all of his school, Anderson has been scornful of prescribed technique. Because laws have been required in the past is reason enough for him why these laws henceforth shall be ignored. He is to express only *himself.* The materials he uses for his work are for the most part as grim and depressing as Tchekov's. He presents life in tragic terms, but he exalts vitality. He works always with the concrete instance, but, unlike Conrad, he is subjective in his analysis, delving always as far as his powers permit into the inner realities. Whether his findings are worth the while, whether he has the power to find the secrets he dissects for, whether he has done anything that will change or even influence the tide of fiction, may seriously be questioned.

DEATH *

The stairway leading up to Dr. Reefy's office, in the Heffner Block above the Paris Dry Goods Store, was but dimly lighted. At the head of the stairway hung a lamp with a dirty chimney that was fastened by a bracket to the wall. The lamp had a tin reflector, brown with rust and covered with dust. The people who went up the stairway followed with their feet the feet of many who had gone before. The soft boards of the stairs had yielded under the pressure of feet and deep hollows marked the way.

At the top of the stairway a turn to the right brought you to the doctor's door. To the left was a dark hallway filled with rubbish. Old chairs, carpenter's horses, step ladders and empty boxes lay in the darkness waiting for shins to be barked. The pile of rubbish belonged to the Paris Dry Goods Co. When a counter or a row of shelves in the store became useless, clerks carried it up the stairway and threw it on the pile.

Dr. Reefy's office was as large as a barn.

* "Death," from *Winesburg, Ohio,* by Sherwood Anderson. New York: The Viking Press. Copyright, 1919, by B. W. Huebsch.

A stove with a round paunch sat in the middle of the room. Around its base was piled sawdust, held in place by heavy planks nailed to the floor. By the door stood a huge table that had once been a part of the furniture of Herrick's Clothing Store and that had been used for displaying custom-made clothes. It was covered with books, bottles and surgical instruments. Near the edge of the table lay three or four apples left by John Spaniard, a tree nurseryman who was Doctor Reefy's friend, and who had slipped the apples out of his pocket as he came in at the door.

At middle age Doctor Reefy was tall and awkward. The gray beard he later wore had not yet appeared, but on the upper lip grew a brown mustache. He was not a graceful man, as when he grew older, and was much occupied with the problem of disposing of his hands and feet.

On summer afternoons, when she had been married many years and when her son George was a boy of twelve or fourteen, Elizabeth Willard sometimes went up the worn steps to Doctor Reefy's office. Already the woman's naturally tall figure had begun to droop and to drag itself listlessly about. Ostensibly she went to see the doctor because of her health, but on the half dozen occasions when she had been to see him the outcome of the visits did not primarily concern her health. She and the doctor talked of that, but they talked most of her life, of their two lives and of the ideas that had come to them as they lived their lives in Winesburg.

In the big empty office the man and the woman sat looking at each other and they were a good deal alike. Their bodies were different, as were also the color of their eyes, the length of their noses and the circumstances of their existence, but something inside them meant the same thing, wanted the same release, would have left the same impression on the memory of an onlooker. Later, and when he grew older and married a young wife, the doctor often talked to her of the hours spent with the sick woman and expressed a good many things he had been unable to express to Elizabeth. He was almost a poet in his old age and his notion of what happened took a poetic turn. "I had come to the time in my life when prayer became necessary and so I invented gods and prayed to them," he said. "I did not say my prayers in words nor did I kneel down, but sat perfectly still in my chair. In the late afternoon when it was hot and quiet on Main Street or in the winter when the days were gloomy, the gods came into the office and I thought no one knew about them. Then I found that this woman Elizabeth knew, that she worshiped also the same gods. I have a notion that she came to the office because she thought the gods would be there, but she was happy to find herself not alone just the same. It was an experience that cannot be explained, although I suppose it is always happening to men and women in all sorts of places."

. . . . . .

On the summer afternoons when Elizabeth and the doctor sat in the office and talked of their two lives they talked of other lives also. Sometimes the doctor made philosophic epigrams. Then he chuckled with amusement. Now and then after a period of silence, a word was said or a hint given that strangely illuminated the life of the speaker, a wish become a desire, or a dream, half dead, flared suddenly into life. For the most part the words came from the woman and she said them without looking at the man.

Each time she came to see the doctor the hotel keeper's wife talked a little more freely and after an hour or two in his presence went down the stairway into Main Street feeling renewed and strengthened against the dullness of her days. With something approaching a girlhood swing to her body she walked along, but when she had got back to her chair by the window of her room and when darkness had come on and a girl from the hotel dining room brought her dinner on a tray, she let it grow cold. Her thoughts ran away to her girlhood with its passionate longing for adventure and she remembered the arms of men that had held her when adventure was a possible thing for her. Particularly she remembered one who had for a time been her lover and who in the moment of his passion had cried out to her more than a hundred times, saying the same words madly over and over: "You dear! You dear! You lovely dear!" The words she thought expressed something she would have liked to have achieved in life.

In her room in the shabby old hotel the sick wife of the hotel keeper began to weep and putting her hands to her face rocked back and forth. The words of her one friend, Doctor Reefy, rang in her ears. "Love is like a wind stirring the grass beneath the trees on a black night," he had said. "You must not try to make love definite. It is the divine accident of life. If you try to be definite and sure about it and to live beneath the trees, where soft night winds blow, the long hot day of disappointment comes swiftly and the gritty dust from passing wagons gathers upon lips inflamed and made tender by kisses."

Elizabeth Willard could not remember her mother, who had died when she was but five years old. Her girlhood had been lived in the most haphazard manner imaginable. Her father was a man who had wanted to be let alone and the affairs of the hotel would not let him alone. He also had lived and died a sick man. Every day he arose with a cheerful face, but by ten o'clock in the morning all the joy had gone out of his heart. When a guest complained of the fare in the hotel dining room or one of the girls who made up the beds got married and went away, he stamped on the floor and swore. At night when he went to bed he thought of his daughter growing up among the stream of people that drifted in and out of the hotel and was overcome with sadness. As the girl grew older and began to walk out in the evening with men she wanted to talk to her, but when he tried was not successful. He always forgot what he wanted to say and spent the time complaining of his own affairs.

In her girlhood and young womanhood Elizabeth had tried to be a real adventurer in life. At eighteen life had so gripped her that she was no longer a virgin but, although she had a half dozen lovers before she married Tom Willard, she had never entered upon an adventure prompted by desire alone. Like all the women in the world, she wanted a real lover. Always there was something she sought blindly, passionately, some hidden wonder in life. The tall beautiful girl with the swinging stride who had walked under the trees with men was forever putting out her hand into the darkness and trying to get hold of some other hand. In all the babble of words that fell from the lips of the men with whom she adventured she was trying to find what would be for her the true word. Elizabeth had married Tom Willard, a clerk in her father's hotel, because he was at hand and wanted to marry at the time when the determination to marry came to her. For a while, like most young girls, she thought marriage would change the face of life. If there was in her mind a doubt of the outcome of the marriage with Tom she brushed it aside. Her father was ill and near death at the time and she was perplexed because of the meaningless outcome of an affair in which she had just been involved. Other girls of her age in Winesburg were marrying men she had always known, grocery clerks or young farmers. In the evening they walked in Main Street with their husbands and when she passed they smiled happily. She began to think that the fact of marriage might be full of some hidden significance. Young wives with whom she talked spoke softly and shyly. "It changes things to have a man of your own," they said.

On the evening before her marriage the perplexed girl had a talk with her father. Later she wondered if the hours alone with the sick man had not led to her decision to marry. The father talked of his life and advised the daughter to avoid being led into another such muddle. He abused Tom Willard, and that led Elizabeth to come to the clerk's defense. The sick man became excited and tried to get out of bed. When she would not let him walk about he began to complain. "I've never been let alone," he said. "Although I've worked hard I've not made the hotel pay. Even now I owe money at the bank. You'll find that out when I'm gone."

The voice of the sick man became tense with earnestness. Being unable to arise, he put out his hand and pulled the girl's head down beside his own. "There's a way out," he whispered. "Don't marry Tom Willard or any one else here in Winesburg. There is eight hundred dollars in a tin box in my trunk. Take it and go away."

Again the sick man's voice became querulous. "You've got to promise," he declared. "If you won't promise not to marry, give me your word that you'll never tell Tom about the money. It is mine and if I give it to you I've the right to make that demand. Hide it away. It is to make up to you for my failure as a father. Some time it may prove to be a door, a great open door to you. Come now, I tell you I'm about to die, give me your promise."

.   .   .   .   .   .

In Doctor Reefy's office, Elizabeth, a tired gaunt old woman at forty-one, sat in a chair near the stove and looked at the floor. By a small desk near the window sat the doctor. His hands played with a lead pencil that lay on the desk. Elizabeth talked of her life as a married woman. She became impersonal and forgot her husband, only using him as a lay figure to give point to her tale. "And then I was married and it did not turn out at all," she said bitterly. "As soon as I had gone into it I began to be afraid. Perhaps I knew too much before and then perhaps I found out too much during my first night with him. I don't remember.

"What a fool I was. When father gave me the money and tried to talk me out of the thought of marriage, I would not listen. I thought of what the girls who were married had said of it and I wanted marriage also. It wasn't Tom I wanted, it was marriage. When father went to sleep I leaned out of the window and thought of the life I had led. I didn't want to be a bad woman. The town was full of stories about me. I even began to be afraid Tom would change his mind."

The woman's voice began to quiver with excitement. To Doctor Reefy, who without realizing what was happening had begun to love her, there came an odd illusion. He thought that as she talked the woman's body was changing, that she was becoming younger, straighter, stronger. When he could not shake off the illusion his mind gave it a professional twist. "It is good for both her body and her mind, this talking," he muttered.

The woman began telling of an incident that had happened one afternoon a few months after her marriage. Her voice became steadier. "In the late afternoon I went for a drive alone," she said. "I had a buggy and a little gray pony I kept in Moyer's Livery. Tom was painting and repapering rooms in the hotel. He wanted money and I was trying to make up my mind to tell him about the eight hundred dollars father had given to me. I couldn't decide to do it. I didn't like him well enough. There was always paint on his hands and face during those days and he smelled of paint. He was trying to fix up the old hotel, make it new and smart."

The excited woman sat up very straight in her chair and made a quick girlish movement with her hand as she told of the drive alone on the spring afternoon.

"It was cloudy and a storm threatened," she said. "Black clouds made the green of the trees and the grass stand out so that the colors hurt my eyes. I went out Trunion Pike a mile or more and then turned into a side road. The little horse went quickly along up hill and down. I was impatient. Thoughts came and I wanted to get away from my thoughts. I began to beat the horse. The black clouds settled down and it began to rain. I wanted to go at a terrible speed, to drive on and on forever. I wanted to get out of town, out of my clothes, out of my marriage, out of my body, out of everything. I almost killed the horse, making him run, and when he could not run any more I got out of the buggy and ran afoot into the darkness until I fell and hurt my side. I wanted to run away from everything but I wanted to run towards something too. Don't you see, dear, how it was?"

Elizabeth sprang out of the chair and began to walk about in the office. She walked as Doctor Reefy thought he had never seen any one walk before. To her whole body there was a swing, a rhythm that intoxicated him. When she came and knelt on the floor beside his chair he took her into his arms and began to kiss her passionately. "I cried all the way home," she said, as she tried to continue the story of her wild ride, but he did not listen. "You dear! You lovely dear! Oh you lovely dear!" he muttered and thought he held in his arms, not the tired-out woman of forty-one but a lovely and innocent girl who had been able by some miracle to project herself out of the husk of the body of the tired-out woman.

Doctor Reefy did not see the woman he had held in his arms again until after her death. On the summer afternoon in the office when he was on the point of becoming her lover a half grotesque little incident brought his love-making quickly to an end. As the man and woman held each other tightly heavy feet came tramping up the office stairs. The two sprang to their feet and stood listening and trembling. The noise on the stairs was made by a clerk from the Paris Dry Goods Store Co. With a loud bang he threw an empty box on the pile of rubbish in the hallway and then went heavily down the stairs. Elizabeth followed him almost immediately. The thing that had come to life in her as she talked to her one friend died suddenly

She was hysterical, as was also Doctor Reefy, and did not want to continue the talk. Along the street she went with the blood still singing in her body, but when she turned out of Main Street and saw ahead the lights of the New Willard House, she began to tremble and her knees shook so that for a moment she thought she would fall in the street.

The sick woman spent the last few months of her life hungering for death. Along the road of death she went, seeking, hungering. She personified the figure of death and made him, now a strong black-haired youth running over hills, now a stern quiet man marked and scarred by the business of living. In the darkness of her room she put out her hand, thrusting it from under the covers of her bed, and she thought that death like a living thing put out his hand to her. "Be patient, lover," she whispered. "Keep yourself young and beautiful and be patient."

On the evening when disease laid its heavy hand upon her and defeated her plans for telling her son George of the eight hundred dollars hidden away, she got out of bed and crept half across the room pleading with death for another hour of life. "Wait, dear! The boy! The boy! The boy!" she pleaded as she tried with all of her strength to fight off the arms of the lover she had wanted so earnestly.

· · · · · · ·

Elizabeth died one day in March in the year when her son George became eighteen, and the young man had but little sense of the meaning of her death. Only time could give him that. For a month he had seen her lying white and still and speechless in her bed, and then one afternoon the doctor stopped him in the hallway and said a few words.

The young man went into his own room and closed the door. He had a queer empty feeling in the region of his stomach. For a moment he sat staring at the floor and then jumping up went for a walk. Along the station platform he went, and around through residence streets past the high school building, thinking almost entirely of his own affairs. The notion of death could not get hold of him and he was in fact a little annoyed that his mother had died on that day. He had just received a note from Helen White, the daughter of the town banker, in answer to one from him. "Tonight I could have gone to see her

and now it will have to be put off," he thought half angrily.

Elizabeth died on a Friday afternoon at three o'clock. It had been cold and rainy in the morning but in the afternoon the sun came out. Before she died she lay paralyzed for six days unable to speak or move and with only her mind and eyes alive. For three of the six days she struggled, thinking of her boy, trying to say some few words in regard to his future, and in her eyes there was an appeal so touching that all who saw it kept the memory of the dying woman in their minds for years. Even Tom Willard who had always half resented his wife forgot his resentment and the tears ran out of his eyes and lodged in his mustache. The mustache had begun to turn gray and Tom colored it with dye. There was oil in the preparation he used for the purpose and the tears, catching in the mustache and being brushed away by his hand, formed a fine mist-like vapor. In his grief Tom Willard's face looked like the face of a little dog that has been out a long time in bitter weather.

George came home along Main Street at dark on the day of his mother's death and, after going to his own room to brush his hair and clothes, went along the hallway and into the room where the body lay. There was a candle on the dressing table by the door and Doctor Reefy sat in a chair by the bed. The doctor arose and started to go out. He put out his hand as though to greet the younger man and then awkwardly drew it back again. The air of the room was heavy with the presence of the two self-conscious human beings, and the man hurried away.

The dead woman's son sat down in a chair and looked at the floor. He again thought of his own affairs and definitely decided he would make a change in his life, that he would leave Winesburg. "I will go to some city. Perhaps I can get a job on some newspaper," he thought, and then his mind turned to the girl with whom he was half angry at the turn of events that had prevented his going to her.

In the dimly lighted room with the dead woman the young man began to have thoughts. His mind played with thoughts of life as his mother's mind had played with the thought of death. He closed his eyes and imagined that the red young lips of Helen White touched his own lips. His body trembled and his hands shook. And then something happened. The boy sprang to his feet and stood stiffly. He looked at the figure of the dead woman under the sheets and shame for his thoughts swept over him so that he began to weep. A new notion came into his mind and he turned and looked guiltily about as though afraid he would be observed.

George Willard became possessed of a madness to lift the sheet from the body of his mother and look at her face. The thought that had come into his mind gripped him terribly. He became convinced that not his mother but some one else lay in the bed before him. The conviction was so real that it was almost unbearable. The body under the sheets was long and in death looked young and graceful. To the boy, held by some strange fancy, it was unspeakably lovely. The feeling that the body before him was alive, that in another moment a lovely woman would spring out of the bed and confront him became so overpowering that he could not bear the suspense. Again and again he put out his hand. Once he touched and half lifted the white sheet that covered her, but his courage failed and he, like Doctor Reefy, turned and went out of the room. In the hallway outside the door he stopped and trembled so that he had to put a hand against the wall to support himself. "That's not my mother. That's not my mother in there," he whispered to himself and again his body shook with fright and uncertainty. When Aunt Elizabeth Swift, who had come to watch over the body, came out of an adjoining room he put his hand into hers and began to sob, shaking his head from side to side, half blind with grief. "My mother is dead," he said, and then forgetting the woman he turned and stared at the door through which he had just come. "The dear, the dear, oh the lovely dear," the boy, urged by some impulse outside himself, muttered aloud.

.   .   .   .   .

As for the eight hundred dollars the dead woman had kept hidden so long and that was to give George Willard his start in the city, it lay in the tin box behind the plaster by the foot of his mother's bed. Elizabeth had put it there a week before her marriage, breaking the plaster away with a stick. Then she got one of the workmen her husband was at that time employing about the hotel to mend the wall. "I jammed the corner of the bed against it," she had explained to her husband, unable at the moment to give up her dream of release, the release that after all came to her but twice in her life, in the moments when her lovers Death and Doctor Reefy held her in their arms.

XLVII

JOSEPH HERGESHEIMER (1880–   )

Hergesheimer represents the East as Cather and Dreiser and Anderson do the near West. He is a Philadelphian from a family of means, reared apart from the coarsening areas of toil, kept from college and even from school by physical frailness. Without profession or trade he became a dilettante, toying with life. Over his Conrad and Turgenev and George Moore he dreamed of novels of his own and he began to work with seriousness, and persevered through much discouragement until he won publication and acclaim. *The Three Black Pennys*, 1917, three novelettes too long to be reckoned short stories, studies of three generations of the iron manufacturing Penny family, was his first really strong work. It is typical of all he has done. A Philadelphian, he is enamored of the past, the American old *régime* era with picturesqueness of setting and costuming and character. He is a connoisseur in brocaded interiors, in bric-a-brac and antiques, in ancient millinery. Like so many others of his generation he is disillusioned even to cynicism, totally unconventional in most things held imperative by his elders, and yet despite all these revolutionary posturings, the Philadelphia "complex" holds him as completely as Old Salem and its puritanism held Hawthorne.

His strength lies in his ability to make alive his characters. In his own words: "I always write about people, men usually near forty, who are not happy. The story at bottom is nearly always the same—a struggle between what is called the spirit and what is called the flesh—the spirit is victorious—that is why it seems to me my books are happy books." Like Dreiser and Willa Cather and many others of his contemporaries, he has expressed himself most often in the longer forms of fiction, but his short-story material is not inconsiderable. In contrast with Dreiser, his art is excellent, and his style is often beautiful—perhaps because he has never corrupted it with the reporter's pencil. Always his characters dominate situation and plot and action. At the close of his tale stands always a haunting personality, like the old musician in "The Thrush in the Hedge." All else—the disgusting realism of the tramp encampment, the doings and the fate of the central character—everything else sinks into insignificance before that one tragic figure. He lingers like a drop of acid on the hand long after even the central story has been forgotten. Hergesheimer's most distinctive collection is his *The Happy End*, 1919.

THE THRUSH IN THE HEDGE *

I

Harry Baggs came walking slowly over the hills in the blue May dusk. He could now see below him the clustered roofs and tall slim stack of a town. His instinct was to avoid it, but he had tramped all day, his blurred energies were hardly capable of a detour, and he decided to settle near by for the night. About him the country rose and fell, clothed in emerald wheat and pale young corn, while trees filled the hollows with the shadowy purple of their darkening boughs. A robin piped a belated drowsy note; the air had the impalpable sweetness of beginning buds.

A vague pleasant melancholy enveloped him; the countryside swam indistinctly in his vision—he surrendered himself to inward sensations, drifting memories, unformulated regrets. He was twenty and had a short powerful body; a broad dusty patient face. His eyes were steady, light blue, and his jaw heavy but shapely. His dress—the forlorn trousers, the odd coat uncomfortably drawn across thick shoulders, and incongruous hat—held patently the stamp of his worldly position: he was a tramp.

He stopped, looking about. The road, white and hard, dipped suddenly down; on the right, windows glimmered, withdrawn behind shrubbery and orderly trees; on the left, a dark plowed field rose to a stiff company of pines and the sky. Harry Baggs stood turned in the latter direction, for he caught the faint odor of wood smoke; behind the field, a newly acquired instinct told him, a fire was burning in the open. This, now, probably meant that other wanderers—tramps—had found a place of temporary rest.

Without hesitation he climbed a low rail fence, found a narrow path trod in the soft loam and followed it over the brow into the hollow beyond. His surmise was correct—a fire smoldered in a red blur on the ground, a few relaxed forms gathered about the wavering smoke, and at their back were grouped four or five small huts.

Harry Baggs walked up to the fire, where, with a conventional sentence, he extended his legs to the low blaze. A man regarded him with a peering suspicious gaze; but any doubts were apparently laid, for the other silently resumed a somnolent indifference. His clothes were an amazing and unnecessary tangle of rags; his stubble of beard and broken black hat had an air of unreality, as though they were the stage properties of a stupid and conventional parody of a tramp.

Another, sitting with clasped knees beyond the fire, interrupted a monotonous whining recital to question Harry Baggs. "Where'd you come from?"

"Somewhere by Lancaster."

"Ever been here before?" And, when Baggs had said no: "Thought I hadn't seen you. Most of us here come back in the spring. It's a comfortable dump when it don't rain cold." He was uncommonly communicative. "The Nursery's here for them that want work; and if not nobody's to ask you reasons."

A third, in a grimy light overcoat, with a short bristling red mustache and morose countenance, said harshly:

"Got any money?"

"Maybe two bits."

"Let's send him in for beer," the other proposed; and a new animation stirred the dilapidated one and the talker.

"You can go to hell!" Baggs responded without heat.

"That ain't no nice way to talk," the second proclaimed. "Peebles, here, meant that them who has divides with all that hasn't."

Peebles directed a hard animosity at Harry Baggs. His gaze flickered over the latter's heavy-set body and unmoved face. "Want your jaw slapped crooked?" he demanded with a degree of reservation.

"No," the boy placidly replied.

A stillness enveloped them, accentuated by the minute crackling of the disintegrating wood. The dark increased and the stars came out; the clip-clip of a horse's hoofs passed in the distance and night. Harry Baggs became flooded with sleep.

"I s'pose I can stay in one of these brownstones?" he queried, indicating the huts.

No one answered and he stumbled toward a small shelter. He was forced to bend, edge himself into the close damp interior, where he collapsed into instant unconsciousness on a heap of bagging. In the night he cried out, in a young strangely distressed voice; and later a drift of rain fell on the roof and ran in thin cold streams over his still body.

II

He woke late the following morning and emerged sluggishly into a sparkling rush of sunlight. The huts looked doubly mean in the pellucid day. They were built of discarded doors and variously painted fragments of lumber, with blistered and unpinned roofs of tin, in which rusted smokepipes had been crazily wired; strips of moldy matting hung over an entrance or so, but the others gaped unprotected. The clay before them was worn smooth and hard; a replenished fire smoked within blackened bricks; a line, stretched from a dead stump to a loosely fixed post, supported some stained and meager red undergarb.

Harry Baggs recognized Peebles and the loquacious tramp at the edge of the clearing. The latter, clad in a grotesquely large and sorry suit of ministerial black, was emaciated and had a pinched bluish countenance. When he saw Baggs he moved forward with a quick uneven step.

"Say," he proceeded, "can you let me have something to get a soda-caffeine at a drug store? This ain't a stall; I got a fierce headache. Come out with a dime, will you? My bean always hurts, but to-day I'm near crazy."

Harry Baggs surveyed him for a moment, and then, without comment, produced the sum in question. The other turned immediately and rapidly disappeared toward the road.

"He's crazy, all right, to fill himself with that dope," Peebles observed; "it's turning him black. You look pretty healthy," he added. "You can work, and they're taking all the men they can get at the Nursery."

The boy was sharply conscious of a crawling emptiness—hunger. He had only fifteen cents; when that was gone he would be without resources.

"I don't mind," he returned; "but I've got to eat first."

"Can't you stick till night?" his companion urged. "There's only half a day left now. If you go later there'll be nothing doing till to-morrow."

"All right," Harry Baggs assented.

The conviction seized him that this dull misery of hunger and dirt had settled upon him perpetually—there was no use in combating it; and, with an animal-like stoicism, he followed the other away from the road, out of the hollow, to where row upon row of young ornamental trees reached in mathematical perspective to broad sheds, glittering expanses of glass, a huddle of toolhouses, and office.

His conductor halted at a shed entrance and indicated a weather-bronzed individual.

"Him," he said. "And mind you come back when you're through; we all dish in together and live pretty good."

Harry Baggs spent the long brilliant afternoon burning bunches of condemned peach shoots. The smoke rolled up in a thick ceaseless cloud; he bore countless loads and fed them to the flames. The hungry crawling increased, then changed to a leaden nausea; but, accepting it as inevitable, he toiled dully on until the end of day, when he was given a dollar and promise of work to-morrow.

He saw, across a dingy street, a small grocery store, and purchased there coffee, bacon and a pound of dates. Then he returned across the Nursery to the hollow and huts. More men had arrived through the day, other fires were burning, and an acrid odor of scorched fat and boiling coffee rose in the delicate evening. A small group was passing about a flasklike bottle; a figure lay in a stupor on the clay; a mutter of voices, at once cautious and assertive, joined argument to complaint.

"Over this way," Peebles called as Harry Baggs approached. The former inspected the purchased articles, then cursed. "Ain't you got a bottle on you?"

But when the bacon had been crisped and the coffee turned into a steaming thick liquid, he was amply appreciative of the sustenance offered. They were shortly joined by Runnel, the individual with the bluish poisoned countenance, and the elaborately ragged tramp.

"Did you frighten any cooks out of their witses?" Peebles asked the last contemptuously. The other retorted unintelligibly in his appropriately hoarse voice. "Dake knocks on back doors," Peebles explained to Harry Baggs, "and then fixes to scare a nickel or grub from the women who open."

Quiet settled over the camp; the blue smoke of pipes and cigarettes merged imperceptibly into the dusk of evening. Harry Baggs was enveloped by a momentary contentment, born of the satisfaction of food, relaxation after toil; and, leaning his head back on clasped hands, he sang:

"I changed my name when I got free
To Mister, like the res'.
But now . . . Ol' Master's voice I hears
Across de river: 'Rome,
You damn ol' nigger, come and bring
Dat boat an' row me home!'"

His voice rolled out without effort, continuous as a flowing stream, grave and round as the deep tone of a temple bell. It increased in volume until the hollow vibrated; the sound, rather than coming from a single throat, seemed to dwell in the air, to be the harmony of evening made audible. The simple melody rose and fell; the simple words became portentous, burdened with the tragedy of vain longing, lost felicity. The dead past rose again like a colored mist over the sordid reality of the present; it drifted desirable and near across the hill; it soothed and mocked the heart—and dissolved.

The silence that followed the song was sharply broken by a thin querulous question; a tenuous bent figure stumbled across the open.

"Whose's singing?" he demanded.

"That's French Janin," Peebles told Harry Baggs; "he's blind."

"I am," the latter responded—"Harry Baggs."

The man came closer, and Baggs saw that he was old and incredibly worn; his skin clung in dry yellow patches to his skull, the temples were bony caverns, and the pits of his eyes blank shadows. He felt forward with a siccated hand, on which veins were twisted like blue worsted over fleshless tendons, gripped Harry Baggs' shoulder, and lowered himself to the ground.

"Another song," he insisted; "like the last. Don't try any cheap show."

The boy responded immediately; his serious voice rolled out again in a spontaneous tide.

"'Hard times,'" Harry Baggs sang, "'hard times, come again no more.'"

The old man said:

"You think you have a great voice, eh? All you have to do to take the great rôles is open your mouth!"

"I hadn't thought of any of that," Baggs responded. "I sing because—well, it's just natural; no one has said much about it."

"You have had no teaching, that's plain. Your power leaks like an old rain barrel. What are you doing here?"

"Tramping."

Harry Baggs looked about, suddenly aware of the dark pit into which he had fallen. The fires died sullenly, deserted except for an occasional recumbent figure. Peebles had disappeared; Dake lay in his rags on the ground; Runnel rocked slowly, like a pendulum, in his ceaseless pain.

"Tramping to the devil!" he added.

"What started you?" French Janin asked.

"Jail," Harry Baggs answered.

"Of course you didn't take it," the blind man commented satirically; "or else you went in to cover some one else."

"I took it, all right—eighteen dollars." He was silent for a moment; then: "There was something I had to have and I didn't see any other way of getting it. I had to have it. My stepfather had money that he put away—didn't need. I wanted an accordion; I dreamed about it till I got ratty, lifted the money, and he put me in jail for a year.

"I had the accordion hid. I didn't tell them where, and when I got out I went right to it. I played some sounds, and—after all I'd done—they weren't any good. I broke it up—and left."

"You were right," Janin told him; "the accordion is an impossible instrument, a thing entirely vulgar. I know, for I am a musician, and played the violin at the Opéra Comique. You think I am lying; but you are young and life is strange. I can tell you this: I, Janin, once led the finale of Hamlet. I saw that the director was pale; I leaned forward and he gave me the baton. I knew music. There were five staves to conduct—at the Opéra Comique."

He turned his sightless face toward Harry Baggs.

"That means little to you," he spoke sharply; "you know nothing. You have never seen a gala audience on its feet; the roses——"

He broke off. His wasted palms rested on knees that resembled bones draped with maculate clothing; his sere head fell forward. Runnel paced away from the embers and returned. Harry Baggs looked, with doubt and wonderment, at the ruined old man.

The mere word musician called up in him an inchoate longing, a desire for something far and undefined. He thought of great audiences, roses, the accompaniment of violins. Subconsciously he began to sing in a whisper that yet reached beyond the huts. He forgot his surroundings, the past without light, the future seemingly shorn of all prospect.

French Janin moved; he fumbled in precarious pockets and at last produced a small bottle; he removed the cork and tapped out on his palm a measure of white crystalline powder, which he gulped down. Then he struggled to his feet and wavered away through the night toward a shelter.

Harry Baggs imagined himself singing heroic measures; he finished, there was a tense pause, and then a thunderous acclamation. His spirit mounted up and up in a transport of emotional splendor; broken visions thronged his mind of sacrifice, renouncement, death. The fire expired and the night grew cold. His ecstasy sank; he became once more aware of the human wreckage about him, the detritus of which he was now a part.

III

He spent the next day moving crated plants to delivery trucks, where his broad shoulders were most serviceable, and in the evening returned to the camp, streaked with fine rich loam. French Janin was waiting for him and consumed part of Harry Baggs' unskilfully cooked supper. The old man was silent, though he seemed continually at the point of bursting into eager speech. However, he remained uncommunicative and followed the boy's movements with a blank speculative countenance. Finally he said abruptly:

"Sing that song over—about the 'damn ol' nigger.'"

Harry Baggs responded; and, at the end, Janin nodded.

"What I should have expected," he pronounced. "When I first heard you I thought: 'Here, perhaps, is a great voice, a voice for Paris;' but I was mistaken. You have some bigness—yes, good enough for street ballads, sentimental popularities; that is all."

An overwhelming depression settled upon Harry Baggs, a sense of irremediable loss. He had considered his voice a lever that might one day raise him out of his misfortunes; he instinctively valued it to an extraordinary degree; it had resembled a precious bud, the possible opening of which would flood his being with its fragrant flowering. He gazed with a new dread at the temporary shelters and men about him, the huts and men that resembled each other so closely in their patched decay.

Until now, except in brief moments of depression, he had thought of himself as only a temporary part of this broken existence. But it was probable that he, too, was done—like Runnel, and Dake, who lived on the fear of women. He recalled with an oath his reception in the village of his birth on his return from jail: the veiled or open distrust of the adults; the sneering of the young; his barren search for employment. He had suffered inordinately in his narrow cell—fully paid, it had seemed, the price of his fault. But apparently he was wrong; the thing was to follow him through life—and he would live a long while—condemning him, an outcast, to the company of his fellows.

His shoulders drooped, his face took on the relaxed sullenness of those about him; curiously, in an· instant he seemed more bedraggled, more disreputable, hopeless.

French Janin continued:

"Your voice is good enough for the people who know nothing. Perhaps it will bring you money, singing at fairs in the street. I have a violin, a cheap thing without soul; but I can get a thin jingle out of it. Suppose we go out together, try our chance where there is a little crowd; it will be better than piggin' in the earth."

It would, Baggs thought, be easier than carrying heavy crates; subtly the idea of lessened labor appealed to him. He signi-

fied his assent and rolled over on his side, staring into nothingness.

French Janin went into the town the following day—he walked with a surprising facility and speed—to discover where they might find a gathering for their purpose. Harry Baggs loafed about the camp until the other returned with the failing of light.

"The sales about the country are all that get the people together now," he reported; "the parks are empty till July. There's to be one to-morrow about eight miles away; we'll try it."

He went to the shelter, where he secured a scarred violin, with roughly shaped pegs and lacking a string. He motioned Harry Baggs to follow him and proceeded to the brow of the field, where he settled down against a fence, picking disconsolately at the burring strings and attempting to tighten an ancient bow. Baggs dropped beside him. Below them night flooded the winding road and deepened under the hedges; a window showed palely alight; the stillness was intense.

"Now!" French Janin said.

The violin went home beneath his chin and he improvised a thin but adequate opening for Harry Baggs' song. The boy, for the first time in his existence, sang indifferently; his voice, merely big, lacked resonance; the song was robbed of all power to move or suggest.

Janin muttered unintelligibly; he was, Harry Baggs surmised, speaking his native language, obscurely complaining, accusing. They tried a second song: "Hard times, hard times, come again no more." There was not an accent of longing nor regret.

"That'll do," French Janin told him; "good enough for cows and chickens."

He rose and descended to the camp, a bowed unsubstantial figure in the gloom.

IV

They started early to the sale. Janin, as always, walked swiftly, his violin wrapped in a cloth beneath his arm. Harry Baggs lounged sullenly at his side. The day was filled with a warm silvery mist, through which the sun mounted rayless, crisp and round. Along the road plum trees were in vivid pink bloom; the apple buds were opening, distilling palpable clouds of fragrance.

Baggs met the morning with a sullen lowered countenance, his gaze on the monotonous road. He made no reply to the blind man's infrequent remarks, and the latter, except for an occasional murmur, fell silent. At last Harry Baggs saw a group of men about the fence that divided a small lawn and neatly painted frame house from the public road. A porch was filled with a confusion of furniture, china was stacked on the grass, and a bed displayed at the side.

The sale had not yet begun. A youth, with a pencil and paper, was moving distractedly about, noting items; a prosperous-appearing individual, with a derby resting on the back of his neck, was arranging an open space about a small table. Beyond, a number of horses attached to dusty vehicles were hitched to the fence where they were constantly augmented by fresh arrivals.

"Here we are!" Baggs informed his companion.

He directed Janin forward, where the latter unwrapped his violin. A visible curiosity held the prospective buyers; they turned and faced the two dilapidated men on the road. A joke ran from laughing mouth to mouth. Janin drew his bow across the frayed strings; Harry Baggs cleared the mist from his throat. As he sang, aware of an audience, a degree of feeling returned to his tones; the song swept with a throb to its climax:

*"'You damn ol' nigger, come and bring
    Dat boat an' row me home!'"*

There was scattered applause.

"Take your hat round," Janin whispered; and the boy opened the gate and moved, with his battered hat extended, from man to man.

Few gave; a careless quarter was added to a small number of pennies and nickels. Janin counted the sum with an unfamiliar oath.

"That other," he directed, and drew a second preliminary bar from his uncertain instrument.

"Here, you!" a strident voice called. "Shut your noise; the sale's going to commence. "

French Janin lowered the violin.

"We must wait," he observed philosophically. "These things go on and on; people come and go."

He found a bank, where he sat, after stumbling through a gutter of stagnant water. Harry Baggs followed and filled a cheap ornate pipe. The voice of the auctioneer rose, tiresome and persistent, punctuated by bids, haggling over minute sums for the absurd flotsam of a small housekeeping square of worn oilcloth, a miscellany of empty jars. A surprisingly passionate argument arose between bidders; personalities and threats emerged. Janin said:

"Listen! That is the world into which musicians are born; it is against such uproar we must oppose our delicate chords —on such hearts." His speech rambled into French and a melancholy silence.

"It's stopped for a little," Baggs reminded him.

Janin rose stiffly and the other guided him to their former place. The voice and violin rose, dominated a brief period, and the boy went among the throng, seeking newcomers. The mist thickened, drops of water shone on his ragged sleeves, and then a fine rain descended. The crowd filled the porch and lower floor, bulged apparently from door and windows. Harry Baggs made a motion to follow with his companion, but no one moved; there was no visible footing under cover. They stayed out stolidly in the wet, by an inadequate tree; and whenever chance offered Harry Baggs repeated his limited songs. A string of the violin broke; the others grew soggy, limp; the pegs would tighten no more and Janin was forced to give up his accompanying.

The activities shifted to a shed and barn, where a horse and three sorry cows and farming implements were sold. Janin and Harry Baggs followed, but there was no opportunity for further melody; larger sums were here involved; the concentration of the buyers grew painful. The boy's throat burned; it was strained, and his voice grew hoarse. Finally he declared shortly that he was going back to the shelter by the Nursery.

As they tramped over the rutted and muddy road, through a steadily increasing downpour, Harry Baggs counted the sum they had collected. It was two dollars and some odd pennies. Janin was closely attentive as the money passed through the other's fingers. He took it from Baggs' hand, recounted it with an unfailing touch, and gave back a half.

The return, even to the younger's tireless being, seemed interminable. Harry Baggs tramped doggedly, making no effort to avoid the deepening pools. French Janin struggled at his heels, shifting the violin from place to place and muttering incoherently.

It was dark when they arrived at the huts; the fires were sodden mats of black ash; no one was visible. They stumbled from shelter to shelter, but found them full. One at last was discovered unoccupied; but they had no sooner entered than the reason was sharply borne upon them —the roof leaked to such an extent that the floor was an uneasy sheet of mud. However, there was literally nowhere else for them to go. Janin found a broken chair on which he balanced his bowed and shrunken form; Harry Baggs sat against the wall.

He dozed uneasily, and, wakened by the old man's babbling, cursed him bitterly. At last he fell asleep; but, brought suddenly back to consciousness by a hand gripping his shoulder, he started up in a blaze of wrath.

He shook off the hand and heard French Janin slip and fall against an insecure wall. The interior was absolutely black; Harry Baggs could see no more than his blind companion. The latter fumbled, at last regained a footing, and his voice fluctuated out of an apparent nothingness.

"There is something important for you to know," Janin proceeded.

"I lied to you about your voice—I, once a musician of the orchestra at the Opéra Comique. I meant to be cunning and take you round to the fairs, where we would make money; have you sing truck for people who know nothing. I let you sing to-day, in the rain, for a dollar—while I, Janin, fiddled.

"I am a *voyou;* there is nothing in English low enough. The thought of it has been eating at me like a rat." The disembodied words stopped, the old man strangled and coughed; then continued gasping: "Attention! You have a supreme barytone, a miracle! I heard all the great voices for twenty years, and know.

"At times there is a voice with perfect pitch, a true art and range; not many— they are cold. At times there is a singer with great heart, sympathy . . . mostly too sweet.

"But once, maybe, in fifty, sixty years, both are together. You are that—I make you amends."

The rain pounded fantastically on the roof a few inches above Harry Baggs' head and the water seeped coldly through his battered shoes; but, in the violent rebirth of the vague glow he had lost a short while before, he gave no heed to his bodily discomfort. "A supreme barytone!" The walls of the hut, the hollow, dissolved before the sudden light of hope that enveloped him; all the dim dreams, the unformulated aspirations on which subconsciously his spirit had subsisted, returned.

"Can you be sure?" he demanded uncertainly.

"Absolutely! You are an artist, and life has wrung you out like a cloth—jail, hungry, outcast; yes, and nights with stars, and water shining; men like old Janin, dead men, begging on the roads—they are all in your voice, jumbled—serious barytone—" The high thin recital stopped, from exhaustion.

Harry Baggs was warm to the ends of his fingers. He wiped his wet brow with a wetter hand.

"That's fine," he said impotently; "fine!"

He could hear French Janin breathing stertorously; and, suddenly aware of the other's age, the misery of their situation, he asked:

"Don't you feel good?"

"I've been worse and better," he replied. "This is bad for your throat, after singing all day in the rain. *Voyou!*" he repeated of himself.

Silence enveloped them, broken by the creaking of the blind man's chair and the decreasing patter of the rain. Soon it stopped and Henry Baggs went outside; stars glimmered at the edges of shifting clouds, a sweet odor rose from the earth, a trailing scent of blossoming trees expanded.

He sang in a vibrant undertone a stave without words. An uneasy form joined him; it was Runnel.

"I b'lieve my head'll burst!" he complained.

"Leave that soda-caffeine be."

He would never forget Runnel with his everlasting pain; or Dake, who lived by scaring women. . . . Great audiences and roses, and the roar of applause. He heard it now.

V

Harry Baggs returned to the Nursery, where, with his visions, his sense of justification, he was happy among the fields of plants. There he was given work of a more permanent kind; he was put under a watchful eye in a group transplanting berry bushes, definitely reassigned to that labor to-morrow. He returned to the camp with a roll of tar paper and, after supper, covered the leaking roof of the shelter. French Janin sat with his blank face following the other's movements. Janin's countenance resembled a walnut, brown and worn in innumerable furrows; his neck was like a dry inadequate stem. As he glanced at him the old man produced a familiar bottle and shook out what little powder, like finely ground glass, it contained. He greedily absorbed what there was and, petulantly exploring the empty container, flung it into the bushes. A nodding drowsiness overtook him, his head rolled forward, he sank slowly into a bowed amorphous heap. Harry Baggs roused him with difficulty.

"You don't want to sit like this," he said; "come up by the field, where it's fresher."

He lifted Janin to his feet, half carried him to the place under the fence. Harry Baggs was consumed by a desire to talk about the future—the future of his voice, he wanted to hear of the triumphs of other voices, of the great stages that they finally dominated. He wanted to know the most direct path there; he was willing that it should not be easy. "I'm as strong as an ox," he thought.

But he was unable to move French Janin from his stupor; in reply to his questions the blind man only muttered, begged to be let alone. Life was at such a low ebb in him that his breathing was imperceptible. Harry Baggs was afraid that he would die without a sound—leave him. He gave up his questioning and sang. He was swept to his feet by a great wave of feeling; with his head back, he sent the resonant volume of his tones toward the stars. Baggs stopped suddenly; stillness once more flooded the plowed hill and he raised imploring arms to the sky in a gust of longing.

"I want to sing!" he cried. "That's all —to sing."

Janin was brighter in the morning.

"You must have some exercises," he told the boy. "I'll get new strings for the violin; it'll do to give you the pitch."

At the day's end they went again to the hilltop. French Janin tightened and tuned his instrument.

"Now!" he measured, with poised bow. "Ah!" Both his voice and violin were tremulous, shrill; but they indicated the pitch of the desired note. "Ah!" the old man quavered, higher.

"Ah!" Harry Baggs boomed in his tremendous round tone.

They repeated the exercises until a slip of a new moon, like a wistful girl, sank and darkness hid the countryside. A palpitating chorus of frogs rose from the invisible streams. Somnolence again overtook Janin; the violin slipped into the fragrant grass by the fence, but his fingers still clutched the bow.

Pity for the other stirred Baggs' heart. He wondered what had ruined him, brought him—a man who had played in an opera house—here. A bony elbow showed bare through a torn sleeve—the blind man had no shirt; the soles of his shoes gaped, smelling evilly. Yet once he had played in an orchestra; he was undoubtedly a musician. Life suddenly appeared grim, a sleepless menace awaiting the first opportune weakness by which to enter and destroy.

It occurred to Harry Baggs for the first time that against such a hidden unsuspected blight his sheer strength would avail him little. He had stolen money; that in itself held danger to his future, his voice. He had paid for it; that score was clear, but he must guard against such stupidities in the years to come. He had now a conscious single purpose—to sing. A new sense of security took the place of his doubts. He stirred Janin from his collapsed sleep, directed him toward their hut.

He returned eagerly in the evening to the vocal exercises. French Janin struggled to perform his part, but mostly Harry Baggs boomed out his Ahs! undirected. The other had been without his white powder for three days; his shredlike muscles twitched continually and at times he was unable to hold the violin. Finally:

"Can you go in to the post-office and ask for a package for me at general delivery?" he asked Harry Baggs. "I'm expecting medicine."

"That medicine of yours is bad as Runnel's dope. I've a mind to let it stay."

The other rose, stood swaying with pinching fingers, tremulous lips.

"I'm afraid I can't make it," he whimpered.

"Sit down," Harry Baggs told him abruptly; "I'll go. Too late now to try pulling you up. Whatever it is, it's got you."

It was warm, almost hot. He walked slowly down the road toward the town. On the left was a smooth lawn, with great stately trees, a long gray stone house beyond. A privet hedge, broken by a drive, closed in the withdrawn orderly habitation. A young moon bathed the scene in a diffused silver light; low cultivated voices sounded from a porch.

Harry Baggs stopped; he had never before seen such a concretely desirable place; it filled him with a longing, sharp like pain. Beyond the hedge lay a different world from this; he could not even guess its wide possession of ease, of knowledge, of facility for song. A voice laughed, gay and untroubled as a bird's note. He wanted to stay, seated obscurely on the bank, saturate himself with the still beauty; but the thought of French Janin waiting for the relief of his drug drove him on.

The maple trees that lined the quiet streets of the town were in full early leaf. Groups paced tranquilly over the brick ways; the houses stood in secure rows. A longing for safety, recognition, choked at Harry Baggs' throat. He wanted to stop at the corner, talk, move home to a shadowy cool porch. He hurried in his ragged clothes past the pools of light at the street crossings into the kinder gloom. At that moment he would have surrendered his voice for a place in the communal peace about him.

He reached the post-office and asked for a package addressed to Janin. The clerk delayed, regarded him with suspicion, but in the end surrendered a small precisely wrapped box. As he returned his mood changed; all he asked, he muttered bitterly, was a fair trial for his voice. He recognized obscurely that a singer's existence must be different from the constricted life of a country town; here were no stage, no audience, for the great harmonies he had imagined himself producing. He had that in his heart which would make mere security, content, forever impossible.

In the dilapidated camp French Janin eagerly clutched the box. He almost filled his palm with the crystalline powder and gulped it hastily. Its effect was produced slowly. . . . Janin waited rigidly for the release of the drug.

The evening following, under the fence on the hill, the blind man dozed while Harry Baggs exercised his voice.

"Good!" the former pronounced unexpectedly. "I know; heard all the great voices for twenty years; a violin in the Opéra Comique. Once I led the finale of Hamlet. I saw the Director stop. . . . He handed me the baton. He died soon after, and that was the beginning of my bad luck. I should have been Director; but I was ignored, and came to America—Buenos Aires; then Washington, and—and morphia."

There was a long silence and then he spoke again with a new energy:

"I'm done, but you haven't started. You're bigger than ever I was; you'll go on and on. I, Janin, will train you; when you sing the great rôles I'll sit in a box, wear diamond studs. Afterward, as we roll in a carriage down the Grandes Boulevards, the people in front of the cafés will applaud; the voice is appreciated in Paris."

"I have a lot to learn first," Baggs put in practically.

The old man recovered his violin. "Ah!" He drew the note tenuous but correct from the uncertain strings. "Ah!" Harry Baggs vociferated to the inattentive frogs, busy with their own chorus.

VI

The practice proceeded with renewed vigor through the evenings that followed; then French Janin sank back into a torpor, varied by acute depression.

"I haven't got the life in me to teach you," he admitted to Harry Baggs. "I'll be dead before you get your chance; besides, you ought to be practising all day, and not digging round plants and singing a little in the evening. You've got the voice, but that's not enough; you've got to work at exercises all your life."

"I'm strong," Harry Baggs told him; "I can work more than most men."

"No, that won't do alone; you've got to go at it right, from the start; the method's got to be good. I'll be dead in

some hospital or field when you'll be hardly starting. But remember it was Janin
who found you, who dug you out of a
set of tramps, gave you your first lessons."
He changed. "Stay along with me, Harry,"
he begged; "take me with you. You're
strong and'll never notice an old man. You
will be making thousands some day. I will
stop the morphia; perhaps I've got a good
bit in me yet. Attention!" He raised the
ow.

"No!" he cried, interrupting. "Breathe
deep, below the chest. Control! Control!
Hold the note steady, in the middle; don't
force it into your head."

His determination soon expired. Tears
crept from under his sunken lids. He
reached furtively into his pocket, took morphia. The conviction seized Harry Baggs
that nothing could be accomplished here.
The other's dejection was communicated
to him. Where could he find the money,
the time for the necessary laborious years
of preparation? He was without credentials, without clothes; there was no one
to whom he could go but the old spent man
beside him. They were adrift together outside life, as the huts they inhabited were
outside the orderly town beyond the hill.

He rose, left Janin, and walked slowly
along the fence to the road. The moon had
increased in size and brilliancy; the apple
trees had bloomed and their fallen petals
glimmered on the ground. He thought of
the house on the smooth sward, with its
hedge and old trees; a sudden longing
seized him to linger at its edge, absorb
again the profound peaceful ease; and
he quickened his pace until he was opposite
the low gray façade.

He sat on the soft steep bank, turned on
his elbow, gazing within. The same voices
drifted from the porch, voices gay or
placid, and contained laughter. A chair
scraped. It was all very close to Harry
Baggs—and in another world. There was
a movement within the house; a window
leaped into lighted existence and then went
out against the wall. Immediately after,
a faint pure harmony of strings drifted
out to the hedge. It was so unexpected,
so lovely, that Harry Baggs sat with suspended breath. The strings made a pattern
of simple harmony; and then, without
warning, a man's voice, almost like his
own, began singing. The tones rose fluid
and perfect, and changed with feeling.
It seemed at first to be a man; and

then, because of a diminuendo of the
voice, a sense of distance not accounted
for by his presence near the hedge, he
knew that he heard a record of the actual
singing.

The voice, except for its resemblance to
his own, did not absorb his attention; it
was the song itself that thrilled and held
him. He had never before heard music
at once so clear and capable of such depths.
He realized instinctively, with a tightening
of his heart, that he was listening to one
of the great songs of which Janin had
spoken. It hung for a minute or more in
his hearing, thrilling every nerve, and then
died away. It stopped actually, but its
harmony rang in Harry Baggs' brain. Instantly it had become an essential, a permanent part of his being. It filled him with
a violent sense of triumph, a richness of
possession that gave birth to a new un-
conquerable pride.

He rose, waited for a short space; but
nothing more followed. He was glad of
that; he had no wish to blur the impressions of the first. Harry Baggs hurried
up the road and crossed the field to where
he had left French Janin. The latter was
still sleeping, crumpled against the vegetation. Baggs grasped the thin shoulder,
shook him into consciousness.

"I have just heard something," he said.
"Listen! What is it?"

He sang without further preliminary,
substituting a blank phrasing for uncom-
prehending words; but the melody swept
without faltering to its conclusion. Janin
answered irritably, disturbed by his rude
awakening:

"The Serenade from Don Giovanni—
Mozart. Well, what about it?"

"It's wonderful!" Harry Baggs declared.
"Are there any more as great?"

"It is good," Janin agreed, his interest
stirred; "but there are better—the Dio
Possente, the Brindisi from Hamlet. Once
I led the finale of Hamlet. I saw the
Director—"

"I'll get every one," the boy interrupted.

"There are others now, newer—finer
still, I'm told; but I don't know." Janin
rose and steadied himself against the fence.
"Give me a start. I've been getting confused lately; I don't seem to keep a direction like I could. From Don Giovanni:
'Deh vieni alla finestra'—'Come to the window' 's about it. I'm glad you're not a
tenor; they're delicate and mean. But you

are a fine boy, Harry; you'll take the old man up along with you!"

He talked in a rapid faint voice, like his breathing. Harry Baggs grasped his arm and led him down to their shanty. French Janin entered first, and immediately the other heard a thin complaint from within:

"Somebody's got that nice bed you made me."

Harry Baggs went into the hut and, stooping, shook a recumbent shape.

"Get out of the old man's place!" he commanded.

A string of muffled oaths responded.

"There's no reserved rooms here."

"Get out!" Baggs insisted.

The shape heaved up obscurely and the boy sent him reeling through the door. French Janin sank with weary relief on the straw and bagging. He grasped the thick young arm above him.

"We won't be long in this," he declared; "diamond studs!"

He fell asleep instantly, with his fingers caught in Harry Baggs' sleeve. The latter, with the supreme egotism of youth, of a single ambition, loosened the hand and moved out of the narrow confinement of the shanty. He wanted space, the sky, into which to sing his imaginary triumphant songs.

VII

The next day moved toward its end without arresting incident. Janin and Harry Baggs had walked to the public road, where they stood leaning against the rail fence. The smoke from Baggs' pipe uprose in unbroken spheres; the evening was definitely hot. French Janin said:

"In the town to-day I asked about that house here at the bend. It seems he's got money; comes for a couple of months in the spring—just like us—and then goes to Europe like as not. Perhaps he knows a voice."

The blind man fell silent, contemplative.

"Trouble is," he broke out fretfully, "we've got nothing to sing. That about the 'damn old nigger' won't do. You ought to know something like the Serenade.

"Well," he added after a moment, "why not? I could teach you the words—it's Italian; you've nearly got the air. It's all wrong and backward; but this isn't the Conservatoire. You can forget it when you have started; sing exercises again."

"When can we begin?" Harry Baggs asked.

"We'll brush our clothes up best we can," Janin proceeded, absorbed in his planning, "and go up to the porch of an evening. 'Mr. Brinton'—that's his name—I'll say, 'I'm M. Janin, once of the orchestra at the Opéra Comique, and I'd like you to listen to a pupil of mine. I've heard them all and this boy is better—'" He stopped; took morphia.

"Can't you stop that for a day?" Harry Baggs demanded desperately. "Can't you?"

He watched with bitter rebellion the inevitable slackening of the other's being, the obfuscation of his mind. Janin hung over the fence, with hardly more semblance of life than an incredibly tattered and empty garment.

"Come on, you old fool!" Baggs exclaimed, burning with impatience, balked desire; he half carried him bruskly to his bed.

Yet, under the old man's fluctuating tuition, he actually began the Serenade within twenty-four hours. *"Deh vieni alla finestra,"* French Janin pronounced. *"Deh vieni—"* Harry Baggs struggled after him. His brow grew wet with the intensity of his effort; his tongue, it seemed to him, would never accomplish the desired syllables.

Janin made a determined effort to live without his drug; the abstinence emphasized his fragility and he was cold, even in the heart of the long sunny day; but the effort stayed him with a flickering vitality, bred visions, renewed hopes of the future. He repeated the names of places, opera houses—the San Carlo, in Naples; the Scala—unknown to Harry Baggs, but which came to him with a strange vividness. The learning of the Serenade progressed slowly; French Janin forgot whole phrases, some of which returned to memory; one entire line he was forced to supply from imagination.

At last the boy could sing it with a degree of intelligence; Janin translated and reconstructed the scene, the characters.

"You ought to have some good clothes," he told Harry Baggs; he spoke again of the necessity of a diamond stud.

"Well, I haven't," the other stated shortly. "They'll have to listen to me without looking."

He borrowed a rusted razor and subjected himself to the pain of an awkward shaving; then inadequately washed his sole shirt and looped the frayed collar with a nondescript tie.

The night was immaculate; the moon, past the full, cast long segments of light and shadow across the countryside. Harry Baggs drew a deep breath:

"We might as well go."

French Janin objected; he wasn't ready; he wasn't quite sure of what he was going to say. Then:

"I haven't anything to show. Perhaps they will laugh at me—at Janin, of the Opéra Comique. I couldn't allow that."

"I'm going to sing," the boy reminded him; "if it's any good they won't laugh. If what you say's right they'll have to believe you."

"I feel bad to-night, too, in my legs."

"Get your violin."

A fresh difficulty arose: French Janin positively refused to play on his present instrument before a critical audience.

"It's as thin as a cat," he protested. "Do you want me to make a show of myself?"

"All right; I'll sing alone. Come on!"

Janin's legs were uncertain; he stumbled over the path to the road and stopped at the fence. He expressed fresh doubts, the hesitation of old age; but Harry Baggs silenced him, forced him on. A cold fear possessed the boy, which he resolutely suppressed: if Janin were wrong, his voice worthless, if they laughed, he was done. Opportunity, he felt, would never return. With his voice scorned, no impetus remained; he had no other interest in life, no other power that could subdue the slight inward flaw.

He saw this in a vivid flash of self-knowledge. . . . If he couldn't sing he would go down, lower than Janin; perhaps sink to the level of Dake.

"Come on!" he repeated grimly, assisting his companion over the luminous white road.

Janin got actually feebler as he progressed. He stopped, gasping, his sightless face congested.

"I'll have to take a little," he whispered, "just a taste. That puts life in me; it needs a good deal now to send me off."

He produced the familiar bottle and absorbed some powder. Its effect was unexpected—he straightened, walked with more ease; but it acted upon his mind with surprising force.

"I want to stop just a little," he proclaimed with such an air of decision that Harry Baggs followed him without protesting to the fragrant bank. "You're a good fellow," Janin went on, seated; "and you're going to be a great artist. It'll take you among the best. But you will have a hard time for a while; you won't want anybody hanging on you. I'd only hurt your chances—a dirty old man, a drug-taker. I would go back to it, Harry; it's got me, like you said. People wouldn't have me round. I doubt if I'd be comfortable with them. They'd ask me why I wasn't Director."

"Come on," Baggs repeated for the third time; "it's getting late."

He lifted French Janin to his feet and forced him on.

"You don't know life," the other continued. "You would get sick of me; you might get influenced to put me in a Home. I couldn't get my breath right there."

Harry Baggs forced him over the road, half conscious of the protesting words. The fear within him increased. Perhaps they wouldn't even listen to him; they might not be there.

His grip tightened on French Janin; he knew that at the first opportunity the old man would sink back into the oblivion of morphia.

"I've done all I could for you, Harry" —the other whimpered. "I've been some —good. Janin was the first to encourage you; don't expect too much."

"If I get anywhere, you did it," Harry Baggs told him.

"I'd like to see it all," French Janin said. "I know it so well. Who'd have thought" —a dull amazement crept into his voice— "that old Janin, the sot, did it? . . . And you'll remember."

They stopped opposite the entrance to the place they sought. Harry Baggs saw people on the porch; he recognized a man's voice that he had heard there before. On the right of the drive a thick maple tree cast a deep shadow, but beyond it a pool of clear moonlight extended to the house. He started forward, but Janin dragged him into the gloom of the maple.

"Sing here," he whispered in the boy's ear; "see, the window—*Deh vieni alla finestra.*"

Harry Baggs stood at the edge of the shadow; his throat seemed to thicken, his voice expire.

"No," he protested weakly; "you must speak first."

He felt the old man shaking under his hand and a sudden desperate calm overtook him.

He moved forward a little and sang the first phrase of the Serenade.

A murmur of attention, of surprised amusement, arose from the porch; then, as his voice gained in bigness, flowed rich and thrilling and without effort from his deep powerful lungs, the murmur died away. The song rose toward its end; Harry Baggs saw nothing but the window above him; he put all the accumulated feeling, the longing, of the past miserable years into his ending.

A silence followed, in which Harry Baggs stood with drooping head. Then an unrestrained patter of applause followed; figures advanced. French Janin gave the boy a sharp unexpected shove into the radiance beyond the tree.

"Go on and on," he breathed; "and never come back any more!"

He turned and shambled rapidly away into the shadows, the obscurity that lined the road.

XLVIII

WILBUR DANIEL STEELE (1886–   )

Although born in the South, in O. Henry's native town, Greensboro, North Carolina, and although educated in the University of Denver where he was graduated in 1907, and although he studied art in Denver, Boston, Paris, and New York, Mr. Steele in his work is neither of the South nor of the West, nor is he a practicer of the graphic arts. His realm as he has finally chosen it is fiction and his locality the sea coast of New England. Though he has demonstrated his power to write the novel, he has succeeded best with the short-story form. He has been, indeed, the most universally successful prize winner in all varieties of short-story contest of all the later writers. In 1925 he was especially mentioned by the O. Henry award committee in connection with maintaining the highest level of the short story during three years.

Steele is typical of that element in the youngest group of writers to-day that seeks for substance rather than form, that has endeavored to shake off the fetters of Bret Harte with his theatric use of locality and of O. Henry with his witchery of technique. With seemingly realistic methods he has sought to find the romance in ordinary life. His best work has been done with New England and Portuguese seamen in the Cape Cod environment, but he makes the local setting always secondary. What he seeks is the hidden, the suggestive, the psychological elements that underlie his situation. The external he makes often picturesque, sometimes with color and with stirring action and with mystery, but always his central *motif* is the dissecting out of the inner meanings, the unseen causes and workings of those forces that brought about the crisis he has chosen to study.

The mystery and the tragedy and the lure of the sea have fastened themselves upon Steele more strongly than upon any one else of his generation. Says O'Brien, "Behind the complications which his men and women weave for one another frequently looms the eternal but ever-changing pattern of the sea. . . . But Mr. Steele's preoccupation is with a more generally shared background, in which wonder is born of ordinary things, whose strangeness has been forgotten through constant surface familiarity. He finds as much drama in the dory life of Portuguese fishermen on Cape Cod as Conrad has found in the southern seas."

While form has been to him always of secondary importance, while the laws of Poe are to him chains that should be shaken off by the creator whose work is to be first of all original, nevertheless unconsciously he has always been true to the great basic fundamentals of short-story art. His tales are single situations handled with economy and compression, often with suggestion rather than expression, and always his tales culminate in endings that are not like final strokes closing everything, but that are suggestive and haunting,—his characters made so compellingly alive that we follow them even beyond the boundaries of the situation.

SIX DOLLARS *

When Tansy Snow was a young man of eighteen or nineteen he went one night to the Stone Fold. The Stone Fold is an islet lying about two miles to the southeast of us. There is a house on it built of stones, and a sheep-shelter, and toward the southern end three thorn-trees.

Tansy took his father's skiff and steered straight through the shoals that lie that way, guided by the lamp in the garret of the house. Donna, who had been in town with her father two days before, told him she would put it there when the old man was asleep and the dogs shut up.

Donna Salisbury wasn't pretty. And she would have been better for a mother's care; better to look at. As you'd expect, living with only a shepherd father, her clothes were heavy, stout things, fitted mostly by guess, and none too clean, and her hair was thick and untended, and the color of her father's sheep. But she was

510

strong, stronger than a boy, and if her face had a dull look, there was something behind the dullness that would make a fellow stop to look again, especially when stars were bright enough to cast shadows among the rocks and the gray grass.

Tansy couldn't understand why he should want to have anything to do with her. He'd been to the Academy and now he had a position in the new bank; he had to wear decent clothes every day, clean collars, and polished boots; it went deeper than that: he had every day to be a decent *man* and wear a clean conscience; otherwise the pointing finger of the banking business would find him out—bound to— in the long run of a man's life.

He had been to the Stone Fold three times, steering by the light. This time he was coming simply to say he wasn't coming. It would be awkward telling the girl. For a day and a night he had been busy trying to think up something humane but at the same time final. Finished. Chopped off.

He hadn't guessed how awkward it would be, after all. They couldn't talk there on the beach on account of the dogs; they had to go along a way. Occasional clouds, great fluffs of things, sailed over the sky, and in the dark when they covered the stars Donna led him, taking his fingers in her strong, dull, warm, eager hand.

He would have said it at the first turn of the shore, but the surf on the bar there was too loud; he didn't want to shout. He would have said it when they started inland toward the thorn-trees, but now they had got into the wind, the full weight of the wind that came in from the open sea and bore the great clouds among the stars and made a living sound among the grasses. He would have said it under the thorn-tree, but under the thorn-tree was Donna.

It was half past two when he left the island, and he hadn't said it yet. What he *had* said he could hardly remember. Sometimes words, fragments of sentences, promises, will come from a man's mouth as if it were some one else speaking: things he doesn't mean at all.

He pushed the skiff off the sand, holding it by the painter.

"When'll you be again?" she whispered.

Now was the time to tell her. She might have seen how pale he was; might have helped him by saying something. But she was a dumb young thing and she hadn't a word. Of a sudden he reached into his pocket and pulled out the money he had there and thrust it into her hands.

She was a dumb one, and she couldn't make it out.

"What's this?"

"I want you should buy yourself some present or other."

"Huh?"

The dogs in the sheepfold began to bark. Tansy jumped into the skiff and pushed off, leaving Donna to stand there, dumber than ever.

He had a fair wind back and put up the sail.

It was six dollars he had given her, a lot of money, the whole of his first week's wages. There were things he could have bought with that: a new tire for his bicycle, and a Young People's Union pin to give Elsie Baker on her birthday. But it was all right. Better to start off clear—not a debt outstanding—no matter what the cost might be.

Even yet, though, he didn't feel quite right. When he got home and up to his room he had three hours to sleep, but he couldn't sleep. He was disgusted with himself. His memory reviewed the night with shame and loathing. He saw the path down which he had started, and even if he had got out of it now, it was disgusting to remember.

All next day he felt drugged and haggard. He made mistakes with figures, so that Mr. Matheson had to speak to him. But what was it? He'd paid, hadn't he? Squared up? Given everything he had to the girl?

Yes, but how about the Lord God? Slowly, as the day went by, he saw this. You can't pay God with **money.**

There was a sociable at Center Church that night. He had asked to see Elsie Baker home. He looked so ill at supper-time that his mother advised him to stay in. To her surprise he acquiesced without trouble. He went upstairs. When he was half undressed for bed, however, he couldn't do it. Getting dressed again, he stole out the back way and went and stood behind a tree near the church and watched the people going in.

The windows were bright and there were sounds of a good time, a hymn, then after a decent interval laughter and runnings about, games. Tansy walked across the street and stood at the steps.

He had given the girl everything he had. Can you give more than you have? And, anyway, any girl that would do that!

Yes, yes; but how about the Lord God?

He went around to the wagon-shed, and in the dark there he fell on his knees. "O Heavenly Father, I've walked in evil; I've committed a grievous sin; I beg Thee to forgive me in Thy mercy. I repent. O God, I repent; I do, I do, honestly! Honestly, God, honestly—"

In the church they were singing "My Country, 'Tis of Thee."

Tansy got up and brushed off his knees. His weariness was gone, like a heavy coat he might have taken off and left there in the shed. In its place there was a sense of security and well-being, such as comes after a bath at the end of a sweaty day. He slipped back to his room and put on his blacks, and, coming down the front way, he said he thought he would go to the sociable. There was no turning him.

Actually he didn't go in, but waited on the steps. There was something about his feelings that would no more have mixed with the romping and the din than oil will mix with water. Yet it was marvelous just to sit apart and listen to it, especially when the organ struck into some familiar air, and all sang, soprano and alto, tenor and bass. It was marvelous to be whiter than snow, one with God, a little child.

He saw Elsie home, after all. It was only a couple of hundred yards, down the shore street and up London Lane, but he would never forget it. It was the first time he'd known that love and reverence could be one and the same thing. Earthly love and religious reverence.

Elsie was so pretty, so enchanting in ribbons and laces, so pure, as pure as a flower on which God's sun shines and God's rain falls unfailingly, as if He were saying in the sun and rain: "Of such is the portion of them that think none but healthy thoughts and dream none but wholesome dreams; yea, even to the third and the fourth generation."

Elsie's great-grandfather it was who gave the land for the Atheneum. Her grandfather rescued the missionaries in Paul Straits, and founded the "Light in Darkness." Her father and mother were in the forefront of everything for decency and right living, and they were well-to-do.

The forefathers of that girl on the Stone Fold—what could they have been? By what steps of wrong thinking, of evil impulses given way to and higher impulses denied, must that strain have come down?

But now, because something had been changed in him, Tansy could think of her with nothing but pity.

In London Lane the lights, shining up under the willows, made it seem the nave of some dim cathedral, in which a boy and a girl walked together. And then Elsie was up on her stoop and he stood at the foot of the steps.

"W-e-l-l?" she said. The light from the two long panes flanking the door fell softly on either side of her figure.

"Elsie," he said, "excepting for my father and mother there's nobody in the world but you amounts to *that,* with me."

"What *are* you saying, you silly?"

She came back down the steps to read the silly's eyes. She was so good she didn't guess the risk. He could have grabbed her and kissed her.

But not he; not now! He kept his hands behind him.

"Elsie, you wait and see. Some day I shall be the biggest man in this town." It wasn't like boasting. "For your sake," he might have said.

He marveled as he walked homeward. On one side there were loveliness, niceness, world's goods; on the other unloveliness, a hard living, the scorn of friends. Yet did God ask him to choose the stony way? By a miracle, no. God asked him to choose the way it would have been the part of even the worldly-wise to choose.

Marveling so, as he crossed above the White Boys' place he spied a pin-prick of light away out beyond the Point. It was as though it rested on the low neck of sand, a fallen star.

"*To-night?*" He felt angry. "She's got her cheek, I must say!"

On impulse he went down to his father's wharf, cast off the skiff's painter, and got in. He would finish *that* off. He would tell Donna what was what. Straight from the shoulder! Then, before he had got the oars out, he realized that it was only the devil tempting him, weaving any arguments at all, just to get him out there to the Stone Fold again.

He made the boat fast and went home. His parents were still up. He shook his father's hand and kissed his mother on the brow. She eyed him with a knowing little smile. "Been seeing Elsie Baker home?"

Tansy stood with his jaw out.

"I've made a decision to-night," he said. "Some day I shall be the biggest man in this town."

He married Elsie Baker on the day he was made assistant cashier at the bank. Within three months he was cashier.

People trusted him. "No need to count your money when it's Tansy passes it out of the till." His word was as good as a bond; better, for bonds can be lost or burned or stolen.

Old man Baker bought the Dow residence in the Brick Walk, had it renovated, and gave it to the couple as a wedding-present. Nothing could have been fitter. It was smallest of the big houses built at the height of the California days, brick for walls, slate for roofing, and a wrought-iron grille around the turf-plot. Four-square with the street, a house of strength and dignity. It was not too large, and that was fit, too. In the great-grandfather's family there were eleven children; in the grandfather's, fourteen; in the father's, three. Elsie herself had none.

It was a town house, pure and simple; the Dows had always been shore folks, lawyers and doctors and the like. From the windows of the guest-chamber up-stairs, full of leafy boughs and neighboring gables, you might have been a thousand miles from the nearest salt; the sewing-room was the same, and so was the west chamber, that had always been known as "the children's room." Yet it is a hard thing to find a house in Urkey without some peep of the water; even at Gramma Pilot's, about as thoroughly shut in as any in town, you've but to climb to the garret to get a sight of blue under the rod of the drug-store chimney. We may wear Brockton shoes, but we're a web-footed race for all that.

And so it was from the "used chamber" in the new Snow home.

The first time they slept there after their wedding-tour to Boston Elsie awoke in the middle of the night. For a moment she couldn't say why. It was too queer. She didn't stir; simply lay there trying to think what it was could be wrong. It wasn't for instants that she recollected where she was, that she was married, that her husband was there beside her. She slid a hand over his pillow to touch his head. There was no head to touch. She was so startled she didn't know what to do or think. She went

cold. Then, of course, when she began to paw around, her hand found Tansy's back. He was sitting up in bed; that was all.

"What *is* the *matter?*" she demanded, she was so upset.

"Nothing. Why, nothing at all." And he lay back on the pillow.

But by and by, when he thought her asleep, he was up again, on an elbow, looking at the window, over the foot of the bed. Like burglars.

You know the feeling of that. Up went Elsie without a word, staring at that window too. And there was nothing there. Nothing but the rear corner of Center Church, one side, and the corner of the Nickerson house, the other, and their one outlook on the harbor in the slit between. By day there would have been a bit of the harbor, a segment of the Point, and out to sea. Now there was nothing but the spark of a chance light; it might have been at the masthead of some vessel at anchor; it was too low for a star.

She was provoked. "What *are* you gawp- ing at?"

"Nothing. Why, nothing in the world. What makes you think I—"

"Is it that light?"

"Wha-what light?"

"Well, I'm all a-fidget now."

He lay back and comforted her. They were young.

Next morning, at the chamber-work, Elsie made a discovery.

"You remember that light last night Tansy?" she laughed at supper-time. "Well, 'twas nothing but old Cabe Sal'sbury's light in his house over to the Stone Fold; you can see how it ranges in daylight. Must be some one sick.

"Or else Cabe's a great student," she modified it when, at bedtime, she saw the lamp burning again in the window on the Stone Fold.

"What you say to closing those blinds?" Tansy suggested. "I vow there's a tang in the air to-night."

No, Elsie wouldn't listen to that.

"The best doctors nowadays say all the air you can have in your bedroom is none too much, even in Winter-time. I'd suffocate."

It was the following day that Tansy began to seem restless. To begin with, he didn't see where they were going to expect much company, overnight, all their friends being local people, with houses of their own. So why didn't they shift into the front chamber, which was roomier, with two closets; and as for air, certainly there was as much air coming up the Brick Walk as there was in the church back yard.

"My *spare* chamber?" was all Elsie could gasp.

"Or even the west chamber—"

"The *children's* room?"

Elsie went straight to her mother about it. Her mother smiled. Phidela Baker had been a young woman once, with a new young husband and a new house of her own. "They're all the same; Providence made 'em so. Ever notice a dog that's made up his mind to lie down in a certain spot? Made up or no, he's got to wander and fidget a dozen times around it first, before he settles down. Don't you take on.

"But over and above everything," was the parting advice, "don't you start out by humoring him too much. Be cheery, but put your foot down."

So when Elsie found Tansy at work one of those days, surreptitiously, trying to get the bureau switched for the bed, and the carpet in a tangle with it, she put her foot down.

He looked foolish to be caught so. His face got redder and redder.

"Light shines in my eyes. That is—in the mornings."

"Can you *imagine* how this room would look?" She demolished him, ruthlessly, but all the while with a smile.

That smile of Elsie Snow's grew famous. No matter if this went bad and that worse, Tansy Snow's wife always had a smile, always seemed to be saying, like her mother before her: "Don't you take on; God will provide."

Her energy was amazing and fruitful. Once she was married and settled down, and since she had no children to stop her, she was able to be a power for good. She was a treasure for Tansy; she saved his pennies; where another in her place might have got trained help from the mainland she did with young girls to come in, carried the bulk of the house herself, and never looked the worse for it.

As she matured she rounded out amazingly; folks wouldn't have believed it, from the slip of a girl she had been. But no matter how full her hands were, they were never too full to spare a finger where help was needed. In the church, in the Dorcases, in the "Light in Darkness," in the Town Farm Association, at Easter, Thanksgiving, Memorial Day, the word came to be: "See Elsie Snow. She'll manage."

There were plenty to say that her capacity for managing didn't go for nothing in Tansy's affairs. Certainly, once, when he wouldn't have foreclosed on Mrs. Hemans's store—which was going to be a valuable property as soon as the fish-freezer was built—certainly then it was his wife showed the common sense of the two, asking him plainly: "Which do you figure you owe the most to, Sarah Hemans or the men and women and children that've got their all in your bank?"

Yet too much may have been made of that. Tansy was honest, and honesty goes a long way. When he made a statement across his desk in the bank-block—it mattered not whether it was to the highest or the humblest—that statement held. And yet, again, in another way, where would he have been if it hadn't been for her? People would really have forgotten that he was alive.

Tansy had turned out a silent and unsociable man. He never went to the post-office; his mail came to the bank. From there home he took the back way; that was about the only place, except church, you'd ever see him, and then half the time he wouldn't see you, walking as he did with his eyes on the ground, studying.

A silent man is a wise one: that's common knowledge. Tansy ought to have been Selectman. Yet he never was. It hurt Elsie. Fall after Fall, as town meeting came and passed, and somehow or other Tansy's name wasn't mentioned, it got deeper and deeper under her skin. Of course nobody ever knew. It wasn't anything you could say anything about. But it was bitter when she recollected the young Tansy standing at the bottom of the steps and vowing: "Some day I shall be the biggest man in this town."

She never mentioned it directly to her husband. The nearest she came was when she would plague him: "Why don't *you* see more of folks? I declare, I can't make you out. What good does it do going to church if you don't take a hand in any of the activities? or in town affairs? See here now, So-and-so and So-and-so are coming in after supper about the cake-sale, and I want you to put on your blacks and stay down a while—and talk. 'Twouldn't harm you to crack a joke, even. Be cheery!"

Tansy would change his collar and put on his blacks. He never crossed his wife; never put *his* foot down. Never but once. That was when Elsie, perceiving at last that there was to be no one for the "children's room," and moved by something too vague to say, suggested they might be more comfortable in the west chamber, after all, as he himself had said. It was the first time she had ever heard him speak as he did. "We'll stay where we are." And they had stayed.

So he would freshen up after supper and come down as she bade him and sit, absent of eye and mind, in a corner of the cake-sale conference. Ten minutes. Half an hour. Then presently, as things warmed up, like dew under the heightening sun, he would be found to be not there. "Studying," his wife would have to tell them with a sigh. "What can a body do with a man whose work is never done? Up there in the dark, from now to bedtime, like as not, studying, studying. You'd never guess. But I declare if some folks were to work the amount Tansy Snow does, and take on so blessed little about it— Well, well. And now, who's it arranged shall get the paper for the streamers and festoons?"

So Tansy would sit there, studying. All alone in the "used chamber," in the dark, in his shirt-sleeves, in the rocker. Studying, studying.

First, in the early days, he thought it was a sin. It seemed to him that it must be Satan himself who was putting that lamp in Donna's garret on the Stone Fold, night after night, to mock him, around the very corner of the church of God, and beckon him from the very pillow where he lay beside his wife.

At first he was angry. "The cheek of her!" She knew he was married, must know it; she had been in town with her father many times; he had seen their boat. Yes, he had seen *her*—at a distance. Angry and scared. Anything to escape that ray that poisoned his thoughts, his dreams! Any room, any window, but that! Angry, scared, and *fascinated!* That was the worst. Fascinated, so that it ate a hole in the fabric of his honesty, like a moth-hole, tiny enough to escape notice, but big enough to let a lie through.

"I've to step up-stairs and get my slippers, wife dear."

"You're tired, Tansy; let me go."

"No, no, you stay by the fire and read; I'll be but a moment, dear."

For a while he was ashamed of himself. He ran to the stairs and started down if he heard Elsie coming. He felt he ought to make up to her somehow, pet her, show himself ten times more fervent than it was his nature to be. But that couldn't last. Nothing that's not in a man's nature can last. What *is* in his nature will out.

It's in the nature of islanders to be weather-vanes. As the weather goes, so do our spirits. There's none that hasn't, in some one of his generations, had a ship. So, even though her husband was a confirmed shore body, Elsie never thought it anything out of the way that he should be weather-tender, and show it by fidgeting and prowling on nights when the fog came and the wind was in the east.

Through the Spring and Summer of their first year there was prevailing fair weather, and only rarely a night like that —a blessed one (at first) when the star on the Stone Fold was blotted out—a torment (later on) when Tansy was upstairs as much as down, stealing peeps, dreading, hoping. In September, though, there came a real spell, five days of it as thick as a hat. In the night of the fourth a lobsterman named Anthony Coral claimed to have seen Mr. Snow of the bank in a dory in Chalk Ground Slough, toward the Stone Fold— was near to running into him—fact!

If a tale like that had been let go far it might have harmed a man in Snow's position. But it didn't go far. Before his mates at the dock had got through guying the credulous "Portuguee," he began to wonder if he hadn't been asleep at his oars, after all, and dreaming dreams, and he never brought it up again.

One thing about that night is certain, however: Tansy wasn't at home. Another thing is certain: it was he that was rowing the dory in Chalk Ground Slough, toward the Stone Fold. And it wasn't above five minutes after he had avoided collision with Coral's lobster-boat that, close aboard the island beach, he made out finally a disk of warm light the size of a penny, up in that part of the vapors where Donna's garret window ought to be.

That settled it. That made it another thing. Had it been no more than spite, Donna wouldn't have wasted oil and wick in weather that would smother the spark in twenty rods, and never a chance in

God's world for Tansy to see and suffer. It was something in *her* made her do it, then; like an act in some ritual of memory. Turning his boat around, he rowed for home. What he had found out filled him with a sense of pity. No, not pity. There was solemnity, tragedy in it, but it wasn't pity, nor sorrow.

After that he began to lose his feeling of shame when he made excuses to slip away up-stairs, till he made them no more. He no longer stole peeps from the window; he sat there brazenly, "studying." As time went by, if the good people gathered in Elsie's parlor—if they could have seen him at the moment of his escape up-stairs —they would never have known him for Tansy Snow. His face was contorted. He shook his fist. "Damn the lot of you, you gabbling, gossiping little parcel of busybodies, you and your holy little schemes, your little brains! The devil! What claim have you on *me?*"

But when he had reached the bedroom and found the rocker and sat down with his back to the bedpost and his sock-feet on the window-sill, little by little the lines would vanish from his face. Little by little as he watched the fallen star, or thought of it shining in secret there, he forgot to hear the busy voices below; he heard the wind running in gray grasses and the living sound of breakers on far-strewn reefs and the dry rustle of leaves in the thorn-tree. And what had happened was that he was no longer surrounded by walls and gables and hemmed in by the thoughts and needs and elbows of hundreds of industrious little two-legged vegetables; the walls had melted, his horizon was the horizon of dark ocean, and he walked in space.

And a girl walked with him—no, a woman—no (as time passed), more than a woman, a kind of goddess, sea-begot, earthborn, the soil of the mother still carelessly on her, and she the stronger for it, and slow, as the tides are slow, and generous, as the earth is generous with the seeds of life, and brooding calm as the sky is, which, knowing nothing, holds within itself all the generations of them that know all. Her hair was thick and tangled, because the grass grows so; eyes heavy, because they looked at things far off; hands large, because the blood that fed them was warm; and her words little words, because only little words can stay in the wind that blows from the caverns among the stars.

"The gray ewe dropped twins in that brush-patch. That's a good ewe."

And Tansy could imagine his own words as simple. "Yes, a good ewe."

"I like the feel of the wind, like to-night; there's rain to come. I like it to blow under my hair, the same as kisses. I love kisses."

"I love to kiss you. I love to be with you with nothing but water roundabout and nothing but stars above, and all on earth asleep, hushed up."

"They're awake in China, though, for the world's round like a ball."

"Most folks know the world's round, yet they think it's flat. I love that in you, Donna; you can *feel* it, you can *see* it being round like a ball. And you can see the stars being round like balls as big as suns, to shine hot on other worlds where there were sheep and people living and having twins and dead under the grass a million centuries before Adam and Eve—and never a thought in all their races whether it should be a thousand or twelve hundred on the Dee Nickerson house, or something useful like aprons or something tasty like doilies at the Dorcas meeting next Tuesday week. You see it. You feel it."

"Yes, Tansy, I see it. I feel it."

"You and I. I love you. And here we are at the tree."

Nor could he any longer, caught in the net of fantasy, recognize the thing as sin. *There's* revenge for you. To have grown to be a man who didn't know right from wrong. Tansy, whose honesty was his strength!

After all, he wasn't a man; he was two men. It was the other that became president of the bank, director in both the new freezers, and owner of considerable property in the town. No one knew his duplicity. How was it possible? Certainly, after living with him ten years, his wife didn't know. Donna *herself*, who might have guessed, might have wished, even Donna couldn't *know*. He could assure himself there was no one. So he had forgotten what happened that night in the wagon-shed behind the church (and almost under his window now). He had forgotten God, who never forgets.

But God moves in a mysterious way. It was a mystery to all "what it was bit Tansy" in his thirty-sixth year. There he was one week, a bit stoop-shouldered perhaps, but wiry for all that and going his way. Honest Tansy, who ought to have been Selectman—and why didn't *somebody* ever put him up? And there he was the next week, and talk of galloping consumption. Or Bright's disease. Or what?

They couldn't have got it out of him; he was too close of mouth. Nor, dig and delve as they would, they couldn't get it out of Mrs. Snow. She didn't know; that's why. He sleeps poorly; that's about all she could say. He would toss, his head as restless on the pillows as if it wore a crown of thorns. Once when he thought her asleep he got up and went into the spare chamber. From the hall where she had stolen she saw him with a candle staring at his own face in the bureau glass. The night-puffed face, the thinning hair, the stooped shoulders—in the mirrored eyes there was the look of a soul in hell, self-pity, self-hate, self-mockery.

Elsie was worried in earnest. When, without warning, a day or so later, he announced, "We'll try the west room a spell for a change," she was quick to humor him. Yet it came to nothing. Before she had so much as a bed-sheet shifted, there he was back, bareheaded: "Let it be as 'twas."

Here are the facts. Tansy oughtn't to have gone near the docks. For years he had kept clear of them, by instinct more than by reason. Now the mysterious way God took was to make him careless. It was a bright and innocent morning anyway; insurance was wanted on a big yawl; it's better to see a risk with your own eyes than to go by hearsay. (If you can see the risk.)

Alongside the yawl three single-handers were lying, the men in them sorting their last night's catch; lusty, brawny young fellows, a pleasure to the eye with their deep color and their flashing grins (more pleasure to the eye than a banker in a nightshirt before a looking-glass). And their voices, in the clear of the morning, were gay and strong.

Five years later Tansy could have repeated every syllable of every word:

"Looks o' that catch o' yourn there, Eddie, you didn't set no very likely place last night, did ye?"

"Aw, leave Eddie be, Sam. Didn't ye hear the terrible thing? Got a good fare o' haddock, Eddie did, only he had to heave the best part away. Turn out to be moth-millers when he come to look. Whatcha make o' that?"

"Laugh, you fellows; I like to hear ye.

But if ye really want to know who 'twas fishin' the Stone Fold las' night, don't ask me; ask Codhead Collins; he's the boy'll know."

"All right, all right, don't jump so. All reminded me was, I was thinking I noted a new little face on the beach over there when I come by the old girl's last week. And a new batch o' wash on the line."

"Godfrey! How many's that she's got now?"

"Don't ask me; I ain't the only dory in the fleet."

It wasn't consumption; Tansy didn't cough. Nor Bright's disease; it didn't act that way. The doctor said it was just insomnia, and it came from too much work. Human flesh can't stand studying at a desk the livelong day and then in a bedroom rocker half the night. He advised, and Elsie insisted, that Tansy ease up, go off somewhere, and take a holiday.

"No, I'll just see it through," was all Tansy would say.

When he said that morning: "We'll try the west room a spell," it was a confession of rout. Once away from that window he might forget; that's how he figured it. He hadn't yet got it through his head that God never forgets. At the bank, who should be waiting to see him but two of those trawlmen, Eddie and Sam. It was something about a loan; Tansy hardly knew; the business was done mechanically; the whole sudden thing *he* saw was that he wasn't to be let escape; that God had sent those wind-browned lusty young fellows as a sign and reminder that by no hiding of his eyes was he to be let forget. He faced it.

When the emissaries were gone he got down on his elbows on his desk and looked at his conscience, and he saw that in all those years of letting his imagination run to that island, instead of keeping it home of nights where it belonged, he had been doing a sinful thing. Now for atonement he was given a cross to bear. In the long run, unless he bore it without flinching, the failure would find him out. It was then, forgetting his hat, he ran home to Elsie with his "Let it be as 'twas."

"As 'twas!" The irony! As though it could be any nearer to what it had been than heaven is to hell.

He tried never to flinch. Shirt-sleeves and sock-feet, "as 'twas," he sat there whole evenings through. No longer did he stride across the wind-blown grass with

Donna by his side. He ran at a crouch under cover of the brush-patches, peeping, spying. Or he lay hidden as near as he dared to the thorn-tree, holding his breath and listening—to youth.

Almost as bad as the jealousy was the shame. Beginning by boasting he would be the biggest man in town, he had ended by being the least in a shady brotherhood, the scummiest of the scum of the water-front.

Sometimes he had to flinch a little; sometimes, reëvoking the image of the goddess he had created, he would rail at them. And now his *"I was the first!"* was the whine of a whip, and he had to grovel:
"Lord, when I have borne enough, in Thy mercy take it away."

There came a time when it seemed it was to be taken away. Mercy's instrument was Austin Dow, the proprietor of the Seaside Lunch that came with the steamer, along with other changes, when the old packet-schooner gave up. More and more excursionists were coming for the day's sail from Gillyport, with an hour ashore at noon, and Dow got to thinking he'd have a sign put on his roof, a big fellow, one you could read from the harbor coming in, with "Shore Dinners Our Specialty" in letters five feet high. And he wanted a license from the town.

It came up in special meeting in January, and it made a stir. There were forward-looking people who realized that times had changed, and they spoke in favor. There were just as many against it, though not quite so apt at saying why; anyway, it would be an eyesore to the worshipers coming out of Center Church, that monstrosity on a roof across the street. And then a man got up in the back of the hall and asked permission to speak.

The man was Tansy Snow. If it had been George True, the town dummy, folks wouldn't have been struck so dead. And that was only the beginning. From the first the thing that had made it look as though Dow might get the vote was that it was the business men that were with him; it was the sentimental old ladies (male and female) that were against.

And now to hear Banker Snow, the busiest business man of them all, the dried-up human calculator, the man with no sentiment, no romance, no imagination beyond set-down-five-and-carry-two—to see him standing there like a born revivalist—and to hear him carrying on—diving back into

history and coming up again—his face running sweat and his eyes as big as quarters with earnestness—reciting the beauty and dignity and grandeur of our island metropolis—recalling the impressions of his boyhood, the simple nobility of that shore-street sky-line, as great epochs had builded it slowly—and then taking the proposed sign-board as a symbol of all the ills the mainland suffers from, making bigness an idol, bustle a religion, the dollar a god to trample them in the dust—it was too much for the town meeting. When it came to a vote, there wasn't a voice for the lunchroom: Dow was too done up even to lift his own.

No one was more amazed than Elsie Snow, or more thrilled. If Tansy didn't fathom what he had done, or what was to follow, she did. As she took him out and home through the streets where people lingered she held him by the arm, "the biggest man in town"; you couldn't fool Elsie Snow.

When they had undressed and she had blown out the light and gone to lift the window, she stood for a moment dreaming down at Dow's lunchroom on the shore, bright in the moonlight in the bottom of the crevice between the Nickerson house and the corner of the church, and, "By gracious," she mused, "it never till this instant occurred to me, but it would've cut off half our one and only sea-view, that monstrosity of his."

No, there was no one more amazed than Elsie.

Staring out through the moonlight, and through the darkness when the moon had set, Tansy Snow was wondering:
"Why in the name of the Eternal did I do that?"

Elsie was right about consequences. The town waked up and rubbed its eyes. Tansy Snow had pulled the wool over them for a couple of decades, but he couldn't do it any more. From the minute he sat down after his speech in meeting there wasn't a question in anybody's mind but what he'd be chosen Selectman the coming Autumn, in place of John Matheson, who was "getting through." If he'd take it, that is.

What a question! As we used to say: "Will a duck swim?" And yet very presently here was Elsie Snow going around with another kind of smile and another and mysterious light in her eye. She was a wonder, Elsie was.

How did she get wind of it? you'll ask. But you must remember that, what with being chairman of this, manager of that, and corresponding secretary of the other, the banker's wife had in her hands the ends of more underground wires than any dozen in Urkey, and under-water wires too, tapping the gossip of all the towns and precincts the length of the Cape. And wise in politics, she knew that two and two, coming at the right time and at all dramatic, are apt to make nearer forty than four. And she knew that there is a tide in the affairs of men. And she knew that it never rains but it pours.

She could hear them at Gillyport: "Well, they say Honest Tansy Snow opened up his mouth at last, and the man's a spellbinder; vow he is." And at Barnstable: "They knew him, and they knew he meant it; he ain't the kind to spout for spoutin' sake, Banker Snow ain't. And they do say there was a good many noses blowed there toward the end."

But Elsie knew more than that. Piecing it together in her astute mind, from a hint here, an allusion there, a slip of somebody's tongue or pen, she knew a thing that only three men in the Congressional District happened yet to know. And this was that "the party," what with the chill of old blood and the heat of bad blood, was secretly in a bad way indeed; that it wanted a doctor, and wanted one quickly—with the Autumn elections coming forward, and a member of Congress to be sent to Washington. No veteran; no silver-trumpeting old warhorse. No, a new name, a fresh fame, a clean slate.

"And where, oh, where," thought Elsie, "where will the lightning strike?"

Selectman? Selectman of a village? That was why she smiled. Since Barlow Atkins left Congress in 1884 people in Urkey had almost forgotten that an islander *could* sit under the dome in Washington. "The biggest man in this town." She remembered the young Tansy standing up straight in London Lane. Well, she'd see.

One afternoon in mid-July the Knights came over in the steamer *Senator Bates* for their annual "time," a clambake at Blue Goat Cove in the evening and the sail back home by moonlight later on. When they had marched the length of the shore street behind their band and got a start for the cove, they took half the population with

them, but they left three of their own number behind.

The sail was all right for these three, but they weren't much on clambakes. They'd rather loaf around the old town, looking at houses. Perhaps they were interested in architecture. Or perhaps it was lightning-rods. They were Mr. Claude Byram of Gillyport, Captain Charlie Slocum of Barnstable, and ex-Senator Bates himself, and they were the three men in the district who knew what Elsie knew. As they strolled they talked. They talked about Henry Poor, the young lawyer in Provincetown, who, unheard of a year ago, had just won the Province-lands suit for the Commonwealth. They talked of the new man who was making such a name for himself as head of the Highmarket Academy—a scholar—no taint of politics there. And once or twice, lingering near the end of the Brick Walk, "Well, here's where *he* lives," they temporized. "What do we say?"

But they couldn't seem quite to say. They had to talk it all over again. Six o'clock passed. They had a snack at Dow's place, and then it was seven, and then it was eight. Elsie Snow wasn't the woman to wait forever. It was in the drug-store, where they had stopped for cigars, that she brought them to earth.

"Captain Slocum, as I live! And *Mr.* Byram! And—*not* Senator *Bates!* Well, I declare, who'd have thought to find *you* drifting around our little town, and without a soul to manage for you? I give you my word—"

She gave them her word it was an outrage, and that even if there wasn't a committee of welcome, it was a home that would be honored by their presence, and a fresh lemon layer-cake, and a drop of rhubarb wine, put down the year she and Tansy were married. And Tansy *would* be tickled.

It seemed providential; seemed to help to clear their minds. When they had arrived, most easily, most pleasantly, at the foot of the Snow steps, they slackened pace and let their hostess go on ahead.

She made it simple for them. "I'll run on and see Tansy's fit to be looked at; he's that much of a home body, he's probably in slippers now."

"I guess, Mrs. Snow," the Senator called after her, spokesman for the three, "I guess you can tell Snow *we*'ll be tickled to see *him.*"

All the woman could think, and that over and over, was, "This is the greatest day in Urkey's history."

Tansy, hearing voices, was half-way up-stairs. She bustled him up the other half, the news on her tongue; but then it was too enormous to tell.

"Get into your blacks, and *hurry*," she bade him; "there's company."

As she turned and swept down-stairs again to put the company at its ease with ash-trays and cake and rhubarb wine, the chosen of fortune felt along the wall with a sigh. Why wouldn't people let him be?

Once inside, he started toward the window, of habit a quarter-century old. Then he remembered he was to hurry. Company. Who? Why had there been that note in her voice? Perhaps at last it was some-body about the Autumn meeting and the Selectmanship. Oh, Tansy knew. He never let on, but he wasn't a fool. And he wanted it—as he'd never wanted anything. Why? For the name? Yes, in a way. More than anything in life, he wanted to be able to go to that window and throw back the taunt of that leering eye of light.

"Yah. Take a look at me—the man that's trusted above all others! Selectman! The biggest man in this island and this town! You, and your 'moth-millers,' you dirty, filthy nobodies, look at me! Yah!"

But he had been told to hurry. In that funny way—*hurry!* It *was* the Selectman-ship! As good as done already. Because he had been an upright citizen and an honest man. Here he was at the window, after all.

It wasn't a "Yah!" It wasn't a sound, nothing formed, just a formless outlashing of a life that was tired in secret; secretly, prematurely old. Then, as he looked again, he lifted a hand and drew it across his eyes.

"Fog coming in. Won't have much of a moonlight sail, that crowd."

He removed his hand and stared. There was no fog. The sky was as clear as glass and full of stars. He put his other hand on the bedpost. The bedpost was solid, any-way.

"Good God! What's—wh-what's hap-pened? What's wrong?"

Elsie couldn't keep them occupied for-ever, even with cake and rhubarb wine. Minutes are minutes to such men. When fifteen had passed, and Slocum had looked at his watch twice, she went to the stairs and called. Then, laughing, "What would you do with such a man?" she marched up to find him. The bedroom was dark, and he wasn't there. She went to the spare chamber, to the west chamber, down the back way to the kitchen. She returned to their bedroom; he *must* be there.

She felt on the bed, the chair; she stood staring out of the window.

She shut her eyes and opened them again. A curious uneasiness, having nothing to do with the company downstairs, seemed to lay hold of her.

"Fog," she said to herself.

She turned around. What was the mat-ter with this room to-night? Why was everything so—so—so wrong—so lost—so funny? She touched the bedpost. It was solid enough. She glanced toward the win-dow again.

She laughed. She saw what was wrong, and it was ridiculous. For two dozen years, without knowing it, she had depended on seeing a light there when the weather was clear. When it was thick, there was no light; no light, it must be thick. And here it was clear, and no light. Absurd, but it had given her the jumps.

That shows what habit is.

Rid of the spell, she remembered what she was about. Her lips whiter and whiter with anger, running on frantic tiptoe, she searched the house.

Coming through the parlor she was all cheer. "Tansy'll be down directly," she promised them, and, slipping out of the door, she was gone.

Time passed. Once or twice they heard a voice calling "Tansy! Tansy!" off in the distance, among the houses and lanes.

They got to talking. "You can't tell me this fellow Poor hasn't made a big im-pression, especially down-Cape." "Yes, but he's a lawyer, and that means politician to lots of people. Now this man McDowell over at the Academy—"

When Mrs. Snow reappeared it was awkward. They didn't want to seem to run, but there was a man Byram ought to see, and there was the boat.

They got out backward, Slocum saying, "We're right sorry not to have seen Snow," and the old Senator adding a word of kind-ness: "The talk's been up our way that your husband's slated for the next Select-man over here. I'm glad of that; he ought to make a good one, from all I hear."

Elsie stood staring at the closed door when they were gone.

"Selectman!" she whispered. "*Select-man!*"

All the poison of all the years came pouring out: "I'll *see* him Selectman! I'd kill myself first! He shall stay a stick till the day of his death, he shall. A dumb, stupid stick—stick-in-the-mud! *Ohhhh!*"

In the kitchen of the house on the Stone Fold they were playing parchisi down on the floor. The board was an old one, held together with court-plaster; most of the men were buttons, and there were only two dice left. Despite these defects, however; despite the two youngest, two babies, creeping in continually and grabbing and getting slapped; and despite the paralytic old shepherd in the chair behind the towel-rack, who wanted attending to now and then—despite these handicaps they played with a quiet concentration, watching each the moves of all the others, alert for cheating, a gamin shrewdness in the eyes narrowed under the forelocks of tangled hair. It was an old game with them; yet to-night there was something new about it; as new as though it had been another game altogether, or the same game transported to heaven, where all is light.

"Better'n that old lantern!"

"Better'n two lanterns!"

"Better'n ten lanterns!"

So, from time to time, between moves, carried away afresh by realization, they joined and gloated.

"Better'n a *hundred* lanterns!"

The dogs were barking outside. An old one from under the stove sniffed toward the door, bristling. The players paid no attention, but the grandfather began to screech at the top of his lungs: "Sha'n't have it! Sha'n't! Ain't nobody no decency? With *her* there? Etta, you tell 'em go way. It's an unholy sin—comin' round a night like to-night—that's what it is! Etta!"

"Shut your face!" Etta threw at him, as, without haste, she got up from the floor. She was a woman of twenty-odd, the mother of one of the infants underfoot. "Remember, you, it's my next move!" she threatened the others; then again to the old man: "Won't you shut up, f'gracious sake!" and finally to the door: "Well, well, 'tain't locked, is it? *Come in!*"

The door opened. Those on the floor sat up straight. Etta retreated a step, taken aback to see a stranger.

"What d'y' want?" she muttered.

The man kept standing there, staring at her; staring at her squat, strong-muscled figure, her lowering face, her hair, thick and matted about her head, the color of unwashed brown sheep. She didn't like it.

"Who are ye, and what d'y' want? Y' dumb?"

But the old shepherd began to screech now: "*I* know 'im! I seen 'im many's the time over to the village. I see ye, Mr. Snow. I know ye well, Banker Snow. Well, I vow! Draw out a chair for Mr. Snow, Etta. Florry! Frank! Scabby! What a parcel o' dummies! Git a chair for Banker Snow."

"What d'y' want?" Etta persisted, unmoved.

Snow lifted a hand and passed it down over his face, which looked drawn and moist. Like a man talking in his sleep, he asked: "What's wrong with Donna?"

That seemed to loosen all tongues at once. The kitchen was as full of voices, of a sudden, as it was of the yellow glare.

"Donna's dead."

"Donna's in there; wanta see 'er?"

"Ma went sick and she got worse and died off."

"Donna ain't boss no longer, she ain't."

"We got the lamp down."

"We gone and got the lamp on 'er now, for *all* 'er."

"At last we got the lamp."

Snow seemed to see the lamp for the first time. Like a man walking in his sleep he went to look at it. It was worth looking at. It stood on its own stand, a good four feet high; its finely swelled reservoir had variegated chasings of brass and nickel all over it; it had an extra-size chimney without a nick, and two wicks, one within the other. A lamp for any parlor in the world. All the parts that could be rubbed were as bright as a new one in the store. It had been looked after, like new; the price-tag, even, had never been taken off. It hung from the stem of the regulator, and the mark was still legible on it amongst the spotting of flies. Tansy read it.

"$6."

Some folks have a God of mercy. And some have a terrible God.

XLIX

CHARLES CALDWELL DOBIE (1881–   )

A more recent "arrival" is C. C. Dobie who must be classed with Steele as one who has sought to free himself from the conventions of the past and to launch out into the unexplored. San Francisco was his birthplace, and it has been his place of residence to the present time, but there is little of California in his tales. "He suffers," says O'Brien, "from lack of sufficient background. While his substance is visualized clearly, it is sometimes deficient in physical grasp." Schooled only through the grammar grade and then for twenty years engrossed with a successful fire insurance business, he has for the most part seen life from the standpoint of the city, from the standpoint of the man of the street. He uses far more of action than Steele. In such stories as "The Hands of the Enemy" we have a combination of Bret Harte and the moving pictures. In others, however, as for instance, "The Cracked Teapot," he is as psychological and as closely concerned with a study of internal rather than external forces as Steele himself. He himself classifies his work as studies in the grotesque vein—stories like "The Open Window," and studies in the dramatic—stories like "The Hands of the Enemy." It is perhaps in the first of these varieties that he has done his best work. He has as yet, however, not fully demonstrated the extent of his powers. For the present he must be labeled as a writer of promise.

THE OPEN WINDOW *

"It happened just as I have said," Fernet reiterated, tossing the wine-dregs from his glass.

The company at the table looked instinctively toward the kitchen. Berthe was bringing a fresh pot of coffee. They all followed Fernet's example, lifting their empty glasses for her to serve them in their turn.

The regular borders of the Hôtel de France, after the fashion of folks who find their meal a duty to be promptly despatched, had departed, but the transients still lingered over their *café noir* and cognac in the hope that something exciting might materialize.

As the sound of Fernet's voice died away, a man who had been sitting in an extreme corner of the room scraped back his chair and rose. Fernet looked up. The man was a hunchback, and, instead of paying for his meal and leaving, he crossed over and said to Fernet, in the most perfect French imaginable:

"I see, my young fellow, that you are discussing something of interest with your

* Published by arrangement with Charles Caldwell Dobie, owner of the copyright.

friends here. Would it be impertinent of me to inquire into the subject?"

Fernet drew out a chair for the newcomer, who seated himself.

"By no means. We were discussing a murder and suicide. The murdered man was an Italian fisherman who lodged at the Hôtel des Alpes Maritimes, the suicide was a musician named Suvaroff."

"Ah," said the hunchback, cracking his fingers. "Why a murder and suicide? Why not two murders?"

"Because," returned Fernet, pompously, "it was abundantly proved to the contrary. This man Suvaroff suffered from neuralgia; the Italian fisherman was given to playing the accordion at all hours of the night. Suvaroff was, in addition, a musician —a high-strung person. The Italian's playing was abominable—even his landlady says as much. In short, Suvaroff deliberately killed this simple-minded peasant because of his music. Then, in a fit of remorse, he killed himself. I leave it to any one here to dispute the fact. Besides, I was on the coroner's jury. I should know what I am talking about."

"Oh, without doubt," agreed the hunchback, smiling amiably. "But, as I remember, the knives in both cases were plunged hilt-deep into the backs of the victims. One does not usually commit suicide in this fashion."

Fernet coldly eyed the curiously handsome face of his antagonist. "It seems you know more about this thing than a coroner's jury," he sneered.

"It seems I do—granting that such an important item was left out of the evidence."

"Then, my good sir, will you be good enough to tell me who *did* kill Suvaroff, since you do not admit that he died by his own hand?"

The hunchback cracked his fingers again. "That is simple enough. Suvaroff was killed by the same person who stabbed the Italian."

"And who might that be, pray?"

The hunchback rose with a malignant smile. "Ah, if I told you that you would know as much as I do, my friend."

And with that he walked calmly over to the proprietor, put down thirty-five cents for his meal upon the counter, and without another word left the room.

A silence fell upon the group. Everybody stared straight ahead, avoiding the eye of his neighbor. It was as if something too terrifying to be remarked had passed them.

Finally, a thick-set man at Fernet's right, with a purple wart on his cheek, said, uneasily, "Come, I must be going."

The others rose; only Fernet remained seated.

"What," said another, "haven't you finished?"

"Yes," returned Fernet, gloomily, "but I am in no hurry."

He sat there for an hour, alone, holding his head between his hands. Berthe cleared off the soiled plates, wiped the oilcloth-covered tables, began noisily to lay the pewter knives and forks for the morning meal. At this Fernet stirred himself and, looking up at her, said:

"Tell me who was the hunchback who came and sat with us? Does he live here —in San Francisco?"

"His name is Flavio Minetti," she replied, setting the lid back upon an uncovered sugar-bowl. "Beyond that I know nothing. But they tell me that he is quite mad."

"Ah, that accounts for many things," said Fernet, smiling with recovered assurance. "I must say he is strangely fascinating."

Berthe looked at him sharply and shrugged. "For my part, he makes me shiver every time I see him come in the door. When I serve him my hand shakes. And he continually cracks his fingers and says to me: "Come, Berthe, what can I do to make you smile? Would you laugh if I were to dance for you? I would give half my life only to see you laughing. Why are you so sad?' . . . No, I wish he would never come again."

"Nevertheless, I should like to see him once more."

"He comes always on Thursday for chicken."

"Thanks," said Fernet, as he put on his hat.

Fernet walked directly to his lodgings that night. He had a room in an old-fashioned house on the east side of Telegraph Hill. The room was shabby enough, but it caught glimpses of the bay and there was a gnarled pepper-tree that came almost to its windows and gave Fernet a sense of eternal, though grotesque, spring. Even his landlord was unusual—a professional beggar who sat upon the curb, with a ridiculous French poodle for company, and sold red and green pencils.

This landlord was sitting out by the front gate as Fernet entered.

"Ah, Pollitto," said Fernet, halting before the old man and snapping his fingers at the poodle who lay crouched before his master, "I see you are enjoying this fine warm night."

"You are wrong," replied the beggar. "I am merely sitting here hoping that some one will come along and rent my front room."

"Then it is vacant?"

"Naturally," replied the old man, with disagreeable brevity, and Fernet walked quickly up to his room.

"Why do I live in such a place?" he asked himself, surveying the four bare walls. "Everything about it is abominable, and that beggar, Pollitto, is a scoundrel. I shall move next week."

He crossed over to the window and flung it open. The pepper-tree lay before him, crouching in the moonlight. He thought at once of Flavio Minetti.

"He is like this pepper-tree," he said, aloud, "beautiful even in his deformity. No,

I would not trade this pepper-tree for a dozen of the straightest trees in the world." He stepped back from the window, and, lighting a lamp, set it upon a tottering walnut table. "Ah, André Fernet," he mused, chidingly, "you are always snared by what is unusual. You should pray to God that such folly does not lead you to disaster."

He went to the window and looked out again. The pepper-tree seemed to be bending close to the ground, as if seeking to hide something. Presently the wind parted its branches and the moonlignt fell at its feet like a silver moth before a blackened candle.

André Fernet shivered and sighed. "Yes," he repeated, again and again, "they are alike. They both are at once beautiful and hideous and they have strange secrets. . . . Well, I shall go on Thursday again, and maybe I shall see him. Who knows, if I am discreet he may tell me who killed this ridiculous musician Suvaroff." And with that he suddenly blew out the light.

On the next Thursday night, when Fernet entered the dining-room of the Hôtel de France his glance rested immediately upon Flavio Minetti. To his surprise the hunchback rose, drawing a chair out as he did so, and beckoning Fernet to be seated next him. For a moment Fernet hesitated. Berthe was just bringing on the soup.

"What! Are you afraid?" she said, mockingly, as she passed.

This decided Fernet. He went and sat beside Minetti without further ado.

"Ah, I was expecting you!" cried the hunchback, genially, as he passed the radishes.

"Expecting *me?*" returned Fernet. His voice trembled, though he tried to speak boldly.

"Yes. Women are not the only inquisitive animals in the world. What will you have—some wine?"

Fernet allowed Minetti to fill his glass. Other boarders began to drift in. Minetti turned his back upon Fernet, speaking to a new-comer at his left. He did not say another word all evening.

Fernet ate and drank in silence. "What did I come for and why am I staying?" he kept asking himself. "This man is mocking me. First of all, he greets me as if I were his boon companion, and next he insults me openly and before everybody in the

room. Even Berthe has noticed it and is smiling. As a matter of fact, he knows no more than I do about Suvaroff's death."

But he continued to sit beside the hunchback all through the meal, and as fruit was put on the table he touched Minetti on the arm and said, "Will you join me in a *café royal?*"

"Not here . . . a little later. I can show you a place where they really know how to make them. And, besides, there are tables for just two. It is much more private."

Fernet's heart bounded and sank almost in one leap. "Let us go now, then," he said, eagerly.

"As you wish," replied Minetti.

Fernet paid for two dinners, and they reached for their hats.

"Where are you going?" asked Berthe, as she opened the door.

Fernet shrugged. "I am in his hands," he answered, sweeping his arm toward Minetti.

"You mean you will be," muttered the hunchback, in an undertone.

Fernet heard him distinctly.

"Perhaps I had better leave him while there is yet time!" flashed through his mind. But the next instant he thought, contemptuously: "What harm can he do me? Why, his wrist is no bigger than a pullet's wing. Bah! You are a fool, André Fernet!"

They stepped out into the street. A languorous note was in the air, the usual cool wind from the sea had not risen. A waning moon silvered the roof-tops, making a pretense of hiding its face in the thin line of smoke above Telegraph Hill.

The hunchback led the way, trotting along in a fashion almost Oriental. At the end of the second block he turned abruptly into a wine-shop; Fernet followed. They found seats in a far corner, away from the billiard-tables. A waiter came forward. They gave their orders.

"Be sure," said Minetti to the waiter, "that we have plenty of anisette and cognac in the coffee."

The man flicked a towel rather contemptuously and made no answer.

"Now," Minetti continued, turning a mocking face toward Fernet, "what can I do for you, my friend?"

Fernet was filled with confusion. "I . . . you . . ." he stammered. "Really, there is nothing. Believe me—"

"Nonsense," interrupted Minetti. "You wish to know who killed Suvaroff. But I warn you, my friend, it is a dreadful thing to share such a secret."

He looked at Fernet intently. The younger man shuddered. "Nevertheless, I should like to know," Fernet said, distinctly.

"Well, then, since you are so determined —it was I who killed him."

Fernet stared, looked again at the hunchback's puny wrists, and began to laugh. "*You!* Do you take me for a fool?" And as he said this he threw back his head and laughed until even the billiard-players stopped their game and looked around at him.

"What are you laughing at?" asked the hunchback, narrowing his eyes.

Fernet stopped. He felt a sudden chill as if some one had opened a door. "I am laughing at you," he answered.

"I am sorry for that," said Minetti, dryly.

"Why?"

The hunchback leaned forward confidentially. "Because I kill every one who laughs at me. It—it is a little weakness I have."

The waiter came with two glasses of steaming coffee. He put them down on the table, together with a bottle of cognac and a bottle of anisette.

"Ah, that is good!" cried the hunchback, rubbing his hands together. "The proprietor is my friend. He is going to let us prepare our own poison!"

Fernet felt himself shivering. "Come," he thought, "this will never do! The man is either mad or jesting." He reached for the anisette.

"Let me pour it for you," suggested Flavio Minetti. "Your hand is shaking, so that you will spill half of it on the floor."

The hunchback's voice had a note of pity in it. Fernet relinquished his hold upon the bottle.

"Don't look so frightened," continued Minetti. "I shall not kill you here. The proprietor is a friend of mine, and, besides—"

"What nonsense!" cried Fernet, with a ghastly smile. "But I must confess you did make my blood run cold for a minute."

Minetti stirred some cognac into his glass. "And, besides," he finished, coldly, "I give everybody a sporting chance. It adds to the game."

That night André Fernet was restless. He lay on his bed looking out at the blinking lights of the harbor. "I must stop drinking coffee," he muttered to himself.

Finally he fell asleep, and when he did he had a strange dream. It seemed that the pepper-tree outside his window suddenly began to move in the night breeze and its long green boughs became alive, twisting like the relentless tentacles of a devil-fish. Its long green boughs became alive, crawling along the ground, flinging themselves into the air, creeping in at André Fernet's open window. He lay upon the bed as he had done earlier in the evening, watching the harbor lights. Slowly the green boughs writhed over the faded carpet, scaled the bedpost and fell upon the bed. André Fernet waited, motionless. He felt the green tentacles close about his legs, clasp his hands, slide shudderingly across his throat. Yet he made no move to free himself. It was only when he felt a breath upon his cheek that he turned slightly, and instead of the tentacle-like boughs of the pepper-tree he fancied himself staring down at the hands of Flavio Minetti. . . . He awoke with a start. The sun was pouring in at the open window. He got up quickly. A noisy clatter issued from the passageway. Fernet opened his door. Two men were carrying a trunk up the stairs. Pollitto, the beggar, walked behind.

"Ah, I see you have rented your front room," said Fernet, stepping out.

"Yes," returned the other. "It was taken as early as six o'clock this morning—by a hunchback."

Fernet stopped breathing. "A hunchback? Was his name Flavio Minetti?"

"Yes. How did you know?"

Fernet tried to smile. "He is a friend of mine," he answered, as he walked back into his room. "Perhaps it would be better if I moved away," he thought. "I do not like this room. Heaven knows why I have stayed this long. Is this fellow Minetti really mad or merely making sport of me? I should like to have him think that I am afraid of him. As for his story about Suvaroff, that is, of course, ridiculous. If I thought otherwise I should go at once to the . . . No, it is all a joke. I shall stay where I am. I shall not have it said that a little, mad, puny, twisted fellow frightened André Fernet out of his lodgings. Besides, it will be curious to watch his little game. What a beautiful morning it is, after all! And the pepper-tree—how it glistens in the sun! I should miss that pepper-tree if I moved away. But I must stop drinking *café royals*. They upset one. I do not know whether it is the coffee, or the cognac, or the anisette, or all three. Of course that dream I had toward morning means nothing—but such dreams are unpleasant. I hate this place. But I shall not move now. No, I shall wait and see what happens."

Fernet did not see Minetti for some days. Indeed, he had dismissed the whole thing from his mind, when one night, returning home early to get out of a drizzle, who should stop him on the stairway but the hunchback.

"Ah, so here you are!" called out Fernet, gaily, in spite of his rapidly beating heart. "I have been waiting for you to call on me ever since I heard that you were lodging under the same roof."

"I have been busy," replied the hunchback, laconically.

Fernet threw open his bedroom door and waved Minetti in.

"Busy?" he echoed, as he struck a light. "And what do you find that is so absorbing, pray?"

"You know my specialty," replied Minetti, flinging off his cap.

Fernet looked up sharply. A malignant look had crept into the hunchback's face.

"Oh, there is no doubt of it, he is quite mad!" said Fernet to himself. Then aloud: "Yes, I have been wanting to talk to you more about this. Take a seat and I shall make some coffee. For instance, do you always employ the knife in despatching your—"

"Scarcely," interrupted Minetti, quickly. "Slow poison has its fascinations. There is a very delicate joy in watching a gradual decline. It is like watching a green leaf fading before the breath of autumn. First a sickly pallor, then a yellowing, finally the sap dries completely, a sharp wind, a fluttering in the air, and it is all over. I have tried nearly every slow way—except mental murder. I fancy that, too, would be exquisite."

"Mental murder. . . . I do not understand."

Minetti stretched himself out and yawned. "Accomplishing the thing without any weapon save the mind."

Fernet picked up the coffee-pot and laughed. "Why, my dear fellow, it is too absurd! The thing cannot be done. You see I am laughing at you again, but no matter."

"No, as you say, it is no matter. You can die only once."

Fernet's laughter stopped instantly. He went on with his preparation for coffee. Minetti changed the subject.

It turned out that there was no sugar in the cracked bowl. Fernet was putting on his hat to go out for some, when the hunchback stopped him.

"Sugar will not be necessary," he said. And as he spoke he drew a vial from his vest pocket and laid it upon the table beside the cups. "You know what these are, of course."

"Saccharine pellets?" inquired Fernet as he threw aside his hat.

Minetti replied with a grunt. Fernet poured out the coffee, set a spoon in each saucer, laid three French rolls upon a blue plate. Then he sat down.

"Permit me!" said Minetti, reaching for the vial and rolling a tiny pellet into his palm.

Fernet held up his cup; the hunchback dropped the pellet into it. Then he corked the vial tightly and laid it aside.

"You forgot to serve yourself," said Fernet.

"So I did!" answered Minetti, nonchalantly. "Well, no matter. I very often drink my coffee so—without sweetening."

Fernet drew back suddenly. Could it be possible that . . . The hunchback was staring at him, an ironical smile was on his lips. Fernet shuddered.

"Drink your coffee!" Minetti commanded, sneeringly. "You are on the verge of a chill."

Fernet obeyed meekly. He felt for all the world like an animal caught in a trap. He tried to collect his thoughts. What had the hunchback been talking about?

"Slow poison!" muttered Fernet, inaudibly to himself.

"What is that you are saying?" demanded the other.

"You were speaking of slow poison. How do you go about it?"

"Oh, that is easy! For instance, once in London I lodged next door to my victim. We became capital friends. And he was always calling me in for a bite of something to eat. Nothing elaborate—a bun and a cup of tea, or coffee and cake. Very much as we are doing now. He died in six months. It is no trick, you know, to poison a man who eats and drinks with you—especially drinks!"

As he said this the hunchback reached for the coffee-pot and poured Fernet another cupful. Then he uncorked the vial again and dropped a pellet into the steaming liquid.

"I do not think that I wish any more," protested Fernet.

"Nonsense! You are still shivering like an old woman with the palsy. Hot coffee will do you good."

"No," said Fernet, desperately, "I never drink more than one cup at a sitting. It keeps me awake, and next morning my hand shakes and I am fit for nothing. I need a steady hand in my business."

"And what may that be, pray?"

"At present I am a draftsman. Some day, if I live long enough, I hope to be an architect."

"If you live long enough? You forget that you have laughed at *me*, my friend."

Fernet tried to appear indifferent. "What a droll fellow you are!" he cried, with sudden gaiety, rubbing his hands together. And without thinking, he reached for his coffee-cup and downed the contents in almost one gulp. He laid the cup aside quickly. He could feel the sweat starting out upon his forehead.

"There, you see," said Minetti, "the coffee has done you good already. You are perspiring, and that is a good sign. A hot drink at the right moment works wonders."

The next morning Pollitto stopped Fernet as he swung out the front gate to his work.

"What is the matter with you?" exclaimed the beggar, in a surprised tone.

"Why . . . what?" demanded Fernet, in a trembling voice. "Do I look so . . .? Pray, tell me, is there anything unusual about me?"

"Why, your face . . . Have you looked at yourself in the glass? Your skin is the color of stale pastry."

Fernet tried to laugh. "It is nothing. I have been drinking too much coffee lately. I must stop it."

It was a fine morning. The sun was shining, and the air was brisk and full of little rippling breezes. The bay lay like a blue-green peacock ruffling its gilded feathers. The city had a genial, smiling countenance. But Fernet was out of humor with all this full-blown content. He had spent a wretched night—not sleepless, but full of disturbing dreams. Dreams about Minetti and his London neighbor and the empty sugar-bowl. All night he had dreamed about this empty sugar-bowl. It seemed that as soon as he had it filled Minetti would slyly empty it again. He tried stowing sugar away in his pockets, but when he put his hand in to draw out a lump a score or more of pellets spilled over the floor. Then he remembered saying:

"I shall call on Minetti's London neighbor. Maybe he will have some sugar."

He walked miles and miles, and finally beat upon a strange door. A man wrapped in a black coat up to his eyebrows opened to his knock.

"Are you Flavio Minetti's London neighbor?" he demanded, boldly.

The figure bowed. Fernet drew the cracked sugar-bowl from under his arm.

"Will you oblige me with a little sugar?" he asked, more politely.

The black-cloaked figure bowed and disappeared. Presently he came back. Fernet took the sugar-bowl from him. It struck him that the bowl felt very light. He looked down at his hands. The bowl had disappeared; only a glass vial lay in his palm. He removed the cork—a dozen or more tiny round pellets fell out. He glanced up quickly at Minetti's London neighbor; a dreadful smile glowed through the black cloak. Fernet gave a cry and hurled the vial in the face of his tormentor. Minetti's London neighbor let the black cloak fall, and André Fernet discovered that he was staring at himself. . . . He awakened soon after that and found that it was morning.

When he brushed his hair his hand had shaken so that the brush fell clattering to the floor. And he had spilled the cream for his morning coffee over the faded strip of carpet before the bureau. It had ended by his eating no breakfast at all. But he had drunk glass after glass of cold water.

After Pollitto's words he trembled more and more like a man with the ague, and before every saloon-door mirror he halted and took a brief survey of his face. Pollitto was right—his skin was dead and full of unhealthy pallor. It was plain that he could not work in his present condition. His trembling fingers could scarcely hold a pencil, much less guide it through the precise demands of a drafting-board. He decided to go to the library and read. But the books on architecture which always enthralled him could not hold his shifting attention. Finally in despair he went up to the librarian and said:

"Have you any books on poison?"

The woman eyed him with a cold, incurious glance.

"Historical or medical?" she snapped out, as she went on stamping mysterious numbers in the pile of books before her.

"Both!"

She consulted a catalogue and made a list for him.

He sat all day devouring books which the librarian had recommended. He did not even go out for lunch. He read historical and romantic instances with a keen, morbid relish; but when it came to the medical books his heart quickened and he followed causes and effects breathlessly. By nightfall he had a relentless knowledge of every poison in the calendar. He knew what to expect from arsenic or strychnine or vitriol. He learned which poisons destroyed tissues, which acted as narcotics, which were irritants. He identified the hemlock, the horse-chestnut, the deadly toadstools. In short, he absorbed and retained everything on the subject. It seemed that the world teemed with poisons; one could be sure of nothing. Even beautiful flowers were not to be trusted.

He was so upset by all he had read that he could scarcely eat dinner. He went to an obscure *pension* in a wretched basement, where he was sure he would be unknown, and, after two or three mouthfuls of soup and a spoonful of rice boiled with tomato, he rose, paid for his meal, and went out to tramp up and down past the tawdry shops of middle Kearny Street. He was trotting aimlessly in the direction of Market Street when he felt a tug at his coat-sleeve. He turned. Minetti was smiling genially up at him.

"Come," said the hunchback, "what is your hurry? Have you had coffee yet? I was thinking that—"

Fernet's heart sank at once. And yet he managed to say boldly: "I have given up drinking coffee. You can see for yourself what a wretched complexion I have. And to-day I have scarcely eaten."

"Pooh!" cried Minetti. "A cup of coffee will do you good."

Fernet began to draw away in futile terror. "No!" he protested, with frightened vehemence. "No, I tell you! I won't drink the stuff! It is useless for you to—"

Minetti began to laugh with scornful good-humor. "What has come over you?" he drawled, half-closing his eyes. "Are you afraid?"

And as he said this Fernet glanced instinctively at the puny wrists, no bigger than a pullet's wing, and replied, boldly:

"Afraid? Of what? I told you last night I need a steady hand in my business, and to-day I have not been able to do any work."

Minetti's mirth softened into genial acquiescence. "Well, maybe you are right. But I must say you are not very companionable. Perhaps the coffee you have been drinking has not been made properly. You should take *something*. You do look badly. A glass of brandy? . . . No? . . . Ah, I have it—coffee made in the Turkish fashion. Have you ever drunk that?"

"No," replied Fernet, helplessly, wondering all the time why he was foolish enough to tell the truth.

"Well, then," announced the hunchback, confidently, "we shall cross over to Third Street and have some Turkish coffee. I know a Greek café where they brew a cup that would tempt the Sultan himself. Have you ever seen it made? They use coffee pounded to a fine powder—a teaspoonful to a cup, and sugar in the same proportion. It is all put together and brought to a boil. The result is indescribable! Really, you are in for a treat."

"If it is sweetened in the making," flashed through Fernet's mind, "at least we shall have no more of that pellet business."

"Yes—the result is quite indescribable," Minetti was repeating, "and positively no bad effects."

And as he said this he slipped his arm into Fernet's and guided him with gentle firmness toward the Greek café in question. Fernet felt suddenly helpless and incapable of offering the slightest objection.

A girl took their orders. She had a freckled nose and was frankly Irish. Naturally, she did not fit the picture, and Fernet could see that she was scornful of the whole business.

"Two coffees . . . medium," Minetti repeated, decisively. "And will you have a sweet with it? They sell taffy made of sesame seeds and honey. Or you can have Turkish delight or a pastry dusted with powdered sugar. Really they are all quite delicious."

Fernet merely shrugged. Minetti ordered Turkish delight. The girl wiped some moisture from the marble table-top and walked toward the coffee-shelf.

"So you were not able to work to-day?" Minetti began, affably. "How did you put in the time?"

"At the library, reading."

"Something droll? A French novel or—"

"Books on *poison!*" Fernet shot out with venomous triumph. "I know more than I did yesterday."

"How distressing!" purred Minetti. "Ignorance is more invulnerable than one fancies. Of course we are taught otherwise, but knowledge, you remember, was the beginning of all trouble. But you choose a fascinating subject. Some day when we get better acquainted I shall tell you all I know about it. Poison is such a subtle thing. It is everywhere—in the air we breathe, in the water we drink, in the food we eat. And it is at once swift and sluggish, painful and stupefying, obvious and incapable of analysis. It is like a beautiful woman, or a great joy, or love itself."

Fernet glanced up sharply. The hunchback had slid forward in his seat and his eyes glowed like two shaded pools catching greedily at the yellow sunlight of midday. Fernet shuddered and looked about the room. Groups of swarthy men were drinking coffee, or sipping faintly red draughts of cherry syrup and sweet soda. At a nearby table a group of six shuffled cards and marked their scores upon a slate. And, of course, there were those who played backgammon, rattling the dice and making exaggerated gestures as they spurred on their adversaries with genial taunts.

The girl came back carrying cups of thick steaming coffee and soft lemon-colored sweetmeats speared with two tiny silver forks. She set the tray down. Minetti reached for his coffee greedily, but Fernet sat back in his seat and allowed the waitress to place the second cup before him. As she did so the table shook suddenly and half of the hot liquid spilled over on the marble table-top. Fernet jumped up to escape the scalding trickle; the girl gave an apologetic scream; Minetti laughed strangely.

"It is all my fault!" cried the hunchback. "What stupidity! Pray be seated. My young woman, will you give the gentleman this coffee of mine? And get me another."

"Pardon me," Fernet protested, "but I cannot think of such a thing!" And with that he attempted to pass the coffee in question back to Minetti. But the hunchback would have none of it. Fernet broke into a terrified sweat.

"He has dropped poison into it!" he thought, in sudden panic. "Otherwise why should he be so anxious to have me drink it? He kicked the table deliberately, too. And this cup of his—why was it not spilled also? No, he was prepared—it is all a trick!"

"Come, come, my friend," broke in Minetti, briskly, "drink your coffee while it is still hot! Do not wait for me. I shall be served presently. And try the sweetmeats; they are delicious."

"I am not hungry," replied Fernet, sullenly.

"No? Well, what of that? Sweetmeats and coffee are not matters of hunger. Really, you are more droll than you imagine!" Minetti burst into a terrifying laugh.

"He thinks I am afraid!" muttered Fernet.

And out of sheer bravado he lifted the cup to his lips. Minetti stopped laughing, but a wide smile replaced his diabolical mirth. The girl brought fresh coffee to the hunchback. He sipped it with frank enjoyment, but he did not once take his gaze from Fernet's pale face.

"Well," thought Fernet, "one cup of poison more or less will not kill me. . . . It is not as if he has made up his mind to finish me at once. He is counting on the exquisite joys of a prolonged agony." And he remembered Minetti's words: "It is like watching a green leaf fading before the breath of autumn. First a sickly pallor, then a yellowing, a sharp wind, a fluttering in the air. . . ." He tossed off the coffee in one defiant gulp. "He thinks that he has me in his power. But André Fernet is not quite a fool. I shall go away to-morrow!"

They went home as soon as Minetti finished his coffee. Fernet felt a sudden nausea; by the time he reached his lodgings his steps were unsteady and his head reeled. Minetti was kindness itself.

"Let me help you into bed," he insisted. "You must have a congestion. Presently I shall heat some water and give you a hot gin."

Fernet was too sick to protest. Minetti

started the gas-stove and filled the kettle and went into his room for gin. Fernet dragged himself out of his clothes and crawled in between the sheets. Minetti came back. Fernet lay with his eyes half-closed, shivering. Finally the water boiled, and the hunchback brought Fernet a huge tumbler of gin and water with bits of lemon-peel and cloves floating in it. It tasted so good that Fernet forgot his terror for the moment. But when the tumbler was empty he felt helpless; he could scarcely lift his arms; so he lay flat upon his back, staring up at the ceiling. He tried to recall scraps of what he had been reading all afternoon. What was the name of the poison that left one paralyzed? He could not remember. He found his movements becoming more and more difficult; he could scarcely turn in bed. Minetti brewed another toddy. Fernet could not hold the glass. He tried to push the tumbler away from his lips, but his efforts were useless. Minetti hovered above him with a bland, gentle smile, and Fernet felt the warm liquid trickling into his mouth and down his throat. In the midst of all this he lost consciousness. . . . Once or twice during the night Fernet had a wakeful interlude. Whenever he opened his eyes he saw Minetti sitting before the open window, gazing down at the twisted pepper-tree.

"Yes, they are both alike!" passed dimly through his mind. "They both are at once beautiful and hideous and they have strange secrets! It is no use, I must go away—to-morrow."

In the morning Minetti was standing by the bed. "I have sent for the doctor," he said. But his voice sounded far away.

The doctor came shortly after ten o'clock. He was a little wizened, dried-up old man with a profound air.

"He is a fraud!" thought Fernet. "He knows nothing!"

"Ah," said the doctor, putting a sly finger against his sharp nose, "our friend here has a nervous collapse. He should have a nurse!"

"A nurse!" exclaimed Minetti, with indignation. "And, pray, what do you call me? Do you not think that—"

"Well, we shall see! we shall see!" replied the doctor, rubbing his hands together. "But he will need all sorts of delicacies and—"

Minetti moistened his lips with sleek satisfaction. "You cannot name a dish that I am not able to prepare."

"How about a custard? To-day he should eat something light."

"A custard is simplicity itself," answered the hunchback, and he cracked his fingers.

Minetti went out with the doctor, and came back shortly, carrying eggs and a bottle of vanilla extract and sugar. Fernet lay helpless, watching him bustling about. Finally the delicacy was made and set away in a pan of water to cool. At noon Minetti brought a blue bowl filled with custard to the bedside. It looked inviting, but Fernet shook his head.

"I am not hungry," he lied.

The hunchback set the bowl down on a chair so that Fernet gazed upon it all day. The hunchback did not leave the room. He sat before the open window, reading from a thick book. Toward nightfall Fernet said to him:

"What do you find so interesting?"

Minetti darted a sardonic glance at his patient. "A book on *poison*. I did not realize that I had grown so rusty on the subject. Why, I remember scarcely enough to poison a field-mouse!"

He rose and crossed over to the bedside. "Do you not feel ready for the custard?"

Fernet cast a longing eye upon the yellow contents of the blue bowl.

"No. To tell the truth, I never eat it."

Minetti shrugged.

"But I should like a glass of water."

The hunchback drew water from the faucet. Fernet watched him like a ferret.

"At least," thought Fernet, "he cannot drop poison in the water secretly. It is well that I can see every move he makes at such a time. I should not like to die of thirst."

A little later Minetti removed the bowl and threw out its contents. Fernet looked on with half-closed eyes.

"What better proof could I have?" he mused. "If the custard were harmless he would eat it himself. I must get away to-morrow."

But the next day he felt weaker than ever, and when the doctor came Minetti said, in answer to questions:

"I made a delicious custard yesterday and he ate every bit. . . . An oyster stew? . . . with milk? I shall see that he has it at noon."

"God help me!" muttered Fernet. "Why does he lie like this? I must get the doctor's ear and tell him how things stand. I shall eat nothing—nothing! Thank Heaven I can drink water without fear."

At noon the oyster stew was ready. But Fernet would have none of it. "Oysters make me ill!" he said.

Minetti merely shrugged as he had done the previous day, and set the savory dish upon a chair before the bed. It exuded tantalizing odors, until Fernet thought he would go mad with longing. Toward evening Minetti threw out the stew. And as before, when the doctor called the hunchback said:

"He ate a quart of stew and there were plenty of oysters in it, I can tell you. Do you think that a chicken fried in olive-oil would be too hearty?"

Fernet groaned. "This is horrible—horrible!" he wept to himself. "I shall die like a starving rat with toasted cheese dangling just beyond reach. God help me to rouse myself! Surely the effects of the poison he has given me must soon wear off. . . . There he is, reading from that big book again. Perhaps he is contriving a way to put poison in my water even though I am able to watch him when he draws me a drink. . . . Poison—poison everywhere. It can even be administered with the prick of a needle. Why did I read about it? Chicken fried in olive-oil . . . what torture!"

The chicken fried in olive-oil was a triumph—Fernet knew all this by the wisps of appetizing fragrance which drifted from the sizzling pan. Minetti made a great stir over the preparations. The tender flesh had to be rubbed thoroughly with garlic and well dusted with salt and pepper. And a quarter of a bottle of yellow-green olive-oil was first placed in the pan. When everything was ready and the chicken cooked to a turn, Minetti carried it to Fernet with a great flourish. Fernet gritted his teeth and turned his face away. He did not have the courage to invent an excuse. Minetti laid it on the chair as usual. For two hours Fernet was tortured with the sight of this tempting morsel, but at the sound of the doctor's step upon the stair the hunchback whisked away the chicken.

"His appetite?" Minetti said, echoing the doctor's query. "Why, one could not wish for better! Only this morning he despatched a chicken as if it had been no more than a soft-boiled egg. As a matter of fact, he is always hungry."

"Well, well," beamed the doctor, "that is the best of signs, and it happens that way very often in nervous cases. You are a capital nurse, my good man, and by the end of the week, if you keep feeding him up in this fashion, he should be as hearty as a school-boy."

At that moment Minetti was called downstairs by his landlord. Fernet struggled to lift himself; the doctor bent toward him.

"This hunchback," Fernet gasped, "he is trying to poison me. Already I have drunk four or five of his concoctions, and that is why I am in this condition . . . helpless. And he is lying when he says that I have eaten. I have touched nothing for three days."

The doctor laid the patient back upon the pillow.

"Poison you, my friend? And for what reason?"

"Because I laughed at him. In God's name, Doctor, see that you keep a straight face in his presence or else—"

The doctor patted Fernet's hand and straightened the sliding bedclothes. By this time Minetti had come back. The doctor and the hunchback whispered together in a far corner. Minetti laughed and tapped his head. At the door Fernet heard the doctor say:

"Just keep up the good work and the idea will pass. It happens that way very often in nervous cases. I shall not look in again until the first of next week unless . . ."

Fernet groaned aloud.

"I must get away to-morrow. . . . I must get away to-morrow!" he kept on repeating.

By the end of the week the smell of food held no temptations for Fernet. Minetti stopped cooking. And when a glass of water was drawn from the faucet Fernet had difficulty in forcing his vision to answer the strain of a searching gaze.

"When my sight fails me." Fernet thought, dimly, "I shall either die of thirst or take the consequences."

When the doctor finally came again Fernet closed his eyes and pretended to be asleep.

"He seems thinner," remarked the doctor, as if he had made an important discovery.

"Well, to tell the truth," replied the hunchback, "he has lost his appetite. I have fed him milk and eggs but—"

"There is nothing to do but be patient," said the doctor. "Medicine will do him no good. Just rest and food. Even a little starvation will not hurt him. People eat too much, anyway."

At this Fernet opened his eyes and broke into a laugh that startled even Minetti. The doctor looked offended.

"Well, he is in your hands," the old fraud said, pompously, to the hunchback. "Just keep up the good work—"

Fernet laughed again.

"He is hysterical," proclaimed the doctor, with an air of supreme wisdom. "It happens that way very often in nervous cases."

And he walked out with great solemnity.

"Ah, I have offended him!" thought Fernet. "Well, now they will finish me—*together!*"

There followed days of delicious weakness. Fernet lay for the most part wrapt in the bliss of silver-blue visions. It seemed as if years were passing. He built shining cities, received the homage of kings, surrendered himself to the joys of ripe-lipped beauties. There were lucid intervals shot through with the malignant presence of Minetti and the puttering visits of the doctor. But these were like waking moments between darkness and dawn, filled with the half-conscious joy of a sleeper secure in the knowledge of a prolonged respite. In such moments Fernet would stir feebly and think:

"I must get away to-morrow!"

And there would succeed almost instantly a languid ecstasy at the thought that to-morrow was something remote and intangible that would never come.

At times the hunchback seemed like nothing so much as a heartless jailer who, if he would, might open the door to some shining adventure. Gradually this idea became fixed and elaborated. Fernet's sight grew dimmer and dimmer until he followed the presence of Minetti by the sounds he made.

"He is jingling something," Fernet would repeat, weakly. "Ah, it must be his keys! He is searching for the one that will set me free! . . . Now he is oiling the lock. . . . He has shut the door again. I am to be held awhile longer. . . . I am a caged bird and just beyond is the pepper-tree. It must be glistening now in the sun-light. Well, let him lock the door, for all the good it will do him. Is not the window always open? When the time comes I shall fly out the window and leave him here—alone. Then we shall see who has the best of this bargain."

And all the silver-blue visions would steal over him again, to be pierced briefly by the arrival of the wizened doctor.

"It is he who keeps me here!" Fernet would say to himself. "If it were not for him I could fly away—forever. Well, presently even he will lose his power."

One day a strange man stood at his bedside. Minetti was there also, and the old fraud of a doctor. The strange man drew back the covers and put his ear to Fernet's fluttering heart and went through other tiresome matters. . . . Finally he smoothed back the covers again, and as he did so he shook his head. He spoke softly, but Fernet heard him distinctly.

"It is too late. . . . You should have called me sooner. He wishes to die. . . . There is nothing to be done."

"Yes, yes—it happens this way very often in nervous cases."

"I have done my best. I have given him food and drink. I have even starved him. But nothing seemed to do any good."

"No," said the stranger; "it is his mind. He has made up his mind that . . . You can do nothing with a man when . . ."

Fernet closed his eyes.

"A man! They think I am a man. What stupidity! Can they not see that I am a bird? . . . They have gone out. He is locking the door again . . . I can hear the keys jingle. . . . Well, let him lock the door if it gives him any pleasure. The window is open and to-night . . ."

The footsteps of the departing visitors died away. A chuckling sound came to André Fernet and the thump of ecstatic fists brought down upon a bare table-top. The voice of Flavio Minetti was quivering triumphantly like the hot whisper of a desert wind through the room:

"Without any weapon save the mind! Ha! ha! ha!"

Fernet turned his face toward the wall. "He is laughing at *me* now. Well, let him laugh while he may. . . . Is not the window open? To-morrow I shall be free and he? . . . No, *he* cannot fly—he has a broken wing. . . . The window is open, André Fernet!"

L

EDNA FERBER (1887-   )

Coming to Edna Ferber we have arrived at the present moment. A native of Wisconsin, educated in the public schools there, employed at seventeen as a newspaper reporter at home and then at Chicago, succeeding sensationally with her first piece of fiction written at twenty-three, she has ever since been a best-seller, sought for eagerly by publishers, and at times reaching the dizziest heights of popularity.

In the short-story areas of her work she began as a disciple of O. Henry,—breezy, thrillingly up to date, unconventional. With her Emma McChesney, self-reliant, efficient, electric, a superwoman surpassing men in their own field, she has added a new character to fiction. She has as much humor as O. Henry and more vivacity, and, like his, always are her stories clean and usually, like his, entertaining—and no more. Sparkling they certainly are, timely, even slangy, but never do they run with any depth. She is an entertainer with saxophone and traps; but thrillingly is she alive and always is she read.

ROAST BEEF, MEDIUM
Served Hot by Emma McChesney *

There is a journey compared to which the travels of Bunyan's hero were a summer-evening's stroll. The Pilgrims by whom this forced march is taken belong to a maligned fraternity, and are known as traveling men. Sample-case in hand, trunk key in pocket, cigar in mouth, brown derby atilt at an angle of ninety, each young and untried traveler starts on his journey down that road which leads through morasses of chicken à la Creole, over greasy mountains of queen fritters made doubly perilous by slippery glaciers of rum sauce, into formidable jungles of breaded veal chops threaded by sanguine and deadly streams of tomato gravy, past sluggish mires of dreadful things en casserole, over hills of corned-beef hash, across shaking quagmires of veal glace, plunging into sloughs of slaw, until, haggard, weary, digestion shattered, complexion gone, he reaches the safe haven of roast beef, medium. Once there, he never again strays, although the pompadoured, white-aproned siren sing-songs in his ear the praises of Irish stew, and pork with apple sauce.

Emma McChesney was eating her soli-

tary supper at the Berger House at Three Rivers, Michigan. She had arrived at the Roast Beef haven many years before. She knew the digestive perils of a small town [5] hotel dining-room as a guide on the snow-covered mountain knows each treacherous pitfall and chasm. Ten years on the road had taught her to recognize the deadly snare that lurks in the seemingly calm [10] bosom of minced chicken with cream sauce. Not for her the impenetrable mysteries of hamburger and onions. It had been a struggle, brief but terrible, from which Emma McChesney had emerged triumphant, her [15] complexion and figure saved.

No more metaphor. On with the story, which left Emma at her safe and solitary supper. She had the last number of the *Dry Goods Review* propped up against the [20] vinegar cruet, and the Worcestershire, and the salt shaker. Between conscientious, but disinterested mouthfuls of medium roast beef, she was reading the snappy ad set forth by her firm's bitterest competitors, [25] the Strauss Sanssilk Skirt Company. It was a good reading ad. Emma McChesney, who had forgotten more about petticoats than the average skirt salesman ever knew, presently allowed her luke-warm beef to [30] grow cold and flabby as she read. Somewhere in her subconscious mind she realized that the lanky head waitress had placed someone opposite her at the table. Also, subconsciously, she heard him order

533

liver and bacon, with onions. She told herself that as soon as she reached the bottom of the column she'd look up to see who the fool was. She never arrived at the column's end.

"I just hate to tear you away from that love lyric; but if I might trouble you for the vinegar—"

Emma groped for it back of her paper and shoved it across the table without looking up.

"—and the Worcester—"

One eye on the absorbing column, she passed the tall bottle. But at its removal her prop was gone. The *Dry Goods Review* was too weighty for the salt shaker alone.

"—and the salt. Thanks. Warm, isn't it?"

There was a double vertical frown between Emma McChesney's eyes as she glanced up over the top of her *Dry Goods Review*. The frown gave way to a half smile. The glance settled into a stare.

"But then, anybody would have stared. He expected it," she said, afterward, in telling about it. "I've seen matinée idols, and tailors' supplies salesmen, and Julian Eltinge, but this boy had any male professional beauty I ever saw, looking as handsome and dashing as a bowl of cold oatmeal. And he knew it."

Now, in the ten years that she had been out representing T. A. Buck's featherloom petticoats, Emma McChesney had found it necessary to make a rule or two for herself. In the strict observance of one of these she had become past mistress in the fine art of congealing the warm advances of fresh and friendly salesmen of the opposite sex. But this case was different, she told herself. The man across the table was little more than a boy—an amazingly handsome, astonishingly impudent, cockily confident boy, who was staring with insolent approval at Emma McChesney's trim, shirt-waisted figure, and her fresh, attractive coloring, and her well-cared-for hair beneath the smart summer hat.

"It isn't in human nature to be as good-looking as you are," spake Emma McChesney, suddenly, being a person who never trifled with half-way measures. "I'll bet you have bad teeth, or an impediment in your speech."

The gorgeous young man smiled. His teeth were perfect. "Peter Piper picked a peck of pickled peppers," he announced, glibly. "Nothing missing there, is there?"

"Must be your morals then," retorted Emma McChesney. "My! My! And on the road! Why, the trail of bleeding hearts that you must leave all the way from Maine to California would probably make the Red Sea turn white with envy."

The Fresh Young Kid speared a piece of liver and looked soulfully up into the adoring eyes of the waitress who was hovering over him.

"Got any nice hot biscuits to-night, girlie?" he inquired.

"I'll get you some; sure," wildly promised his handmaiden, and disappeared kitchenward.

"Brand new to the road, aren't you?" observed Emma McChesney, cruelly.

"What makes you think—"

"Liver and bacon, hot biscuits, Worcestershire," elucidated she. "No old-timer would commit suicide that way. After you've been out for two or three years you'll stick to the Rock of Gibraltar—roast beef, medium. Oh, I get wild now and then, and order eggs if the girl says she knows the hen that layed 'em, but plain roast beef, unchloroformed, is the one best bet. You can't go wrong if you stick to it."

The god-like young man leaned forward, forgetting to eat. "You don't mean to tell me you're on the road!"

"Why not?" demanded Emma McChesney, briskly.

"Oh, fie, fie!" said the handsome youth, throwing her a languishing look. "Any woman as pretty as you are, and with those eyes, and that hair, and figure—Say, Little One, what are you going to do to-night?"

Emma McChesney sugared her tea, and stirred it, slowly. Then she looked up. "To-night, you fresh young kid, you!" she said calmly, "I'm going to dictate two letters, explaining why business was rotten last week, and why it's going to pick up next week, and then I'm going to keep an engagement with a nine-hour beauty sleep."

"Don't get sore at a fellow. You'd take pity on me if you knew how I have to work to kill an evening in one of these little town-pump burgs. Kill 'em! It can't be done. They die harder than the heroine in a ten, twenty, thirty. From supper to bedtime is twice as long as from breakfast to supper. Honest!"

But Emma McChesney looked inexor-

able, as women do just before they relent.
Said she: "O, I don't know. By the time
I get through trying to convince a bunch
of customers that T. A. Buck's featherloom
petticoat has every other skirt in the market looking like a piece of Fourth of July
bunting that's been left out in the rain,
I'm about ready to turn down the spread
and leave a call for six-thirty."

"Be a good fellow," pleaded the un-
quenchable one. "Let's take in all the
nickel shows, and then see if we can't
drown our sorrows in—er—"

Emma McChesney slipped a coin under
her plate, crumpled her napkin, folded her
arms on the table, and regarded the boy
across the way with what our best talent
calls a long, level look. It was so long
and so level that even the airiness of the
buoyant youngster at whom it was directed
began to lessen perceptibly, long before
Emma began to talk.

"Tell me, young 'un, did anyone ever
refuse you anything? I thought not. I
should think that when you realize what
you've got to learn it would scare you to
look ahead. I don't expect you to believe
me when I tell you I never talk to fresh
guys like you, but it's true. I don't know
why I'm breaking my rule for you, unless
it's because you're so unbelievably good-
looking that I'm anxious to know where
the blemish is. The Lord don't make 'em
perfect, you know. I'm going to get out
those letters, and then, if it's just the
same to you, we'll take a walk. These
nickel shows are getting on my nerves.
It seems to me that if I have to look at
one more Western picture about a fool
girl with her hair in a braid riding a show
horse in the wilds of Clapham junction
and being rescued by a band of almost-
Indians by the handsome, but despised
Eastern tenderfoot, or if I see one more
of those historical pictures, with the women
wearing costumes that are a pass between
early Egyptian and late State Street, I
know I'll get hysterics and have to be carried shrieking, up the aisle. Let's walk
down Main Street and look in the store
windows, and up as far as the park and
back."

"Great!" assented he. "Is there a park?"

"I don't know," replied Emma McChesney, "but there is. And for your own good
I'm going to tell you a few things. There's
more to this traveling game than just
knocking down on expenses, talking to

every pretty woman you meet, and learning to ask for fresh white-bread heels at
the Palmer House in Chicago. I'll meet
you in the lobby at eight."

Emma McChesney talked steadily, and
evenly, and generously, from eight until
eight-thirty. She talked from the great
storehouse of practical knowledge which
she had accumulated in her ten years on
the road. She told the handsome young
cub many things for which he should have
been undyingly thankful. But when they
reached the park—the cool, dim, moon-
silvered park, its benches dotted with
glimpses of white showing close beside
a blur of black, Emma McChesney stopped
talking. Not only did she stop talking,
but she ceased to think of the boy seated
beside her on the bench.

In the band-stand, under the arc-light,
in the center of the pretty little square,
some neighborhood children were playing
a noisy game, with many shrill cries, and
much shouting and laughter. Suddenly,
from one of the houses across the way, a
woman's voice was heard, even above the
clamor of the children.

"Fred-dee!" called the voice. "May-
belle! Come, now."

And a boy's voice answered, as boys'
voices have since Cain was a child playing in the Garden of Eden, and as boys'
voices will as long as boys are:

"Aw, ma, I ain't a bit sleepy. We just
begun a new game, an' I'm leader. Can't
we just stay out a couple of minutes
more?"

"Well, five minutes," agreed the voice.
"But don't let me call you again."

Emma McChesney leaned back on the
rustic bench and clasped her strong, white
hands behind her head, and stared straight
ahead into the soft darkness. And if it had
been light you could have seen that the
bitter lines showing faintly about her
mouth were outweighed by the sweet and
gracious light which was glowing in her
eyes.

"Fred-dee!" came the voice of command
again. "May-belle! This minute, now!"

One by one the flying little figures under the arc-light melted away in the direction of the commanding voice and home
and bed. And Emma McChesney forgot
all about fresh young kids and featherloom petticoats and discounts and bills of
lading and sample-cases and grouchy buyers. After all, it had been her protecting

maternal instinct which had been aroused by the boy at supper, although she had not known it then. She did not know it now, for that matter. She was busy remembering just such evenings in her own life—summer evenings, filled with the high, shrill laughter of children at play. She, too, had stood in the doorway making a funnel of her hands, so that her clear call through the twilight might be heard above the cries of the boys and girls. She had known how loath the little feet had been to leave their play, and how they had lagged up the porch stairs, and into the house. Years, whose memory she had tried to keep behind her, now suddenly loomed before her in the dim quiet of the little flower-scented park.

A voice broke the silence, and sent her dream-thoughts scattering to the winds.

"Honestly, kid," said the voice, "I could be crazy about you, if you'd let me."

The forgotten figure beside her woke into sudden life. A strong arm encircled her shoulders. A strong hand seized her own which were clasped behind her head. Two warm, eager lips were pressed upon her lips, checking the little cry of surprise and wrath that rose in her throat.

Emma McChesney wrenched herself free with a violent jerk, and pushed him from her. She did not storm. She did not even rise. She sat very quietly, breathing fast. When she turned at last to look at the boy beside her it seemed that her white profile cut the darkness. The man shrank a little, and would have stammered something, but Emma McChesney checked him.

"You nasty, good-for-nothing, handsome young devil, you!" she said. "So you're married."

He sat up with a jerk. "How did you— what makes you think so?"

"That was a married kiss—a two-year-old married kiss, at least. No boy would get as excited as that about kissing an old stager like me. The chances are you're out of practice. I knew that if it wasn't teeth or impediment it must be morals. And it is."

She moved over on the bench until she was close beside him. "Now, listen to me, boy." She leaned forward, impressively. "Are you listening?"

"Yes," answered the handsome young devil, sullenly.

"What I've got to say to you isn't so much for your sake, as for your wife's.

I was married when I was eighteen, and stayed married eight years. I've had my divorce ten years, and my boy is seventeen years old. Figure it out. How old is Ann?"

"I don't believe it," he flashed back. "You're not a day over twenty-six—anyway, you don't look it. I—"

"Thanks," drawled Emma. "That's because you've never seen me in negligee. A woman's as old as she looks with her hair on the dresser, and bed only three minutes away. Do you know why I was decent to you in the first place? Because I was foolish enough to think that you reminded me of my own kid. Every fond mamma is gump enough to think that every Greek God she sees looks like her own boy, even if her own happens to squint and to have two teeth missing—which mine hasn't, thank the Lord! He's the greatest young—Well, now, look here, young 'un. I'm going to return good for evil. Traveling men and geniuses should never marry. But as long as you've done it, you might as well start right. If you move from this spot till I get through with you, I'll yell police and murder. Are you ready?"

"I'm dead sorry, on the square, I am—"

"Ten minutes late," interrupted Emma McChesney. "I'm dishing up a sermon, hot for once, and you've got to choke it down. Whenever I hear a traveling man howling about his lonesome evenings, and what a dog's life it is, and no way for a man to live, I always wonder what kind of a summer picnic he thinks it is for his wife. She's really a widow seven months in the year, without any of a widow's privileges. Did you ever stop to think what she's doing evenings? No, you didn't. Well, I'll tell you. She's sitting home, night after night, probably embroidering monograms on your shirt sleeves by way of diversion. And on Saturday night, which is the night when every married woman has the inalienable right to be taken out by her husband, she can listen to the woman in the flat upstairs getting ready to go to the theater. The fact that there's a ceiling between 'em doesn't prevent her from knowing just where they're going, and why he has worked himself into a rage over his white lawn tie, and whether they're taking a taxi or the car and who they're going to meet afterward at supper. Just by listening to them coming downstairs she can tell how much Mrs. Third Flat's silk stockings cost, and if she's wearing her new La Valliere or not. Women have that instinct, you know. Or maybe you don't. There's so much you've missed."

"Say, look here—" broke from the man beside her. But Emma McChesney laid her cool fingers on his lips.

"Nothing from the side-lines please," she said. "After they've gone she can go to bed, or she can sit up, pretending to read, but really wondering if that squeaky sound coming from the direction of the kitchen is a loose screw in the storm door, or if it's someone trying to break into the flat. And she'd rather sit there, scared green, than go back through that long hall to find out. And when Tillie comes home with her young man at eleven o'clock, though she promised not to stay out later than ten, she rushes back to the kitchen and falls on her neck, she's so happy to see her. Oh, it's a gay life. You talk about the heroism of the early Pilgrim mothers! I'd iike to know what they had on the average traveling man's wife."

"Bess goes to the matinée every Saturday," he began, in feeble defense.

"Matinée!" scoffed Emma McChesney. "Do you think any woman goes to matinée by preference? Nobody goes but girls of sixteen, and confirmed old maids without brothers, and traveling men's wifes. Matinée! Say, would you ever hesitate to choose between an all-day train and a sleeper? It's the same idea. What a woman calls going to the theater is something very different. It means taking a nap in the afternoon, so her eyes will be bright at night, and then starting at about five o'clock to dress, and lay her husband's clean things out on the bed. She loves it. She even enjoys getting his bath towels ready, and putting his shaving things where he can lay his hands on 'em. and telling the girl to have dinner ready promptly at six-thirty. It means getting out her good dress that hangs in the closet with a cretonne bag covering it, and her black satin coat, and her hat with the paradise aigrettes that she bought with what she saved out of the housekeeping money. It means her best silk stockings, and her diamond sunburst that he's going to have made over into a La Valliere just as soon as business is better. She loves it all, and her cheeks get pinker and pinker, so that she really doesn't need the little dash of

rouge that she puts on 'because everybody does it, don't you know?' She gets ready, all but her dress, and then she puts on a kimono and slips out to the kitchen to 5 make the gravy for the chicken because the girl never can get it as smooth as he likes it. That's part of what she calls going to theater, and having a husband. And if there are children—"

There came a little, inarticulate sound from the boy. But Emma's quick ear caught it.

"No? Well, then, we'll call that one black mark less for you. But if there are 15 children—and for her sake I hope there will be—she's father and mother to them. She brings them up, single-handed, while he's on the road. And the worst she can do is to say to them, 'Just wait until your 20 father gets home. He'll hear of this.' But shucks! When he comes home he can't whip the kids for what they did seven weeks before, and that they've forgotten all about, and for what he never saw, and 25 can't imagine. Besides, he wants his comfort when he gets home. He says he wants a little rest and peace, and he's darned if he's going to run around evenings. Not much, he isn't! But he doesn't object to her 30 making a special effort to cook all those little things that he's been longing for on the road. Oh, there'll be a seat in Heaven for every traveling man's wife—though at that, I'll bet most of 'em will find themselves stuck behind a post."

"You're all right!" exclaimed Emma McChesney's listener, suddenly. "How a woman like you can waste her time on the road is more than I can see. And—I want 40 to thank you. I'm not such a fool——"

"I haven't let you finish a sentence so far, and I'm not going to yet. Wait a minute. There's one more paragraph to this sermon. You remember what I told you 45 about old stagers, and the roast beef diet? Well, that applies right through life. It's all very well to trifle with the little side-dishes at first, but there comes a time when you've got to quit fooling with the minced 50 chicken, and the imitation lamb chops of this world, and settle down to plain, every-day roast beef, medium. That other stuff may tickle your palate for a while, but sooner or later it will turn on you, and 55 ruin your moral digestion. You stick to roast beef, medium. It may sound prosaic, and unimaginative and dry, but you'll find that it wears in the long run. You can take me over to the hotel now. I've lost an hour's sleep, but I don't consider it wasted. And you'll oblige me by putting the stopper on any conversation that may occur to you between here and the hotel. I've talked until I'm so low on words that I'll probably have to sell featherlooms in sign language to-morrow."

They walked to the very doors of the Berger House in silence. But at the foot of the stairs that led to the parlor floor he stopped, and looked into Emma McChesney's face. His own was rather white and tense.

"Look here," he said. "I've got to thank you. That sounds idiotic, but I guess you know what I mean. And I won't ask you to forgive a hound like me. I haven't been so ashamed of myself since I was a kid. Why, if you knew Bess—if you knew——"

"I guess I know Bess, all right. I used to be a Bess, myself. Just because I'm a traveling man it doesn't follow that I've forgotten the Bess feeling. As far as that 5 goes, I don't mind telling you that I've got neuralgia from sitting in that park with my feet in the damp grass. I can feel it in my back teeth, and by eleven o'clock it will be camping over my left eye, with its 10 little brothers doing a war dance up the side of my face. And boy, I'd give last week's commissions if there was someone to whom I had the right to say: 'Henry, will you get up and get me a hot-water bag 15 for my neuralgia? It's something awful. And just open the left-hand lower drawer of the chiffonier and get me out one of those gauze vests and then get me a safety pin from the tray on my dresser. I'm going 20 to pin it around my head.'"

LI

BEN AMES WILLIAMS (1889–   )

The latest depicter of northern New England country and village life has been Ben Ames Williams, a graduate of Dartmouth in the class of 1910. With the small community, "Fraternity," as his center he has depicted seemingly every phase of character and every variety of situation possible for such an environment. He has done this apparently with realism, with intimate knowledge of all his material, yet he has not been depressed like Dreiser and Anderson and Masters. His pictures on the whole are cheerful and clean. He finds village life prevailingly healthful and often ideal. There is an atmosphere in his best work that may even be called romantic: his villains are generally foiled, worth triumphs, and in the end justice usually reigns.

The final place of Williams as a creator of fiction is not yet fully determined. He is in extreme danger of over-production. Having made short-story writing his profession, it has become necessary for him to think constantly in terms of quantity. Almost weekly must come the story for *The Saturday Evening Post* or other magazine. He thus may be taken as a type of the latter-day professional producer of short fiction: the journalizer of the short story. Like many others of the younger group, he has discarded most of the conventional rules, and it is probable that he has discarded too many of them. Often his tales are mere "feature" articles of the newspaper variety dashed off in haste like work for a city daily, to be thrown away with the paper when the day is ended. It is possible that it presages the final fate of the short-story form.

THE ARTIST *

The hotel was so old and so excellent that it was deservedly venerated; it was a local institution and men spoke of it as they did of their clubs. Its accommodations were in many respects archaic; but the cuisine and service were perfection. The main dining-room was largely patronized, and by persons of discrimination; but to the initiate there was a particular charm about the café called The Oak Room, situated below the level of the main floor, where there were soft, leather-padded benches about the walls and long oak tables glossy with the pleasant patina of age and use, and where Hamel was the presiding genius.

Hamel was relatively a young man. Many of us could remember him as bus boy and as waiter. His reign had begun no more than half a dozen years ago, but there was such an air of permanence about him that most people thought he had been where he was for a long time, and if you had asked them to hazard a guess they

would have predicated that he would continue there forever. He was by nature almost startlingly suited to his rôle; and he brought to his responsibilities a definite devotion which ripened in the course of his tenure into a mature and lasting passion.

Like so many men who display this capacity for surrendering themselves to their work, he was small of stature and comparatively insignificent in appearance. He was no doubt of some obscure mid-European blood, since he spoke with a suggestion of accent; but it is usual to think of mid-Europeans as dark, while Hamel was fair. He was small and blond, his hair the color of pale corn, and his eyes a pallid and wistful blue. He wore a mustache; this perhaps in some effort to counteract the ineradicable boyishness of his appearance. But the effect was the contrary of that which he intended; since this mustache, instead of being crisp and curt as he no doubt liked to fancy it was, was soft as down and only a shade darker than his hair. The mouth below it was easy and sensitive, the lower lip so full it seemed always faintly drooping, as though he were a boy wilting under some sharp reproof.

When, as occasionally happens in even the best regulated establishments, some mischance occurred and was brought to his attention, his eyes were apt to assume an expression which accorded with this sensitive and quivering lip, so that you half expected the man to weep. The fact that he never actually reached this emotional pitch failed to nullify the expectation.

He was, for all this apparent sensibility to hurt, the absolute autocrat of his dominion, and wielded an authority which had matured through the years until there were now none to question it. When he first assumed charge of the service in the café, he was in the eyes of the powers an experiment, and even a doubtful one. But he proceeded, during the course of months, to demonstrate his ability. He ruled at first by gentle means, by persuading his subordinates to see the justice of the small changes which he proposed. At the end of some fifteen months, most of those under him were ready enough to let him have the direction of affairs. The only serious opposition came from the cook, a man of parts, but a man who had been in the cafe kitchen for more than twenty years and who was both arrogant and proud. He and Hamel had more than one minor clash; but Hamel always skilfully avoided a major engagement until the time came when he was ready to try his power.

The issue came over the matter of what soup should be served to a private dinner party which had been put in Hamel's hands for arrangement. He ordered clam bisque. The cook argued in favor of a clear soup, but Hamel yielded not an inch. Nevertheless, when the dinner was served, it was clear soup which was delivered to the waiters. Hamel made no comment at the time; he was always careful to do nothing which might disturb his patrons. But after the café was empty he went to the cook and invited the man to join him in taking the matter before their superiors. The cook profanely declined. Hamel replied that if the other refused to accompany him, he would go alone; and under this threat the cook was constrained to agree. Hamel put his case and required either a formal submission and pledge of future obedience or the discharge of the cook.

The victory was not easily won. The cook had friends, and a combative spirit. Negotiations continued for three days; but at the end of that time Hamel delivered a crushing blow. With one hand he produced another cook whose excellence he guaranteed; with the other he offered his own resignation. Victory rested upon his banners, and thereafter his authority was never seriously questioned; his power was absolute.

He deserved the confidence thus bestowed upon him by using his authority, not arrogantly, but with stern justice. A waiter who failed in neatness disappeared within the hour. Clumsy service he sometimes condoned—for a time. Even forgetfulness he could excuse if the culprit showed improvement. But upon neatness and cleanliness he insisted, and upon deference to the patrons of the restaurant. The result was in the first place a steady improvement in the service, and in the second the establishment of a morale, an esprit as a result of which the kitchen and café drew the most efficient servitors from all over the city. To have been employed under Hamel and with honor was to wear a laurel wreath upon the brow.

It was rather curious that, this being the case, Hamel was the object of some mild derision even from his direct subordinates, and in larger measure from the bell boys, the door man, and the other employees. Perhaps his unimpressive stature seemed to make him a fair target; perhaps it was an embarrassed resentment to which his insistence upon perfection provoked them. The little man was not particularly articulate, had not always words to express the ideal toward which he strove. His single and all-embracing phrase was familiar; he used to say:

"We want everything to be nice. You know, nice."

And this phrase was habitually accompanied by a spreading gesture of the hands which was extraordinarily inclusive. But if he could not put into words the essence of his art, he could at least express himself in his work. If you wished to invite a friend to luncheon you had only to telephone Hamel. His voice over the telephone was crisp and efficient.

"Yes, sir." . . . "Luncheon to-day, yes sir." . . . "One thirty." . . . "A gentleman." . . . "Everything will be ready, sir. Yes sir, and I'll see that everything is nice."

You had no need—unless your tastes were particular—to go into details; it was perfectly safe to leave such matters to him.

There would be flowers on the table, relishes, a light soup, fish or perhaps a chop, coffee that was perfection; and cigarettes or the cigars which you were known to prefer would be passed to your guests at the fitting time. At some stage of the luncheon, Hamel himself would appear inconspicuously at your elbow to ask:

"Everything all right, sir?" And to your grateful nod he would respond with pleased humility: "We tried to have everything nice."

He took especial pride in arranging the details of a private dinner party, whether it were to be served in the café or in one of the small dining rooms which were a part of his domain. Pad and pencil in hand he consulted your wishes, suggesting and advising here and there, informing you whether there were particularly choice viands in the larder, recommending this dish, or that, or the other; and when the hour arrived and you were served, he was at hand, in the background but attentive, hungry for what small scrap of thanks or appreciation you were minded to give him. His zeal was not mercenary; he was notorious for his reluctance to accept a tip. The waiters who served under him, knowing quite well that anything given to the head waiter is apt to come out of their pockets, approved of this habit on his part and it was responsible for no small share of the hold he had on them. He was as grateful for a generous tip to one of them as though you had given it to himself, seconded the man's thanks with his own and took so much the greater pains to serve you when next you gave him the opportunity. I once asked him why he refused gratuities; he smiled in a deprecating way as he replied.

"It pleases me to have everything nice, without that," he explained. "I like people to be satisfied, and when they are satisfied, then so am I. That is all. Besides . . ." This with a careless gesture. "I do not need the money."

He managed, at such times, to give a curious impression of affluence and ease, as though his service here were a pleasant hobby rather than a profession.

The high spots of the year were for him those occasions—Christmas, New Year's, Valentine's day or the like—when the café served a special dinner. At such times he even supervised the work of the orchestra; he made sure that you were personally informed of the opportunity for dancing in the assembly hall upstairs; he distributed favors—masks and paper caps or hats, —with a childlike delight; he invited you to take home the flowers that were set upon each table; he beamed upon you with a jovial good cheer almost too great for his small countenance to carry. And now and then you heard his whisper in your ear:

"Everything very nice, isn't it, sir? A nice dinner, yes?" And when you agreed with him he beamed again.

Hamel was an extraordinarily confiding man, and he seemed to find a keen pleasure in telling you about his private affairs. He lived, he used to say, in a beautiful apartment overlooking the river. His wife, he assured those who would listen, was the most beautiful and gracious of women. "She's like me," he would assure you. "She likes everything nice. You wouldn't believe to see how pretty things are at home. Everything just so. She's not satisfied unless it is. I tell her to go out more, to leave things a little, not to work so hard; but she's that way. Hard to please. I tell you, sir, she makes me be careful. You think I am particular and all that, but you should hear the way she talks to me."

This was, we agreed, not incredible. Zealous as Hamel was, he was after all a man; and no man can bring neatness and order to the point which is natural to some women.

He sometimes described the beautiful rugs, the carefully chosen furniture in this apartment of his. He must have known something of such matters, for he spoke of Phyfe and Sheraton; ancient Persian names came trippingly from his tongue; his collection of early glass was, by his own report, small but extraordinarily choice. Now and then the incredulous asked how he could afford such things.

"They're investments, you see," he used to say. "Better than bonds in the bank, because they increase in value faster than the interest on your money. I'm careful when I buy to get everything nice. That's the way, you see."

In the course of half a dozen years he built up in this wise a beautiful and luxurious background for himself. Now and then someone, faintly curious to see the wonders of which Hamel spoke, suggested that he invite some of us to his apartment; but the little man at such suggestions was accustomed to smile in a deprecating way and say humbly:

"But no, you see. It's very nice for me, but that is always another thing. Besides, I must not put more work upon Mrs. Hamel. She is not so well just now."

He was not an inventive man, and this phrase: "Mrs. Hamel is not so well just now," became as much a part of the ritual as his insistence that everything be nice. We got an impression that Mrs. Hamel was a small, energetic, but rather frail woman whose ordinary duties occupied her zealous industry to the point of exhaustion; that she waited upon Hamel and attended his wants with an ardor which left her depleted and weary. I sometimes wondered whether it was in a futile but eternal effort to meet his standards that Mrs. Hamel wore herself out. Hamel was a mild man enough; but he could also be stern. He had the true temperament of an artist, derived from the arrangement and supervision of a beautiful dinner as keen pleasure as a painter derives from the production of a masterpiece. To have "everything nice" was his passion and his creed; and I thought that this insistence on his part might exhaust Mrs. Hamel. But he spoke of her so fondly and so proudly that for the most part we accepted the picture of him basking contentedly in the perfection with which she surrounded him.

One day we missed him, and inquiry revealed the fact that he had suffered an accident. The service elevator, like everything else in the establishment, was old and venerable; but it had the eccentricities of age and Hamel had stepped into it to descend to the basement where the larder was; its mechanism failed and the cage dropped some fifteen feet to the bottom of the shaft. The jar of the fall shattered his right leg above the knee; shock and pain rendered him mercifully unconscious, and he was removed in an ambulance to the nearest hospital. Thence, a few days later, to his home—so we heard—for the lengthy process of recovery. We sent him flowers, a dozen of us subscribing; then the routine of our lives went on very much the same as before.

It was surprising to see how quickly, with Hamel absent, the service in the café began to deteriorate. The man put in his place was one of the waiters who under Hamel had always been efficient and capable; but this man, who had done very well as a subordinate, proved his inadequacy to the position of commander in chief. He showed a gluttinous eagerness for tips; he argued with the other waiters in tones sufficiently loud so that their altercations disturbed our peace; he attempted to chide the cook and was set in his place for his pains. And he confided to us that Hamel would not be able to return for weeks and suggested that he might not return at all. He let us understand quite frankly that he was ambitious to replace the little man and solicited our support even while he failed in his duty to see that we were properly served. For a while we endured; but the contrast between him and Hamel emphasized in our eyes the little man's excellences; and we discussed the situation over the luncheon table. It was Waldron who said one day:

"The plain fact is, I knew Hamel was good, but I didn't realize just how good he was. They say any man's place can be filled; but he's left a hole that is still a hole."

There were eight of us around the board, the big circular table in the middle of the café where the regular luncheon patrons were apt to gather. Ames agreed with Waldron, and proceeded to recount some of Hamel's virtues, while we nodded in assent. Graves said:

"I'm glad we sent him those flowers. But I, for one, am going to see to it that he gets some more of the same, every day or two. The little chap was fond of flowers. Remember how he used to beam when we admired them on the tables."

"I sent him a bunch myself day before yesterday," Ames confessed.

"We'll take turns at it," Graves suggested. "Wonder if he'd like something to read. I expect he's fretting at being kept at home."

"It's probably making things hard for Mrs. Hamel," I reminded them. "A woman like that, a fastidious housekeeper, hates to have her home upset. And there's nothing more upsetting than to have a man around all day."

"We might chip in and send him away somewhere to rest up," Ames suggested.

"Oh, I feel sure he would prefer to stay at home," Randolph urged hurriedly. "Remember how proud he was of his place. Probably he's really having time to enjoy it for the first time in his life."

Some of us smiled at this; for Randolph's frugality was well known. At the same time, what he said accorded with our own estimates of Hamel's character. It was Durkin, big Durkin, who owns an enormous butcher shop in the market district, from which he emerges every noon to lunch with us, who made the next suggestion. I had not given Durkin credit for so much imagination. His business is not an esthetic one; and he wears, somehow, the look of a butcher. A huge, broad man, bulky and thick, with cropped hair above a wide, red face from which gleamed his small blue eyes. Yet he said now:

"I'd like to send him one of these antiques, or a rug, or something; the sort of stuff he likes. If I knew enough about such things to pick 'em out."

A little silence greeted the proposal; a silence in which our thoughts recognized how apt it was, and considered ways and means. Ames was the first to speak. "That beats everything we could do," he agreed. "Durkin, you've hit it."

Randolph, who is New England born and bred, objected: "It would run into money."

"No more than we'd spend on flowers, if he's at home six weeks or so," Ames reminded him.

"The eight of us here could manage some little thing," I urged. "Hamel would appreciate the thought as much as the deed."

"Ought to be something particularly nice," Durkin reminded us. "Something he's maybe wanted."

"We might consult Mrs. Hamel and find out what he has wanted," Graves proposed; but Ames objected to that.

"She'd let it out. We want to surprise him."

"He likes things nice," Durkin said again, unconsciously adopting Hamel's own phrase.

The plan did not mature that day, nor the next. But we discussed it pro and con, and the project grew upon us. Our enthusiasm, perhaps, carried us away. We at first thought of contributing five dollars apiece; it was at once obvious that this was insufficient, that forty dollars would buy nothing of importance. Not from the point of view of a man like Hamel, somewhat of a connoisseur. We considered ten. Then Durkin reminded us that Hamel never accepted tips from any one of us; that we could afford to lump the tips we might

otherwise have given him. Randolph thought ten dollars was enough; Durkin, blushing a little at his own prodigality, suggested fifty. In the end we agreed upon twenty-five dollars as a rough figure; decided we would spend somewhere around two hundred dollars, dividing the sum equally among us. Randolph, the only reluctant one, was brought to agree; but he would, he insisted, go no higher than twenty-five.

The question of what to buy divided us for a long time. Graves knew something about rugs; Martin had some familiarity with Colonial furniture; but it was Durkin again who displayed the practical mind.

"Cross out rugs," he urged. "You know Hamel. A rug from us he'd want to hang on the wall and keep nice. We want something he can use every day, and value too. Who's the best antique dealer in town?"

We looked toward Martin, who answered without hesitation: "Pomeroy! He has the best stuff, and he's honest."

"Let's go to Pomeroy, then," Durkin advised. "Tell him how much we want to spend and put it up to him."

Durkin had this ability to hit upon a suggestion so eminently sensible that there was no opposing it. We at once adopted the measure he proposed, finding reasons to support it, half inclined to believe we had ourselves devised the plan. We thought of going in a body to Pomeroy; but there was no hour convenient for all of us. Durkin said he would not go.

"I don't know anything about things like that," he reminded us.

But we agreed that his judgment was what we needed; and he eventually said he could be at Pomeroy's at four that afternoon. Ames would be there, and Martin, and I saw my way clear to go. The others agreed to leave the decision to us, but Randolph reminded us that we were on no account to exceed the maximum limit. We liked Randolph, in spite of this well recognized trait in the man. Ames and I, departing together, decided that he would probably turn up at Pomeroy's to enforce the limitation.

We were not surprised, therefore, when he appeared at a little past four. Pomeroy had heard our desires and had taken an instant interest; said he knew Hamel himself, and liked him. The dealer was not a regular patron of the café, but I remembered having seen the man there.

"Hamel comes in here sometimes," he explained. "But he's never bought anything of me. Of course, my prices are high. But he likes to look around the shop."

Durkin asked: "Anything here he has particularly wanted?"

So Pomeroy produced the clock. Such matters are Greek to me, but I remember he said this was rare and remarkable. "An antique dealer bought it in Maine," he explained. "Paid fifteen dollars for it. Thought it might be good, so sent Wales a description." Wales, I knew, was the proprietor of another shop in town. "Wales paid him seventy-five dollars, and the Maine man bragged about his deal. But Wales had the clock fixed up and I was glad to pay him two twenty-five. I'm asking four, and it's worth more."

Randolph spoke promptly. "That's over our limit," he said.

"The clock's in running order," Pomeroy rejoined. "I had it overhauled. It's worth five."

"We're not paying over two hundred," Randolph insisted stubbornly.

Durkin spoke. "There are eight of us buying this," he told Pomeroy. "You're in business for a profit, but you can afford to advertise. It would pay you to let us have this at what it cost you.

"I paid thirty dollars to have it overhauled," Pomeroy replied.

"Say two fifty," Durkin suggested.

"We agreed not to go over two hundred," Randolph protested, almost angrily. "That's why I came up here to-day. I expected you to lose your heads."

"I'll take the extra fifty, personally," Durkin said in a mild voice. Martin shook his head.

"We'll split it," he corrected. "Letting Randolph out for his twenty-five, if he wants it that way." Randolph is wealthy; his distress was mildly amusing.

"I didn't say that," he protested, flushing. "Besides, Mr. Pomeroy wants more than two fifty."

Pomeroy may have wished to discomfit Randolph; he may have sought to emulate Durkin's generosity; or he may have been moved by the situation itself. At any rate he said easily: "No, I'll take two fifty. I'm sacrificing that much profit, but after all, I'm not losing anything."

"Wrap it up," said Durkin promptly.

I suggested engraving a legend upon the back of the case; but Martin set me right.

"This is an old clock," he told me. "That's it's charm. Hamel won't need to be reminded who gave it to him; he'll prefer it as it is."

This seemed reasonable, and Pomeroy agreed. He undertook to deliver the clock, cleaned and in order, at the café next day, so that we might inspect it over the luncheon table and plan the presentation. Durkin wrote a check, and the rest of us reached for pocket books to pay our shares. Randolph, now the issue was decided, was the first to speak.

"That's thirty-one and a quarter each," he said, and handed Durkin his full share.

Durkin accepted it without comment; but Randolph seemed to feel easier and we were all glad the matter had been thus adjusted.

The clock was waiting for us next day; we lunched in one of the small private dining rooms so that we might examine it at our ease; and we decided to go with it to Hamel's flat that afternoon. Engagements that interfered were canceled by telephone; we were all, I think, as pleased and eager as children. Ames knew Hamel's address. We took taxicabs and gave the drivers street and number; and during the ride, down into the West End of town, we pleased ourselves by guessing what Hamel's reaction to the gift would be.

The apartment house proved to be a fairly modern structure, not without charm, with letter boxes and speaking tubes in the entrance. Graves, who is the city editor of one of the morning papers, said:

"We'll surprise him, not let him know who we are. His suite's number twelve." And he pressed the button of suite number fourteen. The latch clicked and we went in.

The small automatic elevator would only accommodate four of us at a time. Durkin and Ames and Graves and I went up first, Durkin carrying the clock. Then the cage descended to bring up the others. We found ourselves confronting the door of Hamel's suite, and spoke in whispers while we waited for our companions. No sound came from behind the closed door. The elevator rose again, and Graves knocked, and Hamel's voice from within called us to enter. Graves opened the door and we followed him into the apartment.

I remember quite well the curious sense of incredulity which assailed me in that first moment. I had formed a very definite mental picture of what we should find; expected a small, well appointed flat, beautifully furnished, beautifully kept, quiet and luxurious. But the door let us into a narrow hall, filled with the unmistakable stale odor of fried onions. The hall was dark, shadowed at its inner end by curtains. I saw a hole in one of them, not worn, but torn by some violence; and when I brushed against them, entering the living room, dust filled the air. The living room itself struck me as a whole; remained as a whole in my memories thereafter. Yet I can still see details. A stain of ink upon the floor at one side. An inexpressibly cheap and ugly carpet in need of cleaning, scuffed over at one border so that the lower side showed. A yellow oak writing desk, open, revealing a woman's handkerchief and lip stick, an old newspaper, and some disordered letters. A rocking chair of Mission oak, and a Morris chair, each vaguely dilapidated. Tacked to the walls, Rotogravure pictures from one of the Sunday papers, and a cheaply framed oil painting of two oranges and an apple. A poor reproduction of September Morn with a stocking hanging over the wire at its back. The table in the middle of the room was of oak, littered with the disorderly belongings of a woman. Her high-heeled slipper, in need of polish, lay on its side under the table. The whole room wore an atmosphere of shiftless neglect.

Hamel was not in this room but in the next, the dining room. We had all paused, huddling in an abashed group, till he called to us:

"Who is it? You, Sophie?"

We looked at one another, the same thought, the thought of flight, in every mind. But Durkin was brave.

"No, Hamel," he replied, and stepped toward the connecting door. "Some of us dropped in to see how you were getting along."

There was a moment's silence; the silence, it seemed to me, of consternation. I followed Durkin and saw Hamel's face, drained of color, drawn and ghastly. He lay upon a cot by the window, a pillow under his head, his leg stiffly outstretched in its bandages. The bandages were soiled, as though they needed changing. He stared at us, and I saw his lips work and his lower lip droop and there were tears at last in his eyes. He looked from Durkin to me, and then to each of the others in

turn; and each time his eyes moved with a slow effort, like one forced to look upon fresh horrors while the vision is still shocked with those it has already seen. But he managed at last to speak.

"Your coming . . . You're very nice," he said, huskily.

Durkin wiped his forehead with his handkerchief. "Well, how you feeling?" he inquired.

"Oh, but I am feeling very well," Hamel assured us, seizing at the question, answering almost hungrily, as though the commonplace words were a relief. "Yes, I'm doing nicely."

"You're looking pretty good," Durkin told him.

There was a momentary pause that seemed interminable. I could not speak. My consciousness was filled with the squalor of this room, the soiled dishes still on the table, the chairs in disorder, the linoleum on the floor, the aroma of stale food which came through the open door from the kitchen. Another door revealed a bedroom and I could see the bed, unmade, a woman's stays on the floor by the foot. The others were like me, stunned and silent. Randolph was the first to recover. He had a poise hard to shake; and he stepped into the fearful silence.

"Hamel," he said, in a tone of friendly courtesy. "We have missed you. The Oak Room is not the same without you. We wanted to see you. That's why we came to-day. But also we wanted you to understand the very real regard in which we hold you, and so we have brought you this." He took the clock from Durkin's unresisting hands. "Something to remind you that we are missing you, Hamel." He began to strip away the wrappings, and the crackling of the paper was grateful, since it kept silence at bay. So presently he revealed the clock and set it on the table before Hamel. Hamel, quite obviously, could not speak, so Randolph said quietly: "I think you will find it keeps excellent time."

He stepped back, and I saw his fingers twitch with the strain. His eyes met mine appealingly, and I stammered:

"We miss you every day, Hamel."

Durkin cleared his throat loudly. "You've got to hurry and get back," he urged.

Ames took a hand. "Place isn't the same," he testified.

"No sir," Martin confirmed.

"Anything we can do . . ." Graves seemed pleased with this innovation, this new direction which he had given the conversation. Hamel was crying, and we could not look at him, so we looked at one another. "Yes sir, anything you want," Graves repeated.

"Just let us know," I said.

"Call us up, any of us," Durkin urged.

"Or drop me a line," Ames amended.

The subject exhausted itself. Durkin discovered a new angle.

"If you need a doctor, or anything," he suggested. "We could send some one."

"Or a nurse?" Graves proposed. Then he turned white with horror, because the suggestion seemed to imply a doubt that Hamel was having proper care, and thus to accuse the absent Mrs. Hamel. We looked at Graves ferociously; and Hamel himself was driven to speech by this.

"Mrs. Hamel takes care of me," he said brokenly. "She does everything. She's not very well, and it's hard work for her. . . ."

"You look mighty comfortable," Durkin assured him.

Hamel gathered courage. "The clock's nice," he said. "It's too much. I've seen it, at Pomeroy's. It's too much for me."

We were in the midst of protestations, setting his mind at rest on this point, when Mrs. Hamel returned. The outer door opened with some violence, silencing us; we stood like culprits, and I saw Hamel's eye, full of dread, watching for her appearance. Then she came to the dining room door and saw us. She was a large woman, older than Hamel I should have said. Her hair was unnaturally golden, her garments extravagantly in the mode. There was too much color on her cheeks; and the red upon her lips failed to conceal the cruelty of her mouth. The sight of us silenced her for a moment; then she saw our confusion, as a woman will, and regained her assurance. Looked at Hamel and asked in a harsh voice:

"Who are these guys?"

"They're gentlemen from the café," Hamel said softly. He looked at Durkin and took courage. "My friends," he added. "They came to bring me this clock."

She perceived our gift upon the table and walked toward it, brushing past us, stripping off her gloves; and she picked up the clock and looked at it. "It ain't running," she said accusingly.

"It needs winding only," Randolph assured her gently.

"It looks like a relic to me," she remarked.

"It is an antique, a very nice clock," Hamel protested.

"I been planning to get a clock, one of them under a glass bowl," Mrs. Hamel commented. "Maybe I could exchange this. Do you think?" She set the old clock down jarringly. "Where'd you get it?" she asked us directly.

Hamel said, smiling pitifully: "I expect you'll like it after a while, Sophie." He met our eyes, dignity in his. "It was nice of you to come," he said.

We perceived our dismissal; and, almost defiantly, under that woman's scornful eye, we made our individual farewells to him; and each in turn we bowed politely to her. She followed us only as far as the door between dining room and living room; as we withdrew through the dark little hall she called: "One of you shut the door."

Durkin brought up our rear. Before he drew the door closed, we heard her say to Hamel: "I s'pose I can pawn the damned thing."

No one was willing to wait for a second trip by the elevator; so half of us walked down the sairs to the street floor. Outside the apartment, by common consent we hurried away toward the corner, and not till we were out of sight of Hamel's windoms did we pause.

"We can get taxis here," Graves told us. For a moment we stood still, looking up and down the street.

It was Ames who first made comment. "Poor devil," he murmured.

Graves, a practical man, smiled grimly. "He's an artistic liar, anyway," he suggested.

Martin's remark was more sympathetic. "You know," he reminded us. "The man is an artist. He expresses himself in his work. That sort of thing . . ." He nodded his head back toward Hamel's flat. "It must irk him pretty badly."

"He stood up for her," I reminded them. "He's a loyal little chap."

It was Durkin, as always, who put the thing so clearly that there was nothing more to add.

"He's just a damned brave man," he said.

BARRY BENEFIELD

The short-story work of Barry Benefield, long confined to the magazines and recognized as unusual only by a few judicious readers, came into quick prominence after the success of his first novel, *The Chicken-Wagon Family*, in 1925. The collection of tales which followed in 1926, *Short Turns*, became one of the notable short-story volumes of the year.

Texas is the native state of this new arrival in the fictional field. He was born at Jefferson, Texas, in the area deriving from New Orleans rather than from Dallas or Fort Worth. A year after his graduation from the University of Texas, a year spent as reporter on a local journal, he went to New York, and for eight years was on the staff of the New York *Times*. Later he became advertising manager for a New York publishing house, resigning at length to devote all of his time to fiction.

As a short-story writer Benefield combines the artistry and *finesse* of O. Henry with the sympathy and the human touch of a Sarah Orne Jewett. He uses for his backgrounds the rural areas of the Texas hinterland, but it is a gentle world that he reveals, not the Texas of the cow-boy and the desperado. Like Willa Cather, he deals often with the lowest elements of humanity yet never with coarseness. It is as a lover of his native region that he writes, and it is as a gentle soul seeing good even in the bad that he exhibits to his readers his varied scenes and personalities.

WIND IN THE PINES *

Old Melschott drove his wagon up to the station at 10:15, though the train was not due until 11:30 and was always late; but he wanted to be sure he was there when Myrtle came back. If he should, by any chance, be a few minutes late, she might think he was being revengeful because she had run away with his farm-hand and been away four years.

Besides, in the infinitesimal little town half a mile down the red hill there was nothing and nobody to interest him particularly now. Coming to Crebillon the previous day, and spending the night in the wagon-yard, he had got up early and done his complicated Christmas shopping, including laboriously equalized presents for both Myrtle and Lydia.

His shopping worries were over. He was wondering whether Myrtle, being now forty-five and perhaps worn with remorse and work, were not getting gray and aged; and telling himself that he must not forget to say that she looked fine and fit no matter how she really looked; and resolving that he would act just as if she were returning from an innocent visit somewhere; and trying desperately to prepare for the pas-

* Copyright by the Century Co.

sionate jealous-hearted woman's meeting, down home, with Lydia, of whom she did not know, yet.

The sight of the small red station, 5 through which Myrtle and Luther had no doubt passed in their flight four years before, roused a flare of anger from ashes within him that he had long since thought dead. For a moment he charged himself 10 with being a too soft-hearted fool for jeopardizing the peace and comfort of the tender, trusting Lydia.

Still, he knew that if he had a son or a daughter—if Myrtle had had any chil-15 dren maybe she wouldn't have hated them so much—if he *had* a son or daughter, and they had written that they were homesick, he would also have said to them, "Come home," no matter where they were, or what 20 they had done, or how many others had come in to fill their places, or how much strategic fighting he would have to do to make their coming and their stay as pleasant as possible. And surely she that *had* 25 been his loyal wife for eighteen years— Besides, no matter what had happened, he wanted Myrtle back; only he could *not* give up Lydia now. Lydia he felt sure of; Myrtle filled him with fear. But he was 30 master of his own house.

Old Melschott was not old, very old;

he was forty-nine. The epithet had been applied to him by the predominating Anglo-Saxon population of the upper Louisiana county, partly in affection because of his patient unvarying amiability, partly in derision because, in spite of his twenty-six years on a farm among them, he was still slightly foreign, different from them, therefore inferior. The touch of his Teutonic fathers yet lingered in an occasional turn of speech, and in a naïve habit of deciding on a course of conduct in accordance with reasons entirely his own, and no others, and stubbornly sticking to it.

The tall, thin, brown-faced farmer stopped his wagon in a dusty grove of white-oak trees near the station, and getting down broke a bundle of fodder before each of the mules. He slapped their necks gently, and the big awkward animals rubbed their noses against his shoulder, making away down in their throats the mule's rare approximation of affectionate purring. The little black fise-dog, so fat and aged that her watery brown eyes bulged out of her faintly gray face, stood before the mules barking in feeble asthmatic jealousy.

"Come, Sister," Old Melschott said, bending down and giving her a compensating pat. "We go to de station now. Somebody comes to-day. You know, hey? So-o! You are glad already? Dat is good, Sister. Also we make her glad—if we can."

There was no sun, and the cold December wind, spiked with the freezing moisture in the air, cut Old Melschott to the bone, and he yielded now and then to an attack of coughing. Through the window of the waiting-room he saw a red-hot stove, but he stood his ground outside, stamping his feet and rubbing his hands; for he had a vague fear that if he went inside the train might rush in and discharge Myrtle before he could get out to her, so that for a moment she would be disappointed and worried.

He was presently proud of his caution. A lonely member of that tremendous universal army of train-gazers drifted through the grove of trees and rested his long leaning figure against the station wall several feet away. His eyes rested fondly on the rails in front of him, and on them his imagination slid quickly away to far, mysterious, fascinating countries beyond the distant rim of black forest. After a while he roused himself, effortfully dragging his imagination back to the prosaic little town.

"She goes a-tearin' when she do come," he said grandly, as if somebody had questioned the prodigious powers of the northbound express.

"So?" said Old Melschott uneasily. "But she always stops here, ain't it?"

"Yeah, she stops—if there's anybody to git on or off. But she don't stop nowheres long; except, I reckon, maybe in big cities —Little Rock, Pine Bluff, an' the like of them."

The red stove inside the waiting-room wasted its sweetness on desert air, for the two gray-bearded men stood their ground outside, blowing white shafts of warm breath upon their cold hands, anxiously awaiting their boyhood sweethearts.

The train-gazer's swift sweetheart gave notice finally of her approach. A dim whistle came floating through the woods from the south.

"Carpeaux's Crossin'," the ardent gazer interrupted, lifting himself from against the wall of the station, his greenish-sallow face all aglow with excitement.

Presently there came a series of louder whistles.

"Cow on the track," he said, listening in the strain of suspense at the train's adventurous flight northward.

Then there came two short, snorty, saucy whistles.

"Dead cow," he pronounced with the restraint of infallibility, no grief in his voice, only passionate triumph.

The dull roar of her progress through the wooded flats to the south of the town was suddenly still.

"She waits at the L. P. & T. T. crossin'," said her lover, mortified that she should have to wait at a dinky lumber railroad's intersecting track. But presently she was roaring on again northward. She sent ahead three long blasts.

"My god! She's got a passenger for here!"

When the furious little engine stopped, wheezing, panting, clanking, in front of the Crebillon station, the gazer ran forward to be as near as possible to her dear cylinders and marvelous round wheels that had traveled and would travel so far beyond the rim of the black forest. The station-master rushed out with a truck to the baggage-car. Old Melschott, caught in this tidal wave of activity, went racing along the two passenger-cars looking eagerly up at the faces staring out of the windows.

"Fred!" He heard it back of him, and turning, saw Myrtle standing by the steps of the first coach. Going toward her, he wondered whether he had a right to kiss her.

"Hello, Fred," she said when he came up to her. Her voice was hardly above a whisper, and she was scrutinizing his face anxiously. "How is your cold, Fred?" She merely held out her hand to him. "Are you doin' anything for that cough, Fred?"

"Hel-lo, Myrtle!" Old Melschott almost shouted, beaming upon her. "Ach, me? I am fine. How are you? I *am* glad to see you again, Myrtle. You are good for de sore eyes. You look *fine*, Myrtle, finer as ever. See! Sister is glad also. See how she yump up, Myrtle?"

Paying no attention to the feebly frolicking little dog, twisting her mouth into a faint smile, the faded blond woman handed him her suitcase and stood by his side, intent on getting away from the station as soon as possible. They hurried toward the wagon, leaving the forlorn train-gazer sadly watching his fiery little sweetheart getting in motion to leave him.

On the way out to the grove of trees, Old Melschott noticed, sorrowfully, that Myrtle's pale hair *was* getting gray, that her skin was sallow, that there were baggy puffs under her big pale-blue eyes, and that a flabby fatness was breaking, here and there, the clean lines of that splendid clear-cut figure of which she—and he—had been so proud. And there was an indefinite slovenliness about her clothes and hands and hair that surprised him. He had thought that no matter what happened Myrtle would always be fastidiously tidy. He wondered what kind of work she had been doing since she and Luther had gone their separate ways.

But he determined not to let her see that he was disappointed. Anyway, if she stayed on the farm long, she would have a chance to pick up. Maybe she only needed a rest—yes, he was *sure* of it—to become the massive but magnificent Myrtle of the old days. And he was glad she would not need to do the cooking, or the washing, or any hard work.

But he was not talking enough. "Attention, Friedrich!" he shouted in his mind to himself. "You say somedings now, or she sees dat *you* see and be pained."

"Look, Myrtle!" he said enthusiastically, pointing to the two mules. "See Nell and Minkie; yust de same, yust de same as when—"

"I ran away, like a dog."

"Ach, no, Myrtle; I say as when we bought dem—except a little older."

"Five years older, Fred, five years. They were three then. It don't seem like mules change their looks much, as people do. They go on gettin' old without nobody noticin' it; then they die."

There was something disturbing in the brittle yet faintly tremulous tone of the big blond woman, who was wont to be so independent and self-reliant; and Old Melschott hurried to help her into the wagon and wrap her up warmly in a blanket. When she had convinced him finally that she was comfortable, he smiled up at her rubbed his hands happily together, muttered, "So," several times as if the first stage in a joyous undertaking had been satisfactorily achieved, and bustled around hitching up the traces and wagon-tongue that had been let down for the greater comfort of the mules during their wait.

Presently he was up on the seat beside her, Sister and the trunk were in the back part of the wagon, and the journey home had begun. He noticed fearfully that Myrtle scrupulously kept a space of a few inches between him and her. He remembered that night, twenty-two years before, when he had brought her home from the wedding in the church. *That* night—

He wondered if Myrtle had heard anything about Lydia. Only three letters had passed between him and Myrtle: the one, a month before, in which she had said that she had been by herself for nearly four years and that she was homesick; his answer telling her that his house was always open to her, that he would welcome her, and that she must not hesitate to send for money if she needed it, because he had done even better than usual on the farm in the past few years; and then the third, in which she had merely stated when and by which train she would arrive. He had said nothing about Lydia. He had been afraid to trust himself to tell of her in a letter. It would be better, he had thought, to wait until he and Myrtle met at the station.

Nor could he say anything now. He

would wait until they were all three together. His uneasiness was growing. The
dread of having made a horrible foolish
mistake that might hurt both Lydia and
Myrtle was pressing heavier on him every
minute. It occurred to him that some of
the gossiping neighbors might have found
out Myrtle's address and written to her.
He wished that she would not sit so far
away from him, and so straight and silent
and hard. But he *must* say something. He
braced himself.

"Myrtle!"

"Yes?"

"You look fine, finer as ever."

"Don't Fred, please!" Raising her right
hand in her old vigorous manner, she
swept his words away. He could not compel himself to attempt the conversation
again. He waited, once more making desperate efforts to visualize the meeting of
the passionate Myrtle and the gentle Lydia.

A mile below the station the wagon
rolled out into the gray sandy road leading to the farm, twenty miles southward.
Suddenly the big shabby woman faced
around to him, forcing an aching wavering
smile upon her lips alone.

"Fred, how many other old stray cats
an' dogs an' things have you got around
the place now? I remember you used to
take in ever'thing that came along."

"No cats and dogs, Myrtle, no tramp
ones." He took up the conversation quickly,
glad to drag his mind away from the terrifying problem drawing closer every time
the mules took a step. "But I been afraid
about Sister. She gets old, Myrtle, and
weak. Somedimes, at night, she wakes me
up trying to get her breath, dere by de foot
of de bed. Her lungs and nose get all
stopped up, so de breath must fight its way
out and in. But I buy some liniment day
helps her over de hard places when I get
up and rub it on her."

"Dear little Sister!" The faded blond
woman looked back at the old dog lying
on some fodder in the rear of the wagon.
Having heard her name spoken, Sister
lifted her bulging watery eyes and wagged
her tail weakly in the dry corn-leaves.
"Yes," the woman went on, "she *is* gittin'
old—too."

"Also," the farmer hurried to say, in
order to keep going the safe conversation,
"your red game-rooster, Myrtle, he breaks
his leg off, the left one. It gets caught in
de garden gate; he snatches it off before
I get to him. I make him a wooden one,
and now he lives and walks and fights like
the same little red devil yet."

"He's gittin' on too, then. He was a
year old when—"

Old Melschott's strategic enthusiasm
about the rooster was lost. She asked no
questions about her favorite rooster, nor
about any others down there at home
among the animals about which it was so
safe to talk. The woman beside him had
again lapsed into brooding inattention. Her
rough, red, ungloved hands lay folded in
her lap. The wagon was getting well out
in the country now, and she was staring
straight ahead of her down the gray ribbon
of road wavering savagely at the few old
dead leaves yet clinging frantically to their
trees.

"Myrtle, are you cold?" asked Old Melschott after a while. "I dink I feel you
shiver."

"No, I ain't cold, Fred."

"Are you hungry?"

"No."

"Better let me get out and make a fire
here by the road, Myrtle. It is long after
twelve o'clock now. I got some lunch for
us in dat tin bucket down dere in de wagon
by your suitcase. Den you could get warm
and eat at de same time. What do you
say, Myrtle?"

"Fred, I want to git *home.*"

She fell again into silence, her eyes
greedily watching the road unrolling in
front of her. Old Melschott clucked the
little black mules into a jingling trot.
Gradually the road was rising out of the
timbered lowlands. The swamp-oaks and
stunted cypresses were giving way to
taller and taller pines.

All at once the drooping woman raised
her head, her muscles instantly straining
tight as if to help her eyes to see and her
ears to hear. A long black wedge of wild
ducks slid swiftly across the sunless sky,
trailing their far faint whisper of winter
across the fields and woods.

"This ain't the first time I been homesick, Fred," she said in a level monotone
as if she were merely continuing an old,
old conversation. "But I never could git
up spunk enough to write to you, Fred,
before. It wasn't fair to you, it seemed
like; and it ain't fair now neither; but—"

"I am mighty glad you came back,
Myrtle."

"When we left that night, Fred, we

started straight for New Orleans. After two weeks down there I never seen no more of Luther. I went my way, he his'n. He was no good nohow. My God, Fred, how *could* I—Ne'mind that, though, ne'-mind that. Well I had to git somethin' to do. It was hard to find, work was; an' I got homesick right then, Fred."

"Myrtle!"

"But I jes' *couldn't* write, not much, not a whole letter. We sneaked away that night an' got out of Crebillon on that early mawnin' train for New Orleans. Nobody that knowed us never seen us. I had a woman in the boardin'-house where I was to subscribe for the 'Crebillon Chronicle,' so as I could git the news from home without nobody knowin' where I was.

"Fred, I seen that little piece you had the correspondent from our Silver Shoe Lake section put in, sayin' Mrs. Melschott was gone to Maine, where her grand-mother was sick. Then I seen the others that said I had to stay with her a while longer to nurse her, because she had done become a chronic invalid, an' had no other relatives, an' was so sick she couldn't be moved. Because you done that so soon after we left, Fred, I knowed if I come back it would 'a' been all right with you.

"An' because you done that, I 'lowed, too, that I could come on home without nobody knowin' what had been done by me to you. I cain't tell you, Fred, how many times I set down to write a letter, but I never could bear to finish it before. It wasn't fair to you, it seemed like; an' it ain't fair now neither; but—"

"I am mighty glad you come back, Myrtle."

"If my folks hadn't 'a' died before I left I would 'a' come back to them an' took what talkin' was comin' to me from the neighbors when they found out, jes' to be near home, our home, Fred. Things down there in New Orleans was all the time re-mindin' me; it seemed like ever' day *some-thin'* would set me to thinkin' back an' forwards.

"They eat a lot of fish down there, Fred; an' I—I cooked in a restaurant for over a year—I never fried one but I thought of them we used to ketch out of Silver Shoe Lake right there in front of our house. They never tasted as good as *our* fish, Fred.

"In the summers it was awful hot down there, a lot hotter than it is up here; an' the mosquitos are terribul. Our mosquitos up here ain't nigh as bad as them, Fred. Sometimes in the summer I'd have to set up in bed an' fan an' fan 'em off me, though we did have mosquito-bars. I'd jes' set there a-fannin' an' a-fannin' an' a-wishin' I was home, Fred."

"Myrtle, please!" Old Melschott raised his hand as if to ward off something, and turned his head away.

"There ain't got no trees like ours, Fred, down there. Them squatty little pa'ms settin' around ever'where made me want to see an' listen to our old tall pines again. Fred, if a body puts his hands over both ears, he can hear, any time, how the pines sound away up in their top branches where the wind is always blowin'. I reckon it's the blood always runnin' in the veins does it, Fred, like the wind is always blowin' through the branches away up yonder. I reckon I ain't a cryin' kind of woman, Fred, but sometimes, in the restaurant an' the laundry an' the other places where I worked, when I would close my eyes an' put my hands over my ears an' hear the wind in the pines, I'd jes' have to do it.

"I kept the 'Chronicle' comin' in some-body else's name all the time, except for about three months las' summer. Always after Christmas time I'd see that the cor-respondents from all the little settlements out in the woods were sayin', 'Plowin' is the order of the day now,' or, 'Ever'body is plantin' corn,' or, 'There seems to be a good stand of cotton.' Then I'd remember how it all looked an' felt up here in the spring. I always did like spring, Fred, better than any other time."

"Myrtle—"

"Many a time of nights, Fred, when I'd git home, in January an' February an' March, I'd jes' set by myself in my room a-thinkin' backward an' forward. Seemed like I could jes' see the field back of our house by Silver Shoe Lake all plowed up a-waitin' for the seed; so clean an' black an' fresh, lookin' like it wanted the sun to shine on it an' the seed to drop in it an' the rain to fall on it. An' I could see the chickens an' the turkeys runnin' over the rows huntin' for bugs an' things. An' I could smell the land; an' hear you say, 'Gee, Nell, gee.' In the spring up here it always seemed like ever'body an' ever'-thing was havin' a good time.

"Yeah, Fred, I knowed all about our Silver Shoe Lake section that a body could git out of the 'Chronicle.' I bound I can tell you the names the girls put at the end of their pieces about our settlement. 'Twinkle Star' wrote it up for over a year. Then 'Bright Eyes' done it for nearly two. Since then 'Old Maid' took it, an' has been doin' it ever since.

"An' I watched the 'Chronicle' clost, Fred, to see if you got sick or anything. Last year I came might nigh rushin' home regardless. 'Old Maid' wrote in her 'Silver Shoe Notes' a piece about you like this: 'Mr. Fred Melschott is on the sick list.' But I done been away so long then— An' I didn't know if somebody else wasn't in my— Anyhow, I waited; an' then the next week 'Old Maid' said: 'Mr. Fred Melschott is up an' out again. He said it was jes' a small cold with a hackin' cough.'

"An' ever' winter I'd git skeered about you, Fred, an' your cough. Whenever I'd hear the wild ducks flyin' acrost the sky givin' the sign of winter comin', I'd say to myself, 'Now Fred will be ketchin' cold again an' havin' that nasty little ole cough, because he *won't* take keer of hisself.' You know you won't take keer of yourself, Fred, less'n somebody makes—"

"Ach, Myrtle, I been all right," he interrupted to reassure her; "somebody makes—"

He stopped suddenly. He was committing the mistake he most feared. He did not dare look at the woman there on the seat beside him. He felt that she was drawing even farther away from him than she had been, and that she was shrinking up in the dingy black dress that covered her.

"Who, Fred?" Her voice, in pitiful disproportion to her size, crept around her shoulder to him. "Who is it, Fred? Do I know her? I thought, comin' home, that if anybody had taken my place. . . . But then I was shore no one had, because I watched the 'Chronicle' so clost an' I never seen nothin' about it. Seems like I'd 'a' seen it in the paper if anything had happened.

"But then maybe it was in them three months that I never seen the 'Chronicle' at all. I told you I had watched all the time except for about three months. That was las' summer. That was while I was in the hospital with typhoid fever. I had a terribul time, Fred. I was in the charity part of the hospital. They looked like they kind of got tired of me after the fever was

gone, but it didn't seem somehow like I could git my stren'th back so as I could go out an' work. It hurt, Fred, not to be wanted, an' a body bound to stay anyhow. Ne'mind that, though; ne'mind that—now. Who is she, Fred?"

He felt her waiting. He decided to tell her about Lydia at once; how it had come about; how he had been lonesome, and had not heard from her, and could get no track of her; and how though no one else *could* fill *all* the place left vacant by her, still— No, he couldn't tell her yet. He knew he could not manage the words rightly. He would mix things up. Myrtle would likely as not jump out of the wagon and disappear again, going into more unnecessary hardships. She was like that.

He recollected what she had just said about having been sick, and not getting her strength back. No, he would not take the slightest chance until he had to; he would wait; that would be best. Lydia, he knew, would meet her more than half-way. He knew now how much Myrtle loved the old place down there by the lake, and all the woods and waters around it. Maybe when they were all three together, when she was back home, it would come out straight. Anyway, there was nothing to lose by waiting; there might be in telling now. But how to hold her off in the meantime? He must think that out quickly.

"Who is she, Fred?" He heard her voice ask it again. "Why didn't you write me? Why did you let me come back, like an old stray dog? It's charity, it's hard, when a body ain't needed, when she cain't do nothin'. Stop the wagin, Fred. I'm goin' back to town, back to New Orleans. I ain't goin' home."

"Why, it's only old Ann Weaver," he hurried to say. That was half the truth, anyway. "You remember, Myrtle, de old negro couple dat rented a little piece of de Leete place next to ours. Two years ago Simon dies, and old Ann is homeless. She is sixty-five den; de cabin in our back yard is empty; and so—"

"You took her in of course. Oh, Fred!"

She laid her hand on his arm with a touch of tenderness that made him tremble. He knew that she was looking proudly at him. The undertaking ahead of him was looming larger and more dreadful every minute.

"Well, now I'll look after *her*, Fred. She must be old and weak now, an' I'll make it all up to her, Fred. Would she make you go to bed when you had a cold? *Could* she, Fred?"

"Yes, she could."

"Well, anyway, I notice you've got a little cough right now. But then she's so old; I reckon she done the best she could. An' I'll more'n make it up to her, Fred."

"You will rest yourself, Myrtle. You been working too hard. Why didn't you write sooner? You been sick. I been thinking it was good dat de cooking and everything could go on being done just as it has lately. And you can rest and enjoy yourself. You are tired, a little. I can see it now, I couldn't at first."

"Yes, maybe I am tired, Fred, jes' a little. But I am well an' strong now. I want to work. I been settin' out in my mind all the things I'm a-goin' to do. I aim to make up for the time I been gone, Fred. I don't want my place filled, none of it."

The wagon had reached the crest of a sandy land ridge, and the cold wind of the late afternoon cut across the two big figures on the high spring-seat. Old Melschott tried to smother a slight attack of coughing.

"There!" said his watchful companion almost exultantly. "I knowed it. You've got to stay in bed all day to-morrow, an' I'll make you hot lemonades. You see, Fred, if you will only stay in bed *one* day we can git a good enough holt on that cold to strangle it. Oh, yes, we can; we used to, you know. If I don't, though, you know it will hang on an' on till warm weather comes."

"Ach, Myrtle, I am all right!"

"Yes, that's what you always say. Do you know why I wrote that letter, Fred, at last? It was because I seen that what 'Old Maid' wrote about you in the 'Chronicle': 'Mr. Fred Melschott is on the sick list with a cough an' a cold.' I waited a week, but she never said you had got rid of it. Then I heard the wild ducks flyin' acrost the sky. So I wrote; I couldn't help it this time. That was over a month ago, an' that cough is still with you. Won't you do what I say—jes' to kind of please me, Fred?" She laid her hand on his arm appealingly.

"Yes, I will then." But he had a shuddering suspicion that the next day he would be driving her back to town.

At sundown the wagon was turning out of the main road into the by-road leading to the Silver Shoe Lake neighborhood,

three miles east. There would be no more farms now until the edge of the settlement was reached. Above the road the gigantic pines leaned over, touched, and whispered to the passing night wind.

"Fred!" said the woman by his side after a long silence.

"Yes, Myrtle?"

"I won't never need to put my hands over my ears to hear the pines no more."

"I hope not, Myrtle."

It was after dark when the sure-footed mules, turning a sharp bend in the wooded road, swung into view four little golden squares of light against the black curtain of night. Old Melschott was trying desperately to visualize what would happen within the next hour behind those windows. The woman beside him, whom he could but dimly see now, was trying to visualize all the things she would do in that house to make up for the four hideous years gone by. Old Melschott heard her whisper something.

"What is it, Myrtle?"

"Nothin', Fred. I jes' said, 'Home'!"

At the front gate a negro boy stood waiting to take charge of the wagon and team.

"I heard you all comin', Mr. Fred," he explained. "Aunt Ann say to tell you all supper is ready, an' ef you all don't come right away the biscuits will be ruint an' there'll be trouble from her then. That's what she say. You know how she is, Mr. Fred. I done made a whoppin' big fire in the dinin'-room, like you tole me to."

When the farmer had helped the tremulous excited woman down from the seat she started away from him. "You go on in, Fred, please," she said. "I'm goin' to run down to the boat-landin' to see the lake. I got to have a look at it this minute, *some* kind of a look, even if it is dark. I'll be right back."

She moved off down the descending path, disappearing quickly in the dark.

"Oh, Fred!" she called back.

"Yes, Myrtle? Don't stay long. It's a good supper; all the things you like best —turtle soup, roast wild duck, sweet potatoes, cider—"

"Blow the old deer-horn, Fred, when you want me right bad."

Answering three long blasts, anxious blasts, of the horn fifteen minutes later, she came back up the hill, and found Old Melschott waiting by the front-yard gate.

"I get uneasy, Myrtle," he said.

"About me, Fred? Shucks, the lake wouldn't hurt me. I kind of feel like nobody an' nothin' would hurt me to-night. Did you worry about me shore 'nough, Fred?"

She slid her arm into his, and they walked up the path toward the golden lights, as closely as on that other night twenty-two years before when they were married.

There were three places set on the dining-room table. Old Melschott remained inactive before the steaming bowl of turtle-soup; he kept tapping softly on the table with the end of a fork, and waiting and listening.

"We have company, Fred?" asked the woman across the table, looking hard at him.

"She comes now." He stood up.

There were light footsteps in the adjoining spare room. The door opened and a small white hand came feeling around the jamb. Then a little girl came into the light, standing up very straight to maintain her precarious balance, tilting her chin up and shaking her head as if the mist of black hair about her forehead and temples were impeding her steady gray eyes.

"Uncle Fred?" she called.

"Yes, Lydia."

Reassured, she moved along the wall, and stopped, and walked straight across the room to the table, facing them instinctively in the right direction.

"An' so this is Aunt Myrtle," she said. "I am afraid. Uncle is afraid. Maybe you won't like me. I am blind."

The big blond woman slipped out of her chair on her knees by the side of the table, and the little girl walked forward and put her arms around her neck.

"You like me then, Aunt Myrtle," pronounced Lydia finally. "I see it in your arms when you hug me that way. I like you too. See, uncle, *she* likes me, so I won't have to try hard, like you said for me to do, to make her do it."

"So-o!" said old Melschott, rubbing his hands together triumphantly. "Also Lydia makes you like her, Myrtle? I am glad. I been afraid. I dink all de time you hate children. And my little Lydia—ach, I like her, Myrtle, I like her too. So-o! And I thought you did not like—"

"Oh, Fred! If we 'a' had one, then I—"

"*You* remember her, Myrtle. She is Nick Jamison's Lydia, across de lake. Last summer he dies; den dey are sending her away to an asylum; she is only ten years old; so I ask for her. Also last month when you write I was afraid, so afraid. Ach! but now my little Lydia makes you like her, so quick, so quick. I been afraid. I am glad."

"Fred!" the kneeling woman called across the little girl's shoulder.

"Yes?"

"An' you *do* need me now, Fred, don't you?"

"Ach, Myrtle, you see! More as ever. I been afraid. Now I am glad. So! Come, den, *Liebchen!* De soup gets cold."

The next week, in the "Silver Shoe Notes" of the "Crebillon Chronicle," "Old Maid" said: "Mrs. Fred Melschott is in our midst again. She has been away in Maine nursing an invalid grandmother, who at last has passed to her heavenly reward. Welcome home, Mrs. Melschott! We have missed you!"

LIII

STEPHEN FRENCH WHITMAN (1880–   )

A graduate of Princeton in the class of 1901, trained as a newspaper man, special writer for the New York *Evening Sun*, 1901-1903, Stephen F. Whitman has done literary work in many varied fields. His story "Fear" is reproduced in these Readings to illustrate a late phase of the short story,—"the short short story," the tabloid form of the tale which many believe is to be ultimately the fictional unit of the coming headlong age.

FEAR *

A Short Short Story

The woman and the man, the antagonists 5 who had not met for three years, faced each other in her little living-room. A lamp illuminated their faces; for it was a January evening. The window curtains were drawn: in this cottage, high in a 10 cañon above Hollywood, she always closed them at sunset. Life had made her timorous, even in the apparent security of a new, smiling land. And now, in the country where "such things couldn't happen," her 15 enemy had tracked her down. They had walked up the cañon for the sake of secrecy.

"Have you anything to drink?" he asked. "My heart's not as good as it was." This, 20 then, was why his blond Lettish countenance looked wet and drawn, why his breath still came so fast.

"Some cognac?" she suggested, and went into the kitchen. 25

With a sigh he sat down quickly in the nearest chair.

She returned, bearing two liqueur glasses full to the brim. "I feel a bit faint myself," she murmured. 30

He took the glass she offered him, then paused. A crafty look appeared in the eyes of this man, still young, who had learned in Russia so much about treachery. He reached out for the glass in her hand. 35

A pale smile touched her lips. Disdainful, almost haughty, she resembled an exiled princess, her hair so pallid a gold,

* Published by arrangement with Stephen F. Whitman, owner of the copyright.

her features so delicate, her slender body so fine.

"You suspect my hospitality? Then choose for yourself."

She turned her back. Swiftly he changed the glasses in his hands, drank from hers, held out the other.

Sipping the cognac, she inquired:
"How did you find me, Eiduk?"

He had come from Russia on a secret 10 mission. In San Francisco he had seen her face on the screen. His Helena Feodorovna a cinema actress!

"So little of one, Eiduk. In fact, a failure at it." 15

"But not a failure with this gentleman, eh?" He touched a framed photograph on the table, the likeness of a serious-looking young American.

"It is my fiancé." 20

"Of course you've told him everything?" grinned the Lett, leaning forward to enjoy the effect of that taunt.

She nodded almost joyously. Baffled, he 25 demanded:

"You know why I've come?"

"For the jewels, I suppose."

Helena Feodorovna went slowly into her bedroom.

As she took the jewels from their hiding 30 place, the terrible past reappeared. She saw the revolutionists bursting into the country house, her father, the general, slaughtered, her mother fainting away. 35 Suddenly, amid that pandemonium, Eiduk had appeared, young, bullet-headed, dominant. He had looked into her eyes—had shouted a command. From that moment, for three years, she had belonged to him. 40 She was then only eighteen.

555

An old family servant had sheltered her mother on his tiny farm; Eiduk had vouched for her safety as long as the daughter was docile. Now and then he let Helena write a note to her mother saying that "she was safe." From mother to daughter he allowed no communication. As commissar in the military cheka, the Lett dragged with him everywhere this youthful and beautiful aristocrat, who never dared to escape or kill herself. But sometimes, in private, to redouble his sense of malicious triumph and her preciousness, he bedecked her with her mother's jewels, which he had managed to steal on that day of tragedy.

These were the jewels, impregnated with a thousand hateful memories, that she spread out under the lamp.

The Lett protested:

"Where the devil are all the rest?"

Her blanched lips hardly moving, she retorted:

"Do you think it cost me nothing to give you the slip and get here?" She added, clenching her fists, "When I found out that my mother had already been dead two years!"

He shrugged his shoulders, stared at her young face. Gradually his eyes took on the familiar look of malice.

"Did you expect the broad-minded fiancé to-night?"

"Perhaps."

"If you care for his health, telephone him not to come."

Drawing back his lapel, he revealed the butt of a pistol.

Helena Feodorovna considered the implication impassively, though she became, if possible, paler than before. She regarded with a veiled intensity of thought this foe so strangely debilitated, except in his relentlessness. But a startling smile changed her bleakness as she answered:

"That's hardly necessary. I think that in three or four minutes either you or I will be dead."

His amazed glance followed hers to the two empty little glasses on the table.

"I don't know which you drank," she reminded him. "You had your choice; the odds were equal. I only know that in one of us death is working. Now, either way, I'm free from you forever. Above all, this honorable love I've found here"— she pointed toward the photograph—"will never be debased."

"Poison!" he whispered, his forehead glistening. He pressed his hand to his heart; he could hardly catch his breath.

"Ah!" she triumphed, like a young avenging angel, "do you feel it, Eiduk? Did you really change the glasses? I thought you would!"

Panting faster and faster, he saw her erect, unharmed, transfigured by icy derision; for those who have felt the lash of the Revolution know neither scruple nor pity. Ten minutes later, when there appeared in the doorway a tall American with steady gray eyes, Helena Feodorovna stood awaiting her sentence. She said gently in English:

"To-night, poor dear, you must take this repulsive thing in your car to some deserted place."

The American gazed at the dead body, the jewels, the two glasses. He came to her, took her hands, asked her compassionately:

"Who was he? The one you told me of?" She nodded. "Did you kill him, Helena?"

She laughed hysterically:

"There was no poison. Imagine: this man who amused himself by watching so many die died simply of fear."

NOTES

I

"Rip Van Winkle" appeared in the first number of the *Sketch Book*, 1819. In the *Sketch Book* may be found Irving's acknowledgment of indebtedness to old German legends dealing with situations similar to the "Rip Van Winkle" tale. See *Development of the American Short Story*, p. 11ff.

"The Stout Gentleman" appeared first in *Bracebridge Hall*. In his autobiography the English artist Charles Robert Leslie has given an account of the writing of the story:

"Towards the close of the summer of 1821, I made a delightful excursion with Washington Irving to Birmingham, and thence into Derbyshire. . . . We determined to proceed to Oxford, which we reached about eleven o'clock, and then sat down to a hot supper. The next day it rained unceasingly, and we were confined to the inn, like the nervous traveler whom Irving has described as spending a day in endeavoring to penetrate the mystery of 'the stout gentleman.' This wet Sunday at Oxford did in fact suggest to him that capital story, if story it can be called. The next morning as we mounted the coach, I said something about a *stout gentleman* who had come from London with us the day before, and Irving remarked that 'The Stout Gentleman' would not be a bad title for a tale; as soon as the coach stopped, he began writing with his pencil, and went on at every like opportunity. We visited Stratford-on-Avon, strolled about Charlecot Park and other places in the neighborhood, and while I was sketching, Irving, mounted on a stile or seated on a stone, was busily engaged with 'The Stout Gentleman.' He wrote it with the greatest rapidity, often laughing to himself, and from time to time reading the manuscript to me. We loitered some days in this classic neighborhood, visiting Warwick and Kenilworth; and by the time we arrived at Birmingham, the outline of 'The Stout Gentleman' was completed. The amusing account of 'The Modern Knights Errant' he added at Birmingham, and the inimitable picture of the inn-yard on a rainy day was taken from an inn where we were afterwards quartered at Derby."

II

"Peter Rugg, the Missing Man" appeared in the *New England Galaxy*, September 10, 1824, September 1, 1826, and January 19, 1827. See *William Austin, the Creator of Peter Rugg*, Walter Austin, 1825. Also "A Precursor of Hawthorne," Thomas Wentworth Higginson, *Independent*, March 29, 1888.

III

"The Yankee School Master" first appeared in *The Book of Beauty* annual, 1847. See *James Kirke Paulding*, Amos L. Herold, Columbia University Press, 1926.

1. See *Knickerbocker's History of New York*, Book III, chs. 7 and 8.

2. The influence of Irving's "Legend of Sleepy Hollow" upon this piece is easily detected. See *Development of the American Short Story*, ch. 2.

IV

"The White Old Maid," first published in the *New England Magazine*, 1835.

"At best, Hawthorne's supernatural tales convey a thrilling sense of mystery such that the reader may suspect the author of leading him to the verge of things which neither of them can fathom. 'The Hollow of the Three Hills' and 'The White Old Maid' are both masterpieces of supernatural suggestion. We, as readers, almost grasp what is happening and what the mysterious agents are; then it slips out of our comprehension."—*J. B. Moore*.

"The Prophetic Pictures," published in *The Token*, 1837.

"Mrs. Bullfrog," published in *The Token*, 1837. In this story Hawthorne departed for a moment from his usual manner and put a lightness and levity and surprise ending to it that are N. P. Willis-like and modern. To do such work in the rigorous New England environment was hazardous. It troubled his conscience. In his *American Note-Books*, September 16, 1841, he notes: "As to Mrs. Bullfrog, I give her up to the severest reprehension. The story was written as a mere experiment in that style; it did not come from any depth within me,—neither my heart nor mind had anything to do with it."

The best recent study of Hawthorne is *The Rebellious Puritan*, by Lloyd Morris, 1927. See also *The Development of the American Short Story*, ch. 5.

V

"Hawthorne's Twice-Told Tales," published in *Graham's Magazine*, May, 1842.

Hawthorne's opinion of this critique appears in a letter he wrote to Poe four years later—June, 1846:

"I have read your occasional notices of my productions with great interest—not so much because your judgment was, upon the whole favorable, as because it seemed to be given in earnest. I care for nothing but the truth. I confess, however, that I admire you [more] as a writer of tales than as a critic upon them. I might often—and often do—dissent from your opinions in the latter capacity, but would never fail to recognize your force and originality in the former."

"The Fall of the House of Usher," first published in Burton's *Gentleman's Magazine*, September, 1839.

"The tale predominantly of atmosphere (illustrated in the classic 'Fall of the House of Usher'), revealing whenever found the ability of the author to hold a dominant mood in which as in a calcium light characters and acts are colored, this tale occurs so rarely as to challenge admiration when it does occur."—*Blanche C. Williams*.

1. The couplet from Béranger may be translated, "His heart is a lute suspended; at the slightest touch it resounds."

"The Murders in the Rue Morgue," published in *Graham's Magazine*, April, 1841.

"The primary gift employed in these ingenious narratives is constructiveness; they differ from their predecessors, from 'The Fall of the House of Usher,' for example, not in the intellectual faculties exercised, but in their aim and conduct. In the earlier group Poe gradually worked up to the *dénouement* of a highly complicated series of facts and emotions; in the latter one, stating only the *dénouement* of a similar series, he gradually worked back to its origins: in both cases he first constructed the story, but in telling it he reversed in one the method used in the other. The main difference is that in the old process the emotional element counts for more, while in the new one the incidents are necessarily the important part; indeed, they almost absorb attention. That the ratiocinative tales are on a lower level than the imaginative ones hardly needs to be

said, since it is so conclusively indicated by the fact that later writers have far surpassed Poe in the complexity of this sort of mechanism, and therefore in the apparent miracle of the solution. They come short of Poe only in the original invention of the plot; that is to say, they fail by defects of imagination in the selection, and of artistic power in the grouping, of their facts, for it would be a mistake to suppose that the interest in 'The Murders in the Rue Morgue' is simply the puzzle of detection."—*George E. Woodberry.*
1. To deny what is and to explain what is not. From Rousseau's *Nouvelle Héloïse.*

VI

"Grayling; or, Murder Will Out" was first published in *The Gift* annual, 1842.
The London *Examiner*, 1842, reviewing *The Gift*, singled out "Grayling" for especial praise: "This is an American ghost story, and without exception the best one we ever read. The *rationale* of the whole matter of such appearances is given with fine philosophy and masterly interest. We never read anything more perfect or more consummately told."
And Poe in *The Broadway Journal*, October 4, 1845, reviewing *The Wigwam and the Cabin*, also singled out this story for comment: "We have no hesitation in calling it the best ghost story we ever read. It is full of the richest and most vigorous imagination, is forcibly conceived, and detailed throughout with a degree of artistic skill which has no parallel among American story-tellers since the epoch of Brockden Brown."
Upon this Professor William P. Trent observes: "The tale is certainly well told; but Poe or Hawthorne would have told it better. They would have paid more attention to details, and thus have provided a more artistic setting; in other words they would have thrown an air of glamour over the various events described, and so have strengthened the spell that the successful narrator of a ghost story must cast over his hearers or readers."

VII

"The Spirit-Love of Ione S—" and "Count Potts' Strategy," both from *Dashes at Life with a Free Pencil*, 1845.
1. The old *New York Mirror* of which Willis had been long an editor was discontinued in 1842. On April 8, 1843, appeared the *New Mirror* with Morris and Willis as editors.
2. Wit is a counterfeiter who continually is changing big pennies into gold pieces and who often changes the gold pieces into big pennies.
3. Congress Hall was the most fashionable of the hotels at Saratoga Springs during the period when Saratoga was the leading American "watering place." In "Tom Fane and I" Willis has described the place with minuteness:
"It was soon established, from the plains of Abraham to the savannahs of Alabama, that no person of fashionable taste or broken constitution could exist through the months of July and August without a visit to the chalybeate springs and populous village of Saratoga. . . . I feel called on to describe Congress Hall. Some fourteen or fifteen millions of white gentlemen and ladies consider that wooden and windowed Babylon as the proper palace of delight—a sojourn to be sighed for, and sacrificed for, and economized for—the birthplace of Love, the haunt of Hymen, the arena of fashion. . . . In the strength of the summer solstice, from five hundred to a thousand people dine together at Congress Hall, and after absorbing as many bottles of the best wines of the world, a sunset promenade plays the valve to the sentiment thus generated, and, with a cup of tea, the crowd separates to dress for the nightly ball."
4. As simple as good morning.
The best life of Willis is still Henry A. Beers's in the *American Men of Letters Series.* See *Development of the American Short Story*, pp. 77-90.

VIII

"What Was It?" was first published in *Harper's Monthly Magazine*, 1859.
1. A Mohammedan name for the followers of Zoroaster who worshiped the sun.
2. Tree toad.
3. A journey where it pleases you to go.
The standard authority upon O'Brien is still William Winter's *The Poems and Stories of Fitz-James O'Brien*, 1881. The only other collection is *Collected Stories of Fitz-James O'Brien*, edited by Edward J. O'Brien, 1925. See *Development of the American Short Story*, ch. 7.

IX

"Circumstance" was first published in *The Atlantic Monthly*, 1860, and reissued in *The Amber Gods and Other Stories*, 1863.
The review of Mrs. Spofford by Henry James in *The North American Review*, 1865, is illuminating criticism. See *Development of the American Short Story*, pp. 159-163.

X

"My Double and How He Undid Me," published in *The Atlantic Monthly*, September, 1859, and reissued in *If, Yes, and Perhaps*, 1868, with the note by the author: "A Boston journal, in noticing this story, called it improbable. I think it is. But I think the moral important."
1. "The Sandemanian connection," a religious sect founded by Robert Sandeman (1718-1771), a native of Perth, Scotland. They held to communism of goods, weekly celebration of the communion, and many other strictly-observed rites.
2. "Which means, 'In the thirteenth century,' my dear little bell-and-coral reader. You have rightly guessed what the question means, 'What is the history of the Reformation in Hungary?'"—*Author's Note.*
The best sources for a study of Hale and his work are his autobiographies, *A New England Boyhood* and *Memories of a Hundred Years.* See *Development of the American Short Story*, pp. 183-187.

XI

"The Ghost in the Cap'n Brown House," first published in *The Atlantic Monthly*, December, 1870, and reissued in *Oldtown Fireside Stories*, 1871.
Mrs. Stowe struck the key to the series in her first story, "The Ghost in the Mill":
"In those days we had no magazines and daily papers, each reeling off a serial story. Once a week, 'The Columbian Sentinel' came from Boston with its slender stock of news and editorials; but all the multiform devices—pictorial, narrative, and poetical —which keep the mind of the present generation ablaze with excitement, had not then even an existence. There was no theatre, no opera; there were in Oldtown no parties or balls, except, perhaps, the annual election, or Thanksgiving festival; and when winter came, and the sun went down at half-past four o'clock, and left the long, dark hours of evening to be provided for, the necessity for amusement became urgent. Hence, in those days, chimneycorner story-telling became an art and an accomplishment. Society then was full of traditions and narratives which had all the uncertain glow and shifting mystery of the firelit hearth upon them. They were told to sympathetic audiences, by the rising and falling light of the solemn embers, with the hearth-crickets filling up every pause. Then the aged told their stories to the young,—tales of early life; tales of war and adventure, of forest-days, of Indian captivities and escapes, of bears and wildcats and panthers, of rattlesnakes, of witches and wizards, and strange and wonderful dreams and appearances and providences.
"Sam's method of telling a story was as leisurely as that of some modern novel writers. He would take his time for it and proceed by easy stages. It was like the course of a dreamy, slow-moving river through a tangled meadow flat—not a rush nor a

bush but was repeated in it; in short, Sam gave his philosophy of matters and things in general as he went along, and was especially careful to impress an edifying moral."

See *Development of the American Short Story*, pp. 175, 248.

XII

"Freedom Wheeler's Controversy with Providence," in *The Atlantic Monthly*, July, 1877, reissued in *Somebody's Neighbors*, 1881.

1. Shearjashub. Isaiah 7:3.

The best study as yet of Mrs. Cooke is that by Harriet Prescott Spofford in *Our Famous Women*, 1884. See *Development of the American Short Story*, pp. 173-178; and *A History of American Literature since 1870*, pp. 229-231.

XIII

"Life in the Iron Mills," published in *The Atlantic Monthly*, April, 1861.

"My story is very crude and homely,—only a rough sketch of one or two of those people whom you see every day, and call 'dregs' sometimes—a dull bit of prose, such as you might pick for yourself out of any of these warehouses or back streets. I expect you to call it stale and plebeian, for I know the glimpses of life it pleases you best to find here: New England idyls delightfully tinted; passion-veined hearts, cut bare for curious eyes; prophetic utterances, concrete and clear; or some word of pathos or fun from the old friends who have indenizened themselves in everybody's home. You want something, in fact, to lift you out of this crowded, tobacco-stained commonplace, to kindle and chafe and glow in you. I want you to dig into this commonplace, this vulgar American life, and see what it is. Sometimes I think it has a new and awful significance that we do not see."—Mrs. Davis in A Story of To-day, *The Atlantic Monthly* October, 1861.

See *Development of the American Short Story*, pp. 171-173.

PART II

XIV

"The Rise of the Short Story," published in the *Cornhill Magazine*, July, 1899.

1. Harte was editor of *The Overland Monthly* from the first number, July, 1868, until he left California in 1871. "The Luck of Roaring Camp" appeared in the second number.

2. "Rosamond Grey," a romance by Charles Lamb, 1798.

3. Judge Haliburton of Nova Scotia published his *The Clockmaker, or Sayings and Doings of Sam Slick of Slickville*, in 1837.

4. The Rev. Sylvester Judd's novel, *Margaret, a Tale of the Real and Ideal, Blight and Bloom*, appeared in 1845.

"The Outcasts of Poker Flat," published in *The Overland Monthly*, January, 1869, and reissued in *Luck of Roaring Camp and Other Sketches*, 1870. "An Ingénue of the Sierras," published in the New York *Sun*, May 7, 1893, and reissued in *A Protégé of Jack Hamlin's and Other Stories*, 1894.

The leading authorities on Bret Harte are *The Life of Bret Harte*, T. Edgar Pemberton, 1903; *Bret Harte*, Henry W. Boynton, 1903; *The Life of Bret Harte*, Henry Childs Merwin, 1911; *The Letters of Bret Harte*, Geoffrey Bret Harte. See *A History of American Literature since 1870*, pp. 63-82, and *The Development of the American Short Story*, ch. 10.

XV

"A Struggle for Life," first published in *The Atlantic Monthly*, July, 1867, and reissued in *Marjorie Daw and Other People*, 1873.

The leading authority on Aldrich is *The Life of Thomas Bailey Aldrich*, Ferris Greenslet, 1908. "Mr. Aldrich's Fiction," by William Dean Howells, *The Atlantic Monthly*, November, 1880, is a helpful

study. See *A History of American Literature since 1870*, pp. 126-135, and *The Development of the American Short Story*, pp. 211-219.

XVI

"The Celebrated Jumping Frog of Calaveras County," published in *The New York Saturday Press*, November 18, 1865, and reissued in *The Celebrated Jumping Frog of Calaveras County, and Other Sketches*, 1867.

In the winter of 1864 and 1865 Clemens was a wandering prospector. In January with Jim Gillis he staked out a mine in the Angel's Camp region and started in to work it, but the weather rendered work all but impossible.

"Most of their days were spent in the bar-room of the dilapidated tavern at Angel's Camp, enjoying the company of a former Illinois River pilot, Ben Coon, a solemn, fat-witted person, who dozed by the stove, or told slow, endless stories, without point or application. Listeners were a boon to him, for few came and not many would stay. To Mark Twain and Jim Gillis, however, Ben Coon was a delight. It was soothing and comfortable to listen to his endless narratives, told in that solemn way, with no suspicion of humor. Even when his yarn had a point, he did not recognize it. One dreary afternoon, in his slow, monotonous fashion, he told them about a frog—a frog that had belonged to a man named Coleman, who trained it to jump, but that failed to win a wager because the owner of a rival frog had surreptitiously loaded the trained jumper with shot. The story had circulated among the camps, and a well-known journalist, named Samuel Seabough, had already made a squib out of it, but neither Clemens nor Gillis had ever happened to hear it before. They thought the tale in itself amusing, and the 'spectacle of a man drifting serenely along through such a queer yarn without ever smiling was exquisitely absurd.'" The only thing that came out of this mining adventure of Twain's was this story retold in his own inimitable manner but, continued his biographer Paine, "The hills along the Stanislaus have turned out some wonderful nuggets in their time, but no other of such size as that."

"The Facts Concerning the Recent Carnival of Crime in Connecticut," first published in *The Atlantic Monthly*, June, 1876, and reissued in *The Stolen White Elephant*, 1882.

The chief authority upon Mark Twain is *Mark Twain, a Biography*. Also important is *The Personal and Literary Life of Samuel Langhorne Clemens*, Albert Bigelow Paine, 4 vols., 1912. See *History of American Literature since 1870*, pp. 45-62, and *The Development of the American Short Story*, pp. 297-298.

XVII

"A Day of Days," first published in *The Galaxy*, June, 1866, and reissued in *Stories Revived*, London, 1885, and in *A Landscape Painter*, 1919.

Excellent helps in the study of Henry James are *Henry James*, William C. Brownell, 1909; *Henry James, a Critical Study*, Ford Maddox Hueffer, 1913; *The Method of Henry James*, Joseph Warren Beach, 1918; *The Pilgrimage of Henry James*, Van Wyck Brooks, 1925. See also *The History of American Literature since 1870*, pp. 187-197, and *The Development of the American Short Story*, pp. 194-208.

XVIII

"Devil-Puzzlers," first published in *Old and New*, August, 1871, and reissued in *Devil-Puzzlers and Other Studies*, 1877.

1. Whether a chimera buzzing in a vacuum devours its second intentions.

2. Whether the carriers of a bishop's carriage taken in a forbidden district are not subject to replevin.

XIX

"Posson Jone'," published in *Appleton's Magazine*, April, 1876, and reissued in *Old Creole Days*, 1879.

1. Aunt.
2. Notes.
3. Nobody.
4. American.
5. I say.
6. A kind of liquor.
7. Because.
8. But.
9. One who takes part in a schism or the splitting up of a church into factions.
10. That is all.
11. But come.
12. Literally an embankment; in Creole usage a sidewalk.
13. But certainly.
14. Shops.
15. Jail.
16. Corruption of Monsieur, Mr. or Sir.
17. Come.

XX

"The Lady of Little Fishing," first published in *The Atlantic Monthly*, September, 1874, and reissued in *Castle Nowhere: Lake Country Sketches*, 1875.

Henry James in 1888 devoted one of his *Partial Portraits* to "Miss Woolson." See *A History of American Literature since 1870*, pp. 317-318, and *The Development of the American Short Story*, pp. 250-255.

XXI

"The Lady or the Tiger?" was first published in *The Century Magazine*, November, 1882, and reissued in *The Lady or the Tiger? and Other Stories*, 1884.

See *History of American Literature since 1870*, pp. 358-361, and *The Development of the American Short Story*, pp. 296-298.

XXII

"On an Errand of Mercy," first published in *Vistas of New York*, 1912.

See *Development of the American Short Story*, pp. 293-295.

XXIII

"Banjo Jim's Story," first published in *The Cincinnati Commercial*, October 1, 1876, and reissued in *An American Miscellany*, 1924.

Authorities upon the life and work of Hearn have increased rapidly of late. Perhaps the most helpful are *Lafcadio Hearn*, Nina H. Kennard, 1912; *Lafcadio Hearn's American Days*, Larocque Tinker, 1924; *An American Miscellany*, ed. Albert Mordell, 1924. See *History of American Literature since 1870*.

XXIV

"A Native of Winby," first published in *The Atlantic Monthly*, May, 1891, and reissued in *A Native of Winby and Other Tales*, 1893.

Good authorities are *The Letters of Sarah Orne Jewett*, ed. Annie Fields, 1911; and "Sarah Orne Jewett's Tales," in Edward Garnett's *Friday Nights*, 1922. See also *History of American Literature since 1870*, pp. 231-235, and *The Development of the American Short Story*, pp. 253-263.

XXV

"Way Down in Lonesome Cove," first published in *Harper's Magazine*, December, 1885, and reissued in *Phantoms of the Footbridge and Other Stories*, 1895.

Biographical sketch in *Southern Writers*, Vol. I, Wm. M. Baskerville, 1877. See *History of American Literature since 1870*, pp. 308-316, and *Development of the American Short Story*, pp. 271-275.

XXVI

"Unc' Edinburg's Drowndin'," published in *Harper's Magazine*, January, 1886 and reissued in *In Old Virginia, or "Marse Chan" and Other Stories*, 1887.

The best light on Page's stories is shed by his own volume, *Social Life in Old Virginia before the War*, 1897. A good estimate of Page is to be found in Edwin Mims' "Thomas Nelson Page," *The Atlantic Monthly*, July, 1907. See also *The History of American Literature since 1870*, pp. 265-269, and *The Development of the American Short Story*, pp. 284-286.

XXVII

"Monsieur Motte," published in *The New Princeton Review*, January, 1886, reissued in *Monsieur Motte* [and other stories], 1888.

1. History of France by D. Levy Alvares, Sr.
2. Unexpected.
3. Maid of all work, "factotum."
4. Goodness gracious, what is it?
5. My dear!
6. My goodness!
7. Children.
8. He raised a big row.
9. Waiting room.
10. Carriage entrance.
11. Grating.
12. Oh, I was sure of it.
13. Native of Gascony.
14. So much the worse.
15. I don't care.
16. This is too much!
17. Housekeeper.
18. That negress Marcélite.
19. Aristocrat!
20. Poor trash!
21. It is hot, I tell you.
22. Neckerchief (probably the covering for her hair).
23. Puffs.
24. Hairdresser.
25. Agent, trusty.
26. It was said.
27. Gait.
28. Creole district.
29. Dear!
30. Dearie!
31. Angel!
32. My dearest friend!
33. As usual.
34. At last.
35. Nurse maid.
36. The old man.
37. The Great Musical Concert and Distribution of Prizes.
38. One of the Saint's Days in the French calendar, falling on October 9th.
39. Nobility of birth demands nobility of act.
40. Evening gown.
41. There now!
42. There, my baby; there, my darling!
43. This is the real article.
44. Do you? (Eh?).
45. Muslin from India.
46. Final authority.
47. Madam what's her name?
48. Well, what of it?
49. Oh, my baby; my little darling!
50. Closet.
51. Whom do you mean?
52. Closet.
53. Now don't get impatient, nursie.
54. Mother, "mamma."
55. "The Bronze Horse"—a piece of music for the piano.
56. Examination.
57. Exacting.
58. Good Heavens!
59. Good God, dear Jesus and the Holy Virgin!
60. Care free.
61. Bewitched.
62. Writing desk.
63. Oh, it is you.
64. At heart.
65. Uncertainty is the worst of evils, until the time when reality makes us regret uncertainty.
66. Well, what do you say about it?
67. Bed of justice—the throne which the king occupied in formal sessions of the French parliament.

68. Prayer-desk.
69. Poor little darling!
70. Puny, sickly.
71. 'My good woman.
72. Poor little one!
73. To be sure!
74. A beautiful woman.
75. Don't worry!
76. The pupil.
77. By the way.
78. Believe me!
79. Why.
80. Any way.
81. The selfish fellow!
82. At last.
83. Match.
84. Good-by, my dear.
85. Classroom.
86. I greet you, madam.
87. Refugee.
88. Curtseys.
89. Début, "coming out."
90. "The one (girl) I love," "the one I adore," "my dearest friend."
91. "My very devoted."
92. Tale bearers.
93. Ugly tongues, "gossips."
94. Oh, my God, have pity on me, a poor negress!
95. Dance, sing.
96. Round (dance).
97. Curl papers.
98. But I assure you.
99. Curled.
100. Headache.
101. Cologne water (aromatic spirits).
102. Sedative water (to ease pain).
103. Water from Lourdes, a famous Mecca for religious pilgrims, is considered to have great curative properties.
104. All right.
105. Now.
106. Savage (style).
107. Why, good heavens!
108. I have not slept at all last night.
109. Sends word to you.
110. But this is not bad at all.
111. Greeting! month of vacation! Virgin Mary!
112. To the point of disgust.
113. Private belongings.
114. Dictionary of the (French) Academy (1st edition 1694), considered final authority on vocabulary and word usage, especially by aristocrats.
115. Thank goodness.
116. The old (man).
117. (I) say.
118. Present the old (man).
119. A beautiful evening gown.
120. Curl paper.
121. Patrons.
122. Day pupils.
123. Boarders.
124. But, tell me, my dear.
125. Darling.
126. Grandmother's style.
127. Again; encore.
128. Marchpane—round sweet cake of almonds and sugar.
129. Foolish.
130. Why, this is outrageous!
131. To be sure.
132. Green arbor.
133. But what's the matter now, my child?
134. See 128.
135. Don't speak of it.
136. Even.
137. Really.
138. Finally.
139. Light brown.
140. Carmelite water.
141. The older men are the more wicked they are.
142. Simply and honestly.
143. That's what I call feminine politics.
144. In the slums down town.
145. But, see.
146. Oh, how stupid of me.

147. Unchanging (the state that had been and still is).
148. Reason for existence.
149. Dearest.
150. Anything in the world.
151. Rocking chair.
152. See 67.
153. Point.
154. Just imagine.
155. Boarder.
156. What a good idea!
157. Druggist.
158. That's good!
159. See 144.
160. Oh, these men!
161. Help! Thieves!
162. Wretch! Deceiver! Hussy!
163. Scoundrel!
164. The proud negress.
165. Bunch of hair twisted at her neck.
166. By the grace of God.

XXVIII

"The Mystery of Célestine," published in *Harper's Magazine*, March, 1920.

The autobiography of Mr. Hardy is entitled *Things Remembered*, 1923.

XXIX

"The Love-Letters of Smith," published in *Puck*, July 23, 1890; reissued in *Short Sixes: Stories to be Read While the Candle Burns*, 1891.

Best authorities: "H. C. Bunner," Brander Matthews, *Scribner's Magazine*, September, 1896, reissued in *The Historical Novel and Other Essays*, 1901; "Henry Cuyler Bunner," Benj. W. Wells, *Sewanee Review*, January, 1897; *Development of the American Short Story*, pp. 299-308.

XXX

"A Village Singer," published in *A New England Nun and Other Stories*, 1891.

See "On the Terminal Moraine of New England Puritanism," F. L. Pattee, 1920, introduction to *A New England Nun* in *Harper's Modern Classics* series, republished in *Sidelights on American Literature*, 1922; "Miss Wilkins: An Idealist in Masquerade," Charles Miner Thompson, *The Atlantic Monthly*, May, 1899; *A History of American Literature since 1870*, pp. 235-240; *The Development of the American Short Story*, pp. 317-323.

XXXI

"Among the Corn-Rows," *Harper's Weekly*, June 28, 1890; reissued in *Main Travelled Roads*, 1891.

Introduction to *Main Travelled Roads*, W. D. Howells, 1891, republished from *Harper's Magazine*, September, 1891; *Contemporary American Novelists*, Carl Van Doren; *A History of American Literature since 1870*, pp. 373-377; *The Development of the American Short Story*, pp. 313-317.

XXXII

"An Occurrence at Owl Creek Bridge," first published in the volume *Tales of Soldiers and Civilians*, 1891; republished with the title changed to *In the Midst of Life: Tales of Soldiers and Civilians*, 1892.

See *Ambrose Bierce*, Vincent Starrett, 1920; also *Some American Story Tellers*, Frederic Taber Cooper, 1911; *A History of American Literature since 1870*, pp. 379-380; *The Development of the American Short Story*, pp. 302-306.

XXXIII

"A Leander of the East River," published in *Van Bibber and Others*, 1892.

The best authority is *Adventures and Letters of Richard Harding Davis*, Charles B. Davis, 191; See also *Our Short Story Writers*, Blanche C. Williams, 1920; *A History of American Literature since 1870*, pp. 380-381; *The Development of the American Short Story*, pp. 337-347.

XXXIV

"At the Stuffed-Animal House," published in *Harper's Magazine*, May, 1903; reissued in *Doctor Lavendar's People*, 1903.
See *Our Short Story Writers*, Blanche C. Williams, 1920; "Margaret Deland," Grant M. Overton in *The Women Who Make Our Novels*, 1918; *A History of American Literature since 1870*, pp. 394-396.

XXXV

"The Windigo," published in *The Atlantic Monthly*, April, 1894; reissued in *The Chase of Saint-Castin and Other Stories of the French in the New World*, 1894.
See *Development of the American Short Story*, pp. 329-330.

XXXVI

"Madame Célestin's Divorce," published in *Bayou Folk*, 1894.
See *Library of Southern Literature*, pp. 863-866; *A History of American Literature since 1870*, pp. 364-365; *The Development of the American Short Story*, pp. 324-327.

XXXVII

"A Gray Sleeve," published in *The Little Regiment and other Episodes of the American Civil War*, 1896.
The leading authority is *Stephen Crane: A Study in American Letters*, Thomas Beer, 1923. See *The Development of the American Short Story*, pp. 341-343.

XXXVIII

"Old Lemuel's Journey," published in *The Atlantic Monthly*, June, 1920.
See *A History of American Literature since 1870*, pp. 240-243; *The Development of the American Short Story*, pp. 328-329; *The Women Who Make Our Novels* Grant M. Overton, ch. 2.

XXXIX

"The Choice," published in *The Century Magazine*, November, 1908; reissued in *Xingu, and Other Stories*, 1916.
The best authorities on Mrs. Wharton are : "The Novels of Mrs. Wharton," Henry D. Sedgwick, *The Atlantic Monthly*, August, 1906; *Contemporary American Novelists*, Carl Van Doren, pp. 95-104; *Some American Story Tellers*, Frederic T. Cooper; *The Development of the American Short Story*, pp. 374-379; *The Women Who Make Our Novels*, Grant M. Overton, ch. 1.

XL

"The Madness of John Harned," published in *Everybody's Magazine*, 23:657; reissued in *The Night-Born*, 1913.
See *The American Novel*, Carl Van Doren, pp. 266-270; *The Book of Jack London*, Chairman London, 1921; "The Prophet of the Last Frontier," Fred Lewis Pattee, in *Sidelights on American Literature*, 1922; *The Development of the American Short Story*, pp. 343-353.

XLI

"The Count and the Wedding Guest," published in *The Trimmed Lamp and Other Stories of the Four Million*, 1910.
"The Last Leaf," from the same.
The authorized life of O. Henry is *O. Henry Biography*, C. Alphonso Smith, 1916. See the "Journalization of American Literature," Fred Lewis Pattee, in *Sidelights on American Literature*, 1922; *Our Short Story Writers*, Blanche Colton Williams, 1920; and *Some American Story Tellers*, Frederic T. Cooper, 1911.

XLII

"Emma Blair," published in *Harper's Magazine*, November, 1916.

Criticism in *The Advance of the American Short Story*, Edward J. O'Brien, pp. 205-207.

XLIII

"The Sculptor's Funeral," published in *McClure's Magazine*, June, 1905; reissued in *Troll Garden*, 1905, and *Youth and the Bright Medusa*, 1920.
Criticism of Miss Cather in *The Women Who Make Our Novels*, Grant M. Overton, 1918; *Contemporary American Novelists*, Carl Van Doren, 1922.

XLIV

"Old Rogaum and His Theresa," published in *Free and Other Stories*, 1918.
Much has been written about Dreiser. Of favorable comment, the most significant is "Theodore Dreiser," by Henry L. Mencken in his volume *A Book of Prefaces*, 1917; the opposite view is taken by Stuart P. Sherman in his "Barbaric Naturalism of Theodore Dreiser," in his volume *Our Contemporary Literature*, 1917. See *Contemporary American Novelists*, Carl Van Doren, 1922; *The Men Who Make Our Novels*, George Gordon, ch. 8.

XLV

"A Lady and a Gentleman," from *Gentlemen and Ladies*, 1927.
For criticism of Irvin Cobb see *Our Short Story Writers*, Blanche C. Williams, 1920; *The Life of Irvin S. Cobb*, John W. Townsend, 1923; *Kentucky in American Letters*, John William Townsend, Vol. II, pp. 323-327, 1913; *Contemporary American Novelists*, Carl Van Doren, 1922.

XLVI

"Death," published in *Winesburg, Ohio*, 1919.
For criticism of Anderson see *The Advance of the American Short Story*, Edward J. O'Brien, pp. 247-261. His autobiographical sketch, *A Story-teller's Story*, 1924, is an invaluable introduction to his work. See also *The Men Who Make Our Novels*, George Gordon, ch. 41.

XLVII

"The Thrush in the Hedge," published in *The Saturday Evening Post*, June 10, 1916; reissued in *The Happy End*, 1919.
For criticism of Hergesheimer see *Our Short Story Writers*, Blanche Colton Williams, 1920; *The Advance of the American Short Story*, Edward J. O'Brien, 1923; *The Men Who Make Our Novels*, George Gordon, ch. 5. His narrative, *The Presbyterian Child*, is autobiographical.

XLVIII

"Six Dollars," published in *Urkey Island*, 1926.
For criticism of Steele see *The Advance of the American Short Story*, Edward J. O'Brien. Also *The Bookman*, 46:704.

XLIX

"The Open Window," published in *Harper's Magazine*, August, 1918.
For criticism see *The Advance of the American Short Story*, Edward J. O'Brien.

L

"Roast Beef, Medium," published in *American Magazine*, 73:157, reissued in *Roast Beef, Medium*, 1913.

LI

"The Artist," published in *The Saturday Evening Post*.

LII

"Wind in the Pines," published in *Scribner's Magazine*, October, 1914; reissued in *Short Turns*, 1926.

LIII

"Fear," published in Collier's *National Weekly*, July 31, 1926.